W9-AQR-810

**Putnam's
Contemporary
Dictionaries**

Italian-English
Inglese-Italiano

Putnam's
Contemporary Dictionaries

Italian-English
Inglese-Italiano

ISOPEL MAY, B.A., Ph.D.

Revised by:
ANTONIA SANSICA STOTT, DOTT. LETT.
Lecturer in Italian,
University of Glasgow

CATHERINE WILSON
Special Editor to the American Edition

G. P. PUTNAM'S SONS   New York

First American Edition 1973

Copyright © 1970 by William Collins Sons & Co., Ltd.
Copyright © 1973 by G. P. Putnam's Sons

SBN: 399–11146–8
Library of Congress Catalog Card Number: 72–97576

Published by arrangement
with William Collins Sons & Co., Ltd., London and Glasgow

Printed in the United States of America

General Editor: J. B. Foreman, M.A.
Executive Editor: Isaebail C. Macleod, M.A.

Contents

Introduction	page	vii
Abbreviations used in the Dictionary		ix
Italian Pronunciation		xi
English Pronunciation		xiv
Italian-English Dictionary		1
English-Italian Dictionary		185
Notes on Italian Grammar		396
Italian Verbs		399
Notes on English Grammar		424
English Verbs		425
Numerals		431
Italian Weights and Measures		433
American Weights and Measures		434
Italian Abbreviations		435
American Abbreviations		440

Contenuto

Prefazione	vii
Abbreviazioni usate nel Dizionario	ix
Pronuncia Italiana	xi
Pronuncia Inglese	xiv
Dizionario Italiano-Inglese	1
Dizionario Inglese-Italiano	185
Note sulla Grammatica Italiana	396
Verbi Italiani	399
Note sulla Grammatica Inglese	424
Verbi Inglesi	425
Numeri	431
Misure e Pesi Italiani	433
Misure e Pesi Americani	434
Abbreviazioni Italiane	435
Abbreviazioni Americane	440

v

Introduction

It is opportune to remind the user of the Dictionary that, although a standard pronunciation exists both in English and in Italian—and this we have used here—pronunciation both in Italy and in the English-speaking world varies from one region to another.

Italian Consonants

The consonants s and z may be voiced or unvoiced. When they are voiced this sound is indicated in the Dictionary by a dot under the letters s and z.

Accents used in the Italian-English section of the Dictionary

In this Dictionary, to help the student, the accent has been inserted in all words, marking the open sounds with the 'grave' accent, and the close ones with the 'acute.'

Genders

Rules concerning masculine and feminine forms are indicated in the Supplement. However, to help the student, the feminine form in -trice and exceptions to the rules have been indicated in the Dictionary.

Irregularities and Peculiarities in Italian Plurals

All exceptions in plurals of nouns and adjectives ending in the singular in -cia and -gia and in -io, and the plural of all the words, regular or exceptions, nouns or adjectives, of two or more syllables ending in the singular in -co and -go have been indicated in the Dictionary.

Some nouns in Italian change their gender in the plural. Some nouns have two plurals with different meanings. Some compounds, as well as certain single nouns, have the same form both for the singular and for the plural; some compounds form their plural either changing both parts of the word, or only one. All these plurals are duly indicated in their place in the Dictionary.

English Pronunciation

In the English-Italian section of the Dictionary the letters and symbols of the International Phonetic Association have been used.

English Irregular Plurals

All irregular plurals have been indicated.

vii

Proper Names and Geographical Names

The most important proper names and geographical names have been incorporated in the main part of the Dictionary.

Abbreviations used in the Dictionary—
Abbreviazioni usate nel Dizionario

aggettivo	a	adjective
abbreviazione	abbr	abbreviation
accusativo	acc	accusative
avverbio	ad	adverb
agricoltura	agr	agriculture
anatomia	anat	anatomy
aggettivo e nome femminile	a nf	adjective and noun feminine
aggettivo e nome maschile	a nm	adjective and noun masculine
aggettivo e nome maschile o femminile	a nmf	adjective and noun masculine or feminine
arcaico	arc	archaic
architettura	arch	architecture
astronomia	astr	astronomy
automobile	aut	automobile
ausiliare	aux	auxiliary
aviazione	av	aviation
biblico	Bibl	Biblical
botanico	bot	botanical
chimica	chem	chemistry
cinema	cin	cinema
congiunzione	cj	conjunction
collettivo	coll	collective
commerciale	com	commercial
cucina	cook	cooking
cosmetici	cosm	cosmetics
articolo definito	def art	definite article
dimostrativo	dem	demonstrative
ecclesiastico	eccl	ecclesiastical
economia	econ	economics
elettricità	el	electricity
femminile	f	feminine
familiare	fam	familiar
figurato	fig	figuratively
finanziario	fin	financial
femminile plurale	fpl	feminine plural
geografico	geogr	geographical
geologia	geol	geology
geometria	geom	geometry
grammatica	gram	grammar
storico	hist	historical
impersonale	impers	impersonal
industria	ind	industry
articolo indefinito	indef art	indefinite article
interiezione	interj	interjection
interrogativo	interrog	interrogative
legale	leg	legal
letterario	liter	literary
maschile	m	masculine
matematica	math	mathematics
meccanica	mech	mechanics
medicina	med	medicine
metallurgia	metal	metallurgy
militare	mil	military
minerale	min	mineral
maschile plurale	mpl	masculine plural
musica	mus	music
nome	n	noun

ix

nautico	naut	nautical
nome femminile	nf	noun feminine
nome maschile	nm	noun masculine
nome maschile o femminile	nmf	noun masculine or feminine
nominativo	nom	nominative
nome proprio	n pr	proper noun
nome femminile plurale	nf pl	noun feminine plural
nome maschile plurale	nm pl	noun masculine plural
nome femminile proprio	nf pr	proper noun feminine
nome maschile proprio	nm pr	proper noun masculine
ornitologia	ornit	ornithology
filosofia	phil	philosophy
fotografia	phot	photography
fisica	phys	physics
plurale	pl	plural
poesia	poet	poetry
politico	pol	political
possessivo	poss	possessive
participio passato	pp	past participle
proprio	pr	proper
predicativo	pred	predicative
preposizione	prep	preposition
pronome	pron	pronoun
qualcosa	qc	something
qualcuno	qlcu	someone
radio	rad	radio
reciproco	recip	reciprocal
riflessivo	refl	reflexive
relativo	rel	relative
religione	relig	religion
ferrovia	rly	railway
singolare	sing	singular
gergo	sl	slang
qualcuno	s.o.	someone
qualcosa	sth	something
tecnico	tec	technical
telefono	tel	telephone
teatro	theat	theatre
televisione	tv	television
tipografica	typ	typography
Stati Uniti, americano	US	United States, American
generalmente	usu	usually
vedere	v	see
veterinario	vet	veterinary
verbo intransitivo	vi	verb intransitive
verbo passivo	vp	verb passive
verbo riflessivo	vr	verb reflexive
verbo transitivo	vt	verb transitive
verbo transitivo e intransitivo	vti	verb transitive and intransitive
volgare	vulg	vulgar
zoologia	zool	zoology

x

Italian Pronunciation—Pronuncia Italiana

The Italian alphabet

The Italian alphabet consists of twenty-one letters, of which five are vowels (vocali) a, e, i, o, u; the others are consonants (consonanti).

A	a	G	gi	O	o	U	u
B	bi	H	acca	P	pi	V	vi
C	ci	I	i	Q	qu	Z	zeta
D	di	L	elle	R	erre		
E	e	M	emme	S	esse		
F	effe	N	enne	T	ti		

The letters k, w, x, y (kappa, vi doppio, ics, ipsilon) are used only in words of foreign origin. The letter j (i lungo) is no longer in use.

The Vowels (Le Vocali)

Every vowel in Italian, stressed or unstressed, has a single, distinct sound.

a [ɑ]		as *a* in father	
e	open [ɛ]	as *e* in seven	unaccented e is always close
	close [e]	as *a* in hate	(without the short 'i' sound)
i [i]		as *i* in ravine	
o	open [ɔ]	as *o* in cot	unaccented o is always close
	close [o]	as *o* in note	(without the short 'u' sound)
u [u]		as *oo* in moon	

Stress in Pronunciation

Most words have the stress on the vowel in the last but one syllable; some on the final vowel, others on the vowels in the third last or fourth last syllable. No written (or printed) accent, however, is used except where the final vowel is stressed, and to avoid ambiguity. (See *Written Accents*)

Diphthongs

Diphthongs are made (1) of the combination of a, e, or o with unaccented i or u; (2) when i and u are combined with each other. In (1) the stress falls on a, e, or o; in (2) sometimes on i, sometimes on u; e.g. fiàba, manièra, fióre; lúi, guída.

Hiatus

Hiatus occurs when two vowels are pronounced separately: pa-úra, le-àle.

The Consonants (Le Consonanti)

The consonants b, d, f, l, m, n, p, t, v are pronounced as in English. In double consonants each consonant is distinctly sounded in order to give a double effect within the same sound, as in: bèllo, bírra, còccola, fàccia.

c   is soft, or palatal [tʃ] before e and i (as in cheese): cénere, bàcio, cíbo, fàccia.

c   is hard or guttural [k] before a, o, u and consonants (like k): calamàio, còsa, cuòre, chièsa, clorúro.

ch (only found before e, i) is hard, or guttural (as in chemist): chílo, che.

g   is soft or palatal [dʒ] before e and i (as in general): generàle, gelóso, ginnàsio.

xi

g is hard or guttural [g] before **a, o, u,** : (as in god, gruesome): **gàra, godiménto, gústo, grído.**

gh (only found before **e, i**) is hard, or guttural (as in ghetto, guinea): **ghétto, ghinèa.**

gl is hard or guttural [gl] before **a, o, u, e** (as in gland): **glàndola, glèba, glòbo, glucòsio.**

gli a single, palatal sound [ʎ] (as in brilliant): **gli, fíglio, móglie, màglia.**
Exceptions: **Anglia, glicerína, negligènte, geroglífico, gànglio,** where the sound is guttural.

gn a single, palatal sound [ɲ] (similar to opinion, companion): **campàgna, agnèllo, bàgno, magnífico, sógno.**

h is never pronounced.

qu [kw] (as in question): **quàdro, questióne, quínto, quòta.** If preceded by **c** this sound is kept separate from **qu** giving the effect of a slightly double sound; **àcqua, acquirènte, acquísto, nàcque.**

r [r] must be distinctly pronounced: **ràro, rósso, àrte, tortúra.**

s { unvoiced (s aspra, s sorda) [s] (as in silk): **sèrvo, séta.**
voiced (s dolce, s sonora) [z] (as in rose): **ròsa, úso, spòsa.**
This sound is shown in the Dictionary by a dot under the letter s.

sc before **e, i** has a single, palatal sound [ʃ] (as in shell): **scèna, scéndere.** Before **a, o, u** it has a guttural sound [sk] (as in scholar): **scàtola, scolàro, scuòla.**

z { unvoiced (z aspra, z sorda) [ts]: **zàmpa, zòccolo.**
voiced (z dolce, z sonora) [dz]: **zàino, zèro, zínco, zòtico.**
This sound is shown in the Dictionary by a dot under the letter z.

Written Accents

Three written accents are in use in Italy, the acute (ʹ), the grave (ˋ) and the circumflex (ˆ). The circumflex accent is employed only to indicate that the word has been abbreviated by the omission of part of it. As for the other two accents, there is considerable variation concerning their use. They are invariably indicated as follows: (a) on words in which the accent falls on the last syllable: **città, virtù, caffè** (See *Stress in Pronunciation*); (b) on monosyllables ending with a diphthong: **già, giú, piú;** (c) on monosyllables which, if accented, change meaning; **dà** (part of the verb **dare**), **da** (from, by, to); **sé** (himself), **se** (if) *etc*; (d) on words which change meaning depending on the position of the accent; **àncora** (anchor), **ancóra** (still, yet), **príncipi** (princes), **princípi** (principles). The acute and grave accents are stress marks, the acute over **i** and **u**, the grave over **a**. With **e** and **o** they are pronunciation as well as stress marks, the acute being used for the close sounds, the grave for the open. In many texts, however, only the grave accent is indicated, irrespective of whether the sound may be open or close. In the Italian-English part of this we have inserted the accent in *all* words, marking the open sounds with the 'grave' accent, and the close ones with the 'acute'.

Apostrophe

This indicates the omission of the last vowel of a word and it occurs when the next word begins with a vowel: *eg* **la amíca, l'amíca,** the girl friend; **un bèllo àlbero, un bell'àlbero,** a beautiful tree. The apostrophe is not to be used between plural feminine articles and nouns: *eg* **le èrbe.**

xii

Syllable Division

Italian words are divided into syllables, each syllable normally starting with a consonant.

Double consonants are always separated: ex. màm-ma; pàl-la; sàs-so.

When s is followed by one or more consonants it belongs to the subsequent syllable: eg vi-schio; pò-sta; à-sma.

Vowels in diphthongs are not separated: eg fià-ba; fió-re except when hiatus occurs: eg pa-ú-ra; le-à-le.

When a word is carried from one line to another, if the word is apostrophized the apostrophe cannot be left at the end of the line. The apostrophe must either be accompanied by the first part of the following word, or it must not be used at all and the full, unapostrophized form should be used instead: eg un'a-/mica or una/amica; not un'/amica.

Pronuncia Inglese—English Pronunciation

Vocali e Dittonghi inglesi

Simbolo	Esempio inglese	Esempio italiano o Spiegazione
[ɑː]	father ['fɑːðə]	padre
[ʌ]	but [bʌt] come [kʌm] blood [blʌd]	quasi a
[æ]	man [mæn] cat [kæt]	e molto aperta
[ɛə]	there [ðɛə] bear [bɛə]	e aperta seguita da un suono di a e da una brevissima r
[ai]	fly [flai] high [hai] nine [nain]	mai
[au]	how [hau] house [haus]	fauna
[ei]	day [dei] name [neim] obey [ə'bei]	é[1] e chiusa seguita da un leggero suono di i
[e]	get [get] bed [bed]	petto e breve e stretta
[əː]	bird [bəːd] heard [həːd] word [wəːd]	eu francese
[ə]	ago [ə'gou] concern [kən'səːn]	a brevissima, quàsi priva di suono
[iː]	tea [tiː] see [siː] ceiling ['siːliŋ]	pino, vino
[i]	it, [it] big [big]	i breve e stretta, quasi come in fitto, ritto
[iə]	here [hiə] hear [hiə]	i+a come in zia, mia+ un brevissimo suono di r
[ou]	go [gou] note [nout] slow [slou]	ó[u] o chiusa seguita da un lieve suono di u
[ɔː]	saw [sɔː] all [ɔːl] before [bi'fɔː]	o aperta e prolungata come in mole
[ɔ]	hot [hɔt] wash [wɔʃ] long [lɔŋ]	o aperta e breve come in notte
[ɔi]	boy [bɔi] oil [ɔil]	poi
[uː]	too [tuː] you [juː] shoe [ʃuː] true [truː]	u prolungata, come in fune, luna

xiv

[u]	put [put]	*u* breve, come in t*u*tto, p*u*lpito
	book [buk]	
[uə]	poor [puə]	*u* prolungata +un breve suono
	sure [ʃuə]	di *a* + un brevissimo suono di
		r

Consonanti inglesi

Simbolo	*Esempio inglese*	*Esempio italiano o Spiegazione*
[b]	been [biːn]	*b* italiana
	grab [græb]	
[d]	day [dei]	*d* italiana
	had [hæd]	
[f]	father ['fɑːðə]	*f* italiana
[g]	go [gou]	*g* dura, come in *g*occia,
	big [big]	*gh*iaccio
[ŋ]	long [lɔŋ]	la *n* è prolungata. La *g* non si
	sing [siŋ]	pronuncia
[h]	house [haus]	*h* aspirata
[j]	young [jʌŋ]	*i* italiana
	yes [jes]	
	million ['miljən]	
[k]	come [kʌm]	*c* dura, come in *c*osa, s*c*uola,
	mock [mɔk]	*ch*iosco
	school [skuːl]	
	key [kiː]	
[l]	look [luk]	*l* italiana
[m]	much [mʌtʃ]	*m* italiana
	lamb [læm]	
	column ['kɔləm]	
[n]	noon [nuːn]	*n* italiana
[ŋk]	ink [iŋk]	*n* +*c* dura
	frank [fræŋk]	
[p]	push [puʃ]	*p* italiana
	hope [houp]	
[r]	red [red]	*r* non fortemente
	bread [bred]	marcato
[s]	stand [stænd]	*s* aspra, come in *s*orte
	sand [sænd]	
	yes [jes]	
	decide [di'said]	
[z]	(s between vowels or	*s* dolce e *z* dolce, come in ro*s*a
	at the end of a word)	e *z*aino
	rose [rouz]	
	his [hiz]	
	bases ['beisiz]	
	zeal [ziːl]	
[ʃ]	shall [ʃæl]	*sc* come in *sc*ene, *sci*a, *sci*alle,
	machine [mə'ʃiːn]	*sci*ogliere
	motion ['mouʃən]	
	special ['speʃəl]	
	mission ['miʃən]	

XV

[tʃ]	*ch*in [tʃin] ri*ch* [ritʃ] pi*c*ture ['piktʃə]	*c* palatale, come in *c*ento
[t]	*t*ennis ['tenis] swee*t* [swiːt]	*t* italiana
[v]	*v*ery ['veri] li*v*e [liv]	*v* italiana
[w]	*w*ater ['wɔːtə] *wh*ich [witʃ]	*u* italiana
[ʒ]	vi*s*ion ['viʒən] plea*s*ure ['pleʒə] gara*g*e ['gærɑːʒ]	*j* francese, come in *j*ournal
[dʒ]	*g*erm [dʒəːm] *j*ust [dʒʌst] bri*dg*e [bridʒ]	*g* dolce italiana, come in *g*enio, *g*iusto
[ð]	*th*e [ðə] fa*th*er ['fɑːðə]	Questo suono non esiste in italiano. È un suono dolce che si ottiene mettendo la lingua tra i denti. Potrebbe, approssi- mativamente, rappresentarsi con *dh*
[θ]	*th*ink [θiŋk] me*th*od ['meθəd]	Questo suono non esiste in italiano. È un suono forte, come l'emissione di un soffio tra i denti. Si avvicina alla *c* spagnola, come nella parola *c*e*c*eo
[x]	(Scottish) lo*ch* [lɔx]	suono aspirato duro, come nella parola tedesca na*ch*

ː indica che la vocale precedente è lunga.
L'accento principale è indicato dal simbolo ['] che è posto prima
della sillaba accentata. L'accento secondario è indicato dal
simbolo [ˌ]
Il simbolo fonetico è indicato entro parentesi quadra.

xvi

Italian-English

A

a *prep* at, in, to, by, for, on.
abàte *nm* abbot, abbé.
abbacinàre *vt* to blind, dazzle; deceive.
àbbaco *pl* -chi *nm* elementary arithmetic book; (*arc*) abacus.
abbadéssa *nf* abbess.
abbagliaménto *nm* dazzling, dimness of sight.
abbagliànte *a* dazzling; *nm* (*aut*) driving beam, high beam.
abbagliàre *vt* to dazzle, fascinate, deceive, astonish.
abbaiàre *vi* to bark.
abbaíno *nm* skylight, garret window, garret.
abbandonàre *vt* to leave, quit, abandon; -rsi *vr* to give oneself up to, despair.
abbandonataménte *ad* freely, passionately.
abbandonàto *a* abandoned, forsaken, deserted, desolate.
abbandóno *nm* abandonment, desertion.
abbarbicàre *vi* to take root; -rsi *vr* to cling (as ivy).
abbaruffàre *vt* to ruffle; -rsi *vr* to come to blows.
abbassaménto *nm* lowering, humiliation.
abbassàre *vti* to lower, lessen, abase, humble; -rsi *vr* to humble oneself, fall.
abbàsso *ad* below; *interj* down! down with!
abbastànza *ad* enough, fairly, rather.
abbàttere *vt* to throw down, depress, slaughter; to shoot down (a plane); -rsi *vr* to lose heart, fall.
abbattiménto *nm* knocking down, felling, overthrow, depression.
abbattúto *a* depressed, cast-down.
abbazía *nf* abbey.
abbecedàrio *nm* first spelling book.
abbelliménto *nm* embellishment, ornament.
abbellíre *vt* to adorn, embellish.
abbeveràre *vt* to water (animals).
abbeveratóio *nm* watering place, drinking trough.
abbiccí *nm* alphabet, rudiments.
abbiènte *a* well-to-do.
abbigliaménto *nm* clothes, clothing, finery.
abbigliàre *vt* to deck, dress.
abbinàre *vt* to pair, link together.
abbindolàre *vt* to wind (skeins); cheat, trick.

abbisognàre *vi and impers* to need, want.
abboccaménto *nm* interview, conversation, talk.
abboccàre *vti* to seize with the mouth; (*fig*) to be deceived; -rsi *vr* to have an interview, confer.
abboccàto *a* brimful; (*in speech*) nice; (*of wine*) sweet.
abbonacciàre *vt* to calm, pacify; -rsi *vr* (*sea*) to grow calm.
abbonaménto *nm* subscription, discount, season ticket.
abbonàre *vt* to accept as subscriber; (*com*) to deduct, pass (a doubtful account); -rsi *vr* to subscribe.
abbonàto *nm* subscriber, season-ticket holder, commuter; (*gas, el*) consumer.
abbondànte *a* abundant, plentiful.
abbondànza *nf* abundance, plenty.
abbondàre *vi* to abound.
abbordàbile *a* accessible, approachable.
abbordàggio *nm* (*naut*) boarding.
abbordàre *vt* to board (a ship), accost; -rsi *vr* (*naut*) to collide.
abbórdo *nm* access, approach; (*naut*) boarding.
abbottonàre *vt* to button (up); -rsi *vr* to button up, become secretive.
abbozzàre *vt* to outline, sketch, rough-hew.
abbózzo *nm* rough draft, sketch; a. d'uomo manikin.
abbracciaménto, abbràccio *nm* embrace.
abbracciàre *vt* to embrace, contain, include.
abbrancàre *vt* to grasp, seize; -rsi *vr* to cling to, grasp.
abbreviàre *vt* to abridge, shorten.
abbreviazióne *nf* abbreviation, abridg(e)ment.
abbronzàre *vt* to tan, bronze, make brown.
abbronzatúra *nf* sunburn, tan, bronzing.
abbruciacchiàre *vt* to scorch, burn slightly.
abbrunàre *vt* to brown, darken; -rsi *vr* to go into mourning.
abbruníre *vti* to darken, grow dark, become tanned.
abbrustolíre *vt* to toast, crisp; -rsi *vr* to turn brown.
abbrutíre *vt* to brutalize.
abbuiàre *vt* to obscure; -rsi *vr* to grow dark, cloud over.

I

abbuòno nm discount, deduction.
abburattàre vt to sift.
abdicàre vi to abdicate.
abdicazióne nf abdication.
aberrazióne nf abberration, deviation.
abetàia nf fir-wood.
abéte nm fir-tree.
abiètto a abject, base.
abiezióne nf abjectness, baseness.
àbile a able, capable, clever, skillful.
abilità nf ability, dexterity, skill.
abilitàre vt to enable, qualify.
abilitazióne nf qualification.
Abissínia nf Abyssinia.
abissíno a nm Abyssinian.
abísso nm abyss, chasm; (fig) ruin.
abitàbile a habitable.
abitànte nmf inhabitant.
abitàre vti to inhabit, live in, live.
abitàto a inhabited; nm inhabited place.
abitazióne nf dwelling, house.
àbito nm dress, clothes, suit, habit, custom; a. **borghése** civilian clothes.
abituàle a habitual, customary.
abituàre vt to accustom; -rsi vr to get accustomed.
abitúdine nf habit, custom.
abitúro nm hovel.
abiúra nf abjuration, recantation.
abiuràre vt to abjure, recant.
ablatívo nm ablative case.
abluzióne nf ablution, purification.
abnegazióne nf self-denial, abnegation.
abolíre vt to abolish, repeal.
abolizióne nf abolition, repeal.
abominàre vt to abominate, detest.
abominazióne nf abomination, detestation.
abominévole a abominable.
abomínio nm abomination, shame.
aborígeno a aboriginal.
aborríre vt to abhor.
abortíre vi to miscarry, abort, fail.
abòrto nm miscarriage, abortion, still-born child; failure.
Abràmo nm pr Abraham.
abrasióne nf abrasion, graze.
abrasívo a nm abrasive.
abrogàre vt to abrogate, repeal.
abrogazióne nf abrogation, repeal.
abruzzése a of the Abruzzi; nm native of the A.
Abrúzzi e Molíşe nm pl (geogr) Abruzzi e Molise.
àbside nf apse.
abuşàre vt to abuse, misuse, trespass on.
abuşívo a abusive, improper.
abúşo nm abuse, misuse, infringement (of the law).
A.C. Avànti Crísto ad B.C.
acàcia pl **-cie** nf acacia-tree.
accadèmia nf academy.
accadèmico pl **-ici** a academic; nm academician.
accadére vi to happen, occur.
accadúto nm event.

accagliàre vi -rsi vr to curdle.
accalappiàre vt to catch, ensnare, deceive.
accalcàre vi to crowd up; -rsi vr to crowd.
accaldàrsi vr to get heated, excited.
accaldàto a heated (with running etc).
accaloràre vt to heat; -rsi vr to get heated.
accampaménto nm encampment, camp.
accampàre vi to camp; vt (reasons etc) to adduce; -rsi vr to pitch camp.
accaniménto nm fury, ardor.
accanírsi vr to rage, to concentrate doggedly.
accaníto a pitiless, fierce, obstinate.
accànto ad beside, near.
accantonàre vt to billet.
accaparraménto nm earnest money, deposit; buying up, cornering.
accaparràre vt to conclude (a bargain) by paying earnest money; to buy up, corner.
accapigliàrsi vr to scuffle, to quarrel.
accappatóio nm bathrobe, wrap.
accapponàre vi fàre a. **la pèlle** to make the flesh creep; **la pèlle mi si accappona** I've got gooseflesh.
accarezzaménto nm caress.
accarezzàre vt to caress.
accartocciàre vt to wrap up, to crumple up.
accasàre vt to marry; -rsi vr to marry, set up house.
accasciaménto nm dejection.
accasciàre vt to depress; -rsi vr to fall to the ground, lose heart.
accatastàre vt to heap up, stack.
accattabríghe nm quarrelsome fellow.
accattàre vt to beg.
accattonàggio nm begging.
accattóne nm beggar.
accavalcióne, a cavalcióni ad astride.
accecaménto nm blinding, confusion, obstruction.
accecànte a blinding, dazzling.
accecàre vt to blind: -rsi vr to become blind.
accèdere vi to approach, enter.
acceleràre vt to accelerate, quicken, speed up.
acceleràto a accelerated; (of a train) slow.
acceleratóre nm accelerator.
accelerazióne nf acceleration.
accèndere vt to light, kindle; -rsi vr to catch fire, grow angry.
accendíno nm (cigarette) lighter.
accendisígaro nm cigarette-lighter.
accennàre vti to indicate, hint, nod.
accénno nm sign, hint.
accensióne nf lighting; (aut) ignition.
accènto nm accent.
accentuàre vt to accentuate.
accerchiàre vt to encircle, surround.
accertaménto nm ascertainment,

assurance, check; (of account) settlement.

accertàre vt to ascertain, (com) to settle, to assess; -rsi vr to make sure.

accéso a alight, flushed, bright.

accessíbile a accessible, approachable.

accèsso nm access, fit, paroxysm.

accessòrio a nm accessory.

accétta nf hatchet, axe.

accettàbile a acceptable.

accettàre vt to accept, agree to; **accettànte** nm (com) accepter.

accettazióne nf acceptance.

accètto a received with pleasure, welcome, (com) honored.

acchiappàre vt to catch, trap.

acciaccàre vt to bruise, enfeeble.

acciàcco pl -àcchi nm infirmity, ailment.

acciaieria nf steelworks.

acciàio nm steel.

accidentàle a accidental, casual.

accidentalménte ad accidentally.

accidentàto a (of ground) broken.

accidènte nm accident, misfortune.

accidènti! interj (annoyance) damn it!; (surprise) Good Heavens!

accidia nf idleness, sloth.

accidióso a idle, slothful.

accigliaménto nm frown, sullen air.

accigliàrsi vr to frown, look sullen.

accigliàto a frowning, sullen.

accíngersi vr to set about, prepare oneself.

acciocché cj in order that, so that.

acciuffàre vt to seize by the hair, grasp.

acciúga nf anchovy.

acclamàre vt to acclaim; vi to clap hands, cheer.

acclimàre, acclimatàre vt to acclimatize.

acclimatàrsi vr to grow acclimatized.

acclúdere vt to enclose.

acclúso a enclosed.

accoccolàrsi vr to crouch, squat.

accogliènte a welcoming, cozy.

accogliènza nf reception, welcome.

accògliere vt to receive, welcome.

accollàre vt to put round the neck, yoke; (fig) burden, saddle with; -rsi vr to undertake.

accollàto a high-necked.

accoltellàre vt to stab, knife.

accomandànte nm (com) sleeping partner.

accomandatàrio nm (com) acting partner.

accomàndita nf (com) limited partnership.

accomiatàre vt to dismiss; -rsi vr to take leave of.

accomodaménto nm adjustment, agreement, compromise.

accomodàre vt to repair, mend, arrange, adjust, (com) settle; -rsi vr to sit down, make oneself comfortable, come to terms; **s'accòmodi** take a seat, please.

accompagnaménto nm accompaniment, retinue.

accompagnàre vt to accompany, escort; -rsi vr to keep company, join, match; (mus) accompany oneself.

acconciàre vt to dress (the hair), adorn, arrange; -rsi vr to deck oneself.

acconciatúra nf hair style.

accóncio a fit, suitable.

accondiscéndere vi to consent, condescend.

acconsentíre vi to consent.

accontentàre vt to content; -rsi vr to be satisfied, be content with.

accónto nm (com) part payment.

accoppiàre vt to couple, pair, yoke; -rsi vr to join together, couple.

accoraménto nm grief, affliction.

accoràre vt to grieve deeply; -rsi vr to be grieved to the heart.

accorciàre vt to shorten; -rsi vr to grow shorter.

accordàre vt to grant; (mus) tune, harmonize, (gram) make agree; conciliate; -rsi vr to agree, be in harmony with.

accòrdo nm agreement, arrangement, (mus) chord, (fig) harmony, accord; **èssere d'a.** to agree.

accòrgersi vr to perceive, notice, realize, be aware of.

accorgiménto nm circumspection, prudence, device.

accórrere vi to run up, to go to help.

accortézza nf prudence, sagacity, cunning.

accòrto a wary, shrewd, prudent.

accostàre vt to approach, bring near(er); leave ajar; -rsi vr to approach, draw near.

accòsto ad beside, hard by.

accostumàre vt to train, accustom; -rsi vr to get accustomed.

accovacciàrsi vr to cower, crouch.

accozzàglia nf medley, disorderly mass; **un'a. di gènte** motley crowd.

accreditàre vt to give credit to, to accredit; -rsi to gain credit.

accréscere vt to increase.

accresciménto nm increase, growth.

accudíre vi (of household duties) to attend to.

accumulàre vt to accumulate, heap up; -rsi vr to accumulate.

accumulatóre nm (el) storage cell.

accumulazióne nf accumulation.

accuratézza nf accuracy, care.

accuràto a accurate, neat.

accúsa nf accusation, charge.

accusàre vt to accuse, charge, blame, show, complain of, (com) acknowledge; -rsi vr to accuse oneself, confess.

accusativo a nm accusative.

accusàto nm accused, defendant.

accusatóre nm accuser, prosecutor; **púbblico a.** public prosecutor.

acerbità nf acerbity, asperity.

acèrbo a unripe, sour, (fig) sharp.
àcero nm maple-tree.
acetilène nm acetylene.
acéto nm vinegar.
acetóne nm acetone.
acetóso a vinegary, sourish.
acidità nf acidity, sourness.
àcido a nm acid.
àcino nm grape, grape-stone.
àcne nm acne.
àcqua nf water; **a. corrènte** running water; **a. dólce** fresh water; **a. mineràle** mineral water; **a. potàbile** drinking water; **a. di sèltz** soda-water.
acquafòrte nf etching.
acquàio nm sink.
acquaplàno nm aquaplane.
acquaràgia nf turpentine.
acquartieràre vt (troops) to quarter; -rsi vr to take up quarters.
acquasantièra nf holy water stoup.
acquàta nf heavy shower.
acquàtico pl -ici a aquatic.
acquattàrsi vr to crouch, squat.
acquavíte nf gin, brandy.
acquazzóne nm sudden and heavy shower, downpour.
acquedótto nm aqueduct.
acquerellísta nmf painter in water-colors.
acquerèllo nm water color, water-color painting.
acquerúgiola nf drizzle.
acquiescènza nf acquiescence.
acquietàre vt to appease, pacify.
acquirènte nmf purchaser, buyer.
acquisíre vt to acquire, obtain.
acquistàre vt to acquire, buy; (fig) gain, improve.
acquisto nm acquisition, purchase, gain.
acquitríno nm marsh, swamp.
acquitrinóso a marshy, boggy.
acquolína nf far veníre l'a. in bócca to make somebody's mouth water.
acquóso a watery.
àcre a sharp, sour, harsh.
acrèdine nf bitterness, sourness; (fig) acrimony.
acrimònia nf acrimony.
acrimonióso a acrimonious.
acròbata nmf acrobat.
acrobazía nf acrobatics pl.
acuíre vt to sharpen, whet.
acúme nm quickness of wit, acumen.
acuminàre vt to point, sharpen.
acústica nf acoustics pl.
acutézza nf acuteness, wit, penetration.
acúto a acute, pointed, sharp.
adacquàre vt to water, irrigate.
adagiàre vt to lay down, make comfortable; -rsi vr to arrange oneself comfortably; nm proverb, saying.
adàgio ad slowly, softly, at leisure.
Adàmo nm pr Adam.
adattàbile a adaptable, applicable.
adattabilità nf adaptability.

adattàre vt to fit, adapt, adjust; -rsi vr to adapt oneself.
adàtto a fit, proper, right, suitable.
addebitàre vt to debit.
addensàre vt to make thick; -rsi vr to grow dense, thicken.
addentàre vt to bite.
addentràrsi vr to penetrate, probe.
addéntro ad within, inside.
addestràre vt to train, drill, instruct; (horse) break in; -rsi vr to train oneself, practice.
addétto a belonging to, attached; **a. ad un'ambasciàta** attaché at an embassy.
addí ad on the (day) of.
addiètro ad behind, back(wards), ago.
addío ad nm good-bye.
addirittúra ad downright, immediately, outright.
addírsi vr and impers to suit, become.
additàre vt to point out, show, indicate.
addizionàre vt to add (up).
addizióne nf addition, supplement.
addobbàre vt to furnish, decorate.
addòbbo nm decorative furnishing, hangings.
addolcíre vt to sweeten, soften, alleviate.
addoloràre vt to afflict, grieve; -rsi vr to be grieved, grieve.
Addoloràta (l') nf Our Lady of Sorrows.
addòme nm abdomen.
addomesticàre vt to tame; -rsi to become tame, become more sociable, grow familiar.
addormentàre vt to put to sleep; (fig) calm; -rsi to fall asleep.
addossàre vt to lay upon, place on the back of, place against, charge, load, burden; -rsi vr to undertake, charge oneself with.
addòsso ad on, upon, close by, above; **avére a.** to have on, wear; **tiràrsi a.** to bring upon oneself.
addúrre vt to adduce, cite.
adeguàre vt to equalize, balance, conform.
adeguàto a sufficient.
Adèle nf pr Adela.
adémpiere, adempíre vt to fulfill, perform; -rsi vr to come true.
adempiménto nm fulfillment, accomplishment, execution.
aderènte a adherent, close-fitting; nmf supporter.
aderènza nf adherence, adhesion; (fig pl) high connections.
aderíre vt to adhere, agree.
adescàre vt to lure, entice.
adesióne nf adhesion, adherence, consent.
adesívo a adhesive.
adèsso ad now, at present.
adiacènte a adjacent, adjoining, next.

adiacènza nf adjacency, vicinity.
adibíre vt to destine for use.
àdipe nm fat, grease.
adiposità nf fatness, plumpness.
adipóso a fat, plump.
adiràre vt to make angry, provoke; -rsi vr to get angry.
àdito nm entry, access; **dàre a. a** give rise to.
adocchiàre vt to eye, ogle.
adolescènte a nmf adolescent.
adolescènza nf adolescence, youth.
Adòlfo nm pr Adolph.
adombràre vt to shade, conceal; suggest, symbolize; -rsi vr to take umbrage.
adoperàre vi to use, employ; -rsi vr to exert oneself, endeavor.
adoràbile a adorable, charming.
adoràre vt to adore, worship.
adorazióne nf adoration, worship.
adornàre vt to adorn, deck; -rsi vr to adorn oneself.
adórno a adorned, trimmed.
adottàre vt to adopt.
adottívo a adoptive, adopted.
adozióne nf adoption.
Adriàno nm pr Adrian, Hadrian.
Adriàtico a nm Adriatic.
adulàre vt to flatter.
adulatóre nm -tríce nf flatterer.
adulatòrio a adulatory, flattering.
adulazióne nf adulation, flattery.
adulteràre vt to adulterate, taint, falsify.
adultèrio nm adultery.
adúltero nm adulterer.
adúlto a nm adult, grown-up.
adunànza nf assembly, meeting.
adunàre vt to assemble, bring together, convoke; -rsi vr to come together, assemble, (mil) fall-in.
adunàta nf (mil) fall-in; assembly; **a. popolàre** mass meeting.
adúnco pl -chi a hooked, curved.
aeràre vt to air, aerate.
aèro a of the air, aerial, airy, unsubstantial; nm v aeroplàno.
aerocèntro nm air center.
aerodinàmica nf aerodynamics pl; **aerodinàmico** pl -ici a aerodynamic, streamlined.
aeròdromo nm aerodrome, airfield, airport.
aeronàutica nf aeronautics pl, aviation, air force.
aeroplàno nm flying machine, airplane; **a. da càccia** fighter plane; **a. da bombardaménto** bomber; **a. a reazióne** jet plane; **a. di línea** airliner.
aeropòrto nm airport.
aerosòl nm (chem) aerosol.
àfa nf sultry heat.
affàbile a affable, friendly.
affabilità nf affability.
affaccendàrsi vr to occupy oneself, be very busy.
affaccendàto a busy.
affacciàre vt to bring forward, show;

-rsi vr to show oneself, occur; -rsi su to face (a place).
affamàre vt to starve.
affamàto a hungry, famished, starving.
affannàre vt to trouble, vex; -rsi vr to toil, strive, fret, be anxious.
affannàto a breathless, panting, distressed.
affànno nm shortness of breath, asthma; trouble, anxiety.
affannóso a suffocating, troublesome, wearisome, troubled.
affàre nm affair, matter, business; **uòmo d'affàri** businessman.
affarísta nm unscrupulous businessman.
affaróne nm good bargain.
affascinànte a fascinating.
affascinàre vt to fascinate, enchant.
affastellàre vt to tie up in bundles, jumble up.
affaticàre vt to tire, harass; -rsi vr to get tired, toil, strive.
affàtto ad entirely; **niènte a.** not at all.
affermàre vt to affirm; -rsi vr to assert oneself, make a name for oneself.
affermatíva nf affirmative.
affermatívo a affirmative.
affermazióne nf statement, assertion, achievement.
afferràre vt to seize, grasp, comprehend.
affettàre vt to cut in slices; affect, pretend.
affettàto a sliced; affected, prim; nm sliced ham, salami.
affettazióne nf affectation.
affètto a affected, afflicted; nm affection, love.
affettuosaménte ad lovingly, affectionately.
affettuóso a affectionate.
affezionàre vt to make fond; -rsi vr to become fond of, attached to.
affezióne nf affection, attachment.
affiancàre vt to flank, place side by side.
affiatàre vt to bring together; -rsi vr to get on well together.
affibbiàre vt to buckle, clasp; (fig) give.
affibbiatúra nf buckle, clasp.
affidàre vt to entrust, confide; -rsi vr to trust, rely on.
affievolíre vt to weaken; vi and -rsi vr to grow weak.
affíggere vt to affix, stick (up), attach.
affilàre vt to whet, grind; -rsi vr to become thin.
affiliàre vt to affiliate; -rsi vr to become a member, join.
affiliazióne nf affiliation.
affinàre vt to refine, improve, sharpen, make thin; -rsi vr to become refined, improve, become sharper, become thinner.

affinatóio nm refining furnace.
affinché cj so that, in order that.
affíne a akin, kindred; nm kinsman, relative; **a. di** cj in order to, so as to.
affinità nf affinity, attraction.
affiocàre, affiochíre vt weaken, dim, render hoarse, vi become hoarse.
affiochiménto nm hoarseness.
affioràre vi to come to the surface.
affissàre vt to affix, gaze at.
affissióne nf bill-posting; **vietàta l'a. post** no bills.
affísso a fixed, posted up; nm bill, placard, poster.
affittacàmere nm landlord; nf landlady.
affittàre vt to let, rent, hire, lease.
affítto nm rent, hire; **dàre in a.** to let; **prèndere in a.** to rent.
affliggere vt to afflict, torment; **-rsi** vr to be grieved.
afflítto a afflicted, sad.
afflizióne nf affliction.
affluènza nf crowd, large audience; abundance.
affluíre vi to flow, flock.
affogàre vt to drown, (fig) smother; vi to be drowned; **-rsi** vr to drown oneself; **uòvo affogàto** poached egg.
affollàre vt to crowd, throng; **-rsi** vr to crowd together.
affondàre vti to sink, founder, ruin; **-rsi** vr to sink, founder, go to the bottom.
affossaménto nm trench, entrenchment, sinking.
affrancàre vt to free, exempt; (letter) stamp; **-rsi** vr to be freed; grow strong.
affrancatúra nf postage.
affrànto a broken, crushed, overcome.
affratellàre vt to make as brothers; **-rsi** vr to fraternize.
affrésco pl **-chi** nm fresco.
affrettàre vt to hasten, speed; **-rsi** vr to hurry, make haste.
affrontàre vt to confront, face, attack; **-rsi** to meet face to face fight.
affrónto nm affront, insult.
affumicàre vt to fumigate, smoke-dry, blacken; **-rsi** vr to be smoked, grow black.
affústo nm (mil) gun-carriage.
afóso a sultry, heavy.
Àfrica nf Africa.
africàno a nm African.
Àgata nf pr Agatha.
agènda nf notebook, agenda.
agènte nm agent, factor, manager; **a. di polizía** policeman.
agenzía nf agency; **a. di turísmo** travel agency.
agevolàre vt to facilitate, make easy, help.
agévole a easy, manageable.

agganciàre vt to hook (up).
aggéggio nm gadget, device; trifle.
agghiacciàre vt to freeze, turn to ice; **-rsi** vr to freeze, grow cold.
aggiogàre vt to yoke.
aggiornàre vt to postpone; bring up to date; vi to dawn.
aggiornàto a up-to-date.
aggiotàggio nm stock-jobbing.
aggiràre vt to go round; deceive; **-rsi** vr to wander; deal with.
aggiúngere vt to add; **-rsi** vr to join, be added.
aggiúnta nf addition.
aggiúnto a added, additional; nm adjunct, assistant.
aggiustàre vt to adjust, regulate, set to rights, tidy, settle; **-rsi** vr to adjust oneself, tidy oneself, come to an agreement.
agglomeràre vt **-rsi** vr to agglomerate.
agglomeràto a agglomerate; nm agglomerate, agglomeration.
aggomitolàre vt to wind into a ball; **-rsi** vr to curl up.
aggranchíre vt to benumb.
aggrappàre vt to grapple, grasp; **-rsi** vr to cling to, lay hold (of).
aggravànte a aggravating; nm (leg) aggravating circumstance.
aggravàre vt to aggravate, weigh upon, oppress; **-rsi** vr (illness) to grow worse.
aggràvio nm heavy burden, expense, charge; **a. fiscàle** tax.
aggredíre vt to attack, assault.
aggregàre vt to aggregate.
aggregàto a joint, united; nm aggregate; block of houses; temporary clerk.
aggregazióne nf aggregation.
aggressióne nf aggression, attack.
aggressività nf aggressiveness.
aggressívo a aggressive; nm chemical agent used in warfare.
aggressóre nm aggressor, assailant.
aggrinzàre vt to wrinkle; **-rsi** vr to wrinkle, shrivel (up).
aggrottàre vt to frown; **a. le cíglia** to frown, knit one's brows.
aggrumàre vt to curdle, clot.
aggruppàre vt to group, collect, gather; **-rsi** vr to form a group.
agguàglio nm comparison.
agguantàre vt to seize.
agguàto nm ambush.
agguerríre vt to inure to war, train to arms.
agiatézza nf ease, comfort, easy circumstances pl.
agiàto a in easy circumstances, well-off, comfortable.
àgile a agile, nimble.
agilità nf agility, nimbleness.
àgio nm ease, comfort, leisure.
agíre vi to act, operate, behave; (leg) proceed.
agitàre vt to agitate, upset, excite; **-rsi** vr to get agitated.

agitazióne *nf* agitation, excitement.
àglio *nm* garlic.
agnèllo *nm* lamb.
Agnèse *nf pr* Agnes.
àgo *pl* **àghi** *nm* needle.
agognàre *vt* to yearn for, covet.
agonía *nf* agony, anguish.
agonizzàre *vi* to be in agony, be at the point of death.
agoràio *nm* needle-case.
Agostíno *nm pr* Augustine.
agósto *nm* August.
agràrio *a* agrarian.
agrèste *a* rustic, rural.
agrézza *nf* sourness, tartness.
agrícolo *a* agricultural.
agricoltóre *nm* farmer.
agricoltúra *nf* agriculture.
agrifòglio *nm* holly.
agrimensóre *nm* land surveyor.
àgro *a* sour, sharp; *nm* sourness; field; country surrounding a town.
agrodólce *a* bittersweet; *nm* sweet-and-sour sauce.
agrúmi *nm pl* citrus fruits *pl.*
aguzzàre *vt* to whet, sharpen, point; (*fig*) stimulate, sharpen.
agúzzo *a* sharp-pointed.
ahi *interj* oh!, ouch!
ahimè *interj* alas!
àia *nf* threshing floor.
aitànte *a* strong, sturdy; brave.
aiuòla *nf* flowerbed.
aiutànte *nmf* helper, assistant; (*mil*) **a. di càmpo** aide-de-camp.
aiutàre *vt* to help, assist, lend a hand; **-rsi** *vr* to make use of.
aiúto *nm* help, assistance; helper, assistant.
aizzàre *vt* to instigate, enrage, incite, set on (dogs).
àla *nf* wing; **a. a dèlta** (*av*) delta-wing.
alabàstro *nm* alabaster.
àlacre *a* willing, quick.
alacrità *nf* alacrity, quickness.
alàno *nm* mastiff.
alàre *nm* andiron, firedog.
Alàsca *nf* (*geogr*) Alaska.
alàto *a* winged.
àlba *nf* dawn.
albagía *nf* haughtiness, conceit.
albanése *a nmf* Albanian.
Albanía *nf* (*geogr*) Albania.
àlbatro *nm* albatross; (*tree*) arbutus.
albeggiàre *vi* to dawn.
albergàre *vt* to lodge, to harbor.
albergatóre *nm* hotel-owner.
albèrgo *pl* **-ghi** *nm* hotel.
àlbero *nm* tree; ship's mast.
Albèrto *nm pr* Albert.
albicòcca *nf* apricot.
àlbo *nm* roll, list; **èssere iscrítto all'a. degli avvocàti** to be called (admitted) to the bar.
albóre *nm* dawn.
àlbum *nm* album.
albúme *nm* albumen, white of egg.
alcalíno *a* alkaline.
alcalizzàre *vt* to alkalize.

àlce *nm* elk.
alchímia *nf* alchemy.
alcióne *nm* kingfisher.
àlcool *nm* alcohol; **alcoòlico** *pl* **-ici,** **alcoolizzato** *a nm* alcoholic.
alcoolíşmo *nm* alcoholism.
alcúno *pron* somebody, anybody, (*preceded by* **non**) nobody; *a* any (*preceded by* **non**) no; **alcuni** *a and pron pl* some, a few *pl.*
Aldo *nm pr* Aldous.
àlea *nf* chance, risk; **córrere l'a.** to run the risk.
aleggiàre *vi* to flutter, try to fly.
Alessàndria *nf* (*geogr*) Alexandria (in Egypt).
Alessàndro *nm pr* Alexander.
alétta *nf* fin; (*av*) tab.
alettóne *nm* (*av*) aileron.
alfabètico *pl* **-ici** *a* alphabetical.
alfabèto *nm* alphabet.
alfière *nm* (*mil*) ensign, standard bearer; (*chess*) bishop.
alfíne *ad* at last.
Alfrèdo *nm pr* Alfred.
àlga *nf* seaweed.
àlgebra *nf* algebra.
Algería *nf* Algeria.
Algèrí *nf* Algiers.
algeríno *a nm* Algerian.
aliànte *nm* glider.
àlibi *nm* (*leg*) alibi.
alíce *nf* anchovy.
Alíce *nf pr* Alice.
alienàre *vt* to alienate, estrange; **-rsi** *vr* to be estranged.
alienàto *a* estranged, crazy; *nm* lunatic, mentally deranged person.
alienazióne *nf* alienation, estrangement, mental derangement.
alièno *a* alien, adverse.
alimentàre *a* alimentary; *vt* to feed, nourish.
alimentàrio *a* alimentary.
alimentatóre *nm* nourisher; (*mech*) feeder.
alimentazióne *nf* nourishment, food, diet; (*mech*) feeding.
aliménto *nm* food, nourishment.
alisèi, vènti *nm pl* trade winds *pl.*
aliscàfo *nm* hydrofoil.
àlito *nm* breath, breathing; breeze.
allacciàre *vt* to lace, connect, entangle.
allagaménto *nm* inundation.
allagàre *vt* to inundate, overflow, submerge.
allampanàto *a* emaciated.
allargàre *vt* to enlarge, extend, widen.
allarmàre *vt* to alarm, disturb; **-rsi** *vr* to be alarmed.
allàrme *nm* alarm, alert.
allàto *ad* beside.
allattàre *vt* to suckle, breast-feed.
alleànza *nf* alliance, league.
alleàrsi *vr* to make an alliance.
alleàto *a* allied; *nm* ally.
allegàre *vt* to allege, enclose; (*teeth*) to set on edge.

allegazióne nf allegation.
alleggeríre vt to lighten, relieve; -rsi vr to put on lighter clothing, relieve oneself of.
allegoría nf allegory.
allegraménte ad cheerfully, merrily.
allegrézza nf gaiety, cheerfulness.
allegría nf mirth, gladness.
allégro a gay, cheerful, merry; (mus) allegro.
allenaménto nm training.
allenàre vt to train, strengthen, invigorate.
allenatóre nm trainer, coach.
allentàre vt to slacken, relax, diminish; -rsi vr to get slack; unlace or undo one's clothing.
allergía nf allergy.
allèrgico pl -ici a allergic.
allestíre vt to prepare, make ready.
allettaménto nm allurement.
allettànte a alluring.
allettàre vt to allure, entice; -rsi vr (in illness) to take to one's bed.
allevaménto nm bringing-up, breeding.
allevàre vt to bring up, breed.
allevatóre nm -tríce nf breeder.
alleviàre vt to relieve.
allibíre vi to be amazed.
allietàre vt to gladden.
alliévo nm pupil, student, cadet.
allignàre vi to take root, grow.
allineàre vt to align, set in rows.
allocuzióne nf address, allocution.
allòdola nf skylark.
alloggiàre vti to lodge, stay, billet.
allòggio nm lodgings pl, billet, inn.
allontanaménto nm removal, distance, estrangement.
allontanàre vt to remove, send away; -rsi vr to go away, withdraw.
allóra ad then, at that time.
allorché cj when.
allòro nm laurel.
allucinàre vt to hallucinate; -rsi vr to suffer from hallucination, deceive oneself.
allucinazióne nf hallucination.
allúdere vi to allude, refer, hint.
allumínio nm aluminum.
allungàre vt to lengthen, prolong; (wine etc) water; hand; -rsi vr to grow longer, stretch oneself.
allusióne nf allusion.
almanaccàre vi to fancy, build castles in the air, puzzle one's brain.
almanàcco pl -àcchi nm almanac, calendar.
alméno ad at least.
àlno nm alder-tree.
alóne nm halo.
alpèstre a mountainous, wild.
Àlpi (le) nf pl the Alps pl.
alpigiàno nm inhabitant of a hilly district, mountaineer.
alpinísmo nm mountaineering.
alpíno a alpine; A. nm soldier of a special Italian alpine division.

alquànto a some, a good deal; ad somewhat, rather.
Alsàzia nf (geogr) Alsace.
alsaziàno a nm Alsatian.
alt interj halt, stop.
altaléna nf swing, seesaw.
altaménte ad highly, greatly.
altàre nm altar; a. maggióre high altar.
alteràre vt to alter, change; -rsi vr to get angry, go bad.
alterazióne nf change, deterioration, falsification.
altercare vi to quarrel.
alterézza, alterigia nf haughtiness, pride, insolence.
alternàre vt to alternate.
alternatíva nf alternative, alternation.
alternativaménte ad alternately, alternatively.
alternatívo a alternate, alternative.
altèro a dignified, proud, haughty.
altézza nf height; (of cloth) width; depth; highness; A. Reàle Royal Highness.
altezzóso a haughty, arrogant.
altíccio a tipsy.
altipiàno nm plateau, tableland.
altitúdine nf altitude, height.
àlto a high, tall, loud, deep; (of cloth) wide; (geogr) upper, northern; ad àlta vóce aloud.
Àlto Àdige nm (geogr) South Tyrol.
àlto-atesíno a nm South-Tyrolese.
altofórno nm blast furnace.
altolocàto a high-ranking, important.
altoparlànte nm loudspeaker.
altresí cj likewise, too.
altrettànto ad equally, as much (again); interj the same to you!
àltri pron sing and pl someone, another, some pl.
altrièri, l' ad the day before yesterday.
altriménti ad otherwise.
àltro pron and a (an)other, different, next; (something) else; interj not at all!; per a. anyhow.
altrónde, d' ad besides, on the other hand.
altróve ad elsewhere, somewhere else.
altrúi pron others, other people pl; a. of other people; l'a. nm other people's property.
altúra nf height, elevation.
alúnno nm pupil, schoolboy.
alveàre nm beehive.
àlveo nm channel, bed of a river.
alzàre vt to raise, lift, build; a. le càrte to cut the cards; a. le spàlle to shrug one's shoulders; -rsi vr to get up, rise.
alzàta nf rise, elevation, shrug.
amàbile a amiable, kind, agreeable.
amabilità nf amiability, kindness.
amalgamàre vt to amalgamate.

amànte *a* loving, fond; *nmf* lover, sweetheart.

amàre *vt* to love, like, be fond of.

amareggiáre *vt* to embitter; -rsi *vr* to grow bitter.

amarèna *nf* sour black cherry.

amarézza *nf* bitterness, grief.

amàro *a* bitter, grievous, cruel.

amarràre *vt* to moor.

amatóre *nm* -**tríce** *nf* lover; amateur.

amàzzone *nf* Amazon, horsewoman.

ambascería *nf* embassy, deputation, diplomatic mission.

ambàscia *nf* shortness of breath, anxiety.

ambasciàta *nf* embassy, message.

ambasciatóre *nm* -**tríce** *nf* ambassador.

ambedúe *pron and a pl* both (of).

ambiènte *nm* atmosphere, circle, environment, room.

ambiguità *nf* ambiguity, doubt.

ambíguo *a* ambiguous, doubtful.

àmbio *nm* amble.

ambíre *vt* to long for, covet.

ambizióne *nf* ambition, love of finery, vanity.

ambizióso *a* ambitious, vain, fond of finery.

àmbra *nf* amber.

Ambrógio *nm pr* Ambrose; **ambrosiàno** *a* Ambrosian.

ambulànte *a* walking, itinerant.

ambulànza *nf* ambulance.

ambulatòrio *nm* out-patients' department, first-aid post.

Ambúrgo *nf (geogr)* Hamburg.

àmen *nm* amen.

amenità *nf* amenity, agreeableness.

amèno *a* pleasant, agreeable.

Amèrica *nf* America.

americàna *nf* cycle relay race.

americàno *a nm* American.

ametísta *nf* amethyst.

amíca *nf* (woman) friend.

amichévole *a* friendly, amiable.

amicízia *nf* friendship.

amíco *pl* -**íci** *a* friendly; *nm* friend, boy-friend.

àmido *nm* starch.

Amlèto *nm pr* Hamlet.

ammaccàre *vt* to bruise, crush; -rsi *vr* to get bruised.

ammaestraménto *nm* teaching, instruction, training of animals.

ammaestràre *vt* to teach, instruct; (*animals*) train, tame.

ammainàre *vt* (*sails*) to strike; (*flag*) haul down, lower.

ammalàre *vi* -**rsi** *vr* to fall sick, sicken.

ammalàto *a* sick, ill; *nm* patient.

ammaliàre *vt* to bewitch.

ammànco *pl* -**chi** *nm* shortage, deficit.

ammanettàre *vt* to handcuff.

ammansàre, ammansíre *vt* to make tame, gentle; -rsi *vr* to grow tame, gentle.

ammantàre *vt* to mantle, cover, hide, disguise.

ammaràre *vi* (*av*) to alight (on water).

ammassàre *vt* to amass, heap up; -rsi *vr* to come together, crowd.

ammàsso *nm* heap, accumulation, (*com*) pool.

ammattíre *vi* to go mad.

ammazzàre *vt* to kill, murder; -rsi *vr* to kill oneself; (*fig*) toil hard.

ammazzasètte *nm* braggart, bully.

ammazzatóio *nm* slaughter-house.

ammènda *nf* amends *pl*, fine.

ammendàre *vt* to amend, reform; -rsi *vr* to improve, get better.

ammennícolo *nm* gadget, trinket, trifle, pretext, cavil.

amméttere *vt* to admit, allow, receive.

ammezzàre *vt* to halve.

ammezzàto *nm* mezzanine.

ammiccàre *vt* to wink, beckon, (*with the eyes*) make a signal.

amministràre *vt* to administer, rule.

amministratívo *a* administrative.

amministrazióne *nf* administration, government, trusteeship.

ammiràbile *a* admirable, wonderful.

ammiragliàto *nm* admiralty.

ammiràglio *nm* admiral.

ammiràre *vt* to admire.

ammirazióne *nf* admiration, wonder.

ammissíbile *a* admissible.

ammissióne *nf* admission; tàssa d'a. entrance fee.

ammobiliàre *vt* to furnish.

ammòdo *a* nice-mannered, respectable; *ad* nicely, carefully.

ammogliàre *vt* to give a wife to; -rsi *vr* to take a wife.

ammollàre *vt* to steep, soften; -rsi *vr* to be soaked, get wet.

ammollíre *vt* to soften, move (to compassion); -rsi *vr* to get soft.

ammoníaca *nf* ammonia.

ammoniménto *nm* admonition, warning.

ammoníre *vt* to admonish, warn, advise.

ammonizióne *nf* admonition, reproof, warning.

ammontàre *nm* (*com*) amount; *vt* to heap; *vi* to amount; -rsi *vr* to accumulate.

ammorbidíre *vt* to soften; -rsi *vr* to grow soft.

ammortíre *vt* to weaken, deaden.

ammortizzare *vt* to deaden; (*debt*) redeem.

ammorzàre *vt* to extinguish, put out.

ammostàre *vt* (*grapes*) to press.

ammostatóio *nm* wine-press.

ammucchiàre *vt* to heap up.

ammuffíre *vi* to grow stale.

ammutinaménto *nm* mutiny, revolt.

ammutinàrsi *vr* to mutiny, revolt.

amnesía *nf* amnesia.

amnistía *nf* amnesty.
àmo *nm* fish-hook; **abboccàre all'a** to take the bait; (*fig*) to swallow the bait.
amóre *nm* love, affection; **a. pròprio** self-esteem; **per a. di** for the sake of; **fàre all'a.** to make love.
amoreggiàre *vt* to flirt.
amorétto *nm* flirtation, love affair.
amorévole *a* loving, kind.
amoríno *nm* Cupid, little darling; (*bot*) mignonette.
amorosaménte *ad* lovingly.
amoróso *a* loving; *nm* lover, gallant.
ampiézza *nf* ampleness.
àmpio *a* ample, wide, spacious.
amplèsso *nm* embrace.
ampliàre *vt* to enlarge, extend; **-rsi** *vr* to become larger, extend.
amplificàre *vt* to amplify, exaggerate.
amplificatóre *nm* amplifier.
amplitúdine *nf* amplitude.
ampólla *nf* phial, ampoule.
ampollosità *nf* bombast.
ampollóso *a* bombastic.
amputàre *vt* to amputate.
amputazióne *nf* amputation.
amuléto *nm* amulet, talisman.
anabbagliànte *a* anti-glare.
anacorèta *nm* anchorite, hermit.
anacronísmo *nm* anachronism.
anàgrafe *nf* registry office.
analfabèta *a nmf* illiterate.
analfabetísmo *nm* illiteracy.
anàlisi *nf* analysis.
analizzàre *vt* to analyze.
analogía *nf* analogy.
ananàsso *nm* pineapple.
anarchía *nf* anarchy.
anàrchico *pl* **-ici** *a nm* anarchic, anarchist.
anatomía *nf* anatomy.
anatòmico *pl* **-ici** *a* anatomic(al); *nm* anatomist.
anatomizzàre *vt* to anatomize, dissect.
ànatra *nf* duck.
ànca *nf* hip, haunch.
ànche *ad* also, too, even.
àncora *nf* anchor.
ancóra *ad* yet, still, again, even, more, longer.
ancoràggio *nm* anchorage.
ancoràre *vi* to anchor.
andaménto *nm* gait, carriage, trend.
andànte *a* current, common, cheap, plain; (*style*) flowing; **artícolo a.** cheap article.
andàre *vi* to go, call on, proceed; please, suit, happen; **a. a pièdi** to go on foot; *nm* going, gait; **a lúngo a.** in the long run; **andàrsene** to go away.
andàta *nf* going; **a. e ritórno** (going) there and back; **bigliétto di a.** single ticket.
andatúra *nf* gait.
andàzzo *nm* trend, passing fashion.
Ànde (le) *nf pl* (*geogr*) the Andes *pl*.

andirivièni *nm pl* coming and going of people, digressions, windings *pl*.
àndito *nm* passage, entrance.
Andrèa *nm pr* Andrew.
andróne *nm* portal, entrance (hall).
anèddoto *nm* anecdote.
anelàre *vi* to long for, pant, be breathless.
anèllo *nm* ring, ringlet, thimble; (*of a chain*) link.
anemía *nf* anemia.
anèmico *pl* **-ici** *a* anemic.
anestètico *pl* **-ici** *a nm* anesthetic.
anfíbio *a* amphibious; *nm* amphibian.
anfiteàtro *nm* amphitheatre.
anfràtto *nm* ravine, gorge.
angariàre *vt* to vex, harass, ill-treat.
Àngela *nf pr* Angela.
angèlico *pl* **-ici** *a* angelic.
àngelo *nm* angel.
angheria *nf* vexation, oppression, ill-treatment.
angína *nf* angina, quinsy.
angipòrto *nm* blind alley.
anglicàno *a nm* Anglican.
anglosàssone *a nmf* Anglo-Saxon; British and American.
angolàre *a* angular.
àngolo *nm* angle, corner.
angòscia *nf* anguish, affliction.
angoscióso *a* afflicted, grievous.
anguílla *nf* eel; elusive, nimble person.
angúria *nf* water-melon.
angústia *nf* narrowness; want, distress.
angustiàre *vt* to grieve, vex, harass; **-rsi** *vr* to be distressed, be afflicted.
angústo *a* narrow.
ànice *nm* aniseed.
ànima *nf* soul, spirit, person.
animàle *a nm* animal.
animàre *vt* to animate, enliven; **-rsi** *vr* to grow animated, take courage, get excited.
animàto *a* living, lively, animated; **cartóne a.** animated cartoon.
animèlla *nf* sweetbread.
ànimo *nm* mind, heart, courage; **fàrsi a.** to pluck up courage; **pèrdersi d'a.** to lose heart.
animosità *nf* animosity.
animóso *a* courageous, valiant.
anisétta *nm* anisette.
ànitra *nf* duck.
anitròccolo *nm* duckling.
Ànna *nf pr* Anna, Anne, Ann.
annacquàre *vt* to water, dilute; (*fig*) moderate.
annaffiàre *vt* to water, sprinkle.
annaffiatóio *nm* watering-can.
annàli *nm pl* annals *pl*.
annàta *nf* year; year's profits *pl*, produce *etc*.
annebbiàre *vt* to cloud, dim, darken; **-rsi** *vr* to grow dim, be overcast.
annegàre *vt* to drown; *vi* to be drowned; **-rsi** *vr* to drown oneself.

anneríre *vt* to blacken, tarnish.
annessióne *nf* annexation.
annèsso *a* attached, annexed; *nm* annex.
annèttere *vt* to annex.
annichilíre *vt* to annihilate; (*fig*) dismay.
annidàrsi *vr* to nestle, nest, hide.
annientaménto *nm* annihilation, destruction.
annientàre *vt* to annihilate, destroy; **-rsi** *vr* to come to nothing; (*fig*) abase oneself.
anniversàrio *a nm* anniversary.
ànno *nm* year; **capo d'a.** New Year ('s Day).
annodàre *vt* to knot; **a. amicízie** to make friends.
annoiàre *vt* to bore, vex, tire; **-rsi** *vr* to get tired, be bored.
annòna *nf* victuals *pl*, provisions *pl*.
annonàrio *a* connected with provisions.
annóso *a* old, ancient.
annotàre *vt* to note, annotate.
annotazióne *nf* annotation, note.
annottàre *vi* **-rsi** *vr* to grow dark.
annoveràre *vt* to number, count.
annuàle *a* annual, yearly.
annualità *nf* annuity.
annuàrio *nm* annual, trade directory; (*of members*) list.
annuíre *vi* to nod.
annuità *nf* yearly installment.
annullaménto *nm* annulment, repeal.
annullàre *vt* to repeal, annul.
annunciàre, annunziàre *vt* to announce, predict.
annunciazióne *nf* annunciation; **fèsta dell'A.** Lady Day.
annúncio, annúnzio *nm* announcement, advertisement.
Annunziàta *nf* Our Lady of the Annunciation.
ànnuo *a* annual, yearly.
annusàre *vi* to sniff, smell.
anodíno *a nm* anodyne.
ànodo *nm* (*el*) anode.
anomalía *nf* anomaly.
anòmalo *a* anomalous.
anònimo *a* anonymous.
anormàle *a* abnormal.
anormalità *nf* abnormality.
ànsa *nf* handle.
ansàre *vi* to pant.
ànsia *nf* anxiety.
ansietà *nf* anxiety, anxiousness.
ansimàre *vi* to pant.
ansióso *a* anxious, eager.
antagoníşmo *nm* antagonism.
antagonísta *nmf* antagonist, opponent.
antàrtico *pl* **-ici** *a* antarctic.
antecedènte *a nm* antecedent.
antecedènza *nf* precedence, priority.
antecessóre *nm* predecessor.
antefàtto *nm* preceding event.
anteguèrra *a* pre-war; *nm* pre-war times *pl*.

antemuràle *nm* rampart, bulwark.
antenàto *nm* ancestor.
anténna *nf* feeler, aerial, antenna; **a. d'emissióne** transmitting aerial; **a. di ricezióne** receiving aerial.
antepórre *vt* to put before, prefer.
antepríma *nf* preview.
anterióre *a* prior, former, fore(most).
antiabbagliànte *a* anti-glare.
antiaèreo *a* (*mil*) anti-aircraft.
antibiòtico *pl* **-ici** *a nm* antibiotic.
anticàglia *nf* old rubbish, old curiosity.
anticàmera *nf* anteroom, hall.
anticàrro *a* (*mil*) anti-tank.
antichità *nf* antiquity.
anticipàre *vt* to anticipate, pay in advance, forestall; *vi* arrive earlier.
anticipazióne *nf* anticipation, advance payment.
anticipo *nm* advance, earnest; (*aut*) spark advance.
anticlericàle *a nmf* anti-clerical.
antico *pl* **-ichi** *a* ancient, antique, obsolete.
anticomunísta *a nmf* anti-communist.
antidiluviàno *a* antediluvian.
antídoto *nm* antidote.
antifascísta *a nmf* antifascist.
antifúrto *a nm* antitheft.
antílope *nm* antelope.
antimeridiàno *a* antemeridian.
antimilitaríşmo *nm* antimilitarism.
antipàsto *nm* hors d'œuvres *pl*.
antipatía *nf* antipathy, dislike.
antipàtico *pl* **-ici** *a* unpleasant, disagreeable.
antipodi *nm pl* Antipodes.
antipòrta *nf* outer door.
antiquàrio *nm* antiquarian.
antiquàto *a* antiquated, old-fashioned, out-of-date.
antisemita *nmf* anti-Semite.
antisemítico *pl* **-ici** *a* anti-Semitic.
antisemitíşmo *nm* anti-Semitism.
antisèttico *pl* **-ici** *a nm* antiseptic.
antistànte *a* before, in front of.
antivigília *nf* the day before the eve.
antología *nf* anthology.
Antònia *nf pr* Antonia.
Antònio *nm pr* Ant(h)ony.
antracíte *nf* anthracite.
àntro *nm* cave, den.
antropòfago *pl* **-gi, -ghi** *a nm* man-eater, cannibal.
antropología *nf* anthropology.
anulàre *nm* ring finger.
Anvérsa *nf* (*geogr*) Antwerp.
ànzi *prep* before; *cj* rather, on the contrary.
anzianità *nf* seniority.
anziàno *a* elderly, old, senior; *nm* elder.
anziché *cj* instead of, rather than.
apatía *nf* apathy.
apàtico *pl* **-ici** *a* apathetic.
àpe *nf* bee.
aperitívo *nm* aperitif.

apèrto a open, frank; **all'a.** in the open air; ad frankly.
apertúra nf aperture, opening, hole, span.
apiàrio nm beehive.
àpice nm apex, top, summit.
apocalísse nf Apocalypse.
apòcrifo a apocryphal.
apogèo nm apogee, acme.
apòlide a nmf stateless (person).
apolítico pl -**ici** a non-political.
apología nf apology.
apòlogo pl -**ghi** nm apologue.
apoplessía nf apoplexy.
apoplèttico pl -**ici** a apoplectic.
apòstata nmf apostate.
apostolàto nm apostleship.
apostòlico pl -**ici** a apostolic.
apòstolo nm apostle.
appagàre vt to satisfy, content; -**rsi** vr to be satisfied.
appaiàre vt to pair, match, couple; -**rsi** vr to pair, unite.
appallottolàre vt to roll into a ball; -**rsi** vr to coil up.
appaltàre vt to let out or lease out, farm.
appàlto nm undertaking, contract.
appannàggio nm appanage, inheritance.
appannàre vt to tarnish, dim; -**rsi** vr to grow dim, tarnish.
apparàto nm apparatus, adornment, pomp; (theat) scenery.
apparecchiàre vt to prepare, furnish, lay the cloth; -**rsi** vr to get ready.
apparécchio nm receiver (telephone) apparatus, set; airplane; **a. cinematogràfico** (film) projector; **a. fotogràfico** camera; **a. trasmitténte** transmitting set; **a. televisívo** television set.
apparènte a obvious, visible.
apparènza nf appearance; **in a.** apparently.
apparíre vi to appear, show oneself.
appariscènte a gorgeous.
appariscènza nf appearance, showiness.
apparizióne nf apparition, vision.
appartaménto nm flat, apartment; **a. ammobiliàto** furnished flat.
appartàre vt to set apart, separate; -**rsi** vr to withdraw, retire.
appartàto a secluded, remote, solitary.
appartenére vi to belong, concern.
appassionàre vt to move, excite; -**rsi** vr to be excited, eager (about).
appassionàto a eager, enthusiastic.
appassíre vi to fade, wither.
appellàre vt to call, name; -**rsi** to appeal.
appèllo nm appeal, roll-call; **fare l'a.** to call the roll.
appéna ad hardly, scarcely.
appèndere vt to hang up.
appendíce nf appendix, addition.
appendicite nf appendicitis.
Appenníni nm pl (geogr) the Apennines.

appesantíre vt to make heavy, weigh down; -**rsi** vr to become heavier, stouter.
appetíre vt to long for, desire.
appetito nm appetite, strong desire; **avére a.** to be hungry.
appetitóso a appetizing, tempting.
appianaménto nm leveling.
appianàre vt to level, smooth.
appiattàre vt to flatten, conceal; -**rsi** vr to squat down, hide oneself.
appiccàre vt to join, hang (up), start; infect; -**rsi** vr to cling.
appiccicàre vt to stick; -**rsi** vr to stick together, hang on.
appiccicatíccio a sticky.
appiccicóso a sticky.
appiè ad at the foot, at the bottom.
appièno ad fully, completely.
appigionàre vt to let, rent, (house) lease.
appigliàrsi vt to cling to, hold on to; (advice etc) follow.
appíglio nm pretext.
appiómbo ad perpendicularly; nm perpendicularity; self assurance.
appisolàrsi vr to doze off.
applaudíre vt to applaud.
applàuso nm applause.
applicàre vt to apply, enforce, appoint; -**rsi** vr to apply oneself, study.
appoggiàre vt to lean, prop, support; -**rsi** vr to lean against, depend upon, trust.
appoggiàto a leaning, supported.
appòggio nm prop, support, favor.
appollaiàrsi vr to roost, perch.
appórre vt to affix, insert; (fig) impute.
apportàre vt to bring, cause.
appòsito a special, suitable.
appòsta ad on purpose.
appostaménto nm ambush, (mil) emplacement.
appostàre vt to waylay; -**rsi** vr to lurk.
apprèndere vt to learn, get to know.
apprendísta nmf apprentice.
apprendistàto nm apprenticeship.
apprensióne nf apprehension.
apprensívo a apprehensive, fearful, quick to perceive.
apprèsso prep near, by, after, behind; ad close by, shortly after.
apprestàre vt to prepare; -**rsi** vr to get ready.
apprezzaménto nm appreciation, estimate, appraisement.
apprezzàre vt to value, rate, appreciate.
appròccio nm approach.
approdàre vi to come to shore, land.
appròdo nm landing place.
approfittàre vi to profit; -**rsi** vr to avail oneself, take advantage.
approfondàre, -díre vt to dig, deepen, search out, go into thoroughly.
appropriàre vt to use properly,

adapt; -rsi *vr* to appropriate to oneself.

approssimàre *vt* to place near; -rsi *vr* to approach. draw near.

approssimatívo *a* approximate, rough.

approvàre *vt* to approve, pass.

approvazióne *nf* approval.

approvvigionàre *vt* to victual, provision.

appuntaménto *nm* appointment.

appuntàre *vt* to point, sharpen, pin, tack, blame.

appuntíno *ad* just in time, exactly, neatly.

appúnto *nm* note; *ad* precisely, exactly.

appuràre *vt* to verify, ascertain; (*com*) clear.

apribottíglie *nm* bottle-opener.

apríle *nm* April.

apríre *vt* to open, unlock, split, disclose, begin; -rsi *vr* to open, expand; (*weather*) clear.

apriscàtole *nm* tin-opener, canopener.

aquàrio *nm* aquarium.

àquila *nf* eagle; (*fig*) genius.

aquilóne *nm* north wind; (*toy*) kite.

Aquisgràna *nf* (*geogr*) Aachen.

Aràbia *nf* Arabia.

aràbico *pl* -ici *a* Arabic, Arabian.

àrabo *a* Arab, Arabian; *nm* Arabic, Arab.

aragósta *nf* lobster.

aràldica *nf* heraldry.

aràldo *nm* herald, harbinger.

arància *nf* orange.

aranciàta *nf* orangeade.

aràncio *a nm* orange, orange (tree).

aranción e *a nm* (*color*) orange.

aràre *vt* to plow, cultivate.

aratóre *nm* plowman.

aràtro *nm* plow.

aràzzo *nm* tapestry.

arbitràggio *nm* speculation on the exchange; umpiring.

arbitràre *vi* to arbitrate, umpire, referee; -rsi *vr* to take the liberty (to do).

arbitràrio *a* arbitrary.

arbitràto *nm* arbitration.

arbítrio *nm* will, absolute power.

àrbitro *nm* arbiter, umpire, referee.

arbòreo *a* arboreal.

arboréto *nm* grove.

arboscèllo *nm* small tree, shrub.

arbústo *nm* shrub.

àrca *nf* chest, coffer, tomb; **a. di Noè** Noah's Ark.

arcàico *pl* -ici *a* archaic.

arcaísmo *nm* archaism.

arcàngelo *nm* archangel.

arcàno *a* secret, mysterious; *nm* mystery.

arcàta *nf* archway, arcade.

archeología *nf* archaeology.

archeològico *pl* -ici *a* archaeological.

archeòlogo *pl* -gi, -ghi *nm* archaeologist.

archétto *nm* small arch; (violin) bow.

architettàre *vt* to draw the plan of; (*fig*) plot, contrive.

architétto *nm* architect.

architettúra *nf* architecture.

archívio *nm* archives *pl*, record office.

archivísta *nmf* archivist.

Arcibàldo *nm pr* Archibald.

arcidúca *nm* archduke.

arciduchéssa *nf* archduchess.

arcière *nm* archer.

arcígno *a* gruff, surly.

arcipèlago *pl* -ghi *nm* archipelago.

arciprète *nm* (*eccl*) dean.

arcivescovàdo *nm* archbishopric.

arcivèscovo *nm* archbishop.

àrco *pl* -chi *nm* bow, arch.

arcobaléno *nm* rainbow.

arcuàto *a* arched, bent.

ardènte *a* burning, ardent, eager, spirited.

àrdere *vi* to burn, glow, be on fire, shine.

ardèşia *nf* slate.

ardiménto *nm* boldness, daring.

ardíre *vi* to dare, be bold; *nm* daring, valor.

arditézza *nf* daring, hardihood.

ardíto *a* daring, hardy, bold.

ardóre *nm* ardour, enthusiasm, passion.

àrduo *a* arduous, difficult, dangerous.

àrea *nf* area, surface.

aréna *nf* sand, amphitheatre.

arenàre *vi* to run aground; -rsi *vr* to stick fast, be in difficulties.

argentàre *vt* to silver, silver plate.

argentàto *a* silvery, silver, silverplated.

argentatúra *nf* silver-plating; **a. galvànica** electroplating.

argentería *nf* silverware.

argentiére *nm* silversmith.

Argentína *nf* Argentina.

argentíno *a nm* Argentine.

argentíno *a* silvery.

argènto *nm* silver; **a. vívo** mercury, quicksilver.

argentóne *nm* German silver, nickel silver.

argílla *nf* argil, potter's clay.

argillóso *a* clayey.

arginàre *vt* to dam, dike, embank; (*fig*) stem.

àrgine *nm* bank, embankment, dam (*also fig*).

argomentàre *vt* to argue, reason.

argoménto *nm* argument, subject, topic, occasion, synopsis.

arguíre *vi* to infer.

argutézza *nf* finesse, quibble, witticism.

argúto *a* subtle, witty, ingenious.

argúzia *nf* subtlety, piquancy, joke.

ària *nf* air, wind, appearance, song; **all'a. apèrta** out-of-doors.

aridità *nf* aridity, barrenness.

àrido *a* arid, barren, dry.

arieggiàre vt to air; vi to resemble.
arínga nf herring; **a. affumicàta** kipper, smoked herring.
arióso a airy.
aristocràtico pl **-ici** a aristocratic; nm aristocrat.
aristocrazía nf aristocracy.
aritmètica nf arithmetic.
aritmètico pl **-ici** a arithmetical; nm arithmetician.
arlecchíno nm harlequin, buffoon.
àrma nf weapon; (mil) branch, service; coat of arms.
armacòllo, ad ad in a sling.
armàdio nm cupboard, wardrobe.
armaiuòlo nm gunsmith, armorer.
armaménto nm armament, arming, weapons pl.
armàre vt to arm, equip, provide; **-rsi** vr to arm oneself, take up arms.
armàta nf army, navy; **corpo d'a.** army corps.
armàto a armed, equipped; (el) armored; (building) reinforced; **a màno armàta** by force of arms.
armatúra nf armor, armoring, framework; (el) armature.
Armènia nf (geogr) Armenia.
armèno a nm Armenian.
arménto nm herd of cattle.
armistízio nm armistice.
armonía nf harmony, concord.
armonizzàre vt to harmonize.
Arnàldo nm pr Arnold.
arnése nm tool, utensil.
àrnia nf beehive.
aròma nf aroma, fragrance.
àrpa nf harp.
arpeggiàre vi to play the harp, play in arpeggios.
arpía nf harpy.
arpióne nm hook, hinge.
àrra nf earnest money, pledge.
arrabbiàre vt to make angry; **-rsi** to get angry.
arrabbiàto a furious; rabid.
arrampicàrsi vr to climb.
arrecàre vt to bring, cause.
arredaménto nm furnishings.
arredàre vt to fit out, furnish.
arrèdo nm furniture, furnishings.
arrèndersi vr to surrender, yield, submit.
arrestàre vt to stop, seize, arrest; **-rsi** vr to stop.
arrèsto nm arrest, stop, pause; **in a.** under arrest.
arretràre vt to pull back, withdraw; **-rsi** vr to draw back, recoil.
arretràto a backward; (com) outstanding, in arrears; nm (also pl) arrears pl.
arricchíre vt to enrich, embellish; vi **-rsi** vr to grow rich, thrive.
arricchíto nm profiteer, nouveau riche.
arricciàre vt to curl; **a. il nàso** to frown, show disgust.
arrídere vi to smile upon.
Arrígo nm pr Henry.

arrínga nf harangue, speech.
arringàre vi to harangue.
arrischiàre vt to risk, hazard; **-rsi** vr to venture, dare.
arrischiàto a risky, venturesome, rash.
arrivàre vi to arrive; (fig) to achieve, succeed, happen, understand, fit, be reduced to.
arrivàto a successful; nm a successful man.
arrivedérci(-la) interj goodbye.
arrivísmo nm social climbing.
arrivista nmf social climber, gogetter.
arrívo nm arrival.
arrochíre vt to make hoarse; **-rsi** vr become hoarse.
arrogànte a arrogant, overbearing.
arrogànza nf arrogance.
arrolàre vt to enroll, register; **-rsi** vr to enroll oneself, enlist.
arrossíre vi to blush, be ashamed.
arrostíre vt to roast, toast.
arròsto nm roast meat.
arrotàre vt to whet, grind, wear smooth.
arrotíno nm knife-grinder.
arrotolàre vt to roll up.
arrotondàre vt to round; **-rsi** vr to become round, plump.
arrovellàrsi vr to get angry, worry.
arroventàre vt to make red-hot.
arrovesciàre vt to turn inside out, overthrow; **-rsi** vr to capsize, turn over.
arrovèscio, a rovèscio ad against the grain, on the wrong side, the reverse way.
arruffàre vt to ruffle, tousle, confuse; **-rsi** vr to get ruffled, confused.
arruginíre vi **-rsi** vr to rust, grow rusty.
arsèlla nf mussel.
arsenàle nm arsenal.
arsènico nm arsenic.
àrso a burnt, dried up.
arsúra nf burning heat, drought, thirst.
àrte nf art, skill, profession, artifice.
artéfice nm artificer, artisan, creator.
artèria nf artery; thoroughfare.
àrtico pl **-ici** a arctic, northern.
articolàre vt to articulate, pronounce; a articular.
articolàto a articulate; jointed, hinged.
artícolo nm article; **a. di fóndo** (in newspapers) leading article, leader, editorial; **articoli sportívi** pl sports goods, sporting goods.
artificiàle a artificial.
artifício nm artifice, contrivance, cunning.
artificióso a artful, crafty, sly.
artigianàto nm artisans pl, handicraft, small industry.
artigiàno a (of an) artisan; nm artisan, craftsman.
artiglière nm gunner, artilleryman.

artiglieria nf (mil) artillery.
artiglio nm claw, talon, clutch.
artista nmf artist, artiste, actor, actress, singer.
artistico pl -ici a artistic.
àrto nm (anat) limb.
Artúro nm pr Arthur.
arzigogolàre vt to cavil, follow a fantastic argument.
arzigògolo nm cavil, whim.
arzillo a sprightly, nimble.
ascèlla nf armpit.
ascendènte a ascending, ascendant, -ent; nm ascendency, ascendant, ancestor.
ascendènza nf ancestors pl; ascendancy.
ascéndere vi to ascend, rise; amount to.
ascensióne nf ascent, ascension, Ascension Day.
ascensóre nm lift, elevator.
ascésa nf ascent, accession.
ascèsso nm abscess.
ascèta nm ascetic, recluse.
ascètico pl -ici a ascetic.
ascetismo nm asceticism.
àscia nf axe, hatchet.
asciugacapélli nm hair-drier.
asciugamàno nm towel.
asciugàre vt to dry, wipe.
asciugatríce (automàtica) nf spin-drier.
asciútto a dry, thin, penniless; all'a. in a dry place; restàre all'a. to be without money, news etc.
ascoltàre vt to listen, hear, attend; (med) sound.
ascoltatóre nm -tríce nf listener, hearer.
ascoltazióne nf, **ascólto** nm listening, hearing; (med) auscultation; stàre in ascólto to listen; dàre ascólto to lend an ear.
asfàlto nm asphalt.
asfissía nf asphyxia.
asfissiàre vt to asphyxiate.
Àsia nf Asia.
asiàtico pl -ici a nm Asiatic, Asian.
asilo nm refuge.
asinàta nf foolish action, foolish remark.
asinería nf stupidity, foolish action, foolish remark.
àsino nm ass.
àsma nf asthma.
asmàtico pl -ici a asthmatic.
àsola nf buttonhole.
aspàrago pl -gi nm asparagus.
aspèrgere vt to sprinkle.
asperità nf asperity, harshness.
aspettàre vt to wait for, await; -rsi vr to expect, look for.
aspettativa nf expectation, hope; temporary discharge; in a. ad on the reserve list.
aspettazióne nf expectation.
aspètto nm aspect, appearance, look; sàla d'a. nf waiting room.

aspirànte a aspiring to, sucking up; nmf candidate, competitor.
aspirapólvere nm vacuum cleaner.
aspiràre vt to inhale, suck up; vi aspire to, be a candidate for.
aspirína nf aspirin.
asportàbile a removable.
asportàre vi to remove, extirpate.
asportazióne nf removal.
asprézza nf bitterness, harshness, roughness, sharpness.
asprigno a sourish.
àspro a bitter, rough, sharp, severe, hard.
assaggiàre vt to sample, taste, try.
assàggio nm trial, testing, sampling.
assài nm plenty; ad much, very, enough.
assalíre vt to assail, attack.
assaltàre vt to assault, attack.
assàlto nm assault, attack, onset.
assaporàre vt to savor, taste; (fig) to relish.
assassinàre vt to assassinate, murder.
assassínio nm assassination, murder.
assassíno nm assassin, murderer.
àsse nm axis; nf board, plank.
assecondàre vt to favor, support.
assediàre vt to besiege, crowd round.
assèdio nm siege; (fig) pestering.
assegnaménto nm assignment, allotment; reliance.
assegnàre vt to allow, assign, award, fix.
assegnazióne nf assignment, allotment.
asségno nm allowance, check; a. bancàrio (com) draft; a. postàle money order.
assemblèa nf assembly, meeting.
assembraménto nm throng, concourse, assembling.
assembràre vt to assemble; -rsi vr to assemble.
assennatézza nf commonsense, wisdom, prudence.
assennàto a sensible, wise, prudent.
assènso nm assent, consent.
assènte a absent; nmf absentee.
assentíre vi to assent, consent, approve.
assènza nf absence.
assènzio nm absinthe.
asseríre vt to assert, affirm.
asserragliàre vt to barricade; -rsi vr to barricade oneself.
asserzióne nf assertion, declaration.
assessóre nm assessor, magistrate.
assestaménto, assèsto nm arrangement, settlement.
assestàre vt to arrange, settle, set in order, adjust; deliver (a blow).
assetàto a thirsty, dry, eager.
assettàre vt to arrange, trim, put in order; -rsi vr to adorn oneself, tidy oneself up.
assètto nm good order, trim; méttere in a. to put in order, trim.
asseveràre vi to assert, affirm, declare.

assicuràre *vt* to secure, assure, declare, insure; (*post*) register; -rsi *vr* to fasten oneself, secure for oneself, make sure, insure oneself.

assicurazióne *nf* assurance, insurance, pledge.

assideraménto *nm* **assiderazióne** *nf* frostbite.

assideràre *vt* to chill, benumb; *vi* be benumbed, freeze.

assiduità *nf* assiduity, diligence.

assíduo *a* assiduous, diligent.

assième *ad* together.

assilláre *vt* to urge; harass.

assimiláre *vt* to assimilate, absorb.

assimilazióne *nf* assimilation.

assíse *nf* assizes *pl*.

assistènte *nmf* attendant, assistant; **a. di vólo** air hostess.

assistènza *nf* assistance, aid, help.

assístere *vti* to assist, help; be present.

àsso *nm* ace; **piantàre in a.** to leave in the lurch.

associàre *vt* to associate, join, take into partnership; -rsi *vr* to join, become a partner, subscribe.

associazióne *nf* association.

assodàre *vt* to consolidate, harden; make sure.

assoggettàre *vt* to subject, subdue; -rsi *vr* to subject oneself, submit.

assolàto *a* exposed to the sun, sunny.

assoldàre *vt* to recruit; -rsi *vr* to enlist.

assòlto *a* acquitted, absolved, released.

assolutaménte *ad* absolutely.

assolúto *a* absolute, positive.

assoluzióne *nf* absolution, acquittal.

assòlvere *vt* to acquit, absolve, release.

assomigliàre *vt* to compare; *vi* to resemble; -rsi *vr* to be alike, resemble each other.

assonnàto *a* sleepy, drowsy.

assopíre *vt* to make sleepy, appease; -rsi *vr* to doze off.

assorbènte *a* absorbent; **càrta a.** blotting paper; **a. igiènico** *nm* sanitary towel, sanitary napkin.

assorbíre *vt* to absorb.

assordaménto, *nm* deafening.

assordànte *a* deafening.

assordàre *vt* to stun, deafen.

assordiménto *nm* deafening.

assordíre *vt* to deafen; *vi* to become deaf.

assortiménto *nm* assortment, stock.

assortíre *vt* to stock; (*fig*) to match.

assortíto *a* assorted, stocked, matched.

assòrto *a* absorbed.

assottigliàre *vt* to thin, sharpen, diminish; -rsi *vr* to grow thin, diminish.

assuefàre *vt* to accustom, inure; -rsi *vr* to grow accustomed, inured.

assúmere *vt* to assume, take on, engage, raise (to a dignity), undertake, take up.

assúnto *nm* undertaking, charge, assumption.

assunzióne *nf* assumption, accession, Assumption.

assurdità *nf* absurdity.

assúrdo *a* absurd; *nm* absurdity.

àsta *nf* pole, staff, rod, lance; (*of writing*) stroke; auction.

astànte *a* present, standing by; *nmf* bystander, spectator; **mèdico a.** doctor on duty.

astantería *nf* first-aid post.

astèmio *a* abstemious; *nm* abstainer.

astenérsi *vr* to abstain.

astensióne *nf* abstention.

astinènte *a* abstinent.

astinènza *nf* abstinence.

àstio *nm* hatred, envy, grudge, spite.

astióso *a* rancorous, spiteful.

astràrre *vt* to abstract; -rsi *vr* to turn one's mind from.

astràtto *a* abstract, abstracted; *nm* abstract.

astrazióne *nf* abstraction, absent-mindedness.

astringènte *a* astringent.

àstro *nm* star.

astrología *nf* astrology.

astrològico *pl* -ici *a* astrological.

astròlogo *pl* -gi, -ghi *nm* astrologer.

astronàuta *nm* astronaut.

astronàutica *nf* astronautics.

astronomía *nf* astronomy.

astronòmico *pl* -ici *a* astronomical.

astrònomo *nm* astronomer.

astrúşo *a* abstruse, obscure.

astúccio *nm* box, case, sheath.

astutèzza *nf* astuteness, cunning.

astúto *a* crafty, cunning, deceitful.

astúzia *nf* astuteness, artfulness, trick.

ateíşmo *nm* atheism.

Atène *nf* Athens; **atenièse** *a* *nmf* Athenian.

atenèo *nm* athenaeum, university.

àteo *a* atheistic; *nm* atheist.

atlànte *nm* atlas.

atlàntico *pl* -ici *a* gigantic, Atlantic; *nm* (*geogr*) the Atlantic.

atlèta *nmf* athlete.

atlètica *nf* athletics.

atlètico *a* athletic.

atmosfèra *nf* atmosphere.

atòmico *pl* -ici *a* atomic.

àtomo *nm* atom.

atonía *nf* atony.

àtono *a* unstressed.

àtrio *nm* porch, vestibule.

atróce *a* atrocious, terrible, cruel.

atrocità *nf* atrocity.

atrofía *nf* atrophy.

atrofizzàre *vt* to atrophy; -rsi *vr* to atrophy, waste away.

attaccabottóne *nm* bore, talker.

attaccabríghe *nm* wrangler.

attaccaménto *nm* attachment.

attaccapànni *nm* hatstand, coat-hanger.

attaccàre *vt* to tie, fasten, stick, sew on, attack; (*horses*) harness; hang up; *vi* take root; be contagious; **a. un bottóne** (*fig*) to buttonhole someone; **-rsi** *vr* to stick, to become attached to; quarrel.

attaccatíccio *a* sticky; (*med*) contagious; *nm* burnt taste.

attàcco *pl* **-àcchi** *nm* attack, assault; (*el*) connection, plug.

attecchíre *vi* to take root, thrive.

atteggiaménto *nm* attitude.

atteggiàre *vt* to express in gesture; **-rsi** *vr* to assume an attitude, expression, pose as.

attempàto *a* elderly.

attendàrsi *vr* to camp, pitch tents.

attendènte *nm* (*mil*) orderly, batman.

attèndere *vt* to await, expect; *vi* to wait for, attend to.

attendíbile *a* reliable.

attenérsi *vr* to conform (to).

attentàre *vt* to attempt; **-rsi** *vr* to dare.

attentàto *nm* attempt, outrage.

attènti! *interj* (*mil*) attention!

attènto *a* attentive, careful.

attenuànte *a* extenuating; *nf* extenuating circumstance.

attenuàre *vt* to attenuate, lessen, extenuate.

attenzióne *nf* care, application.

atterràggio *nm* (*av*) landing.

atterràre *vti* to knock down; (*av*) to land; (*fig*) humiliate.

atterríre *vt* to frighten, terrify; **-rsi** *vr* to become terrified.

attésa *nf* waiting, expectation, suspense.

attéso *a* awaited, expected, longed for.

attestàre *vt* to attest, testify.

attestàto *nm* attestation, certificate, proof, token.

attestazióne *nf* attestation, testimony, token.

attiguità *nf* contiguity.

attíguo *a* contiguous, adjacent, next.

attillàrsi *vr* to dress smartly, dress so as to show off one's figure.

attillàto *a* close-fitting, smartly dressed.

àttimo *nm* moment, instant.

attinènte *a* pertaining, belonging to, relating.

attinènza *nf* affinity, relation.

attíngere *vt* (*water etc*) to draw; (*information etc*) to get.

attiràre *vt* to attract, draw, entice; **-rsi** *vr* to draw upon oneself.

attitúdine *nf* aptitude, skill; attitude.

attivaménte *ad* actively, busily.

attivàre *vt* to activate, set in motion.

attivísmo *nm* activism.

attivísta *nmf* activist.

attività *nf* activity, assets *pl*.

attívo *a* active; (*com*) receivable; *nm* (*com*) assets *pl*, credit account.

attizzàre *vt* to stir up, incite.

attizzatóio *nm* poker.

àtto *a* fit, apt; *nm* act, action, deed, gesture, certificate, (*com*) bill; *pl* proceedings, minutes.

attònito *a* astonished, amazed.

attòrcere, attorcigliàre *vt* to twist, wring.

attorcigliaménto *nm* twisting.

attóre *nm* actor.

attorniàre *vt* to enclose, surround.

attórno *prep* about, around; *ad* roundabout.

attossicaménto *nm* poisoning.

attossicàre *vt* to poison.

attraènte *a* attractive.

attràrre *vt* to attract, allure.

attrattíva *nf* attraction, charm.

attraversàre *vt* to cross, pass through; thwart.

attravèrso *prep* across, through.

attrazióne *nf* attraction.

attrezzàre *vt* to equip, fit out, supply with, rig.

attrezzatúra *nf* equipment, plant, organization, rigging.

attrézzo *nm* tool, implement.

attribuíre *vt* to ascribe, attribute, assign; **-rsi** *vr* to claim.

attribúto *nm* attribute.

attríce *nf* actress.

attristàre *vt* to sadden.

attríto *nm* friction, (*fig*) dissension.

attruppàrsi *vr* to gather in crowds, flock together.

attuàbile *a* practicable, feasible.

attuàle *a* present, real, actual.

attualità *nf* actuality, present, reality.

attuàre *vt* to effect, execute, perform, realize.

attuazióne *nf* carrying out, realization.

attuffàre *vt* to immerse, plunge, dip; **-rsi** *vr* to dive, plunge into the water.

attutíre *vt* to calm, ease, deaden.

audàce *a* audacious, bold.

àudio *nm* (*tv*) sound; **a. visívo** *a* audio-visual.

auditóre *nm* hearer, junior judge.

auditòrio *nm* auditorium.

audizióne *nf* audition.

àuge *nm* apogee; **èssere in a.** *vi* to be at the zenith of one's fortune.

auguràre *vt* to wish, augur, foretell; **-rsi** *vr* to hope.

augúrio *nm* good wish, augury, omen.

augústo *a* august, royal.

àula *nf* hall, classroom.

aumentàre *vti* to augment, increase, enlarge, grow.

auménto *nm* growth, increase; (*in pay*) raise.

àureo *a* golden, gold.

aurèola *nf* halo, glory.

auròra *nf* dawn.

ausiliàre *a* *nmf* **-àrio** *a* auxiliary.

auspício *nm* auspice; protection, patronage.

austerità *nf* austerity.

austèro *a* austere, severe.

Austràlia nf Australia.
australiàna nf pursuit cycle race on a track.
australiàno a nm Australian.
Àustria nf Austria.
austríaco pl -aci a nm Austrian.
aut-aut nm dilemma.
autarchía nf autarchy, economic self-sufficiency.
autèntica nf authentication, authoritative approval.
autenticàre vt to authenticate, prove; **còpia autenticàta** certified copy.
autenticità nf authenticity.
autèntico pl -ici a authentic.
autísta nm driver, chauffeur.
àuto nf motor car.
autobiografía nf autobiography.
autoblínda inv, **autoblindàta** nf, **autoblindo** inv armored car.
àutobus nm bus, omnibus.
autocarovàna nf motor convoy.
autocàrro nm lorry, truck.
autocorrièra nf long-distance bus.
autocrazía nf autocracy.
autodidàtta nmf self-taught person.
autodifésa nf self-defense.
autòdromo nm autodrome, circuit.
autògrafo a autographic; nm autograph.
autòma nm automaton.
automàtico pl -ici a automatic.
automazióne nf automation.
automèzzo nm motor vehicle.
automòbile nf motor car, automobile; **a. di piàzza** taxi.
automobilìsmo nm motoring.
automobilìsta nmf motorist.
automobilìstico pl -ici a motor; **còrsa a.** motor race.
autonomía nf autonomy, self-government; (av, aut) range.
autònomo a autonomous, self-governing.
autoparchéggio, autopàrco pl -chi nm car park, parking, parking lot.
autopómpa nf fire-engine.
autopsía nf autopsy.
autóre nm author.
autorespiratóre nm aqualung.
autorévole a authoritative, competent.
autoriméssa nf garage.
autorità nf authority.
autorizzàre vt to authorize.
autorizzazióne nf authorization, permit.
autoscàtto nm (phot) automatic release.
autoscuòla nf driving school.
autostòp nm hitch-hiking; **autostoppísta** nmf hitch-hiker; **fàre l'a.** to thumb a lift, hitch-hike.
autostràda nf motorway.
autotrèno nm motor lorry with trailer, truck.
autríce nf authoress.

autunnàle a autumnal.
autúnno nm autumn, fall.
avallàre vt to guarantee (also fig).
avàllo nm (com) guarantee (also fig).
avambràccio nm forearm.
avàna nm Havana (cigar); a light brown.
avanguàrdia nf vanguard.
avànti ad and prep before, forward, in front of, rather (than); interj forward!
avantièri ad the day before yesterday.
avanzaménto nm advancement, progress, promotion.
avanzàre vt to put forward, advance, promote, surpass, improve, save, put by, be creditor for; vi to advance, be left; **-rsi** vr get on, advance.
avanzàta nf advance.
avànzo nm remainder, remnant, residue, ancient ruin; **d'a.** ad over and above.
avaría nf damage.
avariàre vt to damage.
avarízia nf avarice, niggardliness.
avàro a avaricious, miserly; nm miser.
Àve interj Hail!
avéna nf oats.
avére vt and aux to have, obtain, have on, have to, possess; nm property, wealth, credit.
aviatóre nm airman, **-trice** nf airwoman.
aviazióne nf aviation.
avidaménte ad avidly, greedily, eagerly.
avidità nf avidity, greed, eagerness.
àvido a avid, greedy.
aviolínea nf airline.
avioriméssa nf hangar.
avòrio nm ivory.
avvallaménto nm cavity, subsidence.
avvallàre vt to lower; guarantee; **-rsi** vr to fall in, subside.
avvaloràre vt to strengthen; give value to; **-rsi** to become stronger.
avvampàre vi to burn, be on fire, be inflamed.
avvantaggiàre vt to advantage; **-rsi** vr to better oneself, derive advantage.
avvedérsi vr to perceive, notice.
avvedutézza nf foresight, sagacity.
avvedúto a cautious, provident, sagacious.
avvelenaménto nm poisoning.
avvelenàre vt to poison.
avvenènte a charming, agreeable.
avvenènza nf attractiveness, grace.
avveniménto nm event, incident; (to the throne) accession.
avveníre vi and impers to happen, nm future.
avventàre vt to hurl; vi to be gaudy; **-rsi** vr to throw oneself.
avventàto a imprudent, rash.

avventízio *a* temporary, adventitious.

avvènto *nm* advent, arrival; accession.

avventóre *nm* customer, purchaser.

avventúra *nf* adventure, chance.

avventuràre *vt* -rsi *vr* to venture.

avventurière *nm* adventurer.

avventuróso *a* adventurous, fortunate.

avveràre *vt* to fulfill, prove; -rsi *vr* to come true.

avvèrbio *nm* adverb.

avversàre *vt* to oppose, resist, thwart.

avversàrio *a* contrary, opposing, hostile; *nm* opponent, enemy.

avversióne *nf* aversion, dislike.

avversità *nf* adversity.

avvèrso *a* adverse, contrary.

avvertènza *nf* notice, introduction, care, attention.

avvertiménto *nm* notice, warning.

avvertíre *vt* to inform, advise, warn, perceive; *vi* to take care.

avvezzàre *vt* to accustom.

avvézzo *a* accustomed, used.

avviaménto *nm* setting out, beginning, start.

avviàre *vt* to set going, prepare, begin, start; -rsi *vr* to get going, succeed.

avviàto *a* prosperous.

avvicendàre *vi* to alternate; -rsi *vr* to take turns.

avvicinàre *vt* to put near; -rsi *vr* to approach, draw near.

avviliménto *nm* humiliation, dejection.

avvilíre *vt* to dishearten, abase, humiliate; -rsi *vr* to lose heart, humiliate oneself.

avviluppàre *vt* to entangle, wrap up; -rsi *vr* to wrap oneself up, get entangled.

avvisàglia *nf* skirmish; foreshadowing.

avvişàre *vt* to advise, inform, warn; *vi* to judge, think; -rsi *vr* to think, consider.

avvişàto *a* cautious, prudent.

avvişo *nm* advice, news, bill, advertisement, announcement, warning; **a mío a.** in my opinion.

avvistàre *vt* to sight.

avvitàre *vt* to screw.

avviticchiàre *vt* to twine, twist; -rsi *vr* to be entwined.

avvivàre *vt* to enliven, brighten; -rsi *vr* to become lively, (*of fire and fig*) rekindle.

avvizzíre *vi* to wither, fade.

avvocatéssa *nf* lady lawyer.

avvocàto *nm* lawyer, advocate, solicitor, defender.

avvocatúra *nf* legal profession.

avvòlgere *vt* to wrap round, entwine; -rsi *vr* to wrap oneself, wind round something.

avvoltóio *nm* vulture.

avvoltolàre *vt* to roll up; -rsi *vr* to roll oneself up, wallow.

aziènda *nf* business, firm, management.

azionàre *vt* to set in action, set going.

azióne *nf* action, deed, battle, movement; (*com*) share; **a. ordinària** ordinary share, common stock; **a. preferenziàle** preference share, preferred stock.

azionista *nmf* shareholder, stockholder.

azzannàre *vt* to seize with the teeth.

azzardàre *vt* to hazard, risk; -rsi *vr* to venture.

azzàrdo *nm* hazard, risk; **giuòco d'a.** game of chance.

azzardóso *a* hazardous, risky.

azzeccàre *vt* to hit the mark, guess, chance on.

àzzima *nf* unleavened bread.

azzimàre *vt* to dress smartly; -rsi *vr* to dress oneself up.

azzimàto *a* dressed up.

àzzimo *a* unleavened.

azzittíre *vt* to silence.

azzuffàrsi *vr* to come to blows, scuffle.

azzúrro *a* blue, azure.

B

babbèo *a* silly, foolish; *nm* blockhead.

bàbbo *nm* (*fam*) daddy.

babbúccia *nf* slipper.

babbuíno *nm* baboon; (*fig*) fool.

babórdo *nm* (*naut*) larboard.

bacàre *vi* -rsi *vr* to be worm-eaten, rot.

bàcca *nf* berry.

baccalà *nm* stockfish, cod dried and salted; (*fig*) tall thin person; fool.

baccàno *nm* great noise, tumult.

baccellieràto *nm* bachelor's degree.

baccellière *nm* (*academic*) bachelor.

baccèllo *nm* pod; (*fig*) fool.

bacchétta *nf* rod, staff, stick, wand, maulstick.

bacchettàta *nf* stroke of the cane.

bacchiàre *vt* (*fruit*) to beat down.

Bàcco *nm* *pr* Bacchus; **per B.** by Jove!

bachèca *nf* show-case.

bacheròzzo *nm* grub, worm.

baciàre *vt* to kiss; -rsi *vr* to (exchange a) kiss.

bacíle *nm* basin.

bacíllo *nm* bacillus.

bacinèlla *nf* small basin.

bacíno *nm* basin, wash-hand basin; (*anat*) pelvis; (*naut*) dock; **b. carbonífero** coalfield.

bàcio *nm* kiss.

bàco *pl* **bàchi** *nm* worm, silkworm.

bàda, tenere a *vt* to hold at bay.

badàre *vi* to mind, pay attention to, take care of.

badéssa *nf* abbess.

badía nf abbey.
badíle nm shovel.
bàffo nm moustache, whisker.
baffúto a moustached.
bagagliàio nm luggage car, baggage car; caboose.
bagàglio nm luggage.
bagattèlla nf trifle, small matter.
baggianàta nf foolery.
baggiàno nm fool.
baglióre nm flash of light, gleam.
bagnànte nmf bather.
bagnàre vt to moisten, wet, bath; -rsi vr to get wet; bathe.
bagnatúra nf bathing, bathing season.
bagníno nm bathing attendant.
bàgno nm bath; **fàre un b.** vi to have a bath, to bathe; **stànza da b.** bathroom.
bagórdo nm orgy, reveling.
Bahàma (le) nf pl the Bahamas pl.
bàia nf bay; joke, banter.
bàio a nm (color and horse) bay.
baionétta nf bayonet.
bàita nf (alpine) hut.
balaústra, balaustràta nf balustrade.
balbettàre vi to stammer, stutter.
balbettío nm **balbúzia** nf stammer, stammering.
balbuziènte a stammering; nmf stammerer.
Balcàni nm pl the Balkans pl.
balcànico pl -ici a Balkan.
balconàta nf balcony, (theat) balcony.
balcóne nm balcony.
baldacchíno nm canopy.
baldànza nf boldness, assurance.
baldanzóso a bold, confident.
bàldo a bold, fearless.
baldòria nf bonfire; revel; **fàre b.** vi to feast, make merry.
Baldovíno nm pr Baldwin.
baléna nf whale.
balenàre vi to lighten, flash.
balenièra nf whaler (ship).
balenío nm (continual) lightning.
baléno nm lightning; **in un b.** ad immediately, in a flash.
baléstra nf crossbow.
bàlia nf (wet) nurse.
balía nf power, mercy.
balística nf ballistics.
bàlla nf bale, pack; (sl) fib.
ballàbile a suitable for dancing; nm (mus) dance.
ballàre vi to dance.
ballàta nf ballad, ballade.
ballatóio nm gallery, platform.
ballerína nf dancer, dancing girl, ballet-dancer.
balleríno nm dancer, dancing partner.
ballétto nm ballet, interlude.
bàllo nm ball, dance.
ballonzolàre vi to hop about.
ballòtta nf boiled chestnut; ballot.
ballottàggio nm (second) ballot, ballotage.

balneàre, balneàrio a bathing.
baloccàre vt to amuse; -rsi vr to amuse oneself, dally, toy with.
balòcco pl -òcchi nm plaything, toy.
balordàggine nf stupidity.
balórdo a stupid; nm fool, numskull.
balsàmico pl -ici a balmy.
bàlsamo nm balm, balsam.
Bàltico a nm (geogr) Baltic.
baluàrdo nm bastion, bulwark.
bàlza nf cliff, rock; flounce.
balzàre vi to bounce, jump, spring.
bàlzo nm jump, spring.
bambàgia nf cotton wool.
bambína nf little girl.
bambinàia nf nursery governess.
bambinésco pl -chi a childish.
bambíno nm baby, child, little boy.
bàmbola nf doll.
bambù nm bamboo.
banàle a common, trivial.
banalità nf banality, triviality.
banàna nf banana; **banàno** banana (-tree).
banca nf bank.
bancarèlla nf street stall.
bancàrio a bank, banking.
bancarótta nf bankruptcy; **fàre b.** to go bankrupt.
bancarottière nm bankrupt.
banchétto nm banquet.
banchière nm banker.
banchína nf small bench; quay, wharf, waterfront; platform.
banchísa nf ice-pack.
bànco pl -chi nm bench, counter, desk, bank, stall, (of jury) box; **b. di sàbbia** sand bank; **b. di ghiàccio** ice floe; **b. di ròcce** reef; **b. del lòtto** lottery office.
bancogíro nm (com) clearing.
banconòta nf banknote, note, bill.
bànda nf band, side, stripe, gang; **da b.** ad aside.
banderuòla nf pennon; vane, weathercock.
bandièra nf banner, flag.
bandíre vt to proclaim, announce; banish.
bandíta nf preserve; **b. di càccia** game preserve.
banditismo nm banditry.
bandíto a outlawed, exiled; nm bandit, outlaw.
banditóre nm public crier, auctioneer.
bàndo nm ban, banishment; announcement.
bandolièra nf shoulder belt.
bàndolo nm head of a skein.
bar nm bar.
bàra nf bier, coffin.
baràcca nf booth, stall; barrack, hut.
baraónda nf confusion, disorder, tumult.
baràre vi (at play) to cheat.
bàratro nm abyss, gulf.
barattàre vt to barter, chaffer, exchange.

barattería *nf* embezzlement, swindling.
barattière *nm* barterer; embezzler, swindler.
baràttolo *nm* small can or jar.
bàrba *nf* beard; rootlets *pl*; **fàre la b.** *vi* to shave; **fàrsi la b.** to shave (oneself).
barbabiétola *nf* beet.
barbagiànni *nm* owl; simpleton.
barbàglio *nm* dazzle, glare (*of light*).
Bàrbara *nf pr* Barbara.
barbàrico *pl* **-ici, bàrbaro** *a* barbarous, cruel.
barbàrie, barbarità *nf* barbarity.
barbicàre *vi* to take root.
barbière *nm* barber.
barbóne *nm* long beard, long-bearded man, tramp; poodle.
barbóso *a* boring.
barbugliaménto *nm* stammering, stuttering.
barbugliàre *vi* to stammer, stutter.
barbúto *a* bearded.
bàrca *nf* boat; (*fig*) business.
barcàccia *nf* old boat; (*theat*) stage box.
barcaiuòlo *nm* boatman.
barcamenàrsi *vr* to manage cleverly, steer a middle course.
barcaròla *nf* (*mus*) barcarolle.
Barcellóna *nf* Barcelona.
barchétta *nf* **-o** *nm* small boat.
barcollàre *vi* to rock, sway, totter, waver.
barcollío *nm* rocking.
barcóne *nm* barge, large boat.
bardàre *vt* to harness.
bàrdo *nm* bard.
barèlla *nf* stretcher, handcart.
bargíglio *nm* wattle.
baríle *nm* barrel, cask.
barísta *nmf* barman, barmaid.
barítono *nm* baritone.
barlúme *nm* gleam, glimmer.
bàro *nm* cheat, cardsharper.
barocciàio *nm* carter.
baroccíno *nm* small cart, handcart.
baròccio *nm* cart.
baròcco *pl* **-chi** *a* baroque, bizarre; *nm* baroque.
baròmetro *nm* barometer.
baróne *nm* baron.
baronéssa *nf* baroness.
baronétto *nm* baronet.
bàrra *nf* bar, rod, (*naut*) tiller.
barricàre *vt* to barricade.
barricàta *nf* barricade.
barrièra *nf* barrier, palisade.
Bartolomèo *nm pr* Bartholomew.
barúffa *nf* quarrel, brawl.
barzellétta *nf* joke, funny story.
basàre *vt* to base, ground; **-rsi** *vr* to base oneself.
bàse *nf* base, basis, ground; **b. aèrea** air base.
baseball *nm* baseball.
basétta *nf* side whisker.
Basiléa *nf* (*geogr*) Basle.
basílica *nf* basilica.

basílico *pl* **-ichi** *nm* basil.
bassézza *nf* baseness, meanness.
bàsso *a* low, short, mean, (*price*) cheap, (*of material*) narrow, (*mus*) bass.
bassofóndo *nm* (*naut*) shallow; the underworld.
bassorilièvo *nm* bas-relief.
bassòtto *a* stout and short; *nm* tubby man; basset, dachshund.
bassúra *nf* low ground.
bàsta! *interj* enough, stop, that will do.
bastàrdo *a nm* bastard, illegitimate.
bastàre *v impers* to be enough, suffice.
bastiménto *nm* ship, vessel.
bastióne *nm* bastion, rampart.
bàsto *nm* pack saddle.
bastonàre *vt* to beat, cudgel.
bastonàta, bastonatúra *nf* beating, thrashing.
bastóne *nm* stick, cane; cudgel, truncheon; (*cards*) clubs.
batòsta *nf* blow, misfortune.
battàglia *nf* battle.
battagliàre *vi* to fight, struggle.
battaglièro *a* fighting, warlike.
battàglio *nm* bell-clapper.
battaglióne *nm* battalion.
battàna *nf* punt.
battellière *nm* boatman.
battèllo *nm* boat; **b. a vapóre** steamer.
battènte *nm* (*of a door*) leaf; shutter; doorknocker.
bàttere *vt* to beat, knock, thrash, throb; (*of waves*) wash; (*of clocks*) strike; **b. bandièra** to sail under colors; **b. càssa** to ask for money; **b. i dènti** to chatter (with cold); **b. le màni** to clap; **b. monéta** to mint money; *vi* to knock against, insist; **-rsi** *vr* to fight, duel; **bàttersela** *vr* to run away.
battería *nf* battery; set of kitchen utensils.
battesimàle *a* baptismal.
battésimo *nm* baptism, christening.
battezzàre *vt* to baptize, christen.
battibaléno *nm* **in un b.** in the twinkling of an eye.
battibécco *pl* **-cchi** *nm* quarrel.
batticuòre *nm* palpitation, fear.
battipànni *nm* carpet-beater.
battistèro *nm* baptistery.
battistràda *nm* outrider, guide; (*of tires*) tread.
bàttito *nm* heartbeat, palpitation, throbbing, ticking.
battitóre *nm* beater, thresher; (*sport*) server, batsman, striker.
battúta *nf* beating, remark, cue, (*mus*) bar.
battúto *a* beaten, trodden; (*of iron*) wrought; *nm* (*of meat*) hash, stuffing.
batúffolo *nm* small wad.
baúle *nm* trunk, traveling chest.
bàva *nf* slaver, foam; floss silk.
bavaglíno *nm* child's bib.

bavàglio nm gag.
bavarése a nmf Bavarian.
Bavièra nf Bavaria.
bàvero nm coat collar.
bavóso a slavering.
bazàr nm bazaar.
bàzza nf jutting chin; good luck.
bazzècola nf nonsense, trifle.
bazzicàre vt to frequent, haunt.
beàre vt (poet) to make happy; -rsi vr to delight in.
beatificàre vt to beatify.
beatificazióne nf beatification.
beatitúdine nf beatitude, bliss.
beàto a happy, blissful, blessed.
Beatrìce nf pr Beatrice, Beatrix.
beccàccia nf woodcock.
beccaccíno nm snipe.
beccàio nm butcher.
beccamòrti nm grave-digger.
beccàre vt to peck; -rsi vr to win, get; (fig) to quarrel.
beccheggiàre vi (naut) to pitch.
becchéggio nm (naut) pitching.
becchíme nm birds' food.
becchíno nm sexton.
bécco pl **bécchi** nm beak; (of gas) burner; he-goat; cuckold.
beccúccio nm spout.
bécero nm (fam) low fellow, rascal.
becerúme nm cads pl.
beduíno a nm Bedouin.
Befàna nf Epiphany; old woman taking the place of Father Christmas in Italian tales; ugly deformed woman.
bèffa nf jest, mockery, trick.
beffàrdo a mocking; nm mocker.
beffàre vt to mock, ridicule; -rsi vr to deride, make game of.
beffeggiàre vt to deride, mock.
bèga nf dispute; troublesome business.
beghína nf bigot, pietist.
belàre vi to bleat.
belàto nm bleating.
bèlga pl m **bèlgi** f **bèlghe** a nmf Belgian.
Bèlgio (il) nm Belgium.
Belgràdo nf Belgrade.
bèlla nf belle, sweetheart, girlfriend; (sport) final.
bellétto nm paint, rouge.
bellézza nf beauty; la b. di as much as.
bèllico pl -ici, **bellicóso** a warlike, bellicose.
bellimbústo nm dandy, fop.
bellíno a nice, pretty.
bèllo a beautiful, fine, handsome, nice; nm beautiful; lover, boyfriend, beau; beauty; ad finely, nicely; il b. è the best of it is that.
beltà nf beauty.
bélva nf wild beast.
belvedére nm belvedere; **vettúra b.** observation car.
bemòlle nm (mus) flat.
benché cj although.
bènda nf band, bandage.

bendàre vt to bandage, bind, blindfold.
bène nm good, love, happiness, affection; property, wealth; **bèni mòbili** nm pl movable property; **bèni stàbili** real estate; ad well, quite, right; **per b.** a decent, respectable; **star b.** to be well; **volér b.** a vt to like, be fond of.
benedettíno a nm Benedictine.
benedétto a blessed, holy.
benedíre vt to bless, consecrate.
benedizióne nf benediction, consecration.
beneducàto a well-bred.
benefattóre nm benefactor.
benefattríce nf benefactress.
beneficàre vt to benefit, do good to.
beneficénza nf beneficence, charity.
beneficiàre vi to benefit.
benefício, benefízio nm benefit profit; benefice.
benèfico pl -ici a beneficent, beneficial.
benemerènza nf merit.
benemèrito a deserving, meritorious.
beneplàcito nm approval, consent, convenience, option.
benèssere nm well-being.
benestànte a wealthy, well-to-do.
benestàre nm approval, endorsement.
benevolènza nf benevolence, favor.
benèvolo a benevolent, kind.
Bengàla (il) nm Bengal.
bengalése a nmf Bengali.
Beniamíno nm pr Benjamin.
benignità nf benignity, kindness.
benígno a benignant, benign.
beníno ad pretty well, fairly well.
bentéso ad agreed, understood, of course.
beníssimo ad very well, all right.
benóne ad splendidly, very well.
benpensànte a sensible; nmf orthodox, right-minded person.
benportànte a in good health.
benservíto nm testimonial, dismissal.
bensì cj but, rather.
bentornàto a nm welcome back.
benvenúto a nm welcome.
benvolére vt to like; **fàrsi b.** vr to make oneself liked, win popularity; nm benevolence, affection.
benzína nf petrol, gasoline, benzine.
bére vt to drink, absorb; -rse una còsa vr to believe implicitly in something; nm drinking, drink.
bergamòtto nm bergamot.
berlína nf pillory; (aut) sedan.
Berlíno nf Berlin.
Bèrna nf Berne.
Bernàrdo nm pr Bernard.
bernòccolo nm bump, swelling.
bernoccolúto a bumpy, knotty.
berrétta nf cap, biretta.
berrétto nm cap, beret; **b. bàsco** beret.

bersagliàre *vt* to shoot at, harass.
bersaglière *nm* sharpshooter, bersagliere.
bersàglio *nm* aim, butt, mark, target.
bèrta *nf* raillery, mockery; ram; magpie; **dar la b.** to mock.
Bèrta *nf pr* Bertha.
bertúccia *nf* monkey; ugly woman.
bestémmia *nf* blasphemy, oath.
bestemmiàre *vi* to curse, swear; *vt* to blaspheme.
béstia *nf* animal, beast, brute; idiot.
bestiàle *a* bestial, brutal.
bestialità *nf* bestiality, stupidity.
bestiàme *nm* cattle.
béttola *nf* tavern.
betúlla *nf* birch-tree.
bevànda *nf* drink, beverage.
beveràggio *nm* beverage, potion.
bevíbile *a* drinkable, nice to drink.
bevitóre *nm*, **-tríce** *nf* drinker.
bevúta *nf* draft, drinking.
biàcca *nf* white lead.
biàda *nf* corn, oats.
biancàstro *a* whitish.
biancheggiàre *vi* to grow white, show white.
bianchería *nf* linen; **b. personàle** underwear.
bianchétto *nm* white lead, whitewash, bleaching powder.
bianchézza *nm* whiteness.
biànco *pl* **-chi** *a* white, hoary, fair, pale; *nm* white, whitewash; blank; **lasciàre in b.** to leave blank; **di púnto in b.** *ad* point-blank.
biancospíno *pl* **-íni** *nm* hawthorn.
biancúme *nm* mass of white.
biascicàre *vt* to mumble.
biaşimàbile, biaşimèvole *a* blameworthy, reprehensible.
biaşimàre *vt* to blame, reprove.
biàşimo *nm* blame, reproof.
Bíbbia *nf* Bible.
biberon (*French*) *nm inv* feeding-bottle.
bíbita *nf* drink, refreshments *pl*.
bíblico *a* biblical.
bibliografía *nf* bibliography.
bibliogràfico *pl* **-ici** *a* bibliographical.
bibliògrafo *nm* bibliographer.
bibliotèca *nf* library.
bibliotecàrio *nm* librarian.
bicarbonàto *nm* bicarbonate.
bicchière *nm* drinking glass, tumbler.
bicchieríno *nm* small glass.
biciclétta *nf* bicycle.
bicòcca *nf* small hill fort; hovel.
bidè *nm* bidet.
bidèllo *nm* beadle, janitor, porter, usher.
bidóne *nm* (large metal) receptacle.
bièco *pl* **-chi** *a* grim, squinting; *ad* askance.
biennàle *a* biennial.
biènnio *nm* space of two years.
biètola *nf* beet.
bietolóne *nm* simpleton, fool.

bifólco *pl* **-chi** *nm* plowman, farm laborer, boor.
biforcàrsi *vr* to divide, fork.
bigamía *nf* bigamy.
bígamo *nm* bigamist.
bighellonàre *vi* to idle, loaf, lounge.
bighellóne *nm* idler, loafer.
bígio *a* gray.
bigiotteria *nf* trinkets shop.
bigliettàio *v* **bigliettàrio.**
biglietteria *nf* booking office, ticket office; box office.
bigliettàrio *nm* (*of buses etc*) conductor; ticket collector, booking clerk, (*railroad*) ticket agent; box-office attendant.
bigliétto *nm* card, letter, note; ticket; **b. di andàta e ritórno** return ticket, round-trip ticket; **b. d'abbonaménto** season ticket; **b. circolàre** tourist ticket.
bigodíno *nm* (hair-)curler.
bigotteria *nf* **bigottísmo** *nm* bigotry.
bigòtto *a* bigoted; *nm* bigot.
bikíni *nm* bikini.
bilància *nf* balance, pair of scales.
bilanciàre *vt* to balance, ponder.
bilancière *nm* pendulum, balance wheel, fly press, coining press.
bilàncio *nm* (*com*) balance sheet, budget.
bilateràle *a* bilateral.
bíle *nf* bile, anger.
biliàrdo *nm* billiards, billiard room, billiard table.
bílico *pl* **-chi** *nm* equipoise, balance, pivot.
bilíngue *a* bilingual; deceitful.
bilióso *a* bilious, irascible.
bímba *nf* **bímbo** *nm* child, baby.
bimensíle *a* fortnightly.
bimestràle *a* bimonthly.
bimèstre *nm* period of two months.
bimetallísmo *nm* bimetallism.
bimotóre *nm* two-engined plane.
binàrio *nm* rails, railway track; **único b.** single track; **dóppio b.** double track; *a* binary.
bíndolo *nm* reel, winder, water-wheel; cheat
binòc(c)olo *nm* field-glass, opera-glass, binocular(s).
biòccolo *nm* (*of wool*) flock; (*of cotton*) lump; candle drip; snowflake.
biochímica *nf* biochemistry.
biografía *nf* biography.
biògrafo *nm* biographer.
biología *nf* biology.
biòlogo *pl* **-ogi** *nm* biologist.
biondeggiàre *vi* (*of corn*) to grow yellow, turn golden.
biondézza *nf* fairness, flaxen color.
bióndo *a* blond, fair, flaxen.
biòssido *nm* (*chem*) dioxide.
bipartíre *vt* to halve; **-rsi** *vr* to diverge, branch off.
bipartizióne *nf* division into two parts.
bípede *a nm* biped.
biplàno *nm* biplane.

bírba *nm* hare-brained youngster, rogue.
birbànte *nm* rogue, dishonest fellow.
birbonàta *nf* roguish act.
birbóne *nm* bad fellow, rascal; **fréddo b.** bitter cold.
birbonería *nf* knavery, roguery.
birichinàta *nf* mischievous trick.
birichíno *a* mischievous, cheeky; *nm* little scamp, urchin.
biríllo *nm* skittle, ninepin.
Birmània *nf* Burma.
birmàno *a nm* Burmese, Burman.
bíro *nf* biro, ball(point) pen.
biroccíno *nm* small cart.
biròccio *nm* cart.
bírra *nf* beer.
birràio *nm* brewer, publican.
birrería *nf* alehouse, pub, brewery.
bís *interj* encore.
bişàccia *nf* knapsack.
bisàvo, bisàvolo *nm* great-grandfather.
bişbètico *pl* -ici *a* crabbed, shrewish.
bişbigliàre *vi* to whisper.
bişbíglio *nm* whisper.
bísca *nf* gambling-house, gaming-den.
Biscàglia *nf* Biscay.
biscaiuòlo *nm* gambler.
biscazzière *nm* gambling-house keeper; (*at billiards*) marker; gambler.
bíscia *nf* adder, snake.
biscottíno, biscòtto *nm* biscuit, cookie.
bişestíle *a* bissextile; **ànno b.** *nm* leap year.
bisettimanàle *a* bi-weekly.
bişlàcco *pl* -àcchi *a* queer, odd.
bişlúngo *pl* -ghi *a* oblong.
bişmúto *nm* bismuth.
bişnònno *nm* great-grandfather.
bişógna *nf* business, need.
bişognàre *vi* to need, want, be obliged.
bişognévole *a* needy, necessary; *nm* requisite.
bişógno *nm* need, necessity, poverty.
bişognóso *a* indigent, needy.
bistècca *nf* beefsteak.
bisticciàre *vi* -rsi *vr* to dispute, quarrel.
bistíccio *nm* quarrel; pun.
bistrattàre *vt* to ill-treat, offend, wrong.
bişúnto *a* very greasy.
bitòrzolo *nm* knob, pimple, wart.
bitorzolúto *a* pimply.
bítter *nm inv* bitters.
bitúme *nm* bitumen.
bivaccàre *vi* to bivouac.
bivàcco *nm* bivouac.
bivàlve *a nm* bivalve.
bívio *nm* crossroads *pl.*
bizantino *a* Byzantine.
bízza *nf* freak, whim.
bizzàrro *a* bizarre, odd, queer.
bizzèffe *a ad* galore, in quantity.
bizzóso *a* irascible, wayward.

blandízie *nf* blandishments *pl* wheedling.
blàndo *a* affable, bland, wheedling.
blaşóne *nm* blazonry.
blèşo *a* lisping.
blindaménto *nm* **blindatúra** *n* armor-plating.
blindàre *vt* to armor-plate.
bloccàre *vt* to block, blockade.
blòcco *pl* **blòcchi** *nm* block, blockade; (*com*) bulk.
bloc-nòtes *nm* scribbling pad, scratch pad.
blù *a* blue.
bluàstro *a* bluish.
bluffàre *vti* to bluff.
blúşa *nf* blouse.
bòa *nf* (*serpent, wrap*) boa; (*naut*) buoy.
boàro *nm* cowherd.
boàto *nm* bellowing, thundering.
bobína *nf* reel of cotton, spool, (*el*) bobbin.
bócca *nf* mouth; aperture, opening; **a b. apèrta** *ad* open-mouthed.
boccàle *nm* decanter, jug, mug.
boccapòrto *nm* (*naut*) hatch(way).
boccàta *nf* mouthful.
boccheggiàre *vi* to gasp for air.
bocchíno *nm* pretty mouth; cigarette-holder, mouthpiece.
bòccia *nf* water bottle; bud; (*game*) bowl; **bócce** *nf pl* (*game*) bowls *pl.*
bocciàre *vt* to fail (in an exam).
bocciatúra *nf* failure (in an exam).
bòccio *nm* bud.
bocciòlo *nm* bud.
bocconcíno *nm* titbit.
boccóne *nm* mouthful, bite.
boccóni *ad* prone, face downwards.
Boèmia *nf* Bohemia.
boèmo *a nm* Bohemian.
bofonchiàre *vi* to grumble, mutter.
bòia *nm* executioner, hangman.
boicottàggio *nm* boycotting.
boicottàre *vt* to boycott.
bòlgia *nf* dark hole, pit.
bòlide *nm* meteor, thunderbolt, car driven at great speed.
Bolívia *nf* Bolivia.
boliviàno *a nm* Bolivian.
bólla *nf* blister, bubble; papal bull, seal.
bollàre *vt* to confirm, mark, seal, stamp.
bollatúra *nf* sealing, stamping.
bollènte *a* boiling, fiery.
bollétta *nf* bill, certificate, note, receipt.
bollettíno *nm* bulletin, schedule; **b. meteorològico** weather forecast, weather report.
bollicína *nf* small bubble, pimple.
bollíre *vti* to boil, bubble up.
bollitúra *nf* boiling, bubbling.
bóllo *nm* seal, stamp.
bollóre *nm* boiling, excessive heat.
bolscevíco *pl* -íchi *a nm* Bolshevik.
bólso *a* asthmatic.
bómba *nf* bomb, shell; **b. a màno**

hand-grenade; **b. a scòppio ritardàto** delayed action bomb; **b. chímica** gas bomb; **b. esplosíva** high-explosive bomb; **b. fumògena** smoke bomb; **b. incendiària** incendiary bomb.

bombardaménto *nm* bombardment, bombing.

bombardàre *vt* to bombard, bomb.

bómbola *nf* cylinder, bottle; **b. d'ossigeno** oxygen bottle.

bombolóne *nm* doughnut.

bomboni èra *nf* bonbonniere, candy box.

bonàccia *nf* (*at sea*) calm, tranquillity.

bonaccióne *nm* good-humored fellow.

bonarietà *nf* good humor, good nature.

bonàrio *a* good-humored.

bongustàio *nm* gourmet.

bonifica *nf* land reclamation.

bonificàre *vt* to reclaim land, put under cultivation; (*com*) to grant an allowance.

bonomía *nf* good nature.

bontà *nf* goodness, kindness.

bontempóne *nm* jolly person.

borbogliàre *vi* to rumble, mutter.

borboglío *nm* rumbling, grumbling.

borbottaménto, **borbottío** *nm* grumbling, muttering.

borbottàre *vi* to grumble, mutter.

bòrchia *nf* boss, stud.

bordèllo *nm* uproar; brothel.

bórdo *nm* edge, verge, (*of road*) shoulder; border; rim; (*naut*) board; **a b.** *ad* on board.

bòrea *nm* north wind.

borgàta *nf* village, hamlet.

borghése *a* bourgeois; *nmf* middle-class person.

borghesía *nf* middle class.

bórgo *nm* village.

Borgógna *nf* (*geogr*) Burgundy.

bòria *nf* haughtiness, arrogance.

borióso *a* arrogant, vainglorious.

borotàlco *pl* -**chi** *nm* talcum powder.

borràccia *nf* leather bottle, canteen, water bottle.

borraccína *nf* kind of moss.

bórro *nm* ravine.

bórsa *nf* bag, purse, brief-case, Exchange; **b. di stúdio** bursary, scholarship.

borsaiuòlo *nm* pickpocket.

borsanéra *nf* black market.

borseggiàre *vt* to rob, pick someone's pocket.

borséggio *nm* bag-snatching, robbery.

borsellíno *nm* small purse.

borsétta *nf* handbag.

borsísta *nm* stockbroker, scholarship holder.

boscàglia *nf* underwood, wood.

boscaiuòlo *nm* woodcutter.

boscheréccio *a* woody, sylvan.

boschétto *nm* grove, small wood.

boschívo *a* woody.

bòsco *pl* -**chi** *nm* wood, forest.

boscóso *a* wooded.

bòsso, **bòssolo** *nm* box-plant, boxwood.

botànica *nf* botany.

botànico *pl* -**ici** *a* botanic(al); *nm* botanist.

bòtola *nf* trapdoor.

bòtta *nf* blow; toad.

bottàio *nm* cooper.

bótte *nf* barrel, cask.

bottéga *nf* shop.

bottegàio *nm* shopkeeper.

botteghíno *nm* small shop, box-office, lottery, betting shop.

bottiglia *nf* bottle.

bottiglierìa *nf* bar, wine shop.

bottíno *nm* booty.

bòtto *nm* loud bang; blow; (*of bell*) toll; **di b.** *ad* suddenly, directly.

bottóne *nm* button, cufflink; bud; **b. del collétto** collar stud, collar button.

bòve *v* **búe**.

bovíle *nm* ox-stall, byre.

bovíno *a* bovine.

bòzza *nf* bump, swelling; rough draft, proof sheet, sketch.

bozzétto *nm* outline, sketch.

bòzzolo *nm* cocoon.

bràca *nf* sling, tackle; trouser leg; *pl* **bràche** breeches, trousers *pl*.

braccétto, a *ad* arm in arm.

bracciàle *nm* armlet, bracelet, armband.

braccialétto *nm* bracelet.

bracciànte *nm* laborer.

bracciàta *nf* armful.

bràccio *pl* **bràccia** (*f*), (*fig*) **bràcci** (*m*) *nm* arm; branch, inlet, fathom.

bracciuòlo *nm* elbow-rest, handrail; **sèdia a bracciuòli** armchair.

bràcco *pl* **bràcchi** *nm* hound.

bràce *nf* embers *pl*, charcoal.

braciére *nm* brazier.

braciòla *nf* chop, cutlet, steak.

bràma *nf* desire, longing.

bramàre *vt* to desire, long for.

bramosía *nf* longing.

bramóso *a* eager, longing.

brànchie *nf pl* gills of fishes *pl*.

bcànco *pl* -**chi** *nm* flock, herd, band.

brancolàre *vi* to grope.

brancolóni *ad* gropingly.

brànda *nf* folding bed, camp bed, hammock.

brandèllo *nm* rag, tatter, shred.

brandíre *vt* to brandish.

bràno *nm* piece, extract, passage.

Brasíle *nm* Brazil.

brasiliàno *a nm* Brazilian.

bravàre *vt* to defy; *vi* to boast.

bravàta *nf* bravado, boasting.

bràvo *a* clever, good (at something), honest, brave; *nm* cut-throat; *interj* bravo!

bravúra *nf* skill, bravery.

bréccia *nf* breach.

brefotròfio nm orphanage.
Bretàgna nf Brittany, Britain; **Gran B.** Great Britain.
bretèlle nf pl braces pl, suspenders pl.
brètone a nm Breton.
brève a brief, concise, short; nm brief; **in b.** ad in short.
brevettàre vt to patent.
brevétto nm patent; (mil) commission.
breviàrio nm breviary.
brevità nf brevity, conciseness.
brézza nf breeze.
brícco pl **brícchi** nm kettle, pot, jug.
bricconàta, bricconería nf roguery, trick.
briccóne nm rascal, rogue.
bríciola nf crumb.
bríciolo nm bit, morsel.
bríga nf quarrel, trouble; **attaccàre b.** to quarrel; **dàrsi b.** to take pains.
brigadière nm (mil) brigadier; brigadier general; (carabinieri) sergeant.
brigantàggio nm brigandage.
brigànte nm brigand.
brigantésco pl **-éschi** a of a brigand.
brigàre vt to solicit; vt to intrigue, strive.
brigàta nf brigade, company, party.
Brígida nf pr Bridget, Brigid.
bríglia nf bridle, reins pl.
brillaménto nm glitter; (of mine) explosion.
brillànte a bright, brilliant; nm brilliant.
brillantína nf brilliantine.
brillàre vi to glitter, shine, sparkle.
bríllo a merry, tipsy.
brína, brinàta nf hoar frost.
brinàre vi impers to be white with frost.
brindàre vi to drink a health, toast.
brindèllo nm rag, tatter.
bríndisi nm toast.
brío nm spirit, vivacity.
brióso a lively, spirited, vivacious.
Britànnia nf Britain.
britànnico pl **-ici** a British.
britànno nm Briton.
brívido nm shiver, shudder.
brizzolàto a speckled, growing gray.
bròcca nf jug, jar, pitcher.
broccàto nm brocade.
bròccolo nm broccoli.
brodàglia nf weak broth, tasteless soup.
bròdo nm broth, soup.
brogliàre vt to intrigue.
bròglio nm intrigue.
bròmo, bromúro nm bromide.
bronchiàle a bronchial.
bronchíte nf bronchitis.
bróncio nm pout, sulkiness; **tenére il b.** vi to sulk.
brónco nm stem, trunk; **brónchi** pl bronchi pl.

brontolàre vi to grumble.
brónzo nm bronze.
brucàre vt to browse, nibble at, (leaves) strip off.
bruciacchiàre vt to scorch, singe.
bruciapélo, a ad point-blank, suddenly.
bruciàre vt to burn.
bruciàta nf roast chestnut.
bruciàto a burnt; nm burning; **gioventù bruciàta** (sl) beat generation; **uòmo b.** broken man.
brucióre nm smart, burning.
brúco pl **-chi** nm caterpillar, grub.
brughièra nf heath, moor.
brulicàme nm swarm.
brulicàre vi to swarm, be crawling with.
brulichío nm swarming.
brúllo a bare, sterile.
brúma nf winter mist; ship-worm.
brúno a brown, dark; nm mourning.
Brúno nm pr Bruno.
bruschézza nf brusqueness, rudeness.
brúsco pl **-chi** a brusque, rude, tart.
brúscolo nm mote, speck.
brusío nm hubbub, buzz, whispering.
brutàle a brutal.
brutalità nf brutality.
brúto a brutal, unreasoning; nm brute, wild animal, violent person.
bruttàre vt to dirty, soil, stain.
bruttézza nf ugliness.
brútto a ugly, nasty.
bùbbola nf hoopoe; idle tale.
bùbbolo nm harness bell.
bubbóne nm (med) bubo.
bubbònico pl **-ici** a bubonic.
búca nf hole, cave, cavity; **b. délle lèttere** letter-box.
bucanéve nf snowdrop.
bucàre vt to bore, pierce, puncture.
bucàto a pierced, riddled; nm wash(ing), clean linen.
búccia nf peel, rind, skin, bark.
búccola nf earring, pendant.
bucherellàre vt to riddle with holes.
búco pl **búchi** nm hole, round opening.
budellàme nm bowels pl, entrails pl.
budello pl **-a** (f), (fig) **-i** (m) nm bowel, gut, intestine.
budíno nm pudding.
búe pl **buòi** nm ox; (fig) dunce.
búfalo nm buffalo.
bufèra nf storm, hurricane, whirlwind; **b. di néve** blizzard.
buffet nm sideboard, buffet.
buffétto nm fillip, chuck.
búffo a comical, comic, droll, funny, queer; nm gust, puff.
buffonàta nf buffoonery.
buffóne nm buffoon, untrustworthy person.
bugía nf lie; flat candlestick.
bugiàrdo a lying; nm liar.
bugigàttolo nm very small room, cubby-hole.

búio *a* dark; *nm* dark, darkness; **èssere al b.** *vi* (*fig*) to be in the dark.
búlbo *nm* bulb.
Bulgaría (la) *nf* Bulgaria.
búlgaro *a nm* Bulgarian, Bulgar.
bulíno *nm* (*tec*) graver.
bullóne *nm* bolt.
b(u)ongústo *nm* good taste.
buòno *a* good, sound, kind, right, safe; *nm* good; bond, coupon, permit; **a b. mercàto** *ad* cheap; **di buon'óra** *ad* early; **b. del tesòro** Treasury bill.
burattíno *nm* puppet; flighty person.
burbànza *nf* arrogance, insolent bearing.
búrbero *a* crabbed, morose.
burchièllo, búrchio *nm* small canal boat.
búrla *nf* trick, joke; **per b.** *ad* in fun.
burlàre *vt* to play a trick on, make a fool of; *vi* to joke; **-rsi** *vr* to laugh at, make fun of.
burlésco *pl* **-chi** *a* burlesque, ludicrous.
burlétta *nf* jest, joke.
burlévole *a* laughable, comical, humorous.
burlóne *nm* jester, joker.
buròcrate *nm* bureaucrat.
burocràtico *pl* **-ici** *a* bureaucratic.
burocrazía *nf* bureaucracy.
burràsca *nf* storm, tempest.
burrascóso *a* stormy, tempestuous.
búrro *nm* butter.
burróne *nm* ravine.
búsca *nf* quest, search.
buscàre *vt* to earn, gain; **-rsi** *vr* to bring upon oneself.
busíllis *nm* difficulty; **qui sta il b.** here lies the difficulty.
bussàre *vi* to knock.
bússe *nf pl* beating, blows *pl*.
bússola *nf* mariner's compass; sedan chair; inner door, screen; **pèrdere la b.** to be at one's wits' end.
bussolòtto *nm* dice-box.
bústa *nf* envelope, case.
bustàia *nf* corset-maker.
bústo *nm* bust; corset, stays *pl*.
buttàre *vt* to throw; **b. all'ària** to throw up, upset; **-rsi** *vr* to throw oneself.
butteràto *a* pock-marked.
búttero *nm* pock-mark; mounted herdsman.

C

cabína *nf* cabin; **c. telefònica** telephone booth.
cablogràmma *nm* cablegram.
cabotàggio *nm* coasting trade.
cabotièro *a* coasting; *nm* coaster.
cacào *nm* cacao(-tree), cocoa.
càccia *nf* chase, hunt, pursuit, shooting; **andàre a c.** *vi* to go shooting, go hunting.
cacciagióne *nf* game.

cacciàre *vt* to chase, hunt, go hunting, pursue; thrust; **c. un grído** to utter a cry; **-rsi** *vr* to intrude, thrust one's way into.
cacciatóre *nm* **-trice** *nf* hunter, trapper.
cacciatorpedinière *nf* (torpedoboat) destroyer.
cacciavíte *nm* screwdriver.
càchi *a* khaki; *nm* persimmon (tree).
càcio *nm* cheese.
cadaúno *pron* (*com*) each.
cadàvere *nm* corpse.
cadavèrico *pl* **-ici** *a* cadaverous, corpselike.
cadènte *a* falling, (*of the sun*) setting.
cadènza *nf* cadence, rhythm, time, step, (*mus*) cadenza.
cadenzàto *a* measured, rhythmical.
cadére *vi* to fall.
cadétto *a* younger, cadet; *nm* cadet.
Càdice *nf* (*geogr*) Cadiz.
caducità *nf* frailty, transiency.
cadúco *pl* **-úchi** *a* frail, transient.
cadúta *nf* fall, ruin.
caffè *nm* coffee, café, **c. concèrto** café-chantant.
caffelàtte *nm* white coffee.
caffettièra *nf* coffee-pot.
caffettière *nm* café proprietor.
cafóne *nm* (*south Italy*) peasant; (*fig*) boor.
cagionàre *vt* to cause, occasion.
cagióne *nf* cause, reason, motive; **a c. di** on account of.
cagionévole *a* sickly, weak.
càglio *nm* rennet.
càgna *nf* bitch.
cagnàra *nf* barking, uproar.
cagnésco *pl* **-chi** *a* currish, surly.
cagnolíno *nm* pretty little dog, puppy.
Calàbria *nf* (*geogr*) Calabria.
calabrése *a nmf* Calabrian.
calabróne *nm* hornet.
calamàio *nm* inkstand; cuttlefish.
calamità *nf* calamity, misfortune.
calamíta *nf* magnet, loadstone.
calamitàre *vt* to magnetize.
calamitóso *a* calamitous, disastrous.
càlamo *nm* reed, quill.
calànte *a* sinking, declining, setting, decreasing; **lúna** c. waning moon.
calaprànzi *nm* dumbwaiter.
calàre *vt* to let down, lower; (*sail etc*) strike; *vi* to decrease, descend, sink, set.
càlca *nf* crowd, throng.
calcàgno *nm* heel.
calcàre *vt* to tread on, lay stress on, (*drawing*) trace.
calcàre *nm* limestone.
càlce *nf* lime; *nm* bottom, foot; **in c.** *ad* at the foot of the page.
calcestrúzzo *nm* concrete.
calciàre *vt* to kick; **c. in pòrta** (*sport*) to kick at goal.
calciatóre *nm* footballer.
calcína *nf* lime, mortar.
calcinàccio *nm* flake of dry plaster.

calcinàio *nm* lime-pit.
calcinàre *vt* to calcine.
càlcio *nm* kick; (*sport*) football; butt-end, rifle stock; (*chem*) calcium; c. d'àngolo (*sport*) corner; c. d'inízio (*sport*) kick-off; c. di rigóre (*sport*) penalty; c. di punizióne (*sport*) free kick.
calcístico *pl* -ici *a* football.
càlco *pl* càlchi *nm* cast, imprint, tracing.
calcògrafo *nm* copperplate engraver.
calcolàbile *a* calculable, computable.
calcolàre *vt* to calculate, compute, reckon.
calcolatóre *m* -trice *f a* calculating; *nm* reckoner, computer; (*fig*) shrewd fellow.
calcolatríce *nf* reckoner, computer, calculating machine; (*fig*) shrewd woman.
càlcolo *nm* calculation, reckoning; (*med*) stone, calculus; (*math*) calculus.
caldàia *nf* boiler.
caldalléssa *nf* boiled chestnut.
caldarròsta *nf* roast chestnut.
caldeggiàre *vt* to favor, foster, protect.
calderàio *nm* coppersmith.
calderóne *nm* cauldron; (*fig*) mixture of things.
càldo *a* warm, hot; *nm* heat.
caleidoscòpio *nm* kaleidoscope.
calendàrio *nm* calendar, almanac.
calèsse *nm* gig, carriage.
calettàre *vt* (*mech*) to couple, key on; *vi* to tally, fit.
calía *nf* gold filing; (*fig*) old stuff.
càlibro *nm* caliber.
càlice *nm* goblet, chalice; (*bot*) calyx.
calígine *nf* thick fog, smog, dimness.
caliginóso *a* foggy, dark.
càlle *nf* (*poet*) path; narrow street in Venice.
callífugo *pl* -ghi *nm* corn-plaster.
calligrafía *nf* handwriting.
callísta *nm* chiropodist.
càllo *nm* corn.
callosità *nf* callosity.
callóso *a* callous, hard.
càlma *nf* calm, quiet, tranquillity, quietness.
calmànte *a* soothing; *nm* sedative.
calmàre *vt* to calm, appease, soften; -rsi *vr* to calm down, become smooth.
càlmo *a* calm, tranquil, still, cool, (*sea*) smooth.
càlo *nm* loss of weight, fall in price, shrinkage.
calóre *nm* heat, warmth, feverishness.
caloría *nf* calorie.
calorífero *nm* radiator; impiànto centràle di caloríferi central heating.
caloróso *a* warm, hearty.
calòscia *nf* galosh.

calòtta *nf* skull-cap, calotte; (*mech*) cap.
calpestàre *vt* to trample on, oppress.
calpestío *nm* trampling.
calúnnia *nf* calumny.
calunniàre *vt* to calumniate, slander.
calunniatóre *nm* -tríce *nf* calumniator, slanderer.
calunnióso *a* calumnious, slanderous.
Calvàrio *nm* Calvary, wayside shrine; calvàrio *nm* long suffering.
calvízie *nf* baldness.
càlvo *a* bald; *nm* bald-headed person.
càlza *nf* stocking; fàre la c. *vi* to knit.
calzamàglia *nf* tights *pl*.
calzànte *a* suitable, appropriate.
calzàre *vt* (*shoes*) to put on, wear; *vi* to fit.
calzatóio *nm* shoehorn.
calzatúra *nf* footwear.
calzíno *nm* sock.
calzolàio *nm* bootmaker, shoemaker.
calzolería *nf* shoemaker's shop.
calzóni *nm* trousers *pl*, slacks *pl*; c. córti, calzoncíni shorts *pl*.
camaleónte *nm* chameleon.
cambiàle *nf* (*com*) bill of exchange, draft; eméttere una c. to draw a bill.
cambiaménto *nm* change.
cambiamonéte, cambiavalúte *nm* money changer.
cambiàre *vti* to change, alter, turn, exchange; -rsi *vr* to change.
càmbio *nm* change, exchange; (*tec*) change gear, (*aut*) gear, gearbox.
càmera *nf* chamber, room; c. da lètto bedroom; C. dei Deputàti House of Commons, House of Representatives; C. dei Pàri House of Lords.
cameràta *nm* comrade; *nf* dormitory.
camerièra *nf* maid, servant, waitress; -re *nm* waiter, manservant.
cameríno *nm* (*theat*) dressing room.
càmice *nm* surplice, overall.
camicétta *nf* blouse.
camícia *pl* -ície *nf* shirt, wrapper; (*tec*) jacket; c. da nòtte nightgown, nightdress; c. di fòrza strait-jacket.
caminétto *nm* fireplace.
camíno *nm* fireplace, chimney.
camíon *nm* lorry, truck.
camionétta *nf* (*mil*) jeep.
camioncíno *nm* small van, tradesman's delivery van.
camionísta *nm* lorry driver; truck driver.
cammèllo *nm* camel.
cammèo *nm* cameo.
camminaménto *nm* (*mil*) communication trench.
camminàre *vi* to walk, march; (*of mechanism*) go, work; proceed.
cammíno *nm* way, road, journey; cammín facèndo *ad* on the way.
camomílla *nf* camomile.

camòrra *nf* camorra, secret (criminal) society.
camóscio *nm* chamois, shammy.
campàgna *nf* country, estate; campaign.
campagn(u)òlo *a* rustic, country; *nm* peasant, countryman.
campàle *a* (of the) field; **battàglia c.** *nf* pitched battle.
campàna *nf* bell, bell glass.
campanèlla *nf* small bell; (*bot*) harebell.
campanèllo *nm* (*in the house*) bell.
Campània *nf* (*geogr*) Campania.
campaníle *nm* bell-tower, belfry.
campanilísmo *nm* local patriotism.
campàno *a nm* (inhabitant) of Campania.
campàre *vt* to save, rescue; (*art*) put into relief; *vi* to live.
campeggiàre *vi* to stand out; camp, encamp.
campéggio *nm* camping, camping place.
campèstre *a* rural, rustic.
Campidòglio (il) *nm* the Capitol (in Rome).
campionàrio *a* sample, trade; *nm* pattern book, sample case.
campionàto *nm* championship.
campióne *nm* champion; (*com*) sample.
càmpo *nm* field, camp; **c. d'aviazióne** airfield; **c. di fortúna** emergency landing-ground; **méttere in c.** *vt* to bring forward, propose.
camposànto *nm* burial ground, cemetery.
camuffàre *vt* to disguise, mask.
Canadà *nm* (*geogr*) Canada.
canadése *a nm* Canadian.
canàglia *nf* mob, rabble, riffraff, rogue.
canàle *nm* canal, channel, pipe; **c. navigàbile** waterway.
canalizzàre *vt* to canalize.
cànapa *nf* hemp.
canapè *nm* couch, sofa.
Canàrie (le) *nf pl* (*geogr*) the Canary Islands, the Canaries *pl*.
canaríno *a* canary-colored; *nm* canary.
canàsta *nf* canasta.
cancellàre *vt* to cancel, erase, obliterate.
cancellàta *nf* railing.
cancellatúra *nf* erasure.
cancellería *nf* chancellor's office, chancery; **artícoli di c.** articles of stationery.
cancellière *nm* chancellor, registrar.
cancèllo *nm* gate, railing.
cancrèna *nf* gangrene.
càncro *nm* cancer.
candeggiàre *vt* to bleach.
candeggína *nf* bleach; **candéggio** *nm* bleaching.
candéla *nf* candle, (*aut*) sparking plug, spark plug.
candelàbro *nm* candelabrum.

candelière *nm* candlestick, (*naut*) stanchion.
candelòra *nf* Candlemas.
candidàto *nm* candidate.
candidatúra *nf* candidature.
càndido *a* white; candid, sincere.
candíre *vt* to candy.
candíto *a* candied; *nm* sugar candy.
candóre *nm* whiteness; candor.
càne *nm* dog, (*of a gun*) cock, (*mech*) catch; **c. da càccia** hound, sporting dog; **c. da guàrdia** watchdog; **c. barbóne** poodle; **c. bastàrdo** mongrel.
canèstro *nm* basket, hamper; basketful.
cànfora *nf* camphor.
cangiàbile *a* changeable, fickle.
cangiànte *a* changing, (*of color*) iridescent; **séta c.** shot silk.
cangùro *nm* kangaroo.
canícola *nf* dog-star; dog-days *pl*.
caníle *nm* kennel.
caníno *a* canine; **tósse canína** whooping-cough.
canízie *nf* white hair, old age.
cànna *nf* cane, reed, tube, (*gun*) barrel, (fishing-)rod, stick, (*measure*) rod.
cannèlla *nf* spout, spigot, tap; cinnamon.
cannéto *nm* reed thicket, cane field.
canníbale *nm* cannibal.
cannocchiàle *nm* binoculars *pl*, opera glass, telescope.
cannonàta *nf* cannon-shot.
cannóne *nm* gun, cannon; **c. anticàrro** anti-tank gun; **c. antiaèreo** anti-aircraft gun.
cannoneggiaménto *nm* cannonade, cannonading.
cannoneggiàre *vti* to cannonade.
cannonièra *nf* gunboat.
cannonière *nm* gunner.
cannúccia *nf* thin cane, (*for drinks*) straw, pen-holder, small tube.
canòa *nf* canoe.
cànone *nm* canon, rule; fee, rent.
canònica *nf* vicarage, rectory.
canònico *pl* **-ici** *a* canonical, regular; **dritto c.** canon law; *nm* canon.
canonizzàre *vt* to canonize.
canonizzazióne *nf* canonization.
canottàggio *nm* rowing, canoeing.
canottièra *nf* vest, singlet, undershirt; straw hat.
canòtto *nm* canoe.
cànova *nf* retail shop for wine *etc*.
canovàccio *nm* dishcloth, canvas; plot.
cantànte *a* singing; *nmf* singer.
cantàre *vti* to sing.
cantatóre *a* singing; *nm* singer.
cantatríce *nf* singer.
canterellàre, canticchiàre *vti* to hum, sing softly.
canteríno *a* singing, warbling, chirping.
càntica *nf* poem, song; **càntico** *nm* canticle, hymn.

cantière *nm* dockyard, ship-building yard.
cantilèna *nf* monotonous song, singsong.
cantína *nf* cellar, wine shop.
cànto *nm* singing, song, poem, canto; corner, side, angle.
cantonàta *nf* corner; blunder.
cantóne *nm* corner; canton.
cantonière *nm* maintenance man on roads, railways *etc*; **càsa cantonièra** roadman's house.
cantóre *nm* singer, chorister.
cantoría *nf* choir, chancel.
cantúccio *nm* corner, bit.
canúto *a* gray-headed, hoary.
canzonàre *vt* to make fun of, tease; *vi* to joke.
canzonatòrio *a* mocking, teasing.
canzonatúra *nf* mockery, teasing.
canzóne *nf* song, ode, ballad.
canzonière *nm* collection of lyrical poems, song book.
càos *nm* chaos, confusion.
caòtico *pl* -**ici** *a* chaotic.
capàce *a* able, capable, capacious.
capacità *nf* ability, capacity.
capacitàrsi *vr* to make out, understand.
capànna *nf* -**no** *nm* hut, cabin.
capannèllo *nm* group of persons, small crowd.
caparbietà *nf* obstinacy, stubbornness.
capàrbio *a* obstinate, stubborn.
capàrra *nf* advance payment, earnest money.
capéllo *nm* hair; **capellóne** *nm* (*sl*) beatnik.
capellúto *a* hairy.
capelvènere *nm* (*bot*) maidenhair.
capèstro *nm* halter, rope.
capezzàle *nm* bolster.
capézzolo *nm* nipple.
capigliatúra *nf* hair, head of hair.
capinéra *nf* (*bird*) blackcap.
capire *vt* to understand, realize; *vi* to be contained.
capitàle *a* capital, principal, main; deadly; *nm* capital, wealth, assets *pl*; *nf* capital (city).
capitalísmo *nm* capitalism.
capitalísta *nm* capitalist.
capitanàre *vt* to captain, head.
capitanería *nf* **c. di pòrto** harbor-master's office.
capitàno *nm* captain, commander.
capitàre *vi* to happen, occur, turn up.
capitèllo *nm* (*arch*) capital.
capitolàre *vi* to capitulate; *a* capitular; *nm* capitulary.
capitolíno *a* Capitoline.
capìtolo *nm* chapter, (*of pact or convention*) article.
capitombolàre *vi* to tumble.
capitómbolo *nm* somersault, tumble.
càpo *nm* head; chief, beginning, end, article, item, cape, promontory; **da c.** again; **in c. a** at the end of;

veníre **a c. di** to make out, reason out.
capobànda *pl* **capibànda** *nm* bandmaster, gang leader.
capòcchia *nf* head of a nail, pin *etc*.
capocòmico *pl* -**ici**, **capicòmici** *nm* (*theat*) head of a dramatic company, showman.
capocuòco *pl* **capicuòchi** *nm* head cook, chef.
capofàbbrica *pl* **capifàbbrica** *nm* foreman.
capofítto *ad* head downwards, head foremost.
capogíro *pl* -**íri** *nm* dizziness, giddiness.
capolavóro *pl* -**óri** *nm* masterpiece.
capolínea *pl* **capilínea** *nm* terminus.
capolíno *nm* small head; **fàre c.** to peep in.
capoluògo *pl* -**ghi**, **capiluòghi** *nm* chief town in a district.
capomàstro *pl* -**tri**, **capimàstri** *nm* master builder.
caponàggine *nf* obstinacy.
caporàle *nm* corporal.
caporepàrto *pl* **capirepàrto** *nm* head of a department, shopwalker, floorwalker, foreman.
caporióne *pl* **capirióne** *nm* ringleader.
caposàldo *pl* **capisàldi** *nm* essential point of a speech *etc*; (*mil*) stronghold.
caposquàdra *pl* **capisquàdra** *nm* foreman; (*mil*) squad leader.
capostazióne *pl* **capistazióne** *nm* station-master.
capotàvola *pl* **capitàvola** *nm* head of a table.
capotréno *pl* **capitréno** *nm* guard, conductor.
capovèrso *pl* -**rsi** *nm* beginning of a line or paragraph.
capovòlgere *vt* to overturn, upset; -**rsi** *vr* to capsize, be upset.
càppa *nf* cape, cloak, cope; the letter K.
cappèlla *nf* chapel.
cappellàno *nm* chaplain.
cappellièra *nf* hat-box.
cappèllo *nm* hat.
càpperi! *interj* goodness!
càppero *nm* caper, caper-bush.
càppio *nm* slip-knot, noose.
cappóne *nm* capon.
cappòtto *nm* cloak, overcoat.
cappuccíno *nm* capuchin friar; coffee with a little cream.
cappúccio *nm* cowl, hood.
càpra *nf* she-goat.
caprétto *nm* kid, young goat.
capríccio *nm* caprice, whim.
capriccióso *a* capricious, whimsical.
caprifòglio *nm* honeysuckle.
capriòla *nf* doe, roe; caper, capriole.
capriòlo *nm* roebuck.
càpro *nm* he-goat; **c. espiatório** scapegoat.
càpsula *nf* capsule, percussion cap.

capuffício nm head clerk.
carabína nf carbine.
carabinière nm carabineer, gendarme.
caràffa nf decanter, carafe.
caramèlla nf sweet, candy, toffee, taffy, caramel; monocle.
caràto nm carat; (com) share.
caràttere nm character, quality, style, (typ) type.
caratterística nf characteristic.
caratterístico a characteristic.
caratterizzàre vt to characterize.
carbonàia nf charcoal pit, coalcellar, bunker.
carbonàio nm coalman.
carbònchio nm carbuncle.
carbóne nm coal; c. fòssile pit coal.
carbonèlla nf charcoal, coal cinders.
carbònio nm carbon.
carbonizzàre vt to carbonize.
carburànte nm fuel, petrol, gas, gasoline.
carburatóre nm carburetor.
carcàme nm -àssa nf carcass.
carceràre vt to imprison.
carceràto nm prisoner.
carcerazióne nf imprisonment.
càrcere nm jail, prison.
carcerière nm jailer.
carciòfo nm artichoke.
cardàre vt to card.
cardellíno nm goldfinch.
cardíaco pl -íaci a cardiac.
cardinàle a cardinal, principal; nm cardinal.
càrdine nm hinge; (fig) foundation.
càrdo nm thistle, teasel.
carèna nf (of a ship) keel.
carenàre vt (naut) to careen.
carènza nf lack, scarcity.
carestía nf dearth, famine.
carézza nf caress; high price.
carezzàre vt to caress, fondle, cherish.
carezzévole a caressing, coaxing.
cariàre vt to decay, rot.
càrica nf position, post; (mil) charge; (el) charging; winding.
caricaménto nm loading, charging, winding up.
caricàre vt to charge, load, overburden, exaggerate; c. un orològio to wind up a clock.
caricatóre nm loader, shipper; (of firearms) magazine.
caricatúra nf caricature.
càrico pl -chi a charged, loaded, wound up; nm load, cargo, burden, charge.
càrie nf caries, (of teeth) decay.
caríno a pretty, nice, dear, sweet.
carità nf charity, alms; per c. interj for heaven's sake.
caritatévole a charitable.
carlínga nf (av) cockpit.
Càrlo nm pr Charles.
Carlomàgno nm pr Charlemagne.
carlóna, alla ad in a slovenly manner.

carmelitàno nm Carmelite friar.
carnagióne nf complexion.
carnàle a bodily, physical, carnal, sensual.
carnalità nf carnality, sensuality.
càrne nf flesh, meat.
carnéfice nm executioner, (fig) brutal person.
carneficína nf carnage, slaughter.
carnevàle nm carnival.
Càrniche (Àlpi) nf pl (geogr) Carnic Alps.
carnívoro a carnivorous.
carnóso a fleshy.
càro a dear, expensive; ad dearly, dear; nm high cost; il carovíta the high cost of living; tenér c. to esteem, value.
carógna nf carrion (also fig).
Carolína nf pr Caroline.
caròta nf carrot.
carovàna nf caravan, convoy.
càrpa nf carp.
carpentière nm carpenter.
carpíre vt to seize, snatch; cheat.
carpóne, carpóni ad on all fours.
carradóre nm cartwright.
carràia nf cart road.
carreggiàbile a practicable for carts.
carreggiàta nf track, cart road; gauge; uscíre di c. (fig) to go astray.
carrèllo nm (tec) undercarriage, trolley.
carrétta nf cart.
carrettàta nf cartload.
carrettière nm carrier, carter.
carrétto nm hand-cart.
carrièra nf career, course, speed.
carriòla nf wheelbarrow.
càrro nm cart, wagon, truck; (astr) Great Bear; c. armàto (mil) tank; c. leggèro (mil) light tank; c. fúnebre hearse.
carròzza nf carriage, coach, railway car; c. belvedére observation car; c. ristorànte restaurant car, dining car; c. lètto sleeping car, sleeper.
carrozzàbile a practicable for carriages.
carrozzería nf body of a car, carmaking firm.
carrozzína nf perambulator, (fam) pram, baby carriage.
carrozzino nm light carriage; (motorcycle) sidecar.
carrúcola nf pulley, sheave.
càrsico pl -ici a Karst.
Càrso nm (geogr) Karst.
càrta nf paper, document, writing, charter, playing card, map; c. d'identità identity card; c. igiènica toilet paper; c. da lèttere writing paper, notepaper.
cartacarbóne pl cartecarbóne nf carbon paper.
cartàccia, cartastràccia pl cartestràcce nf waste paper.

cartàio nm papermaker; (at cards) dealer.

cartapècora pl -ore nf parchment.

cartapésta pl **cartapéste, cartepéste** nf papier-mâché.

cartavetràta pl **cartevetràte** nf glass paper, sandpaper.

cartéggio nm correspondence, collection of letters.

cartèlla nf folder, portfolio, writing pad; schoolbag; (of a manuscript) sheet; share, bond, score-card, (lottery) ticket.

cartellièra nf filing cabinet.

cartèllo nm bill, label, signboard, poster.

cartellóne nm placard, playbill.

cartièra nf paper mill.

cartilàgine nf cartilage, gristle.

cartòccio nm cornet, paper bag.

cartolàio nm stationer.

cartolería nf stationer's shop.

cartolína nf card; **c. illustràta** picture postcard; **c. postàle** postcard.

cartóne nm cardboard; cartoon.

cartúccia nf cartridge.

cartuccièra nf cartridge belt.

càsa nf house, home, family, household; religious community; business firm; **c. di salúte** nursing home.

casàccio, a ad at random, haphazard.

casàle nm hamlet.

casalíngo pl **-ghi** a domestic, homely, homemade.

casaménto nm tenement house.

casàta nf lineage, family.

casàto nm surname.

cascàggine nf drowsiness, weariness.

cascàre vi to fall.

cascàta nf fall, waterfall, cascade.

cascemír nm cashmere.

cascína nf dairy farm, dairy.

caseggiàto nm block of houses.

caseifício nm dairy.

casèlla nf pigeonhole, small compartment; (beehive) cell.

casellànte nm level-crossing keeper, signalman.

casellàrio nm set of pigeonholes.

casèrma nf barracks pl.

casétta, casettína nf cottage, small house.

casíno nm little cottage; club, gaming-house.

càso nm case; chance, possibility; **a c.** ad at random.

casolàre nm poor country house.

Càspio, (Mar) nm (geogr) Caspian (Sea).

càssa nf case, chest, coffer, coffin, drum; (of a gun) stock; cash, fund; **c. di rispàrmio** savings bank.

cassafòrte nf safe.

cassapànca nf wooden chest in the form of a bench.

cassàre vt to cancel, annul, quash.

cassazióne nf annulling, cassation; **corte di c.** (leg) court of cassation.

casseruòla nf saucepan.

cassétta nf box, coach-box, collection box, letter-box, mailbox.

cassétto nm drawer.

cassettóne nm chest of drawers.

cassière nm cashier, teller.

càsta nf caste, rank.

castàgna nf chestnut; **castàgno** nm chestnut tree; **c. d'India** horsechestnut(tree).

castagnéto nm chestnut grove.

castàno a chestnut-colored, brown; **c. scúro** dark brown; **c. chiàro** light brown.

castellàno nm lord of a manor.

castèllo nm castle, fortress, (naut) castle.

castigàre vt to punish, chastise, chasten; spoil.

castigàto a chaste, pure; (edition) expurgated.

castígo pl **-ighi** nm punishment.

castità nf chastity, purity.

càsto a chaste, pure.

castòro nm beaver.

castràre vt to castrate, (fig) bowdlerize.

castràto a castrated; nm mutton.

casuàle a casual; accidental.

casualità nf chance.

casúpola nf hovel.

cataclísma nm cataclysm.

catacómba nf catacomb.

catalessi nf catalepsy.

catalizzatóre nm (chem) catalyst.

catalogàre vt to catalogue.

catàlogo pl **-ghi** nm catalogue, list.

catapécchia nf hovel.

cataplàsma nm poultice.

catapulta nf catapult.

catarifrangènte nm reflector, reflex reflector.

catàrro nm catarrh.

catàsta nf pile, heap, stack.

catàsto nm register of lands, land office, land tax.

catàstrofe nf catastrophe.

catechísmo nm catechism.

categoría nf category, class.

categòrico pl **-ici** a categorical.

caténa nf chain, fetter; (of hills) range; **c. cingolàta** (mil) caterpillar track.

catenàccio nm (door) bolt.

catenèlla nf small chain.

cateràtta nf cataract, sluice.

Caterína nf pr Catherine, Katherine.

catinèlla nf wash-hand basin; **piòvere a catinèlle** vi to rain cats and dogs.

catíno nm basin.

catràme nm tar.

càttedra nf desk, teaching post, chair, professorship, pulpit.

cattedràle nf cathedral.

cattivàre vt to captivate; **-rsi** vr to win (love, favor etc).

cattivèria nf naughtiness, wickedness.

cattività nf captivity.

cattívo a bad, naughty, wicked.

Cattolicésimo, Cattolicísmo *nm* (Roman) Catholicism.
cattolicità *nf* Catholicism, Catholic countries *pl.*
cattòlico *pl* **-ici** *a nm* Catholic.
cattúra *nf* capture, arrest; **mandàto di c.** warrant of arrest.
catturàre *vt* to arrest, capture.
Càucaso (il) *nm (geogr)* Caucasus.
caucciù *nm* indiarubber.
càuṣa *nf* cause, origin, reason; *(leg)* law-suit.
cauṣàle *a* causal.
cauṣalità *nf* causality.
cauṣàre *vt* to cause, occasion.
causticità *nf* causticity.
càustico *pl* **-ici** *a nm* caustic.
cautaménte *ad* cautiously.
cautèla *nf* caution, wariness.
càuto *a* cautious, wary.
cauzióne *nf* security, bail, caution money.
càva *nf* quarry, mine.
cavalcàre *vt* to mount *(a horse etc)*; *vi* to ride.
cavalcàta *nf* ride, cavalcade.
cavalcatúra *nf* mount.
cavalcavía *nm* fly-over.
cavalcióni *ad* astride; **a c. di** astride.
cavalière *nm* horseman, knight; escort, dancing partner.
cavàlla *nf* mare.
cavallànte *nm* stable-man, horse-rider.
cavallerésco *pl* **-chi** *a* chivalrous, knightly, noble.
cavallería *nf* cavalry, horse *pl*, chivalry.
cavallerízza *nf* riding school, horse-woman; **cavallerízzo** *nm* rider, riding master, ringmaster.
cavallétta *nf* grasshopper.
cavallétto *nm* small horse; easel, trestle; *(torture)* rack.
cavallína *nf* filly; **córrere la c.** to sow one's wild oats.
cavàllo *nm* horse; *(chess)* knight; **c. vapóre** horse-power.
cavàre *vt* to extract, take out, remove, obtain; **-rsi** *vr* to get out of.
cavatàppi *nm* corkscrew.
cavèrna *nf* cave, cavern.
cavézza *nf* halter.
càvia *nf* guinea-pig.
caviàle *nm* caviar.
cavíglia *nf* ankle (bone).
cavillàre *vi* to carp, cavil, split hairs.
cavíllo *nm* cavil, quibble.
cavillóso *a* caviling, quibbling.
cavità *nf* cavity, hole.
càvo *a* hollow, empty; *nm* cable, rope; **c. di orméggio** mooring cable.
cavolfióre *nm* cauliflower.
càvolo *nm* cabbage; **cavolíni di Bruxelles** brussels sprouts.
cazzòtto *nm* punch, blow.
céce *nm* chick-pea.
Cecília *nf pr* Cecily; **Cecílio** *nm pr* Cecil.
cecità *nf* blindness, ignorance.

cèco *pl* **-chi** *a nm* Czech.
Cecoslovàcchia *nf* Czechoslovakia.
cecoslovàcco *pl* **-chi** *a nm* Czecho-slovak.
cèdere *vi* to give in, yield; cave in; *vt* to give up, cede, surrender, transfer.
cedévole *a* yielding; *(of ground)* sinking.
cedíbile *a* transferable.
cèdola *nf (com)* coupon.
cèdro *nm* cedar, citron.
céfalo *nm* mullet.
cèffo *nm* muzzle, snout.
celàre *vt* to disguise, hide; **-rsi** *vr* to hide (oneself).
celebrànte *nm* officiating priest.
celebràre *vt* to celebrate, praise.
celebrazióne *nf* celebration.
cèlebre *a* celebrated, famous.
celebrità *nf* celebrity.
cèlere *a* nimble, rapid, swift.
celerità *nf* celerity, swiftness.
celèste *a* celestial, divine, heavenly; sky-blue.
cèlia *nf* jest, joke.
celibàto *nm* celibacy.
cèlibe *a* unmarried; *nm* bachelor.
cèlla *nf (of prison, monastery)* cell.
cellofàne *nm* cellophane.
cèllula *nf (anat, el)* cell.
cellulàre *a* cellular, honey-combed; *nm* jail, prison.
cémbalo *nm* tambourine; harpsi-chord, spinet.
cementàre *vt* to cement.
ceménto *nm* cement.
céna *nf* supper.
cenàcolo *nm* supper-room, picture of the Last Supper; artistic circle.
cenàre *vi* to sup.
cenciàia *nf* **-io** *nm* rag-picker.
céncio *nm* dishcloth, rag.
cencióso *a* ragged, in tatters.
cénere *nf* ashes *pl*, cinders *pl*; **giórno delle céneri** *nm* Ash Wednesday.
Cenerèntola *nf* Cinderella.
Cenísio, (Monte) *nm (geogr)* Cenis.
cénno *nm* nod, sign, signal, gesture, hint; notice, outline; **far c.** to beckon, nod.
censiménto *nm* census.
censíre *vt* to take the census.
cènso *nm* income, wealth, life annuity; census.
censóre *nm* censor.
censòrio *a* censorious.
censúra *nf* censure, censorship.
censuràre *vt* to censor, censure.
centellinàre *vt* to sip.
centenàrio *a nm* centenarian; *nm* centenary.
centennàle *a* centennial.
centèsimo *a nm* hundredth; *nm* centesimo, centime, cent.
centígrado *a* centigrade.
centigràmmo *nm* centigram.
centímetro *nm* centimeter.
centinàio *nm* hundred; **a centinàia** in hundreds.

cènto *a* hundred.
centràle *a* central, midland; *nf* c. elèttrica power station; c. telefònica telephone exchange; c. atòmica atomic power station.
centralíno *nm* telephone exchange.
centraliẓẓàre *vt* to centralize.
centràre *vt* to center.
cèntro *nm* center, heart, middle.
centuplicàre *vt* centuplicate, multiply.
cèntuplo *a* centuple, hundredfold.
ceppàia *nf* rooty stump.
céppo *nm* (tree) stump, log, (chopping) block; céppi *pl* shackles *pl* (*also fig*).
céra *nf* wax, polish; aspect, face; c. da scarpe shoe polish.
ceralàcca *nf* sealing wax.
ceràmica *nf* ceramics *pl*.
cérca *nf* quest, search.
cercàre *vt* to look for, seek, strive, try.
cérchia *nf* circle; encircling walls *pl*.
cerchiàre *vt* to hoop.
cerchiàto *a* (*of eyes*) black-ringed.
cérchio *nm* circle, ring, hoop, tire.
cereàle *a nm* cereal.
cerebràle *a* cerebral.
cèreo *a* waxen, wan.
cerimònia *nf* ceremony.
cerimoniàle *a nm* ceremonial.
cerimonióso *a* ceremonious.
ceríno *nm* wax match, taper.
cernièra *nf* hinge (*of a bag, purse etc*), mount; c. làmpo zip-fastener, zipper.
cèrnita *nf* choice, selection, grading.
céro *nm* church candle.
ceròtto *nm* sticking plaster; tedious person.
cèrro *nm* Turkey oak.
certaménte *ad* certainly.
certéẓẓa *nf* assurance, certainty.
certificàre *vt* to certify, confirm.
certificàto *nm* certificate, testimonial.
cèrto *a* certain, positive, sure; *ad* certainly, of course.
certóṣa *nf* Carthusian monastery.
certoṣíno *nm* Carthusian monk.
certúni *pron pl* a few, some *pl*.
cèrva *nf* hind, doe.
cervellíno *nm* hare-brained person.
cervèllo *nm* brain; brains *pl*, judgment, sense.
cervellòtico *pl* -ici *a* fantastic, queer.
Cervíno, (il) *nm* (*geogr*) the Matterhorn.
cèrvo *nm* deer, stag; càrne di c. venison; c. volànte stag-beetle.
Céṣare *nm pr* Caesar.
ceṣellàre *vt* to chisel (*also fig*).
ceṣèllo *nm* chisel.
ceṣóie *nf pl* shears *pl*.
cespúglio *nm* bush, thicket.
cessàre *vti* to cease, end, stop.
cessazióne *nf* cessation, end, (*com*) discontinuance.

cessióne *nf* transfer, assignment.
cèsso *nm* water-closet, toilet.
césta *nf* basket, hamper.
cestinàre *vt* to throw into the waste-paper basket.
cestíno *nm* small basket, waste-paper basket.
césto *nm* (*bot*) head; (*basketball*) basket.
cèto *nm* class, rank.
cetriòlo *nm* cucumber.
che *cj and ad* than, that, whether, but, as soon as, lest; *pron and a* that, what, which, who; che c'è? what is the matter?
che *interj* what! no! never!
checchessía *pron* whatever.
chèrmiṣi *nm* crimson.
chetàre *vt* to quiet, silence; -rsi *vr* to grow quiet, silent.
chetichèlla, àlla *ad* quietly, secretly.
chéto *a* quiet, silent.
chi *pron interrog* who, whom, which; *pron rel* he who, whom *etc*; whoever; some . . . others.
chiàcchiera *nf* gossip, prattle, tittle-tattle.
chiacchieràre *vi* to chat, gossip.
chiacchieràta *nf* chat.
chiacchierío *nm* chattering.
chiacchieróna *nf* -óne *nm* babbler, chatterbox, prattler.
chiàma *nf* rollcall.
chiamàre *vt* to call, name; -rsi *vr* to be called; cóme si chiàma? what is your name?
chiamàta *nf* call, summons.
chiappàre *vt* to catch, seize.
Chiàra *nf pr* Clara, Clare, Claire.
chiaraménte *ad* clearly, frankly.
chiaréẓẓa *nf* clearness, fame.
chiarificàre *vt* to clarify.
chiaríre *vt* to clarify, explain; -rsi *vr* to become clear, (*of the weather*) clear up.
chiàro *a* clear, bright, illustrious, *nm* brightness, light, light color; con quésti chiàri di lúna (*fig*) in these difficult times; *ad* clearly.
chiaróre *nm* brightness, light.
chiaroveggènte *a* clear-sighted, clairvoyant.
chiaroveggènza *nf* clairvoyance.
chiàsso *nm* noise, uproar.
chiassóso *a* noisy.
chiàtta *nf* lighter, barge.
chiavàrda *nf* bolt.
chiàve *nf* key, spanner, (*mus*) clef.
chiavistèllo *nm* bolt.
chiàẓẓa *nf* spot, stain.
chícchera *nf* cup.
chícco *pl* -chi *nm* coffee-bean, grain; hailstone; c. d'úva grape.
chièdere *vt* to ask, beg, inquire.
chiérico *pl* -ici *nm* priest in minor orders; chierichétto *nm* altar-boy, choirboy.
chièṣa *nf* church.
chíglia *nf* (*naut*) keel.

chílo nm chyle; **fàre il c.** to rest after a meal.
chilo(gràmmo) nm kilo(gram).
chilòmetro nm kilometer.
chimèra nf chimera, illusion.
chímica nf chemistry.
chímico pl -ici a chemical; nm chemist.
chína nf declivity, slope; Peruvian bark.
chinàre vt to bend, bow; -rsi vr to bend down, stoop, submit.
chincàglie nf pl **chincaglieria** nf fancy goods pl, knick-knacks pl.
chincaglière nm fancy-goods merchant.
chiníno nm quinine.
chíno a bent.
chiòccia nf broody hen.
chiòcciola nf snail, sea-shell; screwnut; **scàla a c.** spiral stair.
chiòdo nm nail; **ròba da chiòdi** dishonest thing or person, badly done (or made) thing; **piantàre chiòdi** to run up debts.
chiòma nf hair, foliage; (of a comet) tail.
chiòsa nf explanatory note, gloss.
chiosàre vt to comment, gloss.
chiòsco pl -òschi nm kiosk, newsstand.
chiòstra nf enclosure; (of teeth) set; (of mountains) range.
chiòstro nm cloister; (fig) monastic life.
chiòtto a silent.
chirurgía nf surgery.
chirúrgico pl -ici a surgical.
chirúrgo pl -úrgi, -úrghi nm surgeon.
chissà interj who knows!
chitàrra nf guitar.
chitarrísta nmf guitarist.
chiúdere vt to close, enclose, fence; conclude; turn off; -rsi vr close, close over, close in, shut oneself up, withdraw.
chiúnque pron rel indef anyone who, whoever, anyone.
chiúsa nf fence, dam, lock, weir; conclusion, close.
chiúso a closed, enclosed; (sky) overcast; (com) settled; nm enclosure, pen.
chiusúra nf closing, close, fastening, fastener, lock.
ci pron us, to us, each other, one another, this, that, it; ad here, there.
ciabàtta nf slipper.
ciabattíno nm cobbler.
ciàlda nf **cialdóne** nm biscuit, wafer.
cialtróna nf slut.
cialtróne nm blackguard, rascal.
cialtronería nf slatternliness, rascality.
ciambèlla nf ring-shaped cake; name given to many objects similarly shaped, as an air cushion, lifebelt etc.
ciambellàno nm chamberlain.

ciància nf idle talk, gossip; **ciànce!** nonsense!
cianciàre vi to prate, tattle, gossip.
cianfruşàglia nf trash, odds and ends.
cíano nm cornflower.
cianúro nm cyanide; **c. di potàssio** potassium cyanide.
ciào interj hello!, hi!, (leaving) byebye.
ciàrla nf talkativeness, gossip.
ciarlàre vi to talk a lot.
ciarlatanería nf quackery.
ciarlatàno nm quack, charlatan.
ciascúno a and pron each, every, each one, every one.
cibàre vt to feed; -rsi vr to eat, feed upon.
cibària nf food, victuals pl.
cíbo nm food.
cicàla nf cicada, chatterbox.
cicatríce nf scar.
cicatrizzàre vti -rsi vr to cicatrize, heal, skin over.
cícca nf cigar-butt, cigarette-end, quid; (fig) worthless thing.
ciceróne nm cicerone, guide.
cicisbèo nm gallant, lady's man.
ciclamíno nm cyclamen.
ciclísmo nm cycling.
ciclísta nmf cyclist.
ciclóne nm cyclone, hurricane.
ciclostilàre vt to cyclostyle.
ciclostíle nm cyclostyle.
cicógna nf stork.
cicòria nf chicory.
cicúta nf hemlock.
cièco pl -chi a blind; nm blind man.
cièlo nm sky, heaven; atmosphere, climate; ceiling.
cífra nf figure, number, cipher.
cifràre vt to write in cipher; (linen) mark.
cíglio pl ciglia (f), (fig) cigli (m) eyelash, eyebrow, edge; **c. della stràda** roadside.
ciglióne nm bank, edge.
cígno nm swan.
cigolàre vi to creak, squeak.
cigolío nm creaking, squeaking.
Cíle nm (geogr) Chile.
cilécca nf disappointment, failure.
cilèno a nm Chilean.
cilício nm hair-shirt, sackcloth.
ciliègia nf cherry; **ciliègio** nm cherrytree.
cilíndrico pl -ici a cylindrical.
cilíndro nm cylinder, roller.
címa nf top, summit, eminence.
cimèlio nm relic, antique.
cimentàre vt to put to the test, try, risk; -rsi vr to enter into contest with, strive.
ciménto nm test, risk.
címice nf bug, bed-bug; drawing pin, thumbtack.
ciminièra nf smokestack, chimney, funnel.
cimitèro nm cemetery, burial ground.

cimúrro *nm* glanders *pl*; distemper.
Cína *nf* (*geogr*) China.
cinciallégra *nf* tit.
cinedràmma *nm* screenplay.
cinegiornàle *nm* newsreel.
cínema *nm* *inv* *v* **cinematògrafo**.
cinematografàre *vt* to film.
cinematografía *nf* cinematography, cinema.
cinematògrafo *nm* cinema(tograph), picture house, pictures, movies.
cinése *a* *nmf* Chinese.
cingallègra *nf* great tit(mouse).
cíngere *vt* to gird, encircle, surround.
cínghia *nf* belt, strap.
cinghiàle *nm* wild boar.
cíngolo *nm* girdle, (*tec*) caterpillar.
cinguettàre *vi* to chirp, twitter.
cínico *pl* **cínici** *a* cynical; *nm* cynic.
cinísmo *nm* cynicism.
cinquànta *a* fifty.
cinquantèsimo *a* fiftieth.
cinquantína *nf* some fifty, about fifty.
cínque *a* five.
cinquecentísta *nmf* artist or writer of the 16th century.
cinquecènto *a* five hundred; *nm* 16th century.
cinquènnio *nm* period of 5 years.
cínta *nf* city walls *pl*, fence, barrier.
cínto *a* surrounded, girded; *nm* belt; c. erniàrio truss.
cintúra *nf* belt, waistband; **c. di salvatàggio** lifebelt.
cinturíno *nm* strap.
ciò *pron* that, this.
ciòcca *nf* (*of hair*) lock, tuft; cluster.
ciòcco *pl* **ciòcchi** *nm* billet of wood, block, log.
cioccolàta *nf* chocolate (*esp. drink*).
cioccolatíno *nm* chocolate (sweet); *pl* chocolates.
cioccolàto *nm* chocolate.
cioè *ad* i.e., namely, that is.
ciondolàre *vi* to dangle; (*fig*) idle about; *vt* to swing, roll (*head etc*).
cióndolo *nm* pendant, trinket.
ciondolóni *ad* dangling.
ciòtola *nf* bowl.
ciòttolo *nm* pebble.
cipíglio *nm* frown, scowl.
cipólla *nm* onion, bulb.
cipollína *nf* spring onion; **cipollíne sótto acéto** pickled onions.
cíppo *nm* half column, boundary stone.
ciprèsso *nm* cypress.
cípria *nf* face powder.
cipriòta *a* *nmf* Cyprian.
Cípro *nf* (*geogr*) Cyprus.
círca *ad* about, nearly; *prep* as to, concerning, with regard to.
círco *pl* **-chi** *nm* circus.
circolàre *vi* to circulate, go round; *a* *nf* circular.
circolazióne *nf* circulation, traffic.
círcolo *nm* circle, club.
circoncisióne *nf* circumcision.
circondàre *vt* to surround, enclose.

circondàrio *nm* district, neighborhood.
circonferènza *nf* circumference.
circonlocuzióne *nf* circumlocution.
circonvallazióne *nf* belt highway.
circonveníre *vt* to circumvent, entrap.
circoscrívere *vt* to circumscribe, limit.
circoscrizióne *nf* circumscription; area.
circospètto *a* circumspect.
circospezióne *nf* circumspection.
circostànte *a* surrounding.
circostànza *nf* circumstance.
circuíre *vi* to surround, circumvent.
circúito *nm* circuit, compass; **córto c.** (*el*) short circuit.
Cirenàica *nf* (*geogr*) Cirenaica, Cyrenaica.
cisalpíno *a* (*geogr*) cisalpine.
cispadàno *a* (*geogr*) cispadane.
cisposità *nf* bleariness.
cispóso *a* blear-eyed.
císte *nf* cyst.
cistèrna *nf* cistern, tank; tanker.
cistifèllea *nf* gall-bladder.
citàre *vt* to cite, quote, mention; summon.
citazióne *nf* citation, quotation; summons, subpoena.
citòfono *nm* intercom.
citràto *nm* citrate.
città *nf* city.
cittadèlla *nf* citadel.
cittadína *nf* small town.
cittadinànza *nf* citizenship; citizens *pl*.
cittadíno *a* of a town; *nm* citizen, townsman.
ciúco *pl* **ciúchi** *nm* donkey.
ciúffo *nm* forelock, topknot, tuft.
ciúrma *nf* (*naut*) ship's crew.
ciurmàglia *nf* mob, rabble.
ciurmatóre *nm* scoundrel, swindler.
civétta *nf* owl; flirt, coquette.
civettàre *vi* to coquet, flirt.
civettería *nf* coquetry.
cívico *pl* **-ici** *a* civic.
civíle *a* civil, civilian.
civilizzàre *vt* to civilize.
civiltà *nf* civilization, civility.
civísmo *nm* civic virtues *pl*.
clàcson *nm* (*aut*) horn.
clamóre *nm* clamor, outcry.
clamoróso *a* clamorous, noisy.
clandestíno *a* clandestine.
Clàra *nf* *pr* Clara, Clare, Claire.
clarinétto, claríno *nm* clarinet.
clàsse *nf* class, form, rank, grade; schoolroom; **c. operàia** working class.
clàssico *pl* **-ici** *a* classic(al); *nm* classic.
classífica *nf* classification; (*sport*) position, result.
classificàre *vt* to classify.
classificazióne *nf* classification.
Clàudio *nm* *pr* Claud.
clàusola *nf* clause.

claustràle *a* cloistral, claustral.
clausúra *nf* seclusion.
clàva *nf* club, bludgeon.
clavicémbalo *nm* (*mus*) harpsichord.
clavícola *nf* collarbone.
clemènte *a* clement, merciful.
clemènza *nf* clemency, mercy.
clericàle *a* clerical.
clericàto *nm* holy orders *pl*, priesthood.
clèro *nm* clergy.
cliènte *nmf* client, customer.
clientèla *nf* clients *pl*, customers *pl*, patronage, practice.
clíma *nm* climate.
climatèrico *pl* -ici *a* climacteric.
climàtico *pl* -ici *a* climatic; **stazióne climàtica** *nf* health resort.
clínica *nf* clinical medicine; clinic, nursing home.
clínico *pl* **clínici** *a* clinical; *nm* clinical doctor.
clistère *nm* (*med*) enema.
cloàca *nf* sewer, drain.
coabitàre *vi* to live together.
coabitazióne *nf* living together.
coadiuvàre *vt* to assist, help.
coagulàre *vt* to coagulate; -rsi *vr* to coagulate, curdle.
coalizióne *nf* coalition.
coàtto *a* forced, compulsory.
coazióne *nf* compulsion.
cobàlto *nm* cobalt.
còc *nm* coke.
cocaína *nf* cocaine.
cócca *nf* (*arrow*) notch; (*of an apron etc*) corner; pet daughter.
coccàrda *nf* cockade.
cocchière *nm* coachman, driver.
còcchio *nm* carriage, coach.
coccinèlla *nf* ladybird.
cocciníglia *nf* cochineal.
còccio *nm* earthenware pot; potsherd.
cocciutàggine *nf* obstinacy.
cocciúto *a* obstinate.
còcco *pl* **còcchi** *nm* coconut, coconut palm; pet, darling.
coccodríllo *nm* crocodile.
còccola *nf* berry.
coccolàre *vt* to fondle; -rsi *vr* to make oneself snug, nestle.
cocènte *a* hot, burning.
cocómero *nm* watermelon; blockhead.
cocúzzolo *nm* crown of the head; summit, top.
códa *nf* tail, queue; **fàre la c.** to queue, to line up.
codardía *nf* cowardice.
codàrdo *a* cowardly; *nm* coward.
codésto *a and pron* that, that one.
còdice *nm* code, codex.
codicíllo *nm* codicil.
codificàre *vt* to codify.
codíno *nm* small tail, pigtail; reactionary.
coefficiènte *nm* coefficient.
coeguàle *a* co-equal.
coerède *nmf* co-heir(ess).
coerènte *a* coherent, consistent.

coerènza *nf* coherence, consistency.
coesióne *nf* cohesion.
coesístere *vi* to coexist.
coetàneo *a* contemporary.
coèvo *a* coeval.
còfano *nm* coffer, casket; (*aut*) hood.
cogitàre *vi* to cogitate, *v* **ponderàre.**
cògliere *vt* to pick, gather, catch, hit, seize, grasp.
cognàta *nf* sister-in-law; **cognàto** *nm* brother-in-law.
cògnito *a* known.
cognizióne *nf* knowledge.
cognóme *nm* surname.
coincidènza *nf* coincidence; (*of trains*) connection.
coincídere *vi* to coincide.
coinvòlgere *vt* to involve.
colà *ad* there.
colaggiú *ad* below, down there, *v* **laggiù.**
colàre *vt* to strain, sieve, colander; (*metals*) cast; drip; *vi* to drip, trickle, drop, leak.
colassú *ad* up there, *v* **lassù.**
colàta *nf* casting, flow.
colatóio *nm* colander, strainer; crucible.
colazióne *nf* lunch; **príma c.** breakfast.
colèi *pron* she, that woman.
colèra *nf* cholera.
coleróso *nm* cholera patient.
colibrí *nm* humming bird.
còlica *nf* colic.
colíno *nm* strainer.
còlla *nf* glue.
collaboràre *vi* to collaborate.
collaborazióne *nf* collaboration.
collàna *nf* necklace; (*of literary works*) series.
collàre *nm* collar.
collàsso *nm* collapse; **c. cardíaco** heart failure.
collaudàre *vt* to test, try out; approve.
collàudo *nm* test; approval.
collazionàre *vt* to collate, compare.
còlle *nm* hill.
collèga *nmf* colleague.
collegaménto *nm* connection.
collegàre *vt* to connect, join; -rsi *vr* to league, unite.
collègio *nm* boarding school, college; constituency.
còllera *nf* anger, wrath.
collèrico *pl* -ici *a* choleric, irascible.
collètta *nf* (*money*) collection, collect.
collettività *nf* collectivity.
collettívo *a* nm collective.
collétto *nm* collar.
collezionàre *vt* to collect.
collezióne *nf* collection.
collezionìsta *nmf* collector.
collimàre *vi* to agree, tally.
collína *nf* hill.
collinóso *a* hilly.
collírio *nm* collyrium, eyewash.
collisióne *nf* clash, collision.

còllo *nm* neck, collar; piece of luggage; **c. del piède** instep.

collocaménto *nm* placing, employment, situation; **agenzìa di c.** employment bureau.

ollocàre *vt* to place; give in marriage; invest, employ; **-rsi** *vr* to get a position; get married.

collocazióne *nf* placing, arrangement; (*of library books*) press-mark, call number.

collòquio *nm* conversation, interview.

colluttàre *vi* to scuffle, grapple.

colluttazióne *nf* scuffle, grapple.

colmàre *vt* to fill to overflowing, load, overwhelm.

cólmo *a* full, brimful; *nm* summit, limit.

cólo *nm* sieve, strainer.

colómba *nf* dove; **colómbo** *nm* pigeon; **colómbo viaggiatóre** carrier pigeon.

colombàia *nf* dovecot.

Colómbia *nf* (*geogr*) Columbia.

colombiàno *a nm* Columbian.

colònia *nf* colony, settlement.

Colònia *nf* (*geogr*) Cologne; **àcqua di C.** eau-de-Cologne.

colonizzàre *vt* to colonize.

colónna *nf* column, pillar.

colonnello *nm* colonel.

colòno *nm* farmer, colonist, settler.

colorànte *a* coloring; *nm* dye.

coloràre, colorire *vt* to color, dye.

coloràto *pp a* colored.

colòre *nm* color, dye; complection, appearance; pretext; (*cards*) suit.

colorito *a* colored, rosy; *nm* coloring, complexion.

colóro *pron* they, those people.

colossàle *a* colossal.

colossèo *nm* Coliseum, Colosseum.

colòsso *nm* colossus.

cólpa *nf* crime, fault, offense, guilt, blame.

colpabilità *nf* culpability.

colpévole *a* culpable, guilty.

colpíre *vt* to hit, strike.

cólpo *nm* blow, stroke, wound, knock, shot; **ad un c., di c.** *ad* suddenly, unexpectedly.

colpóso *a* (*leg*) culpable, unpremeditated; **omicídio c.** manslaughter.

coltellàta *nf* stab, knife wound.

coltellinàio *nm* cutler.

coltellíno *nm* small knife.

coltèllo *nm* knife.

coltivàre *vt* to cultivate, till.

coltivatóre *nm* **-trice** *nf* cultivator, farmer.

coltivazióne *nf* cultivation.

còlto *a* cultivated, cultured, educated.

cóltre *nf* coverlet, blanket.

coltróne *nm* quilt.

coltúra *nf* cultivation; breeding, culture.

colúi *pron* he, that man.

comandaménto *nm* command, commandment.

comandànte *nm* commander; **c. in secónda** second-in-command.

comandàre *vt* to order, command.

comàndo *nm* order, command, leadership; (*mil*) H.Q.; (*av*) control.

combaciàre *vi* to fit together, tally.

combattènte *nm* combatant, soldier; **ex c.** ex-serviceman, veteran.

combàttere *vti* to fight, oppose.

combattiménto *nm* fight, fighting, battle, action.

combinàre *vt* to combine; conclude, settle; plan; *vi* to agree; **-rsi** *vr* agree, match; happen.

combinazióne *nf* combination, arrangement; chance, coincidence; (*underwear*) combinations *pl*, union suit.

combríccola *nf* band, gang.

combustíbile *a* combustible; *nm* fuel.

combustióne *nf* combustion.

cóme *ad* like, as, how, that, when, why; **interj** what!; **c. sta?** how do you do?

comèta *nf* comet.

comicità *nf* comicality.

còmico *pl* **-ici** *a* comic, comical, funny; *nm* comicality; comedian.

cominciàre *vti* to begin.

comitàto *nm* committee.

comitíva *nf* company, party.

comízio *nm* assembly, meeting.

commèdia *nf* comedy, play.

commediànte *nmf* player, comedian; (*fig*) hypocrite.

commediògrafo *nm* playwright.

commemoràre *vt* to commemorate.

commemorazióne *nf* commemoration.

commènda *nf* allowance, living; civic honor given in Italy.

commendàbile, -dévole *a* commendable, praiseworthy.

commendàre *vt* to commend, praise.

commendatízia *nf* (*com*) letter of recommendation.

commendatóre *nm* special title given in Italy for civic merit.

commensàle *nm* table companion, guest, fellow-boarder.

commentàre *vt* to comment.

comménto *nm* comment.

commerciàle *a* commercial.

commerciànte *nm* dealer, merchant, trader.

commerciàre *vi* to deal, trade; *vt* to deal in.

commèrcio *nm* commerce, trade, business.

commésso *a* committed, entrusted; *nm* shop assistant, store-clerk; **c. viaggiatóre** commercial traveler, representative.

commestíbile *a* eatable, edible; **-ili** *nm pl* eatables *pl*.

comméttere *vt* to commit, entrust, order.

commiàto *nm* dismissal, leave.

commiseràre *vt* to pity, commiserate.
commiserazióne *nf* pity, commiseration.
commissariàto *nm* (*mil*) commissariat, commissary's office, police station.
commissàrio *nm* commissary, commissioner, superintendent.
commissionàrio *nm* commission agent.
commissióne *nf* errand, commission, order, committee; **fare delle commissióni** *vi* to do errands, go shopping.
commòsso *a* moved, touched, affected.
commovènte *a* moving, touching, affecting.
commozióne *nf* emotion; (*med*) concussion.
commuòvere *vt* to move, touch, affect; **-rsi** *vr* to be moved, touched.
commutàre *vt* to commute.
commutatóre *a* commutating; *nm* commutator, switch; **c. lúci anabbagliànti** (*aut*) dimmer switch.
commutatríce *nf* commutator.
comò *nm* chest of drawers.
comodíno *nm* bedside table.
comodità *nf* comfort, convenience, opportunity.
còmodo *a* comfortable, convenient, useful; well-to-do; *nm* comfort, convenience, ease, leisure; **a súo c. at your convenience.**
compaesàno *nm* belonging to the same district or village.
compaginàre *vt* to join firmly together.
compàgine *nf* connection, joining of parts, structure.
compàgna *nf* female companion, wife.
compagnía *nf* company, society.
compàgno *a* like, similar; *nm* companion, comrade, mate, partner; **c. di giuòchi** playmate.
companàtico *pl* **-ici** *nm* food eaten with bread.
comparàre *vt* to compare.
comparatívo *a* comparative.
comparàto *a* comparative; **anatomía c.** comparative anatomy.
comparazióne *nf* comparison, simile.
comparíre *vi* to appear.
compàrsa *nf* appearance; (*theat*) extra.
compartecipàre *vi* to share (in).
compartiménto *nm* compartment, division.
compartíre *vt* to divide, share.
compassàto *a* stiff, formal.
compassionàre *vt* to pity.
compassióne *nf* compassion, pity.
compassionévole *a* exciting or feeling pity, pitiful.
compàsso *nm* compasses *pl*.
compatíbile *a* compatible, excusable.

compatiménto *nm* compassion, forbearance.
compatíre *vt* to pity, excuse.
compatriòta *nmf* compatriot.
compàtto *a* compact, solid.
compendiàre *vt* to abridge.
compèndio *nm* abridgment, compendium.
compensàre *vt* to compensate, indemnify.
compensàto *nm* plywood.
compènso *nm* compensation, reward, indemnity; **in c. in return.**
comperàre *v* **compràre.**
competènte *a* competent, qualified.
competènza *nf* competence, authority; **competenze** *pl* fees *pl*.
compètere *vi* to compete; be due to.
competizióne *nf* competition, contest.
compiacènte *a* obliging, complaisant.
compiacènza *nf* kindness, complaisance; satisfaction.
compiacére *vt* to please, comply with; **-rsi** *vr* to be pleased to, condescend.
compiaciménto *nm* satisfaction, pleasure; congratulation.
compiàngere *vt* to be sorry for, lament, pity.
compiànto *a* lamented, regretted; *nm* regret, pity, lament.
cómpiere *vt* to accomplish, complete, fulfill, finish.
compilàre *vt* to compile.
compilazióne *nf* compilation.
compiménto *nm* accomplishment, completion, fulfillment.
compíre *v* **compiere.**
compitàre *vt* to spell.
compitézza *nf* courtesy, politeness.
cómpito *nm* homework, task.
compíto *a* courteous, polite.
compiúto *a* accomplished, ended, complete.
compleànno *nm* birthday.
complementàre *a* complementary, supplementary.
compleménto *nm* complement; (*mil*) reserve.
complessióne *nf* constitution.
complessità *nf* complexity.
complessívo *a* comprehensive, total.
complèsso *a* complex, compound; *nm* whole, set; (*mus*) band; **in c. in** general, on the whole.
completaménte *ad* completely, entirely.
completàre *vt* to complete.
complèto *a* complete, whole, full; *nm* (*of clothes*) suit.
complicàre *vt* to complicate, make intricate; **-rsi** *vr* to become complicated, difficult.
complicazióne *nf* complication.
còmplice *nm* accomplice.
complimentàre *vt* to compliment.
compliménto *nm* compliment; **compliménti** *pl* congratulations *pl*;

sènza compliménti frankly, without ceremony.

complimentóso *a* obsequious, ceremonious.

complottàre *vti* to plot, conspire.

complòtto *nm* conspiracy, plot.

componènte *a nmf* component, ingredient, member.

componiménto *nm* arrangement, composition.

compórre *vt* to arrange, compose; conciliate; (*type*) set up; **-rsi** *vr* to consist of.

comportàbile *a* bearable, tolerable; convenient.

comportaménto *nm* behavior.

comportàre *vt* to bear, tolerate; allow, involve; **-rsi** *vr* to act, behave.

compòrto *nm* delay, respite.

compoṣitóre *nm* composer; (*typ*) compositor.

compoṣizióne *nf* composition, agreement, arrangement.

compostézza *nf* composure, self-possession.

compósto *a* compound, composed, sedate, self-possessed; *nm* compound, mixture.

cómpra *nf* purchase.

compràre *vt* to buy, purchase.

compratóre *nm* **-tríce** *nf* buyer.

compravéndita *nf* buying and selling.

comprèndere *vt* to understand, comprehend; comprise, include.

comprendònio *nm* (*fam*) understanding.

comprensíbile *a* comprehensible, intelligible.

comprensibilità *nf* comprehensibility, intelligibility.

comprensióne *nf* comprehension, understanding, sympathy.

comprensívo *a* comprehensive, sympathetic.

compréṣo *a* included, inclusive.

comprèssa *nf* compress, lozenge.

comprèsso *a* compressed, oppressed.

comprímere *vt* to compress, restrain.

compromésso *nm* compromise; **mettere in c.** to risk.

compromettènte *a* compromising.

comprométtere *vt* to compromise, involve.

comprovàre *vt* to prove, give evidence of.

compúnto *a* contrite, sorry.

compunzióne *nf* compunction, contrition.

computàre *vt* to compute, reckon.

computísta *nmf* accountant, bookkeeper.

computistería *nf* accountant's office; book-keeping.

còmputo *nm* account, reckoning.

comunàle *a* communal, municipal.

comúne *a* common, ordinary; *nm* commune, municipality; town hall.

comunicàre *vt* to communicate,

announce; administer the Sacrament; **-rsi** *vr* to take the Sacrament.

comunicatíva *nf* facility in explaining and instructing.

comunicàto *nm* bulletin, communiqué.

comunicazióne *nf* communication, connection, message.

comunióne *nf* communion, Communion.

comuníṣmo *nm* Communism.

comuníṣta *a nmf* Communist.

comunità *nf* community.

comúnque *ad* anyhow, however.

con *prep* with, by, at, from, on, against.

conàto *nm* effort, attempt.

cónca *nf* basin, tub; valley; conch.

concatenàre *vt* to link together.

còncavo *a nm* concave, hollow.

concèdere *vt* to grant, concede, allow.

concedíbile *a* allowable, grantable.

concentraménto *nm* **concentrazione** *nf* concentration; **càmpo di concentraménto** concentration camp.

concentràre *vt* to concentrate.

concentràto *a* concentrated; *nm* extract, concentrated food.

concepíbile *a* conceivable.

concepiménto *vt* conception.

concepíre *vt* to conceive, imagine.

concèrnere *vt* to concern, relate.

concertàre *vt* to conduct, arrange, concert, plan; **-rsi** *vr* to agree, be agreed.

concertatóre *nm* **-tríce** *nf* **maéstro c. e direttóre d'orchèstra** conductor.

concertísta *nmf* concert artist.

concèrto *nm* concert, concerto; agreement; **di c.** unanimously.

concessionàrio *nm* (*com*) concessionaire. agent.

concessióne *nf* concession, permission.

concètto *nm* concept, conception, idea, (*lit*) conceit.

concettóso *a* pithy, sententious.

concezióne *nf* conception, idea.

conchíglia *nf* sea-shell, conch.

cóncia *nf* tanning, curing.

conciàre *vt* to dress (*skins*), tan; (*fig*) ill-treat.

conciatóre *nm* **-tríce** *nf* tanner.

conciatúra *nf* tanning, dressing.

conciliàbile *a* compatible, reconcilable.

conciliàbolo *nm* conventicle, secret meeting.

conciliàre *vt* to conciliate, reconcile; **-rsi** *vr* to agree; win (*affection etc*).

conciliazióne *nf* conciliation, reconciliation.

concílio *nm* council.

concimàre *vt* to manure.

concíme *nm* compost, dung, manure.

cóncio *a* tanned; knocked about; *nm* dung.

conciṣióne *nf* concision, conciseness.

concíso *a* concise, brief.
concitaménto *nm* excitement tumult.
concitazióne *nf* excitement, agitation, emotion.
concittadíno *nm* fellow citizen.
concludènte *a* conclusive, decisive, energetic.
conclúdere *vt* to conclude, infer; do; *vi* be conclusive.
conclusióne *nf* conclusion, issue; **in c.** finally.
conclusívo *a* conclusive.
concordàre *vt* to arrange, reconcile; *vi* to agree.
concordàto *a* agreed upon, fixed; *nm* agreement, concordat.
concòrde *a* in agreement, consistent.
concòrdia *nf* harmony, unanimity.
concorrènte *a* concurrent; *nmf* competitor, rival.
concorrènza *nf* concurrence; competition, rivalry.
concórrere *vi* to concur; rival, compete.
concórso *nm* concourse; competition.
concretàre *vt* to make concrete; put into action.
concrèto *a nm* concrete, positive.
concubína *nf* concubine.
concubinàto *nm* concubinage.
concupiscènte *a* covetous.
concupiscènza *nf* concupiscence, lust.
concussióne *nf* concussion; extortion.
condànna *nf* condemnation, conviction.
condannàre *vt* to sentence, condemn.
condensàre *vt* to condense, thicken; **-rsi** *vr* to condense, grow thick.
condensàto *a* condensed.
condensatóre *nm* **-tríce** *nf* condenser.
condensazióne *nf* condensation.
condiménto *nm* seasoning, condiment, dressing, sauce.
condíre *vt* to season, dress.
condiscendènte *a* condescending, compliant.
condiscendènza *nf* compliance, condescension.
condiscéndere *vi* to condescend, yield.
condiscépolo *nm* fellow-disciple, schoolfellow.
condíto *a* seasoned; (*of salad*) dressed.
condivídere *vt* to share.
condizionàle *a* conditional; *nm* (*gram*) conditional; *nf* (*leg*) conditional sentence.
condizionàre *vt* to condition; qualify.
condizionatóre *nm* air conditioner.
condizióne *nf* condition, rank, situation, qualification; **a c.** upon condition.
condogliànza *nf* condolence.
condolérsi *vr* to condole, grieve.
condomínio *nm* joint ownership.
condonàre *vt* to remit, condone.

condótta *nf* conduct, behavior; management; piping system.
condótto *a* **mèdico c.** panel doctor; *nm* duct, conduit, pipe.
conducènte *nmf* driver; leaseholder.
condúrre *vti* to conduct, lead; **-rsi** *vr* to act, behave.
conduttóre *nm* **-tríce** *nf* conductor, driver, guide, leader; (*el*) wire.
conduttúra *nf* conduit, main; **c. d'àcqua** water-pipe.
confabulàre *vi* to confabulate, chat.
confacènte *a* convenient, suitable.
confàrsi *vr* to agree, become, fit, suit.
confederàrsi *vr* to confederate.
confederazióne *nf* confederation.
conferènza *nf* lecture, conference.
conferenzière *nm* lecturer.
conferiménto *nm* bestowal, conferment.
conferíre *vt* to bestow, confer, contribute; *vi* confer (with), agree.
confèrma *nf* confirmation.
confermàre *vt* to confirm, strengthen.
confessàre *vt* to confess, acknowledge; **-rsi** *vr* to go to confession.
confessióne *nf* confession, faith.
confessóre *nm* confessor.
confètto *nm* bonbon, sweet.
confettúra *nf* jam.
confezionàre *vt* to manufacture, prepare, make up; **confezionàto su misúra** made to measure; **artícolo confezionàto** ready-made article.
confezióne *nf* manufacture, preparation; clothes; packing.
conficcàre *vt* to drive in, thrust.
confidàre *vt* to confide, trust; **-rsi** *vr* to confide in.
confidènte *a* confiding, trusting; *nmf* confidant, bosom friend.
confidènza *nf* confidence, secret, intimacy.
confidenziàle *a* confidential, private.
confidenzialménte *ad* confidentially, privately.
confíggere *vt* to nail, thrust.
configuràre *vt* to shape; (*fig*) symbolize.
confinànte *a* bordering, contiguous.
confinàre *vt* to banish, confine; *vi* to border on; **-rsi** *vr* to confine oneself; retire.
confíne *nm* border, frontier, limit.
confíno *nm* political confinement.
confísca *nf* confiscation, forfeiture.
confiscàre *vt* to confiscate, forfeit.
conflagrazióne *nf* conflagration.
conflítto *nm* conflict.
confluíre *vi* to flow together.
confóndere *vt* to confuse, confound; **-rsi** *vr* to get confused; worry.
conformàre *vt* to conform; **-rsi** *vr* to comply (with).
conformazióne *nf* conformation.
confórme *a* conforming, in agreement.
conformísmo *nm* conformism.
conformísta *nmf* conformist.

conformità nf conformity, accordance.

confortàre vt to comfort, console, encourage, fortify; -rsi vr to console oneself, take courage.

confortévole a comforting, comfortable.

confòrto nm comfort, consolation, support.

confratèllo nm (relig) fellow-member.

confratèrnita nf brotherhood, confraternity.

confrontàre vt to compare, confront; vi to agree.

confrónto nm comparison.

confuşióne nf confusion, shame.

confúşo a confused, embarrassed, ashamed; indistinct.

confutàre vt to confute, disprove.

confutazióne nf confutation.

congedàre vt to dismiss; -rsi vr to resign, take leave.

congèdo nm discharge, leave; in c. ad on leave.

congegnàre vt to put together, contrive.

congégno nm appliance, gear.

congelaménto nm congealment, freezing.

congelàre vi to congeal, freeze.

congènere a similar.

congènito a congenital.

congèrie nf heap, mass.

congestionàre vt to congest, crowd.

congettúra nf conjecture, guess.

congetturàre vt to conjecture.

congiúngere vt to connect, join; -rsi vr to join, meet.

congiuntívo a conjunctive, (gram) subjunctive; nm (gram) subjunctive.

congiúnto a joined, connected, combined; nm kinsman, relative.

congiuntúra nf conjuncture, circumstance; predicament.

congiúra nf conspiracy, plot.

congiuràre vi to conspire.

conglomeràre vt to conglomerate.

conglomeràto nm grouping, conglomerate.

conglutinàre vt to conglutinate.

Còngo nm (geogr) Congo.

congolése a nmf Congolese.

congratulàrsi vr to congratulate.

congratulazióne nf congratulation.

congrèga nf gang, set; congregation.

congregàre vt to assemble, call together; -rsi vr to congregate.

congressísta nmf member of a congress.

congrèsso nm congress, conference.

còngruo a congruous, suitable.

conguagliàre vt to balance, equalize.

conguàglio nm adjustment, balancing, leveling.

coniàre vt to coin, (a medal) strike.

coniglièra nf rabbit-hutch.

coníglio nm rabbit.

cònio nm coinage; die, brand.

coniugàre vt to conjugate; -rsi vr to marry.

coniugazióne nf conjugation.

còniuge nm husband; nf wife; còniugi pl married couple.

connazionàle nmf compatriot.

connèttere vt to connect, join, (fig) associate; non c. to have confused ideas.

connivènte a conniving.

connivènza nf connivance.

connotàto nm distinctive mark; connotàti pl description (of a person).

connúbio nm marriage, union.

còno nm cone.

conòcchia nf distaff.

conoscènte nmf acquaintance.

conoscènza nf knowledge, acquaintance; consciousness, cognition.

conóscere vt to know, experience, take cognizance of; farsi c. to make oneself known; -rsi vr to know oneself, know each other.

conoscíbile a knowable, recognizable; nm knowledge.

conosciménto nm knowing, knowledge.

conoscitóre nm -tríce nf connoisseur, good judge.

conosciúto a well-known, famous.

conquísta nf conquest.

conquistàre vt to conquer.

consacràre vt to consecrate, dedicate, devote, ordain.

consacrazióne nf consecration, ordination.

consanguíneo a consanguineous, closely related; nm kinsman.

consapévole a aware, conscious, acquainted.

consapevolézza nf consciousness, knowledge.

cònscio v consapévole.

conségna nf consignment, delivery; lasciàre in c. vt to deposit.

consegnàre vt to consign, deliver.

conseguènte a consequent, consistent.

conseguènza nf consequence; in c. accordingly.

conseguiménto nm attainment.

conseguíre vt to attain, obtain, reach; vi to follow, result.

consènso nm consent, assent.

consensuàle a (leg) by mutual consent.

consentíre vi to consent, agree, yield; vt to permit.

consenziènte a approving, consenting.

consèrva nf jam, preserve, preservation, reservoir.

conservàre vt to keep, preserve; -rsi vr to last, keep in good health.

conservatóre, f -tríce a preserving, preservative, conservative; nm preserver, keeper; (pol) Conservative.

conservatòrio nm academy of music.

conservazióne nf preservation, care, maintenance.

consèsso nm assembly, meeting.

consideràbile *a* considerable.
consideràre *vt* to consider, regard.
consideràto *a* considerate, thoughtful, careful; esteemed.
considerazióne *nf* consideration, esteem.
considerévole *a* considerable, pretty large.
consigliàre *vt* to advise, counsel; -rsi *vr* to ask advice, consult.
consiglière *nm* counselor, councilor.
consiglio *nm* advice, counsel, council.
consímile *a* like, similar.
consistènte *a* consistent; firm, substantial.
consistènza *nf* consistence, consistency.
consístere *vi* to consist.
consòcio *nm* associate, partner.
consolàre *vt* to comfort, console; -rsi *vr* to take comfort.
consolàre *a* consular.
consolàto *nm* consulate.
consolazióne *nf* consolation, comfort, delight.
cònsole *nm* consul.
consolidàre *vt* to consolidate, strengthen; -rsi *vr* to grow firm.
consolidazióne *nf* **consolidaménto** *nm* consolidation, strengthening.
consonànte *a* consonant, agreeing; *nf* consonant.
consonànza *nf* consonance, agreement.
cònsono *a* consonant, agreeing.
consòrte *nmf* consort, husband, wife.
consortería *nf* clique, set.
consòrzio *nm* society, syndicate.
constàre *vi* to consist, be known, be proved.
constatàre *vt* to ascertain, verify, certify.
constatazióne *nf* ascertainment.
consuèto *a* habitual, usual.
consuetúdine *nf* custom, habit, practice.
consulènte *a* consulting, consultant; *nm* consultant, adviser.
consulènza *nf* advice; **c. legàle** legal advice.
consúlta *nf* council.
consultàre *vt* to consult, examine; -rsi *vr* to seek advice, consult.
consultazióne *nf* consultation; **gabinétto di c.** (*med*) consulting room; **libro di c.** reference book.
consúlto *nm* consultation, (medical or legal) opinion.
consumàre *vt* to consume, waste, consummate; -rsi *vr* to wear out, consume, pine away, waste away.
consumatóre *nm* consumer.
consumazióne *nf* consumption, consummation; drink or food (in a café etc).
consúmo *nm* consumption, waste; **úso e c.** wear and tear.
consúnto *a* consumed, worn out; consumptive.

consunzióne *nf* (*med*) consumption.
contàbile *a* book-keeping, calculating; *nm* book-keeper, accountant.
contabilità *nf* book-keeping.
contadína *nf* -no *nm* peasant.
contadinésco *pl* -éschi *a* rustic.
contàdo *nm* country (round a town).
contagiàre *vt* to infect, contaminate.
contàgio *nm* contagion.
contagióso *a* contagious, infectious.
contagócce *nm* dropper.
contaminàre *vt* to contaminate.
contaminazióne *nf* contamination, pollution.
contànte *a* counting, ready; **denàro c.** cash, ready money; *nm* cash.
contàre *vt* to count; relate; consider; *vi* to count, have authority, rely on; **ciò che cónta** what matters.
contatóre *nm* meter, reckoner; **c. a monéta** slot meter; **c. del gas** gasmeter; **c. per parchéggio** parking meter.
contàtto *nm* contact, touch, connection; **spína di c.** contact plug.
cónte *nm* count, earl.
contèa *nf* earldom, county, shire.
conteggiàre *vt* to count, charge.
contéggio *nm* computation, calculation; **c. all'indiètro** countdown.
contégno *nm* behavior, dignity, gravity.
contegnóso *a* dignified, grave, staid.
contemperàre *vt* to proportion, temper.
contemplàre *vt* to contemplate.
contemplatívo *a* contemplative.
contemplazióne *nf* contemplation.
contemporaneità *nf* contemporaneousness.
contemporàneo *a nm* contemporary.
contendènte *a* contending, opposing; *nm* rival, opponent, competitor.
contèndere *vt* to contest; *vi* to contend, quarrel; -rsi *vr* to contend, be rivals for.
contenére *vt* to contain, hold, restrain; -rsi *vr* to behave, control oneself.
contentàre *vt* to content, gratify; -rsi *vr* to be pleased, satisfied.
contentatúra *nf* contentment; **di fàcile c.** *ad* easy to please.
contentézza *nf* contentment, satisfaction.
contènto *a* content, glad, satisfied; *nm* contentment, happiness.
contenúto *a* contained; *nm* contents *pl*, subject.
contenzióso *a* contentious.
conterràneo *a* of the same country; *nm* countryman.
contésa *nf* contest, dispute, contention.
contéssa *nf* countess.
contestàre *vt* to contest, deny.
contestazióne *nf* contest, dispute; notification.
contèsto *a* interwoven; *nm* context.
contézza *nf* knowledge.

contiguità nf contiguity.
contiguo a contiguous, adjoining.
continentàle a continental.
continènte a temperate, continent; nm continent.
continènza nf continence, self-restraint.
contingènte a contingent; nm contingency, contingent; (com) quota.
contingènza nf contingency, emergency, circumstance.
continuaménte ad continuously, continually, constantly.
continuàre vti to continue, pursue, go on, last.
continuazióne, continuità nf continuation, continuity, duration.
continuo a continuous, non-stop, lasting; **di c.** ad non-stop, continuously.
cónto nm account, bill; computation, reckoning; worth.
contòrcere vt to contort; **-rsi** vr to twist, wring, writhe.
contornàre vt to surround, trim.
contórno nm contour, outline; vegetables served with a dish of meat.
contorsióne nf contortion.
contrabbandière nm smuggler.
contrabbàndo nm contraband goods pl, smuggling.
contrabbàsso nm (mus) double bass.
contraccambiàre vt to return, reciprocate.
contraccàmbio nm exchange, return; **rèndere il c.** to give like for like.
contraccólpo nm counter-stroke, rebound.
contràda nf countryside, district, wide street.
contraddíre vt to contradict.
contraddistínguere vt to distinguish, mark.
contraddittòrio a contradictory; nm debate, cross-examination.
contrad(d)izióne nf contradiction.
contraèrea nf anti-aircraft artillery; **contraèreo** a anti-aircraft.
contraffàre vt to counterfeit, forge, imitate; **-rsi** vr to disguise oneself.
contraffàtto a counterfeit, disguised; deformed.
contraffazióne nf counterfeit, forgery.
contrammiràglio nm rear-admiral.
contrappélo nm the wrong way; **a, di c.** (fig) against the grain.
contrappéso nm counter-balance, counterpoise.
contrappórre vt to contrast, oppose; **-rsi** vr to cross, oppose.
contrappúnto nm (mus) counterpoint.
contrariàre vt to thwart, oppose, annoy.
contràrio a contrary, opposite, unfavorable, adverse; nm contrary, opposite; **al c.** on the contrary.

contràrre vt to contract; **-rsi** vr to shrink.
contrasségno nm countersign, badge, mark.
contrastànte a contrasting.
contrastàre vt to contest, oppose, resist; vi to contrast, clash; **-rsi** vr to fight.
contràsto nm contrast, opposition, strife, clash.
contrattàcco nm counter-attack.
contrattàre vti to negotiate, bargain.
contrattèmpo nm mishap, hitch; (mus) syncopation.
contràtto a contracted; nm contract, agreement.
contravveléno nm antidote.
contravveníre vi to contravene, infringe.
contravvenzióne nf contravention, infringement; fine; **fàre una c.** impose a fine.
contrazióne nf contraction.
contribuènte nmf taxpayer.
contribuíre vi to contribute, help, share.
contribúto nm contribution, share.
contristàre vt to afflict, sadden; **-rsi** vr to be afflicted, grieve.
contríto a contrite, penitent.
contrizióne nf contrition, penitence.
cóntro prep against, opposite.
controfirmàre vt to countersign.
controllàre vt to check, control, verify, inspect.
contròllo nm check, control.
controllóre nm controller, ticket-collector, ticket-inspector.
controlúce ad against the light.
contropòrta nf double door.
controproducènte a having the opposite effect.
contropròva nf counter-check, counter-vote, evidence.
contrórdine nm counter-order.
Controrifórma nf Counter-reformation.
controsènso nm misinterpretation, nonsense.
controstòmaco ad unwillingly.
controvèrsia nf controversy, dispute.
controvèrso a controversial, doubtful.
controvèrtere vt to controvert, dispute.
contumàce a contumacious, guilty of default.
contumàcia pl **-àcie** nf default, contumacy; quarantine.
contumèlia nf contumely, abuse.
contundènte a bruising; **àrma c.** blunt weapon.
conturbàre vt to disturb, trouble; **-rsi** vr to be agitated, fret.
contusióne nf bruise, contusion.
contuttochè cj although.
contuttociò ad however, nevertheless.
convalescènte a nmf convalescent.
convalescènza nf convalescence.

convalidàre vt to confirm, corroborate.
convégno nm meeting (place).
convenévole a convenient, proper, suitable; **convenévoli** nm pl compliments, regards, ceremony.
conveniènte a convenient, profitable.
conveniènza nf convenience, advantage, propriety, proportion.
conveníre vi to suit; meet, assemble; agree; vt to summon.
convènto nm convent, monastery.
convenúto a agreed (on), fixed; nm agreement; defendant.
convenzionàle a conventional.
convenzióne nf convention, covenant.
convergènza nf convergence.
convèrgere vi to converge.
convèrsa nf lay sister.
conversàre vi to converse, talk.
conversazióne nf conversation, talk.
conversióne nf conversion.
convèrso a converse, opposite; nm lay brother.
convertíre vt to convert; -**rsi** vr to be converted.
convertíto nm convert.
convessità nf convexity.
convèsso a convex.
convettóre nm convector.
convincènte a convincing.
convíncere vt to convince, persuade.
convinciménto nm **convinzióne** nf conviction, persuasion.
convitàto nm guest.
convíto nm banquet, feast.
convítto nm boarding-school.
convivènte a living together.
convivènza nf cohabitation, living together.
convívere vi to cohabit, live together.
convocàre vt to convoke, summon.
convogliàre vt to convoy, direct.
convòglio nm convoy, train.
convulsióne nf convulsion, spasm.
convulsívo a convulsive, spasmodic.
convúlso a convulsive, jerky; nm convulsion.
cooperàre vi to co-operate.
cooperatíva nf (com) co-operative society.
cooperazióne nf co-operation.
coordinàre vt to co-ordinate.
coordinàta nf co-ordinate.
copèrchio nm cover, lid.
copèrta nf blanket, coverlet, rug, cover; (naut) deck.
copertína nf cover, book-cover, dust-jacket.
copèrto a covered, (of the sky) overcast; clothed, hidden; nm (at table) cover, place.
copertóne nm (tire) cover; tarpaulin.
copertúra nf covering.
còpia nf copy, print; plenty, quantity; **c. fotostàtica (fotocòpia)** photostat (photocopy); **c. carbóne**

carbon copy; **bèlla c.** fair copy; **brútta c.** rough copy.
copialèttere nm letter-book, letterpress.
copiàre vt to copy, imitate, transcribe.
copiatívo a copying.
copiatúra nf copying, transcription.
copióne nm (theat) script.
copióso a abundant, copious.
copísta nmf copyist.
copistería nf copying office, typing office.
cóppa nf cup, goblet; (aut) sump, oil pan.
coppellàre vt (metals) to assay, test.
còppia nf couple, pair.
copricàpo nm headgear, hat.
coprifuòco pl -**fuòchi** nm curfew.
copríre vt to cover, hide, protect, shelter, hold (a post); -**rsi** vr to put on one's hat, wrap oneself up.
copriteièra nm tea-cozy, cap.
coprivivànde nm dishcover.
còpto a Coptic; nm Copt, (language) Coptic.
coràggio nm courage, valor.
coraggiosaménte ad bravely.
coraggióso a courageous, valiant.
coràle a choral; nm chorale.
coràllo nm coral.
Coràno nm Koran.
coràzza nf cuirass, armor-plating.
corazzàre vt to armor.
corazzière nm cuirassier.
còrba nf basket.
corbellàre vt to make a fool of, make fun of.
corbellería nf foolish act.
corbèllo nm (small) basket.
corbézzola nf arbutus-berry; **corbézzolo** nm arbutus-tree.
còrda nf cord, rope, (of a musical instrument) string; (mus) chord.
cordàme nm (naut) cordage, ropes pl.
cordiàle a cordial, hearty, warm; nm cordial.
cordicèlla nf **cordoncíno** nm fine cord, string.
cordòglio nm grief, mourning, sorrow.
cordóne nm cord; cordon.
Corèa nf (geogr) Korea.
coreàno a nm Korean.
coriàndolo nm paper streamer; **coriàndoli** pl confetti.
coricàre vt to lay down; -**rsi** vr to go to bed, lie down.
corísta nm chorister, chorus singer.
cornàcchia nf crow; (fig) croaker.
cornamúṣa nf (mus) bagpipes pl.
cornétta nf (mus) cornet, horn.
cornétto nm ear-trumpet, small horn; pl French beans pl.
cornice nf frame, framework.
cornicióne nm cornice.
corniòla nf (min) cornelian.
còrno pl **còrna** (f), (instruments) **còrni** (m) nm horn.

Cornovàglia nf (geogr) Cornwall.
cornúto a horned; nm cuckold.
còro nm chorus, choir.
coróna nf crown, wreath, garland; (mus) corona.
coronàre vt to crown.
coronàrio a coronary.
coronazióne nf coronation.
corpacciúto a burly, corpulent.
corpétto nm bodice, waistcoat.
còrpo nm body, corpse; mass.
corporàle a bodily, corporal, corporeal.
corporatúra nf size.
corporazióne nf corporation.
corpòreo a corporeal.
corpulènto a corpulent.
corpulènza nf corpulence.
Corràdo nm pr Conrad, Konrad.
corredàre vt to equip, fit up, outfit.
corredíno nm baby's layette.
corrèdo nm equipment, furniture, kit, outfit, trousseau.
corrèggere vt to correct, revise, upbraid; -rsi vr to improve, mend one's ways.
correlazióne nf correlation.
corrènte a running, flowing, current, common; nf stream, current; **tenére al c.** to keep informed.
córrere vi to run, flow, (of time) elapse, circulate, (of distance) intervene.
correttaménte ad correctly, properly.
correttézza nf correctness, propriety, honesty.
corrètto a correct, exact, upright, well-bred.
correttóre nm -tríce nf corrector, (typ) proof-reader.
correzióne nf correction, reform.
corrída nf bullfight.
corridóio nm corridor, passage.
corridóre nm racer, runner.
corrièra nf coach, bus, mail-bus, mail-coach.
corrière nm courier, messenger, carrier, mail, express company; **a vòlta di c.** ad by return of post.
corrispettívo a corresponding; nm equivalent, compensation.
corrispondènte a corresponding, correspondent; nmf correspondent.
corrispondènza nf correspondence, harmony, connection.
corrispóndere vi to correspond, return; vt to pay.
corrívo a easy-going, lenient, rash.
corroboràre vt to corroborate; strengthen.
corroborazióne nf corroboration, support.
corródere vt to corrode, eat away, wear away; -rsi vr to corrode, waste away.
corrómpere vt to corrupt, pollute, bribe; -rsi vr to rot, become corrupt.
corroşívo a nm corrosive.

corrótto a corrupt(ed).
corrucciàre vi -rsi vr to get angry; grieve.
corrúccio nm anger, wrath.
corrugàre vt to corrugate, frown, knit (one's brows); -rsi vr wrinkle.
corruscàre vi to scintillate, flash.
corruttèla nf corruption.
corruttibilità nf corruptibility.
corruzióne nf corruption, decay.
córsa nf race, run, running, trip.
corsàro nm corsair, pirate.
corsía nf passage; (of hospital) ward; dormitory; track.
Còrsica nf (geogr) Corsica.
corsívo a nm cursive, italic, italics pl.
córso a passed, plundered; nm course, main street, flow.
còrso a nm Corsican.
córte nf court, hall, tribunal, yard.
cortéccia nf bark, crust.
corteggiaménto nm courtship, wooing.
corteggiàre vt to court, woo.
corteggiatóre nm suitor, wooer, lover.
cortéggio nm attendants pl, retinue.
cortèo nm procession, train.
cortése a courteous, kind, polite.
cortesía nf courtesy, politeness.
cortézza nf shortness, dullness.
cortigiàna nf courtesan.
cortigiàno nm courtier.
cortíle nm court, courtyard, playground.
cortína nf curtain.
córto a short, brief, deficient; **èssere a c. di** to be short of, lack.
corvétta nf curvet; (naut) corvette.
còrvo nm raven, crow, rook.
còsa nf thing, matter, work; **che còsa?** what?; **tànte còse** regards.
cosàcco a nm Cossack.
còscia nf thigh, haunch.
cosciènte a aware, conscious.
cosciènza nf conscience, consciousness, conscientiousness.
coscienzióşo a conscientious.
cosciòtto nm (of meat) leg.
coscrítto a nm conscript.
coscrizióne nf conscription.
coşí ad as, so, thus, therefore; **c. c. so-so; per c. díre** so to speak.
cosicché cj so that.
cosiddétto a so-called.
coşmètico pl -ici a nm cosmetic.
còşmico pl -ici a cosmic.
còşmo nm cosmos, universe.
coşmòdromo nm cosmodrome, rocket-station.
coşmonàuta nm cosmonaut.
coşmopolita a nm cosmopolitan, cosmopolite.
còşo nm thing, thingummy (word used instead of the real name of something).
cospàrgere vt to sprinkle, strew.
cospètto nm presence.
cospícuo a conspicuous; considerable.
cospiràre vi to conspire, plot.
cospirazióne nf conspiracy.

còsta *nf* coast, declivity; rib; (*of knife, book*) back.
costà *ad* there, in your town.
costaggiù *ad* down there.
costànte *a nf* constant, steady, firm, uniform.
Costantinòpoli *nf* (*geogr*) Constantinople.
costànza *nf* constancy, firmness, perseverance.
Costànza *nf pr* Constance.
Costànza *nf* (*geogr*) lago di C. Lake Constance.
costàre *vt* to cost.
costatàre *v* constatàre.
costatazióne *v* constatazióne.
costàto *nm* flank, ribs *pl*, side.
costeggiàre *vti* to coast, lie along, run along by.
costèi *pron* she, this woman, that woman.
costernàre *vt* to appall, dismay; -rsi *vr* to be dismayed.
costì *ad* there, in your town.
costièra *nf* coast, shore.
costipàre *vt* to constipate, give a cold to; -rsi *vr* to become costive, catch a cold.
costipàto *a* having a cold; constipated.
costipazióne *nf* (*med*) cold; constipation.
costituíre *vt* to constitute, elect; -rsi *vr* to constitute oneself; give oneself up, surrender.
costituzióne *nf* establishment, constitution.
còsto *nm* cost.
còstola *nf* rib; (*of knife, book*) back.
costolétta *nf* chop, cutlet.
costóro *pron pl* they, these (those) people.
costóso *a* costly, expensive.
costringere *vt* to compel, constrain, compress.
costrizióne *nf* constraint, compulsion, constriction.
costruíre *vt* to build, construct.
costruttívo *a* constructive.
costrútto *nm* construction, profit, meaning.
costruzióne *nf* construction, building.
costúi *pron* he, this man, that man.
costumàre *vi and impers* to be usual, be the fashion, be in the habit of.
costumatézza *nf* decency, good manners *pl*, politeness.
costumàto *a* civil, polite.
costúme *nm* custom, morals *pl*; costume.
costúra *nf* seam.
coténna *nf* pigskin, scalp; turf.
cotésto *a and pron* that, *pl* those.
cotidiàno *a nm* daily.
cotógna *nf* quince; cotógno *nm* quince-tree.
cotognàta *nf* quince jam, jelly.
cotolétta *v* costolétta.

cotonàto *nm* cotton; silk and cotton fabric.
cotóne *nm* cotton; c. idròfilo absorbent cotton.
cotonièro *a* cotton.
cotonifício *nm* cotton-mill.
còtta *nf* baking; surplice; prèndere una c. per (*sl*) to have a crush on; get tipsy.
còttimo *nm* job-work, piecework; lavoràre a c. to do piecework.
còtto *a* cooked; (*sl*) madly in love; tipsy.
cottúra *nf* cooking.
covàre *vt* to brood, brood over cherish secretly, smolder, hatch.
covàta *nf* brood, hatch.
covíle *nm* den, hole.
cóvo *nm* den.
covóne *nm* (*of grain*) sheaf.
Còzie, (Àlpi) *nf pl* (*geogr*) Cottian Alps.
còzza *nf* mussel.
cozzàre *vti* to butt, collide.
còzzo *nm* butting, collision, shock.
cràc *nm* crash, (financial) failure.
Cracòvia *nf* (*geogr*) Cracow.
cràmpo *nm* cramp.
crànio *nm* skull.
cràpula *nf* excess guzzling, debauch.
cràsso *a* crass, gross.
cratère *nm* crater.
cravàtta *nf* (neck)tie.
creànza *nf* breeding, manners *pl*.
creàre *vt* to create, cause, appoint.
creatívo *a* creative.
creàto *a* created; *nm* creation universe.
creatóre *nm* -tríce *nf* creator.
creatúra *nf* creature, child.
creazióne *nf* creation, appointment.
credènte *a* believing; *nmf* believer.
credènza *nf* belief, credit; sideboard, pantry.
crédere *vti* to believe, think, trust; -rsi *vr* to believe oneself.
credíbile *a* believable, credible.
credibilità *nf* credibility.
crédito *nm* credit, esteem.
creditóre *nm* -tríce *nf* creditor.
crèdo *nm* creed, credo.
credulità *nf* credulity.
crèdulo *a* credulous.
crèma *nf* cream, custard; (*of society*) élite; c. emolliènte cold cream; c. evanescènte vanishing cream; c. antivàmpa suntan cream.
cremàre *vt* to cremate.
crematóio, fórno crematório *nm* crematorium.
cremazióne *nf* cremation.
crèmisi *a nm* crimson.
crèpa *nf* chink, (*in a wall etc*) crack
crepàccio *nm* crevasse, large crack.
crepacuòre *nm* grief, heartbreak.
crepàre *vi* to burst, crack, split; (fig) die.
crepitàre *vi* to crackle.
crepitio *nm* crackling.

crepuscolàre *a* crepuscular, of twilight.
crepúscolo *nm* dusk, gloaming, twilight.
crescènza *nf* growth, increase.
créscere *vi* to grow, increase, (*of prices or water-level*) rise; *vt* to raise, bring up.
crescióne *nm* watercress.
créscita *nf* growth, rise.
crèṣima *nf* chrism, confirmation.
creṣimàre *vt* to confirm; -rsi *vr* to be confirmed.
créspa *nf* wrinkle, ripple, crease.
créspo *a* crisp, frizzy, wrinkled, pleated; *nm* crêpe.
crèsta *nf* crest.
crestomaziá *nf* anthology.
crèta *nf* chalk, clay.
Crèta *nf* (*geogr*) Crete.
cretineriá *nf* foolish act, nonsense.
cretiníṣmo *nm* cretinism, idiocy.
cretíno *nm* cretin, idiot.
crícca *nf* gang.
crícco *pl* **crícchi** *nm* (*tec*) jack.
Crimèa, (la) *nf* (*geogr*) Crimea.
criminàle *a nmf* criminal, offender.
crímine *nm* crime, offense.
criminologíá *nf* criminology.
crinàle *nm* (*of mountains*) ridge.
críne, críno *nm* horse-hair.
crinièra *nf* mane.
crípta *nf* crypt.
criṣantèmo *nm* chrysanthemum.
críṣi *nf* crisis.
críṣma *nm* chrism, consecrated oil.
cristallàme *nm* crystalware, glassware.
cristalleríá *nf* crystalware, crystal manufactory.
cristallièra *nf* glass case, china cabinet.
cristallíno *a* crystal; crystal-clear; *nm* (*anat*) crystalline lens.
cristalliẓẓàre *vt* -rsi *vr* to crystallize.
cristàllo *nm* crystal, glass.
cristianéṣimo *nm* Christianity.
cristianità *nf* Christendom.
cristiàno *a nm* Christian.
Cristína *nf pr* Christine, Christina.
Cristo *nm pr* Christ.
Cristòforo *nm pr* Christopher.
critèrio *nm* criterion, judgment.
crítica *nf* criticism, critique, censure.
criticàre *vt* to criticize, censure.
crítico *pl* -ici *a* critical, censorious; *nm* critic.
crivellàre *vt* to riddle, sift.
crivèllo *nm* sieve.
cròcchio *nm* gathering, group.
cróce *nf* cross.
crocerossína *nf* Red Cross nurse.
crocevíá *nf* crossroads.
crociàta *nf* crusade.
crociàto *nm* crusader.
crocícchio *nm* crossroads.
crocièra *nf* cruise.
crocifíggere *vt* to crucify.
crocifissióne *nf* crucifixion.
crosifísso *a* crucified; *nm* crucifix.

cròco *pl* **cròchi** *nm* crocus.
crogiuòlo *nm* crucible.
crollàre *vi* to collapse, fall down, slump; *vt* to shake.
cròllo *nm* collapse, fall, ruin, shake.
cròma *nf* (*mus*) quaver, eighth note.
cromàre *vt* to chromium plate.
cromàtico *pl* -ici *a* chromatic.
cromàto *a* chromium-plated.
crònaca *nf* chronicle, news.
crònico *pl* -ici *a* (*med*) chronic.
cronísta *nm* chronicler, reporter .
cronologíá *nf* chronology.
cronològico *pl* -ici *a* chronological.
cronometràre *vt* to time.
cronòmetro *nm* chronometer, stop watch.
cròsta *nf* crust, scab.
crostàceo *nm* crustacean, shellfish.
crostíno *nm* piece of toast, crouton.
crostóso *a* crusty.
cròtalo *nm* rattlesnake.
crucciàre *vt* to irritate, worry; -rsi *vr* to be troubled, worry.
crúccio *nm* grief, trouble, worry.
cruciàle *a* crucial.
crucivèrba *nm* crossword puzzle.
crudèle *a* cruel.
crudelménte *ad* cruelly.
crudeltà *nf* cruelty.
crudézza *nf* crudeness, rawness.
crúdo *a* raw, crude, harsh.
cruènto *a* bloody, dreadful.
crumíro *nm* blackleg, scab, fink, strikebreaker.
crúsca *nf* bran; freckles *pl*.
cruscòtto *nm* (*aut*) dashboard, (*av*) instrument panel.
Cúba *nf* (*geogr*) Cuba.
cubàno *a nm* Cuban.
cúbito *nm* cubit, elbow, forearm.
cúbo *nm* cube.
cuccàgna *nf* abundance, plenty; **paése di C.** land of Cockaigne.
cuccétta *nf* berth, bunk.
cucchiaiàta *nf* spoonful.
cucchiaíno *nm* teaspoon.
cucchiàio *nm* spoon.
cúccia *nf* dog's bed.
cúcciolo *nm* puppy.
cúcco *pl* **cúcchi** *nm* darling, pet; **vècchio c.** childish old man.
cúccuma *nf* coffee pot.
cucína *nf* cooking, kitchen, stove.
cucinàre *vt* to cook.
cuciníno *nm* kitchenette, small kitchen.
cucíre *vt* to sew, stitch.
cucitríce *nf* seamstress; sewing machine.
cucitúra *nf* seam, sewing.
cucú *nm* cuckoo; **orològio a c.** cuckoo clock.
cúculo *nm* cuckoo.
cúffia *nf* bonnet, cap; (*rad*) earphone.
cugína *nf* -o *nm* cousin.
cúi *pron* which, whom, whose.
culinària *nf* cookery.
cúlla *nf* cradle.
cullàre *vt* to rock (a cradle), lull.

culminànte a culminating, highest.
culminàre vi to culminate.
cúlmine nm apex, top.
cúlo nm buttocks pl, rump.
cúlto nm cult, worship.
cultúra nf culture, cultivation.
cumulàre vt to accumulate.
cúmulo nm accumulation, heap, pile.
cúneo nm wedge.
cuòca nf -o nm cook.
cuòcere vt to cook; vi to vex, hurt.
cuoiàio nm tanner, dealer in leather
cuòio nm leather, skin
cuòre nm heart, center; courage.
cupidígia, cupidità nf cupidity, covetousness, greed.
cúpido a eager, covetous, greedy.
Cupído nm pr Cupid.
cúpo a dark; deep, hollow.
cúpola nf cupola, dome.
cúra nf care, cure; parish; (med) treatment.
curànte, mèdico nm doctor in charge of a case.
curàre vt to care, take care of, (med) treat; -rsi vr to take care of oneself, mind.
curàto nm curate, parish priest.
curatóre nm trustee.
cúria nf senate house, court of justice, the bar.
curiàle a curial; nm lawyer.
curiosàre vi to be curious about, pry into.
curiosità nf curiosity, inquisitiveness.
curióso a curious, inquisitive.
cúrva nf bend, curve.
curvàre vt -rsi vr to bend, curve.
curvatúra nf bending, (tec) camber, curvature.
cúrvo a bent, crooked, curved.
cuscinétto nm small cushion; (tec) bearing.
cuscíno nm cushion, pillow; (tec) buffer.
custòde nm attendant, custodian, janitor, door-keeper.
custòdia nf custody, keeping, care; case.
custodíre vt to guard, keep; -rsi vr to take care of oneself.
cúte nf (human) skin.
cutícola nf cuticle.
cutréttola nf wagtail.
czar nm tzar, tsar, czar.
czèco pl -èchi a nm Czech.

D

da prep from, to, at, through, for since, by, in, like, as, when.
dabbàsso, da bàsso ad below, down there, downstairs.
dabbenàggine nf ingenuousness, simplicity, stupidity.
dabbène a good, honest, upright.
daccànto, da cànto ad and prep by, close, near.

daccàpo, da càpo ad again, once more, over again.
dacché, da che cj since, as.
dàdo nm die; (mech) nut; (of soup) cube.
daffàre, da fàre nm occupation, work; un gràn d. a great to-do.
dàino nm fallow deer; buck.
dàma nf lady; (dance) partner; (chess, cards) queen; (game of) draughts, checkers.
dameríno nm dandy, beau.
damigèlla nf maid of honor; young lady.
damigiàna nf demijohn.
danàro v denàro.
danaróso a wealthy.
danése a Danish; nmf Dane.
Danimàrca nf (geogr) Denmark.
dannàre vt to damn; -rsi vr to be damned, strive hard.
dannazióne nf damnation.
danneggiàre vt to damage, harm, impair, injure, spoil.
danneggiàto a damaged, injured; nm (leg) the injured party.
dànno nm damage, injury, loss.
dannóso a harmful, hurtful, detrimental.
dantésco pl -chi a relating to Dante.
dantísta nmf Dante scholar.
Danúbio nm the Danube.
dànza nf dance, dancing.
danzànte a dancing; tratteniménto d. dance, ball.
danzàre vi to dance.
danzatóre nm -trice nf dancer.
dappertútto ad everywhere.
dappocàggine nf worthlessness, ineptitude.
dappòco a inept, worthless.
dappòi ad afterwards, then.
dapprèsso ad by, close by, near.
dappríma, da príma ad at first.
dàre vt to give, produce, yield; vi to hit, stumble, look on to, burst out; -rsi vr to devote oneself, give oneself.
dàre nm (com) debit, liability.
dàrsena nf basin, wet-dock.
dàta nf date; di vècchia d. long-standing.
datàre vi to date.
dàto a given; nm datum; d. che cj since, as.
datóre nm -tríce nf giver; d. di lavóro employer.
dàttero nm date, date-palm.
dattilografàre vt to type.
dattilògrafo nm -fa nf typist.
dattórno, da tórno ad around.
davànti ad and prep before, in front of; a nm front; il d. della càsa the front of the house.
davanzàle nm window-sill.
davànzo, d'avànzo ad more than enough, over.
Dàvide nm pr David.
davvéro ad indeed, really, truly; per d. in earnest.

dazière *nm* exciseman, customs officer.
dàzio *nm* customs duty, excise, toll; **d. doganàle** customs duty.
dèa *nf* goddess.
debilitàre *vt* to debilitate, weaken.
debitaménte *ad* duly, regularly.
débito *a* due; *nm* debt, duty.
debitóre *nm* **-tríce** *nf* debtor.
débole *a* feeble, weak; *nm* weakness.
debolézza *nf* weakness, debility.
debuttànte *nmf* novice, debutante.
debuttàre *vi* to make one's debut.
debútto *nm* debut.
dècade *nf* ten days; decade.
decadènte *a nm* decadent.
decadentísmo *nm* school of decadent poets.
decadènza *nf* decline, decay.
decadére *vi* to decay, decline.
decàno *nm* dean.
decantàre *vt* to extol, praise; decant.
decapitàre *vt* to behead, decapitate.
decapitazióne *nf* beheading.
decarburàre *vt* to decarbonize.
decedúto *a* dead, deceased.
decènne *a* ten years old.
decènnio *nm* decade, period of ten years.
decènte *a* decent, seemly.
decentràre *vt* to decentralize.
decènza *nf* decency, seemliness.
decèsso *nm* death, decease; **àtto di d.** death certificate.
decídere *vt* to decide, settle; **-rsi** *vr* to decide, make up one's mind.
decifràre *vt* to decipher, decode.
dècima *nf* tenth part, tithe.
decimàle *a nm* decimal.
decimàre *vt* to decimate.
dècimo *a* tenth.
decína *nf* about ten.
decisaménte *ad* decidedly, definitely.
decisióne *nf* decision, resolution.
decisívo *a* decisive; critical; **voto d.** casting vote.
deciso *a* decided, determined, resolute.
declamàre *vti* to declaim.
declamatóre *nm* declaimer.
declamazióne *nf* declamation.
declinàre *vt* to decline; *vi* to set, wane, deviate; **d. le pròprie generalità** to give one's particulars.
declíno *nm* decline.
declívio *nm* declivity, slope.
decollàre *vt* to behead; *vi* (*av*) to take off.
decollazióne *nf* decapitation.
decòllo *nm* (*av*) take-off.
decompórre *vt* to decompose; **-rsi** *vr* to decompose, putrefy.
decomposizióne *nf* decomposition.
decoràre *vt* to decorate, adorn.
decorativo *a* decorative.
decoratóre *nm* **-tríce** *nf* decorator.
decorazióne *nf* decoration, ornament.
decòro *nm* decorum, dignity.
decoróso *a* decorous, seemly.

decorrènza *n* (*com*) expiration; **con d. dal** beginning from.
decórrere *vi* to have effect, count from.
decórso *a* expired, passed; *nm* passing, period, course.
decrepitézza *nf* decrepitude.
decrèpito *a* decrepit.
decrescènza *nf* decrease, diminution, wane.
decréscere *vi* to decrease, wane.
decretàre *vt* to decree, award.
decréto *nm* decree.
dècuplo *a nm* ten times, tenfold.
dèdica *nf* dedication.
dedicàre *vt* to dedicate, consecrate, devote; **-rsi** *vr* to devote oneself.
dèdito *a* devoted, addicted.
dedizióne *nf* dedication, devotion.
dedúrre *vt* to deduce, infer.
deduzióne *nf* deduction, inference.
defalcàre *vt* to deduct, subtract.
defenestràre *vt* to throw out of the window; (*fig*) drive out of office.
deferènte *a* deferent, respectful.
deferènza *nf* deference, respect.
deferíre *vi* to defer; *vt* to submit.
defezióne *nf* defection, desertion.
deficiènte *a* insufficient, deficient; *nmf* weak-minded.
deficiènza *nf* deficiency weak-mindedness.
definíre *vt* to define, settle.
definitíva, in *ad* after all.
definíto *a* definite.
definizióne *nf* definition, settlement.
deflagrazióne *nf* deflagration.
deflèttere *vi* to deflect; yield.
deformàre *vt* to deform, deface; **-rsi** *vr* to get deformed, lose one's shape.
defórme *a* deformed, ugly.
deformità *nf* deformity.
defraudàre *vt* to defraud, deprive.
defúnto *a* deceased, late.
degeneràre *vi* to degenerate, get worse.
degenerazióne *nf* degeneration, deterioration.
degènere *a* degenerate.
degènte *a* bedridden; *nmf* in-patient.
degènza *nf* period in bed, stay in hospital.
degnàre *vt* to hold worthy; **-rsi** *vr* to deign.
degnazióne *nf* condescension.
dégno *a* deserving, worthy.
degradàre *vt* to degrade, debase; **-rsi** *vr* to degrade oneself.
degustàre *vt* to taste.
degustazióne *nf* tasting, sipping.
deificàre *vt* to deify.
deità *nf* deity, god, goddess, God.
delatóre *nm* **-tríce** *nf* informer.
delazióne *nf* secret accusation.
dèlega *nf* (*of authority etc*) delegation, proxy.
delegàre *vt* to delegate, depute.
delegàto *a* delegate(d); *nm* delegate, deputy.

delegazióne *nf* delegation, committee.
deletèrio *a* deleterious, harmful.
delfíno *nm* dolphin; Dauphin.
deliberàre *vt* to deliberate, pass (a resolution).
deliberazióne *nf* deliberation, resolution.
delicataménte *ad* delicately, gently.
delicatézza *nf* delicacy, sensibility, tact; luxury.
delicàto *a* delicate, fastidious, discreet.
delimitàre *vt* to fix the boundaries.
delineàre *vt* to delineate, outline, sketch.
delinquènte *a nmf* delinquent, criminal.
delinquènza *nf* delinquency.
delínquere *vi* to commit a crime.
delíquio *nm* swoon, fainting fit.
deliràre *vi* to be delirious, rave.
delírio *nm* delirium, raving.
delítto *nm* crime.
delittuóso *a* criminal.
delízia *nf* delight.
deliziàre *vt* to charm, delight; -rsi *vr* to delight in, take pleasure in.
delizióso *a* charming, delightful.
dèlta *nm* delta; àla a d. (*av*) delta wing.
delucidàre *vt* to explain.
delucidazióne *nf* elucidation, explanation; (*textiles*) decatizing.
delúdere *vt* to disappoint, frustrate; escape.
delusióne *nf* disappointment; deception.
demànio *nm* State property.
demarcazióne *nf* demarcation.
demènte *a nmf* insane, lunatic.
demènza *nf* insanity, lunacy.
demeritàre *vti* to forfeit (one's good opinion), be unworthy of.
democràtico *a* democratic.
democrazía *nf* democracy.
demolíre *vt* to demolish, pull down.
demolizióne *nf* demolition.
dèmone, demònio *nm* demon.
demoníaco *a* demoniac(al).
demoralizzàre *vt* to demoralize.
denàro *nm* money; penny.
denaróso *v* danaróso.
denaturàto *a* methylated; àlcool d. methylated spirit.
denigràre *vt* to defame, disparage.
denigrazióne *nf* disparagement.
denominàre *vt* to denominate, name.
denominazióne *nf* denomination, name.
denotàre *vt* to denote, signify.
densità *nf* density, thickness.
dènso *a* dense, thick.
dentàta *nj* bite, mark of bite.
dentàto *a* toothed, cogged, dentate, serrated.
dentatúra *nf* (set of) teeth.
dènte *nm* tooth, fang; prong.
dentellàre *vt* to indent, notch.

dentièra *nf* denture, dental plate, false teeth *pl*.
dentifrício *nm* toothpaste.
dentísta *nm* dentist.
dentizióne *nf* dentition, teething.
déntro *ad* and *prep* inside, within; *nm* inside.
denudàre *vt* to denude, strip.
denúncia *nf* report, notification; d. di matrimònio marriage banns.
denunciàre *vt* to declare, announce report.
denutríto *a* underfed.
deodorànte *a* deodorizing; *nm* deodorant.
depauperàre *vt* impoverish.
deperiménto *nm* wasting, pining away, decline, deterioration.
deperíre *vi* to waste, pine away, wither, decay.
depilàre *vt* to depilate, remove hairs.
depilatóre *nm* hair remover, depilatory.
depilatòrio *a* depilatory.
depilazióne *nf* hair-removing, depilation.
deploràre *vt* to deplore, lament, blame.
deplorévole *a* deplorable, lamentable, blamable.
depórre *vt* to depose, lay aside, lay down; *vi* to bear witness.
deportàre *vt* to deport, transport.
deportàto *a* deported; *nm* convict.
deportazióne *nf* deportation.
depositàre *vti* to deposit, lodge.
depositàrio *nm* depository.
depòsito *nm* (*mil*) depot; warehouse; deposit; d. bagàgli luggage office, checkroom.
deposizióne *nf* deposition.
depravàre *vt* to corrupt, deprave.
deprecàre *vt* to deprecate; entreat.
depredaménto *nm* depredazióne *nf* depredation, pillage.
depredàre *vt* to pillage, plunder.
depressióne *nf* depression.
deprèsso *a* depressed, low-spirited.
deprezzaménto *nm* depreciation.
deprezzàre *vt* to depreciate, disparage, undervalue.
deprimènte *a* depressing; (*med*) sedative.
deprímere *vt* to depress.
depuràre *vt* to purify, purge.
deputàre *vt* to depute, appoint, fix.
deputàto *a* delegated, deputed; *nm* delegate, deputy.
deputazióne *nf* committee, deputation.
deragliaménto *nm* derailment.
deragliàre *vi* to derail, leave the rails.
derelítto *a* abandoned, derelict.
derídere *vt* to deride, laugh at, ridicule.
derisióne *nf* derision, ridicule.
derisòrio *a* derisive, mocking.
deríva *nf* (*naut*) drift, leeway; alla d. *ad* adrift, astray.

derivàre *vi* to derive, spring, result, follow; *vt* to divert, derive.
derivàto *a* derived; *nm* derivative, by-product.
derivazióne *nf* derivation.
dèroga *nf* derogation.
derogàre *vi* to derogate, deviate from, contravene.
derogazióne *nf* derogation.
derràta *nf* foodstuffs, commodity.
derubàre *vt* to rob.
désco *pl* **déschi** *nm* dinner table, butcher's block, bench, stool.
descrittívo *a* descriptive.
descrívere *vt* to describe, relate.
descrizióne *nf* description.
deṣèrto *a* deserted, desolate, lonely; *nm* desert.
desideràre *vt* to desire, long for, wish, want.
desidèrio *nm* wish, desire.
desideróso *a* eager, longing for.
designàre *vt* to appoint, designate, name.
designazióne *nf* designation.
deṣinàre *vi* to dine; *nm* dinner, meal.
deṣinènza *nf* ending, termination.
deṣístere *vi* to desist, give up.
deṣolàre *vt* to devastate, distress.
deṣolàto *a* desolate, devastated, sorry.
deṣolazióne *nf* desolation, devastation, grief.
dèspota *pl* **-ti** *nm* despot.
destàre *vt* to (a)wake, excite, rouse, stir up; **-rsi** *vr* to (a)wake, be roused.
destinàre *vt* to destine, assign, appoint, address, decide.
destinatàrio *nm* addressee, receiver.
destinazióne *nf* destination.
destíno *nm* destiny, fate.
destituíre *vt* to dismiss, remove (from office).
destituíto *a* deprived of, removed from, destitute.
destituzióne *nf* dismissal, removal.
désto *a* awake, alert.
dèstra *nf* right hand, right side, (*in politics*) Right.
destreggiàre *vi* to act skillfully, be skillful; **-rsi** *vr* to manage, maneuver, steer one's course.
destrézza *nf* dexterity, skill.
dèstro *a* right; clever, dexterous; *nm* opportunity, right moment; **cògliere il d.** to seize the chance.
desúmere *vt* to deduce, infer.
detenére *vt* to hold, keep, detain.
detenúto *a* kept back, imprisoned; *nm* prisoner.
detenzióne *nf* detention, unlawful possession.
detergènte *a nm* detergent.
deterioràre *vt* to deteriorate, damage; **-rsi** *vr* to deteriorate, get worse.
determinàre *vt* to determine, define, cause.

detersívo *a* cleansing; *nm* detergent, detersive, cleansing agent.
detestàre *vt* to detest, hate, loathe.
detonàre *vi* to detonate.
detonazióne *nf* detonation, explosion.
detràrre *vt* to deduct.
detrattóre *nm* **-tríce** *nf* detractor, slanderer.
detrazióne *nf* deduction, detraction, slander.
detriménto *nm* detriment, damage.
detríto *nm* rubbish, sweepings *pl*.
detronizzàre *vt* to dethrone.
détta *nf* **a d. di** according to.
dettàfono *nm* dictaphone.
dettagliàre *vt* to detail.
dettàglio *nm* detail, particular; **commèrcio al d.** (*com*) retail trade.
dettàre *vt* to dictate.
dettàto *nm* **dettatúra** *nf* dictation.
détto *a* called, named; *nm* saying, word, joke.
deturpàre *vt* to deface, disfigure.
devastaménto *nm* devastation, ravage.
devastàre *vt* to devastate, ravage.
devastazióne *nf* devastation.
deviaménto *nm* deviation, derailment; (*of traffic etc*) diversion.
deviàre *vt* to deviate, be diverted, swerve, divert.
deviatóio *nm* (*tec*) points *pl*, switch.
deviazióne *nf* deviation, (*road*) diversion, detour; (*mech*) deflection.
devoluzióne *nf* devolution, transfer.
devòlvere *vt* to devolve, assign, transfer.
devóto *a* devout; *nm* devotee.
devozióne *nf* devotion, piety.
di *prep* of, from, for, with, at, in, some, any, than.
dì *nm* day.
diabète *nm* diabetes.
diabètico *pl* **-ici** *a nm* diabetic.
diabòlico *pl* **-ici** *a* diabolic(al).
diàcono *nm* deacon.
diadèma *nm* diadem, tiara.
diàfano *a* diaphanous.
diafràmma *nm* diaphragm; screen.
diàgnosi *nf* diagnosis.
diagnòstica *nf* diagnostics *pl*.
diagnòstico *a* diagnostic; *nm* diagnostician.
diagonàle *a* diagonal; *nf* (*geom*) diagonal; *nm* (*fabric*) twill.
diagràmma *pl* **-àmmi** *nm* diagram, chart; (*mus*) scale.
dialettàle *a* dialectal.
dialètto *nm* dialect.
diàlogo *pl* **-ghi** *nm* dialogue.
diamànte *nm* diamond.
diàmetro *nm* diameter.
diàmine! *interj* the deuce! of course!
diàna *nf* morning star, reveille.
Diàna *nf pr* Diana.
diànzi *ad* just now, not long ago.
diàpason *nm* tuning fork, diapason, pitch.

diaposítíva nf (phot) transparency, slide; (typ) direct reversal.
diàrio a daily; nm diary.
diarrèa nf diarrhea.
diatríba nf diatribe, quarrel.
diàvolo nm devil.
dibàttere vt to debate, discuss; -rsi vr to struggle.
dibàttito nm debate, discussion, controversy.
dicastèro nm (higher) government office, ministry, department.
dicèmbre nm December.
dicería nf hearsay, rumor.
dichiaràre vt to declare, state; -rsi vr to declare oneself.
dichiarazióne nf declaration.
diciannòve a nineteen; **diciannovèsimo** a nineteenth.
diciassètte a seventeen; **diciassettèsimo** a seventeenth.
diciòtto a eighteen; **diciottèsimo** a eighteenth.
dicitóre nm -tríce nf announcer, speaker, teller.
dicitúra nf wording, words.
didascalía nf captions, directions, subtitles.
didàttico pl -ici a didactic.
didéntro ad nm inside.
dièci a ten.
diecína nf about ten.
dièta nf assembly, diet.
diètro nm back; ad and prep after, behind.
difàtti, difàtto ad as a matter of fact, in fact.
difèndere vt to defend, guard, protect; -rsi vr to defend oneself.
difensíva nf defensive.
difensívo a defensive.
difensóre nm defender.
difésa nf defense.
difettàre vi to be deficient in, lack.
difettívo, difettóso a defective, lacking.
difètto nm defect, flaw, fault.
diffàlco pl -chi nm deduction.
diffamàre vt to defame, libel.
diffamazióne nf defamation.
differènte a different; unlike (s.o., sth.).
differènza nf difference.
differenzíàre vt to differentiate, distinguish (between); -rsi vr to differ (from), be different.
differiménto nm adjournment, deferment.
differíre vt to adjourn, defer, postpone; vi to be different, differ, disagree.
difficíle a difficult, hard; hard to please.
difficoltà nf difficulty, objection.
difficoltóso a full of difficulties, fastidious.
diffída nf intimation, notice.
diffidàre vt to serve a notice; vi to distrust, suspect.
diffidènte a diffident, distrustful.

diffidènza nf diffidence, distrust, suspicion.
diffóndere vi to diffuse, pour, spread; -rsi vr to be diffused, spread.
diffusaménte ad diffusely, abundantly.
diffusióne nf diffusion.
diffúso a diffuse, diffused; longwinded.
difilàto ad at once, forthwith.
difteríte nf diphtheria.
díga nf breakwater, dike.
digerènte a digestive.
digeríbile a digestible.
digeríre vt to digest, assimilate.
digestióne nf digestion.
digestívo a nm digestive.
digèsto nm digest.
digitàle a digital; nf foxglove; digitalis; **imprònte digitàli** fingerprints.
digiunàre vi to fast.
digiúno a fasting, devoid of; nm fast.
dignità nf dignity.
dignitóso a dignified.
digradàre vi to slope down, decline; diminish, (of colors) shade off.
digrassàre vi to remove the fat, skim.
digressióne nf digression.
digrignàre vt to gnash, grind (one's teeth).
digrossàre vt to whittle down, rough-hew; teach the first elements.
diguazzàre vi to splash about, paddle; vi to shake, stir.
dilaceràre, dilaniàre vt to tear (to pieces).
dilagàre vi to overflow, spread.
dilapidàre vt to dilapidate, squander.
dilatàbile a dilatable, extensible.
dilatàre vt -rsi vr to dilate, expand.
dilatàto a dilated, enlarged.
dilatazióne nf dilation, expansion.
dilatòrio a delaying, dilatory.
dilazionàre vt to adjourn, postpone.
dilazióne nf delay, respite.
dileggiàre vt to mock, ridicule.
diléggio nm derision, mockery.
dileguaménto nm disappearance.
dileguàre vt to disperse, dissipate; -rsi vr to dissolve, fade away, vanish.
dilèmma nm dilemma.
dilettànte nmf amateur, dilettante.
dilettàre vt to charm, delight; -rsi vr to delight, take pleasure in.
dilettévole a charming, delightful.
dilètto a beloved, darling; nm delight, pleasure.
diligènte a diligent.
diligènza nf diligence; stagecoach.
dilucidàre vt to elucidate.
diluíre vt to dilute, water.
dilungàre vt to lengthen, prolong; -rsi vr to dwell (on).
dilúngo ad straight on.
diluviàre vi to pour, deluge, rain in torrents.

dilúvio nm deluge, flood.
dimagraménto nm growing thin, slimming; (of ground) impoverishing.
dimagràre, dimagríre vt to make thin; vi to grow thin, lose weight.
dimenàre vt to shake, (tail) wag; -rsi vr to fidget, toss.
dimensióne nf dimension, size.
dimenticànza nf forgetfulness, oblivion.
dimenticàre vt -rsi vr to forget.
diméntico pl -chi a forgetful.
dimésso a humble, modest.
dimestichézza nf familiarity.
diméttere vt to dismiss, remove; forgive; -rsi vr to resign.
dimezzàre vt to halve.
diminuíre vt to abate, diminish, lessen, reduce; vi to decrease.
diminutívo a nm diminutive.
diminuzióne nf diminution, reduction.
dimissióne nf resignation; **dàre le dimissióni** vi to resign.
dimòra nf abode, dwelling, stay; **sènza físsa d.** a homeless, vagabond.
dimoràre vi to live, reside; stay; delay.
dimostràre vt to demonstrate, prove, show; -rsi vr to appear, show oneself.
dimostrazióne nf demonstration.
dinàmica nf dynamics.
dinàmico pl -ici a dynamic, energetic.
dinamíte nf dynamite.
dínamo nf (el) dynamo, generator.
dinànzi ad and prep before, opposite, in front.
dinastía nf dynasty.
diniègo pl -ghi nm denial, refusal.
dinoccolàto a disjointed, loose-limbed, shambling.
dintórno ad and prep about, (a)round; **dintórni** nm pl neighborhood.
Dío nm God.
diòceṣi nf diocese.
Dionígi nm pr Denis, Dennis.
dipanàre vt to wind into a ball; unravel, disentangle.
dipartiménto nm department.
dipartírsi vr to depart, go away.
dipartíta nf (poet) departure, death.
dipendènte a depending, dependent; nmf subordinate, dependant.
dipendènza nf dependence, dependency.
dipèndere vi to depend (on), derive.
dipíngere vt to paint, depict; -rsi vr to paint oneself.
dipínto a painted; nm painting.
diplóma nm diploma, certificate.
diplomàre vt to confer a diploma; -rsi vr to get a diploma, to graduate;
diplomàtico pl -ici a diplomatic; nm diplomat.
diplomazía nf diplomacy.
dipòrto nm amusement, recreation.

diradaménto nm thinning (out), rarefaction.
diradàre vt to thin out; -rsi vr (of hair etc) to get thin.
diramàre vt to lop, prune; send out; -rsi vr to branch out, ramify, spread.
diramazióne nf branching out, branching off, branch, diffusion.
díre vt to say, tell, speak; nm speech, words, statement, saying.
direttaménte ad directly, direct.
direttíssimo nm express train.
direttíva nf direction, instruction.
dirètto a direct, straight; nm fast train; **carròzza dirètta** nf through coach (on a train).
direttóre nm -tríce nf director, directress, headmaster, headmistress, manager(ess), (newspaper) editor.
direzióne nf direction, course; management, leadership, office; (tec) steering-gear.
dirigènte a directing, managing; nm manager, (pol) leader.
dirígere vt to direct, address, manage, regulate; -rsi vr to go towards.
dirigíbile nm airship.
dirimpètto ad opposite; **d.** a prep opposite, in comparison with.
diritta nf right, right hand, right side.
dirítto a straight, upright, erect, plumb, right; nm right, claim, due, law; ad directly, straight (on); **diritti d'autóre** royalties.
dirittúra nf straightness, uprightness.
dirizzàre vi to straighten, prick up (one's ears); -rsi vr to draw oneself up.
diroccàre vt to demolish, dismantle; -rsi vr to fall in ruins.
dirótto a heavy; **piànto d.** nm flood of tears; **piòggia dirótta** heavy rain.
dirozzàre vt to rough-hew, civilize, polish; -rsi vr to become civilized, refined.
dirúpo nm rocky precipice.
diṣabitàto a uninhabited.
diṣabituàre vt to disaccustom; -rsi vr to lose the habit.
diṣaccòrdo nm disagreement, discord.
diṣadàtto a unfit, unsuitable, unbecoming.
diṣadórno a bare, simple, unadorned.
diṣaffezióne nf estrangement, disaffection.
diṣagévole a difficult, uncomfortable.
diṣagevolézza nf difficulty, discomfort.
diṣaggradévole a disagreeable.
diṣagiàto a uncomfortable; poor, needy.
diṣàgio nm discomfort, uneasiness; **sentírsi a d.** to feel uncomfortable.

disàmina *nf* examination, investigation.
disaminàre *vt* examine.
disappetènza *nf* lack of appetite.
disapprèndere *vt* to unlearn, forget.
disapprovàre *vt* to disapprove of, blame.
disappúnto *nm* disappointment.
disarmàre *vt* to disarm; dismantle, *(naut)* lay up (a ship).
disàrmo *nm* disarmament.
disàstro *nm* disaster, accident.
disastróso *a* disastrous, ruinous.
disattènto *a* inattentive.
disattenzióne *nf* inattention, inattentiveness.
disattrezzàre *vt (naut)* to dismantle.
disavànzo *nm* deficiency, deficit.
disavvedutézza, disavvertènza *nf* inadvertency.
disavventúra *nf* misfortune, mishap.
disavvezzàre *vt* to disaccustom.
disbórso *nm* disbursement, outlay.
disbrigàre *vt* to clear off, dispatch; -rsi *vr* to extricate oneself, get out *(of sth)*, make haste.
disbrígo *pl* -ghi *nm* dispatch, settlement.
discàpito *nm* disadvantage, detriment.
discendènte *a* descending; *nmf* descendant.
discendènza *nf* descent; offspring.
discéndere *vi* to descend, go down; spring from; *(of prices, temperature)* fall.
discentràto *a* decentralized; off center.
discépolo *nm* disciple, pupil.
discèrnere *vt* to discern, distinguish.
discerniménto *nm* discernment, judgment.
discésa *nf* descent, fall; *(rad)* lead-in.
dischiúdere *vt* to disclose, reveal.
disciògliere *vt* to dissolve, melt; release, untie; -rsi *vr* to dissolve, melt, get loose.
disciplína *nf* discipline.
disciplinàre *vt* to discipline; *a* disciplinary.
dísco *pl* díschi *nm* disk, disc; *(mus)* record; *(sport)* discus.
díscolo *a* undisciplined, unruly, wild; *nm* rogue, scamp.
discolpàre *vt* to clear from blame, excuse, defend; -rsi *vr* to clear oneself, justify oneself.
disconoscènza *nf* ingratitude.
disconóscere *vt* to disavow, slight, be ungrateful for.
discordànte *a* discordant, clashing, dissonant; disagreeing.
discordànza *nf* discordance, dissonance; disagreement.
discordàre *vi* to disagree; *(mus)* be out of tune.
discòrde *a* d scordant, dissonant.
discòrdia *nf* discord, dissension.
discórrere *vi* to discourse, talk.
discórso *nm* discourse, speech, talk.

discòsto *a* distant, far; *ad* at some distance.
discotéca *nf* discotheque.
discreditàre *vt* to discredit; -rsi *vr* to damage one's reputation.
discrepànza *nf* discrepancy.
discretaménte *ad* discreetly, fairly.
discretézza *nf* discretion, moderation.
discretíva *nf* power of discernment.
discréto *a* discreet; moderate, passable, reasonable.
discrezióne *nf* discretion; a d. according to one's judgment.
discriminàre *vt* to discriminate.
discriminazióne *nf* discrimination.
discussióne *nf* debate, d scussion, dispute.
discútere *vt* to discuss, argue.
discutíbile *a* debatable, questionable.
disdegnàre *v* sdegnàre.
disdégno *nm* contempt, scorn, haughtiness.
disdegnóso *a* contemptuous, scornful.
disdétta *nf* notice to leave; bad luck.
disdíre *vt* to annul, cancel, revoke, unsay; *vi* to be unbecoming; -rsi *vr* to be unbecoming; go back on one's word.
disdòro *nm* dishonor, shame.
disegnàre *vt* to draw, plan.
diségno *nm* design, drawing, plan, purpose.
diseredàre *vt* to disinherit.
disertàre *vt* to desert; lay waste, ruin.
disertóre *a* deserter.
diserzióne *nf* desertion.
disfaciménto *nm* destruction, ruin, decay.
disfàre *vt* to undo, break up, take to pieces, untie; -rsi *vr* to dispose of, get rid of.
disfàtta *nf* defeat.
disfattísta *a nmf* defeatist.
disfàtto *a* undone, defeated, worn-out.
disfída *nf* challenge, duel.
disfunzióne *nf (med)* disorder, irregularity.
disgelàre *vi* to thaw; *vt* to defrost.
disgràzia *nf* misfortune, ill luck, accident.
disgraziàto *a* unfortunate, unlucky; *nm* wretch.
disgregàre *vt* -rsi *vr* to disintegrate, break up.
disguído *nm (of post & fig)* going astray.
disgustàre *vt* to disgust, sicken, vex; -rsi *vr* to take a disgust, dislike for.
disgústo *nm* disgust, dislike, loathing.
disgustóso *a* disgusting.
disillúdere *vt* to disillusion, disenchant.
disillusióne *nf* disillusion, disenchantment.

disimparàre *vt* to unlearn, forget.

disimpegnàre *vt* to redeem, release, fulfill; (*naut*) clear; **-rsi** *vr* to free oneself, manage one's own affairs.

disimpégno *nm* disengagement, release.

disincagliàre *vt* (*naut*) to float (a stranded ship).

disinfettànte *a nm* disinfectant.

disinfettàre *vt* to disinfect.

disinfezióne *nf* disinfection.

disingannàre *vt* to disillusion, undeceive.

disingànno *nm* disillusionment, undeceiving.

disintegràre *vt* **-rsi** *vr* to disintegrate.

disintegrazióne *nf* disintegration.

disinteressàre *vt* (*com*) buy out; to make one lose interest; **-rsi** *vr* to disinterest oneself.

disinteressàto *a* disinterested; unselfish; impartial.

disinterèsse *nm* disinterestedness, unselfishness.

disinvòlto *a* easy, free, sure of oneself, unconstrained, impudent.

disinvoltúra *nf* ease, nonchalance, self-possession, impudence.

disistimàre *vt* not to esteem, to despise.

dislivèllo *nm* difference of level.

dislocàre *vt* to displace.

dismisúra *nf* excess; **a d.** immoderately.

disobbligàre *vt* to free from obligation.

disoccupàto *a* out of work, unemployed; *nm* unemployed person.

disoccupazióne *nf* unemployment.

disonestà *nf* dishonesty.

disonèsto *a* dishonest, indecent.

disonoràre *vt* to disgrace, dishonor.

disonóre *nm* disgrace, dishonor, shame.

disópra *nm* top, upper side; *ad and pron* above, on, over, upstairs; **al d. di** *prep* beyond.

disordinàre *vt* to disorder, disarrange; (*in eating, drinking*) to exceed.

disordinàto *a* disorderly, untidy.

disórdine *nm* disorder, confusion, disorderliness, disturbance.

disorganizzàre *vt* to disorganize.

disorganizzazióne *nf* disorganization.

disorientaménto *nm* disorientation, confusion.

disorientàre *vt* to confuse, disconcert, lead astray, mislead; **-rsi** *vr* to be at a loss, not to know where one is.

disótto *a nm* lower, bottom, lower side; *ad and prep* below, under (neath); **al d. di** inferior to; below.

dispàccio *nm* dispatch; **d. telegràfico** telegram.

disparàto *a* different, disparate, incongruous, unequal.

díspari *a* (*number*) odd; different, unequal.

dispàrte, in *ad* apart, aside, aloof.

dispèndio *nm* expense, outlay.

dispendióso *a* expensive.

dispènsa *nf* distribution; (*of a publication*) number; sideboard, pantry; dispensation, exemption; **dispènse universitàrie** duplicated lecture notes.

dispensàre *vt* to dispense, distribute; exempt.

dispensàrio *nm* dispensary.

dispepsía *nf* dyspepsia.

disperàre *vi* to despair; **-rsi** *vr* to give oneself up to despair.

disperàto *a* despairing, desperate, hopeless, wretched; *nm* destitute creature, desperate creature.

disperazióne *nf* despair, desperation.

dispèrdere *vt* to dispel, disperse, scatter, waste; **-rsi** *vr* to be scattered, disperse.

dispersióne *nf* dispersion, loss; (*el*) leak.

dispèrso *a* missing, dispersed, lost, scattered; *nm* (*mil*) missing soldier.

dispètto *nm* spite, grudge, pique, vexation.

dispettóso *a* spiteful.

dispiacénte *a* sorry; disagreeable.

dispiacére *vi* to dislike, regret; be disagreeable, displease; **mi dispiàce** I am sorry; *nm* displeasure, dissatisfaction, grief, regret.

disponíbile *a* available, free; *nm* (*com*) liquid assets *pl*.

dispórre *vti* to arrange, direct, dispose, order, regulate; **-rsi** *vr* to get ready.

dispositívo *nm* (*mech*) contrivance, appliance; (*phot*) adapter; **d. di sicurezza** safety catch.

disposizióne *nf* arrangement, disposition, disposal, inclination, order; **avére d. per** to have a talent for; **a súa d.** at your disposal.

dispósto *a* willing, inclined, disposed; arranged; **ben d.** in good order, vigorous.

dispregiàre *etc v* **disprezzàre.**

disprezzàbile *a* contemptible, despicable, negligible.

disprezzàre *vt* to despise, scorn.

disprèzzo *nm* contempt, sorrow.

dísputa *nf* debate, dispute, quarrel.

disputàre *vti* to argue, contend, debate, dispute, quarrel; **-rsi** *vr* to contend (for).

dissanguàre *vt* to bleed; (*fig*) impoverish.

dissanguàto *a* drained of blood; (*fig*) impoverished.

dissapóre *nm* disagreement, misunderstanding.

disseminàre *vt* to disseminate, propagate, scatter, sow.

dissennatézza *nf* craziness, foolishness, rashness.

dissènso nm difference of opinion, dissent.
dissentería nf dysentery.
dissentíre vi to disagree (with).
disseppelliménto nm disinterment, exhumation.
disseppellíre vt to disinter.
dissertàre vi to discourse, expatiate.
dissertazióne nf dissertation, thesis.
dissestàre vt to ruin, disarrange, derange; -rsi vr (financially) to ruin oneself.
dissestàto a in financial straits, badly off.
dissèsto nm disorder; financial trouble.
dissetànte a refreshing.
dissetàre vt to quench (thirst).
dissezióne nf dissection.
dissidènte a nmf dissentient, dissenter.
dissídio nm dissension, discord.
dissigillàre vt to unseal.
dissímile a unlike.
dissimulàre vt to dissimulate, conceal.
dissipàre vt to clear up, dissipate, remove; -rsi vr to disappear, vanish.
dissipazióne nf dissipation.
dissociàre vt to dissociate.
dissodàre vt (land) to clear, till.
dissolúbile a dissoluble.
dissolubilità nf dissolubility.
dissolutézza nf dissoluteness, licentiousness.
dissolúto a dissolute, licentious.
dissoluzióne nf disintegration, dissolution; dissoluteness.
dissolvènza nf (cin) fade-out.
dissòlvere vt -rsi vr to dissolve, melt.
dissomigliànza nf unlikeness, difference.
dissonànte a dissonant, discordant.
dissonànza nf dissonance, difference.
dissotterràre vt to disinter.
dissuadére vt to dissuade, deter.
dissuetúdine nf disuse.
distaccaménto nm (mil) detachment.
distaccàre vt to cut off, detach, separate, sever; -rsi vr to become detached, break off.
distàcco pl -chi nm separation, parting, detachment; (fig) indifference.
distànte a distant, far, remote; ad far away.
distànza nf distance; difference.
distanziàre vt to space (out), leave behind.
distàre vi to be distant.
distèndere vt to extend, lay (out), spread, relax; -rsi vr to stretch out.
distendiménto nm **distensióne** nf spreading, stretching, relaxing.
distésa nf expanse, extent.
distillàre vti to distill; trickle.
distillatóio nm still.
distillería nf distillery.

distínguere vt to distinguish; -rsi vr to become famous, distinguish oneself.
distinguíbile a distinguishable.
distínta nf list, note, schedule; **d. dei prèzzi** price list.
distintaménte ad distinctly; (in letters) faithfully.
distintívo a distinctive; nm badge, distinguishing mark.
distínto a distinct; clear; distinguished; **distínti salúti** (in a letter) yours faithfully.
distinzióne nf distinction, regard.
distògliere vt to deter, dissuade, distract.
distorsióne nf distorsion, sprain.
distràrre vi to amuse, distract, divert; -rsi vr to amuse oneself, let one's attention wander.
distràtto a absent-minded, inattentive.
distrazióne nf absent-mindedness, inattention; recreation.
distrétto nm district.
distribuíre vt to distribute, arrange, assign, deliver.
distributívo a distributive.
distributóre a distributing; nm distributor; **d. di benzína** (aut) petrol pump, gasoline pump.
distribuzióne nf distribution, layout.
districàre, distrigàre vt to disentangle, unravel; -rsi vr to extricate oneself, free oneself.
distrúggere vt to destroy, ruin; -rsi vr to destroy oneself (each other).
distruzióne nf destruction.
disturbàre vt to disturb, interrupt, trouble; -rsi vr to put oneself out, take trouble.
distúrbo nm disturbance, trouble, inconvenience, disorder.
disubbidiènte a disobedient.
disubbidiènza nf disobedience.
disubbidíre vi to disobey.
disuguagliànza nf disparity, inequality.
disuguàle a unequal, dissimilar.
disumàno a inhuman.
disunióne nf discord, disunion.
disuníre vt to disjoin, disunite.
disusàre vt to cease using.
disusàto a disused; out-of-date; unaccustomed.
disúso nm disuse; **cadére in d.** to become obsolete.
ditàle nm thimble, finger-stall.
díto pl **díti, díta** (f) nm finger, toe; inch.
dítta nf firm, (commercial) house.
dittàfono nm dictaphone.
dittatóre nm dictator.
dittatúra nf dictatorship.
diúrno a day, diurnal; **albèrgo d.** nm public baths and lavatories pl.
díva nf goddess; great actress or singer.
divagàre vt to amuse, divert; vi to

digress, wander; -rsi *vr* to amuse oneself, relax.

divagazióne *nf* wandering; digression; recreation.

divampàre *vi* to blaze, flare up.

divàno *nm* couch, divan.

divàrio *nm* difference, diversity.

diveníre, diventàre *vi* to become, get, grow, turn.

divèrbio *nm* altercation, dispute.

divergènte *a* divergent, diverging.

divergènza *nf* divergence, divergency.

divèrgere *vi* to diverge, wander from.

diversaménte *ad* differently, otherwise.

diversificàre *vt* to diversify; *vi*, -rsi *vr* to differ.

diversióne *nf* deviation, digression, diversion.

diversità *nf* diversity.

diversívo *a* deviating, diverting; *nm* distraction, amusement.

divèrso *a* different, sundry; **divèrsi** *pl* several; **generi diversi** *nm pl* (com) sundries *pl*.

divertènte *a* amusing, entertaining.

divertiménto *nm* amusement, entertainment, recreation.

divertíre *vt* to divert, amuse, entertain; -rsi *vr* to amuse oneself, have a good time.

divezzàre *vt* to disaccustom, wean; -rsi *vr* to disaccustom oneself.

dividèndo *nm* dividend.

divídere *vt* to divide, share; -rsi *vr* to divide, separate.

divièto *nm* prohibition; **d. d'affissióne** 'post no bills'; **d. di sòsta** 'no parking'.

divinaménte *ad* divinely, beautifully.

divinàre *vt* to divine, foretell.

divincolaménto *nm* wriggle, wriggling, writhing, struggling.

divincolàre *vt* to wriggle; **divincolàrsi** *vr* to writhe, wriggle, struggle free.

divinità *nf* divinity.

divíno *a* divine.

divísa *nf* uniform, livery; (com) currency; hair parting; motto, device; **d. èstera** foreign currency.

divisàre *vti* to devise, p an, resolve.

divisióne *nf* division, department, discord.

divisòrio *a* dividing, separating; **múro d.** nm partition wa l.

dívo *nm* (film)star.

divoràre *vt* to devour eat up.

divorziàre *vti* -rsi *vr* divorce, get a divorce.

divòrzio *nm* divorce.

divulgàre *vt* to divulge, spread; -rsi *vr* to spread.

dizionàrio *nm* dictionary.

dizióne *nf* diction.

do *nm* (mus) C, do.

dóccia *nf* shower(bath), douche;

water-pipe; **fàre la d.** *vi* to take a shower.

docènte *nmf* teacher, university lecturer.

docènza *nf* teaching.

dòcile *a* docile; (of material) easily worked.

docilità *nf* docility, meekness.

documentàre *vt* to bring documentary evidence, document.

documentàrio *a* documentary; *nm* documentary film, newsreel.

documénto *nm* document, evidence.

dodicènne *a* twelve years old; *nmf* twelve-year-old.

dodicèsimo *a* twelfth.

dódici *a* twelve.

dogàna *nf* customs, customs office, custom-house.

doganàle *a* customs.

doganière *nm* customs officer.

dòglia *nf* ache, pain; **dòglie** *pl* labor pains.

dògma *nm* dogma, principle.

dogmàtico *pl* -ici *a* dogmatic.

dólce *a* sweet, mild, soft; *nm* sweetness; pudding, cake.

dolcézza *nf* sweetness, softness.

dolciúmi *nm pl* sweets *pl*, sweetmeats *pl*.

dolènte *a* grieved, sorry; aching.

dolére *vi* to ache; regret; -rsi *vr* to be sorry, complain, grieve, lament, regret.

dòllaro *nm* dollar.

dòlo *nm* fraud.

Dolomíti (le) *nf pl* (geogr) the Dolomites *pl*.

doloorànte *a* aching, painful.

dolóre *nm* ache, grief, pain, regret.

doloróso *a* painful, grievous, sorrowful.

dolóso *a* fraudulent.

domànda *nf* question, request, demand, application; **fàre d.** apply; **fàre una d.** to ask a question, make a request.

domandàre *vt* to ask, demand, request; -rsi *vr* to ask oneself, wonder.

domàni *nm and ad* tomorrow; **d. l'àltro** *ad* the day after tomorrow.

domàre *vt* to break in, tame, conquer, extinguish, subdue, overcome.

domatóre *nm* -trice *nf* tamer.

domatúra *nf* (of horses) breaking, taming.

doménica *nf* Sunday.

domenicàle *a* (of) Sunday.

domenicàno *a nm* Dominican.

domèstica *nf* maid, servant.

domestichézza *nf* domesticity, fam liarity, intimacy.

domèstico *pl* -ici *a* domestic, familiar; *nm* servant.

domiciliàre *vt* to domiciliate, house; -rsi *vr* to live, settle, take up one's abode.

domicílio *nm* abode, domicile.

dominànte *a* dominant; prevailing.
dominàre *vt* to command, dominate, govern, overlook, rule; **-rsi** *vr* to control oneself, master oneself.
dominazióne *nf* domination, rule.
domìnio *nm* dominion, authority, power, territory, domain.
donàre *vt* to bestow, confer, grant; *vi* to be becoming, suit; **-rsi** *vr* to devote oneself.
donatóre *nm* **donatrìce** *nf* donor, giver; **d. di sàngue** blood donor.
donazióne *nf* donation.
dónde *ad* from where, whence, wherefore.
dondolaménto, dóndolo *nm* rocking, swaying, swinging.
dondolàre *vt* **-rsi** *vr* to rock, sway, swing.
dondolóni *ad* dangling.
dònna *nf* woman.
donnaiuòlo *nm* philanderer, ladies' man.
donnésco *pl* **-chi** *a* womanly, feminine, womanish.
dònnola *nf* weasel.
dóno *nm* gift, present; talent.
dópo *ad* and *prep* after, afterwards, next, later; **e d.?** what next?
dopochè *cj* after, when, since.
dopodomàni *nm* the day after tomorrow.
dopoguèrra *nm* the post-war period.
dopoprànzo *nm* afternoon.
doppiàggio *nm* dubbing.
doppiàre *vt* to double; (*cin*) dub.
doppière *nm* two-branched candlestick.
doppiétta *nf* double-barrelled gun.
doppiézza *nf* double-dealing, duplicity.
dóppio *a* double, deceitful, dual; *nm* double, twice as much.
doppióne *nm* duplicate, (*typ*) double.
doràre *vt* to gild; (*cook*) glaze, brown, sugar-coat.
doratúra *nf* gilding.
dormicchiàre *vi* to doze.
dormiglióne *nm* sleepy fellow, lie-a-bed.
dormíre *vti* to sleep; *nm* sleep.
dormitòrio *nm* dormitory; **d. púbblico** doss house, flophouse.
dormivéglia *nf* (state) between sleeping and waking.
Dorotèa *nf pr* Dorothy, Dorothea.
dórso *nm* back; (*of mountain*) crest.
dosàre *vt* to dose.
dòse *nf* dose.
dòsso *nm* back.
dotàre *vt* to endow, give a dowry.
dotàto *a* gifted, endowed, furnished.
dòte *nf* dowry, gift, talent.
dòtto *a* learned; *nm* scholar.
dottoràto *nm* doctor's degree.
dottóre *nm* doctor, physician.
dottoréssa *nf* (female) graduate, lady doctor.
dottrína *nf* doctrine, learning, catechism.

dóve *ad* where, in the case that, whereas; *nm* where.
dovére *vi* to be obliged, have to, must, ought, should, be indebted, owe; *nm* duty, respects.
doveróso *a* right, dutiful.
dovízia *nf* abundance, plenty, wealth.
dovúnque *ad* anywhere, everywhere, wherever.
dozzína *nf* dozen; board and lodgings.
dozzinàle *a* common, ordinary.
dozzinànte *nmf* boarder.
dràga *nf* (*naut*) dredge.
dragamíne *nf* (*naut*) minesweeper.
dragàre *vt* (*naut*) to dredge.
dràgo *pl* **-ghi** *nm* dragon.
dràmma *nf* drachm(a); *nm* drama.
drammàtica *nf* dramatic art.
drammàtico *pl* **-ici** *a* dramatic.
drammatúrgo *pl* **-ghi** *nm* playwright.
drappèllo *nm* squad.
drapperìa *nf* drapery, dry-goods store.
dràppo *nm* silk material.
dràstico *pl* **-ici** *a* drastic.
drenàggio *nm* drainage.
drenàre *vt* to drain.
drítta *nf* right; (*naut*) starboard.
drítto *v* **diritto**.
drizzàre *vt* to straighten, prick up, erect, turn, (*fig*) right; **-rsi** *vr* stand up, straighten up.
dròga *nf* drug, spice.
drogàre *vt* to drug, spice.
drogherìa *nf* grocer's shop, grocery.
droghière *nm* grocer.
dromedàrio *nm* dromedary.
dubbiézza *nf* doubt, uncertainty.
dúbbio *a* doubtful, dubious; *nm* doubt, suspense; **èssere in d.** to be doubtful; **méttere in d.** *vt* to question.
dubbióso *a* doubtful, vague.
dubitàre *vi* to doubt, question, mistrust.
Dublíno *nf* (*geogr*) Dublin.
dublinése *a* of Dublin; *nmf* Dubliner.
dúca *nm* duke.
ducàle *a* ducal.
ducàto *nm* ducat; duchy, dukedom.
dúce *nm* chief, leader.
ducentísta *nm* writer of the thirteenth century.
duchéssa *nf* duchess.
dúe *a* two.
duecènto *a* two hundred; *nm* the thirteenth century.
duellàre *vi* to fight a duel.
duèllo *nm* duel.
duemíla *a nm* two thousand.
duétto *nm* (*mus*) duet.
dúna *nf* dune, sand-hill.
dúnque *cj* so, then, well! what! what about it?
duodècimo *a* twelfth.
duodenàle *a* duodenal; **úlcera d.** duodenal ulcer.

duòmo nm cathedral.
dúplex a **telèfono d.** two-party line telephone.
duplicàre vt to double, duplicate.
duplicatóre nm duplicator, multigraph, (rad) doubler.
dúplice a double, twofold.
duplicità nf duplicity, double-dealing.
duràbile a durable, lasting.
durànte prep during.
duràre vi to last, continue, remain; vt to stand, endure.
duràta nf duration, period, wear, endurance.
duratúro, durévole a durable, lasting.
durézza nf hardness, harshness.
dúro a hard, harsh, severe, insensible, stupid; nm hard, hardship.
dúttile a ductile.

E

e, ed cj and; **e ... e** cj both ... and.
ebanista nm cabinet-maker.
ebanistería nf cabinet-maker's shop, cabinet-making.
èbano nm ebony.
ebbène cj well, well then, what about it?
ebrézza nf drunkenness, intoxication, rapture.
èbbro a drunk, intoxicated, excited, mad.
èbete a dull, stupid; nm feeble-minded person.
ebetísmo nm feeble-mindedness.
ebollizióne nf boiling, ebullition.
ebrèa -o a Hebrew, Jewish; nm Hebrew, Jew; nf Hebrew, Jewess.
ebúrneo a of ivory; ivory-white.
eccedènte a exceeding, excessive.
eccedènza nf excess, surplus.
eccèdere vti to exceed, go too far.
eccellènte a excellent.
eccellènza nf excellence; (title) Excellency.
eccèllere vi to excel.
eccèlso a lofty, sublime.
eccentricità nf eccentricity, strangeness.
eccèntrico pl -ici a eccentric; nm eccentric person; (mech) cam.
eccepíre vt to object, except.
eccessívo a excessive, immoderate.
eccèsso nm excess, overspill.
eccètera nf etcetera.
eccètto prep except(ing), save, unless.
eccettuàre vt to except.
eccezionàle a exceptional.
eccezionalménte ad exceptionally, extraordinarily.
eccezióne nf exception.
eccídio nm massacre, slaughter.
eccitàbile a excitable.
eccitaménto nm **eccitazióne** nf excitement.

eccitànte a exciting, stimulating; nm stimulant.
eccitàre vt to excite, rouse, stimulate; **-rsi** vr to get excited.
ecclesiàstico pl -ici a ecclesiastic(al), nm clergyman, ecclesiastic.
e(c)clissàre vt to eclipse, obscure, outdo; **-rsi** vr to be eclipsed, disappear, slip away.
ècco ad here is, here are, there is (etc); interj see! look!
echeggiàre vi to echo, resound.
eclíssi nf eclipse.
èco pl **èchi** (m) nf echo.
economàto nm stewardship, steward's office, treasureship, treasurer's office.
economía nf economy, saving, thrift; **fàre delle economíe** vi to save money.
econòmico pl -ici; a economic(al).
economizzàre vt to economize, save.
ecònomo a economical, thrifty; nm bursar, steward, treasurer.
édera nf ivy.
Edgàrdo nm pr Edgar.
edicola nf news-stand; small chapel; niche.
edificànte a edifying.
edificàre vt to build; edify.
edifício nm building, edifice.
edíle a building; **ingegnère e.** building engineer.
edilízia nf building, building industry; **edilízio** a building.
Edimbúrgo nf (geogr) Edinburgh.
èdito a published.
editóre nm publisher, editor.
editríce af **càsa e.** publishing house.
edítto nm edict.
edizióne nf edition.
Edmóndo nm pr Edmund, Edmond.
Edoàrdo nm pr Edward.
edòtto a acquainted (with), aware (of), informed (of).
educandàto nm girls' boarding school, convent boarding school.
educàre vt to bring up, train, educate.
educatívo a educational, instructive.
educàto a well-bred, polite, educated.
educazióne nf education, training, upbringing, good breeding.
èffe the letter f.
effeminatézza nf effeminacy.
effemináto a effeminate, unmanly.
efferatézza nf brutality, ferocity.
efferàto a brutal, savage.
effervescènte a effervescent.
effettívo a actual, effective; **effetívi** nm pl (mil) effectives pl.
effètto nm effect, result, impression.
effettuàbile a practicable, feasible.
effettuàre vt to carry out, effect, execute, make, produce; **-rsi** vr to take place, happen.
effettuazióne nf execution, fulfillment.

efficàce *a* effective, effectual, efficacious.
efficàcia *nf* efficacy, efficaciousness, effectiveness.
efficiènte *a* efficient.
efficiènza *nf* effectiveness, efficiency.
effigiàre *vt* to image, make an effigy of, portray, represent.
effígie *nf* effigy.
effímero *a* ephemeral, fleeting.
efflorescènte *a* efflorescent.
efflùsso *a* efflux, outflow.
efflùvio *nm* effluvium.
effóndere *vt* to pour forth, exhale; -rsi *vr* to break out into, burst, flow, spread.
effusióne *nf* effusion, outpouring.
ègida *nf* protection, shelter, shield.
Egídio *nm* *pr* Giles.
Egítto *nm* (*geogr*) Egypt.
egiziàno *a nm* Egyptian.
égli *pron* he.
egoísmo *nm* selfishness, egoism.
egoísta *a* egoistic(al); *nm* egoist.
egrègio *a* egregious, exceptional, remarkable, distinguished.
eguagliànza *nf* equality.
eguagliàre *vt* to (make) equal, level.
eguàle *a* equal, even, like, uniform.
egualménte *ad* equally, alike.
elaboràre *vt* to elaborate, plan, work out.
elargíre *vt* to give liberally, grant, lavish.
elargizióne *nf* donation, generous contribution, gift, grant.
elasticità *nf* elasticity, spring(iness), resilience.
elàstico *pl* -ici *a* elastic; *nm* rubber band.
élce *nm* evergreen oak, holm oak.
elefànte *nm* elephant.
elegànte *a* elegant, graceful, (*of speech*) polished.
eleganza *nf* elegance, polish.
elèggere *vt* to choose, elect.
eleggíbile *a* eligible.
elegía *nf* elegy.
elementàre *a* elementary.
eleménto *nm* element, component; -ívi *pl* rudiments *pl*.
elemòsina *nf* alms *pl*, charity.
elemosinàre *vt* to beg.
elemosinièra *nf* -re *nm* almoner, alms-giver.
Èlena *nf* *pr* Helen, Helena.
elencàre *vt* to list, catalogue.
elènco *pl* -chi *nm* list, catalogue, inventory; e. telefònico telephone directory.
Eleonòra *nf* *pr* Eleanor, Elinor.
elètto *a* chosen, elect, elected.
elettoràle *a* electoral.
elettoràto *nm* electorate, constituency, franchise.
elettóre *nm* elettríce *nf* elector.
elettràuto *nm* (*aut*) electrical repair shop.
elettricísta *nm* electrician.

elettricità *nf* electricity.
elèttrico *pl* -ici *a* electric(al).
elettrificàre *vt* to electrify.
elettrizzàre *vt* to electrify, (*fig*) thrill.
elèttrodo *nm* electrode.
elettrodomèstici *nm* *pl* electrical household appliances *pl*.
elettróne *nm* electron.
elettrotècnica *nf* electrical technology.
elettrotréno *nm* electric train.
elevàre *vt* to elevate, erect, lift, raise; -rsi *vr* to make one's way, raise oneself.
elevatézza *nf* elevation, loftiness, nobility.
elevatóre *nm* (*tec*) elevator.
elevazióne *nf* elevation, raising, rise.
elezióne *nf* election, appointment.
èlica *nf* propeller, screw.
elicòttero *nm* helicopter.
elídere *vt* to elide, suppress.
eliminàre *vt* to eliminate.
eliminatòria *nf* (*sport*) preliminary heat.
eliminazióne *nf* elimination, removal.
elioterapía *nf* heliotherapy, sun treatment.
eliotròpio *nm* heliotrope.
Elísa *nf* *pr* Eliza.
Elisabètta *nf* *pr* Elizabeth, Elisabeth.
elíso *nm* Elysium; *a* Elysian; elided, suppressed.
elisír *nm* elixir.
élla *pron* she.
èlle the letter l.
èlleboro *nm* Christmas rose, hellebore.
ellísse *nf* ellipse.
ellíssi *nf* ellipsis.
ellíttico *pl* -ici *a* elliptic(al).
élmo *nm* helmet.
elocuzióne *nf* elocution.
elogiàre *vt* to praise, commend, eulogize.
elògio *nm* commendation, eulogy.
eloquènte *a* eloquent, fluent.
eloquènza *nf* eloquence.
elòquio *nm* speech.
èlsa *nf* (*of a sword*) hilt.
elucubràre *vt* to meditate on.
elúdere *vt* to avoid, elude, escape.
elusívo *a* elusive, evasive.
elvètico *pl* -ici *a nm* Helvetic, Helvetian, Swiss.
elzevíro *a nm* (*typ*) Elzevir; leading literary article in a newspaper.
emaciàrsi *vr* to become emaciated.
emaciàto *a* emaciated.
emanàre *vt* to issue, exhale; *vi* emanate, proceed.
emanazióne *nf* emanation, efflux, issuing.
emancipàre *vt* to emancipate, free; -rsi *vr* to get emancipated, free oneself.
emancipazióne *nf* emancipation.

Emanuèle nm pr Emmanuel, Immanuel.
embàrgo nm (naut) embargo.
emblèma nm emblem, symbol.
embolía nf (med) embolism.
embolismo nm (astr) embolism.
embrióne nm embryo.
emendaménto nm **emendazióne** nf amendment, amendation, correction.
emendàre vt to amend, emend; **-rsi** vr to amend.
emergènza nf emergency, exigency.
emèrgere vi to emerge, stand out.
emèrito a emeritus.
emètico pl **-ici** a nm emetic.
eméttere vt to emit, express, give out, issue.
emicrània nf headache.
emigrànte a nmf emigrant.
emigràre vi to emigrate.
emigràto nm emigrant, exile, refugee.
emigrazióne nf emigration; migration.
Emília nf pr Emily, Emilia; **Emílio** nm pr Emil.
eminènte a eminent, high.
eminènza nf eminence.
emisfèro nm hemisphere.
emissàrio nm emissary.
emissióne nf emission, issue.
emittènte a issuing; nm issuer; **bànca e.** bank of issue; **stazióne e.** (rad etc) sending station.
èmme the letter m.
emofilía nf hemophilia.
emorragía nf hemorrhage.
emorròidi nm pl (med) hemorrhoids pl, piles pl.
emotívo a emotional, sensitive.
emozionànte a exciting, thrilling.
emozionàre vt to move, excite.
emozióne nf emotion.
émpiere v empíre.
empietà nf impiety, cruelty.
émpio a impious, cruel.
empíre vt to cram, fill (up).
empírico pl **-ici** a empiric(al); nm empiric, empiricist; quack.
empirísmo nm empiricism.
empòrio nm emporium, department store, vast collection.
emulàre vt to emulate, vie (with).
emulazióne nf emulation, rivalry.
èmulo a nm rival, competitor.
emulsióne nf emulsion.
encíclica nf encyclic(al).
enciclopedía nf encyclopedia.
encomiàbile a commendable, praiseworthy.
encòmio nm encomium, praise; (mil) mention in dispatches, citation.
endèmico pl **-ici** a endemic.
endovenóso a intravenous.
Enèa nm pr Aeneas.
energía nf energy.
enèrgico pl **-ici** a energetic, powerful.
energúmeno nm madman, one possessed.

ènfaşi nf emphasis, stress.
enfiagióne nf swelling.
enfiàre vi **-rsi** vr to swell.
enígma nm enigma, riddle.
enigmística nf **libro di e.** book of riddles and puzzles.
ennèşimo a (math) nth.
enòrme a enormous, huge, incredible.
enormità nf hugeness, enormity, nonsense.
Enrichétta nf pr Henrietta.
Enríco nm pr Henry, Harry.
ènte nm being, organization.
entèrico pl **-ici** a enteric.
enteríte nf (med) enteritis.
entità nf entity, existence, importance.
entomología nf entomology.
entràmbi pron and a pl both pl.
entrànte a next, coming.
entràre vi to come in, enter, go in, have to do with.
entràta nf entrance, entry, admission; income, (com) receipts pl, revenue.
entratúra nf entrance; familiar terms.
èntro prep within.
entuşiaşmàre vt to enrapture; **-rsi** vr to become enthusiastic.
entuşiàşmo nm enthusiasm, rapture.
entuşiàsta nmf enthusiast.
entuşiàstico pl **-ici** a enthusiastic.
enumeràre vt to enumerate.
enunciàre vt to enunciate, state, utter.
epàtico pl **-ici** a (med) hepatic, of the liver.
èpico pl **èpici** a epic, heroic.
epicureísmo nm epicureanism.
epicurèo a epicurean; nm epicure.
epidemía nf epidemic.
epidèrmide nf (med) epidermis, (outer) skin.
Epifanía nf Epiphany.
epígono nm imitator, follower; descendant.
epígrafe nf epigraph, inscription.
epigràmma nm epigram.
epilatòrio a depilatory.
epilessía nf (med) epilepsy.
epilèttico pl **-ici** a nm epileptic.
epilogàre v riepilogàre.
epílogo pl **-ghi** nm epilogue.
episcopàle a episcopal.
episcopàto nm episcopacy; episcopate.
episòdio nm episode.
epístola nf epistle.
epíteto nm epithet.
època nf epoch, time.
eppúre cj and yet, however, nevertheless.
epuràre vt to purify, refine, remove, purge.
epurazióne nf purge, removal (from office), purification.
equànime a calm, tranquil, well-balanced.

equanimità *nf* equanimity, composure.
equatóre *nm* equator.
equazióne *nf* equation.
equèstre *a* equestrian.
equilibràre *vt* to balance, poise.
equilíbrio *nm* balance, equilibrium.
equilibrísta *nmf* tightrope-walker.
equinòzio *nm* equinox.
equipaggiaménto *nm* equipment, rigging.
equipaggiàre *vt* to equip, fit out; (*naut*) man.
equipàggio *nm* (*naut*) crew, equipage.
equiparàre *vt* to make equal, compare.
equipollènte *a* equivalent.
equità *nf* equity, fairness, impartiality, justice.
equitazióne *nf* riding, horsemanship.
equivalènte *a nm* equivalent.
equivalènza *nf* equivalence.
equivalére *vi* to be equivalent.
equivocàre *vi* to equivocate, make a mistake, misunderstand.
equívoco *pl* -oci *a* equivocal, ambiguous; *nm* misunderstanding.
èquo *a* equitable, fair, impartial, just.
èra *nf* era, epoch, age.
eràrio *nm* exchequer, public treasury.
èrba *nf* grass, herb; **in e.** *a* green, immature.
erbàccia *nf* weed.
erbàggio *nm* *pl* pot herbs *pl*, vegetables *pl*.
erbaiòlo *nm* costermonger, street vendor of vegetables and fruit.
erbàrio *nm* herbarium.
erbivèndolo *nm* vegetable dealer.
erborísta *nm* herborist.
erbóso *a* grassy.
erède *nm* heir.
eredità *nf* heritage, inheritance, heredity.
ereditàre *vt* to inherit.
ereditàrio *a* hereditary; **príncipe e.** crown prince.
ereditièra *nf* heiress.
eremíta *nm* hermit.
eremitàggio, èremo *nm* hermitage.
eresía *nf* heresy.
erètico *pl* -ici *a* heretical; *nm* heretic.
erètto *a* erect; built; founded.
erezióne *nf* erection.
ergàstolo *nm* galleys *pl*, life sentence.
èrica *nf* heath, heather.
erígere *vt* to erect, raise, institute; **-rsi** *vr* to raise oneself, set up for.
Eritrèa *nf* (*geogr*) Eritrea.
eritrèo *a nm* Eritrean.
ermellíno *nm* ermine.
ermètico *pl* -ici *a* hermetic, airtight; (*fig*) secret.
ermetísmo *nm* obscurity; (*liter*) a modern Italian school of poetry.
èrmo *a* (*poet*) lonely, solitary; *v* **solitàrio.**

Ernèsto *nm* *pr* Ernest.
èrnia *nf* (*med*) hernia, rupture; **e. del dísco** slipped disc.
Eròde *nm* *pr* Herod.
eròe *nm* hero.
erogàre *vt* to bestow, lay out.
eròico *pl* -ici *a* heroic.
eroína *nf* heroine; (*drug*) heroin.
eroísmo *nm* heroism.
erómpere *vi* to break out, burst out, flow, rush out.
erosióne *nf* erosion.
eròtico *pl* -ici *a* erotic.
erotísmo *nm* eroticism.
érpice *nm* harrow.
erràvte *a* errant, wandering.
erràre *vi* to wander, rove, roam, err.
erràto *a* wrong.
èrre the letter r.
erròneo *a* erroneous, faulty, incorrect.
erròre *nm* blunder, error, mistake.
èrta *nf* slope, steep ascent.
èrto *a* steep.
erudíre *vt* to instruct, teach; **-rsi** *vr* to acquire knowledge, become learned.
erudíto *a* learned, scholarly; *nm* scholar.
erudizióne *nf* erudition.
eruttàre *vti* (*of volcano*) erupt, eject, belch.
eruzióne *nf* eruption.
eṣacerbàre *vt* to embitter, exacerbate.
eṣageràre *vti* to exaggerate.
eṣagerazióne *nf* exaggeration.
eṣalàre *vti* to exhale, give out.
eṣalazióne *nf* exhalation.
eṣaltàre *vt* to exalt, praise; **-rsi** *vr* to get excited, become elated.
eṣaltàto *a* excited, elated, hotheaded; *nm* hot-head, fanatic.
eṣàme *nm* examination, investigation; **commissióne di e.** board of examiners.
eṣaminàre *vt* to examine, inspect, investigate, survey, test.
eṣaminatóre, *f* -trice *a* examining; *nm* examiner.
eṣàngue *a* bloodless.
eṣànime *a* lifeless, dead.
eṣasperàre *vt* to exasperate; **-rsi** *vr* to get exasperated.
eṣasperazióne *nf* exasperation.
eṣattézza *nf* accuracy, exactness, exactitude, punctuality.
eṣàtto *a* accurate, exact, precise, punctual.
eṣattóre *nm* -trice *nf* (*of taxes etc*) collector.
eṣattoría *nf* Revenue Office.
eṣaudiménto *nm* satisfaction, fulfillment.
eṣaudíre *vt* to consent, grant, fulfillsatisfy.
eṣauriènte *a* exhaustive.
eṣauriménto *nm* exhaustion, depletion; **e. nervóso** nervous breakdown.
eṣauríre *vt* to exhaust, use up, wear

out; -rsi *vr* to exhaust oneself, run out, run dry.

esauríto *a* exhausted, worn out, sold out, out of print.

esàusto *a* exhausted.

esautoràre *vt* to deprive of authority.

esazióne *nf* collection, exaction.

èsca *nf* bait, decoy, enticement; tinder (for a lighter).

escandescènte *a* choleric, hot-tempered.

escandescènza *nf* outburst, sudden burst of rage.

escavazióne *nf* excavation.

eschimése *a nmf* Eskimo.

esclamàre *vi* to cry out, exclaim.

esclamazióne *nf* exclamation.

esclúdere *vt* to except, exclude, leave out, bar.

esclusióne *nf* exclusion, omission.

esclusíva *nf* patent, exclusive right.

esclusività *nf* exclusiveness.

esclusívo *a* exclusive, sole.

esclúso *a* excluded, excepted.

escogitàre *vt* to contrive, devise, excogitate.

escoriàre *vt* to graze, excoriate.

escoriazióne *nf* abrasion, graze.

escursióne *nf* excursion, trip.

escursionísta *nmf* excursionist.

esecràre *vt* to execrate.

esecrazióne *nf* execration.

esecutívo *a* executive, executory; *nm* executive.

esecutóre *a* executory; *nm* -tríce *nf* executor, performer, executioner.

esecuzióne *nf* **eseguiménto** *nm* execution, performance.

eseguíre *vt* to accomplish, carry out, execute, fulfill, perform.

esémpio *nm* example, instance, pattern, precedent.

esemplàre *a* exemplary, model; *nm* specimen, (*of a book*) copy; model.

esemplificàre *vt* to exemplify.

esentàre *vt* to excuse, exempt, exonerate, free; -rsi *vr* to free oneself.

esènte *a* exempt, free.

esenzióne *nf* exemption (*eccl*) dispensation.

esèquie *nf pl* burial, funeral, obsequies *pl*.

esercènte *nm* dealer, shopkeeper, trader.

esercíre *vt* to carry on, keep, practice; **non e. piú** *vi* to have given up (business or practice).

esercitàre *vt* to exercise, practice, train; -rsi *vr* to practice.

esèrcito *nm* army.

esercízio *nm* exercise, practice, management, drill; (financial) year.

esibíre *vt* to display, exhibit, show; -rsi *vr* to offer oneself, show oneself.

esibizióne *nf* exhibition, show.

esibizionísta *nmf* exhibitionist.

esigènte *a* exacting, exigent, hard to please.

esigènza *nf* exigence, exigency, demand, requirement.

esígere *vt* to exact, require, demand.

esiguità *nf* exiguity, scantiness.

esíguo *a* exiguous, slender, scanty.

esilarànte *a* exhilarating; cheering.

esilaràre *vt* to cheer up, exhilarate.

èsile *a* slender, slim.

esiliàre *vt* to banish, exile; -rsi *vr* to exile oneself, withdraw from.

esiliàto *a* exiled; *nm* exile.

esílio *nm* exile (state).

esilità *nf* slenderness, weakness.

esímere *vt* to exempt, excuse; -rsi *vr* to excuse oneself, evade.

esímio *a* excellent, eminent, distinguished.

esistènte *a* existing, existent, extant.

esistènza *nf* existence, life; (*com*) stock.

esístere *vi* to exist, be, be extant.

esitàre *vi* to hesitate, waver; *vt* (*com*) to sell, dispose of.

èsito *nm* result, outcome, issue, denouement; sale.

esiziàle *a* baneful, fatal.

èsodo *nm* exodus, flight.

esòfago *nm* esophagus, gullet.

esoneràre *vt* to exempt, exonerate, free, release, relieve.

esònero *nm* dispensat on, exemption, exoneration.

esorbitànte *a* exorbitant, excessive.

esorcizzàre *vt* to exorcize.

esordiènte *a* beginning; *nmf* beginner, novice.

esòrdio *nm* beginning, exordium.

esordíre *vi* to begin, start.

esortàre *vt* to admonish, exhort.

esortazióne *nf* exhortation.

esòso *a* greedy, hateful.

esòtico *pl* -ici *a* exotic, foreign.

espàndere *vt* to spread; -rsi *vr* to expand, open one's heart.

espansióne *nf* expansion, demonstration of affection.

espansività *nf* effusiveness.

espansívo *a* expansive, unreserved.

espatriàre *vt* to banish, exile; *vi* to emigrate.

espàtrio *nm* expatriation.

espediènte *a nm* expedient.

espèllere *vt* to expel.

esperiènza *nf* experience; experiment.

esperimentàre *vt* to experience; experiment, test.

esperiménto *nm* experiment, test.

esperíre *vt* to carry out; (*leg*) try.

espèrto *a* experienced; *nm* expert.

espettoràre *vt* to cough up, expectorate.

espiàre *vt* to atone, expiate, make amends for.

espiazióne *nf* amends *pl*, atonement, expiation.

espletàre *vt* to fulfill, accomplish, dispatch.

esplicàre *vt* to develop; explain; e. un'attività to carry on an activity.

esplícito *a* clear, explicit, express.
esplòdere *vi* to blow up, burst out, explode.
esploràre *vt* to examine, explore, search, (*mil*) reconnoiter.
esploratóre *nm* explorer, (*mil*) scout; **gióvane e.** (Boy) Scout; **esploratríce** *nf* explorer; **gióvane e.** Girl Guide, Girl Scout.
esplorazióne *nf* exploration, (*mil*) reconnaissance.
esplosióne *nf* blowing up, discharge, explosion.
esplosívo *a nm* explosive.
esponènte *nm* exponent.
espórre *vt* to show, exhibit, explain, expose, risk; **-rsi** *vr* to expose oneself, run the risk.
esportàre *vt* to export.
esportatóre *a* exporting; *nm* **esportatríce** *nf* exporter.
esportazióne *nf* export, exportation.
esposímetro *nm* (*phot*) exposure meter.
esposizióne *nf* exposure, exhibition, exposition, statement.
espósto *nm* statement, petition; foundling.
espressióne *nf* expression.
espressívo *a* expressive, meaningful.
esprèsso *a* express, expressed, precise; *nm* (*letter, parcel, train*) express, special delivery.
esprímere *vt* to declare, express, signify, utter.
espropriàre *vt* to expropriate, dispossess.
espropriazióne *nf* expropriation.
espugnàre *vt* to (take by) storm.
espulsióne *nf* banishment, expulsion.
espúngere *vt* to expunge, delete.
espurgàre *vt* to expurgate.
espurgazióne *nf* expurgation.
éssa *pron* she.
èsse *nm* the letter s.
essènza *nf* essence.
essenziàle *a* essential, main, principal.
èssere *vi* to be, exist, happen, occur; **e. di** to belong to; **e. per** to be on the point of; *nm* being, state, condition.
essiccàre *vt* to dry; **-rsi** *vr* to dry up.
ésso *pron* he.
èst *nm* east.
èstasi *nf* ecstasy, rapture.
estasiàre *vt* to enrapture, delight; **-rsi** *vr* to be enraptured.
estàte *nf* summer.
estàtico *pl* **-ici** *a* ecstatic.
estemporàneo *a* extemporaneous, extempore, unscripted; **estemporaneamènte** *ad* impromptu, ad lib.
estèndere *vt* to extend, expand; **-rsi** *vr* to extend, stretch.
estensióne *nf* extension, expanse, extent, range.
estenuàre *vt* exhaust; **-rsi** *vr* to become exhausted, weak.

estenuazióne *nf* exhaustion.
Èster *nf pr* Esther.
esterióre *a* exterior, external, outward; *nm* exterior.
esterminàre *vt* to exterminate.
esternàre *vt* to disclose, express, open.
estèrno *a* external, outer; *nm* outside.
èstero *a* foreign; *nm* foreign countries *pl*; **all'e.** abroad.
esterrefàtto *a* terrified, amazed.
estesamènte *ad* extensively.
estéso *a* large, wide, extensive.
estètica *nf* aesthetics *pl*.
estètico *pl* **-ici** *a* aesthetic(al).
èstimo *nm* estimate, valuation, land tax.
estínguere *vt* to extinguish, put out; pay off; **-rsi** *vr* to go out, come to an end, die.
estínto *a* extinguished, deceased; *nm* deceased (person).
estintóre *nm* extinguisher.
estinzióne *nf* extinction, putting out; paying off.
estirpàre *vt* to extirpate, pull out, uproot.
estirpazióne *nf* extirpation, uprooting.
èstone *a nmf* Esthonian.
Estònia *nf* (*geogr*) Esthonia.
estòrcere *vt* to extort.
estorsióne *nf* extortion.
estradizióne *nf* extradition.
estràneo *a* extraneous, not related, alien, foreign; *nm* stranger, foreigner.
estràrre *vt* to dig out, draw out, extract.
estràtto *nm* extract, excerpt, certificate; **e. cónto** (*com*) statement of account.
estrazióne *nf* extraction, digging out; **e. a sòrte** drawing lots.
estremamènte *ad* extremely.
estremità *nf* extremity, end.
estrèmo *a* extreme, farthest; intense, severe; *nm* extremity, extreme.
estrinsecàre *vt* to express, manifest.
estrínseco *pl* **-sechi, -seci** *a* extrinsic.
èstro *nm* inspiration, fancy, freak.
estróso *a* capricious, freakish, whimsical.
estrovèrso *a* extroverted; *nm* extrovert.
estuàrio *nm* estuary, firth.
esuberànte *a* exuberant, overflowing.
esulàre *vi* to go into exile.
esulceràre *vt* to produce sores.
èsule *nmf* exile (person).
esultànte *a* exultant, rejoicing.
esultàre *vi* to exult, rejoice.
esumazióne *nf* exhumation.
età *nf* age.
ètere *nm* ether.
etèreo *a* airy, ethereal, impalpable.
eternàre *vt* to eternalize, make

endless; **-rsi** vr to become eternal, last for ever.
eternità nf eternity.
etèrno a eternal, everlasting.
ètica nf ethics pl.
etichétta nf etiquette; label.
ètico pl **ètici** a ethical; (med) consumptive.
etimología nf etymology.
etimològico pl **-ici** a etymological.
Etiòpia nf (geogr) Ethiopia.
etiòpico pl **-ici** a nm Ethiopian.
etisía nf (med) consumption.
ètnico pl **-ici** a ethnic(al).
etrúsco pl **-chi** a nm Etruscan.
èttaro nm hectare (2.47 acres).
Èttore nm pr Hector.
Eucaristía nf Eucharist.
eufemía nf euphemism.
eufemísmo nm euphemism.
eufonía nf euphony.
euforía nf euphoria, light-heartedness.
eufòrico pl **-ici** a euphoric, elated.
eugàneo a (geogr) Euganean.
Eugènio nm pr Eugene.
eunúco pl **-chi** nm eunuch.
Euròpa nf (geogr) Europe.
europèo a nm European.
Èva nf pr Eve, Eva.
evacuàre vt to clear out, evacuate.
evàdere vt to dispatch; evade; vi to escape.
evanescènte a fading, evanescent.
evanescènza nf evanescence; (rad, tv) fading.
evangelizzàre vt to evangelize.
evangèlo nm gospel.
evaporàre vi to evaporate.
evaporazióne nf evaporation.
evasióne nf escape, evasion.
evasívo a evasive.
eveniènza nf contingency, eventuality.
evènto nm event, result, outcome; **in ógni e.** at all events.
eventuàle a eventual, possible.
evidènte a clear, evident, obvious, plain.
evidènza nf clearness, evidence, obviousness.
evitàbile a avoidable, preventable.
evitàre vt to avoid, escape, spare.
evizióne nf eviction; recovery of possession.
èvo nm age, period, time.
evocàre vt to evoke, recall, conjure up.
evoluzióne nf evolution.
evvíva interj hurrah! long live!
extraconiugàle a extramarital.
extraterritorialità nf extraterritoriality.

F

fa ad ago; nm (mus) fa, F.
fabbisógno nm needs pl, requirement; (com) estimate of expenditure.
fàbbrica nf factory, manufactory, works pl, plant; manufacture; building.
fabbricànte nm manufacturer; builder.
fabbricàre vt to build, manufacture, fabricate.
fabbricàto nm building.
fabbricazióne nf manufacture; building; invention, forgery.
fàbbro nm blacksmith, smith.
fabbroferràio nm blacksmith.
faccènda nf affair, business, matter.
facchinàggio nm porterage.
facchíno nm porter.
fàccia nf face; **f. tòsta** impudence.
facciàta nf façade, front, (of a page) side.
facèto a facetious.
facèzia nf jest, joke, witticism.
fàcile a easy.
facilità nf facility, ease, easiness.
facilitàre vt to facilitate, make easy.
facilménte ad easily.
facoltà nf faculty, authority, power.
facoltativo a optional.
facoltóso a wealthy, well-to-do.
facóndia nf eloquence, fluency.
facóndo a eloquent, fluent, talkative.
fàggio nm beech-tree.
fagiàno nm pheasant.
fagiolíno nm French bean, string bean.
fagiòlo nm kidney-bean; (fig) blockhead.
fàglia nf (silk material) faille.
fagòtto nm bundle; (mus) bassoon; **fàre f.** vi to pack up.
faina nf beech marten.
fàlce nf scythe, sickle.
falciàre vt to cut down, mow.
falciatóre nm mower; **-tríce** nf mower, mowing machine; **f. da pràto** lawn-mower.
fàlco pl **-chi, falcóne** nm falcon, hawk.
falconàra nf falcon-house; loophole.
fàlda nf (snow)flake, layer, slice, slope, (of hat) brim, (of coat) tail, (of mountain) base, foot.
falegnàme nm carpenter, joiner.
falèna nf moth; flake of ashes.
fàlla nf (naut) leak.
fallàce a deceptive, fallacious.
falliménto nm bankruptcy, failure, insolvency.
fallíre vi to fail, go bankrupt; vt to miss.
fallíto a insolvent, unsuccessful; nm bankrupt, failure.
fàllo nm fault, defect.
falò nm bonfire.

falsàre vt to alter, distort, falsify.
falsaríga pl **-ríghe** nf a guide to writing straight; (fig) model, example.
falsàrio nm forger.
falsificàre vt to falsify, forge, misrepresent.
falsificazióne nf falsification, forgery.
falsità nf falsity, falsehood.
fàlso a false, wrong, forged, fictitious, deceitful; (of door etc) blind; nm falsehood, forgery, error.
fàma nf fame, renown, reputation.
fàme nf hunger; **avére f.** to be hungry.
famèlico pl **-ici** a famishing, starving.
famigeràto a notorious.
famíglia nf family, household.
familiàre a domestic, familiar, informal; nm relative, intimate, friend, manservant.
familiarità nf familiarity, intimacy.
familiarizzàre vt to familiarize; **-rsi** vr to become familiar.
famóso a famous, renowned, well-known.
fanàle nm lamp, lantern; (aut) light, lamp; **fanàli di posizióne** parking lights.
fanalíno nm **f. di códa** (av) tail-light; (aut) rear light.
fanàtico pl **-ici** a nm fanatic.
fanatismo nm fanaticism.
fanciúlla nf young girl; **fanciúllo** nm young boy.
fanciullàggine nf childishness.
fanciullésco pl **-chi** a childish.
fanciullézza nf childhood.
fandònia nf lie, idle story, tall tale.
fanfàra nf brass band, fanfare.
fanghíglia nf slush, sludge.
fàngo nm mud, mire.
fangóso a muddy, miry.
fannullóne nm idler, lazybones.
fantasciènza nf science fiction.
fantasía nf imagination, fancy, fantasy; **gioièlli f.** costume jewelry.
fantàsma nm ghost, phantom, phantasm.
fantasticàre vi to build castles in the air, daydream.
fantástico pl **-ici** a fantastic; fanciful; wonderful.
fànte nm foot-soldier; (at cards) jack.
fantería nf infantry.
fantíno nm jockey.
fantòccio nm puppet (also fig).
farabútto nm rascal, scoundrel.
faraóne nm Pharaoh; (game of) faro.
farcíre vt to stuff.
fardèllo nm bundle, burden.
fàre vti to do, make; have, take, take on, appoint, deem, perform, play, bear, cause; **f. attenzióne** to pay attention; **f. bel tèmpo** to be fine; **f. il bàgno** to take a bath; **f. il mèdico** to be a doctor; **f. fàre una còsa** to have a thing done;

f. lavoràre una persóna to make a person work; **-rsi** vr to become, grow, make oneself, turn; **f. fràte** to turn monk; **f. capíre** to make oneself understood; **f. vedére** to show oneself; nm behavior, manner.
farfàlla nf butterfly.
farína nf flour, meal.
farinàceo a farinaceous.
farínge nf pharynx.
farinóso a floury, mealy.
farisèo nm Pharisee.
farmacèutica nf pharmaceutics pl.
farmacía nf chemist's shop, drugstore, pharmacy.
farmacísta nm druggist, pharmacist.
farneticàre vi to be delirious, rave; (fig) talk nonsense.
fàro nm lighthouse.
farràgine nf farrago, medley.
fàrsa nf farce.
farsésco a farcical.
fàscia nf band, bandage, cover, swaddling band.
fasciàme nm (tec) plating, planking.
fasciàre vt to bandage, swaddle, wrap.
fasciatúra nf bandaging, swaddling; (wound) dressing.
fascícolo nm (of a publication) number; dossier.
fascína nf fagot, (mil) fascine.
fàscino nm charm, fascination.
fàscio nm bundle, pile; (of light) beam; **fasces** pl.
fascismo nm Fascism.
fascísta a nmf Fascist.
fàse nf phase, stage, (aut) stroke.
fastèllo nm bundle of wood, faggot.
fastídio nm annoyance, trouble, vexation.
fastidióso a annoying, troublesome, intolerant.
fàsto nm pomp, splendor, display.
fastóso a gorgeous, splendid, ostentatious.
fasúllo a false.
fàta nf fairy; **paése delle fàte** fairyland.
fatàle a fatal; fated, inevitable.
fatalità nf fatality; destiny, fate.
fatíca nf fatigue, weariness, hard work, difficulty; **a f.** with difficulty.
faticàre vi to toil, work hard.
faticóso a exhausting, fatiguing.
fàto nm destiny, doom, fate, lot.
fàtta nf kind, sort; deed.
fattèzze nf pl features pl.
fattíbile a feasible, practicable.
fattívo a effective, active, efficient.
fàtto a done, made; ripe, fullgrown, fit; nm fact, deed, action, event, matter.
fattóre nm, **-tóra**, **-torèssa** nf factor, bailiff, land agent; (in this sense **-tríce** f) maker.
fattoría nf farm, land agency, ranch.
fattoríno nm message-boy, messenger, page, bellboy (bellhop).

fattúra nf make, work, making, workmanship; bill, invoice.
fàtuo a conceited, fatuous; **fuòco f.** will-o'-the-wisp.
fàuna nf fauna.
fàuno nm faun.
fàusto a propitious, happy, lucky.
Fàusto nm pr Faust, Faustus.
fautóre nm -**tríce** nf supporter, favorer, protector.
fàva nf bean, broad bean.
favèlla nf language, speech, tongue.
favellàre vi to speak, talk.
favílla nf spark.
fàvo nm honeycomb.
fàvola nf fable, tale, story; laughing stock.
favolóso a fabulous.
favóre nm favor, kindness, approval; **cambiàle di f.** accommodation bill.
favoreggiàre vt to back, favor, support.
favorévole a favorable, propitious, well-disposed.
favorevoménte ad favorably.
favoríre vt to favor, foster, oblige, promote.
favoríto a favorite; nm favorite; **favoríti** pl side whiskers pl.
fazióne nf faction, party; (mil) guard.
fazióso a factious, seditious.
fazzolétto nm handkerchief.
febbràio nm February.
fébbre nf fever, temperature; **avére la f.** to have (run) a temperature.
febbríle a feverish (also fig).
fèccia nf dregs pl, scum, sediment.
fèci nf pl (med) stool.
fecondàre vt to fecundate, fertilize.
fecondazióne nf fecundation; **f. artificiàle** artificial insemination.
fecóndo a fecund, fertile, fruitful.
féde nf faith, creed, trust, belief, honesty; wedding ring, certificate; **f. di nàscita** birth certificate.
fedéle a faithful, loyal, true; nmf believer, follower.
fedeltà nf faithfulness, fidelity, loyalty.
fèdera nf pillow-case.
federàto a federate.
federazióne nf confederacy, federation.
Federíco nm pr Frederic(k).
fedína nf police record; whisker.
fégato nm liver; (fig) courage.
félce nf fern.
feld-maresciàllo nm (mil) field-marshal.
felíce a happy, lucky.
feliceménte ad happily.
felicità nf happiness, felicity.
felicitàrsi vr to congratulate.
felicitazióne nf congratulation.
felíno a feline.
féltro nm felt.
fémmina nf female, (contemptuous) woman.

femmíneo a womanly, womanish, effeminate.
femminíle a feminine, womanly.
fèndere vt to cleave, cut open, split; -**rsi** vr to burst, crack, split.
fendinébbia nm (aut) fog light.
fenditúra nf cleft, crack, split.
feníce nf (myth) phoenix (also fig).
fènico pl -**ici** a carbolic, phenic.
fenicòttero nm flamingo.
fenòmeno nm phenomenon.
feràce a fertile, fruitful, rich (also fig).
feràle a of death, tragic.
Ferdinàndo nm pr Ferdinand.
fèretro nm bier, coffin.
fèria nf holiday, vacation.
feriàle a working; **giórno f.** working day, weekday.
feriménto nm wounding.
feríre vt to hurt, wound.
feríta nf wound, injury, hurt.
feritóia nf loophole, embrasure; (mech) vent.
fèrma nf (mil) service, term of service; (hunting) pointing.
fermàglio nm brooch, clip, fastener.
fermaménte ad firmly, decidedly, positively.
fermàre vti to stop, fasten, fix, hold; -**rsi** vr to stay, stop, dwell on.
fermàta nf halt, stop, pause.
fermentàre vi to ferment, leaven.
fermentazióne nf fermentation.
ferménto nm ferment, leaven.
fermézza nf firmness, steadiness.
férmo a firm, steady, still; nm firmness; (mech) catch, stop; (leg) provisional arrest; **f. pòsta** poste restante, general delivery.
feróce a ferocious, fierce.
feròcia pl -**cie** nf ferocity, fierceness, savagery.
ferragósto nm August holiday (Aug 15th).
ferraménta nf hardware, ironmongery, iron fittings.
ferraménto nm iron tool.
ferràre vt to add iron fittings, shoe (a horse).
ferràto a iron-plated, shod; **stràda ferràta** railway.
fèrreo a (of) iron; hard, inflexible.
ferrièra nf ironworks pl, iron foundry, iron mine.
fèrro nm iron; pl irons, chains; **f. di cavàllo** horseshoe; **f. da càlza** knitting needle; **f. da stíro** (flat) iron; **età del f.** iron age; **lavóro in f.** ironwork.
ferrovía nf railway, railroad; **f. sotterrànea** underground, subway.
ferroviàrio a (of the) railway; **oràrio f.** nm timetable.
ferrovière nm railwayman, railroader.
fèrtile a fertile, fruitful, prolific.
fertilità nf fertility, fruitfulness (also fig).

fertiliżżànte *a* fertilizing; *nm* fertilizer.
fertiliżżàre *vt* to fertilize.
fervènte *a* burning, ardent, fervent.
fèrvere *vi* to be hot.
fèrvido *a* fervent, ardent, fervid.
fervóre *nm* ardor, fervor, zeal.
fessería *nf* stupidity (in actions or words).
fésso *a* cleft, cracked; *nm* fool.
fessúra *nf* crack, crevice, fissure, split.
fèsta *nf* feast, festivity, holiday, merry-making, saint's day, birthday.
festeggiàre *vt* to celebrate, feast, give a feast for, solemnize, welcome.
festévole *a* festive, joyous.
festíno *nm* entertainment, party.
festivàl *nm* festival.
festività *nf* festivity, gaiety.
festívo *a* festive.
festóso *a* gay, merry.
fetíccio *nm* fetish.
fèto *nm* fetus.
fétta *nf* slice.
fettúccia *nf* tape, ribbon.
fettuccíne *nf pl* noodles.
feudàle *a* feudal.
fèudo *nm* feud, fief.
fiàba *nf* fairy tale, story.
fiàcca *nf* weariness; laziness.
fiaccàre *vt* to exhaust, fatigue, wear out; -rsi *vr* to become tired, weak.
fiaccheràio *nm* cabman.
fiacchézza *nf* fatigue, lassitude, weakness, weariness.
fiàcco *pl* -cchi *a* exhausted, feeble, tired, weary.
fiàccola *nf* torch.
fiaccolàta *nf* torchlight procession.
fiàla *nf* phial, vial.
fiàmma *nf* flame, blaze; (*naut*) pennant.
fiammànte *a* flaming, glowing, bright; nuòvo f. brand new.
fiammàta *nf* blaze, fire.
fiammeggiàre *vi* to blaze, flame, shine.
fiammífero *nm* match.
fiammíngo *pl* -ghi *a* Flemish; *nm* Fleming; (the) Flemish (language).
fiancheggiàre *vt* to flank, help, support, border.
fiànco *pl* -chi *nm* hip, side, flank.
Fiàndre *nf pl* Flanders.
fiàsca *nf* flask.
fiaschettería *nf* wine shop, tavern.
fiàsco *pl* -chi *nm* flask; (*fig*) failure, fiasco; fàre f. to fail.
fiatàre *vi* to breathe, speak.
fiàto *nm* breath.
fíbbia *nf* buckle.
fíbra *nf* fiber, constitution.
ficcàre *vt* to drive in, thrust in; -rsi *vr* to force one's way in, intrude, meddle.
fíco *pl* -chi *nm* fig, fig-tree; f. d'India, ficodíndia prickly pear.

fidanzaménto *nm* betrothal, engagement.
fidanzàre *vt* to betroth; -rsi *vr* to become engaged.
fidanzàto *a* engaged; *nm* fiancé.
fidàre *vt* to entrust; -rsi *vr* to trust, confide, rely on; dare.
fidatézza *nf* reliability.
fidàto, fído *a* faithful, trusty.
fído *a* faithful, loyal; *nm* devoted follower; (*com*) credit.
fidúcia *nf* trust, confidence, reliance.
fiducióso *a* trusting, confident.
fièle *nm* gall, bile; (*fig*) rancor, bitterness.
fieníle *nm* hayloft; (*fig*) shabby place.
fièno *nm* hay.
fièra *nf* fair, exhibition; wild beast.
fieraménte *ad* fiercely, proudly, boldly.
fierézza *nf* fierceness, pride, boldness.
fièro *a* fierce, proud, bold, stern.
fiévole *a* feeble, weak, dim.
fífa *nf* plover, lapwing; (*fam*) funk.
fíggere *vt* to fix, fasten; f. gli òcchi su qualcúno to stare hard at somebody.
fíglia *nf* daughter; (*com*) counterfoil.
figliàstra *nf* stepdaughter; figliàstro *nm* stepson.
fíglio *nm* son, child.
figliòccia *nf* goddaughter; figliòccio *nm* godson.
figúra *nf* figure, illustration; (*of a novel etc*) character; symbol; fàre una bèlla f. to cut a good figure.
figuràccia *nf* poor figure, sorry figure.
figuràre *vti* to figure, represent, symbolize; look smart, appear, pretend; -rsi *vr* to fancy, imagine, picture to oneself.
figuràto *a* figurative; illustrated.
figurinísta *nmf* dress designer.
figuríno *nm* fashion plate, pattern
fíla *nf* line, queue, row.
filànda *nf* spinning mill.
filantropía *nf* philanthropy.
filàntropo *nm* philanthrope, philanthropist.
filàre *vt* to spin; *vi* to run away, take oneself off; *nm* (*of trees etc*) row.
filarmònico *pl* -ici *a nm* philharmonic, music-lover.
filastròcca *nf* nonsense rhyme, rigmarole.
filatelía *nf* philately, stamp collecting.
filatèlico *pl* -ici *a* philatelic; *nm* philatelist.
filàto *a* spun; consequent; *nm* yarn.
filatóio *nm* jenny, spinning-wheel.
filatóre *nm* -tríce *nf* spinner.
filétto *nm* thin thread, border, (*mil*) stripe; (*typ*) rule; fillet.
filiàle *a* filial; *nf* branch, branch-house or office.
filiazióne *nf* filiation.

filibustière *nm* freebooter; (*fig*) adventurer, cad.
filigràna *nf* filigree; (*paper*) watermark.
Filippíne (le) *nf pl* the Philippines.
Filíppo *nm pr* Philip.
film *nm* film, movie.
filmàre *vt* to film.
fílo *nm* thread, flex, wire; trickle; f. spinàto barbed wire; f. flessíbile flex, extension wire; f. di tèrra (*rad*) earth wire, ground wire; *pl* fila *nf* (*fig*) strings.
fílobus *nm* trolley-bus.
filología *nf* philology; study of literary texts.
filóne *nm* (*of mineral*) vein; stream; (*of bread*) long loaf.
filosofía *nf* philosophy.
filosòfico *pl* -ici *a* philosophic(al).
filòsofo *nm* philosopher.
filovía *nf* trolley-bus line.
filtràre *vti* to filter, percolate.
fíltro *nm* filter, philtre, strainer.
filugèllo *nm* silkworm.
fílza *nf* string, series; púnto a f. running stitch.
finàle *a* final, last; *nm* conclusion, finale; *nf* (*sport*) final.
finalménte *ad* finally, at last, lastly.
finalità *nf* finality, aim.
finànche *ad* also, even.
finànza *nf* finance, means.
finanziàrio *a* financial.
finanzière *nm* financier, customs officer.
finchè *cj* as long as; f. non till, until.
fíne *a* thin, fine, delicate, refined; *nm* aim; *nf* conclusion, end.
finèstra *nf* window.
finestríno *nm* (*of train, car*) window.
finézza *nf* fineness, finesse, politeness, shrewdness.
fíngere *vi* -rsi *vr* to pretend, dissemble, feign.
finiménto *nm* finishing; ornament, harness.
finimóndo *nm* end of the world, great uproar, utter ruin.
finíre *vt* to bring to an end, conclude, finish; *vi* to be over, end, finish, give up.
finítimo *a* bordering, neighboring.
finlandése *a nmf* Finnish, Finn.
Finlàndia *nf* Finland.
fíno *a* fine, thin, sharp; *prep* as far as, to, till, until, from, since; *ad* even.
finòcchio *nm* fennel.
finóra *ad* hitherto, so far, up to now.
fínta *nf* pretense, feint; fàre f. *vi* to pretend.
fínto *a* false, sham, artificial; *nm* hypocrite.
finzióne *nf* sham, pretense, fiction.
fío *nm* penalty.
fiocàggine *nf* hoarseness.
fioccàre *vi* to snow in large flakes; (*fig*) shower, abound.
fiòcco *pl* -chi *nm* (*of snow*) flake;

(*of wool*) knot, tassel; coi fiòcchi excellent, first rate.
fiòcina *nf* harpoon.
fiòco *pl* -chi *a* hoarse; weak, (*of light*) dim, (*of sound*) faint.
fiónda *nf* catapult, slingshot.
fioràia *nf* -o *nm* flower-seller.
fiordalíso *nm* cornflower, fleur-de-lis.
fiòrdo *nm* fiord.
fióre *nm* flower, bloom, blossom; (*at cards*) club; f. di làtte cream; f. di quattríni a lot of money; a f. d'àcqua on the surface of the water.
fiorènte *a* blooming, flourishing.
fiorentíno *a nm* Florentine.
fioríre *vi* to flower, thrive.
fiorísta *nmf* florist, flower painter, maker of artificial flowers.
fioríto *a* flowery, full of flowers.
fioritúra *nf* bloom, blossoming; (*fig*) flourishing.
fiòtto *nm* surge, wave.
Firènze *nf* (*geogr*) Florence.
fírma *nf* signature.
firmaménto *nm* firmament.
firmàre *vt* to sign.
fisarmònica *nf* accordion.
fischiàre *vt* to hiss, whistle.
físchio *nm* whistle, hiss; (*in the ears*) buzzing.
físco *nm* Exchequer, Inland Revenue, internal revenue; fisc.
física *nf* physics *pl*.
físico *pl* -ici *a* physical; *nm* physique; physicist.
fisiología *nf* physiology.
fisiològico *pl* -ici *a* physiological.
fisionomía *nf* countenance, physiognomy.
fisioterapía *nf* physiotherapy.
fiso *a* fixed; *ad* fixedly.
fissàre *vt* to fix, fasten; gaze at, appoint, arrange, engage, book; -rsi *vr* to be fixed, settle, set one's heart on.
fissazióne *nf* fixed idea, obsession, fixation.
físso *a* fixed, settled; *nm* fixed salary; *ad* fixedly.
fítta *nf* sharp pain, pang.
fittízio *a* fictitious.
fítto *a* driven in, dense, thick; *nm* lease; rent; a càpo f. headlong.
fiumàna *nf* flood, swollen river, torrent; (*of people*) stream.
fiúme *nm* river.
fiutàre *vt* to smell, sniff, scent; (*fig*) suspect, guess.
fiúto *nm* scent, (sense of) smell.
flagellàre *vt* to flagellate, scourge.
flagèllo *nm* scourge, whip; calamity.
flagrànte *a* flagrant.
flagrànza *nf* flagrancy.
flanèlla *nf* flannel.
flèbile *a* plaintive, feeble.
flèmma *nf* phlegm; calm.
flessíbile *a* flexible, pliable, pliant.
flessióne *nf* flexion, bending.
flessuóso *a* flexuous, supple.
flèttere *vt* to bend, flex.

flirtàre *vi* to flirt.
floreàle *a* floral.
floridézza *nf* floridness, prosperity.
flòrido *a* florid, flourishing, prosperous.
flòscio *a* flabby, flaccid.
flòtta *nf* fleet, navy.
flottíglia *nf* flotilla.
fluidità *nf* fluidity, fluency.
flúido *a nm* fluid.
fluíre *vi* to flow.
fluorescènte *a* fluorescent.
flússo *nm* flood tide, flux, dysentery.
flútto *nm* breaker, surge, wave.
fluttuànte *a* fluctuating, floating.
fluttuàre *vi* to fluctuate, waver.
fluviàle *a* fluvial, river.
fobía *nf* phobia.
fòca *nf* seal.
focàccia *nf* kind of cake.
fóce *nf* river mouth.
focolàio *nm* center of infection.
focolàre *nm* fireplace, hearth.
focóso *a* fiery.
fòdera *nf* lining, sheathing.
foderàre *vt* to line, sheathe.
fòdero *nm* scabbard, sheath.
fòga *nf* impetuosity.
fòggia *nf* fashion, form, manner, way.
foggiàre *vt* to fashion, form, shape.
fòglia *nf* leaf, foil.
fogliàme *nm* foliage, leafage.
fòglio *nm* sheet of paper, bank-note, newspaper, (*of metals*) sheet.
fógna *nf* drain, sewer.
fognatúra *nf* sewage, sewerage.
folclòre *nm* folklore.
folclorísta *nmf* folklorist.
folclorístico *pl* -**ici** *a* pertaining to folklore, folkloristic; (*fam*) folk.
folgoràre *vi* to flash, strike with lightning.
fólgore *nm* thunderbolt.
fòlio *nm* folio.
fòlla *nf* crowd, multitude, throng.
fòlle *a nmf* insane, mad, lunatic; **in f.** (*aut*) in neutral (gear).
follétto *nm* elf, goblin.
follía *nf* folly, insanity, madness.
fólto *a* thick, dense, bushy; *nm* thickness.
fomentàre *vt* to foment, incite, stir up.
fòmite *nm* tinder; (*fig*) cause, source.
fónda *nf* anchorage.
fóndaco *pl* -**achi** *nm* store, warehouse.
fondàle *nm* (*theat*) background.
fondamentàle *a* fundamental, basic, essential.
fondaménto *nm* base, foundation, ground.
fondàre *vt* to build, found, ground, rest; -**rsi** *vr* to be built, founded; rely on.
fondazióne *nf* foundation, institution.
fondènte *a* melting, fusing; *nm* fondant.

fóndere *vt* to melt, fuse, cast, smelt, blend.
fonderìa *nf* foundry.
fondiària *nf* ground tax.
fonditóre *nm* caster, founder, smelter.
fonditúra *nf* melting, casting.
fóndo *a* deep; *nm* bottom, background, end; fund; **artícolo di f.** leading article.
fonètica *nf* phonetics *pl*.
fonètico *pl* -**ici** *a* phonetic.
fonògrafo *nm* gramophone, phonograph; **f. automàtico a gettóne** jukebox.
fonología *nf* phonology.
fontàna *nf* fountain, source, spring.
fónte *nf* spring, source; *nm* font.
foràggio *nm* fodder, forage.
foràre *vt* to bore, pierce; *vi* to puncture; (*ticket*) to punch.
foratúra *nf* piercing; (*aut*) puncture; hole.
fòrbici *nf pl* scissors, pincers, claws.
forbíre *vt* to furbish, polish.
forbitézza *nf* (*of style*) elegance, polish.
fòrca *nf* pitchfork, gallows *pl*.
forcèlla *nf* forked stick; hairpin; (*of chicken*) wishbone; (*of telephone*) cradle; alpine pass.
forchétta *nf* (table) fork.
forcína *nf* hairpin.
forcúto *a* forked.
forènse *a* forensic.
forèsta *nf* forest.
forestàle *a* forestal; **guàrdia f.** forester.
forestière, forestièro *a* foreign, strange; *nm* foreigner, stranger.
fórfora *nf* dandruff, scurf.
fòrgia *nf* forge.
forgiàre *vt* to forge, shape, form.
forièro *a* portending.
fórma *nf* form, shape, figure; formality.
formàggio *nm* cheese; **f. parmigiano** Parmesan cheese.
formàle *a* formal, solemn.
formalità *nf* formality.
formalménte *ad* formally.
formàre *vt* to make, create, fashion, form; -**rsi** *vr* to form, develop.
formàto *a* formed, shaped; *nm* form, size.
formazióne *nf* formation, forming; training.
formíca *nf* ant.
fòrmica *nf* Formica (Registered Trade Name).
formicolàre *vi* to swarm with tingle.
formidàbile *a* formidable, dreadful.
formóso *a* buxom, shapely.
fórmula *nf* formula.
formulàre *vt* to formulate, express.
fornàce *nf* furnace, kiln.
fornàio *nm* baker.
fornèllo *nm* (kitchen) stove.
forniménto *nm* supply, equipment.

forníre *vt* to furnish, provide, supply; -rsi *vr* to provide oneself.
fornitóre *nm* -**trice** *nf* contractor, purveyor, supplier.
fornitúra *nf* stock, supplies *pl*.
fórno *nm* oven, bakery, kiln, furnace.
fóro *nm* hole.
fòro *nm* forum.
fórra *nf* gorge, ravine.
fórse *ad* perhaps.
forsennàto *a* crazy, mad; *nm* madman.
fòrte *a* strong, large, heavy, loud; (*of color*) fast; *nm* fort, forte, sourness; *ad* strongly, loudly, powerfully.
forteménte *ad* strongly, greatly, loudly, bravely.
fortézza *nf* fortress, fortitude.
fortificàre *vt* to fortify, strengthen; -rsi *vr* to acquire strength, grow stronger.
fortúito *a* casual, fortuitous.
fortúna *nf* fortune, luck, chance; **atterràggio di f.** forced landing.
fortunàle *nm* storm at sea.
fortunàto *a* fortunate, lucky.
fortunóso *a* eventful, stormy.
forúncolo *nm* (*med*) boil.
forviàre *vt* to lead astray, mislead, misguide.
fòrza *nf* force, power, strength.
forzàre *vt* to compel, force.
forzàto *a* forced; *nm* convict.
forzière *nm* safe, strong-box.
foschía *nf* haze, mist.
fósco *pl* -**chi** *a* dark, dull, gloomy, somber.
fosfàto *nm* (*chem*) phosphate.
fosforescènte *a* phosphorescent.
fosforescènza *nf* phosphorescence.
fòsforo *nm* phosphorus.
fòssa *nf* hole, pit, grave, den, ditch.
fossàto *nm* ditch, moat.
fossétta *nf* dimple.
fòssile *a nm* fossil.
fossilizzàre *vt* -rsi *vr* to fossilize.
fòsso *nm* ditch.
fotocèllula *nf* photoelectric cell.
fotocòpia *nf* photocopy.
fotocrònaca *nf* photo reportage.
fotocronísta *nmf* press photographer.
fotografàre *vt* to photograph.
fotografía *nf* photograph, photography; **f. istantànea** snapshot.
fotogràfico *pl* -**ici** *a* photographic; **màcchina fotogràfica** camera.
fotògrafo *nm* photographer.
fotorepòrter *mnf* news photographer.
fotoromànzo *nm* photo strip.
fotostàtico *pl* -**ici** *a* photostatic; **còpia fotostàtica** photostat.
foulard (*French*) *nm* silk scarf.
fra *prep* among, amid, between (two); (*time*) in; *nm* Brother.
frac *nm* evening dress; (*fam*) tails.
fracassàre *vt* -rsi *vr* to break in fpieces, smash.
racàsso *nm* crash, fracas, uproar.

fràdicio *a* rotten; wet, wet through.
fradiciúme *nm* mass of wet (or rotten) things.
fràgile *a* brittle, fragile, frail.
fragilità *nf* fragility, brittleness, frailty.
fràgola *nf* strawberry(-plant).
fragóre *nm* crash, loud noise.
fragoróso *a* roaring, very noisy.
fragrànte *a* fragrant, sweet-smelling.
fragrànza *nf* fragrance, aroma.
fraintèndere *vt* to misunderstand.
framassóne *nm* Freemason.
framassonería *nf* Freemasonry.
framménto *nm* fragment.
framméttere *vt* to insert, interpose; -rsi *vr* to interfere, interpose, intrude, meddle.
fràna *nf* **franaménto** *nm* fall of earth or rock, landslide, subsidence.
franàre *vi* to fall, sink, (*earth etc*) slide down.
Francésca *nf pr* Frances; **Francésco** *nm pr* Francis.
francescàno *a nm* Franciscan.
francése *a* French; *nm* Frenchman; *nf* Frenchwoman.
franchézza *nf* candidness, frankness, openness.
franchígia *nf* exemption; franchise; (*mil*) time off duty.
Frància *nf* France.
frànco *pl* -**chi** *a* candid, frank; *nm* franc.
francobóllo *nm* (postage) stamp.
Francofòrte *nf* (*geogr*) Frankfort, Frankfurt.
frangènte *nm* breaker, shoal, reef; (*fig*) difficulty.
fràngere *vt* to break to pieces, crush; -rsi *vr* to break.
frangétta, fràngia *nf* fringe.
frangiflútti *nm* breakwater.
frangitúra *nf* extraction of oil from olives.
frantóio *nm* (*for olives*) oil-press, stone-crusher.
frantumàre *vt* to break, smash.
frantúmi *nm* *pl* fragments *pl*, pieces *pl*.
frappé *nm* shake; **agitatóre per f.** milk shaker.
frappórre *vt* to interpose, insert; -rsi *vr* to interfere.
frasàrio *nm* jargon; phrasing; collection of phrases.
fràsca *nf* spray, twig; inn sign.
fràse *nf* phrase, sentence.
fraseología *nf* phraseology.
fràssino *nm* ash, ash-tree.
frastagliàto *a* indented, irregular, uneven.
frastornàre *vt* to disturb, trouble, distract.
frastuòno *nm* din, hubbub.
fràte *nm* friar, monk, brother.
fratellànza *nf* brotherhood.
fratellàstro *nm* half-brother.
fratèllo *nm* brother.
fratèrno *a* brotherly, fraternal.

fratricída *a* fratricidal; *nmf* fratricide.
fratricídio *nm* fratricide.
fràtta *nf* briar patch, th cket.
frattànto *ad* in the meantime, meanwhile.
frattèmpo *nm* meantime, interval; nel f. meanwhile.
frattúra *nf* fracture, break.
fratturàre *vt* to break, fracture.
fraudolènto *a* fraudulent.
frazióne *nf* fraction; group of houses.
fréccia *nf* arrow; **frecciatína** *nf* pungent remark.
freddaménte *ad* coldly, coolly, calmly.
freddàre *vt* to cool; kill; **-rsi** *vr* to grow cold, cool.
freddézza *nf* coldness, coolness, indifference.
fréddo *a* cold, chilly, cool, indifferent; *nm* coldness, cold; **avére f.** *vi* to be cold.
freddolóso *a* chilly, sensitive to cold.
freddúra *nf* cold; nonsense, silly story, pun.
fregàre *vt* to rub, scrub, cross out; (*vulg*) cheat, swindle; **-rsi** *vr* to rub oneself; (*vulg*) **fregàrsene** not to care.
fregàta *nf* rubbing, scrubbing; (*naut*) frigate.
fregiàre *vt* to decorate, adorn; **-rsi** *vr* to adorn oneself.
frégio *nm* frieze, ornament.
frégola *nf* (*of animals*) heat, (*fig*) mania, immoderate desire.
frèmere *vi* to quiver, thrill, tremble, throb, fume, shudder, rustle.
frèmito *nm* quiver, thrill, throb, roaring.
frenàre *vt* to brake, curb; hinder, repress, restrain; **-rsi** *vr* to keep one's temper; refrain from, restrain oneself.
frenesía *nf* frenzy.
frenètico *pl* **-ici** *a* frantic, raving.
fréno *nm* brake, bridle, curb, restraint; **potènza del f.** brake horsepower.
frenología *nf* phrenology.
frequentàre *vt* to attend, frequent, haunt, consort with.
frequentàto *a* frequented, attended, patronized.
frequènte *a* frequent, quick.
frequenteménte *ad* frequently.
frequènza *nf* frequency, attendance.
frèsa *nf* (milling) cutter.
fresatríce *nf* milling machine.
freschézza *nf* freshness, coolness.
frésco *pl* **-chi** *a* fresh, cool; *nm* coolness, cool; fresco.
frescúra *nf* coolness.
frétta *nf* haste, hurry; **avére f.** *vi* to be in a hurry; **di f., in f.** hastily.
frettolóso *a* hasty, hurried.
fríggere *vt* to fry.
frigidézza frigidità *nf* frigidness, frigidity.

frígido *a* frigid.
frigorífero *nm* refrigerator.
fringuèllo *nm* finch.
frittàta *nf* omelet.
frittèlla *nf* fritter, pancake.
frítto *a* fried; (*fig*) lost, ruined; *nm* fry, fried food.
frittúra *nf* fry, fried food.
frivolézza *nf* frivolity, frivolousness.
frívolo *a* frivolous, trifling.
frizióne *nf* rubbing, massage, friction.
frizzànte *a* sparkling; (*of air*) biting, pungent.
frizzàre *vi* to tingle, sparkle, sting.
frízzo *nm* witticism, gibe.
frodàre *vt* to defraud, swindle.
fròde *nf* fraud, swindle.
fròdo *nm* poaching, smuggling.
fròllo *a* (*of meat*) tender, (*of game*) high; exhausted; **pàsta fròlla** pastry.
frónda *nf* leafy bough, (the) Fronde.
frondóso *a* leafy.
frontàle *a* frontal; *nm* frontal, mantelpiece.
frónte *nf* forehead; *nm* front; **far f. a** to cope with, face, meet.
fronteggiàre *vt* to face, confront.
frontespízio *nm* frontispiece, title page.
frontièra *nf* border, frontier.
frontóne *nm* (*arch*) fronton, gable.
frónzolo *nm* tassel, frill, trinket.
fronzúto *a* leafy.
fròtta *nf* crowd, throng.
fròttola *nf* fib, lie, nonsense; popular song.
frugàle *a* frugal.
frugàre *vt* to rummage; **-rsi** *vr* to search one's pockets.
frúgolo *nm* little, lively child.
fruíre *vi* to make use of, enjoy.
frullàre *vt* to whip, whisk; *vi* to whir, whirl.
frullíno *nm* (*cook*) whisk.
fruménto *nm* wheat.
fruscío *nm* rustle, rustling.
frústa *nf* lash, scourge, whip.
frustàre *vt* to whip, lash, scourge.
frútta *nf* (*coll*) fruit.
fruttàre *vti* to produce, fructify, pay.
fruttéto *nm* orchard.
frutticultóre *nm* fruit-grower.
fruttífero *a* fruit-bearing; fruitful, profitable.
fruttificàre *vi* to fructify.
fruttivéndolo *nm* fruiterer.
frútto *pl* **-i** (*m*), (*table*) **-a** (*f*) *nm* fruit; profit, result, revenue.
fruttuóso *a* fruitful, profitable.
fu *a* late, deceased.
fucilàre *vt* to shoot.
fucilazióne *nf* shooting, execution.
fucíle *nm* gun, rifle.
fucína *nf* forge, smithy.
fucinàre *vt* to forge.
fúga *nf* flight, escape, avoidance; (*mus*) fugue.
fugàce *a* fleeting, transient.
fugàre *vt* to put to flight, rout.

fuggévole *a* fleeting, flying.
fuggiàsco *pl* **-schi** *a nm* fugitive, runaway.
fúggi-fúggi *nm* headlong flight, panic stampede.
fuggíre *vi* to flee, run away, take to flight; *vt* to avoid, shun.
fulgènte *a* shining, refulgent.
fúlgido *a* shining, bright, refulgent.
fulgóre *nm* brightness, splendor, refulgence.
fulíggine *nf* soot.
fulminànte *a* fulminating; *nm* lucifer match, percussion cap.
fulminàre *vt* to strike with lightning, strike dumb; *vi* to flash, lighten.
fúlmine *nm* lightning, thunderbolt.
fulmíneo *a* quick as lightning, sudden.
fúlvo *a* reddish, tawny.
fumai(u)òlo *nm* chimney-pot.
fumànte *a* smoking, steaming.
fumàre *vt* to smoke; **vietàto f.** 'no smoking'.
fumàta *nf* smoke, smoking, puff of smoke, smoke signal.
fumatóre *nm* **-trice** *nf* smoker.
fumétto *nm usu pl* comic strip, cartoon; **romànzo a fumétti** strip cartoon.
fúmo *nm* smoke, fume, steam.
fumògeno *a* smoke-producing.
fumosità *nf* smokiness.
fumóso *a* smoky.
funàmbolo *nm* tight-rope walker.
fúne *nf* cable, rope.
fúnebre *a* funeral, funereal.
funeràle *nm* funeral.
funèreo *a* funereal, gloomy.
funestàre *vt* to desolate, distress, sadden, ruin.
funèsto *a* baneful, disastrous, sorrowful, fatal.
fúngere *vi* to act as, officiate as.
fúngo *pl* **-ghi** *nm* fungus, mushroom, toadstool.
funicolàre *nf* funicular.
funivía *nf* air cable way.
funzionàre *vi* to act, function, run, work.
funzionàrio *nm* functionary, official.
funzióne *nf* function, office, service (in church).
fuochísta *nm* fireman, stoker.
fuòco *pl* **-chi** *nm* fire; (*phot*) focus; **méttere a f.** (*phot*) to focus; **fuochi d'artifízio** firework; **f. di sbarraménto** (*mil*) barrage fire.
fuorché *cj prep* except, but, apart from.
fuòri *ad prep* out, outside, except; **al di f.** *ad* outwards.
fuoribórdo *nm* (*naut*) outboard motor.
fuorilégge *nm* outlaw.
fuorisèrie *nf inv* (*aut*) custom-built.
fuoruscíto *nm* exile, outlaw.
fuorviàre *vt* to mislead; *vi* go astray, stray.
furbería *nf* cunning, slyness.

furbésco *pl* **-schi, furbo** *a* artful, cunning, sly, wily.
furènte *v* furibóndo.
furétto *nm* ferret.
furfànte *nm* rascal, scamp.
furfantería *nf* roguery, piece of roguery.
furgoncíno *nm* small van.
furgóne *nm* van, (*railroad*) caboose.
fúria *nf* fury, rage, hurry; **avére f.** to be in a hurry.
furibóndo, furióso *a* furious, raging.
furóre *nm* frenzy, fury, rage; **fàre f.** to be much admired.
furoreggiàre *vi* to be (all) the rage, make a hit.
furtívo *a* furtive, sly, stealthy.
fúrto *nm* theft, robbery.
fúsa *nf pl* **fare le f.** to purr.
fuscèllo *nm* twig, straw; (*fig*) thin person.
fusièra *nf* spindle-holder.
fusióne *nf* fusion, melting, smelting, casting, merging.
fúso *a* fused, melted.
fúṣo *nm* spindle.
fuṣolièra *nf* fuselage.
fustàgno *nm* fustian; corduroy.
fustigàre *vt* to flog.
fústo *nm* stock, stem, trunk; barrel, cask; frame; (*fam*) he-man.
fútile *a* futile, trifling.
futilità *nf* futility, *pl* trifles.
futúro *a nm* future.

G

gabardína *nf* gabardine, overcoat.
gabbàre *vt* to deceive, mock, swindle.
gabbatóre *nm* **-trice** *nf* deceiver, impostor, swindler.
gàbbia *nf* cage, coop, jail; topsail.
gabbiàno *nm* seagull.
gàbbo *nm* jeering, mockery; **prèndere a g.** to mock.
gabèlla *nf* duty, tax (on goods entering a town).
gabellàre *vt* to tax; (*fig*) **g. per** to pass off as.
gabellière *nm* customs officer.
gabinétto *nm* cabinet; toilet, closet; (*of dentist or doctor*) consulting room, surgery, office; **g. púbblico** public convenience, public comfort station.
Gabrièle *nm pr* Gabriel.
gaèlico *pl* **-ici** *a nm* Gaelic.
gaffe (*French*) *nf* gaffe, blunder.
gaggía *nf* acacia.
gagliardétto *nm* pennon.
gagliàrdo *a* strong, vigorous.
gagliòffo *a* loutish, rascally; *nm* lout, rascal.
gaiaménte *ad* gaily, brightly.
gaiézza *nf* gaiety, brightness.
gàio *a* gay, (*color*) bright.
gàla *nf* finery, gala; **tenúta di g.** (*mil*) full-dress uniform.

galànte a courteous, gallant (towards women); nm gallant, ladies' man.
galanteggiàre vi to play the gallant.
galantería nf courtesy, gallantry; delicacy, dainty.
galantína nf galantine.
galantuòmo nm honest man, man of honor.
galatèo nm code of manners pl, manners.
galèa nf galley.
galeòtto nm convict, galley slave.
galèra nf galley, jail, hard labor.
Galilèa nf (geogr) Galilee.
galilèo a nm Galilean.
gàlla nf gall, blister; **a g.** afloat.
galleggiànte a floating; nm float, buoy, raft.
galleggiàre vi to float.
galleria nf gallery, tunnel; arcade; (theat) gallery, balcony.
Gàlles nm (geogr) Wales.
gallése a Welsh; nm the Welsh language, Welshman; nf Welshwoman.
gallétta nf ship's biscuit, cracker.
gallína nf hen.
gallinàccio nm turkey-cock: chanterelle.
gàllo nm cock, weathercock, Gaul; **g. domèstico** rooster.
gallonàre vt to braid.
gallóne nm braid, (mil) stripe; (measure) gallon.
galoppàre vi to gallop.
galoppàta nf gallop, galloping.
galoppíno nm errand boy, messenger; **g. elettoràle** canvasser.
galòppo nm gallop.
galòscia nf galosh, golosh.
galvànico pl -ici a galvanic.
galvanizzàre vt to galvanize.
gàmba nf leg; **èsser e in g.** vi to be fit active, clever.
gambacórta nm lame man.
gambàle nm legging.
gambàta nf kick.
gàmbero nm crayfish.
gàmbo nm stalk, stem.
gàmma nf gamut, range, scale.
ganàscia nf jaw.
gàncio nm hook, clasp.
gànghero nm hinge; **fuòri dei gàngheri** furious.
gànglio nm ganglion (also fig).
gàra nf competition, contest, match.
garage (Fr) nm garage.
garagísta nm motor mechanic, garage owner.
garànte nm guarantor, surety.
garantíre vt to guarantee, stand surety for, warrant.
garanzía nf guarantee, surety, warrant.
garbàre vi to be agreeable, to be to one's liking, please, suit.
garbatézza nf politeness, kindness.
garbàto a civil, polite.
gàrbo nm courtesy, grace, manner, politeness; **a g.** gracefully, politely.

garbúglio nm entanglement, confusion, disorder.
gareggiàre vi to compete, vie.
garganèlla, bere a vt to gulp down, toss off.
gargarísmo nm gargle.
gargarizzàre vt to gargle.
garibaldíno a nm (one who) fought under Garibaldi.
garítta nf sentry box, look-out turret.
garòfano nm carnation, clove.
garrése nm (of horse) withers pl.
garrétto nm back of the heel, (horse) hock.
garríre vi to chirp, warble, screech; (flag) flap.
garrulità nf garrulity.
gàrrulo a garrulous.
gàrza nf heron; gauze.
garzóne nm apprentice, farm servant, shop-boy.
gas nm inv gas; **fornèllo a g.** gas cooker.
gasàto, gassàto a aerated.
gassísta nm gas-fitter, gasman.
gassómetro nm gasometer.
gassósa nf aerated drink.
gassóso a effervescent, aerated.
gàstrico pl -ici a gastric; **súcco g.** nm gastric juice.
gastríte nf (med) gastritis.
gastronomía nf gastronomy.
gastronòmico pl -ici a gastronomic.
gàtta nf she-cat; **dàre una g. a pelàre** to give a lot of trouble.
gattabúia nf jail, prison.
gattèsco pl -chi a catlike.
gattíno nm kitten.
gàtto nm cat; **èssere quàttro gàtti** to be very few people.
gattóni ad on all fours.
gattopàrdo nm leopard.
gaudènte a jolly, merry; nmf reveler.
gàudio nm joy, bliss, happiness; a joyful, joyous.
gavazzàre vi to revel.
gavétta nf mess tin.
gazósa nf aerated lemonade.
gàzza nf magpie; (fig) babbler, chatterer.
gazzàrra nf uproar.
gazzèlla nf gazelle.
gazzétta nf gazette, newspaper.
gelàre vti to freeze.
gelatería nf ice-cream shop.
gelatière nm ice-cream man.
gelatína nf gelatine, jelly.
gelàto a frozen; nm ice(-cream).
gelidaménte ad icily, coldly.
gèlido a icy, chilly.
gèlo nm freezing weather, frost, ice.
gelóne nm chilblain.
gelosaménte ad jealously.
gelosía nf jealousy, great care; shutter.
gelóso a jealous.
gèlso nm mulberry(-tree).
gelsomíno nm jasmine, jessamine.
Geltrúde nf pr Gertrude.

gemebóndo *a* moaning, plaintive.
gemèllo *a nm* twin; *pl* **gemèlli** twins *pl*; cufflinks *pl*.
gèmere *vi* to groan, moan, trickle, coo.
geminatúra, geminazióne *nf* gemination.
gèmito *nm* groan, moan.
gèmma *nf* gem, jewel; bud.
gemmàre *vt* to bud.
gemmàto *a* full of buds, studded with gems.
gendàrme *nm* gendarme, policeman.
gendarmería *nf* gendarmerie, police.
genealogía *nf* genealogy.
genealògico *pl* -**ici** *a* genealogical.
generàle *a nm* general.
generalità *nf* generality; (*pl*) particulars *pl*.
generalizzàre *vt* to generalize.
generalizzazióne *nf* generalization.
generalménte *ad* generally, in general.
generàre *vt* to generate, beget, breed, cause, engender, produce.
generatóre *nm* generator; (*aut*) dynamo, generator.
generazióne *nf* generation.
gènere *nm* kind, sort, type; gender; **in g.** *ad* in general; **gèneri** *pl* articles, goods *pl*; **g. di prìma necessità** necessaries.
genèrico *pl* -**ici** *a* generic, general.
gènero *nm* son-in-law.
generosaménte *ad* generously.
generosità *nf* generosity.
generóso *a* generous.
gènesi *nf* genesis; **la G.** Book of Genesis.
gengíva *nf* (*in mouth*) gum.
genía *nf* low breed, low set.
geniàle *a* ingenious, clever; genial.
genialità *nf* ingeniousness, talent, genius; geniality.
gènio *nm* genius, talent; **àrma del g.** *nf* (*mil*) engineers *pl*; **andàre a g.** to be to one's liking.
genitàle *a* genital.
gènito *a* born, generated.
genitóre *nm* parent, father; -**tríce** *nf* mother; -**tóri** *pl* parents *pl*.
gennàio *nm* January.
Gènova *nf* (*geogr*) Genoa; **genovése** *a nmf* Genoese.
Genovèffa *nf pr* Genevieve.
gentàccia, gentàglia *nf* mob, rabble.
gènte *nf* people, folk.
gentildònna *nf* gentlewoman, lady of quality.
gentíle *a* courteous, kind, polite; *a nm* Gentile; pagan, heathen.
gentilézza *nf* kindness, politeness, civility.
gentilízio *a* aristocratic, noble; **stèmma gentilízia** *nm* coat of arms.
gentilménte *ad* kindly, politely.
gentiluòmo *nm* gentleman, nobleman.
genuflessióne *nf* genuflection.
genuflèttersi *vr* to genuflect.

genuinità *nf* genuineness.
genuíno *a* genuine, authentic.
genziàna *nf* gentian.
geografía *nf* geography.
geogràfico *pl* -**ici** *a* geographic(al).
geología *nf* geology.
geòmetra *nm* geometer, surveyor.
geometría *nf* geometry.
geomètrico *pl* -**ici** *a* geometric(al).
gerànio *nm* geranium.
geràrca *nm* hierarch; leader.
gerarchía *nf* hierarchy.
gerènte *nm* manager, director.
gerènza *nf* management.
gèrgo *pl* **gèrghi** *nm* jargon, slang.
gèrla *nf* pannier.
Germània *nf* (*geogr*) Germany.
germànico *pl* -**ici** *a* Germanic; *nm* (*language*) Germanic.
germàno *a nm* German; *a* germane; **cugíno g.** first cousin; *nm* blood brother; wild duck.
gèrme *nm* germ, shoot, sprout.
germinàre *vi* to germinate.
germogliàre *vi* to bud, sprout.
germóglio *nm* bud, shoot.
geroglífico *pl* -**ici** *a* hieroglyphic; *nm* hieroglyph(ic).
Geròlamo, Gerònimo *nm pr* Jerome.
Gertrúde *nf pr* Gertrude.
Gerusalèmme *nf* (*geogr*) Jerusalem.
gèsso *nm* chalk, plaster of Paris, gypsum.
gèsta *nf pl* deeds, exploits, feats *pl*.
gestànte *a nf* expectant mother.
gestazióne *nf* gestation, pregnancy.
gesticolàre *vi* to gesticulate.
gesticolazióne *nf* gesticulation.
gestióne *nf* management.
gestíre *vt* to gesticulate; manage.
gèsto *nm* gesture, act, action.
gestóre *nm* manager, (*rly*) traffic manager.
Gesú *nm* Jesus.
gesuíta *nm* Jesuit.
gettàre *vt* to throw, cast, fling; -**rsi** *vr* to jump, throw oneself.
gèttito *nm* (*tax*) yield; (*naut*) jettison.
gètto *nm* throw, throwing, jet, sprout, casting; **a g. contínuo** without a break.
gettóne *nm* counter, token.
ghermíre *vt* to claw, collar, seize.
ghétta *nf* gaiter.
ghétto *nm* ghetto.
ghiacciàia *nf* icebox, refrigerator.
ghiacciàio *nm* glacier.
ghiacciàre *vti* -**rsi** *vr* to freeze.
ghiacciàta *nf* iced drink.
ghiàccio *nm* ice.
ghiacci(u)òlo *nm* icicle.
ghiàia *nf* gravel.
ghiànda *nf* acorn.
ghiandàia *nf* jackdaw, jay.
ghiàndola *nf* gland.
ghibellíno *a nm* Ghibelline.
ghigliottína *nf* guillotine.
ghígna *nf* ugly face, grimace.
ghignàre *vi* to sneer.

ghígno nm sneer, grin.
ghinèa nf guinea.
ghíngeri, in ad finely dressed.
ghiótto a gluttonous, greedy.
ghiottóne nm glutton.
ghiottonería nf gluttony; titbit, dainty, rarity.
ghiribízzo nm freak, whim.
ghiribizzóso a freakish, whimsical.
ghirlànda nf garland, wreath.
ghíro nm dormouse.
ghísa nf cast-iron, pig-iron.
già ad already, formerly, once; **interj** of course, yes.
Giacàrta nf (geogr) Djakarta, Jakarta.
giàcca nf jacket; **g. a vènto** windbreaker, anorak.
giacchè cj as, seeing that, since.
giacènte a lying, lying down, placed; (of capital) unproductive.
giacènza nf stay, demurrage; stock, (of books) unsold copies.
giacére vi to lie, be situated.
giacíglio nm bed, place for lying.
giaciménto nm (geol) layer; (min) deposit.
giacínto nm hyacinth.
Giacòbbe nm pr Jacob.
Giàcomo nm pr James.
giaggi(u)òlo nm Florentine lily, iris.
giaguàro nm jaguar.
giallàstro a yellowish.
giallézza nf yellowness.
giallíno a light yellow.
giàllo a nm yellow; nm thriller; **g. d'uòvo** (egg) yolk.
Giamàica nf Jamaica.
giàmbo nm iambus.
giammài ad never.
Giappóne nm Japan.
giapponése a nmf Japanese.
giàra, giàrra nf jar.
giardinàggio nm gardening.
giardinétta nf (aut) station wagon.
giardinièra nf woman gardener; station wagon; flower stand; pickled vegetables.
giardinière nm gardener.
giardino nm garden.
giarrettièra nf garter; (men's) sock suspender, garter.
giavellòtto nm javelin.
gibbóso a humped, hump-backed.
gibèrna nf cartridge box, pouch.
Gibiltèrra nf Gibraltar.
gigànte nm giant; a gigantic.
giganteggiàre vi to tower, rise like a giant.
gigantésco pl **-schi** a gigantic.
gigantéssa nf giantess.
gíglio nm lily.
gilè nm waistcoat.
gincàna nf (sport) gymkhana.
ginecología nf gynecology.
ginecòlogo pl **-ogi** nm gynecologist.
ginepràio nm thicket of junipers; difficult situation.
ginépro nm juniper.
ginèstra nf broom.

Ginévra nf (geogr) Geneva.
gingillàre vi **-rsi** vr to dawdle, play, trifle.
gingillíno nm dawdler, loiterer.
gingíllo nm knick-knack, trifle.
gingillóne nm dawdler.
ginnaşiàle a of a grammar school, secondary school, high school.
ginnàşio nm grammar school, secondary school, high school.
ginnàsta nmf gymnast, athlete.
ginnàstica nf gymnastics pl.
ginocchièra nf knee-pad.
ginòcchio nm pl **ginòcchi, ginòcchia** f knee.
ginocchióni ad on one's knees.
Gioacchíno nm pr Joachim.
giocàre, giuocàre vti to play, stake, work, make a fool of; **-rsi** vr to make fun of.
giocàta nf game stake.
giocatóre nm **-tríce** nf player.
giocàttolo nm toy, plaything.
giocherellàre vi to play, toy, trifle.
giòco pl **giòchi** nm play, game, sport, gambling, pastime, speculation; (mech) clearance.
giocofòrza, èssere v impers to be necessary.
giocolière nm juggler.
giocondità nf gaiety, cheerfulness.
giocóndo a gay, joyous.
giocosità nf mirth, facetiousness.
giocóso a jocose, facetious.
giogàia nf chain of mountains, (of oxen) dewlap.
giógo pl **gioghi** nm yoke (also fig); mountain ridge, peak.
giòia nf joy, delight; jewel.
gioiellería nf jewelery, jeweler's shop.
gioiellière nm jeweler.
gioièllo nm jewel.
gioiosaménte ad joyfully, joyously.
gioióso a joyful, merry.
gioíre vi to be glad, rejoice.
Giordània nf (geogr) Jordania.
Giordàno nm (geogr) Jordan.
Giórgio nm pr George.
giornalàio nm newsagent, newsboy.
giornàle nm (news)paper, journal, diary; **cíne g.** newsreel; **g. ràdio** news bulletin.
giornalièro a daily; nm day laborer.
giornalíşmo nm journalism.
giornalista nmf journalist, reporter.
giornalístico pl **-ici** a journalistic.
giornalménte ad daily, every day.
giornànte nf cleaning woman.
giornàta nf day, day's work; **vívere alla g.** to live from hand to mouth.
giórno nm day; **èssere a g. di** to be informed of; **di g.** in the daytime.
giòstra nf joust, tournament, merry-go-round, roundabout.
giostràre vi to joust, tilt.
Giosuè nm pr Joshua.
giovaménto nm advantage, benefit.
gióvane, gióvine a young; nm

young man, youth; *nf* young woman.
giovaníle *a* juvenile, youthful.
Giovànna *nf pr* Jane, Jean, Joan.
Giovànni *nm pr* John.
giovanòtto *nm* young man, bachelor.
giovàre *vi* to be of use, be beneficial;
 -rsi *vr* to avail oneself of, benefit by.
giovedì *nm* Thursday.
giovènca *nf* heifer; **giovènco** *pl* **-chi**
 nm bullock, steer.
gioventù *nf* youth, young people.
giovévole *a* beneficial, profitable.
gioviàle *a* jolly, jovial.
giovialità *nf* joviality.
giovinàstro *nm* hooligan, hoodlum.
giovinétta *nf* young girl; **giovinétto**
 nm lad, young fellow.
giovinézza *v* gioventù.
giradíschi *nm* record player.
giràffa *nf* giraffe.
giraménto *nm* turning; **g. di tèsta**
 dizziness.
giramóndo *nm* wanderer, globe-
 trotter.
giràndola *nf* Catherine wheel; (*fig*)
 fickle person.
giránte *a* revolving; *nm* endorser.
giràre *vt* to turn, avoid; (*cin*) shoot,
 act, tour, endorse; *vi* turn, wind,
 wander; **-rsi** *vr* to turn around.
girarròsto *nm* roasting jack, spit,
 turnspit.
girasóle *nm* sunflower.
giràta *nf* turn, walk; endorsement.
giratàrio *nm* (*com*) endorsee.
giravòlta *nf* change of front,
 turning, twirl.
girèlla *nf* pulley, small wheel;
 (*checkers etc*) piece; (*fig*) political
 weathercock.
girellàre *vi* to saunter, stroll.
girèllo *nm* small circle; (*children*)
 go-cart; (*cut of meat*) rump.
girétto *nm* stroll; **fàre un g.** to go
 for a stroll.
girévole *a* revolving, turning.
giríno *nm* tadpole.
gíro *nm* turn, round, circle, tour,
 circulation; endorsement; period of
 time, stroll; **prèndere in g.** to tease.
giróne *nm* (*in Dante's Inferno*)
 circle; (*football*) series (of games).
gironzolàre *vi* to stroll.
giropilòta *nm* automatic pilot,
 gyropilot.
girotóndo *nm* dance in a ring;
 'ring-a-ring-a-roses'.
girovagàre *vi* to roam, wander.
giròvago *pl* **-ghi** *a* roving, wandering; *nm* wanderer, tramp.
gíta *nf* trip, excursion.
gitànte *nmf* tripper, excursionist.
giú *ad* down; **su per g.** approximately,
 roughly.
giúbba *nf* jacket, coat.
giubilàre *vi* to exult, jubilate.
giubilèo *nm* jubilee.
giúbilo *nm* jubilation, rejoicing.
Giúda *nm pr* Judas.
giudàico *pl* **-ici** *a* Judaic; Jewish.

giudaísmo *nm* Judaism.
Giudèa *nf* (*geogr*) Judea, Judaea.
giudèo *a nm* Jewish, Jew, Judean.
giudicàre *vti* to judge, think,
 consider.
giudicàto *a* judged, sentenced; *nm*
 sentence; **passàre in g.** to be beyond
 recall.
giúdice *nm* judge, (*title*) Justice.
Giudítta *nf pr* Judith.
giudiziàle, giudizàrio *a* judicial.
giudízio *nm* judgment, opinion,
 verdict, sentence, prudence; **avére
 g.** to be sensible; **dènte del g.**
 wisdom tooth.
giudizióso *a* judicious, sensible.
giudò *nm* judo.
giúgno *nm* June.
Giuliàno *nm pr* Julian.
Giúlie, (Àlpi) *nf pl* (*geogr*) Julian
 Alps.
Giuliétta *nf pr* Juliet.
Giúlio *nm pr* Julius.
giulívo *a* gay, joyful.
giullàre *nm* jester, minstrel.
giuménta *nf* mare.
giuménto *nm* ass, mule, beast of
 burden.
giuncàia *nf* **giunchéto** *nm* reed bed.
giuncàta *nf* junket.
giunchíglia *nf* jonquil.
giúnco *pl* **giunchi** *nm* reed, rush.
giúngere *vti* to arrive, reach, go as
 far as, succeed, join, get at.
giúngla *nf* jungle.
giúnta *nf* addition, increase, make-
 weight; committee, council; **per g.**
 in addition, moreover.
giuntàre *vt* to join, sew together.
giuntúra *nf* joint, articulation.
giunzióne *nf* junction, connection.
giuocàre *v* giocàre.
giuòco *v* giòco.
giuraménto *nm* oath.
giuràre *vti* to swear, take an oath.
giuràto *a* sworn; *nm* juryman.
giureconsúlto *nm* jurisconsult.
giurí *nm* **giuría** *nf* jury.
giurídico *pl* **-ici** *a* juridical.
giurisdizióne *nf* jurisdiction.
giurisprudènza *nf* jurisprudence.
giurísta *nm* jurist.
Giusèppe *nm pr* Joseph.
Giuseppína *nf pr* Josephine.
giústa *prep* according to.
giustaménte *ad* justly, rightly.
giustézza *nf* exactness, propriety.
giustificàre *vt* to justify; **-rsi** *vr* to
 excuse oneself, justify oneself.
giustificazióne *nf* justification,
 excuse; (*at school*) absence note.
Giustiniàno *nm pr* Justinian.
Giustíno *nm pr* Justin.
giustízia *nf* justice.
giustiziàre *vt* to execute, put to
 death.
giustiziàto *a* executed; *nm* executed
 man.
giustizière *nm* executioner, avenger.

giústo *a* fair, just, lawful, proper, right; *nm* just man; **i giústi** *pl* the just, the right; *ad* just, precisely.
glàbro *a* hairless, smooth.
glaciàle *a* glacial, icy.
gladiatóre *nm* gladiator.
gladíolo *nm* gladiolus.
glàndola *nf* gland.
glandulàre *a* glandular.
glassàre *vt* to ice, glaze.
glàuco *pl* **-chi** *a* glaucous, grayish blue or green.
glèba *nf* glebe, soil, earth; **sèrvo della g.** *nm* serf.
gli *art m pl* the; *pron m (dat)* to him, *(idiom)* to them.
glicerína *nf* glycerin(e).
glícine *nf* wistaria.
globàle *a* global, total, inclusive.
glòbo *nm* globe; **g. dell'òcchio** eyeball.
glòbulo *nm* globule.
glòria *nf* glory.
gloriàrsi *vr* to boast of, be proud of, pride oneself on.
glorificaménto *nm* **glorificazióne** *nf* glorification.
glorificàre *vt* to glorify.
glorióso *a* glorious, proud.
glòssa *nf* gloss, explanation, annotation.
glossàre *vt* to gloss.
glossàrio *nm* glossary.
glucòsio *nm* glucose.
glúteo *a* gluteal; *nm (anat)* gluteus.
glutinàto *a* gluten.
glutinosità *nf* viscosity.
gnaulàre *vi* to mew.
gnòmo *nm* gnome, goblin.
gnòstico *pl* **-ici** *a* gnostic.
gòbba *nf* hump.
gòbbo *a* hump-backed.
góccia, gócciola *nf* drop.
góccio *nm* drop.
gocciolaménto *nm* **gocciolatúra** *nf* dripping, trickling.
gocciolàre *vti* to drip, drop, trickle.
gocciolío *nm* dripping, trickling.
gócciolo *nm* drop.
godè *nm* flare; **gónna a g.** flared skirt.
godére *vti* to enjoy, be glad; **-rsi** *vr* **-rsela** *vr* to enjoy oneself.
goderéccio *a* enjoyable.
godiménto *nm* enjoyment, pleasure; possession, use.
goffàggine *nf* awkwardness, clumsiness.
goffaménte *ad* awkwardly, clumsily.
gòffo *a* awkward, clumsy.
Goffrèdo *nm pr* Geoffrey, Godfrey.
gógna *nf* pillory; **méttere alla g.** to pillory.
góla *nf* throat; gorge; gluttony; **far g.** to be a temptation.
golétta *nf* schooner; narrow gorge; collar.
golf *nm* cardigan, jumper, sweater; golf.
gólfo *nm* gulf.
goliàrdo *nm* university student.

golosaménte *ad* greedily.
golosità *nf* greed, gluttony.
golóso *a* greedy, gluttonous.
gólpe *nf* blight, mildew.
gómena *nf (naut)* cable, hawser.
gomitàta *nf* shove with the elbow.
gómito *nm* elbow.
gomítolo *nm (of thread etc)* ball.
gómma *nf* rubber, gum, resin; tire.
gommapiúma *nf* foam rubber.
gommàto *a* gummed.
gommóso *a* gummy.
góndola *nf* gondola.
gondolière *nm* gondolier.
gonfalóne *nm* flag, standard.
gonfalonière *nm* standard-bearer.
gonfiàre *vt* to inflate, swell; **-rsi** *vr* to swell (up).
gonfiatóio *nm* inflator, tire pump.
gonfiatúra *nf* swelling, inflation, exaggeration, stunt, adulation.
gonfiézza *nf* swelling.
gónfio *a* swollen, inflated.
gonfióre *nm* swelling.
gongolàre *vi* to rejoice, exult.
goniòmetro *nm* protractor.
gónna *nf* skirt; **gonnellíno** *nm* short skirt; **g. scozzése** kilt.
gónzo *nm* blockhead, foo .
gòra *nf* millrace, millpond, pond.
gorgheggiàre *vi* to trill, warble.
gorghéggio *nm* trilling, warbling.
gorgièra *nf* ruff.
górgo *pl* **-ghi** *nm* whirlpool, abyss.
gorgogliàre *vi* to gurgle, bubble.
gorgoglío *nm* gurgling.
gorílla *nm* gorilla.
gòta *nf* cheek.
gòtico *pl* **-ici** *a* Gothic.
gòto *nm* Goth.
gótta *nf* gout.
gottóso *a* gouty.
governànte *nm* ruler, statesman; *nf* governess, housekeeper.
governàre *vt* to govern, rule, *(naut)* steer, *(av)* control; groom, tend.
governatívo *a* government(al).
governatóre *nm* governor, ruler.
govèrno *nm* government, rule; **g. della càsa** housekeeping.
gózzo *nm* goiter; bird's crop.
gozzovíglia *nf* debauch, revelry.
gozzovigliàre *vi* to revel.
gozzúto *a* goitrous, goitered.
gracchiàre *vi* to caw.
gracidaménto *nm* croaking.
gracidàre *vi* to croak.
gràcile *a* weak, delicate, frail.
gracilità *nf* weakness, thinness.
gradàsso *nm* blusterer, braggart.
gradazióne *nf* gradation, shade.
gradévole *a* agreeable, pleasant.
gradiènte *nm* gradient.
gradiménto *nm* liking, pleasure, satisfaction, approval.
gradinàta *nf* flight of steps.
gradíno *nm* step.
gradíre *vt* to like, wish; accept.
gradíto *a* agreeable, pleasant, welcome.

gràdo nm degree, pleasure, rank, will; **èssere in g. di** to be able to.
graduàle a gradual.
gradualménte ad gradually.
graduàre vt to confer (a degree or rank), graduate, grade.
graduàto a graded, progressive, graduated; nm (mil) non-commissioned officer (N.C.O.).
graduatòria nf classification, pass list.
graduazióne nf graduation; scale.
graffiàre vt to scratch.
graffiatúra nf scratch.
gràffio nm scratch; (naut) grapnel.
grafía nf writing, spelling.
gràfico pl -ici a graphic; nm graph.
grafología nf graphology.
gragnuòla nf (fig) hail, shower.
Gràie, (Àlpi) nf pl (geogr) Graian Alps.
gramàglie nf pl deep mourning.
gramígna nf couch-grass, weed.
grammàtica nf grammar.
grammaticàle a grammatical.
gràmmo nm gram.
gràmo a miserable, poor, wretched.
gràna nf (tec) grain; (fam) trouble; Parmesan cheese.
granàglie nf pl wheat, grain.
granàio nm barn, granary.
granàta nf broom, brush; grenade.
granatière nm grenadier.
granàto a garnet red; nm garnet.
grancàssa nf bass drum.
grànchio nm crab; **prèndere un g.** to make a mistake.
grànde a great, big, high, tall, grown up, wide; nm great man, grandee; **i gràndi** pl grown-ups pl.
grandeggiàre vi to rise to a great height, tower above.
grandézza nf greatness, height, size, grandeur; highness.
grandígia nf pomp, arrogance.
grandinàre vti to hail, shower.
grandinàta nf hailstorm (also fig).
gràndine nf hail.
grandiosità nf grandiosity, grandeur.
grandióso a grand, grandiose.
grandúca nm grand duke; **granduchéssa** nf grand duchess.
granducàto nm grand duchy.
granèllo nm grain, seed.
grànfia nf claw, clutch.
granífero a grain-producing.
granire vt to grain; (teeth) cut; vi to seed.
granita nf grated-ice drink, often fruit-flavored.
graníto nm granite.
gràno nm wheat, corn, grain; (necklace) bead; **g. saracèno** buckwheat.
grantúrco pl -chi nm maize, corn.
granulazióne nf granulation.
granulóso a granulous.
gràppa nf clamp, cramp iron, stalk,

(typ) bracket; brandy.
gràppolo nm bunch, cluster.
grassatóre nm highwayman.
grassazióne nf robbery.
grassétto a nm (typ) heavy-faced, heavy type.
grassézza nf fatness, stoutness; greasiness, abundance.
gràsso a fat, abundant, fertile; **martedí g.** Shrove Tuesday.
grassòccio a plump.
grassúme nm fat substance.
gràta nf grating.
graticciàta nf trellis-work, fence.
graticcio nm hurdle, trellis-work.
graticola nf grill, grate, grating.
gratifica nf bonus.
gratificàre vt to gratify.
gratificazióne nf bonus, gratuity.
gràtis ad free, gratis.
gratitúdine nf gratitude.
gràto a grateful, obliged; welcome.
grattacàpo nm problem, trouble.
grattacièlo nm skyscraper.
grattàre vt to scrape, scratch.
grattúgia nf grater.
grattugiàre vt to grate.
gratuitaménte ad free of charge, gratuitously.
gratúito a free, gratuitous.
gravàme nm burden, duty, tax.
gravàre vti to burden, load, weigh on.
gràve a heavy, great, serious, stern, grave; nm (phys) body; seriousness; **èssere g.** to be seriously ill.
graveménte ad gravely, heavily, deeply.
gravézza nf heaviness, gravity, weight; tax.
gravidànza nf pregnancy.
gràvido a pregnant, (fig) full, loaded.
gravità nf gravity, seriousness, weight.
gravitàre vi to gravitate.
gravitazióne nf gravitation.
gravosità nf heaviness, oppressiveness.
gravóso a heavy, oppressive.
gràzia nf grace, favor, mercy.
Gràzia nf pr Grace.
graziàre vt to pardon, grant.
gràzie interj thanks, thank you.
graziosità nf prettiness, graciousness.
grazióso a dainty, pretty, gracious.
Grècia nf (geogr) Greece.
grecísta nmf Hellenist.
grèco pl **grèci** a nm Greek.
gregàrio a gregarious; nm (mil) private, follower.
grégge nm flock, herd.
gréggio a (of materials) coarse; (fig) crude.
Gregòrio nm pr Gregory.
grembiúle nm apron.
grèmbo nm lap, (fig) bosom.
gremíre vt to crowd, fill; **-rsi** vr to fill up, get crowded.

gremíto *a* crowded, packed.
gréppia *nf* crib, manger, rack.
gréppo *nm* cliff, rock; (*of a ditch*) edge.
gréto *nm* pebbly bank.
grettézza *nf* meanness, stinginess.
grétto *a* mean, niggardly, stingy.
grève *a* heavy.
grézzo *v* **gréggio**.
gridàre *vti* to shout, cry, scream, call, proclaim.
grído *nm* cry, shout, scream; **di g.** famous.
grifàgno *a* predatory, fierce.
grífo *nm* snout; griffin, griffon.
grifóne *nm* griffin, griffon.
grigiàstro *a* grayish.
grígio *a nm* gray.
grigiovérde *a* gray-green; *nm* (*mil*) gray-green (Italian) uniform.
gríglia *nf* grate, grating, grill, grid; **alla g.** grilled, broiled.
grillétto *nm* trigger.
gríllo *nm* cricket; (*fig*) whim.
grínfia *nf* claw, clutch.
grínta *nf* forbidding face.
grínza *nf* crease, wrinkle.
grinzóso *a* creased, wrinkled.
grippàre *vi* (*mech*) to seize.
grissíno *nm* breadstick.
grisù *nm* firedamp.
groenlandése *a* (of) Greenland; *nmf* Greenlander.
Groenlàndia *nf* (*geogr*) Greenland.
grónda *nf* eaves *pl*.
grondàia *nf* gutter.
grondàre *vi* to stream, drip; *vt* to pour.
gròppa *nf* back, rump.
gròssa *nf* gross (12 dozen).
grossézza *nf* bigness, size, thickness, dullness, coarseness.
grossísta *nm* wholesale dealer, stockist, distributor.
gròsso *a* big, thick; *nm* main body, chief part; **pèzzo g.** bigwig.
grossolanità *nf* coarseness, grossness.
grossolàno *a* coarse, gross, rude.
gròtta *nf* cave, grotto.
grottésco *pl* **-schi** *a* grotesque; *nm* grotesqueness.
grovíglio *nm* tangle, confusion.
gru *nf* crane.
grúccia *nf* crutch, coathanger; (*for birds*) perch, (*door*) handle.
grugníre *vi* to grunt.
grúgno *nm* muzzle, snout.
grúllo *a nm* foolish, silly, foul.
grúmo *nm* clot.
grumóso *a* clotted.
grúppo *nm* group, knot.
grúzzolo *nm* hoard, savings *pl*.
guadàbile *a* fordable.
guadagnàre *vt* **-rsi** *vr* to earn, gain, acquire, win, reach.
guadàgno *nm* gain, profit.
guadàre *vi* to ford, wade.
guàdo *nm* ford.
guài *interj* woe!
guaína *nf* sheath, case.

guàio *nm* trouble, difficulty, accident, misfortune.
guaíre *vi* to whine, yelp.
guaíto *nm* yelp, whine.
gualcíre *vt* to rumple, crease.
Gualtièro *nm* *pr* Walter.
guància *nf* cheek.
guanciàle *nm* pillow.
guantàio *nm* glover.
guantièra *nf* glove box, tray.
guànto *nm* glove.
guardabòschi *nm* forester.
guardacàccia, guardiacàccia *nm* gamekeeper.
guardacòste *nm* coastguard.
guardàre *vt* to look at, gaze at, watch, consider, protect, guard; **-rsi** *vr* to look at oneself, abstain from, beware of, forbear, look at each other.
guardaròba *nf* cloakroom, wardrobe.
guardarobièra *nf* cloakroom attendant, linen maid.
guardasigílli *nm* Lord Privy Seal.
guardàta *nf* look, glance.
guardatúra *nf* way of looking.
guàrdia *nf* guard, watch, look out; **g. del còrpo** bodyguard.
guardiàno *nm* keeper, watchman.
guardína *nf* guardroom.
guardíngo *pl* **-inghi** *a* cautious.
guarentígia *nf* guarantee.
guaríbile *a* curable.
guarigióne *nf* recovery.
guaríre *vt* to cure, heal; *vi* to recover.
guarnigióne *nf* garrison.
guarníre *vt* to garnish, trim, furnish.
guarnizióne *nf* garnishing, trimming.
Guascógna *nf* (*geogr*) Gascony.
guascóne *a nm* Gascon, (*fig*) gascon, braggart.
guastafèste *nm* spoilsport, wet blanket.
guastamestièri *nm* bungler.
guastàre *vt* to spoil, ruin; **-rsi** *vr* to spoil, be spoiled, quarrel.
guàsto *a* spoiled, damaged, decayed, corrupt; *nm* damage.
guatàre *vt* to gaze, stare.
guàzza *nf* heavy dew.
guazzàre *vi* to paddle, wallow.
guazzétto *nm* stew.
guèlfo *a nm* Guelf, Guelph.
guèrcio *a* squint-eyed.
guèrra *nf* war.
guerrafondàio *nm* warmonger.
guerreggiàre *vi* to (wage) war, fight.
guerrésco *pl* **-chi** *a* (of) war, warlike.
guerrièro *a* warlike; *nm* warrior.
guerríglia *nf* guerrilla war.
gúfo *nm* owl; misanthrope.
gúglia *nf* spire.
Guglièlmo *nm* *pr* William.
guída *nf* guide, guidance, leadership; (*aut*) drive, steering, driving; **g. telefònica** telephone directory;

patènte di g. driving license; scuòla g. driving school.
guidàre vt to guide, lead, manage; drive (a car etc); -rsi vr to conduct oneself, behave.
guiderdóne nm recompense.
Guido nm pr Guy.
guidoṣlítta nf bobsleigh.
guinzàglio nm lead, (for dogs) leash.
guíṣa nf manner, way; a g. di like.
guizzàre vi to dart, flash, flicker, wriggle out.
guízzo nm flash, wriggle.
gúscio nm shell, pod, cover.
gustàre vti to enjoy, taste, like.
gústo nm taste, fancy, liking, relish.
gustosità nf savoriness, delightfulness.
gustóso a tasty, savory, delightful, amusing.
gutturàle a guttural.

I

i art m pl the.
iàrda nf yard.
iàto nm hiatus.
iattànza nf boasting, bragging.
iattúra nf misfortune.
ibèri nm pl Iberians.
Ibèria nf (geogr) Iberia.
ibèrico pl -ici a Iberian.
ibridíṣmo nm hybridism.
íbrido a hybrid.
icàstico pl -ici a figurative, graphic.
icòna, icòne nf icon.
iconoclàsta, iconoclàste nm iconoclast.
Iddío nm God.
idèa nf idea, notion, opinion, ideal, intention.
ideàle a nm ideal.
idealíṣmo nm idealism.
idealista nmf idealist.
idealizzàre vt to idealize.
ideàre vt to imagine, plan.
idèntico pl -ici a identical.
identificàre vt to identify.
identificazióne nf identification.
identità nf identity.
ideología nf ideology.
idillíaco, idíllico a idyllic.
idíllio nm idyll.
idiòma nm language.
idiomàtico pl -ici a idiomatic.
idiosincraṣía nf idiosyncrasy.
idiòta a idiotic; nmf idiot.
idiotíṣmo nm idiom, idiomatic expression.
idiozía nf idiocy.
idolatràre vt to worship, idolize.
idolatría nf idolatry.
idoleggiàre vt to idolize.
ídolo nm idol.
idoneità nf fitness, ability.
idòneo a fit, suitable.
ídra nf hydra.
idrànte nm hydrant, fire-plug, waterplug.

idràulico pl -ici a hydraulic; nm plumber.
ídro nm water snake; (short for) idrovolànte seaplane.
idroelèttrico pl -ici a hydroelectric; centràle idroelèttrica hydroelectric power station.
idròfilo a absorbent; cotóne i. absorbent cotton.
idròfobo a hydrophobic, rabid.
idrògeno nm hydrogen.
ídrope nm idropiṣía nf (med) dropsy.
idròpico pl -ici a nm dropsical, dropsical person.
idroplàno nm seaplane.
idropòrto, idroscàlo nm flying-boat station.
ièna nf hyena.
Ièova nm pr Jehovah.
ièri ad yesterday; i. l'àltro the day before yesterday.
iettatóre nm -tríce nf bringer of ill-luck.
iettatúra nf evil eye, misfortune.
igiène nf hygiene.
igiènico pl -ici a hygienic.
ignàro a ignorant, unaware.
ignàvia nf sloth.
ignàvo a slothful.
ígneo a igneous.
ignizióne nf ignition.
ignòbile a ignoble.
ignomínia nf ignominy.
ignominióso a ignominious.
ignorànte a ignorant.
ignorànza nf ignorance.
ignoràre vt to be ignorant of, ignore.
ignòto a unknown; nm unknown person.
ignúdo a naked, unclothed.
igròmetro nm (phys) hygrometer.
il art m the.
ílare a gay, cheerful.
ilarità nf gaiety, hilarity.
Ílda nf pr Hilda.
ilíaco pl -aci a (anat) iliac; Trojan.
illanguidíre vt to weaken; vi to grow feeble, languish.
illécito a illicit, unlawful.
illegàle a illegal, unlawful.
illegalità nf illegality.
illeggíbile a illegible.
illegittimità nf illegitimacy, unlawfulness.
illegíttimo a illegitimate, unlawful.
illéṣo a unhurt, uninjured.
illetteràto a illiterate, unlettered.
illibatézza nf chastity, purity.
illibàto a chaste, pure.
illiberàle a illiberal.
illimitàto a boundless, unlimited.
illividíre vt to make livid; vi to grow livid.
illògico pl -ici a illogical.
illúdere vt to deceive, delude.
illuminànte a illuminating, (fig) enlightening.
illumináre vt to enlighten, illuminate, light; -rsi vr to light up.

illuminazióne *nf* illumination, lighting.
illuminísmo *nm* illuminism.
illusióne *nf* illusion, dream.
illusòrio *a* deceptive, illusory.
illustràre *vt* to illustrate, explain, make illustrious.
illustratívo *a* illustrative.
illustrazióne *nf* illustration.
illústre *a* famous, illustrious.
imaginífico *pl* -ici *a* with a rich imagination.
Imalàia *nf* (geogr) Himalaya.
imbacuccàre *vt* to muffle up, wrap.
imbaldanzíre *vt* to embolden; -rsi *vr* to grow bold.
imballàggio *nm* packing, wrapping.
imballàre *vt* to pack, wrap.
imbàllo *nm* (aut) racing; packing, wrapping.
imbalsamàre *vt* to embalm, (animals) stuff.
imbambolàto *a* bewildered, stunned, dull, drowsy, confused.
imbandieràre *vt* to beflag.
imbandigióne *nf* preparation of a banquet, dish, table.
imbandíre *vt* to prepare a gala meal, lay (the table).
imbarazzànte *a* embarrassing, awkward.
imbarazzàre *vt* to embarrass, perplex, hamper.
imbaràzzo *nm* embarrassment, difficulty; i. di stòmaco indigestion.
imbarcadèro *nm* landing-place, pier.
imbarcàre *vt* to put (take) on board, ship; -rsi *vr* to embark, take ship.
imbarcatóio *nm* pier.
imbarcazióne *nf* boat.
imbàrco *pl* -chi *nm* embarkation, loading.
imbastíre *vt* (in sewing) to tack; (fig) to improvise, sketch.
imbàttersi *vr* to fall in with.
imbattíbile *a* unbeatable.
imbavagliàre *vt* to gag.
imbeccàre *vt* to feed; (fig) prompt.
imbecílle *a* *nmf* imbecile.
imbèlle *a* cowardly, weak.
imbellettàrsi *vr* to paint one's face.
imbèrbe *a* beardless.
imbestialíre *vi* to grow furious.
imbévere *vt* to imbue, steep; -rsi *vr* to become imbued with.
imbiancaménto *nm* whitewashing, bleaching, whitening; (of hair) graying.
imbiancàre, imbianchíre *vti* to bleach, whiten, whitewash, turn white, grow gray.
imbianchino *nm* house-painter.
imbizzarríre *vi* -rsi *vr* (of horses) to rear, grow furious, spirited.
imboccàre *vti* to feed, prompt, enter, fit, flow into.
imboccatúra *nf* imbócco *pl* -chi *nm* mouth, opening, entrance, mouthpiece.

imboscaménto *nm* hiding, shirking military service.
imboscàre *vt* -rsi *vr* to hide, lie in wait, help evade military service, evade military service.
imboscàta *nf* ambush.
imbottigliàre *vt* to bottle.
imbottíre *vt* to pad, stuff.
imbottitúra *nf* stuffing, wadding, quilting.
imbrattàre *vt* to daub, dirty.
imbrigliàre *vt* to bridle, curb.
imbroccàre *vt* to guess right, hit the mark.
imbrogliàre *vt* to cheat, swindle, muddle, entangle; -rsi *vr* to get confused.
imbróglio *nm* tangle, confused situation, trick, fraud.
imbroglióne *nm* cheat, swindler.
imbronciàre *vi* -rsi *vr* to take offense, sulk.
imbrunàre, imbruníre *vi* to darken, grow dark.
imbruttíre *vt* to disfigure, make ugly; *vi* to grow ugly.
imbucàre *vt* to post, put into a hole; -rsi *vr* to creep into a hole.
imburràre *vt* to butter.
imbúto *nm* funnel.
imitàre *vt* to imitate, copy, mimic.
imitatívo *a* imitative.
imitazióne *nf* imitation.
immacolàto *a* immaculate, spotless.
immagazzinàre *vi* to store.
immaginàre *vt* to imagine, fancy; -rsi *vr* to fancy, imagine, picture.
immaginazióne *nf* imagination, fancy.
immàgine *nf* image, picture.
immancabilménte *ad* unfailingly, certainly.
immàne *a* enormous, huge, frightful.
immangiàbile *a* uneatable.
immantinénte *ad* at once, immediately.
immateriàle *a* immaterial.
immatricolàre *vt* -rsi *vr* to matriculate.
immaturità *nf* immaturity, unripeness.
immatúro *a* unripe, immature.
immedesimàrsi *vr* to identify oneself with.
immediataménte *ad* immediately, directly, forthwith.
immediàto *a* immediate.
immemoràbile *a* immemorial.
immèmore *a* forgetful, unmindful.
immensità *nf* immensity.
immènso *a* immense, vast.
immensuràbile *a* immeasurable.
immèrgere *vt* to immerse, dip, plunge; -rsi *vr* to immerse oneself.
immeritàto *a* undeserved, unmerited.
immeritévole *a* undeserving, unworthy.
immersióne *nf* immersion.
immèrso *a* immersed (also fig).

immigrànte *a nmf* immigrant.
immigràre *vi* to immigrate.
immigrazióne *nf* immigration.
imminènte *a* imminent, impending.
imminènza *nf* imminence.
immischiàre *vt* to bring into, involve; **-rsi** *vr* to interfere, meddle.
immişeríre *vt* to impoverish; *vi* to grow poor.
immissàrio *nm* affluent, tributary.
immòbile *a* immovable, motionless; *nm pl* **gli immòbili** immovables, immovable property, real estate.
immobilità *nf* immobility.
immobilizzàre *vt* to immobilize.
immobilizzazióne *nf* immobilization.
immodèstia *nf* immodesty.
immodèsto *a* immodest.
immolàre *vt* to immolate, sacrifice.
immolazióne *nf* immolation.
immollàre *vt* to wet; **-rsi** *vr* to get wet.
immondézza *nf* uncleanness, filth, garbage.
immondezzàio *nm* garbage heap.
immondízia *nf* garbage, filth.
immóndo *a* unclean, dirty.
immoràle *a* immoral.
immoralità *nf* immorality.
immortalàre *vt* to immortalize.
immortàle *a* immortal.
immortalità *nf* immortality.
immòto *a* motionless.
immúne *a* immune, free, exempt.
immunità *nf* immunity, freedom.
immunizzàre *vt* to immunize; **-rsi** *vr* to become immune.
impaccàre *vt* to pack.
impacchettàre *vt* to make up packets, pack.
impacciàre *vt* to hinder, embarrass, encumber; **-rsi** *vr* to meddle.
impacciàto *a* awkward, embarrassed, self-conscious.
impàccio *nm* encumbrance, obstacle, bother, embarrassment.
impadronírsi *vr* to take possession of, seize, master.
impagàbile *a* priceless, invaluable.
impaginàre *vt (typ)* to make up (a book), page.
impagliàre *vt* to cover with straw.
impalàto *a* rigid, stiff.
impalcàre *vt* to board, plank.
impalcatúra *nf* scaffolding.
impallidíre *vi* to turn pale.
impalpàbile *a* impalpable.
impaludàre *vi* **-rsi** *vr* to grow marshy.
impanàto *a* covered with bread crumbs.
impancàrsi *vr* to presume, act like.
impantanàrsi *vr* to sink in the mud, be bogged.
impappinàrsi *vr* to become confused.
imparàre *vt* to learn.
imparatíccio *nm* thing badly learned, beginner's work.

impareggiàbile *a* incomparable.
imparentàrsi *vr* to become related, marry into.
ímpari *a* odd, uneven, unequal.
impartíre *vt* to impart, bestow, give.
imparziàle *a* impartial, unbiased.
impassíbile *a* impassible, impassive.
impastàre *vt* to knead, mix.
impàsto *nm* mixture.
impastoiàre *vt* to shackle, hinder, impede.
impauríre *vt* to frighten; **-rsi** *vr* to get frightened.
impaziènte *a* impatient.
impazientíre *vi* **-rsi** *vr* to lose one's patience.
impazientíto *a* irritated, annoyed.
impaziènza *nf* impatience.
impazzàre, **impazzíre** *vi* to be crazy about, go mad.
impeccàbile *a* impeccable.
impeciàre *vt* to pitch, tar.
impediménto *nm* impediment, hindrance, obstacle.
impedíre *vt* to prevent, obstruct, hinder.
impegnàre *vt* to bind, engage, pledge, pawn; **-rsi** *vr* to bind, engage oneself, get involved.
impegnatívo *a* binding, exacting.
impègno *nm* engagement, obligation, care.
impenetràbile *a* impenetrable, inscrutable.
impenitènte *a* impenitent.
impenitènza *nf* impenitence.
impensàbile *a* inconceivable, unthinkable.
impensataménte *ad* unexpectedly.
impensàto *a* unthought of, unforeseen, unexpected.
impensieríre *vt* to make uneasy; **-rsi** *vr* to worry.
imperànte *a* ruling, reigning, prevailing.
imperàre *vt* to rule (over).
imperatívo *a nm* imperative.
imperatóre *nm* emperor; **-tríce** *nf* empress.
impercettíbile *a* imperceptible.
imperdonàbile *a* unpardonable.
imperfètto *a nm* imperfect.
imperfezióne *nf* fault, flaw, imperfection.
imperiàle *a* imperial.
imperialísmo *nm* imperialism.
imperiosità *nf* imperiousness.
imperióso *a* domineering, imperious.
imperízia *nf* lack of experience, lack of skill.
impermalírsi *vr* to get cross.
impermeàbile *a nm* waterproof.
impermeabilità *nf* impermeability.
imperniàre *vt* **-rsi** *vr* to pivot, hinge.
impèro *nm* empire, command.
impersonàle *a* impersonal.
impersonàre *vt* to impersonate.
impertèrrito *a* undaunted, fearless.
impertinènte *a* impertinent, saucy.

impertinènza *nf* impertinence.
imperturbàbile *a* imperturbable.
imperversàre *vi* (*of diseases, weather etc*) to rage.
impèrvio *a* hard to reach, inaccessible.
ímpeto *nm* impetus, vehemence, impulse, outburst, transport.
impetràre *vt* to ask for, obtain.
impetuosità *nf* impetuosity, impulsiveness.
impetuóso *a* impetuous, vehement.
impiantàre *vt* to establish, set up.
impiantíto *nm* floor.
impiànto *nm* installation, plant, establishment.
impiastràre *vt* to daub, plaster, smear.
impiàstro *nm* plaster; (*fig*) bore.
impiccagióne *nf* hanging (on the gallows).
impiccàre *vt* to hang; **-rsi** *vr* to hang oneself.
impicciàre *etc v* **impacciare** *etc*.
impiccolíre *vt* to make smaller, diminish, lessen.
impiegàre *vt* to employ, spend, invest; **-rsi** *vr* to get a post.
impiegàto *nm* clerk, employee.
impiègo *pl* **-ghi** *nm* employment, job, position, use.
impietosíre *vt* to move to pity; **-rsi** *vr* to be touched.
impietràre, impietríre *vt* to petrify.
impigliàre *vt* to entangle.
impigríre *vt* to make lazy; **-rsi** *vr* to grow lazy.
impinguàre *vt* to fatten, enrich; **-rsi** *vr* to grow fat, get rich.
impiombàre *vt* to seal with lead, splice (a cable), stop (a tooth), lead.
impiombatúra *nf* sealing with lead, stopping (a tooth), splicing (a cable), leading.
implacàbile *a* implacable, relentless.
implicàre *vt* to implicate, involve, imply.
implicazióne *nf* implication.
implícito *a* implicit.
implorànte *a* imploring.
imploràre *vt* to entreat, implore.
implorazióne *nf* entreaty.
impolítico *pl* **-ici** *a* impolitic.
impoltroníre *vt* to make lazy; **-rsi** *vr* to become lazy.
impolveràre *vt* to cover with dust.
imponderàbile *a nm* imponderable.
imponènte *a* imposing, impressive.
imponènza *nf* grandeur.
imponíbile *a* chargeable, taxable.
impopolàre *a* unpopular.
impopolarità *nf* unpopularity.
impórre *vt* to impose; **-rsi** *vr* to impose oneself, make oneself respected, have success.
importànte *a* important, weighty; *nm* important thing.
importànza *nf* importance.
importàbile *a* importable.

importàre *vt* to import, imply, involve, cost; *v impers* to matter, be of importance.
importazióne *nf* importation, import.
impòrto *nm* amount.
importunaménte *ad* importunately, troublesomely.
importunàre *vt* to importune, bother.
importunità *nf* importunity.
importúno *a* troublesome, importunate, untimely; *nm* intruder.
imposizióne *nf* imposition.
impossessàrsi *vr* to take possession of.
impossíbile *a* impossible.
impossibilità *nf* impossibility.
impossibilitàto *a* unable.
impósta *nf* tax, duty; shutter.
impostàre *vt* to post, mail; set up, lay down.
impostazióne *nf* posting, formulation, general lines.
impostóre *nm* impostor, swindler.
impostúra *nf* imposture, fraud.
impotènte *a* impotent, powerless.
impotènza *nf* impotence, powerlessness.
impoveriménto *nm* impoverishment.
impoveríre *vt* to impoverish; **-rsi** *vr* to grow poor.
impraticàbile *a* impracticable, (*road*) impassable.
impratichíre *vt* to train, exercise; **-rsi** *vr* to practice, exercise oneself.
imprecàre *vt* to curse, swear.
imprecazióne *nf* curse, imprecation.
imprecisióne *nf* inaccuracy, lack of precision.
imprecíso *a* inaccurate, vague.
impregnàre *vt* to impregnate.
impremeditàto *a* unpremeditated.
imprèndere *vt* to begin, undertake.
imprenditóre *nm* contractor; **i. di pómpe fúnebri** funeral undertaker.
impreparàto *a* unprepared.
imprésa *nf* undertaking, enterprise, deed, contract, firm; **i. autotraspòrti** road haulage firm, truck line.
impresàrio *nm* contractor, impresario, undertaker.
imprescindíbile *a* that cannot be ignored, indispensable, absolute.
impressionàbile *a* impressionable.
impressionànte *a* striking, impressive.
impressionàre *vt* to impress, frighten; **-rsi** *vr* to be frightened.
impressióne *nf* impression, sensation, imprint.
impressionísmo *nm* impressionism.
imprestàre *etc v* **prestare** *etc*.
imprevedíbile *a* unforeseeable.
imprevidènte *a* improvident.
imprevidènza *nf* improvidence.
imprevísto *a* unexpected, unforeseen; *nm* unexpected event.

imprigionàre vt to imprison.
imprimé nm printed cloth, print dress.
imprímere vt to impress, imprint, print, engrave.
improbàbile a improbable, unlikely.
improbabilità nf unlikelihood, improbability.
improbità nf dishonesty, wickedness.
ímprobo a dishonest, wicked, hard.
improduttività nf unproductiveness.
produttívo a unproductive.
imprónta nf impression, mark, print, stamp.
improntàto a stamped, marked with.
impropèrio nm abuse, abusive word.
impropriaménte ad incorrectly, improperly.
improprietà nf impropriety, inaccuracy.
impròprio a improper, unsuitable.
improrogàbile a that cannot be postponed.
impròv(v)ido a improvident, rash.
improvvisaménte ad suddenly, unexpectedly.
improvvisàre vti to extemporize, improvise.
improvvisàta nf surprise.
improvvisàto a improvised, extempore, unscripted.
improvvisatóre nm -tríce nf extemporizer, improviser.
improvvisazióne nf improvisation.
improvvíso a sudden, unexpected, unforeseen; **all'i.** suddenly.
imprudènte a imprudent, rash.
imprudènza nf imprudence, rashness.
impudènte a impudent, shameless.
impudènza nf impudence, shamelessness.
impudicízia nf immodesty.
impudíco pl -chi a immodest, shameless.
impugnàre vt to impugn; grip, take up (arms).
impugnatúra nf grip, hilt.
impulsività nf impulsiveness, rashness.
impulsívo a impulsive.
impúlso nm impulse, impetus.
impunità nf impunity.
impuníto a unpunished.
impuntàrsi vr to be stubborn.
impurità nf impurity.
impúro a impure, unclean.
imputàbile a imputable.
imputàre vt to impute, charge, accuse.
imputàto nm accused, defendant.
imputazióne nf imputation, charge.
imputridíre vi to putrefy, rot.
in prep in, into, on, to, by, at.
inàbile a incapable, unable, unfit.
inabilità nf inability, unfitness.

inabilitazióne nf disability, disqualification.
inabissàrsi vr to sink.
inabitàbile a uninhabitable.
inabitàto a uninhabited.
inaccessíbile a inaccessible.
inaccettàbile a unacceptable.
inaccordàbile a ungrantable; (mus) untunable.
inacerbíre vt to embitter, exacerbate.
inacidíre vt to sour; vi to turn sour.
inadattàbile a unadaptable.
inadàtto a unfit, unsuitable, improper.
inadeguatézza nf inadequacy.
inadeguàto a inadequate, insufficient.
inadempiménto nm non-fulfillment.
inafferràbile a unseizable, elusive.
inalberàre vt to hoist, raise; -rsi vr to get angry.
inalienàbile a inalienable.
inalteràbile a unalterable.
inamidàre vt to starch.
inammissíbile a inadmissible.
inamovíbile a irremovable.
inàne a inane, vain.
inanimàto a inanimate.
inanità nf inanity, vanity.
inappagàto a unsatisfied.
inappellàbile a inappellable.
inappetènza nf lack of appetite.
inaridíre vt to parch, dry up; -rsi vr to dry up.
inarrivàbile a unattainable, incomparable.
inarticolàto a inarticulate.
inaspettàto a sudden, unexpected.
inaspriménto nm embitterment, exacerbation.
inasprire vt to embitter, exacerbate; -rsi vr to become embittered.
inastàre vt to hoist.
inattaccàbile a unassailable.
inattendíbile a unreliable, unfounded.
inattéso a unexpected.
inattitúdine nf inaptitude.
inattività nf inactivity.
inattívo a inactive.
inàtto a unapt, unfit; v disadàtto.
inattuàbile a impracticable, unfeasible.
inaudíto a unheard-of.
inauguràle a inaugural.
inauguràre vt to inaugurate, open.
inaugurazióne nf inauguration, opening.
inavvertènza nf inadvertence.
inavvertíto a unobserved, careless.
inazióne nf inaction.
incagliàrsi vr (naut) to run aground.
incalcolàbile a incalculable.
incallíre vi to grow callous, harden.
incaloríre vt to heat.
incalvíre vi to grow bald.
incalzàre vt to chase, press, pursue.
incamminàre vt to set going, start; -rsi vr to set out.
incanalàre vt to canalize, direct.

incancellàbile *a* indelible.
incandescènte *a* incandescent, white-hot.
incandescènza *nf* incandescence.
incannàggio *nm* (*of thread etc*) reeling, winding.
incannàta *nf* spindleful.
incantaménto *nm* enchantment, spell.
incantàre *vt* to charm, enchant; **-rsi** *vr* to be enraptured, stop.
incantéṣimo *nm* charm, enchantment, spell.
incantévole *a* enchanting, charming.
incantevolménte *ad* enchantingly.
incànto *nm* charm, enchantment; (*com*) public sale; **all'i.** by auction.
incanutíre *vi* to grow gray.
incapàce *a* incapable, unable.
incapacità *nf* incapacity.
incappàre *vi* to get into, fall in (with).
incapricciàrsi *vr* to take a fancy, become infatuated.
incarceràre *vt* to imprison.
incaricàre *vt* to charge, entrust; **-rsi** *vr* to take upon oneself.
incaricàto *a* charged with, entrusted with; *nm* deputy, chargé d'affaires.
incàrico *pl* **-chi** *nm* task, appointment, commission.
incarnàre *vt* to incarnate, embody.
incarnàto *a* incarnate; (*of nail*) ingrowing; *nm* rosiness.
incarnazióne *nf* incarnation, embodiment.
incartaménto *nm* dossier, documents *pl.*
incartàre *vt* to wrap in paper.
incàrto *v* **incartaménto.**
incassàre *vt* to box, cash, set, encase.
incàsso *nm* takings *pl.*
incastonàre *vt* to set (jewels).
incastràre *vt* to embed, drive in; **-rsi** *vr* to fit, get stuck.
incatenàre *vt* to chain, fetter, enthrall.
incàuto *a* incautious, rash.
incavàre *vt* to hollow out, excavate.
incàvo *nm* cavity, hollow, groove, notch, socket.
incendiàre *vt* to set on fire; **-rsi** *vr* to catch fire.
incendiàrio *a nm* incendiary.
incèndio *nm* fire.
inceneriménto *nm* incineration, cremation.
inceneríre *vt* to reduce (burn) to ashes.
incensaménto *nm* incensation.
incensàre *vt* to cense; praise.
incènso *nm* incense.
incensuràbile *a* irreproachable.
incentívo *nm* incentive.
inceppàre *vt* to clog, obstruct.
inceràre *vt* to (coat with) wax.
ineràta *nf* oil cloth, tarpaulin.
incertézza *nf* uncertainty, irresolution.
incèrto *a* uncertain, doubtful, irre-

solute; *nm* uncertainty; **incèrti** *pl* incidental profits *pl*, uncertainties.
incespicàre *vi* to stumble, trip.
incessànte *a* incessant, unceasing.
incèsto *nm* incest.
incestuóso *a* incestuous.
incètta *nf* buying up, cornering.
incettàre *vt* (*com*) to buy up, corner.
incettatóre *nm* **-tríce** *nf* monopolizer.
inchiésta *nf* inquest, inquiry.
inchinàre *vt* to incline, bow down; **-rsi** *vr* to bow, stoop.
inchíno *nm* bow, curtsey.
inchiodàre *vt* to nail, rivet, (*also fig*).
inchiòstro *nm* ink.
inciampàre *vi* to stumble, stumble across.
inciàmpo *nm* stumbling block, difficulty.
incidentàle *a* accidental, casual; incidental; parenthetical.
incidènte *nm* accident, incident, dispute.
incidènza *nf* incidence.
incídere *vt* to engrave, etch, record, incise; *vi* to weigh heavily.
incínta *a f* pregnant.
incipiènte *a* incipient.
incipriàre *vt* to powder.
inciṣióne *nf* incision, engraving, recording.
inciṣívo *a* incisive.
incíṣo *a* incised, engraved; *nm* digression, parenthesis.
inciṣóre *nm* engraver, etcher.
incitaménto *nm* incitement, instigation, urge.
incitàre *vt* to incite, spur, urge.
incivíle *a* uncivilized, uncivil.
inciviliménto *nm* civilization, refining.
incivilíre *vt* to civilize, refine; **-rsi** *vr* to become civilized, polite.
inciviltà *nf* incivility, barbarousness.
inclemènte *a* inclement.
inclemènza *nf* inclemency.
inclinàre *vt* to incline, bend; **-rsi** *vr* to incline, lean, slope.
inclinazióne *nf* inclination, slope, propensity.
incline *a* inclined, disposed, prone.
inclito *a* famous, illustrious.
inclúdere *vt* to include, enclose, imply.
incluṣióne *nf* inclusion.
incluṣívo *a* inclusive.
incluṣo *a* included, enclosed.
incoerènte *a* incoherent.
incoerènza *nf* incoherence.
incògnita *nf* (*math*) unknown quantity, unknown factor.
incògnito *a nm* unknown, incognito.
incollàre *vt* to stick, paste, glue.
incolleríre *vi* **-rsi** *vr* to get angry.
incolleríto *a* angry, enraged.
incolóre *a* colorless.
incolpàre *vt* to accuse, inculpate.
incolpévole *a* blameless, innocent.
incólto *a* uncultivated, unkempt.

incòlume *a* unharmed, uninjured, safe.
incolumità *nf* safety.
incombènte *a* impending.
incombènza *nf* errand, charge, task, commission.
incómbere *vi* to impend, hang, fall on.
incominciàre *vt* to begin, commence.
incomodàre *vt* to inconvenience, disturb.
incomodàto *a* indisposed.
incomodità *nf* discomfort, inconvenience.
incòmodo *a* inconvenient, uncomfortable; *nm* inconvenience, trouble.
incomparàbile *a* incomparable, matchless.
incompatíbile *a* incompatible.
incompetènte *a* incompetent, unqualified.
incompetènza *nf* incompetence.
incompiúto *a* unfinished, undone.
incomplèto *a* incomplete.
incompósto *a* disorderly, uncomely, indecent.
incomprensíbile *a* incomprehensible.
incomprensióne *nf* incomprehension.
incompréso *a* not understood.
incomunicabilità *nf* incommunicability.
inconcepíbile *a* inconceivable.
inconciliàbile *a* irreconcilable, incompatible.
inconcludènte *a* inconclusive.
inconclúso *a* unfinished.
incondizionatamènte *ad* unconditionally.
incondizionàto *a* unconditional.
incongruènte *a* incongruous.
incongruènza *nf* incongruency.
incòngruo *a* incongruous.
inconsapévole *a* unconscious, unaware, ignorant.
inconsapevolézza *nf* unconsciousness, ignorance, unawareness.
incònscio *a* unconscious; *nm* the unconscious.
inconseguènte *a* inconsequent.
inconseguènza *nf* inconsequence.
inconsideratézza *nf* inconsiderateness.
inconsideràto *a* inconsiderate, rash.
inconsistènte *a* inconsistent; unsubstantial; unfounded.
inconsolàbile *a* inconsolable.
inconsuèto *a* unusual.
inconsúlto *a* unadvised, rash.
incontentàbile *a* insatiable, exacting.
incontentabilità *nf* insatiability, unappeasability.
incontestàbile *a* indisputable, unquestionable.
incontinènte *a* incontinent.
incontinènza *nf* incontinence.
incontràre *vt* to meet, meet with;

vi to be a success; **-rsi** *vr* to meet, agree, coincide.
incontrastàto *a* uncontested.
incóntro *nm* meeting; match; *ad* towards, opposite; **i. a** *prep* towards, opposite, against.
incontrollàbile *a* uncontrollable.
inconveniènte *a* inconvenient, unseemly; *nm* inconvenience, disadvantage.
inconveniènza *nf* inconvenience.
inconvertíbile *a* inconvertible.
incoraggiaménto *nm* encouragement.
incoraggiàre *vt* to encourage.
incorniciàre *vt* to frame.
incoronàre *vt* to crown.
incoronazióne *nf* coronation.
incorporàre *vt* to incorporate.
incorpòreo *a* incorporeal, immaterial.
incoraggiànte *a* encouraging.
incorreggíbile *a* incorrigible.
incórrere *vt* to incur, fall (into); **i. in débiti** to incur debts.
incorrótto *a* incorrupt.
incorruttíbile *a* incorruptible.
incorruttibilità *nf* incorruptibility.
incosciènte *a* unconscious; lacking conscience, reckless.
incosciènza *nf* unconsciousness; rashness; lack of conscience.
incostànte *a* inconstant, fickle, changeable.
incostànza *nf* inconstancy.
incostituzionàle *a* unconstitutional.
incredíbile *a* incredible, unbelievable.
incredibilménte *ad* incredibly, extraordinarily.
incredulità *nf* incredulity, unbelief.
incrèdulo *a* incredulous, unbelieving.
incrementàre *vt* to increase, promote, encourage.
increménto *nm* increase, increment.
increscióso *a* unpleasant.
increspaménto *nm* **increspatúra** *nf* rippling, ruffling, curling, wrinkling.
increspàre *vt* **-rsi** *vr* to ruffle, ripple, wrinkle, (*of hair*) curl.
incriminàre *vt* to incriminate.
incrinàre *vt* **-rsi** *vr* to crack.
incrociàre *vti* to cross, cruise; **-rsi** *vr* to cross, meet.
incrociatóre *nm* (*naut*) cruiser.
incrócio *nm* crossing, intersection; (*of breeds*) cross.
incrollàbile *a* unshakable.
incrostàre *vt* to encrust; **-rsi** *vr* to crust.
incrudelíre *vi* to be pitiless, commit cruelties.
incrudíre *vi* to grow harsh, rough.
incruènto *a* bloodless.
incubatríce *af* incubating; *nf* incubator.
incubazióne *nf* incubation.
íncubo *nm* nightmare, incubus.
incúdine *nf* anvil.

inculcàre vt to inculcate.
incuràbile a nmf incurable.
incurànte a careless, indifferent, neglectful.
incúria nf carelessness, neglect.
incuriosíre vt to make curious, rouse one's curiosity.
incursióne nf incursion, inroad; **i. aèrea** air raid.
incurvàre vt to bend, curve.
incustodíto a unguarded.
incútere vt to inspire, rouse.
índaco pl **-chi** nm indigo.
indaffaràto a busy.
indagàre vt to inquire, investigate.
indàgine nf inquiry, investigation, research.
indebitàrsi vr to get into debt.
indébito a undue, improper, undeserved, illegal.
indebolíre vt to weaken; **-rsi** vr to flag, grow weak(er).
indecènte a indecent.
indecènza nf indecency.
indecifràbile a indecipherable.
indecisióne nf indecision, hesitation.
indecíso a undecided, hesitant.
indecoróso a indecorous, unseemly.
indefèsso a indefatigable.
indefettíbile a unfailing.
indefiníbile a indefinable.
indefiníto a indefinite.
indegnità nf shame, worthlessness.
indégno a undeserving, unworthy, worthless, contemptible.
indelèbile a indelible.
indelicatézza nf indelicacy.
indelicàto a indelicate, tactless.
indemoniàto a possessed; nm demoniac.
indènne a undamaged, unharmed.
indennità nf **indennízzo** nm indemnity.
indennizzàre vt to indemnify.
indéntro ad inwards.
inderogàbile a that cannot be transgressed.
indescrivíbile a indescribable.
indeterminàto a indeterminate, vague, indefinite.
índi ad afterwards, thence, then.
Índia nf (geogr) India.
indiàno a nm Indian; **fàre l'i.** to feign ignorance.
indiavolàto a demoniac, devilish; (fig) furious, violent.
indicàre vt to indicate, point out, show.
indicatívo a nm indicative.
indicàto a suitable.
indicatóre nm gauge, indicator, guide; **i. stradàle** traffic sign; **i. di velocità** (aut) speedometer.
indicazióne nf indication.
índice nm forefinger, index, pointer, sign.
indicíbile a unspeakable, indescribable.
indietreggiaménto nm withdrawal.

indietreggiàre vi to fall back, recoil.
indiètro ad behind, back, backwards.
indiféso a defenseless.
indifferènte a indifferent, unimportant.
indifferènza nf indifference, unconcern.
indígeno a indigenous; nm native.
indigènte a indigent, needy.
indigènza nf indigence, need.
indigeríbile a indigestible.
indigestióne nf **fàre un' i. di** to eat too much of.
indigèsto a indigestible, tiresome.
indignàre vt to make indignant; **-rsi** vr to grow indignant.
indignazióne nf indignation.
indimenticàbile a unforgettable.
indimostràbile a indemonstrable.
indipendènte a independent, self-reliant; (of flat etc) self-contained.
indipendeménte ad independently.
indipendènza nf independence.
indíre vt to announce, call, fix.
indirètto a indirect.
indirizzàre vt to address, direct; **-rsi** vr to address oneself, have recourse to.
indirízzo nm address.
indiscerníbile a indiscernible.
indisciplína nf indiscipline, unruliness.
indisciplinàto a undisciplined, unruly.
indiscréto a indiscreet, intrusive, prying.
indiscrezióne nf indiscretion, impertinence.
indiscutíbile a unquestionable.
indispensàbile a indispensable, essential.
indispensabilità nf indispensability.
indispensabilménte ad indispensably, most necessarily.
indispettíre vt to vex; **-rsi** vr to be angry, vexed.
indispórre vt to indispose, irritate, upset.
indisposizióne nf indisposition.
indispósto a indisposed, unwell.
indisputàbile a indisputable.
indissolúbile a indissoluble.
indistínto a faint, indistinct, vague.
indistruttíbile a indestructible.
indisturbàto a undisturbed.
individuàle a individual.
individualísmo nm individualism.
individualísta nmf individualist.
individualità nf individuality.
individuàre vt to identify, pick out, specify, characterize.
indivíduo nm individual, fellow.
indivisíbile a indivisible.
indivíso a undivided, whole.
indízio nm indication, sign.
indòcile a unruly, intractable.

índole *nf* nature, disposition, temperament, character.
indolènte *a* indolent, lazy.
indolènza *nf* indolence, laziness.
indolenzíre *vt* to benumb, cramp; **-rsi** *vr* to get numb, get stiff.
indolóre *a* painless.
indomàni, l' *nm* (the) next day.
indòmito *a* indomitable, unconquered, untamed.
Indonèṣia *nf* (*geogr*) Indonesia.
indoneṣiàno *a nm* Indonesian.
indoràre *vt* to gild.
indossàre *vt* to put on, wear.
indossatríce *nf* model, mannequin.
indòsso *ad* on.
indovinàre *vt* to divine, guess, foretell.
indovinàto *a* successful, well-done.
indovinèllo *nm* conundrum, riddle.
indovíno *a* prophetic, foreseeing; *nm* fortune-teller.
indú *a nmf* Hindu, Hindoo.
indubbiaménte *ad* undoubtedly.
indúbbio, indubitàbile *a* undoubted.
indugiàre *vti* to postpone, delay, linger.
indúgio *nm* delay.
indulgènte *a* indulgent.
indulgènza *nf* indulgence, leniency.
indúlgere *vt* to indulge.
induménto *nm* garment.
induríre *vt* to harden; *vi* **-rsi** *vr* to harden, get hard.
indúrre *vt* to inspire, induce; **-rsi** *vr* to decide, resolve.
indústria *nf* industry, skill.
industriàle *a* industrial; *nm* industrialist.
industriàrsi *vr* to do one's best.
industrióso *a* industrious.
induzióne *nf* induction, conjecture.
inebriànte *a* inebriating, intoxicating.
inebriàre *vt* to intoxicate, make drunk; **-rsi** *vr* to get drunk, be enraptured.
ineccepíbile *a* unobjectionable.
inèdia *nf* inanition, starvation, boredom.
inèdito *a* unpublished.
ineducàto *a* ill-bred, impolite.
ineffàbile *a* ineffable.
ineffettuàbile *a* unrealizable.
inefficàce *a* ineffective, ineffectual.
inefficàcia *nf* inefficacy.
inefficiènte *a* inefficient.
ineguagliànza, inegualità *nf* inequality.
ineguàle *a* unlike, unequal, irregular.
inelegànte *a* inelegant.
ineleggíbile *a* ineligible.
ineluttàbile *a* inevitable, inescapable.
inenarràbile *a* unspeakable.
inequivocàbile *a* unequivocal, unmistakable.
inerènte *a* inherent, concerning.
inèrme *a* unarmed, defenseless.

inèrte *a* inert, motionless, limp, lifeless, sluggish.
inèrzia *nf* inertness, idleness, inertia.
ineṣattézza *nf* inexactness, inaccuracy, mistake.
ineṣàtto *a* inaccurate, inexact, (*com*) uncollected.
ineṣaudíto *a* ungranted.
ineṣauríbile *a* inexhaustible.
ineṣàusto *a* unexhausted.
inescuṣàbile *a* inexcusable, unjustifiable.
ineṣeguíto *a* unperformed, unfulfilled.
ineṣistènte *a* non-existent.
ineṣoràbile *a* inexorable, relentless.
ineṣorabilità *nf* inexorability.
ineṣperiènza *nf* inexperience.
ineṣpèrto *a* inexperienced, unskilled.
inesplicàbile *a* inexplicable.
inesploràto *a* unexplored.
inesplóṣo *a* unexploded.
inesprimíbile *a* inexpressible.
inestimàbile *a* inestimable, invaluable.
inettitúdine *nf* ineptitude.
inètto *a* inept, unfit.
inevàṣo *a* (*com*) outstanding.
inevitàbile *a* inevitable, unavoidable.
inevitabilménte *ad* unavoidably.
inèzia *nf* trifle.
infagottàre *vt* to wrap up, muffle.
infallíbile *a* infallible, unfailing.
infallibilità *nf* infallibility.
infamànte *a* disgraceful, shameful.
infamàre *vt* to disgrace, bring shame upon; **-rsi** *vr* to disgrace oneself.
infàme *a* abominable, infamous.
infàmia *nf* infamy, disgrace, shame.
infangàre *vt* to cover with mud.
infànte *nm* infant, child.
infantíle *a* childlike, childish, infantile.
infànzia *nf* infancy.
infarcíre *vt* to stuff, cram.
infarinatúra *nf* covering with flour, (*fig*) smattering.
infàrto *nm i.* (**cardíaco**) heart attack.
infastidíre *vt* to annoy, vex.
infaticàbile *a* indefatigable, untiring.
infàtti *ad* in fact, really.
infatuàre *vt* to infatuate; **-rsi** *vr* to become infatuated.
infatuazióne *nf* infatuation.
infàusto *a* unlucky.
infecóndo *a* barren, unfruitful.
infedèle *a* unfaithful, faithless, false; *nmf* infidel.
infedeltà *nf* unfaithfulness, infidelity.
infelíce *a* unhappy, unlucky, unsuccessful, inappropriate.
infelicità *nf* unhappiness.
inferióre *a* inferior, lower, below, subordinate; *nmf* inferior, subordinate.
inferiorità *nf* inferiority.
inferíre *vt* to infer, deduce, inflict, (*naut*) hoist, bend (a sail).

infermàrsi vr to become an invalid.
infermería nf infirmary, sickroom.
infermièra nf nurse; **infermière** nm hospital attendant, male nurse.
infermità nf illness, infirmity.
inférmo a nm ill, sick, invalid.
infernàle a infernal, hellish.
infèrno nm hell.
inferocíre vti **-rsi** vr to make ferocious, become ferocious.
inferriàta nf grating, railing.
infervoràre vt to fill with fervor; **-rsi** vr to get excited.
infestàre vt to infest.
infèsto a detrimental, harmful.
infettàre vt to infect, pollute.
infettívo a infectious, contagious.
infètto a infected.
infezióne nf infection.
infiacchiménto nm enervation, weakening.
infiacchíre vt to enervate, weaken; **-rsi** vr to grow weak.
infiammàbile a inflammable.
infiammabilità nf inflammability.
infiammàre vt to set on fire, inflame; **-rsi** vr to catch fire, become inflamed.
infiammazióne nf inflammation.
infído a untrustworthy, unfaithful.
infieríre vi to be pitiless, rage.
infievolíre vt to weaken; **-rsi** vr to grow weak.
infilàre vt to thread, string, run through, insert, enter; **-rsi** vr to thread one's way, slip, put on.
infiltràrsi vr to infiltrate, penetrate, seep.
infiltrazióne nf infiltration.
infilzàre vt to pierce, run through, string, stick.
ínfimo a lowest, very low.
infíne ad at last, after all, finally.
infingardàggine nf laziness, slothfulness.
infingàrdo a lazy, slothful.
infíngersi vr to feign, simulate.
infinità nf infinity, large crowd, lot.
infinitèsimo a infinitesimal.
infiníto a nm infinite, boundless, endless, infinity.
infioràre vt to adorn (strew) with flowers.
infirmàre vt to invalidate.
infischiàrsi vr not to care for, make light of.
infittíre vti to make thick, thicken.
inflazióne nf inflation.
inflessíbile a inflexible, unmoved.
inflessióne nf inflection.
inflíggere vt to inflict.
influènte a influential.
influènza nf influence, influenza.
influenzàre vt to influence, affect, bias.
influenzàto a influenced; suffering from influenza.
influíre vi to influence.
influsso nm influx, influence.

infocàre vt to make hot, inflamed.
infondatézza nf groundlessness.
infondàto a groundless.
infóndere vt to infuse, instill.
inforcàre vt to pitchfork, bestride; **i. gli occhiàli** to put on one's spectacles.
informàre vt to acquaint, let (someone) know, inform; **-rsi** vr to find out, inquire.
informatívo a informative.
informatóre a informing; nm **-trice** nf informer.
informazióne nf (piece of) information; **úfficio i.** inquiry office.
infórme a shapeless.
informicolíre vt to cause a tickling sensation, cause pins and needles.
informità nf shapelessness.
infornàta nf batch, ovenful.
infortunàto a injured.
infortúnio nm accident, misfortune.
infossatúra nf hollow, cavity.
infradiciàre vt to drench, soak; **-rsi** vr to get drenched.
inframettènza nf interference, intrusiveness.
infra(m)méttersi vr to meddle.
infràngere vt to break, shatter; **-rsi** vr to break, smash.
infrangíbile a unbreakable.
infrànto a shattered, crushed (also fig).
infrarósso a infra-red.
infrazióne nf infraction, infringement.
infreddàrsi vr to catch a cold.
infreddatúra nf cold.
infreddolíto a cold.
infrequènte a infrequent.
infrequènza nf infrequency.
infrigidíre vt to chill, become cold.
infruttífero a unfruitful, unprofitable.
infruttuóso a fruitless, unsuccessful.
infuòri ad out; **all'i. di** prep except, but, apart from.
infuriàre vt to enrage; vi rage; **-rsi** vr to fly into a passion, lose one's temper.
infusióne nf infusion.
infúso a infused; nm infusion.
ingaggiàre vt to engage, enlist.
ingàggio nm enlistment, engagement.
ingagliardíre vt to invigorate, strengthen; **-rsi** vr to grow strong, strengthen.
ingannàre vt to deceive, beguile, cheat; **-rsi** vr to be mistaken.
ingannatóre a deceiving; nm **-trice** nf deceiver.
ingannévole a deceitful, deceptive.
ingànno nm deceit, fraud.
ingarbugliàre vt to entangle, muddle.
ingegnàrsi vr to do one's best, manage.
ingegnère nm engineer.
ingegnería nf engineering.
ingégno nm talent, genius, intelligence; device.

ingegnosità *nf* ingeniousness, ingenuity.
ingegnóso *a* ingenious, clever.
ingelosíre *vt* to make jealous; **-rsi** *vr* to become jealous.
ingeneràre *vt* to engender, cause.
ingènte *a* enormous, huge.
ingentilíre *vt* to refine; **-rsi** *vr* to become refined.
ingenuità *nf* ingenuousness, naïveté, simple-mindedness.
ingènuo *a* ingenuous, naïve.
ingerènza *nf* interference.
ingeríre *vt* to swallow; **-rsi** *vr* to interfere, meddle.
ingessàre *vt* to (set in) plaster.
ingessatúra *nf* plaster, plastering.
Inghiltèrra *nf* (*geogr*) England.
inghiottíre *vt* to swallow (up).
inghirlandàre *vt* to wreathe, garland.
ingiallíre *vi* to make yellow; *vi* to become yellow.
ingigantíre *vt* to magnify, exaggerate.
inginocchiàrsi *vr* to go on one's knees, kneel down.
inginocchiatóio *nm* kneeling-stool.
ingioiellàrsi *vr* to adorn oneself with jewels.
ingiúngere *vt* to order, command.
ingiunzióne *nf* injunction, order.
ingiúria *nf* insult, affront, damage.
ingiuriàre *vt* to abuse, insult.
ingiurióso *a* insulting, offensive.
ingiustaménte *ad* unjustly, wrong.
ingiustificàbile *a* unjustifiable.
ingiustízia *nf* injustice, unfairness.
ingiústo *a* unjust, unfair.
inglése *a* *nmf* English, the English language, Englishman, Englishwoman.
ingoiàre *vt* to swallow (up).
ingolfàrsi *vr* to form a gulf, plunge into.
ingombrànte *a* cumbersome.
ingombràre *vt* to encumber, obstruct.
ingómbro *a* *nm* encumbered, obstructed, encumbrance, obstruction.
ingommàre *vt* to gum, stick.
ingordígia *nf* greed(iness).
ingórdo *a* *nm* greedy, covetous, glutton.
ingórgo *nm* obstruction; **i. stradàle** traffic jam.
ingranàggio *nm* (*tec*) gear, working.
ingranàre *vti* (*tec*) to put into gear, be in gear; get along.
ingranchíre *vt* to benumb.
ingrandiménto *nm* enlargement.
ingrandíre *vt* to amplify, enlarge, exaggerate, increase; **-rsi** *vr* to grow larger, increase.
ingrassàre *vt* to make fat, lubricate, manure, enrich; *vi* **-rsi** *vr* to grow fat.
ingratitúdine *nf* ingratitude.
ingràto *a* ungrateful, thankless, unpleasant, unprofitable.

ingravidàre *vt* to make pregnant; **-rsi** *vr* to become pregnant.
ingraziàrsi *vr* to ingratiate oneself.
ingrediènte *nm* ingredient.
ingrèsso *nm* entry, entrance, admittance; **ingrèssi** (*theat*) standing room.
ingrossaménto *nm* enlargement, increase, swelling.
ingrossàre *vt* to make big(ger), increase, swell; **-rsi** *vr* to grow big(ger), rise, swell.
ingròsso, all' *ad* wholesale.
ingualcíbile *a* crease-resistant.
inguantàto *a* wearing gloves.
inguaríbile *a* incurable.
ínguine *nm* groin.
inibíre *vt* to inhibit, forbid, restrain.
inibizióne *nf* inhibition, prohibition.
inidòneo *a* unfit, unsuited.
iniettàre *vt* to inject.
iniezióne *nf* injection.
inimicàre *vt* to estrange, alienate; **-rsi** *vr* to become estranged from.
inimicízia *nf* enmity, hostility.
inimitàbile *a* inimitable.
inintelligíbile *a* unintelligible.
ininterrótto *a* uninterrupted, unbroken, non-stop.
iniquaménte *ad* wickedly, unjustly.
iniquità *nf* iniquity, wickedness.
iníquo *a* iniquitous, wicked.
iniziàle *a* *nf* initial.
iniziàre *vt* to begin, initiate.
iniziatíva *nf* initiative, enterprise.
iniziàto *a* *nm* initiated, initiate.
iniziazióne *nf* initiation.
inízio *nm* beginning, commencement.
innacquàre *vt* to water, dilute.
innaffiaménto *nm* watering.
innaffiàre *vt* to water.
innaffiatóio *nm* watering-can.
innalzàre *vt* to raise, heighten; **-rsi** *vr* to rise.
innamoràre *vt* to charm; **-rsi** *vr* to fall in love.
innamoràto *a* in love, loving; *nm* lover, sweetheart.
innànzi *ad* *and prep* before, on, towards, further.
innàto *a* innate.
innegàbile *a* undeniable.
inneggiàre *vt* to celebrate, exalt.
innervosíre *vt* to get on people's nerves.
innestàre *vt* to graft, inoculate, insert, join.
innèsto *nm* graft, insertion, inoculation.
ínno *nm* anthem, hymn.
innocènte *a* *nm* innocent.
innocènza *nf* innocence.
inoculazióne *nf* inoculation.
innòcuo *a* harmless, inoffensive.
innominàbile *a* unnamable, unmentionable.
innominàto *a* unnamed, nameless.
innovàre *vt* to innovate, change.
innovazióne *nf* innovation, change.

innumerévole *a* innumerable, numberless.
inoculàre *vt* to inoculate.
inodóro *a* odorless.
inoffensivo *a* inoffensive, harmless.
inoltràre *vt* to forward, send on; -rsi *vr* to advance, penetrate.
inóltre *ad* besides, moreover, furthermore.
inondàre *vt* to flood, inundate.
inondazióne *nf* flood, inundation.
inoperosità *nf* inactivity, idleness.
inoperóso *a* inactive, idle.
inòpia *nf* indigence, poverty, want.
inopinàto *a* unexpected, unforeseen, sudden.
inopportúno *a* inopportune, untimely.
inoppugnàbile *a* unquestionable.
inorgànico *pl* -ici *a* inorganic.
inorgoglíre *vt* to make proud; -rsi *vr* to become proud.
inorridíre *vt* to horrify; *vi* be horrified.
inosservànte *a* unobservant.
inospitàle, inòspite *a* inhospitable.
inosservànza *nf* non-observance.
inosservàto *a* unobserved.
inossidàbile *a* rustless; acciàio i. stainless steel.
inquadràre *vt* to frame; arrange; set.
inquietànte *a* disquieting.
inquietàre *vt* to worry, alarm; -rsi *vr* to get angry.
inquietézza *nf* uneasiness.
inquièto *a* restless, uneasy, anxious.
inquietúdine *nf* restlessness, uneasiness, apprehension.
inquilíno *nm* tenant, lodger.
inquinaménto *nm* pollution.
inquinàre *vt* to pollute.
inquirènte *a* inquiring, investigating.
inquisíre *vt* to inquire, investigate.
inquisitóre *nm* -tríce *nf* inquisitor; *a* inquiring.
inquisizióne *nf* inquisition.
insaccàre *vt* to put in sacks, stuff.
insaccàto *nm* sausages, salame *etc.*
insalàta *nf* salad.
insalatièra *nf* salad-bowl.
insalúbre *a* unhealthy.
insalubrità *nf* unhealthiness.
insanàbile *a* incurable.
insanguinàre *vt* to cover with blood.
insanguinàto *a* blood-stained.
insània *nf* insanity.
insàno *a* insane, crazy.
insaponàre *vt* to lather, soap.
insapúta, all' (di) *ad* unknown (to).
insaziàbile *a* insatiable.
inscatolàre *vt* to can.
inscenàre *vt* to stage (*also* fig).
inscindíbile *a* inseparable.
inscrutàbile *a* inscrutable.
insediàre *vt* to install; -rsi *vr* to take up office, take possession.
inségna *nf* insignia *pl*, badge; colors *pl*, flag; signboard.
insegnaménto *nm* teaching, tuition.

insegnànte *a* teaching; *nmf* teacher; còrpo i. teaching staff.
insegnàre *vt* to teach.
inseguiménto *nm* chase, pursuit.
inseguíre *vt* to pursue, run after.
inselvatichíre *vt* to make wild; *vi* to grow wild.
insenatúra *nf* inlet.
insensatézza *nf* senselessness, foolishness.
insensàto *a* senseless, foolish.
insensíbile *a* insensible, unfeeling.
insensibilménte *ad* imperceptibly, unfeelingly.
insensibilità *nf* hard-heartedness, insensibility.
inseparàbile *a* inseparable.
inseriménto *nm* insertion.
inseríre *vt* to insert.
inservíbile *a* useless.
inserzióne *nf* inserting, insertion, advertisement.
inserzionísta *nmf* advertiser.
insetticída *a* insecticidal; *nm* insecticide.
insètto *nm* insect, bug.
insídia *nf* ambush, snare.
insidiàre *vti* to lay snares for, make an attempt on.
insidióso *a* insidious.
insième *nm* whole; *ad* together, at the same time.
insígne *a* famous, notorious.
insignificànte *a* insignificant.
insigníre *vt* to decorate, confer (on).
insincerità *nf* insincerity.
insincèro *a* insincere.
insindacàbile *a* that cannot be criticized.
insinuàre *vt* to insinuate, suggest; -rsi *vr* to creep into, penetrate.
insinuazióne *nf* insinuation, suggestion.
insípido *a* insipid, tasteless.
insipiènza *nf* foolishness, ignorance.
insistènte *a* insistent, pressing, urgent.
insistènza *nf* insistence.
insistere *vi* to insist.
ínsito *a* inherent.
insoddisfàtto *a* dissatisfied.
insoddisfazióne *nf* dissatisfaction.
insofferènte *a* intolerant, impatient.
insofferènza *nf* intolerance, impatience.
insolazióne *nf* sunstroke.
insolènte *a* insolent, pert.
insolentíre *vti* to abuse, speak insolently.
insolènza *nf* insolence, pertness.
insòlito *a* unusual.
insolúbile *a* insoluble.
insolúto *a* unsolved, outstanding.
insolvènte *a* insolvent.
insolvènza *nf* insolvency.
insolvíbile *a* unpayable; insolvent.
insómma *ad* in conclusion, in short; *interj* well!
insondàbile *a* unfathomable.
insònne *a* sleepless.

insònnia *nf* insomnia, sleeplessness.
insonnolíto *a* sleepy, drowsy.
insopportàbile *a* insupportable, unbearable.
insórgere *vi* to rebel, rise, arise.
insorgiménto *nm* uprising.
insormontàbile *a* insurmountable.
insórto *nm* rebel, rioter.
insospettàbile *a* beyond suspicion.
insospettàto *a* unsuspected, unexpected.
insospettíre *vt* to make suspicious; **-rsi** *vr* to grow suspicious.
insosteníbile *a* untenable.
insozzàre *vt* to soil, sully.
insperàbile *a* beyond hope.
insperataménte *ad* unexpectedly.
insperàto *a* unhoped-for.
inspiegàbile *a* inexplicable.
inspiràre *vt* to inhale; inspire.
instàbile *a* unstable, variable.
instabilità *nf* instability, variability.
installàre *vt* to install; **-rsi** *vr* to install oneself, settle.
installazióne *nf* installation.
instancàbile *a* untiring, indefatigable, tireless.
instauràre *vt* to set up, establish.
instaurazióne *nf* establishment, foundation.
instillàre *vt* to instill.
instradàre *vt* to set on the right road.
insú *ad* up(wards).
insubordinàto *a* insubordinate.
insubordinazióne *nf* insubordination.
insuccèsso *nm* failure.
insudiciàre *vt* to soil, dirty.
insufficiènte *a* insufficient, inadequate.
insufficiènza *nf* insufficiency.
insulàre *a* insular.
insulína *nf* insulin.
insulsàggine *nf* dullness, foolishness.
insúlso *a* dull, foolish.
insultàre *vt* to abuse, insult.
insúlto *nm* insult, affront; (*med*) attack, stroke.
insuperàbile *a* insuperable.
insuperbíre *vt* to make proud; **-rsi** *vr* to grow proud.
insurrezionàle *a* insurrectionary.
insurrezióne *nf* insurrection, rising.
insussistènte *a* non-existent.
insussistènza *nf* non-existence.
intaccàre *vt* to notch; corrode; injure; begin spending.
intagliàre *vt* to engrave, carve.
intagliatóre *nm* engraver, carver.
intàglio *nm* intaglio, carving.
intangíbile *a* intangible.
intànto *ad* meanwhile; **i. che** *cj* while.
intarsiàre *vt* to inlay.
intàrsio *nm* inlay.
intasàre *vt* to choke, obstruct, stop up; **-rsi** *vr* to get stopped up.
intascàre *vt* to pocket.
intàtto *a* intact, uninjured, unsullied.

intavolàre *vt* to board up; put on a board; begin.
integèrrimo *a* honest, upright.
integràle *a* integral; **pàne i.** wholemeal bread.
integràre *vt* to complete, integrate.
integrazióne *nf* integration.
integrità *nf* integrity, uprightness.
íntegro *a* honest, upright, integral.
intelaiatúra *nf* framework, framing.
intellètto *nm* intellect, mind.
intellettuàle *a* intellectual.
intelligènte *a* intelligent, clever.
intelligènza *nf* intelligence, cleverness, knowledge, understanding.
intelligíbile *a* intelligible, comprehensible.
intemeràta *nf* reproof, tirade.
intemeràto *a* irreproachable.
intemperànte *a* intemperate.
intemperànza *nf* intemperance.
intempèrie *nf pl* inclement weather.
intempestívo *a* unseasonable, untimely.
intèndere *vt* to hear; intend, mean; understand; **-rsi** *vr* to be a good judge of; come to an agreement with; understand (each other).
intendiménto *nm* understanding; intention, purpose.
intenditóre *nm* connoisseur, judge.
inteneríre *vt* to soften, move; **-rsi** *vr* to be moved, feel compassion.
intensaménte *ad* intensely.
intensificàre *vt* to intensify, make more frequent.
intensità *nf* intensity.
intensívo *a* intensive.
intènso *a* intense, violent.
intentàre *vt* (*leg*) to bring (an action).
intènto *a* intent; *nm* aim, intent(ion), purpose.
intenzionàle *a* intentional.
intenzióne *nf* intention, wish.
interaménte *ad* entirely, completely.
intercalàre *vt* to insert; *nm* refrain; pet phrase.
intercèdere *vi* to intercede; (*of distance etc*) exist, intervene.
intercessióne *nf* intercession.
intercettàre *vt* to intercept.
intercettazióne *nf* interception.
intercomunàle *nf* (*tel*) trunk call, long-distance call.
intercomunicànte *a* intercommunicating, communicating.
intercórrere *vi* to elapse, pass, happen.
interdétto *a* interdicted, prohibited, disqualified; disconcerted; *nm* interdict.
interdíre *vt* to forbid, interdict, disqualify.
interdizióne *nf* interdiction, disqualification.
interessaménto *nm* interest, concern.
interessànte *a* interesting.
interessàre *vti* to interest, matter; **-rsi** *vr* to take an interest, care.

interessàto *a* interested; *nm* interested party.
interèsse *nm* interest.
interessènza *nf* (com) co-interest.
interézza *nf* entirety, integrity.
interferènza *nf* interference.
interferíre *vi* to interfere.
interinàle *a* interim, temporary.
interíno *a* provisional.
interióra *nf pl* entrails *pl*, intestines *pl*.
interióre *a* inner; *nm* interior, inside.
interlineàre *vt* to interline; *a* interlinear.
interlocutóre *nm* -**tríce** *nf* interlocutor.
interloquíre *vi* to put in a word, speak.
interlúdio *nm* interlude.
intermediàrio *a* intermediary; *nm* mediator, (com) middleman, go-between.
intermèzzo *nm* interval, intermezzo.
interminàbile *a* interminable, endless.
intermissióne *nf* intermission.
intermittènte *a* intermittent.
intermittènza *nf* intermittence.
internaménte *ad* internally, inwardly.
internàre *vt* to intern; -**rsi** *vr* to enter into, penetrate.
internàto *a* interned; *nm* internee; boarding-school.
internazionàle *a* international.
intèrno *a* internal, interior, inner, inside; *nm* interior, inside; Ministéro degli Intérni Home Office.
intéro *a* entire, whole; honest; *nm* whole.
interpellànza *nf* interpellation.
interpellàre *vt* to interpellate, ask.
interpolàre *vt* to interpolate, insert.
interpórre *vt* -**rsi** *vr* to interpose, intervene.
interposizióne *nf* interposition, intervention.
interpretàre *vt* to interpret, construe.
interpretazióne *nf* interpretation.
intèrprete *nmf* interpreter.
interpunzióne *nf* punctuation.
interraménto *nm* interment, burial.
interràre *vt* to bury, inter; fill with earth.
interrogàre *vt* to interrogate, question, consult, examine; **i. con contradittório** cross-examine.
interrogatívo *a* interrogative, questioning; *nm* question.
interrogatório *nm* interrogation, (cross-)examination.
interrogazióne *nf* interrogation, question.
interrómpere *vt* to interrupt, break (off); -**rsi** *vr* to stop.
interròtto *a* interrupted, cut off; (of road) blocked.
interruttóre *nm* interrupter, (el) switch.

interruzióne *nf* interruption.
intersecàre *vt* to intersect.
interurbàno *a* telefonàta interurbàna long-distance call.
intervàllo *nm* interval, space.
interveníre *vi* to intervene, interfere; be present; happen.
intervènto *nm* intervention, interference; presence; (surgical) operation.
intervenúto *a* present; *nm* person present.
intervísta *nf* interview.
intervistàre *vt* to interview.
intésa *nf* agreement, understanding.
intéso *a* understood, agreed upon; aiming at.
intèssere *vt* to weave.
intestàre *vt* to enter; head; register; -**rsi** *vr* to be obstinate.
intestàto *a* headed; (com) registered; stubborn; intestate.
intestazióne *nf* heading, title, headline.
intestinàle *a* intestinal.
intestíno *a* domestic, internal, civil; *nm* intestine.
intiepidíre *vt* to make lukewarm, warm (up); cool, abate; -**rsi** *vr* to cool down; warm up.
intiéro *v* **intéro**.
intimaménte *ad* intimately, deeply.
intimàre *vt* to intimate, order, notify, enjoin.
intimazióne *nf* order, summons, notification.
intimidazióne *nf* intimidation.
intimidíre *vt* to intimidate; -**rsi** *vr* to become shy, get frightened.
intimità *nf* intimacy, familiarity.
íntimo *a* intimate; inner, deep; private; *nm* intimate friend; heart, depth.
intimoríre *vt* to frighten.
intíngere *vt* to dip.
intíngolo *nm* tasty dish, sauce, gravy.
intirizzíre *vt* to (be)numb, stiffen; -**rsi** *vr* to get benumbed.
intisichíre *vi* to grow consumptive.
intitolàre *vt* to entitle; dedicate.
intitolazióne *nf* entitling, title; dedication.
intolleràbile *a* intolerable.
intollerànte *a* intolerant.
intollerànza *nf* intolerance.
intonacàre *vt* to plaster, whitewash, distemper.
intònaco *pl* -**chi** *nm* plaster, whitewash, distemper.
intonàre *vt* to intone; strike up; -**rsi** *vr* to be in tune (harmony) with, tone with.
intonàto *a* in tune, matching.
intonazióne *nf* intonation, tone.
intònso *a* uncut, unshaven, unshorn.
intontiménto *nm* stupor, daze.
intontíre *vt* to stun, daze; -**rsi** *vr* to be stunned, become dazed.
intòppo *nm* hindrance, obstacle,

hitch; **i. stradàle** (*traffic*) hold up, tie-up, traffic jam.

intorbidàre *vt* to make turbid, confuse, trouble; **-rsi** *vr* to become turbid, troubled, grow dim.

intórno *ad* **i. a** *prep* around, round, about.

intorpidíre *vt* to benumb; *vi* **-rsi** *vr* to grow numb.

intossicàre *vt* to poison.

intossicazióne *nf* poisoning.

intraducíbile *a* untranslatable.

intralciàre *vt* to hinder, interfere with, obstruct.

intràlcio *nm* hindrance, obstruction.

intrallàzzo *nm* plotting, swindle; black market.

intraméttere *v* **introméttere.**

intramezzàre *vt* to interpose, alternate.

intramuscolàre *a* intermuscular.

intransigènte *a* intransigent, uncompromising, unmoved.

intransigènza *nf* intransigence.

intransitívo *a nm* intransitive.

intraprendènte *a* enterprising.

intraprendènza *nf* enterprise.

intraprèndere *vt* to undertake, venture on.

intrattàbile *a* intractable.

intrattenére *vt* to entertain; **-rsi** *vr* to linger, stop, dwell upon.

intratteniménto *nm* entertainment.

intrav(v)edére *vt* to catch a glimpse; have a hazy notion; foresee.

intrecciàre *vt* to entwine, interlace, braid.

intréccio *nm* interlacing; (*of a play*) plot.

intrepidézza, intrepidità *nf* intrepidity, bravery.

intrèpido *a* fearless, intrepid.

intricàto *a* intricate, tangled, complicated.

intrigànte *a* intriguing; *nmf* intriguer.

intrigàre *vi* to intrigue; *vt* to entangle; **-rsi** *vr* to meddle.

intrígo *nm* intrigue.

intrínseco *pl* **-ci** *a* intrinsic.

intríso *a* soaked; *nm* mash, mixture.

intristíre *vt* to decay, pine away, wilt; grow wicked.

introdúrre *vt* to introduce, show in; import; **-rsi** *vr* to get in, introduce oneself.

introduzióne *nf* introduction.

introitàre *vt* (*com*) to cash, get in.

intròito *nm* (*eccl*) introit, (*com*) returns *pl*, revenue.

intromésso *a* interposed, introduced, inserted.

introméttere *vt* to interpose, introduce, insert; **-rsi** *vr* to intervene, intrude, meddle.

intromissióne *nf* intervention, intrusion.

intronàre *vt* to deafen, stun.

introspettívo *a* introspective.

introspezióne *a* introspection.

introvàbile *a* not to be found.

introvèrso *a* introverted; *nm* introvert.

intrúglio *nm* hodgepodge, bad concoction, mess.

intrusióne *nf* intrusion.

intrúso *nm* intruder.

intuíre *vt* to perceive by intuition.

intúito *nm* **intuizióne** *nf* intuition.

inuguàle *etc v* **ineguàle** *etc.*

inumanità *nf* inhumanity.

inumàno *a* inhuman, cruel.

inumàre *vt* to inhume, inter.

inumidíre *vt* to moisten, damp.

inurbanità *nf* incivility.

inurbàno *a* uncivil, rude.

inusàto *a* unusual, obsolete.

inusitàto *a* unusual, obsolete.

inútile *a* useless, unnecessary.

inutilità *nf* uselessness.

inutilmènte *ad* uselessly, in vain.

invadènte *a* intrusive; *nmf* intruder.

invadènza *nf* meddlesomeness.

invàdere *vt* to invade, break into.

invaghírsi *vr* to fall in love with, take a liking to.

invalidàre *vt* to invalidate.

invalidità *nf* invalidity.

invàlido *a* invalid, disabled; *nm* invalid.

invàno *ad* in vain, vainly.

invariàbile *a* invariable, unchangeable.

invariàto *a* unvaried, unchanged.

invasaménto *nm* obsession, excitement, infatuation.

invasàre *vt* to obsess, haunt; put in vases.

invasióne *nf* invasion.

invasóre, f invaditríce *a* invading; *nm* invader.

invecchiàre *vti* to make old, grow old; **-rsi** *vr* to make oneself look old, claim to be older than one is.

invéce *ad* instead, on the contrary; **i. di** *prep* instead of.

inveíre *vi* to inveigh, rail.

inventàre *vt* to invent.

inventàrio *nm* inventory.

inventíva *nf* inventiveness.

inventóre *nm* **-tríce** *nf* inventor.

invenzióne *nf* invention.

inverdíre *vi* to grow green.

inverecóndia *nf* immodesty.

inverecóndo *a* immodest.

invernàle *a* winter, wintry.

inverniciàre *vt* to varnish.

inverniciatúra *nf* varnishing.

invèrno *nm* winter.

invéro *ad* really, truly.

inverosimiglìanza *nf* unlikelihood.

inverosímile *a* unlikely, improbable.

inversióne *nf* inversion.

invèrso *a* inverse, opposite, contrary.

invertebràto *a* invertebrate.

invertíre *vt* to invert, reverse.

invertíto *a* inverted; *nm* invert.

investigàre *vt* to inquire into, investigate.

investigazióne *nf* inquiry, investigation.

investiménto nm investment; collision.
investíre vt to collide with; attack; invest, appoint; **-rsi** vr to take a deep interest in; collide.
invetriàta nf pane of glass.
invettíva nf invective.
inviàre vt to send.
inviàto nm messenger, representative, envoy, correspondent.
invídia nf envy.
invidiàre vt to envy.
invidióso a envious.
invigilàre vt to watch (over).
invigoríre vt to invigorate, strengthen; **-rsi** vr to grow stronger.
inviluppàre vt to envelop, hide; **-rsi** vr to wrap oneself up.
invincíbile a invincible.
invío nm sending, dispatch.
inviolàbile a inviolable.
invişíbile a invisible.
invíşo a disliked, hated.
invitànte a inviting, attractive, tempting.
invitàre vt to invite, ask; (at cards) call.
invitàto nm guest.
invíto nm call, invitation.
invítto a undefeated, unconquered, invincible.
invocàre vt to invoke, appeal to.
invocazióne nf invocation.
invogliàre vt to allure, induce, tempt.
involàre vt to steal; **-rsi** vr to elope, run away.
invòlgere vt to wrap up, envelop, involve.
involontàrio a involuntary.
involtàre vt to wrap up, pack up.
invòlto pp of **invòlgere**; nm bundle, parcel.
invòlucro nm covering, envelope.
invulneràbile a invulnerable.
inzuccheràre vt to sugar.
inzuppàre vt to dip, drench, soak.
ío pron I.
iòdio nm iodine.
iònico pl **-ici** a Ionic.
iònio a Ionian; **l'Iònio** nm (geogr) the Ionian Sea.
iòşa, a ad galore.
ipèrbole nf hyperbole.
ipersensíbile a hypersensitive.
ipertensióne nf (med) hypertension.
ipnòtico pl **-ici** a hypnotic.
ipnotíşmo nm hypnotism.
ipnotizzàre vt to hypnotize.
ipocondría nf hypochondria, spleen.
ipocrişía nf hypocrisy, cant.
ipòcrita nmf hypocrite.
ipotèca nf mortgage.
ipotecàre vt to mortgage.
ipòteşi nf hypothesis.
ìppica nf horse-racing.
íppico pl **-ici** a horse; **còrse ìppiche** horse races.
ippocastàno nm horse-chestnut.
ippòdromo nm racecourse.

ippopòtamo nm hippopotamus.
íra, iracóndia nf anger, rage, wrath.
iracóndo a irascible, choleric.
Iràk nm (geogr) Irak, Iraq.
Iràn nm (geogr) Iran, Persia.
iraniàno a nm Iranian, Persian.
irascíbile a irascible, irritable, hot-tempered.
irascibilità nf irascibility.
iràto a angry, in a rage.
Irène nf pr Irene, Eirene.
íride nf iris; rainbow.
iridescènte a iridescent.
Irlànda nf (geogr) Ireland.
irlandése a Irish; nm Irishman, (language) Irish; nf Irishwoman.
Írma nf pr Irma.
ironía nf irony.
irònico pl **-ici** a ironic(al).
iróşo a angry.
irradiàre vti to (ir)radiate.
irradiazióne nf irradiation, fall-out.
irragionévole a irrational, unreasonable, absurd.
irragionevolézza nf unreasonableness, unfairness.
irrazionàle a irrational.
irrazionalità nf irrationality.
irreàle a unreal.
irrealtà nf unreality.
irreconciliàbile a irreconcilable.
irrecuperàbile a irrecoverable.
irredènto a unredeemed.
irredimíbile a irredeemable.
irrefutàbile a irrefutable.
irregolàre a abnormal, irregular.
irregolarità nf irregularity.
irreligióso a irreligious.
irremissíbile a impossible to remit.
irremovíbile a irremovable, inflexible.
irreparàbile a irreparable.
irreperíbile a that cannot be found.
irreprensíbile a faultless, irreproachable.
irrequietézza nf restlessness.
irrequièto a restless.
irresistíbile a irresistible.
irresolutézza nf irresolution, indecision.
irresolúto a hesitant, irresolute.
irresponsàbile a irresponsible.
irreversíbile a irreversible; direzióne i. (aut) irreversible steering.
irrevocàbile a irrevocable.
irriconoscíbile a unrecognizable.
irrídere vt to deride, laugh at.
irriducíbile a irreducible.
irriflessívo a thoughtless.
irrigàbile a irrigable.
irrigàre vt to irrigate.
irrigazióne nf irrigation.
irrigidiménto nm stiffening.
irrigidíre vt to make stiff; **-rsi** vr to grow (stand) stiff.
irríguo a well-watered.
irrilevànte a insignificant.
irrimediàbile a irremediable.
irrişióne nf derision, mockery.

irrisòrio *a* derisory; paltry.
irrispettóso *a* disrespectful.
irritàbile *a* irritable; (*of skin*) sensitive.
irritabilità *nf* irritability; (*of skin*) sensitiveness.
irritànte *a* irritating.
irritàre *vt* to irritate, inflame; -rsi *vr* to become angry, inflamed.
irritazióne *nf* irritation, inflammation.
irriverènte *a* irreverent.
irriverènza *nf* irreverence.
irrobustíre *vt* to strengthen; -rsi *vr* to grow strong(er).
irrómpere *vi* to break into; swarm; overflow.
irruènte *a* impetuous.
irruènza *nf* impetuosity.
irrugginíre *vti* to make (grow) rusty.
irruzióne *nf* irruption.
irsúto *a* hairy, shaggy.
írto *a* bristling, bushy, shaggy.
Isabèlla *nf pr* Isabella, Isabel.
Isàcco *nm pr* Isaac.
iscrítto *a* enrolled, entered, registered, inscribed.
iscrívere *vt* to enroll, register, inscribe; -rsi *vr* to enter (for).
iscrizióne *nf* inscription, enrollment, matriculation, entry, membership.
Işlàm *nm* Islam.
işlàmico *pl* -ici *a* Islamic.
işlamíşmo *nm* Islamism.
Işlànda *nf* (*geogr*) Iceland.
işlandése *a* Icelandic; *nm* Icelander, Icelandic (language).
íşola *nf* island, isle.
işolaménto *nm* isolation; (*el*) insulation.
işolàno *a* insular; *nm* islander.
işolànte *a* (*el*) insulating; *nm* insulator.
işolàre *vt* to isolate; insulate; -rsi *vr* to shun society.
işolatóre *nm* (*el*) insulator.
Isòtta *nf pr* Isolde.
ispaníşmo *nm* Hispanicism.
ispettoràto *nm* inspector's office, inspectorship, inspectorate.
ispettóre *nm* -tríce *nf* inspector.
ispezionàre *vt* to inspect.
ispezióne *nf* inspection.
íspido *a* bristling, rough, shaggy.
ispiràre *vt* to inspire, instill, infuse into; -rsi *vr* to draw inspiration.
ispirazióne *nf* inspiration.
Işraèle *nm* (*geogr*) Israel.
işraeliàno *a nm* Israeli.
işraelíta *a nmf* Israelite, Jew, Jewess.
işraelítico *pl* -ici *a* Israelite, Jewish.
issàre *vt* to hoist.
istantànea *nf* snapshot.
istantàneo *a* instantaneous, instant.
istànte *a* instant, pressing; *nm* moment; petitioner.
istànza *nf* request, application, petition.

istèrico *pl* -ici *a* hysteric(al).
isteríşmo *nm* hysteria, hysterics *pl*.
istésso *v* stesso.
istigàre *vt* to instigate.
istigazióne *nf* instigation.
istintívo *a* instinctive.
istínto *nm* instinct.
istituíre *vt* to institute, found, appoint.
istitúto *nm* institute, school, bank.
istitutóre *nm* -tríce *nf* founder; tutor, governess.
istituzióne *nf* institution, establishment.
ístmo *nm* isthmus.
istoriàre *vt* to adorn with figures, illustrate.
Ístria *nf* (*geogr*) Istria; istriàno *a nm* Istrian.
ístrice *nf* porcupine.
istrióne *nm* bad actor, charlatan.
istriònico *pl* -ici *a* histrionic.
istruíre *vt* to instruct, teach, inform; -rsi *vr* to acquire knowledge, learn.
istruíto *a* educated, well-read.
istrumentàle *a* instrumental.
istruménto *nm* instrument.
istruttívo *a* instructive.
istruttóre *nm* -tríce *nf* instructor, teacher; giúdice i. examining magistrate.
istruttòria *nf* examination, investigation.
istruttòrio *a* preliminary.
istruzióne *nf* education, instruction, learning, order, teaching; ministèro della Púbblica I. *nm* Ministry of Education.
istupidíre *vt* to make stupid; *vi* to become stupid.
Itàlia *nf* (*geogr*) Italy.
italianaménte *ad* after the Italian fashion, in the Italian way.
italianità *nf* Italian feelings, Italian nationality.
Italiàno *a nm* Italian.
itàlico *pl* -ici *a nm* Italic, Italian, (*typ*) italics.
iteràre *vt* to iterate, repeat.
iterazióne *nf* iteration, repetition.
itineràrio *nm* itinerary, route.
itterízia *nf* (*med*) jaundice.
Iugoslàvia *nf* (*geogr*) Jugoslavia.
iugoslàvo *a nm* Jugoslav.
iunior, iunióre *a* junior.
iúngla *nf* jungle.
iúta *nf* jute.
Iútland *nm* (*geogr*) Jutland.
ívi *ad* there, therein.

L

la *def art f* the; *pron f* (*acc*) her, it, (*mus*) la.
là *ad* there; al di là (di) *ad* and *prep* beyond.
làbbro *nm, pl m* làbbri, *f* làbbra

lip; **i làbbri di una feríta** the lips of a wound; **mòrdersi le làbbra** to bite one's lips.
làbile *a* fleeting, ephemeral, weak.
labirínto *nm* labyrinth, maze.
laboratòrio *nm* laboratory, workroom.
laboriosità *nf* laboriousness, industry.
laborióso *a* laborious, industrious, hard-working; difficult.
laburísmo *nm* Laborism.
laburísta *a* Labor; *nmf* Labour Party member (*Eng.*).
làcca *nf* lacquer.
laccàre *vt* to lacquer, enamel.
lacchè *nm* lackey.
làccio *nm* shoelace, string, snare, noose.
laceránte *a* tearing, rending.
laceràre *v* to lacerate, rend, tear (up); **-rsi** *vr* to tear, get torn.
lacerazióne *nf* laceration, rent.
làcero *a* in rags, rent, torn.
lacònico *pl* **-ici** *a* laconic.
laconísmo *nm* laconism.
làcrima, làgrima *nf* tear; **scoppiàre in làcrime** *vi* to burst into tears.
lacrimàre *vi* to cry, weep, shed tears; water.
lacrimàto *a* lamented, regretted.
lacrimévole *a* tearful.
lacrimògeno *a* lachrymatory.
lacrimóso *a* lachrymose, tearful, weeping.
lacúna *nf* lacuna, blank, gap.
làdro *a* bewitching, thieving; *nm* thief.
ladróne *nm* robber, highwayman.
ladronería *nf* robbery.
laggiú *ad* down there, there below, over there.
lagnànza *nf* complaint.
lagnàrsi *vr* to complain.
làgo *pl* **-ghi** *nm* lake, pool.
làgrima *v* **làcrima.**
lagúna *nf* lagoon.
laicàto *nm* laity.
làico *pl* **-ici** *a* lay; *nm* layman.
laidézza *nf* foulness, obscenity.
làido *a* dirty, foul, obscene.
làma *nf* blade; *nm* (*priest*) Lama; (*zool*) llama.
lambiccàre *vt* to distill; **-rsi il cervèllo** *vr* to cudgel one's brains.
lambícco *pl* **-chi** *nm* still, alembic.
lambíre *vt* to lap, touch lightly.
lamentàre *vt* to lament, mourn, regret; **-rsi** *vr* to complain, mourn.
lamentazióne *nf* lamentation.
laménto *nm* lament, mourning, complaint.
lamentóso *a* mournful, plaintive.
lamièra *nf* plate, sheet iron.
làmina *nf* blade, thin plate (of metal).
laminàto *a* (*metal*) rolled.
laminatóio *nm* rolling-mill.
làmpada *nf* lamp; **l. ad àrco** arclamp.

lampadàrio *nm* chandelier, electriclight pendant.
lampadína *nf* (electric) bulb, small lamp; **l. elèttrica (tascàbile)** torch; flashlight.
lampànte *a* clear, obvious.
lampeggiaménto *nm* lightning; flashing.
lampeggiànte *a* flashing.
lampeggiàre *vi* to lighten; flash.
lampionàio *nm* lamp-lighter.
lampioncíno *nm* Chinese lantern, fairylight.
lampióne *nm* street-lamp.
làmpo *nm* lightning, flash; **chiusúra l.** zip fastener, zipper.
lampóne *nm* raspberry.
lamprèda *nf* lamprey.
làna *nf* wool; **l. di vétro** (*ind*) fiberglass; **di l.** wool(len).
lanaiuòlo *nm* wool-comber, woolworker.
lancétta *nf* (*of watch or clock*) hand; lancet.
lància *nf* lance; (*naut*) launch.
lanciabómbe *nm* trench-mortar.
lanciafiàmme *nm* flamethrower.
lanciàre *vt* to throw, launch; **-rsi** *vr* to fling (launch) oneself.
lanciasilúri *nm* torpedo-tube.
lancière *nm* lancer.
làncio *nm* throwing, launching.
lànda *nf* heath, moor.
lanería *nf* woollens *pl*, woollen goods *pl*.
languènte *a* languishing, pining, drooping.
languidaménte *ad* languidly, languorously.
languidézza *nf* languidness.
lànguido *a* languid, weak; (*of light*) faint.
languíre *vi* to languish, pine; (*of light*) fade.
languóre *nm* languor, weakness, faintness.
lanièro *a* woollen, wool; **commèrcio l.** wool trade.
lanifício *nm* wool factory.
lanóso *a* woolly.
lantèrna *nf* lantern, skylight; **l. di sicurézza** safety-lamp.
lanúgine *nf* down (on the skin).
lapidàre *vt* to stone.
lapidàrio *a* *nm* lapidary.
lapidazióne *nf* stoning.
làpide *nf* memorial tablet, tombstone.
làpin *French nm* cony, cony (skin).
làpis *nm* pencil.
lapislàzzuli *nm* lapis-lazuli.
lappóne *a* Lapp; *nm* (*language*) Lapp(ish); *nmf* Lapp, Laplander.
Lappònia *nf* (*geogr*) Lapland.
làrdo *nm* bacon.
largaménte *ad* largely, abundantly, at length, extensively.
largheggiàre *vi* to be generous, lavish.
larghèzza *nf* breadth, width; **l. di**

mèzzi wealth; **l. di vedúte** broad-mindedness.
largíre vt to give liberally.
largizióne nf donation, gift.
làrgo pl **làrghi** a broad, wide, large, generous; nm breadth, width; **fàrsi l.** to make a way for oneself.
làrice nm larch.
larínge nf larynx.
laringíte nf (med) laryngitis.
làrva nf larva, phantom, sham.
larvataménte ad by innuendo.
larvàto a hidden, latent.
làsca pl **-che** nf roach.
lasciapassàre nm pass, permit.
lasciàre vt to abandon, desert, leave (out), let, permit, quit; **l. cadére** to drop; **l. stàre** to let alone; **-rsi** vr to allow (let) oneself.
làscito nm bequest, legacy.
lascivaménte ad lasciviously, lustfully.
lascívia nf lasciviousness, wantonness.
lascívo a lascivious, wanton.
lassatívo a nm laxative.
làsso a (poet) unhappy, weary; nm (of time) lapse, period.
lassú ad up there.
làstra nf (of glass) pane, plate, slab.
lastricàre vt to pave.
làstrico pl **-chi** nm pavement; **lasciàre sul l.** to leave penniless.
latèbra nf (poet) recess, secret place.
latènte a concealed.
lateràle a side, lateral.
lateranénse a Lateran.
Lateràno a nm pr Lateran.
laterízi nm pl bricks pl.
latifondísta nmf owner of large landed estate.
latifóndo nm large landed estate.
latinísta nmf Latinist, Latin scholar.
latíno a nm Latin.
latitànte a absconding; **rèndersi l.** to abscond.
latitúdine nf latitude.
làto nm side; **a l. di** beside; **dal l. mío** for my part.
latóre nm **-tríce** nf bearer.
latraménto nm barking.
latràre vi to bark.
latràto nm bark, barking.
latrína nf latrine, lavatory, w.c.
làtta nf tin, can; tin plate.
lattàio nm milkman.
lattànte a breast-fed; nm child at the breast, suckling.
làtte nm milk.
lattemièle nm whipped cream.
làtteo a milky.
lattería nf (farm or shop) dairy.
latticínio nm dairy product.
lattièra nf milk-jug, milk-pot, cream-jug, creamer.
lattivéndola nf milk-woman; **lattivéndolo** nm milkman.
lattonière nm tinsmith.
lattòsio nm (chem) lactose.
lattúga nf lettuce.

làuda, làude nf laud, hymn of praise, early religious lyric.
làudano nm laudanum.
Làura nf pr Laura.
làurea nf (university) degree.
laureàndo a nm final-year undergraduate.
laureàre vt to confer a degree on; **-rsi** vr to take one's degree.
laureàto a nm graduate.
làuro nm laurel.
lautaménte ad sumptuously, magnificently.
lautézza nf magnificence, sumptuousness.
làuto a magnificent, sumptuous, abundant.
làva nf lava.
lavabianchería nf washing machine.
lavàbile a washable.
lavàbo nm wash-basin, (eccl) lavabo.
lavàcro nm (liter) bath, font.
lavàggio nm washing; **l. a sècco** dry cleaning.
lavàgna nf slate, blackboard.
lavamàno nm wash-hand basin.
lavànda nf lavender; washing.
lavandàia nf laundress, washer-woman; **lavandàio** nm laundryman.
lavandería nf laundry; **l. automàtica** launderette.
lavandíno nm sink.
lavapiàtti a dish-washing; nmf dishwasher, scullery-boy, scullery-maid.
lavàre vt **-rsi** vr to wash; **l. a sècco** to dry-clean.
lavàta nf wash; (fig) dressing-down, reprimand.
lavatívo nm enema; (vulg) tiresome person, bore.
lavatóio nm wash-house, wash-board.
lavatríce nf washerwoman; washing machine.
lavatúra nf washing; **l. a sècco** dry cleaning.
lavorànte nm workman; nf work-woman.
lavoràre vti to work, labor, till.
lavoratívo a working; **giórno l.** working day, weekday.
lavoràto a worked, processed, manufactured, tilled.
lavoratóre nm **-tríce** nf worker; a working.
lavorazióne nf manufacture, working, workmanship, tilling.
lavorío nm intense activity, intrigue.
lavóro nm work, labor, toil, job; (theat) play.
Làzio nm (geogr) Latium.
Làzzaro nm pr Lazarus.
lazzaróne nm (Neapolitan) beggar; rogue, idler.
le def art f pl the; pron acc f pl them; pron dat f to her.
leàle a loyal, faithful, true, fair.
lealmènte ad loyally, faithfully, fairly.

lealtà nf loyalty, faithfulness, fairness.
lèbbra nf leprosy.
lebbróso a leprous; nm leper.
leccàrda nf dripping-pan.
leccàre vt to lick.
leccàto a affected; **stíle l.** affected style.
léccio nm holm-oak.
leccornía nf dainty, titbit.
lécito a lawful, allowed, right.
lèdere vt to offend, harm, injure.
léga nf league, union, alloy.
legàccio nm string, (of shoes, boots) lace.
legàle a legal, lawful; nm lawyer.
legalità nf legality, lawfulness.
legalizzàre vt to legalize, authenticate.
legalizzazióne nf legalization, authentication.
legalménte ad legally, lawfully.
legàme nm bond, connection, link, tie.
legaménto nm (anat) ligament; binding, linking, connecting.
legàre vt to bind, fasten, alloy, bequeath.
legatàrio nm legatee.
legàto nm ambassador, legate; legacy.
legatóre nm -**trice** nf (book)binder; (leg) testator.
legatoría nf (book)binder's.
legatúra nf binding, fastening, ligature.
legazióne nf legation.
légge nf law, (of parliament) act.
leggènda nf legend.
leggendàrio a legendary.
lèggere vt to read.
leggerézza nf lightness, nimbleness; levity, thoughtlessness.
leggerménte ad lightly; thoughtlessly.
leggéro, leggiéro a light, slight, nimble, thoughtless, frivolous; **péso l.** (boxing) lightweight; **alla leggéra** ad lightly, thoughtlessly; **prèndere alla leggéra** vt to make light of.
leggiadría nf prettiness, grace, gracefulness.
leggiàdro a graceful, charming.
leggíbile a legible, readable.
leggío nm reading-desk, music-stand, lectern.
legióne nf legion.
legislatúra nf legislature.
legislazióne nf legislation.
legittimaménte ad legitimately, lawfully.
legittimità nf lawfulness, legitimacy.
legíttimo a lawful, legitimate.
légna pl **légna** nf wood, firewood; **portàre l. alla sélva** vt to carry coals to Newcastle.
legnai(u)òlo nm woodcutter, joiner, carpenter.
legnàme nm timber, lumber.
legnàta nf blow with a cudgel.
légno nm wood, stick; **di l.** wooden;

l. ricostituíto chipboard; **lavóro in l.** woodwork.
legnóso a woody.
legúme nm vegetable.
lèi pron nom and acc f she, her; you (polite form m and f).
Lèida nf (geogr) Leyden.
lémbo nm edge, hem, strip.
léna nf breath, energy; **di buòna l.** willingly.
Leningràdo nf (geogr) Leningrad.
leníre vt to soften, soothe.
lenitívo a lenitive, palliative.
lenocínio nm pandering; (fig) artifice.
lenóne nm pander, procurer.
lentaménte ad slowly.
lènte nf lentil; lens.
lentézza nf slowness, sluggishness,
lentícchia nf lentil.
lentíggine nf freckle.
lentigginóso a freckled.
lènto a slow, sluggish; loose.
lènza nf fishing-line, line.
lenzuòlo nm pl -**òla** f (bed)sheet.
Leonàrdo nm pr Leonard.
Leóne nm pr Leo, Leon.
leóne nm lion; **leonéssa** nf lioness.
leopàrdo nm leopard.
Leopòldo nm pr Leopold.
lepidézza nf witticism.
lèpido a witty.
Lepontíne, Àlpi nf pl (geogr) Lepontine Alps.
lèpre nf hare.
lércio a dirty, filthy, foul.
lésina nf awl.
lesinàre vi to be stingy; **l sul prézzo** to haggle over the price.
lesióne nf lesion, wound, injury.
léso a hurt, injured, offended.
lessàre vt to boil.
lèssico pl -**ici** nm lexicon.
lessicògrafo nm lexicographer.
lésso a boiled; nm boiled meat.
lestaménte ad quickly, hastily.
lestézza nf agility, quickness, swiftness.
lèsto a agile, quick, swift; ad quickly.
lestofànte nm swindler.
letàle a deadly, lethal.
letamàio nm dung-heap, hovel.
letàme nm dung.
letargía nf **letàrgo** nm pl -**ghi** lethargy.
letàrgico pl -**ici** a lethargic.
letízia nf gladness, joy.
léttera nf letter; **alla l.** literally; **bèlle léttere** pl Arts pl.
letteràle a literal.
letteralménte ad literally.
letteràrio a literary.
letteràto a well-read; nm man of letters.
letteratúra nf literature.
lettièra nf bedstead.
lettíga nf stretcher.
lètto nm bed.
lettóne a nmf Latvian; nm Lettish.
Lettònia nf (geogr) Latvia.
lettoràto nm lectureship.

lettóre nm **-tríce** nf reader, lecturer.
lettúra nf reading; **sàla di l.** reading-room.
leucemía nf leukemia.
lèva nf (mech) lever; (mil) conscription, draft; **èssere di l.** to be liable to call-up; **la l. del 1960** those called up in 1960.
levànte nm East; **vénto di l.** east wind; **il l.** the Levant.
levantíno a nm Levantine.
levàre vt to lift, raise, remove; **-rsi** vr to get out of the way, rise, take off.
levàta nf rising; (postal) collection.
levatóio a **pónte l.** drawbridge.
levatríce nf midwife.
levigàre vt to smooth.
levrière, levrièro nm greyhound.
lèzio nm **leziosàggine** nf affectation, mannerism.
lezióne nf lesson.
lezióso a affected, mincing.
lézzo nm stink, filth.
li pron m acc pl them.
lì ad there; **giù di l.** thereabouts; **l. per l.** immediately; **èssere l. l. per** to be within an ace of.
libanése a nmf Lebanese.
Líbano nm (geogr) Lebanon.
líbbra nf pound (weight).
libéccio nm southwest wind.
libèllo nm libel.
libèllula nf dragonfly.
liberàle a liberal; nm Liberal.
liberalísmo nm liberalism.
liberalità nf liberality.
liberaménte ad freely, frankly.
liberàre vt to free, clear, exempt, release; **-rsi** vr to free oneself, get rid of.
liberazióne nf liberation.
Libèria nf (geogr) Liberia.
liberiàno a nm Liberian.
líbero a free.
libertà nf freedom, liberty.
libertinàggio nm libertinage.
libertíno a nm libertine.
Líbia nf (geogr) Libya.
líbico pl **-ici** a nm Libyan.
libídine nf lust.
libidinóso a lustful.
líbra nf scales.
libràio nm bookseller.
libràre vt to weigh, balance.
librería nf bookshop, |book store; library; bookcase.
librétto nm (mus) libretto; small book; **l. di bànca** bank-book; **l. di circolazióne** (aut) log-book.
líbro nm book; **l. di càssa** cash-book; **l. giàllo** thriller; **l. maèstro** ledger; **l. di preghiére** prayer-book.
liceàle a of a 'liceo'.
licènza nf lease, certificate, license; dismissal.
licenziaménto nm discharge, dismissal.
licenziàre vt to discharge, dismiss; **-rsi** vr to resign; get one's diploma.

licenzióso a licentious.
licèo nm 'Liceo', secondary school.
lído nm shore, beach.
Liègi nf (geogr) Liège.
lietaménte ad happily, merrily.
liéto a glad, happy, cheerful.
liéve a light, slight, easy.
lieveménte ad lightly, gently.
lievitàre vt to leaven; vi (of bread etc) rise.
lièvito nm yeast, leaven; **l. di bírra** yeast.
lígio a faithful, observant.
lignàggio nm lineage.
ligure a nm Ligurian.
Ligúria nf (geogr) Liguria.
lílla nf lilac; nm (color) lilac.
Lílla nf (geogr) Lille.
lillipuziàno a nm Lilliputian.
líma nf (mech) file.
limaccióso a miry, muddy.
limàre vt to file, polish.
límbo nm Limbo.
limitàre vt to limit; nm threshold.
limitazióne nf limitation; **l. dèlle nàscite** birth-control.
límite nm boundary, limit.
limítrofo a adjacent, neighboring.
límo nm mire, mud.
limonàta nf lemonade.
limóne nm lemon (tree).
limpidézza nf clearness, limpidness.
límpido a limpid, clear.
línce nf lynx.
linciàggio nm lynching.
linciàre vt to lynch.
líndo a clean.
línea nf line.
lineaménti nm pl features pl, lineaments pl.
lineétta nf dash, hyphen.
línfa nf lymph, sap.
linfàtico pl **-ici** a lymphatic.
lingòtto nm ingot.
língua nf tongue, language.
linguàggio nm language.
linguísta nmf linguist.
linguística nf linguistics.
linguístico pl **-ici** a linguistic.
líno nm flax, linen; **séme di l.** linseed.
linòleum nm linoleum.
Lióne nf (geogr) Lyon; **lionése** anmf (person from) Lyons.
Lípsia nf (geogr) Leipzig.
liquefàre vt **-rsi** vr to liquefy.
liquidàre vt to liquidate.
liquidàto a liquidated, paid off, ruined.
liquidazióne nf liquidation, winding-up.
líquido a liquid; (money) ready; nm liquid.
liquirízia nf liquorice.
liquóre nm liqueur, liquor.
lira nf (Italian coin) lira; (mus) lyre.
lírica nf lyric, lyrical poem or poetry.
lírico pl **-ici** a lyric, lyrical; nm lyric poet.

lirísmo nm lyricism.
Lisbóna nf (geogr) Lisbon.
lísca nf fishbone.
lisciaménto nm **lisciatúra** nf smoothing, polishing.
lisciàre vt to smooth, polish; (fig) flatter.
líscio a smooth, plain, (of drink) neat, straight; **mèssa líscia** low mass; ad smoothly.
liscíva nf lye.
lísta nf strip; list, menu.
listàre vt to line, border.
listíno nm list, price-list.
litanía nf litany.
líte nf lawsuit, quarrel.
litigànte nmf disputant, litigant.
litigàre vi to dispute, quarrel.
litígio nm dispute, quarrel.
litigióso a quarrelsome.
litografàre vt to lithograph.
litografía nf lithography, lithograph.
litoràle a coastal, coast; nm littoral, coastline.
lítro nm liter.
littorànea nf coast road.
littorína nf diesel rail-car.
Lituània nf (geogr) Lithuania.
lituàno a nm Lithuanian.
liturgía nf liturgy.
litúrgico pl -ici a liturgic(al).
liúto nm (mus) lute.
livellàre vt to level.
livèllo nm level; **passàggio a l.** level-crossing, grade crossing; **l. del màre** sea-level.
lívido a livid; nm bruise.
Lívio nm pr Livy.
livóre nm envy, hatred.
Livórno nf (geogr) Leghorn.
livrèa nf livery.
lízza nf lists pl.
lo def art m the; pron acc m him, it.
lòbo nm lobe.
locàle a local; nm room, premises pl.
località nf locality.
localizzàre vt to locate, localize.
localménte ad locally.
locànda nf inn.
locandièra nf **-re** nm innkeeper.
locatàrio nm lessee, tenant.
locatóre nm **-tríce** nf lessor.
locazióne nf lease.
locomotíva nf locomotive.
locomozióne nf locomotion.
locústa nf locust.
locuzióne nf expression, phrase, idiom.
lodàre vt to praise.
lòde nf praise.
lodévole a praiseworthy, laudable, commendable.
lòdola nf lark, skylark.
Lodovíco nm pr Ludovic(k).
logarítmo nm logarithm.
lòggia nf loggia; (masonic) lodge.
loggióne nm (theat) gallery.
lògica nf logic.
lògico pl -ici a logical; nm logician.
lòglio nm darnel.

logoraménto nm wearing out, wearing down, wasting away.
logoràre vt to wear down, wear out; **-rsi** vr to be worn out.
logorío nm wear and tear.
lógoro a worn down, worn out.
lombàggine nf lumbago.
Lombardía nf (geogr) Lombardy.
lombàrdo a nm Lombard.
lombàta nf (of meat) loin, sirloin.
lómbo nm (human) loin.
lombríco nm earthworm.
Lóndra nf (geogr) London.
londinése a (of) London; nmf Londoner.
longànime a forbearing, patient.
longanimità nf forbearance, patience.
longevità nf longevity.
longèvo a long-lived.
longitudinàle a longitudinal.
longitúdine nf longitude.
lontanaménte ad vaguely, slightly.
lontanànza nf distance; **in l.** at a distance.
lontàno a distant, far; ad far, far away, far off; **da l.** from a distance; **àlla lontàna** at a distance, slightly.
lóntra nf otter.
lónza nf panther; (of meat) loin.
loquàce a loquacious, talkative.
loquacità nf loquacity.
loquèla nf language, way of speaking.
lordàre vt to dirty, soil.
lórdo a dirty; **péso l.** nm (com) gross weight.
lordúra nf dirt, filth.
Lorèna nf (geogr) Lorraine.
lorenése a of Lorraine; nm Lorrainer.
Lorènzo nm pr Laurence, Lawrence.
lóro pron nom pl they, you; acc pl you, them; dat pl to you, to them; poss a pl your, their.
Losànna nf (geogr) Lausanne.
lósco pl -schi a dubious; one-eyed, squint-eyed; **figúra lósca** scoundrel.
lòtta nf fight, struggle.
lottàre vi to fight, struggle, wrestle.
lottería nf lottery.
lòtto nm lot, lottery.
lozióne nf lotion.
lubricità nf lubricity.
lúbrico pl -ici a slippery; indecent.
lubrificànte a lubricating; nm lubricant.
lubrificàre vt to lubricate, oil, grease.
lubrificazióne nf lubrication.
Lúca nm pr Luke.
lucchétto nm padlock.
luccicàre vi to glitter, shine.
luccichío nm glitter, sparkle.
lúccio nm (fish) pike.
lúcciola nf firefly, glowworm.
lúce nf light; **l. abbagliànte** (aut) headlight; **l. anabbagliànte** (aut) anti-glare light; **lúci della ribàlta** pl (theat) footlights; **dare alla l.** to give birth to.
lucènte a shiny, shining, bright.

lucentézza *nf* brightness, shine, sheen.
Lucèrna *nf* (*geogr*) Lucerne.
lucèrna *nf* oil-lamp.
lucernàrio *nm* skylight.
lucèrtola *nf* lizard.
Lucía *nf* pr Lucy.
Luciàno *nm* pr Lucian.
lucidaménto, lucidatúra *nf* polishing.
lucidàre *vt* to polish.
lucidatóre *nm* polisher.
lucidatríce *nf* polisher, polishing machine.
lucidézza *nf* brightness, sheen.
lucidità *nf* lucidity, clearness.
lúcido *a* bright, shiny, lucid.
lucígnolo *nm* wick.
lúcro *nm* profit, gain.
lucróso *a* lucrative, profitable.
ludíbrio *nm* mockery, scorn.
lúe *nf* (*med*) contagion, syphilis.
lúglio *nm* July.
lúgubre *a* lugubrious, dismal.
lúi *pron m* (*nom*) he; (*acc*) him.
Luígi *nm* pr Louis, Lewis.
Luísa *nf* pr Louise, Louisa.
Luisiàna *nf* (*geogr*) Louisana.
lumàca *nf* snail; slow person.
lúme *nm* light, lamp; **a quésti lúmi di lúna** in these hard times.
luminàre *nm* great man, luminary.
luminària *nf* public illumination.
lumíno *nm* night-light.
luminosaménte *ad* brightly, luminously.
luminosità *nf* brightness, luminosity.
luminóso *a* luminous, shining, bright.
lúna *nf* moon; **l. di mièle** honeymoon; **chiàro di l.** moonlight.
lunàre *a* lunar.
lunàrio *nm* almanac; **sbarcàre il l.** to make both ends meet.
lunàtico *pl* **-ici** *a* moody.
lunedí *nm* Monday.
lungaménte *ad* for a long time.
lunghézza *nf* length.
lungimirànte *a* far-seeing.
lúngo *pl* **-ghi** *a* long, tall; slow; weak; *prep* along; **a l.** for a long time; **di gran lúnga** by far; **a l. andàre in the long run.**
lungomàre *nm* sea-front.
lungometràggio *nm* feature film.
luògo *pl* **-ghi** *nm* place; **sul l.** on the spot; **l. comúne** commonplace.
luogotenènte *nm* lieutenant.
lúpa *nf* she-wolf; **lúpo** *nm* wolf.
lupacchiòtto *nm* wolf-cub.
lupanàre *nm* brothel.
lupíno *nm* lupin.
lúppolo *nm* hop (plant).
lúrido *a* dirty, filthy.
luridúme *nm* filth, dirt.
lusínga *nf* allurement, illusion, flattery.
lusingàre *vt* to allure, flatter.
lusinghièro *a* alluring, flattering.
lussàre *vt* (*med*) to dislocate.
lussazióne *nf* dislocation.

Lussembúrgo *nm* (*geogr*) Luxembourg.
lússo *nm* luxury.
lussuóso *a* luxurious.
lussureggiànte *a* luxuriant.
lussureggiàre *vt* to be luxuriant, flourish.
lussúria *nf* lust.
lussurióso *a* lustful.
lustràre *vt* to polish.
lustrascàrpe *nm* shoeblack, shoeshine.
lustríno *nm* sequin.
lústro *a* polished, shining; *nm* luster.
luteràno *a nm* Lutheran.
Lutèro *nm* pr Luther.
lútto *nm* mourning; **a l.** in mourning.
luttuóso *a* mournful, sad.

M

ma *cj* but; **macchè** *interj* not at all.
màcabro *a* macabre.
maccheróni *nm pl* macaroni.
màcchia *nf* spot, stain, blot; bush, woodland; **alla m.** clandestinely.
macchiàre *vt* to soil, spot, stain; **-rsi** *vr* to get dirty, disgrace oneself.
macchiétta *nf* speck; caricature; eccentric person, (*theat*) character study.
màcchina *nf* machine, engine; car; **m. a vapóre** steam engine; **m. da scrívere** typewriter; **m. fuòri série** custom-built car; **m. decapotàbile** convertible; **m. lavapiàtti** dish-washing machine (dishwasher).
macchinalménte *ad* mechanically, automatically.
macchinàre *vt* to plot.
macchinàrio *nm* machinery.
macchinazióne *nf* machination, plot.
macchinísta *nm* engine driver, engineer.
macedònia *nf* fruit salad, macedoine.
macellàio *nm* butcher.
macellàre *vt* to slaughter, butcher.
macellazióne *nf* slaughter(ing).
macellería *nf* butcher's (shop).
macèllo *nm* slaughter-house, slaughtering, slaughter.
maceràre *vt* to soak, macerate; **-rsi** *vr* to wear oneself out.
maceratóio, màcero *nm* macerating vat.
macerazióne *nf* maceration; (*fig*) mortification (of the flesh).
macèrie *nf pl* debris, remains.
macígno *nm* hard stone; boulder.
macilènto *a* emaciated.
màcina *nf* millstone, grindstone.
macinacaffè (*inv*) *nm* coffee-mill.
macinàre *vt* to grind, mill, crush.
macinatóio *nm* mill, press.
macinazióne *nf* grinding, milling.
maciníno *nm* coffee-mill.
maciullàre *vt* to crush, chew.
Maddaléna *nf* pr Magdalene.

Madèra nf (geogr) Madeira.
màdia nf kneading trough, kitchen cupboard.
màdido a wet, soaked.
madònna nf (arc) lady, madonna; **Madònna** the Virgin Mary, (the) Madonna.
madornàle a enormous, gross, huge.
màdre nf mother; **m. lingua** mother tongue; **càsa m.** (com) head office.
madrepàtria nf mother-country, fatherland.
madrepèrla nf mother-of-pearl.
madresélva nf honeysuckle.
Madríd nf (geogr) Madrid; **madrilèno** a nm of Madrid.
madrigàle nm madrigal.
madrína nf godmother.
maestà nf majesty.
maestóso a majestic, stately, magnificent.
maèstra nf (school)mistress, teacher.
maestràle nm mistral.
maestrànza nf skilled workmen pl, skilled hands pl.
maestría nf mastery, skill.
maèstro a main, principal, masterly; nm schoolmaster, teacher, maestro; **àlbero m.** mainmast; **stràda maèstra** highroad.
màfia nf Mafia.
mafióso a nm (member) of the Mafia.
magàgna nf defect, fault, ailment.
magàri interj if only . . . ! ad maybe, perhaps, even.
magazzinàggio nm storage.
magazzinière nm warehouse-man.
magazzíno nm store, warehouse, store-house.
maggése nm fallow land.
màggio nm (month) May.
maggioràna nf marjoram.
maggiorànza nf majority.
maggioràre vt (com) to increase, put up.
maggiorazióne nf (com) increase, additional charge.
maggiordòmo nm butler.
maggióre a bigger, elder, greater, high(er), larger, older, biggest, eldest; nm superior, elder; (mil) major; pl ancestors.
maggiorènne a of age; nm adult.
maggiorménte ad more, much more, all the more.
magía nf magic.
màgico pl -ici a magic(al).
magistèro nm mastery, teaching.
magistràle a magistral, masterly.
magistràto nm magistrate.
magistratúra nf magistracy.
màglia nf stitch; mesh; vest, jersey, (mech) link; mail; **lavoràre a m.** to knit.
magliería nf hosiery, knitted goods pl.
maglifício nm knitwear factory.
màglio nm mallet; (mech) hammer.
maglióne nm jersey, pullover.
magnanimità nf magnanimity.

magnànimo a magnanimous.
magnàno nm locksmith.
magnàte nm magnate, tycoon.
magnèsia nf magnesia.
magnèsio nm magnesium.
magnète nm magnet, magneto.
magnètico pl -ici a magnetic.
magnetísmo nm magnetism.
magnetizzàre vt to magnetize.
magnetòfono nm tape-recorder.
magnificàre vt to extol, magnify.
magnificènza nf grandeur, splendor.
magnífico pl -ici a magnificent, splendid.
magniloquènza nf grandiloquence.
màgno a great.
magnòlia nf magnolia(-tree).
màgo pl -ghi nm sorcerer, wizard; **i Ré Màgi** the Three Kings.
màgra nf shallow water, shortage; **tèmpi di m.** hard times.
magrézza nf thinness, (of soil) poorness.
màgro a thin, poor; **giòrno di m.** day of abstinence.
mài ad ever, never; **cóme m.?** how is that?; **se m.** in case; if anything.
maiàle nm pig, pork.
maiòlica nf majolica.
maionése nf mayonnaise.
Maiòrca nf (geogr) Majorca.
màis nm maize, corn.
maiúscolo a capital; nm capitals pl.
malaccòrto a imprudent, rash.
malacreànza nf ill-breeding.
malaféde nf bad faith.
malaffàre nm **dònna di m.** whore; **gènte di m.** crooks pl, scum.
malagévole a difficult, hard, unmanageable.
malagiàto a uncomfortable, short of money.
malagràzia nf bad grace, rudeness.
malaménte ad badly.
malandàto a in bad repair, in poor health.
malandríno a roguish; nm robber, rogue.
malànimo nm ill will.
malànno nm infirmity, misfortune.
malapéna, a ad hardly, scarcely.
malària nf malaria.
malàrico pl -ici a malarial.
malatíccio a sickly.
malàto a ill, sick, diseased; nm sick person, patient.
malattía nf disease, illness.
malauguràto a unfortunate, ill-omened.
malaugúrio nm bad omen.
malavíta nf (criminal) underworld.
malavòglia nf unwillingness, ill-will.
malavventuràto a ill-fated, unlucky.
malazzàto a sickly.
malcapitàto a unfortunate, unlucky.
malcóncio a in a poor way, in tatters.
malcontènto a discontented, dis-

satisfied; *nm* dissatisfaction, discontent.
malcostúme *nm* immorality, corruption, bad habit.
maldèstro *a* awkward, clumsy.
maldicènza *nf* backbiting, slander.
màle *nm* evil, illness, harm; *ad* badly; **mal di dénti** toothache; **mal di góla** sore throat; **mal di tésta** headache; **méno m.** thank Heavens!; **non c'è m.** pretty good; **restàre m.** to be disappointed; **stàre m.** to be ill.
maledètto *a* cursed, damned.
maledíre *vt* to curse.
maledizióne *nf* curse.
maleducàto *a* rude; *nm* ill-bred person.
maleducazióne *nf* bad manners *pl*, rudeness.
malefàtta *nf* mischief.
malefício *nm* witchcraft, spell, misdeed.
malèfico *pl* **-ici** *a* evil, mischievous.
malèrba *nf* weed.
malése *a nmf* Malay.
Malèsia *nf* (*geogr*) Malaya, Malaysia.
malèssere *nm* indisposition, malaise.
malevolènza *nf* ill will, malevolence.
malèvolo *a* malevolent.
malfamàto *a* ill-famed.
malfattóre *nm* **-tríce** *nf* evil-doer, criminal.
malférmo *a* unsteady, shaky; (*of health*) poor.
malfído *a* unreliable, uncertain.
malgàrbo *nm* bad grace, rudeness.
malgovèrno *nm* misgovernment, mismanagement.
malgradíto *a* unwelcome.
malgràdo *prep* in spite of, notwithstanding; **mío m.** against my will; **m.** (**che**) *cj* although.
malía *nf* witchcraft, charm.
malignità *nf* malignity, wickedness.
malígno *a* evil, malicious, malignant.
malinconía *nf* melancholy, sadness.
malincònico *pl* **-ici** *a* melancholy, sad.
malincuòre, a *ad* unwillingly.
malintenzionàto *a* ill-disposed, malicious.
malintéso *a* mistaken; *nm* misunderstanding.
malízia *nf* malice, cunning, trick.
malizióso *a* mischievous, artful.
mallevadóre *nm* bail, surety.
mallevería, mallevadoría *nf* bail, suretyship.
malmenàre *vt* to ill-treat, ill-use.
malmésso *a* badly dressed, poorly dressed.
malnutríto *a* underfed.
màlo *a* bad, ill, wicked.
malòcchio *nm* evil eye; **vedére di m.** to dislike.
malóra *nf* ruin.
malóre *nm* sudden illness, indisposition.
malsàno *a* unhealthy, unwholesome.

malsicúro *a* unsafe, uncertain, unreliable.
Màlta *nf* (*geogr*) Malta; **maltése** *a nmf* Maltese.
maltalènto *nm* ill-will.
maltèmpo *nm* bad weather.
maltenúto *a* untidy, badly kept.
màlto *nm* malt.
maltòlto *a* ill-gotten; *nm* ill-gotten goods *pl*.
maltrattaménto *nm* ill-treatment.
maltrattàre *vt* to ill-treat, ill-use.
malumóre *nm* ill-humor, spleen.
malvagiaménte *ad* wickedly.
malvàgio *a* wicked.
malvagità *nf* wickedness.
malvísto *a* unpopular.
malvivènte *nm* gangster, criminal.
malvivènza *nf* delinquency, criminality.
malvolentièri *ad* unwillingly.
malvolére *nm* ill-will, dislike, wickedness.
màmma *nf* mama, mum(my), mother.
mammèlla *nf* breast.
mammífero *nm* mammal.
màmmola *nf* violet.
manàta *nf* handful, slap.
mànca *nf* left-hand, left-hand side.
mancànte *a* lacking, missing, deficient; failing, defective.
mancànza *nf* deficiency, lack, shortness, want; **sentíre la m. di** to miss.
mancàre *vi* to lack, be missing, err; **màncano cínque minúti alle dúe** it is five to two; *vt* to miss; **m. il bersàglio** to miss the mark.
mancàto *a* manqué, unsuccessful.
mància *nf* tip, reward.
manciàta *nf* handful.
mancíno *a* left-handed; treacherous.
Manciúria *nf* (*geogr*) Manchuria.
mànco *pl* **-chi** *a* left; *ad* not even.
mandaménto *nm* borough, district.
mandànte *nm* instigator.
mandàre *vt* to send, emit; **m. vía** to send away; **m. all'ària** to ruin.
mandaríno *nm* mandarin; tangerine.
mandàta *nf* batch; (of key) turn.
mandàto *nm* commission, mandate, order, warrant.
mandíbola *nf* jaw.
mandolíno *nm* mandolin.
màndorla *nf* almond; **màndorlo** *nm* almond-tree.
màndra, màndria *nf* flock, herd.
maneggévole *a* easy to handle, manageable.
maneggiàre *vt* to handle, manage, use; **-rsi** *vr* to conduct oneself, manage.
manéggio *nm* handling, use, management; horsemanship, riding-school; intrigue.
manésco *pl* **-chi** *a* ready with one's fists.
manétte *nf pl* handcuffs *pl*.
manganèllo *nm* cudgel.
manganése *nm* manganese.

mangeréccio *a* edible, eatable.
mangiàre *vti* to eat; *nm* eating.
mangiàta *nf* meal, hearty meal.
mangiatóia *nf* crib, manger.
mangiucchiàre *vti* to nibble, pick at one's food.
manía *nf* mania, fixation.
maníaco *pl* -aci *a nm* maniac.
mànica *nf* sleeve; **èssere di m. làrga** to be broad minded; **un àltro pàio di màniche** another kettle of fish; **la M.** the (English) Channel.
mànico *pl* -chi *nm* handle.
manicòmio *nm* (lunatic-)asylum.
manicòtto *nm* muff; (*mech*) coupling.
manicure (Fr) *nmf* manicurist, manicure.
manièra *nf* manner, way; **in qualúnque m.** anyhow.
manieràto *a* affected, mannered.
manifattúra *nf* manufacture, workmanship.
manifestàre *vt* to manifest, show; **-rsi** *vr* to reveal oneself.
manifestazióne *nf* display; demonstration.
manifèsto *a* clear, obvious; *nm* manifesto, bill, placard, leaflet.
maníglia *nf* handle.
manigóldo *nm* rascal, villain.
manipolàre *vt* to handle, manipulate, adulterate.
manipolazióne *nf* handling, preparation, manipulation, adulteration.
maniscàlco *pl* -chi *nm* farrier.
mànna *nf* manna, godsend.
mannàia *nf* axe.
màno *nf* hand; (*of paint*) coat; **a portàta di m.** within reach; **fuòri di m.** out of reach, out of the way; **strétta di m.** handshake; **di secónda m.** second-hand.
manodòpera *nf* labor, workmanship.
manòmetro *nm* manometer, pressure-gauge.
manométtere *vt* to tamper with, violate.
manomissióne *nf* tampering, violation.
manomòrta *nf* (*leg*) mortmain.
manòpola *nf* handle bar grip, knob, fencing glove, cuff.
manoscrítto *a* handwritten; *nm* manuscript.
manovàle *nm* laborer.
manovèlla *nf* crank, handle, winder.
manòvra *nf* maneuver, (*rly*) shunting.
manovràre *vt* to maneuver, shunt, work.
manrovèscio *pl* **manrovèsci** *nm* backhanded blow.
mansàlva *a ad* with impunity.
mansióne *nf* function, duty, office.
mansuefàre *vt* to subdue, tame.
mansuèto *a* meek, mild, docile.
mantèllo *nm* cloak, mantle.
mantenére *vt* to keep (up), maintain; **-rsi** *vr* to keep (oneself).

manteniménto *nm* maintenance' preservation.
màntice *nm* bellows *pl*, (*of a car*) hood.
mànto *nm* cloak, mantle.
Màntova *nf* (*geogr*) Mantua.
mantovàno *a nm* Mantuan.
manuàle *a* manual; *nm* handbook, manual.
manúbrio *nm* handle(-bar), dumbbell.
manufàtto *a* hand-made, manufactured; *nm* hand-made article.
manutenzióne *nf* upkeep, maintenance.
mànzo *nm* steer, beef.
maomettàno *a nm* Mahommedan.
Maométto *nm* *pr* Mohammed, Mahomet.
màppa *nf* map.
mappamóndo *nm* globe of the world.
marachèlla *nf* trick, prank.
maratóna *nf* marathon (race).
màrca *nf* (*com*) brand, mark, make; **m. da bòllo** revenue stamp; **m. di fàbbrica** trade-mark.
marcàre *vt* to mark.
marchésa *nf* marchioness; **marchése** *nm* marquis.
màrchio *nm* brand, mark; **m. di fàbbrica** trade-mark.
màrcia *nf* (*aut*) gear; march; pus.
marciapiède *nm* pavement, sidewalk; platform.
marciàre *vi* to march.
màrcio *a* bad, rotten, tainted; *nm* rottenness, pus.
marcíre *vi* to decay, go bad, rot, waste.
marciúme *nm* rottenness, rotten things *pl*.
màrco *pl* -chi *nm* (*coin*) mark.
Màrco *nm* *pr* Mark.
marconísta *nm* radio operator.
màre *nm* sea; **in àlto m.** on the high seas; **màl di m.** seasickness.
marèa *nf* tide.
mareggiàta *nf* rough sea.
maresciàllo *nm* marshal; warrant-office:.
marétta *nf* choppy sea.
margarína *nf* margarine.
margheríta *nf* daisy.
Margheríta *nf* *pr* Margaret.
marginàle *a* marginal.
màrgine *nm* margin, border, edge.
María *nf* *pr* Mary.
Mariànna *nf* *pr* Marian(ne).
marína *nf* navy; coast, seaside; **régia m.** Royal Navy; **m. mercantíle** merchant navy.
marinàio *nm* sailor, seaman.
marinàra *nf* duffle coat.
marinàre *vt* to pickle, marinate; **m. la scuòla** to play truant.
marináto *a* pickled, soused.
maríno *a* marine, (of the) sea.
Màrio *nm* *pr* Marius.
marionétta *nf* marionette, puppet.

maritàre *vt* to marry; **-rsi** *vr* to get married, marry.
maríto *nm* husband.
maríttimo *a* maritime, marine.
marmàglia *nf* rabble.
marmellàta *nf* jam; **m. d'aràncе** marmalade.
marmítta *nf* saucepan.
màrmo *nm* marble.
marmòcchio *nm* brat.
marmòreo *a* marble, marmoreal.
marmòtta *nf* marmot; (*fig*) lazy-bones.
Màrna *nf* (*geogr*) Marne.
marocchíno *a* Moroccan; *nm* Moroccan, Morocco (leather).
Maròcco *nm* (*geogr*) Morocco.
maróso *nm* billow, wave.
marróne *a* brown; *nm* chestnut; blunder.
Marsíglia *nf* (*geogr*) Marseilles; **marsigliése** *a* *nmf* of Marseilles, Marseillaise.
Màrta *nf* *pr* Martha.
martedí *nm* Tuesday; **m. gràsso** Shrove Tuesday.
martellàre *vti* to hammer, throb.
martèllo *nm* hammer.
martinèllo, martinétto *nm* (*mech*) jack.
Martíno *nm* *pr* Martin.
martín pescatóre *nm* kingfisher.
màrtire *nm* martyr.
martírio *nm* martyrdom.
martirizzàre *vt* to martyrize, torture.
màrtora *nf* marten; (*fur*) sable.
martoriàre *vt* to torment, torture.
marxísmo *nm* Marxism.
marxísta *a* *nm* Marxist, Marxian.
marzapàne *nm* marzipan.
marziàle *a* martial.
marziàno *a* Martian.
màrzo *nm* March.
mascalzóne *nm* rascal, scoundrel.
mascèlla *nf* jaw.
màschera *nf* mask; (*theat*) usher.
mascheràre *vt* to mask; **-rsi** *vr* to disguise oneself.
mascheràta *nf* masquerade.
mascheróne *nm* mask, grotesque face.
maschiètta, alla *ad* **capélli a. m.** shingled hair.
maschíle *a* male, manly, masculine.
màschio *a* male, manly; *nm* male child; inner keep, tower.
masnàda *nf* gang, set.
masnadière *nm* brigand, robber.
màssa *nf* mass, heap.
massacràre *vt* to massacre, slaughter.
massàcro *nm* massacre, slaughter.
massaggiàre *vt* to massage.
massàggio *nm* massage.
massàia *nf* housewife.
masserìa *nf* farm.
masserízie *nf pl* household goods *pl*, household utensils *pl*.
massíccio *a* massy, massive, solid; *nm* massif.

màssima *nf* maxim, rule, saying.
massimaménte *ad* chiefly, especially.
màssimo *a* greatest, highest, utmost, best; *nm* maximum.
màsso *nm* big stone, block, boulder.
massóne *nm* Freemason, mason.
massonería *nf* Freemasonry.
massònico *pl* **-ici** *a* masonic.
masticàre *vt* to chew, masticate; stammer; **m. una língua** to have a smattering of a language.
masticazióne *nf* chewing, mastication.
màstice *nm* mastic, putty.
mastíno *nm* mastiff.
màstio *nm* donjon, keep.
mastodòntico *pl* **-ici** *a* huge, colossal.
màstro *nm* ledger, master.
matàssa *nf* skein.
matemàtica *nf* mathematics.
matemàtico *pl* **-ici** *a* mathematical.
materàsso *nm* mattress.
matèria *nf* matter, material, subject; **m. príma** raw material.
materiàle *a* material, rough; *nm* material.
materialísmo *nm* materialism.
materialísta *a* materialistic; *nmf* materialist.
materialménte *ad* materially, physically.
maternità *nf* maternity, motherhood.
matèrno *a* motherly, mother's, maternal.
Matílde *nf* *pr* Mat(h)ilda.
matíta *nf* pencil.
matríce *nf* matrix, womb, mold; **regístro a m.** (*com*) counterfoil register.
matrícola *nf* register, roll; freshman.
matricolàre *vt* **-rsi** *vr* to matriculate.
matricolíno *nm* (*student*) freshman, beginner.
matrígna *nf* stepmother.
matrimoniàle *a* matrimonial, wedding; **anèllo m.** wedding ring; **caméra m.** double room; **letto m.** double bed.
matrimònio *nm* marriage, wedding.
mattacchióne *nm* joker, wag.
mattànza *nf* (*naut*) slaughter of tunny fish.
Mattèo *nm* *pr* Matthew.
matterèllo *nm* (*cook*) rolling-pin.
mattína *nf* **mattíno** *nm* morning.
mattinàta *nf* forenoon, morning, (*theat*) matinée.
mattinièro *a* early rising.
màtto *a* mad; *nm* madman; **scàcco m.** (*at chess*) checkmate.
mattonàto *nm* brick floor.
mattóne *nm* brick; (*fig*) bore, nuisance.
mattonèlla *nf* tile, briquette.
mattutíno *a* morning; *nm* matins.
maturàre *vti* to ripen, mature.
maturazióne *nf* maturity, ripening, maturation.

maturità *nf* ripeness, maturity; certificàto di **m.** leaving certificate.
matúro *a* ripe, mature, (*com*) fallen due.
Maurízio *nm pr* Maurice; **isola M.** *nf* (*geogr*) Mauritius.
mausolèo *nm* mausoleum.
màzza *nf* mallet, sledge-hammer.
mazzàta *nf* heavy blow (*also fig*).
màzzo *nm* bunch; (*of cards*) pack.
mazzolíno *nm* posy, small bunch, bouquet.
me *pron* (*oblique case*) me, myself.
meccànica *nf* mechanics.
meccànico *pl* **-ici** *a* mechanical; *nm* mechanic, mechanician.
meccaníṣmo *nm* gear, mechanism, works; **m.** di stèrzo (*aut*) steering-gear.
mecenàte *nm* Maecenas, patron.
medàglia *nf* medal.
medaglióne *nm* medallion, locket.
medéṣimo *a and pron* same, -self.
mèdia *nf* average; **in m.** on the average.
mediàno *a* median, mean middle; *nm* (*sport*) halfback.
mediànte *prep* by means of.
mediatóre *nm* mediator, (*com*) broker.
mediazióne *nf* mediation, (*com*) brokerage.
medicàbile *a* curable, medicable.
medicaménto *nm* medicament, medicine.
medicàre *vt* to dress, medicate, treat.
medicàstro *nm* quack.
medicazióne *nm* (*wounds*) dressing, treatment; **pòsto di m.** first-aid post.
medicína *nf* medicine, remedy, drug.
medicinàle *a* medicinal; *nm* medicine, drug.
mèdico *pl* **mèdici** *a* medical; *nm* doctor, physician.
mèdio *a* middle, average, medium; *nm* mean, middle finger; **scuòla mèdia** secondary school, junior high school.
mediòcre *a* mediocre, second-rate.
mediocrità *nf* mediocrity.
medioevàle *a* medieval.
medioèvo *nm* Middle Ages *pl.*
meditabóndo *a* pensive, meditative, thoughtful.
meditàre *vti* to meditate, meditate on.
meditàto *a* deliberate.
meditazióne *nf* meditation.
mediterràneo *a* Mediterranean; *nm* (*geogr*) the Mediterranean.
medúsa *nf* jellyfish, Medusa.
megàfono *nm* megaphone.
mèglio *ad and a* better; *nm* best.
méla *nf* apple; **mélo** *nm* apple-tree.
melacotógna *nf* quince.
melagràna *nf* pomegranate.
melanzàna *nf* eggplant, aubergine.

melarància *nf* orange.
melàssa *nf* molasses, treacle.
melènso *a* sheepish, silly.
mellífluo *a* honeyed, mellifluous.
mélma *nf* mire, mud.
melmóso *a* miry, muddy.
melodía *nf* melody.
melòdico *pl* **-ici** *a* melodic.
melodióso *a* melodious.
melodràmma *nm* opera.
melodrammàtico *a* operatic; (*fig*) melodramatic.
melogràno *nm* pomegranate (tree).
melóne *nm* melon.
membràna *nf* membrane.
membranóso *a* membranous.
mèmbro *nm*, *pl* **-bra** *nf* limb; *pl* **-bri** *m* member.
memoràbile *a* memorable.
memoràndum *nm* memorandum; notebook.
mèmore *a* mindful, grateful.
memòria *nf* memory, remembrance, souvenir, record; **a m.** by heart; **imparàre a m.** to memorize; **memòrie** *pl* memoirs *pl.*
menàre *vt* to lead, take, bring; **m.** càlci to kick; **m. un cólpo** to deal a blow; **m. le màni** to fight; **m. il càne per l'àia** to beat about the bush; **m.** gràmo to bring bad luck; **m. buòno** to bring good luck.
mènda *nf* blemish, slight defect.
mendicànte, *a* begging, mendicant; *nmf* beggar.
mendicàre *vti* to beg.
mendicità *nf* begging; beggars *pl.*
mendíco *a* begging; *nm* beggar.
meningíte *nf* meningitis.
méno *a ad prep* less, minus; least; **fàre a m.** di to do without; **le dúe m. cínque** 5 minutes to 2; **a m. che non** unless.
menomaménte *ad* at all, in the least.
menomàre *vt* to lessen, detract from; disable, impair.
menomazióne *nf* reduction, impairment, disablement.
menopàusa *nf* menopause.
mènsa *nf* table; (*mil*) mess; refectory; (*eccl*) altar.
mensíle *a* monthly; *nm* month's pay.
mensilità *nf* monthly installment, monthly payment, monthly occurrence.
mensilménte *ad* monthly.
mènsola *nf* bracket, console.
mènta *nf* mint.
mentàle *a* mental.
mentalità *nf* mentality.
mènte *nf* mind, intellect, intention, memory; **a m.** *ad* by heart.
mentíre *vi* to lie; *vt* to falsify, misrepresent.
ménto *nm* chin.
méntre *ad and cj* while; **in quél m.** at that moment.
menù *nm* menu, bill of fare.
menzionàre *vt* to mention.

menzióne *nf* mention.
menzógna *nf* falsehood, lie.
menzognèro *a* lying, untrue.
meravíglia *nf* wonder, surprise; a m. *ad* wonderfully well.
meravigliàre *vt* to amaze, surprise; -rsi *vr* to be amazed, wonder.
meravigliosaménte *ad* wonderfully, beautifully.
meraviglióso *a* wonderful; *nm* wonder, the supernatural.
mercànte *nm* merchant, trader; fàre orécchio da m. to turn a deaf ear.
mercanteggiàre *vi* to trade, haggle.
mercantíle *a* mercantile, merchant; plain; *nm* cargo boat.
mercanzía *nf* merchandise, goods *pl*, wares *pl*.
mercàto *nm* market; bargain, price; a buòn m. cheap, cheaply; per sópra m. besides, moreover; M. Comúne Common Market.
mercatúra *nf* trade, commerce.
mèrce *nf* goods *pl*, merchandise; tréno mèrci freight train
mercè *nf* mercy; súa m. thanks to him.
mercéde *nf* pay, reward.
mercenàrio *a nm* mercenary.
mercería *nf* haberdasher's shop; merceríe *pl* haberdashery.
merciàio *nm* merciàia *nf* dry-goods dealer, haberdasher.
mercoledì *nm* Wednesday; m. delle cèneri Ash Wednesday.
mercúrio *nm* mercury, quicksilver.
mèrda *nf* (*vulg*) shit.
merènda *nf* afternoon tea, snack.
meridiàna *nf* sun-dial.
meridiàno *a nm* meridian.
meridionàle *a* south, southern; *nmf* southerner.
meridióne *nm* south.
meríggio *nm* midday, noon.
merínga *nf* meringue.
meritaménte, meritataménte *ad* deservedly, justly.
meritàre *vt* to deserve, earn, be worthwhile, require; -rsi *vr* to deserve.
meritévole *a* deserving, worthy.
mèrito *nm* merit; in m. a as regards, as to.
meritòrio *a* deserving, meritorious.
merlatúra *nf* battlement; lace trimming.
merlétto *nm* lace.
mèrlo *nm* blackbird; (*arch*) merlon; simpleton.
merlúzzo *nm* cod(fish).
mèro *a* mere, pure, simple.
mesàta *nf* month's salary.
méscere *vt* to pour, mix.
meschinería, meschinità *nf* meanness, stinginess.
meschíno *a* poor, mean, wretched.
méscita *nf* wine shop.
mescolànza *nf* mixing, mixture.
mescolàre *vt* to mix, stir, (*cards*) shuffle; -rsi *vr* to mix; interfere.

mése *nm* month, month's pay.
méssa *nf* (*eccl*) Mass; m. in scéna (*theat*) staging; m. in màrcia (*aut*) starter.
messaggería *nf* haulage trade, mailcoach.
messaggèro *nm* -ra *nf* messenger, (*fig*) forerunner.
messàggio *nm* message.
messàle *nm* missal.
mèsse *nf* crop, harvest.
Messía *nm pr* Messiah.
messicàno *a nm* Mexican.
Mèssico *nm* (*geogr*) Mexico.
mésso *a* arranged, disposed, dressed; *nm* messenger, legate.
mestière *nm* trade, occupation, profession, job, craft.
mestízia *nf* sadness.
mèsto *a* sad, sorrowful.
méstola *nf* -lo *nm* ladle, trowel.
mestruazióne *nf* menstruation.
mèta *nf* destination, aim; (*of straw etc*) pile.
metà *nf* half, middle; a m. prèzzo half-price; a m. stràda half-way.
metabolísmo *nm* metabolism.
metafísica *nf* metaphysics *pl*.
metàfora *nf* metaphor.
metafòrico *pl* -ici *a* metaphoric(al).
metàllico *pl* -ici *a* metallic, metal.
metàllo *nm* metal; fatíca del m. metal fatigue.
metallurgía *nf* metallurgy.
metamòrfosi *nf* metamorphosis.
metàno *nm* methane.
metapsíchico *pl* -ici *a* extrasensory.
metèora *nf* meteor.
meteorología *nf* meteorology.
meteorològico *pl* -ici *a* meteorologic(al); bollettíno m. weather report; previsióni meteorologiche weather forecast; uffício m. meteorological office, weather bureau.
metíccio *a nm* half-breed.
meticolóso *a* meticulous.
metíle *nm* methyl.
metòdico *pl* -ici *a* methodical, business-like.
mètodo *nm* method.
metràggio *nm* length (in meters); (*cin*) córto m. short film; lúngo m. feature film.
mètrica *nf* prosody.
mètro *nm* (*measure*) meter.
metronòtte *nm* night watchman.
metròpoli *nf* metropolis.
metropolitàna *nf* underground (railway), subway.
metropolitàno *a* metropolitan; *nm* policeman.
méttere *vt* to put, place, set, cause, put forth; *vi* to lead; -rsi *vr* to put oneself, get into, begin, put on, turn.
mezzadría *nf* metayage, sharecropping.
mezzàdro *nm* métayer, sharecropper.
mezzalàna *nf* mixed wool and cotton cloth; shady person.

mezzalúna nf half-moon, crescent; mincing knife.
mezzanino nm entresol, mezzanine.
mezzàno a nm middle, medium; mediator, pimp.
mezzanòtte pl **mezzenotti** nf midnight, north.
mèzzo a half; ad half; nm middle; **in m.** a prep in the middle of; **mèzza età** middle-age.
mezzodí, mezzogiórno nm midday, noonday, south.
mezzómbra nf half-tone.
mezzotèrmine nm compromise.
mezzúccio nm mean expedient.
mi pron acc and dat (to) me; refl myself; nm (mus) E, mi.
miagolàre vi to mew.
mica nf crumb, grain; ad (fam) not at all.
míccia nf (for explosives etc) fuse.
Michèle nm pr Michael.
micidiàle a deadly, killing.
mício nm tom-cat, (fam) pussy.
microbo nm microbe.
micròfono nm microphone.
micromotóre nm small motor; motor-scooter.
microscòpico pl -ici a microscopic (al).
microscòpio nm microscope.
microsólco pl -chi nm long-playing record, microgroove.
midólla nf (bread)crumb, (fruit) pulp.
midóllo nm marrow, pith.
mièle nm honey.
mìetere vt to reap, mow down.
mietitóre nm -trìce nf reaper, mower.
mietitúra nf reaping.
migliàio nm about a thousand; **a migliàia** by thousands.
míglio nm millet; nm pl **míglia** mile; **distànza in míglia** mileage; pl **mígli** milestone.
miglioraménto nm improvement.
miglioràre vt to improve.
miglióre a better, best.
miglioría nf improvement, amelioration.
mignàtta nf leech (also fig).
mìgnolo nm little finger or toe; olive blossom.
migràre vi to migrate.
migratòrio a migratory.
migrazióne nf migration.
Milàno nf (geogr) Milan; **milanése** a nmf Milanese.
miliardàrio nm multimillionaire, billionaire.
miliàrdo nm billion.
miliàre a milestone; (med) miliary.
milionàrio nm millionaire.
milióne nm million; **milionèsimo** a millionth.
militànte a militant.
militàre vi to serve in the army, militate; a military; nm soldier.
militarménte ad militarily.

mílite nm militiaman, soldier, warrior; **M. Ignòto** Unknown Soldier.
milízia nf army, militia.
millantàre vt -rsi vr to boast (of).
millantatóre nm boaster, braggart.
millantería nf boast(ing).
mílle pl **míla** a thousand; **millèsimo** a thousandth.
millènnio nm millennium.
millepièdi nm millepede.
mílza nf spleen, milt.
mimetísmo nm (mil) camouflage.
mimetizzàre vt -rsi vr to camouflage.
mímica nf gestures pl; mimicry.
mímo nm mime; mimer.
mína nf mine; (of pencil) lead.
minàccia nf threat, menace.
minacciàre vt to threaten, menace.
minaccióso a threatening, menacing.
minàre vt to mine, undermine.
minatóre nm miner, collier.
minatòrio a threatening.
mineràle a mineral; nm mineral, ore.
mineralogía nf mineralogy.
mineràrio a mining.
minèstra nf soup.
mingherlíno a thin, delicate, slender.
miniàre vt to paint in miniature, illuminate (MSS etc).
miniatúra nf miniature.
minièra nf mine; **m. di carbóne** coal-mine.
minimaménte ad at all.
mínimo a least, lowest, smallest; nm minimum.
ministèro nm office, function, ministry; board, department; cabinet; **púbblico m.** public prosecutor, district attorney.
minístro nm minister, secretary of state.
minorànza nf minority.
minoràto a disabled, maimed; nm disabled person, mental deficient.
minorazióne nf diminution, disablement, mental deficiency.
minóre a less(er), smaller, younger, least, minor etc.
minorènne a under age; nm minor; **tribunàle déi minorènni** juvenile court.
minoríle a juvenile; **delinquènza m.** juvenile delinquency; **età m.** minority.
minúscolo a small, minute; **léttera minúscola** small letter; nm (typ) lower-case letter.
minúta nf rough copy, minute.
minúto a minute, small, detailed, petty; nm minute; **al m.** (by) retail.
minúzia nf trifle.
minuzióso a in detail, minute.
minúzzolo nm shred, small bit.
mío a my; pron mine; **i miéi** pl my family, my people.
míope a short-sighted; nm short-sighted person.
miopía nf short-sightedness (also fig).

míra nf aim, target, purpose.
miràbile a admirable, wonderful.
miracolàto a miraculously healed; nm miraculously healed person.
miràcolo nm miracle; wonder.
miracolóso a miraculous, wonderful.
miràggio nm mirage (also fig).
miràre vt to look at, admire, aim.
miríade nf myriad.
miríno nm (of gun etc) (fore)sight, (of camera) view-finder.
mírra nf myrrh.
mirtíllo nm bilberry.
mírto nm myrtle.
misantropía nf misanthropy.
misàntropo nm misanthrope.
miscèla nf mixture, blend; **m. anticongelànte** (aut) antifreeze.
miscellànea nf miscellany.
míschia nf fight, fray.
mischiàre vt to mix, shuffle; **-rsi** vr to mix (with).
miscredènte a unbelieving; nmf unbeliever.
miscredènza nf unbelief, disbelief.
miscúglio nm mixture, medley.
miseràbile a miserable, poor, despicable; nm poor wretch.
miseràndo, miserévole a pitiable.
misèria nf misery, destitution, distress; shortage; trifle; trouble.
misericòrdia nf mercy, pity.
misericordióso a merciful.
mísero a poor, wretched, mean.
misfàtto nm misdeed, crime.
misògino nm misogynist.
missàggio nm (cin) mixing; **tècnico del m.** mixer.
míssile a nm missile; **m. radiocomandàto** radio-controlled missile.
missilística nf rocketry.
missionàrio nm missionary.
missióne nf mission.
misterióso a mysterious.
mistèro nm mystery.
misticísmo nm mysticism.
místico pl **-ici** a nm mystic.
mistificàre vt to mystify, deceive.
místo a mixed; nm mixture; **tréno m.** train for passengers and freight.
mistúra nf mixture.
misúra nf measure(ment), size; moderation.
misuràbile a measurable.
misuràre vt to measure, estimate; limit; try on; pace; **-rsi** vr to compete; try on.
misuràto a measured; moderate, cautious.
míte a gentle, mild, moderate.
mitézza nf gentleness, meekness, mildness, moderation.
mítico a mythical.
mitigàre vt to allay, appease, relieve.
mitigazióne nf mitigation, alleviation.
míto nm myth.
mitología nf mythology.
mítra nf miter, submachine gun.
mitràglia nf (mil) grapeshot.

mitragliàre vt to machine gun.
mitragliatríce nf machine gun.
mitraglière nm machine gunner.
mittènte nmf sender.
mòbile a mobile, moving, movable, changeable, fickle; nm piece of furniture.
mobília nf furniture.
mobilière nm cabinet-maker.
mobilità nf mobility.
mobilitazióne nf mobilization.
moccióso nm snotty-nosed child; brat.
mòccolo nm candle end, small candle; (fam) swear word.
mòda nf fashion; **di m.** ad fashionable.
modalità nf modality, formality.
modèlla nf model; **modèllo** nm model, pattern.
modellàre vt to model, mold, fashion.
modenése a nmf (native) of Modena.
moderàre vt to moderate, curb, reduce; **-rsi** vr to restrain oneself.
moderàto a moderate.
moderazióne nf moderation.
modernità nf modernity.
modernizzàre vt to modernize.
modèrno a modern.
modestaménte ad modestly.
modèstia nf modesty.
modèsto a modest, moderate.
modicità nf moderateness, cheapness.
mòdico pl **-ici** a moderate, cheap.
modífica nf alteration, change.
modificàre vt to modify, mitigate.
modísta nf milliner.
modistería nf milliner's shop.
mòdo nm manner, way; **ad ógni m.** anyhow, anyway; **a m.** carefully, properly; **persóna a m.** well-bred person; **per m. di dire** so to speak.
modulàre vt to modulate, formulate.
modulazióne nf modulation.
mòdulo nm (printed) form, blank.
mògano nm mahogany.
mòggio nm bushel.
mògio a abashed, quiet, crestfallen.
móglie pl **mógli** nf wife.
moina nf blandishment, wheedling.
mòla nf grindstone, millstone.
molàre a nm molar; vt to grind, whet.
mòle nf mass, bulk, size.
molècola nf molecule.
molestàre vt to molest, bother, vex, tease.
molèstia nf trouble, bother.
molèsto a troublesome.
mòlla nf (tec) spring; pl tongs pl.
mollàre vti to loose(n), leave off, yield.
mòlle a soft, wet, pliable, flabby, weak, loose; nm soft part; **méttere in m.** vt to soak, steep.
molléggio nm suspension, springing.
molleménte ad softly, weakly, languidly.

mollétta nf hair-grip, clothespeg, clothespin; pl tongs pl.
mollézza nf softness, feebleness, effeminacy, looseness; pl luxury.
mollíca nf crumb.
mollúsco pl -chi nm mollusc.
mòlo nm pier, quay.
molòsso nm mastiff.
moltéplice a manifold, multiple.
moltiplicàre vt -rsi vr to multiply.
moltiplicazióne nf multiplication.
moltiplicità nf multiplicity.
moltitúdine nf multitude.
mólto a much, (time) long; ad very, much, greatly; nm much, a lot.
momentàneo a temporary, passing.
moménto nm moment, time, chance; un m. ad a while.
mònaca nf nun.
mònaco pl -aci nm monk.
Mònaco nf (geogr) Munich; nm (geogr) Monaco.
monàrca nm monarch.
monarchía nf monarchy.
monàrchico pl -ici a monarchic(al).
monastèro nm monastery.
monàstico pl -ici a monastic.
moncheríno nm stump.
mónco pl -chi a maimed, mutilated; nm maimed person.
moncóne nm stump.
mondanità nf worldliness, society life.
mondàno a mundane, worldly, society; víta mondàna society life; mondàna nf prostitute.
mondàre vt to clean, peel, winnow, (fig) cleanse.
mondaríso nf rice-picker.
mondiàle a worldwide, world, universal.
móndo a clean, pure; nm world, life, everybody; un m. di a world of.
monèlla nf tomboy.
monellería nf prank.
monèllo nm little rogue, street boy, urchin.
monéta nf money, coin, small change.
mòngolo a Mongolian; nm Mongol.
mongolòide a nm mongoloid.
monile nm jewel; necklace.
mònito nm admonition, warning.
monitóre nm monitor, warner.
monòcolo nm monocle; one-eyed person.
monogamía nf monogamy.
monografía nf monograph.
monogràmma nm monogram.
monòlogo pl -ghi nm monologue, soliloquy.
monopàttino nm scooter.
monoplàno nm monoplane.
monopòlio nm monopoly.
monopolizzàre vt to monopolize.
monopósto a nm (aut av) single-seater.
monosíllabo nm monosyllable.
monotonía nf monotony.
monòtono a monotonous.

monsignóre nm monsignor.
montacàrichi nm freight elevator, elevator hoist.
montàggio nm (mech) assembling, glazing; (cin) montage, cutting.
montàgna nf mountain.
montagnóso a mountainous.
montanàro a mountain, of the mountain; nm mountaineer, highlander.
montàno a mountain; paése m. mountain village.
montàre vti to mount, set, furnish; climb, rise; (impers) to matter; -rsi vr to get excited; get swollen-headed.
montatóio nm footboard, running board, stirrup.
montatúra nf fitting, (of spectacles) frame.
montavivànde nm service lift, dumbwaiter.
mónte nm mount, heap; m. di pietà pawnbroker's; andàre a m. to come to nothing.
montóne nm ram, mutton.
montuosità nf hilliness, hill.
montuóso a hilly.
monumentàle a monumental.
monuménto nm monument.
mòra nf blackberry, mulberry; delay, respite; game of mor(r)a.
moràle a moral; nf morals pl, ethics, moral; nm morale.
moralísta nmf moralist.
moralità nf morality, morals pl.
moralizzàre vti to moralize.
morbidaménte ad softly, tenderly.
morbidézza nf softness, leniency.
mòrbido a soft, tender.
morbíllo nm (med) measles.
mòrbo nm disease, plague.
morbosità nf morbidness.
morbóso a morbid.
mordàce a biting, pungent, sarcastic.
mordènte a biting, caustic; nm (chem) mordant; (mus) mordent.
mòrdere vt to bite, sting.
morèllo a jet-black; nm black horse.
morènte a dying, fading; nmf dying man, woman.
morésco pl -chi a Moorish.
morétta nf brunette, Negro girl; morétto Negro boy.
morfína nf morphia, morphine.
moría nf plague, high mortality.
moribóndo a dying, moribund.
morigeràto a temperate, moderate, of good morals.
moríre vi to die; nm death.
mormoràre vti to murmur, whisper, grumble.
mormorío nm murmur, rustling, whisper, complaining, gossip.
mòro a black, dark-skinned; nm mulberry tree, Moor, Negro.
moróso a defaulting, insolvent; nm (fam) sweetheart, boy-friend.
mòrsa nf (mech) vise.
morsicàre vt to bite.

morsicatúra *nf* bite.
mòrso *nm* bite; pang; morsel, bit.
mortàio *nm* mortar.
mortàle *a nm* mortal.
mortalità *nf* mortality.
mortarétto *nm* firecracker.
mòrte *nf* death.
mortèlla *nf* myrtle.
mortificàre *vt* to humiliate, mortify, deaden; **-rsi** *vr* to mortify oneself, be mortified.
mortificazióne *nf* humiliation, mortification.
mòrto *a* dead, deceased.
mortòrio *nm* funeral, burial.
mortuàrio *a* mortuary.
mosàico *pl* **-ici** *nm* mosaic.
mósca *nf* fly.
Mósca *nf* (*geogr*) Moscow; **moscovíta** *a nm* Muscovite.
moscatèllo *nm* muscatel grape.
moscàto *nm* muscat(el); **nóce moscàta** nutmeg.
moscerìno *nm* gnat, midge.
moschèa *nf* mosque.
moschettière *nm* musketeer.
moschétto *nm* musket.
móscio *a* flabby, soft; (*fig*) dispirited.
moscóne *nm* big fly, bluebottle.
Mosè *nm pr* Moses.
Mosèlla *nf pr* (*geogr*) Moselle.
mòssa *nf* move(ment).
mostàrda *nf* Italian sweet fruit pickles; mustard.
mósto *nm* must.
mostóso *a* full of must.
móstra *nf* exhibition, show, display; pretense.
mostràre *vt* to show, display, point out, prove; pretend; **-rsi** *vr* to show oneself, appear.
mostrìna *nf* (*mil*) collar badge.
móstro *nm* monster, prodigy.
mostruosità *nf* monstrosity.
mostruóso *a* monstrous, enormous.
mòta *nf* mire, mud.
motivàre *vt* to give reason for, justify, motivate.
motivazióne *nf* motivation.
motívo *nm* motive, motif; **a m. di** on account of, owing to.
mòto *nm* motion, exercise; revolt; impulse; *nf* motor-cycle.
motocarrozzétta *nf* side-car.
motociclétta *nf* **-cíclo** *nm* motorcycle.
motofurgóne *nm* motorcycle delivery van.
motonàve *nf* motorship.
motopescheréccio *nm* motor trawler.
motóre *nm* motor, engine.
motorìno *nm* **m. d'avviaménto** (*aut*) starter-motor.
motorizzàre *vt* to motorize.
motoscàfo *nm* motor-boat.
motteggiàre *vti* to banter, joke, make fun of.
mòtto *nm* word, saying, motto.
movènte *nm* motive, reason.

movimentàto *a* lively, busy, eventful; **stràda movimentàta** busy street.
moviménto *nm* movement, traffic.
mozióne *nf* motion.
mozzàre *vt* to cut off.
mozzicóne *nm* butt, stub; **m. di sigarétta** cigarette-end.
mózzo *nm* cabin-boy, stable-boy; (*tec*) *a* cut off, docked.
mòzzo *nm* wheel hub.
múcca *nf* cow.
múcchio *nm* heap, pile.
múco *pl* **-chi** *nm* mucus.
múda *nf* molt, molting season.
múffa *nf* mold.
muffíre *vi* to become moldy.
muffíto *a* moldy.
mugghiàre, muggíre *vi* to bellow, howl, roar.
múgghio, muggíto *nm* bellow, roar, howling.
mughétto *nm* lily-of-the-valley.
mugnàio *nm* miller.
mugolàre *vi* to whine, yelp.
mulattièra *nf* mule-track.
mulattière *nm* muleteer.
mulàtto *nm* mulatto.
mulièbre *a* feminine, womanly.
mulinèllo *nm* whirlpool, whirlwind, (*tec*) windlass.
mulíno *nm* mill.
múlo *nm* mule.
múlta *nf* fine.
multàre *vt* to fine.
multicolóre *a* many-colored.
multifórme *a* multiform.
múltiplo *a* multiple.
múmmia *nf* (Egyptian) mummy.
mummificàre *vt* to mummify.
múngere *vt* to milk, (*fig*) exploit.
municipàle *a* municipal, of the town.
município *nm* municipality, town hall.
munificènza *nf* generosity, munificence.
munífico *pl* **-ici** *a* generous, munificent.
muníre *vt* to fortify, furnish; **-rsi** *vr* to equip oneself, fortify oneself.
munizióne *nf* (*mil*) ammunition, munitions *pl*.
muòvere *vt* **-rsi** *vr* to move, stir.
muràglia *nf* wall.
muràle *a* mural, wall.
muràre *vti* to build, wall up; **-rsi** *vr* to shut oneself up.
muratóre *nm* bricklayer, mason.
muratúra *nf* masonry, brickwork.
murèna *nf* moray eel.
múro *nm* wall; *m pl* **múri** walls; *f pl* **múra** (*town*) walls.
Músa *nf* Muse.
muschiàto *a* musky; **ròsa muschiàta** musk-rose.
múschio *nm* musk, moss.
muscolàre *a* muscular.
múscolo *nm* muscle.
muscolóso *a* muscular.
muscóso *a* mossy.

musèo *nm* museum.
museruòla *nf* muzzle.
múṣica *nf* music, band.
muṣicàle *a* musical, music.
muṣicànte *nm* musician, bandsman.
muṣicísta *nmf* musician, composer.
múṣo *nm* muzzle, snout; (*fam*) face; **fàre il m.** to pull a long face; **avere il m.** to sulk.
mussàre *vi* to foam, froth.
mussolína *nf* muslin.
mussulmàno *a nm* Mussulman.
mustàcchi *nm pl* moustache.
múta *nf* change, molt, set; (*of hounds*) pack.
mutàbile *a* changeable.
mutabilità *nf* changeability.
mutaménto *nm* change, alteration, variation.
mutànde *nf pl* drawers *pl*, pants *pl*, underpants; **mutandíne** *nf pl* panties; **m. da bàgno** swimming trunks; **m. da ginnàstica** gym shorts.
mutàre *vt* **-rsi** *vr* to change.
mutévole *a* changeable.
mutilàre *vt* to maim, mutilate.
mutilàto *a* maimed, mutilated; *nm* ripple; **m. di guèrra** war cripple.
mutilazióne *nf* mutilation.
mútiṣmo *nm* dumbness, muteness, taciturnity.
múto *a* dumb, mute.
mútua *nf* (**càssa**) **m.** medical insurance.
mutualménte *a* mutually.
mutuànte *a* lending, loan; *nmf* lender.
mutuàre *vt* to borrow, lend.
mútuo *a* mutual, reciprocal; *nm* loan, mortgage.

N

nàcchere *nf pl* castanets *pl.*
nàfta *nf* naphtha, diesel oil; **a n.** oil-fired.
naftalína *nf* naphthalene; moth-balls *pl.*
nàiade *nf* naiad, water nymph.
nàilon *nm* nylon.
nàno *nm* dwarf; *a* dwarf(ish).
Nàpoli *nf* (*geogr*) Naples; **napoletàno** *a nm* Neapolitan.
nàppa *nf* tassel, tuft.
narcíṣo *nm* daffodil, narcissus.
narcòtico *pl* **-ici** *a nm* narcotic.
naríce *nf* nostril.
narràre *vt* to narrate, relate, tell.
narratíva *nf* narrative, fiction.
narratóre *nm* **-tríce** *nf* narrator, story-teller.
narrazióne *nf* narration, tale.
naṣàle *a* nasal.
nascènte *a* dawning, rising.
nàscere *vi* to be born, originate, rise.
nàscita *nf* birth; extraction, descent.
nascitúro *a nm* unborn (child).
nascóndere *vt* to conceal, hide; **-rsi** *vr* to hide oneself.

nascondíglio *nm* hiding place.
nascostaménte *ad* secretly; stealthily.
nascósto *a* hidden, secret, under-hand; **di n.** secretly, stealthily.
naṣèllo *nm* (*fish*) hake, whiting.
nàṣo *nm* nose; **a lúme di n.** by guesswork.
nàspo *nm* (*tec*) reel, winder.
nàstro *nm* band, ribbon, tape.
nastúrzio *nm* (*bot*) nasturtium, water-cress.
natàle *a* native; **Natàle** *nm* Christ-mas; **natàli** *nm pl* birth.
natalità *nf* birth-rate.
natalízio *a* (of) Christmas; birthday; *nm* birthday.
natànte *a* floating; *nm* craft.
nàtica *nf* buttock.
natío *a* native.
natività *nf* nativity.
natívo *a* native, natural; *nm* native.
nàto *a* born, risen, sprung up; **nàta** née.
nàtta *nf* wen.
natúra *nf* nature, kind; **pagàre in n.** to pay in kind.
naturàle *a* genuine, natural.
naturalézza *nf* naturalness.
naturalizzàre *vt* to naturalize.
naturalizzazióne *nf* naturalization.
naturalménte *ad* naturally, of course.
naufragàre *vi* to be (ship)wrecked.
naufràgio *nm* (ship)wreck, failure.
nàufrago *pl* **-ghi** *a nm* shipwrecked (man).
nàuṣea *nf* nausea, sickness, loathing.
nauṣeabóndo, nauṣeante *a* loath-some, nauseous.
nauṣeàre *vt* to disgust, nauseate.
nàutica *nf* nautical science.
nàutico *pl* **-ici** *a* nautical.
navàle *a* naval.
nàve *nf* ship, vessel.
navétta *nf* shuttle.
navicèlla *nf* bark, small ship.
navigàbile *a* navigable; **canàle n.** waterway.
navigànte *nm* sailor.
navigàre *vti* to navigate, sail; **n. in cattive àcque** to be badly off.
navigàto *a* experienced.
navigatóre *nm* navigator.
navigazióne *nf* navigation.
navíglio *nm* canal; fleet.
nazionàle *a* national; home-grown.
nazionaliṣmo *nm* nationalism.
nazionalità *nf* nationality.
nazionalizzazióne *nf* nationaliza-tion.
nazióne *nf* nation.
naziṣta *a nmf* Nazi.
nazzarèno *a nm* Nazarene.
ne *pron and ad* of him, his, of her, hers; of it, its; of them, theirs; from there; any, some.
né *cj* neither, nor; **né . . . né** neither . . . nor.
neànche *ad* not even; *cj* neither.

nébbia *nf* fog, mist.
nebbióso *a* foggy, hazy.
nebulizzàre *vt* to atomize, vaporize.
nebulizzatóre *nm* atomizer, vaporizer.
nebulósa *nf* nebula.
nebulóso *a* nebulous, hazy.
nécessaire (*Fr*) *nm* beauty case; **n. per únghie** manicure set.
necessariaménte *ad* necessarily.
necessàrio *a* necessary, needful; *nm* what is necessary.
necessità *nf* necessity, need, poverty.
necessitàre *vt* to necessitate; *vi* to be necessary.
necròforo *nm* gravedigger.
necròlògio *nm* obituary, register of deaths.
nefandézza *nf* infamy.
nefàndo *a* abominable, execrable.
nefàsto *a* ill-omened, unlucky.
nefríte *nf* nephritis.
negàbile *a* deniable.
negàre *vt* to deny.
negatíva *nf* denial, negative.
negatívo *a* negative, unfavorable.
negàto *a* denied, unfit; **èssere n. a qc** to be unsuited for sth.
negazióne *nf* denial, negative, negation.
neghittóso *a* slothful.
neglètto *a* neglected, untidy.
negligènte *a* careless, negligent.
negligènza *nf* carelessness, negligence.
negoziàbile *a* negotiable.
negoziànte *nmf* dealer, shopkeeper, tradesman.
negoziàre *vti* to negotiate, deal, trade.
negoziàti *nm pl* negotiation(s).
negózio *nm* shop, store; trade, transaction.
negrièro *nm* slave-trader; (*fig*) slave-driver.
négro *a nm* Negro.
negromànte *nmf* necromancer.
negromanzía *nf* necromancy.
némbo *nm* (storm)cloud.
nemíco *pl* -ici *a* hostile, harmful; *nm* enemy.
nemméno *ad* not even.
nènia *nf* dirge, plaintive song.
nèo *nm* blemish, (*on the skin*) mole.
neologísmo *nm* neologism.
neomicína *nf* neomycin.
nèon *nm* neon; **inségna al n.** neon sign.
neonàto *a nm* newborn (child).
neppúre *ad* not even.
neràstro *a* blackish.
nerbàta *nf* blow with a whip.
nèrbo *nm* nerve; whip; strength.
néro *a* black, dark; *nm* black.
nervatúra *nf* nervous system, nervation; ribbing.
nèrvo *nm* nerve, vigor; **avére i nèrvi** to be in a bad temper.
nervosità *nf* **nervosísmo** *nm* nerves, nervousness.

nervóso *a* nervous, excitable; *nm* irritability.
nèsci: fare il n. to pretend ignorance.
nèspola *nf* medlar; **nèspolo** *nm* medlar-tree.
nèsso *nm* connection, link.
nessúno *pron* nobody, no one; *a* no.
nettaménte *ad* cleanly, clearly.
nettapípe *inv nm* pipe-cleaner.
nettàre *vt* to clean, cleanse.
nèttare *nm* nectar.
nettézza *nf* cleanliness; **n. urbàna** garbage collectors *pl*.
nétto *a* clean; distinct; exact; net.
neuròlogo *pl* -ogi *nm* neurologist.
neutràle *a nm* neutral.
neutralità *nf* neutrality.
neutralizzàre *vt* to neutralize.
nèutro *a* neutral; *nm* neuter.
nevàio *nm* snowfield, glacier.
néve *nf* snow; **fiòcco di n.** snowflake.
nevicàre *vi* to snow.
nevicàta *nf* snowfall, snowstorm.
nevíschio *nm* sleet.
nevóso *a* snowy.
nevralgía *nf* neuralgia.
nevrastenía *nf* neurasthenia.
nevrastènico *pl* -ici *a nm* neurasthenic.
nevròsi *nf* (*med*) neurosis.
nevròtico *pl* -ici *a nm* neurotic.
nevvéro? *interj* isn't it (so)?
níbbio *nm* (*bird*) kite.
nícchia *nf* niche.
nicchiàre *vi* to hesitate.
Niccolò, Nicòla *nm pr* Nicholas.
níchel *nm* nickel.
nicotína *nf* nicotine.
nidiàta *nf* brood, nestful.
nidificàre *vi* to build a nest.
nído *nm* nest, haunt.
niènte *pron and nm* nothing.
nientediméno *ad* no less.
Nigèria *nf* (*geogr*) Nigeria.
Nílo *nm* (*geogr*) Nile.
nínfa *nf* nymph.
ninfèa *nf* water-lily.
ninnanànna *nf* lullaby.
ninnàre *vt* to lull, sing to sleep.
nínnolo *nm* trifle, trinket.
nipóte *nmf* grandson, granddaughter; nephew, niece.
nippònico *pl* -ici *a* Japanese.
nitidézza *nf* clearness.
nítido *a* clear, distinct.
nitóre *nm* neatness, brightness.
nitràto *nm* nitrate.
nitríre *vi* to neigh.
nitríto *nm* neigh.
nítro *nm* niter, saltpeter.
nitrògeno *nm* nitrogen.
níveo *a* snowy, snow-white.
Nízza *nf* (*geogr*) Nice; **nizzàrdo** *a nm* (native) of Nice.
no *ad* no.
nòbile *a nm* noble.
nobiliàre *a* aristocratic.
nobilitàre *vt* to ennoble.
nobilménte *ad* nobly.
nobiltà *nf* nobility, nobleness.

nòcca *nf* knuckle.
nocchièro *nm* pilot, steersman.
nòcciolo *nm* kernel, stone; (*fig*) point, gist.
nocci(u)òla *nf* hazel-nut; **nocci(u)òla** *nm* hazel tree; **nocciolína americàna** peanut.
nòce *nf* walnut; *nm* walnut tree.
nocívo *a* harmful, hurtful.
nòdo *nm* knot.
nodóso *a* gnarled, knotty.
Noè *nm pr* Noah.
nói *pron* we, us.
nòia *nf* boredom, vexation.
noiosità *nf* boredom, bother.
noióso *a* tiresome, boring.
noleggiaménto *nm* hiring, chartering.
noleggiàre *vt* to hire, charter.
noléggio, nòlo *nm* hire, rental; **a n.** for (on) hire.
nolènte *a* unwilling; **volènte o n.** willy-nilly.
nòmade *a* nomadic; *nmf* nomad.
nóme *nm* name, noun; **n. pròprio** first name, Christian name.
nomèa *nf* reputation, notoriety.
nomenclatúra *nf* nomenclature.
nomígnolo *nm* nickname.
nòmina *nf* appointment.
nominàle *a* nominal.
nominàre *vt* to name, appoint.
nominatívo *a* nominative; *nm* nominative, name.
non *ad* not; **non ... che** *ad* but, only.
nonagenàrio *a nm* nonagenarian.
nonagèsimo *a nm* ninetieth.
noncurànte *a* careless, heedless.
noncurànza *nf* carelessness, heedlessness.
nondiméno *ad* nevertheless, still, yet.
nònna *nf* grandmother; **nònno** *nm* grandfather.
nonnúlla *nm* nothing, trifle.
nòno *a* ninth.
nonostànte *prep* in spite of, notwithstanding; *ad* nevertheless.
nonpertànto *ad* nevertheless, still.
nonsènso *nm* nonsense.
nontiscordardimé *nm* forget-me-not.
nòrd *nm* north; **a n.** to the north; **n. est** north-east; **n. òvest** north-west.
nòrdico *pl* **-ici** *a* northern; *nm* northerner.
Norimbèrga *nf* (*geogr*) Nuremberg.
nòrma *nf* rule, standard, directions; **a n. di légge** according to law.
normàle *a nm* normal.
normalità *nf* normality.
normalizzàre *vt* to normalize.
normalménte *ad* normally.
Normandía *nf* (*geogr*) Normandy.
norvegése *a nmf* Norwegian.
Norvègia *nf* (*geogr*) Norway.
nostalgía *nf* homesickness.
nostàlgico *pl* **-ici** *a* nostalgic.
nostràle, nostràno *a* domestic,

home, of one's own country; **prodòtti nostràli** home produce.
nòstro *poss a and pron* our, ours.
nostròmo *nm* boatswain.
nòta *nf* note, mark, list; **n. a piè di pàgina** footnote; **blòcco per nòte** scribbling block, scratch pad.
notàbile *a nm* notable.
notàio *nm* notary.
notàre *vt* to note, notice; **fàrsi n.** *vr* to attract attention.
notaríle *a* notarial.
nòtes *nm* notebook, agenda.
notévole *a* noticeable, remarkable.
notevolménte *ad* considerably, greatly.
notificàre *vt* to notify.
notífica, notificazióne *nf* communication, notification.
notízia *nf* (piece of) news.
notiziàrio *nm* news bulletin; (*cin*) newsreel.
nòto *a* famous, notorious, (well-) known.
notorietà *nf* notoriety.
notòrio *a* notorious.
nottàmbulo *a* night-walking; *nm* night-walker; somnambulist.
nottàta *nf* (duration of a) night.
nòtte *nf* night; **di n.** by night.
nòttola *nf* bat.
nottúrno *a* night(ly), nocturnal; *nm* (*mus*) nocturne.
novànta *a* ninety; **novantènne** 90-year-old; **novantèsimo** ninetieth.
nòve *a* nine.
novecènto *a nm* nine hundred; twentieth century.
novèlla *nf* short story, tale.
novellière *nm* short-story writer.
novellíno *a* inexperienced; *nm* beginner, inexperienced person.
novellística *nf* short-story writing, fiction.
novèllo *a* new.
novèmbre *nm* November.
nòvero *nm* number, class, category.
novilúnio *nm* new moon.
novità *nf* newness, novelty, news.
noviziàto *nm* apprenticeship, novitiate.
novízio *nm* novice, beginner, apprentice.
nozióne *nf* idea, notion.
nòzze *nf pl* wedding, marriage.
núbe *nf* cloud.
nubifràgio *nm* cloudburst, downpour.
núbile *a* (*of women*) unmarried, marriageable; *nf* spinster.
núca *nf* nape (of the neck).
nucleàre *a* nuclear.
núcleo *nm* nucleus.
nudaménte *ad* nakedly, barely, simply, plainly.
nudità *nf* nakedness, nudity.
núdo *a* naked, bare; *nm* nude.
núlla *nm and pron* nothing.
nullaòsta *nm* (*eccl*) nihil obstat; permit; permission.

nullatenènte *nm f* person who owns nothing.
nullità *nf* nonentity, nullity, worthlessness.
núllo *a* null and void.
núme *nm* deity.
numeràle *a nm* numeral.
numeràre *vt* to number.
numerazióne *nf* numbering.
numèrico *pl* -ici *a* numerical.
número *nm* number.
numeróso *a* numerous.
numismàtica *nf* numismatics *pl*.
núnzio *nm* nuncio.
nuòcere *vt* to harm, hurt, damage.
nuòra *nf* daughter-in-law.
nuotàre *vi* to swim.
nuotàta *nf* swim.
nuotatóre *nm* swimmer; **n. subàcqueo** skin-diver.
nuòto *nm* swimming; **passàre a n.** to swim across; **n. subàcqueo** skindiving.
nuòva *nf* (piece of) news.
Nuòva York *nf* (*geogr*) New York.
Nuòva Zelànda *nf* (*geogr*) New Zealand.
nuòvo *a* new; **di n.** again.
nutríce *nf* wet nurse.
nutriènte *a* nourishing, nutritious.
nutriménto *nm* nourishment.
nutríre *vt* to feed, nourish, foster; **-rsi (di)** *vr* to feed (on).
nutritívo *a* nourishing, nutritious.
nutrizióne *nf* feeding, nourishment, nutrition.
nùvola *nf* -lo *nm* cloud.
nùvolo, nuvolóso *a* overcast, cloudy.
nuziàle *a* wedding.

O

o *cj* or, or else; **o ... o** either ... or, whether ... or; **o l'úno o l'àltro** *pron* either; *interj* oh!
òasi *nf* oasis.
obbediènte *etc v* **ubbidiènte** *etc*.
obbligàre (a) *vt* to compel, force, oblige; **-rsi** *vr* to bind oneself, undertake.
obbligazióne *nf* obligation; (*com*) bond, debenture.
òbbligo *pl* -ghi *nm* duty, obligation.
obbròbrio *nm* disgrace.
obesità *nf* obesity.
obèso *a* corpulent, obese.
òbice *nm* (*mil*) howitzer.
obiettàre *vt* to object.
obiettività *nf* objectivity, impartiality.
obiettívo *a* objective, impartial; *nm* objective; lens.
obiezióne *nf* objection.
obitòrio *nm* mortuary, morgue.
oblazióne *nf* donation, oblation.
oblío *nm* forgetfulness, oblivion.
obliquità *nf* obliquity.
oblíquo *a* oblique, underhand.
obliteràre *vt* to obliterate.

oblò *nm* porthole.
òboe *nm* (*mus*) oboe.
òbolo *nm* donation.
òca *nf* goose; **pèlle d'o.** gooseflesh.
occasionàle *a* casual, chance.
occasióne *nf* occasion, opportunity; **d'o.** second-hand.
occhiàia *nf* eye-socket, dark circle under eye.
occhialàio *nm* optician.
occhiàli *nm pl* spectacles *pl*, glasses *pl*.
occhialíno *nm* lorgnette.
occhialúto *a* bespectacled.
occhiàta *nf* glance.
occhieggiàre *vt* to eye, ogle; *vi* to peep, peer.
occhièllo *nm* buttonhole, eyelet.
occhiétto *nm* fàre l'o. a qlcu to wink at s.o.
òcchio *nm* eye; **a còlpo d'o.** at first sight; **in un bàtter d'o.** in a twinkling of an eye; **a quàttro òcchi** *ad* privately.
occidentàle *a* west(ern).
occidènte *nm* west.
occorrènte *a nm* necessary, requisite.
occorrènza *nf* circumstance, necessity, need; **all'o.** in case of need.
occórrere *vi impers* to be necessary, need, happen; **occórre mólto tèmpo** much time is required; **mi occórrono sòldi** I need money.
occúlto *a* hidden, occult.
occupànte *a* occupying; *nmf* occupant, occupier.
occupàre *vt* to occupy; **-rsi (di)** *vr* to attend (to), be busy (with), mind.
occupàto *a* engaged, busy.
occupazióne *nf* occupation.
oceànico *pl* -ici *a* oceanic.
oceàno *nm* ocean.
oculàre *a* eye, ocular; *nm* eye-piece; **testimóne o.** eye-witness.
oculatézza *nf* cautiousness, circumspection, wariness.
oculàto *a* wary, prudent.
oculísta *nm* eye specialist, oculist.
òde *nf* ode.
odiàre *vt* to hate, detest.
odièrno *a* of today, today's, modern.
òdio *pl* òdii *nm* hatred, hate.
odióso *a* hateful, odious.
odissèa *nf* odyssey.
odontoiàtra *nm* odontologist, dentist.
odontoiatría *nf* odontology, dentistry.
odoràre *vti* to smell, scent.
odoràto *nm* (sense of) smell.
odóre *nm* smell, odor, scent.
odoróso *a* fragrant, odorous.
Ofèlia *nf pr* Ophelia.
offèndere *vt* to offend, injure; **-rsi** *vr* to be offended, take offense.
offensíva *nf* (*mil*) offensive.
offensívo *a* offensive, insulting.
offerènte *nmf* bidder, offerer.
offèrta *nf* offer(ing); (*com*) tender, bid.

offertòrio nm offertory.
offésa nf offense, wrong.
offéso a offended, injured.
officína nf works, workshop.
offício v **uffício.**
officióso a obliging; unofficial.
offríre vt to bid, offer.
offuscaménto nm dimming, darkening, obscuring.
oggettivaménte ad objectively.
oggettívo a objective, impartial.
oggètto nm article, object, subject.
òggi ad today; o. a òtto today week.
oggidì, oggigiórno ad nowadays.
ógni a each, every; **in o. luògo** ad everywhere; **in o. mòdo** ad anyhow; **o. tànto** ad every now and then.
Ognissànti nm All Saints' Day.
ognóra ad always.
ognúno pron each, everybody, everyone.
ohibò interj come now!
ohimè interj alas!
olà interj hello!
Olànda nf (geogr) Holland.
olandése a Dutch; nm Dutchman, (the) Dutch (language); nf Dutchwoman.
oleàndro nm oleander.
oleàto a oiled; **càrta oleàta** greaseproof paper, waxed paper.
oleifício nm oil mill.
oleodótto nm (oil) pipeline.
oleóso a greasy, oily.
olfàtto nm (sense of) smell.
oliatóre nm (mech) oil-can, oiler.
olièra nf (oil) cruet.
oligarchía nf oligarchy.
Olímpia nf pr Olympia.
olimpíade nf (usually pl) (sport) Olympic games pl, Olympiad.
olímpico pl **-ici** a Olympic, Olympian; **càlma olímpica** imperturbability.
olimpiónico pl **-ici** a (sport) Olympic; nm (sport) Olympian.
òlio nm oil.
olíva nf olive; **olívo** nm olive tree.
olivàstro a olive(-colored).
olivéto nm olive grove.
Olívia nf pr Olive, Olivia.
ólmo nm elm.
olocàusto nm holocaust, sacrifice.
ològrafo nm holograph.
oltraggiàre vt to outrage, insult.
oltràggio nm outrage, insult.
oltraggióso a outrageous.
oltrànza, ad ad to the bitter end.
óltre ad and prep further, beyond, over; **o. a, che** besides.
oltremàre ad beyond the sea(s), oversea(s).
oltremòdo ad exceedingly.
oltrepassàre vt to go beyond, surpass, outrun, exceed.
oltretómba nm beyond, hereafter.
omàggio nm homage; **còpia in o.** presentation copy; **omàggi** pl respects pl; **in o.** free.
ombelicàle a umbilical.

ombelíco pl **-íchi** nm navel.
ómbra nf shade, shadow; **all'o. in** the shade.
ombreggiàre vt to shade.
ombrellàio nm umbrella maker.
ombrèllo nm umbrella; **ombrellíno** parasol; **ombrellóne** (beach) umbrella.
ombrétto nm (cosm) eye shadow.
ombróso a (places) shady; (people) touchy.
òmero nm shoulder.
Oméro nm pr Homer.
omertà nf (conspiracy of) silence.
ométtere vt to leave out, omit.
omicída a homicidal; nmf homicide, murderer.
omicídio nm homicide, murder.
omissióne nf omission.
òmnibus nm omnibus, bus.
omogèneo a homogeneous.
omòlogo pl **-ghi** a homologous.
omònimo a homonymous; nm homonym, namesake.
omosessuàle a homosexual.
óncia nf ounce.
ónda nf wave; **ondàta** nf big wave (also fig).
ónde ad whence; pron whereby; cj so that, in order that; wherefore.
ondeggiaménto nm rocking, swaying; fluttering, wavering.
ondeggiàre vi to rock, wave; hesitate.
ondóso a undulatory, waving.
ondulàre vt to wave; vi to undulate; **-rsi i capèlli** to wave one's hair.
ondulàto a wavy, undulating, corrugated.
ondulazióne nf undulation; (hair) wave.
ònere nm burden.
oneróso a burdensome, onerous.
onestà nf honesty, uprightness, fairness.
onestaménte ad honestly, modestly, decently.
onèsto a fair, honest, upright.
ònice nf onyx.
onnipossènte, onnipotènte a almighty, omnipotent.
onniscìenza nf omniscience.
onnívoro a omnivorous.
onomàstico pl **-ici** a nm name-day.
onomatopèa nf onomatopoeia.
onorànza nf honor, solemnity.
onoràre vt to honor, do credit to; **-rsi (di)** vr to be proud (of).
onorário a honorary; nm fee, honorarium; **cittadíno o.** freeman.
onorataménte ad honorably.
onoràto a honored; honorable.
onóre nm honor.
onorévole a honorable, (also title of parliamentary deputies).
onorevolménte ad honorably.
onorificènza nf honor, title, decoration.
onorífico pl **-ici** a honorific.
ónta nf disgrace, shame; **ad o. di** in spite of.

ontàno *nm* alder.
opacità *nf* opacity, opaqueness.
opàco *pl* -**chi** *a* opaque, dull, matt.
opàle *nm* opal.
òpera *nf* work, action; opera; institution.
operàbile *a* operable, workable.
operàio *a* working; *nm* workman.
operàre *vti* to work, act, operate; **o. qlcu** operate on s.o.
operàto *a* (*cloth*) fancy; *nm* conduct, action; one who has been operated upon.
operatóre *nm* operator; (*cin*) cameraman.
operatòrio *a* operative; surgical; **sàla operatòria** operating theatre.
operazióne *nf* operation.
operosità *nf* activity, industry.
operóso *a* active, industrious.
opifício *nm* factory, works.
opinàre *vi* to be of the opinion.
opinióne *nf* opinion, contention.
òppio *nm* opium.
opponènte *a* opposing, opponent; *nmf* opponent.
oppórre *vt* -**rsi** *vr* to oppose, object.
opportunaménte *ad* opportunely, appropriately.
opportunísta *nmf* opportunist.
opportunità *nf* opportuneness; opportunity.
opportúno *a* opportune.
opposizióne *nf* opposition.
oppósto *a nm* opposite.
oppressióne *nf* oppression.
oppressívo *a* oppressive.
opprèsso *a* oppressed.
oppressóre *nm* oppressor.
opprimènte *a* oppressive.
opprímere *vt* to oppress, overwhelm.
oppugnàre *vt* to attack; (*fig*) impugn.
oppúre *cj* or (else).
optàre *vi* to opt.
opulènto *a* opulent, rich.
opulènza *nf* opulence, wealth.
opúscolo *nm* pamphlet.
óra *nf* hour, time; **che óre sóno?** what time is it?; *ad* now; presently; **or óra** just now; **óra che** *cj* now that.
oràcolo *nm* oracle.
òrafo *nm* goldsmith.
oràle *a nm* oral.
oralménte *ad* orally, verbally.
oramài *ad* by this time, now; from now on.
oràrio *a* per hour; *nm* timetable; **o. d'ufficio** office hours; **segnàle o.** time signal.
oratóre *nm* -**tríce** *nf* orator, speaker.
oratòria *nf* eloquence, oratory.
oratòrio *a* oratorial; *nm* oratory, Sunday school; (*mus*) oratorio.
Oràzio *nm pr* Horace.
orazióne *nf* oration, prayer.
òrbita *nf* eye-socket, orbit.
òrbo *a* blind.
Òrcadi (le) *nf pl* (*geogr*) the Orkney Islands.

orchèstra *nf* orchestra.
orchidèa *nf* orchid.
órcio *nm* pitcher.
órco *pl* **órchi** *nm* ogre.
òrda *nf* horde.
ordígno *nm* tool, device.
ordinàle *a* ordinal.
ordinaménto *nm* arrangement, disposition.
ordinànza *nf* order; (*mil*) orderly; **o. municipàle** by-law.
ordinàre *vt* to order, arrange, ordain; **gli ordinài di andàre** I ordered him to go.
ordinariamènte *ad* ordinarily, usually.
ordinàrio *a* ordinary, normal; coarse; *nm* professor.
ordinàto *a* orderly, tidy.
ordinazióne *nf* order; (*eccl*) ordination; **fàtto su o.** *a* made to order.
órdine *nm* order; **o. del giòrno** agenda.
ordíre *vt* to weave; plot.
ordíto *nm* warp, web; plot.
orecchíno *nm* earring.
orécchio *nm* ear; **a o.** by ear; **dúro d'o.** hard of hearing.
orecchióni *nm pl* (*med*) mumps.
oréfice *nm* goldsmith.
oreficería *nf* goldsmith's shop; things made of gold.
òrfano *a nm* orphan.
orfanotròfio *nm* orphanage.
Orfèo *nm pr* Orpheus.
òrfico *pl* **òrfici** *a* Orphic.
organétto, organíno *nm* barrel-organ.
organico *pl* -**ici** *a* organic.
organísmo *nm* organism.
organísta *nmf* organist.
organizzàre *vt* to organize.
organizzatóre *a* organizing; *nm* -**tríce** *nf* organizer.
organizzazióne *nf* organization.
òrgano *nm* organ.
orgàsmo *nm* orgasm, excitement.
òrgia *nf* orgy.
orgóglio *nm* pride.
orgogliosaménte *ad* proudly.
orgoglióso *a* proud.
orientàle *a* east(ern), oriental.
orientaménto *nm* orientation, bearings; **o. mediànte ràdio** radio bearing.
orientàre *vt* to set, turn; -**rsi** *vr* to find one's bearings or way.
oriènte *nm* east, orient.
orígano *nm* origan.
originàle *a nm* original, eccentric (person).
originalità *nf* originality, strangeness.
originalménte *ad* originally, ingeniously.
originàre *vti* to give rise to; originate.
originariaménte *ad* originally.
originàrio *a* original, primary.
orígine *nm* origin, beginning, cause.

origliàre *vi* to eavesdrop.
orína *nf* urine.
orinatóio *nm* urinal.
oriúndo *a* native; **èssere o. di Róma** to be of Roman origin.
orizzontàle *a* horizontal.
orizzónte *nm* horizon.
Orlàndo *nm pr* Roland.
orlàre *vt* to edge, hem.
orlatúra *nf* edging, hemming.
órlo *nm* edge, hem.
órma *nf* footprint, mark.
ormài *ad* by now.
ormeggiàre *vt* **-rsi** *vr* to moor.
orméggio *nm* mooring.
ormóne *nm* hormone.
ornamentàle *a* ornamental.
ornaménto *nm* ornament.
ornàre *vt* to adorn, decorate.
ornàto *a* ornate; *nm* decoration.
ornitología *nf* ornithology.
ornitòlogo *pl* **-oghi** *nm* ornithologist.
òro *nm* gold.
orologería *nf* watchmaking, watchmaker's shop, mechanism of a watch (clock).
orologiàio *nm* watchmaker.
orològio *nm* clock, watch.
oròscopo *nm* horoscope.
orrèndo, orríbile *a* horrible, dreadful.
òrrido *a* horrid; *nm* ravine.
orripilànte *a* terrifying; hideous.
orróre *nm* horror, loathing.
orsacchiòtto *nm* bear cub; (*toy*) teddybear.
órso *nm* bear; (*fig*) unsociable person; **Órsa Maggióre** (*astr*) Great Bear; **Órsa Minóre** Little Bear, **o. grígio** grizzly (bear).
Órsola *nf pr* Ursula.
orsù *interj* come on!
ortàggio *nm* vegetable.
ortènsia *nf* hydrangea.
ortíca *nf* nettle.
orticària *nf* nettlerash.
orticultóre *nm* market gardener, truck farmer.
òrto *nm* kitchen garden.
ortodòsso *a* orthodox.
ortografía *nf* orthography, spelling.
ortolàno *nm* vegetable dealer, truck farmer.
ortopedía *nf* orthopedics.
orzaiòlo *nm* stye (on the eyelid).
orzàta *nf* barley water.
òrzo *nm* barley.
osàre *vti* to dare, risk.
Òscar *nm pr* Oscar; **prémio O.** Oscar (prize), (*US*) Academy Award.
oscenità *nf* indecency, obscenity.
oscèno *a* obscene, horrible.
oscillàre *vi* to swing, hesitate, oscillate.
oscillatóre *nm* oscillator.
oscillatòrio *a* oscillatory, oscillating.
oscillazióne *nf* oscillation, swing (ing), fluctuation.
oscuraménto *nm* darkening.

oscuràre *vt* to darken, obscure; **-rsi** *vr* to grow dark, dim.
oscurità *nf* darkness, obscurity.
oscúro *a* dark, obscure, difficult **èssere all'o. di** to be ignorant of.
ospedàle *nm* hospital.
ospitàle *a* hospitable.
ospitalità *nf* hospitality.
ospitàre *vt* to give hospitality to.
òspite *nmf* host(ess); guest.
ospízio *nm* asylum, home.
ossatúra *nf* (bone) structure, framework.
òsseo *a* bony, osseous.
ossequiàre *vt* to pay one's respects to.
ossèquio *nm* homage, obedience; **ossèqui** *pl* regards, respects *pl*.
ossequióso *a* respectful, obsequious.
osservànza *nf* obedience, observance.
osservàre *vt* to observe, watch, examine.
osservatóre *nm* **-trice** *nf* observer.
osservatòrio *nm* observatory; (*mil*) observation post, look-out.
osservazióne *nf* observation, remark.
ossessionàre *vt* to obsess, haunt.
ossessióne *nf* obsession.
ossèsso *nm* person possessed.
ossía *cj* or, or rather.
òssido *nm* oxide.
ossídrico *pl* **-ici** *a* oxyhydrogen.
ossigenàto *a* oxygenized; (*of hair*) peroxided.
ossígeno *nm* oxygen.
òsso *nm*; *m pl* **òssi** (*meat*) bone ; (*fruit*) stone; *f pl* **òssa** (human) bone; **di càrne ed òssa** of flesh and blood.
ossúto *a* big-boned, bony.
ostacolàre *vt* to hinder, interfere with.
ostàcolo *nm* hindrance, obstacle; **córsa ad ostàcoli** hurdle-race, steeplechase.
ostàggio *nm* hostage.
òste *nm* innkeeper, publican, saloon keeper, landlord.
osteggiàre *vt* to be hostile to, oppose.
ostèllo *nm* mansion; inn; hostel.
Ostènda *nf pr* (*geogr*) Ostend.
ostentàre *vt* to show off; feign.
ostentazióne *nf* ostentation; pretense.
ostería *nf* inn, tavern.
ostéssa *nf* innkeeper's wife.
ostètrica *nf* midwife.
òstia *nf* (*eccl*) Host, wafer.
òstico *pl* **-ici** *a* difficult, unpleasant.
ostíle *a* hostile.
ostilità *nf* hostility, enmity.
ostilménte *ad* in a hostile manner, with hostility.
ostinàrsi *vr* to insist, persist.
ostinàto *a* obstinate, stubborn.
ostinazióne *nf* obstinacy, persistence.
ostracísmo *nm* ostracism.
òstrica *nf* oyster.
ostruíre *vt* to obstruct, stop (up).

ostruzióne *nf* obstruction.
Otèllo *nm pr* Othello.
otorinolaringoiàtra *nm* ear, nose and throat specialist.
ótre *nm* (goat)-skin bottle.
ottàgono *nm* octagon.
ottàno *nm* (*chem*) octane.
ottànta *a nm* eighty; **ottanténne** *a* eighty-year-old; **ottantésimo** *a* eightieth; **ottantína** *nf* about eighty.
ottàva *nf* octave; **ottàvo** *a nm* eighth; octavo.
ottemperàre (a) *vi* to comply (with), obey.
ottenebràre *vt* to darken, cloud.
ottenére *vt* to obtain, gain, get.
otteníbile *a* obtainable.
òttica *nf* optics.
òttico *pl* -**ici** *a* optic(al); *nm* optician.
ottimísmo *nm* optimism.
ottimísta *nmf* optimist.
ottimístico *pl* -**ici** *a* optimistic.
òttimo *a* very good, excellent.
òtto *a nm* eight.
ottòbre *nm* October.
ottocènto *a nm* eight hundred; nineteenth century.
ottomàno *a nm* Ottoman.
ottóne *nm* brass, brass instrument.
ottuagenàrio *a nm* octogenarian.
otturàre *vt* to stop (up).
otturazióne *nf* plugging; (*of tooth*) filling, stopping.
ottusità *nf* obtuseness, bluntness.
ottúṣo *a* obtuse, blunt, dull.
ovàia *nf* ovary.
ovàle *a nm* oval.
ovàtta *nf* wadding, cotton wool, absorbent cotton.
ovazióne *nf* ovation.
óve *ad* where; *cj* if, in case.
òvest *nm* west; **a o.** in, to the west.
Ovídio *nm pr* Ovid.
ovíle *nm* fold, sheep-fold.
ovíno *a* ovine; *nm* sheep.
òvolo *nm* a kind of mushroom.
ovúnque *ad* anywhere, everywhere, wherever.
ovvéro *cj* or.
ovviaménte *ad* obviously, evidently.
ovviàre *vt* to obviate, avoid.
òvvio *a* obvious, evident.
oziàre *vi* to idle, loaf.
òzio *nm* idleness, leisure.
oziosità *nf* idleness, laziness.
ozióso *a* idle.
ozòno *nm* ozone.

P

pacataménte *ad* calmly, quietly.
pacatézza *nf* calmness, quietness.
pacàto *a* calm, quiet.
pacchétto *nm* packet, small parcel.
pàcco *pl* **pàcchi** *nm* parcel, package.
pàce *nf* peace.
pachistàno *a nm* Pakistani.
pacière *nm* **pacièra** *nf* peacemaker.

pacificaménte *ad* peacefully, peaceably.
pacificàre *vt* to pacify, reconcile.
pacificazióne *nf* pacification, reconciliation.
pacífico *pl* -**ici** *a* peaceful; **Pacífico** *a nm* (*geogr*) Pacific (Ocean).
padàno *a* (*geogr*) Po; **la Val Padàna** the Po Valley.
padèlla *nf* frying-pan; bed-pan; **dàlla p. nèlla bràge** out of the frying-pan into the fire.
padiglióne *nm* pavilion, tent.
Pàdova *nf* (*geogr*) Padua; **padovàno** *a nm* Paduan.
pàdre *nm* father.
padríno *nm* godfather; (*in a duel*) second.
padróna *nf* landlady, mistress.
padróne *nm* landlord, master, owner, proprietor.
padronànza *nf* command, mastery; **p. di sè** self control.
padronàto *nm* ownership, possession.
padroneggiàre *vt* to command, master; *vi* to play the master.
paeṣàggio *nm* landscape.
paeṣàno *a* country, rustic; *nm* peasant; fellow-townsman.
paéṣe *nm* country; district; village; town.
paeṣísta *nmf* landscape painter.
paffúto *a* chubby, plump.
pàga *nf* pay, wages *pl*.
pagàbile *a* payable.
pagaménto *nm* payment.
paganèṣimo *nm* paganism.
pagàno *a nm* pagan, heathen.
pagàre *vt* to pay, pay for.
pagèlla *nf* (school-)report.
pàggio *nm* pageboy.
pagherò *nm* (*com*) promissory note, I.O.U.
pàgina *nf* leaf, page (of a book).
pàglia *nf* straw; **p. di fèrro** steel wool; **pagliétta** straw-hat.
pagliàccio *nm* buffoon, clown.
pagliàio *nm* straw-rick.
paglieríccio *nm* paillasse.
pagnòtta *nf* loaf.
pàgo *pl* **pàghi** *a* content, satisfied.
pàio *pl f* **pàia** *nm* pair.
Pàkistan *nm* (*geogr*) Pakistan.
pàla *nf* shovel; **ruòta a pàle** paddle-wheel.
palàta *nf* shovelful; blow with a shovel; stroke with an oar.
palatíno *a* Palatine.
palàto *nm* palate.
palàzzo *nm* palace, mansion, building.
pàlco *pl* **pàlchi** *nm* platform, stand; (*theat*) box.
palcoscènico *pl* -**ici** *nm* (*theat*) stage.
paleṣàre *vt* to disclose, reveal.
paléṣe *a* evident, clear, obvious.
Palestína *nf* (*geogr*) Palestine.
palestinése *a nmf* Palestinian.

palèstra *nf* gymnasium.
palétta *nm* small shovel.
palétto *nm* (*of the door*) bolt; small pole.
pàlio *nm* horse-race at Siena; silk banner given to winner.
palizzàta *nf* fence, paling, palisade.
pàlla *nf* ball; **p. a vólo** volleyball; **pallacanèstro** *nf* basketball; **pallacòrda** *nf* lawn tennis; **pallamàglio** *nf* croquet; **pallanuòto** *nf* water polo; **p. da cannóne** shell; **p. da fucíle** bullet.
palleggiaménto, **palléggio** *nm* (*football*) dribbling; (*tennis*) volleying.
palliatívo *a nm* palliative.
pallidézza *nf* paleness, pallor.
pàllido *a* pale, pallid.
pallína *nf* little ball, small shot; **pallíno** *nm* little ball, small shot, pellet; (*bowls*) jack; **avére il p. di** to have a craze for.
palloncíno *nm* balloon, Chinese lantern.
pallóne *nm* ball, balloon, football.
pallóre *nm* paleness, pallor.
pallòttola *nf* bullet, pellet.
pàlma *nf* palm(tree); (*of the hand*) palm.
palméto *nm* palm-grove.
pàlmo *nm* (*of the hand, or measure*) palm.
pàlo *nm* pole, post, pile, pylon.
palombàro *nm* diver.
palómbo *nm* dogfish; wood-pigeon.
palpàbile *a* palpable, obvious.
palpàre *vt* to feel, handle, touch; (*med*) palpate.
pàlpebra *nf* eyelid.
palpitànte *a* palpitating, throbbing.
palpitàre *vi* to palpitate, tremble, throb.
pàlpito *nm* beat, throb.
paltò *nm* overcoat.
palúde *nf* marsh.
paludóso, **palústre** *a* marshy.
Pamèla *nf pr* Pamela.
pàmpino *nm* vine leaf.
Pànama *nm* (*geogr*) Panama.
panàre *vt* to cover with breadcrumbs.
pànca *nf* bench, form.
pancétta *nf* bacon.
panchétto *nf* footstool, small bench.
pància *nf* stomach, belly.
panciòlle, **in** *ad* **stàre in p.** to lounge about.
panciòtto *nm* waistcoat, vest.
Pancràzio *nm pr* Pancras.
pàne *nm* bread, loaf; **buòno cóme il p.** as good as gold.
panegírico *pl* -**ici** *nm* panegyric.
panèllo *nm* oilcake.
panettería *nf* baker's shop.
panettière *nm* baker.
panfrútto *nm* fruitcake.
pània *nf* bird-lime; (*fig*) snare.
pànico *pl* -**ici** *nm* panic.
paníco *pl* -**chi** *nm* millet.

panière *nm* basket.
panifício *nm* bakehouse, bakery.
pànna *nf* cream; (*aut*) breakdown; **p. montàta** whipped cream.
pannéggio *nm* drapery.
pannèllo *nm* (*arch*) panel; **p. di finèstra** window-pane.
pànno *nm* cloth; **pànni** *pl* clothes; **sè ío fóssi néi tuòi pànni** if I were in your place (shoes).
pannolíno *nm* (baby's) diaper; sanitary napkin.
panoràmico *pl* -**ici** *a* panoramic.
panpepàto *nm* gingerbread.
pantalóni *nm pl* trousers.
pantàno *nm* bog, swamp.
panteísmo *nm* pantheism.
pantèra *nf* panther.
pantòfola *nf* slipper.
pantomíma *nf* (*theat*) mime, dumbshow.
Pàola *nf pr* Paula, Pauline.
Pàolo *nm pr* Paul.
papà *nm* daddy, papa.
Pàpa *nm pr* Pope.
papàle *a* papal.
papàto *nm* papacy.
papàvero *nm* poppy.
pàpero *nm* gosling; **Paperíno** *nm* Donald Duck.
papíro *nm* papyrus.
pàppa *nf* pap.
pappagàllo *nm* parrot; **pappagallíno** budgerigar, parakeet.
paràbola *nf* parable; parabola.
parabrézza *nm* (*aut*) windscreen, windshield.
paracadúte *nm* parachute.
paracadutísta *nm* parachutist, paratrooper.
paracénere *nm* fireguard.
paradisíaco *pl* -**íaci** *a* heavenly, paradisiacal.
paradíṣo *nm* heaven, paradise.
paradòsso *nm* paradox.
parafàngo *nm* (*aut*) mudguard, fender.
paraffína *nf* oil, paraffin, kerosene (coal-oil).
paràfraṣi *nf* paraphrase.
parafúlmine *nm* lightning conductor.
parafuòco *pl* -**chi** *nm* fireguard.
paràggi *nm pl* neighborhood.
paragonàre *vt* to compare.
paragóne *nm* comparison; **a p. di** in comparison with.
paràgrafo *nm* paragraph.
paràliṣi *nf* paralysis.
paralítico *pl* -**ici** *a nm* paralytic.
paralizzàre *vt* to paralyze.
parallelaménte *ad* parallel.
parallèlo *a nm* parallel (*also fig*).
paralúme *nm* lampshade.
paraòcchi *nm pl* blinkers *pl*.
parapètto *nm* parapet.
parapíglia *nm* turmoil.
paraPiòggia *nm* umbrella.
paràre *vt* to parry, avert; decorate, lead up to.

parasóle *nm* parasol, (*aut*) sunshield.

parassíta *nm* parasite.

parastatàle *a* state-controlled.

paràta *nf* parade; parry, save; **màla p.** unlucky moment.

paratía *nf* (*naut*) bulkhead.

paratífo *nm* paratyphoid.

paraúrti *nm* (*aut*) bumper.

paravènto *nm* windshield.

parcheggiàre *vt* to park; **parchèggio** *nm* parking (place), parking station, carpark, parking lot.

pàrco *pl* **pàrchi** *a* frugal, moderate; *nm* park.

parécchio *a* a good deal of; *ad* a lot, much; **parècchi** *a* and *pron m pl* **parècchie** *a* and *pron f pl* several.

pareggiàre *vt* to balance, level; *vi* (*sport*) to tie; **una scuòla pareggiàta** an officially recognized school.

paréggio *nm* balance; (*sport*) tie.

parentàdo *nm* **parentèla** *nf* kin *pl*, kindred, relations *pl*, relationship.

parènte *nmf* relation, relative; **p. più strétto** next-of-kin.

parèntesi *nf* brackets *pl*, parenthesis.

parére *vi* to seem, look like; *nm* opinion.

paréte *nf* (internal) wall; (*mountain*) face.

pàri *a* equal, (*number*) even; *nm* (*sing and pl*) equal, peer; **càmera déi p.** House of Lords; *nf* par; **àlla p.** au pair; (*com*) at par.

parificàre *v* **pareggiàre**.

Parígi *nf* (*geogr*) Paris; **parigíno** *a nm* Parisian.

pariglia *nf* (*horses*) pair; tit for tat.

pariménti *ad* likewise.

parità *nf* equality, parity.

parlamentàre *vi* to parley; *a* parliamentary; *nm* Member of Parliament.

parlaménto *nm* parley; parliament.

parlàre *vi* to speak, talk; **p. chiàro** to be plain, speak one's mind.

parmigiàno *a nm* Parmesan (cheese).

parodía *nf* parody.

paròla *nf* word; **p. d'òrdine** (*mil*) password.

parossísmo *nm* paroxysm.

parricída *a* parricidal; *nm* parricide (*criminal*); **parricídio** *nm* parricide (*crime*).

parròcchia *nf* parish, parish church; **parrocchiàle** *a* parish; **parrocchiàno** parishioner.

pàrroco *pl* **-oci** *nm* parish priest; (Protestant) parson, minister.

parrúcca *nf* wig.

parrucchière *nm* **parrucchièra** *nf* hairdresser.

parsimònia *nf* parsimony, sparingness.

pàrte *nf* part, place, share, side; **la màggior p.** the majority; **da p.** aside; **in p.** partly.

partecipàre *vt* to announce; *vi* to share, participate; **p. àgli útili** to share in the profits.

partecipazióne *nf* participation; announcement.

partécipe *a* informed; participating, sharing.

parteggiàre *vi* to side with, take sides.

Partenóne *nm pr* Parthenon.

partenopèo *a* Neapolitan.

partènza *nf* departure, start(ing).

particélla *nf* particle.

particípio *nm* participle.

particolàre *a* particular, special; *nm* particular, detail.

particolareggiàto *a* detailed.

particolarménte *ad* particularly, especially, in particular.

partigiàno *a* partisan; *nm* partisan, supporter.

partíre *vi* to depart, leave, set out, start; **a p. da domàni** starting from tomorrow.

partíta *nf* match; game; party, (*com*) lot, entry.

partíto *nm* (*pol*) party; (*marriage*) match; resolution; **a p. préso** with mind made up.

partitúra *nf* (*mus*) score.

partizióne *nf* division, partition.

pàrto *nm* (child)birth, delivery.

partoríre *vti* to bear, give birth to; *nm* childbearing.

parziàle *a* partial.

parzialità *nf* partiality.

pàscere *vti* **-rsi** *vr* to graze, pasture, feed.

pascolàre *vti* to graze, pasture.

pàscolo *nm* pasture; (*fig*) food.

Pàsqua *nf* Easter; **pasquàle** *a* Easter.

passàbile *a* passable.

passàggio *nm* passage, crossing; (*sport*) pass; **diritto di p.** right of way; **p. a livèllo** level crossing, grade; **p. pedonàle** crossing; pedestrian crossing; **èssere di p.** to be passing through.

passamanería *nf* **passamàno** *nm* trimming.

passamontàgna *nm* Balaclava helmet.

passànte *nmf* passer-by.

passapòrto *nm* passport.

passàre *vti* to pass, spend; **p. da** to call on; **-rsela** *vr* to get on.

passatèmpo *nm* pastime.

passàto *a nm* past.

passeggèro *a* passing, transient; *nm* passenger, traveler.

passeggiàre *vi* to (go for a) walk.

passeggiàta *nf* walk, ride, drive.

passéggio *nm* promenade, walk.

passerèlla *nf* foot-bridge; (*naut*) gangway.

pàssero *nm* sparrow.

passionàle *a* passionate, of passion.

passióne *nf* passion.

passività *nf* passiveness; (*com*) liabilities *pl*.

passívo *a* passive; *nm* passive; (*com*) liabilities *pl*.

pàsso *nm* step, pace; passage; (*geogr*) pass; **a p. d'uòmo** at a walking pace; **di pàri p.** at the same rate.

pàsta *nf* dough, pastry; cake; paste, pulp; **p. dentifrícia** toothpaste; **pastína da tè** teacake, biscuit.

pastèllo *nm* pastel.

pastétta *nf* batter.

pastícca *nf* lozenge, tablet.

pasticceria *nf* confectioner's, confectionary; **pasticcière** *nm* confectioner.

pasticcíno *nm* small cake, tartlet, cookie.

pastíccio *nm* pie; (*fig*) mess; **nèi pastícci** in a fix.

pastíglia *nf* lozenge, pastille.

pàsto *nm* meal.

pastóia *nf* hobble, pastern; (*fig*) fetters.

pastoràle *a* pastoral; *nm* crozier; *nf* pastoral (letter).

pastóre *nm* shepherd, pastor; **pastorèlla** *nf* shepherdess.

pastorizzàre *vt* to pasteurize.

pastóso *a* doughy, soft, mellow.

pastràno *nm* (man's) overcoat.

pastúra *nf* pasture.

patàta *nf* potato; **patàte frítte** chips, French fries; **patatíne frítte** crisps, potato chips.

patènte *a* open, obvious; *nf* license; **patentàto** *a* trained.

paternàle *nf* scolding.

paternaménte *ad* in a fatherly way, paternally.

paternità *nf* paternity; father's name.

patèrno *a* paternal.

patètico *pl* -ici *a* moving, pathetic.

patíbolo *nm* gallows, gibbet.

patiménto *nm* pain, suffering.

patíre *vti* to endure, suffer.

patología *nf* pathology; **patològico** *pl* -ici *a* pathologic(al).

pàtria *nf* (one's own) country, fatherland.

patriàrca *nm* patriarch; **patriarcàle** *a* patriarchal.

patrígno *nm* stepfather.

patrimònio *nm* heritage, estate.

pàtrio *a* of one's own country or home.

patriòt(t)a *nmf* patriot.

patriòttico *pl* -ici *a* patriotic.

Patrízia *nf* *pr* Patricia; **Patrízio** *nm* *pr* Patrick.

patrízio *a* *nm* patrician.

patrocinàre *vt* to defend, support.

patrocinatóre *nm* defender, sponsor, patron.

patrocínio *nm* defense; **p. gratúito** legal aid.

patróno *nm* patron, defending counsel; **patronàto** *nm* patronage.

patteggiàre *vti* come to terms, negotiate.

pattinàggio *nm* skating.

pattinàre *vi* to skate.

pàttino *nm* (ice)skate; **p. a rotèlle** roller skate.

pàtto *nm* pact, condition.

pattúglia *nf* (*mil*) patrol.

pattuíre *vt* to agree (upon), fix.

pattumièra *nf* dustbin, garbage can.

paùra *nf* fear, fright; **avére p.** to be afraid; **far p.** (a) to frighten; **per p. che** lest.

paurosaménte *ad* fearfully, frighteningly.

pauróso *a* fearful, frightful.

pàusa *nf* pause.

pavesàre *vt* to adorn, beflag.

pavése *a* *nm* (inhabitant) of Pavia; *nm* shield.

paviménto *nm* floor.

pavóne *nm* peacock; **pavoneggiàrsi** *vr* to strut.

pazientàre *vi* to be patient, have patience.

paziènte *a* *nmf* patient.

paziènza *nf* patience; **pèrdere la p.** to lose one's temper; *interj* never mind!

pazzésco *a* mad; foolish.

pazzía *nf* madness, foolish action.

pàzzo *a* *nm* mad(man), lunatic.

pècca *nf* blemish, defect, flaw.

peccaminóso *a* sinful, culpable.

peccàre *vi* to sin, err.

peccàto *nm* sin; **che p.!** *interj* what a pity!

peccatóre *nm* -**tríce** *nf* sinner.

pécchia *nf* bee; **pecchióne** *nm* drone.

péce *nf* pitch.

pechinése *a* *nmf* Pekin(g)ese.

pècora *nf* sheep, ewe.

pecoríno *nm* sheep's-milk cheese.

peculàto *nm* peculation.

peculiàre *a* peculiar, special.

peculiarità *nf* peculiarity, characteristic.

pedàggio *nm* toll.

pedagògo *nm* pedagogue.

pedàle *nm* pedal, treadle.

pedàna *nf* dais.

pedànte *a* *nm* pedant(ic).

pedantería *nf* pedantry.

pedàta *nf* kick; footprint.

pedèstre *a* pedestrian; dull.

pediàtra *nmf* pediatrician.

pedicure (*Fr*) *nm* chiropodist.

pedilúvio *nm* foot-bath.

pedína *nf* piece; (*chess*) pawn.

pedinàre *vt* to follow, shadow.

pedóne *nm* **pedonàle** *a* pedestrian.

pèggio *a* *nm* *ad* worse, worst; **àlla p.** if the worst comes to the worst.

peggioraménto *nm* worsening, deterioration.

peggioràre *vt* to make worse; *vi* to worsen.

peggióre *a* worse, worst.

pégno *nm* pawn, pledge, token; **dàre in p.** *vt* to pawn; **giuòco dèi pégni** forfeits *pl*.

pelàre vt to skin, peel; (fig) fleece; -rsi vr to go bald.

pellàme nm hides pl, skins pl.

pèlle nf skin.

pellegrinàggio nm pilgrimage.

pellegrinàre vi to wander.

pellegríno a rare, strange; nm pilgrim.

pelletería nf leather goods pl, leather goods shop.

pellicàno nm pelican.

pelliccería nf furs pl; fur trade; furrier's (shop).

pellíccia nf fur (coat).

pellicciàio nm furrier.

pellícola nf film.

pelliróssa nmf redskin.

pélo nm hair, fur; (cloth) pile; **per un p.** by a hair's breadth.

pelóso a hairy, shaggy.

péltro nm pewter.

pelúria nf down, fluff.

pèlvi nf pelvis.

péna nf punishment; pain; trouble; **in p.** anxious; **far p.** to move to pity; **valére la p.** vi to be worthwhile; **a màla p.** scarcely.

penàle a criminal, penal.

penalísta nm criminal lawyer.

penàre (a) vi to suffer, find difficulty (in).

pendàglio nm pendant.

pendènte a hanging, leaning; nm earring, pendant.

pendènza nf slope, gradient, declivity, grade.

pèndere vi to hang; lean, slope.

pendíce nf **pendío** nm slope, hillside.

pèndolo nm pendulum; **pèndola** nf clock.

pène nm penis.

penetrànte a penetrating, piercing, acute.

penetràre vti to penetrate.

penetrazióne nf penetration.

penicillína nf penicillin.

peninsulàre a peninsular.

penísola nf peninsula.

penitènte a nmf penitent.

penitènza nf penance, penitence.

penitenziàrio a penitentiary; nm prison, penitentiary.

pénna nf feather; pen.

pennàcchio nm plume.

pennellatúra nf brushwork; (med) painting.

pennèllo nm brush, paint-brush; **a p.** perfectly.

Penníne, (Àlpi) nf pl (geogr) Pennine Alps.

penníno nm nib, penpoint.

pennóne nm pennon; (naut) yard.

penóso a painful.

pentàgono nm pentagon.

pensàre vti to think.

pensatóre nm thinker.

pensièro nm thought, idea.

pensieróso a thoughtful.

pènsile a hanging.

pensilína nf (bus etc) shelter; awning.

pensionànte nmf boarder, lodger.

pensionàre vt to pension (off).

pensionàto a retired; nm pensioner; hostel.

pensióne nf pension; board and lodging; boarding house.

pensóso a pensive, thoughtful.

pentàgono nm pentagon.

Pentecòste nf Whitsun(tide), Pentecost.

pentiménto nm repentance.

pentírsi (di) vr to repent.

péntola nf pot, saucepan.

penúltimo a penultimate.

penúria nf lack, shortage.

penzolàre vi to dangle, hang down.

penzolóni, penzolóne ad dangling, hanging.

peònia nf peony.

pepai(u)òla nf pepper-pot.

pépe nm pepper.

peperóne nm chili, pepper.

per prep for, through, by; **p. lo più** generally; **p. l'appúnto** just so; **p. vía aèrea** by airmail.

péra nf pear; (el) pear-switch.

perbène a respectable, nice.

percàlle nm cotton cambric.

percentuàle nf percentage.

percepíre vt to perceive; receive.

percettíbile a perceptible.

percezióne nf perception.

perché cj why?; because; (with subjunctive) in order that; nm reason.

perciò ad therefore, thereby.

percórrere vt to pass through, travel over.

percórso nm distance, route.

percòssa nf blow, stroke.

percuòtere vt to strike.

percussióne nf percussion.

perdènte a losing; nmf loser.

pèrdere vti to lose, miss; **p. di vista** to lose sight of; -rsi vr to get lost, vanish.

pèrdita nf loss, waste; **a p. d'òcchio** as far as the eye can see.

perdizióne nf perdition.

perdonàbile a pardonable.

perdonàre vt to forgive, pardon.

perdóno nm forgiveness, pardon.

perduràre vi to last, persist.

perdutaménte desperately.

perdúto a lost.

peregrinàre v **pellegrinàre.**

peregríno a uncommon.

perènne a everlasting, perennial.

perentòrio a peremptory.

perfètto a perfect.

perfezionaménto nm perfecting; specialization.

perfezionàre vt perfect, improve; -rsi vr to perfect oneself; specialize.

perfezióne nf perfection.

perfídia nf perfidy, wickedness.

pèrfido a perfidious.

perfíno ad even.

perforàre *vt* to perforate, pierce.
perforatríce *nf* drill, drilling machine.
perforazióne *nf* perforation, drilling.
pergamèna *nf* parchment.
pèrgola *nf* **pergolàto** *nm* pergola, arbor.
pericolànte *a* unsafe.
perícolo *nm* danger, peril.
pericolóso *a* dangerous.
periferìa *nf* periphery, outskirts *pl.*
perìfrasi *nf* periphrasis.
perímetro *nm* perimeter.
periòdico *pl* -ici *a nm* periodical.
perìodo *nm* period; (*gram*) sentence.
peripezìa *nf* vicissitude, adventure.
perìre *vi* to die, perish.
periscòpio *nm* periscope.
perìto *a nm* expert.
peritoníte *nf* (*med*) peritonitis.
perìzia *nf* skill; survey.
pèrla *nf* pearl.
perlustràre *vt* to patrol, reconnoiter.
perlustrazióne *nf* patrol, reconnaissance.
permalóso *a* touchy.
permanènte *a* permanent; *nf* permanent wave, perm.
permanènza *nf* stay; **in p.** permanently.
permeàre *vt* to permeate.
permésso *a* permitted; *nm* permission, permit; **p.!** excuse me, allow me.
perméttere (a qlcu di) *vt* to allow (s.o. to); -rsi *vr* to take the liberty.
pèrmuta *nf* exchange.
pernìce *nf* partridge.
pernicióso *a* pernicious.
pèrno, pèrnio *nm* pivot.
pernottaménto *nm* overnight stay.
pernottàre *vi* to spend the night.
però *cj* but, however.
péro *nm* pear tree.
peronòspora *nf* mildew.
peroràre *vti* to plead.
perorazióne *nf* peroration; pleading, defense.
peròssido *nm* peroxide.
perpendicolàre *a nf* perpendicular.
perpetràre *vt* to commit, perpetrate.
perpetuàre *vt* to perpetuate; -rsi *vr* to continue.
perpètuo *a* eternal, perpetual.
perplessità *nf* perplexity.
perplèsso *a* perplexed, puzzled.
perquisíre *vt* to search.
perquisizióne *nf* search.
persecutóre *nm* persecutor.
persecuzióne *nf* persecution.
perseguíre *vt* to follow, pursue.
perseguitàre *vt* to persecute.
perseverànte *a* persevering.
perseverànza *nf* perseverance.
perseveràre *vi* to persevere.
Pèrsia *nf* (*geogr*) Persia, Iran.
persiàna *nf* shutter, shade.
persiàno *a nm* Persian.
persíno *ad* even.
persistènte *a* persistent, persisting.

persístere *vi* to persist.
pèrso *a* lost; **a tèmpo p.** in one's spare time.
persóna *nf* person, body; **di p.** in person.
personàggio *nm* (*theat*) character, personage.
personàle *a* personal; *nm* staff, personnel, body; **questióne p.** private or personal business.
personalità *nf* personality.
personalménte *ad* personally.
personificàre *vt* to personify.
personificàto *a* personified; **è la bontà personificàta** he is goodness itself.
perspicàce *a* shrewd.
perspicàcia *nf* shrewdness.
perspícuo *a* clear.
persuadére *vt* to persuade, convince.
persuasióne *nf* persuasion, conviction.
persuasívo *a* persuasive.
pertànto *cj* therefore.
pèrtica *nf* rod, pole, perch.
pertinàce *a* persistent.
pertinàcia *nf* pertinacity.
pertinènte *a* relevant.
pertinènza *nf* pertinence, relevance; **non è di mìa p.** it is not my business.
perturbàre *vt* to disturb, perturb.
Perú *nm* (*geogr*) Peru; **peruviàno** *a nm* Peruvian.
perugíno *a nm* (inhabitant) of Perugia.
pervàdere *vt* to pervade.
pervenìre *vi* to arrive, reach.
perversióne *nf* perversion.
perversità *nf* wickedness.
pervèrso *a* immoral, wicked.
pervertiménto *nm* perversion.
pervertíre *vt* to lead astray, pervert; -rsi *vr* to go astray; **pervèrto** *a nm* pervert(ed).
pervicàce *a* obstinate.
pesànte *a* heavy; wearisome; weighty.
pesantézza *nf* heaviness.
pesàre *vti* to weigh.
pesàto *a* pondered, well-considered.
pèsca *nf* peach.
pésca *nf* fishery, fishing.
pescàre *vt* to fish, catch, (*fig*) fish out.
pescatóre *nm* fisherman.
pésce *nm* fish; **p. rósso** goldfish; **non sapére che pésci pigliàre** to be at one's wits' end; **p. d'aprìle** April fool.
pescecàne *nm* shark; (*fig*) profiteer.
pescheréccio *a* fishing; *nm* fishing-boat.
pescherìa *nf* fish-market, -shop.
pescivéndolo *nm* fishmonger.
pèsco *nm* peach tree.
péso *nm* weight, burden.
pessimísmo *nm* pessimism.
pessimísta *nmf* pessimist.
pessimístico *pl* -ici *a* pessimistic.

pèssimo *a* very bad.
pésta *nf* footprint, track; trovàrsi nèlle péste to be in difficulties.
pestàre *vt* to crush, pound, tread on.
pèste *nf* plague.
pestèllo *nm* pestle.
pestífero *a* pestilential.
pestilènza *nf* pestilence.
pestilenziàle *a* pestilential.
pésto *a* pounded; búio p. pitch dark; càrta pésta papier-mâché; *nm* Genoese sauce.
pètalo *nm* petal.
petàrdo *nm* petard; (*firework*) cracker.
petizióne *nf* petition.
petrificàre *vt* to petrify.
petrolièra *nf* (oil-)tanker.
petrolífero *a* oil, petroliferous; pòzzo p. oil-well.
petròlio *nm* oil, paraffin, kerosene.
petróso *a* stony.
pettegolàre *vi* to gossip; pettegolézzo *nm* gossiping.
pettégolo *a* gossiping; *nm* (*person*) gossip.
pettinàre *vt* to comb; -rsi *vr* to do one's hair; pettinatríce *nf* hairdresser.
pettinatúra *nf* hairstyle.
pèttine *nm* comb.
pettiròsso *nm* robin(redbreast).
pètto *nm* breast, chest; giàcca a ún (dòppio) pètto single(double)-breasted jacket.
pettorúto *a* proud, haughty; full-breasted.
petulànte *a* cheeky.
petulànza *nf* arrogance, impertinence.
pèzza *nf* patch, cloth, (*material*) bolt.
pezzènte *nm* beggar.
pèzzo *nm* piece; time; p. gròsso bigwig.
piacènte *a* pleasant, attractive.
piacére *vi* to please; quésto mi piàce I like this; *nm* pleasure, favor; avére il p. (di) to be glad (to); per p. please.
piacévole *a* pleasant, enjoyable.
piacevolménte *ad* pleasantly, agreeably.
piàga *nf* sore, evil.
piagnistèo *nm* whine, moaning.
piagnucolàre *vi* to whimper.
piàlla *nf* (*tec*) plane; piallàre *vt* to plane.
piallatríce *nf* planing machine.
piàna *nf* plain.
pianaménte *ad* quietly, slowly.
pianèlla *nf* slipper.
pianeròttolo *nm* landing.
pianéta *nm* planet.
piàngere *vti* to cry, weep, lament.
pianificàre *vt* to plan.
pianísta *nmf* pianist.
piàno *a* flat, smooth, plain; *ad* quietly, slowly; *nm* plain, plane; floor; plan.

piano(fòrte) *nm* piano(forte); p. a códa grand piano.
piànta *nf* plant; plan, map; sole.
piantagióne *nf* plantation.
piantàre *vt* to plant; fix; quit; p. in àsso leave in the lurch; piàntala! cut it out!; -rsi *vr* to place oneself.
piantatóre *nm* -tríce *nf* planter.
pianterréno *nm* ground floor, first floor.
piànto *nm* weeping, tears *pl*.
piantonàre *vt* to keep a watch on, keep under guard.
pianúra *nf* plain.
piàstra *nf* slab, (*of metal*) plate; piastrélla *nf* tile.
piastrína *nf* plaque, (*mil*) badge; p. di riconosciménto identity disk, identification tag.
piattafórma *nf* platform.
piattíno *nm* saucer.
piàtto *a* flat; *nm* dish, plate; p. grànde platter.
piàttola *nf* cockroach; crab-louse; (*fig*) a bore.
piàzza *nf* square; p. del mercàto market-place; p. d'àrmi parade-ground; automòbile da p. taxi; fàre p. pulita to make a clean sweep.
piazzafòrte *nf* stronghold, fort.
piazzàle *nm* large square.
piazzàre *vt* to place, set; -rsi *vr* (*racing*) to be placed.
piazzísta *nm* commercial traveler.
piazzuòla *nf* (*aut*) lay-by.
pícca *nf* pique; (*mil*) pike; *pl* (*cards*) spades *pl*.
piccànte *a* spicy, piquant.
piccàrsi (di) *vr* to claim (to); pride oneself (on); persist (in).
picchétto *nm* tent peg, stake; (*mil*) picket; (*cards*) piquet.
picchiàre *vti* to beat, hit, knock, strike; (*av*) dive; -rsi *vr* come to blows; picchiàta *nf* thrashing; (*av*) dive.
picchiettío *nm* drumming, tapping.
picchio *nm* blow, knock; woodpecker.
piccíno *a* little; *nm* child.
piccionàia *nf* loft, pigeon-loft; (*theat*) gallery.
piccióne *nm* pigeon; p. viaggiatóre carrier pigeon.
pícco *pl* pícchi *nm* peak, top; a p. perpendicularly; andàre a p. (*naut*) to go to the bottom.
piccolézza *nf* smallness, trifle.
píccolo *a* small, young, petty; *nm* child; i píccoli the little ones.
piccóne *nm* pickaxe.
piccòzza *nf* axe; p. da alpinísta ice-axe.
pidocchiería *nf* stinginess, meanness.
pidòcchio *nm* louse.
pidocchióso *a* filthy; stingy.
pième *nm* foot; a pièdi on foot; a pièdi núdi barefoot; stàre in pièdi to stand.

piedistàllo nm pedestal.
pièga nf crease, fold, pleat; **prèndere úna brútta p.** to take a bad turn; **mèssa in p.** nf (hair) set.
piegàre vti to fold (up), bend; subdue; submit; turn; **-rsi** vr to bend, submit.
pieghettàre vt to pleat.
pieghévole a folding, pliable; submissive.
Piemónte nm (geogr) Piedmont; **piemontése** a nmf Piedmontese.
pièna nf flood; crowd.
pienaménte ad fully, completely, entirely.
pienézza nf fullness.
pièno a full; **in p.** completely.
Pièro nm pr Peter.
pietà nf pity, mercy; piety; (art) pietà.
pietànza nf (main) course.
pietóso a merciful; pitiful, wretched.
piètra nf stone.
pietrificàre vt to petrify.
pietrína nf (for lighters) flint.
Piètro nm pr Peter.
pième nf country parish (church).
pìffero nm (mus) fife.
pigiàma nm pajamas pl.
pigiàre vti to crush, press; **-rsi** vr to crowd.
pigióne nf rent; **pigionàle** nm tenant.
pigliàre vt to seize, take.
pigmèo nm pygmy.
pignoraménto nm distraint.
pignoràre vt to distrain.
pigolàre vi to chirp.
pigolío nm chirping, chirruping.
pigraménte ad lazily, sluggishly.
pigrízia nf laziness.
pígro a lazy, sluggish.
píla nf heap, pile; (el) battery; (holy-water) stoup.
pilàstro nm pillar.
Pilàto nm pr Pilate.
píllola nf pill.
pilóne nm pillar; (el) pylon.
pilòta nm pilot.
pilotàre vt to pilot.
pinacotèca nf picture-gallery.
pinéta nf pine-wood.
píngue a fat.
pinguèdine nf corpulence, fatness.
pinguíno nm penguin.
pínna nf fin; (swimming) flipper.
pinnàcolo nm pinnacle.
píno nm pine(-tree).
pínza nf pliers pl, forceps pl; **pinzétta** nf tweezers pl.
Pío nm pr Pius.
pío a pious, charitable.
pioggerèlla nf drizzle, gentle rain.
piòggia nf rain; **p. radioattíva** fallout.
piòlo nm peg; (of ladder) rung.
piombàre vt to seal, cover (with lead); (tooth) stop; vi fall, plunge.
piómbo nm (metal) lead.
pionière nm pioneer.

piòppo nm poplar.
piovàno a **àcqua piovàna** rainwater.
piòvere vti to rain; **p. a dirótto, p. a catinélle** to pour.
piovigginàre vi to drizzle.
piovigginóso, piovóso a drizzling, rainy.
piovosità nf rainfall.
pípa nf (smoker's) pipe.
pipistrèllo nm bat.
píra nf pyre.
piràmide nf pyramid.
piràta nm pirate.
piratería nf piracy.
pírica, pólvere nf gunpowder.
piròfila nf fire-resisting glassware.
piròscafo nm steamer, steamship.
pirotècnica nf fireworks pl, pyrotechnics pl.
piscína nf fish-pond; swimming-pool.
pisèllo nm pea.
pisolíno nm nap, snooze.
pista nf race course, track; (av) runway.
pistàcchio nm pistachio.
pistíllo nm pistil.
pistòla nf pistol.
pistóne nm piston.
pitòcco pl **-òcchi** a stingy; nm beggar; miser.
pittóre nm **-tríce** nf painter.
pittorésco a picturesque.
pittúra nf painting.
pitturàre vti to paint.
più ad longer, more, most; **non ... p.** no longer; **mài p.** never again; **sèmpre p.** more and more; **per di p.** moreover; **per lo p.** generally.
piúma nf feather, plume.
piumíno nm eiderdown; powder-puff.
piuttòsto (che, di) ad rather (than).
píva nf bagpipe.
pivière nm plover.
pizzería nf pizza shop, pizza restaurant.
pizzicàgnolo nm delicatessen seller.
pizzicàre vti to nip; itch.
pizzichería nf delicatessen shop.
pízzico pl **-chi** nm pinch; **pizzicóre** nm itch.
pízzo nm lace; pointed beard; (mountain) peak.
placàre vt to appease, soothe; **-rsi** vr subside.
plàcca nf plate, plaque; (in throat) spot.
plàcido a placid, peaceful.
plafóne nm ceiling.
plagiàrio nm plagiarist.
plàgio nm plagiarism.
planàre vi (av) to glide down.
planetàrio a planetary; nm planetarium.
plasmàre vt to mold.
plàstica nf plastic; modelling; plastic surgery.
plàtano nm plane (tree).

platèa nf (theat) orchestra seats pl.
plàtino nm platinum.
plauṣíbile a acceptable, reasonable.
plàuṣo nm applause, praise.
plebàglia nf mob, rabble.
plèbe nf common people.
plebèo a plebeian, vulgar; nm commoner.
plebiscíto nm plebiscite.
plenàrio a plenary.
plenilúnio nm full moon.
plenipotenziàrio a nm plenipotentiary.
pleuríte nf (med) pleurisy.
plíco pl **plíchi** nm envelope, packet.
plotóne nm (mil) platoon, squad.
plúmbeo a leaden.
pluràle a nm plural.
pneumàtico pl **-ici** a pneumatic; nm tire.
po' v **pòco.**
pòco pl **pòchi** a pron little (pl few); ad (very) little, a little while; **fra p.** soon; **p. fa** not long ago; **un po' per** what with . . .
podàgra nf (med) gout.
podére nm farm.
poderóso a mighty, powerful.
podestà nm mayor.
podíṣmo nm (sport) walking.
poèma nm long poem.
poeṣía nf poem, poetry.
poèta nm poet.
poetéssa nf poetess.
poètico pl **-ici** a poetical.
poggiàre vi to rest; (mil) move.
pòggio nm hillock, knoll.
poggiòlo nm balcony.
pòi ad afterwards, then; **da óra in p.** from now on; **da allóra in p.** from that time on; **o príma o p.** sooner or later.
poichè cj since, as, for, after, when.
polàcco pl **-àcchi** a Polish; nm Pole.
polàre a polar.
polèmica nf controversy, polemic(s).
polènta nf corn meal.
poligamía nf polygamy.
polígamo a polygamous; nm polygamist.
poliglòtta a nm polyglot.
polígono nm polygon.
polímero nm (chem) polymer.
poliomielíte nf poliomyelitis.
pòlipo nm polyp; (med) polypus.
politeàma nm theater.
politècnico pl **-ici** a nm polytechnic.
politène nm polythene.
política nf politics, policy.
político pl **-ici** a politic(al); nm politician.
poliviníle nm (chem) polyvinyl.
polizía nf police.
poliziésco pl **-chi** a police; **film p.** detective film.
poliziòtto nm policeman, constable, patrolman.
pòlizza nf (com) policy, bill.
pollàio nm hen-house, poultry-yard.
pollàme nm poultry.

pollàstra nf pullet; **pollàstro** nm cockerel.
pollería nf poultry shop.
pòllice nm thumb, big toe; inch.
pòlline nm pollen.
póllo nm chicken, fowl.
polluzióne nf pollution.
polmonàre a pulmonary.
polmóne nm lung.
polmoníte nf pneumonia.
pòlo nm (el and geogr) pole.
Polònia nf (geogr) Poland.
pólpa nf (fruit) pulp; boned meat.
polpétta nf rissole.
pólpo nm octopus.
polsíno nm cuff.
pólso nm pulse; wrist; **di p.** energetic.
poltíglia nf mush, mud, slush.
poltríre vi to lie lazily in bed, idle.
poltróna nf armchair, easy chair; orchestra seat; **p. a dondolo** rocking chair; **poltroncina** nf back orchestra seat.
poltróne nm idler.
poltronería nf laziness.
pólvere nf dust, powder; **p. néra da spàro** gunpowder; **caffè in p.** ground coffee.
polverizzàre vt to pulverize.
polveróne nm cloud of dust.
polveróso a dusty.
pomàta nf ointment.
pomèllo nm knob, grip; cheek-bone.
pomeridiàno a (in the) afternoon.
pomeríggio nm afternoon.
pómice nf pumice(-stone).
pómo nm apple(-tree); head; knob.
pomodòro, pomidòro pl **pomodòri, pomidòri** nm tomato.
pomogranàto nm pomegranate.
pómpa nf pump; pomp, display; **far p. di** to display, show off.
pompàre vt to pump (up).
pompèlmo nm grapefruit.
pompière nm fireman; **pompièri** (córpo dèi) fire brigade, fire department.
pompóso a pompous.
pònce nm (drink) punch.
ponderàre vti to ponder, consider.
ponderazióne nf cautious deliberation, reflection.
ponènte nm west.
pónte nm bridge; (naut) deck.
pontéfice nm pontiff, pope.
pontifício a papal.
pontíle nm landing-stage.
pontóne nm pontoon.
popolàno a of the (common) people; nm man of the people.
popolàre vt to populate, people; **-rsi** vr to become populated; a popular, working-class; **cànto p.** folksong.
popolarésco pl **-chi** a popular.
popolarizzàre vt to popularize.
popolazióne nf people, population.
pòpolo nm nation, people.
popolóso a populous.
popóne nm melon.

póppa *nf* (woman's) breast; (*naut*) stern.
poppàre *vti* to suck.
porcellàna *nf* china, porcelain.
porchería *nf* dirt, dirty trick.
porcíle *nm* (pig)sty.
pòrco *pl* -ci *nm* pig, swine; *a* dirty, horrible.
porcospíno *nm* hedgehog; porcupine.
pòrfido *nm* porphyry.
pòrgere *vt* to give, hand, offer, present, tender.
pòro *nm* pore.
porosità *nf* porousness.
poróso *a* porous.
pórpora *nf* purple.
pórre *vt* to place, put, set.
pòrro *nm* leek; wart.
pòrta *nf* door, gate, gateway, (*football*) goal.
portabagàgli *nm* porter; luggage rack, baggage rack.
portacénere *nm* ashtray.
portacípria *nm* powder-compact.
portaèrei *nf* aircraft carrier.
portafògli *nm* wallet, pocketbook; portafòglio *nm* wallet, pocketbook, portfolio.
portafortúna *nm* mascot.
portalèttere *nm* postman.
portaménto *nm* bearing, carriage.
portamonéte *nm* purse.
portaombrèlli *nm* umbrella stand.
portàre *vt* to bear, bring, carry, take; wear.
portaritràtti *nm* photograph frame.
portasapóne *nm* soap-dish.
portasigarétte *nm* cigarette case.
portàta *nf* capacity; course, dish, importance; range; **a p. di màno** (with)in reach; **di gràn p.** far reaching.
portàtile *a* portable.
portatóre *nm* bearer, holder.
portauòvo *nm* eggcup.
portavivànde *nm* dumbwaiter.
portavóce *nm* mouthpiece; megaphone; spokesman.
portènto *nm* marvel, prodigy.
portentóso *a* prodigious, wonderful.
pòrtico *pl* -ici *nm* porch, portico; *pl* arcade.
portièra *nf* door curtain; doorkeeper('s wife); (*aut*) door.
portière *nm* caretaker, (hotel-) porte doorman, janitor; (*sport*) goal-keeper.
portinàio *v* portière.
portinería *nf* porter's lodge.
pòrto *nm* port, harbor; (*com*) carriage; **p. frànco** carriage free.
Portogàllo *nm* (*geogr*) Portugal.
portoghése *a nmf* Portuguese; (*sl*) gatecrasher.
portóne *nm* main door, front door.
porzióne *nf* portion, share.
pòsa *nf* pause; pose; laying; (*phot*) exposure.
posamíne *nm* (*naut*) mine-layer.

posàre *vt* to lay, put (down); *vi* to pose; rest; **-rsi** *vr* to alight, stay.
posàta *nf* article of cutlery.
posàto *a* sedate, calm.
poscrítto *nm* postscript, footnote.
poṣdomàni *ad* the day after tomorrow.
poṣitíva *nf* (*phot*) positive.
poṣitívo *a* certain, matter-of-fact, positive.
poṣizióne *nf* position.
pospórre *vt* to place after, postpone.
posposizióne *nf* postponement.
possedére *vt* to possess.
possediménto *nm* possession, property.
possènte *a* powerful.
possèsso *nm* possession, property.
possessóre *nm* owner, possessor.
possíbile *a* possible; **fàre tútto il p.** to do one's best.
possibilità *nf* possibility, power.
possidènte *nmf* landowner, property owner.
pòsta *nf* mail, post (office); stake, bet; **p. per l'intèrno** inland mails, domestic mails; **a bèlla p.** on purpose.
postàle *a* post, postal; **vagóne p.** mail van, mail car (railway post office).
postàre *vt* to place, station.
postéggio *nm* park, parking; **p. di tassì** cabrank, cabstand.
pòsteri *nm pl* descendants *pl*, posterity.
posterióre *a* back, hind, posterior.
posterità *nf* posterity.
postíccio *a* artificial, false.
posticipazióne *nf* delay, postponement.
postílla *nf* (foot)note.
postíno *nm* postman.
pósto *a* placed, situated; *nm* place, room, seat; job; **c'è p.?** is there any room?
postulànte *nmf* applicant, petitioner.
pòstumo *a* posthumous.
potàbile *a* drinkable, drinking; **àcqua non p.** water unfit for drinking.
potàre *vt* to lop, prune.
potàssio *nm* potassium.
potènte *a* mighty, powerful.
potènza *nf* might, power, strength.
potenziàle *a nm* potential.
potére *vi* to be able (can), be allowed (may); *nm* authority, power; **può dàrsi** it may be.
pòvero *a* poor; *nm* poor man, beggar.
povertà *nf* poverty.
pozióne *nf* draft, potion.
pózza *nf* puddle, pool.
pozzànghera *nf* puddle.
pózzo *nm* well; mine-shaft.
pranzàre *vi* to dine; lunch.
prànzo *nm* lunch, dinner; **sàla da p.** *nf* dining room; **dópo p.** in the afternoon.

Pràga *nf* (*geogr*) Prague.
pratería *nf* grassland, prairie.
pràtica *nf* practice, training; affair; **pràtiche religióse** *nf pl* religious observances.
praticàbile *a* practicable; **stràda p.** passable road.
praticànte *a nmf* practicing, regular church-goer.
praticàre *vt* to practice; frequent.
pràtico *pl* -**ici** *a* practical, experienced; **èssere p. di** *vi* to be familiar with.
pràto *nm* meadow, lawn.
pratolìna *nf* daisy.
Preàlpi (le) *nf pl* (*geogr*) the Pre-Alps.
preàmbolo *nm* preamble.
preavvíso *nm* forewarning, notice.
precàrio *a* precarious.
precauzióne *nf* care, precaution.
precedènte *a* preceding, previous; *nm* precedent; **buòni precedènti** good record.
precedenteménte *ad* previously, formerly.
precedènza *nf* precedence, priority; **in p.** in advance; previously.
precèdere *vt* to go before, precede; *vi* to come first, precede.
precètto *nm* precept, rule, order.
precettóre *nm* -**trìce** *nf* teacher, tutor.
precipitàre *vt* to fling down; *vi* to crash, fall; -**rsi** *vr* to rush, throw oneself.
precipitazióne *nf* fall; haste.
precipitóso *a* hasty, steep.
precipízio *nm* precipice.
precípuo *a* principal, main.
precisaménte *ad* precisely, exactly.
precisàre *vt* to specify.
precisióne *nf* accuracy, exactness.
precíso *a* accurate, precise, punctual.
preclúdere *vt* to preclude, bar.
precòce *a* precocious, premature.
precocità *nf* precociousness, prematureness.
preconcètto *a* preconceived; *nm* preconception, prejudice.
precursóre *nm* forerunner, precursor.
prèda *nf* prey, plunder.
predatòrio *a* predatory.
predàre *vt* to pillage, plunder, sack.
predecessóre *nm* predecessor.
predestinàre *vt* to predestine.
predétto *a* above-mentioned; foretold.
prèdica *nf* preaching, sermon.
predicàre *vti* to preach.
predicàto *a* preached; exalted; *nm* predicate.
predicatóre *nm* preacher.
predilètto *a nm* favorite.
predilezióne *nf* partiality, fondness.
predilígere *vt* to like better, prefer.
predíre *vt* to foretell, predict.
predispórre *vt* to predispose, arrange.

predizióne *nf* prediction; **p. dell'avvenìre** fortune-telling.
predominàre *vti* to (pre)dominate.
predomínio *nm* predominance, supremacy.
predóne *nm* marauder, plunderer.
preesistènza *nf* pre-existence.
prefabbricàre *vt* to prefabricate.
prefazióne *nf* preface, introduction.
preferènza *nf* preference; **a p. di** rather than; **di p.** preferably.
preferenziàle *a* preferential; **azióni preferenziàli** preference shares, preferred stock.
preferíbile *a* preferable.
preferíre *vt* to prefer, like better.
preferíto *a nm* favorite.
prefètto *nm* prefect.
prefettúra *nf* prefecture.
prefíggersi (di) *vr* to intend (to).
prefiggiménto *nm* determination, resolve.
prefísso *a* intended; *nm* prefix.
pregàre *vti* to pray, ask; **prègo!** *interj* not at all, don't mention it.
pregévole *a* valuable.
preghièra *nf* prayer, request.
pregiàre *vt* to appreciate, esteem, value; -**rsi** *vr* to be honored, have the honor.
pregiàto *a* esteemed; (*com*) favor; valuable; **Pregiatíssimo Signóre** (*in letters*) Dear Sir.
prègio *nm* good merit, value.
pregiudicàre *vt* to injure; prejudice.
pregiudicàto *a* bound to fail; *nm* previous offender.
pregiudiziévole *a* prejudicial, detrimental.
pregiudízio *nm* prejudice; detriment.
pregnànte *a* (*lit and fig*) pregnant.
prégno *a* full, impregnated; pregnant.
pregustàre *vt* to anticipate, look forward to.
preistòrico *pl* -**ici** *a* prehistoric.
prelàto *nm* prelate.
prelevaménto *nm* drawing; (*com*) withdrawal.
prelevàre *vt* to draw; withdraw.
prelibàto *a* delicious, excellent.
preliminàre *a nm* preliminary.
prelúdio *nm* prelude.
prematúro *a* premature, untimely.
premeditàre *vt* to plan, premeditate.
premeditazióne *nf* premeditation.
prèmere *vt* to press; *vi* to press; matter.
premèssa *nf* premise, previous statement.
preméttere *vt* to premise, say first, state in advance.
premiàre *vt* to award a prize, reward.
premiazióne *nf* prizegiving.
preminènte *a* pre-eminent.
prèmio *nm* prize, reward; (*com*) premium.
premunìre *vt* to fortify; -**rsi** *vr* to take precautions.

premúra *nf* attention, care; haste.
premurosaménte *ad* solicitously, kindly.
premuróso *a* attentive, solicitous, kind.
prèndere *vt* to take, catch, seize.
prendisóle *nm* sun-suit.
prenotàre *vt* to book, engage.
prenotazióne *nf* booking.
preoccupàre *vt* to make anxious, trouble; **-rsi** *vr* to worry.
preoccupàto *a* anxious, worried.
preoccupazióne *nf* anxiety, care, preoccupation.
preordinàre *vt* to predetermine, prearrange.
preparàre *vt* **-rsi** *vr* to get ready, prepare.
preparatívo *nm* preparation.
preparàto *a* prepared; *nm* (*chemical etc*) preparation.
preparazióne *nf* preparation.
preponderànte *a* predominant, prevailing.
prepórre *vt* to place before, prefer.
preposizióne *nf* preposition.
prepósto *nm* (*eccl*) rector, vicar.
prepotènte *a* overbearing; *nm* bully.
prepotènza *nf* arrogance, bullying.
prerogatíva *nf* prerogative.
présa *nf* grip, hold; seizure; (*el*) (wall-)plug; **màcchina da p.** (*cin*) camera.
preşàgio *nm* omen, presage.
preşagíre *vt* to foretell, presage.
preşàgo *pl* **-ghi** *a* foreboding, having a presentiment of.
prèşbite *a* long-sighted.
prescégliere *vt* to choose, select.
prescíndere *vi* to leave out of account.
prescrívere *vt* to prescribe, order.
prescrizióne *nf* prescription; regulation.
preşentàre *vt* to present, introduce; **-rsi** *vr* to present oneself, appear; occur.
preşentatóre *nm* (*rad and tv*) announcer, (*theat*) master of ceremonies.
preşentazióne *nf* presentation, introduction.
preşènte *a nm* present; **tenèr p.** to bear in mind; **i presènti** those present.
presentiménto *nm* presentiment.
presentíre *vt* to have a presentiment, foresee.
preşènza *nf* presence; **p. di spírito** presence of mind.
preşèpio *nm* crib.
preservàre *vt* to preserve.
prèside *nm* headmaster, principal.
presidènte *nm* president, chairman.
presidenziàle *a* presidential.
presidiàre *vt* to garrison.
presídio *nm* garrison, defense.
presièdere (a) *vi* to preside (at), be in charge (of).
prèssa *nf* (*mech*) press.

pressànte *a* pressing, urgent.
prèssi *nm pl* neighborhood.
pressióne *nf* pressure.
prèsso *ad* close by, near; *prep* near, beside, with; (*address*) care of; **p. a pòco** *ad* approximately.
pressochè *ad* almost, nearly.
prestabilíre *vt* to pre-arrange.
prestànte *a* good-looking.
prestàre *vt* to lend; pay (*attention etc*); **fàrsi p.** *vt* to borrow; **-rsi** *vr* to be fit for, lend oneself.
prestazióne *nf* performance; **prestazióni** *pl* services.
prestigiatóre *nm* conjurer, juggler.
prestígio *nm* prestige, conjuring.
prèstito *nm* loan; **avére in p.** to borrow; **dàre in p.** to lend.
prèsto *ad* soon, early, quickly; *interj* (be) quick! **far p.** to make haste; **al piú p.** as soon as possible.
preşúmere *vi* to presume, suppose.
preşumíbile *a* presumable.
preşuntuóso *a* conceited, presumptuous.
preşunzióne *nf* presumption.
presuppórre *vti* to (pre)suppose.
presuppósto *a* presupposed; *nm* presupposition.
prète *nm* priest.
pretendènte *nmf* claimant, suitor.
pretèndere *vt* to claim, want; *vi* to claim, pretend.
pretensióne *nf* pretention, claim.
pretésa *nf* claim; pretense; pretension; **sènza pretése** unpretentious.
pretèsto *nm* pretext, occasion.
pretóre *nm* magistrate.
prètto *a* pure, real.
pretúra *nf* magistrate's court.
prevalènte *a* prevalent, prevailing.
prevalènza *nf* prevalence, supremacy.
prevalére *vi* to prevail.
prevedére *vt* to foresee.
prevedíbile *a* to be expected.
preveggènza *nf* foresight.
preveníre *vt* to precede, forestall, prevent, warn.
preventivàre *vt* (*com*) to estimate.
preventívo *a* preventive; *nm* (*com*) estimate.
prevenzióne *nf* bias, prejudice, prevention.
previdènte *a* provident.
previdènza *nf* foresight; **p. sociàle** social security.
prèvio *a* previous, subject to.
previşióne *nf* forecast, expectation.
preziosísmo *nm* (*liter*) preciosity.
preziosità *nf* preciousness, preciosity.
prezióso *a* precious, valuable.
prezzémolo *nm* parsley.
prèzzo *nm* price.
prigióne *nf* jail, prison, penitentiary.
prigionía *nf* imprisonment.
prigionièro *nm* prisoner.
prima *ad* before, sooner, first,

formerly; **quànto p.** very soon; **p. di** *prep*, **p. che** *cj* before.
primàrio *a* primary, chief; *nm* chief physician.
primatíccio *a* early.
primàto *nm* pre-eminence; (*sport*) record.
primavèra *nf* spring, springtime.
primaveríle *a* (of the) spring.
primeggiàre *vi* to excel.
primièro *a* first, former, previous.
primitívo *a* primitive, original.
primízia *nf* early fruit or vegetable; novelty.
prímo *a nm* first, former; **di príma màno** first hand; **di prím'órdine** first rate.
primogènito *a nm* first-born.
primòrdio *nm* beginning.
prímula *nf* primrose.
principàle *a* principal, main; *nm* principal, employer, manager.
principalménte *ad* mainly, chiefly.
principàto *nm* principality.
príncipe *nm* prince; **principéssa** *nf* princess.
principiànte *nmf* beginner.
principiàre *vt* to begin, start.
princípio *nm* beginning; principle.
prióre *nm* prior.
privàre *vt* to deprive, strip.
privataménte *ad* privately.
privatísta *nmf* external student.
privatíva *nf* monopoly; tobacconist's.
privàto *a* private; *nm* private citizen.
privazióne *nf* (de)privation.
privilegiàto *a* privileged; (*com*) preference.
privilègio *nm* privilege.
prívo (di) *a* devoid (of), lacking (in).
prò *nm* advantage, benefit, profit; **a che p.?** what is the use?; **buòn p. gli fàccia!** much good may it do him!
probàbile *a* probable, likely.
probabilità *nf* probability, chance.
probità *nf* honesty, probity.
problèma *nm* problem.
problemàtico *pl* **-ici** *a* difficult, uncertain.
pròbo *a* honest, upright.
probòscide *nf* trunk; proboscis.
procacciàre *vt* **-rsi** *vr* to get, procure, earn.
procàce *a* provocative.
procacità *nf* procacity, sauciness, impudence.
procèdere *vi* to proceed; behave; *nm* process; behavior.
procediménto *nm* conduct; course; process.
processàre *vt* (*leg*) to try; **far p.** to bring to trial.
processióne *nf* procession.
procèsso *nm* process; (*leg*) trial.
procínto *nm* **èssere in p. di** to be on the point of.
proclàma *nm* proclamation.

proclamàre *vt* to proclaim.
proclíve *a* inclined; **proclività** *nf* tendency.
procrastinàre *vti* to postpone, put off.
procreàre *vt* to procreate, generate.
procreazióne *nf* procreation.
procúra *nf* power of attorney, proxy.
procuràre *vt* to get; cause; provide; try; **-rsi** *vr* to get, procure.
procuratóre *nm* attorney, solicitor; (*eccl*) procurator; **P. Generàle** Attorney General.
pròde *a* brave, valiant; *nm* hero.
prodézza *nf* gallant deed, gallantry.
prodigalità *nf* lavishness, prodigality.
prodigàre *vt* to lavish, pour out; **-rsi** *vr* to do one's best.
prodígio *nm* marvel, prodigy.
pròdigo *pl* **-ghi** *a* lavish, prodigal; *nm* prodigal.
proditoriaménte *ad* treacherously.
prodòtto *a* produced; *nm* product, produce.
prodúrre *vt* to produce, yield; cause; **-rsi** *vr* to appear in public; happen.
produttività *nf* productiveness, productivity.
produttívo *a* productive, fruitful.
produttóre *a* producing; *nm* **-trice** *nf* producer, maker.
produzióne *nf* production, manufacture; exhibition.
proèmio *nm* introduction, preface.
profanàre *vt* to profane, debase.
profanazióne *nf* profanation.
profàno *a* profane, secular; *nm* profane, layman.
proferíre *vt* to utter.
professàre *vt* to profess.
professióne *nf* profession, trade, occupation; **di p.** by profession.
professionista *nm* professional man; (*sport*) professional.
professóre *nm* (school)master, teacher, (*university*) professor; **professoréssa** *nf* professor, mistress.
profèta *nm* prophet; **profetéssa** *nf* prophetess.
profetàre, profetizzàre *vt* to prophesy.
profezía *nf* prophecy.
profferíre *vt* to offer; utter.
profferta *nf* offer.
profícuo *a* profitable, useful.
profilàssi *nf* (*med*) prophylaxis.
profílo *nm* profile, outline.
profittàre *vi* to profit, make progress.
profítto *nm* profit, benefit.
proflúvio *nm* overflow, abundance.
profondaménte *ad* deeply, profoundly.
profóndere *vt* to lavish, squander; **-rsi** *vr* to be lavish.
profondità *nf* depth, profundity.
profóndo *a* deep, profound; *nm* depth.

pròfugo pl -ghi nm refugee.
profumàre vt to perfume, scent; -rsi vr to put on scent.
profumería nf perfumer's shop; perfumery.
profumière nm perfumer; negòzio di p. perfumer's shop.
profúmo nm perfume, scent.
profusióne nf abundance, profusion.
progènie nf progeny, descendants pl, issue.
progenitóre nm ancestor, forefather -trìce nf ancestor.
progettàre vt to plan.
progètto nm plan, project, scheme; p. di lègge bill.
prògnoṣi nf (med) prognosis.
progràmma nm program, prospectus, syllabus.
progredíre vi to advance, (make) progress.
progredíto a advanced, civilized.
progrèsso nm progress, headway.
proibíre vi to forbid, prohibit, prevent.
proibitívo a prohibitive.
proibizióne nf prohibition.
proiettàre vti to project, cast; (cin) to screen.
proièttile nm projectile, shell.
proiettóre nm searchlight, floodlight; projector; (aut) headlight.
proiezióne nf projection; (film) showing, slide.
pròle nf pl children, issue.
proletariàto nm proletariat.
proletàrio a nm proletarian.
prolífico pl -ici a prolific.
prolísso a long-winded, prolix.
pròlogo pl -ghi nm prologue.
prolungaménto nm prolongation, extension, continuation.
prolungàre vt to extend, prolong; -rsi vr to continue, extend.
prolusióne nf inaugural lecture.
proméssa nf promise.
promettènte a promising.
prométtere vti to promise.
prominènte a prominent, jutting.
prominènza nf prominence.
promíscuo a promiscuous, mixed.
promontòrio nm headland, promontory.
promòsso a promoted, (of candidate in exam) successful.
promozióne nf promotion; avére la p. to pass (exam).
promulgàre vt to promulgate.
promuòvere vt to promote, pass; cause.
pròno a prone.
pronóme nm pronoun.
pronòstico pl -ici nm forecast.
prontaménte ad readily, immediately, promptly.
prontézza nf quickness, readiness, promptitude.
prónto a ready, prompt; (on telephone) hello!; prónta càssa ready cash.

pronúncia nf pronunciation.
pronunciàre vt to pronounce, utter; -rsi vr to express one's opinion.
propagànda nf propaganda, advertising.
propagàre vt -rsi vr to propagate, spread.
propàggine nf ramification, lineage; (agr) layer.
propalàre vt to divulge, spread.
propèndere vi to incline.
propensióne nf propensity.
propènso a inclined, ready.
propiziàre vt -rsi vr to propitiate.
propízio a favorable, propitious.
proponiménto nm resolution, resolve.
propórre vt to propose, suggest; -rsi vr to intend, resolve.
proporzionàle a proportional.
proporzionàto a proportioned, proportionate; suitable.
proporzióne nf proportion.
propòsito nm purpose; a p. by the by, by the way; di p. on purpose.
propósta nf proposal, proposition.
propriaménte ad properly, really, exactly.
proprietàrio nm owner, proprietor; (newspaper) publisher.
pròprio a (one's) own, characteristic; nm one's own; ad exactly, just, really.
propugnàre vt to plead for, support.
propulsióne nf propulsion.
pròra nf (naut) bow, prow.
pròroga nf adjournment, postponement, extension, respite.
prorogàre vt to postpone, put off, extend.
prorómpere vi to burst (out), gush.
pròṣa nf prose; (theat) drama.
prosàico pl -ici a prosaic.
prosciògliere vt to release; (leg) acquit.
prosciugaménto nm draining, reclamation; drying up.
prosciugàre vt to drain, dry, reclaim; vi and -rsi vr to dry (up).
prosciútto nm ham.
proscrítto a outlawed, exile; nm outlaw, exile.
proscrizióne nf proscription, banishment.
proseguiménto nm continuation.
proseguíre vt to continue, go on, pursue.
prosèlito nm proselyte.
proṣodía nf prosody.
prosperàre vi to prosper, thrive.
prosperità nf prosperity, wealth.
pròspero a prosperous, fortunate.
prosperóso a prosperous; healthy, plump.
prospettìva nf perspective; prospect, view, outlook.
prospètto nm prospect, view; prospectus.
prospiciènte a facing, opposite.
prossimaménte ad before long, in

the near future; (in film programs) coming shortly; nm trailer.
prossimità nf nearness, proximity, vicinity.
pròssimo a near, next; nm neighbor; **in un p. avveníre** in the near future.
prostituíre vt to prostitute; **-rsi** vr to prostitute oneself, sell oneself.
prostitúta nf prostitute.
prostituzióne nf prostitution.
prostràre vt to prostrate, overwhelm; exhaust; **-rsi** vr to bow down; get exhausted.
prostrazióne nf prostration, exhaustion.
protagonísta nmf chief character, protagonist.
protèggere vt to protect, defend, support.
proteína nf protein.
protèndere vt to hold out, stretch; **-rsi in avànti** vr to lean forward.
protèsta nf protest(ation).
protestànte a nmf Protestant.
protestàre vti to protest.
protestàto a protested (also com); **protèsto** nm (com) protest.
protètto a protected, sheltered; nm favorite, protégé.
protettóre nm **-tríce** nf patron, protector.
protezióne nf protection, patronage.
protocòllo nm protocol; record; **formàto p.** foolscap (size).
protòtipo nm prototype.
protràrre vt to protract, put off.
protrazióne nf protraction, deferment.
protruberànza nf protruberance.
protuberànte a protuberant, bulging.
pròva nf proof; evidence; test; rehearsal.
provàre vt to prove; show; try (on); feel; rehearse; **-rsi** vr to endeavor, try.
proveniènza nf origin, source.
proveníre vi to come (from); be caused (by).
provènto nm income, proceeds pl.
Provènza nf (geogr) Provence.
provenzàle a nmf Provençal.
proverbiàle a proverbial.
provèrbio nm proverb, saying.
provètta nf test-tube.
provètto a experienced, skilled.
província nf province, district.
provinciàle a provincial; **stràda p.** nf highway, main road.
províno nm test-tube; (cin) film-test.
provocànte a provocative.
provocàre vt to provoke, cause, stir up.
provocazióne nf provocation.
provolóne nm a kind of cheese.
provvedére (di) vt to provide (with); **p. a** vi to provide (for); **-rsi** vr to provide oneself.

provvediménto nm measure, provision.
provvidènza nf providence; (fig) boon.
provvidenziàle a providential.
pròvvido a provident, thrifty.
provvigióne nf (com) commission; provision.
provvisòrio a provisional, temporary.
provvísta nf supply.
prúa v **próra**.
prudènte a prudent, careful.
prudènza nf prudence, caution.
prúdere vi to itch.
prúgna nf plum; **prúgno** nm plum-tree.
prúno nm thorn-bush; thorn.
pruríto nm itch(ing).
pseudònimo a pseudonymous; nm pseudonym, pen-name.
psicanàlisi nm psychoanalysis.
psicanalísta nmf psychoanalyst.
psichiàtra nmf psychiatrist; **psichiatría** nf psychiatry.
psicología nf psychology; **psicològico** pl **-ici** a psychological; **psicòlogo** pl **-ogi** nm psychologist.
pubblicàre vt to publish, issue.
pubblicazióne nf publication, issue.
pubblicità nf publicity, advertising.
pubblicitàrio a advertising.
púbblico pl **-ici** a public; nm audience, public.
pubertà nf puberty.
pudicízia nf modesty.
pudíco pl **-chi** a modest, bashful.
pudóre nm decency, modesty.
pueríle a childish, puerile.
puerízia nf childhood.
pugilàto nm boxing.
púgile nm boxer, pugilist.
Púglia nf (geogr) Apulia.
pugliése a nm (inhabitant) of Apulia.
pugnalàre vt to stab.
pugnalàta nf stab.
pugnàle nm dagger.
púgno nm fist; blow; handful; **in p.** in one's hands; **fàre a púgni** fight, clash.
púlce nf flea.
puicíno nm chick(en).
pulédro nm colt, foal.
puléggia nf pulley.
pulíre vt to clean, polish, wash.
pulíto a clean, clear, neat.
pulizía nf cleaning; cleanliness, cleanness.
pullman nm motor-coach; (rly) Pullman car.
pullóver nm pullover.
pullulàre di vi to be full of, swarm with, pullulate with.
pulvíscolo nm fine dust, motes pl.
púlpito nm pulpit.
pulsànte a pulsating, throbbing; nm push-button; **p. da campanèllo** bell push.
pulsàre vi to beat, pulsate, throb.

pulsazióne *nf* beat, pulsation, throb.
pungènte *a* prickly, stinging, pungent.
púngere *vt* to prick, sting.
pungiglióne *nm* sting.
púngolo *nm* goad, spur.
punìre *vt* to punish.
punizióne *nf* punishment.
púnta *nf* point, tip, end; top; headland; a little; in p. di pièdi on tiptoe.
puntàre *vt* to point, aim; push; bet; p. i pièdi to dig one's heels in; *vi* to head for.
puntàta *nf* installment; stake; thrust.
punteggiatúra *nf* punctuation.
puntéggio *nm* (*sport*) score.
puntellàre *vt* to prop, support.
puntèllo *nm* prop, support.
puntíglio *nm* punctilio, obstinacy; spite.
puntiglióso *a* punctilious, obstinate.
puntína *nf* (*of record player*) stylus; p. da disègno drawing pin, thumbtack.
púnto *nm* point, dot, mark, full stop; stitch; spot; *a* any; non ... p. no, none; *ad* at all; in p. exactly; di p. in biànco point-blank; p. e vírgola semicolon; dúe púnti colon.
puntuàle *a* punctual.
puntualità *nf* punctuality.
puntúra *nf* prick, sting; injection.
punzecchiàre *vt* to prick, sting; tease.
pupàzzo *nm* puppet.
pupílla *nf* (*eye*) pupil.
pupíllo *nm* pupília *nf* ward.
púpo *nm* puppet; (*fam*) baby.
purchè *cj* on condition that, provided (that).
púre *ad* also, too; however, yet.
purézza *nf* purity.
púrga *nf* purgative.
purgànte *a nm* purgative, laxative.
purgàre *vt* to purge, purify, expurgate.
purgatívo *a* laxative, purgative.
purgatòrio *nm* Purgatory.
purificàre *vt* to purify, cleanse.
purificazióne *nf* purification.
purità *nf* purity.
puritàno *a nm* Puritan (*also fig*).
púro *a* pure; p. sàngue thoroughbred.
purpúreo *a* deep red, purple.
purtròppo *ad* unfortunately.
pusillànime *a* cowardly, faint-hearted; *nm* coward.
putifèrio *nm* uproar, hullabaloo.
putrèdine *nf* putridity, rottenness.
putrefàre *vi* -rsi *vr* to go bad, putrefy, rot.
putrefazióne *nf* decomposition.
pútrido *a* putrid, rotten.
puttàna *nf* whore.
pútto *nm* (*art*) cherub, child's figure.
puzzàre *vi* to smell bad, stink.
púzzo *nm* bad smell, stench, stink.
púzzola *nf* polecat.
puzzolènte *a* fetid, stinking.

Q

qua *ad* here; da quàndo in q.? since when?
quadèrno *nm* exercise book.
quadràngolo *nm* quadrangle.
quadrànte *nm* quadrant, dial, clock-face, sun-dial.
quadràre *vt* to square; *vi* to suit.
quadràto *a* square, strong; *nm* square.
quàdro *nm* picture; painting, description; (*mil*) cadre; quàdri *pl* (*cards*) diamonds; a quàdri (*cloth etc*) checked.
quaggiù *ad* down here.
quàglia *nf* quail.
quàlche *a* some, any; q. còsa *pron* something, anything; in q. luògo somewhere, anywhere.
qualcòsa *pron* something, anything.
qualcúno *pron* someone, somebody, anyone, anybody; *pl* some, any.
quàle *a pron* which?, what?; as; that, who, whom, whose.
qualífica *nf* qualification; title.
qualificàre *vt* to qualify; call; describe.
qualità *nf* quality, capacity.
qualóra *cj* if.
qualsíasi, qualúnque *a* any, whatever, whichever; un uòmo q. an ordinary man.
qualvòlta, ògni *cj* whenever.
quàndo *ad cj* when, if, since; di q. in q. from time to time; quand'ànche even if.
quantità *nf* quantity, amount.
quànto *a ad pron* how, how much; as, as much as, what; q. príma as soon as possible; per q. though; quànti *pl* as (many), how many.
quantúnque *cj* (al)though.
quarànta *a* forty; quarantèna *nf* quarantine; quarantènne *a* forty-year-old; quarantèsimo *a* fortieth; quarantína *nf* some forty.
quarésima *nf* Lent.
quaresimàle *a* Lenten.
quartière *nm* (*city*) quarter, district; flat, apartment; (*mil*) quarters *pl*; q. generàle (*mil*) H.Q.
quartíno *nm* quarter of a liter, about half a pint.
quàrto *a* fourth; *nm* quarter; quarto.
quàsi *ad* almost, nearly; hardly; *cj* as if; quàsi che as if.
quassù *ad* up here.
quàtto *a* cowering, crouching; q. q. very quietly.
quattórdici *a* fourteen; quattordicènne *a nmf* fourteen-year-old; quattordicèsimo *a* fourteenth.
quattríno *nm* farthing; quattríni *pl* money.
quàttro *a* four.
quattrocènto *a* four hundred; *nm* the 15th century.

quél(lo) *dem a pron* that, that one; whoever; he; the former; **q. che** what.

quèrcia *nf* oak(tree).

querèla *nf* complaint.

querelàre *vt* (*leg*) to proceed against, prosecute; **-rsi** *vr* (*leg*) to bring a complaint.

quésti *dem pron* this man, the latter.

questionàre *vi* to dispute, quarrel.

questionàrio *nm* questionnaire.

questióne *nf* question; dispute, lawsuit.

quésto *dem a pron* this, this one, he, the latter.

questóre *nm* superintendent of police.

quèstua *nf* begging, (*for charity*) collection.

questúra *nf* police station.

questuríno *nm* policeman.

qui *ad* here; **q. vicíno** close by; **fin q.** so far, till now.

quietànza *nf* receipt.

quietàre *vt* to quiet; **-rsi** *vr* to quiet down.

quiète *nf* quiet, calm, peace, silence, rest.

quièto *a* quiet, calm, still, tranquil.

quíndi *ad* hence, therefore, then, thereby.

quíndici *d* fifteen; **quindicènne** *a nmf* fifteen-year-old; **quindicèsimo** *a* fifteenth.

quindicína *nf* some fifteen; **una q. di giórni** a fortnight or so.

quindicinàle *a nm* fortnightly (*magazine*).

quinquennàle *a* quinquennial.

quínta *nf* (*theat*) wing; **diétro le quínte** *ad* behind the scenes.

quintàle *nm* quintal (100 kilos).

quínto *a* fifth.

Quirinàle *nm* Quirinal.

quòta *nf* share, installment; (*av*) altitude, (*naut*) depth.

quotàre *vt* (*com*) to quote; **-rsi** *vr* to subscribe (a sum).

quotàto *a* (*com*) quoted; esteemed, well-liked.

quotazióne *nf* (*com*) quotation; **quotazióni di Bórsa** Stock-Exchange quotations.

quotidiàno *a* daily; *nm* daily paper.

quoto, quoziènte *nm* quotient.

R

rabàrbaro *nm* rhubarb.

rabberciàre *vt* to botch; patch (up).

ràbbia *nf* anger, fury; hydrophobia, rabies.

rabbíno *nm* Rabbi.

rabbióso *a* furious, angry; rabid.

rabboníre *vt* to calm, pacify; **-rsi** *vr* to calm down.

rabbrividíre *vi* to shiver, shudder.

rabbúffo *nm* rebuke, reprimand.

rabbuiàre *vi* **-rsi** *vr* to grow dark.

rabdomànte *nm* dowser, water diviner.

raccapezzàre *vt* to collect, put together; **-rsi** *vr* to find one's way, make out.

raccapricciànte *a* horrifying, terrifying.

raccapricciàre *vt* to horrify; *vi* **-rsi** *vr* to be horrified, shudder.

raccapríccio *nm* horror.

raccattàre *vt* to pick up, collect.

racchétta *nf* racquet; **r. del tergicristàllo** (*aut*) windscreen wiper, windshield wiper; **r. per la nève** snowshoes.

racchiúdere *vt* to contain, hold.

raccògliere *vt* to pick up; assemble, gather, collect; receive; fold; **-rsi** *vr* to gather, collect one's thoughts.

raccogliménto *nm* concentration, meditation.

raccòlta *nf* collection, gathering; harvest, harvesting.

raccòlto *a* picked, collected; (*fig*) engrossed; cozy, curled up; *nm* crop, harvest.

raccomandàbile *a* reliable, recommendable.

raccomandàre *vt* to recommend; (*mail*) register; **-rsi** *vr* to entreat; commend oneself; **mi raccomàndo** please.

raccomandàta *nf* registered letter; person recommended.

raccomandàto *a* recommended; registered; *nm* protégé.

raccomandazióne *nf* recommendation; registration.

raccomodàre *vt* to mend, repair; arrange; revive.

raccontàre *vt* to narrate, relate, tell.

raccónto *nm* story, tale, report.

raccorciàre *vt* to shorten; **-rsi** *vr* to grow short(er), shrink.

Rachèle *nf pr* Rachel.

rachítico *pl* **-ici** *a* rickety, stunted.

rachítide *nf* **rachitísmo** *nm* rickets.

racimolàre *vt* to scrape together, glean.

ràda *nf* (*naut*) roads *pl*, roadstead.

ràdar *nm* radar.

raddolcíre *vt* to soften, soothe, sweeten; **-rsi** *vr* to soften; (*of weather*) become milder.

raddoppiàre *vt* to (re)double.

raddrizzàre *vt* to straighten; correct; **-rsi** *vr* to draw oneself up; improve.

radènte *a* shaving, grazing; **vòlo r.** (*av*) hedgehopping.

ràdere *vt* **-rsi** *vr* to shave (oneself).

radiàre *vt* to expel, strike off.

radiatóre *nm* radiator.

radiazióne *nf* radiation; expulsion.

ràdica *nf* briarwood, root.

radicàle *a nm* radical.

radicàre *vi* **-rsi** *vr* to (take) root.

radíce *nf* root; horse-radish.

radiestesía *nf* sensitivity to radiation.

ràdio *nf* radio, wireless; *nm* radium.

radioascoltatóre nm -tríce nf, **radioauditóre** nm -tríce nf radio listener.
radioattívo a radioactive; **piòggia radioattíva** fall-out; **rèndere r.** to activate.
radiocomandàto a remote controlled.
radiocronísta nmf radio commentator.
radiodiffusióne nf broadcasting, broadcast.
radiofònico pl -ici a wireless; **apparècchio r.** wireless set.
radiografía nf radiography.
radiología nf X-ray treatment.
radioscòpico pl -ici a radioscopic **esàme r.** X-ray examination.
radióso a beaming, radiant, bright.
radiotelegrafísta nm wireless operator.
radiotrasmissióne nf broadcasting, broadcast.
radiotrasmittènte a broadcasting; nf broadcasting station.
ràdo a rare, thin, infrequent; **di r.** seldom.
radunàre vt -rsi vr to assemble, gather.
radúno nm meeting, gathering, rally.
radúra nf glade, clearing.
ràfano nm horse-radish.
Raffaèle nm pr Raphael.
raffermàre vt to confirm, renew.
rafférmo a stale.
ràffica nf gust of wind, squall.
raffiguràre vt to represent.
raffilàre vt to sharpen, whet; pare.
raffinaménto nm refining.
raffinàre vt to refine, thin.
raffinatézza nf refinement.
raffinería nf refinery.
rafforzàre vt to reinforce, strengthen; -rsi vr to get stronger.
raffreddaménto nm cooling, coolness.
raffreddàre vt to chill, cool; -rsi vr to cool, get cold; catch a cold.
raffreddóre nm (med) cold.
raffrenàre vt to check, curb, restrain; -rsi vr to check oneself.
raffrontàre vt to compare.
raffrónto nm comparison.
raganèlla nf tree-frog; rattle.
ragàzza nf girl.
ragàzzo nm boy; lad.
raggiànte a radiant.
ràggio nm ray, beam; radius; spoke.
raggiràre vt to cheat, swindle, trick.
raggíro nm trick.
raggiúngere vt to reach; join; achieve; hit.
raggiustàre vt to mend; set in order.
raggranellàre vt to scrape together.
raggrinzíre vt to wrinkle (up).
raggruppaménto nm cluster, group (ing).
raggruppàre vt to collect, set in

groups; -rsi vr to cluster, form groups.
raggruzzolàre vt to put together, save.
ragguagliàre vt to balance, compare; inform.
ragguàglio nm balance; comparison; information.
ragguardévole a considerable, notable.
ràgia nf rosin, resin; **àcqua r.** turpentine.
ragionaménto nm reasoning, argument.
ragionàre vi to reason, argue, discuss.
ragióne nf reason, right; **avèr r.** to be right.
ragionería nf accountancy, bookkeeping.
ragionévole a reasonable.
ragionevolézza nf reasonableness.
ragionière nm (certified) accountant, book-keeper.
ragliàre vi to bray.
ràglio nm braying.
ragnatéla nf **ragnatélo** nm spider's web.
ràgno nm spider.
ragú nm ragout.
Raimóndo nm pr Raymond.
rallegraménto nm rejoicing; congratulation.
rallegràre vt to cheer, make glad; -rsi vr to rejoice; congratulate.
rallentàre vt to slacken, lessen; **r. il pàsso** to slacken down one's pace; vi to slow down.
ramaiòlo nm ladle.
ramanzína nf telling-off, scolding.
ramàrro nm green lizard.
ràme nm copper.
ramificàre vi -rsi vr to branch (out), ramify.
ramificazióne nf ramification.
ramíngo pl -ghi a roaming, wandering.
ramíno nm copper kettle; (card game) rummy.
rammaricàrsi vr to be sorry, grieve, regret.
rammàrico pl -chi nm grief, regret, bitterness.
rammendàre vt to darn, mend.
ramméndo nm darn, mending.
rammentàre vt to recall, remind; -rsi vr to recollect, remember.
rammolliménto nm softening.
rammollíre vt to soften (also fig); move to pity.
ràmo nm branch; (com) line; arm; antler.
ramoscèllo nm spray, twig.
ramóso a branchy.
ràmpa nf flight of steps; steep slope; ramp.
rampicànte a climbing, creeping; nm (zool) climber; (plant) creeper.
rampógna nf rebuke, reproof.
rampóllo nm offspring, shoot.

rampóne nm harpoon; crampon.
ràna nf frog.
rancidézza nf rancidness.
ràncido a rancid, rank.
ràncio nm (mil) rations, mess.
rancóre nm grudge, rancor.
randàgio a stray, wandering.
randèllo nm cudgel.
ranèlla nf (mech) washer.
Randòlfo nm pr Randolph.
ràngo pl **rànghi** nm rank.
rannicchiàrsi vr to crouch, curl up.
rannuvolàre vi -rsi vr to cloud over, grow dark.
ranòcchia nf **ranòcchio** nm frog.
rantolàre vi to breathe heavily, have the death-rattle in one's throat.
ràntolo nm heavy breathing, (death-) rattle.
ranúncolo nm buttercup.
ràpa nf turnip.
rapàce a greedy, predatory.
rapacità nf greed, rapaciousness.
rapàre vt to crop the hair of.
rapidaménte ad rapidly.
rapidità nf rapidity, swiftness.
ràpido a quick, speedy, fast; nm express train.
rapiménto nm kidnapping; (fig) rapture.
rapína nf robbery, plunder.
rapinàre vt to rob, plunder.
rapinatóre nm robber.
rapíre vt to abduct, steal, carry off; (fig) ravish.
rappacificàre vt to pacify, reconcile.
rappezzàre vt to patch (up).
rappèzzo nm patch.
rappòrto nm report, relation, connection; éssere in buòni rappòrti to be on good terms.
rappresàglia nf reprisal, retaliation.
rappreṣentànte nm representative, agent.
rappreṣentànza nf agency; deputation; representation.
rappreṣentàre vt to represent; (theat) perform; -rsi vr to picture to oneself.
rappreṣentatívo a representative.
rappreṣentazióne nf description; performance.
raraménte ad seldom.
rarefàre vt -rsi vr to rarefy.
rarità nf rarity; scarcity.
ràro a rare.
rasàre vt to shave; smooth; -rsi vr to shave.
raschiàre vt to scrape, scratch.
ràschio nm irritation in the throat.
raṣentàre vt to graze; border upon.
raṣènte (a) prep close to.
ràso a smooth, shaven; **r. a** prep close to; nm satin.
rasóio nm razor.
raspàre vt to rasp, scratch; search through.
rasségna nf review, parade.
rassegnàre vt to resign; pass in

review; -rsi vr to resign oneself, submit.
rassegnazióne nf resignation.
rasserenàre vt to brighten, calm; -rsi vr to clear up, brighten up.
rassettàre vt to tidy, mend.
rassicurànte a reassuring.
rassicuràre vt to (re)assure; -rsi vr to make sure, be reassured.
rassicurazióne nf assurance, reassurance.
rassodaménto nm hardening, (fig) consolidation.
rassodàre vti to harden, strengthen.
rassomigliànza nf likeness, resemblance.
rassomigliàre vi -rsi vr to be alike, resemble.
rastrellàre vt to rake; ransack; (mil) mop up, comb.
rastrellièra nf rack; crib.
rastrèllo nm (tool) rake.
ràta nf installment; vèndita a ràte hire-purchase system, installment plan.
rateàle a by installments, partial.
ratífica nf ratification.
ratificàre vt to ratify.
ràtto nm abduction, kidnapping, theft; rat; a quick, swift.
rattoppàre vt to mend, patch (up).
rattòppo nm patch.
rattrappíre vti to benumb; contract.
rattristàre vt to sadden; -rsi vr to grieve.
raucèdine nf hoarseness.
ràuco pl **ràuchi** a hoarse.
ravanèllo nm radish.
ravvedérsi vr to reform, repent.
ravvediménto nm reformation, repentance.
ravviàre vt to (re)arrange, tidy.
ravvicinàre vt to bring closer; reconcile; compare.
ravviṣàbile a recognizable.
ravviṣàre vt to recognize.
ravvivàre vt to revive (also fig).
ravvòlgere etc v **avvòlgere** etc.
raziocínio nm reason(ing), common sense.
razionàle a rational.
razióne nf ration, portion.
ràzza nf race, kind.
ràzza nf (fish) ray.
razzía nf raid; insect-powder.
razziàle a racial.
razziàre vti to raid, plunder.
ràzzo nm rocket, missile; spoke.
razzolàre vi to scratch about, rummage.
ré nm king.
rè nm (mus) D, re.
reagíre vi to react.
reàle a real; royal; nm the real, reality.
realíṣmo nm realism.
realíṣta nmf realist; royalist.
realístico pl -ici a realistic.
realizzàre vt to realize; -rsi vr to come true.

realizzazióne *nf* fulfillment; realization; (*theat*) production.
realménte *ad* really, in reality.
realtà *nf* reality.
reàme *nm* kingdom.
reàto *nm* crime.
reattívo *a* reactive; *nm* (*chem*) reagent.
reattóre *nm* reactor; (*av*) jet plane; **r. sperimentàle** breeder reactor.
reazionàrio *a nm* reactionary.
reazióne *nf* reaction; **aèreo a r.** (*av*) jet; **motóre a r.** jet engine.
recapitàre *vt* to deliver.
recàpito *nm* address, delivery.
recàre *vt* to bring, carry; cause; **-rsi** *vr* to go.
recensióne *nf* review.
recensíre *vt* to review.
recènte *a* recent, new.
recenteménte *ad* recently.
recèsso *nm* recess.
recídere *vt* to cut off.
recidíva *nf* relapse.
recíngere *vt* to enclose, fence in.
recínto *a* enclosed; *nm* enclosure.
recipiènte *nm* container, vessel.
recíproco *pl* **-oci** *a* mutual, reciprocal.
recíso *a* cut off; resolute; curt.
rècita *nf* performance, recital.
recitàre *vt* to recite, act, play.
recitazióne *nf* recitation; acting.
reclamàre *vt* to claim; *vi* complain.
réclame *nf* (*Fr*) advertising, advertisement.
reclàmo *nm* complaint.
reclusióne *nf* seclusion; imprisonment.
reclusòrio *nm* penitentiary, prison.
rècluta *nf* (*mil*) recruit.
reclutaménto *nm* recruiting.
reclutàre *vt* to recruit.
recòndito *a* hidden, innermost.
recriminàre *vi* to recriminate.
recriminazióne *nf* recrimination.
recrudescénza *nf* recrudescence.
redarguíre *vt* to reproach.
redattóre *nm* **-trice** *nf* compiler; journalist, writer; (*newspaper*) sub-editor, copyreader.
redazióne *nf* compiling; editing; editorial staff; editor's office.
redditízio *a* paying, profitable.
rèddito *nm* income, revenue.
redènto *a* redeemed.
redentóre *nm* **-trice** *nf* redeemer; *a* redeeming; **il R.** the Redeemer.
redenzióne *nf* redemption.
redígere *vt* to compile, draw up.
redímere *vt* to redeem.
rèdini *nf pl* reins *pl*.
redivívo *a* risen from the dead; new.
rèduce *a* returning; *nm* survivor; ex-serviceman.
réfe *nm* thread.
referènza *nf* reference, testimonial.
refettòrio *nm* refectory.
refezióne *nf* light meal; **r. scolàstica** school meal.

refrattàrio *a* refractory; fireproof.
refrigerànte *a* refrigerating, refrigerant; *nm* refrigerator, icebox.
refrigèrio *nm* cool; relief.
refurtíva *nf* stolen goods *pl*.
regàglie *v* **rigàglie**.
regalàre *vt* to make a present of, present.
regàle *a* regal, royal.
regàlo *nm* gift, present.
regàta *nf* regatta.
reggènte *nm* regent.
reggènza *nf* regency.
règgere *vti* to bear, carry; govern; hold; **-rsi** *vr* to stand; be ruled.
règgia *nf* royal palace.
reggicàlze *nm* suspender belt, garter belt, girdle.
reggiménto *nm* regiment; government.
reggipètto, reggiséno *nm* brassière.
regía *nf* state monopoly; (*theat*) production; (*cin*) direction.
regíme *nm* regime; regimen, diet; **stàre a r.** to be on a diet.
regína *nf* queen.
règio *a* royal.
regióne *nf* region, district.
regista *nmf* (*theat*) producer, (*cin*) director.
registràre *vt* (*com*) to enter; record, register.
registratóre *nm* **-trice** *nf* registrar, recorder; **r. su nàstro** tape-recorder.
registrazióne *nf* (*com*) entry; recording, registration.
regístro *nm* register; registry.
regnàre *vi* to reign.
régno *nm* reign; kingdom.
règola *nf* rule; moderation; **di r.** as a rule; **in r.** in order.
regolamentàre *a* regulation.
regolaménto *nm* regulation; (*of accounts*) settlement.
regolàre *a* regular; *vt* to regulate; settle; **-rsi** *vr* to act, behave.
regolarità *nf* regularity.
regolarizzàre *vt* to regularize.
regolatézza *nf* orderliness, moderation.
regolàto *a* orderly, regular, moderate.
regolazióne *nf* regulation; adjustment.
règolo *nm* (*for lines*) ruler; **r. calcolatóre** sliding rule.
reiètto *a* rejected; *nm* castaway, outcast.
reintegràre *vt* to reinstate, restore; compensate.
relativaménte *ad* relatively, comparatively; **r. a** with regard to.
relatívo *a* relative; comparative; **r. a** concerning.
relatóre *nm* reporter.
relazióne *nf* report; relation; acquaintance; affair; **avèr mólte relazióni** to know many people.
relegàre *vt* to confine, relegate.

religióne nf religion.
religióso a religious; nm member of a religious order.
relíquia nf relic.
relítto nm wreckage.
remàre vi to row, paddle.
rematóre nm rower, oarsman.
reminiscènza nf reminiscence.
remissióne nf remission.
remissívo a meek, submissive.
rèmo nm oar.
remòto a distant, remote, secluded.
réna nf sand(s).
rèndere vt to give back, repay; yield, render; make; -rsi vr to become, make oneself; -rsi cónto di to realize.
rendicónto nm report, statement.
rendiménto nm rendering, returning (thanks); yield; efficiency.
rèndita nf income, revenue.
rène nm kidney.
renitènte a unwilling, recalcitrant; r. alla lèva (mil) failing to appear at the call up.
rènna nf reindeer.
Rèno nm (geogr) Rhine.
rèo a guilty.
repàrto nm department; (mil) detachment, party.
repellènte a repellent, repulsive.
repentàglio nm danger, risk.
repènte, repentíno a sudden.
reperíbile a to be found.
repèrto nm report, evidence, exhibit.
repertòrio nm repertory, inventory.
rèplica nf reply, retort; repetition.
replicàre vt to reply, retort; repeat.
repressióne nf repression.
reprímere vt to repress, check.
rèprobo a nm reprobate.
repúbblica nf republic.
repubblicàno a nm republican.
reputàre vt to consider, deem.
reputàto a esteemed, well thought of.
reputazióne nf reputation.
rèquie nf rest, peace.
requisíre vt to requisition.
requisitòria nf charge, indictment.
requisizióne nf requisition.
résa nf surrender; rendering, return, yield.
residènte a residing; nmf resident.
residènza nf residence, residency.
residuo a residual; nm residue.
rèsina nf resin.
resistènte a resistant, strong; (color) fast; r. a proof against.
resistènza nf resistance, endurance.
resístere vi to resist, hold out, be proof against.
resocónto nm report; account.
respíngere vt to drive back, reject.
respiràre vti to breathe.
respirazióne nf respiration, breathing.
respíro nm breath; respite.
responsàbile a responsible.
responsabilità nf responsibility.
respònso nm response, answer.

rèssa nf crowd, throng.
restàre v rimanére.
restauràre vt to restore.
restàuro nm restoration, repair.
restío a restive, reluctant, unmanageable.
restituíre vt to return, restore.
restituzióne nf restitution, reinstatement.
rèsto nm remainder, rest; (money) change; rèsti pl remains pl; del r. besides.
restríngere vt to narrow, contract, restrict, tighten; -rsi vr to contract, narrow, shrink.
restrizióne nf restriction.
resurrezióne nf risurrezióne.
retàggio nm heritage, inheritance.
réte nf net, network, share.
reticènza nf reticence.
Rètiche, (Àlpi) nf pl (geogr) Rhaetian Alps.
reticolàto nm barbed wire entanglement; wire-netting.
retòrica nf rhetoric.
retòrico a rhetorical.
retribuíre vt to pay, reward.
retribuzióne nf pay; retribution.
rètro ad behind; nm back; védi r. please turn over (P.T.O.).
retrobottéga nf back-shop.
retrocèdere vt to degrade, reduce in rank; vi to retreat.
retrocucína nm scullery.
retrògrado a nm retrograde, reactionary.
retroscèna nm behind the scenes; underhand dealing.
retrotèrra nf hinterland.
rètta nf charge, terms pl; (geom) straight line; dàr r. a qlcu to follow s.o.'s advice.
rettàngolo nm rectangle.
rettífica nf amendment; alteration.
rettificàre vt to rectify, correct.
rettificazióne nf rectification, correction.
rèttile nm reptile.
rettitúdine nf honesty, uprightness.
rètto a straight; honest, right.
rettóre nm rector.
reumatísmo nm rheumatism.
reverèndo a reverend; nm padre.
revisióne nf revision; r. dèi cónti audit.
rèvoca nf revocation, repeal.
revocàbile a revokable.
revocàre vt to repeal, revoke.
revòlver nm revolver.
revolveràta nf revolver shot.
ri: common prefix to Italian verbs meaning again or back; thus: **richiúdere** to shut again; **ridàre** to give back etc. For verbs with prefix **ri-** not given below, see entries without prefix.
riabilitàre vt to rehabilitate, requalify; -rsi vr to regain one's good name.

riabilitazióne nf rehabilitation.
rialzàre vt to lift up again, heighten; vi go up.
riàlzo nm rise.
riàrso a dry, parched.
riassúnto nm summary, summing-up.
riavérsi vr to recover.
ribadíre vt to clinch, fix; rivet.
ribaldería nf foul deed, knavish trick.
ribàldo nm rascal, scoundrel.
ribàlta nf (theat) footlights, front of the stage.
ribaltàre vti to capsize, overturn.
ribassàre vt to lower, reduce.
ribàsso nm fall, decline; reduction.
ribàttere vt to beat again; repel; (fig) confute.
ribellàrsi vr to rebel, rise (against).
ribèlle a nm rebel.
ribellióne nf rebellion.
ríbes nm redcurrant; blackcurrant.
ribrézzo nm horror, loathing.
ributtànte a revolting.
ricadére vi to fall down again; (have a) relapse.
ricadúta nf relapse.
ricamàre vt to embroider.
ricamatríce nf embroiderer.
ricambiàre vt to change again, reciprocate, repay, return.
ricàmbio nm exchange, return; pèzzo di r. (tec) spare (part).
ricàmo nm embroidery.
ricapitolàre vti to recapitulate, sum up.
ricattàre vt to blackmail.
ricattatóre nm blackmailer.
ricàtto nm blackmail(ing).
ricavàre vt to draw, extract; gain.
ricàvo, ricavàto nm proceeds pl, return.
Riccàrdo nm pr Richard.
ricchézza nf riches pl, richness, wealth.
ríccio a curly; nm lock; hedgehog; sea urchin.
ricciúto a curly.
rícco pl **ricchi** a rich.
ricérca nf search, pursuit, research, inquiry, demand; àlla r. di in search of.
ricercàre vt to look for again, seek, pursue, investigate.
ricercatézza nf affectation.
ricètta nf prescription; recipe.
ricettàcolo nm receptacle.
ricettàre vt to shelter; receive (stolen goods).
ricettazióne nf receiving stolen goods.
ricévere vt to receive, welcome.
riceviménto nm receiving, reception.
ricevitóre nm receiver.
recevúta nf receipt.
richiamàre vt to (re)call; reprimand.
richiàmo nm recall, call; admonition.

richièdere vt to ask again for; require; send for; apply for.
richièsta nf demand, request.
richièsto a in demand, required, sought after.
rícino, òlio di nm castor oil.
ricognizióne nf (mil) reconnaissance.
ricolmàre vt to fill, overload (with).
ricólmo a brimful.
ricompènsa nf recompense, reward.
ricompensàre vt to recompense, reward.
ricompórre vt to reassemble; (re)compose; -rsi vr to recover oneself.
riconciliàre vt to reconcile.
riconfèrma nf confirmation.
riconoscènte a grateful, thankful.
riconoscènza nf gratitude.
riconóscere vt to recognize, acknowledge.
riconosciménto nm recognition, acknowledgment; identification.
ricopríre vt to cover, hide.
ricordànza nf (poet) recollection, remembrance.
ricordàre vti to remember, recall; remind; mention; -rsi vr to remember, recall.
ricòrdo nm memory, record, souvenir; pl memories pl.
ricorrènza nf recurrence; anniversary; occasion.
ricórrere vi to apply, resort; recur; occur.
ricórso nm petition, claim; recurrence.
ricostituènte a nm tonic.
ricostruzióne nf rebuilding, reconstruction.
ricòtta nf buttermilk curd.
ricoveràre vt to shelter, admit (into hospital); -rsi vr to find shelter.
ricóvero nm refuge, shelter.
ricreàre vt to recreate, refresh; -rsi vr to find recreation.
ricreazióne nf pastime, recreation.
ricrédersi vr to change one's mind.
ricuperàre vt to recover; salvage; make up for.
ricúpero nm recovery; rescue.
ricusàre vt to refuse, reject.
rídda nf confusion, turmoil.
ridènte a smiling, pleasant, bright.
rídere vi to laugh; -rsi (di) vr to laugh (at).
ridícolo a ridiculous; nm ridicule.
ridíre, trovàre da vi to find fault.
ridondànte a redundant.
ridòsso, a ad close by, very near.
ridòtta nf (mil) redoubt.
ridúrre vt to reduce.
riduzióne nf reduction; adaptation, (mus) arrangement.
rielezióne nf re-election.
rièmpiere, riempíre vt to fill, stuff; -rsi vr to fill (oneself).
rientràre vi to re-enter, return; be part of; r. in sè to come to oneself.
riepilogàre vti to recapitulate.

riepílogo *pl* **-ghi** *nm* recapitulation.
rifaciménto *nm* remaking, recon-struction.
rifàre *vt* to do again, (re)make; **-rsi** *vr* to make up one's losses.
rifàtto *a* done again, rebuilt, remade.
riferíre *vt* to relate, report, attribute; **-rsi** *vr* to refer, relate.
rifiatàre *vi* to breathe (*also* *fig*); utter a word.
rifiníre *vt* to finish, give the last touch to; satisfy.
rifioríre *vi* to bloom again, (*fig*) flourish again.
rifiutàre *vti* **-rsi** *vr* to refuse, deny.
rifiúto *nm* refusal; **rifiúti** *pl* refuse, scum.
riflessióne *nf* reflection, deliber-ation.
riflessívo *a* thoughtful; (*gram*) reflexive.
riflèttere *vti* to reflect.
riflettóre *nm* searchlight, floodlight, reflector.
rifluíre *vi* to flow back, ebb.
riflússo *nm* ebb(-tide), reflux.
rifocillàre *vt* to supply (with food and drink); **-rsi** *vr* to take refresh-ment.
rifóndere *vt* to refund; melt again.
rifórma *nf* reform(ation).
riformàre *vt* to amend, reform; (*mil*) to declare unfit for service.
riforniménto *nm* supplying, supply; (*av*, *aut*) refuelling; **stazióne di r.** (*aut*) filling station, gas station.
riforníre *vt* to provide, supply; **-rsi** *vr* to take in a fresh supply.
rifràngere *vt* to refract.
rifrazióne *nf* refraction.
rifréddo *nm* cold dish.
rifugiàrsi *vr* to hide oneself, take refuge.
rifugiàto *nm* refugee.
rifúgio *nm* refuge, shelter.
rifúlgere *vi* to shine brightly.
ríga *nf* line; ruler; row, stripe; (hair) parting.
rigàglie *nf* *pl* giblets *pl*.
rigàgnolo *nm* brook; gutter.
rigàre *vt* to rule (lines).
rigattière *nm* second-hand dealer.
rigeneràre *vt* **-rsi** *vr* to regenerate.
rigenerazióne *nf* regeneration.
rigettàre *vti* to throw again, throw back, reject; vomit; bud again.
rigidézza, rigidità *nf* rigidity; strictness.
rígido *a* rigid; severe, strict; very cold.
rigiràre *vt* to turn again; surround; trick; **-rsi** *vr* to turn around.
rigiro *nm* turning around; trick.
rígo *pl* **ríghi** *nm* line.
rigóglio *nm* bloom, luxuriance.
rigoglióso *a* luxuriant, flourishing.
rigónfio *a* puffed up, swollen; *nm* swelling.
rigóre *nm* rigor, severity, strict-ness; **a r. di tèrmini** in the strict sense.
rigorosità *nf* rigorousness, strictness.
rigoróso *a* rigorous, severe, strict.
rigovernàre *vti* to clean, wash up.
riguardànte *a* regarding, concerning.
riguardàre *vt* to look at again; regard; concern; **-rsi** *vr* to take care of oneself.
riguàrdo *nm* care, consideration, regard, respect; **r. a** concerning.
rigurgitànte *a* overflowing, swarm-ing.
rigurgitàre *vi* to flow back, over-flow; regurgitate; swarm with.
rilasciàre *vt* to leave again; release, grant, issue; relax.
rilassaménto *nm* slackening, relaxa-tion.
rilassàre *vt* **-rsi** *vr* to loosen, relax, slacken.
rilegàre *vt* to bind (again).
rilegatóre *nm* **-tríce** *nf* bookbinder.
rilegatúra *nf* binding, bookbinding.
rilevànte *a* considerable, important.
rilevàre *vt* to take away again; raise; notice, point out; survey; take; call for.
rilièvo *nm* relief; importance; re-mark.
rilúcere *vi* to glitter, shine.
riluttànte *a* reluctant.
ríma *nf* rhyme; **rispóndere per le ríme** to give as good as one gets.
rimandàre *vt* to send again; send back; defer; reject; refer.
rimaneggiàre *vt* to rearrange, alter, (*pol*) shuffle.
rimanènte *a* remaining; *nm* re-mainder.
rimanènza *nf* remainder, remnant.
rimanére *vi* to remain; be located; be surprised; rest with.
rimasúglio *nm* remainder; **rimasúgli** *pl* remains *pl*.
rimbàlzo *nm* rebound; **di r.** on the rebound.
rimbambíre *vi* to grow childish.
rimbeccàre *vt* to retort.
rimboccàre *vt* (*trousers*) to turn up; (*sheets*) turn down; (*sleeves*) roll up.
rimbombàre *vi* to roar, thunder.
rimbómbo *nm* roar.
rimborsàbile *a* repayable.
rimborsàre *vt* to reimburse, repay.
rimbórso *nm* reimbursement, repay-ment.
rimbròtto *nm* rebuke, reproach.
rimediàre *vti* to remedy; **r. a** find a remedy for.
rimédio *nm* cure, remedy.
rimembrànza *nf* remembrance.
rimeritàre *vt* to recompense, reward.
rimescolàre *vt* to mix up, (*cards*) shuffle; **-rsi** *vr* to be upset.
riméssa *nf* garage, shed; remittance.
rimésso *a* fit again; remitted; meek; **r. a nuòvo** done up; **dénte r.** false tooth.
rimestàre *vt* to stir up.

riméttere *vt* to put again, put back, return; remit; lose; defer, refer; vomit; **-rsi** *vr* to recover; resume; improve; rely on.
rimodernàre *vt* to modernize, remodel.
rimontàre *vti* to remount; go up; date back, go back.
rimorchiàre *vt* to tow.
rimorchiatóre *nm* (*naut*) tug(boat).
rimòrchio *nm* tow; trailer.
rimòrso *nm* remorse.
rimostrànza *nf* complaint, protest.
rimostràre *vt* to show again; *vi* to remonstrate.
rimozióne *nf* removal.
rimpàsto *nm* rearrangement, (*pol*) shuffle.
rimpatriàre *vti* to repatriate.
rimpàtrio *nm* repatriation.
rimpètto *v* **dirimpètto.**
rimpiàngere *vt* to lament, regret.
rimpiànto *nm* regret.
rimpicciolíre *vti* to lessen.
rimproveràre *vt* to reproach, blame; grudge; **-rsi** *vr* to blame oneself, repent.
rimpròvero *nm* rebuke, reproach.
rimuneràre *vt* to remunerate, reward.
rimunerazióne *nf* remuneration, reward.
rimuòvere *vt* to remove; deter, dissuade.
Rinàldo *nm pr* Reginald, Ronald.
Rinascènza *nf v* **Rinasciménto.**
rinàscere *vi* to be born again, revive.
rinasciménto *nm* rebirth; **R.** Renaissance.
rinàscita *nf* rebirth, revival.
rincalzàre *vt* (*a plant*) to earth up; (*bedclothes*) tuck in.
rincantucciàrsi *vr* to creep into a corner, hide oneself.
rincaràre *vt* (*prices*) to raise; *vi* to grow dearer.
rincàro *nm* rise in prices.
rincasàre *vi* to return home.
rinchiúdere *vt* to shut up.
rincórrere *vt* to chase, pursue.
rincórsa *nf* run-up.
rincréscere *v impers* to be sorry, regret, mind.
rincresciménto *nm* regret.
rincrudíre *vt* to aggravate, embitter; *vi* to get worse.
rinculàre *vi* to draw back, recoil.
rinfacciàre *vt* to cast in s.o.'s teeth, taunt.
rinforzàre *vt* to make stronger, reinforce; *vi* to strengthen.
rinfòrzo *nm* reinforcement.
rinfrancàre *vt* to reanimate; **-rsi** *vr* to take heart again; improve.
rinfrescànte *a* refreshing.
rinfrescàre *vt* to cool; refresh, restore; *vi* to get cooler; **-rsi** *vr* to take refreshment.
rinfrésco *pl* **-éschi** *nm* refreshments *pl*.

rinfuṣa, àlla *ad* higgledy-piggledy, in confusion.
ringalluzzíre *vt* to elate, make cocky.
ringentilíre *vt* to refine.
ringhiàre *vi* to growl, snarl.
ringhièra *nf* banisters *pl*, railing.
ringhióso *a* snarling.
ringiovaníre *vt* to make young(er), rejuvenate; *vi* to grow young again.
ringraziaménti *nm pl* thanks *pl*.
ringraziàre *vt* to thank.
rinnegaménto *nm* disowning, denial.
rinnegàre *vt* to disown, deny.
rinnegàto *a nm* renegade.
rinnovàbile *a* renewable.
rinnovaménto *nm* renewal; revival.
rinnovàre *vt* to renew; revive.
rinnòvo *nm* renewal.
rinocerónte *nm* rhinoceros.
rinomànza *nf* fame, renown.
rinomàto *a* famous, renowned.
rinsavíre *vi* to return to reason.
rintanàrsi *vr* to hide, shut oneself up.
rintoccàre *vi* (*of clock*) to strike, (*of bell*) toll.
rintócco *pl* **-ócchi** *nm* (*clock*) stroke, (*bell*) tolling, knell.
rintracciàre *vt* to trace, find (out).
rintronàre *vt* to deafen; *vi* resound.
rintuzzàre *vt* to blunt, abate, retort.
rinúncia, rinúnzia *nf* renunciation, renouncement.
rinunciàre, rinunziàre *vti* to give up, renounce.
rinveniménto *nm* discovery; recovery.
rinveníre *vt* to discover, find (out); *vi* to recover one's senses.
rinviàre *vt* to put off, postpone, adjourn; send back.
rinvigoríre *vt* to make strong(er); **-rsi** *vr* to grow strong(er).
rinvío *nm* adjournment, postponement; sending back.
Río délle Amàzzoni (il) *nm* (*geogr*) the river Amazon.
rióne *nm* (*town*) part, quarter, ward.
riordinàre *vt* to put in order, rearrange, reorganize.
riorganizzàre *vt* reorganize.
rípa *nf* bank, escarpment.
riparàbile *a* (that) can be mended, repairable.
riparàre *vt* to shelter, protect; repair, make good; repeat (*an exam*); *vi* to make up for, remedy; take shelter, **-rsi** *vr* to protect oneself.
riparazióne *nf* reparation; repair; **esàmi di r.** *pl* (*exams*) second session.
ripàro *nm* cover, shelter, defense.
ripartíre *vt* to distribute, divide, share; *vi* to start again.
ripartizióne *nf* distribution, division.
ripercussióne *nf* repercussion.
ripètere *vt* to repeat.
ripetitóre *nm* **-trice** *nf* repeater; coach, private teacher.

ripetizióne *nf* repetition; coaching, private lesson.
ripiàno *nm* shelf; (*stair*) landing; level place.
ripícco *pl* **-pícchi** *nm* pique.
rípido *a* steep.
ripiegàre *vt* to fold (again); *vi* to bend; give ground, retire; **-rsi** *vr* become bent.
ripiègo *pl* **-ghi** *nm* expedient, remedy.
ripièno *a* full, stuffed (with); *nm* stuffing.
ripórre *vt* to put away, put back, place; conceal.
riportàre *vt* to bring again, bring back, report; receive; (*com*) carry forward; **-rsi** *vr* to go back, refer.
ripórto *nm* (*com*) balance forward.
riposàre *vt* to rest; put down again; *vi* **-rsi** *vr* to rest.
ripóso *nm* rest, quiet, pause.
ripostíglio *nm* lumber-room; hiding-place.
riprèndere *vt* to take again, resume, take back; recover; reprove; *vi* to begin again; revive; **-rsi** *vr* to recover, collect oneself; correct oneself.
riprésa *nf* resumption, revival; recapture, recovery; (*cin*) shot; (*aut*) acceleration; recording; (*boxing*) round.
ripristinàre *vt* to restore.
riprístino *nm* restoration.
riprodúrre *vt* to reproduce; **-rsi** *vr* to reproduce.
riproduttóre, *f* **-tríce** *a* reproducing; *nm* r. acústico pick-up.
riproduzióne *nf* reproduction.
ripromèttersi *vr* to intend, propose, expect.
ripròva *nf* new evidence; confirmation.
riprovàre *vt* to try again; criticize; (*in exams*) fail.
ripudiàre *vt* to repudiate, (*leg*) renounce.
ripugnànte *a* disgusting, repugnant.
ripugnànza *nf* aversion, reluctance.
ripugnàre *vi* to be repugnant, disgust.
ripúlsa *nf* refusal, repulse.
risàia *nf* rice-field.
risalíre *vti* to go up (again), go back.
risaltàre *vt* to jump again; *vi* stand out.
risàlto *nm* prominence, relief; **dàre r. a** to show up.
risanaménto *nm* healing, recovery, reformation; (*of marsh land*) reclamation.
risanàre *vt* to cure, heal; reclaim, reform.
risarciménto *nm* compensation, indemnity.
risarcíre *vt* to compensate, indemnify.
risàta *nf* laugh(ter).
riscaldaménto *nm* heating.

riscaldàre *vt* to heat, warm; **-rsi** *vr* to warm up, get warm.
riscaldatóre *nm* **-tríce** *nf* heater, radiator.
riscattàre *vt* to ransom, redeem.
riscàtto *nm* redemption, ransom.
rischiaràre *vt* to illuminate, light up, enlighten; **-rsi** *vr* to brighten, clear up.
rischiàre *vt* to risk; *vi* to run the risk.
ríschio *nm* risk.
rischióso *a* risky, dangerous, daring.
risciacquàre *vt* to rinse.
riscontràre *vt* to check, compare; find.
riscóntro *nm* checking, comparison; reply.
riscòssa *nf* insurrection, recovery.
riscuòtere *vt* (*money*) to draw, get, receive; rouse, shake; **-rsi** *vr* to start, be startled.
risentiménto *nm* resentment.
risentíre *vt* to feel again, hear again; experience, feel, suffer; *vi* to feel, show traces; **-rsi** *vr* to take offense; come to oneself, wake up; **-rsi di** *vr* to resent.
risentíto *a* angry, resentful; heard again.
risèrbo *nm* reserve, discretion, self-restraint.
risèrva *nf* reserve, reservation; stock, preserve.
riservàre *vt* to reserve, put off; **-rsi** *vr* to reserve (to) oneself; intend.
riservatézza *nf* reserve, prudence.
riservàto *a* reserved; confidential, private.
riservísta *nm* reservist.
risíbile *a* laughable, ridiculous.
risièdere *vi* to reside.
ríso *pl f* **rísa** *nm* laughter.
ríso *nm* rice.
risolúto *a* determined, resolute, resolved.
risoluzióne *nf* resolution; solution.
risòlvere *vt* to resolve, settle, solve; **-rsi** *vr* to decide, make up one's mind, be resolved.
risonànza *nf* resonance, sound.
risonàre *vi* to resound, echo, ring; *vt* to ring again; play again.
risórgere *vi* to rise (again), revive.
risorgiménto *nm* renascence, revival.
risórsa *nf* resource.
risparmiàre *vt* to save, spare.
rispàrmio *nm* saving.
rispecchiàre *vt* to reflect; (*fig*) to mirror.
rispettàbile *a* respectable, considerable.
rispettàre *vt* to respect.
rispètto *nm* respect; regard.
rispettóso *a* respectful.
risplèndere *vi* to shine, glitter.
rispondènte *a* answering, in keeping, in conformity.
rispondènza *nf* correspondence, agreement.

rispóndere *vi* to answer, reply, respond.
rispósta *nf* answer, reply, response.
ríssa *nf* brawl, fray.
ristabilíre *vt* to re-establish, restore; -rsi *vr* to recover one's health.
ristàmpa *nf* reprint, new impression; il líbro è in r. the book is being reprinted.
ristampàre *vt* to reprint.
ristorànte *a* restorative; *nm* restaurant, refreshment room.
ristoràre *vt* to refresh, restore; -rsi *vr* to refresh oneself.
ristoratóre, *f* -tríce *a* restorative; *nm* restorer, restaurant.
ristòro *nm* relief, refreshment.
ristrettézza *nf* narrowness, meanness, lack; r. di mèzzi lack of means, straitened circumstances.
ristrétto *a* narrow, limited, restricted, condensed.
risúcchio *nm* eddy, swirl.
risultàre *vi* to result, follow; appear, become known.
risultàto *nm* result.
risurrezióne *nf* resurrection.
risuscitàre *vti* to resuscitate, revive.
risvegliàre *vt* to (a)wake, excite, rouse, stir up; -rsi *vr* to wake up, be roused.
risvéglio *nm* awakening, revival.
risvòlto *nm* lapel, cuff; (*pocket*) flap; (*trousers*) turn-up, cuff.
ritàglio *nm* (*of material*) length, remnant; (*newspaper*) clipping, cutting; ritàgli di témpo *pl* spare time.
ritardàre *vt* to delay, put off, retard; *vi* to be late, delay.
ritardatàrio *nm* latecomer.
ritàrdo *nm* delay; èssere in r. to be late.
ritégno *nm* reserve, restraint.
ritempràre *vt* to fortify, restore, retemper.
ritenére *vt* to keep back, hold; consider, think; -rsi *vr* to consider oneself; restrain oneself.
ritenúta *nf* deduction.
ritiràre *vt* to retract, take back, withdraw; -rsi *vr* to retire, retreat, withdraw; subside; shrink.
ritiràta *nf* retreat; lavatory, rest room.
ritíro *nm* retreat, withdrawal.
rítmo *nm* rhythm.
ríto *nm* rite, custom.
ritócco *pl* -ócchi *nm* (finishing) touch.
ritornàre *vi* to return, come (go) back, recur; *vt* to return.
ritornèllo *nm* refrain.
ritórno *nm* return, recurrence; bigliétto di andàta e r. round-trip ticket; èssere di r. to be back.
ritorsióne *nf* retort, retaliation.
ritràrre *vt* to withdraw, draw back; get; represent; deduce; *vr* to withdraw; represent oneself.
ritrattàre *vt* to treat again; retract;

portray; -rsi *vr* to recant; draw oneself.
ritràtto *nm* portrait.
ritrosía *nf* reluctance, shyness.
ritróso *a* bashful, reluctant; a r. backwards.
ritrovàre *vt* to find again, recover; -rsi *vr* to find oneself; meet again; see one's way.
ritrovàto *nm* invention; discovery; device, gadget.
ritròvo *nm* meeting-place, haunt.
rítto *a* erect, straight; *nm* (*of material*) right side.
rituàle *a nm* ritual.
riunióne *nf* gathering, meeting.
riuníre *vt* to re-unite, gather, combine, bring together; -rsi *vr* to come together again, unite.
riuscíre *vi* to succeed, manage, be able; be good at; be, arrive; go out again.
riuscíta *nf* result; success; riuscíto *a* successful.
ríva *nf* bank, shore.
rivàle *a nmf* rival.
rivaleggiàre *vi* to rival, compete.
rivalérsi *vr* to make good one's losses.
rivalità *nf* rivalry.
rivàlsa *nf* revenge.
rivedére *vt* to see again, meet again; revise, check; r. bòzze to read proofs.
rivelàre *vt* to reveal, show, display.
rivelazióne *nf* revelation.
rivéndere *vt* to resell, retail.
rivendicàre *vt* to claim, vindicate.
rivéndita *nf* resale; shop.
rivèrbero *nm* reflection; reverberation.
riverènte *a* reverent, respectful.
riverènza *nf* reverence, respect; bow, curtsey.
riveríre *vt* to respect, venerate, pay one's respects to.
riversàre *vt* to pour (again), pour out (again); throw; -rsi *vr* to flow, pour, rush.
riversíbile *a* reversible.
riversióne *nf* reversion.
rivèrso *a* on one's back.
rivestiménto *nm* covering, coating, lining.
rivestíre *vt* to dress again; clothe, cover, line; (*fig*) hold.
rivièra *nf* coast.
rivíncita *nf* return match; revenge.
rivísta *nf* revision; magazine; parade, review.
rívo *nm* (*poet*) brook, stream.
rivòlgere *vt* to turn; r. la paròla *a* to address; -rsi *vr* to apply, turn.
rivolgiménto *nm* upheaval, change.
rivòlta *nf* revolt, insurrection.
rivoltàre *vt* to turn (over) (again), turn inside out; mix, upset; -rsi *vr* to turn; rebel, revolt.
rivoltèlla *nf* revolver.
rivoluzionàrio *a nm* revolutionary.

rivoluzióne nf revolution.
ròba nf stuff, things pl; **r. da chiòdi** (person) bad lot, (things) rubbish.
Robèrto nm pr Robert.
robustézza nf robustness, strength.
robústo a robust, strong, sturdy.
rócca nf distaff.
ròcca nf fortress, rock, stronghold.
rocchétto nm reel; (eccl) surplice.
ròccia nf cliff, rock.
roccióso a rocky.
ròco pl **ròchi** a hoarse.
rodàggio nm (aut) running in.
Ròdano nm (geogr) Rhone.
ròdere vt to gnaw, nibble; corrode; -rsi vr to worry, be consumed with.
Rodèsia nf (geogr) Rhodesia.
rodiménto nm gnawing; erosion, worry.
rododèndro nm rhododendron.
Rodòlfo nm pr Rudolph, Rudolf.
Rodrígo nm pr Roderick.
rógna nf scabies, mange; (fig) nuisance.
rognóne nm kidney of animals.
rognóso a scabby, mangy.
rògo pl **ròghi** nm stake, pyre, bonfire.
Róma nf (geogr) Rome; **romàno** a nm Roman.
romanésco a nm Roman dialect.
Romanía nf (geogr) Rumania.
romànico pl -ici a (arch) Romanesque; (language) Romance.
romanticísmo nm Romanticism.
romàntico pl -ici a romantic.
romànza nf ballad, song.
romanzésco pl -chi a romantic, adventurous.
romanzière nm novelist.
romànzo nm romance, novel; a (language) Romance.
rombàre vi to roar.
rómbo nm roar; thunder.
romitàggio nm hermitage.
romíto a lonely, solitary; nm hermit.
rómpere vti to break.
rompicàpo nm puzzle; worry.
rompicòllo nm thoughtless person; **a r.** headlong.
rompighiàccio nm ice-breaker.
rompiscàtole inv nmf bore, tiresome person.
róncola nf pruning knife.
rónda nf (mil) patrol, rounds.
róndine nf swallow.
rondóne nm (bird) swift.
ronzàre vi to buzz, hum.
ronzíno nm jade, worn-out horse.
ronzío nm buzzing, humming.
ròrido v rugiadóso.
ròsa nf rose; colór **r.** pink.
rosàio nm rose-bush.
rosàrio nm rosary.
ròseo a rosy.
roséto nm rose-garden.
rosicchiàre vt to gnaw, nibble.
rosmaríno nm rosemary.
róso a corroded, gnawed.
rosolàccio nm field poppy.

rosolàre vt to brown.
rosolía nf German measles.
rosóne nm rose window, rosette.
ròspo nm toad.
rossàstro, rossíccio a reddish.
rossétto nm lipstick, rouge; **r. indelèbile** kiss-proof lipstick.
rósso a nm red.
rossóre nm flush, blush, redness; shame.
rosticcería nf cook shop.
ròstro nm dais, rostrum.
rotàia nf rail.
rotàre vi to rotate, revolve.
rotazióne nf rotation.
rotèlla nf small wheel, castor; (anat) kneecap; **pàttini a rotèlle** roller skates.
rotocàlco nm rotogravure process.
rotolàre vti to roll (up); -rsi vr to roll, wallow.
ròtolo nm roll; **andàre a ròtoli** to go to rack and ruin.
rotolóne nm tumble.
rotondàre vt to make round.
rotondeggiànte a roundish.
rotondità nf roundness, rotundity.
rotóndo a round, plump, rotund.
rótta nf course; breach; rout; **a r. di còllo** at breakneck speed.
rottàme nm wreck, fragment; **rottàmi** pl scraps pl, rubbish.
rótto a broken; addicted to, accustomed; nm break; **per il r. dèlla cúffia** by the skin of one's teeth.
rottúra nf breakage, break, breaking-off, rupture.
rovènte a red-hot, fiery.
róvere nm oak.
rovesciàre vt to overthrow, overturn; pour; upset; -rsi vr to be overturned, capsize; fall (down).
rovèscio a inside out; upside down; supine; nm reverse, opposite; set back; (tennis) backhand; **a r.** inside out, upside down, the wrong way.
rovína nf ruin.
rovinàre vt to ruin: vi to fall with a crash; -rsi vr to ruin oneself.
rovinóso a ruinous.
rovistàre vti to rummage, search.
róvo nm blackberry bush, bramble.
rozzaménte ad roughly, clumsily, rudely.
rozzézza nf roughness, rudeness.
rózzo nm rough, rude.
rúba, a ad in great quantities.
rubacuòri inv nm ladykiller.
rubàre vt to steal (from).
rubicóndo a rubicund, ruddy.
Rubicóne nm (geogr) Rubicon.
rubinétto nm tap, faucet.
rubíno nm ruby.
rúblo nm rouble.
rubríca nf newspaper column; address book; rubric.
rúde a rough, harsh, hard.
rúdere nm remains, ruin pl.
rudimentàle a rudimentary.

rudiménto nm first principle, rudiment.
ruffiàno nm pander, procurer.
rúga nf wrinkle.
rúggine nf rust, blight; ill-feeling.
rugginóso a rusty.
ruggíre vi to roar.
ruggíto nm roar(ing).
rugiàda nf dew.
rugiadóso a dewy.
rugóso a wrinkled.
ruína etc v **rovína** etc.
rullàre vi to roll.
rullío nm rolling.
rúllo nm (drum etc) roll; (mech) drumroller, cylinder.
rumèno a nm R(o)umanian.
ruminànte a nm ruminant.
ruminàre vti to ruminate.
rumóre nm noise, rumor.
rumoreggiàre vi to make a noise, rumble.
rumoróso a noisy, loud.
ruòlo nm list, roll, role; **di r.** regular, on the staff.
ruòta nf wheel.
rúpe nf cliff, rock.
ruràle a rural; nm countryman.
ruscèllo nm brook.
russàre vi to snore.
Rússia nf (geogr) Russia.
rússo a nm Russian.
rústico pl **-ici** a country, rustic; unsociable.
ruttàre vi to belch.
rútto nm belching.
ruvidézza nf roughness, coarseness.
rúvido a rough, coarse.
ruzzàre vi to romp.
ruzzolàre vi to roll, tumble down.
ruzzolóne nm fall, tumble; **ruzzolóni**, (a) ad headlong.

S

sàbato nm Saturday.
sàbbia nf sand.
sabotàggio nm sabotage.
saccarína nf saccharine.
saccheggiàre vt to sack, plunder.
sacchéggio nm plunder, sack.
sàcco pl **sàcchi** nm bag, sack; **un s. di** a lot of; **mèttere nel s.** to outwit; **vuotàre il s.** to speak one's mind.
saccóne nm straw mattress.
sacerdòte nm priest.
sacerdotéssa nf priestess.
sacerdòzio nm priesthood.
sacramentàle a sacramental.
sacramentàre vi to swear.
sacraménto nm sacrament.
sacrificàre vti to sacrifice.
sacrifício, sacrifízio nm sacrifice.
sacrilègio nm sacrilege.
sacrílego pl **-eghi** a impious, sacrilegious.
sàcro a holy, sacred.
sacrosànto a sacrosanct; indisputable; well-merited.

sàdico pl **-ici** a nm sadist(ic).
sadísmo nm sadism.
saétta nf arrow; lightning, thunderbolt.
saettàre vti to dart, shoot.
sagàce a sagacious, shrewd, wise.
sagàcia, sagacità nf sagacity, shrewdness.
saggézza nf wisdom.
saggiàre vt to assay, test.
sàggio a wise, sensible; nm wise man; (liter) essay; test, example, sample.
sàgoma nf shape; outline; pattern; character.
sàgra nf annual festival.
sagràto nm hallowed ground (in front of church).
sagrestàno nm sexton.
sagrestía nf sacristy, vestry.
sàio nm sackcloth; (eccl) monk's habit.
sàla nf hall, room; **s. d'aspètto** waiting room.
salamàndra nf salamander.
salàme nm sausage, salami.
salamòia nf brine, pickle.
salàre vt to salt.
salariàre vt to pay wages to.
salariàto a wage-earning; nm wage-earner.
salàrio nm pay, wages.
salàsso nm blood-letting; extortion.
salàto a salty, salted.
saldàre vt to solder, weld, join; (com) to settle.
saldatúra nf soldering, welding.
saldézza nf firmness, steadiness.
sàldo a firm, steady; nm (com) balance; settlement.
sàle nm salt; common-sense; **s. inglése** Epsom salts.
salgèmma nm rock-salt.
sàlice nm willow.
salièra nf salt-cellar.
salína nf salt-mine, salt-pan.
salíno a saline, salt(y).
salíre vi to rise, climb, go up, mount; vt to climb, go up.
Salisbúrgo nf (geogr) Salzburg.
saliscéndi (inv) nm latch.
salíta nf ascent, slope.
salíva nf saliva.
sàlma nf corpse.
salmàstro a brackish.
sàlmo nm psalm.
salmóne nm salmon.
salnítro nm saltpeter.
Salomóne nm pr Solomon.
salóne nm hall, reception room.
salòtto nm drawing room, sitting room.
salpàre vi to (set) sail, weigh anchor.
sàlsa nf sauce.
salsèdine nf salt(iness).
salsíccia nf sausage.
sàlso a salt, salty.
saltàre vt to clear, jump (over), skip, miss out; vi to jump, leap, spring.

salterellàre *vi* to hop (about), skip (about).

saltimbànco *pl* -**chi** *nm* acrobat; mountebank.

sàlto *nm* jump, leap; **s. mortàle** somersault.

saltuàrio *a* desultory.

salúbre *a* healthy, wholesome.

salúme *nm* salt meat.

salumería *nf* pork-butcher's (shop); **salumière** *nm* pork-butcher.

salutàre *vt* to greet, salute, say good-bye to, welcome; *a* healthy, salutary.

salúte *nf* health, safety, salvation; **s.!** bless you!; **alla s.!** here's health!; **càsa di s.** nursing-home.

salúto *nm* greeting, salute; **salúti** *pl* regards *pl.*

sàlva *nf* salvo, volley.

salvacondótto *nm* safe-conduct.

salvadanàio *nm* money-box.

salvagènte (*inv*) *nm* lifebelt, life preserver; traffic island.

salvaguardàre *vt* to safeguard.

salvaguàrdia *nf* protection, safeguard.

salvàre *vt* to rescue, save; **-rsi** *vr* to save oneself, escape.

salvatàggio *nm* rescue, salvage.

salvatóre *a* saving; *nm* rescuer, saver, savior.

salvazióne *nf* salvation.

salvézza *nf* salvation, safety, escape.

sàlvia *nf* (*plant*) sage.

salviétta *nf* napkin, serviette.

sàlvo *a* safe, secure; **sàno e s.** safe and sound; **in s.** in a safe place; *prep* except, save.

samaritàno *a nm* Samaritan.

sambúco *pl* -**chi** *nm* elder-tree.

Samuèle *nm pr* Samuel.

san *a* Saint.

sanàre *vt* to heal.

sanatòrio *nm* sanatorium.

sancíre *vt* to sanction; ratify.

sàndalo *nm* sandal; sandalwood.

sàngue *nm* blood; **s. fréddo** composure.

sanguígno *a* (of) blood; blood-red; sanguine.

sanguinàrio *a* bloodthirsty; sanguinary.

sanguinàccio *nm* blood sausage.

sanguinàre *vi* to bleed.

sanguinolènto *a* bleeding; blood-stained.

sanguinóso *a* bloody.

sanguisúga *nf* leech; (*fig*) extortioner.

sanità *nf* health, sanity, soundness.

sanitàrio *a* medical, sanitary; *nm* physician.

sàno *a* healthy, sane; sound, wholesome.

santificàre *vt* to consecrate, hallow, sanctify.

santità *nf* holiness, sanctity.

sànto *a* holy, hallowed; *nm* saint.

santuàrio *nm* sanctuary, shrine.

sanzionàre *vt* to authorize, sanction.

sanzióne *nf* sanction, approval.

sapére *vt* to be able; be acquainted with, get to know; hear; know (how to); learn; smell (of), taste (of); *nm* knowledge, learning.

sapiènte *a nm* learned, wise (man).

sapiènza *nf* learning, wisdom.

saponàta *nf* lather, soapsuds.

sapóne *nm* soap; **saponétta** *nf* cake of soap.

sapóre *nm* taste, flavor.

saporitaménte *ad* tastily; **pagàre s.** to pay a very high price.

saporíto, saporóso *a* delicious, savory.

Sàra *nf pr* Sara(h).

saracinésca *nf* rolling shutter; portcullis.

sarcàsmo *nm* sarcasm.

sarcàstico *pl* -**ici** *a* sarcastic.

sàrchio, sarchièllo *nm* hoe.

sarcòfago *pl* -**gi, -ghi** *nm* sarcophagus.

Sardégna *nf* (*geogr*) Sardinia.

sardína *nf* sardine.

sàrdo *a nm* Sardinian.

sàrta *nf* dressmaker.

sàrtie *nf pl* (*naut*) rigging, shrouds *pl.*

sàrto *nm* tailor.

sartoría *nf* tailor's shop.

sassàta *nf* blow from a stone.

sàsso *nm* stone; **rimanére di s.** to be astonished.

sassòfono *nm* saxophone.

Sàtana *nm pr* Satan.

satèllite *a nm* satellite.

sàtira *nf* satire, lampoon.

satireggiàre *vt* to satirize.

satírico *pl* -**ici** *a* satiric(al); *nm* satirist.

satollàre *vt* to fill up, satiate.

satóllo *a* full, overfed, satiated.

saturàre *vt* to saturate, glut.

Satúrno *nm* Saturn.

sàturo *a* saturated.

Sàul *nm pr* Saul.

Savèrio *nm pr* Xavier.

sàvio *a* wise; *nm* sage.

Savòia *nf* (*geogr*) Savoy.

saziàre *vt* to satiate, satisfy; **-rsi** *vr* to get tired of.

sazietà *nf* satiety.

sàzio *a* sated; satiated.

şbadatàggine *nf* carelessness, thoughtlessness.

şbadàto *a* careless, heedless.

şbadigliàre *vi* to yawn.

şbadíglio *nm* yawn.

şbagliàre *vt* to mistake; **s. stràda** to take the wrong turning; *vi and* -**rsi** *vr* to be mistaken, make a mistake.

şbàglio *nm* error, mistake.

şbalestràto *a* unbalanced, wild.

şballàre *vt* to unpack; *vi* to tell tall tales.

şbalordiménto *nm* astonishment, bewilderment, daze.

şbalordíre *vt* to amaze, astound.

şbalorditívo *a* amazing.

şbalzàre *vt* to throw, toss, emboss.

sbàlzo nm bound; sudden change; a sbàlzi by fits and starts; lavóro a s. embossed work.

sbandàre vt to disband; vi to skid; (naut) list.

sbaragliàre vt to rout.

sbaràglio nm rout; risk.

sbarazzàre vt to rid; -rsi vr to get rid of.

sbarazzíno nm scamp.

sbarbàre vt -rsi vr to shave.

sbarbàto a clean-shaven.

sbarcàre vi to disembark, land; s. il lunàrio to make both ends meet.

sbàrco pl sbàrchi nm landing, unloading.

sbàrra nf bar.

sbarraménto nm (mil) barrage; obstruction.

sbarràre vt to bar, obstruct; (eyes) open wide; (check) cross.

sbassàre vt to lower.

sbatacchiàre vt to slam, bang.

sbàttere vti to knock, bang, shake.

sbiadíre vti to fade.

sbièco pl -chi a awry, oblique; di s. askance.

sbigottiménto nm dismay, astonishment.

sbigottíre vt to dismay, bewilder.

sbilanciàre vt to unbalance, unsettle; -rsi vr to speak freely; spend beyond one's means.

sbilàncio nm lack of balance, disproportion.

sbilènco pl -chi a crooked, twisted.

sbirciàre vti to cast a sidelong glance.

sbloccàre vt to unblock, clear; decontrol.

sblòcco nm unblocking; (fig) unfreezing.

sboccàre vi to flow into, open into.

sboccàto a foul-mouthed.

sbocciàre vi to blossom, open.

sbócco pl sbócchi nm outlet; (river) mouth; (road) end.

sbòrnia nf drunkenness.

sborsàre vt pay out, spend.

sbórso nm disbursement, outlay, payment.

sbottonàre vt to unbutton; -rsi vr to unbutton one's clothes; unbosom oneself.

sbozzàre vt to sketch out; sbòzzo nm rough draft, sketch.

sbraitàre vi to bawl, shout.

sbranàre vt to tear to pieces.

sbriciolàre vt -rsi vr to crumble.

sbrigàre vt to dispatch, finish; -rsi vr to hurry up, make haste.

sbrigatívo a hasty, summary.

sbrigliàto a lively, unbridled, wild.

sbrogliàre vt to disentangle, extricate.

sbucàre vi to come out, spring out.

sbucciàre vt to pare, peel, shell, skin.

sbuffàre vi to pant, puff, snort.

scàbbia nf scabies, mange.

scabróso a difficult, rough, rugged.

scacchièra nf chessboard, checker-

board; scacchière nm Exchequer; Cancellière dello s. Chancellor of the Exchequer.

scacciàre vt to dispel, drive out.

scàcco pl scàcchi nm square, check; s. (màtto) check(mate); scàcchi chess; a s. checked, checkered.

scadènte a inferior, of poor quality.

scadènza nf (com) maturity; a brève s. in a short time.

scadére vi (com) to be due; expire; lose value; sink.

scafàndro nm diving suit.

scaffàle nm shelf; bookcase.

scàfo nm hull.

scagionàre vt to exculpate, justify.

scàglia nf flake, chip, scale.

scagliàre vt to fling, hurl, throw; -rsi vr to hurl oneself, rush.

scaglióne nm echelon.

scàla nf ladder; staircase, stairs pl; scale.

scalàre vt to climb up, to scale; (com) scale down.

scalàta nf climbing.

scalatóre nm -tríce nf climber.

scalcinàto a seedy, shabby.

scaldabàgno nm water-heater.

scaldàre vt to heat, warm; -rsi vr to warm oneself; get excited.

scaldavivànde (inv) nm dish-warmer.

scaldíno nm hand-warmer, portable warming-pan.

scalfíre vt to graze, scratch.

scalinàta nf (flight of) steps.

scalíno nm step.

scalmanàrsi vr to get agitated.

scàlmo nm (naut) rowlock, oarlock.

scàlo nm landing-place, stop; (rly) s. mèrci freight station.

scaloppína nf veal cutlet.

scalpellíno nm stone-cutter, small chisel.

scalpèllo nm chisel.

scalpóre nm fuss.

scàltro a shrewd, crafty.

scàlzo a barefoot(ed).

scambiàre vt to exchange; mistake.

scambiévole a mutual, reciprocal.

scàmbio nm exchange; (rly) points pl, switch.

scamiciàto a shirt-sleeved; nm revolutionary.

scamosciàto a chamois, suède.

scampagnàta nf country excursion.

scampàre vt to rescue, save; vi to escape; scampàrela bèlla to have a narrow escape.

scàmpo nm escape, safety; shrimp.

scàmpolo nm remnant.

scancellàre v cancellàre.

scandagliàre vt to sound.

scandàglio nm sounding, sounding-rod.

scandalizzàre vt to scandalize, shock.

scàndalo nm scandal.

scandalóso a scandalous, shocking.

Scandinàvia nf (geogr) Scandinavia.

scandínavo *a nm* Scandinavian.
scandíre *vt* to scan; pronounce clearly.
scannàre *vt* to butcher, cut someone's throat.
scannellatúra *nf* groove, fluting.
scànno *nm* bench, seat.
scansafatíche *inv nmf* loafer.
scansàre *vt* to avoid, shun; **-rsi** *vr* to step aside.
scansía *nf* bookcase, set of shelves.
scansióne *nf* scansion.
scantonàre *vi* to turn the corner; sneak off.
scanzonàto *a* free and easy, unconventional.
scapestràto *a* wild, dissolute; *nm* waster.
scapigliàre *vt* to ruffle; **scapigliàto** *a* dishevelled, disorderly, unconventional.
scapitàre *vi* to lose, suffer loss.
scàpito *nm* detriment, loss.
scàpola *nf* shoulder-blade.
scàpolo *a* single; *nm* bachelor.
scappàre *vi* to escape, run away.
scappàta *nf* escapade; short call; trip.
scappaménto *nm* (*mech*) exhaust.
scappatóia *nf* loophole, way out.
scarabèo *nm* beetle; scarab.
scarabocchiàre *vt* to scrawl, scribble.
scarabòcchio *nm* scribble, scribbling.
scarafàggio *nm* cockroach, roach.
scaramúccia *nf* skirmish.
scaramucciàre *vt* to skirmish.
scaraventàre *vt* to fling, hurl.
scarceràre *vt* to release (from prison).
scardinàre *vt* to unhinge.
scàrica *nf* volley, shower; (*el*) discharge.
scaricàre *vt* to discharge, unload.
scàrico *pl* **-chi** *a* unloaded, discharged, (*clock*) run down; light; *nm* discharge, unloading, waste; túbo di s. exhaust-pipe, waste-pipe.
scarlattína *nf* scarlet fever.
scarlàtto *a nm* scarlet.
scarmigliàre *vt* to ruffle.
scàrno *a* lean, thin.
scàrpa *nf* shoe; scarpóne *nm* boot; s. da sci ski-boot.
scarseggiàre *vi* to be scarce, lack.
scarsézza, scarsità *nf* scarcity, lack.
scàrso *a* scanty, scarce, short.
scartàre *vt* unwrap, reject, discard.
scàrto *nm* discard(ing), refuse; *nm* swerve; di s. of inferior quality.
scassinàre *vt* to force open.
scassinatóre *nm* burglar, housebreaker.
scàsso *nm* housebreaking.
scatenàre *vt* to unchain, let loose; cause; **-rsi** *vr* to break out.
scàtola *nf* box, tin, can, case; in s. canned.
scatolàme *nm* tins *pl*, cans *pl*, canned food.
scattàre *vi* to be released, go off,

spring (up); get angry; *vt* (*phot*) to shoot.
scàtto *nm* click, jerk; impulse; (*tec*) release.
scaturíre *vi* to gush, spring.
scavalcàre *vt* to climb over; oust; excel.
scavàre *vt* to dig out, excavate.
scavezzacòllo *nm* (*fig*) reckless person.
scàvo *nm* excavation.
scégliere *vt* to choose, pick out, select.
scelleratézza *nf* wickedness, crime.
scelleràto *a nm* wicked (man).
scellíno *nm* shilling.
scélta *nf* choice, selection; di prima s. choice, top quality.
scélto *a* choice, picked, select(ed).
scemàre *vti* to diminish, lessen.
scèmo *a* foolish, stupid; *nm* fool.
scémpio *a* silly; single; *nm* slaughter.
scèna *nf* scene, stage; mèttere in s. (*theat*) to produce, stage.
scenàta *nf* scene; row.
scenàrio *nm* scenario; scenery.
scéndere *vti* to come (go) down, descend.
sceneggiatúra *nf* staging; (*cin*) scenario.
scènico *pl* **-ici** scenic; stage.
sceríffo *nm* sheriff.
scervellàrsi *vr* to cudgel (rack) one's brains.
scèttico *pl* **-ici** *a* skeptical; *nm* skeptic.
scèttro *nm* scepter.
scévro *a* exempt, free (from).
schèda *nf* card, file-card; voting paper.
schedàre *vt* to file, catalogue.
schedàrio *nm* card-index.
schéggia *nf* splinter.
scheggiàre *vt* **-rsi** *vr* to splinter.
schèletro *nm* skeleton.
schèma *nm* plan, scheme; diagram.
schérma *nf* fencing.
schermírsi *vr* to defend oneself.
schérmo *nm* protection; (*cin*, *tv*) screen; (*phot*) filter.
scherníre *vt* to despise, flout, scoff at.
schérno *nm* derision, taunt.
scherzàre *vi* to jest, joke, make fun.
schérzo *nm* jest, joke, trick.
scherzóso *a* facetious, joking, playful.
schettinàre *vi* to roller-skate.
schettíno *nm* roller skate.
schiaccianóci *nm* nutcrackers *pl*.
schiacciànte *a* crushing, overwhelming.
schiacciàre *vt* to crush, squash.
schiaffeggiàre *vt* to slap, smack.
schiàffo *nm* box on the ear, slap; insult.
schiamazzàre *vi* to make a din.
schiamàzzo *nm* din, uproar.
schiantàre *vt* **-rsi** *vr* to break.
schiànto *nm* crash; pang; di s. suddenly.

schiariménto nm clearing up; explanation.
schiaríre vt to clear up; explain; -rsi vr to become clear, light, brighten, light up.
schiaríta nf clearing; (fig) improvement.
schiàtta nf race, stock.
schiavitú nf slavery.
schiàvo a slave; nm slave, bondsman.
schièna nf back.
schièra nf band, group; mèttersi in s. to fall in.
schieràre vt -rsi vr to draw up, side with.
schiettézza nf purity, frankness.
schiètto a pure, unadulterated; frank.
schifézza nf disgusting thing, disgust.
schifiltóso a fastidious, hard to please.
schífo nm disgust.
schifosàggine nf disgusting action (thing), loathsomeness.
schifóso a disgusting, loathsome.
schiòppo nm gun.
schiúdere vt -rsi vr to open.
schiúma nf foam, froth; scum.
schivàre vt to avoid.
schívo a shy; averse.
schizzàre vt to splash, squirt; sketch; vi spurt, rush.
schízzo nm splash; sketch.
sci nm ski; s. nàutico waterski.
scía nf track, wake.
sciàbola nf saber.
sciacàllo nm jackal.
sciacquàre vt to rinse; sciàcquo nm gargling, mouthwash.
sciagúra nf disaster, misfortune.
sciagurataménte ad unfortunately, miserably; wickedly.
sciaguràto a unlucky, wretched; nm wretch.
scialacquàre vt to squander, waste.
scialàre vi to be wasteful, dissipate; enjoy oneself.
sciàlbo a pale, wan.
sciàlle nm shawl.
scialúppa nf (naut) launch.
sciàme nm crowd, swarm.
sciancàto a lame.
Sciangai nf (geogr) Shanghai.
sciàre vi to ski.
sciàrpa nf scarf, sash.
sciàtto a slovenly, untidy, careless.
scíbile nm knowledge.
scienteménte ad knowingly.
scientificaménte ad scientifically.
scientífico pl -ici a scientific.
sciènza nf science, knowledge.
scienziàto nm scientist.
scímmia nf ape, monkey.
scimmiottàre vt to ape, mimic.
scimunito a foolish, silly.
scíndere vt to divide, separate.
scintílla nf spark.
scintillàre vi to sparkle, glitter.
scintillío nm sparkling, twinkling.

sciocchézza nf foolishness, nonsense, trifle.
sciòcco pl sciòcchi a foolish, silly; nm fool.
sciògliere vt to dissolve, melt; release, untie; -rsi vr to dissolve, melt; free oneself.
scioglilíngua inv nm tonguetwister.
sciòlto a melted; loose, free; nimble.
scioperànte nm striker.
scioperàre vi to (go on) strike.
scioperàto a lazy; nm loafer.
sciòpero nm strike.
sciorinàre vt (clothes) hang out; display.
scipíto a insipid, tasteless.
siròcco pl -chi nm south-east wind.
sciròppo nm syrup.
scísma nm schism.
scissióne nf division, split.
sciupàre vt to ruin, spoil, waste.
sciupío nm waste.
sciupóne nm waster, spendthrift.
scivolàre vi to slide, slip, skid; scívolo nm chute.
scoccàre vt to dart, to throw; vi to strike.
scocciàre vt (fam) to bore, bother.
scocciatóre nm -tríce nf (fam) bore.
scodèlla nf bowl, soup plate.
scodellàre vt to dish up, serve out; (fig) pour out.
scodinzolàre vi to wag (the tail).
scoglièra nf cliff.
scòglio nm rock, reef; stumbling-block.
scoiàttolo nm squirrel.
scolàre vti to drain, drip.
scolàstico pl -ici a scholastic.
scolàro nm pupil, schoolboy.
scollàto a (dress) low-necked.
scollatúra nf neckline.
scòllo nm neck-opening.
scólo nm drainage; drain-pipe.
scoloríre vt to discolor; vi to fade.
scolpàre vt to exculpate, justify; -rsi vr to apologize; justify oneself.
scolpíre vt sculpture, carve, engrave.
scombinàre vt to disarrange.
scombussolàre vt to disturb, upset.
scomméssa nf bet, wager.
scomméttere vt to bet, wager.
scomodàre vt -rsi vr to trouble, bother.
scomodità nf inconvenience.
scòmodo a uncomfortable, inconvenient; nm trouble.
scompaginàre vt to upset.
scomparíre vi disappear, be lost.
scompàrsa nf disappearance, death.
scompartiménto nm compartment.
scompigliàre vt to upset, confuse.
scompíglio nm confusion, fuss.
scompórre vt to take to pieces, disarrange; -rsi vr to be upset, lose one's temper.
scompósto a dismantled, disordered; upset.
scomúnica nf excommunication.
scomunicàre vt to excommunicate.

sconcertàre *vt* to baffle, disconcert, puzzle.
sconcézza *nf* obscenity, disgusting thing.
scóncio *a* indecent, nasty.
sconclusionàto *a* rambling.
sconfessàre *vt* to disavow, disown.
sconfíggere *vt* to defeat.
sconfinàto *a* boundless, unlimited.
sconfítta *nf* defeat.
sconfortàto *a* discouraged, disheartened.
sconfòrto *nm* discouragement, dejection.
scongiuràre *vt* to implore; remove.
scongiúro *nm* exorcism.
sconnèttere *vt* to disconnect.
sconoscènte *a* ungrateful.
sconosciúto *a nm* unknown.
sconquassàre *vt* to smash.
sconquassàto *a* rickety, tumbledown.
sconsideràto *a* thoughtless.
sconsigliàre *vt* to advise against, dissuade.
sconsolàto *a* disconsolate, depressed.
scontàre *vt* (*com*) to deduct, discount; to expiate, pay for; to take for granted.
scontentézza *nf* discontent.
scontènto *a* disappointed, dissatisfied; *nm* discontent.
scónto *nm* discount.
scontràrsi *vr* to clash, crash, collide.
scontríno *nm* check, receipt, ticket.
scóntro *nm* collision.
scontrosàggine, scontrosità *nf* cantankerousness, bad temper, peevishness.
scontróso *a* sulky, peevish, bad-tempered.
sconveniènte *a* unseemly, unprofitable.
sconveniènza *nf* unseemliness, discourtesy.
sconvòlgere *vt* to derange, upset.
sconvolgiménto *nm* upset, confusion.
scópa *nf* broom.
scopàre *vi* to sweep.
scopèrta *nf* discovery.
scopèrto *a* bare, open, unprotected.
scòpo *nm* aim, end, object, purpose.
scoppiàre *vi* to burst (out), explode.
scòppio *nm* burst(ing), explosion; outburst, outbreak.
scopríre *vt* to discover, find out; reveal; **-rsi** *vr* to uncover oneself.
scoraggiàre *vt* to dishearten; **-rsi** *vr* to get disheartened.
scorbutíco *pl* **-ici** *a* scorbutic; cantankerous; awkward.
scorciàre *vt* to shorten; **scorciatóia** *nf* short-cut.
scórcio *nm* foreshortening; end.
scordàre *vt* **-rsi** *vr* to forget; untune.
scòrgere *vt* to discern, perceive.
scornàto *a* humiliated, ridiculed, disgraced.
scòrno *nm* disgrace, shame.

scorpacciàta *nf* bellyful.
scorpióne *nm* scorpion.
scorrazzàre *vi* to run about.
scórrere *vt* to run through; raid; glance over; *vi* to run, slide, flow.
scorrería *nf* incursion, raid.
scorrettézza *nf* mistake; bad manners; dishonesty.
scorrètto *a* incorrect; improper; dishonest, dissolute.
scorrévole *a* flowing, fluent, gliding.
scorrevolézza *nf* fluency, smoothness.
scórsa *nf* glance.
scórso *a* last, past.
scorsóio *a* running; **nódo s.** slip-knot.
scòrta *nf* escort; supply.
scortàre *vt* to escort.
scortecciàre *vt* to strip, peel.
scortése *a* discourteous, rude, uncivil.
scortesía *nf* rudeness, rude act.
scorticàre *vt* to flay, fleece, skin.
scorticatúra *nf* scratch, graze.
scòrza *nf* bark, peel, rind, skin.
scoscéso *a* steep.
scòssa *nf* shake, shock.
scòsso *a* shaken, upset.
scostàre *vt* **-rsi** *vr* to move (away), shift (aside).
scostumàto *a* dissolute; rude.
scottàre *vt* to burn, scald, scorch.
scottatúra *nf* burn, scald.
scòtto *a* (*cook*) overdone; *nm* score, reckoning.
scovàre *vt* to dislodge, rouse, find out.
Scòzia *nf* (*geogr*) Scotland.
scozzése *a* Scottish; *nm* Scot, Scotsman, (*language*) Scots.
screditàre *vt* to discredit.
scrédito *nm* discredit, disgrace.
scremàre *vt* to skim.
screpolàre *vt* **-rsi** *vr* to chap, crack.
scrèzio *nm* dispute, quarrel.
scribacchiàre *vi* to scribble.
scricchiolàre *vi* to creak.
scricchiolío *nm* creaking.
scrígno *nm* casket, jewel-case.
scriminatúra *nf* (*hair*) parting.
scrítta *nf* inscription, notice.
scrítto *a* written; *nm* writing; document.
scrittóio *nm* writing desk.
scrittóre *nm* **-tríce** *nf* writer.
scrittúra *nf* (hand)writing; contract.
scritturàre *vt* (*theat*) to engage.
scrivanía *nf* (writing-)desk.
scrívere *vt* to write.
scroccàre *vt* to scrounge.
scròcco *pl* **scròcchi** *nm* scrounging; swindle.
scròfa *nf* sow.
scrollàre *vt* to shake, shrug.
scrosciàre *vi* (*rain*) to pelt; (*fig*) thunder.
scròscio *nm* roar; downpour; **piòvere a s.** to pour.
scrúpolo *nm* scruple.
scrupolóso *a* scrupulous.

scrutàre *vt* to investigate, scan.
scrutinàre *vt* to scrutinize.
scrutínio *nm* list of marks; voting; scrutiny.
scucíre *vt* to unstitch.
scuderia *nf* stable.
scudíscio *nm* lash, whip.
scúdo *nm* shield, protection.
scultóre *nm* sculptor.
scultúra *nf* carving, sculpture.
scuòla *nf* school, schoolhouse; **s. diúrna** day-school; **s. seràle** night school.
scuòtere *vt* to shake; stir up; **-rsi** *vr* to rouse oneself, stir.
scúre *nf* ax, hatchet.
scúro *a* dark; grim; *nm* darkness; shutter.
scurríle *a* scurrilous.
scúşa *nf* excuse, pretext.
scuşàre *vt* to excuse, forgive, justify; **-rsi** *vr* to apologize, justify oneself; **scúsi** excuse me; I beg your pardon.
şdebitàrsi *vr* to pay one's debts.
şdegnàre *vt* to disdain, scorn; **-rsi** to get angry.
şdégno *nm* disdain; indignation.
şdegnóso *a* disdainful, haughty.
şdentàto *a* toothless.
şdoganàre *vt* to clear (through the customs).
şdolcinàto *a* maudlin, sugary, affected.
şdraiàre *vt* to stretch at full length; **-rsi** *vr* to lie down, stretch oneself out; **sdràio** *nm* deck chair.
şdrucciolàre *vi* to slip, slide.
şdrucíre *vt* to tear, unstitch.
se *cj* if, whether; **se no** or else, otherwise.
sè *refl pron* oneself, himself, herself, itself, themselves *pl*.
sebbène *cj* although, though.
Sebastiàno *nm pr* Sebastian.
seccaménte *ad* drily, bluntly.
seccànte *a* tiresome, irritating; **persóna s.** a nuisance.
seccàre *vt* to dry; bother, irritate; **-rsi** *vr* to dry (up); get tired, get annoyed.
seccatúra *nf* nuisance, bother; desiccation.
sécchia *nf* **-o** *nm* bucket, pail.
sécco *pl* **sécchi** *a* dry; thin; **lavàre a s.** to dry-clean.
secolàre *a* age-old; secular, lay; *nm* layman.
sècolo *nm* century, age.
secondàre *v* assecondàre.
secondàrio *a* secondary.
secóndo *a* second; favorable; *nm* second, main dish; **di secónda màno** second-hand; *prep* according to; **s. me** in my opinion.
sèdano *nm* celery.
sedàre *vt* to soothe, calm.
sedatívo *a nm* sedative.
sède *nf* center, seat; residence; office; see.
sedentàrio *a* sedentary.

sedére *vi* to sit; **-rsi** *vr* to sit down, take a seat.
sèdia *nf* chair.
sedicènte *a* self-styled.
sédici *a* sixteen; **sedicènne** sixteen-year-old; **sedicèsimo** sixteenth.
sedíle *nm* seat, bench.
sedizióne *nf* sedition.
sedizióso *a* seditious.
sedúrre *vt* to seduce; entice, charm.
sedúta *nf* sitting; meeting.
seduttóre *nm* **-tríce** *nf* seducer.
seduzióne *nf* seduction, enticement; charm.
séga *nf* saw.
ségala, ségale *nf* rye.
segàre *vt* to saw.
segatúra *nf* sawing; sawdust.
sèggio *nm* chair, seat; see.
sèggiola *v* **sèdia**.
segnalàre *vt* to signal; point out; **-rsi** *vr* to distinguish oneself.
segnalazióne *nf* signal(ling).
segnàle *nm* signal.
segnalíbro *nm* bookmark.
segnàre *vt* to mark, note; (*sport*) score; **-rsi** *vr* to cross oneself.
ségno *nm* sign, mark.
ségo *pl* **séghi** *nm* tallow.
segregaménto *nm* **segregazióne** *nf* segregation, isolation.
segregàre *vt* to isolate, segregate.
segretàrio *nm* **-ria** *nf* secretary.
segreteria *nf* secretary's office.
segretézza *nf* secrecy.
segréto *a nm* secret.
seguàce *nmf* follower, supporter.
seguènte *a* following; next.
seguire *vt* to follow; supervise; *vi* to follow; result.
seguitàre *vi* to continue, go on, keep on.
séguito *nm* continuation; followers *pl*, retinue; sequel; series; succession; **di s.** in succession; **in s.** later on; **in s. a** *prep* owing to.
sèi *a* six.
seicènto *a* six hundred; *nm* 17th century.
sèlce *nf* flint(stone).
selciàto *nm* pavement; road surface.
selezionàre *vt* to select, choose.
selezióne *nf* selection; digest.
sèlla *nf* saddle.
sellàre *vt* to saddle.
seltz *nm* soda(-water), seltzer.
sélva *nf* forest, wood.
selvaggína *nf* game.
selvàggio *a* savage; wild; rough; *nm* savage.
selvatichézza *nf* wildness; unsociability; uncouthness.
selvàtico *pl* **-ici** *a* wild, rough.
semàforo *nm* traffic lights.
sembiànte *nm* **sembiànza** *nf* appearance.
sembràre *v* **parére**.
sème *nm* seed; cause; **semènza** seeds *pl*; (*liter*) progeny.
semestràle *a* half-yearly.

semèstre *nm* half-year.
semi- *prefix* half-, semi-.
semicúpio *nm* hip-bath.
sémina, seminagióne *nf* sowing; sowing season.
seminàre *vt* to sow; scatter.
seminàrio *nm* seminary; seminar.
seminàto *a* sown; strewn; *nm* sown field.
seminterràto *nm* basement.
sémola *nf* bran; fine flour; freckles *pl.*
semovènte *a* self-moving, self-propelled.
Sempióne *nm* (*geogr*) Simplon.
sempitèrno *a* everlasting.
sémplice *a* simple, easy; mere, plain; soldàto s. *nm* private (soldier).
semplicità *nf* simplicity.
semplificàre *vt* to simplify.
sèmpre *ad* always, ever; still; per s. forever; s. méno less and less; s. piú more and more; s. che *cj* provided (that).
sènapa, sènape *nf* mustard.
senàto *nm* senate.
senatóre *nm* senator.
senése *a nmf* Sienese.
seníle *a* senile.
senilità *nf* senility.
senióre *a nm* senior.
Sènna *nf* (*geogr*) Seine.
sénno *nm* judgment, sense, wisdom.
séno *nm* bosom, breast; cove, inlet.
sensàle *nm* broker, middleman.
sensàto *a* sensible, judicious.
sensazionàle *a* sensational, thrilling.
sensazióne *nf* sensation, feeling.
sensería *nf* brokerage.
sensíbile *a* sensitive; considerable.
sensibilità *nf* sensitiveness, feeling, sensitivity.
sensitívo *a* sensory; sensitive.
sènso *nm* sense; feeling; meaning; sensation; s. único one way; privo di sènsi unconscious; sensòrio *a* sensory; *nm* sense organ.
sensuàle *a* sensual.
sensualità *nf* sensuality.
sentènza *nf* decree; judgment; maxim.
sentenziàre *vi* to judge; talk sententiously.
sentièro *nm* footpath, path(way).
sentimentàle *a* sentimental.
sentiménto *nm* sentiment; feeling; *pl* senses *pl.*
sentína *nf* bilge.
sentinèlla *nf* (*mil*) sentinel, sentry.
sentíre *vi* to feel; hear, listen to; -rsi *vr* to feel; *nm* feelings *pl.*
sentíto *a* heart-felt, sincere.
sentóre *nm* vague suspicion, inkling.
sènza *prep* without; sènz'àltro *ad* immediately; of course.
separàre *vt* to separate, divide; -rsi *vr* to part, separate.
separataménte *ad* separately.
separazióne *nf* separation, parting.
sepólcro *nm* sepulcher, grave.

sepoltúra *nf* burial; grave; luògo di s. burial place.
seppelliménto *nm* interment, burial.
seppellíre *vt* to bury.
séppia *nf* cuttlefish.
sequèla *nf* series, sequence.
sequestràre *vt* to sequester, sequestrate, distrain upon.
sequèstro *nm* sequestration, distraint.
séra *nf* evening.
seràle *a* evening.
seràta *nf* evening; evening party; (*theat*) evening performance.
serbàre *vt* to put aside; to keep.
serbatóio *nm* reservoir, tank.
sèrbo *nm* in s. in reserve; aside.
serenàta *nf* serenade.
serenità *nf* serenity, calmness.
seréno *a* serene, clear, calm.
sergènte *nm* sergeant.
sèriaménte *ad* seriously, gravely.
sèrie *nf* series; set; succession; in s. mass-produced; fuòri s. special, custom-built.
serietà *nf* seriousness, gravity.
sèrio *a* serious, earnest; grave; reliable; sul s. in earnest.
sermóne *nm* sermon; reproof.
sèrpe *nf* -pènte *nm* serpent, snake.
serpeggiàre *vi* to meander, wind; spread.
sèrra *nf* greenhouse, hothouse.
serràglio *nm* menagerie; seraglio.
serramànico, coltèllo a claspknife.
serrànda *nf* (*of a shop*) shutter.
serràre *vt* to lock (up); shut, close; clench; -rsi *vr* to stand close; close up.
serratúra *nf* lock.
sèrva *nf* maid, (woman)servant.
servíle *a* servile, slavish.
servíre *vti* to serve; -rsi *vr* to (make) use (of); help oneself.
servitóre *nm* servant.
servitú *nf* servitude; servants *pl,* staff.
serviziévole *a* obliging.
servízio *nm* service; favor; kindness; di s. on duty; fuòri s. off duty; dònna di s. *nf* maid; mezzo s. part-time service.
sèrvo *nm* (man)servant.
sessànta *a nm* sixty; sessantènne *a nmf* sixty-year-old (person); sessantèsimo *a* sixtieth; sessantína *nf* about sixty.
sessióne *nf* session.
sèsso *nm* sex.
sessuàle *a* sexual.
sèsto *a* sixth; *nm* order; méttere in s. to put in order, tidy.
séta *nf* silk.
setàccio *nm* sieve.
séte *nf* thirst; avèr s. to be thirsty.
setería *nf* silk shop; silk goods.
sétola *nf* bristle.
setolóso *a* bristly.
sètta *nf* sect.
settànta *a nm* seventy; settantènne

a nmf seventy-year-old (person); **settantèsimo** *a* seventieth; **settantìna** *nf* about seventy.
sètte *a* seven; **settènne** seven-year-old.
settecènto *a* seven hundred; *nm* 18th century.
settèmbre *nm* September.
settentrionàle *a* north(ern), northerly; *nm* northerner.
settentrióne *nm* north.
sèttico *pl* -ici *a* septic.
settimàna *nf* week.
settimanàle *a nm* weekly.
sèttimo *a* seventh.
settóre *nm* sector.
settuagenàrio *a nm* septuagenarian.
severaménte *ad* severely, sternly.
severità *nf* severity, strictness, sternness.
sevèro *a* severe, strict, stern.
sevízie *nf pl* cruelty, ill-treatment.
sezionàre *vt* to cut up, dissect.
sezióne *nf* section; department.
sfaccendàre *vi* to bustle about.
sfaccendàto *nm* idler, loafer.
sfacchinàre *vi* to drudge.
sfacchinàta *nf* heavy piece of work.
sfacciatàggine *nf* impudence, insolence.
sfacciàto *a* impudent, shameless.
sfacèlo *nm* break-up, collapse, ruin.
sfamàre *vt* to appease someone's hunger.
sfàrzo *nm* pomp, splendor.
sfarzóso *a* gorgeous, sumptuous.
sfasàto *a* (*el*) out of phase; (*fig*) inconsistent, inconsequent.
sfasciàre *vt* to unbandage; demolish, dismantle.
sfatàre *vt* to disprove, discredit.
sfavillàre *vi* to sparkle, shine.
sfavorévole *a* unfavorable.
sfèra *nf* sphere, circle, globe.
sfèrico *pl* -ici *a* spherical.
sferràre *vt* (*a horse*) to unshoe; (*a blow*) deliver; (*an attack*) launch.
sfèrza *nf* lash, whip.
sferzàre *vt* to whip, lash, scourge.
sfiatàrsi *vr* to talk oneself hoarse.
sfìda *nf* challenge, defiance.
sfidàre *vt* to challenge, dare, defy; **sfìdo!** *interj* of course.
sfidúcia *nf* distrust, mistrust, lack of confidence.
sfiduciàto *a* discouraged, disheartened.
sfiguràre *vt* to disfigure; *vi* to cut a poor figure.
sfilàre *vt* to unstring, unthread; *vi* to file (past).
sfilàta *nf* row, parade.
sfìnge *nf* sphinx.
sfiniménto *nm* exhaustion.
sfiníto *a* exhausted, worn out.
sfioràre *vt* to graze, skim over, touch lightly, touch on.
sfioríre *vi* to wither, fade.
sfoderàre *vt* to remove the lining; (*sword etc*) draw, display, show off.

sfogàre *vt* to vent, let out; **-rsi** *vr* to give vent to one's feelings, speak frankly.
sfoggiàre *vti* to show off, flaunt.
sfòggio *nm* show, display.
sfogliàre *vt* to pick off leaves; turn over the pages of, run through (a book).
sfógo *pl* **sfóghi** *nm* vent, outlet; eruption.
sfolgorànte *a* blazing, flaming.
sfolgoràre *vi* to blaze, flash.
sfollàre *vt* to disperse; *vi* to disperse, evacuate.
sfondàre *vt* to break (down), knock the bottom out.
sfóndo *nm* background.
sformàto *a* shapeless; *nm* pie, pudding.
sfornàre *vt* to take out of the oven, bring out.
sfortúna *nf* ill-luck, misfortune.
sfortunàto *a* unlucky.
sforzàre *vt* to force strain; **-rsi** *vr* to strive, try hard.
sfòrzo *nm* effort, strain.
sfracellàre *vt* to shatter, smash.
sfrattàre *vt* to turn out, evict.
sfràtto *nm* notice to quit, eviction.
sfrégio *nm* disfigurement; affront.
sfrenatézza *nf* wildness, licentiousness.
sfrenàto *a* unbridled, unrestrained, wild.
sfrontatézza *nf* effrontery, impudence.
sfrontàto *a* brazen, impudent.
sfruttaménto *nm* exploitation.
sfruttàre *vt* to exploit.
sfuggíre *vi* to escape.
sfumàre *vi* to end in smoke, vanish; *vt* (*of colors*) to shade.
sfumatúra *nf* nuance; shade, shading.
sgabèllo *nm* stool.
sgabuzzíno *nm* closet.
sgambettàre *vi* to kick the legs about; toddle.
sgambétto *nm* caper, jump; **fàre uno s.** a to trip (s.o.) up.
sganciàre *vt* to unhook.
sgangheràto *a* ramshackle, rickety, unhinged.
sgarbatézza *nf* rudeness; clumsiness.
sgarbàto *a* rude, unmannerly.
sgarbería *nf* **sgàrbo** *nm* rudeness, offense.
sgargiànte *a* gaudy, showy.
sgelàre *vti* to melt, thaw.
sghèmbo *a* crooked, oblique, slanting.
sghignazzàre *vi* to guffaw.
sgobbàre *vi* to drudge, toil, work hard.
sgobbóne *nm* slogger.
sgocciolàre *vi* to drip, trickle.
sgomb(e)ràre *vt* to clear; (*mil*) to abandon; *vi* to clear out, move out.
sgómb(e)ro *a* clear, empty, free; *nm* removal.

şgomentàre vt to dismay, frighten.
şgoménto a dismayed, frightened; nm dismay, fright.
şgominàre vt to rout.
şgonfiàre vt to deflate.
şgòrbio nm scrawl; (fig) ugly dwarf.
şgorgàre vi to gush, spout (out).
şgozzàre vt to cut s.o.'s throat.
şgradévole a disagreeable, unpleasant.
şgrammaticàto a ungrammatical.
şgranàre vt to shell, husk; s. gli òcchi to open the eyes wide.
şgranchíre vt -rsi vr to stretch.
şgravàre vt to lighten, relieve, unload; -rsi vr to relieve oneself, bring forth.
şgraziàto a ungraceful, clumsy.
şgretolàre vt to crumble, grind, smash.
şgridàre vt to rebuke, scold.
şgridàta nf rebuke, scolding.
şguaiàto a unbecoming, uncomely, coarse.
şgualcíre vt to crumple; -rsi vr to crease.
şgualdrína nf strumpet.
şguàrdo nm glance, look.
şguarníre vt to untrim; (mil) withdraw the garrison.
şguàttera nf scullery-maid; sguàttero nm scullery-boy.
şguazzàre vi to wallow (also fig).
şgusciàre vt to hull, shell; vi to slip away, steal away.
sí ad yes; díre di s. to agree.
sì $refl$ $pron$ oneself, himself, herself, itself, themselves pl; $indef$ $pron$ one, people, they; $pron$ each other, one another.
sía . . . sía cj whether . . . or; both . . . and.
siamése a nmf Siamese.
siberiàno a nm Siberian.
sibilàre vi to hiss, whizz.
síbilo nm hiss, whistle, whizzing.
sicàrio nm hired assassin.
sicchè cj so that.
siccità nf drought, dryness.
siccóme ad cj as.
Sicília nf (geogr) Sicily; siciliàno a nm Sicilian.
sicomòro nm sycamore.
sicuraménte ad certainly; safely.
sicurézza nf certainty, safety, security; s. di sè self-possession.
sicúro a sure, certain; safe, secure, trusty; $interj$ quite so; al s. in safety.
sicurtà nf security, guarantee; insurance.
siderúrgico pl -ici a iron; stabiliménto s. ironworks.
sièpe nf hedge.
sièro nm serum; whey.
sifílide nf syphilis.
sifóne nm siphon.
sigarétta nf cigarette.
sígaro nm cigar.
Sigfrído nm pr Siegfried.

sigillàre vt to seal.
sigíllo nm seal.
Sigişmóndo nm pr Siegmund.
sígla nf monogram, initials.
significànte, significativo a significant; expressive.
significàre vt to mean, signify.
significàto nm meaning, significance.
signóra nf lady; madam, Mrs; signóre nm gentleman; Mr; sir; vívere da s. to live like a lord.
signoreggiàre vti to rule, dominate.
signoría nf lordship; dominion, rule.
signoríle a gentlemanly; ladylike; high-class.
signorína nf miss, young lady; signorino nm (young) master.
silenziatóre nm silencer, (aut) muffler.
silènzio nm silence.
silenzióso a silent, quiet.
sílice nf silica.
síllaba nf syllable.
sillabàre vt to spell out.
sílo nm silo.
sillogísmo nm syllogism.
siluràre vt to torpedo; (fig) give the sack.
silúro nm torpedo.
silvèstre a sylvan.
Silvèstro nm pr Silvester; la nòtte di San S. New Year's Eve.
Sílvia nf pr Sylvia, Silvia.
simboleggiàre vti to symbolize.
simbòlico pl -ici a symbolical.
símbolo nm symbol.
similàre a similar.
símile a alike, such, like; nm fellow-creature, like.
similitúdine nf simile; similitude.
similménte ad the same, likewise.
simmetría nf symmetry.
Simóne nm pr Simon.
simpatía nf liking, attraction; sympathy.
simpàtico pl -ici a agreeable, congenial, nice, pleasant; sympathetic.
simpatizzànte a sympathizing; nmf sympathizer.
simpatizzàre vi to sympathize; take a liking.
simpòsio nm symposium, conference.
simulàcro nm image, shadow.
simulàre vt to simulate, feign, sham.
simulazióne nf simulation, shamming.
simultàneo a simultaneous.
sinagòga nf synagogue.
sinceraménte ad sincerely, honestly.
sinceràrsi vr to make sure.
sincerità nf sincerity, truthfulness, candor.
sincèro a sincere, candid, frank.
sincopàto a syncopated.
sincronizzatóre nm synchronizer.
sindacàto nm syndicate, trade union.
síndaco pl -aci nm mayor, (Scotland) provost; (com) auditor.
sinfonía nf symphony.

sinfònico *pl* **-ici** *a* symphonic, symphony.

singhiozzàre *vi* to sob.

singhiózzo *nm* hiccup; sob.

singolàre *a* singular; peculiar, eccentric; rare; single.

singolarità *nf* singularity, strangeness.

síngolo *a* single, each, individual.

sinístra *nf* left (hand).

sinistràto *a* homeless; injured.

sinístro *a* left; ominous, sinister; *nm* accident, mishap.

síno *v* **fíno.**

sínodo *nm* synod.

sinònimo *a* synonymous; *nm* synonym.

sintàssi *nf* syntax.

síntesi *nf* synthesis.

sintètico *pl* **-ici** *a* synthetic(al); concise.

síntomo *nm* symptom.

sinuosità *nf* sinuosity.

sinuóso *a* sinuous, winding.

sinusíte *nf* sinusitis.

sipàrio *nm* (*theat*) (drop) curtain.

Siracúṣa *nf* (*geogr*) Syracuse; **siracuṣàno** *a* *nm* Syracusan.

sirèna *nf* mermaid; siren, hooter.

Síria *nf* (*geogr*) Syria.

siriàno *a* *nm* Syrian.

sirínga *nf* (*med*) syringe.

sistèma *nm* system.

sistemàre *vt* to arrange, settle.

sistemàtico *pl* **-ici** *a* systematic, methodical, businesslike.

sistemazióne *nf* arrangement, settlement; position.

síto *nm* place, site, spot.

situàto *a* placed.

situazióne *nf* situation, set-up, position, site.

ṣlacciàre *vt* to unbind, undo, unlace, untie.

ṣlanciàre *vt* to fling, hurl; **-rsi** *vr* to hurl oneself, rush upon, venture.

ṣlanciàto *a* slim, slender.

ṣlàncio *nm* impetus, enthusiasm, impulse.

ṣlattàre *vt* to wean.

ṣlavàto *a* (*of color*) washed out, pale; dull, insipid.

ṣlàvo *a* *nm* Slav.

ṣleàle *a* disloyal; unfair.

ṣlealtà *nf* disloyalty.

ṣlegàre *vt* to untie.

ṣlegàto *a* untied, unbound; 'incoherent.

ṣlítta *nf* sledge, sleigh.

ṣlittaménto *nm* skidding, skid; (*mech*) slipping.

ṣlittàre *vi* to skid; sleigh; slip.

ṣlogàre *vt* to dislocate.

ṣlogatúra *nf* dislocation.

ṣloggiàre *vt* to dislodge, drive out; *vi* to clear out, decamp.

ṣmacchiàre *vt* to clean, remove stains.

ṣmàcco *pl* **ṣmàcchi** *nm* humiliation, let down.

ṣmagliànte *a* dazzling, gaudy.

ṣmagliàrsi *vr* (*stockings*) to run; (*knitting*, *net*) to get undone.

ṣmagliatúra *nf* (*of stocking*) ladder, run.

ṣmaltàre *vt* to enamel, glaze.

ṣmaltíre *vt* to digest, work off.

ṣmàlto *nm* enamel.

ṣmània *nf* longing, mania, frenzy.

ṣmaniàre *vi* to long for, fret.

ṣmarriménto *nm* loss; bewilderment.

ṣmarríre *vt* to lose, mislay; **-rsi** *vr* to lose one's way, stray; get confused.

ṣmascheràre *vt* to unmask.

ṣmembràre *vt* to dismember.

ṣmemoràto *a* absent-minded, forgetful.

ṣmentíre *vt* to deny; **-rsi** *vr* to eat one's words; **smentíta** *nf* denial, refutation.

ṣmeràldo *nm* emerald.

ṣmèrcio *nm* sale.

ṣmerigliàto *a* **càrta smerigliàta** emery paper; **vètro s.** frosted glass.

ṣmeríglio *nm* emery.

ṣméttere *vt* to give up, stop wearing; *vi* to give up, leave off, stop.

ṣmílzo *a* slender, slim.

ṣminuzzàre *vt* to cut up, chop finely.

ṣmistaménto *nm* clearing; (*rly*) shunting, switching; (*letters*) sorting.

ṣmistàre *vt* to clear; (*letters*) sort; (*rly*) shunt, switch.

ṣmiṣuràto *a* enormous, immeasurable.

ṣmobiliàre *vt* to strip of furniture.

ṣmobilitàre *vt* to demobilize.

ṣmodàto, ṣmoderàto *a* excessive, immoderate.

ṣmòking *nm* dinner-jacket, tuxedo.

ṣmontàre *vt* to take down, take to pieces; discourage; *vi* to alight, get out of.

ṣmórfia *nf* grimace, wry face.

ṣmorfióso *a* mincing, affected.

ṣmòrto *a* pale, wan.

ṣmorzàre *vt* to dim, tone down; quench.

ṣmúnto *a* pale, emaciated.

ṣmuòvere *vt* to shift, move; affect.

ṣmussàre *vt* to bevel, blunt, smooth.

ṣnaturàre *vt* to alter the nature of, pervert.

ṣnellézza *nf* slimness; agility, nimbleness.

ṣnèllo *a* slim; nimble, agile.

ṣnervàre *vt* to enervate, exhaust.

ṣnobbàre *vt* to look down on, cut.

ṣnobíṣmo *nm* snobbery.

ṣnodàre *vt* to loosen, untie; make supple; **-rsi** *vr* to get untied; wind.

ṣnudàre *vt* to bare, unsheathe.

soàve *a* sweet, soft, gentle.

soavità *nf* sweetness, softness, gentleness.

sobbalzàre *vi* to start, jump.

sobbarcàrsi *vr* to take on oneself.
sobbórgo *pl* **-ghi** *nm* suburb.
sobillàre *vt* to incite, instigate, stir up.
sobrietà *nf* sobriety, temperance.
sòbrio *a* sober, temperate.
socchiúdere *vt* to leave ajar.
soccómbere *vi* to give in, succumb, yield.
soccórrere *vt* to help, relieve, succor.
soccórso *nm* aid, help, relief.
sociàle *a* social; (*com*) of partnership.
socialísmo *nm* socialism.
socialísta *nm* socialist; **socialístico** *a* socialist.
società *nf* society, community; (*com*) company, partnership; **s. a responsabilità limitàta** limited liability company, corporation.
sociévole *a* companionable, sociable.
sòcio *nm* member, fellow, associate, partner.
sociología *nf* sociology.
sociòlogo *pl* **-gi, -ghi** *nm* sociologist.
sodalízio *nm* association, guild, society.
soddisfacènte *a* satisfactory.
soddisfàre *vt* to satisfy, fulfill; make amends.
soddisfazióne *nf* satisfaction.
sòdio *nm* sodium.
sòdo *a* solid, hard, sound, firm.
sofà *nm* sofa.
sofferènte *a* suffering, poorly.
sofferènza *nf* suffering, endurance.
soffermàrsi *vr* to linger, pause.
soffiàre *vti* to blow.
sòffice *a* soft.
soffiétto *nm* bellows; *pl* (*of carriage*) folding top, puff; (*fig*) blurb.
sóffio *nm* puff, whiff, breath.
soffítta *nf* attic, garret.
soffítto *nm* ceiling.
soffocàre *vti* to choke, suffocate.
soffocazióne *nf* choking, suffocation.
soffríre *vti* to suffer, bear.
Sòfia *nf pr* (*geogr*) Sofia.
Sofía *nf pr* Sophia, Sophie, Sophy.
sofísma *nm* sophism.
sofisticàre *vi* to sophisticate, quibble; *vt* to adulterate.
soggettísta *nmf* (*cin*) scenario writer.
soggettívo *a* subjective.
soggètto *a* subject, liable; *nm* subject, topic; **s. agli incidènti** accident-prone.
soggezióne *nf* awe, timidity; subjection.
sogghignàre *vi* to sneer, grin.
soggiacére *vi* to be subjected, be liable; succumb.
soggiogàre *vt* to subdue, subjugate.
soggiornàre *vi* to sojourn, stay.
soggiórno *nm* sojourn, stay; **permèsso di s.** permission to stay.
soggiúngere *vti* to add, reply.
sòglia *nf* threshold.
sògliola *nf* (*fish*) sole.
sognànte *a* dreaming, dreamy.

sognàre *vt* to dream of; **-rsi** *vr* to imagine, fancy.
sognatóre *nm* **-tríce** *nf* dreamer.
sógno *nm* dream, fancy.
sol *nm* (*mus*) sol, G.
solàio *nm* loft.
solaménte *ad* only, solely.
solcàre *vt* to furrow, plow.
sólco *pl* **-chi** *nm* furrow, track, wrinkle, groove.
soldatésca *nf* soldiery.
soldatésco *pl* **-chi** *a* soldierly.
soldàto *nm* soldier.
sòldo *nm* (*old Italian coin*) soldo; **sòldi** *pl* pay, money.
sóle *nm* sun(shine); **al s.** in the sun.
soleggiàto *a* sunny.
solènne *a* solemn.
solennità *nf* solemnity.
solére *vi* to use, be in the habit of.
solèrte *a* active, attentive, zealous.
solèrzia *nf* diligence, industriousness.
solétto *a* alone; **sólo s.** all alone.
solfàto *nm* sulphate.
solidàle *a* joint; loyal to.
solidarietà *nf* solidarity.
solidità *nf* solidity; (*of colors*) fastness.
sòlido *a* solid; (*of colors*) fast; sound, reliable.
solilòquio *nm* soliloquy.
solísta *nmf* soloist.
solitàrio *a* solitary, lonely; *nm* hermit; (*gem and game*) solitaire; (*game*) patience.
sòlito *a* usual, **di s.** usually.
solitúdine solitude.
sollàzzo *nm* amusement, pastime, laughing-stock.
sollecitàre *vt* to urge, solicit; hasten.
sollécito *a* prompt; solicitous; *nm* soliciting (*payment etc*).
sollecitúdine *nf* diligence, speed; attention.
solleóne *nm* dog-days *pl*.
solleticàre *vt* to tickle; stimulate.
sollético *pl* **-ichi** *nm* tickle.
sollevàre *vt* to lift, raise; relieve; **-rsi** *vr* to rise.
sollevàto *a* relieved, cheered up.
sollièvo *nm* relief, comfort.
sólo *a* alone, only, sole; **da s.** by oneself; *ad* but, only.
solstízio *nm* solstice.
soltànto *ad* only, solely.
solúbile *a* soluble.
solubilità *nf* solubility.
soluzióne *nf* solution.
solvènte *a nm* solvent.
solvènza, solvibilità *nf* solvency.
sòma *nf* load, burden.
Somàlia *nf* (*geogr*) Somaliland.
somàro *nm* ass, donkey.
somigliànte *a* like, resembling.
somigliànza *nf* likeness, resemblance.
somigliàre *vi* to be like, look like, resemble.
sómma *nf* addition, sum, amount.

sommaménte *ad* extremely, highly.
sommàre *vt* to add up; *vi* to amount to.
sommàrio *a nm* summary.
sommèrgere *vt* to submerge, flood; **-rsi** *vr* to sink, dive.
sommergíbile *a* submergible; *nm* submarine.
sommésso *a* meek, subdued.
somministràre *vt* to administer.
somministrazióne *nf* administration; provision, supply.
sommità *nf* summit, top.
sómmo *a* highest, very great; *nm* summit.
sommòssa *nf* rising, rebellion.
sommozzatóre *nm* frogman, skindiver.
sommuòvere *vt* to excite, rouse, stir up.
sonàglio *nm* harness-bell; rattle.
sonàre *v* **suonàre**.
sónda *nf* sounding line; probe, feeler; drill.
sondàggio *nm* sounding.
sondàre *vt* to sound, probe.
sonería *nf* striking mechanism; alarm-bell.
sonétto *nm* sonnet.
sonnàmbulo *nm* sleepwalker, somnambulist.
sonnecchiàre *vi* to doze.
sonnellíno *nm* doze, nap.
sonnífero *nm* soporific, narcotic.
sónno *nm* sleep; **avér s.** to be sleepy.
sonnolènto *a* drowsy, sleepy.
sonnolènza *nf* drowsiness.
sonorità *nf* sonorousness, sonority.
sonòro *a* resonant, sonorous; sound.
sontuosità *nf* sumptuousness.
sontuóso *a* sumptuous.
sopíre *vt* to make drowsy; calm.
sopóre *nm* drowsiness, light sleep.
soporífero *a nm* soporific.
sopperíre a *vi* to provide for.
soppiantàre *vt* to oust, supplant.
sopportàbile *a* bearable, endurable.
sopportàre *vt* to bear, endure, tolerate.
soppressióne *nf* suppression, abolition.
sopprímere *vt* to suppress, abolish, kill.
sópra *prep* above, on, over; **di s.** upstairs.
soprabbondàre *etc v* **sovrabbondàre** *etc.*
sopràbito *nm* overcoat.
sopraccíglio *nm* eyebrow.
sopraddétto *a* above-mentioned.
sopraffàre *vt* to overcome, overwhelm.
sopraffazióne *nf* act of tyranny, abuse of power.
sopraffíno *a* first-class, superfine, exceptional.
sopraggiúngere *vi* to arrive, come up, happen.
sopr(a)intendènte *nm* superintendent.

sopraluògo *pl* **-òghi** *nm* investigation on the spot.
soprammòbile *nm* knick-knack.
soprannaturàle *a nm* supernatural.
soprannóme *nm* nickname.
soprannúmero *nm* excess, surplus.
sopràno *nm (mus)* soprano.
soprappassàggio *nm* overpass.
soprappensièro *ad* sunk in thought.
soprappiù *nm* extra.
soprapprèzzo *nm* increase in price, surcharge.
soprascàrpa *nf* overshoe, galosh.
soprascrítta *nf* address; superscription.
soprascrítto *a* above(-written).
soprassàlto *nm* start; **di s.** with a start.
soprassedére *vi* to wait, postpone.
soprattàssa *nf* surtax.
soprattútto *ad* above all, especially.
sopravanzàre *vt* to surpass, exceed; *vi* to be left over.
sopravveníre *vi* to turn up, happen, occur.
sopravvènto *nm* advantage, superiority.
sopravvívere *vi* to outlive, survive.
soprúso *nm* abuse of power; insult, outrage.
soqquàdro *nm* confusion, disorder; **a s.** topsy-turvy.
sorbíre *vt* to sip; **-rsi** *vr* to put up with; swallow.
Sorbóna *nf pr* Sorbonne.
sórcio *nm* mouse.
sordaménte *ad* with a dull sound, with a thud; secretly.
sòrdido *a* dirty, filthy.
sordità *nf* deafness.
sórdo *a* deaf; hollow, dull.
sordomúto *a* deaf-and-dumb; *nm* deaf-mute.
sorèlla *nf* sister.
sorellàstra *nf* half-sister.
sorgènte *nf* spring, source; cause.
sórgere *vi* to (a)rise, rise up.
sormontàre *vt* to overcome, surmount.
sornióne *a* sly.
sorpassàre *vt* to overtake; excel, outdo; **sorpàsso** *nm (aut)* overtaking.
sorpassàto *a* out of date.
sorprendènte *a* surprising, astonishing.
sorprèndere *vt* to surprise; catch.
sorprésa *nf* surprise.
sorrèggere *vt* to support.
sorridènte *a* smiling.
sorrídere *vi* to smile (at); appeal.
sorríso *nm* smile.
sórso *nm* draft; drop; sip.
sòrta *nf* kind, sort.
sòrte *nf* destiny, fortune; lot.
sorteggiàre *vt* to draw by lot.
sortéggio *nm* draw.
sortilègio *nm* witchcraft.
sortíre *vi* to be drawn (by lot); to go out.
sortíta *nf* sally, witty remark.

sorvegliànza *nf* surveillance, supervision.

sorvegliàre *vt* to oversee, watch (over).

sorvolàre *vt* to fly over, pass over.

sospèndere *vt* to suspend; hang; adjourn, interrupt.

sospensióne *nf* suspension.

sospéso *a* hanging, suspended; in suspense, uncertain.

sospettàre *vti* to suspect.

sospètto *a* suspicious; suspect; *nm* suspicion.

sospettóso *a* suspicious, distrustful.

sospiràre *vt* to long for, sigh for; *vi* to sigh.

sospíro *nm* sigh.

sossópra *ad* topsy-turvy, upside-down.

sòsta *nf* halt, stop; respite.

sostantívo *nm* noun, substantive.

sostànza *nf* substance; **in s.** essentially, in short.

sostanziàle *a* substantial, fundamental.

sostanzióso *a* substantial, nourishing.

sostàre *vi* to pause, stop.

sostégno *nm* support.

sostenére *vt* to support, sustain, carry, maintain, keep up, endure, hold; **-rsi** *vr* to lean on, support oneself.

sosteníbile *a* sustainable, tenable; bearable.

sostentaménto *nm* sustenance, support.

sostentàre *vt* to support.

sostenúto *a* stiff, reserved, distant.

sostituíre *vt* to replace, take the place of.

sostitúto *nm* substitute.

sostituzióne *nf* replacement, substitution.

sottacéti *nm pl* pickles *pl.*

sottàna *nf* skirt, petticoat; (*eccl*) cassock.

sottentràre (a) *vi* to take the place (of).

sotterfúgio *nm* subterfuge.

sottèrra *ad* underground.

sotterràneo *a* subterranean, underground; *nm* cave, vault, dungeon.

sotterràre *vt* to bury.

sottigliézza *nf* thinness, fineness; subtlety, quibble.

sottíle *a* thin, slender; subtle.

sottintèndere *vt* to imply, understand.

sottintéso *a* understood, implied; *nm* allusion.

sótto *ad prep* under(neath), below; **al di s.** di below.

sottòcchio *ad* before one's eyes.

sottochiàve *ad* under lock and key.

sottocommissióne *nf* sub-commission.

sottolineàre *vt* to underline; emphasize.

sottomàno, di *ad* underhand(edly).

sottomaríno *a nm* submarine.

sottomésso *a* subject; submissive, respectful.

sottométtere *vt* to conquer, subdue, subject; **-rsi** *vr* to give in, submit, yield.

sottomissióne *nf* submission, subjection.

sottopassàggio *nm* subway, underpass.

sottopórre *vt* to subject; submit; **-rsi** *vr* to submit.

sottoscrívere *vt* to sign, underwrite; *vi* subscribe; **-rsi** *vr* to sign.

sottoscrizióne *nf* subscription.

sottosegretàrio *nm* under-secretary.

sottosópra *ad* topsy-turvy, upside-down.

sottostànte *a* below.

sottostàre *vi* to be subjected; lie below; submit.

sottosuòlo *nm* subsoil.

sottotenènte *nm* second lieutenant.

sottovèste *nf* petticoat, slip.

sottovóce *ad* in a low voice, in an undertone.

sottràrre *vt* to subtract; steal; take away, deduct; **-rsi** *vr* to escape from, evade.

sottrazióne *nf* subtraction, taking away.

sottufficiàle *nm* non-commissioned officer.

sovènte *ad* often.

soverchiàre *vt* to overflow; overcome; surpass.

soverchieria *nf* insolence, imposition.

sovèrchio *a* excessive.

soviètico *pl* **-ici** *a* Soviet.

sóvra *v* **sópra.**

sovrabbondànza *nf* superabundance.

sovrabbondàre *vi* to superabound.

sovraccàrico *pl* **-ichi** *a* overloaded; *nm* overload; **per s.** in addition, moreover.

sovranità *nf* sovereignty.

sovrannaturàle *v* **soprannaturàle.**

sovràno *nm* sovereign.

sovrastàre *vi* to hang over, surpass.

sovrumàno *a* superhuman.

sovveníre *vti* to assist, help; **far s.** to remind; **-rsi** *vr* to remember.

sovvenzióne *nf* subsidy, subvention.

sovversióne *nf* overthrow, subversion.

sovversívo *a* subversive; *nm* subverter.

sovvertíre *vt* to overthrow, subvert.

sózzo *a* filthy, loathsome.

sozzúra *nf* filth.

spaccalégna (*inv*) *nm* wood-cutter.

spaccapiètre (*inv*) *nm* stone-breaker.

spaccàre *vt* to cleave, split, break.

spaccatúra *nf* crack, split.

spacciàre *vt* to sell; pass off; dispatch; **-rsi** *vr* to set up as.

spacciàto *a* done for.

spàccio *nm* sale; shop.

spàcco *pl* **spàcchi** *nm* cleft, split.

spaccóne nm boaster, braggart.
spàda nf sword; pl (cards) spades pl.
Spàgna nf (geogr) Spain.
spagnolétta nf spool; (fam) peanut.
spagn(u)òlo a Spanish; nm Spaniard.
spàgo pl spàghi nm string, twine.
spaiàre vt to uncouple.
spalancàre vt to open wide, throw open.
spàlla nf shoulder, back.
spalleggiàre vt to back, support.
spallièra nf (of chair) back.
spallína nf epaulet, shoulder-strap.
spalmàre vt to spread, smear.
spàlto nm glacis.
spàndere vt to spread, divulge; shed; squander.
spànna nf span.
sparàre vt to shoot, fire, discharge.
sparàto a shot; nm shirt-front.
sparatòria nf shooting, exchange of shots.
sparecchiàre vt to clear (away).
spàrgere vt to scatter, shed, spread.
sparíre vi to disappear.
sparizióne nf disappearance.
sparlàre vi to speak ill.
spàro nm shot.
sparpagliàre vt to scatter, spread.
spàrso a shed, loose.
spartiàcque (inv) nm watershed, divide.
spartíre vt to divide, separate.
spartíto nm (mus) score.
spartitràffico (inv) nm traffic island.
spartizióne nf distribution, division, partition.
sparúto a gaunt, lean, thin.
sparvière, sparvièro nm hawk.
spaṣimànte nm lover, wooer.
spaṣimàre vi to suffer terribly; yearn.
spàṣimo nm pang, (med) spasm.
spassàrsi vr to amuse oneself, enjoy oneself; spassàrsela to have a very good time.
spassionàto a dispassionate, impartial.
spàsso nm amusement, pastime; andàre a s. to go for a walk.
spassóso a amusing.
spatriàre v espatriàre.
spauràcchio nm scarecrow; bugbear.
spauríre vt to frighten.
spavaldería nf boldness, defiance; boast.
spavàldo a bold, defiant; nm bold fellow, braggart.
spaventapàsseri (inv) nm scarecrow.
spaventàre vt to frighten, scare.
spaventévole a dreadful, frightful.
spaziàle a space.
spavènto nm fright, fear.
spaventóso a dreadful, frightful.
spaziàre vi to soar.
spazientírsi vr to lose one's patience.
spàzio nm space, distance; interval; room; period of time.
spazióso a broad, roomy, spacious.

spazzacamíno pl -íni nm chimney-sweep.
spazzamíne inv nm minesweeper.
spazzanéve (inv) nm snowplow.
spazzàre vt to sweep.
spazzatúra nf sweeping; sweepings pl.
spazzaturàio, spazzíno nm sweeper; garbageman.
spàzzola nf brush.
spazzolàre vt to brush.
spazzolíno nm small brush; s. da dènti toothbrush.
specchiàrsi vr to look at oneself in the glass, be reflected.
specchièra nf looking-glass, dressing-table.
spècchio nm mirror, looking-glass.
speciàle a special, particular.
specialísta nmf specialist.
specialità nf speciality.
specializzàrsi vr to specialize.
specializzazióne nf specialization.
specialménte ad especially.
spècie (inv) nf kind, species, sort; far s. to amaze; in s. especially.
specífica nf (com) detailed list.
specificàre vt to specify.
specificazióne nf specification.
specífico pl -ici a nm specific.
specióso a specious.
speculàre vti to speculate (upon).
speculazióne nf speculation.
spedíre vt send, mail, dispatch, forward.
speditaménte ad quickly, promptly; fluently.
speditézza nf expedition, quickness; fluency.
spedíto a prompt, quick; fluent.
spedizióne nf dispatch, expedition, forwarding, consignment.
spedizionière nm forwarding agent, shipping agent, carrier, express company.
spègnere vt to extinguish, put out, switch off; stifle; kill; -rsi vr to be extinguished, go out; fade away, pass away.
spelàto a hairless; threadbare, worn.
spelónca nf cave, den.
spèndere vti to spend.
spennàre vt to pluck (poultry).
spensieratézza nf light-heartedness.
spensieràto a light-hearted, care-free.
spènto a extinguished; extinct; (of colors, eyes etc) dull.
speràbile a to be hoped for.
sperànza nf hope, expectation.
speranzóso a hopeful.
speràre vt to hope for, expect.
spèrdersi vr to get lost, go astray.
sperdúto a secluded, wild; lost (also fig); ill at ease.
spergiuràre vi to perjure oneself, swear falsely.
spergiúro a perjured; nm perjurer; perjury.
sperimentàle a experimental.

sperimentàre *vt* to experiment with.
speróne *nm* spur.
sperperàre *vt* to dissipate, squander, waste.
spèrpero *nm* dissipation, waste.
spésa *nf* expense, cost; shopping; purchase; **spése generàli** running cost, operating cost.
spèsso *a* dense; thick; *ad* frequently, often.
spessóre *nm* thickness.
spettàcolo *nm* sight, spectacle; performance.
spettànza *nf* concern; *pl* dues *pl*; **èssere di s. di** to be the duty of, concern.
spettàre *vi* to be the duty of; be the turn of.
spettatóre *nm* **-tríce** *nf* spectator, bystander, onlooker.
spettinàto *a* dishevelled, unkempt.
spèttro *nm* ghost, specter.
spettràle *a* ghostly, spectral.
spettroscòpio *nm* spectroscope.
spèzie *nf pl* spices *pl*.
spezzàre *vt* to break.
spezzóne *nm* incendiary bomb.
spía *nf* spy; telltale.
spiacènte *a* sorry.
spiacére *v* **dispiacére**.
spiacévole *a* unpleasant.
spiàggia *nf* beach, shore.
spianàre *vt* to level, raze, smooth.
spianàta *nf* open space, clearing; esplanade.
spiantàre *vt* to uproot; ruin.
spiantàto *nm* penniless person.
spiàre *vt* to spy upon, watch for.
spiccàre *vt* to pick; *vi* stand out; **s. un salto** to leap; **s. le paròle** to enunciate clearly.
spícchio *nm* (*of garlic*) clove, (*of fruit*) segment, quarter.
spicciàre *vt* to dispatch; **-rsi** *vr* to hurry up, make haste.
spicciolàta, alla *ad* a few at a time.
spícciolo *a* small; *nm* small coin; *pl* change.
spíder *nm* (*aut*) two-seater sports car.
spièdo *nm* spit.
spiegàbile *a* explicable, justifiable.
spiegàre *vt* to explain; spread out, display; **-rsi** *vr* to make oneself understood; open out.
spiegazióne *nf* explanation.
spietàto *a* pitiless, ruthless.
spíffero *nm* draft (of air).
spíga *nf* stalk of wheat.
spighétta *nf* braid.
spigliatézza *nf* ease, nimbleness.
spigliàto *a* easy, nimble.
spígo *pl* **spíghi** *nm* lavender.
spigolàre *vt* to glean.
spígolo *nm* (*of table etc*) corner.
spílla *nf* pin, brooch.
spillàre *vt* to broach, tap, draw.
spíllo *nm* pin; **spillóne** brooch, (hat-)pin.
spilòrcio *a* miserly, niggardly, stingy; *nm* miser.

spína *nf* thorn; (*fish*) bone; (*elec*) plug; **s. dorsàle** backbone, spine.
spinàci *nm pl* spinach.
spíngere *vt* to push; drive, induce.
spíno *nm* thorn.
spinóso *a* thorny.
spínta *nf* push, shove.
spinterògeno *nm* (*aut*) coil ignition.
spínto *a* pushed, driven; excessive; daring.
spionàggio *nm* espionage, spying.
spiovènte *a* drooping, sloping.
spiòvere *vi* to stop raining.
spíra *nf* coil.
spiràglio *nm* air-hole; gleam of light; breath of air.
spiràle *a nf* spiral.
spiràre *vi* to blow; die, expire; *vt* to exhale.
spiritàto *a* possessed.
spiritísmo *nm* spiritualism.
spírito *nm* spirit, ghost; wit.
spiritóso *a* witty; alcoholic.
spirituàle *a* spiritual.
splendènte *a* bright, brilliant, shining.
splèndere *vt* to shine, glitter.
splèndido *a* gorgeous, magnificent, splendid.
splendóre *nm* splendor, magnificence.
Splúga, (Pàsso déllo) *nm* (*geogr*) Splugen Pass.
spodestàre *vt* to dispossess, oust.
spòglia *nf* booty, spoil; **spòglie** *pl* remains *pl*.
spogliàre *vt* to strip, undress; despoil; **-rsi** *vr* to strip oneself, undress.
spogliarèllo *nm* striptease.
spogliatóio *nm* dressing-room, cloakroom.
spòglio *a* bare, undressed; *nm* examination; **spògli** *pl* cast-off clothes *pl*.
spòla *nf* shuttle; **fàre la s.** to go to and fro, commute.
spolétta *nf* reel of cotton, spool; (*mil*) fuse.
spolpàre *vt* to remove flesh; bleed white.
spolveràre *vt* to dust; eat up.
spolveràta *nf* dust(ing), brush(ing).
spónda *nf* bank, edge.
sponsàli *nm pl* (*poet*) wedding.
spontaneità *nf* spontaneousness, spontaneity.
spontàneo *a* spontaneous.
spopolàre *vt* to depopulate.
sporàdico *pl* **-ici** *a* sporadic.
sporcàre *vt* to dirty, soil.
sporcízia *nf* dirt, filth.
spòrco *pl* **spòrchi** *a* dirty, unclean.
sporgènte *a* jutting out.
spòrgere *vt* to put out; *vi* to jut out; **-rsi** *vr* to lean out.
spòrta *nf* (shopping)basket.
sportèllo *nm* (*of carriage etc*) door, (*of booking office*) window; counter.

sportívo a sporting, sports, sportsmanlike; nm sportsman.
spòṣa nf bride, young wife; **spòso** nm bridegroom.
sposalízio nm wedding.
spoṣàre vt to marry, wed; **-rsi** vr to get married.
spossànte a exhausting, enervating.
spossàre vt to exhaust, wear out.
spossatézza nf exhaustion, weariness.
spossessàre vt to dispossess.
spostaménto nm shifting, displacement, change.
spostàre vt to shift, displace, change.
spostàto a out of its place; illadjusted; nm misfit.
spràuga nf bolt, (cross-)bar.
spràzzo nm flash, gleam.
sprecàre vt to waste, squander.
sprèco pl **sprèchi** nm waste.
sprecóne nm waster, squanderer.
spregévole a despicable, mean.
spregiàre v **sprezzàre**.
sprègio nm disdain, scorn.
spregiudicatézza nf open-mindedness.
spregiudicàto a unbiased, unprejudiced.
sprèmere vt to squeeze (also fig).
spremúta nf squash.
sprezzànte a scornful, contemptuous.
sprigionàre vt to give off, release; **-rsi** vr to spring out, burst forth.
sprizzàre vi to spout, spurt.
sprofondaménto nm sinking, subsidence, collapse.
sprofondàre vi to founder, sink; **-rsi** vr to sink, collapse; be absorbed.
spronàre vt to spur, urge.
spróne nm spur.
sproporzionàto a disproportionate.
sproporzióne nf disproportion.
spropòsito nm blunder, gaffe.
sprovvedére vt to leave unprovided; **-rsi** vr to deprive oneself.
sprovvísta, alla ad unawares, unexpectedly.
sprovvísto a lacking, unprovided with, unprepared.
spruzzàre vt to spray, sprinkle.
sprúzzo nm spray, sprinkling.
ṣpudoràto a shameless, impudent.
spúgna nf sponge.
spugnosità nf sponginess.
spugnóso a spongy.
spumànte a foaming, frothing; nm sparkling wine.
spuntàre vt to blunt; cut off the end; vi to appear, rise.
spuntíno nm snack.
sputàre vti to spit.
spúto nm spit, spittle.
squàdra nf square; squad, team.
squadràre vt to look up and down; square.
squadríglia nf squadron.
squagliàrsi vr to melt, thaw; steal away.

squàllido a dismal, dreary.
squallóre nm dreariness, gloom.
squàlo nm shark.
squàma nf (of fish etc) scale.
squamóso a scaly.
squarciagóla, a ad at the top of one's voice.
squarciàre vt to rend, tear asunder; dispel.
squàrcio nm gash, rent, tear; (of a book etc) passage.
squartàre vt to quarter, cut up.
squassàre vt to shake.
squattrinàto a penniless.
squilibràto a unbalanced.
squilíbrio nm want of balance; **s. mentàle** madness.
squílla nf (small) bell; ring.
squillànte a blaring, shrill.
squillàre vi to blare; ring, peal.
squíllo nm blare, ring.
squiṣitézza nf exquisiteness, deliciousness.
squiṣito a exquisite, delicious.
squittíre vi to squeak.
ṣradicàre vt to eradicate, uproot.
ṣragionàre vi to talk nonsense, reason falsely.
ṣregolatézza nf disorder, dissoluteness.
ṣregolàto a disorderly, dissolute.
stàbile a stable, firm, lasting.
stabiliménto nm factory, works, plant, establishment.
stabilíre vt to establish, fix; ascertain; decide; set; **-rsi** vr to settle.
stabilità nf stability, firmness.
stabilizzatóre nm (av naut) stabilizer.
staccaménto nm detachment.
staccàre vt to detach, remove, separate; **-rsi** vr to be different; become detached, break off; leave.
stacciàre vt to sieve, sift.
stàccio nm sieve.
stàcco pl **stàcchi** nm separation.
stadèra nf (tec) steelyard.
stàdio nm stadium, sports-ground; phase.
stàffa nf footboard; stirrup; **pèrdere le stàffe** to lose one's temper.
staffière nm groom.
staffilàre vt to whip, lash.
staffíle nm whip, lash.
stagionàle a seasonal.
stagionàre vi to season.
stagióne nf season.
stagnàio, stagníno nm tin-smith.
stagnànte a stagnant.
stagnàre vt to solder, tin; vi to stagnate.
stàgno nm tin; pond, pool.
stàio pl m **stài** f **stàia** nm bushel.
Stalingràdo nf (geogr) Stalingrad.
stàlla nf stable, cowshed.
stallàggio nm stabling.
stallière nm groom, stableman.
stallóne nm stallion.
stamàne, stamàni, stamattína ad this morning.

stambúgio *nm* cubby-hole, little dark room.

stàmpa *nf* press, print; **stàmpe** *pl* printed matter.

stampàre *vt* to print, publish; coin; -rsi *vr* to impress.

stampatèllo *nm* block letters.

stampàto *a* printed; *nm* printed matter; form.

stampèlla *nf* crutch.

stampería *nf* printing press, printing works.

stàmpo *nm* die, stamp, kind, sort.

stancàre *vt* to tire; bore.

stanchézza *nf* tiredness, weariness.

stànco *pl* -chi *a* tired, weary.

stànga *nf* bar; (*of carriage*) shaft.

stangàre *vt* to bar; thrash.

stanòtte *ad* last night; tonight.

stànte *a* being; **sedúta s.** during the sitting; at once.

stantío *a* stale.

stantúffo *nm* piston.

stànza *nf* room; (*poet*) stanza; **èssere di s.** (*mil*) to be stationed.

stanziàre *vt* to set apart (funds).

stappàre *vt* to uncork.

stàre *vi* to stay, remain; stand; live; be.

stàrna *nf* partridge.

starnutíre *vi* to sneeze.

starnúto *nm* sneeze.

staséra *ad* this evening, tonight.

statàle *a* (of the) state; *nm* civil servant.

Stàti Uníti *nm pl* United States *pl.*

stàtico *pl* -ici *a* static.

statísta *nm* statesman.

statística *nf* statistics.

statístico *pl* -ici *a* statistical.

stàto *nm* state, condition, situation; **s. maggióre** (*mil*) general staff.

stàtua *nf* statue.

statuària *nf* statuary.

statunitènse *a nmf* United States (citizen).

statúra *nf* height, size, stature.

statúto *nm* statute; constitution.

stazionàrio *a* stationary.

stazióne *nf* station; **s. climàtica** health resort.

stàzza *nf* (*naut*) tonnage.

stazzàre *vt* to gauge, measure; *vi* (*naut*) to have a tonnage of.

stécca *nf* (*billiards*) cue; (*mus*) false note; small stick; (*umbrella*) rib.

steccàto *nm* fence, paling, rails *pl.*

stecchíno *nm* toothpick.

stecchíto *a* dried up; skinny; stiff and stark.

Stéfano *nm pr* Stephen.

stélla *nf* star.

stellàto *a* starry.

stellétta *nf* asterisk; (*mil*) star.

stèlo *nm* stalk, stem.

stèmma *nm* coat of arms.

stemperàre *vt* to melt; mix.

stempiàrsi *vr* to lose one's hair at the temples, to go bald.

stendàrdo *nm* standard.

stèndere *vt* to spread, lay out, hang out, (out)stretch; draw up.

stenografàre *vt* to write in shorthand.

stenografía *nf* shorthand.

stenògrafo *nm* **stenògrafa** *nf* shorthand-writer, stenographer.

stentàre *vi* to find it hard to.

stènto *nm* difficulty; privation, suffering; **a s.** hardly, with difficulty.

stéppa *nf* steppe.

stereofònico *pl* -ici *a* stereophonic.

stèrile *a* sterile, barren, unproductive.

sterilità *nf* sterility, barrenness.

sterilizzàre *vt* to sterilize.

sterlína *nf* pound (sterling).

sterminàre *vt* to exterminate.

sterminàto *a* exterminated; boundless.

stermínio *nm* extermination.

sterràre *vt* to dig up, excavate.

sterzàre *vt* (*aut*) to steer; **stèrzo** *nm* (*aut*) steering wheel, steering.

stésso *a pron* same, self; *nm* same.

stesúra *nf* drawing up, drafting.

stilàre *vt* to draw up.

stíle *nm* style.

stílla *nf* drop.

stillàre *vti* to drip, ooze, exude.

stílo *nm* stylus.

stilogràfica, (pénna) *nf* fountain pen.

stíma *nf* estimate, estimation, valuation; esteem.

stimàre *vt* to estimate, value; esteem; consider; -rsi *vr* to think oneself.

stimolànte *a* stimulating; *nm* stimulant.

stimolàre *vt* to drive, goad, stimulate, urge.

stímolo *nm* goad, spur, stimulus.

stínco *pl* -chi *nm* shin, shinbone.

stipàre *vt* -rsi *vr* to crowd, throng.

stipèndio *nm* salary, wages *pl;* **s. ridótto** (**mèzzo s.**) half-pay.

stípite *nm* (door-)post; (*family*) stock.

stipulàre *vt* to stipulate.

stipulazióne *nf* stipulation.

stiracchiàre *vt* to stretch; bargain over.

stiracchiàto *a* forced, unconvincing.

stiràre *vt* to iron; stretch (out); -rsi *vr* to stretch (oneself).

stíro, fèrro da *nm* iron.

stírpe *nm* birth, descent, race.

stitichézza *nf* constipation.

stítico *pl* -ici *a* constipated.

stíva *nf* (*naut*) hold.

stivàle *nm* boot; **stivalétto** *nm* ankle-boot.

stivàre *vt* to stow.

stízza *nf* anger.

stizzírsi *vr* to get angry, get cross.

stizzóso *a* irritable, ill-tempered.

stoccafísso *nm* stockfish.

Stoccólma *nf* (*geogr*) Stockholm.

stòffa *nf* material, stuff.

stòico *pl* **-ici** *a* stoical; *nm* stoic.
stòla *nf* stole.
stolidità, stolidézza *nf* stolidity; stupidity.
stòlido *a* stolid; stupid.
stoltézza *nf* foolishness, folly.
stólto *a* foolish; *nm* fool.
stomacàre *vt* to disgust, sicken; **-rsi** *vr* to be disgusted with, be sick of.
stomachévole *a* disgusting, loathsome.
stòmaco *pl* **-chi** *nm* stomach.
stonàre *vi* to be out of tune; be out of place.
stonatúra *nf* false note (*also fig*).
stóppa *nf* tow, oakum.
stóppia *nf* stubble.
stoppíno *nm* wick.
stòrcere *vt* to twist, distort; **-rsi** *vr* to twist, writhe.
stordiménto *nm* dazed state, dizziness.
stordíre *vt* to daze, stun, stupefy.
storditàggine *nf* absent-mindedness, carelessness, foolishness.
stòria *nf* history, story, tale.
stòrico *pl* **-ici** *a* historical; *nm* historian.
storióne *nm* sturgeon.
stormíre *vi* to rustle.
stórmo *nm* flight, flock; **suonàre a s.** to sound the tocsin.
stornàre *vt* to avert, ward off.
stórno, stornèllo *nm* starling.
storpiàre *vt* to cripple, maim, mangle.
storpiatúra *nf* crippling, maiming, mangling.
stórpio *a* crippled; *nm* cripple.
stòrta *nf* sprain.
stòrto *a* twisted, crooked; wrong.
stovíglie *nf pl* crockery.
stra- *prefix* over.
stràbico *pl* **-ici** *a* squint-eyed.
strabiliàre *vi* to be amazed, be astounded.
strabísmo *nm* squint, squinting.
straboccàre *vi* to overflow.
stracciàre *vt* to tear.
stràccio *a* ragged, torn; *nm* rag.
straccióne *nm* ragamuffin.
stràda *nf* road, street, way; **s.** facèndo on the way.
stradàle *a* road, of the road; *nm* road.
stradóne *nm* large street, main road.
strafalcióne *nm* blunder.
strafàre *vi* to overdo.
stràge *nf* massacre, slaughter, havoc.
stralunàre *vt* to open wide, roll (one's eyes).
stramazzàre *vi* to fall heavily.
strambería *nf* eccentricity, oddity.
stràmbo *a* odd, eccentric.
stràme *nm* litter, straw.
strampalàto *a* odd, eccentric.
stranézza *nf* oddness, strangeness.
strangolàre *vt* to strangle, throttle, choke.
stranièro *a* foreign; *nm* foreigner.

stràno *a* strange, odd, queer, funny.
straordinariaménte *ad* extraordinarily, unusually, enormously.
straordinàrio *a* extraordinary, astonishing, unusual; **edizióne** straordinària *nf* (*newspaper*) special edition; **lavóro s.** *nm* overtime work.
strapazzàre *vt* to ill-treat, ill-use; **-rsi** *vr* to overwork oneself.
strapazzàta *nf* scolding; overwork.
strapàzzo *nm* overwork, over-exertion.
strappàre *vt* to tear, wrench, snatch; **-rsi** *vr* to get torn; tear oneself away.
stràppo *nm* tear, jerk; infringement; **fàre úno s. àlla règola** to make an exception.
straripàre *vi* to overflow.
Strasbúrgo *nf* (*geogr*) Strasbourg.
strascicàre *vt* to drag, shuffle; drawl.
stràscico *pl* **-ichi** *nm* train; sequel.
stratagèmma *nm* stratagem.
strategía *nf* strategy.
stratègico *pl* **-ici** *a* strategic.
stràto *nm* layer, stratum.
stravagànte *a* odd, strange; *nm* eccentric.
stravagànza *nf* eccentricity, oddness.
straviziàre *vi* to be intemperate.
stravízio *nm* excess, intemperance.
stravòlto *a* twisted, convulsed.
straziàre *vt* to rend, torture.
stràzio *nm* torment, torture; heartbreak, trouble.
stréga *nf* witch; **stregóne** *nm* wizard.
stregàre *vt* to bewitch.
stregonería *nf* witchcraft.
strégua *nf* standard, way.
stremàre *vt* to exhaust.
strènna *nf* Christmas box; gift.
strènuo *a* brave; strenuous, vigorous.
strepitàre *vi* to make an uproar, shout.
strèpito *nm* din, uproar.
strepitóso *a* uproarious, clamorous.
streptocòcco *pl* **-còcchi** *nm* streptococcus.
streptomicína *nf* streptomycin.
strétta *nf* clasp, embrace, grasp, hold; **s. di màno** handshake.
strettézza *nf* narrowness; poverty; **in strettézze** hard up.
strétto *a* narrow, tight; strict; *nm* strait.
strettóia *nf* difficult situation.
strettóio *nm* (*mech*) press.
stricnína *nf* strychnine.
stridènte *a* shrill, sharp, strident; jarring, clashing.
stridere *vi* to creak, screech, jar.
strído *nm* cry, screech.
stridóre *nm* screeching, jarring.
strídulo *a* piercing, shrill.
stríglia *nf* curry-comb.
strigliàre *vt* to curry; rebuke.
strillàre *vi* to scream, shout.

stríllo *nm* scream, shriek, cry.
strillóne *nm* (news)paper-boy.
striminzíto *a* thin, stunted.
strimpellàre *vt* to strum, thrum.
strinàto *a* singed.
strínga *nf* (shoe)lace.
stringàto *a* laced; tight; (*of style*) concise.
stríngere *vt* to press, tighten, grasp; **-rsi** *vr* to press (against); shrug; squeeze.
stríscia *nf* strip, stripe.
strisciàre *vt* to drag, shuffle; graze; *vi* to crawl, creep.
stríscio *nm* graze; **di s.** grazingly.
stritolàre *vt* to crush.
strizzàre *vt* to squeeze, wring; **s. l'òcchio** to wink.
stròfa *nf* strophe.
strofinàccio *nm* duster, floor-cloth.
strofinàre *vt* to rub.
strombazzàre *vt* to trumpet; boast.
stroncàre *vt* to break (off); criticize harshly.
stroncatúra *nf* devastating criticism.
stropicciàre *vt* to rub, shuffle.
stròzza *nf* throat.
strozzàre *vt* to strangle, throttle, suffocate; (*fig*) fleece.
strozzinàggio *nm* usury.
strozzíno *nm* usurer.
strúggere *vt* to melt; consume; **-rsi** *vr* to be consumed; long (for); melt.
struggiménto *nm* torment; longing.
struménto *nm* implement, tool, instrument.
strútto *nm* lard.
struttúra *nf* structure.
strúzzo *nm* ostrich.
stuccàre *vt* to coat with stucco, plaster; surfeit; **-rsi** *vr* to grow weary.
stuccatúra *nf* plastering.
stucchévole *a* filling; sickening, tedious.
stúcco *pl* **-chi** *nm* plaster, stucco; **rimanére di s.** to be dumbfounded; *a* fed-up, sick.
studènte *nm* **studentéssa** *nf* student.
studentésco *pl* **-chi** *a* student, student-like.
studiàre *vti* to study; **-rsi** *vr* to do one's best, try.
studiataménte *ad* deliberately; with affectation.
stúdio *nm* study; plan; office; studio; **a bèllo s.** on purpose.
studióso *a* studious; *nm* scholar.
stúfa *nf* stove; **s. elèttrica** electric fire, electric heater.
stufàto *nm* stew.
stúfo *a* bored, sick, tired.
stuòia *nf* mat, matting.
stuòlo *nm* band, group, troop.
stupefacènte *a* stupefying; *nm* drug, narcotic.
stupefàre *vt* to astonish, stupefy.
stupefazióne *nf* astonishment, stupefaction.
stupèndo *a* splendid, stupendous.

stupidàggine *nf* foolishness; nonsense.
stupidità *nf* stupidity.
stúpido *a* stupid; *nm* fool.
stupíre *vt* to amaze, astound.
stupóre *nm* amazement, stupor, daze.
stupràre *vt* to rape, violate.
stúpro *nm* rape.
sturàre *vt* to uncork.
stuzzicadènti (*inv*) *nm* toothpick.
stuzzicànte *a* appetizing.
stuzzicàre *vt* to prod, pick; tease; whet.
su *prep* on, upon, over, above; about; towards; *ad* up, upstairs; on.
subàcqueo *a* underwater, subaqueous; **pésca subàcquea** underwater fishing.
subaltèrno *a nm* subordinate.
subbúglio *nm* turmoil, upheaval.
subcosciènte *a nm* subconscious.
súbdolo *a* shifty, underhand.
subentràre *vi* to take the place of.
subíre *vt* to undergo, suffer.
subissàre *vt* to sink, ruin, overwhelm; *vi* to sink, fall into ruin.
subitàneo *a* sudden.
súbito *a* sudden; *ad* at once, immediately.
sublimàre *vt* to sublimate.
sublimàto *nm* sublimate.
sublíme *a* sublime.
subodoràre *vt* to get wind of, suspect.
subordinàre *vt* to subordinate.
subordinazióne *nf* subordination.
subornàre *vt* to suborn, bribe.
subornazióne *nf* subornation.
suburbàno *a* suburban.
subúrbio *nm* suburb(s).
subúrra *nf* slums *pl*.
succèdere *vi* to succeed; follow; happen; **-rsi** *nm* succession.
successióne *nf* succession.
successívo *a* following, subsequent.
succèsso *nm* success.
successóre *nm* successor.
succhiàre *vt* to suck.
succhièllo *nm* gimlet.
succínto *a* scanty, succinct.
súcco *pl* **súcchi** *nm* juice, essence.
succóso *a* juicy.
súccubo *a* (entirely) dominated; *nm* succubus.
succulènto *a* succulent.
succursàle *nf* branch (office).
sud *nm* (*geogr*) south; **s. est** south-east; **s. ovest** south-west.
sudafricàno *a nm* South African.
sudamericàno *a nm* South American.
sudàre *vti* to perspire, sweat.
súddito *nm* subject.
súdicio *a* dirty, filthy.
sudiciúme *nm* dirt, filth.
sudóre *nm* perspiration, sweat.
sufficiènte *a* sufficient, enough; *nm* haughty person.
sufficiènza *nf* enough, sufficient

quantity; (in *exams*) pass mark; self-sufficiency.
suffísso *nm* suffix.
suffragàre *vt* to support.
suffragétta *nf* suffragette.
suffràgio *nm* suffrage; approval; **mèssa in s.** Mass for the repose of a soul.
suggellàre *vt* to seal (up).
suggèllo *nm* seal.
suggeriménto *nm* suggestion.
suggeríre *vt* to suggest; (*theat*) prompt.
suggeritóre *nm* (*theat*) prompter.
suggestionàre *vt* to hypnotize; influence.
suggestióne *nf* suggestion; influence.
suggestívo *a* evocative, suggestive.
súghero *nm* cork, cork-tree.
súgo *pl* **-ghi** *nm* gravy, juice; (*fig*) pleasure.
suicída *a* suicidal; *nm* suicide (*person*).
suicidàrsi *vr* to commit suicide.
suicídio *nm* suicide (*act*).
suíno *a nm* swine.
sulfamídico *pl* **-ici** *a* sulphamidic; *nm* sulphonamide.
sulfúreo *a* sulphureous.
sultàno *nm* sultan.
súo *nm* property; *poss a and pron* his, hers, its, one's.
suòcero *nm* father-in-law; **suòcera** *nf* mother-in-law.
suòla *nf* (*of a shoe*) sole.
suòlo *nm* soil, ground.
suonàre *vti* to sound, play, strike, ring.
suòno *nm* sound.
suòra *nf* nun, sister.
superàre *vt* to outrun; excel; get over, get through; surpass, exceed; **s. di número** outnumber.
supèrbia *nf* arrogance, pride.
supèrbo *a* arrogant, proud; superb; lofty.
superficiàle *a* superficial.
superficialità *nf* superficiality.
superfície *pl* **-ci** *nf* surface, area.
supèrfluo *a* superfluous, unnecessary; *nm* surplus.
superióre *a* higher; superior; upper; above; senior; *nm* superior.
superiorità *nf* superiority.
superlatívo *a* superlative.
supermercàto *nm* supermarket.
supersònico *pl* **-ici** *a* supersonic.
supèrstite *a* surviving; *nmf* survivor.
superstizióne *nf* superstition.
superstizióso *a* superstitious.
supíno *a* supine.
suppellèttili *nf* *pl* equipment; fittings *pl*, furnishings *pl*.
suppergiú *ad* approximately, nearly, roughly.
supplementàre *a* supplementary, additional.
suppleménto *nm* supplement, addition, extra.

supplènte *a* *nmf* substitute, temporary (teacher).
supplènza *nf* temporary post.
súpplica *nf* entreaty, petition.
supplicàre *vt* to entreat, implore.
supplichévole *a* imploring, entreating.
supplíre *vi* to make up for, replace, substitute for.
supplízio *nm* torture, torment.
suppórre *vt* to suppose.
suppòrto *nm* support; (*of an object*) rest, stand, bracket, mount.
supposizióne *nf* supposition.
suppuràre *vi* to suppurate.
supremazía *nf* supremacy.
suprèmo *a* supreme, extraordinary, greatest, highest, last.
surgelaménto *nm* deep freeze.
surgelàto *a nm* deep frozen food.
surrealísmo *nm* surrealism.
surrealísta *a nm* surrealist.
surriscaldàre *vt* to overheat.
surrogàre *vt* to replace, substitute.
surrogàto *nm* substitute.
Susànna *nf* *pr* Susan.
suscettíbile *a* susceptible, touchy.
suscettibilità *nf* susceptibility, touchiness.
suscitàre *vt* to give rise to, provoke, rouse.
susína *nf* plum; **susíno** *nm* plumtree.
susseguènte *a* subsequent, successive.
sussidiàre *vt* to subsidize, support, help.
sussídio *nm* subsidy, aid.
sussiègo *pl* **-ghi** *nm* exaggerated dignity, haughtiness.
sussistènza *nf* existence, subsistence.
sussístere *vi* to exist, subsist.
sussultàre *vi* to start, tremble.
sussúlto *nm* start, tremor.
sussurràre *vti* to whisper, murmur.
sussúrro *nm* whisper, murmur.
şvagàre *vt* to amuse; distract someone's attention.
şvagàto *a* absent-minded.
şvàgo *pl* **-ghi** *nm* amusement, recreation.
şvaligiàre *vt* to rob, burgle.
şvalutàre *vt* to depreciate, undervalue.
şvalutazióne *nf* depreciation, devaluation.
şvaníre *vi* to disappear, vanish.
şvaníto *a* vanished, faded; feebleminded.
şvantàggio *nm* disadvantage.
şvantaggióso *a* unfavorable, detrimental.
şvaporàre *vi* to evaporate, vanish, lose strength.
şvariàto *a* varied, various.
şvedése *a* Swedish; *nmf* Swede.
şvéglia *nf* waking-up; alarm clock; (*mil*) reveille.
şvegliàre *vt* to (a)rouse, wake (up); **-rsi** *vr* to wake (up).

şvegliatézza nf alertness, readiness of mind.
şvéglio a awake; quick-witted, alert.
şvelàre vt to reveal, disclose.
şvèllere vt to extirpate, eradicate.
şveltézza nf quickness, rapidity.
şveltíre vt to make lively, nimble, quick, slender.
şvèlto a quick, alert; slender; ad fast, quickly.
şvéndere vt to undersell; sell below cost.
şvéndita nf clearance sale.
şveniménto nm fainting fit, swoon.
şveníre vi to faint, swoon.
şventàre vt to baffle, foil, thwart.
şventatézza nf thoughtlessness, rashness.
şventàto a thwarted; heedless, scatter-brained; nm scatter-brain.
şventolàre vt to wave, flutter.
şventràre vt to disembowel; destroy.
şventúra nf bad luck, misfortune, mishap.
şventuràto a unfortunate, unlucky.
şvergognàre vt to disgrace.
şvergognàto a shameless.
şvernàre vi to winter.
şvestíre vt to undress.
Şvezia nf (geogr) Sweden.
şvezzàre vt to wean.
şviaménto nm deviation; leading astray; going astray.
şviàre vt to divert; lead astray; **-rsi** vr to diverge; go astray.
şvignàrsela vr to slip away.
şviluppàre vt to develop, work out; **-rsi** vr to develop, grow; break out.
şvilúppo nm development, growth, increase.
şvincolàre vt to free, redeem, clear.
şvişàre vt to disfigure, misrepresent.
şvişceràre vt to disembowel; examine thoroughly.
şvişceràto a ardent, passionate.
şvísta nf oversight.
şvitàre vt to unscrew.
Şvízzera nf (geogr) Switzerland.
şvízzero a nm Swiss.
şvogliatézza nf listlessness, laziness.
şvogliàto a lazy, listless; nm lazybones.
şvolazzàre vi to fly about, flit, flutter.
şvòlgere vt to unwind, unroll; develop; carry out; **-rsi** vr to unfold, unroll; happen, take place.
şvolgiménto nm unwinding, unrolling; treatment; development.
şvòlta nf turn, turning point; winding, bend.
şvoltàre vi to turn, bend.
şvoltolàre vt to roll; **-rsi** vr to roll about, wallow.
şv(u)otàre vt to empty.

T

tabaccàio nm **-àia** nf tobacconist.
tabacchería nf tobacconist's shop; cigar store.
tabacchièra nf snuff-box.
tabàcco pl **-chi** nm tobacco; **t. da nàso** snuff.
tabèlla nf table; list, schedule.
tabellóne nm notice board, bulletin board; **t. d'affissióne** billboard.
tabernàcolo nm tabernacle, shrine.
tabù nm taboo.
tàcca nf notch; defect.
taccàgno a miserly, stingy.
tacchíno nm turkey.
tàccia nf bad reputation; accusation, charge.
tacciàre vt to accuse (of), charge (with).
tàcco pl **-chi** nm (of a shoe) heel; **t. a spíllo** stiletto heel.
taccuíno nm memorandum book, notebook, pocket-book.
tacére vi to be silent, keep silence; vt to be silent about, leave out, conceal.
tachímetro nm (aut) speedometer.
tàcito a tacit; silent.
tacitúrno a taciturn, sulky.
tafàno nm gadfly.
tafferúglio nm brawl, fray.
tàglia nf ransom, tribute, price on someone's head; size.
tagliabòschi (inv) nm woodcutter, woodman.
tagliacàrte (inv) nm paper-cutter, paperknife.
tagliàndo nm coupon.
tagliàre vt to cut, cut off, cut out.
tagliatèlle nf pl noodles.
tagliàto a cut; cut out; fit.
tagliènte a cutting; sharp.
tàglio nm cut; (of bills etc) denomination; dress length, (of knife etc) edge.
tagli(u)òla nf trap.
tailleur (Fr) nm costume
tàlamo nm nuptial bed.
tàlco pl **-chi** nm talc, talcum powder.
tàle a such, like, similar; pron someone; **tal dei tàli** so-and-so.
talènto nm talent; intelligence; will.
talismàno nm talisman.
tallóne nm heel.
talménte ad so, so much, to such a degree.
talóra v **talvòlta**.
tàlpa nf mole.
talúno a some, certain; pron somebody, someone.
talvòlta ad sometimes.
tamaríndo nm tamarind.
tamburíno nm drummer.
tambúro nm drum; cylinder.
tameríce nf tamarisk.
tamponàre vt to stop, plug.
tampóne nm stopper; (med) tampon.
tàna nf den, hole, lair.

tànfo nm bad smell, stench.
Tanganíca nm (geogr) Tanganyika.
tangènte a tangent.
Tàngeri nf (geogr) Tangier.
tànghero nm boor, bumpkin.
tangíbile a tangible.
tànto a so much, as much; ad so, so long, so much; t.... quànto as ... as, both ... and; **tànti** a and pron pl as many.
tapíno a miserable, wretched; nm wretch.
tàppa nf halting place; stage; lap.
tappàre vt to cork, plug, stop (up); -rsi vr to shut oneself up; to stop one's ears.
tapparèlla nf rolling shutter.
tappéto nm carpet, rug.
tappezzàre vt to upholster; paper.
tappezzería nf wallpaper; hangings; upholstery.
tappezzière nm paper-hanger; upholsterer.
tàppo nm cork, plug, stopper.
tàra nf tare; defect.
tarchiàto a thickset.
tardàre vi to be late, be long, delay; vt to defer.
tàrdi ad late; far t. to be late.
tàrdo a slow; dull; tardy, late.
tàrga nf nameplate, number-plate.
tarìffa nf tariff.
tarlàto a worm-eaten.
tàrlo nm woodworm, clothes moth.
tàrma nf moth.
taròcchi nm pl tarot.
tàrsia nf inlaid work, marquetry.
tartagliàre vi to stammer, stutter.
tartaglióne nm stammerer.
tàrtaro nm tartar; a nm Tartar.
tartarúga nf tortoise, turtle.
tartassàre vt to harass, bully.
tartína nf canapé.
tartúfo nm truffle.
tàsca nf pocket.
tascàbile a pocket.
tàssa nf tax; (school etc) fee.
tassàmetro nm (aut) taximeter; t. di parchéggio parking meter.
tassàre vt to tax; assess.
tassatìvo a definite, compulsory.
tassì nm taxi, taxicab.
tassìsta nm taxidriver, taximan.
tàsso nm badger; (com) rate; yew-tree.
tastàre vt to touch; feel; sound.
tastièra nf keyboard.
tàsto nm (of musical instrument, typewriter etc) key; touch; subject.
tastóni, a ad gropingly.
tàttica nm tactics pl.
tàttico pl -ici a tactical; nm tactician.
tàtto nm touch; tact.
tatuàggio nm tattoo, tattooing.
tatuàre vt to tattoo.
taumatúrgo nm miracle-worker.
tavèrna nf public house.
tàvola nf table; board; slab.
tavolétta nf tablet, small board; t. di cioccolàta bar of chocolate.

tavolíno nm small table, writing-desk.
tàvolo nm table.
tavolòzza nf palette.
tàzza nf cup.
te pron 2nd pers sing oblique case and object you, yourself.
tè nm tea; pastína da t. teacake, scone, biscuit.
teatràle a theatrical.
teàtro nm theater; t. di varietà music-hall, vaudeville theater.
tècnica nf technique.
tècnico pl -ici a technical; nm technician.
tedésco pl -chi a nm German.
tediàre vt to bore, tire, weary.
tèdio nm boredom, tedium, weariness.
tedióso a tedious, irksome, tiresome.
tegàme nm pan.
téglia nf oven-pan.
tégola nf -olo nm brickbat, tile.
teièra nf teapot.
téla nf cloth; linen; (painter's) canvas; (theat) curtain; painting.
telàio nm loom; frame.
teleàrma pl -i nf guided missile.
telecàmera nf (tv) telecamera.
telefèrica nf cable way.
telefonàre vt to telephone.
telefonàta nf telephone call; t. urbàna local call; t. interurbàna long-distance call.
telefònico pl -ici a telephone.
telèfono nm telephone.
telegiornàle nm television news.
telegrafàre vt to telegraph, cable.
telegràfico pl -ici a telegraph(ic).
telegràmma nm telegram, cable.
telepatía nf telepathy.
telería nf linen and cotton goods pl; negoziànte di telerìe (linen-)draper.
telescòpio nm telescope.
telescrivènte a nf teletype; tele-printer.
televisióne nf television; t. a gettóne coin television, pay tele-vision; trasmèttere per t. to televise.
televisóre nm television set.
tellína nf cockle.
télo nm (of material) length, width.
telóne nm (theat) drop-curtain.
tèma nm theme; composition.
temeràrio a rash, arrogant, fool-hardy.
temére vti to be afraid of, dread, fear.
temerità nf rashness, temerity.
tèmpera nf (painting) tempera; distemper; (metal) temper.
temperaménto nm temperament; mitigation.
temperànza nf temperance, modera-tion.
temperàre vt to mitigate; (pencil) sharpen; temper.
temperatúra nf temperature.
temperíno nm penknife.
tempèsta nf storm, tempest.

tempestàre *vi* to storm; *vt* to harass, assail (*also fig*); adorn.
tempestívo *a* opportune, timely.
tempestóso *a* stormy.
tèmpia *nf* (*anat*) temple.
tèmpio *pl* -**pii** *nm* temple.
tèmpo *nm* time; weather; (*gram*) tense; stage; **che t. fa?** what kind of weather is it?
temporàle *nm* storm.
temporalésco *pl* -**chi** *a* stormy.
temporàneo *a* temporary.
temporeggiàre *vi* to temporize.
tèmpra *nf* temper; character; timbre.
tempràre *vt* to temper; strengthen; mold.
tenàce *a* tenacious, persevering; obstinate.
tenàcia *nf* tenacity, stubbornness.
tenàglia *nf pl* tongs *pl*; pincers *pl*; pliers *pl*.
tènda *nf* curtain; tent; awning.
tendàggio *nm* curtain, drape.
tendènza *nf* tendency, trend.
tèndere *vt* to hold out; stretch (out); *vi* to be inclined to; aim.
tendína *nf* curtain.
tènebre *nf pl* darkness.
tenebróso *a* dark; obscure; mysterious.
tenènte *nm* lieutenant.
teneraménte *ad* tenderly, gently.
tenére *vt* to hold, keep; **t. a** to be proud of, care for, like; **t. da** to take after; **t. per** to side with; -**rsi** *vr* to consider oneself; keep to.
tenerézza *nf* tenderness, affection.
tènero *a* tender, loving; *nm* tender part; affection.
tènia *nf* tapeworm.
tènnis *nm* tennis; **t. su pràto** lawn-tennis; **tennísta** tennis-player.
tenóre *nm* tenor; **t. di víta** standard of living; way of living.
tensióne *nf* tension, strain.
tentàcolo *nm* tentacle.
tentàre *vt* to try, attempt; tempt; (*med*) probe.
tentatívo *nm* attempt, endeavor; trial.
tentatóre *f* -**tríce** *a* tempting; *nm* tempter; *nf* temptress.
tentazióne *nf* temptation.
tentennaménto *nm* wavering.
tentennàre *vi* to stagger; waver.
tènue *a* slight, thin, fine; soft.
tenuità *nf* thinness, smallness, slightness; softness.
tenúta *nf* estate; uniform.
teología *nf* theology.
teològico *pl* -**ici** *a* theological.
teòlogo *pl* -**ogi** *nm* theologian.
teorèma *nm* theorem.
teoría *nf* theory.
teòrico *pl* -**ici** *a* theoretical; *nm* theorist.
tèpido *v* **tièpido**.
tepóre *nm* warmth.
terapèutico *pl* -**ici** *a* therapeutic.
terapía *nf* therapy.

Terèsa *nf pr* T(h)eresa.
tèrgere *vt* to wipe off, dry.
tergicristàllo *nm* (*aut*) windshield wiper.
tergiversàre *vi* to beat about the bush, hesitate.
tergiversazióne *nf* hesitation.
tèrgo *nm* back; **a t.** overleaf; **da t.** from behind.
termàle *a* thermal.
tèrme *nf pl* hot baths *pl*; hot springs *pl*; spa.
terminàre *vti* to finish, end.
tèrmine *nm* boundary; date; term; limit; **a rigór di tèrmini** strictly speaking.
termoconvettóre *nm* convector.
termòforo *nm* warming pad.
termòmetro *nm* thermometer.
tèrmos *nm* thermos.
termosifóne *nm* radiator.
tèrno *nm* treble; jackpot.
tèrra *nf* earth, land, ground.
terracòtta *nf* terracotta; baked clay.
terraférma *nf* mainland.
terràglia *nf* earthenware, pottery.
terramicína *nf* terramycin.
Terranòva *nf* Newfoundland.
terrapièno *nm* bank, earthwork.
terràzza *nf* -**àzzo** *nm* terrace.
terremòto *nm* earthquake.
terréno *a* earthly, worldly; *nm* ground, soil; land; **pian t.** ground floor.
terrèstre *a* earthly, terrestrial.
terríbile *a* terrible, awful, frightful.
territòrio *nm* territory.
terróre *nm* terror, dread.
tèrso *a* clear, terse.
terziàrio *a nm* tertiary.
tèrzo *a* third; *nm* third party.
tésa *nf* (*of hat*) brim; (*of cap*) visor; (*of nets*) cast.
tèschio *nm* skull.
tèsi *nf* thesis.
téso *a* taut, tight, strained.
tesorería *nf* treasury.
tesorière *nm* treasurer.
tesòro *nm* treasure; treasury.
tèssera *nf* card; ticket; (*mosaic*) tessera.
tesseraménto *nm* rationing.
tesseràre *vt* to ration.
tèssere *vt* to weave.
tèssile *a nm* textile.
tessitóre *nm* -**tríce** *nf* weaver.
tessitúra *nf* weaving.
tessúto *nm* cloth, fabric; tissue; web; **negòzio di tessúti** dry-goods store; **un t. de menzogne** a tissue of lies.
tèsta *nf* head; **t. càlda** hot-head.
testaménto *nm* testament, will.
testàrdo *a* headstrong, stubborn.
testàta *nf* (*of bed, bridge etc*) head; (*newspaper*) heading; butt.
tèste *nmf* witness; **bànco dei tèsti** witness box, witness stand.
testícolo *nm* testicle.
testimòne *nmf* witness; **t. oculàre** eyewitness.

testimoniànza *nf* evidence, testimony, witness.
testimoniàre *vti* to testify, witness.
tèsto *nm* text.
testuàle *a* exact, precise; textual.
testúggine *nf* tortoise, turtle.
tètano *nm* tetanus.
tètro *a* dismal, gloomy.
tétto *nm* roof; house; **sènza t.** homeless.
tettóia *nf* penthouse; (*of market, station etc*) roof.
teutònico *pl* **-ici** *a* Teutonic.
Tévere *nm* (*geogr*) Tiber.
ti *pron* 2nd *pers sing object and oblique* you, yourself.
tiàra *nf* tiara.
Tíbet *nm* (*geogr*) Tibet.
tibetàno *a nm* Tibetan.
tíbia *nf* (*mus*) pipe; (*anat*) shinbone, tibia.
ticchettío *nm* ticking.
tícchio *nm* caprice, whim.
tiepidézza *nf* (*fig*) lukewarmness.
tièpido *a* lukewarm (*also fig*).
tífo *nm* (*med*) typhus; **fàre il t. per** to be a fan of.
tifòide *nf* (*med*) typhoid.
tifóne *nm* typhoon.
tifóso *a* typhous; *nm* (*fig cinema, football etc*) fan.
tíglio *nm* lime(tree); fiber.
tígna *nf* ringworm.
tignòla *nf* moth.
tigràto *a* striped, tabby (cat).
tígre *nf* tiger, tigress.
timbràre *vt* to stamp, postmark.
tímbro *nm* stamp; **t. postàle** postmark; timbre.
timidézza *nf* shyness, timidity.
tímido *a* bashful, shy, timid.
tímo *nm* thyme.
timóne *nm* (*naut*) helm, rudder.
timonière *nm* helmsman, steersman.
timoràto *a* respectful; scrupulous; devout.
timóre *nm* fear, awe.
timoróso *a* timorous, timid.
Timòteo *nm* *pr* Timothy.
tímpano *nm* eardrum; (*mus*) kettledrum.
tínca *nf* tench.
tinèllo *nm* breakfast room; small vat.
tíngere *vt* to dye, paint, stain.
tíno *nm* tub, vat.
tinòzza *nf* (bath-)tub, wash-tub.
tínta *nf* color, dye, hue, tint.
tintarélla *nf* (*fam*) sun-tan.
tintinnàre *vi* to tinkle, jingle.
tintóre *nm* dyer.
tintoría *nf* dyer's, dye-works; cleaners' shop.
tintúra *nf* dyeing; tincture.
típico *pl* **-ici** *a* typical.
típo *nm* type; model; specimen; **un bel t.** a queer fellow.
tipografía *nf* typography; printing works.
tipogràfico *pl* **-ici** *a* typographical.
tipògrafo *nm* printer, typographer.

tiranneggiàre *vt* to oppress, tyrannize.
tirànnico *pl* **-ici** *a* tyrannical.
tirànnide, tirannía *nf* tyranny.
tirànno *nm* tyrant.
tiràre *vt* to draw, pull, drag; throw; (*typ*) print; *vi* shoot at; blow; **tíra vènto** it is windy; **quèsta màcchina tíra béne** this car goes like a bird.
tiràta *nf* draw, pull; stretch; tirade.
tiratóre *nm* marksman, shooter.
tiratúra *nf* drawing, pulling; (*typ*) circulation; edition.
tirchiería *nf* stinginess.
tírchio *a* miserly, stingy; *nm* miser.
tíro *nm* draft; fire; throw; trick; **animàle da t.** draft animal.
tirocínio *nm* apprenticeship; training.
tiròide *nf* thyroid.
Tiròlo *nm* (*geogr*) Tyrol; **tirolése** *a nm* Tyrolese.
Tirrèno *a nm* (*geogr*) Tyrrhenian.
tìşi *nf* (*med*) consumption.
tìşico *pl* **-ici** *a nm* consumptive.
titillàre *vt* to titillate, tickle.
titolàre *a* regular; titular; *nm* regular holder; owner; (*of a chair*) professor.
títolo *nm* title; headline; right; qualification; (*com*) security; stock.
titubànte *a* hesitating, undecided.
titubànza *nf* hesitation.
titubàre *vi* to hesitate, waver.
tízio *nm* fellow; **Tízio, Càio e Semprónio** Tom, Dick and Harry.
tízzo, tizzóne *nm* (fire)brand.
toccàre *vt* to touch, handle; strike; move; (*naut*) call at; *vi* to fall on; be the duty of.
tócco *pl* **-chi** *nm* touch; knock; stroke; piece; **al t.** at one o'clock.
tòga *nf* toga; gown.
tògliere *vt* to take (away); take off; free; prevent; **t. di mèzzo** to get rid of; **-rsi** *vr* to get away, get off, get out.
tolétta, toilette (*Fr*) dressing table; toilet.
tolleràbile *a* tolerable.
tollerànte *a* indulgent, tolerant.
tollerànza *nf* tolerance, endurance; **càsa di t.** brothel.
tolleràre *vt* to bear, tolerate.
tómba *nf* grave, tomb.
tómbola *nf* bingo.
Tommàşo *nm* *pr* Thomas.
tòmo *nm* tome, volume.
tònaca *nf* (monk's) habit, (priest's) cassock; tunic.
tonàre *v* tuonàre.
tondíno *nm* saucer, small plate.
tóndo *a* round; *nm* round; circle; **chiàro e t.** plainly.
tónfo *nm* splash; thud.
tònico *pl* **-ici** *a nm* tonic.
tonificànte *a* tonic, bracing.
tonnellàggio *nm* tonnage.
tonnellàta *nf* ton.
tónno *nm* tuna.

tòno *nm* tone; èssere fuòri t. to be out of tune.
tonsílla *nf* tonsil.
tonsillíte *nf* tonsillitis.
tonsúra *nf* tonsure.
tónto *a nm* stupid, simpleton.
topàia *nf* rats' nest; hovel.
topàzio *nm* topaz.
tòpica *nf* blunder, gaffe.
tòpo *nm* mouse, rat; t. di bibliotèca bookworm.
topografía *nf* topography.
tòppa *nf* patch; door-lock.
toràce *nm* thorax.
tórba *nf* peat.
tórbido *a* turbid, muddy; gloomy; *nm* disorder, trouble.
tòrcere *vt* to wring, twist.
tòrchio *nm* press.
tòrcia *nf* torch, candle.
torcicòllo *nm* stiff neck.
tórdo *nm* thrush.
Toríno *nf* (*geogr*) Turin; torinése *a nm* Torinese.
tórma *nf* crowd; swarm; herd.
torménta *nf* blizzard, snowstorm.
tormentàre *vt* to torment, torture, worry; -rsi *vr* to worry.
torménto *nm* torment, torture.
tormentóso *a* tormenting, vexing.
tornacónto *nm* profit.
tornànte *a* returning; *nm* bend, turning.
tornàre *vi* to return; turn out; be correct; fit.
tornèo *nm* tournament.
tórnio *nm* (*tec*) turning lathe.
torníre *vt* (*tec*) to turn.
tornitóre *nm* turner.
tórno *nm* period; in quél t. thereabouts; tórno tórno all round.
tòro *nm* bull.
torpedinàre *vt* to torpedo.
torpèdine *nm* torpedo.
torpedinièra *nf* torpedo boat.
torpedóne *nm* (motor) coach.
tòrpido *a* torpid, sluggish, dull.
torpóre *nm* torpor, sluggishness.
tórre *nf* tower.
torrefazióne *nf* coffee roasting; coffee store.
torreggiàre *vi* to loom, tower.
torrènte *nm* torrent, stream, flood.
torrenziàle *a* torrential.
tòrrido *a* torrid; scorching.
torróne *nm* nougat.
torsióne *nf* torsion, twist.
tórso *nm* torso, trunk.
tórsolo *nm* (*fruit*) core, (*vegetable*) stump.
tórta *nf* cake, tart, pie.
tortièra *nf* baking tin.
tòrto *nm* wrong, fault; avér t. to be wrong; a t. unjustly, wrongly; bent, crooked.
tórtora *nf* turtle-dove.
tortuóso *a* tortuous, crooked.
tortúra *nf* torture.
torturàre *vt* to torture.
torvaménte *ad* grimly, surlily.

tórvo *a* grim, surly.
tosàre *vt* to clip, cut (s.o.'s) hair, shear.
tosatúra *nm* (sheep-)shearing.
Toscàna *nf* Tuscany; toscàno *a nm* Tuscan.
tósse *nf* cough.
tòssico *pl* -ici *a* poisonous; *nm* poison.
tossíre *vi* to cough.
tostapàne *nm* toaster; pàne tostàto toast.
tostàre *vt* to roast (*coffee*); toast.
tòsto *a* hard; fàccia tòsta impudence; *ad* immediately; t. che *cj* as soon as.
totàle *a nm* total.
totalità *nf* totality, whole.
totalitàrio *a* absolute, totalitarian.
totalizzàre *vt* to totalize, score.
totalménte *ad* totally, completely.
tòtano *nm* cuttlefish.
tovàglia *nf* (table)cloth.
tovagliòlo *nm* napkin, serviette.
tòzzo *a* squat, stocky, thickset; *nm* piece; un t. di pàne a piece of bread.
tra *prep* among, between; t. pòco in a short time.
traballànte *a* unsteady, staggering.
traballàre *vi* to stagger, totter; jolt.
trabíccolo *nm* bed-warmer; rickety vehicle.
traboccàre *vi* to brim over, overflow.
trabocchétto *nm* trap.
tracannàre *vt* to gulp down.
tràccia *nf* trail, trace, track; outline.
tracciàre *vt* to trace, draw, mark out, sketch.
tracòlla *nf* shoulder-belt.
tracòllo *nm* breakdown, collapse; ruin.
tracotànte *a* arrogant, overbearing.
tracotànza *nf* arrogance.
tradiménto *nm* treason, betrayal, treachery; a t. treacherously.
tradíre *vt* to betray, deceive, be unfaithful to.
traditóre *nm* -tríce *nf* traitor; *a* treacherous.
tradizionàle *a* traditional.
tradizióne *nf* tradition.
tradúrre *vt* to translate; bring into effect; take to; turn.
traduttóre *nm* -tríce *nf* translator.
traduzióne *nf* translation.
trafelàto *a* breathless, panting.
trafficànte *nm* dealer, trafficker.
trafficàre *vi* to deal, trade, traffic.
tràffico *pl* -ichi, -ici *nm* traffic; trade, trading.
trafíggere *vt* to transfix, pierce.
trafítta *nf* pang, stabbing pain.
traforàre *vt* to bore, perforate, pierce.
trafóro *nm* boring, piercing; tunnelling; tunnel.
trafugàre *vt* to steal, purloin.
tragèdia *nf* tragedy.
traghettàre *vt* to ferry.

traghétto nm ferry.
tràgico pl -ici a tragic; nm tragedian.
tragítto nm passage, way, journey.
traguàrdo nm winning post; (fig) goal.
trainàre v **trascinàre**.
tràino nm haulage; truck; load.
tralasciàre vt to omit; interrupt.
tràlcio nm vine-shoot.
tralíccio nm trellis; ticking.
tralignàre vi to degenerate.
tram nm tram(car), streetcar.
tràma nf weft; plot.
tramandàre vt to hand down.
tramàre vt to weave; plot.
trambústo nm bustle.
tramestío nm stir, bustle.
tramezzàre vt to partition off; interpose.
tramèzzo nm partition.
tràmite nm way; **per t. di** through.
tramontàna nf north wind.
tramontàre vi to set, fade, wane.
tramónto nm setting, sunset; end.
tramortíre vt to stun; vi to faint.
trampolíno nm springboard; (fig) stepping stone.
tràmpolo nm stilt.
tramutàre vt to alter, change, transform.
tranèllo nm snare, trap.
trangugiàre vt to bolt, gulp down, swallow.
trànne prep but, except, save.
tranquillànte a tranquilizing; nm tranquilizer.
tranquillizzàre vt to tranquillize.
tranquillità nf calm, tranquillity.
tranquíllo a calm, quiet, tranquil.
transatlàntico pl -ici a transatlantic; nm liner.
transazióne nf arrangement; composition; transaction.
transígere vi to come to terms; yield; (com) compound.
transistor nm transistor.
transitàbile a (of a road etc) practicable.
transitàre vi to pass (through).
trànsito nm transit; **t. interrótto** road closed; **vietàto il t.** no thoroughfare.
transitòrio a transitory, transient.
transizióne nf transition.
tranvài v **tram**.
tranvière nm tram conductor; tram driver; streetcar operator.
trapanàre vt to drill; (med) trepan.
tràpano nm drill; (med) trepanning saw.
trapassàre vt to pierce, run through; vi to pass (away).
trapàsso nm death; passage; transfer.
trapelàre vi to transpire, leak out.
trapèzio nm trapeze.
trapiantàre vt to transplant; **-rsi** vr to emigrate, settle.
trapiànto nm transplantation, grafting.
tràppola nf snare, trap.

trapúnta nf quilt, comforter.
trapúnto a quilted.
tràrre vt to draw; get; lead; **tràrsi** vr to draw; get (out); stand (back).
trasalíre vi to start, startle.
trasandàre vt to neglect.
trasandàto a careless, slatternly.
trasbordàre vt to transship, transfer; (train etc) change.
trascèndere vti to transcend, go beyond; lose one's control.
trascinàre vt to drag, trail; fascinate.
trascórrere vt to pass, spend; vi to elapse, pass.
trascórso a past; nm fault, slip.
trascrívere vt to transcribe.
trascrizióne nf transcription.
trascuràbile a negligible.
trascurànza nf carelessness, negligence, slovenliness.
trascuràre vt to neglect, disregard.
trascuràto a careless, negligent, indifferent, slovenly.
trasecolàre vi to be amazed, startled.
trasferíbile a transferable.
trasferiménto nm change; removal; transfer.
trasferíre vt **-rsi** vr to transfer, remove.
trasfèrta nf transfer; travelling allowance.
trasfiguràre vt to transfigure.
trasfigurazióne nf transfiguration.
trasfóndere vt to transfuse, instill.
trasformàre vt to transform.
trasformatóre nm (elec) transformer.
trasformazióne nf transformation.
trasfusióne nf transfusion.
trasgredíre vti to infringe, transgress.
trasgressióne nf infringement, transgression.
trasgressóre nm infringer, transgressor, offender.
traslocàre vti to move; change one's address.
traslòco pl -chi nm removal.
trasméttere vt to pass on, send, transmit; **t. per ràdio** to broadcast.
trasmissióne nf transmission; broadcast.
trasmodàre vi to exaggerate; exceed.
trasmodàto a excessive, immoderate.
trasmutàre vt to transmute, transform.
trasognàre vi to (day)dream.
trasognàto a dreamy, lost in reverie.
trasparènte a transparent.
trasparíre vi to appear (through); be evident; **lasciàre t.** to betray, reveal.
traspiràre vi to perspire; transpire, leak out.
traspirazióne nf perspiration.
trasportàbile a transportable.
trasportàre vt to carry, convey, transport; transfer.

traspòrto *nm* transport (*also fig*).
trastullàrsi *vr* to amuse oneself, toy with.
trastúllo *nm* plaything, amusement; (*fig*) laughing stock.
trasversàle *a* transverse, cross; *nf* transversal line, side street.
trasvolàta *nf* flight across.
trasvolàre *vt* to fly across.
tràtta *nf* (*com*) draft; trade.
trattaménto *nm* treatment; reception; salary.
trattàre *vti* to deal with; treat; deal in; discuss; **-rsi** *vr impers* to be a question (of).
trattativa *nf* negotiation.
trattàto *nm* treaty; treatise.
tratteggiàre *vt* to outline, sketch.
trattenére *vt* to keep (back); restrain; deduct; entertain; **-rsi** *vr* to stay; stop; restrain oneself; help (doing).
tratteniménto *nm* entertainment; party.
trattenúta *nf* deduction.
trattíno *nm* hyphen; dash.
tràtto *nm* pull; stroke; line, stretch; trait, feature; way of dealing; **tútt'ad un tràtto** all of a sudden.
trattóre *nm* tractor.
trattoría *nf* eating house, restaurant.
travagliàre *vt* to torment, trouble; **-rsi** *vr* to worry, toil.
travàglio *nm* labor, toil; trouble.
travasàre *vt* to decant, pour off.
tràve *nf* beam.
travèrsa *nf* crossbar; side street; (*rly*) sleeper, tie.
traversàle *a* transversal.
traversàre *vt* to cross.
traversàta *nf* crossing, passage.
traversía *nf* misfortune, trouble.
travèrso *a* oblique, transverse; **di t.** askance, the wrong way.
travertíno *nm* travertine.
travestiménto *nm* disguise; travesty.
travestíre *vt* to disguise, travesty.
traviaménto *nm* going astray; corruption.
traviàre *vt* to mislead; pervert; **-rsi** *vr* to go astray.
travicèllo *nm* joist.
travisàre *vt* to distort, misrepresent.
travolgènte *a* overwhelming, overpowering.
travòlgere *vt* to carry away; overcome, overwhelm; sweep away.
travolgiménto *nm* overthrow.
trazióne *nf* traction.
tre *a* three.
trebbiàre *vt* to thrash, thresh.
trebbiatríce *nf* thresher, threshing machine.
trebbiatúra *nf* threshing.
tréccia *nf* plait, pigtail, tress.
trecentísta *nm* painter or writer of the 14th century.
trecènto *a* three hundred; *nm* 14th century.
trédici *a* thirteen; **tredicènne**

thirteen-year-old; **tredicèsimo** thirteenth.
trégua *nf* truce, respite.
tremànte *a* trembling, quivering, shuddering.
tremàre *vi* to tremble, quake, shake.
tremèndo *a* awful, dreadful, tremendous; **tremendaménte** *ad* awfully, dreadfully.
trementína *nf* turpentine.
trèmito *nm* shaking, tremble, trembling.
tremolàre *vi* to quiver, flicker.
tremolío *nm* quivering, flickering.
trèmulo *a* tremulous, trembling.
trèno *nm* train; **t. di víta** way of living.
trénta *a* thirty; **trentènne** thirty-year-old; **trentèsimo** thirtieth; **trentína** some thirty.
Trènto *nf* (*geogr*) Trent, Trento.
trepidàre *vi* to be anxious; be in a flutter; tremble.
trepidazióne *nf* anxiety, trepidation.
trèpido *a* anxious; fluttering, trembling.
treppièdi (*inv*) *nm* trivet, tripod.
trésca *nf* intrigue.
tréspolo *nm* trestle; rickety vehicle.
triangolàre *a* triangular.
triàngolo *nm* triangle.
tribolàre *vi* to suffer, toil; **far t.** to vex.
tribolazióne *nf* suffering, tribulation.
tríbolo *nm* suffering, tribulation.
tribórdo *nm* (*naut*) starboard.
tribú *nf* tribe.
tribúna *nf* platform; gallery; stand.
tribunàle *nm* (law) court; tribunal.
tribúno *nm* tribune.
tributàre *vt* to give; offer; pay.
tributàrio *a* fiscal; *nm* tributary.
tribúto *nm* tribute; tax.
trichèco *pl* **-chi** *nm* walrus.
tricolóre *a nm* tricolor; (*usu*) Italian flag.
tricòrno *nm* three-cornered hat.
tridènte *nm* hay-fork; trident.
triennàle *a* triennial.
trifòglio *nm* clover; shamrock; trefoil.
tríglia *nf* mullet.
tríllo *nm* trill.
trimestràle *a* quarterly.
trimèstre *nm* quarter; term.
trína *nf* lace.
trincèa *nf* trench.
trinceraménto *nm* entrenchment.
trinceràre *vt* to entrench; **-rsi** *vr* to take refuge.
trinchétto, àlbero di *nm* (*naut*) foremast.
trinciànte *a nm* carving (knife).
trinciàre *vt* to cut.
trinciàto *a* cut up; *nm* cut tobacco.
Trinità *nf* Trinity.
trionfàle *a* triumphal.
trionfànte *a* exultant, triumphal.

trionfàre *vi* to be triumphant, triumph over.
trionfo *nm* triumph.
tríplice *a* threefold, treble, triple.
tríplo *a* triple; *nm* triple the amount.
trípode *nm* tripod.
tríppa *nf* tripe; (*vulg*) paunch.
tripudiàre *vi* to exult.
tripúdio *nm* exultation.
tríste *a* sad, sorrowful; depressing.
tristézza *nf* sadness, sorrow; gloominess.
trísto *a* wicked, wretched; *nm* rogue.
tritàre *vt* to mince; pound.
tritàto *a* minced; *nm* mince.
tritatútto *inv nm* mincing machine.
tríto *a* minced; worn out; trite.
tríttico *pl* -ici *nm* triptych.
trivèlla *nf* (*tec*) borer.
trivellàre *vt* (*tec*) to bore.
triviàle *a* low; vulgar.
trivialità *nf* coarseness, vulgarity; vulgar expression.
trívio *nm* crossroad(s).
trofèo *nm* trophy.
trògolo *nm* trough.
tròia *nf* sow.
trómba *nf* trumpet; bugle; (*anat*) tube; (*of staircase*) well.
trombettière *nm* trumpeter.
troncaménto *nm* cutting off; breaking off.
troncàre *vt* to break off; cut off; cut short; interrupt.
trónco *pl* -chi *a* broken; truncated; *nm* trunk.
trónfio *a* puffed up; conceited.
tròno *nm* throne.
tròpico *pl* -ici *nm* tropic.
tròppo *ad* too (much); *a and pron* too much; **tròppi** *pl* too many.
tròta *nf* trout.
trottàre *vi* to trot; walk fast.
tròtto *nm* trot.
tròttola *nf* (whipping) top.
trovàre *vt* to find (out); meet (with); **andàre a t.** to go and see; -rsi *vr* to be, find oneself, meet.
trovàta *nf* invention, expedient.
trovatèllo *nm* foundling.
trovatóre *nm* troubadour.
truccàre *vt* to make up; -rsi *vr* to make up one's face.
trúcco *pl* -cchi *nm* trick, deceit, make-up.
trúce *a* fierce, grim.
trucidàre *vt* to slay, murder.
trúciolo *nm* chip, shaving.
trucolènto, truculènto *a* truculent.
trúffa *nf* cheat, swindle; **t. alla americàna** confidence trick, confidence game.
truffàre *vt* to cheat, swindle.
truffatóre *nm* -trice *nf* cheat, swindler.
trúppa *nf* troop, band, troupe.
tu *pron* thou, you (*sing*); **dàre del t.** to be on first name terms.
tubàre *vi* to coo.

tubercolàre *a* tubercular.
tubercolòsi *nf* consumption, tuberculosis.
tubercolóso, tubercolòtico *a nm* consumptive.
túbero *nm* tuber.
túbo *nm* pipe, tube.
tubolàre *a* tubular.
tuffàre *vt* to plunge; -rsi *vr* to dive, plunge.
túffo *nm* dive, plunge.
túfo *nm* tufa; tuff.
tugúrio *nm* hovel.
tulipàno *nm* tulip.
túmido *a* tumid, swollen; (*style*) pompous.
tumóre *nm* tumor.
tumulàre *vt* to bury, inter.
túmulo *nm* grave; tumulus.
tumúlto *nm* tumult, uproar; riot.
tumultuóso *a* tumultuous; riotous.
túnica *nf* tunic.
Túnisi *nf* (*geogr*) Tunis; **tunisíno** *a nm* Tunisian.
Tunisía *nf* (*geogr*) Tunisia.
túo *poss a* thy, your; *poss pron* thine, yours.
tuonàre *vi* to thunder.
tuòno *nm* thunder.
t(u)órlo *nm* (egg) yolk.
turàcciolo *nm* cork, stopper.
turàre *vt* to stop, plug, fill up.
túrba *nf* crowd, mob, rabble.
turbaménto *nm* perturbation; excitement; commotion.
turbànte *nm* turban.
turbàre *vt* to upset, trouble, disturb; -rsi *vr* to get upset.
turbína *nf* turbine; **t. idràulica** waterwheel.
turbinàre *vi* to eddy; whirl.
túrbine *nm* whirl, eddy (*also fig*); hurricane.
turbinío *nm* whirling.
turbolènto *a* turbulent; riotous, stormy.
turchése *nf* turquoise.
Turchía *nf* (*geogr*) Turkey.
turchíno *nm* dark blue.
túrco *pl* -chi *a* Turkish; *nm* Turk.
túrgido *a* turgid; pompous.
turísmo *nm* tourism.
turísta *nmf* tourist.
turístico *pl* -ici *a* tourist.
túrno *nm* turn; **di t.** on duty.
túrpe *a* base, vile; disgraceful.
turpitúdine *nf* baseness, turpitude.
túta *nf* mechanic's overall.
tutèla *nf* guardianship, tutelage; defense.
tutelàre *vt* to guard, defend, protect.
tutóre *nm* -trice *nf* guardian.
tutòrio *a* tutelar; tutorial.
tuttavía *ad and cj* nevertheless, still, yet.
tútto *a* all, whole; *pron* all, everything; **tútti** *pl* all *pl*, everyone; *ad* wholly, all; *nm* whole; **del t.** quite; **t. ad un tràtto** all of a sudden.
tuttóra *ad* still.

U

ubbía *nf* false idea; superstition; nonsense.
ubbidiènte *a* obedient.
ubbidiènza *nf* obedience.
ubbidíre *vti* to obey.
ubertà *nf* fertility.
ubertóso *a* fertile, fruitful.
ubicazióne *nf* position, situation.
ubiquità *nf* ubiquity, omnipresence.
ubriacàre *vt* to intoxicate, make drunk; **-rsi** *vr* to get drunk.
ubriacatúra, ubriachézza *nf* drunkenness, intoxication.
ubriàco *pl* **-chi** *a* drunk.
ubriacóne *nm* drunkard.
uccellàre *vi* to go fowling.
uccellatóre *nm* fowler.
uccèllo *nm* bird; **u. di bòsco** fugitive from the law.
uccídere *vt* to kill.
uccisióne *nf* killing, murder.
Ucràina *nf* (*geogr*) Ukraine.
udiènza *nf* audience; hearing; **dàre u.** to receive.
udíre *vt* to hear, listen to.
udíto *nm* (sense of) hearing.
uditóre *nm* **-tríce** *nf* listener, hearer.
uditório *nm* audience, hearers *pl.*
ufficiàle *a* official; formal; *nm* officer; official.
ufficialménte *ad* officially.
ufficiàre *vi* to officiate.
uffício *nm* office; agency; department; duty; **d'u.** officially.
ufficióso *a* unofficial.
uffízio *nm* (religious) office.
úfo, a *ad* gratis.
úggia *nf* boredom; dislike; **avére in u.** to dislike.
uggióso *a* tiresome; dull; gloomy.
Úgo *nm* *pr* Hugh.
ugonòtto *nm* Huguenot.
uguagliànza *nf* equality.
uguagliàre *vt* to (be) equal (to); equalize; **-rsi** *vr* to claim equality; compare oneself.
uguàle *a* equal; same; like, similar.
ugualménte *ad* equally.
uh! *interj* ah!
úlcera *nf* ulcer.
ulíva *etc* *v* **olíva** *etc.*
ulterióre *a* further; ulterior.
ultimaménte *ad* lately; recently.
ultimàre *vt* to complete, finish.
ultimàtum *nm* ultimatum.
último *a* last, latest; utmost; lowest; ultimate.
últra *prefix* ultra, extremely; **non plus últra** *nm* height, acme.
ultrasònico *pl* **-ici** *a* ultrasonic.
ultraviolétto *a* ultra-violet.
ululàre *vi* to howl.
ululàto, úlulo *nm* howl, howling.
umanaménte *ad* humanly, humanely.

umanésimo *nm* humanism.
umanísta *nm* humanist.
umanità *nf* humanity; mankind.
umanitàrio *a* humanitarian.
umàno *a* human; humane.
Umbèrto *nm* *pr* Humbert.
umidità *nf* dampness, moisture.
úmido *a* damp, moist; *nm* dampness; stew.
úmile *a* humble; modest.
umiliànte *a* humiliating.
umiliàre *vt* to humble; humiliate; mortify; **-rsi** *vr* to abase oneself, humble oneself.
umiliazióne *nf* humiliation, mortification.
umilménte *ad* humbly; modestly.
umiltà *nf* humility; humbleness.
umóre *nm* humor; mood; **di buòn u.** in a good humor.
umorísmo *nm* humor.
umorísta *nm* humorist.
umorístico *pl* **-ici** *a* humorous, funny.
un *v* **úno.**
unànime *a* unanimous.
unanimità *nf* unanimity.
uncinétto *nm* crochet hook.
uncíno *nm* hook.
úndici *a* eleven; **undicènne** eleven-year-old; **undicèsimo** eleventh.
úngere *vt* to grease; smear; anoint.
ungherése *a* *nmf* Hungarian.
Ungheria *nf* (*geogr*) Hungary.
únghia *nf* nail; claw; hoof.
unguènto *nm* ointment.
único *pl* **-ici** *a* only, single, sole; unique.
unificàre *vt* to unify.
unificazióne *nf* unification.
uniformàre *vt* to conform; make uniform; **-rsi (a)** *vr* to comply (with), conform (to).
unifórme *a* *nf* uniform.
uniformità *nf* uniformity.
unigènito *a* only-begotten.
unióne *nf* union, harmony.
uníre *vt* to unite, join; enclose.
unísono *nm* unison; harmony.
unità *nf* unity; unit.
uníto *a* united; **tínta uníta** plain color.
universàle *a* universal; **giudízio u.** the Last Judgment.
universalità *nf* universality.
università *nf* university.
universitàrio *a* (of a) university; *nm* university student.
univèrso *nm* universe.
úno *indef art* a(n), one; *a* one; *indef pron* one, someone; **l'úno e l'àltro** both.
únto *nm* grease; fat; *a* greasy.
untuóso *a* greasy, oily; unctuous.
unzióne *nf* unction.
uòmo *nm* man.
uòpo *nm* necessity, need; **èssere d'u.** *impers* to be necessary; **fàre all'u.** to meet the case.
uòvo *pl* *f* **uòva** *nm* egg.

uragàno nm hurricane.
Uràli (gli) nm pl (the) Urals.
uràngo pl **-ghi** nm orangutang.
urànio nm uranium.
urbanística nf town planning.
urbanità nf civility; courtesy; urbanity.
urbaniẓẓàre vt to urbanize.
urbàno a urban; urbane; civil, courteous.
Úrbe (l') nf the 'city', Rome.
urgènte a urgent, pressing.
urgènza nf urgency.
úrgere vi to be urgent, be pressing.
urína v **orína**.
urlàre vt to shout, howl, shriek.
úrlo pl **úrli** or f (of humans) **úrla** nm cry; shout; howl, shriek.
úrna nf urn; ballot-box; **andàre àlle úrne** to go to the polls.
urtànte a irritating, annoying.
urtàre vti to knock against; (fig) annoy; hit.
urticària nf nettle-rash, urticaria.
úrto nm collision; push, shove; **èssere in u.** to be at variance, be on bad terms.
uṣànza nf usage; custom.
uṣàre vt to use, make use of; vi to be accustomed; be fashionable.
uṣàto a second-hand; usual; in use.
uscière nm usher.
úscio nm door.
uscíre vi to go (come) out; go off; get out; retire.
uscíta nf going (coming) out; exit; outlet; witty remark; **vía di u.** escape.
uṣign(u)òlo nm nightingale.
úṣo a used; accustomed; nm usage; custom.
ússaro,ússero nm hussar.
ustionàre vt to burn, scorch.
ustióne nf burn.
uṣuàle a usual.
uṣualménte ad usually.
uṣufruíre vi to benefit by; take advantage of.
uṣufrútto nm usufruct.
uṣúra nf usury.
uṣuràio nm usurer.
uṣurpàre vt to usurp.
uṣurpazióne nf usurpation.
utensíle nm implement, tool, utensil.
utènte nm user; consumer.
útero nm uterus, womb.
útile a useful; nm profit; interest.
utilità nf utility, usefulness, benefit.
utilitària nf (aut) minicar, compact.
utilitàrio a utilitarian.
utilitaríṣmo nm utilitarianism.
utiliẓẓàbile a utilizable, that can be made use of.
utiliẓẓàre vt to make use of, utilize.
utiliẓẓazióne nf utilization, use.
utilménte ad usefully.
utopía nf utopia; chimerical project.
úva nf grapes pl; **u. spína** gooseberry.
úẓẓolo nm whim, fancy.

V

vacànte a vacant.
vacànza nf holiday, vacation; vacancy; **v. scolàstica** school holidays, recess.
vàcca nf cow.
vaccàro nm cowherd.
vaccinàre vt to vaccinate.
vaccinazióne nf vaccination.
vaccíno nm vaccine.
vacillaménto nm staggering, wobbling; unsteadiness; (fig) hesitation.
vacillànte a tottering, unsteady; wavering, irresolute.
vacillàre vi to totter; be irresolute.
vàcuo a empty; vacuous; vain.
vagabondàggio nm vagabondage, vagrancy; wandering.
vagabondàre vi to roam, rove, wander.
vagabóndo a wandering; nm vagabond; wanderer.
vagaménte ad vaguely; prettily.
vagànte a wandering, roving.
vagàre vi to wander, ramble.
vagheggiàre vt to cherish; long for; look lovingly at; **-rsi** vr to look at oneself complacently.
vagheggíno nm dandy, beau.
vaghéẓẓa nf beauty; longing; delight; vagueness.
vagíre vi to wail, whimper.
vagíto nm wail(ing), whimper(ing).
vàglia nf ability; merit; worth; **v. postàle** nm postal order.
vagliàre vt to sift; (fig) weigh.
vàglio nm sieve.
vàgo pl **-ghi** a vague; pretty.
vagóne nm (rly) coach, car; **v. letto** sleeping car; **v. mèrci** freight car; **v. ristorante** dining car.
vainíglia v **vaníglia**.
vaiòlo nm smallpox.
valànga nf avalanche.
valdéṣe a nmf Waldensian.
valènte a skillful, clever; valiant.
valentía nf skill, ability, worth.
Valentíno nm pr Valentine.
valentuòmo pl **-uòmini** nm worthy man.
Valènza nf (geogr) Valencia.
valére vi to be worth; be valid; **v. la péna** to be worth while; **vàle a díre** that is to say; **-rsi** vr to avail oneself, make use.
Valèria nf pr Valerie.
valetudinàrio a nm valetudinarian.
valévole a valid; efficacious.
valicàre vt to cross, pass.
vàlico pl **-ichi** nm crossing; passage; pass.
validità nf validity.
vàlido a valid, efficacious.
valigería nf leather-goods shop; trunk manufactory.
valígia pl **-ie** nf suitcase.
valigiàio nm trunk-maker; leatherware merchant.

vallàta, vàlle nf valley.
vallétto nm valet.
valligiàno nm dalesman, inhabitant of a valley.
valóre nm value, worth; valor.
valorizzàre vt to employ to advantage, turn to account.
valorosaménte ad bravely.
valoróso a brave, valiant.
valsènte nm value, price.
valúta nf value; money.
valutàre vt to value, appraise.
valutazióne nf estimation, valuation.
vàlva nf valve.
vàlvola nf (el) fuse; valve.
vàlzer nm waltz.
vàmpa nf flame; flush.
vampàta nf blaze; blast; flush.
vampíro nm vampire.
vanaglòria nf vainglory, conceit.
vanaglorióso a vainglorious, conceited.
vanaménte ad in vain, vainly.
vandalísmo nm vandalism.
vàndalo nm vandal.
vaneggiàre vi to be delirious, rave.
vànga nf spade.
vangàre vt to dig.
vangélo nm Gospel.
vaníglia nf vanilla.
vanità nf vanity.
vanitóso a vain, conceited.
vàno a vain, useless; nm space, room.
vantàggio nm advantage; profit; odds.
vantaggiosaménte ad advantageously, to good profit.
vantaggióso a advantageous, profitable.
vantàre vt to boast of; -rsi vr to be proud, boast.
vantería nf boast(ing), brag(ging).
vànto nm boast.
vànvera, a ad at random, nonsensically.
vapóre nm vapor, steam; fume; bastiménto a v. steamer; màcchina a v. steam-engine.
vaporétto nm steamboat.
vaporizzatóre nm vaporizer, atomizer.
vaporóso a airy, filmy, vaporous.
varàre vt to launch.
varcàre vt to cross, pass.
vàrco pl -chi nm passage, way; aspettàre al v. to lie in wait for.
varechína nf chlorine; àcqua di v. bleach.
variàbile a variable, changeable; unsettled.
variaménte ad variously.
variànte a varying; nf variant.
variàre vti to vary, change.
variazióne nf variation, change.
varicèlla nf chicken-pox.
varicóso a varicose.
variegàto a variegated.
varietà nf variety, (theat) vaudeville.

vàrio a varied, various.
variopínto a many-colored.
vàro nm launch(ing).
Varsàvia nf (geogr) Warsaw.
vàsca nf basin; tub; bath; pond.
vascèllo nm vessel, ship.
vascolàre a vascular.
vaṣelína nf vaseline.
vaṣellàme nm crockery, china.
vàṣo nm vase; pot; vessel; v. da nòtte chamber-pot.
vassàllo a nm vassal, subject.
vassóio nm tray.
vastità nf vastness; expanse, extent.
vàsto a vast, wide.
vàte nm (poet) bard, poet; prophet.
Vaticàno nm Vatican.
vaticínio nm prophecy.
vecchiàia, vecchiézza nf old age.
vècchio a old.
véccia nf tare, vetch.
véce nf stead, place; in mía v. in my stead; in v. di instead of; fàre le véci di to act as.
vedére vt to see; fàrsi v. to appear, show oneself.
vedétta nf look-out, sentinel.
védova nf widow; védovo nm widower.
vedovànza nf widowhood.
vedovíle a widower's, widow's.
vedúta nf sight, view.
veemènte a vehement.
veemènza nf vehemence.
vegetàle a nm vegetable.
vegetàre vi to vegetate.
vegetariàno a nm vegetarian.
vegetazióne nf vegetation.
vègeto a strong, thriving, vigorous.
veggènte a seeing: nmf seer, prophet, prophetess.
véglia nf waking; watch; wake.
vegliàrdo nm old man.
vegliàre vi to be awake; watch over; watch by.
veglióne nm masked ball.
veícolo nm vehicle.
véla nf sail; a gónfie véle very well.
velàre vt to veil; cloud; conceal.
velataménte ad covertly, by allusions.
velàto a veiled; (fig) covert; (of voice) husky.
veleggiàre vti to sail.
veléno nm poison, venom.
velenóso a poisonous.
velièro nm sailing-boat.
velína, nf flimsy; càrta v. tissue-paper.
velívolo nm airplane.
velleità nf foolish ambition, foolish idea.
vèllo nm fleece.
vellutàto a velvety, velvet-like.
vellúto nm velvet.
vélo nm veil.
velóce a swift, quick, rapid.
veloceménte ad swiftly, quickly, fast.
velocità nf speed, velocity.
velòdromo nm cycle-racing track.

véltro *nm* greyhound.
véna *nf* vein; **èssere in v.** to be in form; be in the mood.
venàle *a* venal; market(able).
venatúra *nf* vein; (*of wood*) grain.
vendémmia *nf* grape-gathering; vintage.
vendemmiàre *vi* to gather grapes.
vendemmiatóre *nm* **-tríce** *nf* vine-harvester.
véndere *vt* to sell.
vendétta *nf* revenge, vengeance.
vendicàre *vt* to avenge, revenge.
vendicatívo *a* revengeful, vindictive.
véndita *nf* sale.
venditóre *nm* **-tríce** *nf* seller, vendor; **v. ambulànte** hawker, peddler.
veneràbile *a* venerable.
veneràre *vt* to worship; venerate.
venerazióne *nf* veneration; worship.
venerdì *nm* Friday; **gli mànca un v.** he has a screw loose.
venèreo *a* venereal.
Vèneto *nm* (*geogr*) Venetia; *a* of Venetia.
Venèzia *nf* (*geogr*) Venice; **veneziàno** *a nm* Venetian.
veniàle *a* venial.
veníre *vi* to come; **v. méno** to faint.
ventàglio *nm* fan.
ventàta *nf* gust of wind.
vénti *a* twenty; **ventènne** twenty-year-old; **ventènnio** *nm* period of twenty years; **ventèsimo** twentieth; **ventína** *nf* a score.
ventilàre *vt* to ventilate.
ventilatóre *nm* ventilator; (*aut*) fan.
ventilazióne *nf* ventilation.
vènto *nm* wind.
ventósa *nf* sucker.
ventóso *a* windy.
vèntre *nm* abdomen, belly.
ventúra *nf* chance, luck.
ventúro *a* next, coming, future.
venúta *nf* arrival, coming.
veràce *a* truthful; true.
veracità *nf* veracity.
vераménte *ad* really, truly, indeed.
verànda *nf* veranda(h), porch.
verbàle *a* verbal; *nm* minutes *pl*.
verbalménte *ad* verbally, orally.
verbèna *nf* vervain, verbena.
vèrbo *nm* verb; word.
verbosità *nf* verbosity, prolixity.
verbóso *a* verbose, prolix.
verdàstro *a* greenish.
vérde *a nm* green; **èssere al v.** to be penniless.
verdeggiànte *a* verdant.
verdeggiàre *vi* to be (grow) green.
verdétto *nm* verdict.
verdúra *nf* vegetables *pl*; verdure.
verecóndia *nf* modesty, bashfulness.
verecóndo *a* modest, bashful.
vérga *nf* rod; **v. pastoràle** (*eccl*) crozier.
verginàle *a* maidenly, virgin.
vérgine *nf* virgin.

verginità *nf* virginity.
vergógna *nf* shame; shyness.
vergognàrsi *vr* to be ashamed; be shy.
vergognóso *a* shameful; shy; ashamed.
verífica *nf* check; verification; (*com*) audit.
verificàre *vt* to check; verify; (*com*) audit; **-rsi** *vr* to come to pass; come true.
verisímile *etc v* **verosímile.**
verísmo *nm* realism.
verità *nf* truth.
veritièro *a* truthful.
vèrme *nm* worm.
vermíglio *a* vermilion.
vèrmut *nm* vermouth.
vernàcolo *a nm* vernacular.
verníce *nf* paint, varnish; (*fig*) smattering; patent leather; **úna màno di v.** a coat of paint.
verniciàre *vt* to paint, varnish; polish.
verniciatúra *nf* painting, varnishing; polishing.
véro *a* true *nm* truth; **dàl v.** from life, from nature.
verosimigliànza *nf* likelihood; verisimilitude.
verosímile *a* likely, probable.
verrúca *nf* wart.
versaménto *nm* pouring; spilling; payment.
versànte *nm* side; slope; (*com*) depositor; payer.
versàre *vt* to pour; spill; shed; pay; *vi* to be, live.
versàtile *a* versatile.
versàto *a* poured out; spilled; shed; versed; paid.
verseggiàre *vti* to versify.
versióne *nf* version; translation.
vèrso *nm* line; verse; sound; note; way; **non c'è v.** it is impossible; *prep* towards.
vertènte *a* regarding.
vertènza *nf* dispute.
vèrtere *vi* to be about, concern, regard.
verticàle *a* vertical.
vèrtice *nm* vertex; top; height.
vertígine *pl* **-ini** *nf* dizziness, giddiness.
vertiginóso *a* dizzy.
vescíca *nf* bladder; blister.
vescovàdo *nm* bishopric; bishop's palace.
vescovíle *a* episcopal, of a bishop.
véscovo *nm* bishop.
vèspa *nf* wasp; (*motor-scooter*) 'Vespa'.
vespàio *nm* wasp's nest; (*fig*) hornet's nest.
vespasiàno *nm* (public) urinal.
vèspro *nm* evening; evensong; vespers.
vessàre *vt* to vex; oppress.
vessazióne *nf* vexation.
vessíllo *nm* flag, standard.

vestàglia *nf* dressing-gown, bath-robe.
vestàle *nf* vestal.
vèste *nf* dress; guise; (*fig*) capacity;
vèsti *pl* clothes *pl*.
vestiàrio *nm* clothes *pl*, clothing.
vestíbolo *nm* hall, vestibule.
vestígio *pl* *f* -**gia** *f* footprint, track, vestige, trace.
vestíre *vt* to dress, clothe; -**rsi** *vr* to dress.
vestíto *nm* dress; suit.
veteràno *a* veteran; *nm* (*mil*) ex-serviceman, veteran.
veterinària *nf* veterinary science.
veterinàrio *a* veterinary; *nm* veterinary surgeon.
vèto *nm* veto.
vetràio *nm* glass-blower; glazier.
vetràta *nf* glass door; (stained-)glass window.
vetrería *nf* glass manufactory; glassware.
vetrína *nf* shop-window; glass case, showcase.
vetriòlo *nm* vitriol.
vétro *nm* glass; window-pane.
vétta *nm* summit, top.
vettovàglie *nf* *pl* provisions *pl*, victuals *pl*.
vettúra *nf* car; cab; carriage; coach; (*rly*) **v. ristorànte** restaurant car, diner (dining-car).
vetturíno *nm* driver, cabby.
vetústo *a* ancient, old.
vezzeggiàre *vt* to fondle.
vézzo *nm* (bad) habit; charm; neck-lace.
vezzóso *a* charming; pretty.
vi *pron acc and dat* you, to you; *ad* there.
vía *nf* street; road; way; **v. di mézzo** compromise.
viabilità *nf* condition of a road.
viadótto *nm* viaduct.
viaggiàre *vt* to travel, journey.
viaggiatóre *nm* -**tríce** *nf* traveler; passenger.
viàggio *nm* journey; tour; voyage; **viàggi** *pl* travels *pl*.
viàle *nm* avenue.
viandànte *nm* passer-by; traveler.
viavài *nm* coming and going.
vibràre *vti* to vibrate; strike; quiver.
vibrazióne *nf* vibration; quivering.
vicàrio *nm* vicar.
více *prefix* vice-, assistant, deputy.
vicènda *nf* event; vicissitude; **a v.** in turn; reciprocally.
vicendévole *a* mutual; reciprocal.
vicendevolménte *ad* mutually, each other, one another.
vichíngo *pl* -**ghi** *nm* Viking.
vicinànza *nf* closeness, nearness; neighborhood, vicinity.
vicinàto *nm* neighborhood; neighbors *pl*.
vicíno *a* near, neighboring; *nm* neighbor; *ad* close by, near; **v. a** *prep* beside, close to, near.

vicissitúdine *nf* vicissitude.
vícolo *nm* alley, lane.
vídeo *inv* *nm* (*tv*) video.
vidimàre *vt* to authenticate; visa.
vidimazióne *nf* authentication; visa.
viennése *a* *nmf* Viennese.
vieppiù *ad* more (and more).
vietàre *vt* to forbid, prohibit.
vigènte *a* in force.
vígere *vi* to be in force.
vigilànte *a* vigilant, watchful.
vigilànza *nf* vigilance, watchfulness; look-out.
vigilàre *vt* to watch over, to keep an eye on; *vi* to be on one's guard; keep watch.
vígile *a* watchful, vigilant; *nm* policeman.
vigília *nf* eve; vigil.
vigliaccheria *nf* cowardice, cowardly action.
vigliàcco *pl* -**àcchi** *a* cowardly; *nm* coward.
vígna *nf* **vignéto** *nm* vineyard.
vignétta *nf* vignette; cartoon.
vigóre *nm* vigor; strength; force.
vigoría *nf* vigor; strength.
vigoróso *a* vigorous; strong.
víle *a* cowardly; vile; *nm* coward.
vilipèndere *vt* to despise, scorn.
vílla *nf* villa, country house.
villàggio *nm* village.
villanía *nf* rudeness, abuse.
villàno *a* rude, uncivil; *nm* boor, ill-bred fellow; peasant.
villeggiànte *nmf* holidaymaker, vacationer.
villeggiàre *vi* to spend one's summer holidays.
villeggiatúra *nf* holiday (in the country); **luògo di v.** holiday resort.
villeréccio *a* rustic, rural.
villíno *nm* small villa.
vilménte *ad* cowardly; meanly.
viltà *nf* cowardice; meanness.
vímine *nm* osier, withy; **di vímini** wicker.
vinàio *nm* wine merchant.
Vincènzo *nm* *pr* Vincent.
víncere *vt* to win; defeat, overcome, vanquish; -**rsi** *vr* to master oneself.
víncita *nf* winning(s).
vincitóre *nm* -**tríce** *nf* winner, conqueror.
vincolàre *vt* to bind; (*com*) tie up.
víncolo *nm* bond, tie.
vinícolo *a* wine.
viníle *nm* (*chem*) vinyl.
víno *nm* wine.
viòla *nf* (*mus*) viola, viol; (*bot*) viola; **v. del pensièro** pansy; *a* *nm* (*color*) violet.
violacciòcca *nf* wallflower.
violàre *vt* to violate.
violazióne *nf* violation.
violentàre *vt* to rape; violate.
violènto *a* violent.
violènza *nf* violence.
violétta *nf* violet.
violinísta *nmf* violinist.

violíno nm violin, fiddle.
violoncèllo nm violoncello.
viòttola nf -olo nm lane.
vípera nf viper.
viràre vi (naut) to tack, turn.
viràta nf tacking, turn.
Virgílio nm pr Virgil.
vírgola nf comma; púnto e vírgola semi-colon; virgolétte nf pl quotation marks.
viríle a manly, virile.
virilità nf manliness, virility; manhood.
virtù nf virtue.
virtualménte ad virtually.
virtuosísmo nm virtuousness; virtuosity.
virtuóso a virtuous; virtuoso.
virulènto a virulent.
víscere nm (anat) vital organ; vísceri m pl viscera pl; víscere f pl bowels (fig).
víschio nm mistletoe; bird-lime.
vischióso a viscous; slimy.
víscido a sticky; slippery.
viscónte nm viscount.
visíbile a visible.
visibílio nm a lot; andàre in v. to go into raptures.
visibilità nf visibility.
visibilménte ad visibly; clearly.
visièra nf visor; (of cap) peak.
visionàrio a nm visionary.
visióne nf vision; préndere in v. to examine.
vísita nf visit; v. mèdica medical examination.
visitàre vt to visit; to call on; (med) examine.
visitatóre nm -tríce nf visitor.
visívo a visual.
víso nm face; a v. apèrto frankly, openly.
visóne nm mink.
víspo a brisk, lively.
vísta nf sight; outlook, view; conóscere di v. to know by sight; fàr v. di to pretend.
vistàre vt to visa.
vísto a seen; nm visa; méttere il v. to visa.
vistóso a gaudy, showy; large.
visuàle a visual; nf sight; view.
víta nf life; living; waist.
vitàlba nf (bot) traveler's joy, clematis.
vitàle a vital.
vitalità nf vitality.
vitalízio a lasting for life; nm life annuity.
vitamína nf vitamin(e).
vitamínico pl -ici a vitaminic.
víte nf vine; (tec) screw.
vitèllo nm calf; càrne di v. veal.
vitellóne nm bullock; (fig) representative of contemporary jeunesse dorée.
víttima nf victim.
vítto nm food; board; living.
vittòria nf victory.
Vittòrio nm pr Victor.

vittorióso a victorious.
vituperàre vt to vituperate.
vitupèrio nm insult, shame, disgrace.
viúzza nf narrow street, lane.
víva interj hurrah, hurray.
vivàce a lively, live; bright; quick.
vivacità nf vivacity; quickness; brightness.
vivàio nm (of fish or plants) nursery.
vivaménte ad deeply, warmly.
vivànda nf food; dish.
vivènte a living.
vívere vti to live; nm life, living; v. àlla giornàta to live from hand to mouth.
víveri nm pl provisions pl, supplies pl, victuals pl.
vivézza nf liveliness; brightness; vividness.
vívido a vivid.
vivificàre vt to enliven; give life to.
vivisezióne nf vivisection.
vívo a living; alive; lively; bright; deep; a víva vóce orally; toccàre nel v. to pierce to the quick.
viziàre vt to spoil, vitiate.
viziàto a spoilt, vitiated.
vízio nm vice; bad habit; defect.
vizióso a vicious, depraved.
vízzo a withered.
vocabolàrio nm vocabulary; dictionary.
vocàbolo nm word; term.
vocàle a vocal; nf vowel.
vocazióne nf calling, vocation.
vóce nf voice; rumor; a v. orally; ad àlta v. loudly.
vociferàre vi to shout; vociferate; rumor.
vociferazióne nf shouting; vociferation.
vóga nf fashion, vogue; energy; in v. fashionable.
vogàre vi to row.
vòglia nf desire, wish; will; birthmark.
vói pron 2nd pers pl nom and oblique you.
volàno nm badminton; shuttlecock; flywheel.
volànte a flying; nm (aut) steering-wheel; nf (police) flying-squad.
volantino nm leaflet.
volàre vi to fly.
volàta nf flight; rush.
volàtile a winged; volatile.
volenteróso v. volonteróso.
volentièri ad willingly; màl v. unwillingly.
volére vti to will; want; wish; like; take, require; nm wish; will.
volgàre a vulgar; nm vernacular.
volgarità nf vulgarity.
vòlgere vti -rsi vr to turn.
vólgo pl -ghi nm common herd; populace.
volitívo a strong-willed.
vólo nm flight; a v. immediately.
volontà nf will.

volontàrio *a* voluntary; *nm* volunteer.
volonteróso *a* willing.
vólpe *nf* fox.
volpíno *a* foxy; crafty; *nm* Pomeranian dog.
vòlta *nf* time; turn; **úna v.** once; **dúe vòlte** twice; (*arch*) vault.
voltàggio *nm* (*el*) voltage.
voltàre *vti* **-rsi** *vr* to turn.
voltàta *nf* turn(ing), bend.
volteggiàre *vi* to fly about, whirl; vault.
vólto *nm* face, countenance; *a* turned.
volúbile *a* fickle, inconstant.
volúme *nm* volume, quantity.
voluminóso *a* voluminous, bulky.
volutaménte *ad* intentionally, deliberately.
voluttà *nf* delight, pleasure; voluptuousness.
voluttuóso *a* voluptuous.
vómere *nm* plowshare.
vomitàre *vt* to vomit.
vòmito *nm* vomiting.
vóngola *nf* clam.
voràce *a* voracious, greedy.
voracità *nf* voracity, greed(iness).
voràgine *nf* gulf, abyss.
vòrtice *nm* vortex; whirl(pool).
vorticóso *a* whirling, swirling.
vòstro *poss a* your; *poss pron* yours.
votànte *a* voting; *nm* voter.
votàre *vi* to vote; *vt* to approve; consecrate; offer; **-rsi** *vr* to devote oneself.
votazióne *nf* voting.
votívo *a* votive.
vóto *nm* vow; votive offering; prayer; (*school*) mark; vote.
vulcànico *pl* **-ici** *a* volcanic.
vulcanizzàre *vt* to vulcanize.
vulcàno *nm* volcano.
vulneràbile *a* vulnerable.
vuotàre *vt* to empty.
vuòto *a* empty; vacant; *nm* empty space; vacuum; void; **andàre a v.** to fail.

Z

zafferàno *nm* saffron.
zàffiro *nm* sapphire.
zàino *nm* knapsack, pack.
zàmpa *nf* paw.
zampillànte *a* gushing.
zampillàre *vi* to spurt; spring.
zampíllo *nm* spurt, jet.
zampíno *nm* little paw; (*fig*) finger.
zampógna *nf* bagpipes *pl*; reedpipe.
zampognàro *nm* piper.
zàna *nf* basket; cradle.
zàngola *nf* churn.
zànna *nf* fang; tusk.
zanzàra *nf* mosquito.
zanzarièra *nf* mosquito net.
zàppa *nf* hoe.
zappàre *vt* to dig; hoe.
zappatóre *nm* hoer; (*mil*) pioneer.
zar *nm* czar, tzar.

zàttera *nf* (*naut*) lighter; raft.
zavòrra *nf* ballast.
zàzzera *nf* shock of hair; mane.
zèbra *nf* zebra.
zécca *nf* mint; **nuòvo di z.** brand-new.
zecchíno *nm* sequin.
zèffiro *nm* zephyr.
Zelànda *nf* (*geogr*) Zealand; **Nuòva Z.** New Zealand.
zelànte *a* zealous.
zèlo *nm* zeal.
zènit *nm* zenith.
zènzero *nm* ginger; **pàn di z.** gingerbread.
zéppo *a* full; **piéno z.** crowded, packed.
zerbíno *nm* doormat; dandy.
zerbinòtto *nm* beau, dandy.
zèro *nm* zero, nought.
zía *nf* aunt.
zibaldóne *nm* miscellany, medley.
zibellíno *nm* sable.
zígomo *nm* cheek-bone.
zigzagàre *vi* to zigzag.
zimbèllo *nm* decoy(-bird); laughing-stock.
zincàto *a* zinc plated.
zínco *pl* **-chi** *nm* zinc.
zíngaro *nm* gypsy.
zío *nm* uncle.
zitèlla *nf* spinster; old maid.
zittíre *vti* to hiss.
zitto *a* silent; **stàre z.** to keep quiet.
zizzània *nf* darnel; **seminàre z.** to sow dissension.
zoccolàio *nm* clog-maker.
zòccolo *nm* clog, wooden shoe; hoof; skirting-board.
zodíaco *pl* **-chi** *nm* zodiac.
zolfanèllo *nm* (sulphur) match.
zólfo *nm* sulphur.
zòlla *nf* clod; lump; **zollétta di zúcchero** lump of sugar.
zóna *nf* zone, area.
zónzo, a *ad* idling; strolling.
zoología *nf* zoology.
zoològico *pl* **-ici** *a* zoological.
zoppicànte *a* limping, lame.
zoppicàre *vi* to limp.
zòppo *a* lame, limping.
zòtico *pl* **-ici** *a* boorish, rough; *nm* boor, uncouth fellow.
zúcca *nf* pumpkin; squash; (*fig*) pate.
zuccheràre *vt* to sugar; sweeten (*also fig*).
zuccherièra *nf* sugar-basin.
zuccherifício *nm* sugar-refinery.
zúcchero *nm* sugar.
zucchíno *nm* zucchini, Italian squash.
zúffa *nf* brawl, scuffle.
zufolàre *vi* to whistle.
zúfolo *nm* whistle.
zulú *nm* Zulu.
zúppa *nf* soup; **z. inglése** trifle.
zuppièra *nf* (soup) tureen.
zúppo *a* drenched, soaked.
Zurigo *nf* (*geogr*) Zurich.

English-Italian

A

a [ə] *indef art* un(o), una.
aback [ə'bæk] *ad* all'indietro; **taken a.** sconcertato.
abandon [ə'bændən] *n* abbandono, trasporto; *vt* abbandonare.
abandonment [ə'bændənmənt] *n* abbandono.
abase [ə'beis] *vt* abbassare, umiliare.
abasement [ə'beismənt] *n* umiliazione.
abash [ə'bæʃ] *vt* confondere.
abate [ə'beit] *vt* diminuire, abbassare; *vi* calmarsi, indebolirsi.
abatement [ə'beitmənt] *n* diminuzione, riduzione.
abbé ['æbei] *n* abate.
abbess ['æbis] *n* badessa.
abbey ['æbi] *n* badia.
abbot ['æbət] *n* abate.
abbreviate [ə'briːvieit] *vt* abbreviare.
abbreviation [ə,briːvi'eiʃən] *n* abbreviazione.
abc ['eibiː'siː] *n* abbiccì.
abdicate ['æbdikeit] *vti* abdicare.
abdomen ['æbdəmen] *n* addome.
abdominal [æb'dɔminl] *a* addominale.
abduct [æb'dʌkt] *vt* rapire.
abduction [æb'dʌkʃən] *n* ratto.
Abel ['eibəl] *nm pr* Abele.
aberration [,æbə'reiʃən] *n* aberrazione.
abet [ə'bet] *vt* favoreggiare, incitare.
abeyance [ə'beiəns] *n* sospensione.
abhor [əb'hɔː] *vt* aborrire, detestare.
abhorrence [əb'hɔrəns] *n* odio, ripugnanza.
abhorrent [əb'hɔrənt] *a* ripugnante, contrario a.
abide [ə'baid] *vti* sopportare; **a. by** conformarsi a; tener fede a, attenersi a.
ability [ə'biliti] *n* abilità, talento.
abject ['æbdʒekt] *a* abietto, reietto, vile.
abjuration [,æbdʒuə'reiʃən] *n* abiura.
abjure [əb'dʒuə] *vt* abiurare, ripudiare.
ablative ['æblətiv] *a n* ablativo.
ablaze [ə'bleiz] *a* in fiamme; risplendente.
able ['eibl] *a* abile, capace, in grado di.
ablution [ə'bluːʃən] *n* abluzione.
abnegation [,æbni'geiʃən] *n* abnegazione, rinunzia.
abnormal [æb'nɔːməl] *a* anormale.
abnormality [,æbnɔː'mæliti] *n* anormalità; anomalia.

aboard [ə'bɔːd] *ad prep* (*naut*) a bordo.
abode [ə'boud] *n* dimora, domicilio.
abolish [ə'bɔliʃ] *vt* abolire.
abolition [,æbə'liʃən] *n* abolizione.
abominable [ə'bɔminəbl] *a* abominevole.
abomination [ə,bɔmi'neiʃən] *n* abominazione, disgusto.
aboriginal [,æbə'ridʒənl] *a n* aborigeno, indigeno.
abortion [ə'bɔːʃən] *n* aborto.
abortive [ə'bɔːtiv] *a* abortivo, prematuro; (*fig*) fallito.
abound [ə'baund] *vi* abbondare.
abounding [ə'baundiŋ] *a* abbondante, ricco.
about [ə'baut] *prep* circa, intorno a, per; *ad* intorno, presso, qua e là; **to be about to** stare per.
above [ə'bʌv] *ad prep* in alto, al di sopra di; più (alto) che, lassù, più in alto, sopra.
Abraham ['eibrəhæm] *nm pr* Abramo.
abrasion [ə'breiʒən] *n* abrasione, scalfittura.
abreast [ə'brest] *ad* di fianco.
abridge [ə'bridʒ] *vt* abbreviare, ridurre.
abridg(e)ment [ə'bridʒmənt] *n* abbreviazione, compendio.
abroad [ə'brɔːd] *ad* all'estero, fuori.
abrogate ['æbrougeit] *vt* abrogare.
abrogation [,æbrou'geiʃən] *n* abrogazione.
abrupt [ə'brʌpt] *a* brusco, improvviso; ripido.
abscess ['æbsis] *n* ascesso.
abscond [əb'skɔnd] *vi* rendersi latitante, fuggire.
absence ['æbsəns] *n* assenza, mancanza; **a. of mind** distrazione.
absent ['æbsənt] *a* assente; *vr* [əb'sent] **to absent oneself** assentarsi.
absentee [,æbsən'tiː] *n* persona abitualmente assente dal suo domicilio o dal lavoro, scuola, etc.
absently ['æbsəntli] *ad* distrattamente.
absinthe ['æbsinθ] *n* assenzio.
absolute ['æbsəluːt] *a* assoluto, completo; puro.
absolutely ['æbsəluːtli] *ad* assolutamente.
absoluteness ['æbsəluːtnis] *n* assolutezza.
absolution [,æbsə'luːʃən] *n* assoluzione.

185

absolutism ['æbsəlu:tizəm] n assolutismo.
absolve [əb'zɔlv] vt assolvere.
absorb [əb'sɔ:b] vt assorbire.
absorbed [əb'sɔ:bd] a assorbito, assorto.
absorbent [əb'sɔ:bənt] a n assorbente; **a. cotton** (US) cotone idrofilo.
absorbing [əb'sɔ:biŋ] a assorbente, interessante.
absorption [əb'sɔ:pʃən] n assorbimento.
abstain [əb'stein] vi astenersi.
abstemious [æb'sti:miəs] a astemio, frugale, moderato.
abstention [æb'stenʃən] n astensione.
abstinence ['æbstinəns] n astinenza.
abstinent ['æbstinənt] a astinente, sobrio.
abstract ['æbstrækt] a astratto; n astrazione, astratto; vt [æb'strækt] astrarre; sottrarre.
abstraction [æb'strækʃən] n astrazione; distrazione; sottrazione.
abstruse [æb'stru:s] a astruso.
absurd [əb'sə:d] a assurdo, ridicolo.
absurdity [əb'sə:diti] n assurdità.
absurdly [əb'sə:dli] ad assurdamente.
abundance [ə'bʌndəns] n abbondanza.
abundant [ə'bʌndənt] a abbondante.
abuse [ə'bju:s] n abuso, cattivo uso; insulto; vt [ə'bju:z] abusare di, far cattivo uso; insultare.
abusive [ə'bju:siv] a abusivo; ingiurioso.
abysmal [ə'bizməl] a abissale.
abyss [ə'bis] n abisso.
Abyssinia [,æbi'siniə] n Abissinia.
Abyssinian [æbi'siniən] a n abissino.
acacia [ə'keiʃə] n acacia.
academic [,ækə'demik] a n accademico.
academician [ə,kædə'miʃən] n accademico.
academy [ə'kædəmi] n accademia.
accede [æk'si:d] vi accedere; aderire.
accelerate [æk'seləreit] vti accelerare.
acceleration [æk,selə'reiʃən] n accelerazione.
accelerator [æk'seləreitə] n acceleratore.
accent ['æksənt] n accento, tono; **accent, accentuate** vt accentuare.
accentuation [æk,sentju'eiʃən] n accentuazione.
accept [ək'sept] vt accettare, approvare.
acceptable [ək'septəbl] a accetto, gradevole.
acceptance [ək'septəns] n accettazione, accoglienza.
accepter, acceptor [ək'septə] n (com) accettante.
access ['ækses] n accesso.
accessible [æk'sesəbl] a accessibile.

accession [æk'seʃən] n accessione; aggiunta.
accessory [æk'sesəri] a n accessorio; complice.
accident ['æksidənt] n accidente, caso; incidente; **by a.** per caso; **a.-prone** soggetto agli incidenti.
accidental [,æksi'dentl] a casuale, fortuito; n (mus) accidente.
accidentally [,æksi'dentəli] ad accidentalmente, per caso.
acclaim [ə'kleim] vt acclamare.
acclamation [,æklə'meiʃən] n acclamazione.
acclimatization [ə,klaimətai'zeiʃən] n acclimatazione.
acclimatize [ə'klaimətaiz] vt acclimatare.
accommodate [ə'kɔmədeit] vt accomodare, comporre; alloggiare.
accommodating [ə'kɔmədeitiŋ] a accomodante; compiacente.
accommodation [ə,kɔmə'deiʃən] n accomodamento, adattamento; alloggio; sistemazione.
accompaniment [ə'kʌmpənimənt] n accompagnamento.
accompanist [ə'kʌmpənist] n accompagnatore, -trice.
accompany [ə'kʌmpəni] vt accompagnare.
accomplice [ə'kʌmplis] n complice.
accomplish [ə'kʌmpliʃ] vt compiere, completare, effettuare.
accomplishment [ə'kʌmpliʃmənt] n compimento, realizzazione; dote.
accord [ə'kɔ:d] n accordo, consenso; vti accordare, concedere.
accordance [ə'kɔ:dəns] n accordo, conformità.
according to [ə'kɔ:diŋtu] prep secondo.
accordingly [ə'kɔ:diŋli] ad in conseguenza, in conformità.
accordion [ə'kɔ:diən] n (mus) fisarmonica.
accost [ə'kɔst] vt rivolgere la parola a, abbordare.
account [ə'kaunt] n conto; acconto; importanza; relazione; **on a. of** a causa, (motivo) di; **on no a.** a nessun patto.
account [ə'kaunt] vt considerare, stimare; **a. for** spiegare la ragione di.
accountability [ə,kauntə'biliti] n responsabilità.
accountable [ə'kauntəbl] a responsabile.
accountant [ə'kauntənt] n contabile; **certified public a.** ragioniere.
accredit [ə'kredit] vt accreditare, fornire di credenziali.
accretion [æ'kri:ʃən] n accrescimento.
accrue [ə'kru:] vi derivare, provenire; accumularsi.
accumulate [ə'kju:mjuleit] vt accumulare, ammassare; vi accumularsi.

accumulation [ə‚kjuːmju'leiʃən] *n* accumulamento, ammasso.
accumulative [ə'kjuːmjulətiv] *a* accumulativo.
accumulator [ə'kjuːmjuleitə] *n* accumulatore.
accuracy ['ækjurəsi] *n* esattezza, precisione.
accurate ['ækjurit] *a* esatto, preciso.
accursed [ə'kəːsid] *a* maledetto.
accusation [‚ækju'zeiʃən] *n* accusa.
accusative [ə'kjuːzətiv] *a n* accusativo.
accuse [ə'kjuːz] *vt* accusare.
accustom [ə'kʌstəm] *vt* abituare; **a.** oneself *vr* abituarsi.
ace [eis] *n* asso; **within an a.** lì per lì.
acerbity [ə'səːbiti] *n* acerbità, asprezza.
acetate ['æsitit] *n* acetato.
acetone ['æsitoun] *n* acetone.
acetylene [ə'setiliːn] *n* acetilene.
ache [eik] *n* dolore, male; *vi* dolere.
achieve [ə'tʃiːv] *vt* compiere, condurre a termine; raggiungere.
achievement [ə'tʃiːvmənt] *n* compimento; raggiungimento; successo.
aching ['eikiŋ] *a* dolorante.
acid ['æsid] *a n* acido.
acidify [ə'sidifai] *vt* acidificare.
acidity [ə'siditi] *n* acidità.
acknowledge [ək'nɔlidʒ] *vt* ammettere; riconoscere; accusare (ricezione di).
acknowledgment [ək'nɔlidʒmənt] *n* ammissione; riconoscimento; l'accusare ricezione
acme ['ækmi] *n* acme, culmine.
acne ['ækni] *n* acne.
acolyte ['ækəlait] *n* accolito.
acorn ['eikɔːn] *n* ghianda.
acoustic [ə'kuːstik] *a* acustico; **acoustics** *n pl* acustica.
acquaint [ə'kweint] *vt* informare, mettere al corrente.
acquaintance [ə'kweintəns] *n* conoscenza; conoscente.
acquiesce [‚ækwi'es] *vi* accettare, acconsentire tacitamente.
acquiescence [‚ækwi'esns] *n* acquiescenza.
acquiescent [‚ækwi'esnt] *a* acquiescente, rassegnato.
acquire [ə'kwaiə] *vt* acquisire, acquistare.
acquisition [‚ækwi'ziʃən] *n* acquisizione; acquisto.
acquit [ə'kwit] *vt* assolvere; **a.** oneself *vr* comportarsi.
acquittal [ə'kwitl] *n* assoluzione.
acre ['eikə] *n* acro.
acrid ['ækrid] *a* acre, aspro.
acrimonious [‚ækri'mouniəs] *a* aspro, astioso.
acrimony ['ækriməni] *n* acrimonia.
acrobat ['ækrəbæt] *n* acrobata.
across [ə'krɔs] *ad prep* attraverso, da un lato all'altro, dall'altra parte.
acrostic [ə'krɔstik] *n* acrostico.
act [ækt] *n* atto; azione; *vti* agire,

fare, comportarsi; rappresentare, recitare.
acting ['æktiŋ] *a* facente; avente funzione di; *n* rappresentazione; modo di recitare.
action ['ækʃən] *n* azione; combattimento; gesto; processo.
activate ['æktiveit] *vt* attivare; rendere radioattivo.
active ['æktiv] *a* attivo, energico.
actively ['æktivli] *ad* attivamente.
activity [æk'tiviti] *n* attività, energia.
actor ['æktə] *n* attore; **actress** *n* attrice.
actual ['æktjuəl] *a* reale, effettivo.
actuality [‚æktju'æliti] *n* realtà.
actually ['æktjuəli] *ad* realmente, effettivamente.
actuate ['æktjueit] *vt* mettere in azione; trascinare.
acumen ['ækjumən] *n* acume.
acute [ə'kjuːt] *a* acuto; perspicace.
acuteness [ə'kjuːtnis] *n* acutezza; perspicacia.
adage ['ædidʒ] *n* adagio, detto, proverbio.
Adam ['ædəm] *nm pr* Adamo.
adamant ['ædəmənt] *a* adamantino, inflessibile.
adapt [ə'dæpt] *vt* adattare, modificare.
adaptability [ə‚dæptə'biliti] *n* adattabilità.
adaptable [ə'dæptəbl] *a* adattabile.
adaptation [‚ædæp'teiʃən] *n* adattamento.
adapter [ə'dæptə] *n* (*phot*) adattatore; (*el*) pezzo di raccordo.
add [æd] *vti* aggiungere, soggiungere; addizionare, sommare; **to a. up** fare la somma.
adder ['ædə] *n* vipera.
addict ['ædikt] *n* tossicomane; [ə'dikt] *vt* abituare, dedicare.
addiction [ə'dikʃən] *n* dedizione, inclinazione.
addition [ə'diʃən] *n* addizione, somma; aggiunta; **in a. to** oltre a.
additional [ə'diʃənl] *a* aggiunto; supplementare.
additionally [ə'diʃnəli] *ad* in aggiunta; inoltre.
addled ['ædld] *a* guasto; confuso.
address [ə'dres] *n* indirizzo; discorso; destrezza; *vt* indirizzare; rivolgere la parola o lo scritto a.
addressee [‚ædre'siː] *n* destinatario.
adduce [ə'djuːs] *vt* addurre; citare.
Adela ['ædilə] *nf pr* Adele.
adenoids ['ædinɔidz] *n pl* adenoidi.
adept ['ædept] *a n* esperto.
adequate ['ædikwit] *a* adeguato.
adhere [əd'hiə] *vi* aderire, attaccarsi.
adherence [əd'hiərəns] *n* aderenza.
adherent [əd'hiərənt] *a* aderente, attaccato; *n* partigiano, seguace.
adhesion [əd'hiːʒən] *n* adesione.
adhesive [əd'hiːsiv] *a* adesivo, appiccicaticcio; **a. paper** carta gom-

mata; **a. plaster** cerotto adesivo.
adieu [ə'djuː] *interj* n addio.
adipose ['ædipous] *a* adiposo.
adjacent [ə'dʒeisənt] *a* adiacente, attiguo.
adjective ['ædʒiktiv] n aggettivo.
adjoin [ə'dʒɔin] *vti* essere adiacente.
adjoining [ə'dʒɔiniŋ] *a* adiacente, contiguo.
adjourn [ə'dʒəːn] *vt* aggiornare; rimandare.
adjournment [ə'dʒəːnmənt] n rinvio.
adjudge [ə'dʒʌdʒ] *vt* aggiudicare; assegnare.
adjudicate [ə'dʒuːdikeit] *vt* giudicare; aggiudicare.
adjudication [ə,dʒuːdi'keiʃən] n aggiudicazione; sentenza.
adjudicator [ə'dʒuːdikeitə] n giudice; arbitro.
adjunct ['ædʒʌŋkt] n aggiunta; aggiunto.
adjure [ə'dʒuə] *vt* implorare, scongiurare.
adjust [ə'dʒʌst] *vt* aggiustare; adattare; regolare.
adjustable [ə'dʒʌstəbl] *a* aggiustabile; regolabile.
adjustment [ə'dʒʌstmənt] n adattamento; regolamento.
adjutant ['ædʒutənt] n aiutante.
ad lib [æd'lib] *ad* all'impronto, estemporaneamente; *vti* improvvisare; *n*. improvvisazione.
adman ['ædmæn] n agente pubblicitario.
admass ['ædmæs] n 'il grosso pubblico'.
administer [əd'ministə] *vt* amministrare; somministrare.
administration [əd,minis'treiʃən] n amministrazione; somministrazione.
administrative [əd'ministrətiv] *a* amministrativo.
administrator [əd'ministreitə] n amministratore.
admirable ['ædmərəbl] *a* ammirabile, ammirevole.
admiral ['ædmərəl] n ammiraglio.
admiralty ['ædmərəlti] n ammiragliato; Ministero della Marina.
admiration [ædmə'reiʃən] n ammirazione.
admire [əd'maiə] *vt* ammirare.
admirer [əd'maiərə] n ammiratore; corteggiatore.
admiring [əd'maiəriŋ] *a* ammirativo.
admissible [əd'misəbl] *a* ammissibile.
admission [əd'miʃən] n ammissione.
admit [əd'mit] *vt* ammettere; riconoscere; lasciar entrare; **a. of** *vi* permettere.
admittance [əd'mitəns] n ammissione; ingresso.
admittedly [əd'mitidli] *ad* certo, certo che.
admonish [əd'mɔniʃ] *vt* ammonire.
admonishment [əd'mɔniʃmənt] n ammonimento; esortazione.

ado [ə'duː] n confusione, trambusto; difficoltà.
adolescence [,ædou'lesns] n adolescenza.
adolescent [,ædou'lesnt] *a* n adolescente.
adopt [ə'dɔpt] *vt* adottare; **adopted** *a* adottato; **adopted son** figlio adottivo.
adoption [ə'dɔpʃən] n adozione.
adoptive [ə'dɔptiv] *a* adottivo.
adorable [ə'dɔːrəbl] *a* adorabile.
adoration [,ædɔː'reiʃən] n adorazione; venerazione.
adore [ə'dɔː] *vt* adorare, venerare.
adorer [ə'dɔːrə] n adoratore.
adorn [ə'dɔːn] *vt* adornare.
adornment [ə'dɔːnmənt] n ornamento.
Adrian ['eidriən] nm pr Adriano.
Adriatic [,eidri'ætik] *a* n Adriatico.
adrift [ə'drift] *ad* alla deriva.
adroit [ə'drɔit] *a* destro, abile.
adroitness [ə'drɔitnis] n destrezza, abilità.
adulation [,ædju'leiʃən] n adulazione.
adult ['ædʌlt] *a* n adulto.
adulterate [ə'dʌltəreit] *vt* adulterare.
adulteration [ə,dʌltə'reiʃən] *a* adulterazione, sofisticazione.
adulterer [ə'dʌltərə] n adultero; **adulteress** n adultera.
adultery [ə'dʌltəri] n adulterio.
advance [əd'vaːns] n avanzamento, marcia in avanti, progresso; (com) rialzo; anticipo; *vt* avanzare; aumentare; anticipare; *vi* avanzare; progredire.
advanced [əd'vaːnst] *a* avanzato, progredito.
advancement [əd'vaːnsmənt] n avanzamento, progresso, promozione.
advantage [əd'vaːntidʒ] n vantaggio.
advantageous [,ædvən'teidʒəs] *a* vantaggioso.
advent ['ædvənt] n avvento.
adventitious [,ædven'tiʃəs] *a* avventizio, casuale.
adventure [əd'ventʃə] n avventura, impresa.
adventurer [əd'ventʃərə] n avventuriero.
adventurous [əd'ventʃərəs] *a* avventuroso.
adverb ['ædvəːb] n avverbio.
adverbial [əd'vəːbial] *a* avverbiale.
adversary ['ædvəsəri] n avversario, antagonista.
adverse ['ædvəːs] *a* avverso, contrario, opposto.
adversity [əd'vəːsiti] n avversità.
advertise ['ædvətaiz] *vti* fare della pubblicità per; mettere annunci, rendere noto.
advertisement [əd'vəːtismənt] n annuncio, avviso; inserzione; reclame.

advertiser ['ædvətaizə] n inserzionista; **advertising** a pubblicitario; n pubblicità.
advice [əd'vais] n consigli(o), avviso.
advisable [əd'vaizəbl] a consigliabile, raccomandabile.
advise [əd'vaiz] vt consigliare; avvisare.
advisedly [əd'vaizidli] ad consideratamente, giudiziosamente.
adviser [əd'vaizə] n consigliere.
advisory [əd'vaizəri] a che consiglia; consultivo.
advocate ['ædvəkit] n avvocato; vt ['ædvəkeit] difendere, patrocinare; sostenere.
Aegean [i'dʒiːən] a n (geogr) Egeo.
aerated ['eiəreitid] a gassoso.
aerial ['ɛəriəl] a aereo, etereo; n (rad) antenna.
aerobatics ['ɛərou'bætiks] n pl acrobazie aeree.
aerodrome ['ɛərədroum] n aerodromo.
aerodynamics ['ɛəroudai'næmiks] n aerodinamica; **aerodynamic** a aerodinamico.
aeronaut ['ɛərənɔːt] n aeronauta.
aeronautics [ˌɛərə'nɔːtiks] n aeronautica.
aerosol ['ɛərəsɔl] n aerosol.
aerostat ['ɛərostæt] n aerostato.
aerostatics [ˌɛero'stætiks] n pl aerostatica.
aesthete ['iːsθiːt] n esteta.
aesthetic [iːs'θetik] a estetico; **aesthetics** n estetica.
afar, afar off [ə'fɑː, ə'fɑːr'ɔf] ad lontano, in lontananza; **from a.** da lontano.
affability [ˌæfə'biliti] n affabilità.
affable ['æfəbl] a affabile.
affair [ə'fɛə] n affare; avventura, relazione.
affect [ə'fekt] vt affettare; riguardare; influire su; commuovere.
affectation [ˌæfek'teiʃən] n affettazione.
affected [ə'fektid] a affettato; affetto; commosso.
affection [ə'fekʃən] n affetto, affezione.
affectionate [ə'fekʃnit] a affettuoso.
affidavit [ˌæfi'deivit] n deposizione scritta e giurata, affidavit.
affiliate [ə'filieit] vt affiliare, associare.
affiliation [əˌfili'eiʃən] n affiliazione.
affinity [ə'finiti] n affinità; parentela.
affirm [ə'fəːm] vt affermare, confermare.
affirmation [ˌæfəː'meiʃən] n affermazione, asserzione.
affirmative [ə'fəːmətiv] a affermativo; n affermativa.
affix [ə'fiks] vt affiggere, apporre, attaccare; ['æfiks] n affisso.
afflict [ə'flikt] vt affliggere.
affliction [ə'flikʃən] n afflizione.
affluence ['æfluəns] n affluenza, abbondanza.

affluent ['æfluənt] a ricco; n affluente.
afford [ə'fɔːd] vt fornire, offrire; permettersi il lusso di.
afforestation [æ'fɔris'teiʃən] n imboschimento.
affranchise [ə'fræntʃaiz] vt affrancare, liberare.
affront [ə'frʌnt] n affronto; insulto; vt affrontare; insultare.
afloat [ə'flout] ad a galla.
afoot [ə'fut] ad (fig) in moto, in ballo.
aforesaid [ə'fɔːsed] a predetto.
afraid [ə'freid] a impaurito, pauroso; **to be a.** aver paura.
afresh [ə'freʃ] ad di nuovo, un'altra volta.
Africa ['æfrikə] n Africa.
African ['æfrikən] a n africano.
Afrikan(d)er [ˌæfri'kæn(d)ə] a n sud-africano, di origine olandese.
aft [ɑːft] ad (naut) a poppa.
after ['ɑːftə] ad prep cj dopo, dietro, in seguito a; ad imitazione di; dopo che; **a. all** in fin dei conti.
after-effect ['ɑːftəri'fekt] n conseguenza.
aftermath ['ɑːftəmæθ] n secondo taglio del fieno; (fig) conseguenze pl, risultati pl.
afternoon ['ɑːftə'nuːn] n pomeriggio.
afterthought ['ɑːftəθɔːt] n riflessione, ripensamento.
afterwards ['ɑːftəwədz] ad dopo, più tardi.
again [ə'gen] ad ancora, di nuovo; altrettanto; **a. and a.** ripetutamente; **now and a.** di quando in quando.
against [ə'genst] prep contro, in opposizione a; di fronte a; **a. the grain** (fig) contro voglia.
agate ['ægət] n agata.
Agatha ['ægəθə] nf pr Agata.
age ['eidʒ] n età; periodo; **of a.** maggiorenne; **under a.** minorenne.
age ['eidʒ] vti invecchiare.
aged ['eidʒid] a vecchio; ['eidʒd] dell'età di.
ageless ['eidʒlis] a di età invariata, sempre giovane.
agency ['eidʒənsi] n agenzia, rappresentanza.
agenda [ə'dʒendə] n ordine del giorno.
agent ['eidʒənt] n agente, rappresentante.
agglomeration [əˌglɔmə'reiʃən] n agglomerazione.
aggrandizement [ə'grændizmənt] n accrescimento (di potenza).
aggravate ['ægrəveit] vt aggravare; (fam) esasperare.
aggravating ['ægrəveitiŋ] a (fam) irritante, insopportabile.
aggregate ['ægrigit] a n aggregato; **in the a.** nel complesso.
aggregation [ˌægri'geiʃən] n aggregazione.
aggression [ə'greʃən] n aggressione.

aggressive [ə'gresiv] *a* aggressivo.
aggressiveness [ə'gresivnis] *n* aggressività.
aggressor [ə'gresə] *n* aggressore.
aghast [ə'gɑːst] *a* stupefatto; terrorizzato.
agile ['ædʒail] *a* agile.
agility [ə'dʒiliti] *n* agilità.
agitate ['ædʒiteit] *vt* agitare; commuovere; discutere.
agitation [ˌædʒi'teiʃən] *n* agitazione, commozione.
agitator ['ædʒiteitə] *n* agitatore.
Agnes ['ægnis] *nf pr* Agnese.
agnostic [æg'nɔstik] *a n* agnostico.
ago [ə'gou] *ad* fa.
agog [ə'gɔg] *a* ansioso, desideroso; *ad* con ansia.
agonized ['ægənaizd] **agonizing** ['ægənaiziŋ] *a* angoscioso.
agony ['ægəni] *n* agonia; angoscia.
agrarian [ə'grɛəriən] *a* agrario.
agree [ə'griː] *vi* accordarsi, convenire; acconsentire; confarsi.
agreeable [ə'griəbl] *a* piacevole, simpatico; disposto; conveniente.
agreeableness [ə'griəblnis] *n* piacevolezza, conformità.
agreement [ə'griːmənt] *n* accordo, contratto, patto.
agricultural [ˌægri'kʌltʃərəl] *a* agricolo.
agriculture ['ægrikʌltʃə] *n* agricoltura.
aground [ə'graund] *ad a (naut)* in secco; **to run a.** incagliarsi.
ahead [ə'hed] *ad* (in) avanti.
aid [eid] *n* aiuto, assistenza, sussidio; **first a.** pronto soccorso; *vt* aiutare.
aide-de-camp ['eiddə'kãːŋ] *n* aiutante di campo.
ail [eil] *vi* sentirsi male; *vt* affliggere.
ailing ['eiliŋ] *a* sofferente.
ailment ['eilmənt] *n* indisposizione, malattia.
aim [eim] *n* mira, scopo, proposito; *vti* puntare; *vi* mirare a; aspirare a.
aimless ['eimlis] *a* senza scopo.
air [ɛə] *n* aria; aspetto; atmosfera; *(mus)* aria; *vt* arieggiare, ventilare; **a.-hostess** assistente di volo, 'hostess'; **a. conditioner** condizionatore dell'aria; **a. station** scalo aereo; **a.-raid** incursione aerea.
aircraft *(inv)* ['ɛəkrɑːft] *n* aereo, aerei; **a .carrier** porta erei.
airdrome ['ɛədroum] *n* aerodromo.
air force ['ɛəfɔːs] *n* aeronautica, aviazione.
airily ['ɛərili] *ad* gaiamente; spensieratamente.
airiness ['ɛərinis] *n* leggerezza; spensieratezza.
airing ['ɛəriŋ] *n* ventilazione; giretto all'aria aperta.
airless ['ɛəlis] *a* privo d'aria.
airline ['ɛəlain] *n* aviolinea.
airmail ['ɛəmeil] *n* posta aerea.
airman ['ɛəmən] *n* aviatore.
airplane ['ɛəplein] *n* aeroplano;

fighter a. aeroplano da caccia.
airport ['ɛəpɔːt] *n* aeroporto.
air-pump ['ɛəpʌmp] *n* pompa pneumatica.
airship ['ɛəʃip] *n* dirigibile.
airtight ['ɛətait] *a* a tenuta d'aria.
airway ['ɛəwei] *n* via aerea.
airy ['ɛəri] *a* arioso; leggero; spensierato: aereo; vano.
aisle [ail] *n* navata.
ajar [ə'dʒɑː] *ad* socchiuso.
akimbo [ə'kimbou] *ad* le mani su i fianchi e i gomiti in fuori.
akin [ə'kin] *a* affine, parente.
alabaster ['æləbɑːstə] *a n* (di) alabastro.
alacrity [ə'lækriti] *n* alacrità.
Alan ['ælən] *nm pr* Alano.
alarm [ə'lɑːm] *n* allarme; *vt* allarmare, spaventare.
alarm-clock [ə'lɑːmklɔk] *n* (orologio a) sveglia.
alas! [ə'læs] *interj* ahimè!
Albania [æl'beiniə] *n (geogr)* Albania.
Albanian [æl'beiniən] *a n* albanese.
albatross ['ælbətrɔs] *n* albatro.
albeit [ɔːl'biːit] *cj* quantunque.
Albert ['ælbət] *nm pr* Alberto.
albino [æl'biːnou] *pl* **albinos** albino.
album ['ælbəm] *n* album.
albumen ['ælbjumin] *n* albume.
alchemy ['ælkimi] *n* alchimia.
alcohol ['ælkəhɔl] *n* alcool.
alcoholic [ˌælkə'hɔlik] *a* alcoolico; *n* alcoolizzato.
alcoholism ['ælkəhɔlizəm] *n* alcoolismo.
alcove ['ælkouv] *n* alcova, recesso.
alder ['ɔːldə] *n* ontano.
alderman ['ɔːldəmən] *n* assessore comunale.
ale [eil] *n* birra; **a.-house** birreria.
alert [ə'ləːt] *a* vigilante, attento; *n* allarme; **on the a.** all'erta.
alertness [ə'ləːtnis] *n* vigilanza; vivacità.
Alexander [ˌælig'zɑːndə] *nm pr* Alessandro.
Alexandria [ˌælig'zɑːndriə] *n (geogr)* Alessandria (d'Egitto).
Alfred ['ælfrid] *nm pr* Alfredo.
algebra ['ældʒibra] *n* algebra.
Algeria [æl'dʒiəriə] *n (geogr)* Algeria.
Algerian [æl'dʒiəriən] *a n* algerino.
alias ['eiliæs] *ad* alias; *n* falso nome.
alibi ['ælibai] *n* alibi.
Alice ['ælis] *nf pr* Alice.
alien ['eiliən] *a* estraneo; *n* straniero.
alienate ['eiliəneit] *vt* alienare.
alienation [ˌeiliə'neiʃən] *n* alienazione.
alight [ə'lait] *a* acceso; illuminato; infiammato; *vi* scendere; atterrare.
alike [ə'laik] *a* simile; *ad* parimenti.
alimentary [ˌæli'mentəri] *a* alimentare; alimentario.
alimentation [ˌælimen'teiʃən] *n* alimentazione.
alimony ['æliməni] *n* alimonia, alimenti.

alive [ə'laiv] a vivo, vivente; vivace.
alkaline ['ælkəlain] a alcalino.
all [ɔːl] a tutto; n pron tutto; ad completamente, del tutto; not at all! niente affatto!
allay [ə'lei] vt calmare; alleviare; diminuire.
allegation [,æle'geiʃən] n allegazione, asserzione.
allege [ə'ledʒ] vt allegare, asserire.
allegiance [ə'liːdʒəns] n fedeltà, obbedienza (al sovrano etc).
allegorical [,æle'gɔrikəl] a allegorico.
allegory ['æligəri] n allegoria.
allergic [ə'ləːdʒik] a allergico.
allergy ['ælədʒi] n allergia.
alleviate [ə'liːvieit] vt alleviare, mitigare.
alley ['æli] n vicolo.
alliance [ə'laiəns] n alleanza; unione.
allied ['ælaid] a alleato.
alligator ['æligeitə] n alligatore.
alliteration [ə,litə'reiʃən] n allitterazione.
allocate ['æləkeit] vt assegnare; distribuire.
allocation [,ælə'keiʃən] n assegnazione.
allot [ə'lɔt] vt distribuire; assegnare.
allotment [ə'lɔtmənt] n assegnazione, lotto; piccolo pezzo di terreno da coltivare.
allow [ə'lau] vt permettere, accordare; to a. for tener conto di.
allowable [ə'lauəbl] allowed [ə'laud] a lecito.
allowance [ə'lauəns] n assegno; indennità; riduzione, sconto.
alloy ['ælɔi] n lega (metallica); vt fondere, mescolare.
All Saints' Day ['ɔːl'seintsdei] n Ognissanti.
All Souls' Day ['ɔːl'soulzdei] n giorno dei morti.
allude [ə'luːd] vi alludere.
allure [ə'ljuə] vt allettare, sedurre.
allurement [ə'ljuəmənt] n allettamento.
alluring [ə'ljuəriŋ] a allettante, seducente.
allusion [ə'luːʒən] n allusione.
ally ['ælai] n alleato; vt [ə'lai] alleare, collegare, unire.
almanac ['ɔːlmənæk] n almanacco.
almighty [ɔːl'maiti] a onnipotente; the A. Dio.
almond ['aːmənd] n mandorla; a.-tree mandorlo.
almoner ['aːmənə] n elemosiniere.
almost ['ɔːlmoust] ad quasi.
alms [aːmz] (inv) n elemosina; a.-house ospizio di mendicità.
aloft [ə'lɔft] ad in alto.
alone [ə'loun] a solo; to let a. lasciar stare.
along [ə'lɔŋ] ad prep avanti, lungo, per; come a.! su via!; a. with con.
aloof [ə'luːf] ad a distanza; in disparte; a freddo, distante, sostenuto.

aloud [ə'laud] ad a voce alta, forte.
alphabet ['ælfəbit] n alfabeto.
alpine ['ælpain] a alpino.
Alps [ælps] n pl (geogr) Alpi.
already [ɔːl'redi] ad già, di già.
Alsace ['ælzæs] n Alsazia.
Alsatian [æl'seiʃjən] a n alsaziano; A. (dog) cane lupo.
also ['ɔːlsou] ad anche, inoltre, pure.
altar ['ɔːltə] n altare; high a. altare maggiore.
alter ['ɔːltə] vti cambiare, cambiarsi, alterare.
alterable ['ɔːltərəbl] a alterabile.
alteration [,ɔːltə'reiʃən] n modificazione, alterazione.
altercation [,ɔːltə'keiʃən] n alterco.
alternate [ɔːl'təːnit] a alternato, alterno; vti ['ɔːltəneit] alternar(si), avvicendar(si); alternately vicendevolmente.
alternation [,ɔːltəː'neiʃən] n alternazione.
alternative [ɔːl'təːnətiv] a alternativo; n alternativa; alternatively ad alternativamente.
although [ɔːl'ðou] cj sebbene, quantunque, benché.
altitude ['æltitjuːd] n altitudine, altezza; (av) quota.
altogether [,ɔːltə'gəðə] ad completamente, nell'insieme.
altruism ['æltruizəm] n altruismo.
altruistic [,æltru'istik] a altruistico.
alum ['æləm] n allume.
aluminum [ə'luːminəm] n alluminio.
alveolar ['ælviolə] a alveolato.
always ['ɔːlwəz] ad sempre.
amalgam [ə'mælgəm] n amalgama.
amalgamate [ə'mælgəmeit] vti amalgamar(si).
amalgamation [ə,mælgə'meiʃən] n amalgamazione, fusione.
amass [ə'mæs] vt accumulare, ammassare.
amateur ['æmətə] a n dilettante.
amaze [ə'meiz] vt meravigliare, stupire.
amazement [ə'meizmənt] n meraviglia.
amazing [ə'meiziŋ] a sorprendente.
Amazon ['æməzən] n (geogr) Rio delle Amazzoni.
ambassador [æm'bæsədə] n ambasciatore.
ambassadress [æm'bæsədris] n ambasciatrice.
amber ['æmbə] n ambra.
ambiguity [,æmbi'gjuiti] n ambiguità.
ambiguous [æm'bigjuəs] a ambiguo.
ambition [æm'biʃən] n ambizione.
ambitious [æm'biʃəs] a ambizioso.
amble ['æmbl] vi andare lemme lemme; n passo lento.
Ambrose ['æmbrouz] nm pr Ambrogio; Ambrosian a ambrosiano.
ambulance ['æmbjuləns] n ambulanza.

ambush ['æmbuʃ] n agguato, imboscata.
ameliorate [ə'miːliəreit] vti migliorare.
amelioration [ə,miːliə'reiʃən] n miglioramento.
amen ['ɑːmen] interj amen, così sia.
amenable [ə'miːnəbl] a trattabile.
amend [ə'mend] vti emendare, emendarsi.
amendment [ə'mendmənt] n emendamento.
amends [ə'mendz] n pl compenso, riparazione; **to make a.** fare ammenda.
amenity [ə'miːniti] n amenità; **amenities** n pl comodità pl.
America [ə'merikə] n America.
American [ə'merikən] a n americano.
amethyst ['æmiθist] n ametista.
amiability [,eimiə'biliti] n amabilità.
amiable ['eimiəbl] a amabile.
amicable ['æmikəbl] a amichevole.
amid(st) [ə'mid(st)] prep fra, in mezzo a, tra.
amiss [ə'mis] a sbagliato; ad inopportunamente, in mala parte.
amity ['æmiti] n amicizia.
ammonia [ə'mouniə] n ammoniaca.
ammunition [,æmju'niʃən] n munizioni pl.
amnesia [æm'niːziə] n amnesia.
amnesty ['æmnesti] n amnistia.
amok [ə'mɔk] v **amuck.**
among(st) [ə'mʌŋ(st)] prep fra, in mezzo a, tra.
amoral [æ'mɔrəl] a amorale.
amorous ['æmərəs] a amoroso.
amorphous [ə'mɔːfəs] a amorfo.
amount [ə'maunt] n ammontare, quantità, somma; vi ammontare.
amphibious [æm'fibiəs] a anfibio.
amphitheatre ['æmfi,θiətə] n anfiteatro.
ample ['æmpl] a ampio; abbondante.
amplification [,æmplifi'keiʃən] n amplificazione.
amplifier ['æmplifaiə] n amplificatore.
amplify ['æmplifai] vti ampliare, amplificare.
amputate ['æmpjuteit] vt amputare.
amputation [,æmpju'teiʃən] n amputazione.
amuck [ə'mʌk] ad in un accesso di pazzia sanguinaria.
amulet ['æmjulit] n amuleto.
amuse [ə'mjuːz] vt divertire, svagare.
amusement [ə'mjuːzmənt] n divertimento, svago.
amusing [ə'mjuːziŋ] a divertente; faceto.
an [æn] indef art un(o), una.
anachronism [a'nækrənizəm] n anacronismo.
anagram ['ænəgræm] n anagramma.
analogous [ə'næləgəs] a analogo.
analogy [ə'nælədʒi] n analogia.
analysis [ə'næləsis] pl **analyses** n

analisi; analyst n analizzatore.
analytic(al) [,ænə'litik(əl)] a analitico.
analyze ['ænəlaiz] vt analizzare.
anarchist ['ænəkist] n anarchico.
anarchy ['ænəki] n anarchia.
anathema [ə'næθimə] n anatema.
anatomical [,ænə'tɔmikəl] a anatomico.
anatomy [ə'nætəmi] n anatomia.
ancestor ['ænsistə] n antenato.
ancestral [æn'sestrəl] a avito.
ancestry ['ænsistri] n lignaggio, stirpe.
anchor ['æŋkə] n àncora, (fig) salvezza; **at a.** ancorato; vti ancorar (si).
anchorage ['æŋkəridʒ] n ancoraggio.
anchovy ['æntʃəvi] n acciuga.
ancient ['einʃənt] a antico, venerabile.
and [ænd, ənd, ən] cj e, ed.
andiron ['ændaiən] n alare.
Andrew ['ændruː] nm pr Andrea.
anecdote ['ænikdout] n aneddoto.
anemia [ə'niːmiə] n anemia.
anemone [ə'neməni] n anemone; **sea a.** attinia.
anesthetic [,ænis'θetik] a n anestetico.
anew [ə'njuː] ad di nuovo.
angel ['eindʒəl] n angelo; **guardian a.** angelo custode.
angelic [æn'dʒelik] a angelico.
anger ['æŋgə] n ira, rabbia; vt adirare, far arrabbiare.
angle ['æŋgl] n angolo; punto di vista; vi pescare all'amo.
angler ['æŋglə] n pescatore.
Anglican ['æŋglikən] a n anglicano.
angling ['æŋgliŋ] n pesca all'amo.
Anglo-Saxon ['æŋglou'sæksən] a n anglo-sassone.
angry ['æŋgri] a arrabbiato, irato.
anguish ['æŋgwiʃ] n angoscia.
angular ['æŋgjulə] a angolare.
aniline ['æniliːn] n anilina.
animadversion [,ænimæd'vəːʃən] n censura, critica.
animal ['æniməl] a n animale.
animate ['ænimit] a animato; vt animare.
animation [,æni'meiʃən] n animazione.
animosity [,æni'mɔsiti] n animosità.
aniseed ['ænisiːd] n seme di anice.
anisette [,æni'zet] n anisetta.
ankle ['æŋkl] n caviglia.
Ann(e) [æn] nf pr Anna.
annals ['ænlz] n pl annali.
annex ['æneks] n annesso; edificio supplementare.
annex [ə'neks] vt annettere.
annexation [,ænek'seiʃən] n annessione.
annihilate [ə'naiəleit] vt annichilire.
annihilation [ə,naiə'leiʃən] n annientamento.
anniversary [,æni'vəːsəri] a n anniversario.

annotate ['ænouteit] vt annotare.
announce [ə'nauns] vt annunciare.
announcement [ə'naunsmənt] n annuncio, avviso.
announcer [ə'naunsə] n annunziatore, -trice; (rad) annunciatore, -trice, presentatore, -trice.
annoy [ə'nɔi] vt disturbare, irritare.
annoyance [ə'nɔiəns] n fastidio, irritazione.
annoying [ə'nɔiiŋ] a noioso, fastidioso.
annual ['ænjuəl] a annuale, annuo; n annuario; pianta annuale.
annuity [ə'njuiti] n annualità.
annul [ə'nʌl] vt annullare, abolire.
annulment [ə'nʌlmənt] n annullamento.
annunciation [ə'nʌnsi'eiʃən] n annunciazione.
anodyne ['ænoudain] a anodino.
anoint [ə'nɔint] vt ungere; consacrare.
anomalous [ə'nɔmələs] a anomalo, irregolare.
anomaly [ə'nɔməli] n anomalia, irregolarità.
anon [ə'nɔn] ad subito; **ever and a.** di quando in quando.
anonymous [ə'nɔniməs] a anonimo.
anorak ['ænəræk] n giacca a vento.
another [ə'nʌðə] a pron (un) altro; (un) secondo; **one a.** l'un l'altro.
Anselm ['ænselm] nm pr Anselmo.
answer ['ɑːnsə] n risposta; vt rispondere a; **to answer for** rispondere di.
answerable ['ɑːnsərəbl] a responsabile.
answering ['ɑːnsəriŋ] a in risposta; corrispondente.
ant [ænt] n formica.
antagonism [æn'tægənizəm] n antagonismo, opposizione.
antagonist [æn'tægənist] n antagonista.
Antarctic [ænt'ɑːktik] a antartico; n Antartico, Antartide.
antecedent [.ænti'siːdənt] a n antecedente.
antechamber ['ænti.tʃeimbə] n anticamera.
antedate ['ænti'deit] vt anticipare, antidatare.
antediluvian ['æntidi'luːviən] a n antidiluviano.
antelope ['æntiloup] n antilope.
antenatal ['ænti'neitl] a prenatale.
anteroom ['æntirum] n anticamera.
anthem ['ænθəm] n antifona; inno.
anthology [æn'θɔlədʒi] n antologia.
Anthony ['æntəni] nm pr Antonio.
anthracite ['ænθrəsait] n antracite.
anthropologist [.ænθrə'pɔlədʒist] n antropologo.
anthropology [.ænθrə'pɔlədʒi] n antropologia.
anti-aircraft ['ænti'ɛəkrɑːft] a anti-aereo.
antibiotic ['æntibai'ɔtik] a n antibiotico.

antics ['æntiks] n pl stramberie, eccessi pl.
antichrist ['æntikraist] n anticristo.
anticipate [æn'tisipeit] vt anticipare; aspettarsi; pregustare.
anticipation [æn.tisi'peiʃən] n anticipazione, anticipo; previsione.
anticlimax ['ænti'klaimæks] n improvviso crollo discesa nel banale.
antidote ['æntidout] n antidoto.
antifogging ['æntifɔgiŋ] a n antiappannante, antinebbia.
antifreeze ['æntifriːz] n (aut) anticongelante.
antifriction ['ænti'frikʃən] n antiattrito.
anti-glare ['ænti'glɛə] a antiabbagliante; a. **headlights** (aut) fari anabbaglianti.
antihistamine ['ænti'histəmiːn] n antistamina.
antimacassar ['æntimə'kæsə] n copridivano, copripoltrona.
antimilitarism ['ænti'militərizəm] n antimilitarismo.
antimony ['æntiməni] n antimonio.
antipathy [æn'tipəθi] n antipatia, avversione.
antipodes [æn'tipədiːz] n pl antipodi pl.
antipope ['æntipoup] n antipapa.
antiquarian [.ænti'kwɛəriən] a n antiquario.
antiquated ['æntikweitid] a antiquato, fuori uso.
antique [æn'tiːk] a antico; n oggetto antico.
antiquity [æn'tikwiti] n antichità, tempi antichi pl.
anti-rust ['æntirʌst] a n antiruggine.
antiseptic [.ænti'septik] a n antisettico.
antisocial ['ænti'souʃəl] a antisociale.
anti-theft ['ænti'θeft] a n antifurto.
antithesis [æn'tiθisis] pl **antitheses** n antitesi.
antler ['æntlə] n corno di cervo.
Antwerp ['æntwəːp] n (geogr) Anversa.
anvil ['ænvil] n incudine.
anxiety [æŋ'zaiəti] n ansia, ansietà.
anxious ['æŋkʃəs] a ansioso, preoccupato; desideroso.
any ['eni] a alcuno, -ni, del, dei, nessuno, qualche, un po' di; ogni, qualsiasi, qualunque; pron alcuno, nessuno.
anybody ['eni.bɔdi], **anyone** ['eniwʌn] pron alcuno, qualcuno; nessuno; chiunque.
anyhow ['enihau] ad in ogni caso, ad ogni modo; in qualsiasi modo.
anything ['eniθiŋ] pron qualche cosa, alcuna cosa; qualunque cosa.
anyway ['eniwei] ad in ogni caso, ad ogni modo.
anywhere ['eniwɛə] ad dovunque, in qualsiasi luogo.
apart [ə'pɑːt] ad a parte, in disparte.

apartheid [ə'pɑːtheit] *n* segregazione razziale.
apartment [ə'pɑːtmənt] *n* stanza, appartamento; **a. hotel** appartamento d'affitto con servizio.
apathetic [,æpə'θetik] *a* apatico, indifferente.
apathy [ˈæpəθi] *n* apatia, indifferenza.
ape [eip] *n* scimmia; *vt* imitare, scimmiottare.
Apennines [ˈæpinainz] *n pl* Appennini.
aperient [ə'piəriənt] *a n* lassativo.
aperitif [ə'peritif] *n* aperitivo.
aperture [ˈæpətjuə] *n* apertura, foro.
apex [ˈeipeks] *pl* **apexes, apices** *n* apice, vertice.
aphorism [ˈæfərizəm] *n* aforisma.
apiary [ˈeipjəri] *n* apiario.
apiece [ə'piːs] *ad* per ognuno, a testa.
aplomb [ˈæpləm] *n* perpendicolarità; sicurezza di sè.
apocalypse [ə'pɔkəlips] *n* apocalisse.
apocryphal [ə'pɔkrifəl] *a* apocrifo.
apogee [ˈæpoudʒiː] *n* apogeo.
apologetic [ə,pɔlə'dʒetik] *a* pieno di scuse.
apologize [ə'pɔledʒaiz] *vi* scusarsi.
apology [ə'pɔlədʒi] *n* scusa, giustificazione; apologia.
apoplectic [,æpə'plektik] *a* apoplettico.
apoplexy [ˈæpəpleksi] *n* apoplessia.
apostle [ə'pɔsl] *n* apostolo.
apostolic [,æpəs'tɔlik] *a* apostolico.
apostrophe [ə'pɔstrəfi] *n* apostrofe; (*gram*) apostrofo.
apostrophize [ə'pɔstrəfaiz] *vt* apostrofare.
appall [ə'pɔːl] *vt* spaventare, atterrire.
appalling [ə'pɔːliŋ] *a* spaventoso.
apparatus [,æpə'reitəs] *n* (*anat*) apparato; (*tec*) apparecchio.
apparent [ə'pærənt] *a* chiaro, manifesto; **heir a.** *n* erede legittimo.
apparition [,æpə'riʃən] *n* apparizione, fantasma.
appeal [ə'piːl] *n* appello; attrattiva; *vi* appellarsi; attrarre.
appealing [ə'piːliŋ] *ad* supplichevole; attraente.
appear [ə'piə] *vi* apparire; comparire; sembrare.
appearance [ə'piərəns] *n* apparenza; aspetto; apparizione; comparizione.
appease [ə'piːz] *vt* calmare; pacificare.
appeasement [ə'piːzmənt] *n* pacificazione; appagamento.
append [ə'pend] *vt* apporre, aggiungere.
appendicitis [ə pendi'saitis] *n* appendicite.
appendix [ə'pendiks] *pl* **appendixes, appendices** *n* appendice.
appertain [,æpə'tein] *vi* appartenere; riferirsi.
appetite [ˈæpitait] *n* appetito.

appetizing [ˈæpitaiziŋ] *a* appetitoso.
applaud [ə'plɔːd] *vti* applaudire.
applause [ə'plɔːz] *n* applauso, -si *pl.*
apple [ˈæpl] *n* mela; **a.-tree** melo.
appliance [ə'plaiəns] *n* apparecchio; applicazione.
applicable [ˈæplikəbl] *a* applicabile.
applicant [ˈæplikənt] *n* candidato.
application [,æpli'keiʃən] *n* applicazione; domanda; diligenza.
apply [ə'plai] *vti* applicare; applicarsi; rivolgersi, fare domanda.
appoint [ə'pɔint] *vt* stabilire; nominare.
appointed [ə'pɔintid] *a* fissato; arredato, equipaggiato.
appointment [ə'pɔintmənt] *n* appuntamento; nomina; impiego; decreto.
apportion [ə'pɔːʃən] *vt* distribuire.
apportionment [ə'pɔːʃənmənt] *n* ripartizione.
apposite [ˈæpəzit] *a* apposito, appropriato.
apposition [,æpə'ziʃən] *n* apposizione.
appraisal [ə'preizəl] *n* stima, valutazione.
appraise [ə'preiz] *vt* stimare, valutare.
appreciable [ə'priːʃəbl] *a* apprezzabile; considerevole.
appreciate [ə'priːʃieit] *vt* apprezzare; tenere in giusto conto; *vi* aumentare di valore.
appreciation [ə,priːʃi'eiʃən] *n* apprezzamento; stima; rivalutazione.
apprehend [,æpri'hend] *vt* arrestare; comprendere; temere.
apprehension [,æpri'henʃən] *n* comprensione; apprensione; timore; arresto.
apprehensive [,æpri'hensiv] *a* timoroso; perspicace.
apprentice [ə'prentis] *n* apprendista.
apprenticeship [ə'prentiʃip] *n* apprendistato, tirocinio.
approach [ə'proutʃ] *n* avvicinamento; approccio; accesso; *vti* avvicinare, avvicinarsi.
approachable [ə'proutʃəbl] *a* avvicinabile, accessibile.
approbation [,æprə'beiʃən] *n* approvazione, sanzione.
appropriate [ə'proupriit] *a* appropriato, proprio; [ə'proupreit] *vt* appropriarsi; stanziare denaro.
appropriately [ə'proupriitli] *ad* appropriatamente.
appropriation [ə,proupri'eiʃən] *n* appropriazione; stanziamento.
approval [ə'pruːvəl] *n* approvazione, (*com*) prova.
approve [ə'pruːv] *vt* approvare, sanzionare.
approximate [ə'prɔksimit] *a* approssimativo; *vti* approssimar(si).
approximately [ə'prɔksimitli] *ad* approssimativamente.

apricot ['eiprikɔt] n albicocca; **a. tree** albicocco.
April ['eiprəl] n aprile.
apron ['eiprən] n grembiule.
apropos ['æprəpou] ad a proposito.
apse [æps] n abside.
apt [æpt] a adatto, atto; **a. at** bravo in; **a. to** avente tendenza a.
aptitude ['æptitjuːd] n attitudine.
Apulia [ə'pjuːliə] n (geogr) Puglia; **Apulian** a n pugliese.
aqualung ['ækwəlʌŋ] n autorespiratore.
aquarium [ə'kwɛəriəm] n acquario.
aquatic [ə'kwætik] a acquatico.
aqueduct ['ækwidʌkt] n acquedotto.
aquiline ['ækwilain] a aquilino.
Arab ['ærəb] a n arabo.
arabesque [ˌærə'besk] a arabesco.
Arabia [ə'reibiə] n (geogr) Arabia.
Arabian [ə'reibiən] a n arabo, arabico; **Arabic** a n arabico, la lingua araba.
arable ['ærəbl] a arabile.
arbiter ['ɑːbitə] n arbitro, giudice.
arbitrary ['ɑːbitrəri] a arbitrario.
arbitrate ['ɑːbitreit] vti arbitrare.
arbitration [ˌɑːbi'treiʃən] n arbitrato.
arbor ['ɑːbə] n pergolato.
arc [ɑːk] n arco; **a. lamp** lampada ad arco.
arcade [ɑː'keid] n galleria; porticato; portici pl.
arch [ɑːtʃ] a birichino, furbetto; n arco, volta; vti arcuar(si).
archaeologist [ˌɑːki'ɔlədʒist] n archeologo.
archaeology [ˌɑːki'ɔledʒi] n archeologia.
archaic [ɑː'keiik] a arcaico.
archangel ['ɑːkˌeindʒəl] n arcangelo.
archbishop ['ɑːtʃ'biʃəp] n arcivescovo.
archbishopric [ɑːtʃ'biʃəprik] n arcivescovado.
archdeacon ['ɑːtʃ'diːkən] n arcidiacono.
archduke ['ɑːtʃ'djuːk] n arciduca.
arched [ɑːtʃt] a ad arco, arcuato.
archer ['ɑːtʃə] n arciere.
archery ['ɑːtʃəri] n tiro con l'arco.
archetype ['ɑːkitaip] n archetipo.
Archibald ['ɑːtʃibəld] nm pr Archibaldo.
archipelago [ˌɑːki'peligou] pl **archipelagoes** n arcipelago.
architect ['ɑːkitekt] n architetto.
architecture ['ɑːkitektʃə] n architettura.
archives ['ɑːkaivz] n pl archivi.
archway ['ɑːtʃwei] n arcata.
Arctic ['ɑːktik] a n artico.
Ardennes [ɑː'den] pl (geogr) Ardenne.
a:dent ['ɑːdənt] a ardente.
ardor ['ɑːdə] n ardore.
arduous ['ɑːdjuəs] a arduo; strenuo.
area ['ɛəriə] n area; zona.
arena [ə'riːnə] n arena.

Argentina [ˌɑːdʒən'tiːnə] n (geogr) Argentina.
Argentine ['ɑːdʒəntain] n (geogr) Argentina.
Argentinian [ˌɑːdʒən'tiniən] a n argentino.
argue ['ɑːgjuː] vti argomentare, discutere.
argument ['ɑːgjumənt] n discussione, ragionamento.
argumentative [ˌɑːgju'mentətiv] a polemico.
arid ['ærid] a arido.
aridity [æ'riditi] n aridità.
aright [ə'rait] ad bene, giustamente.
arise [ə'raiz] vi alzarsi; sorgere.
aristocracy [ˌæris'tɔkrəsi] n aristocrazia.
aristocrat ['æristəkræt] n nobile, aristocratico.
aristocratic [ˌæristə'krætik] a aristocratico.
arithmetic [ə'riθmətik] n aritmetica.
arithmetical [ˌæriθ'metikəl] a aritmetico.
ark [ɑːk] n arca.
arm [ɑːm] n braccio; bracciuolo; pl **arms** (mil) armi pl; vti armar(si).
armament ['ɑːməmənt] n armamento.
armchair ['ɑːm'tʃɛə] n poltrona.
Armenia [ɑː'miniə] n (geogr) Armenia.
Armenian [ɑː'miːniən] a n armeno.
armful ['ɑːmful] n bracciata.
armistice ['ɑːmistis] n armistizio.
armlet ['ɑːmlit] n bracciale.
armor ['ɑːmə] n armatura, corazza; blindatura; forze corazzate pl.
armored ['ɑːməd] a corazzato, blindato; **a. car** autoblindo.
armory ['ɑːməri] n arsenale; armeria.
armpit ['ɑːmpit] n ascella.
army ['ɑːmi] n esercito; armata.
Arnold ['ɑːnld] nm pr Arnaldo, Arnoldo.
aromatic(al) [ˌærou'mætik(əl)] a aromatico.
around [ə'raund] ad all'intorno, in ogni parte; prep intorno a.
arouse [ə'rauz] vt (ri)svegliare; suscitare.
arraign [ə'rein] vt accusare, chiamare in giudizio.
arrange [ə'reindʒ] vt accomodare; disporre; ordinare; (mus) adattare; vi prendere accordi.
arrangement [ə'reindʒmənt] n accomodamento; accordo.
array [ə'rei] n ordine, schiera; mostra; abbigliamento.
arrears [ə'riəz] n pl arretrati.
arrest [ə'rest] n arresto, fermata; vt arrestare, fermare.
arrival [ə'raivəl] n arrivo.
arrive [ə'raiv] vi arrivare, giungere.
arrogance ['ærəgəns] n arroganza.
arrogant ['ærəgənt] a arrogante.

arrogate ['ærougeit] *vt* arrogarsi, pretendere.
arrow ['ærou] *n* freccia.
arsenal ['ɑːsinl] *n* arsenale.
arsenic ['ɑːsnik] *n* arsenico.
arson ['ɑːsn] *n* incendio doloso.
art [ɑːt] *n* arte; **fine arts** *pl* belle arti *pl*; **Arts** *pl* lettere *pl*.
artery ['ɑːtəri] *n* arteria.
artesian [ɑː'tiːziən] *a* artesiano.
artful ['ɑːtful] *a* abile; astuto; ingannevole.
arthritis [ɑː'θraitis] *n* artrite.
Arthur ['ɑːθə] *nm pr* Arturo.
artichoke ['ɑːtitʃouk] *n* carciofo.
article ['ɑːtikl] *n* articolo; **leading a.** articolo di fondo; *vt* mettere come apprendista.
articulate [ɑː'tikjulit] *a* articolato; distinto, chiaro; *n* animale articolato; *vti* [ɑː'tikjuleit] articolare; pronunciare distintamente; esprimersi.
articulation [ɑː.tikju'leiʃən] *n* articolazione; pronuncia distinta.
artifice ['ɑːtifis] *n* artificio, astuzia.
artificial [ɑːti'fiʃəl] *a* artificiale; artificioso.
artificiality [.ɑːtifiʃi'æliti] *n* artificiosità.
artillery [ɑː'tiləri] *n* artiglieria.
artilleryman [ɑː'tilərimən] *a* artigliere.
artisan [.ɑːti'zæn] *n* artigiano.
artist ['ɑːtist] *n* artista; pittore.
artistic [ɑː'tistik] *a* artistico.
artless ['ɑːtlis] *a* ingenuo, semplice.
artlessness ['ɑːtlisnis] *n* ingenuità, semplicità.
as [æz] *ad cj* come, nello stesso modo in cui; siccome, mentre; *rel pron* che; **as ... as** così ... come, tanto ... quanto; **as for** in quanto a; **as long as** finchè, purchè.
asbestos [æz'bestəs] *n* amianto.
ascend [ə'send] *vti* ascendere, salire.
ascendency [ə'sendənsi] *n* ascendente, influenza.
ascension [ə'senʃən] *n* ascensione.
ascent [ə'sent] *n* ascesa, salita.
ascertain [.æsə'tein] *vt* accertarsi, scoprire.
ascetic [ə'setik] *a* ascetico; *n* asceta.
ascribe [əs'kraib] *vt* ascrivere; attribuire.
ash [æʃ] *n* cenere.
ash(tree) ['æʃ(triː)] *n* frassino.
ashamed [ə'ʃeimd] *a* vergognoso; **to be a. of** vergognarsi.
ashen ['æʃn] *a* cinereo, di color cinerino.
ashore [ə'ʃɔː] *ad* a riva, a terra.
ashtray ['æʃtrei] *n* portacenere.
Asia ['eiʃə] *n (geogr)* Asia.
Asian ['eiʃən], **Asiatic** [.eiʃi'ætik] *a n* asiatico.
aside [ə'said] *n* parole pronunziate a parte; *ad* a parte; in disparte.
ask [ɑːsk] *vti* chiedere; invitare; informarsi.

askance [əs'kæns] *ad* obliquamente.
asleep [ə'sliːp] *a* addormentato; **to fall a.** addormentarsi.
asparagus [əs'pærəgəs] *n (coll)* asparago, asparagi.
aspect ['æspekt] *n* apparenza, aspetto; *(of houses etc)* esposizione.
aspen ['æspən] *n* pioppo tremulo.
asperity [æs'periti] *n* asperità; asprezza; rigore.
asperse [əs'pəːs] *vt* aspergere; calunniare, denigrare.
aspersion [əs'pəːʃən] *n* aspersione; calunnia.
asphalt ['æsfælt] *n* asfalto.
asphodel ['æsfədel] *n* asfodelo.
asphyxiate [æs'fiksieit] *vt* asfissiare.
aspirate ['æspəreit] *vt* aspirare.
aspiration [.æspə'reiʃən] *n* aspirazione.
aspire [əs'paiə] *vi* aspirare, bramare.
aspirin ['æspərin] *n* aspirina.
aspiring [əs'paiəriŋ] *a* ambizioso.
ass [æs] *n* asino; **to make an a. of oneself** rendersi ridicolo.
assail [ə'seil] *vt* assalire, attaccare.
assailant [ə'seilənt] *n* assalitore.
assassin [ə'sæsin] *n* assassino.
assassinate [ə'sæsineit] *vt* assassinare.
assassination [ə.sæsi'neiʃən] *n* assassinio.
assault [ə'sɔːlt] *vt* assalire; *n* assalto.
assemble [ə'sembl] *vti* riunir(si); *(mech)* montare.
assembly [ə'sembli] *n* assemblea, riunione; *(mech)* montaggio.
assent [ə'sent] *n* assenso, consenso; *vi* acconsentire, approvare.
assert [ə'səːt] *vt* asserire; rivendicare (un diritto).
assertion [ə'səːʃən] *n* asserzione, rivendicazione.
assess [ə'ses] *vt* valutare, stimare; tassare.
assessable [ə'sesəbl] *a* tassabile, imponibile.
assessment [ə'sesmənt] *n* tassa; valutazione.
assessor [ə'sesə] *n* assessore; agente del fisco.
asset [æset] *n* bene, vantaggio; *pl (com)* attivo.
assiduity [.æsi'djuiti] *n* assiduità, diligenza.
assiduous [ə'sidjuəs] *a* assiduo, diligente.
assign [ə'sain] *vt* assegnare; fissare.
assignee [.æsi'niː] *n (com)* mandatario.
assignment [ə'sainmənt] *n* assegnazione; stanziamento; nomina, incarico.
assimilate [ə'simileit] *vt* assimilare.
assimilation [ə.simi'leiʃən] *n* assimilazione.
assist [ə'sist] *vt* assistere, aiutare.
assistance [ə'sistəns] *n* assistenza, aiuto.
assistant [ə'sistənt] *a n* assistente; aiuto, aggiunto.

assizes [ə'saiziz] n pl corte d'assise.
associate [ə'souʃiit] a associato n; socio; vti [ə'souʃieit] associar(si).
association [ə,sousi'eiʃən] n associazione; A. football giuoco del calcio.
assort [ə'sɔːt] vt assortire.
assortment [ə'sɔːtmənt] n assortimento.
assuage [ə'sweidʒ] vt calmare, mitigare.
assume [ə'sjuːm] vt assumere; arrogarsi; presumere.
assuming [ə'sjuːmiŋ] a presuntuoso.
assumption [ə'sʌmpʃən] n assunto; assunzione; supposizione.
assurance [ə'ʃuərəns] n assicurazione; certezza; fiducia in sè.
assure [ə'ʃuə] vt assicurare; rassicurare.
assuredly [ə'ʃuəridli] ad certamente.
asterisk ['æstərisk] n asterisco.
astern [əs'təːn] ad (naut) a poppa.
asthma ['æsmə] n asma.
asthmatic [æs'mætik] a asmatico.
astigmatism [æs'tigmətizəm] n astigmatismo.
astir [ə'stəː] ad a in moto.
astonish [əs'tɔniʃ] vt sorprendere; stupire.
astonishing [əs'tɔniʃiŋ] a sorprendente, straordinario.
astonishingly [əs'tɔniʃiŋli] ad sorprendentemente.
astonishment [əs'tɔniʃmənt] n sorpresa, stupore.
astound [əs'taund] vt stupefare.
astrakhan [,æstrə'kæn] n astracan.
astral ['æstrəl] a astrale.
astray [əs'trei] ad fuori della giusta via; to go a. sviarsi.
astride [əs'traid] ad a cavalcioni.
astringent [əs'trindʒənt] a n astringente.
astrologer [əs'trɔlədʒə] n astrologo.
astrology [əs'trɔlədʒi] n astrologia.
astronaut ['æstrənɔːt] n astronauta.
astronautics [,æstrə'nɔːtiks] n astronautica.
astronomer [əs'trɔnəmə] n astronomo.
astronomical ['æstrə'nɔmikəl] a astronomico.
astronomy [əs'trɔnəmi] n astronomia.
astute [əs'tjuːt] a astuto, sagace.
astuteness [əs'tjuːtnis] n astuzia, scaltrezza.
asunder [ə'sʌndə] ad a pezzi; separatamente.
asylum [ə'sailəm] n asilo; casa di ricovero; lunatic a. manicomio.
at [æt] prep a, da, di, in.
atheism ['eiθiizəm] n ateismo.
atheist ['eiθiist] n ateo.
Athenian [ə'θiːniən] a n ateniese.
Athens ['æθinz] n (geogr) Atene.
athlete ['æθliːt] n atleta.
athletic [æθ'letik] a atletico.
athletics [æθ'letiks] n atletica.

at-home [ət'houm] n ricevimento (a casa).
Atlantic [ət'læntik] a n atlantico.
atlas ['ætləs] n atlante.
atmosphere ['ætməsfiə] n atmosfera.
atmospherics [,ætməs'feriks] n pl (rad) scariche pl.
atom ['ætəm] n atomo.
atomic [ə'tɔmik] a atomico.
atomize ['ætəmaiz] vt atomizzare.
atomizer ['ætəmaizə] n polverizzatore; spruzzatore.
atone [ə'toun] vi espiare.
atonement [ə'tounmənt] n espiazione, riparazione.
atrocious [ə'trouʃəs] a atroce.
atrocity [ə'trɔsiti] n atrocità.
atrophy ['ætrəfi] n atrofia.
attach [ə'tætʃ] vt attaccare; attribuire; fissare; vi attaccarsi, aderire.
attaché [ə'tæʃei] n diplomatico, addetto ad un'ambasciata; a.-case valigetta.
attached [ə'tætʃt] a addetto, assegnato; affezionato.
attachment [ə'tætʃmənt] n attaccamento; affetto; (mech) accessorio.
attack [ə'tæk] n attacco, offensiva; accesso; vt attaccare, assalire.
attain [ə'tein] vt conseguire, ottenere, raggiungere; vi arrivare.
attainable [ə'teinəbl] a conseguibile, raggiungibile.
attainment [ə'teinmənt] n conseguimento; pl cultura.
attempt [ə'tempt] n tentativo; attentato; vt provare, tentare; attentare.
attend [ə'tend] vi attendere a; prestare attenzione; dare assistenza; essere presente; vt accompagnare, frequentare.
attendance [ə'tendəns] n servizio; assistenza; frequenza; persone presenti.
attendant [ə'tendənt] n servitore, custode; (theat) maschera. pl seguito.
attention [ə'tenʃən] n attenzione, premura; to pay a. stare attento.
attentive [ə'tentiv] a attento; premuroso.
attenuate [ə'tenjueit] vt attenuare.
attest [ə'test] vti attestare, testimoniare.
attestation [,ætes'teiʃən] n attestazione, conferma.
attic ['ætik] n soffitta, solaio; attico.
attire [ə'taiə] n abbigliamento.
attitude ['ætitjuːd] n atteggiamento; posa.
attorney [ə'təːni] n procuratore, procura; A. General Procuratore Generale; Ministro della Giustizia; district a. pubblico ministero.
attract [ə'trækt] vt attirare.
attraction [ə'trækʃən] n attrazione, attrattiva.
attractive [ə'træktiv] a attraente, attrattivo.

attribute ['ætribjuːt] *n* attributo, qualità; *vt* [ə'tribju(ː)t] attribuire.
attrition [ə'triʃən] *n* attrito.
attune [ə'tjuːn] *vt* armonizzare.
aubergine ['oubəʒiːn] *n* melanzana.
auburn ['ɔːbən] *a* color rame, ramato.
auction ['ɔːkʃən] *n* asta, vendita all'incanto; *vt* vendere all'asta.
auctioneer [,ɔːkʃə'niə] *n* banditore.
audacious [ɔː'deiʃəs] *a* audace.
audacity [ɔː'dæsiti] *n* audacità.
audibility [,ɔːdi'biliti] *n* udibilità.
audible ['ɔːdəbl] *a* udibile.
audibly ['ɔːdəbli] *ad* distintamente.
audience ['ɔːdiəns] *n* pubblico; udienza.
audio-visual [,ɔːdiou'vizjuəl] *a* audiovisivo.
audit ['ɔːdit] *n* controllo; *vt* rivedere (conti).
audition [ɔː'diʃən] *n* audizione; *vti* ascoltare, esibirsi in audizione.
auditor ['ɔːditə] *n* revisore di conti.
auditorium [,ɔːdi'tɔːriəm] *n* sala, auditorio.
auger ['ɔːgə] *n* succhiello.
augment [ɔːg'ment] *vt* aumentare; *vi* crescere.
augmentation [,ɔːgmen'teiʃən] *n* aumento.
augur ['ɔːgə] *n* augure; *vti* predire, presagire.
augury ['ɔːgjuri] *n* presagio, pronostico.
August ['ɔːgəst] *n* agosto.
august [ɔː'gʌst] *a* augusto, maestoso.
Augustin(e) [ɔː'gʌstin] *nm pr* Agostino.
Augustus [ɔː'gʌstəs] *nm pr* Augusto.
aunt [ɑːnt] *n* zia.
aureomycin [,ɔːriou'maisin] *n* aureomicina.
auspice ['ɔːspis] *n* auspicio, augurio.
auspicious [ɔːs'piʃəs] *a* di buon augurio.
austere [ɔs'tiə] *a* austero.
austerity [ɔs'teriti] *n* austerità.
Australia [ɔs'treiliə] *n* (*geogr*) Australia.
Australian [ɔs'treiliən] *a n* australiano.
Austria ['ɔstriə] *n* (*geogr*) Austria.
Austrian ['ɔstriən] *a n* austriaco.
authentic [ɔː'θentik] *a* autentico.
authenticate [ɔː'θentikeit] *vt* autenticare.
authentication [ɔː,θenti'keiʃən] *n* autenticazione.
authenticity [,ɔːθen'tisiti] *n* autenticità.
author ['ɔːθə] *n* autore.
authoritative [ɔː'θɔritətiv] *a* autorevole, autoritario.
authority [ɔː'θɔriti] *n* autorità.
authorization [,ɔːθərai'zeiʃən] *n* autorizzazione.
authorize ['ɔːθəraiz] *vt* autorizzare.
autobiography [,ɔːtoubai'ɔgræfi] *n* autobiografia.
autobus ['ɔːtoubʌs] *n* autobus.

autocamp ['ɔːtoukæmp] *n* accampamento per automobilisti.
autocrat ['ɔːtəkræt] *n* autocrate.
autodrome ['ɔːtoudroum] *n* autodromo.
autograph ['ɔːtəgrɑːf] *n* autografo; *vt* firmare; (*typ*) autografare.
automatic [,ɔːtə'mætik] *a* automatico; *n* rivoltella.
automatically [,ɔːtə'mætikəli] *ad* automaticamente.
automation [,ɔːtə'meiʃən] *n* automazione.
automobile ['ɔːtəməbiːl] *n* automobile.
autonomy [ɔː'tɔnəmi] *n* autonomia.
autopsy ['ɔːtəpsi] *n* autopsia.
autumn ['ɔːtəm] *n* autunno.
autumnal [ɔː'tʌmnəl] *a* autunnale, d'autunno.
auxiliary [ɔːg'ziljəri] *a* ausiliario, -re; *n* ausiliare; *pl* milizie ausiliarie.
avail [ə'veil] *n* utilità, vantaggio; *vi* giovare (a), essere utile (a); *vt* aiutare, favorire; **to a. oneself of** valersi di.
availability [ə'veilə'biliti] *n* disponibilità.
available [ə'veiləbl] *a* disponibile.
avalanche ['ævəlɑːnʃ] *n* valanga.
avarice ['ævəris] *n* avarizia.
avaricious [,ævə'riʃəs] *a* avaro.
avenge [ə'vendʒ] *vt* vendicare.
avenger [ə'vendʒə] *n* vendicatore.
avenue ['ævinjuː] *n* viale; accesso.
aver [ə'vəː] *vt* affermare, asserire.
average ['ævəridʒ] *a* di media categoria, medio; *n* media; (*naut*) avaria; *vt* fare la media.
averse [ə'vəːs] *a* avverso, contrario.
aversion [ə'vəːʃən] *n* avversione, antipatia.
avert [ə'vəːt] *vt* schivare; distogliere.
aviary ['eivjəri] *n* aviario.
aviation [,eivi'eiʃən] *n* aviazione.
avid ['ævid] *a* avido.
avidity [ə'viditi] *n* avidità.
avoid [ə'vɔid] *vt* evitare, schivare.
avoidance [ə'vɔidəns] *n* l'evitare; fuga, scampo.
avowed [ə'vaud] *a* manifesto, aperto, dichiarato.
await [ə'weit] *vt* aspettare.
awake [ə'weik] *a* sveglio; *vti* svegliar(si).
awaken [ə'weikən] *vti* risvegliare, risvegliarsi.
awakening [ə'weikniŋ] *n* risveglio (*also fig*).
award [ə'wɔːd] *n* giudizio; ricompensa; *vt* aggiudicare, assegnare.
aware [ə'wɛə] *a* conscio.
away [ə'wei] *ad* lontano, via.
awe [ɔː] *n* timore misto a venerazione.
awful ['ɔːful] *a* terribile, spaventevole.
awfully ['ɔːfuli] *ad* terribilmente; straordinariamente, molto.
awhile [ə'wail] *ad* un momento.
awkward ['ɔːkwəd] *a* goffo; imbarazzante; imbarazzato; scomodo.

awkwardly ['ɔːkwədli] *ad* goffamente; in modo imbarazzato.
awkwardness ['ɔːkwədnis] *n* goffaggine; difficoltà.
awl [ɔːl] *n* lesina.
awning ['ɔːniŋ] *n* tenda.
awry [ə'rai] *n* storto.
ax [æks] *n* ascia.
axiom ['æksiəm] *n* assioma.
axis ['æksis] *pl* **axes** ['æksiːz] *n* asse.
axle ['æksl] *n* (*mech*) asse.
ay(e) [ai] *ad* sì.
azalea [ə'zeiliə] *n* azalea.
azure ['eiʒə] *a* azzurro.

B

babble ['bæbl] *vti* balbettare; parlare scioccamente.
babbling ['bæbliŋ] *n* balbettio; discorso senza senso.
Babel ['beibəl] *n* Babele; **babel** *n* confusione.
baboon [bə'buːn] *n* babuino.
baby ['beibi] *n* neonato, bimbo; **b. carriage** carrozzina.
babyhood ['beibihud] *n* prima infanzia.
babyish ['beibiiʃ] *a* bambinesco, infantile, puerile.
bachelor ['bætʃələ] *n* celibe, scapolo; baccelliere.
bachelorhood ['bætʃələhud] *n* celibato.
bacillus [bə'siləs] *pl* **bacilli** *n* bacillo.
back [bæk] *n* dorso, parte posteriore, schiena; schienale; spalle *pl*; spalliera; *a* posteriore, di dietro, indietro, di ritorno; **be b.** essere di ritorno; **come b.** ritornare.
back [bæk] *vti* spalleggiare; indietreggiare; (*com*) avallare; **b. a horse** puntare su un cavallo.
backbite ['bækbait] *vti* calunniare.
backbone ['bækboun] *n* spina dorsale.
background ['bækgraund] *n* sfondo; ambiente.
backslider ['bæk'slaidə] *n* recidivo.
backward ['bækwəd] *a* riluttante; tardivo.
backwardness ['bækwədnis] *n* lentezza d'intelligenza, ritardo di sviluppo.
backwards ['bækwəds] *ad* (all') indietro, a ritroso.
bacon ['beikən] *n* lardo affumicato, pancetta.
bacterium [bæk'tiəriəm] *pl* **bacteria** *n* batterio.
bacteriology [bæk,tiəri'ɔlədʒi] *n* batteriologia.
bad [bæd] *a* cattivo, colpevole, dannoso, grave, sfavorevole; *n* male; **to go b.** andare a male; **badly** *ad* male, malamente.
badge [bædʒ] *n* distintivo, emblema.

badger ['bædʒə] *n* (*zool*) tasso; *vt* tormentare, molestare.
badness ['bædnis] *n* cattiveria; (*quality*) inferiorità.
baffle ['bæfl] *vt* impedire, frustrare; sconcertare; rendere vano.
baffling ['bæfliŋ] *a* sconcertante.
bag [bæg] *n* borsa, borsetta, sacco, carniere; pesci o selvaggina presi; *vt* insaccare, prendere, rubare.
baggage ['bægidʒ] *n* bagagli(o); **b. car** bagagliaio.
bagpipe(s) ['bægpaip(s)] *n* (*usu pl*) cornamusa.
bagpiper ['bægpaipə] *n* suonatore di cornamusa.
bail [beil] *n* cauzione, garanzia, garante; **to go b. for** essere garante di; *vt* procurare la libertà provvisoria a; aggottare (una barca).
bailiff ['beilif] *n* ufficiale giudiziario; fattore di campagna.
bait [beit] *n* esca; *vt* fornire di esca, adescare; tormentare; alimentare; *vi* prendere cibo.
bake [beik] *vt* cuocere al forno; *vi* indurirsi per effetto del calore.
bake-house ['beikhaus] **bakery** ['beikəri] *n* forno.
baker ['beikə] *n*ˈ fornaio; **b.'s (shop)** panetteria.
baking ['beikiŋ] *n* cottura al forno; **b. powder** lievito.
balance ['bæləns] *n* bilancia; equilibrio; armonia; (*com*) bilancio, saldo; **b. sheet** bilancio; **to lose one's b.** perdere l'equilibrio; *vti* pesare, bilanciare, mantener l'equilibrio.
balcony ['bælkəni] *n* balcone.
bald [bɔːld] *a* calvo; (*style*) disadorno.
baldness ['bɔːldnis] *n* calvizie *pl*.
Baldwin ['bɔːldwin] *nm pr* Baldovino.
bale [beil] *n* balla; *vt* imballare.
balk [bɔːk] *n* trave rozzamente digrossata; *vt* evitare, ostacolare.
Balkan ['bɔːlkən] *a* balcanico.
Balkans ['bɔːlkəns] *n* Balcani.
ball [bɔːl] *n* palla, pallone, (*thread*) gomitolo; (*dance*) ballo; **ballpoint** (**pen**) penna a sfera.
ballad ['bæləd] *n* ballata.
ballast ['bæləst] *n* (*naut*) zavorra.
ballet ['bælei] *n* balletto, danza classica.
balloon [bə'luːn] *n* pallone; pallone aerostatico; (*cartoons*) fumetto.
ballot ['bælət] *n* scheda (di votazione), scrutinio; *vi* votare a scrutinio segreto; **b. box** urna.
balm [bɑːm] *n* balsamo.
balmy ['bɑːmi] *a* balsamico, fragrante.
balsam ['bɔːlsəm] *n* balsamo.
Baltic ['bɔːltik] *a n* Baltico.
Baltimore ['bɔːltimɔː] *n* Baltimora.
balustrade [,bæləs'treid] *n* balustrata.
bamboo [bæm'buː] *n* bambù.

bamboozle [bæm'buːzl] *vt* (*sl*) ingannare, mistificare.

ban [bæn] *n* bando; scomunica; *vt* proibire, mettere all'indice.

banal [bə'nɑːl] *a* banale.

banality [bə'næliti] *n* banalità.

banana [bə'nɑːnə] *n* banana.

band [bænd] *n* banda; legame; striscia; *vt* legare insieme; *vi* unirsi.

bandage ['bændidʒ] *n* benda, fascia.

bandbox ['bændbɔks] *n* cappelliera.

bandit ['bændit] *n* bandito.

bandolier [‚bændə'liə] *n* bandoliera.

bandsman ['bændzmən] *n* bandista.

bandy ['bændi] *a* curvo, storto; *vt* ribattere, disputare, scambiare parole.

baneful ['beinful] *a* dannoso, velenoso.

bang [bæŋ] *n* colpo rumoroso, esplosione, fracasso; *vt* colpire rumorosamente, sbatacchiare.

bangle ['bæŋgl] *n* braccialetto.

banish ['bæniʃ] *vt* bandire, esiliare.

banishment ['bæniʃmənt] *n* bando, esilio.

banister ['bænistə] *n* ringhiera, balaustra.

bank [bæŋk] *n* argine, riva; banca, banco; *vt* depositare in una banca; **b.-note, b. bill** banconota; **to b. on** contare su.

banker ['bæŋkə] *n* banchiere.

bank holiday ['bæŋk'hɔlədi] *n* festa civile.

banking ['bæŋkiŋ] *n* professione bancaria; *a* bancario.

bankrupt ['bæŋkrəpt] *a n* fallito; **to go b.** fallire.

bankruptcy ['bæŋkrəptsi] *n* fallimento, bancarotta.

banner ['bænə] *n* bandiera, stendardo.

banns [bænz] *n pl* pubblicazioni matrimoniali *pl*.

banquet ['bæŋkwit] *n* banchetto; *vi* banchettare.

banter ['bæntə] *n* beffa; *vti* prendere in giro, beffarsi.

baptism ['bæptizəm] *n* battesimo.

baptismal [bæp'tizməl] *a* battesimale.

baptist(e)ry ['bæptist(ə)ri] *n* battistero.

baptize [bæp'taiz] *vt* battezzare.

bar [bɑː] *n* (s)barra; ostacolo; bar; **the bar** ordine degli avvocati; *vt* (s)barrare; escludere; ostacolare; **b. tender** barista; **to be called to the b. to be admitted to the b.** essere iscritto all'albo degli avvocati.

barbarian [bɑː'bɛəriən] *n* barbaro.

barbaric [bɑː'bærik] *a* barbarico, primitivo.

barbarism ['bɑːbərizem] *n* barbarie, barbarismo.

barbarity [bɑː'bæriti] *n* barbarie, crudeltà.

barbarous ['bɑːbərəs] *a* barbaro.

barbecue ['bɑːbikjuː] *n* animale arrostito intero; festa campestre.

barbed [bɑːbd] *a* dentellato, spinato; pungente; **b. wire** filo di ferro spinato.

barber ['bɑːbə] *n* barbiere, parrucchiere.

barbiturate [bɑː'bitjurit] *n* barbiturico.

bare [bɛə] *a* nudo, spoglio, scoperto; *vt* denudare, scoprire.

barefaced ['bɛəfeist] *a* sfacciato.

barefoot(ed) ['bɛə'fut(id)] *a* scalzo; *ad* a piedi nudi.

bareheaded ['bɛə'hedid] *a ad* a capo scoperto.

barely ['bɛəli] *ad* appena.

bareness ['bɛənis] *n* nudità.

bargain ['bɑːgin] *n* affare; occasione; **into the b.** per giunta, in più; *vi* contrattare; **to b. for** aspettarsi.

barge [bɑːdʒ] *n* chiatta; lancia di parata; *vi* **to b. into** urtare.

baritone ['bæritoun] *a n* baritono.

bark [bɑːk] *n* latrato; corteccia, scorza; *vi* abbaiare; *vt* scorticare, scorzare.

barley ['bɑːli] *n* orzo.

barm [bɑːm] *n* fermento, lievito di birra.

barmaid ['bɑːmeid] *n* barista.

barman ['bɑːmən] *n* barista.

barn [bɑːn] *n* granaio; **barnyard** aia, cortile (di fattoria).

barnacle ['bɑːnəkl] *n* cirripede.

barometer [bə'rɔmitə] *n* barometro.

baron(ess) ['bærən(is)] *n* barone(ssa).

baronet ['bærənit] *n* baronetto.

baroque [bə'rouk] *a n* barocco.

barrack ['bærək] *n usu pl* caserma; *vt* alloggiare in caserma; schernire, fischiare.

barrage ['bærɑːʒ] *n* (*mil*) sbarramento.

barrel ['bærəl] *n* barile, botte; (*gun*) canna.

barren ['bærən] *a* sterile.

barrenness ['bærɔnnis] *n* sterilità.

barricade [‚bæri'keid] *n* barricata; *vt* barricare, ostruire.

barrier ['bæriə] *n* barriera; **sound b.** muro del suono.

barrister ['bæristə] *n* avvocato.

barrow ['bærou] *n* carriola, carretto.

barter ['bɑːtə] *n* baratto; *vt* barattare, scambiare.

Bartholomew [bɑː'θɔləmjuː] *nm pr* Bartolomeo.

basalt ['bæsɔːlt] *n* basalto.

base [beis] *n* base, fondamento; *a* basso, indegno, vile; *vt* basare, fondare.

baseball ['beisbɔːl] *n* 'baseball', palla a basi.

baseless ['beislis] *a* infondato, senza base.

basement ['beismənt] *n* seminterrato.

baseness ['beisnis] *n* bassezza, viltà.

bash [bæʃ] *n* colpo forte; *vt* colpire violentemente.

bashful ['bæʃful] *a* timido.
bashfulness ['bæʃfulnis] *n* timidezza.
basic ['beisik] *a* basilare, fondamentale.
basil ['bæzl] *n* basilico.
basin ['beisn] *n* bacino, bacinella; scodella; lavabo; **sugar b.** zuccheriera.
basis ['beisis] *pl* **bases** *n* base, fondamento.
bask [bɑːsk] *vi* godersi il caldo o il sole.
basket ['bɑːskit] *n* cesta, cesto, paniere; **b.ball** pallacanestro.
Basle [bɑːl] *n* (*geogr*) Basilea.
Basque [bæsk] *a n* basco.
bas-relief ['bæsri,liːf] *n* basso rilievo.
bass [bæs] *n* (*fish*) pesce persico; (*mus*) basso.
bassoon [bə'suːn] *n* (*mus*) fagotto.
bastard ['bæstəd] *a n* bastardo.
baste [beist] *vt* imbastire; spruzzare di grasso l'arrosto; bastonare.
bastion ['bæstiən] *n* bastione.
bat [bæt] *n* (*zool*) pipistrello; (*cricket etc*) mazza, (*ping-pong*) racchetta.
batch [bætʃ] *n* (*bread*) infornata; (*goods*) lotto.
bath [bɑːθ] *n* bagno *anche di mare*), tinozza; **to take a b.** fare il bagno; *vt* bagnare; *vi* bagnarsi, fare un bagno; **bathrobe** accappatoio.
bathe [beið] *n* (*di mare etc*) bagno; *vti* bagnar(si), (*nel mare etc*) fare il bagno.
bather ['beiðə] *n* bagnante.
bathing ['beiðiŋ] *n* bagnare, bagno, bagni *pl*; **b. costume, b. suit** costume da bagno; **b. cap** cuffia da bagno.
bathos ['beiθɔs] *n* discesa dal sublime al ridicolo.
bathysphere ['bæθisfiə] *n* batiscafo.
baton ['bætən] *n* bacchetta; bastone di comando.
battalion [bə'tæljən] *n* battaglione.
batten ['bætn] *n* assicella, traversa in legno; *vt* rinforzare con legno; **to b. down** (*naut*) chiudere un boccaporto.
batter ['bætə] *n* pastella; *vti* battere violentemente; cannoneggiare.
battering-ram ['bætəriŋræm] *n* ariete.
battery ['bætəri] *n* (*mil, el*) batteria, pila.
battle ['bætl] *n* battaglia, combattimento; *vi* combattere, lottare.
battlement ['bætlmənt] *n* merlo, bastione.
bauble ['bɔːbl] *n* ornamento di poco valore; bastone del buffone.
Bavaria [bə'vɛəriə] *n* (*geogr*) Baviera.
Bavarian [bə'vɛəriən] *a n* bavarese.
bawd [bɔːd] *n* mezzana.
bawdiness ['bɔːdinis] *n* oscenità.
bawdy ['bɔːdi] *a* osceno.
bawl [bɔːl] *vi* gridare ad alta voce, schiamazzare.

bay [bei] *n* baia, insenatura del mare; (*bot*) lauro; (*window*) recesso; latrato di grosso cane; *vi* abbaiare, latrare; **to hold at b.** tenere a bada.
bayonet ['beiənit] *n* baionetta.
bazaar [bə'zɑː] *n* bazar.
be [biː] *vi and aux* essere, esistere, vivere, stare, dovere, costare; **to b. in** essere in casa; **to b. long** tardare; **to be two years old** avere due anni,
beach [biːtʃ] *n* lido, spiaggia.
beacon ['biːkən] *n* faro, segnale.
bead [biːd] *n* (*necklace etc*) grano; (*liquids*) goccia; (*rifle*) mirino; **beads** *pl* rosario.
beadle ['biːdl] *n* bidello, sagrestano.
beagle ['biːgl] *n* piccolo cane da caccia.
beak [biːk] *n* becco, rostro.
beaker ['biːkə] *n* coppa, bicchiere.
beam [biːm] *n* trave; (*light*) raggio; sorriso; *vi* risplendere; sorridere.
beaming ['biːmiŋ] *a* raggiante.
bean [biːn] *n* fagiolo, fava; **full of beans** (*sl*) energico, vivace.
bear [bɛə] *n* orso.
bear [bɛə] *vt* portare, sopportare; produrre; *vi* dirigersi, inclinare; **to b. oneself** comportarsi.
bearable ['bɛərəbl] *a* sopportabile.
beard [biəd] *n* barba *vt* sfidare.
bearded ['biədid] *a* barbuto.
beardless ['biədlis] *a* imberbe.
bearer ['bɛərə] *n* latore, portatore.
bearing ['bɛəriŋ] *n* portamento, contegno; **bearings** *pl* orientamento; (*mech*) cuscinetto.
beast [biːst] *n* bestia, animale.
beastly ['biːstli] *a* bestiale; (*sl*) orribile.
beat [biːt] *n* battito, palpito; (*of policeman etc*) giro; *vti* battere, vincere; palpitare; **to b. about the bush** menare il can per l'aia.
beatification [bi,ætifi'keiʃən] *n* beatificazione.
beatify [biː'ætifai] *vt* beatificare.
beating ['biːtiŋ] *n* azione del battere, busse *pl*; sconfitta.
beatitude [biː'ætitjuːd] *n* beatitudine.
beatnik ['biːtnik] *n* beatnik, capellone.
Beatrice ['biətris] **Beatrix** ['biətrix] *nf* Beatrice.
beau [bou] *pl* **beaux** *n* damerino; cicisbeo.
beautician [bjuː'tiʃən] *n* estetista.
beautiful ['bjuːtəful] *a* bello.
beautifully ['bjuːtəfli] *ad* meravigliosamente, perfettamente.
beautify ['bjuːtifai] *vt* abbellire.
beauty ['bjuːti] *n* bellezza.
beaver ['biːvə] *n* castoro, castorino.
becalm [bi'kɑːm] *vt* abbonacciare.
because [bi'kɔz] *cj* perchè; **b. of a** causa di.
beckon ['bekən] *vti* chiamare con un cenno.
become [bi'kʌm] *vi* divenire, acca-

dere; *vt* convenire a, star bene a.
becoming [bi'kʌmiŋ] *a* conveniente, che s'addice a.
bed [bed] *n* letto; **bedding** biancheria da letto; (*of animals*) lettiera.
bedclothes ['bedklouðz] *n pl* coperte e biancheria da letto.
bedlam ['bedləm] *n* grande confusione; manicomio.
bedouin ['beduin] *a n* beduino.
bedraggle [bi'drægl] *vt* inzaccherare.
bedridden ['bed,ridn] *a* allettato.
bedroom ['bedrum] *n* camera (da letto).
bedside ['bedsaid] *n* capezzale.
bedstead ['bedsted] *n* fusto del letto.
bee [biː] *n* ape; **beeline** linea diretta.
beech [biːtʃ] *n* faggio.
beef [biːf] *n* manzo; **beefsteak** bistecca; **b. tea** brodo ristretto.
beehive ['biːhaiv] *n* alveare.
beer [biə] *n* birra; **b.-house** birreria.
beeswax ['biːzwæks] *n* cera vergine.
beet ['biːt] *n* barbabietola, bietola.
beetle ['biːtl] *n* scarabeo, scarafaggio.
befall [bi'fɔːl] *vti* accadere a, capitare a, succedere.
befit [bi'fit] *vt* essere adatto a, andar bene per.
befitting [bi'fitiŋ] *a* adatto, conveniente.
before [bi'fɔː] *ad* prima, già, avanti; *prep* prima di, davanti a; *cj* prima che.
beforehand [bi'fɔːhænd] *ad* in anticipo.
befriend [bi'frend] *vt* mostrarsi amico di, aiutare.
beg [beg] *vti* domandare, pregare; elemosinare.
beget [bi'get] *vt* generare.
beggar ['begə] *n* mendicante.
beggarly ['begəli] *a* meschino, gretto.
beggary ['begəri] *n* mendicità.
begin [bi'gin] *vti* cominciare, iniziare, intraprendere, mettersi a.
beginner [bi'ginə] *n* principiante.
beginning [bi'giniŋ] *n* principio.
begonia [bi'gouniə] *n* begonia.
begrudge [bi'grʌdʒ] *vt* invidiare, lesinare.
beguile [bi'gail] *vt* ingannare.
behalf [bi'hɑːf] *n* **on b. of** da parte di.
behave [bi'heiv] *vi* comportarsi; (*machines*) funzionare.
behavior [bi'heivjə] *n* comportamento, condotta; funzionamento.
behead [bi'hed] *vt* decapitare.
behind [bi'haind] *ad* indietro; *prep* dietro a; **b. time** in ritardo; **b. the times** antiquato.
behindhand [bi'haindhænd] *ad a* in arretrato, in ritardo.
behold [bi'hould] *vt* guardare, vedere, contemplare.
beholder [bi'houldə] *n* osservatore, spettatore.
being ['biːiŋ] **for the time b.** per ora;

n essere vivente, ente, esistenza.
belabor [bi'leibə] *vt* bastonare.
belated [bi'leitid] *a* tardivo, in ritardo.
belch [beltʃ] *vti* (e)ruttare; *n* rutto.
beleaguer [bi'liːgə] *vt* assediare.
belfry ['belfri] *n* campanile.
Belgian ['beldʒən] *a n* belga.
Belgium ['beldʒəm] *n* Belgio.
Belgrade [bel'greid] *n* Belgrado.
belief [bi'liːf] *n* credenza, fede, opinione.
believable [bi'liːvəbl] *a* credibile.
believe [bi'liːv] *vti* aver fede, credere, pensare, supporre.
believer [bi'liːvə] *n* credente.
belittle [bi'litl] *vt* denigrare.
bell [bel] *n* campana, campanello; **bellboy, bellhop** fattorino d'albergo.
bellicose ['belikous] *a* bellicoso.
belligerent [bi'lidʒərənt] *a n* belligerante.
bellow ['belou] *vi* mugghiare, muggire, ruggire; *n* muggito.
bellows ['belouz] *n pl* mantice, soffietto.
belly ['beli] *n* pancia, ventre.
belong [bi'lɔŋ] *vi* appartenere, spettare.
belongings [bi'lɔŋiŋs] *n pl* effetti *pl.*
beloved [bi'lʌv(i)d] *a n* amato, diletto.
below [bi'lou] *prep* sotto (a); al di sotto di; *ad* (al di) sotto, giù.
belt [belt] *n* cinghia, cintura; zona; regione.
bemoan [bi'moun] *vt* compiangere; *vi* lamentarsi.
bench [bentʃ] *n* banco, panca, seggio; ufficio di giudice.
bend [bend] *n* curva, inclinazione; *vt* curvare, piegare; *vi* chinarsi, piegarsi.
beneath [bi'niːθ] *ad prep* al di sotto (di), in basso, sotto.
Benedictine [[,beni'diktin] *a n* benedettino.
benediction [,beni'dikʃən] *n* benedizione.
benefaction [,beni'fækʃən] *n* beneficenza.
benefactor ['benifæktə] *n* benefattore.
beneficence [bi'nefisəns] *n* beneficenza.
beneficent [bi'nefisənt] *a* benefico.
beneficial [,beni'fiʃəl] *a* benefico, utile, vantaggioso.
beneficiary [,beni'fiʃəri] *n* beneficiario.
benefit ['benifit] *n* vantaggio, profitto, (*leg*) beneficio; *vt* beneficare; *vi* trarre profitto.
benevolence [bi'nevələns] *n* benevolenza.
benevolent [bi'nevələnt] *a* benevolo, caritatevole.
benign [bi'nain] **benignant** [bi'nignənt] *a* benevolo, benigno.

Benjamin ['bendʒəmin] *nm pr* Beniamino.
bent [bent] *n* curva, inclinazione naturale, tendenza; *a* curvo, deciso; **to be b.** on essere deciso a.
benumb [bi'nʌm] *vt* intorpidire.
benzine ['benziːn] *n* benzina.
bequeath [bi'kwiːð] *vt* lasciare per testamento.
bequest [bi'kwest] *n* lascito, eredità.
bereave [bi'riːv] *vt* privare, spogliare.
bereavement [bi'riːvmənt] *n* perdita di parente, lutto.
beret ['berei] *n* berretto, basco.
bergamot ['bəːgəmɔt] *n* (*bot*) bergamotto.
Berlin [bəː'lin] *n* (*geogr*) Berlino; **Berliner** berlinese.
Bermuda [bəː'mjuːdə] *n* 1. (le) Bermude 2. *pl.*
Bernard ['bəːnəd] *nm pr* Bernardo.
berry ['beri] *n* bacca.
berserk ['bəːsəːk] **to go b.** abbandonarsi a violenza cieca.
berth [bəːθ] *n* cuccetta; (*fig*) impiego; (*naut*) posto d'ancoraggio d'una nave; *vi* (*naut*) ancoreggiare.
Bertha ['bəːθə] *nf pr* Berta.
beryl ['beril] *n* (*min*) berillo.
beseech [bi'siːtʃ] *vt* implorare, supplicare.
beset [bi'set] *vt* assediare, assalire.
beside [bi'said] *prep* accanto a, vicino a; **b.** oneself fuori di sè.
besides [bi'saidz] *ad prep* inoltre, per di più, oltre a.
besiege [bi'siːdʒ] *vt* assediare.
besom ['bizəm] *n* granata, scopa.
best [best] *a* il migliore; *ad* il meglio, nel miglior modo, nel più alto grado; *n* il meglio.
bestial ['bestiəl] *a* bestiale, brutale.
bestiality [ˌbestiˈæliti] *n* bestialità, brutalità.
bestir [bi'stəː] *vi* **b.** oneself muoversi, scuotersi.
bestow [bi'stou] *vt* conferire, dare, depositare.
bestowal [bi'stouəl] *n* donazione, concessione.
bestride [bi'straid] *vt* stare a cavallo (a cavalcioni) di.
bet [bet] *n* scommessa; *vti* scommettere.
Bethlehem ['beθlihem] *n* Betlemme.
betoken [bi'touken] *vt* indicare, presagire.
betray [bi'trei] *vt* tradire, palesare.
betrayal [bi'treiəl] *n* tradimento.
betrothal [bi'trouðəl] *n* fidanzamento.
betrothed [bi'trouðd] *a n* fidanzato.
better ['betə] *a* migliore; *ad* meglio; **our betters** *pl* i nostri superiori; *vti* migliorar(e).
betting ['betiŋ] *n* lo scommettere.
between [bi'twiːn] *prep* fra, tra; **betwixt and b.** mezzo e mezzo.
beverage ['bevəridʒ] *n* bevanda.

bevy ['bevi] *n* compagnia; stormo.
bewail [bi'weil] *vti* lamentar(si), deplorare.
beware [bi'wɛə] *vi* stare in guardia.
bewilder [bi'wildə] *vt* confondere, rendere perplesso.
bewildering [bi'wildəriŋ] *a* sbalorditivo, sconcertante.
bewilderment [bi'wildəmənt] *n* confusione.
bewitch [bi'witʃ] *vt* ammaliare, stregare.
beyond [bi'jɔnd] *prep ad n* al di là (di); **the back of b.** il più remoto angolo della terra.
bias ['baiəs] *n* inclinazione, pregiudizio; **on the b.** per sbieco; *vt* far inclinare; influenzare.
bib [bib] *n* bavaglino.
Bible ['baibl] *n* Bibbia.
biblical ['biblikəl] *a* biblico.
bibliography [ˌbibliˈɔgrəfi] *n* bibliografia.
bibliophile ['biblioufail] *n* bibliofilo.
bicarbonate [bai'kaːbənit] *n* bicarbonato.
biceps ['baiseps] *n* bicipite.
bicker ['bikə] *vi* litigare, altercare.
bicycle ['baisikl] *n* bicicletta; *vi* andare in bicicletta.
bid [bid] *n* (*at an auction*) offerta, proposta; *vti* comandare; dire.
bidder ['bidə] *n* (*at an auction*) offerente.
biennial [bai'eniəl] *a* biennale.
bier [biə] *n* bara.
big [big] *a* grosso, grande, importante; **bigwig** (*sl*) pezzo grosso.
bigamist ['bigəmist] *n* bigamo.
bigamous ['bigəməs] *a* bigamo.
bigamy ['bigəmi] *n* bigamia.
bigot ['bigət] *n* **bigoted** ['bigətid] *a* bigotto.
bigotry ['bigətri] *n* bigottismo.
bike [baik] *n* (*fam*) bicicletta.
bilateral [bai'lætərəl] *a* bilaterale.
bilberry ['bilbəri] *n* mirtillo.
bile [bail] *n* bile.
bilge [bildʒ] *n* (*naut*) sentina; (*sl*) sciocchezze.
bilingual [bai'liŋwəl] *a* bilingue.
bilious ['biljəs] *a* biliare; bilioso.
bill [bil] *n* (*bird*) becco; (*notice etc*) cartellone, cartello; (*account*) conto, fattura; biglietto di banca, banconota; (*com*) cambiale; (*leg*) progetto di legge; **billboard** spazio per la pubblicità.
billet ['bilit] *n* (*mil*) accantonamento; *vt* accantonare truppe.
billiards ['biljəds] *n pl* biliardo; **billiard saloon** sala del biliardo.
billion ['biljən] *n* bilione, miliardo.
billow ['bilou] *n* flutto, maroso.
billowy ['biloui] *a* pieno di marosi; ondeggiante.
bimetallism [bai'metəlizem] *n* bimetallismo.

bin [bin] *n* recipiente per grano, carbone *etc.*

binary ['bainəri] *a* binario.

bind [baind] *vti* (ri)legare; obbligare; **it was bound to happen** doveva accadere.

binding ['baindiŋ] *a* obbligatorio, impegnativo; *n* legatura, rilegatura.

bindweed ['baindwiːd] *n* convolvolo.

binoculars [bi'nɔkjuləz] *n pl* binocolo.

biographer [bai'ɔgrəfə] *n* biografo.

biographical [baiou'græfikəl] *a* biografico.

biography [bai'ɔgrəfi] *n* biografia.

biological [baiə'lɔdʒikəl] *a* biologico.

biology [bai'ɔlədʒi] *n* biologia.

biped ['baiped] *a n* bipede.

birch [bəːtʃ] *n* (*bot*) betulla; sferza.

bird [bəːd] *n* uccello.

bird-lime ['bəːdlaim] *n* vischio.

bird's-eye view ['bəːdzai'vjuː] *n* panorama a volo d'uccello.

birth [bəːθ] *n* nascita; origine.

birthday ['bəːθdei] *n* compleanno.

birthplace ['bəːθpleis] *n* luogo di nascita.

birthright ['bəːθrait] *n* diritto ereditario; primogenitura.

Biscay ['biskei] *n* Biscaglia.

biscuit ['biskit] *n* biscotto, pastina da tè; **soda b.** galletta, 'cracker'.

bisect [bai'sekt] *vt* bisecare.

bishop ['biʃəp] *n* vescovo; (*chess*) alfiere.

bismuth ['bizmэθ] *n* bismuto.

bison ['baisn] *n* bisonte.

bit [bit] *n* pezzo, pezzetto; (*bread*) boccone; (*bridle*) morso; (*tec*) morsa; punta.

bitch [bitʃ] *n* cagna; lupa; volpe femmina.

bite [bait] *n* morsicatura, morso; boccone; *vt* mordere; abboccare.

biting ['baitiŋ] *a* pungente; sarcastico.

bitter ['bitə] *a* amaro, aspro.

bitterness ['bitənis] *n* amarezza; rancore; (*of climate*) rigidità.

bitumen ['bitjumin] *n* bitume.

bivouac ['bivuæk] *n* bivacco.

bizarre [bi'zɑː] *a* bizzarro, eccentrico.

blab [blæb] *vt* rivelare indiscretamente; *vi* chiacchierare.

black [blæk] *a* nero; minaccioso; oscuro; triste.

blackberry ['blæk.beri] *n* mora.

blackbird ['blækbəːd] *n* merlo.

blackboard ['blækbɔːd] *n* lavagna.

blacken ['blækən] *vt* annerire; diffamare.

blackguard ['blægɑːd] *n* mascalzone.

blacking ['blækiŋ] *n* lucido nero per scarpe.

blackish ['blækiʃ] *a* nerastro.

blackleg ['blækleg] *n* crumiro.

blackmail ['blækmeil] *n* ricatto; *vt* ricattare; **blackmailer** ricattatore.

blackness ['blæknis] *n* nerezza, oscurità.

blackout ['blækaut] *n* oscuramento; perdita temporanea dei sensi.

blacksmith ['blæksmiθ] *n* fabbroferraio.

bladder ['blædə] *n* vescica.

blade [bleid] *n* filo (d'erba); lama.

blame [bleim] *n* biasimo, censura; colpa; *vt* biasimare, censurare.

blameless ['bleimlis] *a* irreprensibile, innocente.

blameworthy ['bleim.wəːði] *a* biasimevole.

blanch [blɑːntʃ] *vt* scolorire; *vi* impallidire.

Blanche [blɑːntʃ] *nf pr* Bianca.

blancmange [blə'mɔnʒ] *n* biancomangiare.

bland [blænd] *a* blando.

blandishment ['blændiʃmənt] *n* blandizia.

blank [blæŋk] *a* bianco; vuoto; *n* lacuna; spazio in bianco; modulo; **b. check** assegno in bianco; **b. verse** verso sciolto.

blanket ['blæŋkit] *n* coperta; copertura.

blankly ['blæŋkli] *ad* senza espressione; recisamente.

blare [bleə] *n* squillo; *vi* squillare; *vt* annunciare a gran voce.

blaspheme [blæs'fiːm] *vti* bestemmiare.

blasphemous ['blæsfiməs] *a* blasfemo; empio.

blasphemy ['blæsfimi] *n* bestemmia.

blast [blɑːst] *n* raffica, colpo di vento; esplosione; squillo; *vt* far esplodere; distruggere; maledire; **b. off** blast-off; **b. furnace** altoforno.

blasting ['blɑːstiŋ] *n* esplosione.

blatant ['bleitənt] *a* rumoroso; sguaiato; evidente.

blaze [bleiz] *n* fiamma, vampata; *vi* divampare, fiammeggiare.

blazer ['bleizə] *n* giacca sportiva; giacca di uniforme scolastica.

bleach [bliːtʃ] *vt* imbiancare.

bleak [bliːk] *a* esposto al vento; squallido; desolato; triste.

blear [bliə] *a* oscuro, confuso; **b.-eyed** dagli occhi cisposi.

bleat [bliːt] *vi* belare; **bleat(ing)** *n* belato.

bleed [bliːd] *vi* sanguinare; *vt* salassare; **bleeding** *n* emorragia.

blemish ['blemiʃ] *n* macchia; difetto (morale o fisico).

blench [blentʃ] *vi* indietreggiare.

blend [blend] *n* miscela, mistura; *vti* mescolar(si).

bless [bles] *vt* benedire, consacrare.

blessed ['blesid] *a* benedetto; beato, santo.

blessing ['blesiŋ] *n* benedizione.

blight [blait] *n* golpe, carbonchio; (*fig*) influenza maligna; *vt* inaridire.

blind [blaind] *a* cieco; *n* tendina, persiana; finzione; *vt* accecare.

blindfold ['blaindfould] *ad* ad occhi bendati; *vt* bendare gli occhi.

blindly ['blaindli] *ad* ciecamente, alla cieca.

blindness ['blaindnis] *n* cecità; mancanza di discernimento.

blink [bliŋk] *n* occhiata, sguardo rapido; guizzo di luce; *vi* battere le palpebre; ammiccare.

blinker ['bliŋkə] *n (aut)* lampeggiatore; paraocchi.

bliss [blis] *n* beatitudine; felicità.

blissful ['blisful] *a* beato; delizioso.

blister ['blistə] *n* bolla, vescica; *vt* far venire vesciche a; *vi* coprirsi di vesciche.

blithe [blaið] *a* giocondo.

blitheness ['blaiðnis] *n* giocondità.

blizzard ['blizəd] *n* bufera di neve, tormenta.

bloat [blout] *vti* gonfiar(si).

bloater ['bloutə] *n* aringa affumicata.

blob [blɔb] *n* goccia; macchia.

block [blɔk] *b* blocco; ceppo; gruppo di case; ostacolo; *vt* bloccare, ostacolare.

blockade [blɔ'keid] *n* blocco, assedio.

blockhead ['blɔkhed] *n* stupido.

blond(e) [blɔnd] *a n* biondo.

blood [blʌd] *n* sangue; discendenza, parentela, bellimbusto; **b.-donor** donatore di sangue; **b.-curdling** raccapricciante; **b.-stained** macchiato di sangue.

bloodhound ['blʌdhaund] *n* segugio.

bloodless ['blʌdlis] *a* esangue, pallido.

bloodshed ['blʌdʃed] *n* spargimento di sangue.

bloodshot ['blʌdʃɔt] *a* iniettato di sangue.

bloody ['blʌdi] *a* sanguinoso; sanguinario; insanguinato; *(vulg)* maledetto; *ad (vulg)* maledettamente, molto.

bloom [bluːm] *n* fiore, fioritura; incarnato; *vi* fiorire, sbocciare.

blooming ['bluːmiŋ] *a* fiorente.

blossom ['blɔsəm] *n* fiore, fioritura; *vi* fiorire.

blot [blɔt] *n* macchia; cancellatura; difetto, colpa; *vt* macchiare; asciugare con carta assorbente; **b. out** cancellare.

blotch [blɔtʃ] *n* macchia, chiazza; sgorbio; pustola; **blotched, blotchy** chiazzato; bitorzoluto.

blotting-paper ['blɔtiŋ,peipə] *n* carta assorbente.

blouse [blauz] *n* blusa, camicetta.

blow [blou] *n* colpo; raffica, soffio; soffiata; *vti* soffiare; suonare *(a wind instrument)*; ansare.

blowy ['bloui] *a* ventoso.

blowzy ['blauzi] *a* scapigliato.

blubber ['blʌbə] *n* grasso di balena; *vi* piangere rumorosamente.

bludgeon ['blʌdʒən] *n* randello.

blue [bluː] *a n* azzurro, blu, celeste; turchino; *a* nervoso, depresso, triste;

to have the blues essere depresso.

bluebell ['bluːbel] *n* giacinto selvatico; campanula.

bluebottle ['bluː,bɔtl] *n* moscone.

blue-stocking ['bluː,stɔkiŋ] *n* donna intellettuale, donna saccente.

bluff [blʌf] *a* brusco, franco; *n* inganno, montatura; *vt* ingannare.

bluish ['blu(ː)iʃ] *a* bluastro, azzurrognolo.

blunder ['blʌndə] *n* errore grossolano, sbaglio; *vti* condurre maldestramente (un affare); fare un errore.

blunt [blʌnt] *a* smussato; franco; rude; ottuso; *vt* smussare; ottundere.

bluntly ['blʌntli] *ad* bruscamente; esplicitamente.

bluntness ['blʌntnis] *n* rudezza; franchezza; ottusità.

blur [bləː] *n* macchia; offuscamento; *vt* macchiare; offuscare.

blurb [bləːb] *n* soffietto editoriale.

blurt out ['bləːt'aut] *vt* spifferare, riferire senza discrezione.

blush [blʌʃ] *n* rossore; *vi* arrossire.

bluster ['blʌstə] *n* fanfaronata; millanteria; *vi* tempestare; smargiassare; **blusterer** *n* spaccone.

boar [bɔə] *n* verro; cinghiale.

board [bɔːd] *n* asse, tavola; comitato, commissione; ministero; *(naut)* bordo; **above b.** a carte scoperte; pensione; *pl (theat)* palcoscenico; *vti* coprire di assi; prendere a pensione, tenere a pensione; salire a bordo.

boarder ['bɔːdə] *n* convittore, pensionante.

boarding house ['bɔːdiŋhaus] *n* pensione.

boarding school ['bɔːdiŋskuːl] *n* convitto.

boast [boust] *n* vanteria, vanto; *vti* vantar(si).

boastful ['boustful] *a* millantatore.

boat [bout] *n* barca; battello, vapore; **in the same b.** trovarsi nelle stesse condizioni.

boatman ['boutmən] *n* barcaiuolo.

boatswain ['boutswein, 'bousn] *n (naut)* nostromo.

bob [bɔb] *vt* tagliare corti (i capelli); *vi* fare inchini; muoversi in su e in giù; **b. up** tornare a galla.

bobbin ['bɔbin] *n* bobina, rocchetto.

bobsled ['bɔbsled] *n* bob, guidoslitta.

bodice ['bɔdis] *n* corpetto.

bodiless ['bɔdilis] *a* incorporeo.

bodily ['bɔdili] *a* corporeo; *ad* corporalmente; di peso, in massa.

bodkin ['bɔdkin] *n* punteruolo, passanastro.

Bodleian [bɔd'li(ː)ən] *a* bodleiano.

body ['bɔdi] *n* corpo; torso; cadavere; ente; **in a b.** tutti insieme.

bodyguard ['bɔdigɑːd] *n* guardia del corpo.

Boer ['bouə] *a n* boero.

bog [bɔg] *n* palude, pantano.

boggle ['bɔgl] *vi* trasalire; esitare.
boggy ['bɔgi] *a* paludoso.
bogie ['bougi] *n* carrello.
bogus ['bougəs] *a* falso, finto; simulato.
Bohemia [bou'hiːmiə] *n* Boemia.
Bohemian [bou'hiːmiən] *a n* boemo; 'bohemien'.
boil [bɔil] *n* (punto di) ebollizione; foruncolo; *vti* (far) bollire; lessare.
boiler ['bɔilə] *n* bollitore; caldaia.
boisterous ['bɔistərəs] *a* chiassoso; turbolento.
bold [bould] *a* audace, temerario; sfacciato; vigoroso; **boldly** *ad* arditamente; sfacciatamente.
boldness ['bouldnis] *n* audacia; sfacciataggine.
bole [boul] *n* tronco d'albero.
bolshevik ['bɔlʃivik] *a n* bolscevico.
bolshevism ['bɔlʃivizəm] *n* bolscevismo.
bolster ['boulstə] *n* cuscino, traversino; *vt* sostenere.
bolt [boult] *n* bullone, catenaccio; spranga; freccia; fulmine; *vt* chiudere a catenaccio; inghiottire in fretta; *vi* darsela a gambe.
bomb [bɔm] *n* bomba; *vti* bombardare.
bombard [bɔm'bɑːd] *vt* bombardare.
bombardment [bɔm'bɑːdmənt] *n* bombardamento.
bombast ['bɔmbæst] *n* linguaggio ampolloso.
bombastic [bɔm'bæstik] *a* ampolloso.
bomber ['bɔmə] *n* bombardiere.
bombshell ['bɔmʃel] *n* obice, granata; notizia, evento sconvolgente.
bond [bɔnd] *n* legame, vincolo; obbligazione; (com) deposito doganale.
bondage ['bɔndidʒ] *n* schiavitù, servitù.
bondsman ['bɔndzmən] *n* (com) garante.
bone [boun] *n* osso; *vt* disossare.
boneless ['bounlis] *a* senz'osso.
bonfire ['bɔn faiə] *n* falò.
Boniface ['bɔnifeis] *nm pr* Bonifazio.
bonnet ['bɔnit] *n* berretto scozzese, cappellino legato con nastri sotto il mento.
bonny ['bɔni] *a* bello, grazioso.
bonus ['bounəs] *n* compenso; gratifica; extradividendo.
bony ['bouni] *a* ossuto.
boo [buː] *vti* fischiare.
booby ['buːbi] *n* individuo sciocco.
book [buk] *n* libro; *vt* prendere nota di; prenotare; registrare; *vi* fare un biglietto (ferroviario).
book-binder ['buk baində] *n* rilegatore di libri.
book-binding ['buk baindiŋ] *n* rilegatura di libri.
book case ['bukkeis] *n* libreria, scaffale.
booking ['bukiŋ] *n* prenotazione; **b.**

clerk bigliettario; **b. office** biglietteria.
book-keeper ['buk kiːpə] *n* contabile.
book-keeping ['buk kiːpiŋ] *n* contabilità.
booklet ['buklit] *n* libretto, opuscolo.
bookmaker ['buk meikə] *n* allibratore.
bookmark(er) ['buk mɑːk(ə)] *n* segnalibro.
bookseller ['buk selə] *n* libraio.
bookshop ['bukʃɔp] *n* libreria.
bookstall ['bukstɔːl] *n* edicola, chiosco; bancarella.
bookworm ['bukwəːm] *n* tignuola; (fig) topo di biblioteca.
boom [buːm] *n* rimbombo; palo che tien tesa una rete; barriera galleggiante in un porto; improvviso aumento di attività commerciale; *vi* rimbombare; avere un improvviso aumento di attività.
boon [buːn] *n* dono, favore, vantaggio.
boor [buə] *n* persona zotica, villana.
boorish ['buəriʃ] *a* rozzo, zotico.
boost [buːst] *vt* lanciare un prodotto con gran pubblicità; (el) elevare la tensione di.
boot [buːt] *n* stivale; (aut) portabagagli.
booth [buːð] *n* baracca; **telephone b.** cabina telefonica.
booty ['buːti] *n* bottino.
booze [buːz] *n* (fam) bevande alcooliche *pl*; *vi* bere all'eccesso.
borax ['bɔːræks] *n* borace.
border ['bɔːdə] *n* bordo; confine; *a* di confine; *vti* confinare (con); orlare; rasentare.
borderer ['bɔːdərə] *n* abitante di confine.
bordering ['bɔːdəriŋ] *a* di confine, limitrofo.
bore [bɔː] *n* buco, foro; calibro di fucile; noia, seccatura; seccatore; *vt* (per)forare; seccare, annoiare.
boredom ['bɔːdəm] *n* noia.
boric ['bɔːrik] *a* borico.
boring ['bɔːriŋ] *a* noioso.
born [bɔːn] *a* nato; nativo.
borough ['bʌrə] *n* città avente amministrazione autonoma; collegio elettorale; mandamento.
borrow ['bɔrou] *vt* prendere a prestito.
bosom ['buzəm] *n* petto, seno; il davanti di una camicia; **b. friend** amico intimo.
boss [bɔs] *n* borchia, ornamento in rilievo; (sl) padrone; capo.
bossy ['bɔsi] *a* prepotente; autoritario.
botanic [bə'tænik] *a* botanico.
botanist ['bɔtənist] *n* botanico.
botany ['bɔtəni] *n* botanica.
botch [bɔtʃ] *vt* rappezzare inabilmente.
both [bouθ] *a pron* ambedue, l'uno e

l'altro; **both** . . . **and** tanto . . . quanto.
bother ['bɔðə] n fastidio; vt seccare; vi preoccuparsi.
bothersome ['bɔðəsəm] a seccante, noioso.
bottle ['bɔtl] n bottiglia; fascio di fieno; vt imbottigliare.
bottom ['bɔtəm] n fondo, base; sedere; **at b.** in fondo.
bottomless ['bɔtəmlis] a senza fondo.
bough [bau] n ramo d'albero.
boulder ['bouldə] n masso roccioso.
bounce [bauns] n rimbalzo, salto; vi (rim)balzare.
bouncer ['baunsə] n (sl) chi getta fuori da un locale gli intrusi.
bouncing ['baunsiŋ] a vigoroso; vivace.
bound [baund] n confine; limite; salto, rimbalzo; a diretto; connesso con; destinato a; vt limitare; vi saltare, rimbalzare.
boundary ['baundəri] n linea di confine.
boundless ['baundlis] a illimitato.
bounteous ['bauntiəs] a benefico, generoso.
bountiful ['bauntiful] a generoso, liberale.
bounty ['baunti] n generosità; premio d'incoraggiamento.
bouquet ['bukei] n mazzolino; profumo.
bourgeois ['buəʒwɑ:] a n borghese; **bourgeoisie** borghesia.
bout [baut] n assalto; accesso; partita.
bovine ['bouvain] a bovino.
bow [bou] n arco; nodo.
bow [bau] n inchino; (ship) prua; vi inchinarsi; sottomettersi.
bowel ['bauəl] n budello; **bowels** pl budella pl; (fig) viscere.
bowl [boul] n ciotola; vaso; recipiente; boccia; palla di legno; vti rotolare.
bowler ['boulə] n bombetta, cappello duro; giocatore di bocce; (cricket) giocatore che serve la palla.
bowling ['bouliŋ], **bowls** [boulz] n gioco delle bocce.
bowsprit ['bousprit] n (naut) bompresso.
box [bɔks] n scatola; cassetta; (driver's) cassetta; (jury) banco; (theat) palco; schiaffo; **b. car** vagone merci chiuso; vt mettere in scatola; vi fare del pugilato.
boxer ['bɔksə] n pugilatore, pugile.
boxing ['bɔksiŋ] n pugilato; **b. match** partita di pugilato.
box number ['bɔks,nʌmbə] n casella postale.
box-office ['bɔks'ɔfis] n botteghino del teatro, biglietteria.
boy [bɔi] n ragazzo.
boycott ['bɔikət] vt boicottare.
boyhood ['bɔihud] n fanciullezza.
boyish ['bɔiiʃ] a fanciullesco.

brace [breis] n qualunque cosa che tiene unito; paio; **braces** pl bretelle pl; vt assicurare strettamente.
bracelet ['breislit] n braccialetto.
bracing ['breisiŋ] a invigorante, salubre.
bracken ['brækən] n felce.
bracket ['brækit] n mensola; parentesi; vt mettere fra parentesi.
brackish ['brækiʃ] a salso, salmastro.
brag [bræg] n millanteria, vanteria; vi vantarsi.
braggart ['brægət] n millantatore, spaccone.
braid [breid] n (of hair) treccia; gallone; vt intrecciare; guarnire.
brain [brein] n cervello; (fig, usu pl) intelligenza; **b. washing** lavaggio del cervello; **b.-drain** emigrazione pesante di studiosi e scienziati.
brain [brein] vt accoppare.
brainy ['breini] a (fam) intelligente.
braise [breiz] vt brasare.
brake [breik] n macchia di cespugli; (mech) freno; vt frenare; **b. horse-power** potenza del freno; **foot b.** (aut) freno a pedale; **hand b.** freno a mano.
bramble ['bræmbl] n pruno, rovo.
bran [bræn] n crusca.
branch [brɑ:ntʃ] n ramo; diramazione; filiale; vi ramificarsi; **to b. off** biforcarsi; **to b. out** estendersi.
brand [brænd] n marchio; tizzone; vt marchiare; stigmatizzare; imprimere.
brandish ['brændiʃ] vt brandire.
brandy ['brændi] n acquavite, cognac.
brash [bræʃ] a impudente; fragile.
brass [brɑ:s] n ottone; (fig) sfrontatezza.
brassiere ['bræsiə] n reggipetto, reggiseno.
brassy ['brɑ:si] a di ottone; impudente.
brat [bræt] n marmocchio; monello.
bravado [brə'vɑ:dou] n bravata, spavalderia.
brave [breiv] a coraggioso; n prode; vt affrontare, sfidare.
bravely ['breivli] ad coraggiosamente.
bravery ['breivəri] n coraggio.
brawl [brɔ:l] n rissa; vi rissare.
brawn [brɔ:n] n muscolo, forza muscolare; soprassata.
brawny ['brɔ:ni] a forte, muscoloso.
bray [brei] vi ragliare.
brazen ['breizn] a d'ottone; impudente; **b.-faced** sfrontato.
brazenly ['breiznli] ad sfacciatamente.
brazier ['breiziə] n braciere.
Brazil [brə'zil] n Brasile.
Brazilian [brə'ziljən] a n brasiliano.
breach [bri:tʃ] n breccia, rottura; vt far breccia in, rompere.
bread [bred] n pane.

breadth [bredθ] *n* ampiezza, larghezza; (*of material*) altezza.

break [breik] *n* rottura; intervallo; *vti* rompere, spezzare; rompersi, spezzarsi; venir meno a.

breakable ['breikəbl] *a* fragile.

breakage ['breikidʒ] *n* rottura.

breakaway ['breikəwei] *n* separazione; (*rly*) sbandamento.

breakdown ['breikdaun] *n* collasso; crollo; esaurimento nervoso; (*aut*) panna, guasto.

breaker ['breikə] *n* rompitore; violatore; (*of horses*) domatore; maroso.

breakfast ['brekfəst] *n* (prima) colazione.

breaking ['breikiŋ] *n* rottura; interruzione; infrazione.

breakneck ['breiknek] *a* rompicollo.

breakwater ['breik,wɔːtə] *n* frangiflutti, diga.

breast [brest] *n* mammella; petto; seno; *vt* affrontare, lottare con.

breath [breθ] *n* respiro; fiato; soffio.

breathalyser ['breθəlaizə] *n* analizzatore del tasso alcoolico.

breathe [briːð] *vti* respirare; prender fiato; mormorare; infondere; **b. forth** esalare.

breathing ['briːðiŋ] *n* respiro, respirazione.

breathless ['breθlis] *a* ansimante, senza fiato.

breathlessly ['breθlisli] *ad* con il fiato sospeso.

breathlessness ['breθlisnis] *n* mancanza di respiro, affanno.

breeches ['britʃiz] *n pl* calzoni *pl*, brache *pl*.

breed [briːd] *n* discendenza, razza; *vti* generare; partorire; (ri)prodursi; allevare.

breeder ['briːdə] *n* allevatore; **b. reactor** reattore nucleare autofertilizzante.

breeding ['briːdiŋ] *n* allevamento; educazione, buone maniere *pl*.

breeze [briːz] *n* brezza, vento leggero.

breezy ['briːzi] *a* battuto dal vento, fresco; gioviale.

brethren ['breðrən] *n pl* confratelli *pl*.

breviary ['briːvjəri] *n* breviario.

brevity ['breviti] *n* brevità, concisione.

brew [bruː] *vt* fare (*un infuso*); fare (*la birra*); (*fig*) tramare; *vi* essere in fermentazione; prepararsi.

brewer ['bru(ː)ə] *n* fabbricante di birra.

brewery ['bruəri] *n* fabbrica di birra.

briar *v* **brier**

bribe [braib] *n* dono (per corrompere o influenzare); *vt* corrompere (per mezzo di doni).

bribery ['braibəri] *n* corruzione.

brick [brik] *n* mattone; *a* di mattoni;

to drop a b. commettere un'indiscrezione.

bridal ['braidl] *a* nuziale; *n* sposalizio.

bride [braid] *n* sposa; **bridegroom** sposo.

bridesmaid ['braidzmeid] *n* damigella d'onore della sposa.

bridge [bridʒ] *n* ponte, (*naut*) ponte di comando; (*cards*) 'bridge', ponte.

Bridget ['bridʒit] *nf pr* Brigida.

bridle ['braidl] *n* briglia, freno.

brief [briːf] *a* breve, conciso; *n* (*leg*) riassunto.

briefness ['briːfnis] *n* brevità.

brier ['braiə] *n* rosa di macchia, rovo; (pipa di) radica.

brig [brig] *n* brigantino.

brigade [bri'geid] *n* brigata.

brigadier [,brigə'diə] *n* comandante di brigata.

brigand ['brigənd] *n* bandito, brigante.

brigandage ['brigəndidʒ] *n* brigantaggio, banditismo.

bright [brait] *a* brillante, luminoso, risplendente; gaio, vivace; sveglio, intelligente.

brighten ['braitn] *vt* rallegrare, rendere più brillante; *vi* illuminarsi, rischiararsi.

brightness ['braitnis] *n* splendore; vivacità.

brilliancy ['briljənsi] *n* splendore.

brilliant ['briljənt] *a* brillante, lucente; *n* brillante.

brim [brim] *n* orlo; bordo, margine; (*of hat*) tesa, ala; *vti* colmar(si); **to b.** over traboccare.

brimless ['brimlis] *a* senza orlo, senz'ala.

brindled ['brindld] *a* chiazzato.

brine [brain] *n* acqua salata.

bring [briŋ] *vt* portare; procurare; addurre; causare; indurre; **to b.** up educare.

brink [briŋk] *n* orlo; limite estremo.

brisk [brisk] *a* vivace, svelto.

briskly ['briskli] *ad* vivacemente; speditamente.

briskness ['brisknis] *n* vivacità, sveltezza.

bristle ['brisl] *n* setola, pelo duro e rado; *vi* andare in collera.

bristly ['brisli] *a* setoloso.

Britain ['britn] *n* Britannia; **Great B.** Gran Bretagna.

Britannic [bri'tænik] *a* britannico.

British ['britiʃ] *a* britannico, inglese.

Briton ['britn] *n* britanno.

brittle ['britl] *a* fragile, friabile.

brittleness ['britlnis] *n* fragilità, friabilità.

broach [broutʃ] *n* spiedo; *vt* spillare; cominciare una discussione.

broad [brɔːd] *a* ampio, largo; indelicato, volgare, (*accent*) marcato.

broadcast ['brɔːdkɑːst] *n* trasmissione radiofonica; *vt* trasmettere per radio; *vi* parlare alla radio; **broad-**

caster apparecchio trasmittente; chi parla alla radio; **broadcasting** radiodiffusione.
broaden ['brɔːdn] vti allargar(si), estender(si).
broadly ['brɔːdli] ad largamente; b. speaking generalmente parlando.
broadness ['brɔːdnis] n larghezza, ampiezza; grossolanità; accento marcato.
brocade [brə'keid] n broccato.
brochure ['brouʃjuə] n opuscolo.
broil [brɔil] n lite, tumulto; vt arrostire alla griglia o allo spiedo.
broken ['broukən] a rotto; (of weather) incerto; (of ground) accidentato; scoraggiato; scorretto.
broker ['broukə] n mediatore, sensale.
bromide ['broumaid] n bromuro.
bronchial ['brɔnkiəl] a bronchiale.
bronchitis [brɔŋ'kaitis] n bronchite.
bronze [brɔnz] n bronzo; a bronzeo, di bronzo; vti abbronzar(si).
brooch [broutʃ] n spilla.
brood [bruːd] n covata; vti covare; meditare, preoccuparsi.
brook [bruk] n ruscello.
broom [brum] n ginestra; scopa.
broomstick ['brumstik] n manico di scopa.
broth [brɔθ] n brodo.
brothel ['brɔθl] n bordello.
brother ['brʌðə] n fratello; confratello (pl **brethren**); b. in arms compagno d'armi; b. in law cognato.
brotherhood ['brʌðəhud] n fratellanza, fraternità; confraternita.
brotherly ['brʌðəli] a fraterno.
brow [brau] n fronte; sopracciglio; (cliff) orlo; (hill) sommità.
browbeat ['braubiːt] vt intimidire.
brown [braun] a marrone, scuro, abbronzato; n color marrone; vti rendere (divenire) marrone, abbronzare; rosolare.
brownie ['brauni] n folletto; giovane esploratrice.
browse [brauz] vti brucare; scorrere libri.
bruise [bruːz] n contusione, ammaccatura, livido; vt ammaccare.
brunette [bruː'net] a n bruna.
brunt [brʌnt] n urto; **to bear the b.** sopportare il peso.
brush [brʌʃ] n spazzola; spazzolata; pennello; vt spazzolare; sfiorare.
brushwood ['bruʃwud] n macchia.
brusque [brusk] a brusco, rude.
Brussels ['brʌslz] n (geogr) Bruxelles; B. sprouts cavolini di Bruxelles.
brutal ['bruːtl] a brutale.
brutality [bruː'tæliti] n brutalità.
brutalize ['bruːtəlaiz] vt abbrutire.
brute [bruːt] a brutale; n bruto.
brutish ['bruːtiʃ] a brutale, bestiale.
bubble ['bʌbl] n bolla; progetto vano; rumore di liquido che bolle; vi gorgogliare; far bolle; bollire.
buccaneer [ˌbʌkə'niə] n pirata.

Bucharest ['bjuːkərest] n (geogr) Bucarest.
buck [bʌk] n daino; coniglio; leprotto; maschio di molti animali; (sl) dollaro.
bucket ['bʌkit] n secchia, secchio.
buckle ['bʌkl] n fibbia; vt affibbiare, fermare; piegare.
buckler ['bʌklə] n scudo rotondo; (fig) protettore.
buckwheat ['bʌkwiːt] n grano saraceno.
bucolic [bjuː'kɔlik] a bucolico, pastorale.
bud [bʌd] n bocciolo; gemma; germoglio; vi germogliare.
Buddha ['budə] n Budda.
Buddhist ['budist] a buddistico; n buddista.
budge [bʌdʒ] vi fare un piccolo movimento, muoversi.
budgerigar ['bʌdʒərigɑː] n pappagallino.
budget ['bʌdʒit] n bilancio preventivo; vi fare un bilancio preventivo.
buff [bʌf] a scamosciato, marrone; n pelle di bufalo; color camoscio.
buffalo ['bʌfəlou] a bufalo.
buffer ['bʌfə] n (mec) respingente.
buffet ['bʌfit] n schiaffo; vt schiaffeggiare.
buffet ['bufei] n credenza, 'buffet'.
buffoon [bʌ'fuːn] n buffone.
buffoonery [bʌ'fuːnəri] n buffoneria.
bug [bʌg] n cimice; (sl) virus; piccolo insetto; **big bug** (sl) persona importante.
bugbear ['bʌgbeə] n spauracchio.
buggy ['bʌgi] n carrozzino scoperto, calesse.
bugle ['bjuːgl] n buccina.
bugler ['bjuːglə] n sonatore di buccina.
build [bild] n costruzione; corporatura; vt costruire; edificare, fabbricare; vi nidificare.
builder ['bildə] n costruttore; impresario di costruzioni.
building ['bildiŋ] a edile, edilizio; n edificio, costruzione.
built [bilt] a costruito, formato; **well-b.** ben messo, ben piantato.
bulb [bʌlb] n bulbo; lampadina elettrica.
bulbous ['bʌlbəs] a bulboso.
Bulgaria [bʌl'gɛəriə] n (geogr) Bulgaria.
Bulgarian [bʌl'gɛəriən] a n bulgaro.
bulge [bʌldʒ] n gonfiore, protuberanza; vi gonfiarsi.
bulging ['bʌldʒiŋ] a sporgente, protuberante.
bulk [bʌlk] n massa; la maggior parte; vi ammontare, essere voluminoso.
bulkiness ['bʌlkinis] n voluminosità.
bulky ['bʌlki] a ingombrante, voluminoso.
bull [bul] n toro; bolla papale.
bulldog ['buldɔg] n bulldog, mastino.

bulldozer ['bul,douzə] n 'bulldozer', scavatrice.
bullet ['bulit] n pallottola; proiettile.
bulletin ['bulitin] n bollettino, notiziario; **news b.** giornale radio; **b. board** tabellone per affissi.
bullfight ['bulfait] n corrida.
bullfinch ['bulfintʃ] n ciuffolotto.
bullion ['buljən] n oro o argento in verghe.
bullock ['bulək] n bue giovane.
bull's eye ['bulzai] n oblò; lente convessa; centro del bersaglio.
bully ['buli] n prepotente, tiranno; manzo lesso in scatola; vt tiranneggiare, fare il bravaccio con.
bulrush ['bulrʌʃ] n giunco.
bulwark ['bulwək] n baluardo; bastione; (naut) parapetto.
bum-boat ['bʌmbout] n battello di rifornimento viveri.
bump [bʌmp] n collisione, colpo, urto; bernoccolo, gonfiore; vti urtare, collidere.
bumper ['bʌmpə] a pieno, abbondante; n (aut) paraurti; (rly) respingente.
bumpkin ['bʌmpkin] n zotico.
bumptious ['bʌmpʃəs] a presuntuoso.
bumpy ['bʌmpi] a (of road) sassoso, ineguale; bernoccoluto.
bun [bʌn] n panetto, piccola focaccia; crocchia di capelli.
bunch [bʌntʃ] n fascio, mazzo; grappolo; vi raggrupparsi.
bundle ['bʌndl] n fagotto, fastello; vt affastellare; **b. off** mandare via senza cerimonie.
bung [bʌŋ] n tappo, grosso turacciolo; vt tappare, otturare.
bungalow ['bʌŋgəlou] n 'bungalow', casetta di costruzione leggera, a un piano.
bungle ['bʌŋgl] n lavoro malfatto, pasticcio; vti fare o aggiustare malamente, guastare.
bunion ['bʌnjən] n callo, infiammazione ai piedi.
bunk [bʌŋk] n cuccetta; sciocchezze.
bunny ['bʌni] n coniglietto.
buoy [bɔi] n boa, gavitello.
buoyancy ['bɔiənsi] n galleggiabilità; (fig) elasticità, brio.
buoyant ['bɔiənt] a capace di stare a galla; leggero; vivace.
burden ['bə:dn] n peso, carico, fardello, onere; ritornello; (naut) tonnellaggio; vt caricare, gravare.
burdensome ['bə:dnsəm] a gravoso, opprimente.
burdock ['bə:dɔk] n (bot) lappola.
bureau [bjuə'rou] pl **bureaus** n scrittoio; ufficio.
bureaucracy [bjuə'rɔkrəsi] n burocrazia.
bureaucrat ['bjuəroukræt] n burocrate.
bureaucratic [,bjuərou'krætik] a burocratico.

burglar ['bə:glə] n scassinatore; **b. alarm** campanello antifurto.
burglary ['bə:gləri] n furto mediante scasso.
burgle ['bə:gl] vt scassinare.
Burgundy ['bə:gəndi] n (geogr) Borgogna; **b.** vino di Borgogna.
burial ['beriəl] n sepoltura; **b. ground** cimitero; **b. place** sepoltura, tomba.
burlesque [bə:'lesk] a burlesco; n 'burlesque'; farsa.
burly ['bə:li] a grosso e robusto.
Burma ['bə:mə] n Birmania.
Burmese [bə:'mi:z] a n birmano.
burn [bə:n] n bruciatura, scottatura; (scozzese) ruscello; vti bruciare, ardere.
burner ['bə:nə] n becco di lampada o di fornello a gas.
burning ['bə:niŋ] a bruciante, ardente; n bruciatura.
burnish ['bə:niʃ] vt brunire, lustrare.
burrow,['bʌrou] n tana; vi rintanarsi; investigare.
bursar ['bə:sə] n economo; borsista.
bursary ['bə:səri] n borsa di studio.
burst [bə:st] n esplosione, scoppio; vti (far) esplodere, (far) scoppiare; rompere.
bury ['beri] vt seppellire; (fig) dimenticare, nascondere alla vista.
bus [bʌs] pl **buses** n autobus.
busman ['bʌsmən] pl **busmen** n conducente di autobus.
bush ['buʃ] n cespuglio, macchia; (mech) boccola.
bushel ['buʃel] n staio.
bushy ['buʃi] a folto; cespuglioso.
busily ['bizili] ad attivamente.
business ['bizinis] n affare, affari pl; commercio; occupazione; azienda commerciale; **business-like** metodico, pratico; **b. suit** abito maschile da passeggio.
bust [bʌst] n busto; petto.
bustard ['bʌstəd] n ottarda.
bustle ['bʌsl] n andirivieni, tramestio; vi agitarsi, affaccendarsi.
busy ['bizi] a occupato, affaccendato.
busybody ['bizi,bɔdi] n ficcanaso.
but [bʌt] cj ma, però, se non che; ad prep eccetto, fuorchè, non . . . che; n ma.
butane ['bju:tein] n (chem) butano.
butcher ['butʃə] n macellaio; vt macellare; massacrare.
butchery ['butʃəri] n macello; strage.
butler ['bʌtlə] n maggiordomo.
butt [bʌt] n barile, botte; calcio di fucile; bersaglio; zimbello; cozzo, cornata; vt cozzare.
butter ['bʌtə] n burro; vt imburrare.
buttercup ['bʌtəkʌp] n ranuncolo.
butterfly ['bʌtəflai] n farfalla.
buttock ['bʌtək] n natica.
button ['bʌtn] n bottone; **collar b.** bottoncino per colletto; **b. hook** allacciabottoni; vt abbottonare; **to b. oneself up** abbottonarsi.

buttonhole ['bʌtnhoul] n occhiello; fiore portato all'occhiello; vt far occhielli; (fig) attaccar bottone; **buttonholer** attaccabottoni.

buttress ['bʌtris] n contrafforte; sostegno.

buxom ['bʌksəm] a grassoccio; formoso.

buy [bai] vt acquistare, comp(e)rare.

buyer ['baiə] n acquirente, compratore.

buzz [bʌz] vi ronzare; n ronzio.

buzzing ['bʌziŋ] a ronzante; n ronzio.

by [bai] prep da, di, a fianco di, per, vicino a; non più tardi di; **by the way, by the** by a proposito; ad vicino, da parte; **to stand by** stare vicino, parteggiare per, essere spettatore; **to put by** metter via.

bye-bye ['baibai] interj addio, arrivederci, ciao; n (fam) nanna.

bygone ['baigon] a finito, passato.

bye-law ['bailɔ:] n regolamento locale.

by-pass ['baipɑ:s] n strada che evita il passaggio per una città.

byre ['baiə] n stalla per buoi.

by-road ['bairoud] **byway** ['baiwei] n strada secondaria.

bystander ['bai‚stændə] n spettatore.

by-word ['baiwɔːd] n detto comune; oggetto di rimprovero.

Byzantine [bi'zænti:n] a n bizantino.

Byzantium [bi'zæntiəm] n Bisanzio.

C

cab [kæb] n vettura pubblica; **taxi-c.** tassì; **c. rank, c. stand** posteggio di tassì.

cabbage ['kæbidʒ] n cavolo.

cabin ['kæbin] n cabina, capanna; **c. boy** mozzo di nave.

cabinet ['kæbinit] n gabinetto, armadietto, stipo; **c.-maker** ebanista; **C.** Consiglio dei Ministri.

cable ['keibl] n cavo; cablogramma; vi spedire un cablogramma; **c. car** funicolare.

caboose [kə'bu:s] n (naut) cucina, cambusa, (rly) furgone.

cacao [kə'kɑːou] n cacao.

cackle ['kækl] n schiamazzo; vi schiamazzare.

cactus ['kæktəs] pl **cactuses, cacti** n cactus, pianta grassa.

cad [kæd] n furfante.

caddy ['kædi] n scatola per custodire il tè; (golf) porta-mazze.

cadence ['keidəns] n cadenza.

cadet [kə'det] n cadetto.

cadge [kædʒ] vti scroccare.

Caesar ['si:zə] nm pr Cesare.

café ['kæfei] n caffè, ristorante.

cafeteria [‚kæfi'tiəriə] n ristorante 'self-service'.

cage [keidʒ] n gabbia.

Cain [kein] nm pr Caino.

caique [kai'i:k] n caicco, scialuppa.

cairngorm ['kɛən'gɔːm] n quarzo giallo.

cajole [kə'dʒoul] vt blandire, lusingare.

cajolery [kə'dʒouləri] n adulazione, allettamento.

cake [keik] n torta, dolce, pasticcino; **c. of soap** saponetta; vti incrostar (si).

Calabrian [kə'læbriən] a n calabrese.

calamitous [kə'læmitəs] a calamitoso, disastroso.

calamity [kə'læmiti] n calamità, sventura.

calcium ['kælsiəm] n (chem) calcio.

calculable ['kælkjuləbl] a calcolabile.

calculate ['kælkjuleit] vti calcolare; contare (su).

calculation [‚kælkju'leiʃən] n calcolo; previsione.

calculator ['kælkjuleitə] n calcolatore; macchina calcolatrice.

calculus ['kælkjuləs] pl **calculi** n (math, med) calcolo.

Caledonia [‚kæli'douniə] n Caledonia, Scozia; **Caledonian** caledone, scozzese.

calendar ['kælində] n calendario; annuario; lista.

calender ['kælində] n (mech) cilindratoio; calandra; vt calandrare.

calf [kɑːf] pl **calves** n vitello; pelle di vitello; piccolo di elefante e di altri mammiferi.

caliber ['kælibə] n calibro.

calipers ['kælipəz] n pl compassi.

call [kɔːl] n chiamata, richiamo; grido; breve visita; diritto; **within c.** a portata di voce; **c. boy** (theat) buttafuori; **c. up** chiamata alle armi; **telephone c.** telefonata; vti chiamare; gridare; chiamarsi; invocare; fare una breve visita.

caller ['kɔːlə] n visitatore.

calling ['kɔːliŋ] n occupazione, professione; vocazione.

callous ['kæləs] a calloso; insensibile.

callow ['kælou] a implume; inesperto; imberbe.

calm [kɑːm] a calmo, sereno; n calma, tranquillità; vt calmare, tranquillare.

calmly ['kɑːmli] ad tranquillamente, con calma.

calmness ['kɑːmnis] n calma, tranquillità.

calomel ['kæloumel] n calomelano.

calorie ['kæləri] n caloria.

calumniate [kə'lʌmnieit] vt calunniare.

calumny ['kæləmni] n calunnia.

Calvary ['kælvəri] n Calvario; **c.** Via Crucis, calvario.

Calvinism ['kælvinizəm] n calvinismo.

calypso [kæ'lipso] n calipso.

camber ['kæmbə] n curvatura, inarcamento; vt curvare.

cambric ['keimbrik] *n* cambrì, batista.

camel ['kæməl] *n* cammello.

cameo ['kæmiou] *n* cammeo.

camera ['kæmərə] *n* macchina fotografica; **cameraman** fotoreporter; operatore cinematografico, televisivo; **in c.** a porte chiuse.

camomile ['kæməmail] *n* camomilla.

camouflage ['kæmuflɑːʒ] *n* camuffamento, mimetizzazione.

camp [kæmp] *n* campeggio; campo; accampamento; *vi* accamparsi, attendarsi; **camp site** camping.

campaign [kæm'pein] *n* campagna; *vi* fare una campagna.

camphor ['kæmfə] *n* canfora.

campus ['kæmpəs] *n* insieme di terreni, campi di gioco, edifici universitari.

can [kæn] *n* bidone; scatola di latta per cibi conservati.

can [kæn] *vi* (*3rd sing*) essere in grado di; potere; sapere; *vt* mettere in scatola.

Canada ['kænədə] *n* Canadà.

Canadian [kə'neidiən] *a n* canadese.

canal [kə'næl] *n* canale.

canary [kə'nɛəri] *n* canarino.

Canary (Islands) [kə'nɛəri ('ailəndz)] *n* (Isole) Canarie.

cancel ['kænsəl] *vt* annullare; cancellare; sopprimere.

cancellation [ˌkænse'leiʃən] *n* annullamento, soppressione.

cancer ['kænsə] *n* cancro.

candid ['kændid] *a* franco, sincero.

candidate ['kændidit] *n* candidato.

candidature ['kændiditʃə] *n* candidatura.

candidness ['kændidnis] *n* franchezza.

candied ['kændid] *a* candito.

candle ['kændl] *n* candela.

Candlemas ['kændlməs] *n* Candelora.

candlestick ['kændlstik] *n* candeliere.

candor ['kændə] *n* franchezza, sincerità.

candy ['kændi] *n* candito; dolciumi *pl*; **c. floss, cotton c.** zucchero filato.

cane [kein] *n* bastone da passeggio; canna; bacchetta; **sugar c.** canna da zucchero; *vt* bastonare.

canine ['keinain] *a* canino.

canister ['kænistə] *n* barattolo.

canker ['kæŋkə] *n* cancro; brutto difetto; influenza corruttrice; *vti* corromper(si).

cankerous ['kæŋkərəs] *a* cancrenoso.

canned [kænd] *a* conservato in scatola; **c. meat** carne in scatola.

cannibal ['kænibəl] *n* cannibale.

cannon ['kænən] *n* cannone, cannoni *pl*; (*billiards*) carambola.

cannonade [ˌkænə'neid] *n* bombardamento, cannoneggiamento.

canny ['kæni] *a* astuto, abile.

canoe [kə'nuː] *n* canoa.

canon ['kænən] *n* canone; canonico.

canonical [kə'nɔnikəl] *a* canonico.

canonization [ˌkænənai'zeiʃən] *n* canonizzazione.

canonize ['kænənaiz] *vt* canonizzare.

canopy ['kænəpi] *n* baldacchino.

cant [kænt] *n* pendenza, inclinazione; gergo; ipocrisia.

cantankerous [kən'tæŋkərəs] *a* intrattabile, litigioso.

canteen [kæn'tiːn] *n* borraccia da soldato; cantina militare; cassetta per posateria.

canter ['kæntə] *n* piccolo galoppo; *vi* andare a piccolo galoppo.

canticle ['kæntikl] *n* cantico.

cantilever ['kæntiliːvə] *n* mensola che regge balconi *etc*; modiglione; **c. bridge** ponte a mensola.

canton ['kæntɔn] *n* cantone.

canvas ['kænvəs] *n* canovaccio, tela; vele *pl*.

canvass ['kænvəs] *vti* sollecitare voti, ordini *etc*.

canvasser ['kænvəsə] *n* galoppino elettorale.

canyon ['kænjən] *n* 'canyon', burrone.

cap [kæp] *n* berretto, copricapo, cuffietta; *vt* coprire; superare.

capability [ˌkeipə'biliti] *n* capacità, abilità.

capable ['keipəbl] *a* abile, capace.

capacious [kə'peiʃəs] *a* spazioso, capace.

capaciousness [kə'peiʃəsnis] *n* spaziosità, capacità.

capacity [kə'pæsiti] *n* capacità; competenza; ufficio.

cape [keip] *n* capo, promontorio; cappa, mantello.

caper ['keipə] *n* cappero; capriola; (*fig*) stramberia.

Capetown ['keiptaun] *n* *pr* (*geogr*) Città del Capo.

capillary [kə'piləri] *a* capillare.

capital ['kæpitl] *a* capitale; eccellente; maiuscolo; *n* capitale; lettera maiuscola; (*arch*) capitello.

capitalism ['kæpitəlizəm] *n* capitalismo.

capitalist ['kæpitəlist] *n* capitalista.

capitalize [kə'pitəlaiz] *vt* capitalizzare.

Capitol ['kæpitl] **(the)** *n* Campidoglio; **Capitoline** *a* capitolino.

capitulate [kə'pitjuleit] *vi* capitolare, arrendersi.

capitulation [kəˌpitju'leiʃən] *n* capitolazione, resa.

capon ['keipən] *n* cappone.

caprice [kə'priːs] *n* capriccio.

capricious [kə'priʃəs] *a* capriccioso; volubile.

capriciousness [kə'priʃəsnis] *n* capricciosità.

capsize [kæp'saiz] *vti* capovolger(si).

capstan ['kæpstən] *n* (*naut*) argano.

capsule ['kæpsju:l] *n* capsula; schema.

captain ['kæptin] *n* capitano, comandante; capo.

caption ['kæpʃən] *n* intestazione, titolo; (*cin*) didascalia.

captious ['kæpʃəs] *a* capzioso; sofistico.

captiousness ['kæpʃəsnis] *n* capziosità.

captivate ['kæptiveit] *vt* attrarre; cattivarsi.

captivating ['kæptiveitiŋ] *a* seducente, affascinante.

captive ['kæptiv] *a n* prigioniero.

captor ['kæptə] *n* chi fa prigioniero, catturatore.

capture ['kæptʃə] *n* cattura; *vt* catturare.

Capuchin ['kæpjuʃin] *n* frate cappuccino.

car [ka:] *n* automobile; carro; (*rly*) vagone, (*rly*) carrozza; **armored c.** (*mil*) autoblinda; **baggage c.** bagagliaio; **cable c.** funicolare; **freight c.** vagone merci; **mail c.** vagone postale; **restaurant c., dining c.** vagone ristorante; **sleeping c.** vagone letto; **carpark** parcheggio.

carafe [kə'ra:f] *n* caraffa.

caramel ['kærəmel] *n* caramello; caramella.

carat ['kærət] *n* carato.

caravan ['kærəvæn] *n* carovana, carrozzone; (*aut*) roulotte.

caraway ['kærəwei] *n* (*bot*) comino.

carbine ['ka:bain] *n* carabina.

carbohydrate ['ka:bou'haidreit] *n* (*chem*) carboidrato.

carbolic [ka:'bɔlik] *a* fenico.

carbon ['ka:bən] *n* carbonio; **c. paper** carta carbone.

carbonate ['ka:bənit] *n* carbonato.

carbonic [ka:'bɔnik] *a* carbonico.

carboniferous [,ka:bə'nifərəs] *a* carbonifero.

carbonize ['ka:bənaiz] *vt* carbonizzare.

carbuncle ['ka:bʌŋkl] *n* carbonchio.

carburetor ['ka:bjuretə] *n* carburatore.

carcass ['ka:kəs] *n* carcassa.

card [ka:d] *n* biglietto da visita; cartoncino; carta da giuoco; cartolina; tessera; *vt* cardare.

cardboard ['ka:dbɔ:d] *n* cartone.

cardiac ['ka:diæk] *a* cardiaco.

cardigan ['ka:digən] *n* giacca a maglia.

cardinal ['ka:dinl] *a n* cardinale.

care [kɛə] *n* cura, attenzione; preoccupazione; (**in**) **c. of** (*in indirizzi*) presso; *vi* importare; interessarsi; **to care for** voler bene a; curare; piacere.

careen [kə'ri:n] *vti* (*naut*) carenare.

career [kə'riə] *n* carriera; corsa.

careful ['kɛəful] *a* accurato; attento, premuroso.

carefully ['kɛəfuli] *ad* attentamente; con cura.

carefulness ['kɛəfulnis] *n* accuratezza; attenzione.

careless ['kɛəlis] *a* negligente, trascurato.

carelessness ['kɛəlisnis] *n* negligenza, trascuratezza.

caress [kə'res] *n* carezza; *vt* accarezzare.

caretaker ['kɛə,teikə] *n* custode, guardiano, portiere.

cargo ['ka:gou] *pl* **cargoes** *n* (*d'una nave*) carico.

Caribbean [,kæri'bi:ən] *a* caraibico.

caricature [,kærikə'tjuə] *n* caricatura; *vt* caricaturare.

caricaturist [,kærikə'tjuərist] *n* caricaturista.

Carmelite ['ka:milait] *a n* carmelitano.

carnage ['ka:nidʒ] *n* carneficina, strage.

carnal ['ka:nl] *a* carnale, sensuale.

carnation [ka:'neiʃən] *n* garofano.

carnival ['ka:nivəl] *n* carnevale.

carnivorous [ka:'nivərəs] *a* carnivoro.

carob ['kærəb] *n* (*bot*) carruba; **c.-tree** carrubo.

carol ['kærəl] *n* carola, inno natalizio.

Caroline ['kærəlain] *nf pr* Carolina.

carotid [kə'rɔtid] *n* (*anat*) carotide.

carouse [kə'rauz] *vi* far baldoria, gozzovigliare.

carousel [kə'rauzəl] *n* carosello.

carp [ka:p] *n* carpa; **c. at** *vi* trovare sempre da ridire su.

carpenter ['ka:pintə] *n* carpentiere, falegname.

carpentry ['ka:pintri] *n* carpenteria.

carpet ['ka:pit] *n* tappeto.

carping ['ka:piŋ] *a* cavilloso.

carriage ['kæridʒ] *n* carrozza, vettura; (*com*) trasporto, prezzo di trasporto; portamento; **baby c.** carrozzina per bambini.

carrier ['kæriə] *n* portatore; corriere, spedizioniere; portapacchi di bicicletta.

carrion ['kæriən] *n* carogna.

carrot ['kærət] *n* carota.

carry ['kæri] *vti* portare; trasportare; riportare; raggiungere; **to carry oneself** comportarsi.

cart [ka:t] *n* carro, calesse; *vt* trasportare con carro.

cartage ['ka:tidʒ] *n* trasporto con carri; prezzo di trasporto.

carter ['ka:tə] *n* carrettiere.

Carthusian [ka:'θju:ziən] *a n* certosino.

cartilage ['ka:tilidʒ] *n* cartilagine.

carton ['ka:tən] *n* cartone; scatola.

cartoon [ka:'tu:n] *n* cartone; vignetta; cartone animato; **cartoonist** vignettista; disegnatore di cartoni animati.

cartridge ['ka:tridʒ] *n* cartuccia.

carve [kɑːv] *vt* intagliare, scolpire; trinciare.

carving ['kɑːviŋ] *n* scultura, intaglio; il trinciare; **c. knife** trinciante.

cascade [kæs'keid] *n* cascata; *vi* scrosciare; sparpagliarsi.

case [keis] *n* caso, avvenimento; causa; cassa; astuccio, fodero; valigia.

casement ['keismənt] *n* finestra a due battenti.

cash [kæʃ] *n* cassa; contanti *pl*; *vt* incassare, prelevare.

cashier [kæ'ʃiə] *n* cassiere; *vt* (*mil*) destituire.

cashmere ['kæʃmiə] *n* cachemire, cashmere.

cask [kɑːsk] *n* barile.

casket ['kɑːskit] *n* cofanetto, scrigno.

casserole ['kæsəroul] *n* casseruola.

cassock ['kæsək] *n* tunica del clero anglicano.

cast [kɑːst] *n* getto, lancio; stampo; insieme degli attori in una rappresentazione; *vti* gettare, lanciare; dedurre; distribuire parti agli attori.

castanets [ˌkæstə'nets] *n pl* nacchere *pl*.

castaway ['kɑːstəwei] *n* naufrago; reietto.

caste [kɑːst] *n* casta.

castigate ['kæstigeit] *vt* castigare, punire.

Castile [kæs'tiːl] *n* Castiglia; **Castilian** *a n* castigliano.

casting ['kɑːstiŋ] *n* getto; colata; distribuzione di parti ad attori.

cast iron ['kɑːst'aiən] *n* ghisa.

castle ['kɑːsl] *n* castello; (*chess*) torre.

castor ['kɑːstə] *n* rotella da mobili; saliera; ampolla; **c. sugar** zucchero raffinato.

castor oil ['kɑːstər'ɔil] *n* olio di ricino.

castrate [kæs'treit] *vt* castrare.

castration [kæs'treiʃən] *n* castrazione.

casual ['kæʒjuəl] *a* casuale, fortuito; (*clothes*) semplice, sportivo.

casually ['kæʒjuəli] *ad* per caso; con noncuranza.

casualty ['kæʒjuəlti] *n* disgrazia; vittima; **c. list** lista delle vittime.

casuist ['kæzjuist] *n* casista.

casuistry ['kæzjuistri] *n* casistica.

cat [kat] *n* gatto.

cataclysm ['kætəklizəm] *n* cataclisma.

catacomb ['kætəkoum] *n* catacomba.

Catalan ['kætələn] *a n* catalano.

catalepsy ['kætəlepsi] *n* catalessi.

catalogue ['kætələg] *n* catalogo; *vt* catalogare.

Catalonia [ˌkætə'louniə] *n* Catalogna.

catapult ['kætəpʌlt] *n* catapulta; fionda; *vti* catapultare.

cataract ['kætərækt] *n* cateratta; (*falls*) cascata.

catarrh [kə'tɑː] *n* catarro.

catastrophe [kə'tæstrəfi] *n* catastrofe.

catch [kætʃ] *n* presa, cattura; preda; guadagno fatto; pesca; trappola; paletto di porta; *vti* acchiappare, afferrare; sorprendere; capire.

catching ['kætʃiŋ] *a* contagioso; orecchiabile.

catchword ['kætʃwəːd] *n* richiamo, slogan.

catechism ['kætikizəm] *n* catechismo.

catechize ['kætikaiz] *vt* catechizzare.

categorical [ˌkæti'gɔrikəl] *a* categorico.

category ['kætigəri] *n* categoria.

cater ['keitə] *vi* provvedere cibo; procurare divertimento.

caterer ['keitərə] *n* provveditore di cibo *etc*.

caterpillar ['kætəpilə] *n* bruco (*mech*) cingola.

catgut ['kætgʌt] *n* minugia.

cathedral [kə'θiːdrəl] *n* cattedrale, duomo.

Catherine ['kæθərin] *nf pr* Caterina.

cathode ['kæθoud] *n* catodo.

catholic ['kæθəlik] *a n* cattolico.

Catholicism [kə'θɔlisizəm] *n* cattolicismo.

cattle ['kætl] *n pl* bestiame.

catty ['kæti] *a* (*fig*) sarcastico, acido.

Caucasus ['kɔːkəsəs] *n* Caucaso; **Caucasian** *a n* caucasico.

cauldron ['kɔːldrən] *n* caldaia.

cauliflower ['kɔliflauə] *n* cavolfiore.

cause [kɔːz] *n* causa, motivo, ragione; *vt* causare, produrre.

causeway ['kɔːzwei] *n* strada rialzata.

caustic ['kɔːstik] *a n* caustico.

causticity [kɔːs'tisiti] *n* causticità.

cauterize ['kɔːtəraiz] *vt* cauterizzare.

caution ['kɔːʃən] *n* prudenza, cautela; avvertimento; cauzione; *vt* mettere in guardia.

cautious ['kɔːʃəs] *a* cauto, prudente.

cautiously ['kɔːʃəsli] *ad* cautamente, con prudenza.

cautiousness ['kɔːʃəsnis] *n* cautela.

cavalcade [ˌkævəl'keid] *n* cavalcata.

cavalier [ˌkævə'liə] *a* brusco, scortese; *n* cavaliere.

cavalry ['kævəlri] *n* cavalleria.

cave [keiv] *n* cava, caverna; **to cave in** cedere schiacciare.

cavern ['kævən] *n* caverna, grotta.

cavernous ['kævənəs] *a* cavernoso.

caviar(e) ['kæviɑː] *n* caviale.

cavil ['kævil] *n* cavillo; *vi* cavillare.

cavity ['kæviti] *n* cavità.

caw [kɔː] *n* gracchiamento; *vi* gracchiare.

Cayenne [kei'en] *n* Caienna; **c. (pepper)** pepe di Caienna.

cease [siːs] *vti* cessare, fermarsi, finire.

ceaseless ['siːslis] *a* continuo, incessante.

ceaselessly ['siːslisli] *ad* incessantemente, di continuo.

Cecil [sesl] *nm pr* Cecilio.
Cecilia [sə'siːliə] **Cecily** ['sesili] *nf pr* Cecilia.
cedar ['siːdə] *n* cedro.
ceiling ['siːliŋ] *n* soffitto.
celebrate ['selibreit] *vti* celebrare.
celebrated ['selibreitid] *a* celebre, famoso.
celebration [ˌseli'breiʃən] *n* celebrazione.
celebrity [si'lebriti] *n* celebrità.
celerity [si'leriti] *n* celerità, rapidità.
celery ['seləri] *n* sedano.
celestial [si'lestiəl] *a* celeste; celestiale.
celibacy ['selibəsi] *n* celibato.
celibate ['selibit] *a n* celibe.
cell [sel] *n* cella; (*anat*) cellula; (*el*) pila; **fuel c.** pila a combustibile.
cellar ['selə] *n* cantina.
cellarer ['selərə] *n* cantiniere.
cellist ['tʃelist] *n* violoncellista.
cello ['tʃelou] *n* violoncello.
cellophane ['seləfein] *n* cellofane.
cellular ['seljulə] *a* cellulare.
celluloid ['seljulɔid] *a n* (di) celluloide.
cellulose ['seljulous] *a* celluloso; *n* cellulosa.
Celtic ['keltik] *a* celtico.
cement [si'ment] *n* cemento; *vt* cementare.
cemetery ['semitri] *n* cimitero.
censer ['sensə] *n* incensiere, turibolo.
censor ['sensə] *n* censore; *vt* censurare; **censorship** censura, censorato.
censorious [sen'sɔːriəs] *a* ipercritico.
censurable ['senʃərəbl] *a* censurabile.
censure ['senʃə] *n* censura, giudizio avverso; *vt* censurare, criticare.
census ['sensəs] *n* censimento, censo.
cent [sent] *n* centesimo di dollaro; (*fam*) soldo.
centaur ['sentɔː] *n* centauro.
centenarian [ˌsenti'nɛəriən] *a n* (*persona*) centenario.
centenary [sen'tiːnəri] *a n* centenario.
centennial [sen'teniəl] *a* centennale.
center ['sentə] *n* centro; *vti* concentrar(si); (*sport*) centrare.
centigrade ['sentigreid] *a* centigrado.
centimeter ['senti'miːtə] *n* centimetro (0.393 *inches*).
centipede ['sentipiːd] *n* millepiedi.
central ['sentrəl] *a* centrale.
centralization [ˌsentrəlai'zeiʃən] *n* accentramento.
centralize ['sentrəlaiz] *vt* accentrare.
centrifugal [sen'trifjugəl] *a* centrifugo.
centuple ['sentjupl] *a n* centuplo.
century ['sentʃuri] *n* secolo.
ceramics [si'ræmiks] *n* ceramica.
cereal ['siəriəl] *a n* cereale.
cerebral ['seribrəl] *a* cerebrale.
ceremonial [ˌseri'mouniəl] *a* da cerimonia; *n* cerimoniale, etichetta.

ceremonious [ˌseri'mouniəs] *a* cerimonioso.
ceremony ['seriməni] *n* cerimonia; **to stand on c.** fare complimenti.
certain ['səːtn] *a* certo, sicuro; **for c.** sicuramente; **to make c.** assicurarsi.
certainly ['səːtnli] *ad* certamente, sicuramente.
certainty ['səːtnti] *n* certezza, sicurezza.
certifiable ['səːtifaiəbl] *a* attestabile; che dovrebbe essere attestato pazzo.
certificate [sə'tifikit] *n* certificato.
certification [ˌsəːtifi'keiʃən] *n* certificazione.
certify ['səːtifai] *vt* attestare, certificare; (*leg*) autenticare, legalizzare.
certitude ['səːtitjuːd] *n* certezza.
cervical ['səːvikəl] *a* (*anat*) cervicale.
cessation [se'seiʃən] *n* cessazione.
cession ['seʃən] *n* cessione.
cesspit ['sespit] **cesspool** ['sespuːl] *n* pozzo nero.
cetacean [si'teiʃjən] *n* cetaceo.
Ceylonese [si'lɔniːz] *a n* cingalese.
chafe [tʃeif] *n* irritazione; *vti* irritar(si) (la pelle); frizionare; (*fig*) irritare, irritarsi.
chaff [tʃɑːf] *n* pula; paglia; (*fam*) burla.
chaffer ['tʃæfə] *vi* comprare lesinando sul prezzo.
chaffinch ['tʃæfintʃ] *n* fringuello.
chagrin ['ʃægrin] *n* cruccio, dispetto.
chain [tʃein] *n* catena; *vt* incatenare.
chair [tʃɛə] *n* sedia; seggio; cattedra; **chairlift** seggiovia; **to take the c.** assumere la presidenza.
chairman ['tʃɛəmən] *n* presidente, presidentessa.
chairmanship ['tʃɛəmənʃip] *n* presidenza.
chalice ['tʃælis] *n* calice.
chalk [tʃɔːk] *n* gesso; (*min*) calcare; **by a long c.** di gran lunga.
chalky ['tʃɔːki] *a* gessoso; calcareo; pallido, terreo.
challenge ['tʃælindʒ] *n* sfida; *vt* sfidare; obbiettare; provocare.
chamber ['tʃeimbə] *n* aula, sala; (*tec*) camera; **Chamber** Camera; **c. music** musica da camera.
chamberlain ['tʃeimbəlin] *n* ciambellano.
chambermaid ['tʃeimbəmeid] *n* cameriera d'albergo.
chameleon [kə'miːliən] *n* camaleonte.
chamois ['ʃæmwɑː] *n* camoscio.
champagne [ʃæm'pein] *n* sciampagna.
champion ['tʃæmpiən] *n* campione; *vt* sostenere (una causa); **championship** campionato.
chance [tʃɑːns] *a* fortuito, casuale; *n* caso, sorte, fortuna; occasione; **by c.** per caso; *vti* accadere; (*fam*) arrischiare.
chancel ['tʃɑːnsəl] *n* presbiterio, coro.
chancellor ['tʃɑːnsələ] *n* cancelliere.

chancery ['tʃɑːnsəri] n cancelleria.
chancy ['tʃɑːnsi] a incerto, rischioso.
chandelier [ˌʃændi'liə] n lampadario.
chandler ['tʃɑːndlə] n droghiere, fornitore.
change [tʃeindʒ] n cambio, mutamento; danaro spicciolo; resto; vti cambiar(si).
changeable ['tʃeindʒəbl] a mutabile, incostante.
changeableness ['tʃeindʒəblnis] n inconstanza.
changeless ['tʃeindʒlis] a costante, immutabile.
changeling ['tʃeindʒliŋ] n (poet) bimbo sostituito.
changing ['tʃeindʒiŋ] a cangiante, mutevole; n cambio.
channel ['tʃænl] n canale, stretto; the (English) C. la Manica; (fig) via; vt incanalare, (arch) scanalare.
chant [tʃɑːnt] n canto, recitativo monotono.
chaos ['keiɔs] n caos.
chaotic [kei'ɔtik] a caotico.
chap [tʃæp] n screpolatura; (fam) ragazzo, individuo; vti screpolar(si).
chapel ['tʃæpəl] n cappella.
chaperon ['ʃæpəroun] n 'chaperon', accompagnatrice di signorine; vt scortare.
chaplain ['tʃæplin] n cappellano.
chaplaincy ['tʃæplinsi] n carica di cappellano.
chaplet ['tʃæplit] n corona, ghirlanda.
chapter ['tʃæptə] n capitolo.
char [tʃɑː] vti carbonizzar(si).
char(woman) ['tʃɑː(wumən)] n domestica a ore.
character ['kæriktə] n carattere, caratteristica; scrittura; attestato di servizio; individuo eccentrico; personaggio.
characteristic [ˌkæriktə'ristik] a caratteristico; n caratteristica.
characterize ['kæriktəraiz] vt caratterizzare; definire.
charade [ʃə'rɑːd] n sciarada.
charcoal ['tʃɑːkoul] n carbone di legna; (drawing) carboncino.
charge [tʃɑːdʒ] n prezzo, spesa; carica; incarico, cura; accusa; attacco; vti far pagare; incaricare; accusare; caricare di; attaccare.
chargeable ['tʃɑːdʒəbl] a a carico di, addebitabile.
charger ['tʃɑːdʒə] n destriero; (of gun) caricatore; accumulatore elettrico.
chariot ['tʃæriət] n cocchio.
charitable ['tʃæritəbl] a caritatevole.
charitableness ['tʃæritəblnis] n filantropia.
charity ['tʃæriti] n carità, beneficenza.
charlatan ['ʃɑːlətən] n ciarlatano.
Charles [tʃɑːlz] nm pr Carlo.
Charlotte ['ʃɑːlət] nf pr Carlotta.
charm [tʃɑːm] n attrattiva, fascino;

incantesimo; amuleto, ciondolo; vt affascinare, incantare.
charmer ['tʃɑːmə] n incantatore, incantatrice.
charming ['tʃɑːmiŋ] a incantevole.
chart [tʃɑːt] n carta nautica, quadro statistico; vt fare la carta di.
charter ['tʃɑːtə] n carta, documento; vt concedere statuto; noleggiare.
chary ['tʃɛəri] a cauto, prudente, parco di.
chase [tʃeis] n caccia, inseguimento; vt cacciare, inseguire; cesellare.
chasing ['tʃeisiŋ] n cesellatura.
chasm ['kæzəm] n abisso, baratro.
chassis ['ʃæsiː] n inv chassis, telaio, intelaiatura.
chaste [tʃeist] a casto, puro.
chastise [tʃæs'taiz] vt castigare.
chastisement ['tʃæstizmənt] n castigo, punizione.
chastity ['tʃæstiti] n castità, purezza.
chat [tʃæt] n chiacchierata; vi chiacchierare.
chattels ['tʃætls] n pl beni mobili pl.
chatter ['tʃætə] vi chiacchierare; (teeth) battere.
chatterbox ['tʃætəbɔks] n chiacchierone, chiacchierona.
chatty ['tʃæti] a ciarliero, chiacchierone.
chauffeur ['ʃoufə] n autista.
cheap [tʃiːp] a a buon mercato; cheaply ad a buon mercato.
cheapen ['tʃiːpən] vt diminuire il prezzo; screditare, sottovalutare.
cheapness ['tʃiːpnis] n basso prezzo, buon mercato.
cheat [tʃiːt] n inganno; ingannatore, imbroglione; vti ingannare, truffare.
cheating ['tʃiːtiŋ] n inganno, truffa.
check [tʃek] n scacco; arresto; freno; controllo; quadretto su stoffa o carta; scontrino; conto; assegno bancario; **check room** deposito bagagli; vt controllare; far arrestare, fermare; (chess) dare scacco.
checkers ['tʃekəz] n giuoco della dama.
checkmate ['tʃek'meit] n scacco matto; vt dare scacco matto a.
checkpoint ['tʃekpɔint] n posto di controllo.
cheek [tʃiːk] n guancia, gota; sfrontatezza.
cheer [tʃiə] n disposizione d'animo, buon umore; applauso; vivande pl; vti applaudire; incoraggiare rallegrare.
cheerful ['tʃiəful] a allegro, di buon umore.
cheerfully ['tʃiəfuli] ad allegramente.
cheerfulness ['tʃiəfulnis] n allegria, buon umore.
cheering ['tʃiəriŋ] a incoraggiante; n acclamazioni.
cheerio ['tʃiəri'ou] interj (fam) ciao, arrivederci!
cheerless ['tʃiəlis] a triste.
cheery ['tʃiəri] a allegro.

cheese [tʃiːz] n formaggio.
chemical ['kemikəl] a chimico.
chemicals ['kemikəlz] n pl prodotti chimici.
chemist ['kemist] n chimico; farmacista.
chemistry ['kemistri] n chimica.
chenille [ʃə'niːl] n ciniglia.
cherish ['tʃeriʃ] vt nutrire; curare con affetto, tener caro.
cherry ['tʃeri] n ciliegia; **c.-tree** ciliegio.
cherub ['tʃerəb] n cherubino.
chess [tʃes] n (gioco degli) scacchi.
chessboard ['tʃesbɔːd] n scacchiera.
chessman ['tʃesmæn] n scacco.
chest [tʃest] n petto, torace; cassa, cassetta; **c. of drawers** cassettone.
chestnut ['tʃesnʌt] n castagna; **c.-tree** castagno; **horse c.** ippocastano.
chew [tʃuː] vt masticare; **to c. the cud** ruminare; **to c. over** meditare.
chick [tʃik] n pulcino.
chicken ['tʃikin] n pollastro, pollo.
chicken-pox ['tʃikinpɔks] n varicella.
chicory ['tʃikəri] n cicoria.
chide [tʃaid] vt sgridare, biasimare.
chief [tʃiːf] a principale, il più importante; n capo.
chiefly ['tʃiːfli] ad sopratutto, principalmente.
chieftain ['tʃiːftən] n (di tribù, clan) capo.
chilblain ['tʃilblein] n gelone.
child [tʃaild] pl **children** ['tʃildrən] n bambino, figlio; **c.-bearing** gravidanza.
childbirth ['tʃaildbəːθ] n parto.
childhood ['tʃaildhud] n infanzia.
childish ['tʃaildiʃ] a infantile, puerile.
childless ['tʃaildlis] a senza figli.
childlike ['tʃaildlaik] a infantile, da bambino.
Chile ['tʃili] n Cile.
Chilean ['tʃiliən] a n cileno.
chili ['tʃili] n pepe di Caienna.
chill [tʃil] a freddo; n colpo di freddo; sensazione di freddo; vt raffreddare.
chilly ['tʃili] a freddoloso, piuttosto freddo.
chime [tʃaim] n scampanio armonioso; vti battere, scampanare.
chimney ['tʃimni] n camino, fumaiuolo; **c.-corner** angolo del focolare.
chimneysweep ['tʃimniswiːp] n spazzacamino.
chimpanzee [ˌtʃimpən'ziː] n (zool) scimpanzè.
chin [tʃin] n mento.
China ['tʃainə] n Cina.
china ['tʃainə] n porcellana.
Chinese ['tʃai'niːz] a n cinese.
chink [tʃiŋk] n crepa, fessura.
chintz [tʃints] n cotone stampato.
chip [tʃip] n frammento, scheggia, truciolo; patata fritta; vt scheggiare, tagliare a piccoli pezzi.

chipboard ['tʃipbɔːd] n legno ricostituito.
chipmunk ['tʃipmʌŋk] n (zool) tamia orientale.
chiropodist [ki'rɔpədist] n pedicure, callista.
chirp [tʃəːp] n cinguettio; vi cinguettare.
chisel ['tʃizl] n cesello, scalpello; vi cesellare.
chivalrous ['ʃivəlrəs] a cavalleresco.
chivalry ['ʃivəlri] n (fig) cavalleria.
chive [tʃaiv] n aglio di serpe.
chloride ['klɔːraid] n cloruro.
chlorine ['klɔːriːn] n cloro.
chloroform ['klɔrəfɔːm] n cloroformio; vt cloroformizzare.
chlorophyl(l) ['klɔrəfil] n (bot) clorofilla.
chocolate ['tʃɔkəlit] n cioccolata; cioccolato, cioccolatino.
choice [tʃɔis] a prelibato, scelto, squisito; n scelta.
choir ['kwaiə] n coro; **choirmaster** maestro di cappella.
choke [tʃouk] n soffocazione; strozzameeto; (mech) regolatore; vti soffocare, soffocarsi; ingombrare.
cholera ['kɔlərə] n colera.
choleric ['kɔlərik] a collerico, irascibile.
choose [tʃuːz] vti scegliere.
choos(e)y ['tʃuːzi] a (fam) schizzinoso, pignolo.
chop [tʃɔp] n colpo d'ascia; costoletta di maiale o di montone; vt tagliare, tagliuzzare.
chopper ['tʃɔpə] n corta ascia, mannaia.
choppy ['tʃɔpi] a increspato, mosso.
choral ['kɔːrəl] a n corale.
chord [kɔːd] n (mus) corda, (mus) accordo.
choreographer [ˌkɔri'ɔgræfə] n coreografo.
choreography [ˌkɔri'ɔgrəfi] n coreografia.
chorister ['kɔristə] n corista.
chorus ['kɔːrəs] n coro; ritornello.
Christ [kraist] nm pr Cristo.
christen ['krisn] vt battezzare.
Christendom ['krisndəm] n cristianità.
christening ['krisniŋ] n battesimo.
Christian ['kristjən] a n cristiano; **C. name** nome proprio; nome di battesimo.
Christianity ['kristi'æniti] n cristianesimo.
christianize ['kristjənaiz] vt convertire al cristianesimo.
Christina [kris'tiːnə] **Christine** ['kristiːn] nf pr Cristina.
Christmas ['krisməs] n Natale; **C. gift** [gift] strenna natalizia.
Christopher ['kristəfə] nm pr Cristoforo.
chromatic [krə'mætik] a cromatico.
chrome [kroum] n cromo; vt cromare.

chromium ['kroumiəm] n (chem) cromo.

chromosome ['kroumǝsoum] n cromosoma.

chronic ['krɔnik] a cronico; (sl) terribile.

chronicle ['krɔnikl] n cronaca.

chronicler ['krɔniklǝ] n cronista.

chronological [,krɔnǝ'lɔdʒikǝl] a cronologico.

chronology [krǝ'nɔlǝdʒi] n cronologia.

chronometer [krǝ'nɔmitǝ] n cronometro.

chrysalis ['krisǝlis] n crisalide.

chrysanthemum [kri'sænθǝmǝm] n crisantemo.

chubby ['tʃʌbi] a paffuto, pienotto.

chuck [tʃʌk] vt dare un buffetto a; (fam) gettare; (fam) sperperare; c. **out** (fam) mettere alla porta; **chucker-out** chi getta fuori da un locale gli intrusi.

chuckle ['tʃʌkl] n riso soffocato; vi ridere sotto i baffi.

chum [tʃʌm] n (fam) amico intimo, compagno; vi (fam) essere amici.

chunk [tʃʌŋk] n grosso pezzo, tozzo.

church [tʃǝːtʃ] n chiesa.

churchman ['tʃǝːtʃmǝn] n ecclesiastico.

churchyard ['tʃǝːtʃ'jɑːd] n campo santo.

churl [tʃǝːl] n zotico, uomo sgarbato o tirchio.

churlish ['tʃǝːliʃ] a rozzo, sgarbato, tirchio.

churlishness ['tʃǝːliʃnis] n sgarbatezza, tirchieria.

churn [tʃǝːn] n zangola; vti battere il latte dentro la zangola per farne burro; agitar(si).

chute [ʃuːt] n canale di scolo.

ciborium [si'bɔːriǝm] n ciborio.

cicada [si'kɑːdǝ] n cicala.

cicatrize ['sikǝtraiz] vti cicatrizzar (si).

cider ['saidǝ] n sidro.

cigar [si'gɑː] n sigaro; c. **store** tabaccheria.

cigarette [,sigǝ'ret] n sigaretta; c. **case** portasigarette.

cinder ['sindǝ] n brace, cenere.

Cinderella [,sindǝ'relǝ] n Cenerentola.

cine-camera [sini'kæmǝrǝ] n macchina da presa, cinepresa.

cinema ['sinimǝ] n cinema(tografo).

cinematographic [sini,mætǝ'græfik] a cinematografico.

cinematography [,sinimǝ'tɔgrǝfi] n cinematografia.

cinnamon ['sinǝmǝn] n cannella, cinnamomo.

cipher ['saifǝ] n zero; nulla, nullità; cifrario, cifra.

circle ['sǝːkl] n cerchio, circolo; orbita; (theat) galleria; vti circondare, girare intorno a.

circuit ['sǝːkit] n circuito; giro; circoscrizione.

circuitous [sǝ'kjuːitǝs] a tortuoso, indiretto.

circular ['sǝːkjulǝ] a n circolare.

circularize ['sǝːkjulǝraiz] vt inviare circolari a.

circulate ['sǝːkjuleit] vti (far) circolare.

circulation [,sǝːkju'leiʃǝn] n circolazione.

circulatory ['sǝːkjuːlǝtǝri] n circolatorio.

circumcise ['sǝːkǝmsaiz] vt circoncidere.

circumcision [,sǝːkǝm'siʒǝn] n circoncisione.

circumference [sǝ'kʌmfǝrǝns] n circonferenza.

circumflex ['sǝːkǝmfleks] a circonflesso.

circumlocution [,sǝːkǝmlǝ'kjuːʃǝn] n circonlocuzione, perifrasi.

circumscribe ['sǝːkǝmskraib] vt circoscrivere.

circumspect ['sǝːkǝmspekt] a circospetto, cauto.

circumspection [,sǝːkǝm'spekʃǝn] n circospezione.

circumstance ['sǝːkǝmstǝns] n circostanza, condizione.

circumstantial [,sǝ'kǝm'stænʃǝl] a circostanziato; indiziario.

circumvent [,sǝːkǝm'vent] vt ingannare, circuire.

circumvention [,sǝːkǝm'ventʃǝn] n circonvenzione, raggiro.

circus ['sǝːkǝs] n circo.

Cistercian [sis'tǝːʃǝn] a n cistercense.

cistern ['sistǝn] n cisterna, serbatoio.

citadel ['sitǝdl] n cittadella, fortezza.

cite [sait] vt citare.

citizen ['sitizn] n cittadino; **citizenship** n cittadinanza.

citrate ['sitrit] n (chem) citrato.

citric ['sitrik] a citrico.

citron ['sitrǝn] n cedro.

city ['siti] n città, centro d'una grande città.

civet ['sivit] n zibetto.

civic ['sivik] a civico.

civil ['sivl] a civile, educato, gentile.

civilian [si'viljǝn] n civile, borghese.

civility [si'viliti] n cortesia, educazione.

civilization [,sivilai'zeiʃǝn] n civilizzazione, civiltà.

civilize ['sivilaiz] vt incivilire, civilizzare.

claim [kleim] n diritto, pretesa; reclamo, rivendicazione; concessione mineraria; vt pretendere; reclamare, rivendicare; asserire.

claimant ['kleimǝnt] n pretendente.

clairvoyance [klɛǝ'vɔiǝns] n chiaroveggenza.

clairvoyant [klɛǝ'vɔiǝnt] a n chiaroveggente.

clam [klæm] *n* mollusco bivalve; (*mech*) grappa, morsa.

clamant ['kleimənt] *a* insistente, rumoroso.

clamber ['klæmbə] *vi* arrampicarsi.

clamminess ['klæminis] *n* viscosità.

clammy ['klæmi] *a* freddo umido; viscoso.

clamor ['klæmə] *vi* chiedere clamorosamente, fare molto rumore.

clamorous ['klæmərəs] *a* clamoroso.

clamp [klæmp] *n* pinza, morsa; *vt* tener fermo, assicurare.

clan [klæn] *n* tribù, 'clan'.

clandestine [klæn'destin] *a* clandestino.

clang [klæŋ] **clangor** ['klæŋgə] *n* fragore.

clang [klæŋ] *vti* far risuonare con fragore.

clank [klæŋk] *n* suono metallico, clangore; *vi* produrre un rumore secco, metallico.

clap [klæp] *n* battimano; colpo; *vti* battere le mani, applaudire.

clapper ['klæpə] *n* applauditore; battente, battaglio.

Clara ['klɛərə] **Clare** [klɛə] *n f pr* Clara, Chiara.

claret ['klærət] *n* bordò.

clarification [ˌklærifi'keiʃən] *n* chiarificazione.

clarify ['klærifai] *vt* chiarire; raffinare.

clarinet [ˌklæri'net] *n* (*mus*) clarinetto.

clarity ['klæriti] *n* chiarezza.

clash [klæʃ] *n* collisione, scontro; conflitto; rumore, strepito; *vti* urtar (si), fare strepito.

clashing ['klæʃiŋ] *a* opposto, contrastante.

clasp [klɑːsp] *n* fermaglio, gancio; stretta di mano, abbraccio; *vt* agganciare; stringere, abbracciare.

class [klɑːs] *n* classe; *vt* classificare.

classic ['klæsik] *a n* classico.

classical ['klæsikəl] *a* classico.

classicism ['klæsisizəm] *n* classicismo.

classification [ˌklæsifi'keiʃən] *n* classifica, classificazione.

classify ['klæsifai] *vt* classificare.

clatter ['klætə] *n* acciottolio, fracasso; *vti* far fracasso.

Claud(e) [klɔːd] *nm pr* Claudio.

clause [klɔːz] *n* clausola.

claustrophobia [ˌklɔːstrə'foubiə] *n* claustrofobia.

claw [klɔː] *n* artiglio; *vti* artigliare.

clay [klei] *n* argilla, creta.

clean [kliːn] *a* pulito, netto; innocente, puro; completo; *vt* pulire.

cleaning ['kliːniŋ] *n* pulitura, pulizia; **dry-c.** lavaggio a secco; **spring c.** pulizia di Pasqua.

cleanliness ['klenlinis] *n* pulizia.

cleanly ['klenli] *a* pulito; ['kliːnli] *ad* in modo pulito.

cleanness ['kliːnnis] *n* pulizia, chiarezza, purezza.

cleanse [klenz] *vt* purificare; pulire.

cleansing ['klenziŋ] *a* purificante; *n* purificazione; detersione; **c. cream** crema detergente.

clear [kliə] *a* chiaro, evidente; libero da ostacoli; *vti* chiarire, chiarificare, schiarir(si); sdoganare.

clearance ['kliərəns] *n* liquidazione; sdoganamento.

clearing ['kliəriŋ] *n* tratto di terreno disboscato per la coltivazione; **c. house** (*com*) stanza di compensazione.

clearly ['kliəli] *ad* chiaramente, distintamente.

clearness ['kliənis] *n* chiarezza.

cleavage ['kliːvidʒ] *n* sfaldamento.

cleaver ['kliːvə] *n* mannaia del macellaio.

clef [klef] *n* (*mus*) chiave.

cleft [kleft] *n* spaccatura, fessura.

clemency ['klemənsi] *n* clemenza.

clement ['klemənt] *a* clemente, mite.

clench [klentʃ] *vt* stringere; (*tec*) ribadire; (*fig*) definire.

clergy ['kləːdʒi] *n* clero.

clergyman ['kləːdʒimən] *n* pastore evangelico, ecclesiastico.

cleric ['klerik] *n* ecclesiastico.

clerical ['klerikəl] *a* clericale; di impiegato; **c. work** lavoro d'ufficio.

clerk [kləːk] *n* impiegato d'ufficio; commesso.

clever ['klevə] *a* intelligente, abile, ingegnoso.

cleverness ['klevənis] *n* intelligenza, abilità, ingegnosità.

click [klik] *n* suono metallico; scatto.

client ['klaiənt] *n* cliente.

clientele [ˌkliːɑ̃ːn'teil] *n* clientela.

cliff [klif] *n* rupe a picco, scarpata.

climate ['klaimit] *n* clima.

climatic [klai'mætik] *a* climatico.

climax ['klaimæks] *n* culmine, punto culminante.

climb [klaim] *vti* arrampicarsi, scalare; *n* salita; scalata.

climber ['klaimə] *n* scalatore, (*bot*) pianta rampicante; (*fig*) arrivista.

clinch [klintʃ] *v* **clench.**

cling [kliŋ] *vi* avvitticchiarsi, aggrapparsi.

clinic ['klinik] *n* clinica.

clinical ['klinikəl] *a* clinico.

clink [kliŋk] *n* tintinnio; (*sl*) prigione; *vti* (far) tintinnare.

clip [klip] *n* fermaglio, gancio; taglio, tosatura; ritaglio; *vt* tagliare, tosare.

clipper ['klipə] *n* goletta; forbici per tosare.

clipping ['klipiŋ] *n* taglio, tosatura; ritaglio di un giornale.

clique [kliːk] *n* cricca.

cloak [klouk] *n* mantello; (*fig*) pretesto; *vt* (*fig*) mascherare.

clock [klɔk] *n* orologio (da muro), pendola; *vti* cronometrare.

clockwork ['klɔkwəːk] n meccanismo d'orologio.
clod [klɔd] n zolla di terra.
clog [klɔg] n zoccolo; intoppo; vt ingombrare, ostruire.
cloister ['klɔistə] n chiostro, convento.
close [klous] a chiuso, rinchiuso; afoso; fitto, stretto; vicino; ad (da) vicino; prep vicino a; n recinto.
close [klouz] n conclusione, fine; vt chiudere, concludere, finire; **closed-circuit television** n televisione a circuito chiuso.
closely ['klousli] ad strettamente; attentamente.
closeness ['klousnis] n prossimità, vicinanza; pesantezza dell'aria.
closet ['klɔzit] n gabinetto, salotto privato, studio; armadio a muro.
closing ['klouziŋ] a di chiusura, ultimo; n chiusura.
closure ['klouʒə] n chiusura, fine.
clot [klɔt] n coagulo, grumo; vi coagularsi, raggrumarsi.
cloth [klɔθ] n stoffa, tela, tessuto; tovaglia.
clothe [klouð] vt (ri)vestire.
clothes [klouðz] n pl indumenti, vestiti pl; **clothespeg, clothespin** molletta ferma-bucato.
clothier ['klouðiə] n commerciante in vestiti e stoffe.
clothing ['klouðiŋ] n vestiario, indumenti.
cloud [klaud] n nube, nuvola; vi rannuvolarsi; vt annuvolare, oscurare.
cloudless ['klaudlis] a senza nubi, sereno.
cloudy ['klaudi] a nuvoloso, oscuro.
clove [klouv] n chiodo di garofano.
clover ['klouvə] n trifoglio.
clown [klaun] n buffone, pagliaccio.
clownish ['klauniʃ] a pagliaccesco; rustico.
cloy [klɔi] vt saziare, nauseare.
club [klʌb] n bastone, randello; circolo; (cards) fiori; vt bastonare; **to c. together** pagare il proprio tributo.
cluck [klʌk] vi chiocciare.
clue [kluː] n bandolo, indizio.
clump [klʌmp] n gruppo d'alberi o di cespugli; vi camminare pesantemente.
clumsiness ['klʌmzinis] n goffaggine, mancanza di tatto.
clumsy ['klʌmzi] a goffo, senza tatto.
cluster ['klʌstə] n grappolo, gruppo, sciame; vi crescere in grappoli; raccogliersi in gruppo.
clutch [klʌtʃ] n presa fortissima, stretta; (mech) innesto; vti afferrare, agguantare; **clutches** pl artigli, grinfie pl.
clutter ['klʌtə] n confusione, massa confusa; vti far confusione, ingombrare.

coach [koutʃ] n carrozza, (rly) carrozza, vagone, vettura; pullman; insegnante privato, ripetitore; allenatore di atleti; vt allenare; dare ripetizioni a; **baby c.** carrozzina per bambini.
coagulate [kou'ægjuleit] vti coagulare, coagularsi.
coagulation [kou,ægju'leiʃən] n coagulazione.
coal [koul] n carbone; **c. field** bacino carbonifero.
coalesce [,kouə'les] vi fondersi, unirsi.
coalition [,kouə'liʃən] n coalizione.
coal-mine ['koulmain] n miniera di carbone.
coarse [kɔːs] a ruvido, rozzo, grossolano, volgare.
coarseness ['kɔːsnis] n ruvidezza, grossolanità.
coast [koust] n costa; vt costeggiare.
coastal ['koustl] a costiero.
coastguard ['koustgɑːd] n guardiacoste.
coat [kout] n giacca; mantello; paltò; mano (di vernice); vt rivestire; verniciare; **c.-of-arms** stemma.
coating ['koutiŋ] n rivestimento, strato.
coax [kouks] vt persuadere con le moine, blandire.
cob [kɔb] n cavallo da tiro; cigno maschio; pannocchia di frumentone.
cobalt ['koubɔːlt] n cobalto.
cobble ['kɔbl] n ciottolo; vt selciare con ciottoli; rattoppare.
cobbler ['kɔblə] n ciabattino.
cobra ['koubrə] n (zool) cobra.
cobweb ['kɔbweb] n ragnatela.
cocaine [kə'kein] n cocaina.
cochineal ['kɔtʃiniːl] n cocciniglia.
cock [kɔk] n gallo, maschio di uccelli; rubinetto, spina; mucchio di fieno; cane di fucile; vti drizzar(si); ammucchiare fieno; **c.-eyed** strabico.
cockade [kɔ'keid] n coccarda.
cockchafer ['kɔk,tʃeifə] n maggiolino.
cockerel ['kɔkərəl] n galletto.
cockle ['kɔkl] n (zool) cardio; (bot) loglio; **c.-shell** conchiglia.
cockney ['kɔkni] a n londinese (spesso con senso spregiativo).
cockpit ['kɔkpit] n arena da combattimento; (av) carlinga.
cockroach ['kɔkroutʃ] n scarafaggio.
cockscomb ['kɔkskoum] n cresta di gallo; (bot) amaranto.
cocksure ['kɔk'ʃuə] a presuntuoso.
cocktail ['kɔkteil] n 'cocktail'; **c. cabinet** mobile bar.
cocky ['kɔki] a impertinente, presuntuoso.
cocoa ['koukou] n cacao.
coconut ['koukənʌt] n noce di cocco.
cocoon [kə'kuːn] n bozzolo.
cod [kɔd] n (inv) merluzzo.

coddle ['kɔdl] *vt* vezzeggiare, coccolare.
code [koud] *n* codice, cifrario.
codeine ['koudiːn] *n* codeina.
codex ['koudeks] *pl* **codices** *n* codice.
codicil ['kɔdisil] *n* codicillo.
codification [ˌkɔdifi'keiʃən] *n* codificazione.
codify ['kɔdifai] *vt* codificare.
coeducation ['kouˌedjuː'keiʃən] *n* istruzione in scuola mista.
coefficient [ˌkoui'fiʃənt] *n* coefficiente.
coerce [kou'əːs] *vt* costringere.
coercion [kou'əːʃən] *n* coercizione.
coercive [kou'əːsiv] *a* coercitivo.
coexistence ['kouig'zistəns] *n* coesistenza.
coffee ['kɔfi] *n* caffè; **c. mill** macinino da caffè; **c. pot** caffettiera; **ground c.** caffè tostato; **white c.** caffellatte.
coffer ['kɔfə] *n* cofano, scrigno.
coffin ['kɔfin] *n* cassa da morto, bara.
cog [kɔg] *n* dente d'una ruota; *vt* dentare una ruota.
cogency ['koudʒənsi] *n* forza di persuasione.
cogent ['koudʒənt] *a* convincente, persuasivo.
cogitate ['kɔdʒiteit] *vti* cogitare, ponderare.
cogitation [ˌkɔdʒi'teiʃən] *n* cogitazione.
cognate ['kɔgneit] *a n* congiunto, parente.
cognizance ['kɔgnizəns] *n* conoscenza, percezione.
cohabit [kou'hæbit] *vi* coabitare.
cohabitation [ˌkouhæbi'teiʃən] *n* coabitazione.
co-heir ['kou'ɛə] (*m*) **co-heiress** ['kou'ɛəris] (*f*) *n* coerede.
cohere [kou'hiə] *vi* aderire; essere coerente.
coherence [kou'hiərəns] *n* coerenza.
coherent [kou'hiərənt] *a* coerente.
cohesion [kou'hiːʒən] *n* coesione.
cohesive [kou'hiːsiv] *a* coesivo.
coiffure [kwɑː'fjuə] *n* pettinatura, acconciatura.
coil [kɔil] *n* rotolo, gomitolo; (*snake*) spira; (*el*) bobina; *vt* arrotolare, avvolgere in spire.
coin [kɔin] *n* moneta; *vt* coniare.
coinage ['kɔinidʒ] *n* conio; sistema monetario.
coincide [ˌkouin'said] *vi* coincidere.
coincidence [ˌkou'insidəns] *n* coincidenza; combinazione.
coincidental [kouˌinsi'dentl] *a* coincidente, di coincidenza.
coke [kouk] *n* carbone coke.
colander ['kʌləndə] *n* colapasta, colatoio.
cold [kould] *a* freddo; *n* freddo; raffreddore; **to be c.** aver freddo; **to catch a c.** infreddarsi.
coldly ['kouldli] *ad* freddamente.
coldness ['kouldnis] *n* freddezza.

colic ['kɔlik] *n* colica.
collaborate [kə'læbəreit] *vi* collaborare.
collaboration [kəˌlæbə'reiʃən] *n* collaborazione.
collaborator [kə'læbəreitə] *n* collaboratore.
collapse [kə'læps] *n* crollo, caduta; (*med*) collasso; *vi* crollare; avere un collasso.
collar ['kɔlə] *n* colletto; (*dogs*) collare; **c. stud, c. button** bottone del colletto; *vt* afferrare, prendere per il collo.
collate [kɔ'leit] *vt* collazionare.
collateral [kɔ'lætərəl] *a n* collaterale.
collation [kɔ'leiʃən] *n* collazione.
colleague ['kɔliːg] *n* collega.
collect ['kɔlekt] *n* colletta; [kə'lekt] *vt* raccogliere, mettere insieme, radunare, fare una collezione; *vi* radunarsi; **to c. oneself** riprendersi.
collected [kɔ'lektid] *a* raccolto, riunito; padrone di sè.
collection [kə'lekʃən] *n* riunione, raccolta, colletta, collezione.
collective [kə'lektiv] *a* collettivo.
collectivity [kəlek'tiviti] *n* collettività.
collector [kə'lektə] *n* collezionista; esattore.
college ['kɔlidʒ] *n* collegio; università.
collide [kə'laid] *vi* scontrarsi.
collier ['kɔliə] *n* minatore; nave carboniera.
collision [kə'liʒən] *n* collisione, scontro.
colloquial [kə'loukwiəl] *a* usato nella conversazione familiare, d'uso corrente; **colloquialism** espressione familiare.
colloquy ['kɔləkwi] *n* colloquio.
collusion [kə'luːʒən] *n* collusione.
Colombia [kə'lʌmbiə] *n* (*geogr*) Colombia.
colon ['koulən] *n* due punti; **semi-c.** punto e virgola.
colonel ['kəːnl] *n* colonnello.
colonial [kə'louniəl] *a* coloniale.
colonist ['kɔlənist] *n* abitante di colonia.
colonization [ˌkɔlənai'zeiʃən] *n* colonizzazione.
colonize ['kɔlənaiz] *vti* colonizzare.
colonnade [ˌkɔlə'neid] *n* colonnato.
colony ['kɔləni] *n* colonia.
color ['kʌlə] *n* colore, colorito, tinta; apparenza; pretesto; **colors** *pl* bandiera; *vti* colorare, colorire, colorirsi, dipingere; arrossire.
colored ['kʌləd] *a* colorato, colorito, di colore; **c. person** persona di colore.
colorful ['kʌləful] *a* pieno di colore, pittoresco.
coloring ['kʌləriŋ] *n* colorante; colorito; arrossimento.
colorless ['kʌləlis] *a* incolore, pallido; insipido.

colossal [kə'lɔsl] *a* colossale.
Colosseum [,kɔlə'siəm] *n* Colosseo.
colt [koult] *n* puledro.
column ['kɔləm] *n* colonna.
columnist ['kɔləmnist] *n* giornalista, cronista.
coma ['koumə] *n* coma, torpore.
comb [koum] *n* pettine; (*crest*) cresta; favo; *vt* pettinare, strigliare; (*fig*) rastrellare, perlustrare.
combat ['kɔmbət] *n* combattimento, lotta; *vti* combattere, lottare.
combatant ['kɔmbətənt] *a n* combattente.
combination [,kɔmbi'neiʃən] *n* combinazione.
combine ['kɔmbain] *n* associazione, sindacato; [kəm'bain] *vti* combinar-(si).
combined [kɔm'baind] *a* combinato, congiunto; **c. ticket** biglietto misto.
combing ['koumiŋ] *n* pettinata; (*fig*) rastrellamento, perlustramento.
combustible [kəm'bʌstəbl] *a n* combustibile.
combustion [kəm'bʌstʃən] *n* combustione.
come [kʌm] *vi* venire, arrivare, giungere; accadere; **to c. back** ritornare; **to c. in** entrare; **to c. around** passare da; riprendere i sensi.
comedian [kə'miːdiən] *n* commediante, (attore) comico.
comedown ['kʌmdaun] *n* (*fig*) crollo.
comedy ['kɔmidi] *n* commedia.
comeliness ['kʌmlinis] *n* avvenenza.
comely ['kʌmli] *a* avvenente.
comet ['kɔmit] *n* cometa.
comfort ['kʌmfət] *n* conforto, consolazione, comodità, agio; *vt* confortare, consolare.
comfortable ['kʌmfətəbl] *a* comodo, confortevole; adeguato.
comfortably ['kʌmfətəbli] *ad* comodamente, con agio.
comforter ['kʌmfətə] *n* consolatore; lunga sciarpa di lana; trapunta.
comic(al) ['kɔmik(l)] *a* comico, buffo; *n pl* giornale a fumetti.
coming ['kʌmiŋ] *a* venturo, prossimo; *n* venuta, arrivo.
comma ['kɔmə] *n* virgola.
command [kə'mɑːnd] *n* comando, ordine; dominio; *vti* comandare, ordinare; controllare, dominare.
commandant [,kɔmən'dænt] *n* comandante.
commandeer [,kɔmən'diə] *vt* requisire.
commander [kɔ'mɑːndə] *n* comandante.
commanding [kɔ'mɑːndiŋ] *a* che comanda; maestoso, dominante.
commandment [kɔ'mɑːndmənt] *n* comandamento.
commemorate [kə'meməreit] *vt* commemorare.
commemoration [kə,memə'reiʃən] *n* commemorazione.
commence [kə'mens] *vti* cominciare.

commencement [kə'mensmənt] *n* principio; cerimonia per il conferimento di lauree.
commend [kə'mend] *vt* lodare; raccomandare.
commendable [kə'mendəbl] *a* lodevole.
commendation [,kɔmen'deiʃən] *n* elogio, raccomandazione.
commensurable [kə'menʃərəbl] *a* commensurabile.
commensurate [kə'menʃərit] *a* adeguato, commisurato.
comment [kɔment] *n* commento; *vi* commentare.
commentary ['kɔməntəri] *n* commentario, commento.
commentator ['kɔmenteitə] *n* commentatore, radiocronista.
commerce ['kɔməːs] *n* commercio.
commercial [kɔ'məːʃəl] *a* commerciale; (*tv etc*) pubblicità.
commercialize [kə'məːʃəlaiz] *vt* rendere commerciabile.
commiserate [kə'mizəreit] *vt* compiangere.
commiseration [kə,mizə'reiʃən] *n* commiserazione, pietà.
commissariat [,kɔmi'sɛəriət] *n* (*mil*) commissariato.
commission [kə'miʃən] *n* commissione, incarico, mandato; brevetto da ufficiale; *vt* incaricare, dare una carica a, armare, equipaggiare (una nave).
commissionaire [kə,miʃə'nɛə] *n* portiere gallonato.
commissioned [kə'miʃənd] *a* delegato; **non-c. officer** sottufficiale.
commissioner [kə'miʃənə] *n* commissario.
commit [kə'mit] *vt* affidare. consegnare, mandare in prigione, commettere **to c. oneself** impegnarsi.
commitment [kə'mitmənt] *n* impegno.
committal [kə'mitl] *n* consegna, perpretazione; il mandare in prigione.
committee [kə'miti] *n* comitato, commissione.
commode [kə'moud] *n* cassettone.
commodious [kə'moudiəs] *a* spazioso.
commodity [kə'mɔditi] *n* merce, prodotto, genere di prima necessità.
commodore ['kɔmədɔː] *n* (*naut*) commodoro.
common ['kɔmən] *a* comune, usuale, ordinario; *n* terreno demaniale; **c. market** mercato comune; **c.-sense** buonsenso, senso comune; **c. stock** (*com*) azioni ordinarie; **in c.** in comune.
commoner ['kɔmənə] *n* borghese o popolano.
commonly ['kɔmənli] *ad* comunemente.
commonplace ['kɔmənpleis] *a* banale, trito; *n* banalità, luogo comune.
commons ['kɔmənz] *n pl* popolo;

House of C. Camera dei Comuni; (*food*) cibo, razioni *pl*; **short c.** scarse razioni *pl*.

commonwealth ['kɔmənwelθ] *n* comunità indipendente.

commotion [kə'mouʃən] *n* agitazione, trambusto.

communal ['kɔmjunl] *a* della comunità, comunale.

communicant [kə'mjuːnikənt] *n* (*eccl*) comunicando; informatore.

communicate [kə'mjuːnikeit] *vti* comunicar(si).

communication [kə͵mjuːni'keiʃən] comunicazione.

communicative [kə'mjuːnikətiv] *a* comunicativo.

communion [kə'mjuːnjən] *n* comunione, comunanza.

communiqué [kə'mjuːnikei] *n* comunicato ufficiale.

communism ['kɔmjunizəm] *n* comunismo.

communist ['kɔmjunist] *n* comunista.

community [kə'mjuːniti] *n* comunità.

commutation [͵kɔmjuː'teiʃən] *n* commutazione; **c. passenger** (*rly*) abbonato; **c. ticket** (*rly*) biglietto di abbonamento.

commute [kə'mjuːt] *vt* commutare; *vi* fare la spola.

commuter [kə'mjuːtə] *n* (*rly*) abbonato.

compact ['kɔmpækt] *n* patto, contratto; portacipria.

compact [kəm'pækt] *a* compatto, conciso.

compactness [kəm'pæktnis] *n* compattezza, concisione.

companion [kəm'pænjən] *n* compagno, socio; dama di compagnia.

companionable [kəm'pænjənəbl] *a* socievole.

companionship [kəm'pænjənʃip] *n* amicizia, compagnia.

company ['kʌmpəni] *n* compagnia, associazione, società; (*naut*) ciurma; **joint stock c.** società per azioni; **limited liability c.** società a responsabilità limitata.

comparable ['kɔmpərəbl] *a* paragonabile.

comparative [kəm'pærətiv] *a n* comparativo; comparato; relativo; **comparatively** relativamente, comparativamente.

compare [kəm'pɛə] *vti* paragonare, confrontare.

comparison [kəm'pærisn] *n* paragone, confronto.

compartment [kəm'paːtmənt] *n* scompartimento.

compass ['kʌmpəs] *n* circonferenza, spazio, portata; bussola; *vt* circondare; realizzare.

compasses ['kʌmpəsiz] *n pl* compasso.

compassion [kəm'pæʃən] *n* compassione, pietà.

compassionate [kəm'pæʃənit] *a* pieno di compassione; *vt* compassionare.

compatibility [kəm͵pætə'biliti] *n* compatibilità.

compatible [kəm'pætəbl] *a* compatibile.

compatriot [kəm'pætriət] *n* compatriota.

compel [kəm'pel] *vt* costringere, forzare.

compelling [kəm'peliŋ] *a* irresistibile.

compendious [kəm'pendiəs] *a* compendioso.

compendium [kəm'pendiəm] *pl* **compendiums, compendia** *n* compendio.

compensate ['kɔmpenseit] *vti* compensare, ricompensare.

compensation [͵kɔmpen'seiʃən] *n* compenso, indennità.

compère ['kɔmpɛə] *n* (*theat*) presentatore, gareggiare, concorrere.

compete [kəm'piːt] *vi* competere; *vti* presentare.

competence ['kɔmpitəns] *n* competenza, capacità.

competent ['kɔmpitənt] *a* competente, capace.

competition [͵kɔmpi'tiʃən] *n* competizione, concorso, gara; (*com*) concorrenza.

competitive [kəm'petitiv] *a* di competizione, di concorso; (*com*) di concorrenza; **c. prices** prezzi di concorrenza.

competitor [kəm'petitə] *n* competitore, concorrente.

compilation [͵kɔmpi'leiʃən] *n* compilazione.

compile [kəm'pail] *vt* compilare.

complacency [kəm'pleisnsi] *n* compiacenza, compiacimento.

complacent [kəm'pleisnt] *a* compiaciuto, compiacente.

complain [kəm'plein] *vi* lamentarsi.

complaint [kəm'pleint] *n* lagnanza, reclamo; malattia.

complaisance [kəm'pleizəns] *n* compiacenza, cortesia.

complement ['kɔmplimənt] *n* complemento.

complementary [͵kɔmpli'mentəri] *a* complementare.

complete [kəm'pliːt] *a* completo, intero, perfetto; *vt* completare, finire; riempire.

completely [kəm'pliːtli] *ad* completamente.

completion [kəm'pliːʃən] *n* completamento; compimento.

complex ['kɔmpleks] *a* complesso, complicato; *n* complesso.

complexion [kəm'plekʃən] *n* carnagione, colorito.

complexity [kəm'pleksiti] *n* complessità.

compliance [kəm'plaiəns] *n* condiscendenza; **in c. with** d'accordo con.

compliant [kəm'plaiənt] *a* accondiscendente.

complicate ['komplikeit] *vt* complicare.

complicated ['komplikeitid] *a* complicato.

complication [‚kompli'keiʃən] *n* complicazione.

complicity [kəm'plisiti] *n* complicità.

compliment ['komplimənt] *n* complimento; *vt* [‚kompli'ment] congratularsi con.

complimentary [‚kompli'mentəri] *a* di complimento, di omaggio, di favore; **c. tickets** biglietti di omaggio.

comply [kəm'plai] *vi* accondiscendere, conformarsi.

component [kəm'pounənt] *a n* componente.

compose [kəm'pouz] *vt* comporre; calmare.

composed [kəm'pouzd] *a* composto, calmo.

composer [kəm'pouzə] *n* compositore.

composite ['kompəzit] *a* composto, composito.

composition [‚kompə'ziʃən] *n* composizione; concordato; tema.

compositor [kəm'pozitə] *n* (*typ*) compositore.

compost ['kompost] *n* composto, concime; *vt* concimare.

composure [kəm'pouʒə] *n* calma, compostezza.

compound ['kompaund] *a* composto; *n* miscela, composto; *vt* [kom'paund] comporre, mescolare; *vi* accordarsi.

comprehend [‚kompri'hend] *vt* comprendere, includere.

comprehensible [‚kompri'hensəbl] *a* comprensibile.

comprehension [‚kompri'henʃən] *n* comprensione.

comprehensive [‚kompri'hensiv] *a* comprensivo.

compress ['kompres] *n* compressa.

compress [kəm'pres] *vt* comprimere; condensare.

compression [kəm'preʃən] *n* compressione; (*fig*) concentrazione.

comprise [kəm'praiz] *vt* comprendere, includere.

compromise ['komprəmaiz] *n* compromesso; *vti* compromettere, accomodare, sistemare.

comptometer [komp'tomitə] *n* macchina calcolatrice.

compulsion [kəm'pʌlʃən] *n* costrizione, obbligo.

compulsive [kəm'pʌlsiv] *a* coercitivo.

compulsory [kəm'pʌlsəri] *a* obbligatorio, forzato.

compunction [kəm'pʌŋkʃən] *n* compunzione.

computation [‚kompju:'teiʃən] *n* computo, calcolo.

compute [kəm'pju:t] *vt* computare.

computer [kəm'pju:tə] *n* calcolatore, (macchina) calcolatrice.

comrade ['komrid] *n* camerata, compagno.

con [kon] *vt* imparare a memoria.

concave ['kon'keiv] *a* concavo, a volta.

conceal [kən'si:l] *vt* celare, nascondere.

concealment [kən'si:lmənt] *n* occultamento, nascondiglio.

concede [kən'si:d] *vt* ammettere; concedere.

conceit [kən'si:t] *n* vanità, presunzione; ricercatezza; concettismo.

conceited [kən'si:tid] *a* presuntuoso, vanesio, affettato.

conceivable [kən'si:vəbl] *a* concepibile.

conceive [kən'si:v] *vt* concepire.

concentrate ['konsentreit] *vti* concentrar(si).

concentration [‚konsen'treiʃən] *n* concentramento, concentrazione.

concentric [kon'sentrik] *a* concentrico.

concept ['konsept] *n* concetto.

conception [kən'sepʃən] *n* concezione.

concern [kən'sə:n] *n* ansietà, faccenda, ditta, impresa; *vt* avere a che fare con, concernere, riguardare.

concerned [kən'sə:nd] *a* interessato; preoccupato.

concerning [kən'sə:niŋ] *prep* riguardo a, circa.

concert ['konsət] *n* concerto; accordo.

concert [kən'sə:t] *vt* concertare.

concertina [‚konsə'ti:nə] *n* piccola fisarmonica.

concerto [kən'tʃə:tou] *n* (*mus*) concerto; **piano c.** concerto per pianoforte.

concession [kən'seʃən] *n* concessione; **concessionary** *a* concessionario.

concession(n)aire [kən seʃə'nɛə] *n* concessionario.

conciliate [kən'silieit] *vt* conciliare, guadagnarsi.

conciliation [kən‚sili'eiʃən] *n* conciliazione.

conciliatory [kən'siliətəri] *a* conciliante.

concise [kən'sais] *a* breve, conciso.

conciseness [kən'saisnis] *n* concisione, brevità.

concision [kən'siʒən] *n* concisione.

conclave ['konkleiv] *n* conclave.

conclude [kən'klu:d] *vti* concludere, finire.

concluding [kən'klu:diŋ] *a* finale, ultimo.

conclusion [kən'klu:ʒən] *n* conclusione, fine.

conclusive [kən'kluːziv] *a* conclusivo.

concoct [kən'kɔkt] *vt* mescolare ingredienti; architettare, tramare.

concoction [kən'kɔkʃən] *n* miscuglio, macchinazione.

concomitance [kən'kɔmitəns] *n* concomitanza.

concomitant [kən'kɔmitənt] *a* concomitante; *n* fatto concomitante.

concord ['kɔŋkɔːd] *n* concordia; (*mus*) accordo.

concordance [kən'kɔːdəns] *n* accordo; concordanza; indice alfabetico.

concordant [kən'kɔːdənt] *a* concorde, armonioso.

concourse ['kɔŋkɔːs] *n* affluenza, concorso.

concrete ['kɔnkriːt] *a* concreto; *n* calcestruzzo; **reinforced c.** cemento armato.

concubine ['kɔŋkjubain] *n* concubina.

concur [kən'kəː] *vi* concorrere, accordarsi.

concurrence [kən'kʌrəns] *n* concorso, consenso.

concurrent [kən'kʌrənt] *a* concorrente; concorde.

concussion [kən'kʌʃən] *n* scossa, urto; **c. (of the brain)** commozione cerebrale.

condemn [kən'dem] *vt* condannare, biasimare; confiscare.

condemnation [.kɔndem'neiʃən] *n* condanna, biasimo.

condensation [.kɔnden'seiʃən] *n* condensazione.

condense [kən'dens] *vti* condensar(si); (*fig*) compendiare.

condescend [.kɔndi'send] *vi* (ac) condiscendere, degnarsi.

condescending [.kɔndi'sendiŋ] *a* condiscendente.

condescension [.kɔndi'senʃən] *n* condiscendenza.

condiment ['kɔndimənt] *n* condimento.

condition [kən'diʃən] *n* condizione, stato, patto; *vt* condizionare, porre condizioni; rimandare (uno studente).

conditional [kən'diʃənl] *a n* condizionale.

condole [kən'doul] *vi* fare le condoglianze.

condolence [kən'douləns] *n* condoglianza.

condone [kən'doun] *vt* condonare, perdonare.

conducive [kən'djuːsiv] *a* contribuente, tendente.

conduct ['kɔndəkt] *n* condotta, direzione *vt* [kən'dʌkt] condurre, dirigere.

conductor [kən'dʌktə] *n* conduttore, guida, (*tram etc*) bigliettario, (*rly*) capotreno; controllore; direttore d'orchestra.

conductress [kən'dʌktris] *n* bigliettaria.

conduit ['kɔndit] *n* condotto.

cone [koun] *n* cono (*bot*) pigna.

confection [kən'fekʃən] *n* confezione, composizione; *vt* preparare, confezionare.

confectioner [kən'fekʃənə] *n* pasticciere.

confectionery [kən'fekʃnəri] *n* dolci *pl*, pasticceria.

confederacy [kən'fedərəsi] *n* confederazione; lega; cospirazione.

confederate [kən'fedərit] *a n* confederato, alleato.

confederation [kən.fedə'reiʃən] *n* confederazione.

confer [kən'fəː] *vti* conferire.

conference ['kɔnfərəns] *n* conferenza, abboccamento, congresso.

conferment [kən'fəːmənt] *n* conferimento.

confess [kən'fes] *vti* confessar(si).

confession [kən'feʃən] *n* confessione.

confessional [kən'feʃənl] *a n* confessionale.

confessor [kən'fesə] *n* confessore.

confetti [kən'feti] *n pl* coriandoli.

confidant(e) [.kɔnfi'dænt] *n* confidente.

confide [kən'faid] *vti* confidare.

confidence ['kɔnfidəns] *n* fiducia, confidenza; **self-c.** sicurezza di sè; **c. trick, c. game** truffa all'americana.

confident ['kɔnfidənt] *a* fiducioso, presuntuoso.

confidently ['kɔnfidəntli] *ad* con sicurezza, con fiducia.

confidential [.kɔnfi'denʃəl] *a* confidenziale, privato.

confidentially [.kɔnfi'denʃəli] *ad* confidenzialmente.

configuration [kən.figju'reiʃən] *n* configurazione.

confine [kən'fain] *vti* confinare; limitar(si).

confines ['kɔnfainz] *n pl* confini *pl*.

confinement [kən'fainmənt] *n* confino, reclusione; parto.

confirm [kən'fəːm] *vt* confermare, ratificare; cresimare.

confirmation [.kɔnfə'meiʃən] *n* conferma, ratifica; cresima.

confirmed [kən'fəːmd] *a* inveterato, convinto; cresimato.

confiscate ['kɔnfiskeit] *vt* confiscare.

confiscation [.kɔnfis'keiʃən] *n* confisca.

conflagration [.kɔnflə'greiʃən] *n* conflagrazione.

conflict ['kɔnflikt] *n* conflitto, lotta, urto; *vi* [kən'flikt] lottare, urtarsi.

conflicting [kən'fliktiŋ] *a* opposto, in conflitto.

confluence ['kɔnfluəns] *n* confluenza.

confluent ['kɔnfluənt] *a n* confluente.

conform [kən'fɔːm] *vti* conformar(si).

conformation [kɔn.fɔː'meiʃən] *n* conformazione, adattamento.

conformist [kən'fɔːmist] *n* conformista.
conformity [kən'fɔːmiti] *n* conformità.
confound [kən'faund] *vt* confondere; mandare al diavolo; **c. it!** accidenti!
confounded [kən'faundid] *a* confuso, sconcertato; (*fam*) maledetto.
confraternity [ˌkɔnfrə'təːniti] *n* confraternita.
confront [kən'frʌnt] *vt* affrontare, mettere a confronto.
confrontation [ˌkɔnfrʌn'teiʃən] *n* confronto.
confuse [kən'fjuːz] *vt* confondere, sconcertare.
confused [kən'fjuːzd] *a* confuso, disorientato.
confusion [kən'fjuːʒən] *n* confusione, disordine; imbarazzo.
confute [kən'fjuːt] *vt* confutare.
congeal [kən'dʒiːl] *vti* congelar(si).
congealment [kən'dʒiːlmənt] *n* congelamento.
congenial [kən'dʒiːniəl] *a* affine; simpatico; adatto.
congenital [kən'dʒenitl] *a* congenito.
congest [kən'dʒest] *vt* congestionare; ingorgare.
congested [kən'dʒestid] *a* congestionato; sovrappopolato.
congestion [kən'dʒestʃən] *n* congestione; ingorgamento.
conglomerate [kən'glɔməreit] *vti* conglomerar(si).
conglomeration [kənˌglɔmə'reiʃən] *n* conglomerazione, conglomerato.
congratulate [kən'grætjuleit] *vt* congratularsi con, rallegrarsi con.
congratulation [kənˌgrætju'leiʃən] *n* congratulazione, rallegramento.
congregate ['kɔŋgrigeit] *vti* congregare, unirsi.
congregation [ˌkɔŋgri'geiʃən] *n* congregazione, riunione.
congress ['kɔŋgres] *n* congresso.
congruous ['kɔŋgruəs] *a* congruo.
conic(al) ['kɔnik(əl)] *a* conico.
conjectural [kən'dʒektʃərəl] *a* congetturale.
conjecture [kən'dʒektʃə] *n* congettura; *vti* congetturare.
conjoin [kən'dʒɔin] *vti* congiunger(si).
conjoint ['kɔndʒɔint] *a* congiunto, unito.
conjugal ['kɔndʒugəl] *a* coniugale.
conjugate ['kɔndʒugeit] *vti* coniugar (si).
conjugation [ˌkɔndʒu'geiʃən] *n* coniugazione.
conjunction [kən'dʒʌŋkʃən] *n* congiunzione, unione.
conjunctive [kən'dʒʌŋktiv] *a* *n* congiuntivo.
conjuncture [kən'dʒʌŋktʃə] *n* congiuntura.
conjure ['kʌndʒə] *vti* evocare; far giochi di prestigio; **c. up** evocare; [kən'dʒuə] scongiurare.
conjurer ['kʌndʒərə] *n* prestigiatore.

connect [kə'nekt] *vti* connetter(si), far coincidenza; associare; **connected** connesso, imparentato.
connectedly [kə'nektidli] *ad* coerentemente, logicamente.
connecting [kə'nektiŋ] *a* che connette; di comunicazione, di collegamento.
connection, [kə'nekʃən] *n* collegamento, connessione; legame, rapporto; parentela; (*rly*) coincidenza; **in this c.** a questo proposito.
connective [kə'nektiv] *a* connettivo.
connivance [kə'naivəns] *n* connivenza.
connive [kə'naiv] *vi* essere connivente.
connoisseur [ˌkɔni'səː] *n* conoscitore, intenditore.
connotation [ˌkɔnou'teiʃən] *n* significato implicito.
conquer ['kɔŋkə] *vti* conquistare, vincere; **conquering** vincente, vittorioso.
conqueror ['kɔŋkərə] *n* conquistatore.
conquest ['kɔŋkwest] *n* conquista.
Conrad ['kɔnræd] *nm pr* Corrado.
conscience ['kɔnʃəns] *n* coscienza.
conscientious [ˌkɔnʃi'enʃəs] *a* coscienzioso.
conscientiousness [ˌkɔnʃi'enʃəsnis] *n* coscienziosità.
conscious ['kɔnʃəs] *a* consapevole, conscio, cosciente.
consciousness ['kɔnʃəsnis] *n* consapevolezza, coscienza, conoscenza.
conscript ['kɔnskript] *a n* coscritto.
conscription [kən'skripʃən] *n* coscrizione, leva.
consecrate ['kɔnsikreit] *vt* consacrare.
consecration [ˌkɔnsi'kreiʃən] *n* consacrazione.
consecutive [kən'sekjutiv] *a* consecutivo.
consensus [kən'sensəs] *n* consenso unanime.
consent [kən'sent] *n* consenso, accordo; *vi* acconsentire.
consequence ['kɔnsikwəns] *n* conseguenza, effetto; importanza.
consequent ['kɔnsikwənt] *a* conseguente.
consequently ['kɔnsikwəntli] *ad cj* di conseguenza, conseguentemente.
conservative [kən'səːvətiv] *a* conservatore.
conservatory [kən'səːvətri] *n* serra, conservatorio.
conserve [kən'səːv] *n* conserva; *vt* conservare.
consider [kən'sidə] *vti* considerare, riflettere.
considerable [kən'sidərəbl] *a* considerevole.
considerate [kən'sidərit] *a* riguardoso; premuroso.
consideration [kənˌsidə'reiʃən] *n*

considerazione; importanza; ricompensa.

considering [kən'sidəriŋ] prep tenuto conto di, visto che.

consign [kən'sain] vt consegnare, mandare.

consignee [.kɔnsai'niː] n (com) destinatario.

consignment [kən'sainmənt] n consegna; (com) partita di merci.

consignor [kən'sainə] n (com) mittente.

consist [kən'sist] vi consistere.

consistence [kən'sistəns] **consistency** [kən'sistənsi] n consistenza, densità.

consistent [kən'sistənt] a coerente; costante.

consolation [.kɔnsə'leiʃən] n consolazione.

console [kən'soul] vt consolare.

consoling [kən'souliŋ] a consolante.

consolidate [kən'sɔlideit] vti consolidar(si).

consolidation [kən.sɔli'deiʃən] n consolidamento.

consonance ['kɔnsənəns] n consonanza, armonia, accordo.

consonant ['kɔnsənənt] a consono, armonioso; n (gram) consonante.

consort ['kɔnsɔːt] n consorte, compagno; [kən'sɔːt] vi accompagnar(si).

conspicuous [kən'spikjuəs] a cospicuo, eminente.

conspiracy [kən'spirəsi] n cospirazione, congiura.

conspirator [kən'spirətə] n cospiratore.

conspire [kən'spaiə] vti cospirare, tramare.

constable ['kʌnstəbl] n conestabile, guardia, poliziotto.

Constance ['kɔnstəns] nf pr Costanza.

constancy ['kɔnstənsi] n costanza, perseveranza.

constant ['kɔnstənt] a costante, fedele.

Constantinople [.kɔnstænti'noupl] n Costantinopoli.

constantly ['kɔnstəntli] ad costantemente, continuamente.

constellation [.kɔnstə'leiʃən] n costellazione.

consternation [.kɔnstər'neiʃən] n costernazione.

constipate ['kɔnstipeit] vt costipare.

constipated ['kɔnstipeitid] a stitico.

constipation [.kɔnsti'peiʃən] n stitichezza.

constituency [kən'stitjuənsi] n circoscrizione elettorale.

constituent [kən'stitjuənt] a costituente; n elettore.

constitute ['kɔnstitjurt] vt costituire.

constitution [.kɔnsti'tjurʃən] n costituzione, legge.

constitutional [.kɔnsti'tjurʃənl] a costituzionale; n passeggiata igienica.

constrain [kən'strein] vt costringere; reprimere.

constraint [kən'streint] n costrizione, repressione; imbarazzo.

constrict [kən'strikt] vt comprimere, contrarre.

constriction [kən'strikʃən] n costrizione, contrazione.

construct [kən'strʌkt] vt costruire.

construction [kən'strʌkʃən] n costruzione.

constructive [kən'strʌktiv] a costruttivo.

construe [kən'struː] vt (gram) analizzare; tradurre; interpretare.

consul ['kɔnsəl] n console.

consular ['kɔnsjulə] a consolare.

consulate ['kɔnsjulit] n consolato.

consult [kən'sʌlt] vti consultar(si).

consultant [kən'sʌltənt] n consulente.

consultation [.kɔnsəl'teiʃən] n consultazione, consulto.

consulting [kən'sʌltiŋ] a di consultazione.

consume [kən'sjuːm] vti consumar (si).

consumer [kən'sjuːmə] n consumatore, utente.

consummate [kən'sʌmit] a consumato, perfetto.

consummate ['kɔnsʌmeit] vt compiere, consumare.

consummation [.kɔnsʌ'meiʃən] n consumazione.

consumption [kən'sʌmpʃən] n consumo; (med) consunzione, tisi.

consumptive [kən'sʌmptiv] a n tisico.

contact ['kɔntækt] n contatto; vti [kən'tækt] metter(si) in contatto con; essere in contatto.

contagion [kən'teidʒən] n contagio.

contagious [kən'teidʒəs] a contagioso.

contain [kən'tein] vt contenere, includere; reprimere.

container [kən'teinə] n recipiente.

contaminate [kən'tæmineit] vt contaminare, infettare.

contamination [kən.tæmi'neiʃən] n contaminazione.

contemplate ['kɔntempleit] vt contemplare, meditare; progettare.

contemplation [.kɔntem'pleiʃən] n contemplazione; progetto.

contemplative [kən'templətiv] a contemplativo, meditativo.

contemporary [kən'tempərəri] a n contemporaneo; coetaneo.

contempt [kən'tempt] n disprezzo.

contemptible [kən'temptəbl] a spregevole.

contemptuous [kən'temptjuəs] a sprezzante.

contend [kən'tend] vi contendere, lottare; contestare; sostenere.

content [kən'tent] a contento, soddisfatto; n contentezza, soddisfazione; vt accontentare, soddisfare.

contented [kən'tentid] *a* contento.
contention [kən'tenʃən] *n* contesa, discordia, opinione.
contentious [kən'tenʃəs] *a* litigioso; controverso; (*leg*) contenzioso.
contentment [kən'tentmənt] *n* il contentarsi; contentezza.
contents ['kɔntents] *n pl* contenuto.
contest ['kɔntest] *n* competizione; contesa; *vt* [kən'test] contestare, disputare.
contestant [kən'testənt] *n* competitore, concorrente.
context ['kɔntekst] *n* contesto.
contiguous [kən'tigjuəs] *a* contiguo.
continence ['kɔntinəns] *n* continenza.
continent ['kɔntinənt] *a* casto, continente, moderato; *n* continente.
continental [ˌkɔnti'nentl] *a n* continentale.
contingency [kən'tindʒənsi] *n* contingenza.
contingent [kən'tindʒənt] *a n* contingente.
continual [kən'tinjuəl] *a* continuo.
continuation [kənˌtinju'eiʃən] *n* continuazione, seguito.
continue [kən'tinjuː] *vti* continuare, persistere, proseguire.
continuity [ˌkɔnti'njuːiti] *n* continuità.
continuous [kən'tinjuəs] *a* continuo, ininterrotto.
continuously [kən'tinjuəsli] *ad* continuamente, ininterrottamente.
contort [kən'tɔːt] *vt* contorcere.
contortion [kən'tɔːʃən] *n* contorsione.
contour ['kɔntuə] *n* contorno, profilo.
contraband ['kɔntrəbænd] *a n* (di) contrabbando.
contract ['kɔntrækt] *n* contratto, appalto; *vt* [kən'trækt] contrarre; contrattare, appaltare.
contraction [kən'trækʃən] *n* contrazione.
contractor [kən'træktə] *n* contraente; appaltatore; imprenditore.
contradict [ˌkɔntrə'dikt] *vt* contraddire.
contradiction [ˌkɔntrə'dikʃən] *n* contraddizione.
contradictory [ˌkɔntrə'diktəri] *a* contraddittorio.
contralto [kən'træltou] *n* (*mus*) contralto.
contrariety [ˌkɔntrə'raiəti] *n* contrarietà, opposizione.
contrary ['kɔntrəri] *a* contrario; ostinato; *n* contrario; *ad* contrariamente; **on the c.** al contrario.
contrast ['kɔntræst] *n* contrasto; *vt* [kən'træst] mettere in contrasto, confrontare; *vi* contrastare.
contravene [ˌkɔntrə'viːn] *vt* contravvenire.
contravention [ˌkɔntrə'venʃən] *n* contravvenzione.

contribute [kən'tribjuːt] *vti* contribuire.
contribution [ˌkɔntri'bjuːʃən] *n* contributo; collaborazione.
contributor [kən'tribjutə] *n* contributore; collaboratore.
contrite ['kɔntrait] *a* contrito.
contrition [kən'triʃən] *n* contrizione.
contrivance [kən'traivəns] *n* invenzione, congegno.
contrive [kən'traiv] *vt* inventare; escogitare, fare in modo di.
control [kən'troul] *n* controllo, freno, autorità; *vt* controllare, frenare, dirigere.
controversial [ˌkɔntrə'vəːʃəl] *a* controverso.
controversy ['kɔntrəvəːsi] *n* controversia.
contumacious [ˌkɔntjuː'meiʃəs] *a* contumace.
contuse [kən'tjuːz] *vt* ammaccare, contundere.
contusion [kən'tjuːʒən] *n* contusione.
conundrum [kə'nʌndrəm] *n* indovinello.
convalesce [ˌkɔnvə'les] *vi* rimettersi in salute.
convalescence [ˌkɔnvə'lesns] *n* convalescenza.
convalescent [ˌkɔnvə'lesnt] *a n* convalescente.
convector [kən'vektə] *n* convettore, termo convettore.
convene [kən'viːn] *vti* convocare; convenire.
convenience [kən'viːniəns] *n* comodità, convenienza, vantaggio; **public c.** gabinetto pubblico.
convenient [kən'viːniənt] *a* comodo, conveniente, adatto.
convent ['kɔnvənt] *n* convento.
conventicle [kən'ventikl] *n* conventicola.
convention [kən'venʃən] *n* convenzione.
conventional [kən'venʃənl] *a* convenzionale.
conventual [kən'ventjuəl] *a* conventuale.
converge [kən'vəːdʒ] *vi* convergere.
convergent [kən'vəːdʒənt] *a* convergente.
conversant [kən'vəːsənt] *a* versato (in), bene informato.
conversation [ˌkɔnvə'seiʃən] *n* conversazione.
converse ['kɔnvəːs] *a n* converso, contrario; *vi* [kən'vəːs] conversare.
conversely ['kɔnvəːsli] *ad* viceversa.
conversion [kən'vəːʃən] *n* conversione.
convert ['kɔnvəːt] *n* convertito; *vt* [kən'vəːt] convertire.
convertible [kən'vəːtəbl] *a* convertibile; **c. car** automobile decappottabile.
convex ['kɔn'veks] *a* convesso.
convey [kən'vei] *vt* portare, trasportare; trasmettere; esprimere.

conveyance [kən'veiəns] n mezzo di trasporto.
conveyor [kən'veiə] n portatore; c.-belt (ind) trasportatore a cinghia.
convict ['kɔnvikt] n ergastolano; vt [kən'vikt] dichiarare colpevole.
conviction [kən'vikʃən] n condanna; convinzione.
convince [kən'vins] vt convincere.
convincing [kən'vinsiŋ] a convincente.
convivial [kən'viviəl] a conviviale.
convocation [ˌkɔnvə'keiʃən] n convocazione, assemblea.
convoke [kən'vouk] vt convocare.
convoy ['kɔnvɔi] n convoglio, scorta; vt convogliare, scortare.
convulse [kən'vʌls] vt sconvolgere, agitare, mettere in convulsioni.
convulsion [kən'vʌlʃən] n convulsione.
convulsive [kən'vʌlsiv] a convulsivo.
coo [kuː] vi tubare.
cook [kuk] n cuoco, cuoca; vti cucinare, cuocere; **cookbook** libro di cucina.
cooker ['kukə] n fornello, cucina; pentola.
cookery ['kukəri] n arte culinaria; c. book libro di cucina.
cookie ['kuki] n biscotto.
cooking ['kukiŋ] n cottura; arte culinaria; cucina.
cool [kuːl] a fresco; calmo; impudente; n fresco, frescura; vti rinfrescar(si).
cooler ['kuːlə] n refrigerante; (sl) gattabuia; air c. condizionatore dell'aria.
cooling ['kuːliŋ] a rinfrescante.
coolly ['kuːlli] ad freddamente, con calma.
coolness ['kuːlnis] n fresco; sangue freddo; sfacciataggine.
coop [kuːp] n stia; vt mettere nella stia, rinchiudere.
co-operate [kou'ɔpəreit] vi cooperare.
co-operation [kouˌɔpə'reiʃən] n cooperazione.
co-operative [kou'ɔpərətiv] a cooperativo.
co-operator [kou'ɔpəreitə] n cooperatore.
co-ordinate [kou'ɔːdineit] vt coordinare; n coordinata.
co-ordination [kouˌɔːdi'neiʃən] n coordinazione.
co-owner ['kou'ounə] n comproprietario.
copartner ['kou'pɑːtnə] n (com) consocio; **copartnership** società in nome collettivo.
cope [koup] n cappa di ecclesiastico; c. with vi far fronte a, lottare contro.
Copenhagen [ˌkoupn'heigən] n Copenaghen.
co-pilot ['kou'pailət] n (av) secondo pilota.

copious ['koupiəs] a abbondante, copioso.
copiousness ['koupiəsnis] n abbondanza.
copper ['kɔpə] a di rame, color di rame; n rame, moneta di rame, caldaia; (sl) poliziotto; **coppers** pl moneta spicciola; **copperplate** engraving incisione su rame.
coppice ['kɔpis] n bosco ceduo.
copulate ['kɔpjuleit] vi accoppiarsi.
copulation [ˌkɔpju'leiʃən] n copulazione, accoppiamento.
copy ['kɔpi] n copia; trascrizione; (journalism) materiale; c. book quaderno; c. reader revisore di stampa; fair c. bella copia; rough c. brutta copia; vt copiare; imitare; trascrivere.
copyright ['kɔpirait] n diritti d'autore pl, proprietà letteraria.
coquet(te) [kou'ket] vi civettare.
coquette [kou'ket] n (donna) civetta.
coral ['kɔrəl] a n (di) corallo.
cord [kɔːd] n corda, funicella; spinal c. spina dorsale; vt legare con una corda.
cordial ['kɔːdiəl] a n cordiale.
cordiality [ˌkɔːdi'æliti] n cordialità.
cordially ['kɔːdiəli] ad cordialmente.
cordon ['kɔːdn] n cordane; vt cordonare.
corduroy ['kɔːdərɔi] n velluto a coste.
core [kɔː] n torsolo; (fig) centro, cuore.
cork [kɔːk] n sughero; tappo, turacciolo; vt tappare, turare.
corkscrew ['kɔːk'skruː] n cavatappi.
corn [kɔːn] n mais, granturco; callo durone; c.-cob pannocchia; **cornflakes** fiocchi di granturco; **cornflour, cornmeal** farina di gran turco, polenta.
cornelian [kɔː'niːliən] n (min) corniola.
corner ['kɔːnə] n angolo; spigolo; (com) accaparramento; vt (fig) mettere alle strette; svoltare; accaparrare; **cornerstone** pietra angolare.
cornet ['kɔːnit] n (mus) cornetta; cartoccio conico.
cornflower ['kɔːnflauə] n fiordaliso.
cornice ['kɔːnis] n cornicione.
Cornwall ['kɔːnwəl] n Cornovaglia; **Cornish** a n della Cornovaglia.
coronary ['kɔrənəri] a (anat) coronario; c. thrombosis trombosi delle coronarie.
coronation [ˌkɔrə'neiʃən] n incoronazione.
coroner ['kɔrənə] n magistrato inquirente nei casi di sospetta morte violenta.
coronet ['kɔrənit] n corona nobiliare, diadema.
corporal ['kɔːpərəl] a n corporale; a corporeo; n caporale.

corporate ['kɔ:pərit] a corporativo.
corporation [,kɔ:pə'reiʃən] n corporazione, (com) società a responsabilità limitata, azienda municipale; (fam) pancia.
corporative ['kɔ:pərətiv] a corporativo.
corporeal [kɔ:'pɔ:riəl] a corporeo.
corps [kɔ:] pl **corps** n (mil) corpo.
corpse [kɔ:ps] n cadavere.
corpulence ['kɔ:pjuləns] n corpulenza.
corpulent ['kɔ:pjulənt] a corpulento.
corpuscle ['kɔ:pʌsl] n corpuscolo.
correct [kə'rekt] a corretto, esatto, giusto; vt correggere.
correction [kə'rekʃən] n correzione; punizione.
correctly [kə'rektli] ad correttamente.
correctness [kə'rektnis] n correttezza.
correlate ['kɔrileit] vti essere, mettere in correlazione.
correlation [,kɔri'leiʃən] n correlazione.
correspond [,kɔris'pɔnd] vi corrispondere.
correspondence [,kɔris'pɔndəns] n corrispondenza.
correspondent [,kɔris'pɔndənt] a n corrispondente.
corresponding [,kɔris'pɔndiŋ] a corrispondente.
corridor ['kɔridɔ:] n corridoio.
corroborate [kə'rɔbəreit] vt corroborare.
corroboration [kə,rɔbə'reiʃən] n conferma, corroborazione.
corrode [kə'roud] vti corroder(si).
corrosive [kə'rousiv] a n corrosivo.
corrugate ['kɔrugeit] vti corrugar(si); **corrugated iron** lamiera ondulata; **corrugated paper** carta increspata.
corrupt [kə'rʌpt] a corrotto, depravato; vti corromper(si).
corruption [kə'rʌpʃən] n corruzione.
corsair ['kɔ:seə] n corsaro.
corset ['kɔ:sit] n corsetto, busto; c.-maker bustaia.
Corsican ['kɔ:sikən] a n corso, corsa.
cosmetic [kɔz'metik] a n cosmetico.
cosmic ['kɔzmik] a cosmico.
cosmodrome ['kɔzmədroum] n cosmodromo.
cosmogony [kɔz'mɔgəni] n cosmogonia.
cosmography [kɔz'mɔgrəfi] n cosmografia.
cosmonaut ['kɔzmənɔ:t] n cosmonauta.
cosmopolitan [,kɔzmə'pɔlitən] a n cosmopolita.
cosmos ['kɔzmɔs] n cosmo.
Cossack ['kɔsæk] n cosacco.
cost [kɔst] n costo, prezzo; **costs** pl spese processuali pl; vt costare; (com) fissare il prezzo; **running c.** spese generali.

costermonger ['kɔstə,mʌŋgə] n venditore ambulante di frutta etc.
costive ['kɔstiv] a stitico.
costiveness ['kɔstivnis] n stitichezza.
costliness ['kɔstlinis] n costosità.
costly ['kɔstli] a costoso.
costume ['kɔstju:m] n costume; completo.
cot [kɔt] n lettino per bambini.
coterie ['koutəri] n circolo.
cottage ['kɔtidʒ] n casetta di campagna, 'cottage'.
Cottian Alps ['kɔtiən,ælps] n pl Alpi Cozie.
cotton ['kɔtn] n cotone, tela di cotone; a di cotone; **absorbent c.** cotone idrofilo.
couch [kautʃ] n divano.
cough [kɔf] n tosse; vti tossire.
council ['kaunsl] n consiglio, concilio.
councilor ['kaunsilə] n consigliere.
counsel ['kaunsəl] n consigli(o), parere; consulente legale.
counselor ['kaunslə] n consigliere, avvocato.
count [kaunt] n conto, conteggio; conte; **c. of indictment** capo d'accusa; **countdown** conteggio all'indietro; vti contare, numerare, includere.
countenance ['kauntinəns] n viso, espressione; vt approvare, incoraggiare.
counter ['kauntə] n gettone; (in a shop etc) banco, cassa; ad contro, in opposizione.
counteract [,kauntə'rækt] vt agire in opposizione a, neutralizzare.
counter-attack ['kauntərə,tæk] n (mil) contrattacco.
counterbalance ['kauntə,bæləns] n contrappeso.
counterfeit ['kauntəfit] a contraffatto, falsificato; n contraffazione, falsificazione; vt contraffare, falsificare, fingere.
counterfoil ['kauntəfɔil] n (com) matrice.
countermand [,kauntə'ma:nd] vt disdire, revocare.
counterpane ['kauntəpein] n copriletto.
counterpart ['kauntəpa:t] n controparte, doppio, duplicato.
counterpoint ['kauntəpɔint] n (mus) contrappunto.
counterpoise ['kauntəpɔiz] n contrappeso; vt controbilanciare.
countersign ['kauntəsain] n contrassegno; controfirma; parola d'ordine; vt controfirmare.
counterweight ['kauntəweit] n contrappeso.
countess ['kauntis] n contessa.
counting-house ['kauntiŋhaus] n ufficio contabile, amministrazione.
countless ['kauntlis] a innumerevole.
country ['kʌntri] n paese, nazione, patria; campagna; **countryman** compatriota; contadino.

county ['kaunti] n contea
coup [kuː] n colpo.
couple ['kʌpl] n coppia, paio; vti accoppiar(si); (rly) agganciare.
coupling ['kʌpliŋ] n accoppiamento, (tec) agganciamento.
coupon ['kuːpɔn] n cedola, tagliando, buono.
courage ['kʌridʒ] n coraggio.
courageous [kə'reidʒəs] a coraggioso.
courageously [kə'reidʒəsli] ad coraggiosamente.
courier ['kuriə] n corriere, messaggero.
course [kɔːs] n corso, direzione; pista; (meal) portata.
court [kɔːt] n corte; tribunale; (tennis) campo; vt corteggiare.
courteous ['kəːtiəs] a cortese.
courteousness ['kəːtiəsnis] n cortesia.
courtesan [ˌkɔːti'zæn] n cortigiana, prostituta.
courtesy ['kəːtisi] n cortesia, gentilezza.
courtier ['kɔːtiə] n cortigiano.
courtly ['kɔːtli] a cortigianesco, cerimonioso.
courtship ['kɔːtʃip] n corte, corteggiamento.
courtyard ['kɔːtjaːd] n corte, cortile.
cousin ['kʌzn] n cugino, cugina.
cove [kouv] n insenatura, piccola baia.
covenant ['kʌvinənt] n convenzione, patto; vti stipulare, convenire.
cover ['kʌvə] n coperta; copertura; coperchio; copertina; riparo; vt coprire, nascondere, ricoprire, proteggere; far la cronaca di.
coverage ['kʌvəridʒ] n copertura; (journalism) servizio d'informazione.
covering ['kʌvəriŋ] n coperta; (com) garanzia.
coverlet ['kʌvəlit] n copriletto.
covet ['kʌvit] vt bramare.
covetous ['kʌvitəs] a cupido, avido.
covey ['kʌvi] n covata (di uccelli).
cow [kau] n vacca, mucca, (di mammiferi) femmina; vt intimidire.
coward ['kauəd] n codardo.
cowardice ['kauədis] n codardia.
cowardly ['kauədli] a codardo; ad vilmente.
cower ['kauə] vi acquattarsi, farsi piccolo, tremare.
cowl [kaul] n cappuccio.
coxcomb ['kɔkskoum] n damerino, zerbinotto.
coxswain ['kɔkswein, 'kɔksn] n timoniere.
coy [kɔi] a ritroso, timido.
coyness ['kɔinis] n timidezza, ritrosia.
coziness ['kouzinis] n agio, tepore confortevole, intimità.
cozy ['kouzi] a comodo, intimo; **tea c.** n copriteiera.
crab [kræb] n granchio; (mech) argano; **c. apple** mela selvatica.

crabbed ['kræbid] a ruvido, sgarbato; (writing) illegibile.
crack [kræk] n fessura, crepa, spacco; incrinatura; schianto, schiocco; a di prim'ordine, ottimo; vti spaccar(si); **to c. a joke** dire una spiritosaggine.
cracked ['krækt] a fesso, incrinato; scervellato.
cracker ['krækə] n petardo; galletta.
crackle ['krækl] vi crepitare, scricchiolare.
crackling ['krækliŋ] n crepitio, scoppiettio.
cracknel ['kræknl] n biscotto croccante.
Cracow ['krækou] n Cracovia.
cradle ['kreidl] n culla; (for broken limbs) gabbia, alzacoperte; vt cullare.
craft [kraːft] n abilità; arte; furberia, inganno; piccola imbarcazione.
craftily ['kraːftili] ad abilmente, astutamente.
craftiness ['kraːftinis] n furbizia.
craftsman ['kraːftsmən] n artigiano; **craftsmanship** arte dell'artigiano.
crafty ['kraːfti] a furbo, abile.
crag [kræg] n picco, roccia scoscesa.
craggy ['krægi] a roccioso, dirupato.
cram [kræm] vti rimpinzar(si); (fam) imbottirsi di nozioni in vista di un esame.
cramp [kræmp] n crampo; vt impacciare; cagionare crampi a; impedire nei movimenti.
cranberry ['krænbəri] n mirtillo nero.
crane [krein] n gru; vti allungare il collo, sporgersi.
cranium ['kreiniəm] pl **crania** n cranio.
crank [kræŋk] n manovella; (fig) individuo eccentrico.
cranny ['kræni] n fessura.
crape [kreip] n crespo, gramaglie pl.
crash [kræʃ] n schianto, crollo; cozzo; scontro; vi crollare con fracasso, precipitare; urtare (contro).
crass [kræs] a crasso, grossolano.
crate [kreit] n cassa da imballaggio.
crater ['kreitə] n cratere.
cravat [krə'væt] n fazzoletto da collo, cravatta.
crave [kreiv] vti bramare, implorare.
craven ['kreivn] a n codardo.
craving ['kreiviŋ] a ardente, insaziabile; n brama, voglia.
crawl [krɔːl] vi strisciare, andare carponi.
crayfish ['kreifiʃ] n gambero d'acqua dolce.
crayon ['kreiən] n pastello.
craze [kreiz] n mania, pazzia; passione; moda.
craziness ['kreizinis] n follia; instabilità d'un edificio.
crazy ['kreizi] a folle, pazzo; instabile.
creak [kriːk] n cigolio; vi cigolare, scricchiolare.

cream [kriːm] n panna, crema; (fig) fior fiore; **c. jug** lattiera.
creamer ['kriːmə] n lattiera.
creamery ['kriːməri] n caseificio, latteria.
crease [kriːs] n grinza, piega; vt piegare; sgualcir(si).
create [kriː'eit] vt creare.
creation [kriː'eiʃən] n creazione, creato.
creative [kriː'eitiv] a creativa.
creator [kri'eitə] n creatore.
creature ['kriːtʃə] n creatura.
credentials [kri'denʃəls] n pl credenziali pl.
credibility [ˌkredi'biliti] n credibilità.
credible ['kredəbl] a credibile.
credit ['kredit] n credito, fiducia; reputazione, onore, merito; vt credere, prestar fede a; attribuire, accreditare a.
creditable ['kreditəbl] a degno di fede, di stima, che torna all'onore di.
creditor ['kreditə] n creditore.
credulity [kri'djuːliti] n credulità.
credulous ['kredjuləs] a credulo.
creed [kriːd] n credo, somma degli articoli di fede.
creek [kriːk] n cala, piccola baia, insenatura.
creep [kriːp] vi (of plants) arrampicarsi; insinuarsi; strisciare; n strisciamento; pl brividi pl, pelle d'oca.
creeper ['kriːpə] n pianta rampicante; (fig) persona strisciante.
creepy ['kriːpi] a strisciante, che dà i brividi.
cremate [kri'meit] vt cremare.
cremation [kri'meiʃən] n cremazione.
crematorium [ˌkremə'tɔːriəm] pl **crematoria** forno crematorio.
creole ['kriːoul] a n creolo.
creosote ['kriəsout] n (chem) creosoto.
crêpe [kreip] n crespo, tessuto di seta.
crescent ['kresnt] a crescente, a mezzaluna; n fila di case disposte a semicerchio.
cress [kres] n crescione.
crest [krest] n cresta, ciuffetto, criniera.
crestfallen ['krestˌfɔːlən] a abbattuto, mortificato.
crevasse [kri'væs] n crepaccio.
crevice ['krevis] n crepa, fessura.
crew [kruː] n ciurma, equipaggio.
crib [krib] n lettino per bimbo; mangiatoia, presepio; (fam) plagio; (sl) traduttore, bigino; vt copiare, plagiare.
cricket ['krikit] n grillo; (sport) 'cricket'.
crime [kraim] n delitto, misfatto.
criminal ['kriminl] a criminale, penale; n criminale, delinquente.
criminology [ˌkrimi'nolədʒi] n criminologia.
crimson ['krimzn] a n cremisi.

cringe [krindʒ] vi essere servile, comportarsi servilmente.
crinkle ['kriŋkl] n grinza, crespa; vti increspar(si), spiegazzare.
crinoline ['krinəlin] n crinolina.
cripple ['kripl] n sciancato, zoppo, invalido; vt azzoppare; (fig) diminuire la capacità di.
crisis ['kraisis] n crisi.
crisp [krisp] a croccante; (hair) crespo; (air) frizzante; (style) incisivo.
crispness ['krispnis] n friabilità; cresposità; freddo intenso; chiarezza.
criterion [krai'tiəriən] pl **criteria** n criterio.
critic ['kritik] n critico.
critical ['kritikəl] a critico.
criticism ['kritisizəm] n critica, giudizio critico.
criticize ['kritisaiz] vt criticare, fare la critica a.
croak [krouk] vi gracchiare, gracidare; (fig) predire malanni.
croaky ['krouki] a rauco.
crochet ['krouʃei] n lavoro ad uncinetto.
crockery ['krokəri] n terraglie pl, vasellame.
crocodile ['krokədail] n coccodrillo.
crocus ['kroukəs] n croco.
croft [krɔft] n piccolo podere, campicello.
crone [kroun] n vecchia rugosa.
crony ['krouni] n (fam) vecchio amico.
crook [kruk] n ricurvatura; gancio; bastone da pastore; (sl) malvivente; vti curvar(si).
crooked ['krukid] a curvo, storto; disonesto.
crookedness ['krukidnis] n tortuosità, disonestà.
croon [kruːn] vi canticchiare sotto voce.
crop [krɔp] n raccolto; gozzo d'uccello; frusta; capelli corti; vt mozzare, tosare; mietere, raccogliere; brucare.
croquet ['kroukei] n (sport) 'croquet', pallamaglio.
crosier ['krouʒə] n pastorale.
cross [krɔs] a obliquo, trasversale; di cattivo umore; n croce; incrocio; vt attraversare; incrociare; segnare con una croce; vi incrociarsi.
cross-examine ['krɔsig'zæmin] vt interrogare a contraddittorio.
crossing ['krɔsin] n traversata; incrocio; **level c., grade c.** passaggio a livello.
crossroads ['krɔsroudz] n pl crocevia.
crossword ['krɔswəːd] n cruciverba.
crotchet ['krɔtʃit] n capriccio; crotchety capriccioso.
crouch [krautʃ] vi accucciarsi, rannicchiarsi.
croup [kruːp] n groppa; (med) crup, difterite.

crow [krou] *n* cornacchia, corvo; (*cock's*) canto; *vi* cantare; **c. over** vantarsi sopra.

crowd [kraud] *n* folla, massa; *vti* affollar(si); **crowded** affollato, popoloso.

crown [kraun] *n* corona; (*head*) sommità; (*hat*) fondo; coronamento; *vt* (in)coronare; **to c. it all** per colmo (di fortuna, di disgrazia).

crucial ['kruːʃəl] *a* cruciale, critico.

crucible ['kruːsibl] *n* crogiuolo.

crucifix ['kruːsifiks] *n* crocifisso.

crucifixion [ˌkruːsi'fikʃən] *n* crocifissione.

crucify ['kruːsifai] *vt* crocifiggere.

crude [kruːd] *a* crudo, grezzo, immaturo, primitivo.

cruel ['kruəl] *a* crudele.

cruelly ['kruəli] *ad* crudelmente.

cruelty ['kruəlti] *n* crudeltà.

cruet ['kruːit] *n* ampolla, ampollina; **c.-stand** ampolliera.

cruise [kruːz] *n* crociera; *vi* fare una crociera; incrociare.

cruiser ['kruːzə] *n* incrociatore; automobile della polizia.

crumb [krʌm] *n* briciola, mollica.

crumble ['krʌmbl] *vti* sbriciolar(si), sgretolar(si).

crumple ['krʌmpl] *vti* raggrinzar(si), sgualcir(si).

crunch [krʌntʃ] *vti* sgranocchiare rumorosamente, scricchiolare.

crusade [kruːˈseid] *n* crociata.

crusader [kruːˈseidə] *n* crociato.

crush [krʌʃ] *n* compressione, schiacciamento; calca; (*sl*) infatuazione, cotta; *vt* schiacciare, frantumare; sgualcire; annientare.

crushing ['krʌʃiŋ] *a* schiacciante; **c. mill** frantoio; **c. plant** impianto di frantumazione.

crust [krʌst] *n* crosta, incrostazione; *vti* incrostar(si).

crustiness ['krʌstinis] *n* irascibilità.

crusty ['krʌsti] *a* crostoso; irritabile.

crutch [krʌtʃ] *n* gruccia, stampella; forcella; inforcatura.

crux [krʌks] *n* punto, nodo.

cry [krai] *n* grido, richiamo, urlo, pianto; *vti* gridare, piangere.

crying ['kraiiŋ] *a* evidente, patente; *n*. pianto.

crypt [kript] *n* cripta.

cryptic ['kriptik] *a* misterioso, nascosto.

crystal ['kristl] *a* di cristallo; *n* cristallo.

crystalline ['kristəlain] *a n* cristallino.

crystallize ['kristəlaiz] *vti* cristallizzar(si).

cub [kʌb] *n* cucciolo di animali selvatici; **c. scout** lupetto.

Cuba ['kjuːbə] *n* Cuba: **Cuban** *a n* cubano, cubana.

cube [kjuːb] *n* cubo.

cubic ['kjuːbik] *a* cubico.

cubicle ['kjuːbikl] *n* stanzetta, piccolo locale, cubicolo.

cuckold ['kʌkəld] *n* becco, cornuto.

cuckoo ['kukuː] *n* cuculo, cucù; (*sl*) mezzo scemo.

cucumber ['kjuːkəmbə] *n* cetriolo.

cud [kʌd] *n* bolo alimentare di ruminante.

cuddle ['kʌdl] *vt* abbracciare stretto.

cudgel ['kʌdʒəl] *n* clava, randello; *vt* picchiare con la clava, randellare; **to c. one's brains** scervellarsi.

cue [kjuː] *n* (*theat*) battuta d'entrata; suggerimento; stecca da biliardo.

cuff [kʌf] *n* polsino; risvolto dei pantaloni; pugno, scapaccione; *vt* percuotere, picchiare.

cuisine [kwiːˈziːn] *n* cucina, modo di cucinare.

cul-de-sac ['kuldəˈsæk] *n* vicolo cieco.

culinary ['kʌlinəri] *a* culinario.

culminate ['kʌlmineit] *vi* culminare.

culmination [ˌkʌlmiˈneiʃən] *n* culminazione, culmine.

culpable ['kʌlpəbl] *a* colpevole.

culprit ['kʌlprit] *n* colpevole; imputato.

cult [kʌlt] *n* culto, venerazione.

cultivate ['kʌltiveit] *vt* coltivare.

cultivated ['kʌltiveitid] *a* coltivato; colto, educato.

cultivation [ˌkʌltiˈveiʃən] *n* coltivazione; cultura.

cultivator ['kʌltiveitə] *n* coltivatore, cultore.

cultural ['kʌltʃərəl] *a* culturale.

culture ['kʌltʃə] *n* coltura, allevamento; (*of the mind*) cultura.

cultured ['kʌltʃəd] *a* colto.

cumber ['kʌmbə] *vt* impacciare, ingombrare.

cumbersome ['kʌmbəsəm] *a* ingombrante, poco maneggevole.

cumulative ['kjuːmjulətiv] *a* cumulativo.

cunning ['kʌniŋ] *a* astuto, furbo; *n* astuzia, furberia, accortezza.

cup [kʌp] *n* tazza, calice, coppa.

cupboard ['kʌbəd] *n* armadio.

cupidity [kjuːˈpiditi] *n* cupidigia.

cur [kəː] *n* cane bastardo.

curable ['kjuərəbl] *a* guaribile.

curate ['kjuərit] *n* curato.

curative ['kjuərətiv] *a* curativo.

curator [kjuəˈreitə] *n* sovrintendente.

curb [kəːb] *n* costrizione, freno; bordo di marciapiede; *vt* frenare, soggiogare.

curds [kəːdz] *n pl* latte cagliato.

curdle ['kəːdl] *vti* cagliare, coagular (si); (*fig*) agghiacciar(si).

cure [kjuə] *n* cura, guarigione, rimedio; *vt* guarire; (*fish*) affumicare.

curfew ['kəːfjuː] *n* coprifuoco.

curio ['kjuəriou] *pl* **curios** *n* oggetti rari.

curiosity [ˌkjuəriˈɔsiti] *n* curiosità.

curious ['kjuəriəs] curioso, raro, singolare.

curiously ['kjuəriəsli] *ad* curiosamente, stranamente; **c. enough** strano a dirsi.

curl [kə:l] *n* ricciolo; curva; *vt* arricciare, arricciarsi, sollevarsi in onde, in spire.

curler ['kə:lə] *n* bigodino, ferro per arricciare i capelli; giocatore di 'curling'.

curly ['kə:li] *a* ricciuto.

currant ['kʌrənt] *n* uva sultanina; ribes.

currency ['kʌrənsi] *n* circolazione monetaria, moneta circolante; corso.

current ['kʌrənt] *a n* corrente.

curry ['kʌri] *n* salsa fatta di spezie e di aromi; *vt* stufare con aromi; (*leather*) conciare; (*horse*) strigliare; **to c. favor with** adulare, ingraziarsi.

currycomb ['kʌri,koum] *n* striglia.

curse [kə:s] *n* imprecazione, maledizione; sventura, calamità; *vti* bestemmiare, maledire; (*passive*) essere afflitto.

cursed [kə:st] *a* maledetto.

cursive ['kə:siv] *a n* corsivo.

cursory ['kə:səri] *a* frettoloso, rapido.

curt [kə:t] *a* asciutto, brusco.

curtail [kə:'teil] *vt* abbreviare, accorciare.

curtain ['kə:tn] *n* cortina, tenda, sipario.

curtsey ['kə:tsi] *n* inchino, riverenza.

curve [kə:v] *n* curva; *vti* curvar(si).

cushion ['kuʃən] *n* cuscino; (*mech*) cuscinetto.

custard ['kʌstəd] *n* crema.

custody ['kʌstədi] *n* custodia, imprigionamento.

custom ['kʌstəm] *n* uso, costume, abitudine, clientela; *pl* dazio, dogana; **customhouse** dogana.

customary ['kʌstəməri] *a* abituale, consueto.

customer ['kʌstəmə] *n* avventore, cliente; (*sl*) tipo, individuo.

cut [kʌt] *n* taglio, ferita; affronto; riduzione; (*meat, material etc*) pezzo; *vt* tagliare, trinciare; togliere il saluto a; (*prices*) ridurre; (*cards*) alzare; **short c.** scorciatoia; **cutoff** scorciatoia; ritaglio di giornale.

cuticle ['kju:tikl] *n* cuticola.

cutler ['kʌtlə] *n* coltellinaio.

cutlery ['kʌtləri] *n* posateria.

cutlet ['kʌtlit] *n* cotoletta.

cutter ['kʌtə] *n* tagliatore; (*mech*) fresa.

cut-throat ['kʌtθrout] *a* accanito; *n* assassino.

cutting ['kʌtiŋ] *a* tagliente; (*fig*) pungente, mordace; *n* taglio; ritaglio, riduzione.

cuttle ['kʌtl] *n* **cuttlefish** seppia; **c.-bone** osso di seppia.

cyanide ['saiənaid] *n* (*chem*) cianuro.

cycle ['saikl] *n* ciclo, bicicletta; *vi* andare in bicicletta.

cyclist ['saiklist] *n* ciclista.

cyclone ['saikloun] *n* ciclone.

cylinder ['silində] *n* cilindro.

cylindrical [si'lindrikəl] *a* cilindrico.

cynic ['sinik] *n* cinico.

cynical ['sinikəl] *a* cinico.

cynicism ['sinisizəm] *n* cinismo.

cypress ['saipris] *n* cipresso.

Cyprus ['saiprəs] *n* Cipro; **Cyprian, Cypriot** *n* cipriota.

cyst [sist] *n* ciste.

czar [za:] *n* zar.

Czechoslovakia ['tʃekouslou'vækiə] *n* Cecoslovacchia; **Czech** *a n* ceco; **Czechoslovak** *a n* cecoslovacco.

D

dab [dæb] *n* pezzettino, spalmatina, tocco, schizzo; *vt* toccare leggermente.

dabble ['dæbl] *vi* sguazzare; **to d. in** fare una cosa da dilettante.

dachshund ['dækshund] *n* cane bassotto.

dad [dæd] **daddy** ['dædi] *n* (*fam*) babbo, papà.

daffodil ['dæfədil] *n* narciso.

daft [da:ft] *a* pazzerello, sciocco.

dagger ['dægə] *n* daga, pugnale.

dahlia ['deiliə] *n* (*bot*) dalia.

daily ['deili] *a* giornaliero, quotidiano; *n* (*giornale*) quotidiano.

daintiness ['deintinis] *n* delicatezza, raffinatezza, ricercatezza.

dainty ['deinti] *a* squisito, delicato, grazioso; schizzinoso; *n* leccornia.

dairy ['dɛəri] *n* latteria, cascina, caseificio; **dairymaid** lattaia; **dairyman** lattaio.

dais ['deiis] *n* pedana.

daisy ['deizi] *n* margherita, pratolina.

dale [deil] *n* vallata.

dally ['dæli] *vi* perdere tempo, gingillarsi, trastullarsi.

Dalmatia [dæl'meiʃə] *n* Dalmazia.

Dalmatian [dæl'meiʃjən] *a n* dalmata.

dam [dæm] *n* argine, diga; (*of animals*) madre; *vt* arginare.

damage ['dæmidʒ] *n* danno, danni *pl*; perdita; *vt* danneggiare.

damaged ['dæmidʒd] *a* guastato, avariato.

damaging ['dæmidʒiŋ] *a* dannoso, nocivo.

damask ['dæməsk] *n* damasco.

dame [deim] *n* dama, nobildonna.

damn [dæm] *vt* dannare, maledire.

damnation [dæm'neiʃən] *n* dannazione.

damned [dæmd] *a* dannato, maledetto; *ad* (*sl*) maledettamente; molto.

damning ['dæmiŋ] *a* che condanna, schiacciante; che maledice; *n* condanna; maledizione.

damp [dæmp] *a* umido; *n* umidità; *vt* inumidire; (*fig*) scoraggiare.

dampness ['dæmpnis] *n* umidità.

damsel ['dæmzəl] n (poet) donzella.
damson ['dæmzən] n susina damascena.
dance [dɑ:ns] n ballo, danza; vi ballare, danzare.
dancer ['dɑ:nsə] n ballerino, ballerina.
dancing ['dɑ:nsiŋ] a danzante; n il ballo, la danza.
dandelion ['dændilaiən] n (bot) tarassico, (fam) soffione.
dandle ['dændl] vt dondolare, far ballare sulle ginocchia, vezzeggiare.
dandruff ['dændrif] n forfora.
dandy ['dændi] n bellimbusto, damerino.
Dane [dein] n danese.
danger ['deindʒə] n pericolo.
dangerous ['deindʒrəs] a pericoloso.
dangle ['dæŋgl] vti (far) dondolare.
dangling ['dæŋgliŋ] a ciondolante, penzoloni.
Daniel ['dænjəl] nm pr Daniele.
Danish ['deiniʃ] a n danese.
dank [dæŋk] a umido e freddo.
Danube ['dænju:b] n Danubio.
dapper ['dæpə] a arzillo, vivace.
dappled ['dæpld] a chiazzato, pomellato.
dare [dɛə] vi osare; vt sfidare; I dare say forse, probabilmente; dare-devil scavezzacollo.
daring ['dɛəriŋ] a audace, intrepido; n audacia.
dark [dɑ:k] a buio, (o)scuro, tenebroso; n oscurità, tenebre pl.
darken ['dɑ:kən] vti oscurar(si).
darkness ['dɑ:knis] n oscurità, tenebre pl, buio.
darling ['dɑ:liŋ] a caro, diletto; n prediletto.
darn [dɑ:n] n rammendo; vt rammendare.
darning ['dɑ:niŋ] n rammendo; d. needle ago da rammendo; d. wool lana da rammendo.
dart [dɑ:t] n dardo; balzo, movimento rapido; vt dardeggiare, lanciare; vi balzare, slanciar(si).
dash [dæʃ] n slancio, impeto, attacco, colpo; goccio; lineetta; dashboard (aut) cruscotto; vti precipitarsi, urtare violentemente, frantumare, frantumarsi, distruggere; to d. off fare qualcosa velocemente, scappar via.
dashing ['dæʃiŋ] a impetuoso; sgargiante.
dastard ['dæstəd] n codardo, vile; dastardly a vile, codardo.
dastardliness ['dæstədlinis] n viltà.
data ['deitə] n pl dati, elementi.
date [deit] n dattero; data, scadenza; appuntamento; out of d. antiquato; up to d. aggiornato; vti datare; avere (fissare) un appuntamento.
dative ['deitiv] a n dativo.
daub [dɔ:b] n imbrattamento, pittura malfatta, intonaco; vt imbrattare, impiastrare.

daughter ['dɔ:tə] n figlia; d.-in-law nuora.
daunt [dɔ:nt] vt scoraggiare, spaventare.
dauntless ['dɔ:ntlis] a intrepido.
David ['deivid] nm pr Davide.
dawdle ['dɔ:dl] vi bighellonare.
dawn [dɔ:n] n alba, aurora; inizio; vi albeggiare, cominciare ad apparire.
day [dei] n giorno, giornata, dì; d. boy allievo esterno; d. school scuola diurna.
daybreak ['deibreik] n alba.
daydream ['deidri:m] n sogno ad occhi aperti.
day-laborer '['dei,leibərə] n lavoratore a giornata.
daylight ['deilait] n (luce del) giorno.
daytime ['deitaim] n il giorno, la giornata.
daze [deiz] n intontimento, stupore.
dazzle ['dæzl] vt abbagliare.
deacon ['di:kən] n diacono.
dead [ded] a morto; completo, assoluto; n morto, morti, (fig) profondità; at d. of night nel cuor della notte; ad completamente, assolutamente.
deaden ['dedn] vt ammortire, smorzare; vi affievolirsi.
deadlock ['dedlɔk] n punto morto.
deadly ['dedli] a mortale; ad mortalmente.
deadness ['dednis] n ammortimento, stato di torpore.
deaf [def] a sordo.
deafen ['defn] vt assordare, stordire; deafening assordante.
deaf-mute ['def'mju:t] n sordomuto.
deafness ['defnis] n sordità.
deal [di:l] n affare, accordo; (at cards) mano; legno d'abete o di pino; quantità; a good d. (of) molto; vi commerciare, trattare; comportarsi; vt distribuire; assestare (un colpo).
dealer ['di:lə] n commerciante, negoziante.
dealing ['di:liŋ] n commercio; distribuzione; condotta; pl rapporti pl.
dean [di:n] n arciprete, decano; preside di facoltà.
dear [diə] a caro, costoso; dear me! interj Dio mio!
dearly ['diəli] ad teneramente; a caro prezzo.
dearness ['diənis] n caro prezzo.
dearth [də:θ] n carestia, scarsità.
death [deθ] n morte; deathbed letto di morte; d.-rate mortalità.
debar [di'bɑ:] vt escludere.
debase [di'beis] vt abbassare, svilire.
debatable [di'beitəbl] a discutibile, contestabile.
debate [di'beit] n dibattito, discussione; vti dibattere, discutere.
debauch [di'bɔ:tʃ] n crapula, orgia; vt pervertire.

debauchery [di'bɔːtʃəri] n pervertimento, scostumatezza.
debenture [di'bentʃə] n (com) obbligazione.
debilitate [di'biliteit] vt debilitare.
debility [di'biliti] n debolezza, languore.
debit ['debit] n (com) debito; vt addebitare.
debris ['debri] n macerie, detriti.
debt [det] n debito.
debtor ['detə] n debitore.
debunk [diː'bʌŋk] vt ridurre alle giuste proporzioni.
debut ['deibuː] n debutto.
débutante ['debjuːtɑːnt] n debuttante.
decade ['dekeid] n decade, decennio.
decadence ['dekədəns] n decadenza.
decadent ['dekədənt] a n decadente.
decalogue ['dekəlɔg] n decalogo.
decant [di'kænt] vt versare, travasare.
decanter [di'kæntə] n caraffa.
decapitate [di'kæpiteit] vt decapitare.
decasyllable ['dekəsiləbl] a n (poet) decasillabo.
decay [di'kei] n decomposizione, decadenza, rovina; vi decadere, decomporsi, deperire, (teeth) cariarsi.
decease [di'siːs] vi decedere, morire.
deceased [di'siːst] a n deceduto, defunto, fu.
deceit [di'siːt] n inganno, frode, falsità.
deceitful [di'siːtful] a ingannevole, falso.
deceitfulness [di'siːtfulnis] n doppiezza, falsità.
deceive [di'siːv] vt ingannare, deludere.
decelerate [diː'seləreit] vti rallentare.
December [di'sembə] n dicembre.
decency ['diːsnsi] n decenza, decoro.
decent ['diːsnt] a decente, decoroso, onesto, per bene.
decentralize [di'sentrəlaiz] vt decentrare.
deception [di'sepʃən] n inganno; illusione.
deceptive [di'septiv] a ingannevole.
deceptiveness [di'septivnis] n carattere ingannevole, fallacia.
decibel ['desibel] n (phys) decibel.
decide [di'said] vti decidere.
decided [di'saidid] a deciso, risoluto, inconfutabile.
decidedly [di'saididli] ad decisamente, indubbiamente.
decimal ['desiməl] a n decimale.
decimate ['desimeit] vt decimare.
decimation [ˌdesi'meiʃən] n decimazione.
decipher [di'saifə] vt decifrare.
deciphering [di'saifəriŋ] n decifrazione.
decision [di'siʒən] n decisione, giudizio; risolutezza.
decisive [di'saisiv] a decisivo; deciso.

decisiveness [di'saisivnis] n risolutezza.
deck [dek] n (naut) ponte, coperta; mazzo di carte da gioco; vt ornare, coprire, rivestire; d. chair sedia a sdraio.
declaim [di'kleim] vti declamare.
declamation [ˌdeklə'meiʃən] n declamazione.
declamatory [di'klæmətəri] a declamatorio.
declaration [ˌdeklə'reiʃən] n dichiarazione.
declare [di'klɛə] vt dichiarare, proclamare; vi dichiararsi.
declension [di'klenʃən] n (gram) declinazione.
decline [di'klain] n declino, decadimento; declivio; (price) ribasso; vti declinare, rifiutare; inclinarsi; diminuire.
declivity [di'kliviti] n declivio.
decode [diː'koud] vt decifrare, tradurre.
décolleté [dei'kɔltei] a n scollato; scollatura.
decompose [ˌdiːkəm'pouz] vti decomporre, decomporsi; scomporre, scomporsi.
decomposition [ˌdiːkɔmpə'ziʃən] n decomposizione.
decontrol ['diːkən'troul] vt togliere i controlli a.
decorate ['dekəreit] vt decorare, ornare, (a room) verniciare.
decoration [ˌdekə'reiʃən] n decorazione, ornamento.
decorator ['dekə'reitə] n (pittore) decoratore; interior d. arredatore.
decorous ['dekərəs] a decoroso.
decorum [di'kɔːrəm] n decoro.
decoy [di'kɔi] n esca, richiamo; vt allettare, adescare.
decrease ['diːkriːs] n diminuzione; vti [diː'kriːs] diminuire.
decree [di'kriː] n decreto: vt decretare.
decrepit [di'krepit] a decrepito.
decry [di'krai] vt denigrare, screditare.
dedicate ['dedikeit] vt dedicare.
dedicated [di'dedikeitid] a dedicato; votato, consacrato; scrupoloso.
dedication [ˌdedi'keiʃən] n dedica; dedicazione.
deduce [di'djuːs] vt dedurre, desumere.
deduct [di'dʌkt] vt dedurre, sottrarre.
deduction [di'dʌkʃən] n deduzione.
deed [diːd] n azione, atto, fatto, impresa; titolo, contratto.
deem [diːm] vti giudicare, stimare, pensare.
deep [diːp] a profondo; alto; sprofondato; cupo; ad profondamente; n abisso, alto mare.
deep-freeze [diːp'friːz] n surgelamento.
deepen ['diːpən] vti approfondir(si).
deeply ['diːpli] ad profondamente.

deepness ['di:pnis] n profondità.
deer [diə] n (inv) cervo, daino.
deface [di'feis] vt sfigurare; cancellare.
defacement [di'feismənt] n sfregio, cancellazione.
defamation [,defə'meiʃən] n diffamazione, calunnia.
defamatory [di'fæmətəri] a diffamatorio, calunnioso.
defame [di'feim] vt diffamare, calunniare.
default [di'fɔ:lt] n mancanza; insolvenza contumacia; vti render(si) contumace, mancare di pagare.
defaulter [di'fɔ:ltə] n debitore moroso; imputato contumace.
defeat [di'fi:t] n disfatta, sconfitta; vt sconfiggere.
defeatist [di'fi:tist] n disfattista.
defect [di'fekt] n difetto, imperfezione.
defection [di'fekʃən] n defezione.
defective [di'fektiv] a difettoso, imperfetto; **mentally d.** infermo di mente.
defend [di'fend] vt difendere.
defendant [di'fendənt] n convenuto, imputato.
defender [di'fendə] n difensore.
defense [di'fens] n difesa.
defenseless [di'fenslis] a indifeso.
defensive [di'fensiv] a difensivo; n difensiva.
defer [di'fə:] vt differire, rimandare; essere deferente.
deference ['defərəns] n deferenza.
deferent ['defərənt] a deferente.
deferentially [,defə'renʃəli] ad con deferenza.
deferment [di'fə:mənt] n differimento, rimando; dilazione.
defiance [di'faiəns] n sfida; spavalderia.
defiant [di'faiənt] a ardito, provocante; spavaldo.
deficiency [di'fiʃənsi] n deficienza; (com) disavanzo.
deficient [di'fiʃənt] a deficiente, difettoso, insufficiente.
deficit ['defisit] n disavanzo, deficit.
defile ['di:fail] n gola di montagna, stretto passaggio; vt [di'fail] insozzare; violare; vi procedere in fila, sfilare.
defilement [di'failmənt] n contaminazione, violazione.
define [di'fain] vt definire, determinare, delimitare.
definite ['definit] a definito, preciso.
definition [,defi'niʃən] n definizione.
definitive [di'finitiv] a definitivo; decisivo.
deflate [di'fleit] vt (tire) sgonfiare; (fin) deflazionare.
deflect [di'flekt] vt (far) deflettere.
deflection [di'flekʃən] n deviazione.
deforest [di'fɔrist] vt disboscare.
deform [di'fɔ:m] vt deformare.
deformed [di'fɔ:md] a deforme.

deformity [di'fɔ:miti] n deformità.
defraud [di'frɔ:d] vt defraudare.
defray [di'frei] vt pagare, sostenere le spese.
defrost [di'frɔst] vt (also com) sgelare; disgelare; (refrigerator) sbrinare; **defroster** (aut) riscaldatore.
deft [deft] a lesto; agile; abile.
defunct [di'fʌŋkt] a n defunto, deceduto.
defy [di'fai] vt sfidare.
degenerate [di'dʒenərit] a n degenerato; vi [di'dʒenəreit] degenerare.
degradation [,degrə'deiʃən] n degradazione.
degrade [di'greid] vt degradare.
degrading [di'greidiŋ] a degradante.
degree [di'gri:] n grado, laurea.
deign [dein] vti degnar(si).
deity ['di:iti] n deità, divinità.
deject [di'dʒekt] vt deprimere, scoraggiare.
dejected [di'dʒektid] a abbattuto, scoraggiato.
dejection [di'dʒekʃən] n scoraggiamento.
delay [di'lei] n ritardo, indugio; vt ritardare; vi indugiare.
delegate ['deligit] n delegato; ['deligeit] vt delegare.
delegation [,deli'geiʃən] n delegazione.
delete [di'li:t] vt cancellare.
deleterious [,deli'tiəriəs] a deleterio.
deletion [di'li:ʃən] n cancellatura.
deliberate [di'libərit] a cauto, deliberato, misurato; vti [di'libəreit] deliberare.
deliberately [di'libəritli] ad deliberatamente, apposta.
deliberation [di,libə'reiʃən] n deliberazione; decisione.
delicacy ['delikəsi] n delicatezza; leccornia.
delicate ['delikit] a delicato.
delicately ['delikitli] ad delicatamente.
delicious [di'liʃəs] a delizioso, squisito.
deliciousness [di'liʃəsnis] n squisitezza.
delight [di'lait] n diletto, gioia; vti dilettar(si), divertir(si).
delightful [di'laitful] a delizioso, dilettevole, incantevole, molto piacevole.
delightfully [di'laitfuli] ad deliziosamente.
delineate [di'linieit] vt delineare.
delineation [di,lini'eiʃən] n delineazione.
delinquency [di'liŋkwənsi] n delinquenza.
delinquent [di'liŋkwənt] n delinquente.
delirious [di'liriəs] a delirante.
delirium [di'liriəm] n delirio.
deliver [di'livə] vt liberare, salvare;

(*med*) partorire; consegnare; (*speech*) pronunciare; (*blow*) vibrare.

deliverance [di'livərəns] *n* liberazione; parto; consegna; pronunziamento.

deliverer [di'livərə] *n* liberatore, salvatore.

delivery [di'livəri] *n* consegna, distribuzione di posta; parto; il pronunciare un discorso; **cash on d.** (**C.O.D.**) contro assegno; **delivery-man** fattorino, ragazzo; **general d.** fermo posta.

dell [del] *n* valletta, conca.

delphinium [del'finiəm] *n* (*bot*) fiorcappuccio.

delta ['deltə] *n* delta; **d.-wing** (*av*) ala a delta.

delude [di'ljuːd] *vt* illudere, ingannare.

deluge ['deljuːdʒ] *n* diluvio.

delusion [di'luːʒən] *n* illusione; allucinazione.

delusive [di'ljuːsiv] *a* ingannevole, illusorio.

delve [delv] *vt* zappare; (*fig*) penetrare, sondare.

demagogue ['deməgɔg] *n* demagogo.

demand [diː'maːnd] *n* domanda, richiesta; *vt* richiedere; domandare, esigere.

demeanor [di'miːnə] *n* comportamento.

demented [di'mentid] *a* demente, pazzo.

demise [di'maiz] *n* decesso; cessione.

demobilization ['diː.moubilai'zeiʃən] *n* smobilitazione.

demobilize [diː'moubilaiz] *vt* smobilitare.

democracy [di'mɔkrəsi] *n* democrazia.

democrat ['deməkræt] *n* democratico.

democratic [.demə'krætik] *a* democratico.

demolish [di'mɔliʃ] *vt* demolire.

demolition [.demə'liʃən] *n* demolizione.

demon ['diːmən] *n* demonio, spirito maligno.

demoniac [di'mouniæk] *a* demoniaco; *n* indemoniato.

demonstrate ['demənstreit] *vti* dimostrare.

demonstration [.deməns'treiʃən] *n* dimostrazione.

demonstrative [di'mɔnstrətiv] *a* dimostrativo; espansivo.

demoralization [di.mɔrəlai'zeiʃən] *n* demoralizzazione.

demoralize [di'mɔrəlaiz] *vt* demoralizzare.

demur [di'məː] *n* esitazione, irresolutezza; *vi* esitare; obiettare.

demure [di'mjuə] *a* affettatamente modesto.

demureness [di'mjuənis] *n* modestia, affettato candore.

den [den] *n* covo, tana; (*fam*) studiolo.

denationalize [diː'næʃnəlaiz] *vt* snazionalizzare.

denial [di'naiəl] *n* diniego, rifiuto.

denigrate ['denigreit] *vt* denigrare.

denigration [.deni'greiʃən] *n* denigrazione.

denim ['denim] *n* tessuto di cotone; *pl* tuta.

Denis ['denis] *nm pr* Dionigi.

denizen ['denizn] *n* abitante; straniero naturalizzato.

Denmark ['denmaːk] *n* Danimarca.

denominate [di'nɔmineit] *vt* denominare.

denomination [di.nɔmi'neiʃən] *n* denominazione; (*com*) taglio, valore.

denote [di'nout] *vt* denotare, indicare.

denounce [di'nauns] *vt* denunciare.

dense [dens] *a* denso, spesso; ottuso.

density ['densiti] *n* densità; stupidità.

dent [dent] *n* incavo, intaccatura; (*mech*) dente; *vt* intaccare; *vi* dentellarsi.

dental ['dentl] *a n* dentale.

dentifrice ['dentifris] *n* dentifricio.

dentist ['dentist] *n* dentista.

denture ['dentʃə] *n* dentiera.

denude [di'njuːd] *vt* denudare.

denunciation [di.nʌnsi'eiʃən] *n* denuncia, accusa.

deny [di'nai] *vt* negare; rifiutare.

deodorant [diː'oudərənt] *n* deodorante.

depart [di'paːt] *vi* partire; (*fig*) derogare da; **departed** *a* passato; **the departed** il defunto, i defunti.

department [di'paːtmənt] *n* dipartimento, reparto; **d. store** emporio.

departure [di'paːtʃə] *n* partenza; allontanamento; **new d.** nuovo orientamento.

depend [di'pend] *vi* dipendere, contare su.

dependability [di'pendəbiliti] *n* fidatezza; (*of machine etc*) sicurezza di funzionamento.

dependable [di'pendəbl] *a* fidato, sicuro, attendibile.

dependant, dependent [di'pendənt] *n* dipendente.

dependence [di'pendəns] *n* dipendenza; fiducia.

depict [di'pikt] *vt* dipingere, descrivere.

depilate ['depileit] *vt* depilare.

depilatory [di'pilətəri] *a n* depilatorio.

deplete [di'pliːt] *vt* esaurire, vuotare.

deplorable [di'plɔːrəbl] *a* deplorevole.

deplore [di'plɔː] *vt* deplorare.

deploy [di'plɔi] *vti* (*mil*) spiegar(si).

depopulate [di'pɔpjuleit] *vt* spopolare.

depopulation [diː.popju'leiʃən] *n* spopolamento.

deport [di'pɔːt] vt deportare, esiliare.
deportation [ˌdiːpɔː'teiʃən] n deportazione.
deportment [di'pɔːtmənt] n portamento, contegno.
depose [di'pouz] vt deporre, togliere di carica.
deposit [di'pɔzit] n deposito; versamento; vt depositare; versare.
depositary [di'pɔzitəri] n depositario.
deposition [ˌdepə'ziʃən] n deposizione.
depositor [di'pɔzitə] n depositante.
depository [di'pɔzitəri] n deposito.
depot ['depou] n deposito, magazzino.
depravation [ˌdeprə'veiʃən] n corruzione, depravazione.
deprave [di'preiv] vt corrompere, depravare.
depravity [di'præviti] n depravazione.
deprecate ['deprikeit] vt deprecare.
deprecation [ˌdepri'keiʃən] n deprecazione.
depreciate [di'priːʃieit] vt deprezzare, screditare; vi diminuire di valore.
depreciation [diˌpriːʃi'eiʃən] n deprezzamento.
depredation [depri'deiʃən] n depredazione.
depress [di'pres] vt deprimere.
depressing [di'presiŋ] a deprimente.
depression [di'preʃən] n depressione.
deprivation [ˌdepri'veiʃən] n privazione.
deprive [di'praiv] vt privare.
depth [depθ] n profondità, fondo;
 d.-charge bomba di profondità;
 d.-finder scandaglio.
deputation [ˌdepjuː'teiʃən] n deputazione.
depute [di'pjuːt] vt deputare.
deputize ['depjutaiz] vi sostituire, fare le veci di.
deputy ['depjuti] n delegato, deputato, rappresentante.
derail [di'reil] vt far deragliare; vi deragliare.
derailment [di'reilmənt] n deragliamento.
derange [di'reindʒ] vt disordinare, scombussolare.
derangement [di'reindʒmənt] n sconvolgimento, confusione.
derelict ['derilikt] a abbandonato, derelitto; n relitto.
dereliction [ˌderi'likʃən] n abbandono; negligenza.
deride [di'raid] vt deridere.
derision [di'riʒən] n derisione, sarcasmo.
derisive [di'raisiv] a derisorio.
derivation [ˌderi'veiʃən] n derivazione.
derivative [di'rivətiv] a n derivato.
derive [di'raiv] vti derivare.
derogate ['derəgeit] vi derogare.
derogation [ˌderə'geiʃən] n deroga.

derogatory [di'rɔgətəri] a derogatorio.
derrick ['derik] n argano, gru.
descend [di'send] vti scendere, discendere; trasmettersi.
descendant [di'sendənt] a n discendente.
descent [di'sent] n discesa, pendio; discendenza, lignaggio.
describe [dis'kraib] vt descrivere.
description [dis'kripʃən] n descrizione; genere, specie.
descriptive [dis'kriptiv] a descrittivo.
descry [dis'krai] vt discernere, scorgere.
desecrate ['desikreit] vt profanare.
desecration [ˌdesi'kreiʃən] n profanazione.
desert [di'zəːt] vti disertare.
desert ['dezət] n deserto.
desert [di'zəːt] n (usu pl) merito.
deserted [di'zəːtid] a deserto, abbandonato.
deserter [di'zəːtə] n disertore.
desertion [di'zəːʃən] n diserzione.
deserve [di'zəːv] vt meritare.
deserving [di'zəːviŋ] a degno, meritevole.
desiccate ['desikeit] vt essiccare.
design [di'zain] n disegno, proposito; vt disegnare, proporsi.
designate ['dezigneit] vt designare.
designation [ˌdezig'neiʃən] n designazione.
designer [di'zainə] n disegnatore, modellista.
designing [di'zainiŋ] a astuto, intrigante.
desirable [di'zaiərəbl] a desiderabile.
desire [di'zaiə] n desiderio, passione, voglia, preghiera; vt desiderare, pregare.
desirous [di'zaiərəs] a desideroso.
desist [di'zist] vi desistere.
desk [desk] n tavolo, scrittoio, scrivania; cattedra, banco di scuola.
desolate ['desəlit] a desolato; ['desəleit] vt desolare, devastare.
desolation [ˌdesə'leiʃən] n desolazione, distruzione.
despair [dis'pɛə] n disperazione; vi disperar(si).
despairing [dis'pɛəriŋ] a disperato, che fa disperare.
despatch [dis'pætʃ] v dispatch.
desperate ['despərit] a disperato; furioso.
desperately ['despəritli] ad disperatamente; gravemente.
desperation [ˌdespə'reiʃən] n disperazione, accanimento.
despicability [ˌdespikə'biliti] n spregevolezza.
despicable ['despikəbl] a spregevole.
despise [dis'paiz] vt disprezzare.
despite [dis'pait] n dispetto; prep a dispetto di, nonostante, malgrado.
despoil [dis'pɔil] vt derubare, spogliare.

despondency [dis'pɔndənsi] n abbattimento, scoraggiamento.
despondent [dis'pɔndənt] a abbattuto, scoraggiato.
despot ['despɔt] n despota.
despotic [des'pɔtik] a dispotico.
despotism ['despətizəm] n dispotismo.
dessert [di'zə:t] n 'dessert', dolci e frutta (alla fine del pasto) pl.
destination [,desti'neiʃən] n destinazione.
destine ['destin] vt destinare.
destiny ['destini] n destino, fato.
destitute ['destitju:t] a bisognoso, privo di mezzi.
destitution [,desti'tju:ʃən] n destituzione, miseria.
destroy [dis'trɔi] vt distruggere.
destroyer [dis'trɔiə] n distruttore; (naut) cacciatorpediniere.
destruction [dis'trʌkʃən] n distruzione, rovina.
destructive [dis'trʌktiv] a distruttivo.
destructiveness [dis'trʌktivnis] n potenza distruttiva, mania distruttiva.
desultory ['desəltəri] a saltuario, sconnesso.
detach [di'tætʃ] vt (di)staccare, separare.
detached [di'tætʃt] a distaccato, isolato, obiettivo.
detachment [di'tætʃmənt] n distacco; (mil) distaccamento.
detail ['di:teil] n dettaglio, particolare; vt dettagliare; (mil) distaccare.
detain [di'tein] vt detenere, trattenere.
detect [di'tekt] vt scoprire.
detection [di'tekʃən] n scoperta, rivelazione.
detective [di'tektiv] n 'detective', agente investigativo.
detention [di'tenʃən] n detenzione.
deter [di'tə:] vt distogliere, scoraggiare.
detergent [di'tə:dʒənt] a n detergente; detersivo.
deteriorate [di'tiəriəreit] vti deteriorar(si).
deterioration [di,tiəriə'reiʃən] n deterioramento.
determinate [di'tə:minit] a determinato, definito, deciso.
determination [di,tə:mi'neiʃən] n determinazione, risolutezza.
determine [di'tə:min] vt determinare, decidere; vi decidersi.
determined [di'tə:mind] a deciso, risoluto.
deterrent [di'terənt] n azione avente un effetto preventivo, freno.
detest [di'test] vt detestare.
detestable [di'testəbl] a detestabile.
detestation [,di:test'teiʃən] n avversione, odio.
dethrone [di'θroun] vt detronizzare.

detonate ['detouneit] vti (far) detonare.
detonation [,detou'neiʃən] n detonazione.
detonator ['detouneitə] n detonatore.
detour ['deituə] n deviazione d'itinerario, giro; deviazione stradale.
detract [di'trækt] vti detrarre, sottrarre.
detraction [di'trækʃən] n detrazione; diffamazione.
detractor [di'træktə] n detrattore; diffamatore.
detriment ['detrimənt] n detrimento, danno.
detrimental [,detri'mentl] a dannoso.
deuce [dju:s] n diavolo, diamine; (cards) due; (tennis) quaranta pari.
devaluate [di:'væljueit] vt svalutare.
devaluation [,di:vælju'eiʃən] n svalutazione.
devalue [di:'vælju:] v devaluate.
devastate ['devəsteit] vt devastare.
devastating ['devəsteitiŋ] a rovinoso, devastante.
devastation [,devəs'teiʃən] n devastazione.
develop [di'veləp] vt sviluppare; vi svilupparsi.
development [di'veləpmənt] n sviluppo.
deviate ['di:vieit] vti (far) deviare.
deviation [,di:vi'eiʃən] n deviazione.
device [di'vais] n mezzo, espediente, progetto, stratagemma; aggeggio; dispositivo.
devil ['devl] n diavolo.
devilish ['devliʃ] a diabolico.
devilry ['devlri] n diavoleria.
devious ['di:viəs] a indiretto, tortuoso, falso.
devise [di'vaiz] vt escogitare, progettare; lasciare per testamento.
devoid [di'vɔid] a privo.
devolution [,di:və'lu:ʃən] n devoluzione.
devolve [di'vɔlv] vt devolvere; vi ricadere.
devote [di'vout] vt consacrare, dedicare.
devoted [di'voutid] a devoto, votato.
devotee [,devou'ti:] n devoto.
devotion [di'vouʃən] n devozione, dedizione.
devour [di'vauə] vt divorare.
devout [di'vaut] a devoto, pio.
devoutness [di'vautnis] n religiosità.
dew [dju:] n rugiada.
dewy ['dju:i] a rugiadoso.
dexterity [deks'teriti] n destrezza.
dexterous ['dekstərəs] a destro, abile.
diabetes [,daiə'bi:ti:z] n diabete.
diabetic [,daiə'betik] a diabetico.
diabolic(al) [,daiə'bɔlik(əl)] a diabolico.
diadem ['daiədem] n diadema.
diagnose ['daiəgnouz] vt diagnosticare.

diagnosis [‚daiəg'nousis] n diagnosi.
diagonal [dai'ægənl] a n diagonale.
diagram ['daiəgræm] n diagramma.
dial ['daiəl] n meridiana, (clock etc) quadrante; (tel) disco combinatore.
dialect ['daiəlekt] n dialetto.
dialectal [‚daiə'lektəl] a dialettale.
dialogue ['daiələg] n dialogo.
diameter [dai'æmitə] n diametro.
diametrically [‚daiə'metrikəli] ad diametralmente.
diamond ['daiəmənd] n diamante, brillante; (geom) rombo; diamonds pl (cards) quadri.
diaper ['daiəpə] n tela operata; pannolino.
diaphanous [dai'æfənəs] a diafano.
diaphragm ['daiəfræm] n diaframma.
diarrhea [‚daiə'riə] n diarrea.
diatribe ['daiətraib] n diatriba.
diary ['daiəri] n diario; agenda.
dictaphone ['diktəfoun] n dittafono.
dictate ['dikteit] vti dettare.
dictation [dik'teiʃən] n dettatura; comando.
dictator [dik'teitə] n chi detta; dittatore.
dictatorial [‚diktə'tɔːriəl] a dittatorio, dittatoriale.
dictatorship [dik'teitəʃip] n dittatura.
diction ['dikʃən] n dizione.
dictionary ['dikʃənri] n dizionario, vocabolario.
didactic [di'dæktik] a didattico.
die [dai] pl dice n dado; pl dies n (tec) conio, stampo; vi morire; to d. out scomparire.
diesel ['diːzəl] n pr diesel; d. oil nafta.
diet ['daiət] n dieta, regime; vt mettere a dieta, a regime; vi seguire una dieta.
differ ['difə] vi differire; dissentire.
difference ['difrəns] n differenza; contesa.
different ['difrənt] a differente, diverso.
differential [‚difə'renʃəl] a differenziale.
differentiate [‚difə'renʃieit] vti differenziar(si).
difficult ['difikəlt] a difficile.
difficulty ['difikəlti] n difficoltà; ostacolo.
diffidence ['difidəns] n diffidenza, sfiducia in sè, timidezza.
diffident ['difidənt] a diffidente, timido.
diffuse [di'fjuːs] a diffuso; vti diffonder(si).
diffusion [di'fjuːʒən] n diffusione.
dig [dig] vti scavare, vangare.
digest ['daidʒest] n riassunto, digesto; vti [dai'dʒest] digerire, assimilare.
digestible [di'dʒestəbl] a digeribile.
digestion [di'dʒestʃən] n digestione.
digestive [di'dʒestiv] a digestivo.

digger ['digə] n scavatore.
digit ['didʒit] n dito, cifra.
dignified ['dignifaid] a composto, dignitoso.
dignify ['dignifai] vt investire di dignità.
dignitary ['dignitəri] n dignitario.
dignity ['digniti] n dignità.
digress [dai'gres] vi fare delle digressioni.
digression [dai'greʃən] n digressione.
dike [daik] n diga.
dilapidate [di'læpideit] vt dilapidare; dilapidated in rovina.
dilate [dai'leit] vti dilatar(si).
dilatory ['dilətəri] a dilatorio.
dilemma [di'lemə] n dilemma.
diligence ['dilidʒəns] n diligenza.
diligent ['dilidʒənt] a diligente.
dilute [dai'ljuːt] vt diluire a diluito.
dilution [dai'ljuːʃən] n diluzione.
dim [dim] a indistinto, oscuro; appannato; debole; (intelligence) ottuso; vti offuscar(si), oscurar(si).
dime [daim] n moneta d'argento equivalente ad un decimo di dollaro.
dimension [di'menʃən] n dimensione.
dimensional [di'menʃənl] a di dimensioni; (phys) dimensionale.
diminish [di'miniʃ] vti diminuire.
diminution [‚dimi'njuːʃən] n diminuzione.
diminutive [di'minjutiv] a n diminutivo.
dimness ['dimnis] n oscurità, offuscamento; imprecisione.
dimple ['dimpl] n fossetta.
din [din] n frastuono, rumore; assordante.
dine [dain] vi pranzare.
diner ['dainə] a commensale; (rly) vagone ristorante.
dinette [di'net] n saletta da pranzo.
dinginess ['dindʒinis] n squallore; sudiciume.
dingy ['dindʒi] a scuro, sporco.
dining ['dainiŋ] n il pranzare; d. car vagone ristorante; d. room sala da pranzo.
dinner ['dinə] n desinare, pranzo, cena
dint [dint] n tacca, ammaccatura; by d. of prep a forza di.
diocese ['daiəsis] n diocesi.
dioxide [dai'ɔksaid] n (chem) biossido.
dip [dip] n immersione; inclinazione; candela di sego; vti immerger(si), inclinar(si); abbassarsi.
diphtheria [dif'θiəriə] n difterite.
diphthong ['difθɔŋ] n dittongo.
diplomacy [di'plouməsi] n diplomazia.
diplomat ['dipləmæt] n diplomatico.
diplomatic [‚diplə'mætik] a diplomatico.
dipper ['dipə] n chi (s')immerge; mestolo; Big Dipper or Great Bear l'Orsa Maggiore.

dire ['daiə] *a* spaventoso, terribile.
direct [di'rekt] *a* diretto; esplicito; *ad* immediatamente; *vt* avviare, dirigere, indirizzare.
direction [di'rekʃən] *n* direzione, indicazione.
directive [di'rektiv] *a* direttivo; *n* direttiva, istruzione.
directly [di'rektli] *ad cj* immediatamente, appena che.
directness [di'rektnis] *n* franchezza.
director [di'rektə] *n* direttore.
directory [di'rektəri] *n* (*tel*) elenco, guida, consiglio d'amministrazione.
dirge [dəːdʒ] *n* canto funebre, nenia.
dirt [dəːt] **dirtiness** ['dəːtinis] *n* sporcizia, sudiciume.
dirty ['dəːti] *a* sporco, sudicio; *vt* insudiciare, sporcare.
disability [ˌdisə'biliti] *n* incapacità, invalidità.
disable [dis'eibl] *vt* inabilitare, rendere incapace.
disabled [dis'eibld] *a* incapace, invalido.
disabuse [ˌdisə'bjuːz] *vt* disingannare.
disadvantage [ˌdisəd'vɑːntidʒ] *n* svantaggio.
disadvantageous [ˌdisædvɑːn'teidʒəs] *a* svantaggioso.
disagree [ˌdisə'griː] *vi* dissentire, non andar d'accordo; nucere.
disagreeable [ˌdisə'griəbl] *a* sgradevole, antipatico.
disagreement [ˌdisə'griːmənt] *n* disaccordo, dissenso.
disallow ['disə'lau] *vt* non permettere, non ammettere.
disappear [ˌdisə'piə] *vi* scomparire, svanire.
disappearance [ˌdisə'piərəns] *n* scomparsa.
disappoint [ˌdisə'point] *vt* deludere.
disappointed [ˌdisə'pointid] *a* deluso, scontento.
disappointing [ˌdisə'pointiŋ] *a* deludente, spiacevole.
disappointment [ˌdisə'pointmənt] *n* delusione, disappunto.
disapproval [ˌdisə'pruːvəl] *n* disapprovazione.
disapprove [ˌdisə'pruːv] *vt* disapprovare.
disapproving [ˌdisə'pruːviŋ] *a* di disapprovazione.
disapprovingly [ˌdisə'pruːviŋli] *ad* con disapprovazione.
disarm [dis'ɑːm] *vti* disarmare.
disarmament [dis'ɑːməmənt] *n* disarmo.
disarrange ['disə'reindʒ] *vt* scompigliare, scomporre, disorganizzare.
disarray ['disə'rei] *n* disordine, scompiglio.
disarray ['disə'rei] *vt* scompigliare.
disaster [di'zɑːstə] *n* disastro.
disastrous [di'zɑːstrəs] *a* disastroso.

disavow ['disə'vau] *vt* disconoscere, sconfessare, ripudiare.
disavowal ['disə'vauəl] *n* rinnegazione, disconoscimento.
disband [dis'bænd] *vti* sbandar(si).
disbelief ['disbi'liːf] *n* incredulità.
disbelieve ['disbi'liːv] *vt* non credere a; **disbeliever** *n* miscredente.
disburden [dis'bəːdn] *vt* alleggerire d'un peso.
disburse [dis'bəːs] *vt* sborsare.
disbursement [dis'bəːsmənt] *n* sborso.
disc [disk] *n* disco; **d.-brake** (*aut*) freno a disco; **identity d.** (*mil*) piastrina d'identità; **slipped d.** (*med*) ernia del disco.
discard [dis'kɑːd] *vt* scartare.
discern [di'səːn] *vt* discernere.
discerning [di'səːniŋ] *a* acuto, penetrante.
discernment [di'səːnmənt] *n* discernimento, acutezza di giudizio.
discharge [dis'tʃɑːdʒ] *n* scarico, scarica; emissione; suppurazione; liberazione; pagamento; adempimento; *vi* scaricarsi; suppurare; *vt* scaricare, emettere; liberare; licenziare.
disciple [di'saipl] *n* discepolo.
disciplinarian [ˌdisipli'neəriən] *n* chi mantiene una rigida disciplina.
disciplinary ['disiplinəri] *a* disciplinare.
discipline ['disiplin] *n* disciplina; *vt* disciplinare, castigare.
disclaim [dis'kleim] *vt* negare, ripudiare, non riconoscere.
disclose [dis'klouz] *vt* dischiudere, rivelare.
disclosure [dis'klouʒə] *n* rivelazione.
discolor [dis'kʌlə] *vt* scolorire, macchiare; *vi* scolorirsi, macchiarsi.
discoloration [disˌkʌlə'reiʃən] *n* scoloramento, macchia.
discomfiture [dis'kʌmfitʃə] *n* sconfitta, scoraggiamento.
discomfort [dis'kʌmfət] *n* disagio, incomodo.
disconcert [ˌdiskən'səːt] *vt* sconcertare.
disconcerting [ˌdiskən'səːtiŋ] *a* sconcertante.
disconnect ['diskə'nekt] *vt* sconnettere, staccare.
disconsolate [dis'kɔnsəlit] *a* sconsolato, triste.
discontent(ment) ['diskən'tent (mənt)] *n* scontento.
discontented ['diskən'tentid] *a* malcontento.
discontinuance [ˌdiskən'tinjuəns] *n* cessazione, interruzione.
discontinue ['diskən'tinjuː] *vt* cessare, interrompere.
discord ['diskɔːd] *n* discordia; (*mus*) dissonanza.
discordance [dis'kɔːdəns] *n* discordanza.
discordant [dis'kɔːdənt] *a* di-

scorde, dissenziente; discordante; dissonante.
discotheque ['diskɔtek] n discoteca.
discount ['diskaunt] n sconto, tara; vt [dis'kaunt] scontare, fare la tara a.
discourage [dis'kʌridʒ] vt scoraggiare, dissuadere.
discouragement [dis'kʌridʒmənt] n scoraggiamento.
discouraging [dis'kʌridʒiŋ] a scoraggiante.
discourse ['diskɔːs] n discorso; vi [dis'kɔːs] discorrere.
discourteous [dis'kəːtiəs] a scortese.
discover [dis'kʌvə] vt scoprire.
discoverer [dis'kʌvərə] n scopritore.
discovery [dis'kʌvəri] n scoperta.
discredit [dis'kredit] n discredito; vt screditare.
discreditable [dis'kreditəbl] a vergognoso.
discreet [dis'kriːt] a discreto, prudente, riservato.
discrepancy [dis'krepənsi] n discrepanza.
discretion [dis'kreʃən] n discrezione, prudenza.
discriminate [dis'krimineit] vti discriminare.
discrimination [dis.krimi'neiʃən] n discriminazione.
discursive [dis'kəːsiv] a discorsivo, digressivo, saltuario.
discus ['diskəs] n (sport) disco.
discuss [dis'kʌs] vt discutere.
discussion [dis'kʌʃən] n discussione.
disdain [dis'dein] n sdegno; vt sdegnare.
disdainful [dis'deinful] a sdegnoso.
disdainfully [dis'deinfuli] ad sdegnosamente.
disease [di'ziːz] n malattia.
diseased [di'ziːzd] a malato.
disembark ['disim'baːk] vti sbarcare.
disembarkation [.disembə'keiʃən] n sbarco.
disenchant ['disin'tʃɑːnt] vt disincantare, disilludere.
disengage ['disin'geidʒ] vt svincolare, liberare.
disentangle ['disin'tæŋgl] vt districare, sbrogliare.
disfavor ['dis'feivə] n disistima, sfavore.
disfigure [dis'figə] vt deturpare, sfregiare.
disfigurement [dis'figəmənt] n deturpazione, sfregio.
disgorge [dis'gɔːdʒ] vt buttar fuori.
disgrace [dis'greis] n disonore, vergogna, disgrazia; vt disonorare, far cadere in disgrazia.
disgraceful [dis'greisful] a vergognoso, disonorevole.
disgruntled [dis'grʌntld] a malcontento, di cattivo umore, irritato.
disguise [dis'gaiz] n travestimento, maschera; vt travestire, mascherare.
disgust [dis'gʌst] n disgusto; vt disgustare.

disgusted [dis'gʌstid] a disgustato, indignato.
disgusting [dis'gʌstiŋ] a disgustoso.
dish [diʃ] n piatto; portata; recipiente; **dishwasher** lavapiatti; vt mettere nel piatto, servire.
dishearten [dis'haːtn] vt scoraggiare.
dishevel [di'ʃevəl] vt scapigliare.
disheveled [di'ʃevəld] a scarmigliato, arruffato; disordinato.
dishonest [dis'ɔnist] a disonesto.
dishonesty [dis'ɔnisti] n disonestà.
dishonor [dis'ɔnə] n disonore; (com) mancato pagamento; vt disonorare; (com) rifiutarsi di pagare.
dishonorable [dis'ɔnərəbl] a disonorevole.
disillusion [disi'luːʒən] n disillusione; vt disilludere.
disinclination [.disinkli'neiʃən] n antipatia, avversione.
disincline ['disin'klain] vt rendere avverso a.
disinfect [.disin'fekt] vt disinfettare.
disinfectant [.disin'fektənt] n disinfettante.
disinherit ['disin'herit] vt diseredare.
disintegrate [dis'intigreit] vti disintegrar(si).
disinterested [dis'intristid] a disinteressato, imparziale.
disjointed [dis'dʒɔintid] a disarticolato; incoerente; sconnesso.
disk [disk] v **disc.**
dislike [dis'laik] n antipatia; vt sentire antipatia per; **I d.** it non mi piace.
dislocate ['disləkeit] vt slogare.
dislocation [.dislə'keiʃən] n dislocazione, slogatura.
dislodge [dis'lɔdʒ] vti sloggiare.
disloyal ['dis'lɔiəl] a sleale, infedele.
disloyalty ['dis'lɔiəlti] n slealtà, infedeltà.
dismal ['dizməl] a tetro, triste, squallido.
dismantle [dis'mæntl] vt smantellare.
dismay [dis'mei] n costernazione, sbigottimento; vt costernare, sbigottire.
dismember [dis'membə] vt smembrare.
dismiss [dis'mis] vt licenziare, bandire, allontanare.
dismissal [dis'misəl] n licenziamento, rigetto.
dismount ['dis'maunt] vi smontare.
disobedience [.disə'biːdjəns] n disobbidienza.
disobedient [.disə'biːdjənt] a disubbidiente.
disobey ['disə'bei] vti disubbidire (a).
disoblige ['disə'blaidʒ] vt rifiutare un favore a.
disorder [dis'ɔːdə] n disordine; indisposizione; vt disordinare; far ammalare.
disorderly [dis'ɔːdəli] a disordinato, sregolato.

disorganization [dis.ɔːgənaiˈzeiʃən] n disorganizzazione.

disorganize [disˈɔːgənaiz] vt disorganizzare.

disown [disˈoun] vt rinnegare, disconoscere.

disparage [disˈpæridʒ] vt deprezzare, screditare.

disparagement [disˈpæridʒmənt] n denigrazione.

disparaging [disˈpæridʒiŋ] a sprezzante, spregiativo.

disparagingly [disˈpæridʒiŋli] ad con disprezzo, in modo spregiativo.

disparity [disˈpæriti] n disparità, differenza.

dispassionate [disˈpæʃnit] a spassionato, imparziale.

dispatch [disˈpætʃ] n dispaccio; spedizione; prontezza; vt spedire, sbrigare.

dispel [disˈpel] vt dissipare, scacciare.

dispensary [disˈpensəri] n dispensario.

dispensation [dispenˈseiʃən] n dispensa, dispensazione.

dispense [disˈpens] vt dispensare; distribuire.

disperse [disˈpəːs] vt disperdere; vi disperdersi.

dispersion [disˈpəːʃən] n dispersione.

displace [disˈpleis] vt spostare, sostituire; (naut) dislocare, stazzare; **displaced person** profugo.

displacement [disˈpleismənt] n spostamento, sostituzione; (naut) dislocamento.

display [disˈplei] n mostra, esibizione, ostentazione; vt mettere in mostra, esporre, ostentare.

displease [disˈpliːz] vt displacere, offendere.

displeasure [disˈpleʒə] n displacere, scontento.

disposal [disˈpouzəl] n disposizione; eliminazione; **at your d.** a sua disposizione.

disposable [disˈpouzəbl] a disponibile.

dispose [disˈpouz] vt disporre; **to d. of** disfarsi di, vendere.

disposition [ˌdispəˈziʃən] n disposizione, carattere, temperamento.

dispossess [ˈdispəˈzes] vt privare, spossessare.

disproportion [ˈdisprəˈpɔːʃən] n sproporzione.

disproportionate [ˌdisprəˈpɔːʃnit] a sproporzionato.

disprove [ˈdisˈpruːv] vt confutare.

disputable [disˈpjuːtəbl] a discutibile, disputabile; contestabile.

dispute [disˈpjuːt] n disputa, controversia, vertenza; vti disputare.

disqualification [disˌkwɔlifiˈkeiʃən] n squalifica.

disqualify [disˈkwɔlifai] vt squalificare.

disquieting [disˈkwaiətiŋ] a inquietante.

disregard [ˌdisriˈgaːd] n noncuranza; vt ignorare, trascurare, non curarsi di.

disregardful [ˌdisriˈgaːdful] a noncurante.

disrepair [ˈdisriˈpɛə] n cattivo stato, rovina.

disreputable [disˈrepjutəbl] a disonorevole, losco, malfamato.

disrepute [ˈdisriˈpjuːt] n scredito; disistima; cattiva fama.

disrespect [ˈdisrisˈpekt] n mancanza di rispetto, irriverenza.

disrupt [disˈrʌpt] vt rompere, disorganizzare.

disruption [disˈrʌpʃən] n rottura, scissione.

dissatisfaction [ˈdisˌsætisˈfækʃən] n malcontento.

dissatisfied [ˈdisˈsætisfaid] a insoddisfatto, scontento.

dissatisfy [ˈdisˈsætisfai] vt non soddisfare.

dissect [diˈsekt] vt sezionare; (fig) criticare.

dissection [diˈsekʃən] n dissezione.

dissemble [diˈsembl] vti simulare, nascondere.

disseminate [diˈsemineit] vt disseminare, diffondere.

dissemination [diˌsemiˈneiʃən] n disseminazione; (fig) divulgazione.

dissension [diˈsenʃən] n discordia, dissenso.

dissent [diˈsent] n dissenso, dissentimento; vt dissentire.

dissenter [diˈsentə] n dissidente.

disservice [ˈdisˈsəːvis] n disservizio.

dissident [ˈdisidənt] a n dissidente.

dissimilar [diˈsimilə] a dissimile.

dissimilarity [ˌdisimiˈlæriti] n dissomiglianza.

dissipate [ˈdisipeit] vti dissipar(si).

dissipated [ˈdisipeitid] a dissoluto, dissipato.

dissipation [ˌdisiˈpeiʃən] n dissipazione, dispersione.

dissociate [diˈsouʃieit] vti dissociar(si).

dissociation [diˌsousiˈeiʃən] n dissociazione, sdoppiamento.

dissoluble [diˈsɔljubl] a dissolubile.

dissolute [ˈdisəluːt] a dissoluto.

dissolution [ˌdisəˈluːʃən] n dissoluzione, scioglimento.

dissolve [diˈzɔlv] vti discioglier(si), dissolver(si), disfar(si); n (cin) dissolvenza.

dissolvent [diˈzɔlvənt] a n dissolvente.

dissonance [ˈdisənəns] n dissonanza.

dissonant [ˈdisənənt] a dissonante; discordante.

dissuade [diˈsweid] vt dissuadere.

dissuasion [diˈsweiʒən] n dissuasione.

distaff [ˈdistaːf] n conocchia.

distance [ˈdistəns] n distanza.

distant [ˈdistənt] a distante, remoto; (fig) freddo, riservato.

distaste ['dis'teist] n ripugnanza.
distasteful [dis'teistful] a ripugnante, sgradevole.
distemper [dis'tempə] n indisposizione; (vet) cimurro.
distemper [dis'tempə] vt dipingere a tempera, intonacare.
distend [dis'tend] vti gonfiar(si), dilatar(si).
distill [dis'til] vt distillare; vi stillare.
distillation [,disti'leifən] n distillazione.
distillery [dis'tiləri] n distilleria.
distinct [dis'tiŋkt] a ben definito, distinto, diverso.
distinction [dis'tiŋkfən] n distinzione.
distinctive [dis'tiŋktiv] a distintivo, caratteristico.
distinguish [dis'tiŋgwif] vti distinguere, differenziare.
distinguished [dis'tiŋgwifd] a distinto, insigne.
distinguishing [dis'tiŋgwifiŋ] a distintivo, caratteristico.
distort [dis'tɔːt] vt distorcere, deformare; svisare.
distortion [dis'tɔːfən] n distorsione, deformazione.
distract [dis'trækt] vt distrarre; far impazzire.
distracted [dis'træktid] a sconvolto, pazzo.
distraction [dis'trækfən] n distrazione, svago; follia; disperazione.
distrain [dis'trein] vi sequestrare, fare un sequestro.
distraught [dis'trɔːt] a sconvolto, disperato.
distress [dis'tres] n dolore; miseria, difficoltà; vt affliggere.
distressed [dis'trest] n angustiato, afflitto, in angustie.
distressing [disː'tresiŋ] a penoso, doloroso.
distribute [dis'tribju(ː)t] vt distribuire.
distribution [distri'bjuːfən] n distribuzione.
distributor [dis'tribjutə] n distributore, distributrice; (merchandise) grossista.
district ['distrikt] n distretto; quartiere.
distrust [dis'trʌst] n diffidenza, sfiducia; vt diffidare di.
distrustful [dis'trʌstful] a diffidente, sospettoso.
disturb [dis'təːb] vt disturbare.
disturbance [dis'təːbəns] n agitazione, tumulto.
disunion ['dis'juːnjən] n disunione.
disuse ['dis'juːs] n disuso.
ditch [ditf] n fossa, fossato.
ditto ['ditou] n lo stesso; ad come sopra.
ditty ['diti] n canzone popolare, ritornello.
divan [di'væn] n divano.
dive [daiv] n tuffo; **d. bombing**

bombardamento in picchiata; vi immergersi, tuffarsi; (av) scendere in picchiata.
diver ['daivə] n tuffatore; palombaro; **skin d.** nuotatore subacqueo, sommozzatore.
diverge [dai'vəːdʒ] vi divergere.
divergence [dai'vəːdʒəns] **divergency** [dai'vəːdʒənsi] n divergenza.
divergent [dai'vəːdʒənt] a divergente.
diverse ['daivə(ː)z] a diverso.
diversify [dai'vəːsifai] vt diversificare, variare.
diversion [dai'vəːfən] n diversione; **road d., traffic d.** deviazione stradale.
diversity [dai'vəːsiti] n diversità.
divert [dai'vəːt] vt deviare, divertire.
divest [dai'vest] vt spogliare, svestire.
divide [di'vaid] vti divider(si).
dividend ['dividend] n (com) dividendo.
dividers [di'vaidəz] n pl compasso a punte fisse.
divine [di'vain] a divino; n teologo; vti divinare, predire.
diviner [di'vainə] n indovino; **water d.** rabdomante.
diving ['daiviŋ] n il tuffarsi, immersione; **d. board** trampolino; **d. suit** scafandro.
divinity [di'viniti] n divinità; teologia.
divisible [di'vizəbl] a divisibile.
division [di'viʒən] n divisione.
divorce [di'vɔːs] n divorzio; vt divorziare da.
divorcee [di'vɔːsei] n divorziato, divorziata.
divulge [dai'vʌldʒ] vt divulgare.
dizziness ['dizinis] n capogiro, vertigine.
dizzy ['dizi] a vertiginoso;'preso da vertigine; **to feel d.** sentirsi girar la testa.
do [duː] vt fare, compiere, eseguire; cucinare; (sl) ingannare; vi comportarsi; stare di salute; andar bene; bastare.
docile ['dousail] a docile.
docility [dou'siliti] n docilità.
dock [dɔk] n bacino portuario; **dockyard** arsenale; vt mozzare; (fam) ridurre; vi entrare in porto.
docker ['dɔkə] n scaricatore di porto.
doctor ['dɔktə] n dottore, medico.
doctrine ['dɔktrin] n dottrina.
document ['dɔkjumənt] n documento.
documentary [,dɔkju'mentəri] a n documentario.
dodge [dɔdʒ] vti scansare, schivare, eludere.
doe [dou] n (deer) daina, (hare) lepre femmina, (rabbit) coniglia; **doeskin** pelle di daino.
dog [dɔg] n cane; **d. days** pl la canicola; **top d.** (fam) persona autorevole; **dogfish** pescecane; **d.**

rose rosa canina; *vt* seguire, pedinare.
dogged ['dɔgid] *a* ostinato, tenace.
doggedly ['dɔgidli] *ad* ostinatamente, indefessamente.
dogma ['dɔgmə] *n* dogma.
dogmatic [dɔg'mætik] *a* dogmatico.
dogmatize ['dɔgmətaiz] *vi* dogmatizzare.
doings ['du(ː)iŋz] *n pl* fatti, azioni, occupazioni.
dole [doul] *n* distribuzione caritatevole; **the d.** sussidio dato ai disoccupati; *vt* distribuire in piccole quantità, dare in elemosina.
doleful ['doulful] *a* malinconico, triste.
doll [dɔl] *n* bambola.
dollar ['dɔlə] *n* dollaro.
Dolomites ['dɔləmaits] *n pl* le Dolomiti.
dolphin ['dɔlfin] *n* delfino.
dolt [doult] *n* individuo ottuso.
domain [də'mein] *n* dominio, proprietà terriera.
dome [doum] *n* cupola.
domestic [də'mestik] *a n* domestico, domestica; **d. mail** posta per l'interno.
domicile ['dɔmisail] *n* domicilio.
dominant ['dɔminənt] *a* dominante.
dominate ['dɔmineit] *vti* dominare.
domination [ˌdɔmi'neiʃən] *n* dominazione, dominio.
domineer [ˌdɔmi'niə] *vi* spadroneggiare, tiranneggiare.
domineering [ˌdɔmi'niəriŋ] *a* dispotico, imperioso, prepotente.
Dominic ['dɔminik] *nm pr* Domenico.
Dominican [də'minikən] *a n* domenicano.
dominion [də'minjən] *n* dominio.
domino ['dɔminou] *pl* dominoes *n* domino.
don [dɔn] *n* insegnante universitario; *vt* indossare, mettersi.
donate [dou'neit] *vt* donare.
donation [dou'neiʃən] *n* donazione.
donkey ['dɔŋki] *n* asino, somaro; **d.-engine** locomotiva di manovra.
donor ['dounə] *n* donatore; **blood d.** donatore di sangue.
doom [duːm] *n* condanna; destino, sorte; *vt* condannare.
doomsday ['duːmzdei] *n* giorno del giudizio.
door [dɔː] *n* porta, uscio; **doorway** vano della porta.
dope [doup] *n* lubrificante; stimolante; narcotico.
dormant ['dɔːmənt] *a* assopito; inattivo; caduto in disuso; **d. partner** (*com*) socio occulto.
dormitory ['dɔːmitri] *n* dormitorio.
dormouse ['dɔːmaus] *n* ghiro.
dorsal ['dɔːsəl] *a* dorsale.
dose [dous] *n* dose; *vt* dosare, somministrare a dosi; (*drinks*) adulterare.
dot [dɔt] *n* punto, puntino.

dotage ['doutidʒ] *n* rimbambimento.
dotard ['doutəd] *n* vecchio rimbambito.
dote [dout] *vi* essere rimbambito, essere infatuato.
double ['dʌbl] *a* doppio; finto; *n* doppio; *ad* due volte; *vt* raddoppiare; passar intorno a; *vi* voltare improvvisamente.
doubt [daut] *n* dubbio, incertezza; sospetto; *vti* dubitare; sospettare.
doubtful ['dautful] *a* incerto, dubbio, dubbioso.
doubtless ['dautlis] *ad* indubbiamente, senza dubbio.
dough [dou] *n* pasta.
dove [dʌv] *n* colomba.
dowager ['dauədʒə] *n* vedova (che ha un titolo o un patrimonio ereditato dal marito).
dowdy ['daudi] *a* sciatto, trasandato.
down [daun] *n* duna, collinetta; lanugine, peluria; piumino; *a* depresso; *prep* in basso, giù per; *ad* giù, in basso, in giù; **d. with . . .** *interj* a abbasso; *vt* (*fam*) abbattere, gettare terra.
downcast ['daunkɑːst] *a* abbattuto.
downfall ['daunfɔːl] *n* caduta, rovescio di fortuna.
downhearted ['daun'hɑːtid] *a* scoraggiato, abbattuto.
downhill ['daun'hil] *a* discendente; *n* discesa; *ad* in discesa.
downpour ['daunpɔː] *n* acquazzone.
downright ['daunrait] *a* netto, chiaro; onesto *ad* categoricamente.
downstairs ['daun'stɛəz] *a* del (al) piano di sotto; *ad* giù.
downward ['daunwəd] *a* verso il basso, discendente; **downwards** *ad* in giù, in basso.
dowry ['dauəri] *n* dote.
doze [douz] *n* sonnellino; *vt* sonnecchiare.
dozen ['dʌzn] *n* dozzina.
drab [dræb] *a* grigio, scialbo.
draft [drɑːft] *n* (*outline*) abbozzo; brutta copia; assegno, tratta; (*mil*) distaccamento; bevanda, pozione; corrente d'aria, (*naut*) pescaggio; trazione; *vt* redigere; abbozzare; arruolare.
draftsman ['drɑːftsmən] *n* disegnatore.
drafty ['drɑːfti] *a* pieno di correnti d'aria.
drag [dræg] *n* (*naut*) draga; (*agr*) erpice; carrozza a quattro cavalli; (*fig*) ostacolo, peso; *vt* trascinare, dragare.
dragon ['drægən] *n* drago(ne); **dragonfly** libellula.
dragoon [drə'guːn] *n* (*mil*) dragone.
drain [drein] *n* canale di scolo, fogna, tubo di scarico, tubo per drenaggio; *vt* prosciugare per drenaggio; scolare, bere fino in fondo.
drainage ['dreinidʒ] *n* fognatura,

drenaggio, prosciugamento.
drake [dreik] n anitra maschio.
drama ['drɑːmə] n dramma.
dramatic [drə'mætik] a drammatico.
dramatist ['dræmətist] n drammaturgo.
dramatize ['dræmətaiz] vt drammatizzare; adattare per il teatro.
drape [dreip] vt coprire, drappeggiare.
draper ['dreipə] n merciaio, negoziante in tessuti.
drapery ['dreipəri] n tessuti, drappeggi, commercio in tessuti.
drastic ['dræstik] a drastico, energico.
draught [drɑːft] v draft.
draughts [drɑːfts] n pl (game) gioco della dama.
draw [drɔː] n trazione; attrazione; sorteggio; (sport) pareggio; vti tirare, (ri)tirarsi, attirare, trascinare; disegnare; tirare a sorte; (com) emettere; riscuotere, (sport) pareggiare.
drawback ['drɔːbæk] n inconveniente, svantaggio.
drawbridge ['drɔːbridʒ] n ponte levatoio.
drawer ['drɔːə] n disegnatore; redattore; (com) traente; cassetto; **drawers** pl mutande pl.
drawing ['drɔːiŋ] n disegno; sorteggio; tiraggio; d. room salotto.
drawl [drɔːl] n pronuncia strascicata; vi strascicare le parole.
dray [drei] n carro pesante.
dread [dred] n terrore; vt temere.
dreadful ['dredful] a terribile.
dreadnought ['drednɔːt] n (naut) supercorazzata.
dream [driːm] n sogno: vti sognare.
dreamer ['driːmə] n sognatore.
dreamy ['driːmi] a sognante, vago.
dreary ['driəri] a triste, cupo.
dredge [dredʒ] n draga; vt dragare; (with flour, sugar etc) spolverizzare (di).
dregs [dregz] n pl feccia, fondo, sedimento.
drench [drentʃ] vt bagnare, inzuppare; **drenching rain** pioggia dirotta.
dress [dres] n abito, vestito, veste, modo di vestirsi; vti vestire, vestirsi; (mil) allineare; medicare; (dish) guarnire.
dresser ['dresə] n assistente chirurgo; (theat) vestiarista; credenza, dispensa; toletta.
dressing ['dresiŋ] n abbigliamento; medicazione; condimento.
dressing-gown ['dresiŋgaun] n vestaglia.
dressmaker ['dres,meikə] n sarta.
dribble ['dribl] n gocciolamento; bava; (football) palleggio; vi gocciolare; sbavare; (football) palleggiare, dribblare.
drift [drift] n spinta, direzione, velocità; deriva; vti lasciarsi trasportare, andare alla deriva, ammucchiare.
drifter ['driftə] n (naut) motopeschereccio con tramaglio.
drill [dril] n (mech) perforatrice, trapano; (mil) esercitazioni pl; vt trapanare; esercitare; vi fare esercitazioni.
driller ['drilə] n macchina perforatrice.
drilling ['driliŋ] n trapanazione; (mil) esercitazione; d. machine trapano.
drink [driŋk] n bevanda, bibita; intemperanza nel bere; vti bere.
drinkable ['driŋkəbl] a bevibile, potabile.
drinking ['driŋkiŋ] a da bere, potabile; n il bere, alcoolismo.
drip [drip] n gocciolamento, stillicidio; vi gocciolare.
dripping ['dripiŋ] n grasso sciolto di carne.
drive [draiv] n passeggiata in carrozza o in auto; viale; spinta, propulsione; (aut) guida; vt condurre, guidare; costringere; trasportare; vi andare in carrozza, in auto.
drivel ['drivl] n bava, saliva; insulsaggine; vi sbavare; parlare da sciocco.
driver ['draivə] n autista, conducente, conduttore, guidatore, vetturino.
driving ['draiviŋ] a propulsore; dinamico; sferzante; d. rain pioggia sferzante; n (aut) guida; (mech) comando; d. school scuola guida; d. wheel (aut) volante.
drizzle ['drizl] n pioggerella; vi piovigginare.
droll [droul] a buffo, divertente.
drollery ['drouləri] n buffoneria.
dromedary ['drɔmədəri] n dromedario.
drone [droun] n (bee) fuco; ronzio; fannullone; vi ronzare, parlare con tono monotono.
droop [druːp] n portamento curvo; accasciamento; vi pendere, curvarsi, abbassare, languire.
drop [drɔp] n goccia, goccio; caduta; (prices) ribasso; (temperature) abbassamento; vt lasciar cadere; vi cadere, diminuire.
dropper ['drɔpə] n contagocce.
dropsy ['drɔpsi] n (med) idropisia.
dross [drɔs] n scoria; (fig) rifiuto.
drought [draut] n siccità.
drove [drouv] n branco, gregge, mandria.
drover ['drouvə] n mandriano.
drown [draun] vti affogare, annegare;
drowning annegamento, sommersione.
drowse [drauz] vi assopirsi, sonnecchiare.
drowsiness ['drauzinis] n sonnolenza.
drowsy ['drauzi] a sonnolento.
drudge [drʌdʒ] n schiavo; sgobbone.

drudge [drʌdʒ] *vi* sfacchinare.
drudgery ['drʌdʒəri] *n* lavoro faticoso, ingrato.
drug [drʌg] *n* droga, prodotto farmaceutico; stupefacente; **drugstore** farmacia.
druggist ['drʌgist] *n* farmacista.
drum [drʌm] *n* tamburo; (*anat*) timpano; (*mech*) rullo; *vi* suonare il tamburo, tamburellare; *vt* inculcare.
drummer ['drʌmə] *n* tamburino, batterista; viaggiatore di commercio; propagandista.
drunk [drʌŋk] *a* ubriaco.
drunkard ['drʌŋkəd] *n* ubriacone.
drunken ['drʌŋkən] *a* ubriaco.
drunkenness ['drʌŋkənnis] *n* ubriachezza.
dry [drei] *a* asciutto, arido, secco; privo d'interesse; *vt* asciugare, seccare, esaurire; *vi* evaporare completamente, seccarsi; **to d. clean** lavare a secco; **d.-goods store** negozio di tessuti.
dryly ['draili] *ad* seccamente.
dryness ['drainis] *n* aridità, secchezza.
dual ['djuːəl] *a* doppio, duplice; **d. highway** strada a doppia carreggiata.
dub [dʌb] *vt* (*cin*) doppiare; **dubbing** *n* doppiaggio.
dubious ['djuːbiəs] *a* dubbio, equivoco, incerto.
Dublin ['dʌblin] *n* Dublino.
duchess ['dʌtʃis] *n* duchessa.
duchy ['dʌtʃi] *n* ducato.
duck [dʌk] *n* anitra, anatra; *vti* immerger(si), tuffar(si); *vi* abbassare il capo improvvisamente.
duckling ['dʌkliŋ] *n* anatroccolo.
duct [dʌkt] *n* canale, tubo, condotto; (*anat*) vaso.
due [djuː] *a* dovuto, debito, adeguato; *n* dovuto, quota, tassa; **to be d.** dover arrivare.
duel ['djuːəl] *n* duello.
duet [djuː'et] *n* duetto.
duke [djuːk] *n* duca.
dukedom ['djuːkdəm] *n* ducato.
dull [dʌl] *a* tardo, lento; (*color*) smorto; (*sound*) sordo; triste, monotono; *vt* intorpidire, smorzare, istupidire.
dullard ['dʌləd] *n* individuo ottuso.
dullness ['dʌlnis] *n* lentezza, mancanza di vivacità, monotonia, ottusità.
duly ['djuːli] *ad* debitamente, a tempo debito.
dumb [dʌm] *a* muto; **dumbwaiter** montavivande.
dumbfound [dʌm'faund] *vt* stupefare, confondere.
dumbness ['dʌmnis] *n* mutismo.
dummy ['dʌmi] *n* fantoccio, manichino, uomo di paglia; **baby's d.** succhiotto, tettarella.
dump [dʌmp] *n* deposito di rifiuti;

(*mil*) deposito di munizioni; *vt* scaricare.
dumpling ['dʌmpliŋ] *n* grossa polpetta di pasta bollita; (*sl*) individuo, animale piccolo e rotondetto.
dumpy ['dʌmpi] *a* tarchiato, tozzo.
dun [dʌn] *a* grigio scuro; *n* creditore importuno; *vt* domandare insistentemente il pagamento.
dunce [dʌns] *n* ignorante, stupido.
dune [djuːn] *n* duna.
dung [dʌŋ] *n* letame, sterco.
dungarees [ˌdʌŋgə'riːz] *n pl* tuta.
dungeon ['dʌndʒən] *n* prigione sotterranea, segreta.
dupe [djuːp] *n* credulone, gonzo; *vt* gabbare, ingannare.
duplicate ['djuːplikit] *a n* duplicato; *vt* ['djuplikeit] duplicare.
duplicator ['djuːplikeitə] *n* copialettere.
duplicity [djuː'plisiti] *n* doppiezza.
durability [ˌdjuərə'biliti] *n* durabilità.
durable ['djuərəbl] *a* durevole.
duration [djuə'reiʃən] *n* durata.
duress [djuə'res] *n* costrizione, violenza, imprigionamento.
during ['djuəriŋ] *prep* durante.
dusk [dʌsk] *n* crepuscolo.
dusky ['dʌski] *a* oscuro, fosco.
dust [dʌst] *n* polvere; **dustbin** pattumiera; *vt* spolverare; impolverare, cospargere di.
duster ['dʌstə] *n* strofinaccio.
dusting ['dʌstiŋ] *n* spolverare, spolveratura; (*fig*) bastonatura.
dusty ['dʌsti] *a* polveroso.
Dutch [dʌtʃ] *a n* olandese; **D. courage** finto coraggio, coraggio dato da stimolanti.
dutiful ['djuːtiful] *a* ubbidiente, rispettoso.
duty ['djuːti] *n* dovere; rispetto; servizio; imposta, tassa.
dwarf [dwɔːf] *a n* nano; *vt* rimpicciolire.
dwell [dwel] *vi* dimorare, abitare; soffermarsi.
dwelling ['dweliŋ] *n* abitazione, dimora.
dwindle ['dwindl] *vi* consumarsi, rimpicciolirsi.
dye [dai] *n* tintura, tinta; *vt* tingere; *vi* tingersi, prendere il colore di.
dyer ['daiə] *n* tintore.
dying ['daiiŋ] *a* morente, moribondo.
dynamic [dai'næmik] *a* dinamico; **dynamics** *n pl* dinamica.
dynamite ['dainəmait] *n* dinamite.
dynamo ['dainəmou] *pl* **dynamos** *n* dinamo.
dynasty ['dinəsti] *n* dinastia.
dysentery ['disntri] *n* dissenteria.
dyspepsia [dis'pepsiə] *n* dispepsia.

E

each [iːtʃ] *a pron* ciascuno, ogni, ognuno; **e. other** l'un l'altro.

eager ['iːgə] *a* ardente, avido.

eagerly ['iːgəli] *ad* ardentemente, avidamente.

eagerness ['iːgənis] *n* premura, ansia, brama.

eagle ['iːgl] *n* aquila.

ear [iə] *n* orecchio, orecchia; spiga.

earl [əːl] *n* conte dell'aristocrazia inglese.

earldom ['əːldəm] *n* contea.

earliness ['əːlinis] *n* ora mattutina; precocità.

early ['əːli] *a* primo; mattutino, prossimo, prematuro; *ad* di buon'ora, presto.

earn [əːn] *vt* guadagnare, meritare.

earnest ['əːnist] *a* serio, fervido; *n* anticipo, caparra, pegno; **in e.** seriamente, sul serio.

earnestness ['əːnistnis] *n* serietà.

earnings ['əːniŋz] *n pl* guadagni *pl.*

ear-ring ['iəːriŋ] *n* orecchino.

earth [əːθ] *n* terra, suolo; tana; **e. wire** (*el*) filo di terra.

earthen ['əːθən] *a* di terra, di terra-cotta.

earthenware ['əːθənwɛə] *n* terraglia.

earthly ['əːθli] *a* terreno, terrestre.

earthquake ['əːθkweik] *n* terremoto.

earthworm ['əːθwəːm] *n* lombrico.

earthy ['əːθi] *a* di terra, terroso; grossolano.

earwig ['iəwig] *n* forfecchia.

ease [iːz] *n* agio, comodo, riposo; *vt* calmare, dar sollievo a, allentare, alleggerire.

easel ['iːzl] *n* cavalletto.

easily ['iːzili] *ad* facilmente, comoda-mente.

easiness ['iːzinis] *n* disinvoltura, facilità.

east [iːst] *n* est, oriente; *a* orientale.

Easter ['iːstə] *n* Pasqua.

easterly ['iːstəli] *a* (*vento, direzione*) d'est, dell'est.

eastern ['iːstən] *a* orientale, dell'est.

eastward ['iːstwəd] *a ad* est, verso est.

easy ['iːzi] *a* agevole, comodo, disin-volto, facile.

eat [iːt] *vti* mangiare.

eatable ['iːtəbl] *a* mangiabile; *a n* commestibile.

eating ['iːtiŋ] *a* che consuma, (*fig*) che rode; *n* il mangiare.

eaves [iːvz] *n pl* gronda.

eavesdrop ['iːvzdrɔp] *vi* origliare.

ebb [eb] *n* riflusso; **e.-tide** bassa marea; *vi* rifluire, abbassarsi.

ebony ['ebəni] *a* d'ebano; *n* ebano.

eccentric [ik'sentrik] *a n* eccentrico.

eccentricity [.eksen'trisiti] *n* eccen-tricità.

ecclesiastic [i.kliːzi'æstik] *a n* eccle-siastico.

echelon ['eʃələn] *n* (*mil*) scaglione.

echo ['ekou] *n* eco; *vt* ripetere; *vi* echeggiare.

eclectic [ek'lektik] *a n* eclettico.

eclipse [i'klips] *n* eclissi; *vt* eclissare.

economic [.iːke'nɔmik] *a* economico; **economical** economico, economo; **economics** *n pl* economia, scienze economiche.

economist [iː'kɔnəmist] *n* econo-mista.

economize [iː'kɔnəmaiz] *vti* econo-mizzare.

economy [iː'kɔnəmi] *n* economia.

ecstasy ['ekstəsi] *n* estasi.

ecstatic [eks'tætik] *a* estatico.

eczema ['eksimə] *n* eczema.

eddy ['edi] *n* vortice; *vi* girar vorticosamente, turbinare.

Eden ['iːdn] *n* Eden, Paradiso Ter-restre.

Edgar ['edgə] *nm pr* Edgardo.

edge [edʒ] *n* bordo, margine, orlo, filo tagliente; *vt* bordare, orlare; *vi* avanzare obliquamente; **to be on e.** avere i nervi tesi.

edgeways ['edʒweiz] **edgewise** ['edʒ-waiz] *ad* di taglio; a mala pena.

edgy ['edʒi] *a* affilato, tagliente; (*fig*) nervoso.

edible ['edibl] *a* commestibile, man-gereccio.

edict ['iːdikt] *n* editto.

edification [.edifi'keiʃən] *n* edifica-zione.

edifice ['edifis] *n* edificio.

edify ['edifai] *vt* (*fig*) edificare.

edifying ['edifaiiŋ] *a* edificante.

Edinburgh ['edinbərə] *n* Edimburgo.

edit ['edit] *vt* curare l'edizione di; (*cin*) curare il montaggio.

edition [i'diʃən] *n* edizione.

editor ['editə] *n* editore, direttore, redattore d'un giornale *etc.*

editorial [.edi'tɔːriəl] *a* editoriale; redazionale; *n* articolo di fondo.

educate ['edjuːkeit] *vt* istruire, edu-care.

education [.edjuː'keiʃən] *n* istru-zione.

educational [.edjuː'keiʃənl] *a* educa-tivo.

Edward ['edwəd] *nm pr* Edoardo.

eel [iːl] *n* anguilla.

eerie ['iəri] *a* misterioso, che ispira paura, soprannaturale.

efface [i'feis] *vt* cancellare.

effect [i'fekt] *n* effetto, conseguenza; significato; **effects** *pl* beni, effetti, oggetti personali *pl*; *vt* effettuare, compiere.

effective [i'fektiv] *a* efficace, effetti-vo.

effectively [i'fektivli] *ad* efficace-mente, effettivamente.

effectual [i'fektjuəl] *a* efficace, valido.

effectuate [i'fektjueit] *vt* effettuare.

effeminacy [i'feminəsi] *n* effemina-tezza.

effeminate [i'feminit] *a* effeminato.

effervesce [,efə'ves] *vi* essere effervescente, spumare.
effervescence [,efə'vesns] *n* effervescenza.
effervescent [,efə'vesnt] *a* effervescente; vivace, spumeggiante.
effete [e'fiːt] *a* indebolito, esausto.
efficacious [,efi'keiʃəs] *a* efficace.
efficacy ['efikəsi] *n* efficacia.
efficiency [i'fiʃənsi] *n* efficienza.
efficient [i'fiʃənt] *a* efficiente.
efficiently [i'fiʃəntli] *ad* con competenza, efficacemente.
effigy ['efidʒi] *n* effigie.
effort ['efət] *n* sforzo.
effortless ['efətlis] *a* senza sforzo, agevole, piano; passivo.
effrontery [e'frʌntəri] *n* sfrontatezza.
effusion [i'fjuːʒən] *n* effusione.
effusive [i'fjuːsiv] *a* espansivo, esuberante.
egg [eg] *n* uovo; *vt* incitare, istigare; **eggcup** porta-uovo.
egoism ['egouizəm] *n* egoismo.
egoist ['egouist] *n* egoista.
egotism ['egoutizəm] *n* egotismo.
egotist ['egoutist] *n* egotista.
Egypt ['iːdʒipt] *n* Egitto.
Egyptian [i'dʒipʃən] *a n* egiziano.
eight [eit] *a n* otto; **eighth** *a n* ottavo.
eighteen ['ei'tiːn] *a n* diciotto; **eighteenth** *a n* diciottesimo.
eighty ['eiti] *a n* ottanta; **eightieth** *a n* ottantesimo.
Eire ['ɛərə] *n* Irlanda.
either ['aiðə] *a pron* l'uno o l'altro, ognuno dei due; *ad* neanche, nemmeno; **e. . . . or** *cj* o . . . o.
ejaculate [i'dʒækjuleit] *vt* emettere; *vi* esclamare.
ejaculation [i,dʒækju'leiʃən] *n* esclamazione.
eject [iː'dʒekt] *vt* emettere, espellere.
elaborate [i'læbərit] *a* elaborato; *vt* [i'læbəreit] elaborare.
elaboration [i,læbə'reiʃən] *n* elaborazione.
elapse [i'læps] *vi* passare, trascorrere.
elastic [i'læstik] *a n* elastico.
elasticity [,elæs'tisiti] *n* elasticità.
elate [i'leit] *vt* esaltare, inebriare.
elation [i'leiʃən] *n* esaltazione, esultanza.
elbow ['elbou] *n* gomito; *vt* prendere a gomitate; *vi* farsi largo a gomitate; **e. room** spazio, agio.
elder ['eldə] *a* più vecchio, maggiore; *n* maggiore; dignitario della chiesa; *(bot)* sambuco.
elderly ['eldəli] *a* anziano.
Eleanor ['elinə] *nf pr* Eleonora.
elect [i'lekt] *a* eletto, scelto; *vti* eleggere, scegliere.
election [i'lekʃən] *n* elezione.
elector [i'lektə] *n* elettore.
electoral [i'lektərəl] *a* elettorale.
electorate [i'lektərit] *n* elettorato, elettori *pl.*

electric [i'lektrik] *a* elettrico; **e. heater** stufa elettrica.
electrical [i'lektrikəl] *a* elettrico.
electrician [ilek'triʃən] *n* elettricista.
electricity [ilek'trisiti] *n* elettricità.
electrification [i,lektrifi'keiʃən] *n* elettrificazione.
electrify [i'lektrifai] *vt* elettrificare; elettrizzare.
electrocardiogram [i'lektrou'kɑːdiogram] *n* elettrocardiogramma.
electrocute [i'lektrəkjuːt] *vt* fulminare; giustiziare sulla sedia elettrica.
electrocution [i,lektrə'kjuːʃən] *n* elettroesecuzione.
electronic [ilek'trɔnik] *a* elettronico.
electronics [ilek'trɔniks] *n* elettronica.
elegance ['eligəns] *n* eleganza.
elegant ['eligənt] *a* elegante.
elegy ['elidʒi] *n* elegia.
element ['elimənt] *n* elemento.
elemental [,eli'mentl] *a* degli elementi; fondamentale.
elementary [,eli'mentəri] *a* elementare, rudimentale.
elephant ['elifənt] *n* elefante.
elevate ['eliveit] *vt* elevare, innalzare.
elevation [,eli'veiʃən] *n* elevazione.
elevator [,eli'veitə] *n* ascensore, montacarichi.
eleven [i'levn] *a n* undici; **eleventh** *a n* undicesimo.
elf [elf] *n* elfo, folletto.
Elia(h) Elias ['iːliə, i'laiəs] *nm pr* Elia.
elicit [i'licit] *vt* tirar fuori, attirare.
elide [i'laid] *vt* elidere.
eligibility [,elidʒə'biliti] *n* eleggibilità.
eligible ['elidʒəbl] *a* eleggibile, desiderabile.
eliminate [i'limineit] *vt* eliminare.
elimination [i,limi'neiʃən] *n* eliminazione.
elision [i'liʒən] *n* elisione.
Elizabeth [i'lizəbəθ] *nf pr* Elisabetta.
Elizabethan [i,lizə'biːθən] *a* elisabettiano.
elk [elk] *n* alce.
ellipse [i'lips] *n* ellisse.
ellipsis [i'lipsis] *pl* **ellipses** *n* ellissi.
elliptic(al) [i'liptik(əl)] *a* ellittico.
elm [elm] *n* olmo.
elocution [,elə'kjuːʃən] *n* elocuzione.
elongate ['iːlɔŋgeit] *vti* allungar(si); prolungare.
elope [i'loup] *vi* fuggire (con un amante).
elopement [i'loupmənt] *n* fuga di amanti.
eloquence ['eləkwəns] *n* eloquenza.
eloquent ['eləkwənt] *a* eloquente.
eloquently ['eləkwəntli] *ad* con eloquenza, con calore.
else [els] *ad* altrimenti; *a* altro.
elsewhere ['els'wɛə] *ad* altrove.
elucidate [i'luːsideit] *vt* delucidare, chiarire.

elucidation [i.luːsi'deiʃən] n delucidazione, (s)chiarimento.

elude [i'luːd] vt eludere, sfuggire a.

elusive [i'luːsiv] a evasivo, sfuggevole.

emaciate [i'meiʃieit] vt emaciare, far dimagrire.

emaciation [i.meisi'eiʃən] n macilenza.

emanate ['eməneit] vti emanare.

emanation [.emə'neiʃən] n emanazione.

emancipate [i'mænsipeit] vt emancipare.

emancipation [i.mænsi'peiʃən] n emancipazione.

Emanuel [i'mænjuəl] nm pr Emanuele.

embalm [im'baːm] vt imbalsamare.

embankment [im'bæŋkmənt] n argine, diga.

embargo [em'baːgou] n embargo.

embark [im'baːk] vti imbarcar(si); (fig) intraprendere.

embarkation [embaːˈkeiʃən] n imbarco.

embarrass [im'bærəs] vt imbarazzare.

embarrassing [im'bærəsiŋ] a imbarazzante.

embarrassment [im'bærəsmənt] n imbarazzo.

embassy ['embəsi] n ambasciata.

embellish [im'beliʃ] vt abbellire.

embellishment [im'beliʃmənt] n abbellimento.

ember ['embə] n (usu pl) brace, ceneri ardenti pl; e. days i tre giorni di digiuno delle quattro Tempora.

embezzle [im'bezl] vt appropriarsi fraudolentemente.

embezzlement [im'bezlmənt] n appropriazione indebita.

embitter [im'bitə] vt amareggiare, inasprire.

emblem ['embləm] n emblema, simbolo.

embody [im'bɔdi] vt incarnare, personificare; includere.

embolden [im'bouldən] vt incoraggiare, imbaldanzire.

embolism ['embəlizəm] n (med) embolia.

emboss [im'bɔs] vt ornare con rilievi.

embrace [im'breis] n abbraccio; vt abbracciare; comprendere.

embrasure [im'breiʒə] n (mil) feritoia; (arch) strombatura di porta (o finestra).

embroider [im'brɔidə] vt ricamare.

embroidery [im'brɔidəri] n ricamo.

embroil [im'brɔil] vt imbrogliare.

embryo ['embriou] pl **embryos** n embrione.

emerald ['emərəld] n smeraldo.

emerge [i'məːdʒ] vi emergere; sbucare.

emergence [i'məːdʒəns] n emersione, apparizione improvvisa.

emergency [i'məːdʒənsi] n emergenza.

emergent [i'məːdʒənt] a emergente, sorgente.

emery ['eməri] n smeriglio; e. paper carta smerigiata.

emetic [i'metik] a n emetico.

emigrant ['emigrənt] a n emigrante.

emigrate ['emigreit] vi emigrare.

emigration [.emi'greiʃən] n emigrazione.

Emily ['emili] nf pr Emilia.

eminence ['eminəns] n eminenza; altura.

eminent ['eminənt] a eminente.

emissary ['emisəri] a n emissario.

emission [i'miʃən] n emissione.

emit [i'mit] vt emettere.

Emmanuel [i'mænjuəl] nm pr Emanuele.

emollient [i'mɔliənt] a n emolliente.

emolument [i'mɔljumənt] n emolumento.

emotion [i'mouʃən] n commozione, emozione.

emotional [i'mouʃənəl] a emotivo, impressionabile, commovente.

emperor ['empərə] n imperatore.

emphasis ['emfəsis] n enfasi.

emphasize ['emfəsaiz] vt dare enfasi a, mettere in rilievo, sottolineare.

emphatic [im'fætik] a enfatico.

empire ['empaiə] n impero.

empirical [em'pirikəl] a empirico.

employ [im'plɔi] n impiego; vt impiegare.

employee [.emplɔi'iː] n impiegato.

employer [im'plɔiə] n datore di lavoro, padrone.

employment [im'plɔimənt] n impiego, occupazione.

emporium [em'pɔːriəm] n emporio.

empower [im'pauə] vt autorizzare.

empress ['empris] n imperatrice.

emptiness ['emptinis] n vuoto, vacuità.

empty ['empti] a vuoto, vacante; n pl i vuoti; to return the empties restituire i vuoti; vti vuotar(si).

emulate ['emjuleit] vt emulare.

emulation [.emju'leiʃən] n emulazione.

emulsion [i'mʌlʃən] n emulsione.

enable [i'neibl] vt mettere in grado (di), permettere.

enact [i'nækt] vt mettere in atto; recitare.

enactment [i'næktmənt] n decreto, legge.

enamel [i'næməl] n smalto; vt smaltare.

enamor [i'næmə] vt innamorare.

encamp [in'kæmp] vti accampar(si).

encampment [in'kæmpmənt] n accampamento.

enchant [in'tʃaːnt] vt incantare.

enchanter [in'tʃaːntə] n incantatore, mago.

enchanting [in'tʃaːntiŋ] a incantevole, affascinante.

enchantment [in'tʃɑːntmənt] *n* incantesimo, incanto.
enchantress [in'tʃɑːntris] *n* incantatrice, maga.
encircle [in'səːkl] *vt* accerchiare.
enclose [in'klouz] *vt* accludere; rinchiudere, circondare.
enclosure [in'klouʒə] *n* recinto; *(com)* allegato.
encompass [in'kʌmpəs] *vt* circondare, abbracciare.
encore [ɔŋ'kɔː] *interj n* bis; *vt* chiedere il bis (di).
encounter [in'kauntə] *n* incontro; scontro; *vt* incontrare, affrontare.
encourage [in'kʌridʒ] *vt* incoraggiare.
encouragement [in'kʌridʒmənt] *n* incoraggiamento.
encroach [in'kroutʃ] *vi* intromettersi illegalmente, usurpare i diritti altrui.
encroachment [in'kroutʃmənt] *n* usurpazione, abuso.
encumber [in'kʌmbə] *vt* ingombrare, gravare.
encumbrance [in'kʌmbrəns] *n* impedimento, ingombro; ipoteca.
encyclical [en'siklikəl] *a (eccl)* enciclico; *n (eccl)* enciclica.
encyclopedia [en,saiklou'piːdiə] *n* enciclopedia.
end [end] *n* fine; scopo; morte; estremità; *vti* finire.
endanger [in'deindʒə] *vt* mettere in pericolo.
endear [en'diə] *vt* rendere caro.
endearing [en'diəriŋ] *a* tenero, affettuoso.
endearment [en'diəmənt] *n* tenerezza, carezza; **term of e.** vezzeggiativo.
endeavor [in'devə] *n* sforzo, tentativo; *vi* sforzarsi, tentare.
endemic [en'demik] *a* endemico.
ending ['endiŋ] *n* conclusione, termine; *(gram)* desinenza.
endive ['endiv] *n* indivia.
endless ['endlis] *a* interminabile.
endorse [in'dɔːs] *vt* firmare, girare, confermare, sanzionare.
endorsement [in'dɔːsmənt] *n (com)* girata; approvazione.
endow [in'dau] *vt* dotare.
endowment [in'daumənt] *n* dotazione; dote, pregio.
endurance [in'djuərəns] *n* resistenza, pazienza, sopportazione.
endure [in'djuə] *vt* sopportare, tollerare; *vi* durare, continuare.
enduring [in'djuəriŋ] *a* tollerante, paziente; durevole.
enema ['enimə] *n* clistere.
enemy ['enimi] *a n* nemico.
energetic [,enə'dʒetik] *a* energico.
energy ['enədʒi] *n* energia.
enervate ['enəːveit] *vt* snervare.
enfeeble [in'fiːbl] *vt* indebolire.
enfold [in'fould] *vt* avvolgere, abbracciare.

enforce [in'fɔːs] *vt* imporre, far osservare.
enforcement [in'fɔːsmənt] *n* imposizione; applicazione.
enfranchise [in'fræntʃaiz] *vt* affrancare, liberare; dare il diritto di voto.
enfranchisement [in'fræntʃizmənt] *n* affrancamento, liberazione.
engage [in'geidʒ] *vt* impegnare, prenotare; assumere in servizio; *vi* entrare in, occuparsi di, impegnarsi.
engaged [in'geidʒd] *a* impegnato; fidanzato; occupato.
engagement [in'geidʒmənt] *n* impegno; fidanzamento.
engaging [in'geidʒiŋ] *a* attraente.
engender [in'dʒendə] *vt* generare, produrre.
engine ['endʒin] *n* macchina, motore.
engineer [,endʒi'niə] *n* ingegnere; macchinista; *(mil)* soldato del Genio.
engineer [,endʒi'niə] *vt (fam)* macchinare, architettare.
engineering [,endʒi'niəriŋ] *n* ingegneria.
England ['iŋglənd] *n* Inghilterra.
English ['iŋgliʃ] *a n* inglese; **Englishman** Inglese.
engrave [in'greiv] *vt* incidere; *(fig)* imprimere.
engraving [in'greiviŋ] *n* incisione.
engross [in'grous] *vt* assorbire (attenzione); **to become engrossed** astrarsi.
engulf [in'gʌlf] *vt* inghiottire, sommergere.
enhance [in'hɑːns] *vt* aumentare, intensificare.
enigma [i'nigmə] *n* enigma.
enigmatic [,enig'mætik] *a* enigmatico.
enjoin [in'dʒɔin] *vt* ingiungere, ordinare.
enjoy [in'dʒɔi] *vt* divertirsi, godere.
enjoyable [in'dʒɔiəbl] *a* piacevole, divertente.
enjoyment [in'dʒɔimənt] *n* godimento, piacere.
enlarge [in'lɑːdʒ] *vt* espandere, estendere, ingrandire; *vi* allargarsi; dilungarsi.
enlargement [in'lɑːdʒmənt] *n* allargamento, ingrandimento.
enlighten [in'laitn] *vt (fig)* illuminare.
enlightenment [in'laitnmənt] *n* spiegazione, schiarimento.
enlist [in'list] *vti* arruolar(si).
enlistment [in'listmənt] *n* arruolamento.
enliven [in'laivn] *vt* ravvivare.
enmity ['enmiti] *n* inimicizia, ostilità.
ennoble [i'noubl] *vt* nobilitare.
ennui [ɑː'nwi] *n* noia.
enormity [i'nɔːmiti] *n* enormità.
enormous [i'nɔːməs] *a* enorme.
enough [i'nʌf] *a* sufficiente; *ad* abbastanza, sufficientemente; *n* il necessario, sufficienza.
enquire [in'kwaiə] *v* **inquire**.

enrage [in'reidʒ] *vt* far arrabbiare, imbestialire.
enrapture [in'ræptʃə] *vt* estasiare, incantare.
enrich [in'ritʃ] *vt* arricchire.
enroll [in'roul] *vt* iscrivere, registrare; arruolare.
enrollment [in'roulmənt] *n* iscrizione, registrazione; arruolamento.
enshrine [in'ʃrain] *vt* custodire come cosa sacra, rinchiudere.
ensign ['ensain] *n* bandiera, insegna.
enslave [in'sleiv] *vt* asservire, fare schiavo.
enslavement [in'sleivmənt] *n* asservimento, schiavitù.
ensnare [in'snɛə] *vt* irretire, prendere al laccio.
ensue [in'sjuː] *vi* risultare, seguire.
ensure [in'ʃuə] *vt* assicurare.
entail [in'teil] *n* assegnazione, eredità inalienabile; *vt* comportare, implicare; intestare a.
entangle [in'tæŋgl] *vt* aggrovigliare, impegolare.
entanglement [in'tæŋglmənt] *n* groviglio, imbroglio.
enter ['entə] *vt* entrare; iscrivere; **to e. into** (*fig*) entrare in, iniziare.
enterprise ['entəpraiz] *n* impresa.
enterprising ['entəpraiziŋ] *a* intraprendente.
entertain [ˌentə'tein] *vt* divertire, intrattenere, ricevere; nutrire (sospetti).
entertaining [ˌentə'teiniŋ] *a* divertente, piacevole.
entertainment [ˌentə'teinmənt] *n* divertimento, trattenimento.
enthralling [in'θrɔːliŋ] *a* ammaliante, incantevole.
enthusiasm [in'θjuːziæzəm] *n* entusiasmo.
enthusiast [in'θjuːziæst] *n* entusiasta.
enthusiastic [inˌθjuːzi'æstik] *a* entusiastico.
entice [in'tais] *vi* adescare, allettare.
enticement [in'taismənt] *n* seduzione, allettamento, lusinga.
enticing [in'taisiŋ] *a* seducente, attraente.
entire [in'taiə] *a* completo, intero.
entirely [in'taiəli] *ad* interamente, completamente.
entirety [in'tairəti] *n* interezza; integrità.
entitle [in'taitl] *vt* intitolare, aver diritto a.
entity ['entiti] *n* entità.
entomb [in'tuːm] *vt* inumare.
entombment [in'tuːmmənt] *n* inumazione.
entrails ['entreilz] *n pl* intestini, viscere *pl*.
entrance ['entrəns] *n* entrata, ingresso; **e. fee** tassa d'iscrizione.
entrance [in'trɑːns] *vt* incantare, estasiare.

entrap [in'træp] *vt* intrappolare, raggirare.
entreat [in'triːt] *vt* implorare, supplicare.
entreaty [in'triːti] *n* preghiera, supplica.
entrench [in'trentʃ] *vt* trincerare.
entrenchment [in'trentʃmənt] *n* trinceramento.
entrust [in'trʌst] *vt* affidare, commettere.
entry ['entri] *n* entrata, ingresso, iscrizione, annotazione.
entwine [in'twain] *vt* intrecciare.
enumerate [i'njuːməreit] *vt* enumerare.
enunciate [i'nʌnsieit] *vt* enunciare.
enunciation [iˌnʌnsi'eiʃən] *n* enunciazione.
envelop [in'veləp] *vt* avvolgere; (*mil*) accerchiare.
envelope ['enviloup] *n* busta, involucro.
enviable ['enviəbl] *a* invidiabile.
envious ['enviəs] *a* invidioso.
environment [in'vaiərənmənt] *n* ambiente.
environs [in'vaiərənz] *n pl* dintorni *pl*.
envisage [in'vizidʒ] *vt* immaginare, vedere, figurarsi.
envoy ['envɔi] *n* inviato, ministro plenipotenziario.
envy ['envi] *n* invidia; *vt* invidiare.
epaulet(te) ['epoulet] *n* (*mil*) spallina.
ephemeral [i'femərəl] *a* effimero, fuggevole.
epic ['epik] *a* epico; *n* epica.
epicure ['epikjuə] *n* epicureo.
epicurean [ˌepikjuə'riːən] *a n* epicureo.
epidemic [ˌepi'demik] *a* epidemico; *n* epidemia.
epigram ['epigræm] *n* epigramma.
epigraph ['epigrɑːf] *n* epigrafe.
epilepsy ['epilepsi] *n* epilessia.
epileptic [ˌepi'leptik] *a n* epilettico.
epilogue ['epilɔg] *n* epilogo.
Epiphany [i'pifəni] *n* Epifania.
episcopacy [i'piskəpəsi] *n* episcopato.
episcopal [i'piskəpəl] *a* episcopale.
episode ['episoud] *n* episodio.
epistle [i'pisl] *n* epistola.
epitaph ['epitɑːf] *n* epitaffio.
epithet ['epiθet] *n* epiteto.
epitome [i'pitəmi] *n* epitome, compendio.
epitomize [i'pitəmaiz] *vt* compendiare, riassumere.
epoch ['iːpɔk] *n* epoca.
equable ['ekwəbl] *a* equo.
equal ['iːkwəl] *a n* uguale; *vt* uguagliare.
equality [iː'kwɔliti] *n* uguaglianza.
equalize ['iːkwəlaiz] *vt* uguagliare, pareggiare.
equally ['iːkwəli] *ad* ugualmente.
equanimity [ˌiːkwə'nimiti] *n* equanimità.

equate [i'kweit] vt uguagliare; paragonare.
equation [i'kweiʃən] n equazione.
equator [i'kweitə] n equatore.
equatorial [ˌekwə'tɔːriəl] a equatoriale.
equerry [i'kweri] n scudiero.
equestrian [i'kwestriən] a equestre.
equilibrium [ˌiːkwi'libriəm] n equilibrio.
equinox ['iːkwinɔks] n equinozio.
equip [i'kwip] vt equipaggiare, attrezzare.
equipage ['ekwipidʒ] n attrezzatura; equipaggio.
equipment [i'kwipmənt] n equipaggiamento, attrezzatura.
equitable ['ekwitəbl] a equo, giusto.
equity ['ekwiti] n equità.
equivalent [i'kwivələnt] a n equivalente.
equivocal [i'kwivəkəl] a ambiguo, equivoco, sospetto.
era ['iərə] n era.
eradicate [i'rædikeit] vt sradicare.
erase [i'reiz] vt cancellare, raschiare.
eraser [i'reizə] n raschietto; gomma per cancellare.
erasure [i'reiʒə] n cancellatura.
erect [i'rekt] a eretto, ritto; vt erigere, innalzare.
erection [i'rekʃən] n elevazione, erezione.
ermine ['əːmin] n ermellino.
Ernest ['əːnist] nm pr Ernesto.
erode [i'roud] vt erodere, consumare.
erosion [i'rouʒən] n erosione.
erotic [i'rɔtik] a erotico.
err [əː] vi errare, sbagliare.
errand ['erənd] n commissione, incarico.
errant ['erənt] a errante.
erratic [i'rætik] a irregolare; eccentrico; erratico.
erroneous [i'rouniəs] a erroneo, scorretto.
error ['erə] n errore, sbaglio; colpa.
erudite ['erjuːdait] a erudito.
erudition [ˌerjuː'diʃən] n erudizione.
erupt [i'rʌpt] vi (volcano) eruttare, entrare in eruzione.
eruption [i'rʌpʃən] n eruzione, scoppio.
erysipelas [ˌeri'sipiləs] n erisipela.
escalator ['eskəleitə] n scala meccanica; scala mobile.
escapade [ˌeskə'peid] n (fig) scappata.
escape [is'keip] n fuga, scampo, scappamento; vti fuggire; evitare; sfuggire.
escapism [is'keipizəm] n evasione (dalla realtà).
eschew [is'tʃuː] vt astenersi da, evitare.
escort ['eskɔːt] n scorta; [is'kɔːt] vt scortare.
Eskimo ['eskimou] pl **Eskimoes** a n esquimese.
especial [is'peʃəl] a speciale.

especially [is'peʃəli] ad specialmente, sopratutto.
espionage [ˌespiə'nɑːʒ] n spionaggio.
esplanade [ˌesplə'neid] n spianata; lungomare.
esquire [is'kwaiə] n signore (usato negli indirizzi dopo il cognome); **John Smith Esq.** Egregio Signor John Smith.
essay ['esei] n saggio; tema; prova; vt tentare, provare.
essence ['esns] n essenza.
essential [i'senʃəl] a n essenziale.
essentially [i'senʃəli] ad essenzialmente, fondamentalmente.
establish [is'tæbliʃ] vt stabilire, fondare, istituire; constatare; **established** stabilito, affermato.
establishment [is'tæbliʃmənt] a stabilimento, istituzione; ordine costituito; accertamento.
estate [is'teit] n tenuta, proprietà; stato.
esteem [is'tiːm] n considerazione, stima; vt considerare, stimare.
Esther ['estə] nf pr Ester.
estimable ['estiməbl] a stimabile, degno di stima.
estimate ['estimit] n stima, valutazione, preventivo; ['estimeit] vt stimare, valutare.
estimation [ˌesti'meiʃən] n stima, valutazione.
estrange [is'treindʒ] vt alienare, estraniare, inimicarsi.
estrangement [is'treindʒmənt] n alienazione, allontanamento.
estuary ['estjuəri] n estuario.
etch [etʃ] vt incidere all'acquaforte.
etching ['etʃiŋ] n acquaforte, incisione.
eternal [iː'təːnl] a eterno.
eternity [iː'təːniti] n eternità.
ether ['iːθə] n etere.
ethereal [iː'θiəriəl] a etereo.
ethics ['eθiks] n etica.
Ethiopia [ˌiːθi'oupiə] n Etiopia.
Ethiopian [ˌiːθi'oupiən] a etiopico; n etiope.
etiquette [ˌeti'ket] n etichetta.
Etna ['etnə] n Etna.
Etruscan [i'trʌskən] a n etrusco.
etymology [ˌeti'mɔlədʒi] n etimologia.
Eucharist ['juːkərist] n Eucarestia.
Eugene [juː'ʒein] nm pr Eugenio.
eulogy ['juːlədʒi] n elogio.
eunuch ['juːnək] n eunuco.
euphemism ['juːfimizəm] n eufemismo.
euphony ['juːfəni] n eufonia.
Europe ['juərəp] n Europa.
European [ˌjuərə'piːən] a n europeo.
euthanasia [ˌjuːθə'neiziə] n eutanasia.
evacuate [i'vækjueit] vt evacuare, sfollare.
evacuation [iˌvækju'eiʃən] n evacuazione, sfollamento.
evacuee [iˌvækjuː'iː] n sfollato.

evade [i'veid] vt evitare, schivare.
evaluate [i'væljueit] vt valutare.
evanescence [,i:və'nesns] n evanescenza.
evanescent [,i:və'nesnt] a evanescente.
evangelic(al) [,i:væn'dʒelikəl] a evangelico; **evangelist** n evangelista.
evaporate [i'væpəreit] vti (far) evaporare.
evaporation [i,væpə'reiʃən] n evaporazione.
evasion [i'veiʒən] n evasione, sotterfugio.
evasive [i'veisiv] a evasivo.
Eve [i:v] nf pr Eva.
eve [i:v] n vigilia.
even ['i:vən] a pari; uguale; piatto; uniforme; ad anche, perfino; vt uguagliare, uniformare.
evening ['i:vəniŋ] n sera.
evenly ['i:vənli] ad uniformemente; in parti uguali; pianamente; con calma.
evenness ['i:vənnis] n uguaglianza, uniformità.
event [i'vent] n avvenimento, evento.
eventful [i'ventful] a pieno di avvenimenti, memorabile.
eventual [i'ventjuəl] a finale, eventuale; **eventually** ad finalmente.
ever ['evə] ad mai, sempre.
evergreen ['evəgri:n] a n sempreverde.
everlasting [,evə'la:stiŋ] a eterno; n eternità.
evermore [,evə'mɔ:] ad sempre; **for e.** per sempre.
every ['evri] a ogni, ciascuno, tutti; **e. now and then** di quando in quando; **e. other day** un giorno sì, e un giorno no.
everybody ['evribɔdi] **everyone** ['evriwʌn] pron ognuno, tutti pl.
everyday ['evridei] a di ogni giorno, quotidiano.
everything ['evriθiŋ] pron ogni cosa, tutto.
everywhere ['evriwɛə] ad in ogni luogo, ovunque.
evict [i:'vikt] vt espellere, sfrattare.
eviction [i:'vikʃən] n espulsione, sfratto.
evidence ['evidəns] n evidenza, prova, testimonianza; **to give e.** deporre.
evident ['evidənt] a evidente, chiaro.
evil ['i:vl] a cattivo, maligno, funesto; ad male; n male.
evince [i'vins] vt manifestare, dimostrare.
evocative [i:'vɔkətiv] a evocatore.
evoke [i'vouk] vt evocare.
evolution [,i:və'lu:ʃən] n evoluzione, sviluppo.
evolve [i'vɔlv] vti evolver(si).
ewe [ju:] n pecora (femmina).
ewer ['ju:ə] n brocca.
exact [ig'zækt] a esatto, preciso; vt esigere.

exacting [ig'zæktiŋ] a esigente, impegnativo.
exactitude [ig'zæktitju:d] **exactness** [ig'zæktnis] n esattezza, precisione.
exactly [ig'zæktli] ad esattamente; proprio; precisamente.
exaggerate [ig'zædʒəreit] vt esagerare.
exaggeration [ig,zædʒə'reiʃən] n esagerazione.
exalt [ig'zɔ:lt] vt esaltare.
exaltation [,egzɔ:l'teiʃən] n esaltazione.
examination [ig,zæmi'neiʃən] n esame; visita (medica).
examine [ig'zæmin] vt esaminare; visitare.
examiner [ig'zæminə] n esaminatore.
example [ig'za:mpl] n esempio.
exasperate [ig'za:spəreit] vt esasperare.
exasperation [ig,za:spə'reiʃən] n esasperazione.
excavate ['ekskəveit] vt scavare.
excavation [,ekskə'veiʃən] n scavo.
exceed [ik'si:d] vti eccedere, superare.
exceedingly [ik'si:diŋli] ad estremamente.
excel [ik'sel] vi eccellere, essere superiore a.
excellence ['eksələns] n eccellenza, superiorità.
excellency ['eksələnsi] n (titolo) eccellenza.
excellent ['eksələnt] a eccellente, ottimo.
except [ik'sept] prep eccetto, eccettuato, ad eccezione di, tranne; vt eccettuare; vi obiettare; **excepting** eccetto, tranne.
exception [ik'sepʃən] n eccezione, obiezione.
exceptional [ik'sepʃənl] a eccezionale.
exceptionally [ik'sepʃənəli] ad eccezionalmente, in via eccezionale.
excerpt ['eksə:pt] n estratto, citazione.
excess [ik'ses] n eccesso; **e. fare** supplemento.
excessive [ik'sesiv] a eccessivo, smoderato.
exchange [iks'tʃeindʒ] n cambio, scambio; borsa; (tel) centrale telefonica; vt (s)cambiare.
exchequer [iks'tʃekə] n Scacchiere, Tesoro, Fisco.
excise [ek'saiz] n imposta indiretta, dazio sul consumo.
exciseman [ek'saizmæn] pl **-men** n daziere.
excitable [ik'saitəbl] a eccitabile, impressionabile.
excite [ik'sait] vt eccitare, provocare, entusiasmare.
excitement [ik'saitmənt] n agitazione, eccitazione; trambusto.
exciting [ik'saitiŋ] a eccitante, emozionante.
exclaim [iks'kleim] vi esclamare.

exclamation [ˌekskləˈmeiʃən] n esclamazione.

exclude [iksˈkluːd] vt escludere.

exclusion [iksˈkluːʒən] n esclusione.

exclusive [iksˈkluːsiv] a esclusivo, scelto.

excommunicate [ˌekskəˈmjuːnikeit] vt scomunicare.

excommunication [ˈekskəˌmjuːniˈkeiʃən] n scomunica.

excrement [ˈekskrimənt] n escremento.

excrete [eksˈkriːt] vt espellere, secernere.

excruciating [iksˈkruːʃieitiŋ] a atroce, lancinante.

excursion [iksˈkəːʃən] n escursione, gita.

excusable [iksˈkjuːzəbl] a scusabile, perdonabile.

excuse [iksˈkjuːz] n scusa, pretesto; vt scusare, perdonare, dispensare da.

execrable [ˈeksikrəbl] a esecrabile.

execrate [ˈeksikreit] vt esecrare.

execute [ˈeksikjuːt] vt eseguire, mettere in esecuzione; giustiziare.

execution [ˌeksiˈkjuːʃən] n esecuzione; sequestro.

executioner [ˌeksiˈkjuːʃənə] n boia, carnefice.

executive [igˈzekjutiv] a esecutivo; n direzione, dirigente.

executor [igˈzekjutə] n esecutore.

exemplar [igˈzemplə] n esemplare, modello.

exemplary [igˈzempləri] a esemplare.

exemplify [igˈzemplifai] vt illustrare con esempi; fare copia autentica di.

exempt [igˈzempt] a esente; vt esentare.

exemption [igˈzempʃən] n esenzione.

exercise [ˈeksəsaiz] n esercizio, esercitazione; vti esercitar(si).

exert [igˈzəːt] vt esercitare, fare uso di; to e. oneself sforzarsi.

exertion [igˈzəːʃən] n sforzo; impiego, uso.

exhalation [ˌekshəˈleiʃən] n esalazione.

exhale [eksˈheil] vt esalare.

exhaust [igˈzɔːst] n (mech) scarico, scappamento; vt esaurire, vuotare; (gas etc), aspirare; vi (gas etc) scaricarsi.

exhauster [igˈzɔːstə] n aspiratore; ventilatore di scarico.

exhaustion [igˈzɔːstʃən] n esaurimento.

exhaustive [igˈzɔːstiv] a esauriente.

exhibit [igˈzibit] n oggetto mandato ad un'esposizione; (leg) reperto; vt esibire, esporre.

exhibition [ˌeksiˈbiʃən] n esibizione, esposizione, mostra; borsa di studio.

exhibitioner [ˌeksiˈbiʃenə] n chi usufruisce di una borsa di studio.

exhibitor [igˈzibitə] n espositore.

exhilarate [igˈziləreit] vt esilarare.

exhilaration [igˌziləˈreiʃən] n eccitazione, entusiasmo, allegria.

exhort [igˈzɔːt] vt esortare.

exhortation [ˌegzɔːˈteiʃən] n esortazione.

exigency [ekˈsidʒənsi] n esigenza.

exigent [ˈeksidʒənt] a esigente.

exile [ˈeksail] n esilio; esule; vt bandire, esiliare.

exist [igˈzist] vi esistere.

existence [igˈzistəns] n esistenza.

existentialism [ˌegzisˈtenʃəlizəm] n esistenzialismo.

existentialist [ˌegzisˈtenʃəlist] a n esistenzialista.

existing [igˈzistiŋ] a esistente, attuale.

exit [ˈeksit] n uscita.

exodus [ˈeksədəs] n esodo.

exonerate [igˈzɔnəreit] vt esonerare.

exoneration [igˌzɔnəˈreiʃən] n esonero.

exorbitant [igˈzɔːbitənt] a esorbitante.

exorcism [ˈeksɔːsizəm] n esorcismo.

exorcize [ˈeksɔːsaiz] vt esorcizzare.

exotic [egˈzɔtik] a esotico; n pianta esotica.

expand [iksˈpænd] vti espander(si), sviluppar(si).

expanse [iksˈpæns] n spazio, distesa.

expansion [iksˈpænʃən] n espansione, estensione.

expansive [iksˈpænsiv] a espansivo.

expatiate [eksˈpeiʃieit] vi diffondersi, spaziare.

expatriate [eksˈpætrieit] vt espatriare.

expect [iksˈpekt] vt aspettar(si); prevedere; supporre; sperare.

expectancy [iksˈpektənsi] n aspettativa, attesa; aspettazione.

expectant [iksˈpektənt] a in attesa; e. mother donna incinta.

expectation [ˌekspekˈteiʃən] n aspettativa, speranza.

expectorate [eksˈpektəreit] vt espettorare.

expediency [iksˈpiːdiənsi] n convenienza, opportunità.

expedient [iksˈpiːdiənt] a conveniente; n espediente, mezzo ingegnoso.

expedite [ˈekspidait] vt accelerare, sbrigare.

expedition [ˌekspiˈdiʃən] n impresa, spedizione; prontezza.

expel [iksˈpel] vt espellere, cacciare.

expend [iksˈpend] vt consumare, spendere.

expenditure [iksˈpenditʃə] n spesa.

expense [iksˈpens] n spesa.

expensive [iksˈpensiv] a costoso, dispendioso.

experience [iksˈpiəriəns] n esperienza; vt provare, sperimentare.

experiment [iksˈperimənt] n esperimento, prova; vi sperimentare.

experimental [eksˌperiˈmentl] a sperimentale.

expert [ˈekspəːt] a abile, esperto; n esperto, perito, specialista.

expertise ['ekspəːtiːz] n abilità, pratica (di).
expertly ['ekspəːtli] ad espertamente, abilmente.
expiate ['ekspieit] vt espiare.
expiation [ˌekspi'eiʃən] n espiazione.
expiration [ˌekspaiə'reiʃ-n] n scadenza, termine.
expire [iks'paiə] vti scadere, spirare.
expiry [iks'paiəri] n termine, scadenza.
explain [iks'plein] vti spiegare.
explanation [ˌeksplə'neiʃən] n spiegazione, chiarimento.
explanatory [iks'plænətəri] a esplicativo, chiarificatore.
explicit [iks'plisit] a esplicito, chiaro.
explode [iks'ploud] vti (far) esplodere; (fig) rivelare la falsità di.
exploit ['eksplɔit] n gesta, impresa; [iks'plɔit] vt sfruttare, utilizzare.
exploitation [ˌeksplɔi'teiʃən] n sfruttamento, utilizzazione.
exploration [ˌeksplɔː'reiʃən] n esplorazione.·
explore [iks'plɔː] vt esplorare.
explorer [iks'plɔːrə] n esploratore, esploratrice.
explosion [iks'plouʒən] n esplosione, scoppio.
explosive [iks'plousiv] a n esplosivo.
exponent [eks'pounənt] n esponente, interprete.
export ['ekspɔːt] n esportazione, genere esportabile; vt [eks'pɔːt] esportare.
expose [iks'pouz] vt esporre, smascherare.
exposition [ˌekspə'ziʃən] n esposizione.
expostulate [iks'pɔstjuleit] vi fare rimostranze, protestare.
expostulation [iks'pɔstju'leiʃən] n rimostranza, protesta.
exposure [iks'pouʒə] n esposizione, (phot) esposizione, posa; smascheramento, scandalo.
expound [iks'paund] vt commentare, spiegare.
express [iks'pres] a esplicito, espresso; n (letter) espresso; (train) direttissimo; vt esprimere; spremere; spedire per espresso; e. company servizio corriere.
expression [iks'preʃən] n espressione.
expressive [iks'presiv] a espressivo.
expropriate [eks'prouprieit] vt espropriare.
expulsion [iks'pʌlʃən] n espulsione.
expurgate ['ekspəːgeit] vt (es)purgare.
expurgation [ˌekspəː'geiʃən] n espurgazione.
exquisite ['ekskwizit] a squisito; (pain) acuto.
exquisiteness ['ekskwizitnis] n squisitezza.
ex-service ['eks'səːvis] a che ha prestato servizio militare; **exserviceman** n ex-combattente.

extant [eks'tænt] a esistente ancora.
extemporary [iks'tempərəri] a estemporaneo, improvvisato.
extempore [eks'tempəri] a improvvisato, estemporaneo; ad estemporaneamente.
extemporize [iks'tempəraiz] vt improvvisare.
extend [iks'tend] vti estender(si); prolungare; prorogare; porgere.
extension [iks'tenʃən] n estensione, prolungamento; proroga; e. wire (el) filo flessibile.
extensive [iks'tensiv] a esteso, largo.
extensively [iks'tensivli] ad ampiamente, estensivamente.
extent [iks'tent] n estensione; grado; punto; portata.
extenuate [eks'tenjueit] vt attenuare, scusare.
extenuating [eks'tenjueitiŋ] a attenuante.
extenuation [eks,tenju'eiʃən] n attenuazione.
exterior [eks'tiəriə] a n esterno, esteriore.
exterminate [eks'təːmineit] vt sterminare.
extermination [eks,təːmi'neiʃən] n sterminio.
external [eks'təːnl] a n esterno.
extinct [iks'tiŋkt] a estinto, spento.
extinction [iks'tiŋkʃən] n estinzione.
extinguish [iks'tiŋgwiʃ] vt estinguere, spegnere.
extinguisher [iks'tiŋgwiʃə] n spegnitoio, estintore.
extirpate ['ekstəːpeit] vt estirpare.
extirpation [ˌekstəː'peiʃən] n estirpazione.
extol [iks'tɔl] vt esaltare, estollere.
extort [iks'tɔːt] vt estorcere.
extortion [iks'tɔːʃən] n estorsione.
extortionate [iks'tɔːʃnit] a (price) eccessivo, esorbitante.
extra ['ekstrə] a extra, straordinario; superiore; ad extra, in più; straordinariamente n extra; supplemento; (theat) comparsa; e.-postage soprattassa.
extract ['ekstrækt] n estratto; vt [iks'trækt] estrarre.
extraction [iks'trækʃən] n estrazione, origine.
extradite ['ekstrədait] vt (leg) estradare.
extradition [ˌekstrə'diʃən] n estradizione.
extraneous [eks'treiniəs] a estraneo.
extraordinary [iks'trɔːdnri] a straordinario.
extrasensory ['ekstrə'sensəri] a al di là dei sensi.
extraterritorial ['ekstrə,teri'tɔːriəl] a estraterritoriale.
extravagance [iks'trævigəns] n prodigalità; stravaganza.
extravagant [iks'trævigənt] a prodigo; stravagante.
extreme [iks'triːm] a n estremo.

extremely [iks'tri:mli] *ad* estremamente.
extremism [iks'tri:mizəm] *n* (*pol*) estremismo.
extremity [iks'tremiti] *n* estremità; estremo; eccesso; estremo pericolo; bisogno; dolore.
extricate ['ekstrikeit] *vt* districare.
extrinsic [eks'trinsik] *a* estrinseco.
extrovert ['ekstrouvə:t] *n* estroverso.
exuberance [ig'zju:bərəns] *n* esuberanza.
exuberant [ig'zju:bərənt] *a* esuberante.
exult [ig'zʌlt] *vi* esultare.
exultation [ˌegzʌl'teiʃən] *n* esultanza.
eye [ai] *n* occhio; sguardo; vista.
eyeball ['aibɔ:l] *n* bulbo oculare.
eyebrow ['aibrau] *n* sopracciglio.
eyelash ['ailæʃ] *n* ciglio.
eyelid ['ailid] *n* palpebra.
eyesight ['aisait] *n* vista, potere visivo.
eyewitness ['æˌwitnis] *n* testimonio oculare; *vt* guardare, osservare.

F

fable ['feibl] *n* favola.
fabric ['fæbrik] *n* tessuto; struttura.
fabricate ['fæbrikeit] *vt* inventare, (*fig*) fabbricare.
fabrication [ˌfæbri'keiʃən] *n* contraffazione, invenzione.
fabulous ['fæbjuləs] *a* favoloso.
façade [fə'sɑ:d] *n* facciata.
face [feis] *n* faccia, viso; facciata; faccetta; (*of a watch*) quadrante; *vt* affrontare, fronteggiare; guardare verso.
facet['fæsit] *n* sfaccettatura, faccetta.
facetious [fə'si:ʃəs] *a* faceto, gioviale.
facial ['feiʃəl] *a* facciale.
facile ['fæsail] *a* facile; scorrevole; superficiale; affrettato.
facilitate [fə'siliteit] *vt* facilitare, agevolare.
facility [fə'siliti] *n* facilità; destrezza; *pl* agevolazioni; attrezzature.
facing ['feisiŋ] *a* che sta di fronte; *n* (*buildings*) rivestimento; (*dress*) risvolto.
facsimile [fæk'simili] *n* facsimile.
fact [fækt] *n* fatto, realtà.
faction ['fækʃən] *n* fazione.
factious ['fækʃəs] *a* fazioso.
factor ['fæktə] *n* fattore.
factory ['fæktəri] *n* fabbrica, manifattura.
factual ['fæktjuəl] *a* effettivo, reale.
faculty ['fækəlti] *n* facoltà.
fad [fæd] *n* mania.
fade [feid] *n* (*cin*) dissolvenza; *vi* appassire; sbiadire; dileguarsi; svanire.
faded ['feidid] *a* appassito; sbiadito.
fag [fæg] *n* lavoro faticoso; (*sl*) sigaretta.
fag(g)ot ['fægət] *n* fascina.

fail [feil] *n* fallo; *vt* abbandonare; mancare a; bocciare; *vi* fallire; mancare, essere insufficiente; (*com*) fallire.
failing ['feiliŋ] *a* debole, scarso; *n* debolezza, difetto, mancanza; *prep* in mancanza di.
faille [feil] *n* faglia, tessuto di seta.
failure ['feiljə] *n* fallimento, fiasco, insuccesso; mancanza.
faint [feint] *a* debole, lieve, (*of colors*) pallido; *n* svenimento; *vi* svenire.
faintness ['feintnis] *n* debolezza, languore.
fair [fɛə] *a* bello; biondo; chiaro; sereno; giusto; leale; onesto; *ad* bene, onestamente; *n* fiera, mercato.
fairly ['fɛəli] *ad* lealmente; abbastanza.
fairness ['fɛənis] *n* bellezza; bianchezza, biondezza; onestà, equità.
fairy ['fɛəri] *a* fatato; *n* fata; **fairy tale** fiaba.
fairyland ['fɛərilænd] *n* paese delle fate.
faith [feiθ] *n* fede, fiducia.
faithful ['feiθful] *a* fedele, leale.
faithfully ['feiθfəli] *ad* fedelmente; **Yours f.** distinti saluti.
faithless ['feiθlis] *a* miscredente; sleale, falso.
fake [feik] *n* contraffazione, falso; *vti* falsificare; fingere.
falcon ['fɔ:lkən] *n* falcone.
fall [fɔ:l] *n* caduta; abbassamento; ribasso; rovina; cascata; autunno; *vi* cadere; diminuire; toccare in sorte.
fallacious [fə'leiʃəs] *a* fallace.
fallacy ['fæləsi] *n* errore; sofisma; fallacia.
fallibility [ˌfæli'biliti] *n* fallibilità.
fallible ['fæləbl] *a* fallibile.
falling ['fɔ:liŋ] *a* cadente; *n* caduta; scadenza.
fall-out ['fɔ:laut] *n* pioggia radioattiva.
fallow ['fælou] *a* incolto; *n* maggese.
false ['fɔ:ls] *a* falso, finto, ingannevole.
falsehood ['fɔ:lshud] *n* menzogna.
falsify ['fɔ:lsifai] *vt* falsificare.
falsity ['fɔ:lsiti] *n* falsità.
falter ['fɔ:ltə] *vi* balbettare; esitare; vacillare.
fame [feim] *n* fama.
famed [feimd] *a* rinomato, famoso, celebre.
familiar [fə'miljə] *a n* familiare.
familiarity [fəˌmili'æriti] *n* familiarità.
familiarize [fə'miljəraiz] *vt* familiarizzare.
family ['fæmili] *n* famiglia; **f. name** cognome.
famine ['fæmin] *n* carestia.
famish ['fæmiʃ] *vti* affamare; morire di fame.
famous ['feiməs] *a* famoso, celebre.

fan [fæn] n ventaglio, ventilatore; (sl) tifoso d'uno sport; vt sventolare, ventilare; (fig) stimolare, alimentare.
fanatic [fə'nætik] a n fanatico.
fanaticism [fə'nætisizəm] n fanatismo.
fanciful ['fænsiful] a capriccioso, fantasioso; immaginario.
fancy ['fænsi] n fantasia, capriccio, desiderio; vt creare con la fantasia, immaginare, desiderare.
fanfare ['fænfɛə] n fanfara.
fang [fæŋ] n zanna.
fantastic [fæn'tæstik] a fantastico.
fantasy ['fæntəsi] n fantasia, immaginazione.
far [fɑ:] a lontano, remoto; ad a grande distanza; di gran lunga, molto; so **f.** finora, fin qui; **faraway** lontano; **f.-fetched** esagerato, ricercato, stiracchiato; **f. off** molto lontano; **f.-reaching** di lunga portata.
farce [fɑ:s] n farsa.
farcical ['fɑ:sikəl] a farsesco.
fare [fɛə] n cibo, nutrimento; (train etc) prezzo di una corsa, passeggero; vi stare, trovarsi, vivere, mangiare.
farewell ['fɛə'wel] n addio.
farm [fɑ:m] n fattoria, podere; **farmyard** aia; vt coltivare, prendere, dare in appalto; vi fare l'agricoltore.
farmer ['fɑ:mə] n agricoltore, fittavolo.
farming ['fɑ:miŋ] n il lavoro dei campi; agricoltura; coltivazione.
farrier ['færiə] n maniscalco.
farther ['fɑ:ðə] a più lontano, ulteriore ad anche, inoltre, più a lungo; più lontano.
farthest ['fɑ:ðist] a il più lontano, estremo; ad più lontano.
farthing ['fɑ:ðiŋ] n quarto di 'penny'; (fig) cosa di nessun valore.
fascinate ['fæsineit] vt affascinare.
fascination [,fæsi'neiʃən] n fascino.
fascism ['fæʃizəm] n (pol) fascismo.
fascist ['fæʃist] a n fascista.
fashion ['fæʃən] n moda, modello; modo, stile; vt fare, foggiare, creare secondo un modello.
fashionable ['fæʃnəbl] a alla moda, di moda; elegante.
fast [fɑ:st] a fermo, fisso, saldo; rapido, veloce; (fig) dissoluto; n astinenza, digiuno; ad rapidamente; fermamente, saldamente; vi digiunare.
fasten ['fɑ:sn] vt assicurare, attaccare, fissare; vi attaccarsi.
fastener ['fɑ:snə] n chiusura, fermaglio; **zip f.** chiusura lampo.
fastening ['fɑ:sniŋ] n chiusura, fermatura.
fastidious [fæs'tidiəs] a di gusti difficili, schizzinoso.
fastidiousness [fæs'tidiəsnis] n l'essere di gusti difficili.
fasting ['fɑ:stiŋ] a di digiuno; n digiuno.

fat [fæt] a grasso; corpulento; ricco, fertile; n grasso.
fatal ['feitl] a fatale, funesto.
fatalism ['feitəlizəm] n fatalismo.
fatality [fə'tæliti] n fatalità, sventura, morte accidentale.
fate [feit] n fato, destino.
fated ['feitid] a destinato.
fateful ['feitful] a fatale, decisivo.
father ['fɑ:ðə] n padre; vt procreare; **f.-in-law** suocero.
fatherhood ['fɑ:ðəhud] n paternità.
fatherless ['fɑ:ðəlis] a orfano di padre.
fatherly ['fɑ:ðəli] a paterno.
fathom ['fæðəm] n misura di profondità (metri 1,83 circa); vt scandagliare; (fig) capire.
fathomless ['fæðəmlis] a incommensurabile, impenetrabile.
fatigue [fə'ti:g] n fatica; vt affaticare, stancare.
fatiguing [fə'ti:giŋ] a faticoso, sfibrante.
fatness ['fætnis] n grassezza.
fatten ['fætn] vti ingrassare.
fatty ['fæti] a adiposo, grasso.
fatuity [fə'tju:iti] n fatuità.
fatuous ['fætjuəs] a fatuo.
faucet ['fɔ:sit] n rubinetto.
fault [fɔ:lt] n difetto, colpa, fallo; **to a f.** all'eccesso.
faultless ['fɔ:ltlis] a irreprensibile, perfetto.
faulty ['fɔ:lti] a difettoso, imperfetto.
faun [fɔ:n] n fauno.
favor ['feivə] n favore, parzialità; vt favorire.
favorable ['feivərəbl] a favorevole, propizio.
favorite ['feivərit] a n favorito.
fawn [fɔ:n] a n cerbiatto; color fulvo; vi accarezzare, adulare.
fear [fiə] n paura, timore; vti temere, aver paura.
fearful ['fiəful] a spaventoso, timoroso.
fearless ['fiəlis] a ardimentoso, impavido.
fearsome ['fiəsəm] a spaventoso.
feasible ['fi:zəbl] a fattibile, possibile.
feast [fi:st] n festa, festino, vt festeggiare; vi banchettare, far festa.
feat [fi:t] n atto eroico, prodezza.
feather ['feðə] n penna, piuma.
feature ['fi:tʃə] n fattezza, lineamento; configurazione; caratteristica.
February ['februəri] n febbraio.
feckless ['feklis] a inefficiente.
fecund ['fi:kənd] a fecondo.
fecundity [fi'kʌnditi] n fecondità.
federal ['fedərəl] a federale.
federate ['fedərit] a (con)federato.
federation [,fedə'reiʃən] n (con)federazione.
fee [fi:] n onorario, emolumento; (enrollment, examination etc) tassa; vt pagare un onorario a.
feeble ['fi:bl] a debole.

feebleness ['fi:blnis] n debolezza.

feed [fi:d] n alimento, (fam) mangiata; (mech) alimentazione, rifornimento; vti nutrir(si).

feeder ['fi:də] n alimentatore; (bib) bavaglino; (stream) affluente; (rly) linea secondaria; (feeding bottle) biberon, poppatoio.

feeding ['fi:diŋ] n alimentazione, nutrimento.

feel [fi:l] n sensazione (tattile); vti sentir(si), avere la sensazione di, percepire.

feeler ['fi:lə] n antenna; tentacolo; (fig) sondaggio, approccio; (mech) sonda.

feeling ['fi:liŋ] a sensibile; n sentimento, sensazione, sensibilità.

feign [fein] vti fingere, simulare.

feint [feint] n finta; (mil) finto attacco; vi fare una finta.

felicitate [fi'lisiteit] vt felicitarsi con, congratularsi con.

felicitation [fi,lisi'teiʃən] n felicitazione, congratulazione.

felicitous [fi'lisitəs] a felice, appropriato.

felicity [fi'lisiti] n felicità.

feline ['fi:lain] a n felino.

fell [fel] n collina brulla; pelle, vello; a feroce vt abbattere.

fellow ['felou] n individuo; camerata, compagno, socio; fellowship compagnia; amicizia; associazione; borsa di studio.

felon ['felən] n criminale.

felony ['feləni] n crimine.

felt [felt] n feltro.

female ['fi:meil] a femminile, di sesso femminile; n femmina.

feminine ['feminin] a femminile.

fen [fen] n terreno acquitrinoso.

fence [fens] n recinto, stecconato; ricettatore; vt chiudere con un recinto; ricettare; vi tirar di scherma; (fig) schermirsi.

fencing ['fensiŋ] n scherma; recinto.

fend [fend] vt f. off parare; f. for oneself provvedere a se stesso.

fender ['fendə] n paraurti; parafuoco; (aut) parafango.

fennel ['fenl] n finocchio.

Ferdinand ['fə:dinənd] nm pr Ferdinando.

ferment ['fə:ment] n fermento; [fə:'ment] vti (far) fermentare; (fig) fomentare.

fermentation [,fə:men'teiʃən] n fermentazione.

fern [fə:n] n felce.

ferocious [fə'rouʃəs] a feroce.

ferocity [fə'rɔsiti] n ferocia.

ferret ['ferit] n furetto; f. out vt scoprire.

ferrule ['feru:l] n ghiera.

ferry ['feri] n traghetto, ferryboàt; vt traghettare.

fertile ['fə:tail] a fertile.

fertility [fə:'tiliti] n fertilità.

fertilize ['fə:tilaiz] vt fertilizzare.

fervent ['fə:vənt] a fervente.

fervid ['fə:vid] a fervido.

fervor ['fə:və] n fervore.

fester ['festə] vi suppurare.

festival ['festivəl] n festa, celebrazione; (mus etc) festival.

festive ['festiv] a festivo, gioioso.

festivity [fes'tiviti] n festività, festa.

festoon [fes'tu:n] n festone; vt adornare con festoni.

fetch [fetʃ] vt andare a prendere; valere, fruttare.

fête [feit] n festa; vt festeggiare.

fetid ['fetid] a fetido.

fetish ['fi:tiʃ] n feticcio.

fetter ['fetə] n catena; fetters pl ceppi pl; vt mettere in ceppi; intralciare.

fettle ['fetl] n condizione, stato.

feud [fju:d] n contesa, inimicizia.

feudal ['fju:dəl] a feudale.

feudalism ['fju:dəlizəm] n feudalismo.

fever ['fi:və] n febbre.

feverish ['fi:vəriʃ] a febbricitante, febbrile.

few [fju:] a pron pl pochi; a f. alcuni, un certo numero; the f. la minoranza.

fiancé [fi'ɑ:nsei] n fidanzato; fiancée fidanzata.

fiasco [fi'æskou] n insuccesso, fiasco.

fib [fib] n (fam) piccola bugia.

fiber ['faibə] n fibra.

fiberglass ['faibəglɑ:s] n lana di vetro.

fibrous ['faibrəs] a fibroso.

fickle ['fikl] a incostante, volubile.

fickleness ['fiklnis] n incostanza, volubilità.

fiction ['fikʃən] n prosa narrativa; finzione, invenzione.

fictitious [fik'tiʃəs] a fittizio.

fiddle ['fidl] n (fam) violino; vti (fam) suonare il violino; gingillarsi

fidelity [fi'deliti] n fedeltà.

fidget ['fidʒit] n irrequietezza; vi essere irrequieto, agitarsi.

fidgety ['fidʒiti] a irrequieto.

field [fi:ld] n campo.

fiend [fi:nd] n demonio, spirito maligno.

fiendish ['fi:ndiʃ] a demoniaco, diabolico.

fiendishly ['fi:ndiʃli] ad diabolicamente.

fierce [fiəs] a feroce, violento; ardente.

fiercely ['fiəsli] ad ferocemente; ardentemente; furiosamente.

fierceness ['fiəsnis] n ferocia; ardore, furia.

fiery ['faiəri] n infiammato, focoso.

fife [faif] n piffero.

fifteen ['fif'ti:n] a n quindici; fifteenth a n quindicesimo, decimo quinto.

fifth [fifθ] a n quinto.

fifty ['fifti] a n cinquanta; fiftieth a n cinquantesimo.

fig (tree) ['fig(triː)] n (pianta di) fico.
fight [fait] n battaglia, combattimento; vti combattere, lottare.
fighter ['faitə] n combattente; (av) caccia.
figment ['figmənt] n finzione, invenzione.
figurative ['figjurətiv] a figurativo; figurato; ornato.
figure ['figə] n cifra; figura; vti figurarsi, raffigurare; f. out calcolare; figurehead uomo di paglia.
filament ['filəmənt] n filamento.
filch [filtʃ] n refurtiva; vt rubacchiare.
file [fail] n lima; fila; filza, schedario; vti archiviare, ordinare; (far) marciare in fila; limare.
filial ['filiəl] a filiale.
filibuster ['filibʌstə] n ostruzionista; vi ostruzionare.
filigree ['filigriː] n filigrana.
fill [fil] n sazietà; vt riempire; (position) occupare; (tooth) otturare; vi riempirsi.
fillet ['filit] n nastro; filetto.
filling ['filiŋ] n riempitura; ripieno; (tooth) otturazione; f. station (aut) stazione di rifornimento.
fillip ['filip] n lo schioccare delle dita; (fig) stimolo; vti schioccare le dita; (fig) stimolare.
filly ['fili] n puledra.
film [film] n film, pellicola; patina; (fig) velo; vt filmare.
filmy ['filmi] a velato, vaporoso.
filter ['filtə] n filtro; vti filtrare; f.-tip cigarette sigaretta con filtro.
filth [filθ] filthiness ['filθinis] n sudiciume; oscenità.
filthy ['filθi] a sudicio; osceno.
fin [fin] n pinna.
final ['fainl] a finale, ultimo, decisivo; n (sport) gara finale; pl esami finali pl; finalist n (sport) finalista.
finale [fi'naːli] n (mus) finale.
finally ['fainəli] ad finalmente, alla fine; definitivamente.
finance [fai'næns] n finanza; vt finanziare.
financial [fai'nænʃəl] a finanziario.
financier [fai'nænsiə] n finanziere.
finch [fintʃ] n fringuello.
find [faind] n scoperta, ritrovamento; vt trovare; f. out scoprire.
fine [fain] a bello; delicato; fine, raffinato; ad bene; n multa; vt multare.
fineness ['fainnis] n bellezza; finezza.
finery ['fainəri] n abiti delle feste pl, fronzoli pl.
finesse [fi'nes] n finezza, sottigliezza.
finger ['fiŋgə] n dito; vt tastare, toccare delicatamente; fingerprint impronta digitale.
finical ['finikəl], finicky ['finiki] a pignolo, affettato, schizzinoso.
finish ['finiʃ] n rifinitura, ultimo tocco; fine; vti finire, perfezionare.

finite ['fainait] a definito, limitato; (gram) finito.
Finland ['finlənd] n Finlandia.
Finn [fin] n finlandese.
Finnish ['finiʃ] a finlandese.
fiord [fjɔːd] n fiordo.
fir (tree) ['fəː(triː)] n abete.
fire ['faiə] n fuoco, incendio; (gun) tiro; vt incendiare; sparare.
firearms ['faiəraːmz] n pl armi da fuoco pl.
fire brigade ['faiəbri,geid] n corpo dei pompieri.
fire department ['faiədiː'paːtmənt] n corpo dei pompieri.
fire-escape ['faiəris,keip] n uscita di sicurezza.
fire-extinguisher ['faiəriks,tiŋgwiʃə] n estintore, pompa antincendio.
firefly ['faiəflai] n lucciola.
fireman ['faiəmən] pl firemen n pompiere.
fireplace ['faiəpleis] n caminetto, camino.
fireproof ['faiəpruːf] a incombustibile.
fireside ['faiəsaid] n focolare.
firewood ['faiəwud] n legna da ardere.
firework ['faiəwəːk] n fuoco d'artifizio.
firing ['faiəriŋ] n combustione; scarica, sparo; f. party, f. squad (mil) plotone d'esecuzione.
firm [fəːm] a duro; saldo, stabile; deciso; n ditta.
firmament ['fəːməmənt] n firmamento.
firmly ['fəːmli] ad fermamente; saldamente.
firmness ['fəːmnis] n fermezza; stabilità.
first [fəːst] n primo; ad prima, in primo luogo.
firth [fəːθ] n (scozzese) estuario.
fish [fiʃ] pl fishes, fish n pesce; vti pescare.
fisher(man) ['fiʃə(mən)] pl fishermen n pescatore.
fishery ['fiʃəri] n pesca; riserva di pesca; vivaio.
fishing ['fiʃiŋ] a di pesca, per la pesca; n pesca; f. hook amo; f. line lenza; f. rod canna da pesca.
fishmonger ['fiʃ,mʌŋgə] n pescivendolo.
fish-pond ['fiʃpɔnd] n vasca per pesci.
fishy ['fiʃi] a di pesce; (fig) dubbio, equivoco.
fission ['fiʃən] n fissione.
fissure ['fiʃə] n crepa, fessura.
fist [fist] n pugno.
fit [fit] a adatto, appropriato, conveniente, idoneo; in buona salute; n misura; accesso, convulsione; vti adattare; prepararsi a; convenire, star bene.
fitful ['fitful] a spasmodico, irregolare.

fitfully ['fitfuli] *ad* a sbalzi; irregolarmente.
fitness ['fitnis] *n* opportunità; buona salute.
fitting ['fitiŋ] *a* adatto, conveniente; *n* (*of a dress etc*) prova; (*usu pl*) accessori, arredi, infissi *pl*.
fittingly ['fitiŋli] *ad* convenientemente.
five [faiv] *a n* cinque.
fix [fiks] *n* (*fam*) dilemma, difficoltà; *vt* fissare, aggiustare; stabilire; **to f. up** accomodare.
fixation [fik'seiʃən] *n* fissazione.
fixative ['fiksətiv] *a* fissativo; *n* fissativo, fissatore.
fixed [fikst] *a* fisso, fissato.
fixing ['fiksiŋ] *n* (*phot*) fissaggio.
fixture ['fikstʃə] *n* infisso; (*sport*) data fissata; impianto di gas, luce *etc*.
fizz [fiz] *n* (*sl*) spumante, bevanda effervescente; *vi* frizzare.
fizzle ['fizl] *vi* frizzare, sibilare; **to f. out** far fiasco.
flabbergast ['flæbəgɑ:st] *vt* (*fam*) sbalordire.
flabbiness ['flæbinis] *n* flaccidezza.
flabby ['flæbi] *a* cascante, floscio.
flaccid ['flæksid] *a* flaccido.
flag [flæg] *n* bandiera; (*bot*) iride; (*stone*) pietra da lastrico; *vi* perdere le forze.
flagellate ['flædʒileit] *vt* flagellare.
flagellation [flædʒe'leiʃən] *n* flagellazione.
flagon ['flægən] *n* bottiglione.
flagrancy ['fleigrənsi] *n* flagranza.
flagrant ['fleigrənt] *a* flagrante.
flair [flɛə] *n* fiuto, intuizione.
flake [fleik] *n* fiocco; lamina, scaglia; *vti* sfaldar(si).
flaky ['fleiki] *a* scaglioso; fioccoso; (*pastry*) sfogliato.
flamboyant [flæm'bɔiənt] *a* sgargiante.
flame [fleim] *n* fiamma; *vi* fiammeggiare.
flaming ['fleimiŋ] *a* infuocato, ardente.
Flanders ['flɑ:ndəz] *n* (*geogr*) Fiandre.
flank [flæŋk] *n* fianco; *vt* fiancheggiare.
flannel ['flænl] *a n* (di) flanella.
flap [flæp] *n* falda, lembo, tesa, colpo d'ala; *vt* agitare, sbattere.
flare [flɛə] *n* chiarore intenso, fiammata improvvisa; (*av*) razzo; *vi* brillare di luce viva, avvampare.
flash [flæʃ] *n* baleno, lampo, vampata; **flashback** (*cin*) scena retrospettiva; **flashbulb** lampada per fotolampo; **flashlight** lampadina elettrica; (*naut*) luce intermittente; **flashpoint** temperatura di infiammabilità; *vti* lanciare, balenare, sfavillare.
flashy ['flæʃi] *a* (*fam*) sgargiante, vistoso, appariscente.
flask [flɑ:sk] *n* fiasco.
flat [flæt] *a* piano, piatto; monotono,

uniforme; reciso; *n* appartamento; piano di casa; **service flats** appartamenti di affitto con servizio.
flatly ['flætli] *ad* freddamente, recisamente.
flatness ['flætnis] *n* monotonia, uniformità.
flatten ['flætn] *vt* appiattire.
flatter ['flætə] *vt* adulare, lusingare.
flattering ['flætəriŋ] *a* adulatorio.
flattery ['flætəri] *n* adulazione.
flatulence ['flætjuləns] *n* flatulenza.
flaunt [flɔ:nt] *vt* ostentare.
flautist ['flɔ:tist] *n* flautista.
flavor ['fleivə] *n* aroma, gusto, sapore; *vt* dare gusto a, aromatizzare.
flaw [flɔ:] *n* difetto, pecca.
flax [flæks] *n* lino.
flaxen ['flæksən] *a* di lino; biondo.
flay [flei] *vt* scorticare, pelare.
flea [fli:] *n* pulce.
fleck [flek] *n* lentiggine; macchietta; particella.
fledge [fledʒ] *vi* mettere le ali.
fledged [fledʒd] *a* (*of bird*) pennuto; piumato.
fledgling ['fledʒliŋ] *n* uccellino appena uscito dal nido.
flee [fli:] *vi* fuggire.
fleece [fli:s] *n* vello; *vt* (*sl*) pelare, derubare.
fleecy ['fli:si] *a* lanoso, velloso.
fleet [fli:t] *n* flotta.
fleeting ['fli:tiŋ] *a* fugace, transitorio.
Fleming ['flemiŋ] *n* fiammingo.
Flemish ['flemiʃ] *a n* fiammingo.
flesh [fleʃ] *n* carne.
fleshy ['fleʃi] *a* polposo, grasso.
flex [fleks] *n* (*el*) filo flessibile.
flexibility [,fleksə'biliti] *n* flessibilità.
flexible ['fleksəbl] *a* flessibile.
flick [flik] *n* colpetto, schiocco; buffetto; (*sl*) cinema; *vt* colpire; dare un buffetto; **f. knife** coltello a molla.
flicker ['flikə] *n* barlume; tremolio; battito; *vi* tremolare, vacillare; brillare debolmente.
flight [flait] *n* volo; stormo; (*av*) squadriglia; rampa di scale; fuga.
flightily ['flaitili] *ad* capricciosamente, leggermente.
flighty ['flaiti] *a* frivolo, incostante.
flimsiness ['flimzinis] *n* tenuità, inconsistenza; frivolezza.
flimsy ['flimzi] *a* tenue, leggero; frivolo.
flinch [flintʃ] *vi* indietreggiare, ritirarsi.
fling [fliŋ] *n* getto, lancio; godimento completo; baldoria; *vt* gettare, lanciare.
flint [flint] *n* pietra focaia, selce; (*of cigarette lighter*) pietrina.
flinty ['flinti] *a* petroso; crudele, duro.
flip [flip] *vt* sbattere leggermente; **egg-flip** uova sbattute, zabaione.

flippancy ['flipənsi] n leggerezza, mancanza di serietà.

flippant ['flipənt] a leggero, irrispettoso.

flipper ['flipə] n pinna, ala natatoria.

flirt [fləːt] n ragazza civettuola; damerino; amoreggiamento, 'flirt'; vt agitare; vi civettare, 'flirtare'.

flirtation [fləːˈteiʃən] n amoreggiamento, 'flirt'.

flit [flit] vi volare, svolazzare; sloggiare.

float [flout] n galleggiante; carro per processione; vti galleggiare, far galleggiare.

floater ['floutə] n galleggiante.

floating ['floutiŋ] a galleggiante, fluttuante; f. capital (com) capitale circolante.

flock [flɔk] n branco, gregge; bioccolo, fiocco di lana; vi riunirsi a stormi.

floe [flou] n banchisa.

flog [flɔg] vt frustare.

flogging ['flɔgiŋ] n bastonatura, fustigazione.

flood [flʌd] n diluvio, inondazione, allagamento; vt inondare, sommergere.

floodlight ['flʌdlait] n riflettore; vt illuminare con riflettori.

floor [flɔː] n pavimento; piano (di casa); vt pavimentare, ridurre al silenzio; atterrare.

flop [flɔp] n tonfo; fiasco, insuccesso; vi camminare (sedersi) goffamente; (sl) far fiasco; flophouse dormitorio pubblico.

floral ['flɔːrəl] a floreale.

Florence ['flɔːrəns] n (geogr) Firenze; Florentine a n fiorentino, fiorentina.

florid ['flɔrid] a florido, prosperoso.

florin ['flɔrin] n fiorino (in Inghilterra, moneta da due scellini).

florist ['flɔrist] n fiorista, fioraio, floricultore.

flotilla [flouˈtilə] n flottiglia.

flotsam ['flɔtsəm] n relitti pl; merci ritrovate galleggianti sul mare pl.

flounce [flauns] n falpalà; vt ornare di volani; vi dimenarsi, muoversi in modo agitato.

flounder ['flaundə] n (fish) passerino; vi agitarsi, dibatersi; condurre una cosa male, fare errori.

flour ['flauə] n (fior di) farina.

flourish ['flʌriʃ] n fioritura; (of trumpets) squillo; (writing) svolazzo; vi fiorire; (fig) prosperare; vt (stick etc) brandire.

flout [flaut] vt insultare, schernire.

flow [flou] n flusso, corso, corrente; abbondanza; f. of words facilità; vi fluire, scorrere.

flower ['flauə] n fiore; flowerbed aiuola; fiorire, produrre fiori.

flowery ['flauəri] a fiorito.

flowing ['flouiŋ] a fluente, corrente, sciolto, fluido; n flusso, corso.

flu [fluː] n (fam) influenza.

fluctuate ['flʌktjueit] vi fluttuare.

fluctuation [ˌflʌktjuˈeiʃən] n oscillazione, fluttuazione.

flue [fluː] n conduttura d'un camino, tubo.

fluency ['fluːənsi] n fluidità, scioltezza, facilità (di parola).

fluent ['fluːənt] a fluente, scorrevole, dalla parola facile.

fluff [flʌf] n lanugine, peluria.

fluid ['fluːid] a n fluido.

fluke [fluːk] n (naut) marra; (zool) distoma epatico; (fam) vantaggio inaspettato, colpo di fortuna.

flunkey ['flʌŋki] n valletto.

fluorescent [fluəˈresnt] a fluorescente.

flurry ['flʌri] n agitazione; improvviso colpo di vento, o scroscio di pioggia.

flush [flʌʃ] n rossore, afflusso di sangue al volto; vt sciacquare (con acqua abbondante); vi arrossire.

fluster ['flʌstə] n agitazione, eccitazione; vti agitare, agitarsi.

flute [fluːt] n flauto.

flutter ['flʌtə] n svolazzamento; agitazione; (sl) speculazione; vt agitare; vi agitarsi, svolazzare.

flux [flʌks] n flusso.

fly [flai] n mosca; vti (far) volare.

flying ['flaiiŋ] a volante, sventolante; breve.

foal [foul] n puledro.

foam [foum] n schiuma, spuma; vi schiumare, spumeggiare.

fob (off) [fɔb] vt imbrogliare, appioppare qc a qlcu.

focus ['foukəs] n fuoco; in f. a fuoco; out of f. fuori fuoco, sfocato.

fodder ['fɔdə] n foraggio.

foe [fou] n avversario, nemico.

fog [fɔg] n nebbia.

foggy ['fɔgi] a nebbioso.

foible ['fɔibl] n lato debole.

foil [fɔil] n foglia sottile di metallo; cosa che serve a porre in risalto; vt frustrare; far perdere le tracce.

foist [fɔist] vt introdurre di nascosto, far accettare con un trucco.

fold [fould] n piega, spira; ovile; (fig) Chiesa; vt piegare; (arms) incrociare; vi ripiegarsi.

folder ['fouldə] n (manifestino) pieghevole; cartella, cartellatta; piegatore.

folding ['fouldiŋ] a pieghevole; n piega; f. bed branda.

foliage ['fouliidʒ] n fogliame.

folk [fouk] n gente, popolo; (fam) la propria famiglia.

folklore ['fouklɔː] n folclore.

follow ['fɔlou] vt seguire; inseguire; vi conseguire, derivare.

follower ['fɔlouə] n seguace, discepolo, pl ammiratori pl; following a seguente; n seguito.

folly ['fɔli] n follia.

foment [fouˈment] vt fomentare.

fond [fɔnd] *a* affezionato, appassionato; **to be f. of** voler bene a, amare.

fondle ['fɔndl] *vt* accarezzare.

fondly ['fɔndli] *ad* appassionatamente, amorevolmente.

fondness ['fɔndnis] *n* affettuosità indulgente, tenerezza, passione.

font [fɔnt] *n* fonte battesimale.

food [fuːd] *n* cibo, alimento, nutrimento.

fool [fuːl] *n* idiota, sciocco; (*court*) buffone; *vt* imbrogliare, ingannare; *vi* fare lo sciocco.

foolery ['fuːləri] *n* buffonata, sciocchezza.

foolhardy ['fuːl͵hɑːdi] *a* temerario.

foolish ['fuːliʃ] *a* sciocco, stolto.

foolishness ['fuːliʃnis] *n* sciocchezza, stoltezza.

foot [fut] *pl* **feet** *n* piede; fanteria; misura lineare corrispondente a 30,5 cm. circa.

football ['futbɔːl] *n* calcio, pallone per il calcio; **association f.** gioco del calcio; **Rugby f.** pallovale, rugby; **footballer** giocatore di calcio.

foot-bridge ['futbridʒ] *n* ponte per soli pedoni, cavalcavia.

foothold ['futhould] *n* punto d'appoggio; (*fig*) piede.

footlights ['futlaits] *n pl* (*theat*) luci della ribalta.

footman ['futmən] *n* servo in livrea.

footnote ['futnout] *n* poscritto, postilla.

footpath ['futpɑːθ] *n* sentiero.

footprint ['futprint] *n* orma, impronta.

footstep ['futstep] *n* passo, suono di passi.

footstool ['futstuːl] *n* sgabello.

for [fɔː] *prep* per, a, di, a causa di; *cj* perchè.

forage ['fɔridʒ] *n* foraggio.

foray ['fɔrei] *n* incursione, scorreria.

forbear [fɔːˈbɛə] *vi* trattenersi da.

forbearance [fɔːˈbɛərəns] *n* pazienza, sopportazione.

forbearing [fɔːˈbɛəriŋ] *a* paziente.

forbid [fəˈbid] *vt* proibire, vietare.

forbidding [fəˈbidiŋ] *a* severo; ripugnante.

force [fɔːs] *n* forza, violenza; (*of law*) vigore; **forces** *pl* truppe *pl*; *vt* costringere, forzare.

forceful ['fɔːsful] *a* energico.

forceps ['fɔːseps] *n pl* pinze chirurgiche *pl*, forcipe.

forcible ['fɔːsəbl] *a* impetuoso, violento.

ford [fɔːd] *n* guado; *vt* passare a guado.

fordable ['fɔːdəbl] *a* guadabile.

fore [fɔː] *a* anteriore; *n* davanti, parte anteriore.

fore-arm ['fɔːrɑːm] *n* avambraccio.

forebear ['fɔːbɛə] *n* antenato.

foreboding [fɔːˈboudiŋ] *n* presagio, presentimento.

forecast ['fɔːkɑːst] *n* previsione; *vt* pronosticare.

forecastle ['fouksl] *n* (*naut*) castello di prua.

forefather ['fɔː͵fɑːðə] *n* antenato.

forefinger ['fɔː͵fiŋgə] *n* indice.

forefront ['fɔːfrʌnt] *n* prima linea; posizione d'importanza.

foregoing ['fɔːgouiŋ] *a* precedente; **foregone** *a* previsto.

foreground ['fɔːgraund] *n* primo piano.

forehead ['fɔrid] *n* fronte.

foreign ['fɔrin] *a* estero, straniero, forestiero, estraneo.

foreigner ['fɔrinə] *n* straniero, (*fam*) forestiero.

foreman ['fɔːmən] *pl* **foremen** *n* capo-officina; capomastro; capo dei giurati.

foremost ['fɔːmoust] *a* primo; *ad* in testa, in avanti.

forenoon ['fɔːnuːn] *n* mattino.

forensic [fəˈrensik] *a* forense.

forerunner ['fɔː͵rʌnə] *n* precursore.

foresee [fɔːˈsiː] *vt* prevedere.

foreshadow [fɔːˈʃædou] *vt* adombrare; presagire.

foresight ['fɔːsait] *n* preveggenza; prudenza.

forest ['fɔrist] *a* forestale; *n* foresta; **forestry** silvicultura.

forestall [fɔːˈstɔːl] *vt* prevenire, anticipare; (*com*) fare incetta.

forester ['fɔristə] *n* guardia forestale.

foretaste ['fɔːteist] *n* pregustazione.

foretell [fɔːˈtel] *vt* predire, pronosticare.

forethought ['fɔːθɔːt] *n* previdenza.

forever [fəˈrevə] *ad* per sempre, eternamente.

forewarn [fɔːˈwɔːn] *vt* (pre)avvertire.

foreword ['fɔːwəːd] *n* prefazione.

forfeit ['fɔːfit] *n* multa, pegno; perdita; *vt* perdere il diritto a, dover pagare, essere privato di.

forfeiture ['fɔːfitʃə] *n* multa, perdita.

for(e)gather [fɔːˈgæðə] *vi* adunarsi; incontrarsi, fraternizzare.

forge [fɔːdʒ] *n* fornace, fucina; *vt* forgiare, contraffare, falsificare; **to f. ahead** avanzare.

forger ['fɔːdʒə] *n* falsificatore.

forgery ['fɔːdʒəri] *n* contraffazione, documento falso.

forget [fəˈget] *vti* dimenticare.

forgetful [fəˈgetful] *a* dimentico, distratto, immemore.

forgetfulness [fəˈgetfulnis] *n* smemorataggine, oblio.

forgivable [fəˈgivəbl] *a* perdonabile.

forgive [fəˈgiv] *vt* perdonare.

forgiveness [fəˈgivnis] *n* perdono, remissione.

forgiving [fəˈgiviŋ] *a* clemente, indulgente.

forgo [fɔːˈgou] *vt* rinunziare a, privarsi di.

fork [fɔːk] *n* forchetta; *vi* biforcarsi.

forlorn [fəˈlɔːn] *a* abbandonato,

infelice; **f. hope** vana speranza, impresa disperata.

form [fɔːm] n forma; modulo; banco di scuola, classe; covo di lepre; vti formar(si).

formal ['fɔːməl] a formale, cerimonioso.

formality [fɔː'mæliti] n formalità.

formally ['fɔːməli] ad formalmente.

formation [fɔː'meiʃən] n formazione.

former ['fɔːmə] a precedente, primo, antico; pron (di due persone) il primo.

formerly ['fɔːməli] ad già, un tempo.

formidable ['fɔːmidəbl] a formidabile.

formula ['fɔːmjulə] pl **formulae**, **formulas** n formula.

formulate ['fɔːmjuleit] vt formulare.

forsake [fə'seik] vt abbandonare.

fort [fɔːt] n forte, fortezza.

forte ['fɔːti] n attitudine speciale, forte; (mus) forte.

forth [fɔːθ] ad (in) avanti, fuori.

forthcoming [fɔːθ'kʌmiŋ] a prossimo, presso a venire, vicino alla pubblicazione.

forthright ['fɔːθrait] a franco; esplicito; ad immediatamente, esplicitamente.

forthwith ['fɔːθ'wiθ] ad immediatamente, senz'altro.

fortification [,fɔːtifi'keiʃən] n fortificazione.

fortify ['fɔːtifai] vt fortificare.

fortitude ['fɔːtitjuːd] n forza d'animo.

fortnight ['fɔːtnait] n due settimane pl, quindici giorni, quindicina.

fortnightly ['fɔːt,naitli] a quindicinale; ad ogni quindici giorni.

fortress ['fɔːtris] n fortezza, roccaforte.

fortuitous [fɔː'tjuːitəs] a fortuito, casuale.

fortunate ['fɔːtʃnit] a fortunato, favorevole.

fortune ['fɔːtʃən] n fortuna, destino; **f.-telling** predizione dell'avvenire.

forty ['fɔːti] a n quaranta; **fortieth** a n quarantesimo.

forward ['fɔːwəd] a avanzato; precoce; spinto; ad (in) avanti, in poi; vt far proseguire, spedire, promuovere.

forwarding ['fɔːwədiŋ] n spedizione; **f. agent** (com) spedizioniere.

forwards ['fɔːwədz] ad v **forward**.

fossil ['fɔsl] n fossile.

fossilize ['fɔsilaiz] vti fossilizzar(si).

foster ['fɔstə] vt allevare, nutrire; incoraggiare.

foul [faul] a sporco, sudicio, osceno; (sport) sleale; **f. play** intrigo, azione disonesta; n (sport) fallo.

foully ['faulli] ad sudiciamente; ignobilmente.

foulness ['faulnis] n sporcizia, oscenità.

found [faund] vt fondare; fondere; vi fondarsi.

foundation [faun'deiʃən] n fondazione; fondamenta pl; istituzione.

founder ['faundə] n fondatore; fonditore.

founder ['faundə] vt affondare, (a horse) azzoppare; vi affondare, sprofondarsi.

foundling ['faundliŋ] n trovatello.

foundry ['faundri] n fonderia.

fountain ['fauntin] n fontana, fonte; **f. pen** penna stilografica.

four [fɔː] a n quattro; **fourth** a n quarto.

fourfold ['fɔːfould] a quadruplo.

fourteen ['fɔː'tiːn] a n quattordici; **fourteenth** a n quattordicesimo.

fowl [faul] n pollo, uccello.

fox [fɔks] n volpe.

foxhound ['fɔkshaund] n bracco.

foxy ['fɔksi] a (fig) astuto, scaltro.

fraction ['frækʃən] n frazione.

fractious ['frækʃəs] a litigioso, permaloso.

fracture ['fræktʃə] n frattura; vti fratturar(si).

fragile ['frædʒail] a fragile.

fragment ['frægmənt] n frammento.

fragrance ['freigrəns] n fragranza.

fragrant ['freigrənt] a fragrante.

frail [freil] a fragile, debole.

frailty ['freilti] n fragilità.

frame [freim] n cornice; struttura, intelaiatura; (bicycle) telaio; (spectacles) montatura; vt incorniciare; dar forma a; inventare.

framework ['freimwəːk] n struttura, ossatura.

franc [fræŋk] n franco (moneta).

France [frɑːns] n Francia.

Frances ['frɑːnsis] nf pr Francesca.

franchise ['fræntʃaiz] n franchigia, diritti di voto pl.

Francis ['frɑːnsis] nm pr Francesco.

Franciscan [fræn'siskən] a n francescano.

Frank [fræŋk] nm pr Franco.

frank [fræŋk] a aperto, franco, schietto.

frankness ['fræŋknis] n franchezza, schiettezza.

frantic ['fræntik] a fuori di sè, frenetico.

frantically ['fræntikəli] ad freneticamente; terribilmente.

fraternal [frə'təːnəl] a fraterno.

fraternity [frə'təːniti] n fraternità, confraternità.

fraternize ['frætənaiz] vi fraternizzare.

fratricide ['frætrisaid] n fratricida, fratricidio.

fraud [frɔːd] n frode, truffa; impostore.

fraudulent ['frɔːdjulənt] a fraudolento.

fraught [frɔːt] a carico (di).

fray [frei] n zuffa, rissa; vti logorar(si).

freak [friːk] *n* capriccio, anomalia.
freakish ['friːkiʃ] *a* capriccioso.
freckle ['frekl] *n* lentiggine; *vti* macchiar(si) di lentiggini.
Frederic(k) ['fredrik] *nm pr* Federico.
free [friː] *a* libero; gratis, gratuito; (*com*) franco; *vt* liberare.
freedom ['friːdəm] *n* libertà; disinvoltura; familiarità.
freely ['friːli] *ad* liberamente; gratuitamente.
freeman ['friːmən] *pl* **freemen** *n* cittadino onorario.
freemason ['friː‚meisn] *n* frammassone.
freemasonry ['friː‚meisnri] *n* frammassoneria.
freethinker ['friː'θiŋkə] *n* libero pensatore.
freeze [friːz] *n* (*of prices etc*) congelamento, blocco; *vti* congelar(si), gelare, irrigidir(si).
freezer ['friːzə] *n* congelante; frigorifero; cella frigorifera.
freezing ['friːziŋ] *a* gelido, glaciale; *n* congelamento; **below f. point** sotto zero.
freight [freit] *n* nolo, carico; *vt* (*ship*) caricare, noleggiare; **f. car** vagone merci.
French [frentʃ] *a n* francese; **Frenchman** *n* francese; **F. fries** patate fritte.
frenzied ['frenzid] *a* frenetico.
frenzy ['frenzi] *n* frenesia.
frequency ['friːkwənsi] *n* frequenza.
frequent ['friːkwənt] *a* frequente; *vt* [fri'kwent] frequentare.
frequently ['friːkwəntli] *ad* frequentemente.
fresco ['freskou] *pl* **frescos, frescoes** *n* affresco.
fresh [freʃ] *a* fresco; nuovo; (*of water*) dolce; inesperto.
freshen ['freʃn] *vti* rinfrescar(si), rinvigorir(si).
freshly ['freʃli] *ad* in modo fresco; di fresco, recentemente.
freshness ['freʃnis] *n* freschezza.
fret [fret] *n* inquietudine, irritazione; (*arch*) fregio, greca; *vt* agitare, irritare; fregare, rodere; *vi* impazientirsi, irritarsi.
fretful ['fretful] *a* irritabile.
fretwork ['fretwəːk] *n* lavoro d'intaglio, lavoro a greca.
friar ['fraiə] *n* frate.
friction ['frikʃən] *n* attrito, frizione.
Friday ['fraidi] *n* venerdì.
friend [frend] *n* amico; **F.** quacchero.
friendless ['frendlis] *a* senza amici.
friendliness ['frendlinis] *n* cordialità.
friendly ['frendli] *a* amichevole, amico; *ad* amichevolmente.
friendship ['frendʃip] *n* amicizia.
frieze [friːz] *n* fregio.
frigate ['frigit] *n* fregata.
fright [frait] *n* spavento, paura.
frighten ['fraitn] *vt* spaventare.

frightful ['fraitful] *a* spaventoso.
frigid ['fridʒid] *a* glaciale, frigido, freddo.
frigidity [fri'dʒiditi] *n* freddezza, frigidità.
frill [fril] *n* frangia, gala increspata.
fringe [frindʒ] *n* frangia, frangetta; bordo, limite; *vt* ornare di frangia.
frisk [frisk] *vi* far salti, salterellare.
frisky ['friski] *a* saltellante, vivace.
fritter ['fritə] *n* frittella; frammento; *vt* suddividere in frammenti; (*time*) sciupare.
frivolity [fri'vɔliti] *n* frivolezza, vanità.
frivolous ['frivələs] *a* frivolo.
frizzle ['frizl] *vti* arricciar(si); sfriggere.
fro [frou] *ad* indietro; **to and f.** avanti e indietro.
frock [frɔk] *n* veste, vestito intero; (*monk's*) tonaca.
frog [frɔg] *n* rana; alamaro.
frolic ['frɔlik] *n* scherzo, spasso; *vi* far salti, scherzare.
frolicsome ['frɔliksəm] *a* allegro, gaio.
from [frɔm] *prep* da, per.
front [frʌnt] *a* di fronte, davanti; *n* parte anteriore, facciata; (*mil*) fronte; *vti* essere di fronte a; affrontare.
frontage ['frʌntidʒ] *n* facciata, prospetto.
frontal ['frʌntl] *a n* frontale.
frontier ['frʌntiə] *a n* (di) frontiera.
frontispiece ['frʌntispiːs] *n* frontespizio.
frost [frɔːst] *n* gelo; (*sl*) fiasco; **hoar-f.** brina.
frostbite ['frɔstbait] *n* congelamento.
frosty ['frɔsti] *a* gelato, gelido.
froth [frɔθ] *n* schiuma, spuma; chiacchierata vuota.
frothy ['frɔθi] *a* schiumoso, spumoso; vuoto.
frown [fraun] *n* aggrottamento delle ciglia, cipiglio; *vi* aggrottare le ciglia.
frowsy ['frauzi] *a* sciatto, sporco; di cattivo odore.
fructify ['frʌktifai] *vi* fruttificare.
frugal ['fruːgəl] *a* frugale.
fruit [fruːt] *n* frutto, frutta *pl*.
fruit dealer ['fruːt diːla] *n* commerciante in frutta, fruttivendolo.
fruitful ['fruːtful] *a* fruttifero, produttivo, fecondo.
fruitfulness ['fruːtfulnis] *n* fertilità, fecondità.
fruition [fruː'iʃən] *n* fruizione; (*fig*) godimento.
fruitless ['fruːtlis] *a* infruttuoso, sterile.
fruity ['fruːti] *a* che sa di frutta; (*fig*) piccante.
frump [frʌmp] *n* donna vestita di abiti fuori moda.
frustrate [frʌs'treit] *vt* frustrare.

frustration [frʌs'treiʃən] *n* frustrazione, delusione.

fry [frai] *n* fritto, frittura; (*zool*) avannotto; (*fig*) persone di poca importanza; **small f.** *vti* friggere.

frying pan ['fraiiŋ,pæn] *n* padella.

fuddle ['fʌdl] *vt* confondere, intontire, ubriacare.

fuel [fjuəl] *n* combustibile, carburante; (*fig*) esca, alimento.

fueling ['fjuəliŋ] *n* approvvigionamento, rifornimento combustibili.

fugitive ['fjuːdʒitiv] *a n* fuggitivo.

fugue [fjuːg] *n* (*mus*) fuga.

fulfill [ful'fil] *vt* soddisfare, compiere.

fulfillment [ful'filmənt] *n* adempimento, realizzazione, compimento.

full [ful] *a* pieno; *ad* completamente, perfettamente, in pieno; *n* pieno, colmo; *vt* follare, gualcare.

fuller ['fulə] *n* follatore.

fullness ['fulnis] *n* pienezza, abbondanza.

fully ['fuli] *ad* completamente, interamente.

fulminate ['fʌlmineit] *vti* fulminare.

fulsome ['fulsəm] *a* disgustoso, nauseante.

fumble ['fʌmbl] *vti* frugare, maneggiare senza abilità, annaspare.

fume [fjuːm] *n* fumo, vapore; accesso di rabbia; *vt* sottoporre a vapori chimici; *vi* emettere vapori; essere in collera.

fumigate ['fjuːmigeit] *vt* fumigare.

fumigation [,fjuːmi'geiʃən] *n* fumigazione.

fun [fʌn] *n* allegria, divertimento, svago.

function ['fʌnkʃən] *n* funzione; cerimonia; *vi* funzionare.

functional ['fʌnkʃənl] *a* funzionale.

fund [fʌnd] *n* fondo, capitale.

fundamental [,fʌndə'mentl] *a* fondamentale.

funeral ['fjuːnərəl] *a* funebre, funerario; *n* funerale.

funereal [fjuː'niəriəl] *a* funereo, lugubre, funebre.

fungus ['fʌŋgəs] *n* fungo.

funicular [fju'nikjulə] *a n* funicolare.

funk [fʌŋk] *n* (*sl*) panico, timore.

funnel ['fʌnl] *n* imbuto; ciminiera di nave.

funny ['fʌni] *n* buffo, comico, strano.

fur [fəː] *n* pelliccia, pelo; incrostazione.

furbish ['fəːbiʃ] *vt* forbire, lustrare.

furious ['fjuəriəs] *a* furioso, furibondo.

furl [fəːl] *vt* ammainare, chiudere.

furlough ['fəːlou] *n* (*mil etc*) licenza, permesso.

furnace ['fəːnis] *n* fornace; caldaia di termosifone.

furnish ['fəːniʃ] *vt* fornire, rifornire; ammobiliare.

furnishings ['fəːniʃiŋs] *n pl* arredamento.

furniture ['fəːnitʃə] *n* mobilia, mobili *pl.*

furrier ['fʌriə] *n* pellicciaio.

furrow ['fʌrou] *n* solco; ruga; traccia; *vt* solcare.

furry ['fəːri] *a* peloso; di pelliccia; coperto di pelliccia; patinoso.

further ['fəːðə] *a* altro, ulteriore; *ad* oltre, più avanti; *vt* favorire, promuovere.

furthermore ['fəːðə'mɔː] *ad* per di più, inoltre.

furtive ['fəːtiv] *a* furtivo.

fury ['fjuəri] *n* furore, furia.

furze [fəːz] *n* ginestra spinosa.

fuse [fjuːz] *n* spoletta, (*el*) valvola; *vti* fonder(si), far esplodere.

fuselage ['fjuːzilɑːʒ] *n* (*av*) fusoliera.

fusillade [,fjuːzi'leid] *n* scarica di fucili.

fusion ['fjuːʒən] *n* fusione.

fuss ['fʌs] *n* trambusto, scalpore; *vi* agitarsi; far confusione.

fussily ['fʌsili] *ad* con esagerata attenzione; con inutile indaffaramento.

fussy ['fʌsi] *a* brontolone; di difficile contentatura.

fustian ['fʌstiən] *n* fustagno.

fusty ['fʌsti] *a* ammuffito, che sa di muffa.

futile ['fjutail] *a* futile.

future ['fjuːtʃə] *a n* futuro, avvenire.

futurity ['fjuːtuəriti] *n* avvenire.

fuzz [fʌz] *n* lanugine; increspatura di capelli.

fuzzy ['fʌzi] *a* lanuginoso; dai capelli crespi; confuso; (*phot*) sfocato.

G

gabardine ['gæbədiːn] *n* gabardina.

gabble ['gæbl] *n* barbugliamento; *vt* pronunciare in modo inarticolato o confuso; *vi* parlare indistintamente.

gable ['geibl] *n* (*arch*) timpano, frontone; **g. roof** tetto a due spioventi.

Gabriel ['geibriəl] *nm pr* Gabriele.

gad [gæd] *vi* bighellonare; **g. about** *a n* vagabondo.

gadfly ['gædflai] *n* tafano.

gadget ['gædʒit] *n* (*fam*) congegno, aggeggio.

Gaelic ['geilik] *a* gaelico.

gag [gæg] *n* bavaglio; (*sl*) battuta improvvisata; *vt* imbavagliare; *vi* (*sl*) improvvisare battute.

gage [geidʒ] *n* pegno.

gaiety ['geiəti] *n* gaiezza.

gaily ['geili] *ad* gaiamente.

gain [gein] *n* guadagno; *vt* guadagnare; *vi* (*clock*) andare avanti.

gainings ['geiniŋz] *n pl* utili, profitti.

gainsay [gein'sei] *vt* contraddire.

gait [geit] *n* andatura.

gaiter ['geitə] *n* ghetta.

galaxy ['gæləksi] *n* galassia; (*fig*) assemblea brillante.

gale [geil] *n* bufera di vento.

gall [gɔːl] *n* bile, fiele; malignità; *vt*

irritare; scorticare; **gallstone** calcolo biliare.

gallant ['gælənt] *a* intrepido, valoroso; galante; *n* galante, cavaliere.

gallantry ['gæləntri] *n* valore; galanteria.

galleon ['gæliən] *n* (*naut*) galeone.

gallery ['gæləri] *n* galleria; (*theat*) loggione.

galley ['gæli] *n* galea; (*naut*) cambusa.

gallivant [ˌgæli'vænt] *vi* andare a zonzo.

gallon ['gælən] *n* gallone (*misura inglese di capacita = litri* 4,543).

gallop ['gæləp] *n* galoppo; *vti* (far) galoppare.

gallows ['gælouz] *n* *pl* forca, patibolo.

galore [gə'lɔː] *n* abbondanza; *ad* a bizzeffe.

galosh [gə'lɔʃ] *n* galoscia; soprascarpa.

galvanic [gæl'vænik] *a* (*el*) galvanico; (*fig*) galvanizzante.

galvanize ['gælvənaiz] *vt* galvanizzare.

gambit ['gæmbit] *n* (*chess*) gambetto; (*fig*) iniziativa, attacco.

gamble ['gæmbl] *n* gioco d'azzardo; *vti* giocare d'azzardo, speculare rischiosamente.

gambler ['gæmblə] *n* giocatore d'azzardo, speculatore.

gambling ['gæmbliŋ] *n* giochi d'azzardo *pl*, **g. house** bisca.

gambol ['gæmbəl] *n* piroetta, capriola; *vi* piroettare.

game [geim] *n* gioco, partita; caccia, selvaggina.

gamekeeper ['geimˌkiːpə] *n* guardacaccia.

gammon ['gæmən] *n* parte più bassa d'un prosciutto, prosciutto affumicato; (*fig*) inganno.

gamut ['gæmət] *n* gamma, serie completa.

gander ['gændə] *n* papero.

gang [gæŋ] *n* banda; squadra; combriccola.

ganglion ['gæŋgliən] *n* ganglio.

gangrene ['gæŋgriːn] *n* cancrena.

gangster ['gæŋstə] *n* 'gangster', bandito.

gangway ['gæŋwei] *n* corridoio, passaggio; passerella.

gannet ['gænit] *n* gabbiano.

gantry ['gæntri] *n* gru a cavalletto.

gap [gæp] *n* breccia, fenditura; passo di montagna; (*fig*) divergenza; lacuna.

gape [geip] *n* spaccatura; apertura della bocca; sbadiglio; *vi* sbadigliare; spalancare la bocca.

garage ['gærɑːʒ] *n* autorimessa, 'garage'.

garb [gɑːb] *n* abbigliamento

garbage ['gɑːbidʒ] *n* rifiuti *pl*; **g. can** pattumiera.

garble ['gɑːbl] *vt* falsificare (una storia).

garden ['gɑːdn] *n* giardino; *vi* lavorare di giardinaggio.

gardener ['gɑːdnə] *n* giardiniere.

gardening ['gɑːdniŋ] *n* giardinaggio.

gargle ['gɑːgl] *n* gargarismo; *vi* fare gargarismi.

gargoyle ['gɑːgɔil] *n* gargolla; figura grottesca.

garish ['geəriʃ] *a* abbagliante, sgargiante.

garland ['gɑːlənd] *n* ghirlanda.

garlic ['gɑːlik] *n* aglio.

garment ['gɑːmənt] *n* articolo di vestiario, indumento.

garnish ['gɑːniʃ] *n* (*cook*) guarnizione, contorno; *vt* guarnire, ornare.

garret ['gærət] *n* abbaino, soffitta.

garrison ['gærisn] *n* guarnigione; *vt* fornire di guarnigione.

garrulity [gæ'ruːliti] *n* loquacità.

garrulous ['gæruləs] *a* garrulo, loquace.

garter ['gɑːtə] *n* giarrettiera.

gas [gæs] *pl* **gases** *n* gas; **g. cooker** cucina a gas, fornello a gas; **g. meter** contatore del gas; **g. stove** cucina a gas.

gash [gæʃ] *n* squarcio; *vt* fare uno squarcio.

gasoline ['gæsəliːn] benzina.

gasp [gɑːsp] *n* respiro affannoso, rantolo; sussulto; *vti* boccheggiare, ansare; soffocare un'esclamazione.

gassy ['gæsi] *a* gassoso.

gastric ['gæstrik] *a* gastrico.

gastritis [gæs'traitis] *n* gastrite.

gastronomical [ˌgæstrə'nɔmikəl] *n* gastronomico.

gastronomy [gæs'trɔnəmi] *n* gastronomia.

gate [geit] *n* cancello, (*of town*) porta.

gateway ['geitwei] *n* portone, entrata.

gather ['gæðə] *vt* (rac)cogliere, radunare; fare le pieghe; *vi* radunarsi; (*med*) venire a suppurazione.

gathering ['gæðəriŋ] *n* adunata, assemblea; (*med*) ascesso.

gaudy ['gɔːdi] *a* sfarzoso e di cattivo gusto.

gauge [geidʒ] *n* apparecchio misuratore, misura base, stima; *vt* misurare con esattezza; (*fig*) formarsi un concetto di.

gauger ['geidʒə] *n* collaudatore.

gaunt [gɔːnt] *a* macilento, sparuto.

gauntlet ['gɔːntlit] *n* grosso guanto che copre il polso, guanto di armatura.

gauntness ['gɔːntnis] *n* macilenza.

gauze [gɔːz] *n* garza, velo.

gawky ['gɔːki] *a* goffo, sguaiato, balordo.

gay [gei] *a* allegro, gaio; vistoso; brillante; (*fig*) dissoluto.

gaze [geiz] *n* sguardo fisso; *vi* guardare fisso.

gazelle [gə'zel] *n* gazzella.

gazette [gə'zet] *n* gazzetta.

gazetteer [ˌgæzi'tiə] *n* dizionario geografico.
gear [giə] *n* equipaggiamento, congegno, ingranaggio, meccanismo, (*aut*) marcia; **in g.** in marcia.
gelatin(e) ['dʒelətiːn] *n* gelatina.
geld [geld] *vt* castrare.
gelding ['geldiŋ] *n* cavallo castrato.
gelignite ['dʒelignait] *n* (*chem*) nitroglicerina.
gem [dʒem] *n* gemma, gioiello.
gender ['dʒendə] *n* genere; sesso.
genealogical [ˌdʒiːniə'lɔdʒikəl] *a* genealogico.
genealogy [ˌdʒiːni'ælədʒi] *n* genealogia.
general ['dʒenərəl] *a n* generale.
generality [ˌdʒenə'ræliti] *n* generalità, maggioranza.
generalization [ˌdʒenərəlai'zeiʃən] *n* generalizzazione.
generalize ['dʒenərəlaiz] *vti* generalizzare.
generally ['dʒenərəli] *ad* generalmente, di solito.
generate ['dʒenəreit] *vt* generare.
generation [ˌdʒenə'reiʃən] *n* generazione.
generative ['dʒenərətiv] *a* generativo, produttivo.
generator ['dʒenəreitə] *n* generatore, (*aut*) dinamo, generatore.
generosity [ˌdʒenə'rɔsiti] *n* generosità.
generous ['dʒenərəs] *a* generoso.
generously ['dʒenərəsli] *ad* generosamente.
genetic [dʒi'netik] *a* genetico.
Geneva [dʒi'niːvə] *n* Ginevra.
Genevieve [ˌdʒenə'viːv] *nf pr* Genoveffa.
genial ['dʒiːniəl] *a* amabile, piacevole; (*climate*) mite.
geniality [ˌdʒiːni'æliti] *n* amabilità, giovialità.
genital ['dʒenitl] *a* genitale.
genitals ['dʒenitlz] *n pl* organi genitali.
genitive ['dʒenitiv] *a n* genitivo.
genius ['dʒiːniəs] *n* genio, talento.
Genoa ['dʒenouə] *n* Genova; **Genoese** *a n* genovese.
genocide ['dʒenousaid] *n* genocidio.
genteel [dʒen'tiːl] *a* (*ironic*) compito, manieroso.
gentle ['dʒentl] *a* dolce, mite; nobile.
gentlefolk ['dʒentlfouk] *n* gente che appartiene alle classi elevate.
gentleman ['dʒentlmən] *n* gentiluomo, signore.
gentlemanly ['dʒentlmənli] *a* da gentiluomo, signorile.
gentleness ['dʒentlnis] *n* dolcezza, tenerezza, grazia.
gentlewoman ['dʒentlˌwumən] *n* gentildonna, signora.
gently ['dʒentli] *ad* con delicatezza, dolcemente.
gentry ['dʒentri] *n* piccola nobiltà.
genuine ['dʒenjuin] *a* genuino.

genuineness ['dʒenjuinis] *n* genuinità.
geodesy [dʒiː'ɔdisi] *n* geodesia.
Geoffrey ['dʒefri] *nm pr* Goffredo.
geographic(al) [dʒiə'græfik(əl)] *a* geografico.
geography [dʒi'ɔgrəfi] *n* geografia.
geology [dʒi'ɔlədʒi] *n* geologia.
geometric [dʒiə'metrik] *a* geometrico.
geometry [dʒi'ɔmitri] *n* geometria.
George [dʒɔːdʒ] *nm pr* Giorgio.
Georgian ['dʒɔːdʒiən] *a n* georgiano, georgiana.
geranium [dʒi'reiniəm] *n* geranio.
geriatric [ˌdʒeri'ætrik] *a* geriatrico.
geriatrics [ˌdʒeri'ætriks] *n* geriatria.
germ [dʒəːm] *n* germe.
German ['dʒəːmən] *a n* tedesco.
Germany ['dʒəːməni] *n* Germania.
germinate ['dʒəːmineit] *vi* germinare.
germination [ˌdʒəːmi'neiʃən] *n* germinazione.
Gertrude ['gəːtruːd] *nf pr* Gertrude.
gestation [dʒes'teiʃən] *n* gestazione.
gesticulate [dʒes'tikjuleit] *vi* gesticolare.
gesticulation [dʒesˌtikju'leiʃən] *n* il gesticolare.
gesture ['dʒestʃə] *n* gesto; *vi* gestire.
get [get] *vt* ottenere, ricevere, guadagnare, prendere, portare, persuadere; *vi* arrivare, raggiungere, divenire.
gewgaw ['gjuːgɔː] *n* ninnolo.
geyser ['giːzə] *n* sorgente calda; apparecchio scaldabagno.
ghastly ['gɑːstli] *a* spaventoso, spettrale.
gherkin ['gəːkin] *n* cetriolino.
ghetto ['getou] *pl* **ghettos** *n* ghetto.
ghost [goust] *n* spirito, fantasma; **The Holy G.** lo Spirito Santo.
ghostly ['goustli] *a* spettrale.
ghoul [guːl] *n* spirito maligno che divora i cadaveri; (*fig*) persona orribile e crudele.
ghoulish ['guːliʃ] *a* demoniaco, macabro.
giant ['dʒaiənt] *a n* gigante; **giantess** *n* gigantessa.
gibber ['dʒibə] *vi* parlare rapidamente e senza senso.
gibberish ['gibəriʃ] *n* parole senza senso.
gibbet ['dʒibit] *n* forca, patibolo.
gibe [dʒaib] *n* beffa, scherno; *vti* beffar(si), schernire.
giblets ['dʒiblits] *n pl* rigaglie *pl*.
Gibraltar [dʒi'brɔːltə] *n* Gibilterra.
giddiness ['gidinis] *n* vertigine; incostanza.
giddy ['gidi] *a* in preda a vertigini, incostante.
gift [gift] *n* dono, regalo, donazione.
gig [gig] *n* calessino; (*naut*) lancia.
gigantic [dʒai'gæntik] *a* gigantesco.

giggle ['gigl] *n* risatina sciocca; *vi* ridere scioccamente.
gigue [ʒiːg] *n* (*mus*) giga.
gild [gild] *vt* (in)dorare.
gilding ['gildiŋ] *n* doratura.
Giles [dʒailz] *nm pr* Egidio.
gill [gil] *n* misura di capacità liquida (*litri* ,0142).
gilt [gilt] *a* dorato; *n* doratura.
gimcrack ['dʒimkræk] *a* appariscente e di nessun valore; *n* cianfrusaglia.
gimlet ['gimlit] *n* succhiello.
gin [dʒin] *n* gin; trappola.
ginger ['dʒindʒə] *n* zenzero; **gingerbread** pan di zenzero.
gingerly ['dʒindʒəli] *a* guardingo; *ad* con precauzione.
gingham ['giŋəm] *n* percalle a righe o quadretti, rigatino.
gipsy, gypsy ['dʒipsi] *n* zingaro, zingara; *a* zingaresco.
giraffe [dʒi'rɑːf] *n* giraffa.
gird [gəːd] *vt* cingere, circondare; *vi* beffare.
girder ['gəːdə] *n* (*mech*) trave maestra, putrella.
girdle ['gəːdl] *n* cintura; cerchia; busto; *vt* recingere; chiudere con una cintura.
girl [gəːl] *n* ragazza, fanciulla.
girlhood ['gəːlhud] *n* adolescenza (di ragazza).
girlish ['gəːliʃ] *a* di (da) ragazza.
girth [gəːθ] *n* circonferenza; sottopancia; *vt* cingere.
gist [dʒist] *n* punto essenziale, sostanza.
give [giv] *vti* dare, cedere; **g. and take** *n* compromesso, concessione reciproca.
gizzard ['gizəd] *n* (*of birds*) ventriglio.
glacial ['gleisiəl] *a* glaciale.
glacier ['glæsiə] *n* ghiacciaio.
glad [glæd] *a* contento, lieto.
glade [gleid] *n* radura.
gladiator ['glædieitə] *n* gladiatore.
gladiolus [,glædi'ouləs] *pl* **gladioli** *n* gladiolo.
gladly ['glædli] *ad* con piacere, volentieri.
gladness ['glædnis] *n* contentezza.
glamor ['glæmə] *n* fascino, magia.
glamorous ['glæmərəs] *a* affascinante.
glance [glɑːns] *n* occhiata, sguardo; *vi* dare un'occhiata, gettare uno sguardo.
glancing ['glɑːnsiŋ] *a* fugace, rapido.
gland [glænd] *n* glandola.
glanders ['glændəz] *n pl* cimurro.
glandular ['glændjulə] *a* glandolare.
glare [glɛə] *n* bagliore, luce abbagliante; sguardo furibondo; *vi* risplendere di luce abbagliante; guardare con rabbia.
glaring ['glɛəriŋ] *a* abbagliante; manifesto.
glass [glɑːs] *n* vetro, vetri *pl*; bic-

chiere; cristallo; telescopio; **glasses** *pl* occhiali *pl*.
glassy ['glɑːsi] *a* vitreo.
Glaswegian [glæs'wiːdʒən] *a n* abitante di Glasgow.
glaze [gleiz] *n* smalto, vernice; *vt* fornire di vetri; smaltare, verniciare.
glazier ['gleiziə] *n* vetraio.
gleam [gliːm] *n* barlume, debole raggio di luce; *vi* luccicare, baluginare.
glean [gliːn] *vti* spigolare, raccogliere.
gleaning ['gliːniŋ] *n* spigolatura.
glebe [gliːb] *n* gleba.
glee [gliː] *n* giubilo; (*mus*) canone.
glen [glen] *n* valletta.
glib [glib] *a* liscio, scorrevole, pronto.
glide [glaid] *vi* scivolare, trascorrere.
glider ['glaidə] *n* (*av*) aliante; (*naut*) idroplano.
gliding ['glaidiŋ] *a* scorrevole, (*av*) che plana; *n* (*av*) volo a vela.
glimmer ['glimə] *n* luce debole e incerta; *vi* mandare una luce fioca.
glimpse [glimps] *n* rapida visione; *vt* intravvedere.
glint [glint] *n* luccichio; *vi* luccicare.
glisten ['glisn] *n* scintillio, luccichio; *vi* scintillare, luccicare.
glitter ['glitə] *n* scintillio; *vi* scintillare.
glittering ['glitəriŋ] *a* scintillante, brillante; *n* scintillio.
gloaming ['gloumiŋ] *n* crepuscolo.
gloat [glout] *vi* guardare con gioia perversa, gongolare.
globe [gloub] *n* globo.
gloom [gluːm] *n* tenebre *pl*, tristezza.
gloomy ['gluːmi] *a* fosco, tetro, triste.
glorification [,glɔːrifi'keiʃən] *n* glorificazione.
glorify ['glɔːrifai] *vt* glorificare.
glorious ['glɔːriəs] *a* glorioso, magnifico.
gloriously ['glɔːriəsli] *ad* gloriosamente, splendidamente.
glory ['glɔːri] *n* gloria, splendore; *vi* esultare, gloriarsi.
gloss [glɔs] *n* chiosa, glossa; lucentezza; (*fig*) vernice; *vt* lucidare; chiosare.
glossary ['glɔsəri] *n* glossario.
glossy ['glɔsi] *a* lucido, lucente.
glove [glʌv] *n* guanto.
glow [glou] *n* incandescenza, calore; ardore; *vi* rosseggiare; essere incandescente; ardere.
glow-worm ['glouwəːm] *n* lucciola.
glower ['glauə] *vi* guardare con cipiglio.
glucose ['gluːkous] *n* (*chem*) glucosio.
glue [gluː] *n* colla; *vt* incollare.
glum [glʌm] *a* accigliato, taciturno.
glut [glʌt] *n* sovrabbondanza, sazietà.
glutinous ['gluːtinəs] *a* gluttinoso.
glutton ['glʌtn] *n* ghiottone.
gluttonous ['glʌtənəs] *a* ghiotto, goloso.

gluttony ['glʌtni] n golosità, ingordigia.

glycerine ['glisəriːn] n glicerina.

gnarled [naːld] a nodoso, nocchieruto, pieno di nodi.

gnash [næʃ] vt digrignare (i denti).

gnat [næt] n moscerino.

gnaw [nɔː] vt rodere, rosicchiare.

gnome [noum] n gnomo.

go [gou] vi andare, farsi; **g.-ahead** a (fam) intraprendente; n segnale di passare all'azione; **g.-between** intermediario; **g.-getter** (fam) arrivista.

goad [goud] n pungolo, stimolo; vt mandar avanti col pungolo, stimolare.

goal [goul] n meta, traguardo; (football) porta, rete; "gol."

goat [gout] n capra; **g.-herd** capraio.

gobble ['gɔbl] vt ingoiare a grossi bocconi.

goblet ['gɔblit] n calice, coppa.

goblin ['gɔblin] n folletto, spirito maligno.

god [gɔd] n dio, divinità; idolo.

godchild ['gɔdtʃaild] n figlioccio.

goddess ['gɔdis] n dea.

godfather ['gɔd,faːðə] n padrino.

godhead ['gɔdhed] n divinità.

godless ['gɔdlis] a ateo, empio.

godlessness ['gɔdlisnis] n ateismo; empietà.

godliness ['gɔdlinis] n devozione, religiosità.

godly ['gɔdli] a devoto, religioso.

godmother ['gɔd,mʌðə] n madrina.

godsend ['gɔdsend] n dono del cielo, fortuna inaspettata.

godson ['gɔdsʌn] n figlioccio.

goggle ['gɔgl] vi stralunare (gli occhi).

goggles ['gɔglz] n pl occhiali di protezione; (sl) occhialoni.

going ['gouiŋ] n partenza; l'andare; andamento; a ben avviato.

goiter ['gɔitə] n gozzo.

gold [gould] a aureo, d'oro; n oro, danaro.

golden ['gouldən] a aureo, d'oro, dorato.

goldfinch ['gouldfintʃ] n cardellino.

goldfish ['gouldfiʃ] n pesce rosso.

goldsmith ['gouldsmiθ] n orefice.

golosh [gə'lɔʃ] v galosh.

gondolier [,gɔndə'liə] n gondoliere.

gong [gɔŋ] n gong.

good [gud] a buono; n bene; **g. day** buon giorno; **g. night** buona sera, buona notte.

good-bye ['gud'bai] interj addio, arrivederci.

good-for-nothing ['gudfə,nʌθiŋ] a inutile; n buono a nulla.

goodly ['gudli] a bello, buono; considerevole.

good-natured ['gud'neitʃəd] a di buon carattere.

goodness ['gudnis] n bontà, generosità.

goods ['gudz] n pl beni pl, effetti pl, merci pl.

goodwill ['gud'wil] n buona volontà, benevolenza, favore.

goose [guːs] pl geese n oca; **g. flesh** pelle d'oca.

gooseberry ['guzbəri] n uva spina.

gorge ['gɔːdʒ] n strozza; vt ingozzare; vi rimpinzarsi; gola di montagna.

gorgeous ['gɔːdʒəs] a magnifico, sontuoso, sgargiante.

gorilla [gə'rilə] n gorilla.

gorse [gɔːs] n ginestra spinosa.

gory ['gɔːri] a insanguinato.

gosling ['gɔzliŋ] n paperetto.

gospel ['gɔspəl] n vangelo.

gossamer ['gɔsəmə] n sottile filo di ragnatela, velo finissimo.

gossip ['gɔsip] n chiacchiera, pettegolezzo; individuo pettegolo; vi pettegolare.

Gothic ['gɔθik] a gotico.

gouache [gu'aːʃ] n guazzo.

gourd [guəd] n zucca.

gourmet ['guəmei] n buongustaio, conoscitore.

gout [gaut] n gotta.

gouty ['gauti] a gottoso.

govern ['gʌvən] vti governare.

governable ['gʌvənəbl] a docile.

governess ['gʌvənis] n istitutrice.

governing ['gʌvəniŋ] a governante, dirigente.

government ['gʌvənmənt] n governo.

governor ['gʌvənə] n governatore; (sl) padrone, capo, padre.

gown [gaun] n veste, vestito, toga; dressing g. veste da camera, vestaglia.

grab [græb] vt afferrare, impadronirsi con la violenza di.

grabble ['græbl] vi andare a tastoni.

grace [greis] n grazia, favore; vt adornare, favorire.

Grace [greis] nf pr Grazia.

graceful ['greisful] a aggraziato, grazioso.

gracefulness ['greisfulnis] n grazia.

gracious ['greiʃəs] a condiscendente, grazioso.

gradation [gre'deiʃən] n gradazione.

grade [greid] n grado; pendenza; classe; classificazione; vt classificare, graduare; **g. crossing** passaggio a livello.

gradient ['greidiənt] n pendenza, gradiente.

gradual ['grædjuəl] a n graduale.

gradually ['grædjuəli] ad gradualmente, gradatamente; a poco a poco.

graduate ['grædjuit] n laureato; diplomato; ['gradjueit] vt graduare; vi laurearsi.

graduation [,grædju'eiʃən] n laurea, licenza, diploma; graduazione.

graft [graːft] n innesto; vt innestare.

grain [grein] n grano; grana; venatura.

gram [græm] *n* grammo.
grammar ['græmə] *n* grammatica.
grammarian [grə'mɛəriən] *n* grammatico.
grammatical [grə'mætikəl] *a* grammaticale.
gramophone ['græməfoun] *n* grammofono.
granary ['grænəri] *n* granaio.
grand [grænd] *a* grande, grandioso, imponente, maestoso, principale.
grandchild ['græntʃaild] *pl* **grandchildren** *n* nipote, nipotino, nipotina.
granddaughter ['græn,dɔːtə] *n* nipote, nipotina.
grandeur ['grændʒə] *n* magnificenza, splendore.
grandfather ['grænd,fɑːθə] *n* nonno.
grandiose ['grændious] *a* grandioso, pomposo.
grandmother ['græn,mʌðə] *n* nonna.
grandparent ['græn,pɛərənt] *n* nonno, nonna.
grandson ['grænsʌn] *n* nipote, nipotino.
grandstand ['grænstænd] *n* tribuna d'onore.
grange [greindʒ] *n* fattoria, casa signorile di campagna.
granite ['grænit] *n* granito.
grant [grɑːnt] *n* concessione, borsa di studio, donazione; *vt* ammettere, concedere.
grape [greip] *n* (acino d') uva; (*mil*) carica di mitraglia; **grapefruit** pompelmo.
graph [grɑːf] *n* grafico.
graphic ['græfik] *a* grafico.
graphite ['græfait] *n* grafite.
grapnel ['græpnəl] *n* ancoretta, uncino.
grapple ['græpl] *n* ancoretta, rampone; lotta corpo a corpo; *vt* assicurare con l'ancoretta; *vi* venire alle prese; lottare.
grasp [grɑːsp] *n* presa, stretta; comprensione; *vt* afferrare.
grasping ['grɑːspiŋ] *a* avaro, avido.
grass [grɑːs] *n* erba.
grasshopper ['grɑːs,hɔpə] *n* grillo, saltamartino; (*av mil*) apparecchio di collegamento.
grassy ['grɑːsi] *a* erboso.
grate [greit] *n* grata, griglia, inferriata; *vt* munire di grata; grattugiare; *vi* stridere; irritare.
grateful ['greitful] *a* grato, riconoscente.
grater ['greitə] *n* grattugia.
gratification [,grætifi'keiʃən] *n* gratificazione, soddisfazione.
gratify ['grætifai] *vt* gratificare.
grating ['greitiŋ] *a* irritante; stridente; *n* grata, inferriata.
gratitude ['grætitjuːd] *n* gratitudine, riconoscenza.
gratuitous [grə'tjuːitəs] *a* gratuito, ingiustificato.

gratuity [grə'tjuːiti] *n* gratifica, mancia.
grave [greiv] *a* austero, grave, serio; *n* tomba.
gravel ['grævəl] *n* ghiaia; *vt* ricoprire di ghiaia; (*fig*) imbarazzare.
graveyard ['greivjɑːd] *n* camposanto, cimitero.
gravitate ['græviteit] *vi* gravitare.
gravitation [,grævi'teiʃən] *n* gravitazione.
gravity ['græviti] *n* gravità.
gravy ['greivi] *n* sugo di carne, salsa.
gray [grei] *a n* grigio.
grayness ['greinis] *n* grigiore.
graze [greiz] *n* abrasione; *vt* escoriare, scalfire, sfiorare; *vt* pascere, pascolare.
grazing ['greiziŋ] *n* pascolo, pastura.
grease [griːs] *n* grasso, unto; materia lubrificante; *vt* lubrificare, ungere.
greasy ['griːzi] *a* grasso, unto, untuoso.
great [greit] *a* grande, nobile.
Great Britain ['greit'britn] *n* Gran Bretagna.
greatly ['greitli] *ad* grandemente, molto.
greatness ['greitnis] *n* grandezza.
Greece [griːs] *n* Grecia.
greed [griːd] *n* bramosia, cupidigia.
greedily ['griːdili] *ad* avidamente, golosamente.
greediness ['griːdinis] *n* avidità, golosità.
greedy ['griːdi] *a* ghiotto, goloso, avido.
Greek [griːk] *a n* greco.
green [griːn] *a* verde; *n* verde, verzura; **greens** *pl* erbaggi *pl*, verdura.
greenery ['griːnəri] *n* verdura.
greenfinch ['griːnfintʃ] *n* verdone.
greengage ['griːngeidʒ] *n* susina claudia.
greengrocer ['griːn,grousə] *n* erbivendolo, ortolano.
greenhouse ['griːnhaus] *n* serra.
Greenland ['griːnlənd] *n* Groenlandia.
Greenlander ['griːnləndə] *n* groenlandese.
greenness ['griːnnis] *n* color verde; (*fig*) immaturità, inesperienza.
greet [griːt] *vt* salutare (all'arrivo).
greeting ['griːtiŋ] *n* saluto.
Gregory ['gregəri] *nm pr* Gregorio.
grenade [gre'neid] *n* (*mil*) granata.
grenadier [,grenə'diə] *n* granatiere.
grey [grei] *v* **gray.**
greyhound ['greihaund] *n* levriero.
grid [grid] *n* grata, griglia; (*map*) quadrettatura.
grief [griːf] *n* afflizione, dolore.
grievance ['griːvəns] *n* lagnanza; torto.
grieve [griːv] *vti* addolorar(si), affligger(si).
grievous ['griːvəs] *a* doloroso, penoso, grave, serio.

grill [gril] n (vivanda alla) griglia; vt arrostire alla griglia; sottoporre ad un severo interrogatorio; vi esser tormentato (dal caldo).

grim [grim] a fosco, torvo, severo.

grimace [gri'meis] n smorfia.

grime [graim] n sudiciume.

grimy ['graimi] a sudicio.

grin [grin] n sogghigno, largo sorriso; vi sogghignare.

grind [graind] n lavoro faticoso e ingrato; vt arrotare, macinare; (fig) opprimere; vi sgobbare.

grinder ['graində] n arrotino; macina, dente molare.

grindstone ['graindstoun] n macina, mola.

grip [grip] n presa, stretta; controllo; impugnatura; capacità di fermare l'attenzione; vi afferrare, tenere fermo.

gripe [graip] vt afferrare; causare dolori al ventre.

grisly ['grizli] a orribile, spaventoso.

grist [grist] n grano da macinare, malto preparato per la fabbricazione della birra.

gristle ['grisl] n cartilagine.

grit [grit] n sabbia, grana; (fam) forza di carattere.

grizzled ['grizld] a brizzolato.

groan [groun] n gemito, lamento; vi gemere, lamentarsi.

grocer ['grousə] n droghiere.

grocery ['grousəril n (generi di) drogheria, (negozio, generi di) drogheria.

grog [grɔg] n (fam) bevanda alcoolica calda, 'grog'.

groggy ['grɔgi] a brillo; barcollante; vacillante; malfermo.

groin [grɔin] n inguine.

groom [grum] n stalliere; palafreniere; vt strigliare.

groove [gru:v] n scanalatura, solco; vt scanalare, solcare.

grope [group] vi andare tentoni, brancolare.

groping(ly) ['groupiŋ(li)] ad (a) tentoni.

gross [grous] a grossolano, volgare, (com) lordo, complessivo; n grossa.

grossness ['grousnis] n grossolanità, volgarità.

grotesque [grou'tesk] a n grottesco; **grotesqueness** n bizzarria, grottesco.

grotto ['grɔtou] pl **grottos, grottoes** n grotta.

ground [graund] n terra, terreno, suolo; base; motivo; sfondo; vt basare, fondare; istruire bene; vi incagliarsi; **grounds** pl deposito, fondi pl; (of mansion) parco, giardini pl; g. **floor** pianterreno; g. **wire** (rad) filo di terra.

grounding ['graundiŋ] n base, conoscenza.

groundless ['graundlis] a infondato.

group [gru:p] n gruppo; vti raggruppar(si).

grouse [graus] n gallo di montagna; vi (fam) brontolare.

grove [grouv] n boschetto.

grovel ['grɔvl] vi strisciare a terra, umiliarsi.

grow [grou] vi crescere, aumentare, svilupparsi, divenire; vt coltivare.

grower ['grouə] n coltivatore.

growl [graul] n borbottio rabbioso; vi brontolare, borbottare irosamente.

grown-up ['grounʌp] a n adulto.

growth [grouθ] n crescita, sviluppo, progresso; (med) escrescenza morbosa, tumore.

grub [grʌb] n larva, bruco; (sl) cibo; vt zappare, sgobbare.

grubby ['grʌbi] a sporco, verminoso.

grudge [grʌdʒ] n astio, rancore; vt lesinare;, invidiare.

grudgingly ['grʌdʒiŋli] ad a malincuore, malvolentieri.

gruel ['gruəl] n pappa d'avena; to give s.o. his g. darne un fracco a qlcu.

grueling ['gruəliŋ] a estenuante.

gruesome ['gru:səm] a orribile, orripilante.

gruff [grʌf] a burbero, sgarbato.

gruffness ['grʌfnis] n burbanza.

grumble ['grʌmbl] vi borbottare, brontolare.

grumpy ['grʌmpi] a (fam) irritabile, bisbetico.

grunt [grʌnt] n grugnito, brontolio; vti grugnire, brontolare.

guarantee [ˌgærən'ti:] n garanzia, garante; vt garantire, essere garante per.

guarantor [ˌgærən'tɔ:] n garante; (com) avallante.

guard [gɑ:d] n guardia; (rly) capotreno; vt custodire, proteggere, sorvegliare.

guarded ['gɑ:did] a prudente, guardingo, cauto.

guardedly ['gɑ:didli] ad in modo guardingo, con circospezione.

guardian ['gɑ:diən] n guardiano, tutore; **guardianship** protezione, tutela.

guerrilla [gə'rilə] pl **guerrillas** n guerriglia; guerrigliere.

guess [ges] n congettura, supposizione; vti congetturare, indovinare, supporre.

guest [gest] n ospite.

guffaw [gʌ'fɔ:] n risata fragorosa.

guidance ['gaidəns] n guida, direzione.

guide [gaid] n guida, cicerone; vt guidare, dirigere.

guild [gild] n corporazione.

guile [gail] n artificio, astuzia, inganno.

guileless ['gaillis] a semplice, ingenuo.

guillotine [ˌgilə'ti:n] n ghigliottina; vt ghigliottinare.

guilt [gilt] n colpa, colpevolezza.

guiltless ['giltlis] *a* innocente.
guilty ['gilti] *a* colpevole.
Guinea ['gini] *n* Guinea.
guinea ['gini] *n* ghinea (*moneta inglese antica, che valeva ventun scellini*).
guinea-pig ['ginipig] *n* porcellino d'india, cavia.
guise [gaiz] *n* apparenza, foggia, guisa.
guitar [gi'tɑ:] *n* chitarra.
gulf [gʌlf] *n* golfo; abisso; vortice.
gull [gʌl] *n* gabbiano; *vt* gabbare, ingannare.
gullet ['gʌlit] *n* gola, esofago.
gully ['gʌli] *n* burrone.
gulp [gʌlp] *n* atto dell'inghiottire, quantità inghiottita in una volta; *vt* inghiottire voracemente, trangugiare.
gum [gʌm] *n* gomma; gengiva; *vt* ingommare.
gun [gʌn] *n* cannone, fucile, arma da sparo; **gunfire** sparatoria, cannoneggiamento; **gunman** (*sl*) rapinatore.
gunboat ['gʌnbout] *n* (*naut*) cannoniera.
gunner ['gʌnə] *n* artigliere.
gunpowder ['gʌn,paudə] *n* polvere da sparo.
gunshot ['gʌnʃɔt] *n* colpo di arma da fuoco.
gunsmith ['gʌnsmiθ] *n* armaiolo.
gurgle ['gəːgl] *n* gorgoglio; *vi* gorgogliare.
gush [gʌʃ] *n* fiotto, zampillo; effusione sentimentale; *vti* sgorgare in gran copia, zampillare; fare esagerate effusioni.
gushing ['gʌʃiŋ] *a* zampillante; espansivo.
gust ['gʌst] *n* (*of wind, rain*) raffica, (*of wind*) colpo; (*of rage*) scoppio.
gusto ['gʌstou] *n* entusiasmo, piacere.
gusty ['gʌsti] *a* burrascoso.
gut [gʌt] *n* budello, intestino; *vt* sbudellare, sventrare.
gutter ['gʌtə] *n* grondaia, cunetta.
guttural ['gʌtərəl] *a* gutturale.
Guy [gai] *nm pr* Guido.
guy [gai] *n* (*mech*) cavo; figura grottesca, spauracchio; individuo.
guzzle ['gʌzl] *vti* mangiare o bere a crepapelle.
gymnasium [dʒim'neiziəm] *n* palestra.
gymnast ['dʒimnæst] *n* ginnasta.
gymnastics [dʒim'næstiks] *n pl* ginnastica.
gypsy ['dʒipsi] *v* gipsy.
gyrate [,dʒaiə'reit] *vi* girare, turbinare.

H

haberdasher ['hæbədæʃə] *n* merciaio.

haberdashery ['hæbədæʃəri] *n* merceria.
habit ['hæbit] *n* abitudine; abito.
habitable ['hæbitəbl] *a* abitabile.
habitation [,hæbi'teiʃən] *n* abitazione.
habitual [hə'bitjuəl] *a* abituale.
hack ['hæk] *n* intaccatura, taglio; cavallo da nolo; individuo sfruttato in un lavoro gravoso; *vt* colpire con arma da taglio; tagliuzzare; *vi* tossire a colpi secchi.
hackney ['hækni] *n* h. **cab** vettura da nolo; **hackneyed** *a* banale.
haddock ['hædək] *n* specie di merluzzo.
haft [hɑ:ft] *n* elsa, manico.
hag [hæg] *n* megera, strega.
haggard ['hægəd] *a* magro, sparuto; **haggardness** sparutezza, pallore, magrezza.
haggle ['hægl] *vi* disputare, lesinare sul prezzo, contrattare.
Hague (the) [ðə'heig] *n* l'Aja.
hail [heil] *n* grandine; saluto; *vi* grandinare; *vt* chiamare a gran voce.
hair [hɛə] *n* capello, capelli *pl*; pelo; **h.'s breadth** spessore di un capello, distanza minima; **haircut** taglio di capelli; **hairline** corda di crine; **hairpin** forcina.
hairdresser ['hɛə,dresə] *n* parrucchiere, parrucchiera.
hairless ['hɛəlis] *a* calvo, senza peli.
hairy ['hɛəri] *a* peloso, irsuto.
halcyon ['hælsiən] *a* calmo; *n* alcione.
hale [heil] *a* robusto, sano, vigoroso.
half [hɑ:f] *pl* **halves** *a* mezzo; *n* metà, mezzo; *ad* a metà, (a) mezzo; **half-brother** fratellastro; **half-hour** mezz'ora; **half-pay** mezzo stipendio; **half-way** a mezza strada; **half-witted** corto d'intelletto; **half-yearly** semestrale, due volte all'anno.
halfpenny ['heipni] *pl* **halfpennies, halfpence** *n* mezzo penny.
halibut ['hælibət] *n* (*fish*) passera.
hall [hɔ:l] *n* aula, salone, sala di ricevimento; vestibolo.
hallo(a)! [hə'lou] *interj* salve!; (*tel*) pronto!
hallow ['hælou] *vt* consacrare; **hallowed** *a* santo, benedetto.
hallucination [hə,luːsi'neiʃən] *a* allucinazione.
halo ['heilou] *pl* **halos, haloes** *n* alone, aureola.
halt [hɔ:lt] *n* sosta, fermata; *vi* fare una sosta, fermarsi; esitare; zoppicare.
halter ['hɔːltə] *n* capestro; cavezza.
halve [hɑːv] *vt* dimezzare.
ham [hæm] *n* prosciutto; coscia.
Hamburg ['hæmbəːg] *n* Amburgo.
hamburger ['hæmbəːgə] *n* polpetta di carne e cipolla tritata; panino imbottito di tale polpetta.
hamlet ['hæmlit] *n* piccolo villaggio.
hammer ['hæmə] *n* martello; (*gun*)

cane; *vt* martellare; (*fam*) ficcare in testa; battere.

hammering ['hæmərɪŋ] *a* martellamento, battuta.

hammock ['hæmək] *n* amaca.

hamper ['hæmpə] *n* cesta; (*naut*) accessori ingombranti; *vt* impedire, ostacolare.

hamster ['hæmstə] *n* criceto.

hand [hænd] *n* mano; (*of clocks etc*) lancetta; calligrafia; (*cards*) mano; (*worker*) operaio; *vt* consegnare, porgere.

handbag ['hændbæg] *n* borsetta.

handbill ['hændbil] *n* volantino.

handbook ['hændbuk] *n* manuale.

handcuff ['hændkʌf] *n usu pl* manette *pl*; *vt* mettere le manette a.

handful ['hændful] *n* manata, pugno; (*fam*) persona, cosa difficile da trattarsi.

handicap ['hændikæp] *n* ostacolo; (*sport*) 'handicap', corsa pareggiata.

handicraft ['hændikrɑːft] *n* arte, lavoro dell'artigiano.

handiwork ['hændiwəːk] *n* lavoro (a mano).

handkerchief ['hæŋkətʃif] *n* fazzoletto.

handle ['hændl] *n* manico; maniglia; (*fig*) occasione; *vt* maneggiare, manipolare.

handlebar ['hændlbɑː] *n* manubrio di bicicletta.

handshake ['hændʃeik] *n* stretta di mano.

handsome ['hænsəm] *a* bello, ben proporzionato; generoso.

handwriting ['hænd,raitiŋ] *n* calligrafia, scrittura.

handy ['hændi] *a* abile, destro; a portata di mano.

hang [hæŋ] *vt* appendere, attaccare, impiccare; *vi* dipendere, pendere.

hangar ['hæŋə] *a* aviorimessa, 'hangar'.

hangman ['hæŋmən] *pl* -men *n* boia, carnefice.

hank [hæŋk] *n* matassa; (*naut*) anello della randa.

hanker ['hæŋkə] *vi* bramare.

haphazard ['hæp'hæzəd] *n* puro caso; *ad* a caso.

hapless ['hæplis] *a* sfortunato.

happen ['hæpən] *vi* accadere, avvenire, capitare, succedere.

happening ['hæpəniŋ] *n* avvenimento.

happily ['hæpili] *ad* felicemente, fortunatamente.

happiness ['hæpinis] *n* felicità.

happy ['hæpi] *a* felice, propizio.

harangue [hə'ræŋ] *n* arringa; *vt* arringare.

harass ['hærəs] *vt* seccare, tormentare.

harbinger ['hɑːbindʒə] *n* messaggero; precursore.

harbor ['hɑːbə] *n* porto, rifugio; *vt* accogliere, albergare; (*fig*) nutrire.

hard [hɑːd] *a* duro, difficile; *ad* con insistenza, con difficoltà, molto.

harden ['hɑːdn] *vt* indurire, rendere insensibile; *vi* indurirsi, diventare insensibile.

hardihood ['hɑːdihud] *n* ardimento, arditezza.

hardiness ['hɑːdinis] *n* robustezza, resistenza fisica.

hardly ['hɑːdli] *ad* appena, a mala pena, scarsamente.

hardness ['hɑːdnis] *n* durezza.

hardship ['hɑːdʃip] *n* avversità, disagio, privazione.

hardware ['hɑːdwɛə] *n* ferramenta *pl*.

hardy ['hɑːdi] *a* ardito; resistente.

hare [hɛə] *n* lepre.

harem ['hɛərem] *n* harem.

haricot ['hærikou] *n* fagiolo.

hark! [hɑːk] *interj* ascolta(te)!

harlequin ['hɑːlikwin] *n* arlecchino.

harlot ['hɑːlət] *n* prostituta.

harm [hɑːm] *n* danno, male; *vt* danneggiare, far male a.

harmful ['hɑːmful] *a* dannoso, nocivo.

harmless ['hɑːmlis] *a* innocuo.

harmlessly ['hɑːmlisli] *ad* in modo innocuo.

harmonica [hɑː'mɔnikə] *n* armonica; armonica a bocca.

harmonics [hɑː'mɔniks] *n pl* armonia.

harmonious [hɑː'mouniəs] *a* armonioso.

harmonium [hɑː'mouniəm] *n* armonium.

harmonize ['hɑːmənaiz] *vti* armonizzare.

harmony ['hɑːməni] *n* armonia.

harness ['hɑːnis] *n* bardatura, finimenti *pl*; *vt* bardare; (*fig*) utilizzare.

harp [hɑːp] *n* arpa; *vi* insistere fino ad annoiare.

harpoon [hɑː'puːn] *n* fiocina; *vt* fiocinare.

harpsichord ['hɑːpsikɔːd] *n* clavicembalo.

harpy ['hɑːpi] *n* arpia; (*fig*) megera.

harrow ['hærou] *n* erpice; *vt* erpicare; (*fig*) straziare.

harsh [hɑːʃ] *a* aspro, crudele, severo.

harshness ['hɑːʃnis] *n* asprezza, severità.

hart [hɑːt] *n* cervo, daino.

harum-scarum ['hɛərəm'skɛərəm] *a* avventato, irresponsabile.

harvest ['hɑːvist] *n* messe, raccolto; *vt* mietere, raccogliere.

harvester ['hɑːvistə] *n* mietitore.

hash [hæʃ] *n* specie di ragù; (*fig*) pasticcio; *vt* sminuzzare; (*fig*) fare un pasticcio di.

hasp [hɑːsp] *n* fermaglio.

hassock ['hæsək] *n* grosso cuscino usato come inginocchiatoio.

haste [heist] *n* fretta, furia.

hasten ['heisn] *vti* affrettar(si).

hastily ['heistili] *ad* frettolosamente, di furia.

hastiness ['heistinis] *n* fretta, precipitazione; irritabilità.

hasty ['heisti] *a* frettoloso, avventato; irritabile.

hat [hæt] *n* cappello; **hatbox** cappelliera.

hatch [hætʃ] *n* mezza porta; (*naut*) boccaporto; covata; *vt* covare; macchinare; *vi* (*of eggs*) schiudersi; (*of birds*) nascere.

hatchet ['hætʃit] *n* accetta.

hate [heit] *n* odio; *vt* odiare.

hateful ['heitful] *a* odioso.

hatpin ['hætpin] *n* spillone (da cappello).

hatred ['heitrid] *n* odio; astio.

hatter ['hætə] *n* cappellaio.

haughtiness ['hɔːtinis] *n* arroganza, superbia.

haughty ['hɔːti] *a* arrogante, superbo.

haul [hɔːl] *n* retata; tirata; (*fig*) guadagno; refurtiva; *vt* tirare, trascinare, rimorchiare.

haulage ['hɔːlidʒ] *n* trasporto.

haulier ['hɔːliə] *n* imprenditore di trasporti, impresa autotrasporti.

haunch [hɔːntʃ] *n* anca, coscia.

haunt [hɔːnt] *n* ritrovo; *vt* frequentare; ossessionare, perseguitare; **haunted** *a* frequentato, perseguitato, infestato da fantasmi.

Havana [hə'vænə] *n* Avana.

have [hæv] *vt aux* avere, ricevere, fare; **h. to** dovere.

haven ['heivn] *n* porto, rifugio.

haversack ['hævəsæk] *n* zaino, sacco da montagna.

havoc ['hævək] *n* devastazione, distruzione.

hawk [hɔːk] *n* falco; *vt* portare in giro (merci) per la vendita; *vi* cacciare col falco.

hawker ['hɔːkə] *n* venditore ambulante.

hawser ['hɔːzə] *n* (*naut*) gomena, piccolo cavo.

hawthorn ['hɔːθɔːn] *n* biancospino.

hay [hei] *n* fieno.

haycock ['heikɔk] **haystack** ['heistæk] *n* mucchio di fieno.

hazard ['hæzəd] *n* azzardo, rischio; *vt* arrischiare, azzardare.

hazardous ['hæzədəs] *a* rischioso.

haze [heiz] *n* nebbia, nebbiolina; (*fig*) confusione di mente.

hazel [heizl] *n* nocciolo, nocciola.

hazy ['heizi] *a* nebbioso, indistinto, vago.

he [hiː] *pron* egli, lui; (*prefix with names of animals*) maschio.

head [hed] *n* capo, testa; (*arrow*) punta; (*bed*) capezzale; (*page*) testata; *vt* capeggiare; intestare; *vi* colpire con la testa; dirigersi; **headmaster** n direttore di scuola, preside.

headache ['hedeik] *n* male di capo, emicrania.

heading ['hediŋ] *n* intestazione, titolo, (*av*) rotta.

headland ['hedlənd] *n* capo, promontorio.

headlight ['hedlait] *n* (*aut*) faro (anteriore).

headlong ['hedlɔŋ] *a* impetuoso, precipitoso; *ad* (a) capofitto.

headmost ['hedmoust] *a* il più avanzato.

headquarters ['hed'kwɔːtəz] *n pl* Quartier Generale.

headstrong ['hedstrɔŋ] *a* ostinato, testardo.

headway ['hedwei] *n* progresso, cammino.

heady ['hedi] *a* violento; testardo; inebriante.

heal ['hiːl] *vt* guarire, sanare.

healing ['hiːliŋ] *a* salutare; *n* guarigione.

health ['helθ] *n* salute.

healthy ['helθi] *a* sano, salutare, salubre.

heap [hiːp] *n* cumulo, mucchio; *vt* accumulare, ammucchiare.

hear [hiə] *vt* ascoltare; *vti* sentire, udire; apprendere.

hearing ['hiəriŋ] *n* udito; udienza; ascolto; **within h.** a portata di voce.

hearsay ['hiəsei] *n* diceria, voce.

hearse [həːs] *n* carro funebre.

heart [haːt] *n* cuore; **heartbeat** pulsazione; **heartbreak** crepacuore.

heartache ['haːteik] *n* crepacuore.

heartbroken ['haːt,broukən] *a* straziato.

heartburn ['haːtbəːn] *n* bruciore di stomaco.

hearten ['haːtn] *vt* incoraggiare, rincorare.

heartening ['haːtniŋ] *a* incoraggiante.

hearth [haːθ] *n* focolare.

heartily ['haːtili] *ad* cordialmente; vigorosamente.

heartless ['haːtlis] *a* senza cuore, insensibile.

hearty ['haːti] *a* cordiale; vigoroso.

heat [hiːt] *n* calore, caldo; *vt* riscaldare, infiammare.

heater ['hiːtə] *n* riscaldatore; **electric h.** stufetta elettrica.

heath [hiːθ] *n* brughiera, erica.

heathen ['hiːðən] *a n* pagano.

heather ['heðə] *n* erica.

heating ['hiːtiŋ] *n* riscaldamento; **h. element** resistenza.

heave [hiːv] *n* spinta; conato di vomito; *vt* alzare con fatica; (far) sollevare; *vi* spingere; ansimare; sollevarsi.

heaven ['hevn] *n* cielo.

heavenly ['hevnli] *a* celeste, celestiale, divino.

heavily ['hevili] *ad* pesantemente; molto.

heaviness ['hevinis] *n* pesantezza; oppressione.

heavy ['hevi] *a* pesante, opprimente;

h. sea mare grosso; **h.-hearted** col cuore triste; **heavyweight** (*boxing*) peso massimo.

Hebrew ['hiːbruː] *a n* ebraico, ebreo.

Hebrides ['hebridiz] *n* (isole) Ebridi.

heckle ['hekl] *n* carda; *vt* cardare; tempestare di domande.

hectic ['hektik] *a* (*med*) etico, tisico; agitato; febbrile.

Hector ['hektə] *nm pr* Ettore.

hedge [hedʒ] *n* siepe.

hedgehog ['hedʒhɔg] *n* porcospino, riccio (*also fig*).

heed [hiːd] *n* attenzione; *vt* fare attenzione a, badare a.

heedful ['hiːdful] *a* attento, cauto.

heedless ['hiːdlis] *a* disattento, incurante.

heel [hiːl] *a* calcagno, tacco, tallone; *vt* mettere i tacchi a.

hefty ['hefti] *a* forte, vigoroso; piuttosto pesante.

hegemony [hiː'geməni] *n* egemonia.

heifer ['hefə] *n* giovenca.

height [hait] *n* altezza, altura; culmine.

heighten ['haitn] *vt* innalzare, intensificare.

heinous ['heinəs] *a* atroce, odioso.

heir [ɛə] *n* erede; **heiress** ereditiera.

heirloom ['ɛəluːm] *n* cimelio di famiglia.

Helen ['helin] *nf pr* Elena.

helicopter ['helikɔptə] *n* elicottero.

hell [hel] *n* inferno.

hello [he'lou] *interj* salve!; (*tel*) pronto!

helm [helm] *n* (*naut*) timone.

helm(et) ['helm(it)] *n* elmetto, casco.

helmsman ['helmzmən] *pl* -men *n* timoniere.

help [help] *n* aiuto, assistenza, rimedio; *vt* aiutare, soccorrere; evitare; servire (cibo a tavola).

helper ['helpə] *n* aiuto, aiutante, soccorritore, soccorritrice.

helpful ['helpful] *a* servizievole, utile.

helping ['helpiŋ] *n* (*food*) porzione.

helpless ['helplis] *a* impotente.

helplessness ['helplisnis] *n* impotenza; mancanza di iniziativa.

helpmate ['helpmeit] *n* collaboratore, compagno.

helter-skelter ['heltə'skeltə] *ad* alla rinfusa.

hem [hem] *n* orlo, bordura; *vt* orlare; **to h. in** circondare.

hemisphere ['hemisfiə] *n* emisfero.

hemlock ['hemlɔk] *n* cicuta.

hemorrhage ['heməridʒ] *n* emorragia.

hemp [hemp] *n* canapa.

hemstitch ['hemstitʃ] *n* orlo a giorno.

hen [hen] *n* gallina; femmina di vari uccelli.

hence [hens] *ad* di qui a, perciò, quindi.

henceforth ['hens'fɔːθ] *ad* d'ora in avanti.

henchman ['hentʃmən] *pl* **henchmen** *n* (*pol*) seguace, accolito.

Henry ['henri] *nm pr* Enrico.

her [həː] *pron* a la, lei; di lei, suo (sua, sue, suoi); **to h.** le, a lei; **herself** *pron* ella medesima, lei stessa.

herald ['herəld] *n* araldo; *vt* annunciare, proclamare.

heraldry ['herəldri] *n* araldica.

herb [həːb] *n* erba aromatica.

herbalist ['həːbəlist] *n* erborista.

herd [həːd] *n* branco, gregge, mandria; *vt* custodire bestiame; *vi* formare gregge.

herdsman ['həːdzmən] *pl* -men *n* mandriano.

here [hiə] *ad* qui, costì.

hereabout(s) ['hiərə,baut(s)] *ad* all'intorno, qui vicino.

hereafter [hiər'aːftə] *n* vita futura; *ad* d'ora in poi.

hereditary [hi'reditəri] *a* ereditario.

heredity [hi'rediti] *n* eredità.

heresy ['herəsi] *n* eresia.

heretic ['herətik] *a n* eretico.

herewith ['hiə'wið] *ad* con questo, qui accluso.

heritage ['heritidʒ] *n* eredità (*also fig*).

hermetically [həː'metikəli] *ad* ermeticamente.

hermit ['həːmit] *n* eremita.

hermitage ['həːmitidʒ] *n* eremitaggio.

hernia ['həːniə] *n* ernia.

hero ['hiərou] *n* eroe; protagonista.

heroic [hi'rouik] *a* eroico.

heroine ['herouin] *n* eroina; protagonista.

heroism ['herouizəm] *n* eroismo.

heron ['herən] *n* airone.

herring ['heriŋ] *n* aringa; **smoked h.** aringa affumicata.

hers [həːz] *pron* il suo, la sua, i suoi, le sue; di lei.

hesitant ['hezitənt] *a* esitante, titubante.

hesitate ['heziteit] *vi* esitare.

hesitation [,hezi'teiʃən] *n* esitazione.

heterogeneous ['hetərou'dʒiːniəs] *a* eterogeneo.

hew [hju:] *vt* abbattere; spaccare.

heyday ['heidei] *n* apogeo, apice.

hiatus [hai'eitəs] *n* iato; lacuna.

hibernate ['haibəneit] *vi* svernare, essere in ibernazione.

hiccup, hiccough ['hikʌp] *vi* (avere il) singhiozzo; *n* singhiozzo.

hide [haid] *n* cuoio, pelle; *vti* nasconder(si), celar(si).

hideous ['hidiəs] *a* mostruoso, ripugnante.

hideousness ['hidiəsnis] *n* mostruosità.

hideout ['haidaut] *n* nascondiglio.

hiding ['haidiŋ] *n* nascondiglio; (*fam*) fustigazione.

hierarchy ['haiəraːki] *n* gerarchia.

higgledy-piggledy ['higldi'pigldi] *ad* alla rinfusa.

high [hai] a alto; importante; (time) avanzato; (color) acceso; **h. altar** altare maggiore; **h. school** scuola media; **h. water** alta marea.

highbrow ['haibrau] an intellettuale.

highland ['hailənd] a montanaro; n usu pl regione montuosa.

highlander ['hailəndə] n montanaro.

highly ['haili] ad molto, estremamente.

highness ['hainis] n (title) altezza.

highway ['haiwei] n strada maestra; autostrada; **highwayman** bandito.

hike [haik] vi n (fare una) escursione a piedi.

hiker ['haikə] n escursionista (a piedi).

hilarious [hi'lɛəriəs] a ilare, allegro.

hill [hil] n colle, collina.

hilliness ['hilinis] n natura collinosa.

hillock ['hilək] n collinetta, poggio.

hillside ['hilsaid] n pendio.

hilltop ['hiltɔp] n sommità della collina.

hilly ['hili] a collinoso.

hilt [hilt] n elsa, impugnatura.

him [him] pron lui, lo; **to h.** gli, a lui; **himself** egli stesso, proprio lui, si, se stesso, quello.

Himalaya [ˌhiməˈleiə] n Imalaia.

Himalayan [ˌhiməˈleiən] a n imalaiano, imalaiana.

hind [haind] n cerva, daina; a posteriore.

hinder ['haində] a posteriore; vt ['hində] impedire, ostacolare.

hindrance ['hindrəns] n impedimento, ostacolo.

hinge [hindʒ] n cardine; vt munire di cardini; vi dipendere.

hint [hint] n allusione, accenno; vti alludere, accennare.

hinterland ['hintəlænd] n retroterra.

hip [hip] n anca, fianco.

hippopotamus [ˌhipəˈpɔtəməs] n ippopotamo.

hire ['haiə] n nolo, affito; vt affittare, noleggiare; **for h.** da nolo; **to h. out** dare a nolo.

hireling ['haiəliŋ] n mercenario.

hirsute ['həːsjuːt] a irsuto, ispido.

his [hiz] a pron (il) suo, di lui.

hiss [his] n fischio, sibilo; vti fischiare, sibilare.

historian [his'tɔːriən] n storico.

historic [his'tɔrik] a importante; (gram) storico.

historical [his'tɔrikəl] a storico.

history ['histəri] n storia.

histrionic [ˌhistri'ɔnik] a istrionico.

hit [hit] n colpo; successo; tentativo fortunato; vt colpire.

hitch [hitʃ] n nodo, impedimento, ostacolo.

hitch-hike ['hitʃhaik] vi fare l'autostop.

hitch-hiker ['hitʃˌhaikə] n chi fa l'autostop.

hitch-hiking ['hitʃˌhaikiŋ] n autostop.

hither ['hiðə] ad qui, qua; **h. and thither** qua e là.

hitherto ['hiðə'tuː] ad finora.

hive [haiv] n alveare.

hoar [hɔː] a canuto, grigio; **h.-frost** n brina.

hoard [hɔːd] n ammasso, tesoro; vti ammassare, fare incetta di.

hoarder ['hɔːdə] n risparmiatore.

hoarding ['hɔːdiŋ] n accumulazione, incetta, risparmio.

hoarse [hɔːs] a rauco.

hoarsely ['hɔːsli] ad raucamente.

hoarseness ['hɔːsnis] n raucedine.

hoary ['hɔːri] a canuto, venerabile.

hoax [houks] n inganno, tiro scherzoso; vt ingannare.

hobble ['hɔbl] n zoppicamento, pastoia; vi zoppicare; vt impastoiare.

hobbledehoy ['hɔbldi'hɔi] n adolescente goffo.

hobby ['hɔbi] n svago preferito, 'hobby'.

hock [hɔk] n garretto (di cavallo).

hockey ['hɔki] n pallamaglio, 'hockey'; **ice h.** hockey sul ghiaccio.

hoe [hou] n zappa; vti zappare.

hog [hɔg] n maiale, porco.

hogmanay [ˌhɔgməˈnei] n (in Scozia) ultimo giorno dell'anno.

hogshead ['hɔgzhed] n grossa botte della capacità di galloni 52½ (= litri 238,5).

hoist [hɔist] n montacarichi; vt innalzare, sollevare.

hold [hould] n presa, stretta; luogo fortificato; (naut) stiva; vt contenere; tenere; trattenere; vi tenere (duro).

holder ['houldə] n detentore, possessore.

holding ['houldiŋ] n possesso, tenuta.

hole [houl] n buca, buco, cavità; tana; (sl) situazione difficile.

holiday ['hɔlidei] n giorno festivo, vacanza; **holidaymaker** villeggiante.

holiness ['houlinis] n santità.

Holland ['hɔlənd] n Olanda.

hollow ['hɔlou] a cavo, vuoto; (fig) falso; n cavità, buca; vt incavare, scavare.

holly ['hɔli] n agrifoglio.

holm [houm] n leccio.

holster ['houlstə] n fondina di pistola.

holy ['houli] n sacro, santo.

homage ['hɔmidʒ] n omaggio.

home [houm] n casa, focolare domestico, patria; a domestico, familiare, nazionale; **homecoming** ritorno al focolare.

homeland ['houmlænd] n patria.

homeless ['houmlis] a senza tetto, senza patria.

homely ['houmli] a casalingo; insignificante; semplice.

home-made ['houm'meid] a fatto in casa.

homesick ['houmsik] a nostalgico.

homesickness ['houmsiknis] n nostalgia.

homeward ['houmwəd] a ad verso casa, verso il proprio paese.

homework ['houmwəːk] n compito per casa.

homicide ['hɔmisaid] n omicida; omicidio.

homogeneous [,hɔmə'dʒiːniəs] a omogeneo.

homosexual ['houmou'seksjuəl] a omosessuale.

hone [houn] n cote; vt affilare.

honest ['ɔnist] a onesto, leale.

honestly ['ɔnistli] ad onestamente, sinceramente.

honesty ['ɔnisti] n onestà, lealtà.

honey ['hʌni] n miele.

honeycomb ['hʌnikoum] n favo.

honeymoon ['hʌnimuːn] n luna di miele; viaggio di nozze.

honeysuckle ['hʌni,sʌkl] n caprifoglio.

honor ['ɔnə] n onore, onoranza; (title) eccellenza; vt onorare.

honorable ['ɔnərəbl] a onorevole.

honorary ['ɔnərəri] a onorario.

hood [hud] n cappuccio; cofano di automobile; mantice di carrozza; vt incappucciare.

hoodwink ['hudwiŋk] vt bendare gli occhi a; (fig) ingannare.

hoof [huːf] pl hoofs, hooves n zoccolo.

hook [huk] n uncino, gancio, amo; vt agganciare, prendere all'amo.

hooked [hukt] a adunco.

hooligan ['huːligən] n giovinastro.

hoop [huːp] n cerchio.

hoot [huːt] n grido della civetta; schiamazzo; (train) fischio; vi gridare; suonare il clacson; vt deridere.

hooter ['huːtə] n sirena; clacson.

hop [hɔp] n balzo, salto su un piede; luppolo; vi saltare su un piede.

hope [houp] n speranza; vti sperare.

hopeful ['houpful] a speranzoso, ottimista.

hopeless ['houplis] a disperato, senza rimedio, senza speranza.

hopelessly ['houplisli] ad irrimediabilmente, senza speranza.

Horace ['hɔrəs] nm pr Orazio.

horde [hɔːd] n orda.

horizon [hə'raizn] n orizzonte.

horizontal [,hɔri'zɔntl] a orizzontale.

hormone ['hɔːmoun] n ormone.

horn ['hɔːn] n corno; (insect) antenna; (aut) clacson.

hornet ['hɔːnit] n calabrone.

horoscope ['hɔrəskoup] n oroscopo.

horrible ['hɔrəbl] a orribile.

horrid ['hɔrid] a orrido, odioso.

horrify ['hɔrifai] vt far inorridire.

horror ['hɔrə] n orrore.

horse [hɔːs] n cavallo, pl cavalleria; horseshoe ferro di cavallo.

horseback ['hɔːsbæk] n groppa; on h. ad a cavallo, in sella.

horseman ['hɔːsmən] n cavaliere; horsewoman amazzone.

horsemanship ['hɔːsmənʃip] n equitazione.

horticultural [,hɔːti'kʌltʃərəl] a riguardante l'orticultura.

horticulture ['hɔːtikʌltʃə] n orticultura.

hose [houz] n tubo flessibile; idrante; calze pl.

hosiery ['houʒəri] n maglieria.

hospice ['hɔspis] n ospizio.

hospitable ['hɔspitəbl] a ospitale.

hospital ['hɔspitl] n (o)spedale.

hospitality [,hɔspi'tæliti] n ospitalità.

host [houst] n ospite (che ospita); albergatore, oste; moltitudine, schiera; ostia.

hostage ['hɔstidʒ] n ostaggio.

hostel ['hɔstəl] n pensionato; ostello.

hostess ['houstis] n padrona di casa, ospite; (av) "hostess."

hostile ['hɔstail] a ostile.

hostility ['hɔs'tiliti] n ostilità.

hot [hɔt] a caldo, ardente, veemente, (food) piccante; hothead testa calda, persona impulsiva; h. line linea diritta; hotplate fornello, piastra riscaldante; h.-water bottle borsa dell'acqua calda.

hotel [hou'tel] n albergo; hotelier albergatore.

hound [haund] n cane da caccia; vt inseguire, perseguitare.

hour ['auə] n ora.

hourly ['auəli] a ad ogni ora.

house [haus] n casa; vt alloggiare; (harvest) portare dentro il raccolto; full h. (theat) tutto esaurito.

housebreaker ['haus,breikə] n scassinatore.

housecoat ['hauskout] n vestaglia.

household ['haushould] n famiglia, compresi i domestici; a di (da) famiglia, casalingo, domestico.

householder ['haus,houldə] n capofamiglia.

housekeeper ['haus,kiːpə] n governante, di casa.

housekeeping ['haus,kiːpiŋ] n governo della casa.

housetop ['haustɔp] n tetto della casa.

housewife ['hauswaif] n massaia, casalinga; astuccio da lavoro tascabile.

housework ['hauswəːk] n lavoro domestico.

housing ['hauziŋ] n l'accogliere, l'alloggiare; alloggio, abitazione.

hovel ['hɔvəl] n casupola, tugurio.

hover ['hɔvə] vi librarsi, gravitare; ronzare intorno; sorvolare.

how [hau] ad come, quanto.

however [hau'evə] ad cj comunque, però, tuttavia.

howitzer ['hauitsə] n obice.

howl [haul] n ululato, urlo; vi ululare, urlare.

hub [hʌb] n (mech) mozzo di ruota; (fig) punto centrale.

hubbub ['hʌbʌb] n suono confuso, tumulto.

huddle ['hʌdl] n folla disordinata; vti ammucchiare confusamente, affollarsi, accalcarsi, stringersi insieme.

hue [hju:] n colore, tinta; clamore.

huff [hʌf] n risentimento, stizza.

hug [hʌg] n (fam) abbraccio, stretta; vt (fam) abbracciare stretto; (fig) restare attaccato a.

huge [hju:dʒ] a enorme.

hugeness ['hju:dʒnis] n grandezza smisurata.

Hugh [hju:] nm pr Ugo.

Huguenot ['hju:gənɔt] n ugonotto.

hulk [hʌlk] n (naut) carcassa.

hull [hʌl] n baccello; (naut) scafo.

hullabaloo ['hʌləbə'lu:] n fracasso, baccano, confusione.

hullo [hʌ'lou] interj ciao, salve!; (tel) pronto!

hum [hʌm] n ronzio; vi ronzare; canticchiare a labbra chiuse; (fam) essere in grande attività.

human ['hju:mən] a umano.

humane [hju:'mein] a umano, umanitario.

humanism ['hju:mənizəm] n umanesimo.

humanist ['hju:mənist] n umanista.

humanitarian [hju:,mæni'tɛəriən] a filantropico, umanitario; n filantropo.

humanity [hju:'mæniti] n umanità.

humanly ['hju:mənli] ad umanamente.

humble ['hʌmbl] a umile; vt umiliare; **to eat h. pie** scusarsi umilmente.

humbly ['hʌmbli] ad umilmente, con sottomissione.

humbug ['hʌmbʌg] n (fam) frottola, inganno, ipocrisia; impostore, ipocrita; interj sciocchezze!

humdrum ['hʌmdrʌm] a noioso, monotono.

humid ['hju:mid] a umido.

humidity [hju:'miditi] n umidità.

humiliate [hju:'milieit] vi umiliare.

humiliation [hju:,mili'eifən] n umiliazione.

humility [hju:'militi] n umiltà.

humor ['hju:mə] n senso dell'umorismo, vena; vt assecondare.

humorist ['hju:mərist] n umorista.

humorous ['hju:mərəs] a umoristico, spiritoso.

hump [hʌmp] n gobba, protuberanza; (fig) malumore; **humpbacked** gobbo.

hunch [hʌntʃ] n gobba, protuberanza; (fig) impressione, sospetto; **hunchbacked** gobbo.

hundred ['hʌndrəd] a n cento.

hundredfold ['hʌndrədfould] a n centuplo.

hundredth ['hʌndrədθ] a n centesimo.

hundredweight ['hʌndrədweit] n (cwt) misura di peso di 112 libbre (=chili 50,8).

Hungarian [hʌŋ'gɛəriən] a n ungherese.

Hungary ['hʌŋgəri] n Ungheria.

hunger ['hʌŋgə] n fame; vi bramare; vt affamare.

hungry ['hʌŋgri] a affamato, desideroso; **be h.** aver fame.

hunk [hʌŋk] n grosso pezzo.

hunt [hʌnt] n caccia, gruppo di cacciatori; vti cacciare.

hunter ['hʌntə] n cacciatore.

hunting ['hʌntiŋ] n caccia.

huntsman ['hʌntsmən] pl -men n cacciatore.

hurdle ['hə:dl] n graticcio, ostacolo; **h. race** corsa ad ostacoli.

hurdy-gurdy ['hə:di,gə:di] n organetto a manovella.

hurl [hə:l] vt scagliare.

hurly-burly ['hə:li,bə:li] n mischia, tumulto.

hurrah [hu'rɑ:] interj urrah!

hurricane ['hʌrikən] n ciclone, uragano.

hurriedly ['hʌridli] ad in gran fretta, precipitosamente.

hurry ['hʌri] n fretta, premura; vti affrettarsi.

hurt [hə:t] n ferita, danno; vti far male a, danneggiare, dolere.

hurtful ['hə:tful] a dannoso, nocivo.

hurtle ['hə:tl] vti scagliar(si). precipitarsi.

husband ['hʌzbənd] n marito; vt amministrare con parsimonia, risparmiare.

husbandman ['hʌzbəndmən] pl -men n agricoltore.

husbandry ['hʌzbəndri] n agricoltura; amministrazione domestica.

hush [hʌʃ] n silenzio, quiete; vti (far) tacere.

husk [hʌsk] n buccia.

husky ['hʌski] a pieno di bucce; (voice) rauco, velato.

hussar [hu'zɑ:] n ussaro.

hussy ['hʌsi] n civetta, donna leggera.

hustle ['hʌsl] n spinta, trambusto; vt spingere.

hut [hʌt] n capanna; (mil) baracca.

hutch [hʌtʃ] n conigliera; gabbia; casotto.

hyacinth ['haiəsinθ] n giacinto.

hybrid ['haibrid] a n ibrido.

hydrant ['haidrənt] n idrante.

hydrate ['haidreit] n idrato.

hydroelectric ['haidroui'lektrik] a idroelettrico.

hydroplane ['haidrouplein] n idroplano, idrovolante.

hydrogen ['haidridʒən] n idrogeno.

hydropsy ['haidrɔpsi] n idropisia.

hyena [hai'i:nə] n iena.

hygiene ['haidʒi:n] n igiene.

hygienic [hai'dʒiːnik] *a* igienico.
hymn [him] *n* inno.
hyperbole [hai'pəːbəli] *n* iperbole.
hypersensitive ['haipəːˈsensitiv] *a* ipersensibile, ipersensitivo.
hyphen ['haifən] *n* lineetta, tratto d'unione.
hypnotism ['hipnətizəm] *n* ipnotismo.
hypochondriac [ˌhaipou'kɔndriæk] *a n* ipocondriaco.
hypocrisy [hi'pɔkrəsi] *n* ipocrisia.
hypocrite ['hipəkrit] *n* ipocrita.
hypocritical [ˌhipə'kritikəl] *a* ipocrita.
hypodermic [ˌhaipə'dəːmik] *a* ipodermico.
hypothesis [hai'pɔθisis] *pl* **hypotheses** *n* ipotesi.
hypothetical [ˌhaipou'θetikəl] *a* ipotetico.
hysteria [his'tiəriə] *n* isterismo.
hysterical [his'terikəl] *a* isterico.
hysterics [his'teriks] *n* attacco isterico.

I

I [ai] *pron* io.
Ia(i)n [iən] *nm pr* (*scozzese*) Giovanni.
ice [ais] *n* ghiaccio, gelato; *vt* ghiacciare; (*cook*) glassare.
iceberg ['aisbəːg] *n* massa di ghiacci galleggianti, 'iceberg'.
ice-cream ['ais'kriːm] *n* gelato.
Iceland ['aislənd] *n* Islanda.
Icelander ['aisləndə] *n* islandese.
Icelandic [ais'lændik] *a n* islandese.
icicle ['aisikil] *n* ghiacciolo.
icing ['aisiŋ] *a* (*sugar*) al velo; *n* (*cook*) glassa.
icy ['aisi] *a* gelato, gelido, ghiacciato.
idea [ai'diə] *n* idea.
ideal [ai'diəl] *a n* ideale.
idealism [ai'diəlizəm] *n* idealismo.
idealist [ai'diəlist] *n* idealista.
identikit [ai'dentikit] *n* identi-kit.
identic(al) [ai'dentik(əl)] *a* identico.
identification [ai,dentifi'keiʃən] *n* identificazione, riconoscimento; **i. tag** (*mil*) piastrina di riconoscimento.
ideology [ˌaidi'ɔlədʒi] *n* ideologia.
idiocy ['idiəsi] *n* idiozia.
idiom ['idiəm] *n* idiotismo, espressione idiomatica; idioma.
idiomatic [ˌidiə'mætik] *a* idiomatico.
idiot ['idiət] *n* idiota.
idiotic [ˌidi'ɔtik] *a* idiota, stupido.
idle ['aidl] *a* indolente, ozioso, inutile, vano; *vi* oziare; *vt* sprecare (tempo) in ozio.
idleness ['aidlnis] *n* indolenza, ozio.
idly ['aidli] *ad* pigramente, inutilmente.
idol ['aidl] *n* idolo.
idolater [ai'dɔlətə] *n* idolatra.
idolatry [ai'dɔlətri] *n* idolatria.
idolize ['aidəlaiz] *vt* idolatrare.

idyll ['idil] *n* idillio.
if [if] *cj* se; **if anything** se mai; **if so** in tal caso.
ignition [ig'niʃən] *n* ignizione, accensione; **i. key** (*aut*) chiavetta dell'accensione.
ignoble [ig'noubl] *a* ignobile.
ignominious [ˌignə'miniəs] *a* ignominioso.
ignominy ['ignəmini] *n* ignominia.
ignoramus [ˌignə'reiməs] *n* ignorante.
ignorance ['ignərəns] *n* ignoranza.
ignorant ['ignərənt] *a* ignorante.
ignore [ig'nɔː] *vt* far finta di non sentire, di non vedere, ignorare, trascurare.
ill [il] *a* (am)malato; dannoso, malefico; *ad* male; *n* male, danno.
illegal [i'liːgəl] *a* illegale.
illegality [ˌiliː'gæliti] *n* illegalità.
illegible [i'ledʒəbl] *a* illeggibile.
illegitimacy [ili'dʒitiməsi] *n* illegittimità.
illegitimate [ˌili'dʒitimit] *a* illegittimo.
illiberal [i'libərəl] *a* illiberale, tirchio.
illicit [i'lisit] *a* illecito.
illiterate [i'litərit] *a n* analfabeta.
illness ['ilnis] *n* malattia.
illogical [i'lɔdʒikəl] *a* illogico.
illuminate [i'ljuːmineit] *vt* illuminare; miniare.
illumination [i,ljuːmi'neiʃən] *n* illuminazione; miniatura.
illusion [i'luːʒən] *n* illusione.
illusive [i'luːsiv] *a* illusorio.
illustrate ['iləstreit] *vt* illustrare.
illustration [ˌiləs'treiʃən] *n* illustrazione.
illustrious [i'lʌstriəs] *a* illustre.
image ['imidʒ] *n* immagine.
imagery ['imidʒəri] *n pl* immagini; linguaggio figurato.
imaginable [i'mædʒinəbl] *a* immaginabile.
imaginary [i'mædʒinəri] *a* immaginario.
imagination [i,mædʒi'neiʃən] *n* immaginazione.
imaginative [i'mædʒinətiv] *a* immaginativo, fantasioso.
imagine [i'mædʒin] *vti* immaginare, figurarsi, farsi un'idea.
imbecile [i'mbisiːl] *a n* imbecille.
imbibe [im'baib] *vt* assimilare, assorbire, bere.
imbue [im'bjuː] *vt* imbevere, impregnare.
imitate ['imiteit] *vt* imitare.
imitation [ˌimi'teiʃən] *n* imitazione.
immaculate [i'mækjulit] *a* immacolato.
immaterial [ˌimə'tiəriəl] *a* immateriale, di nessuna importanza.
immature [ˌimə'tjuə] *a* immaturo.
immeasurable [i'meʒərəbl] *a* incommensurabile.

immediacy [i'mi:diəsi] n immedia-
tezza.
immediate [i'mi:diet] a immediato.
immediately [i'mi:diətli] ad immediatamente.
immemorial [,imi'mɔːriəl] a im-
memorabile.
immense [i'mens] a immenso.
immensity [i'mensiti] n immensità.
immerse [i'məːs] vt immergere.
immersion [i'məːʃən] n immersione.
immigrant ['imigrənt] a n immi-
grante.
immigrate ['imigreit] vi immigrare.
immigration [,imi'greiʃən] n immi-
grazione.
imminent ['iminənt] a imminente.
immobility [,imou'biliti] n immobilità.
immobilize [i'moubilaiz] vt immobilizzare.
immoderate [i'mɔdərit] a smodato.
immodest [i'mɔdist] a immodesto,
impudico.
immolate ['imouleit] vt immolare.
immoral [i'mɔrəl] a immorale.
immorality [,imə'ræliti] a immoralità.
immortal [i'mɔːtl] a n immortale.
immortality [,imɔː'tæliti] n immortalità.
immortalize [i'mɔːtəlaiz] vt im-
mortalare.
immovable [i'muːvəbl] a immobile,
inamovibile.
immune [i'mjuːn] a immune.
immunity [i'mjuːniti] n immunità.
immunization [,imjuːnai'zeiʃən] n
immunizzazione.
immutability [i,mjuːtə'biliti] n im-
mutabilità.
immutable [i'mjuːtəbl] a immutabile.
imp [imp] n diavoletto.
impact ['impækt] n collisione, urto.
impair [im'pɛə] vt danneggiare,
menomare.
impalpable [im'pælpəbl] a impalpa-
bile.
impart [im'paːt] vt impartire, comunicare.
impartial [im'paːʃəl] a imparziale.
impartiality ['im,paːʃi'æliti] n im-
parzialità.
impassible [im'paːsəbl] a impassibile.
impassioned [im'pæʃənd] a appassionato, eloquente.
impassive [im'pæsiv] a impassibile.
impatience [im'peiʃəns] n impa-
zienza.
impatient [im'peiʃənt] a impaziente.
impeach [im'piːtʃ] vt accusare,
imputare.
impeccable [im'pekəbl] a impecca-
bile.
impecunious [,impi'kjuːniəs] a senza
denaro, povero.
impede [im'piːd] vt impedire, ostacolare.
impediment [im'pedimənt] n impedimento, ostacolo.

impel [im'pel] vt costringere, spingere.
impend [im'pend] vi sovrastare,
incombere.
impenetrable [im'penitrəbl] a impenetrabile.
impenitent [im'penitənt] a impeni-
tente.
imperative [im'perətiv] a n impera-
tivo.
imperceptible [,impə'septəbl] a impercettibile.
imperfect [im'pəːfikt] a n imperfetto.
imperfection [,impə'fekʃən] n imperfezione.
imperial [im'piəriəl] a imperiale; n
(beard) pizzo; imperiale.
imperialism [im'piəriəlizəm] n im-
perialismo.
imperil [im'peril] vt mettere in
pericolo.
imperious [im'piəriəs] a imperioso.
imperishable [im'periʃəbl] a im-
perituro.
impermeable [im'pəːmiəbl] a impermeabile.
impersonal [im'pəːsnl] a impersonale.
impersonate [im'pəːsəneit] vt interpretare, impersonare.
impertinence [im'pəːtinəns] n impertinenza.
impertinent [im'pəːtinənt] a impertinente.
imperturbable [,impəː'təːbəbl] a
imperturbabile.
impervious ['im'pəːviəs] a impervio,
inaccessibile (also fig).
impetuosity [im,petju'ɔsiti] n impetuosità.
impetuous [im'petjuəs] a impetuoso.
impetus ['impitəs] n impeto.
impiety [im'paiəti] n empietà.
impinge [im'pindʒ] vi venire in urto
(con); interferire (in).
impious ['impiəs] a empio.
implacable [im'plækəbl] a implaca-
bile.
implant [im'plaːnt] vt impiantare,
instillare.
implement ['implimənt] n arnese,
utensile; vt ['impliment] effettuare,
completare.
implicate ['implikeit] vt implicare.
implication [,impli'keiʃən] n impli-
cazione; by i. implicitamente, per
induzione.
implicit [im'plisit] a implicito.
implicitly [im'plisitli] ad implicitamente.
implied [im'plaid] a implicito, sottinteso.
imploration [,implɔː'reiʃən] n im-
plorazione.
implore [im'plɔː] vt implorare.
imply [im'plai] vt implicare, significare; insinuare.
impolite [,impə'lait] a scortese,
sgarbato.
import ['impɔːt] n (articolo di)
importazione; importanza; significa-

to; *vt* [im'pɔːt] significare; (*com*) importare.

importance [im'pɔːtəns] *n* importanza.

important [im'pɔːtənt] *a* importante.

importation [ˌimpɔː'teiʃən] *n* importazione.

importer [im'pɔːtə] *n* importatore.

importunate [im'pɔːtjunit] *a* importuno, insistente.

importune [ˌimpɔː'tjuːn] *vt* importunare.

impose [im'pouz] *vt* imporre.

imposing [im'pouziŋ] *a* maestoso, imponente.

imposition [ˌimpə'ziʃən] *n* imposizione, imposta; inganno.

impossibility [im.pɔsə'biliti] *n* impossibilità.

impossible [im'pɔsəbl] *a* impossibile.

impostor [im'pɔstə] *n* impostore.

imposture [im'pɔstʃə] *n* impostura, inganno.

impotence ['impətəns] *n* impotenza.

impotent ['impətənt] *a* impotente.

impound [im'paund] *vt* sequestrare, confiscare.

impoverish [im'pɔvəriʃ] *vt* impoverire.

impracticable [im'præktikəbl] *a* impraticabile.

impregnable [im'pregnəbl] *a* impregnabile.

impregnate [im'pregneit] *vt* impregnare.

impress [im'pres] *vt* imprimere, impressionare.

impression [im'preʃən] *n* impressione, impronta; stampa.

impressionability [im.preʃnə'biliti] *n* impressionabilità, sensibilità.

impressionable [im'preʃnəbl] *a* impressionabile.

impressive [im'presiv] *a* impressionante, solenne.

imprint [im'print] *vt* imprimere, stampare; *n* ['imprint] impressione; impronta; stampa.

imprison [im'prizn] *vt* imprigionare.

imprisonment [im'priznmənt] *n* prigionia, carcere.

improbable [im'prɔbəbl] *a* improbabile.

impromptu [im'prɔmptjuː] *a* improvvisato, estemporaneo; *ad* all'impronto, estemporaneamente.

improper [im'prɔpə] *a* improprio, sconveniente, scorretto.

impropriety [ˌimprə'praiəti] *n* improprietà, sconvenienza.

improve [im'pruːv] *vti* migliorare.

improvement [im'pruːvmənt] *n* miglioramento, progresso, progressi *pl*.

improvidence [im'prɔvidəns] *n* improvidenza.

improvident [im'prɔvidənt] *a* improvidente.

improvise ['imprəvaiz] *vt* improvvisare.

imprudence [im'pruːdəns] *n* imprudenza.

imprudent [im'pruːdənt] *a* imprudente.

impudence ['impjudəns] *n* impudenza, sfacciataggine.

impudent ['impjudənt] *a* impudente, sfacciato.

impulse ['impʌls] *n* impulso.

impulsive [im'pʌlsiv] *a* impulsivo.

impulsiveness [im'pʌlsivnis] *n* impulsività.

impunity [im'pjuːniti] *n* impunità.

impure [im'pjuə] *a* impuro.

impurity [im'pjuəriti] *n* impurità.

imputation [ˌimpuː'teiʃən] *n* imputazione.

impute [im'pjuːt] *vt* imputare, attribuire.

in [in] *prep* ad a, in, entro, dentro, durante, secondo.

inability [ˌinə'biliti] *n* inabilità.

inaccessible [ˌinæk'sesəbl] *a* inaccessibile.

inaccuracy [in'ækjurəsi] *n* inaccuratezza, imprecisione.

inaccurate [in'ækjurit] *a* inaccurato, impreciso.

inaction [in'ækʃən] *n* inattività.

inactive [in'æktiv] *a* inattivo.

inadequate [in'ædikwit] *a* inadeguato, insufficiente.

inadmissible [ˌinəd'misəbl] *a* inammissibile.

inadvertent [ˌinəd'vəːtənt] *a* involontario.

inane [i'nein] *a* inane, sciocco, vacuo.

inanimate [in'ænimit] *a* inanimato.

inanity [i'næniti] *n* inanità, vacuità.

inapplicable [in'æplikəbl] *a* inapplicabile.

inappropriate [ˌinə'proupriit] *a* non appropriato, improprio.

inapt ['in'æpt] *a* inadatto, inetto.

inarticulate [ˌinɑː'tikjulit] *a* inarticolato, indistinto.

inasmuch as [inəz'mʌtʃæz] *ad* visto che, poichè, in quanto che.

inattention [ˌinə'tenʃən] *n* disattenzione, distrazione.

inattentive [ˌinə'tentiv] *a* disattento, distratto.

inaudible [in'ɔːdəbl] *a* impercettibile, inafferabile.

inaugurate [i'nɔːgjureit] *vt* inaugurare.

inborn ['in'bɔːn] *a* innato.

inbreeding ['in'briːdiŋ] *n* incrocio tra animali affini.

incalculable [in'kælkjuləbl] *a* incalcolabile.

incandescence [ˌinkæn'desns] *n* incandescenza.

incandescent [ˌinkæn'desnt] *a* incandescente.

incantation [ˌinkæn'teiʃən] *n* incantesimo, parole magiche.

incapability [in.keipə'biliti] *n* incapacità, inettitudine.

incapable [in'keipəbl] *a* incapace, inetto.

incapacitate [,inkə'pæsiteit] *vt* rendere inabile, incapace.

incapacity [,inkə'pæsiti] *n* inabilità, incapacità.

incarcerate [in'kɑːsəreit] *vt* incarcerare.

incarceration [in,kɑːsə'reiʃən] *n* incarcerazione.

incarnate [in'kɑːnit] *a* incarnato; *vt* [inkɑːneit] incarnare.

incautious [in'kɔːʃəs] *a* incauto.

incendiary [in'sendjəri] *a n* incendiario.

incense ['insens] *n* incenso; *vt* [in'sens] incensare; *vi* fare arrabbiare.

incentive [in'sentiv] *n* incentivo, motivo.

incessant [in'sesnt] *a* continuo, incessante.

incest ['insest] *n* incesto.

incestuous [in'sestjuəs] *a* incestuoso.

inch [intʃ] *n* pollice (*misura lineare* = cm 2,54); *vt* spostarsi gradatamente.

incidence ['insidəns] *n* incidenza.

incident ['insidənt] *n* avvenimento, episodio, incidente; *a* incidente, inerente.

incidental [,insi'dentl] *a* casuale, fortuito.

incision [in'siʒən] *n* incisione.

incisive [in'saisiv] *a* incisivo, penetrante.

incite [in'sait] *vt* incitare, stimolare.

incitement [in'saitmənt] *n* incitamento, stimolo.

incivility [,insi'viliti] *n* scortesia.

inclemency [in'klemənsi] *n* inclemenza.

inclement ['inklemənt] *a* inclemente.

inclination [,inkli'neiʃən] *n* inclinazione, propensità; pendio.

incline [in'klain] *n* pendio, piano inclinato; *vti* inclinare, essere incline.

include [in'kluːd] *vt* includere, comprendere.

inclusion [in'kluːʒən] *n* inclusione.

inclusive [in'kluːsiv] *a* compreso, inclusivo.

incoherence [,inkou'hiərəns] *n* incoerenza.

incoherent [,inkou'hiərənt] *a* incoerente.

income ['inkəm] *n* reddito, entrata.

incoming ['in,kʌmiŋ] *a* entrante, che succede ad altri; *n* l'entrare, il flusso; *pl* entrate.

incommunicability [,inkə'mjuːnikəbiliti] *n* incomunicabilità.

incomparable [in'kɔmpərəbl] *a* incomparabile.

incompatible [,inkəm'pætəbl] *a* incompatibile.

incompetence [in'kɔmpitəns] *n* incompetenza.

incompetent [in'kɔmpitənt] *a* incompetente.

incomplete [,inkəm'pliːt] *a* incompleto, incompiuto.

incomprehensible [in,kɔmpri'hensəbl] *a* incomprensibile.

inconceivable [,inkən'siːvəbl] *a* inconcepibile.

inconclusive [,inkən'kluːsiv] *a* inconcludente.

incongruous [in'kɔŋgruəs] *a* incongruo.

inconsequent [in'kɔnsikwənt] *a* illogico, inconseguente.

inconsequential [in'kɔnsikwəntʃəl] *a* inconseguente, irrilevante.

inconsiderable [,inkən'sidərəbl] *a* trascurabile.

inconsiderate [,inkən'sidərit] *a* sconsiderato; senza riguardi.

inconsistent [,inkən'sistənt] *a* inconsistente, incompatibile.

inconsolable [,inkən'souləbl] *a* inconsolabile.

inconspicuous [,inkən'spikjuəs] *a* incospicuo, insignificante.

inconstancy [in'kɔnstənsi] *n* incostanza.

inconstant [in'kɔnstənt] *a* incostante.

incontinent [in'kɔntinənt] *a* incontinente.

inconvenience [,inkən'viːniəns] *n* disturbo, inconveniente, disagio; *vt* incomodare, disturbare.

inconvenient [,inkən'viːniənt] *a* incomodo, scomodo.

inconvertible [,inkən'vəːtəbl] *a* inconvertibile.

incorporate [in'kɔːpəreit] *vt* incorporare; *a* [in'kɔːpərit] unito in corporazione.

incorporeal [,inkɔː'pɔːriəl] *a* immateriale, incorporeo.

incorrect [,inkə'rekt] *a* inesatto, scorretto, sbagliato..

incorrectness [,inkə'rektnis] *n* inesattezza, scorrettezza.

incorrigible [in'kɔridʒəbl] *a* incorreggibile.

incorruptible [,inkə'rʌptəbl] *a* incorruttibile.

increase ['inkriːs] *n* aumento, incremento; *vti* [in'kriːs] aumentare, (far) crescere.

incredible [in'kredəbl] *a* incredibile.

incredulity [,inkri'djuːliti] *n* incredulità.

incredulous [in'kredjuləs] *a* incredulo.

increment ['inkrimənt] *n* incremento, guadagno.

incriminate [in'krimineit] *vt* incriminare, incolpare.

incubate ['inkjubeit] *vti* covare; essere in incubazione.

incubation [,inkju'beiʃən] *n* incubazione.

incubator ['inkjubeitə] *n* incubatrice.

inculcate ['inkʌlkeit] *vt* inculcare.

inculpate ['inkʌlpeit] *vt* incolpare.

incumbent [in'kʌmbənt] *a* incombente, obbligatorio; *n* titolare d'un beneficio ecclesiastico.

incur [in'kə:] *vt* incorrere in.
incurable [in'kjuərəbl] *a* incurabile.
incursion [in'kə:ʃən] *n* incursione.
indebted [in'detid] *a* indebitato, grato.
indecency [in'di:snsi] *n* indecenza.
indecent [in'di:snt] *a* indecente.
indecipherable ['indi'saifərəbl] *a* indecifrabile.
indecision [.indi'siʒən] *n* indecisione.
indecisive [.indi'saisiv] *a* indeciso, non decisivo.
indecorous [in'dekərəs] *a* indecoroso, sconveniente.
indeed [in'di:d] *ad* davvero, infatti, in realtà.
indefatigable [.indi'fætigəbl] *a* instancabile.
indefensible [.indi'fensəbl] *a* indefensibile.
indefinite [in'definit] *a* indefinito.
indelible [in'delibl] *a* indelebile.
indelicacy [in'delikəsi] *n* indelicatezza.
indelicate [in'delikit] *a* indelicato.
indemnify [in'demnifai] *vt* indennizzare, risarcire.
indemnity [in'demniti] *n* indennità, risarcimento.
indent ['indent] *n* dentellatura, tacca; contratto, documento; requisizione; *vti* [in'dent] dentellare, intaccare; stendere un documento in due copie; requisire.
indentation [.inden'teiʃən] *n* dentellatura.
indenture [in'dentʃə] *n* dentellatura; contratto.
independence [.indi'pendəns] *n* indipendenza.
independent [.indi'pendənt] *a* indipendente.
independently [.indi'pendəntli] *ad* indipendentemente, separatamente.
indescribable [indis'kraibəbl] *a* indescrivibile.
indestructible [.indis'trʌktəbl] *a* indistruttibile.
indeterminate [.indi'tə:minit] *a* indeterminato.
index ['indeks] *n* indice.
India ['indiə] *n* India.
Indian ['indiən] *a n* indiano.
indicate ['indikeit] *vt* indicare.
indication [.indi'keiʃən] *n* indicazione, segno, sintomo.
indicative [in'dikətiv] *a* indicativo, che indica.
indicator ['indikeitə] *n* indicatore; **mileage i.** contachilometri.
indict [in'dait] *vt* accusare.
indictment [in'daitmənt] *n* accusa, imputazione.
indifference [in'difrəns] *n* indifferenza.
indifferent [in'difrənt] *a* indifferente, mediocre.
indigence ['indidʒəns] *n* indigenza.
indigenous [in'didʒinəs] *a* indigeno.
indigent ['indidʒənt] *a* indigente.

indigestible [.indi'dʒestəbl] *a* indigeribile, indigesto.
indigestion [.indi'dʒestʃən] *n* imbarazzo di stomaco; dispepsia.
indignant [in'dignənt] *a* indignato, sdegnato.
indignantly [in'dignəntli] *ad* con indignazione, con sdegno.
indignation [.indig'neiʃən] *n* indignazione, sdegno.
indignity [in'digniti] *n* offesa, trattamento indegno.
indigo ['indigou] *n* indaco.
indirect [.indi'rekt] *a* indiretto.
indiscernible [.indi'sə:nəbl] *a* indiscernibile.
indiscreet [.indis'kri:t] *a* indiscreto; sconsiderato.
indiscretion [.indis'kreʃən] *n* indiscrezione; imprudenza.
indiscriminate [.indis'kriminit] *a* indiscriminato.
indispensable [.indis'pensəbl] *a* indispensabile.
indispose [.indis'pouz] *vt* indisporre.
indisposed [.indis'pouzd] *a* indisposto; maldisposto.
indisposition [.indispə'ziʃən] *n* indisposizione.
indisputable ['indis'pju:təbl] *a* indiscutibile, sicuro.
indisputed ['indis'pju:tid] *a* indiscusso.
indissoluble [.indi'sɔljubl] *a* indissolubile.
indistinct [.indis'tiŋkt] *a* indistinto, confuso.
indistinctness [.indis'tiŋktnis] *n* mancanza di chiarezza.
indistinguishable [.indis'tiŋgwiʃəbl] *a* indistinguibile.
indite [in'dait] *vt* comporre, redigere.
individual [.indi'vidjuəl] *a* singolo, individuale; *n* individuo.
individuality [.indi.vidju'æliti] *n* individualità.
indivisible [.indi'vizəbl] *a* indivisibile.
Indo-China ['indou'tʃainə] *n* Indocina.
Indo-Chinese ['indou'tʃai'ni:z] *a n* indocinese.
indolence ['indələns] *n* indolenza.
indolent ['indələnt] *a* indolente.
indomitable [in'dɔmitəbl] *a* indomabile; indomito.
indoor ['indɔ:] *a* che ha luogo in casa, da eseguirsi in casa; **indoors** *ad* dentro, in casa.
indrawn ['in'drɔ:n] *a* chiuso in se stesso, introverso.
indubitable [in'dju:bitəbl] *a* indubitabile.
induce [in'dju:s] *vt* indurre.
inducement [in'dju:smənt] *n* allettamento, incentivo.
induction [in'dʌkʃən] *n* induzione; investitura.
inductive [in'dʌktiv] *a* induttivo.
indulge [in'dʌldʒ] *vti* indulgere,

lasciar libero corso a; abbandonarsi.
indulgence [in'dʌldʒəns] n indulgenza, compiacenza; licenza.
indulgent [in'dʌldʒənt] a indulgente.
industrial [in'dʌstriəl] a industriale.
industrialist [in'dʌstriəlist] n industriale.
industrialization [in'dʌstriəlai'zeiʃən] n industrializzazione.
industrious [in'dʌstriəs] a attivo, operoso.
industry ['indəstri] n industria, attività.
inebriate [i'niːbriit] vt inebriare, ubriacare.
ineffable [in'efəbl] a ineffabile.
ineffective [,ini'fektiv] a inefficace.
ineffectual [,ini'fektjuəl] a inefficace, vano.
inefficacy [in'efikəsi] n inefficacia.
inefficiency [,ini'fiʃənsi] n inefficienza; inefficacia; incapacità.
inefficient [,ini'fiʃənt] a inefficiente, poco capace.
inelegant [in'eligənt] a inelegante.
ineligible [in'elidʒəbl] a ineleggibile.
inept [i'nept] a inetto.
ineptitude [i'neptitjuːd] n inettitudine.
inequality [,iniː'kwɔliti] n ineguaglianza.
inert [i'nəːt] a inerte.
inertia [i'nəːʃjə] n inerzia.
inertness [i'nəːtnis] n inerzia, apatia.
inestimable [in'estiməbl] a inestimabile.
inevitability [in,evitə'biliti] n inevitabilità.
inevitable [in'evitəbl] a inevitabile.
inexact [,inig'zækt] a inesatto.
inexcusable [,iniks'kjuːzəbl] a imperdonabile.
inexhaustible [,inig'zɔːstəbl] a inesauribile.
inexorable [in'eksərəbl] a inesorabile.
inexpensive [,iniks'pensiv] a poco costoso, a buon mercato.
inexperience [,iniks'piəriəns] n inesperienza.
inexperienced [,iniks'piəriənst] a inesperto.
inexplicable [in'eksplikəbl] a inesplicabile, inspiegabile.
inexpressible [,iniks'presəbl] a inesprimibile.
inexpressive [,iniks'presiv] a inespressivo.
infallibility [in,fælə'biliti] n infallibilità.
infallible [in'fæləbl] a infallibile.
infamous ['infəməs] a infame.
infamy ['infəmi] n infamia.
infancy ['infənsi] n infanzia.
infant ['infənt] a infantile, nascente; n neonato, bambino, infante.
infantry ['infəntri] n fanteria.
infatuate [in'fætjueit] vt infatuare.
infatuated [in'fætjueitid] a infatuato; fanatico di.

infatuation [in,fætju'eiʃən] n infatuazione.
infect [in'fekt] vt infettare.
infection [in'fekʃən] n infezione.
infectious [in'fekʃəs] a infettivo, contagioso.
infer [in'fəː] vt inferire, dedurre.
inference ['infərəns] n conclusione, deduzione.
inferior [in'fiəriə] a n inferiore.
inferiority [in,fiəri'ɔriti] n inferiorità.
infernal [in'fəːnl] a infernale.
infertile [in'fəːtail] a improduttivo, non fertile.
infest [in'fest] vt infestare.
infidel ['infidəl] a n infedele, miscredente.
infidelity [,infi'deliti] n infedeltà.
infiltrate ['infiltreit] vti infiltrar(si).
infinite ['infinit] a n infinito.
infinitive [in'finitiv] a n (gram) infinito.
infinity [in'finiti] n infinità.
infirm [in'fəːm] a infermo, debole; irresoluto.
infirmary [in'fəːməri] n infermeria, ospedale.
infirmity [in'fəːmiti] n infermità; irresolutezza.
inflame [in'fleim] vt infiammare.
inflammable [in'flæməbl] a infiammabile.
inflammation [,inflə'meiʃən] n infiammazione.
inflammatory [in'flæmətəri] a infiammatorio.
inflate [in'fleit] vti gonfiare, gonfiarsi.
inflation [in'fleiʃən] n gonfiamento; inflazione.
inflect [in'flekt] vt inflettere.
inflection [in'flekʃən] n inflessione.
inflexible [in'fleksəbl] a inflessibile rigido.
inflict [in'flikt] vt infliggere.
infliction [in'flikʃən] n inflizione.
influence ['influəns] n ascendente, influenza, influsso; vt influenzare.
influential [,influ'enʃəl] a influente, autorevole.
influenza [,influ'enzə] n (med) influenza.
influx ['inflʌks] n afflusso, flusso.
inform [in'fɔːm] vt informare.
informal [in'fɔːml] a non ufficiale, senza formalità; irregolare.
informality [,infɔː'mæliti] n assenza di formalità; (leg) irregolarità.
informant [in'fɔːmənt] n informatore.
information [,infə'meiʃən] n informazione, informazioni pl; accusa.
informer [in'fɔːmə] n delatore.
infrequent [in'friːkwənt] a infrequente, raro.
infringe [in'frindʒ] vt trasgredire.
infringement [in'frindʒmənt] n infrazione, trasgressione.
infuriate [in'fjuərieit] vt infuriare, rendere furioso.

infuse [in'fjuːz] *vt* infondere, instillare, mettere in infusione; stare in infusione.

infusion [in'fjuːʒən] *n* infusione, infuso.

ingenious [in'dʒiːniəs] *a* ingegnoso.

ingenuity [ˌindʒi'njuːiti] *n* abilità inventiva, ingegnosità.

ingenuous [in'dʒenjuəs] *a* ingenuo; **ingenuousness** *n* ingenuità.

ingle-nook ['iŋglnuk] *n* angolo del focolare.

inglorious [in'glɔːriəs] *a* inglorioso.

ingot ['iŋgət] *n* lingotto.

ingrained ['in'greind] *a* radicato; inveterato.

ingratiate [in'greiʃieit] *vt* ingraziarsi.

ingratitude [in'grætitjuːd] *n* ingratitudine.

ingredient [in'griːdiənt] *n* ingrediente.

inhabit [in'hæbit] *vt* abitare, occupare.

inhabitable [in'hæbitəbl] *a* abitabile.

inhabitant [in'hæbitənt] *n* abitante.

inhale [in'heil] *vt* aspirare.

inhaler [in'heilə] *n* inalatore.

inhere [in'hiə] *vi* essere inerente.

inherent [in'hiərənt] *a* inerente, intrinseco.

inherit [in'herit] *vti* ereditare.

inheritance [in'heritəns] *n* eredità.

inhibit [in'hibit] *vt* inibire, impedire.

inhibition [ˌinhi'biʃən] *n* inibizione.

inhospitable [in'hɔspitəbl] *a* inospitale.

inhuman [in'hjuːmən] *a* barbaro, inumano.

inhumanity [ˌinhuː'mæniti] *n* inumanità.

inimical [i'nimikəl] *a* nemico, ostile.

inimitable [i'nimitəbl] *a* inimitabile.

iniquity [i'nikwiti] *n* iniquità.

initial [i'niʃəl] *a n* iniziale; *vt* firmare con le sole iniziali.

initiate [i'niʃiit] *n* iniziato; *vt* [i'niʃieit] iniziare.

initiation [iˌniʃi'eiʃən] *n* iniziazione.

initiative [i'niʃiətiv] *n* iniziativa.

inject [in'dʒekt] *vt* iniettare.

injection [in'dʒekʃən] *n* iniezione.

injudicious [ˌindʒuː'diʃəs] *a* sconsiderato, avventato.

injunction [in'dʒʌŋkʃən] *n* ingiunzione.

injure ['indʒə] *vt* danneggiare, ferire, nuocere a.

injurious [in'dʒuəriəs] *a* nocivo, ingiurioso.

injury ['indʒəri] *n* ferita, torto, danno.

injustice [in'dʒʌstis] *n* ingiustizia.

ink [iŋk] *n* inchiostro; **inkstand** calamaio; **inkwell** calamaio, infisso.

inkling ['iŋkliŋ] *n* indizio, sospetto.

inky ['iŋki] *a* d'inchiostro, nero come l'inchiostro, macchiato d'inchiostro.

inland ['inlənd] *a n* (di un paese) interno, nell'interno, verso l'interno; **i. revenue** fisco.

inlay ['inlei] *n* intarsio; *vt* intarsiare.

inlet ['inlet] *n* insenatura, piccola baia.

inmate ['inmeit] *n* inquilino; persona alloggiata in un istituto.

inmost ['inmoust] *a* il più interno, profondo.

inn [in] *n* albergo, locanda; **innkeeper** locandiere, oste.

innate ['i'neit] *a* innato, istintivo.

inner ['inə] *a* interiore, interno.

innocence ['inəsns] *n* innocenza.

innocent ['inəsnt] *a n* innocente.

innocuous [i'nɔkjuəs] *a* innocuo.

innovate ['inouveit] *vt* innovare.

innovation [ˌinou'veiʃən] *n* innovazione.

innuendo [ˌinjuː'endou] *n* allusione, insinuazione.

innumerable [i'njuːmərəbl] *a* innumerevole.

inoculate [i'nɔkjuleit] *vt* inoculare; vaccinare; innestare; inculcare.

inoculation [iˌnɔkju'leiʃən] *n* inoculazione.

inoffensive [ˌinə'fensiv] *a* inoffensivo.

inopportune [in'ɔpətjuːn] *a* inopportuno, intempestivo.

inordinate [i'nɔːdinit] *a* eccessivo, smoderato.

in-patient ['inˌpeiʃənt] *n* ammalato degente in ospedale.

input ['input] *n* (*mech, el*) entrata, alimentazione; **i. energy** energia immessa.

inquest ['inkwest] *n* inchiesta.

inquire [in'kwaiə] *vt* domandare; *vi* indagare, informarsi, fare ricerche *pl*.

inquiringly [in'kwaiəriŋli] *ad* interrogativamente, con aria interrogativa.

inquiry [in'kwaiəri] *n* investigazione, inchiesta.

inquisition [ˌinkwi'ziʃən] *n* inquisizione.

inquisitive [iŋ'kwizitiv] *a* curioso, indagatore.

inquisitively [in'kwizitivli] *ad* con curiosità; indiscretamente.

inquisitor [in'kwizitə] *n* inquisitore.

inroad ['inroud] *n* incursione; scorreria, sottrazione.

insane [in'sein] *a* folle, pazzo.

insanity [in'sæniti] *n* follia, pazzia.

insatiable [in'seiʃjəbl] *a* insaziabile.

inscribe [in'skraib] *vt* iscrivere; incidere.

inscription [in'skripʃən] *n* iscrizione.

inscrutable [in'skruːtəbl] *a* inscrutabile.

insect ['insekt] *n* insetto.

insecticide [in'sektisaid] *n* insetticida.

insecure [ˌinsi'kjuə] *a* malsicuro.

insecurity [ˌinsi'kjuəriti] *n* mancanza di sicurezza.

insemination [inˌsemi'neiʃən] *n*

(*med*) fecondazione; **artificial i.** fecondazione artificiale.

insensibility [in‚sensə'biliti] *n* incoscienza, insensibilità.

insensible [in'sensəbl] *a* inconscio; insensibile; privo di sensi.

insensitive [in'sensitiv] *a* insensibile.

inseparable [in'sepərəbl] *a* inseparabile.

insert [in'sə:t] *vt* inserire.

insertion [in'sə:ʃən] *n* inserzione, aggiunta.

inside ['in'said] *a* interno, interiore; *n* interno; *ad* dentro; *prep* dentro; **i. out** rivoltato, a rovescio.

insider ['in'saidə] *n* chi è addentro, iniziato.

insidious [in'sidiəs] *a* insidioso.

insight ['insait] *n* penetrazione, intuito.

insignificant [‚insig'nifikənt] *a* insignificante.

insincere [‚insin'siə] *a* insincero, falso.

insincerity [‚insin'seriti] *n* insincerità, falsità.

insinuate [in'sinjueit] *vt* insinuare; introdurre.

insinuation [in‚sinju'eiʃən] *n* insinuazione.

insipid [in'sipid] *a* insipido, insulso.

insipidity [‚insi'piditi] *n* insipidezza; insulsaggine.

insist [in'sist] *vi* insistere.

insistence [in'sistəns] *n* insistenza.

insistent [in'sistənt] *a* insistente.

insolence ['insələns] *n* insolenza.

insolent ['insələnt] *a* insolente.

insoluble [in'sɔljubl] *a* insolubile.

insolvency [in'sɔlvənsi] *n* insolvenza.

insolvent [in'sɔlvənt] *a* insolvente.

insomnia [in'sɔmniə] *n* insonnia.

inspect [in'spekt] *vt* ispezionare, controllare.

inspection [in'spekʃən] *n* ispezione, controllo.

inspector [in'spektə] *n* ispettore, controllore.

inspiration [‚inspə'reiʃən] *n* ispirazione.

inspire [in'spaiə] *vt* ispirare.

instability [‚instə'biliti] *n* instabilità.

install [in'stɔ:l] *vt* installare, insediare.

installation [‚instə'leiʃən] *n* insediamento; (*el etc*) impianto, installazione.

installment [in'stɔ:lmənt] *n* rata; puntata; **i. plan** (sistema di) vendita a rate.

instance ['instəns] *n* esempio, istanza; **for i.** ad esempio.

instant ['instənt] *a* immediato; (*month*) corrente; *n* istante, momento.

instantaneous [‚instən'teiniəs] *a* istantaneo.

instantly ['instəntli] *ad* immediatamente.

instead [in'sted] *ad* invece (di).

instep ['instep] *n* collo del piede.

instigate ['instigeit] *vt* istigare.

instigation [‚insti'geiʃən] *n* istigazione.

instigator ['instigeitə] *n* istigatore, istigatrice.

instill [in'stil] *vt* instillare.

instinct ['instiŋkt] *n* istinto.

instinctive [in'stiŋktiv] *a* istintivo.

institute ['institju:t] *n* istituto, istituzione; *vt* istituire.

institution [‚insti'tju:ʃən] *n* istituzione, ente; (*eccl*) nomina.

instruct [in'strʌkt] *vt* istruire, informare.

instruction [in'strʌkʃən] *n* istruzione, insegnamento; *pl* istruzione, disposizione.

instructive [in'strʌktiv] *a* istruttivo.

instructor [in'strʌktə] *n* istruttore, maestro, lettore universitario; **instructress** maestra, insegnante.

instrument ['instrumənt] *n* strumento; arnese.

instrumental [‚instru'mentl] *a* strumentale.

insubordinate [‚insə'bɔ:dnit] *a* insubordinato, indisciplinato.

insufficiency [‚insə'fiʃənsi] *n* insufficienza.

insufficient [‚insə'fiʃənt] *a* insufficiente.

insular ['insjulə] *a* insulare.

insulate ['insjuleit] *vt* isolare.

insulation [‚insju'leiʃən] *n* isolamento.

insult ['insʌlt] *n* insulto; *vt* [in'sʌlt] insultare.

insuperable [in'sju:pərəbl] *a* insuperabile, insormontabile.

insurance [in'ʃuərəns] *n* (*com*) assicurazione.

insure [in'ʃuə] *vt* assicurare.

insurer [in'ʃuərə] *n* (*com*) assicuratore.

insurgency [in'sə:dʒənsi] *n* sollevarsi; insurrezione.

insurgent [in'sə:dʒənt] *a n* insorto.

insurmountable [‚insə'mauntəbl] *a* insormontabile.

insurrection [‚insə'rekʃən] *n* insurrezione.

intact [in'tækt] *a* intatto, intero.

intake ['inteik] *n* immissione; presa (*pump*) aspirazione.

intangible [in'tændʒəbl] *a* intangibile.

integer ['intidʒə] *n* numero intero.

integral ['intigrəl] *a n* integrale.

integrate ['intigreit] *a* integrale, intero; *vt* integrare, completare.

integration [‚inti'greiʃən] *n* integrazione.

integrity [in'tegriti] *n* integrità.

intellect ['intilekt] *n* intelletto.

intellectual [‚inti'lektjuəl] *a n* intellettuale.

intelligence [in'telidʒəns] *n* intelligenza; informazioni *pl*, notizie *pl*.

intelligent [in'telidʒənt] *a* intelligente.

intelligentsia [in,teli'dʒentsiə] *n* intellettuali, classe colta.

intelligibility [in,telidʒə'biliti] *n* intelligibilità.

intelligible [in'telidʒəbl] *a* intelligibile; comprensibile; chiaro.

intemperance [in'tempərəns] *n* intemperanza.

intemperate [in'tempərit] *a* smoderato, violento; dedito al bere; (*climate*) rigido.

intend [in'tend] *vti* intendere, proporsi.

intended [in'tendid] *a* intenzionale, deliberato.

intense [in'tens] *a* intenso; (*fig*) profondo, ipersensibile.

intensification [in,tensifi'keiʃən] *n* intensificazione.

intensify [in'tensifai] *vti* intensificar(si).

intensity [in'tensiti] *n* intensità.

intensive [in'tensiv] *a* intensivo, intenso.

intent [in'tent] *a* intento; *n* scopo.

intention [in'tenʃən] *n* intenzione, proposito.

intentional [in'tenʃənl] *a* intenzionale, premeditato.

inter [in'tə:] *vt* interrare, seppellire.

interact [,intər'ækt] *vt* esercitare azione reciproca.

interaction [,intər'ækʃən] *n* azione reciproca.

intercede [,intə:'si:d] *vi* intercedere.

intercept [,intə:'sept] *vt* intercettare.

interception [,intə:'sepʃən] *n* intercettamento; interruzione.

interchange ['intə:'tʃeindʒ] *n* scambio; *vti* scambiar(si).

interchangeable [,intə:'tʃeindʒəbl] *a* scambievole.

intercourse ['intə:kɔ:s] *n* relazione, rapporto; **sexual i.** rapporti sessuali *pl.*

interdependent [,intədi'pendənt] *a* interdipendente.

interdict ['intə:dikt] *n* interdetto (papale); *vt* [,intə:'dikt] interdire, vietare.

interdiction [,intə:'dikʃən] *n* divieto, interdizione, interdetto.

interest ['intrist] *n* interesse, interessi *pl,* interessamento; *vt* interessare.

interesting ['intristiŋ] *a* interessante.

interfere [,intə'fiə] *vi* intervenire, intromettersi, ostacolare, interferire.

interference [,intə'fiərəns] *n* interferenza, ingerenza, intralcio.

interim ['intərim] *n* interim, lasso di tempo; *ad* nel frattempo; *a* provvisorio, temporaneo.

interior [in'tiəriə] *a* interiore, interno; *n* interno.

interject [,intə:'dʒekt] *vti* interporre.

interjection [,intə:'dʒekʃən] *n* interiezione; (*fig*) intromissione.

interlace [,intə:'leis] *vt* intrecciare.

interleave ['intəli:v] *vt* interfogliare.

interlock [,intə:'lɔk] *n* (*cin*) sincro-

nizzazione; *vti* allacciar(si); (*cin*) sincronizzare.

interlocutor [,intə:'lɔkjutə] *n* interlocutore.

interloper ['intə:loupə] *n* intruso.

interlude ['intə:lu:d] *n* interludio, intervallo.

intermediate [,intə:'mi:diət] *a* intermedio.

interment [in'tə:mənt] *n* inumazione, seppellimento.

interminable [in'tə:minəbl] *a* interminabile.

intermingle [,intə:'miŋgl] *vti* inframmischiar(si).

intermission [,intə:'miʃən] *n* intervallo, interruzione, pausa.

intermittent [,intə:'mitənt] *a* intermittente.

intern [in'tə:n] *vt* internare.

internal [in'tə:nl] *a* interno; **i. revenue** fisco.

international [,intə:'næʃənl] *a n* internazionale.

internment [in'tə:nmənt] *n* internamento.

interpellation [in,tə:pe'leiʃən] *n* interpellanza.

interplay ['intə:'plei] *n* gioco (di colori etc.); azione reciproca.

interpolate [in'tə:pouleit] *vt* interpolare.

interpose [,intə:'pouz] *vti* interpor(si).

interpret [in'tə:prit] *vti* interpretare; fare da interprete.

interpreter [in'tə:pritə] *n* interprete.

interrogate [in'terəgeit] *vt* interrogare.

interrogation [in,terə'geiʃən] *n* interrogazione.

interrogative [,intə'rɔgətiv] *a n* interrogativo.

interrogatory [,intə'rɔgətəri] *a n* interrogatorio.

interrupt [,intə'rʌpt] *vt* interrompere.

interruption [,intə'rʌpʃən] *n* interruzione.

intersect [,intə:'sekt] *vti* intersecar(si).

intersection [,intə:'sekʃən] *n* intersecazione.

intersperse [,intə:'spə:s] *vt* spargere qua e là, disseminare, inframmezzare.

intertwine [,intə:'twain] *vti* intrecciar(si).

interval ['intəvəl] *n* intervallo.

intervene [,intə:'vi:n] *vi* intervenire, intromettersi; **intervening** interveniente; **in the intervening time** nel frattempo.

intervention [,intə:'venʃən] *n* intervento.

interview ['intəvju:] *n* intervista, abboccamento; *vt* intervistare.

intestate [in'testit] *a* intestato, senza disposizioni testamentarie.

intestinal [in'testinl] *a* intestinale.
intestine [in'testin] *a* intestino, interno; *n* intestino; *n pl* intestino.
intimacy ['intiməsi] *n* intimità.
intimate ['intimit] *a* intimo; *vt* ['intimeit] intimare, comunicare, suggerire.
intimation [,inti'meiʃən] *n* intimazione, avviso.
intimidate [in'timideit] *vt* intimidire.
intimidation [in,timi'deiʃən] *n* intimidazione.
into ['intu] *prep* in.
intolerable [in'tɔlərəbl] *a* intollerabile.
intolerance [in'tɔlərəns] *n* intolleranza.
intolerant [in'tɔlərənt] *a* intollerante.
intonation [,intou'neiʃən] *n* intonazione.
intone [in'toun] *vt* intonare.
intoxicate [in'tɔksikeit] *vt* ubriacare, inebriare.
intoxication [in,tɔksi'keiʃən] *n* ubriachezza, ebbrezza.
intransigent [in'trænsidʒənt] *a* intransigente.
intrepid [in'trepid] *a* intrepido.
intrepidity [,intri'piditi] *n* intrepidità.
intricacy ['intrikəsi] *n* groviglio, viluppo.
intricate ['intrikit] *a* intricato, involuto.
intrigue [in'triːg] *n* intrigo, macchinazione; *vi* intrigare, macchinare; *vt (sl)* stuzzicare la curiosità di.
intriguing [in'triːgiŋ] *a* intrigante; interessante.
intrinsic [in'trinsik] *a* intrinseco.
introduce [,intrə'djuːs] *vt* introdurre, presentare.
introduction [,intrə'dʌkʃən] *n* introduzione, presentazione.
introductory [,intrə'daktəri] *a* introduttivo, preliminare.
introspection [,introu'spekʃən] *n* introspezione.
introspective [,introu'spektiv] *a* introspettivo.
introvert ['introuvəːt] *a n* introvertito, introverso.
intrude [in'truːd] *vti* intromettersi.
intruder [in'truːdə] *n* intruso.
intrusion [in'truːʒən] *n* intrusione.
intuition [,intjuː'iʃən] *n* intuito, intuizione.
intuitive [in'tjuːitiv] *a* intuitivo.
inundate ['inʌndeit] *vt* inondare.
inure [i'njuə] *vt* indurire, abituare.
invade [in'veid] *vt* invadere.
invader [in'veidə] *n* invasore.
invalid ['invɔliːd] *a n* invalido, infermo; *vt (mil)* riformare; [in'vælid] *a* non valido, nullo.
invalidate [in'vælideit] *vt* infirmare.
invalidity [,invə'liditi] *n* invalidità.
invaluable [in'væljuəbl] *a* inestimabile.

invariable [in'vɛəriəbl] *a* invariabile.
invasion [in'veiʒən] *n* invasione.
invective [in'vektiv] *n* invettiva.
inveigh [in'vei] *vi* inveire.
inveigle [in'viːgl] *vt* adescare, sedurre.
invent [in'vent] *vt* inventare.
invention [in'venʃən] *n* invenzione.
inventive [in'ventiv] *a* inventivo.
inventor [in'ventə] *n* inventore.
inventory [in'invəntri] *n* inventario; *vt* inventariare.
inversion [in'vəːʃən] *n* inversione.
invert [in'vəːt] *vt* invertire.
invest [in'vest] *vt* investire.
investigate [in'vestigeit] *vti* investigare.
investigation [in,vesti'geiʃən] *n* investigazione, indagine.
investigator [in'vestigeitə] *n* investigatore, investigatrice.
investiture [in'vestitʃə] *n* investitura.
investment [in'vestmənt] *n (com)* investimento.
inveterate [in'vetərit] *a* inveterato, ostinato.
invidious [in'vidiəs] *a* sgradevole, odioso.
invigorate [in'vigəreit] *vt* invigorire, rinforzare.
invincible [in'vinsəbl] *a* invincibile.
inviolate [in'vaiəlit] *a* inviolato.
invisible [in'vizəbl] *a* invisibile.
invitation [,invi'teiʃən] *n* invito.
invite [in'vait] *vt* invitare.
inviting [in'vaitiŋ] *a* invitante, attraente.
invocation [,invou'keiʃən] *n* invocazione.
invoice ['invɔis] *n (com)* fattura; *vt (com)* fatturare.
invoke [in'vouk] *vt* invocare.
involuntary [in'vɔləntəri] *a* involontario.
involve [in'vɔlv] *vt* implicare, coinvolgere, comportare.
inward ['inwəd] *a* interno, intimo; verso l'interno.
inwardly ['inwədli] *ad* internamente, *(fig)* intimamente.
iodine ['aiədiːn] *n* iodio.
Ionian [ai'ouniən] *a n* Ionio.
irascible [i'ræsibl] *a* irascibile; irritabile.
irate [ai'reit] *a* irato.
Ireland ['aiəːlənd] *n* Irlanda.
iris ['aiəris] *n* iride, *(bot)* iris, giaggiolo.
Irish ['aiəriʃ] *a n* irlandese
irksome ['əːksəm] *a* fastidioso, tedioso.
iron ['aiən] *a* ferreo, di ferro, in ferro; *n* ferro; ferro da stiro; *vt* stirare; ferrare; **i. age** età del ferro; **i. industry** industria siderurgica; **i. foundry** fonderia; **i. ore** minerale di ferro.
ironclad ['aiənklæd] *a* corazzato; *n* corazzata.
ironical [ai'rɔnikəl] *a* ironico.

ironmonger ['aiən,mʌŋgə] n negoziante in ferramenta.

ironmongery ['aiən,mʌŋgəri] n ferramenta.

ironwork ['aiənwəːk] n lavoro in ferro, costruzione in ferro.

irony ['aiərəni] n ironia.

irradiate [i'reidieit] vti irradiare.

irrational [i'ræʃənl] a irrazionale.

irreconcilable [i'rekənsailəbl] a irreconciliabile.

irrefutable [i'refjutəbl] a irrefutabile.

irregular [i'regjulə] a irregolare, anormale.

irrelevant [i'relivənt] a non appropriato, non pertinente.

irremovable [,iri'muːvəbl] a irremovibile.

irreparable [i'repərəbl] a irreparabile.

irreplaceable [,iri'pleisəbl] a insostituibile.

irrepressible [,iri'presəbl] a irreprimibile, irrefrenabile.

irreproachable [,iri'proutʃəbl] a irreprensibile.

irresistible [,iri'zistəbl] a irresistibile.

irresolute [i'rezəluːt] a irresoluto.

irresolution ['i,rezə'luːʃən] n irresolutezza.

irrespective [,iris'pektiv] a senza riguardo a.

irresponsible [,iris'pɔnsəbl] a irresponsabile.

irreverent [i'revərənt] a irriverente.

irrevocable [i'revəkəbl] a irrevocabile.

irrigate ['irigeit] vt irrigare.

irrigation [,iri'geiʃən] n irrigazione.

irritable ['iritəbl] a irritabile.

irritably ['iritəbli] ad irritabilmente.

irritant ['iritənt] a n irritante.

irritate ['iriteit] vt irritare.

irritation [,iri'teiʃən] n irritazione.

irruption [i'rʌpʃən] n irruzione.

Isabel ['izəbel] nf pr Isabella.

Islam ['izlɑːm] n pr Islam.

Islamic [iz'læmik] a islamico, maomettano.

island ['ailənd] n isola; (road) salvagente.

islander ['ailəndə] n isolano.

isolate ['aisəleit] vt isolare.

isolation [,aisə'leiʃən] n isolamento.

Israel ['izreiəl] n Israele.

Israeli [iz'reili] a n israeliano.

Israelite ['izriəlait] n israelita.

issue ['isjuː] n uscita, sbocco; (notes etc) emissione; (publication) tiratura, edizione; (offspring) discendenza; vt pubblicare; rilasciare; vi uscire.

isthmus ['isməs] n istmo.

it [it] pron esso, essa, lo, la; **its** a (il) suo, (la) sua; **itself** pron si, se stesso, se stessa.

Italian [i'tæliən] a n italiano.

italics [i'tæliks] n pl corsivo.

Italy ['itəli] n Italia.

itchy ['itʃi] a che prude.

itch [itʃ] n prurito, scabbia; vi prudere.

item ['aitəm] n articolo, numero; (com) voce.

iterate ['itəreit] vt ripetere.

itinerant [i'tinərənt] a ambulante, girovago.

itinerary [ai'tinərəri] n itinerario.

ivory ['aivəri] a di (in) avorio; n avorio.

ivy ['aivi] n edera.

J

jab [dʒæb] vt colpire con oggetto appuntito.

jabber ['dʒæbə] vti pronunciare rapidamente e indistintamente, mormorare, borbottare.

jack [dʒæk] n (naut) bandiera; (mech) cricco; (spit) girarrosto; (cards) fante; (bowls) boccino; **j. of all trades** factotum.

jackal ['dʒækɔːl] n sciacallo.

jackass ['dʒækæs] n somaro.

jackdaw ['dʒækdɔː] n cornacchia, taccola.

jacket ['dʒækit] n giacca, giacchetta; buccia; rivestimento; copertina di libro.

jackknife ['dʒæknaif] n coltello a serramanico.

jackpot ['dʒækpɔt] n (poker) posta; **to hit the j.** fare una grossa vincita.

Jacob ['dʒeikəb] nm pr Giacobbe.

Jacobite ['dʒækəbait] n giacobita.

jade [dʒeid] n giada; vecchia cavalla; donnaccia.

jag [dʒæg] n punta di roccia, sporgenza appuntita.

jagged ['dʒægid] a dentellato, frastagliato.

jail [dʒeil] n carcere, prigione; vt incarcerare.

jailer ['dʒeilə] n carceriere.

jam [dʒæm] n conserva di frutta, marmellata; blocco; compressione; ingorgo di traffico; vt comprimere, bloccare, bloccarsi.

Jamaica [dʒə'meikə] n Giamaica.

Jamaican [dʒə'meikən] a n giamaicano.

James [dʒeimz] nm pr Giacomo.

Jane [dʒein] nf pr Giovanna, Gianna.

jangle ['dʒæŋgl] n suono aspro e discordante; vti (far) fare rumori discordanti; vociare sgarbatamente, berciare.

janitor ['dʒænitə] n bidello; portiere.

January ['dʒænjuəri] n gennaio.

Japan [dʒə'pæn] n Giappone.

Japanese [,dʒæpə'niːz] a n giapponese.

jar [dʒɑː] n giara, vaso, barattolo; suono aspro; vi vibrare; discordare; produrre un'impressione sgradevole; vt scuotere.

jargon ['dʒɑːgən] n gergo, linguaggio professionale.
jasmine ['dʒæsmin] n gelsomino.
jasper ['dʒæspə] n diaspro.
jaundice ['dʒɔːndis] n itterizia.
jaunt [dʒɔːnt] n gita, scampagnata.
jaunty ['dʒɔːnti] a arzillo, vivace.
javelin ['dʒævlin] n giavellotto.
jaw [dʒɔː] n mascella; **jaws** pl fauci pl, mandibola.
jay [dʒei] n ghiandaia.
jealous ['dʒeləs] a geloso.
jealousy ['dʒeləsi] n gelosia.
Jean [dʒiːn] nf pr Giovanna.
jeans [dʒiːnz] n pl calzoni di tela; tuta.
jeer [dʒiə] n derisione, scherno; vti beffarsi, deridere, schernire.
Jeffrey ['dʒefri] nm pr Goffredo.
jelly ['dʒeli] n gelatina.
jellyfish ['dʒelifiʃ] n medusa.
jeopardize ['dʒepədaiz] vt mettere in pericolo.
jeopardy ['dʒepədi] n repentaglio, pericolo.
Jericho ['dʒerikou] n Gerico.
jerk [dʒəːk] n scatto, strattone; vti dare uno strattone; sobbalzare.
jerkin ['dʒəːkin] n giacca a vento; giustacuore.
Jerome [dʒə'roum] nm pr Gerolamo.
jersey ['dʒəːzi] n camicetta a maglia; maglione; maglia sportiva.
Jerusalem [dʒə'ruːsələm] n Gerusalemme.
jest [dʒest] n scherzo, beffa, zimbello; vi scherzare.
jester ['dʒestə] n burlone, buffone.
Jesuit ['dʒezjuit] n gesuita; ipocrita.
Jesus ['dʒiːzəs] nm pr Gesù.
jet [dʒet] n zampillo, getto; (chem) becco; giaietto.
jetsam ['dʒetsəm] n (naut) relitti pl di mare.
jettison ['dʒetisn] vt gettare in mare (un carico); (fig) disfarsi di.
jetty ['dʒeti] n gettata, molo.
Jew [dʒuː] n ebreo, giudeo, israelita.
jewel ['dʒuːəl] n gioiello.
jeweler ['dʒuːələ] n gioielliere.
jewelry ['dʒuːəlri] n gioielli pl, gioielleria.
Jewess ['dʒu(ː)is] n ebrea, israelita.
Jewish ['dʒu(ː)iʃ] a ebreo, giudaico, israelitico.
jib [dʒib] vi recalcitrare; vt (naut) orientare.
jig [dʒig] n giga.
jigsaw ['dʒigsɔː] n sega da traforo; j. puzzle gioco di pazienza.
jilt [dʒilt] n donna capricciosa; vt abbandonare il fidanzato o la fidanzata.
jingle ['dʒiŋgl] n tintinnio; vti far tintinnare.
Joan [dʒoun] nf pr Giovanna.
job [dʒɔb] n lavoro, occupazione, posto, faccenda.
jockey ['dʒɔki] n fantino.
jocose [dʒə'kous] a giocoso.

jocular ['dʒɔkjulə] a allegro, scherzoso.
jocund ['dʒɔkənd] a giocondo.
jog [dʒɔg] n gomitata, spinta; andatura lenta; vti urtare col gomito, spingere; procedere adagio.
joggle ['dʒɔgl] n leggera scossa.
John [dʒɔn] nm pr Giovanni.
join [dʒɔin] n giuntura, congiunzione; vti associarsi a, congiungere, unirsi a; raggiungere.
joiner ['dʒɔinə] n falegname.
joint [dʒɔint] a articolazione, giuntura; parte di bestia macellata.
jointly ['dʒɔintli] ad unitamente, assieme, collettivamente.
joke [dʒouk] n facezia, scherzo, tiro, barzelletta, burla; vi scherzare.
jolly ['dʒɔli] a allegro, festoso, giovanile.
jolt [dʒoult] n scossa, sobbalzo; vti (far) sobbalzare.
Jonathan ['dʒɔnəθən] nm pr Gionata.
Jordan ['dʒɔːdn] n Giordano, Giordania.
Jordanian [dʒɔː'deiniən] a n giordanico, giordano.
Joseph ['dʒouzif] nm pr Giuseppe; **Josephine** nf pr Giuseppina.
Joshua ['dʒɔʃwə] nm pr Giosuè.
jostle ['dʒɔsl] vt spingere, urtare col gomito; vi lottare.
jot [dʒɔt] n iota, particella minima.
journal ['dʒəːnl] n giornale, periodico; diario.
journalism ['dʒəːnəlizəm] n giornalismo.
journalist ['dʒəːnəlist] n giornalista.
journalistic [.dʒəːnə'listik] a giornalistico.
journey ['dʒəːni] n viaggio; vi viaggiare, fare un viaggio.
journeyman ['dʒəːnimən] n meccanico o operaio qualificato che lavora a giornata.
joust [dʒaust] n torneo.
jovial ['dʒouviəl] a allegro, gioviale.
joviality [.dʒouvi'æliti] n giovialità.
joy [dʒɔi] n gioia.
Joy [dʒɔi] nf pr Gioia.
joyful ['dʒɔiful] a gioioso.
joyfully ['dʒɔifuli] ad gioiosamente, allegramente.
joyfulness ['dʒɔifulnis] n allegrezza, gioia.
joyless ['dʒɔilis] a senza gioia, triste.
joyous ['dʒɔiəs] a gioioso, gaio.
jubilant ['dʒuːbilənt] a esultante, giubilante.
jubilation [.dʒuːbi'leiʃən] n esultanza, giubilo.
jubilee ['dʒuːbiliː] n giubileo.
Judaic [dʒu(ː)'deiik] a giudaico, ebraico.
Judaism ['dʒuːdeiizəm] n giudaismo.
Judas ['dʒuːdəs] nm pr Giuda.
judge [dʒʌdʒ] n giudice; vti giudicare.
judgment ['dʒʌdʒmənt] n giudizio, sentenza, punizione divina.

judicial [dʒu(ː)'diʃəl] *a* giudiziario, imparziale.
judicious [dʒu(ː)'diʃəs] *a* giudizioso.
Judith ['dʒuːdiθ] *nf pr* Giuditta.
jug [dʒʌg] *n* brocca, caraffa, boccale.
juggle ['dʒʌgl] *n* gioco di prestigio; *vi* far giochi di destrezza o di prestigio, raggirare.
juggler ['dʒʌglə] *n* prestigiatore; impostore.
Jugoslav ['juːgouˈslɑːv] *a n* iugoslavo.
Jugoslavia ['juːgouˈslɑːviə] *n* Iugoslavia.
jugular ['dʒʌgjulə] *a n* (vena) giugulare.
juice [dʒuːs] *n* succo; (*sl*) benzina.
juicy ['dʒuːsi] *a* succoso; (*sl*) interessante.
jukebox ['dʒuːkbɔks] *n* grammofono a gettone, 'jukebox'.
Juliet ['dʒuːliət] *nf pr* Giulietta.
Julius ['dʒuːliəs] *nm pr* Giulio.
July [dʒu(ː)'lai] *n* luglio.
jumble ['dʒʌmbl] *n* confusione, mescolanza; *vt* mescolare, gettare insieme alla rinfusa.
jump [dʒʌmp] *n* salto; *vti* saltare, fare un salto.
jumper ['dʒʌmpə] *n* saltatore; maglione, golf.
jumpy ['dʒʌmpi] *n* nervoso, irrequieto, teso.
junction ['dʒʌŋkʃən] *n* congiunzione, unione; nodo ferroviario.
juncture ['dʒʌŋktʃə] *n* congiuntura, giuntura, stato di cose.
June [dʒuːn] *n* giugno.
jungle ['dʒʌŋgl] *n* giungla.
junior ['dʒuːniə] *a n* chi è più giovane, chi ha grado o posizione inferiore.
juniper ['dʒuːnipə] *n* ginepro.
junk [dʒʌŋk] *n* articoli marinareschi *pl*, articoli *pl* di scarto.
junket ['dʒʌŋkit] *n* giuncata.
jurisdiction [ˌdʒuəris'dikʃən] *n* giurisdizione.
jurisprudence ['dʒuərisˌpruːdəns] *n* giurisprudenza.
jurist ['dʒuərist] *n* giurista.
juror ['dʒuərə] *n* giurato.
jury ['dʒuəri] *n* giuria.
just [dʒʌst] *a* giusto, retto; *ad* appena; esattamente, proprio; **j. now** or ora.
justice ['dʒʌstis] *n* giustizia, giudice.
justifiable ['dʒʌstifaiəbl] *a* giustificabile.
justification [ˌdʒʌstifi'keiʃən] *n* giustificazione.
justify ['dʒʌstifai] *vt* giustificare.
justly ['dʒʌstli] *ad* giustamente, a buon diritto.
justness ['dʒʌstnis] *n* giustizia.
jut [dʒʌt] *n* sporgenza; *vi* sporgere.
juvenile ['dʒuːvenail] *a* giovane, giovanile; *n* giovane, minorenne.
juxtaposition [ˌdʒʌkstəpə'ziʃən] *n* giustapposizione.

K

kale, kail [keil] *n* cavolo riccio.
kangaroo [ˌkæŋgə'ruː] *n* canguro.
kapok ['keipɔk] *n* capoc.
Katharine, Katherine ['kæθərin]
Kathleen ['kæθliːn] *nf pr* Caterina.
kedge [kedʒ] *n* (*naut*) ancorotto.
keel [kiːl] *n* (*naut*) chiglia; chiatta; *vt* (*naut*) carenare.
keen [kiːn] *a* acuminato, acuto; amante, appassionato, forte, intenso; **be keen on** essere amante di.
keenness ['kiːnnis] *n* acutezza, perspicacia; passione; entusiasmo.
keep [kiːp] *n* mantenimento; (*of castle*) torrione; *vt* tenere, mantenere, conservare, trattenere; festeggiare; *vi* continuare, conservarsi, mantenersi.
keeper ['kiːpə] *n* custode, guardiano.
keeping ['kiːpiŋ] *n* custodia, armonia.
keepsake ['kiːpseik] *n* ricordo, pegno d'affetto.
keg [keg] *n* bariletto.
ken [ken] *n* comprensione, conoscenza.
kennel ['kenl] *n* canile.
Kenya ['kenjə] *n* Kenia.
kerchief ['kəːtʃif] *n* fazzoletto da capo, fisciù.
kernel ['kəːnl] *n* mandorla, gheriglio; (*fig*) nocciolo.
kerosene ['kerəsiːn] *n* petrolio raffinato.
kestrel ['kestrəl] *n* gheppio.
kettle ['ketl] *n* bollitore, bricco.
key [kiː] *n* chiave; (*mus*) chiave, tasto.
kick [kik] *n* calcio; (*mil*) rinculo; *vti* dare (tirare) calci (a).
kid [kid] *n* capretto; (*fam*) ragazzino; *vti* (*sl*) prendere in giro, scherzare.
kidnap ['kidnæp] *vt* rapire una persona.
kidney ['kidni] *n* rene, rognone; carattere, tipo.
kill [kil] *vt* ammazzare, uccidere.
killer ['kilə] *n* uccisore, assassino; **lady k.** dongiovanni.
killing ['kiliŋ] *a* mortale, distruttivo; (*fam*) affascinante; *n* uccisione, carneficina.
kiln [kiln] *n* fornace.
kilogram ['kilogræm] *n* chilo (grammo).
kilometer ['kiloˌmiːtə] *n* chilometro.
kilt [kilt] *n* 'kilt', gonnellino degli scozzesi.
kin [kin] *n* parentela, congiunti, parenti *pl*.
kind [kaind] *a* buono, gentile; *n* genere, sorta, specie, tipo.
kindergarten ['kindəˌgɑːtn] *n* giardino d'infanzia.
kindle ['kindl] *vt* accendere, destare, infiammare, suscitare.

kindly ['kaindli] a benevolo, gentile; ad benevolmente, gentilmente.
kindness ['kaindnis] n benevolenza, bontà, gentilezza.
kindred ['kindrid] a affine; n affinità, parentela, parenti pl.
king [kiŋ] n re.
kingdom ['kiŋdəm] n regno, reame.
kingfisher ['kiŋ,fiʃə] n martin pescatore.
kingly ['kiŋli] a da re, regale.
kink [kiŋk] n nodo; (fig) capriccio, ghiribizzo.
kinsfolk ['kinzfouk] n congiunti, parenti pl.
kinsman ['kinzmən] n congiunto, parente.
kiosk ['kiːɔsk] n chiosco, edicola.
kipper ['kipə] n aringa salata e affumicata.
kiss [kis] n bacio; vt baciare.
kit [kit] n utensili, attrezzi pl; borsa utensili; kitbag sacco militare.
kitchen ['kitʃin] n cucina.
kitchenette [,kitʃin'et] n cucinino.
kite [kait] n nibbio; aquilone.
kitten ['kitn] n gattino, micino.
knack [næk] n abilità, facoltà.
knapsack ['næpsæk] n zaino.
knave [neiv] n briccone, furfante; (cards) fante.
knavery ['neivəri] n bricconeria.
knavish ['neiviʃ] a da briccone, disonesto.
knead [niːd] vt impastare; massaggiare.
knee [niː] n ginocchio.
kneel [niːl] vi inginocchiarsi.
knell [nel] n rintocco funebre.
knickerbockers ['nikəbɔkəz] n pl calzoni pl alla zuava.
knickers ['nikəz] n pl mutande da donna pl; v also knickerbockers.
knick-knack ['niknæk] n ninnolo.
knife [naif] n coltello; vt accoltellare.
knight [nait] n cavaliere; (chess) cavallo.
knighthood ['naithud] n titolo di cavaliere.
knightly ['naitli] a cavalleresco.
knit [nit] vti lavorare a maglia; saldar(si); corrugare (la fronte); congiunger(si).
knitting ['nitiŋ] n lavoro a maglia; k. needle, k. pin ferro da calza.
knob [nɔb] n bernoccolo; pomo.
knock [nɔk] n colpo, urto; il bussare (alla porta); vti bussare; colpire, urtare, picchiare; to k. down abbattere; assegnare all'asta; to k. out mettere fuori combattimento.
knocker ['nɔkə] n battente.
knoll [noul] n collinetta, poggio.
knot [nɔt] n nodo, groviglio; vti annodar(si).
knotty ['nɔti] a nodoso; ingarbugliato.
know [nou] vti conoscere, sapere.
knowing ['nouiŋ] a abile, accorto.

knowingly ['nouiŋli] ad scientemente, a bello studio.
knowledge ['nɔlidʒ] n conoscenza, cognizioni pl, sapere.
knowledgeable ['nɔlidʒəbl] a intelligente, ben informato.
knuckle ['nʌkl] n nocca (delle dita), articolazione, giuntura; k.-duster pugno di ferro.

L

label ['leibl] n cartellino, etichetta; vt mettere le etichette a, classificare.
labor ['leibə] n fatica, lavoro faticoso; doglie del parto pl; vi affaticarsi, lavorare faticosamente; hard l. n lavori forzati pl; L. Party partito laburista.
laboratory [lə'bɔrətəri] n laboratorio.
laborer ['leibərə] n bracciante.
laborious [lə'bɔːriəs] a faticoso; laborioso.
laboriousness [lə'bɔːriəsnis] n laboriosità; fatica.
laburnum [lə'bəːnəm] n avorno, laburno.
labyrinth ['læbərinθ] n labirinto.
lace [leis] n merletto, pizzo; laccio da scarpe; vt allacciare; guarnire con merletti.
lacerate ['læsəreit] vt lacerare.
laceration [,læsə'reiʃən] n lacerazione.
lachrymose ['lækrimous] a lacrimoso.
lack [læk] n mancanza; vt mancare di; vi mancare.
lackadaisical [,lækə'deizikəl] a affettato, languido.
lackey ['læki] n lacchè.
laconic [lə'kɔnik] a laconico.
lacquer ['lækə] n lacca.
lad [læd] n giovanetto, ragazzo.
ladder ['lædə] n scala a piuoli.
lade [leid] vt caricare una nave.
lading ['leidiŋ] n carico.
ladle ['leidl] n mestolo.
lady ['leidi] n signora, gentildonna; L. Day Festa dell'Annunciazione.
ladybird ['leidibəːd] n coccinella.
ladylike ['leidilaik] a da signora, distinto, signorile.
ladyship ['leidiʃip] n Eccellenza (titolo delle signore dell'aristocrazia).
lag [læg] vi indugiare; farsi tirare; to l. behind restare indietro.
lagoon [lə'guːn] n laguna.
lair [lɛə] n covo, tana.
laird [lɛəd] n (scozzese) proprietario terriero.
laity ['leiiti] n laicato.
lake [leik] n lago.
lamb [læm] n agnello.
lame [leim] a zoppo; vt azzoppare.
lameness ['leimnis] n zoppaggine.
lament [lə'ment] n lamento, pianto.

elegia funebre; *vt* lamentar(si), rimpiangere.

lamentable ['læməntəbl] *a* lamentevole, deplorevole.

lamentation [,læmen'teiʃən] *n* lamentazione, lamento.

lamented [lə'mentid] *a* deplorato; compianto.

lamp [læmp] *n* lampada, lampione, lucerna, fanale; (*fig*) lume.

lampoon [læm'puːn] *n* satira, pasquinata.

lamprey ['læmpri] *n* lampreda.

lance [lɑːns] *n* lancia; rampone; *vt* tagliare col bisturi.

lancer ['lɑːnsə] *n* lanciere.

lancet ['lɑːnsit] *n* bisturi.

land [lænd] *n* terra, suolo, terreno; paese; *vt* sbarcare, atterrare; porsi (in una situazione).

landed ['lændid] *a* terriero.

landing ['lændiŋ] *n* approdo, sbarco; atterraggio; pianerottolo.

landlord ['lænlɔːd] **landlady** ['lænd,leidi] *n* padrone, padrona di terre o case affittate, locandiere, locandiera.

landmark ['lænmɑːk] *n* punto di riferimento, pietra miliare, pietra di confine.

landowner ['lænd,ounə] *n* proprietario di terre.

landscape ['lænskeip] *n* paesaggio.

lane [lein] *n* vicolo, viottolo.

language ['læŋgwidʒ] *n* lingua, linguaggio.

languid ['læŋgwid] *a* languido.

languish ['læŋgwiʃ] *vi* languire.

languor ['læŋgə] *n* languore.

lank [læŋk] **lanky** ['læŋki] *a* alto e magro.

lanolin(e) ['lænəlin] *n* lanolina.

lantern ['læntən] *n* lanterna.

lap [læp] *n* grembo; lembo, falda; (*races*) giro di pista; *vt* lambire; avvolgere, ripiegare; bere rumorosamente; (*of dogs*) lappare; **to l. up** leccare il piatto, mangiar tutto; **lapping waves** maretta.

lapdog ['læpdɔg] *n* cagnolino.

lapel [lə'pel] *n* risvolto.

Lapland ['læplænd] *n* Lapponia.

Lapp [læp] **Laplander** ['læplændə] *a n* lappone.

lapse [læps] *n* decorso, lasso (di tempo), intervallo; errore; perdita di validità; *vi* passare, trascorrere, decadere; (*fig*) cadere.

larboard ['lɑːbəd] *n* (*naut*) babordo.

larceny ['lɑːsni] *n* furto, ladrocinio.

larch [lɑːtʃ] *n* larice.

lard [lɑːd] *n* lardo.

larder ['lɑːdə] *n* dispensa.

large [lɑːdʒ] *a* grande, ampio, spazioso; considerevole; numeroso.

largely ['lɑːdʒli] *ad* largamente, in gran misura.

largeness ['lɑːdʒnis] *n* grandezza, estensione.

lark [lɑːk] *n* allodola; (*fam*) burla, scherzo.

larynx ['læriŋks] *n* laringe.

lascivious [lə'siviəs] *a* lascivo.

lasciviousness [lə'siviəsnis] *n* lascivia.

lash [læʃ] *n* ciglio; frusta(ta), sferza(ta); sarcasmo; *vt* frustare, sferzare, incitare; assicurare con una corda; **to l. its tail** agitare la coda; **to l. out** prorompere (in); (*horse*) sferrare calci.

lashing ['læʃiŋ] *n* frustata; *pl* (*fam*) abbondanza.

lass [læs] *n* fanciulla, ragazza.

last [lɑːst] *n* ultimo, scorso, estremo; *ad* per ultimo; l'ultima volta; finalmente; *n* ultimo; fine; (*shoe*) forma; *vi* durare.

lasting ['lɑːstiŋ] *a* duraturo, durevole.

lastly ['lɑːstli] *a* in conclusione, per ultimo.

latch [lætʃ] *n* saliscendi, serratura a scatto; *vt* chiudere con saliscendi.

late [leit] *a* tardivo; in ritardo; recente; ultimo; fu, defunto; *ad* tardi; **latecomer** ritardatario.

lately ['leitli] *ad* recentemente, ultimamente.

latent ['leitənt] *a* latente.

lateral ['lætərəl] *a* laterale.

latest ['leitist] *a* recentissimo, ultimo.

lathe [leið] *n* tornio.

lather ['lɑːðə] *n* schiuma, saponata; sudore schiumoso; *vt* insaponare, coprir(si) di schiuma.

latin ['lætin] *a n* latino.

latitude ['lætitjuːd] *n* latitudine; (*fig*) larghezza, libertà.

latrine [lə'triːn] *n* latrina.

latter ['lætə] *a pron* (*di due*) quest'ultimo, il secondo.

latterly ['lætəli] *ad* di recente.

lattice ['lætis] *n* gɪata, traliccio.

laudable ['lɔːdəbl] *a* lodevole.

laugh(ter) ['lɑːf(tə)] *n* risata, riso.

laugh [lɑːf] *vi* ridere.

laughable ['lɑːfəbl] *a* buffo, comico.

launch [lɔːntʃ] *n* (*naut*) lancia, varo; *vt* varare; *vti* lanciar(si) in.

launder ['lɔːndə] *vti* lavare e stirare, fare il bucato.

launderette [lɔːnd'ret] *n* lavanderia automatica (dove il cliente fa il bucato da sè).

laundress ['lɔːndris] *n* lavandaia.

laundry ['lɔːndri] *n* lavanderia, bucato; **laundryman** lavandaio.

Laura ['lɔːrə] *nf pr* Laura.

laurel ['lɔrəl] *n* alloro, lauro.

Laurence ['lɔrəns] *nm pr* Lorenzo.

lavatory ['lævətəri] *n* gabinetto, latrina.

lavender ['lævində] *n* lavanda.

lavish ['læviʃ] *a* generoso, prodigo; *vt* prodigare, profondere.

law [lɔː] *n* diritto, legge.

lawful ['lɔːful] *a* legale, legittimo.

lawfully ['lɔːfuli] *ad* legittimamente, legalmente.

lawfulness ['lɔːfulnis] n legalità, legittimità.

lawgiver ['lɔːˌgivə] n legislatore.

lawless ['lɔːlis] a illegale, illegittimo.

lawn [lɔːn] n prato; batista; **lawn-mower** falciatrice per prati; **l. tennis** tennis su prato.

Lawrence ['lɔrəns] nm pr Lorenzo.

lawsuit ['lɔːsuːt] n causa, procedimento legale.

lawyer ['lɔːjə] n avvocato.

lax [læks] a negligente, rilassato.

laxative ['læksətiv] n lassativo.

lay [lei] a laico, secolare; n (of ground) configurazione; vti collocare, (de)porre, stendere, adagiare; coricarsi; scommettere; **to l. down** deporre; (law) dettare; (project) tracciare; (life) fare sacrifizio di; **to l. out** spendere; spiegare; **to l. up** ammassare; **laid up** allettato; **to l. waste** devastare.

layer ['leiə] n strato; (agr) propaggine.

layette [lei'et] n corredino da neonato.

layman ['leimən] n laico, secolare.

laze [leiz] vi passare (il tempo) in ozio, oziare.

laziness ['leizinis] n indolenza, pigrizia.

lazy ['leizi] a indolente, pigro.

lead [liːd] n direzione, guida; (dog) guinzaglio; vt condurre, dirigere, guidare; vi fare da guida.

lead [led] n piombo, scandaglio; vt impiombare, saldare col piombo.

leaden ['ledn] a di piombo, plumbeo.

leader ['liːdə] n capo, duce; articolo di fondo d'un giornale.

leadership ['liːdəʃip] n direzione, comando.

leading ['liːdiŋ] a dominante, eminente, principale; **l. article** articolo di fondo.

leaf [liːf] pl **leaves** n foglia; foglio, pagina; (door) battente; (table) asse.

leafless ['liːflis] a senza foglie, sfrondato.

leaflet ['liːflit] n manifestino, volantino.

leafy ['liːfi] a coperto di foglie, fronzuto.

league [liːg] n lega, società; vt unir(si) in lega.

leak [liːk] n falla; vi far acqua, perdere; **to l. out** trapelare.

leakage ['liːkidʒ] n perdita, indiscrezione.

leaky ['liːki] a che perde, che cola.

lean [liːn] a magro, scarno; vti appoggiare, appoggiarsi, inclinarsi.

leaning ['liːniŋ] a pendente, inclinato; n inclinazione; **the Leaning Tower of Pisa** la Torre pendente di Pisa.

leanness ['liːnnis] n magrezza.

leap [liːp] n balzo, salto; vi balzare, saltare; **l. year** anno bisestile.

learn [ləːn] vt imparare.

learned ['ləːnid] a dotto, erudito.

learning ['ləːniŋ] n erudizione, sapere.

lease [liːs] n contratto d'affitto; vt affittare; **leasehold** a in affitto; n durata di un contratto d'affitto; **leaseholder** n affittuario.

leash [liːʃ] n guinzaglio.

least [liːst] a il più piccolo, il minimo; n il meno; ad meno, minimamente; **at l.** almeno.

leather ['leðə] n cuoio, pelle; a di cuoio, di pelle.

leave [liːv] n licenza, permesso; congedo, commiato; vt abbandonare, lasciare; vi partire.

leaven ['levn] n lievito; vt far lievitare.

leaving ['liːviŋ] n partenza; pl avanzi, rifiuti.

Lebanese [ˌlebə'niːz] a n libanese.

Lebanon ['lebənən] n Libano.

lecherous ['letʃərəs] a lascivo, vizioso.

lechery ['letʃəri] n lascivia; libertinaggio.

lecture ['lektʃə] n conferenza; lezione universitaria; ramanzina; vti tenere una conferenza, o lezione; ammonire.

lecturer ['lektʃərə] n conferenziere; libero docente.

lectureship ['lektʃəʃip] n carica di libero docente.

ledge [ledʒ] n ripiano, sporgenza.

ledger ['ledʒə] n (com) libro mastro.

lee [liː] n (naut) sottovento.

leech [liːtʃ] n sanguisuga.

leek [liːk] n porro.

leer [liə] n occhiata bieca, occhiata maliziosa; vi guardar di traverso.

leeward ['liːwəd] a di sottovento; ad in direzione di sottovento.

left [left] a sinistro, manco, mancino; n sinistra; ad a sinistra; **l.-handed** mancino.

leftovers ['leftˌouvəz] n pl rimasugli, resti pl.

leg [leg] n gamba; (fowl) coscia; (birds etc) zampa; (table etc) piede.

legacy ['legəsi] n legato, lascito.

legal ['liːgəl] a legale.

legality [liː(ː)'gæliti] n legalità.

legalization [ˌligəlai'zeiʃən] n legalizzazione.

legalize ['liːgəlaiz] vt legalizzare.

legate ['legit] n legato.

legatee [ˌlegə'tiː] n legatario.

legation [li'geiʃən] n legazione.

legend ['ledʒənd] n leggenda.

legendary ['ledʒəndəri] a leggendario.

legging ['legiŋ] n gambale; pl ghette pl.

Leghorn ['leg'hɔːn] n Livorno.

legible ['ledʒəbl] a leggibile.

legion ['liːdʒən] n legione.

legionary ['liːdʒənəri] a legionario.

legislation [ˌledʒis'leiʃən] n legislazione.

legislative ['ledʒislətiv] a legislativo.

legislator ['ledʒisleitə] n legislatore.
legislature ['ledʒisleitʃə] n legislatura, corpo legislativo.
legitimacy [li'dʒitiməsi] n legittimità.
legitimate [li'dʒitimit] a legittimo.
leisure ['leʒə] n agio, ozio, comodo, ritagli di tempo.
leisurely ['leʒəli] a fatto con comodo, a proprio agio; ad senza fretta.
lemon ['lemən] n limone.
lemonade ['lemə'neid] n limonata.
lend [lend] vt prestare; vi fare un prestito.
lending ['lendiŋ] n prestito.
length [leŋθ] n lunghezza; taglio di stoffa.
lengthen ['leŋθən] vti allungar(si).
lengthy ['leŋθi] a lungo, prolisso.
lenient ['li:niənt] a indulgente.
lens [lenz] n lente.
Lent [lent] n quaresima.
Lenten ['lentən] a quaresimale, da quaresima.
lentil ['lentl] n lenticchia.
Leo ['li(:)ou] nm pr Leone.
Leonard ['lenəd] nm pr Leonardo.
leopard ['lepəd] n leopardo.
Leopold ['liəpould] nm pr Leopoldo.
leper ['lepə] n lebbroso.
leprosy ['leprəsi] n lebbra.
lesbian ['lezbiən] a lesbico; n lesbica.
lesion ['li:ʒən] n lesione.
less [les] a meno, minore; n meno; ad prep meno.
lessee [le'si:] n locatario.
lessen ['lesn] vti diminuire, rimpicciolir(si).
lessening ['lesniŋ] n diminuzione, attenuazione.
lesser ['lesə] a minore.
lesson ['lesn] n lezione.
lest [lest] cj per paura che.
let [let] vt lasciare, permettere; dare in affitto; l. down abbassare; allungare; sciogliere; deludere; l. off lasciar andare; perdonare, (a shot etc) far partire.
lethal ['li:θəl] a letale, mortale.
lethargic [le'θɑ:dʒik] a letargico.
lethargy ['leθədʒi] n letargo.
letter ['letə] n lettera.
lettuce ['letis] n lattuga.
leukemia [lju'ki:miə] n leucemia.
Levantine ['levəntain] a levantino.
level ['levl] a livellato, orizzontale, pari; n spianata, livello; l. crossing passaggio a livello; vt livellare, spianare, pareggiare; (fig) dirigere.
lever ['li:və] n (mech) leva.
leverage ['li:vəridʒ] n (mech) azione d'una leva, sistema di leve.
levity ['leviti] n frivolezza, leggerezza.
levy ['levi] n leva; imposta, tributo; vt arruolare; (tax etc) imporre.
lewd [lju:d] a impudico, lascivo.
lewdness ['lju:dnis] n lascivia.
Lewis ['lu(:)is] nm pr Luigi.

lexicographer [‚leksi'kɔgrəfə] n lessicografo.
lexicon ['leksikən] n lessico.
liability [‚laiə'biliti] n obbligo; disposizione a; responsabilità; pl (com) passività.
liable ['laiəbl] a soggetto, responsabile.
liar ['laiə] n bugiardo.
libation [lai'beiʃən] n libagione.
libel ['laibəl] n libello, calunnia, diffamazione; vt diffamare a mezzo di libello.
libelous ['laibləs] a diffamatorio.
liberal ['libərəl] a n liberale.
liberality [‚libə'ræliti] n liberalità.
liberate ['libəreit] vt liberare.
liberation [‚libə'reiʃən] n liberazione.
Liberia [lai'biəriə] n Liberia.
libertine ['libə(:)ti:n] a n libertino.
liberty ['libəti] n libertà; licenza.
librarian [lai'brɛəriən] n bibliotecario.
library ['laibrəri] n biblioteca.
libretto [li'bretou] ol **librettos** n libretto (d'opera).
Libya ['libiə] n Libia.
Libyan ['libiən] a libico.
license ['laisəns] n licenza, patente, permesso.
license ['laisəns] vt autorizzare, dar permesso a.
licentious [lai'senʃəs] a licenzioso.
lichen ['laiken] n lichene.
lick [lik] n leccata; vt leccare, lambire.
lid [lid] n coperchio.
lie [lai] n bugia, menzogna; (of ground) configurazione; vi mentire; giacere, stare, trovarsi; l. down sdraiarsi.
lieutenant [lu:'tenənt] n luogotenente, tenente.
life [laif] n vita; l. insurance assicurazione sulla vita; l. preserver salvagente; bastone sfollagente.
lifebelt ['laifbelt] n cintura di salvataggio, salvagente.
lifeboat ['laifbout] n scialuppa di salvataggio.
life-giving ['laif‚giviŋ] a vivificante.
lifeguard ['laifgɑ:d] n bagnino.
lifeless ['laiflis] a inanimato, senza vita.
lifelike ['laiflaik] a realistico, vivido.
life-long ['laiflɔŋ] a che dura tutta la vita.
lifetime ['laiftaim] n durata della vita.
lift [lift] n ascensore, montacarichi; passaggio; vt alzare, elevare, sollevare; vi (of weather) schiarire.
ligament ['ligəmənt] n legamento.
ligature ['ligətʃuə] n legatura.
light [lait] a chiaro, biondo, luminoso; leggero; n luce, lampada, lume; finestra; vt accendere; vi illuminar (si).
lighten ['laitn] vti alleggerir(si), accender(si), rischiararsi.

lighter ['laitə] *n* accendisigaro, accendino; (*naut*) chiatta.
light-hearted ['lait'hɑːtid] *a* allegro, ottimista.
lighthouse ['laithaus] *n* faro.
lighting ['laitiŋ] *n* illuminazione.
lightless ['laitlis] *a* privo di luce.
lightly ['laitli] *ad* leggermente; agilmente; un poco.
light-minded ['lait'maindid] *a* frivolo, sconsiderato.
lightning ['laitniŋ] *n* lampi *pl*; (flash of) l. lampo.
lightsome ['laitsəm] *a* allegro, gaio.
lightweight ['laitweit] *n* peso leggero.
Ligurian [li'gjuəriən] *a n* ligure.
like [laik] *a* simile, uguale, somigliante; *prep* come, a somiglianza di; *n* altrettanto, la stessa cosa, *pl* simpatia; *vti* amare, piacere, volere; **I l. that** ciò mi piace; **as you l.** come vuoi.
likelihood ['laiklihud] *n* verosimiglianza, probabilità.
likely ['laikli] *a* probabile, verosimile; *ad* probabilmente.
liken ['laikən] *vt* paragonare.
likeness ['laiknis] *n* somiglianza, aspetto, ritratto.
likewise ['laikwaiz] *ad* parimenti, inoltre, altrettanto.
liking ['laikiŋ] *n* gusto, inclinazione, simpatia.
lilac ['lailək] *a* (di) color lilla; *n* lilla.
lilt [lilt] *n* cadenza, ritmo.
lily ['lili] *n* giglio.
limb [lim] *n* arto, membro; ramo; (*sl*) ragazzo sventato.
limber ['limbə] *vt* **l. up** (*sport*) scaldarsi i muscoli, mettersi in forma.
lime [laim] *n* calce; vischio; tiglio; cedro.
limelight ['laimlait] *n* (*theat*) luce della ribalta.
limit ['limit] *n* limite; (*sl*) il colmo; *vt* limitare.
limitation [ˌlimi'teiʃən] *n* limitazione.
limited ['limitid] *a* limitato; **l. liability company** (*com*) società a responsabilità limitata.
limp [limp] *a* debole, floscio, inerte; *n* andatura zoppicante; *vi* zoppicare.
limpet ['limpit] *n* patella.
limpid ['limpid] *a* limpido.
linden ['lindən] *n* tiglio.
line [lain] *n* linea; equatore; limite; lenza; ruga; (*com*) ramo; *pl* (*of an actor*) parte.
line [lain] *vt* rigare, segnare; foderare; riempire; **to l. up** allinear(si), fare la coda.
lineage ['liniidʒ] *n* lignaggio.
lineal ['liniəl] *a* diretto, in linea diretta.
lineament ['liniəmənt] *n* lineamento, tratto.
linear ['liniə] *a* lineare.

linen ['linin] *n* biancheria, tela di lino; *a* di lino.
liner ['lainə] *n* (*naut*) transatlantico.
linger ['liŋgə] *vi* indugiare, andare lentamente, attardarsi.
linguist ['liŋgwist] *n* linguista, poliglotta.
linguistics [liŋ'gwistiks] *n* linguistica.
lining ['lainiŋ] *n* fodera.
link [liŋk] *n* anello (di catena), legame, vincolo; *vt* congiungere, vincolare; *vi* collegarsi; **cufflinks** gemelli per polsini.
links [liŋks] *n* *pl* (*costruzione sing.*) campo da golf.
linnet ['linit] *n* fanello.
linoleum [li'nouliəm] *n* linoleum.
linseed ['linsiːd] *n* seme di lino.
lint [lint] *n* filaccia, garza.
lintel ['lintl] *n* architrave, mensola di caminetto.
lion ['laiən] *n* leone; (*fig*) celebrità.
lioness ['laiənis] *n* leonessa.
lip [lip] *n* labbro; (*sl*) discorso impudente; **l. service** fedeltà a parole, ipocrisia.
lipstick ['lipstik] *n* rossetto, matita per labbra.
liquefy ['likwifai] *vti* liquefar(si).
liqueur [li'kjuə] *n* liquore.
liquid ['likwid] *a n* liquido.
liquidate ['likwideit] *vti* liquidare.
liquidation [ˌlikwi'deiʃən] *n* liquidazione.
liquor ['likə] *n* bevanda alcoolica.
liquorice ['likəris] *n* liquiriza.
Lisbon ['lizbən] *n* Lisbona.
lisp [lisp] *n* pronuncia blesa; *vi* parlare bleso.
lissom(e) ['lisəm] *a* flessibile, pieghevole.
list [list] *n* elenco, lista, ruolo; (*prices etc*) bollettino; (*naut*) sbandamento; *vt* elencare.
listen ['lisn] *vi* ascoltare.
listener ['lisnə] *n* ascoltatore.
listless ['listlis] *a* indifferente, svogliato.
listlessness ['listlisnis] *n* svogliatezza.
litany ['litəni] *n* litania.
liter ['liːtə] *n* litro.
literacy ['litərəsi] *n* grado di istruzione.
literal ['litərəl] *a* letterale.
literary ['litərəri] *a* letterario.
literate ['litərit] *a* non analfabeta; letterato.
literature ['litəritʃə] *n* letteratura.
lithe [laið] *a* flessibile, flessuoso.
lithograph ['liθəgrɑːf] *n* litografia.
lithography [li'θɔgrəfi] *n* litografia.
Lithuania [ˌliθju(ː)'einiə] *n* Lituania.
Lithuanian [ˌliθju(ː)'einiən] *a n* lituano.
litigant ['litigənt] *n* litigante, parte in causa.
litigate ['litigeit] *vti* essere in causa, contestare.
litigation [ˌliti'geiʃən] *n* lite, causa.

litter ['litə] n lettiera, lettiga; (of animals) figliata; scarti e rifiuti pl; confusione; vt spargere disordinatamente; apprestare la lettiera per; vt (of animals) figliare.
little ['litl] a piccolo, breve, poco, un po' di; ad poco; n poco.
live [laiv] a vivente, vivo; [liv] vi vivere, abitare.
livelihood ['laivlihud] n mezzi di sussistenza pl, mantenimento.
liveliness ['laivlinis] n vivacità, animazione.
lively ['laivli] a vivo, vivace.
liven ['laivn] vt ravvivare.
liver ['livə] n fegato.
livery ['livəri] n livrea; l.-stable stallaggio.
livid ['livid] a livido; (fam) furioso.
living ['liviŋ] a vivente; n (mezzi per vivere) vita; beneficio ecclesiastico.
lizard ['lizəd] n lucertola.
llama ['lɑːmə] n (zool) lama.
load [loud] n carico, peso; vt caricare, colmare.
loaf [louf] pl **loaves** n pane in cassetta; pagnotta; (sl) testa; vi oziare.
loafer ['loufə] n fannullone.
loam [loum] n argilla sabbiosa.
loan [loun] n prestito.
loath [louθ] a restio, riluttante.
loathe [louð] vt detestare, sentire ripugnanza per.
loathing ['louðiŋ] n ripugnanza.
loathsome ['louðsəm] a nauseante, ripugnante.
lobby ['lɔbi] n corridoio (in un pubblico edificio).
lobster ['lɔbstə] n aragosta.
local ['loukəl] a locale, del luogo.
locality [lou'kæliti] n località.
localize ['loukəlaiz] vt localizzare.
locally ['loukəli] ad localmente.
locate [lou'keit] vt individuare, situare.
location [lou'keiʃən] n posizione, (com) locazione.
lock [lɔk] n serratura; (canal) chiusa; (hair) ciocca, ciuffo; vt chiudere a chiave, serrare.
locker ['lɔkə] n armadietto.
locket ['lɔkit] n medaglione.
locksmith ['lɔksmiθ] n fabbro.
locomotion [,loukə'mouʃən] n locomozione.
locomotive ['loukə,moutiv] a locomotivo, locomotore; n locomotiva.
locust ['loukəst] n locusta.
lode [loud] n filone metallifero.
lodge [lɔdʒ] n casetta (spesso al cancello d'un parco); (freemasons) loggia; vti alloggiare; collocare; (appeal) presentare, sporgere.
lodger ['lɔdʒə] n inquilino.
lodging ['lɔdʒiŋ] n alloggio, usu pl stanze prese in affitto.
loft [lɔft] n abbaino, solaio.

loftiness ['lɔftinis] n altezza, elevatezza, nobiltà; superbia.
lofty ['lɔfti] a alto; altero; elevato, nobile.
log [lɔg] n ceppo, tronco; (naut) diario di bordo.
logarithm ['lɔgəriθəm] n logaritmo.
loggerhead ['lɔgəhed] at loggerheads with ad in urto con.
logic ['lɔdʒik] n logica.
logical ['lɔdʒikəl] a logico.
logician [lou'dʒiʃən] n logico.
loin [lɔin] n lombo, lombata; pl (poet) fianchi, lombi pl.
loiter ['lɔitə] vi bighellonare, indugiare.
loiterer ['lɔitərə] n bighellone, perdigiorno.
loll [lɔl] vi adagiarsi; pigramente; (tongue) penzolare.
lollipop ['lɔlipɔp] n lecca-lecca.
Lombard ['lɔmbəd] a n lombardo.
Lombardy ['lɔmbədi] n Lombardia.
London ['lʌndən] n Londra; **Londoner** n Londinese.
lone [loun] a solitario, solo, isolato.
loneliness ['lounlinis] n solitudine.
lonely ['lounli] a solo, solitario; desolato.
lonesome ['lounsəm] a solitario, malinconico.
long [lɔŋ] a lungo; ad a lungo, lungamente, per molto tempo; n molto tempo; vi bramare, desiderare ardentemente; l.-sighted presbite; preveggente; l.-suffering paziente, tollerante; l.-standing di lunga data.
longing ['lɔŋiŋ] n brama, desiderio ardente.
longitude ['lɔnitjuːd] n longitudine.
longwinded ['lɔŋ'windid] a prolisso, noioso.
look [luk] n sguardo, occhiata, espressione; aspetto; bellezza; vi guardare, sembrare; to l. for cercare; to l. like somigliare a.
looking-glass ['lukiŋglɑːs] n specchio.
lookout ['luk'aut] n guardia; vigilanza; vista; (fig) prospettiva.
loom [luːm] n telaio; vi apparire all'orizzonte.
loop [luːp] n cappio, laccio, nodo scorsoio; gancio; punto a maglia; vti far cappio, annodare.
loophole ['luːphoul] n feritoia; (fig) scappatoia.
loose [luːs] a sciolto, libero, slegato, rilassato; scorretto; sfrenato; vt sciogliere, slegare, liberare.
loosen ['luːsn] vti allentar(si).
looseness ['luːsnis] n scioltezza; (fig) rilassatezza; libertinaggio; (style etc) imprecisione.
loot [luːt] n bottino; vt saccheggiare.
lop [lɔp] vt potare, tagliare.
lopsided ['lɔp'saidid] a asimmetrico, sbilenco.
loquacious [lou'kweiʃəs] a loquace.
loquacity [lou'kwæsiti] n loquacità.

lord [lɔːd] n signore.
lordly ['lɔːdli] a signorile; altero; sontuoso.
lordship ['lɔːdʃip] n signoria.
lore [lɔː] n tradizioni pl.
lorry ['lɔri] n autocarro, camion.
lose [luːz] vti perdere, perdersi; sciupare.
loser ['luːzə] n chi perde, perdente; **to be a good l.** saper perdere.
loss [lɔs] n perdita.
lot [lɔt] n destino, sorte; lotto, quantità, quota.
lotion ['louʃən] n lozione.
lottery ['lɔtəri] n lotteria.
lotus ['loutəs] n loto.
loud [laud] a rumoroso, sonoro, alto, forte; (colors) vistoso; ad ad alta voce, forte.
loudness ['laudnis] n frastuono, rumorosità, vistosità.
Louis ['lu(ː)i] nm pr Luigi.
Louisa [lu(ː)'iːzə] **Louise** [lu(ː)'iːz] nf pr Luisa, Luigia.
lounge [laundʒ] n (theat) ridotto; (hotel) salone, vestibolo; salotto; **l. suit** abito maschile da passeggio; vi andare a zonzo, bighellonare, poltrire.
lour ['lauə] vi corrugare le sopracciglia; (weather) minacciare, oscurarsi.
louse [laus] pl **lice** n pidocchio.
lousy ['lauzi] a pidocchioso; (fig) sporco, vile, schifoso.
lout [laut] n zoticone.
lovable ['lʌvəbl] a amabile.
love [lʌv] n amore; saluti affettuosi pl; vti amare.
loveliness ['lʌvlinis] n leggiadria.
lovely ['lʌvli] a bello, attraente.
lover ['lʌvə] n amante; innamorato, innamorata.
loving ['lʌviŋ] a affettuoso, tenero; d'amore.
lovingly ['lʌviŋli] ad amorosamente, affettuosamente, teneramente.
low [lou] a basso, abbattuto, depresso; ad in basso, a voce bassa; vi muggire.
lower ['louə] vti abbassar(si).
lowering ['louəriŋ] n abbassamento, ribasso.
lowland ['loulənd] n bassopiano, pianura.
Lowlands ['louləndz] n pl Scozia meridionale.
lowly ['louli] a basso, umile; ad umilmente.
loyal ['lɔiəl] a leale, fedele.
loyalty ['lɔiəlti] n lealtà, fedeltà.
lozenge ['lɔzindʒ] n pasticca, losanga.
lubricant ['luːbrikənt] n lubrificante.
lubricate ['luːbrikeit] vt lubrificare.
lubrication [ˌluːbri'keiʃən] n lubrificazione.
lucid ['luːsid] a chiaro, lucido.
lucidity [luː'siditi] n lucidità.
Lucie, Lucy ['luːsi] nf pr Lucia.
luck [lʌk] n fortuna, sorte.
luckless ['lʌklis] a sfortunato.

lucky ['lʌki] a fortunato, propizio.
lucrative ['luːkrətiv] a lucrativo.
lucre ['luːkə] n lucro.
ludicrous ['luːdikrəs] a ridicolo, comico.
luff [lʌf] n (naut) orzata; vi (naut) orzare.
lug [lʌg] vti trascinare, tirare.
luggage ['lʌgidʒ] n bagagli(o); **l. office (room)** deposito bagagli; **l. rack** portabagagli.
lugubrious [luː'guːbriəs] a lugubre.
Luke [luːk] nm pr Luca.
lukewarm ['luːkwɔːm] a tiepido; indifferente.
lull [lʌl] n calma, tregua; vti acquietar(si); cullare.
lullaby ['lʌləbai] n ninna-nanna.
lumbago [lʌm'beigou] n lombaggine.
lumber ['lʌmbə] n legname da costruzione; mobili pl; di scarto; cianfrusaglie.
luminary ['luːminəri] n luminare.
luminous ['luːminəs] a luminoso.
lump [lʌmp] n massa, pezzo, pezzetto, blocco; gonfiore; vt ammassare, riunire in blocco.
lumpy ['lʌmpi] a grumoso, bernoccoluto.
lunacy ['luːnəsi] n demenza, pazzia.
lunar ['luːnə] a lunare.
lunatic ['luːnətik] a n demente, pazzo.
lunch [lʌntʃ] n (seconda) colazione; vi fare (la seconda) colazione; fare uno spuntino.
luncheon ['lʌntʃən] n seconda colazione, pasto del mezzogiorno; spuntino.
lung [lʌŋ] n polmone.
lupin(e) ['luːpin] n (bot) lupino.
lurch [ləːtʃ] n traballamento; vi traballare; **to leave in the l.** lasciare nelle peste.
lure [ljuə] n adescamento; vt adescare.
lurid ['ljuərid] a livido, spettrale, terribile.
lurk [ləːk] vi appiattarsi, stare in agguato.
luscious ['lʌʃəs] a dolce, succolento, delizioso.
lush [lʌʃ] a lussureggiante; succoso.
lust [lʌst] n lussuria, concupiscenza, brama; vi desiderare ardentemente, bramare.
luster ['lʌstə] n lucentezza, lustro; lampadario a gocce.
lustful ['lʌstful] a lussurioso, bramoso.
lustrous ['lʌstrəs] a lustro, rilucente.
lusty ['lʌsti] a sano e robusto, vigoroso.
lute [luːt] n (mus) liuto.
Lutheran ['luːθərən] a n luterano.
Luxemburg ['lʌksəmbəːg] n Lussemburgo.
luxuriance [lʌg'zjuəriəns] n esuberanza, rigoglio.

luxuriant [lʌg'zjuəriənt] *a* lussureggiante, rigoglioso.
luxurious [lʌg'zjuəriəs] *a* lussuoso.
luxury ['lʌkʃəri] *n* lusso.
lyceum [lai'siəm] *n* liceo.
lye [lai] *n* lisciva.
lying ['laiiŋ] *a* bugiardo, menzognero; *n* menzogna.
lying-in ['laiiŋ'in] *n* parto.
lymph [limf] *n* linfa, vaccino.
lynch [lintʃ] *vt* linciare.
lynx [liŋks] *n* lince.
Lyons ['laiənz] *n* Lione.
lyre ['laiə] *n* (*mus*) lira.
lyric ['lirik] *n* lirica, poesia lirica.
lyrical ['lirikəl] *a* lirico.

M

macabre [mə'kɑːbr] *a* macabro.
macadam [mə'kædəm] *n* macadam.
macadamize [mə'kædəmaiz] *vt* macadamizzare.
macaroon [ˌmækə'ruːn] *n* amaretto, spumiglia.
macaroni [ˌmækə'rouni] *n* maccheroni *pl*, pasta.
mace [meis] *n* mazza; (*chem*) macis.
macerate ['mæsəreit] *vt* macerare.
machination [ˌmæki'neiʃən] *n* macchinazione, trama.
machine [mə'ʃiːn] *n* macchina.
machinery [mə'ʃinəri] *n* macchinario, meccanismo; (*fig*) macchina.
mackerel ['mækrəl] *n* sgombro.
mackintosh ['mækintɔʃ] *n* impermeabile.
mad [mæd] *a* matto, furioso; (*of dog*) idrofobo.
madam ['mædəm] *n* (*vocative*) signora.
madden ['mædn] *vt* far impazzire.
maddening ['mædniŋ] *a* che fa impazzire; esasperante.
Madeira [mə'diərə] *n* Madera.
madly ['mædli] *ad* pazzamente, alla follia.
madness ['mædnis] *n* pazzia, follia.
madrigal ['mædrigəl] *n* madrigale.
maecenas [mi'siːnæs] *n* mecenate.
magazine [ˌmægə'ziːn] *n* magazzino; periodico, rivista; caricatore di arma.
Magdalen(e) ['mægdəlin] *nf pr* Maddalena.
maggot ['mægət] *n* baco; (*fig*) capriccio, ubbia.
magic ['mædʒik] *n* magia; **magic(al)** *a* magico.
magician [mə'dʒiʃən] *n* mago.
magistrate ['mædʒistrit] *n* magistrato.
magnanimous [mæg'næniməs] *a* magnanimo.
magnate ['mægnit] *n* magnate.
magnesia [mæg'niːʃə] *n* magnesia.
magnesium [mæg'niːziəm] *n* magnesio.
magnet ['mægnit] *n* magnete, calamita.

magnetic [mæg'netik] *a* magnetico.
magnetism ['mægnitizəm] *n* magnetismo.
magnetize ['mægnitaiz] *vt* magnetizzare.
magnificence [mæg'nifisns] *n* magnificenza.
magnificent [mæg'nifisnt] *a* magnifico, sontuoso.
magnify ['mægnifai] *vt* ampliare, ingrandire; **magnifying glass** *n* lente d'ingrandimento.
magnitude ['mægnitjuːd] *n* grandezza, vastità.
magnolia [mæg'nouliə] *n* magnolia.
magpie ['mægpai] *n* gazza.
mahogany [mə'hɔgəni] *n* mogano.
maid [meid] *n* domestica; fanciulla; zitella; **old m.** vecchia zitella.
maiden ['meidn] *a* verginale, nubile; *n* fanciulla, vergine.
maidenhood ['meidnhud] *n* verginità.
maidenly ['meidnli] *a* di fanciulla, delicato, modesto.
mail [meil] *n* posta, corrispondenza; maglia di ferro; **m. car** vagone postale; **mailman** portalettere; *vt* mandare per posta.
maim [meim] *vt* mutilare, storpiare.
main [mein] *a* principale; *n* conduttura principale; l'essenziale.
mainland ['meinlənd] *n* continente.
mainly ['meinli] *ad* per lo più, principalmente.
maintain [men'tein] *vt* mantenere, sostenere.
maintenance ['meintinəns] *n* mantenimento, manutenzione.
maize [meiz] *n* granturco, mais.
majestic [mə'dʒestik] *a* maestoso.
majesty ['mædʒisti] *n* maestà.
major ['meidʒə] *a* maggiore; *n* (*mil*) maggiore.
Majorca [mə'dʒɔːkə] *n* Maiorca.
majority [mə'dʒɔriti] *n* maggioranza; maggiore età.
make [meik] *n* fabbricazione, fattura, marca; *vt* fare, creare, fabbricare; rendere; **m. for** *vi* dirigersi; **m.-believe** finta, finzione.
maker ['meikə] *n* creatore, fabbricante.
makeshift ['meikʃift] *a* improvvisato; *n* espediente, ripiego.
make-up ['meikʌp] *n* confezione, composizione; comportamento; trucco, cosmetici.
making ['meikiŋ] *n* creazione, fattura, confezione.
maladjusted ['mælə'dʒʌstid] *a* disadatto, incapace di inserirsi (in una società *etc*).
maladjustment ['mælə'dʒʌstmənt] *n* incapacità di adattamento, inadattabilità.
malady ['mælədi] *n* malattia.
malaise [mæ'leiz] *n* malessere.
malaria [mə'lɛəriə] *n* malaria.
Malay [mə'lei] *a n* malese.

male [meil] a maschile; n maschio.
malevolence [mə'levələns] n malevolenza.
malevolent [mə'levələnt] a malevolo.
malice ['mælis] n malizia, malignità.
malicious [mə'liʃəs] a maligno, malevolo.
malign [mə'lain] a maligno; vti calunniare, malignare.
malignant [mə'lignənt] a maligno, malevolo.
malinger [mə'liŋgə] vi fingersi malato.
malleable ['mæliəbl] a malleabile.
mallet ['mælit] n mazzuolo, martello di legno.
mallow ['mælou] n malva.
malnutrition ['mælnju(:)'triʃən] n malnutrizione; denutrizione.
malt [mɔːlt] n malto.
Malta ['mɔːltə] n Malta; **Maltese** a n maltese.
maltreat [mæl'triːt] vt maltrattare.
mamma [mə'maː] n (fam) mamma.
mammal ['mæməl] n mammifero.
man [mæn] pl **men** n uomo, persona, essere umano; (checkers) pedina; (chess) pezzo; vt presidiare; far funzionare; farsi coraggio.
manacle ['mænəkl] n usu pl manetta; restrizione, impedimento; vt ammanettare.
manage ['mænidʒ] vt amministrare, dirigere, gestire; riuscire.
manageable ['mænidʒəbl] a trattabile, maneggevole.
management ['mænidʒmənt] n amministrazione, gestione, direzione.
manager ['mænidʒə] n amministratore, direttore.
managing ['mænidʒiŋ] a dirigente; **m. director** consigliere delegato.
Manchuria [mænt'tʃuəriə] n Manciuria.
mandarin ['mændərin] n mandarino; (bot) mandarino.
mandate ['mændeit] n mandato.
mandolin ['mændəlin] n mandolino.
mane [mein] n criniera.
maneuver [mə'nuːvə] n manovra; vti manovrare.
manful ['mænful] a maschio, virile.
mange [meindʒ] n rogna, scabbia.
manger ['meindʒə] n greppia, mangiatoia.
mangle ['mæŋgl] n mangano; vt manganare, maciullare, straziare.
mangy ['meindʒi] a rognoso.
manhole ['mænhoul] n botola.
manhood ['mænhud] n età virile, virilità.
mania ['meiniə] n mania.
maniac ['meiniæk] a n pazzo furioso; maniaco.
manicure ['mænikjuə] n manicure.
manifest ['mænifest] a manifesto, evidente; n (com) manifesto, nota di carico; vti manifestar(si), rivelare.
manifestation [ˌmænifes'teiʃən] n manifestazione

manifesto [ˌmæni'festou] n manifesto, pl **manifesto(e)s** n manifesto, proclama.
manifold ['mænifould] a molteplice, multiforme.
manikin ['mænikin] n nano, omino; manichino.
manipulate [mə'nipjuleit] vt manipolare, maneggiare.
manipulation [məˌnipju'leiʃən] n manipolazione.
mankind [mæn'kaind] n genere umano, umanità.
manliness ['mænlinis] n virilità, mascolinità.
manly ['mænli] a maschio, virile.
mannequin ['mænikin] n indossatore, indossatrice.
manner ['mænə] n maniera, modo; **manners** pl buone maniere pl, educazione.
mannerism ['mænərizəm] n manierismo; affettazione; (fam) gesto consueto, ticchio.
mannerly ['mænəli] a cortese, educato.
mannish ['mæniʃ] a mascolino.
manor ['mænə] n grande proprietà terriera; maniero.
manse [mæns] n (Scozia) residenza d'un parroco presbiteriano.
mansion ['mænʃən] n palazzo, villa.
manslaughter ['mænˌslɔːtə] n omicidio colposo.
mantelpiece ['mæntlpiːs] n mensola del camino, caminetto.
mantle ['mæntl] n mantello, manto.
Mantua ['mæntjuə] n Mantova; **Mantuan** a n mantovano.
manual ['mænjuəl] a n manuale.
manufactory ['mænju'fæktəri] n fabbrica.
manufacture [mænju'fæktʃə] n fabbricazione, manifattura; manufatto; vt fabbricare, confezionare.
manufacturer [ˌmænju'fæktʃərə] n fabbricante; industriale.
manure [mə'njuə] n concime; vt concimare.
manuscript ['mænjuskript] a n manoscritto.
many ['meni] a pl molti, -te pl; n molti; **a good m.** un buon numero di; **a great m.** moltissimi; **the m.** la folla.
map [mæp] n carta geografica, mappa; vt rappresentare su una carta; **to m. out** progettare in ogni particolare.
maple ['meipl] n acero; **m. sugar** zucchero d'acero.
mar [maː] vt guastare, sciupare.
marble ['maːbl] n marmo, pallina (di vetro).
March [maːtʃ] n marzo.
march [maːtʃ] n frontiera, confine; (mil) marcia; (mus) marcia; vi confinare, (far) marciare.
marchioness ['maːʃənis] n marchesa.
mare [mɛə] n cavalla, giumenta;

shank's m. il cavallo di S. Francesco.
Margaret ['mɑːgərit] **Marguerite** [ˌmɑːgəˈriːt] nf pr Margherita.
margarine [ˌmɑːdʒəˈriːn] n margarina.
margin ['mɑːdʒin] n bordo, margine.
marginal ['mɑːdʒinəl] a marginale; di confine.
marigold ['mærigould] n calendula.
marinade ['mærineid] n (cook) salsa marinata; vt marinare.
marine [məˈriːn] a marino, marittimo; n marina.
mariner ['mærinə] n marinaio.
marionette [ˌmæriəˈnet] n marionetta.
marital ['mæritl] a coniugale.
maritime ['mæritaim] a marittimo.
marjoram ['mɑːdʒərəm] n maggiorana.
mark [mɑːk] n segno, marca, marchio; bersaglio; (school) voto, (German coin) marco; vt marcare, segnare; prestare attenzione a.
Mark [mɑːk] nm pr Marco.
market ['mɑːkit] n mercato; vt esporre o vendere in mercato; **m.** gardener ortolano, orticoltore.
marketable ['mɑːkitəbl] a vendibile.
marketing ['mɑːkitiŋ] n compravendita.
marking-ink ['mɑːkiŋˈiŋk] n inchiostro indelebile.
marksman ['mɑːksmən] n tiratore scelto.
marl [mɑːl] n marna.
marmalade ['mɑːməleid] n marmellata (di agrumi).
marmot ['mɑːmət] n marmotta.
maroon [məˈruːn] a marrone rossastro; n individuo abbandonato su qualche isola o spiaggia deserta; vt abbandonare su un'isola o spiaggia deserta.
marquess, -quis ['mɑːkwis] n marchese.
marriage ['mæridʒ] n matrimonio, nozze.
marriageable ['mæridʒəbl] a ammogliabile, maritabile.
marrow ['mærou] n midollo; zucchino.
marry ['mæri] vti maritar(si), sposar(si).
Marseilles [mɑːˈseilz] n Marsiglia.
marsh [mɑːʃ] n acquitrino, palude.
marshal ['mɑːʃəl] n maresciallo; vt ordinare, disporre per ordine.
marshy ['mɑːʃi] a paludoso.
marten ['mɑːtin] n martora.
Martha ['mɑːθə] nf pr Marta.
martial ['mɑːʃəl] a marziale.
Martin ['mɑːtin] nm pr Martino.
martin ['mɑːtin] n rondicchio.
martinet [ˌmɑːtiˈnet] n zelante della disciplina, castigamatti.
martyr ['mɑːtə] n martire.
martyrdom ['mɑːtədəm] n martirio.
marvel ['mɑːvəl] n meraviglia; vi meravigliarsi.

marvelous ['mɑːviləs] a meraviglioso.
Marxist ['mɑːksist] a n marxista.
Mary ['meəri] nf pr Maria.
mascot ['mæskət] n portafortuna, mascotte.
masculine ['mɑːskjulin] a maschile; mascolino; (fig) maschio.
mash [mæʃ] vt mescolare, schiacciare; **mashed potatoes** purè di patate; **potato masher** schiacciapatate.
mask [mɑːsk] n maschera; vt mascherare.
masochism ['mæzəkizəm] n masochismo.
mason ['meisn] n muratore; massone.
masonic [məˈsɔnik] a massonico.
masonry ['meisnri] n lavoro in muratura; massoneria.
masque [mɑːsk] n rappresentazione allegorica.
masquerade [ˌmæskəˈreid] n mascherata; vi mascherarsi, travestirsi.
mass [mæs] n messa; massa; vti ammassar(si); **m. meeting** adunata popolare, comizio.
massacre ['mæsəkə] n massacro; vt massacrare.
massage ['mæsɑːʒ] n massaggio.
massive ['mæsiv] a compatto, massiccio.
massy ['mæsi] a massiccio, imponente.
mast [mɑːst] n (naut) albero.
master ['mɑːstə] n signore, signorino; professore, maestro; **M. of Arts** laureato in lettere; **m. of ceremonies** (theat) presentatore; vt dominare, impadronirsi (di).
masterful ['mɑːstəful] a imperioso.
masterly ['mɑːstəli] a abile.
masterpiece ['mɑːstəpiːs] n capolavoro.
mastery ['mɑːstəri] n maestria, padronanza, supremazia.
masticate ['mæstikeit] vt masticare.
mastiff ['mæstif] n mastino.
mat [mæt] a opaco; n stuoia, sottopiatto, sottovaso etc; vt coprire con stuoie; **matted hair** capelli arruffati.
match [mætʃ] n fiammifero; uguale; gara, partita; matrimonio, partito; avversario; vti accoppiare, maritare; armonizzare; opporre; uguagliare.
matchless ['mætʃlis] a incomparabile, senza pari.
mate [meit] n compagno; (naut) secondo; scacco matto; vti accoppiar(si); dare scacco matto.
material [məˈtiəriəl] a materiale, essenziale; n materiale, materia.
materialism [məˈtiəriəlizəm] n materialismo.
materialistic [məˌtiəriəˈlistik] a materialistico.
materialize [məˈtiəriəlaiz] vti materializzare, materializzarsi, avverarsi.

materially [mə'tiəriəli] *ad* materialmente, fisicamente.
maternal [mə'tə:nl] *a* materno.
maternity [mə'tə:niti] *n* maternità; **m. hospital** casa di maternità.
mathematical [,mæθi'mætikəl] *a* matematico.
mathematician [,mæθimə'tiʃən] *n* matematico.
mathematics [,mæθi'mætiks] *n* matematica.
matin ['mætin] *n* mattutino.
matinée['mætinei]*n*(theat)'matinée', mattinata.
matriculate [mə'trikjuleit] *vti* immatricolar(si).
matriculation [mə,trikju'leiʃən] *n* immatricolazione.
matrimonial [,mætri'mouniəl] *a* matrimoniale, coniugale.
matrimony ['mætriməni] *n* matrimonio.
matron ['meitrən] *n* matrona, capoinfermiera; vigilatrice.
matter ['mætə] *n* affare, faccenda; materia, questione; *vi* importare; (med) emettere pus; **m.-of-fact** *a* positivo, pratico; **what is the m.?** che c'è?
Matterhorn ['mætəhɔ:n] *n* Monte Cervino.
Matthew ['mæθju:] *nm pr* Matteo.
mattress ['mætris] *n* materasso.
mature [mə'tjuə] *a* maturo; (com) scaduto; *vti* (far) maturare; (com) scadere.
maturation [,mætju'reiʃən] *n* maturazione.
maturity [mə'tjuəriti] *n* maturità; (com) scadenza.
maudlin ['mɔ:dlin] *a* brillo e piagnucoloso.
maul [mɔ:l] *n* maglio; *vt* malmenare, percuotere.
Maurice ['mɔris] *nm pr* Maurizio.
mauve [mouv] *a n* (color) ciclamino.
mawkish ['mɔ:kiʃ] *a* sdolcinato, sentimentale.
mawkishness ['mɔ:kiʃnis] *n* sentimentalità sdolcinata.
maxim ['mæksim] *n* massima.
maximum ['mæksiməm] *a* massimo.
May [mei] *n* maggio; **M. Day** il 1 maggio.
may [mei] *v* difettivo potere, avere il permesso di.
mayflower ['mei'flauə] *n* biancospino.
mayonnaise [,meiə'neiz] *n* (cook) maionese.
mayor [mɛə] *n* sindaco.
maze [meiz] *n* labirinto.
me [mi:] *pron* mi, me.
meadow ['medou] *n* prato.
meager ['mi:gə] *a* povero, scarso, scarno.
meal [mi:l] *n* pasto; farina.
mean [mi:n] *a* basso, vile, gretto, mediocre; (average) medio; *n* mezzo;

media; *vti* significare, proporsi, destinare.
meander [mi'ændə] *n* meandro, tortuosità; *vi* vagare; (fig) divagare.
meaning ['mi:niŋ] *a* espressivo, significativo; *n* significato, intenzione.
meaningful ['mi:niŋful] *a* pieno di significato, significativo, espressivo.
meanness ['mi:nnis] *n* bassezza, tirchieria.
meantime, -while [mi:n'taim, -wail] *n* frattempo; *ad* nel frattempo, intanto.
measles ['mi:zlz] *n* (med) morbillo.
measurable ['meʒərəbl] *a* misurabile.
measure ['meʒə] *n* misura; *vti* misurare.
measured ['meʒəd] *a* misurato, cadenzato, ritmico.
measurement['meʒəmənt]*n* misura.
meat [mi:t] *n* carne; cibo.
meaty ['mi:ti] *a* carnoso, polposo; sostanzioso.
mechanic [mi'kænik] *n* meccanico.
mechanical [mi'kænikəl] *a* meccanico.
mechanics [mi'kæniks] *n pl* meccanica.
mechanism ['mekənizəm] *n* meccanismo.
medal ['medl] *n* medaglia.
medallion [mi'dæliən] *n* medaglione.
meddle ['medl] *vi* immischiarsi, intromettersi.
meddler ['medlə] *n* persona inframettente.
meddlesome ['medlsəm] *a* inframettente.
mediate ['mi:dieit] *vi* far da mediatore, interporsi.
mediation [,mi:di'eiʃən] *n* mediazione, intervento.
medical ['medikəl] *a* medico; *n* (fam) studente di medicina.
medicate ['medikeit] *vt* medicare.
medicinal [me'disinl] *a* medicinale.
medicine ['medsin] *n* medicina.
medieval [,medi'i:vəl] *a* medi(o)evale.
mediocre [,mi:di'oukə] *a* mediocre.
mediocrity [,mi:di'ɔkriti] *n* mediocrità.
meditate ['mediteit] *vti* macchinare; meditare.
meditation [,medi'teiʃən] *n* meditazione.
mediterranean [,meditə'reiniən] *a* mediterraneo; *a n* Mediterraneo.
medium ['mi:djəm] *a* medio; *n* mezzo, strumento; medium
medlar ['medlə] *n* (bot) nespola, -o.
medley ['medli] *n* miscellanea, miscuglio.
meek [mi:k] *a* mite, remissivo.
meekness ['mi:knis] *n* mansuetudine, sottomissione.
meet [mi:t] *n* riunione di cacciatori; *vti* incontrar(si), far la conoscenza di.

meeting ['miːtiŋ] *n* incontro, riunione, duello; **m. place** luogo di ritrovo.

megalomania ['megəlou'meiniə] *n* megalomania.

megaphone ['megəfoun] *n* megafono.

melancholy ['melənkəli] *a* malinconico; *n* malinconia.

mellifluous [me'lifluəs] *a* mellifluo.

mellow ['melou] *a* maturo, succoso, tenero; *vti* ammorbidir(si), maturar(si).

mellowness ['melounis] *n* maturità, succosità; (*fig*) comprensione, maturità.

melodious [mi'loudiəs] *a* melodioso.

melodrama ['melə,drɑːmə] *n* dramma a lieto fine.

melodramatic [,melədrə'mætik] *a* melodrammatico.

melody ['melədi] *n* melodia.

melon ['melən] *n* melone, popone; **water m.** anguria, cocomero.

melt [melt] *n* fusione; *vt* fondere, sciogliere; *vi* fondersi, sciogliersi, dissolversi; (*fig*) intenerirsi.

member ['membə] *n* membro.

membership ['membəʃip] *n* insieme dei membri di una associazione, funzione di membro.

membrane ['membrein] *n* membrana.

memento [mə'mentou] *n* memento; oggetto ricordo.

memoir ['memwɑː] *n* (*pl book*) ricordi *pl*.

memorable ['memərəbl] *a* memorabile.

memorandum [,memə'rændəm] *pl* **memoranda** *n* memorandum, appunto; **m. book** taccuino, agenda.

memorial [mi'mɔːriəl] *a* commemorativo; *n* memoriale, monumento (alla memoria).

memorize ['meməraiz] *vt* imparare a memoria.

memory ['meməri] *n* memoria, ricordo.

menace ['menəs] *n* minaccia; *vt* minacciare.

menacing ['menisiŋ] *a* minaccioso, torvo.

mend [mend] *n* rammendo; riparazione; *vt* accomodare, rammendare, riparare, correggere; *vi* correggersi; rimettersi (in salute).

mendacious [men'deiʃəs] *a* mendace.

mendicant ['mendikənt] *a n* mendicante.

menial ['miːniəl] *a* servile, umile; *n* servo.

menstruation [,menstru'eiʃən] *n* mestruazione.

mental ['mentl] *a* mentale.

mentality [men'tæliti] *n* mentalità.

mention ['menʃən] *n* accenno, menzione; *vt* accennare a, menzionare; **don't m. it!** *interj* di niente!

mercantile ['məːkəntail] *a* mercantile.

mercenary ['məːsinəri] *a n* mercenario.

merchandise ['məːtʃəndaiz] *n* mercanzie *pl*, merce.

merchant ['məːtʃənt] *n* mercante, commerciante.

merciful ['məːsiful] *a* misericordioso, pietoso.

merciless ['məːsilis] *a* spietato.

mercurial [məː'kjuəriəl] *a* mutevole, eccitabile.

mercury ['məːkjuri] *n* mercurio.

mercy ['məːsi] *n* misericordia, pietà, carità.

mere [miə] *a* mero, puro, schietto, semplice.

merely ['miəli] *ad* puramente, semplicemente.

merge [məːdʒ] *vti* immergersi, assorbire, amalgamarsi.

meridian [mə'ridiən] *a n* meridiano.

meringue [mə'ræŋ] *n* meringa.

merit ['merit] *n* merito; *vt* meritare.

meritorious [,meri'tɔːriəs] *a* meritorio.

mermaid ['məːmeid] *n* sirena.

merriment ['merimənt] *a* allegria.

merry ['meri] *a* allegro, brioso.

mesh [meʃ] *n* maglia, rete; *vt* prendere nella rete; (*mech*) ingranare.

mesmerize ['mezməraiz] *vt* ipnotizzare.

mess [mes] *n* confusione, pasticcio; mensa, pasto preso da una comunità; *vt* fare confusione in, un pasticcio di; *vi* mangiare alla mensa.

message ['mesidʒ] *n* ambasciata, messaggio.

messenger ['mesindʒə] *n* messaggero.

Messiah [me'saiə] *n* Messia.

metal ['metl] *n* metallo; **m. fatigue** fatica del metallo.

metallic [mi'tælik] *a* metallico, di metallo.

metallurgy [me'tælədʒi] *n* metallurgia.

metamorphosis [,metə'mɔːfəsis] *n* metamorfosi.

metaphor ['metəfə] *n* metafora.

metaphoric(al) [,metə'fɔrik(əl)] *a* metaforico.

metaphysical [,metə'fizikəl] *a* metafisico.

metaphysics [,metə'fiziks] *n pl* metafisica.

meteor ['miːtiə] *n* meteora.

meteorological [,miːtiərə'lɔdʒikəl] *a* metereologico; **m. office** ufficio metereologico.

meter ['miːtə] *n* contatore, misuratore; metro; metro poetico; ritmo.

method ['meθəd] *n* metodo.

methodical [mi'θɔdikəl] *a* metodico; **methodically** metodicamente.

Methodist ['meθədist] *n* metodista.

methyl ['meθil] *n* (*chem*) metile.

meticulous [me'tikjuləs] *a* meticoloso.

metric ['metrik] *a* metrico.
metrical['metrikəl] *a* (*linear measure*) metrico.
metropolis [mi'trɔpəlis] *n* metropoli.
metropolitan [‚metrə'pɔlitən] *a n* metropolitano.
mettle ['metl] *n* ardore, coraggio, foga.
mew [mju:] *n* miagoliò; gabbia (per falchi); **mews** *pl* scuderie, stalle *pl* (disposte intorno ad un cortile).
mew [mju:] *vi* miagolare.
Mexican ['meksikən] *a n* messicano.
Mexico ['meksikou] *n* Messico.
Michael ['maikl] *nm pr* Michele.
Michaelmas ['miklməs] *n* festa di S. Michele.
microbe ['maikroub] *n* microbo.
microgroove ['maikrou‚gru:v] *n* microsolco.
microphone ['maikrəfoun] *n* microfono.
microscope ['maikrəskoup] *n* microscopio.
microscopic(al) [‚maikrə'skɔpik(əl)] *a* microscopico.
mid [mid] *a* medio, mezzo.
midday ['middei] *n* mezzogiorno.
middle ['midl] *a* intermedio, medio, di mezzo; *n* mezzo, centro; **M. Ages** Medioevo; **m.-aged** di mezza età; **m. class** borghesia.
middleman ['midlmæn] *pl* -men *n* (*com*) intermediario.
middling ['midliŋ] *a* medio, mediocre; *ad* discretamente.
midge [midʒ] *n* moscerino.
midget ['midʒit] *n* omiciattolo, cosa piccolissima.
midland ['midlənd] *a* centrale; **the Midlands** *pl* contee dell'Inghilterra centrale.
midnight ['midnait] *a n* (di) mezzanotte.
midshipman ['midʃipmən] *pl* -men *n* (*naut*) cadetto.
midst [midst] *n* mezzo, centro.
midsummer ['mid‚sʌmə] *n* periodo del solstizio d'estate.
midway ['mid'wei] *ad* a metà strada.
midwife ['midwaif] *n* levatrice.
midwifery ['midwifəri] *n* ostetricia.
might [mait] *past tense of* **may**; *n* forza, potenza.
mighty ['maiti] *a* possente, potente; *ad* (*fam*) molto.
mignonette [‚minjə'net] *n* reseda.
migraine ['mi:grein] *n* emicrania.
migrate [mai'greit] *vi* emigrare, trasmigrare.
migration [mai'greiʃən] *n* migrazione, emigrazione.
migratory ['maigrətəri] *a* migratore, migratorio.
Milan [mi'læn] *n* Milano; **Milanese** *a n* milanese.
mild [maild] *a* dolce, mite, blando.
mildew ['mildju:] *n* muffa.
mildness ['maildnis] *n* dolcezza, mitezza.

mile [mail] *n* miglio (= *metri* 1609).
mileage ['mailidʒ] *n* distanza in miglia; **m. recorder** contachilometri.
milestone ['mailstoun] *n* pietra miliare.
militant ['militənt] *a* militante; *n* attivista.
military ['militəri] *a* militare; **the m.** i militari.
militate ['militeit] *vi* **m. against** opporsi a.
militia [mi'liʃə] *n* milizia.
milk [milk] *n* latte; *vti* mungere.
milkmaid ['milkmeid] *n* mungitrice.
milkman ['milkmən] *n* lattaio.
milky ['milki] *a* latteo, di latte; **the M. Way** la Via Lattea.
mill [mil] *n* mulino, fabbrica; *vt* macinare.
millennium [mi'leniəm] *n* millennio.
millepede ['milipi:d] *n* millepiedi.
miller ['milə] *n* mugnaio.
millet ['milit] *n* miglio.
milliard ['miliɑ:d] *n* miliardo, bilione.
milliner ['milinə] *n* modista.
million ['miljən] *a n* milione; **millionaire** milionario.
millpond ['milpɔnd] *n* gora di mulino.
millstone ['milstoun] *n* macina di mulino.
mimic ['mimik] *a* imitativo; *n* mimo; imitatore; contraffazione.
mimicry ['mimikri] *n* mimesi; mimica; mimetismo.
mince [mins] *n* carne tritata; *vt* tritare; abbreviare; (*fig*) mitigare; parlare con affettazione.
mincing ['minsiŋ] *a* affettato.
mind [maind] *n* mente, intelligenza; animo, opinione; memoria; *vt* badare a, occuparsi di, fare attenzione a, importare; spiacere.
mindful ['maindful] *a* attento, memore.
mine [main] *n* mina, miniera; *pron* (il) mio *etc*; *vti* scavare, estrarre; minare.
miner ['mainə] *n* minatore.
mineral ['minərəl] *a n* minerale.
mingle ['miŋgl] *vti* mescolar(si), mischiar(si).
miniature ['minətʃə] *a n* (in) miniatura.
minim ['minim] *n* (*mus*) minima.
minimize ['minimaiz] *vt* minimizzare.
minimum ['miniməm] *a n* minimo.
mining ['mainiŋ] *a* minerario; *n* lavoro nelle miniere.
minion ['minjən] *n* favorito; **m. of the law** (*fam*) poliziotto.
miniskirt ['miniskə:t] *n* minigonna.
minister ['ministə] *n* ministro; *vi* dare aiuto.
ministration [‚minis'treiʃən] *n* aiuto, assistenza.
ministry ['ministri] *n* ministero.
mink [miŋk] *n* visone.

minnow ['minou] n pesciolino d'acqua dolce.

minor ['mainə] a minore; n minorenne.

minority [mai'nɔriti] n minoranza; minorità.

minster ['minstə] n chiesa d'un monastero, cattedrale.

minstrel ['minstrəl] n menestrello.

mint [mint] n zecca; (fig) grossa somma; menta; vt coniare.

minuet [‚minju'et] n minuetto.

minus ['mainəs] prep meno, privo di; a n meno.

minute [mai'nju:t] a minuto, piccolissimo; ['minit] n minuto; nota, minuta; **minutes** pl verbale.

minuteness [mai'nju:tnis] n minutezza, piccolezza.

minx [miŋks] n ragazza sfacciata.

miracle ['mirəkl] n miracolo.

miraculous [mi'rækjuləs] a miracoloso.

mirage [mi'rɑ:ʒ] n miraggio.

mire ['maiə] n fango, pantano.

mirror ['mirə] n specchio; vt rispecchiare.

mirth [mə:θ] n allegria.

miry ['maiəri] a fangoso.

misadventure ['misəd'ventʃə] n disgrazia.

misanthrope ['mizənθroup] n misantropo.

misanthropy [mi'sænθrəpi] n misantropia.

misapply ['misə'plai] vt applicare erroneamente.

misapprehend ['mis‚æpri'hend] vt fraintendere.

misbehave ['misbi'heiv] vi comportarsi male.

misbehavior ['misbi'heivjə] n cattivo contegno.

miscalculate ['mis'kælkjuleit] vti calcolare male.

miscarriage [mis'kæridʒ] n aborto; disguido postale; insuccesso; errore.

miscarry [mis'kæri] vi abortire; andare smarrito; fallire.

miscellaneous [‚misi'leiniəs] a miscellaneo.

miscellany [mi'seləni] n miscellanea.

mischance [mis'tʃɑ:ns] n disgrazia, sventura.

mischief ['mistʃif] n male, danno, malizia, birichinata.

mischievous ['mistʃivəs] a cattivo, dannoso; malizioso, furbo.

misconception ['miskən'sepʃən] n concetto erroneo, malinteso.

misconduct [mis'kɔndəkt] n cattiva condotta; cattiva amministrazione; adulterio.

misconstrue ['miskən'stru:] vt fraintendere.

misdeed ['mis'di:d] n misfatto.

misdemeanor [‚misdi'mi:nə] n cattiva condotta, infrazione alla legge.

misdirection ['misdi'rekʃən] n indirizzo sbagliato, informazione sbagliata.

miser ['maizə] n avaro.

miserable ['mizərəbl] a triste, infelice; miserabile.

miserly ['maizəli] a avaro, sordido.

misery ['mizəri] n infelicità; indigenza, pl avversità.

misfire ['mis'faiə] vi far cilecca (also fig).

misfit ['misfit] n indumento mal riuscito; (fam) individuo spostato.

misfortune [mis'fɔ:tʃən] n disgrazia, sfortuna.

misgiving [mis'giviŋ] n apprensione; presentimento.

mishap ['mishæp] n disgrazia, incidente.

misinform ['misin'fɔ:m] vt informar male.

misinterpret ['misin'tə:prit] vt interpretar male.

misjudge ['mis'dʒʌdʒ] vt giudicare male.

mislay [mis'lei] vt smarrire, metter fuori posto.

mislead [mis'li:d] vt sviare, ingannare.

misleading [mis'li:diŋ] a ingannevole, che fa sbagliare.

mismanage ['mis'mænidʒ] vt amministrar male, dirigere male.

mismanagement ['mis'mænidʒmənt] n cattiva amministrazione.

misplace ['mis'pleis] vt collocare male.

misprint ['mis'print] n errore di stampa; [mis'print] vt stampare con errori.

misrepresent ['mis‚repri'zent] vt travisare.

misrule ['mis'ru:l] n malgoverno.

miss [mis] n signorina (premesso al nome di donna non sposata); colpo mancato, insuccesso; vti non afferrare, non colpire, perdere, sbagliare; sentire la mancanza di; (fig) far cilecca, mancare; to m. out tralasciare, saltare.

missal ['misəl] n messale.

missile ['misail] n proiettile, missile; **guided m.** missile teleguidato.

missing ['misiŋ] a mancante, assente, disperso.

mission ['miʃən] n missione.

missionary ['miʃnəri] a n missionario.

misspell ['mis'spel] vt sbagliar l'ortografia di, scrivere erratamente.

mist [mist] n foschia, caligine; **Scotch m.** pioggia leggera.

mistake [mis'teik] n errore, sbaglio; vti scambiare, fraintendere, sbagliarsi.

mistaken [mis'teikən] a erroneo, sbagliato.

Mister ['mistə] n Mr Signor(e).

mistletoe ['misltou] n vischio.

mistress ['mistris] n padrona; maestra; amante; **Mrs** ['misiz] Signora.

mistrust ['mis'trʌst] *n* diffidenza, sfiducia; *vt* diffidare di.
mistrustful ['mis'trʌstful] *a* diffidente.
misty ['misti] *a* nebbioso.
misunderstand ['misʌndə'stænd] *vt* capir male, fraintendere.
misunderstanding ['misʌndə'stændiŋ] *n* malinteso; dissapore.
misuse ['mis'juːs] *n* abuso, uso sbagliato; maltrattamento; *vt* ['mis'-juːz] maltrattare; usar male; abusare di.
mite [mait] *n* piccola moneta, piccolo contributo; (*child*) piccino.
miter ['maitə] *n* mitra.
mitigate ['mitigeit] *vt* mitigare, attenuare.
mitten ['mitn] *n* mezzo guanto, manopola.
mix [miks] *vti* mescolare, mescolarsi, armonizzare, associarsi; **to m. up** confondere.
mixture ['mikstʃə] *n* miscela, miscuglio, mistura.
mix-up ['miks'ʌp] *n* confusione, baruffa.
moan [moun] *n* gemito, lamento; *vi* gemere, lamentarsi.
moat [mout] *n* fosso, fossato.
mob [mɔb] *n* folla tumultuante, plebaglia; *vt* assalire, accalcarsi.
mobile ['moubail] *a* mobile.
mobility [mou'biliti] *n* mobilità.
mobilization [ˌmoubilai'zeiʃən] *n* mobilitazione.
mobilize ['moubilaiz] *vt* mobilitare.
mock [mɔk] *a* falso, finto, imitato; *vti* ingannare; deridere, burlarsi di.
mockery ['mɔkəri] *n* derisione, scherno, beffa.
mode [moud] *n* modo, maniera, moda.
model ['mɔdl] *a* modello; *n* modello, modella; *vt* modellare.
moderate ['mɔdərit] *a* moderato, modico; *vti* ['mɔdəreit] moderare, moderarsi, (*weather*) calmarsi.
moderation [ˌmɔdə:'reiʃən] *n* moderazione.
modern ['mɔdən] *a* moderno.
modernity [mɔ'dəːniti] *n* modernità.
modernization [ˌmɔdə:nai'zeiʃən] *n* rimodernamento.
modernize ['mɔdə:naiz] *vt* rimodernare.
modest ['mɔdist] *a* modesto.
modesty ['mɔdisti] *n* modestia.
modification [ˌmɔdifi'keiʃən] *n* modificazione.
modify ['mɔdifai] *vt* modificare.
modulation [ˌmɔdju'leiʃən] *n* modulazione.
Mohammed [mou'hæmid] *nm pr* Maometto.
Mohammedan [mou'hæmidən] *a n* maomettano.
moist [mɔist] *a* umido.
moisten ['mɔisn] *vti* inumidir(si).

moistness ['mɔistnis] **moisture** ['mɔistʃə] *n* umidità.
molar ['moulə] *a n* molare.
mold [mould] *n* muffia; terriccio; modello, forma, stampo; *vt* formare, modellare, plasmare.
moldy ['mouldi] *a* ammuffito.
mole [moul] *n* molo, talpa.
molest [mou'lest] *vt* molestare.
mollify ['mɔlifai] *vt* addolcire, ammollire.
mollusc ['mɔləsk] *n* mollusco.
molt [moult] *n* muda; *vi* mudare.
moment ['moumənt] *n* momento; importanza.
momentary ['moumətəri] *a* momentaneo, transitorio.
momentous [mou'mentəs] *a* grave, importante.
Monaco ['mɔnəkou] *n* Monaco (Principato di).
monarch ['mɔnək] *n* monarca.
monarchy ['mɔnəki] *n* monarchia.
monastery ['mɔnəstəri] *n* monastero.
monastic [mə'næstik] *a* monastico.
Monday ['mʌndi] *n* lunedì.
monetary ['mʌnitəri] *a* monetario.
money ['mʌni] *n* denaro, moneta, soldi *pl.*
Mongol ['mɔŋgɔl] *a n* mongolo.
Mongolian [mɔŋ'gouliən] *a* mongolo; *n* lingua mongolica.
mongoloid ['mɔŋˌgɔlɔid] *a n* mongoloide.
mongoose ['mɔŋguːs] *n* mangosta.
mongrel ['mʌŋgrəl] *n* meticcio; cane bastardo; *a* ibrido, misto.
monitor ['mɔnitə] *n* consigliere; (*el*) monitore; dispositivo di controllo.
monk [mʌŋk] *n* monaco.
monkey ['mʌŋki] *n* scimmia.
monocle ['mɔnəkl] *n* monocolo.
monogram ['mɔnəgræm] *n* monogramma.
monograph ['mɔnəgraːf] *n* monografia.
monologue ['mɔnələg] *n* monologo.
monopolize [mə'nɔpəlaiz] *vt* monopolizzare; **monopoly** *n* monopolio.
monosyllable ['mɔnəˌsiləbl] *n* monosillabo.
monotonous [mə'nɔtənəs] *a* monotono.
monotony [mə'nɔtəni] *n* monotonia.
monsoon [ˌmɔn'suːn] *n* monsone.
monster ['mɔnstə] *a* enorme, mostruoso; *n* mostro.
monstrance ['mɔnstrəns] *n* ostensorio.
monstrosity [mɔns'trɔsiti] *n* mostruosità.
monstrous ['mɔnstrəs] *a* mostruoso.
Mont Blanc [mɔ̃:m'blɑ̃:ŋ] *n* Monte Bianco.
Mont Cenis [ˌmɔ̃:nsə'ni:] *n* Moncenisio.
month [mʌnθ] *n* mese.
monthly ['mʌnθli] *a* mensile; *ad* mensilmente; *n* rivista mensile.

monument ['mɔnjumənt] n monumento.

monumental [,mɔnju'mentl] a monumentale.

mood [mu:d] n stato d'animo, umore; (verb) modo.

moody ['mu:di] a di malumore; lunatico.

moon [mu:n] n luna.

moonlight ['mu:nlait] n chiaro di luna.

moor [muə] n brughiera; vt (naut) ormeggiare.

Moor [muə] n moro, marocchino.

mooring ['muəriŋ] n (naut) ormeggio.

Moorish ['muərij] a moro, moresco.

mop [mɔp] n scopa di stracci, strofinaccio; vt pulire, asciugare (un pavimento).

mope [moup] vi essere abbattuto, depresso.

moral ['mɔrəl] a n morale; **morals** pl condotta, costumi pl.

morale [mɔ'rɑ:l] n il morale, lo stato d'animo.

moralist ['mɔrəlist] n moralista.

morality [mə'ræliti] n morale, moralità.

moralize ['mɔrəlaiz] vi moralizzare.

morass [mə'ræs] n palude.

morbid ['mɔ:bid] a morboso.

morbidity [mɔ:'biditi] n morbosità.

mordant ['mɔ:dənt] a pungente, acuto.

more [mɔ:] a più; ad più, di più.

moreover [mɔ:'rouvə] ad inoltre, per di più.

morganatic [,mɔ:gə'nætik] a morganatico.

morgue [mɔ:g] n 'morgue', obitorio.

moribund ['mɔribʌnd] a n morente, moribondo.

Mormon ['mɔ:mən] a n mormone.

morning ['mɔ:niŋ] n mattina, -no, mattinata.

Moroccan [mə'rɔkən] a n marocchino.

Morocco [mə'rɔkou] n (geogr) Marocco.

morocco [mə'rɔkou] n (leather) marocchino.

moron ['mɔ:rɔn] n deficiente, idiota.

morose [mə'rous] a tetro, imbronciato, non socievole.

moroseness [mə'rousnis] n tetraggine.

morphia ['mɔ:fiə] **morphine** ['mɔ:fi:n] n (chem) morfina.

Morris ['mɔris] nm pr Maurizio.

morsel ['mɔ:səl] n boccone, pezzetto.

mortal ['mɔ:tl] a n mortale.

mortality [mɔ:'tæliti] n mortalità.

mortar ['mɔ:tə] n mortaio, calcina.

mortgage ['mɔ:gidʒ] n ipoteca; vt ipotecare.

mortify ['mɔ:tifai] vti mortificar(si); incancrenire.

mortmain ['mɔ:tmein] n (leg) manomorta.

mortuary ['mɔ:tjuəri] a mortuario; n camera mortuaria.

mosaic [mə'zeiik] a n (di) mosaico.

Moscow ['mɔskou] n Mosca.

Moses ['mouziz] nm pr (Bibl) Mosè.

Moslem ['mɔzlem] **Muslim** ['mʌzlim] a n musulmano.

mosque [mɔsk] n moschea.

mosquito [məs'ki:tou] n zanzara.

moss [mɔs] n muschio; terreno paludoso.

most [moust] a il più, la maggior parte; ad il più, di più, molto; **mostly** principalmente, per lo più.

mote [mout] n bruscolo, pagliuzza.

motel [mou'tel] n 'motel', autostello.

moth [mɔθ] n falena; tarma, tignola.

mother ['mʌðə] n madre; **m.-in-law** suocera; **m.-of-pearl** madreperla; **m. tongue** madre lingua.

motherhood ['mʌðəhud] n maternità.

motherly ['mʌðəli] a materno.

motif [mou'ti:f] n motivo, idea dominante.

motion ['moujən] n moto, movimento; mozione; vi fare cenno a.

motionless ['moujənlis] a senza moto, immobile.

motivation [,mouti'veijən] n motivazione; motivo, movente.

motive ['moutiv] a motore; n motivo, movente; causa.

motley ['mɔtli] a multicolore, eterogeneo.

motor ['moutə] a motore; n motore, macchina; **m. car** automobile; **motorway** autostrada.

motorcade ['moutəkeid] n sfilata di automobili.

motoring ['moutəriŋ] a automobilismo.

motorist ['moutərist] n automobilista.

mottle ['mɔtl] vt chiazzare, macchiare.

motto ['mɔtou] pl **mottoes** n motto.

mound [maund] n montagnola; tumulo, mucchio.

mount [maunt] n colle, monte; cavallo, montatura; vt ascendere, salire, montare, far salire su; incorniciare.

mountain ['mauntin] n montagna, monte.

mountaineer [,maunti'niə] n montanaro, alpinista.

mountainous ['mauntinəs] a montuoso.

mountebank ['mauntibæŋk] n ciarlatano, saltimbanco.

mourn [mɔ:n] vti piangere, lamentarsi, portare il lutto.

mourner ['mɔ:nə] n persona in lutto; chi accompagna un funerale; prefica.

mournful ['mɔ:nful] a lugubre, triste.

mourning ['mɔːniŋ] n lutto.
mouse [maus] pl **mice** n topo, sorcio.
moustache [məs'tɑːʃ] n baffo, baffi pl.
mousy ['mausi] a grigio topo; scialbo, insignificante, (person) timido, silenzioso.
mouth [mauθ] n bocca; foce; apertura.
mouthful ['mauθful] n boccone.
mouthpiece ['mauθpiːs] n (mus instrument) imboccatura; bocchino; (fig) portavoce.
movable ['muːvəbl] a mobile, (leg) mobiliare; **movables** n pl beni mobili.
move [muːv] n movimento; mossa; vti muovere, muoversi, traslocare; commuovere; spingere; procedere.
movement ['muːvmənt] n movimento, moto.
movies ['muːviz] n pl (fam) cinematografo.
moving ['muːviŋ] a commovente; mobile.
mow [mou] vt falciare, mietere.
mower ['mouə] n falciatore; (mech) falciatrice.
Mr v **Mister.**
Mrs v **mistress.**
much [mʌtʃ] ad molto, pressappoco; a pron molto.
muck [mʌk] n concime, letame; sudiciume.
mud [mʌd] n fango; **m.-bath** (med) fangature pl; **mudguard** (aut) parafango; **m.-pie** formina di terra, di sabbia.
muddle ['mʌdl] n confusione, disordine; vt confondere, guastare; **muddler** n confusionario, pasticcione.
muddy ['mʌdi] a fangoso.
muff [mʌf] n manicotto.
muffin ['mʌfin] n piccola focaccia.
muffle ['mʌfl] vt imbacuccare, avvolgere, bendare, coprire, soffocare.
muffler ['mʌflə] n sciarpa pesante; (aut) silenziatore.
mufti ['mʌfti] n abito borghese.
mug [mʌg] n bicchiere, boccale; (sl) faccia.
muggy ['mʌgi] a afoso, umido.
mulberry ['mʌlbəri] n gelso moro, mora.
mule [mjuːl] n mulo; pianella.
mull [mʌl] vt **mulled wine** vino caldo.
mullet ['mʌlit] n triglia; muggine.
mullion ['mʌliən] n (arch) colonnina divisoria d'una finestra bifora.
multiform ['mʌltifɔːm] a multiforme.
multiple ['mʌltipl] a n multiplo.
multiplication [.mʌltipli'keiʃən] n moltiplicazione.
multiplicity [.mʌlti'plisiti] n moltiplicità.
multiply ['mʌltiplai] vti moltiplicar(si).

multiracial ['mʌlti reiʃəl] a dalle molte razze, plurirazziale.
multitude ['mʌltitjuːd] n moltitudine.
mumble ['mʌmbl] n borbottio; vi borbottare.
mummy ['mʌmi] n mummia; (fam) mamma.
mumps [mʌmps] n parotite, (fam) orecchioni.
munch [mʌntʃ] vt masticare, sgranocchiare.
mundane ['mʌndein] a mondano, del mondo.
Munich ['mjuːnik] n Monaco (di Baviera).
municipal [mjuː'nisipəl] a municipale.
municipality [mjuː.nisi'pæliti] n municipalità.
munificent [mjuː'nifisnt] a munifico.
munitions [mjuː'niʃəns] n pl munizioni pl.
mural ['mjuərəl] a murale; n affresco.
murder ['məːdə] n assassinio; vt assassinare.
murderer ['məːdərə] n assassino.
murderous ['məːdərəs] a assassino, micidiale.
murky ['məːki] a fosco, tenebroso.
murmur ['məːmə] n mormorio; vi mormorare.
muscle ['mʌsl] n muscolo.
Muscovite ['mʌskəvait] a n moscovita.
muscular ['mʌskjulə] a muscolare; muscoloso.
muse [mjuːz] n musa; vi meditare, essere assorto in un pensiero.
museum [mjuː'ziəm] n museo.
mushroom ['mʌʃrum] n fungo.
music ['mjuːzik] n musica; **m.-hall** teatro di varietà.
musical ['mjuːzikəl] a musicale.
musician [mjuː'ziʃən] n musicista.
musk [mʌsk] n muschio.
musket ['mʌskit] n moschetto.
musketeer [.mʌski'tiə] n moschettiere.
musketry ['mʌskitri] n moschetteria, fucileria.
Muslim ['muslim] a n musulmano.
muslin ['mʌzlin] n mussola.
mussel ['mʌsl] n arsella, cozza, muscolo.
Mussulman ['mʌslmən] a n musulmano.
must [mʌst] n mosto, muffa.
must [mʌst] v dovere.
mustard ['mʌstəd] n senape; difettivo mostarda.
muster ['mʌstə] a adunata, parata; vti raccoglier(si), radunar(si).
mustiness ['mʌstinis] n muffa.
musty ['mʌsti] a ammuffito.
mute [mjuːt] a n muto.
mutilate ['mjuːtileit] vt mutilare.
mutilation [.mjuːti'leiʃən] n mutilazione.

mutineer [‚mjuːti'niə] n ammutinato.

mutinous ['mjuːtinəs] a ammutinato, rivoltoso; ribelle.

mutiny ['mjuːtini] n ammutinamento; vi ammutinarsi.

mutter ['mʌtə] n borbottio; vi borbottare.

mutton ['mʌtn] n carne di montone o di pecora.

mutual ['mjuːtjuəl] a mutuo, reciproco.

muzzle ['mʌzl] n muso; museruola; (gun etc) bocca; vt mettere la museruola a; (fig) costringere al silenzio.

muzzy ['mʌzi] a confuso, inebetito; instupidito (dall'alcool).

my [mai] a (il) mio, (la) mia etc; **myself** pron io stesso, mi, me stesso.

myriad ['miriəd] a n miriade.

myrrh [məː] n mirra.

myrtle ['məːtl] n mirto.

mysterious [mis'tiəriəs] a misterioso.

mystery ['mistəri] n mistero.

mystic(al) ['mistik(əl)] a n mistico.

mystify ['mistifai] vt mistificare; ingannare; disorientare.

myth [miθ] n mito.

mythological [‚miθə'lɔdʒikəl] a mitologico.

mythology [mi'θɔlədʒi] n mitologia.

N

nag [næg] n (fam) cavallo, -lino; vti (fam) brontolare; tormentare.

nail [neil] n unghia; artiglio; chiodo; vt inchiodare; **on the n.** puntualmente, senz'indugio.

naïve [nai'iːv] a ingenuo, semplice.

naked ['neikid] a nudo, disadorno; evidente; indifeso.

nakedness ['neikidnis] n nudità.

name [neim] n nome; reputazione; vt chiamare, designare, nominare.

nameless ['neimlis] a senza nome, anonimo, innominato; indicibile.

namely ['neimli] ad cioè.

namesake ['neimseik] n omonimo.

nanny ['næni] n bambinaia, balia.

nap [næp] n pisolino, sonnellino; (of material) pelo; vi fare un pisolino, sonnecchiare.

nape [neip] n nuca.

naphtha ['næfθə] n nafta.

napkin ['næpkin] n tovagliolo, pannolino.

Naples ['neiplz] n Napoli.

Napoleon [nə'pouliən] nm pr Napoleone.

narcissus [naː'sisəs] n narciso.

narcotic [naː'kɔtik] a n narcotico.

narrate [næ'reit] vt narrare.

narration [næ'reiʃən] n narrazione.

narrative ['nærətiv] a narrativo; n narrazione, racconto.

narrator [næ'reitə] n narratore.

narrow ['nærou] a stretto, ristretto;

minuzioso; n (usu pl) stretto, gola; vt restringere.

narrowly ['nærouli] ad a stento; minuziosamente.

narrowness ['nærounis] n strettezza, ristrettezza.

nasal ['neizəl] a n nasale.

nastiness ['naːstinis] n cattiveria; sporcizia; indecenza.

nasturtium [nəs'təːʃəm] n nasturzio.

nasty ['naːsti] a disgustoso; cattivo; indecente.

nation ['neiʃən] n nazione.

national ['næʃənl] a nazionale.

nationalism ['næʃnəlizəm] n nazionalismo.

nationality [‚næʃə'næliti] n nazionalità.

nationalization [‚næʃnəlai'zeiʃən] n nazionalizzazione.

nationalize ['næʃnəlaiz] vt nazionalizzare.

native ['neitiv] a n indigeno, nativo.

nativity [nə'tiviti] n natività, nascita.

natty ['næti] a ben aggiustato, in ghingheri.

natural ['nætʃrəl] a naturale.

naturalist ['nætʃrəlist] n naturalista.

naturalization [‚nætʃrəlai'zeiʃən] n naturalizzazione.

naturalize ['nætʃrəlaiz] vt naturalizzare.

naturally ['nætʃrəli] ad naturalmente, per natura.

nature ['neitʃə] n natura.

naught [nɔːt] n nulla, zero.

naughtiness ['nɔːtinis] n cattiveria, disubbidienza, impertinenza.

naughty ['nɔːti] a cattivo, disubbidiente.

nausea ['nɔːsiə] n nausea.

nauseate ['nɔːsieit] vt nauseare.

nauseous ['nɔːsiəs] a disgustoso, nauseante.

nautical ['nɔːtikəl] a nautico.

naval ['neivəl] a navale.

nave [neiv] n navata.

navel ['neivəl] n ombelico.

navigability [‚nævigə'biliti] n navigabilità.

navigable ['nævigəbl] a navigabile.

navigate ['nævigeit] vti navigare.

navigation [‚nævi'geiʃən] n navigazione.

navigator ['nævigeitə] n navigatore.

navy ['neivi] n flotta; marina; **n. yard** arsenale marittimo.

Nazarene [‚næzə'riːn] a n nazzareno.

Nazareth ['næzəriθ] n Nazaret.

Nazi ['naːtsi] a n nazista.

Neapolitan [niə'pɔlitən] a n napoletano.

near [niə] a vicino, intimo; ad presso, vicino; prep vicino a; vti approssimar(si), avvicinar(si).

nearby ['niəbai] a ad prep vicino.

nearly ['niəli] ad quasi; da vicino, strettamente.

nearness ['niənis] *n* prossimità, vicinanza, intimità.

neat [niːt] *a* lindo, accurato; (*of drinks*) liscio; chiaro e conciso.

neatly ['niːtli] *ad* accuratamente; abilmente; elegantemente.

neatness ['niːtnis] *n* pulizia, ordine, accuratezza, proprietà.

necessarily ['nesisərili] *ad* necessariamente.

necessary ['nesisəri] *a n* necessario.

necessitate [ni'sesiteit] *vt* richiedere, necessitare.

necessity [ni'sesiti] *n* necessità.

neck [nek] *n* collo.

neckerchief ['nekətʃif] *n* fazzoletto da collo.

necklace ['neklis] *n* collana.

necktie ['nektai] *n* cravatta.

necrology [ne'krɔlədʒi] *n* necrologia; necrologio.

necromancer ['nekroumænsə] *n* negromante.

necromancy ['nekroumænsi] *n* negromanzia.

nectar ['nektə] *n* nettare.

need [niːd] *n* bisogno; *vti* aver bisogno di; essere necessario, occorrere.

needful ['niːdful] *a* necessario.

neediness ['niːdinis] *n* indigenza, miseria.

needle ['niːdl] *n* ago; **knitting n.** ferro da calza.

needless ['niːdlis] *a* inutile.

needy ['niːdi] *a* bisognoso, indigente.

nefarious [ni'feəriəs] *a* abominevole.

negation [ni'geiʃən] *n* negazione.

negative ['negətiv] *a* negativo; *n* negativa.

neglect [ni'glekt] *n* negligenza, trascuratezza; *vi* negligere, trascurare.

neglectful [ni'glektful] *a* negligente, trascurato.

negligence ['neglidʒəns] *n* negligenza, trascuratezza.

negligent ['neglidʒənt] *a* negligente, trascurato.

negligible ['neglidʒəbl] *a* trascurabile.

negotiate [ni'gouʃieit] *vti* negoziare, trattare.

negotiation [ni,gouʃi'eiʃən] *n* trattativa, negoziati *pl*.

Negro ['niːgrou] *n* negro; **Negro woman** negra.

neigh [nei] *vi* nitrire.

neighbor ['neibə] *n* prossimo, vicino.

neighborhood ['neibəhud] *n* vicinato, dintorni, vicinanze *pl*.

neighboring ['neibəriŋ] *a* limitrofo, vicino.

neighborly ['neibərli] *a* amichevole, da buon vicino.

neither ['naiðə] *a pron* nè l'uno nè l'altro; *cj* nè, neppure; **neither . . . nor** nè . . . nè.

neon ['niːɔn] *n* (*chem*) neon; **n. lights** luci al neon.

nephew ['nevju] *n* nipote (di zio).

nerve [nəːv] *n* nervo; *pl* nervi *pl*; sangue freddo; (*fam*) sfrontatezza.

nervous ['nəːvəs] *a* eccitabile, nervoso; pauroso, timido.

nervousness ['nəːvəsnis] *n* nervosismo; timidezza.

nervy ['nəːvi] *a* (*fam*) eccitabile, nervoso.

nest [nest] *n* nido; covo; *vi* nidificare.

nestle ['nesl] *vi* annidarsi; accoccolarsi.

nestling ['nesliŋ] *n* uccellino di nido.

net [net] *a* netto; *n* rete; *vt* prendere con la rete, pescare; (*fig*) irretire; *vi* far le reti.

Netherlands ['neðələndz] *n pl* Paesi Bassi.

netting ['netiŋ] *n* rete; reticolato.

nettle ['netl] *n* ortica.

network ['netwəːk] *n* rete, reticolato.

neuralgia [njuə'rældʒə] *n* nevralgia.

neurasthenia [,njuərəs'θiniə] *n* neurastenia, nevrastenia.

neurasthenic [,njuərəs'θenik] *a* nevrastenico.

neurosis [njuə'rousis] *n* neurosi, nevrosi.

neurotic [njuə'rɔtik] *a* nervoso; *n* neurotico, neuropatico.

neuter ['njuːtə] *a* neutrale, neutro; *n* neutro; individuo che si tiene neutrale.

neutral ['njuːtrəl] *n* neutrale; *a* neutro.

neutrality [nju'træliti] *n* neutralità.

neutralize ['njuːtrəlaiz] *vt* neutralizzare.

never ['nevə] *ad* non . . . mai, mai.

nevertheless [,nevəðə'les] *ad cj* nondimeno, ciò nonostante, tuttavia.

new [njuː] *a* nuovo, fresco, novello; **n.-born child** neonato.

New Guinea [nju'gini] *n* Nuova Guinea.

New Hebrides [nju'hebrədiːz] *n pl* Nuove Ebridi.

newly ['njuːli] *ad* di fresco, di recente.

news [njuːz] *n* (*sing*) notizie *pl*; **a piece of n.** una notizia; **newsagent** giornalaio; **newsreel** cinegiornale; **newsstand** edicola.

newspaper ['njuːs,peipə] *n* giornale.

newt [njuːt] *n* (*zool*) tritone.

New York ['njuː'jɔːk] *n* Nuova York.

New Zealand [njuː'ziːlənd] *n* Nuova Zelanda.

New Zealander [njuː'ziːləndə] *n* neozelandese.

next [nekst] *a* prossimo, seguente, più vicino; *ad* poi, subito, dopo; *prep* accanto a, vicino a.

nib [nib] *n* pennino.

nibble ['nibl] *vti* rosicchiare; abboccare.

Nice [niːs] *n* Nizza.

nice [nais] *a* buono; amabile, simpatico; grazioso, bello; esatto, scrupoloso; difficile (di gusti); sottile.

nicety ['naisiti] *n* delicatezza; sotti-

gliezza; **to a n.** con estrema esattezza.
niche [nitʃ] n nicchia.
Nicholas ['nikələs] nm pr Nicola, Niccolò.
nick [nik] n tacca; **in the n.** of time appena in tempo.
nickel ['nikl] n nichel.
nickname ['nikneim] n nomignolo, soprannome.
niece [niːs] n nipote (di zio).
Nigeria [nai'dʒiəriə] n (geogr) Nigeria.
Nigerian [nai'dʒiəriən] a n (abitante) della Nigeria.
niggard ['nigəd] n avaro.
niggardliness ['nigədlinis] n avarizia.
niggardly ['nigədli] a avaro.
niggling ['niglin] a insignificante.
night [nait] n notte, sera.
nightfall ['naitfɔːl] n tramonto, crepuscolo; **at n.** sull'imbrunire.
nightingale ['naitingeil] n usignuolo.
nightly ['naitli] a notturno; di ogni notte; ad di notte; ogni notte.
nightmare ['naitmɛə] n incubo.
nihilist ['naiilist] n nichilista.
Nile [nail] n Nilo.
nimble ['nimbl] a agile; svelto, sveglio.
nimbleness ['nimblnis] n agilità, sveltezza.
nine [nain] a n nove; **ninth** a nono.
nineteen ['nain'tiːn] a n diciannove; **nineteenth** a diciannovesimo.
ninetieth ['naintiiθ] a novantesimo.
ninth [nainθ] a n nono.
ninety ['nainti] a n novanta.
nip [nip] n morso, pizzicotto, detto sarcastico, aria gelida, (of liquor) goccia.
nip [nip] vt pizzicare; mordere; stroncare.
nipper ['nipə] n pinza, pinzetta; (sl) monello, ragazzo.
nipple ['nipl] n capezzolo.
nippy ['nipi] a pungente; (sl) svelto.
niter ['naitə] n nitrato di potassio.
nitrate ['naitreit] n nitrato.
no [nou] a nessuno; ad no, non, niente.
nobility [nou'biliti] n nobiltà.
noble [noubl] a n nobile.
nobleman ['noublmən] pl -men n nobile, nobiluomo.
nobleness ['noublnis] n nobiltà.
nobody ['noubədi] pron nessuno.
nocturnal [nɔk'təːnl] a notturno.
nocturne ['nɔktəːn] n (mus) notturno.
nod [nɔd] n cenno affermativo del capo; vti annuire; chinare il capo; sonnecchiare.
noise [nɔiz] n rumore, chiasso, clamore.
noiseless ['nɔizlis] a senza rumore, silenzioso.
noisily ['nɔizili] ad rumorosamente.
noisiness ['nɔizinis] n rumorosità.
noisy ['nɔizi] a rumoroso; turbolento.

nomad ['nouməd] n nomade.
nomadic [nou'mædik] a nomade.
nominal ['nɔminl] a nominale.
nominate ['nɔmineit] vt designare, proporre, nominare.
nomination [ˌnɔmi'neiʃən] n designazione, nomina.
nominative ['nɔminətiv] a n nominativo.
nonchalant ['nɔnʃələnt] a noncurante, indifferente.
nonconformist ['nɔnkən'fɔːmist] a n anticonformista.
nonconformity ['nɔnkən'fɔːmiti] n anticonformismo.
nondescript ['nɔndiskript] a non classificabile, qualunque.
none [nʌn] pron nessuno; ad niente, affatto, per nulla; **n. the less** nondimeno.
nonentity [nɔ'nentiti] n persona insignificante, nullità.
non-existent ['nɔnig'zistənt] a inesistente.
nonsense ['nɔnsəns] n assurdità, schiocchezza.
nonsensical [nɔn'sensikəl] a assurdo, privo di senso.
non-stop ['nɔn'stɔp] a ininterrotto; ad ininterrottamente.
noodle ['nuːdl] n semplicione; (cook) taglierini.
nook [nuk] n angolo, cantuccio, recesso.
noon [nuːn] n mezzogiorno; **noonday** a n mezzogiorno.
noose [nuːs] n nodo scorsoio; (fig) trappola.
nor [nɔː] cj nè, neppure, nemmeno.
Nordic ['nɔːdik] a nordico.
normal ['nɔːməl] a normale; perpendicolare; n perpendicolare; norma.
Norman ['nɔːmən] a n normanno.
Normandy ['nɔːməndi] n Normandia.
Norse [nɔːs] a n norvegese, lingua norvegese.
Norseman ['nɔːsmən] pl -men n norvegese.
north [nɔːθ] a nordico, settentrionale; ad a (verso) nord; n nord, settentrione; **n.-east** nord-est; **n.-west** nord-ovest.
northerly ['nɔːðəli] a del nord.
northern ['nɔːðən] a del nord nordico.
northward(s) ['nɔːθwəd(s)] ad verso nord.
Norway ['nɔːwei] n Norvegia.
Norwegian [nɔː'wiːdʒən] a n norvegese.
nose [nouz] n naso.
nosegay ['nouzgei] n mazzolino di fiori.
nostalgia [nɔs'tældʒiə] n nostalgia.
nostalgic [nɔs'tældʒik] n nostalgico.
nostril ['nɔstril] n narice.
not [nɔt] ad non.

notable ['noutəbl] *a* notevole; *n* notabile.
notably ['noutəbli] *ad* notevolmente; considerevolmente; sensibilmente.
notary ['noutəri] *n* notaio.
notation [nou'teiʃən] *n* notazione.
notch [nɔtʃ] *n* incisione, tacca; *vt* dentellare.
note [nout] *n* (*mus*) nota; segno; appunto, biglietto; *vt* notare, prender nota di; **notepaper** carta da lettere.
notebook ['noutbuk] *n* taccuino, bloc-notes.
noted ['noutid] *a* noto, rinomato.
noteworthy ['nout‚wəːði] *a* degno di nota.
nothing ['nʌθiŋ] *pron* niente, nulla; *ad* per nulla; *n* zero, niente.
nothingness ['nʌθiŋnis] *n* il nulla, inesistenza.
notice ['noutis] *n* avviso; notifica; preavviso; disdetta; recensione; **noticeboard** tabellone per affissi.
noticeable ['noutisəbl] *a* notevole, visibile.
noticeably ['noutisəbli] *ad* notevolmente; percettibilmente.
notification [‚noutifi'keiʃən] *n* notificazione, notifica.
notify ['noutifai] *vt* notificare.
notion ['nouʃən] *n* nozione, idea, opinione.
notoriety [‚noutəː'raiəti] *n* notorietà.
notorious [nou'tɔːriəs] *a* notorio.
notwithstanding ['nɔtwiθ'stændiŋ] *ad prep* nonostante, malgrado, tuttavia.
nougat ['nuːgɑː] *n* torrone.
nought [nɔːt] *n* niente, zero.
noun [naun] *n* nome, sostantivo.
nourish ['nʌriʃ] *vt* nutrire.
nourishment ['nʌriʃmənt] *n* nutrimento, nutrizione.
novel ['nɔvəl] *a* nuovo, insolito; *n* romanzo.
novelist ['nɔvəlist] *n* romanziere.
novelty ['nɔvəlti] *n* novità.
November [nou'vembə] *n* novembre.
novice ['nɔvis] *n* novizio.
noviciate, novitiate [nou'viʃiit] *n* noviziato.
now [nau] *ad cj* ora, allora, ora che; *n* questo momento.
nowadays ['nauədeiz] *ad* al giorno d'oggi.
nowhere ['nouwɛə] *ad* in nessun luogo, da nessuna parte.
noxious ['nɔkʃəs] *a* dannoso, nocivo.
nozzle ['nɔzl] *n* becco, beccuccio; (*pump*) beccaglio.
nuance [nju'ɑːns] *n* sfumatura.
nuclear ['njuːkliə] *a* nucleare.
nucleus ['njuːkliəs] *n* nucleo.
nude [njuːd] *a n* nudo.
nudge [nʌdʒ] *n* gomitata; *vt* toccare col gomito.
nudist ['njuːdist] *n* nudista.
nudity ['njuːditi] *n* nudità.
nugget ['nʌgit] *n* pepita d'oro.

nuisance ['njuːsns] *n* fastidio, seccatura.
null [nʌl] *a* nullo.
nullify ['nʌlifai] *vt* annullare.
nullity ['nʌliti] *n* nullità.
numb [nʌm] *a* intorpidito.
number ['nʌmbə] *n* numero.
numbness ['nʌmnis] *n* intorpidimento, torpore.
numeral ['njuːmərəl] *a n* numerale.
numerous ['njuːmərəs] *a* numeroso.
nun [nʌn] *n* monaca, suora.
nunnery ['nʌnəri] *n* convento (di monache).
nuptial ['nʌpʃəl] *a* nuziale; *n pl* nozze *pl*.
Nuremberg ['njuərəmbəːg] *n* Norimberga.
nurse [nəːs] *n* infermiera; bambinaia, balia, nutrice; *vt* assistere, curare, nutrire; (*fig*) covare (*hatred etc*); coltivare, accarezzare.
nursery ['nəːsri] *n* stanza dei bambini; (*of plants*) vivaio.
nursing ['nəːsiŋ] *a* che allatta, nutre; *n* allattamento, nutrire; professione di infermiera.
nurture ['nəːtʃə] *n* allevamento, cura, educazione; *vt* nutrire, allevare, educare.
nut [nʌt] *n* noce, nocciola; (*mech*) dado; **a hard n.** (*sl*) un osso duro.
nutcracker ['nʌt‚krækə] *n* (*usu pl*) schiaccianoci.
nutmeg ['nʌtmeg] *n* noce moscata.
nutrition [nju'triʃən] *n* nutrizione.
nutritious [nju'triʃəs] *a* nutriente.
nutshell ['nʌtʃel] *n* guscio di noce; **in a n.** in poche parole.
nuzzle ['nʌzl] *vti* frugare (col muso); accoccolarsi (vicino a).
nylon ['nailən] *n* nailon.
nymph [nimf] *n* ninfa.

O

oaf [ouf] *pl* **oafs**, *n* persona goffa, semplicione.
oak [ouk] *n* quercia.
oakum ['oukəm] *n* stoppa.
oar [ɔː] *n* remo; **oarlock** scalmo; *vt* remare.
oarsman ['ɔːzmən] *n* rematore.
oasis [ou'eisis] *pl* **oases** *n* oasi.
oat [out] *n* (*usu pl*) avena.
oath [ouθ] *n* bestemmia, giuramento.
oatmeal ['outmiːl] *n* farina d'avena.
obduracy ['ɔbdjurəsi] *n* ostinazione.
obdurate ['ɔbdjurit] *a* ostinato.
obedience [ə'biːdiəns] *n* ubbidienza.
obedient [ə'biːdiənt] *a* ubbidiente.
obeisance [ou'beisəns] *n* inchino; omaggio.
obelisk ['ɔbilisk] *n* obelisco.
obey [ə'bei] *vti* ubbidire a; ubbidire.
obituary [ə'bitjuəri] *n* necrologia.
object ['ɔbdʒikt] *n* oggetto; fine, scopo; persona o cosa di aspetto

ridicolo; vti [əb'dʒekt] obiettare, opporre, opporsi.
objection [əb'dʒekʃən] n obiezione.
objectionable [əb'dʒekʃnəbl] a offensivo.
objective [əb'dʒektiv] a n obiettivo, oggettivo.
oblation [ou'bleiʃən] n oblazione.
obligation [,ɔbli'geiʃən] n obbligo, debito, dovere, impegno.
obligatory [ɔ'bligətəri] a obbligatorio.
oblige [ə'blaidʒ] vt obbligare; fare un favore a.
obliging [ə'blaidʒiŋ] a gentile, compiacente.
oblique [ə'bli:k] a obliquo.
obliterate [ə'blitəreit] vt cancellare.
obliteration [ə,blitə'reiʃən] n obliterazione, cancellatura.
oblivion [ə'bliviən] n oblio.
oblivious [ə'bliviəs] a dimentico, immemore.
oblong ['ɔblɔŋ] a oblungo.
obnoxious [əb'nɔkʃəs] a detestabile; nocivo.
oboe ['oubou] n (mus) oboe.
obscene [ɔb'si:n] a osceno.
obscenity [ɔb'seniti] n oscenità.
obscure [əb'skjuə] a oscuro; vt oscurare.
obscurity [əb'skjuəriti] n oscurità.
obsequies ['ɔbsikwiz] n pl esequie, funerali pl.
obsequious [əb'si:kwiəs] a ossequioso, servile.
observance [əb'zə:vəns] n osservanza; (religious) pratica.
observant [əb'zə:vənt] a n osservante; a attento, rispettoso.
observation [,ɔbzə'veiʃən] n osservazione.
observatory [əb'zə:vətri] n osservatorio.
observe [əb'zə:v] vti osservare, praticare; rilevare.
observer [əb'zə:və] n osservatore.
obsess [əb'ses] vt ossessionare.
obsession [əb'seʃən] n ossessione.
obsolete ['ɔbsəli:t] a caduto in disuso, antiquato.
obstacle ['ɔbstəkl] n ostacolo, impedimento.
obstetrics [ɔb'stetriks] n ostetricia.
obstinacy ['ɔbstinəsi] n ostinazione.
obstinate ['ɔbstinit] a ostinato.
obstinately ['ɔbstinitli] ad ostinatamente.
obstreperous [əb'strepərəs] a indisciplinato, rumoroso.
obstruct [əb'strʌkt] vt ostruire; ritardare, impedire.
obstruction [əb'strʌkʃən] n ostacolo, ostruzione.
obstructive [ɔb'strʌktiv] a ostruente, ostruttivo.
obtain [əb'tein] vt ottenere.
obtrude [əb'tru:d] vti imporre, imporsi, intromettersi.
obtuse [əb'tju:s] a ottuso.

obviate ['ɔbvieit] vt ovviare a.
obvious ['ɔbviəs] a ovvio, evidente.
occasion [ə'keiʒən] n occasione; motivo.
occasional [ə'keiʒənl] a occasionale, accidentale, di quando in quando.
occasionally [ə'keiʒənli] ad di quando in quando, occasionalmente.
occult [ɔ'kʌlt] a occulto.
occupancy ['ɔkjupənsi] n occupazione, presa di possesso.
occupant ['ɔkjupənt] n occupante, locatario.
occupation [,ɔkju'peiʃən] n occupazione; impiego, professione.
occupy ['ɔkjupai] vt occupare, prendere possesso di; impiegare.
occur [ə'kə:] vi accadere; venire in mente a; ricorrere.
occurrence [ə'kʌrəns] n avvenimento, evento.
ocean ['ouʃən] n oceano.
ocher ['oukə] n ocra.
o'clock [ə'klɔk] it is two o. sono le due.
octave ['ɔktiv] n ottava.
October [ɔk'toubə] n ottobre.
octopus ['ɔktəpəs] n piovra, polipo.
octosyllable ['ɔktou,siləbl] a ottosillabico; n ottonario.
ocular ['ɔkjulə] a oculare.
oculist ['ɔkjulist] n oculista.
odd [ɔd] a dispari, scompagnato; occasionale; bizzarro, strano.
oddity ['ɔditi] n stranezza, singolarità; persona eccentrica.
oddment ['ɔdmənt] n (usu pl) scampoli, rimanenze.
oddness ['ɔdnis] n disparità; bizzarria; stranezza.
odds [ɔdz] n pl differenza; disaccordo; probabilità; vantaggio; o. and ends pl avanzi, resti, cianfrusaglie pl.
ode [oud] n ode.
odious ['oudiəs] a odioso.
odium ['oudiəm] n odio, odiosità.
odor ['oudə] n odore; reputazione.
odorous ['oudərəs] a fragrante, odoroso.
odyssey ['ɔdisi] n odissea.
of [ɔv] prep di; a, in; da; of course per certo.
off [ɔf] ad via, lontano, a distanza; prep (via) da, distante da; a esterno; laterale; remoto; libero; o.-peak di consumo ridotto.
offal ['ɔfəl] n regaglie; rifiuti pl.
offend [ə'fend] vti offendere; trasgredire.
offender [ə'fendə] n offensore, delinquente, reo.
offense [ə'fens] n offesa; colpa, reato, trasgressione.
offensive [ə'fensiv] n offensiva; a offensivo; aggressivo.
offer ['ɔfə] n offerta, proposta; vti offrir(si), presentar(si).
offering ['ɔfəriŋ] n offerta; sacrificio.
offertory ['ɔfətəri] n offertorio; (collection) colletta.

offhand ['ɔf'hænd] *a* casuale; improvvisato; alla buona; *ad* lì per lì.
office ['ɔfis] *n* ufficio, carica, ministero; gabinetto medico.
officer ['ɔfisə] *n* ufficiale.
official [ə'fiʃəl] *a* ufficiale; *n* funzionario, impiegato, ufficiale.
officiate [ə'fiʃieit] *vi* esercitare le funzioni di; (*eccl*) officiare.
officious [ə'fiʃəs] *a* intromettente; ufficioso.
offing ['ɔfiŋ] *n* largo, mare aperto, distanza dalla costa; **in the o.** al largo; (*fig*) in vista.
offset ['ɔfsət] *n* compenso, equivalente; germoglio; rampollo; *vt* controbilanciare.
offshoot ['ɔfʃuːt] *n* germoglio; derivato.
offside ['ɔf'said] *n* (*football etc*) fuori gioco.
offspring ['ofspriŋ] *n* prole, rampollo; prodotto.
often ['ɔfn] *ad* spesso.
ogle ['ougl] *vt* adocchiare, guardare sottecchi.
ogre ['ougə] *n* orco.
oil [ɔil] *n* olio; petrolio; *vt* lubrificare, ungere; **oilcloth** tela cerata; **o. pan** (*aut*) coppa; **oilskin** tela impermeabile; **fuel o.** nafta.
oily ['ɔili] *a* oleoso, untuoso.
ointment ['ɔintmənt] *n* unguento, pomata.
old [ould] *a* vecchio; antico; usato; **o.-fashioned** antiquato.
olden ['ouldən] *a* antico.
oleander [,ouli'ændə] *n* oleandro.
oligarchy ['ɔligɑːki] *n* oligarchia.
olive ['ɔliv] *a* d'oliva; d'olivo; olivastro; *n* olivo, oliva.
omelet(te) ['ɔmlit] *n* frittata.
omen ['oumen] *n* augurio, presagio.
ominous ['ɔminəs] *a* sinistro, infausto.
omission [ou'miʃən] *n* omissione.
omit [ou'mit] *vt* omettere.
omnibus ['ɔmnibəs] *pl* **-buses** *n* (*usu* bus) autobus, omnibus.
omnipotence [ɔm'nipətəns] *n* onnipotenza.
omnipotent [ɔm'nipətənt] *a* onnipotente.
on [ɔn] *prep* su, sopra; a; di; in; per; *ad* addosso; indosso; avanti; in poi; **off and o.** di quando in quando, intermittentemente.
once [wʌns] *ad* una volta, un tempo; *cj* una volta che.
on-coming ['ɔn,kʌmiŋ] *a* prossimo, che si avvicina.
one [wʌn] *a* uno; unico, uno solo; *pron* uno; si; questo, quello, codesto; **o. another** l'un l'altro; si; **o.-sided** unilaterale; **o.-way ticket** biglietto d'andata; **o.-way traffic** circolazione a senso unico.
oneness ['wʌnnis] *n* identità, unione, accordo.
onerous ['ɔnərəs] *a* oneroso.

onion ['ʌnjən] *n* cipolla.
onlooker ['ɔn,lukə] *n* spettatore.
only ['ounli] *a* solo, unico; *ad* solo, solamente, soltanto, unicamente: *cj* eccetto che.
onset ['ɔnset] *n* inizio.
onslaught ['ɔnslɔːt] *n* aggressione, assalto.
onto ['ɔntu] *prep* su, sopra.
onus ['ounəs] *n* peso, onere, responsabilità.
onward ['ɔnwəd] *a* avanzato; progressivo; *ad* (in) avanti.
onyx ['ɔniks] *n* onice.
ooze [uːz] *n* melma, fango; *vi* colare, fluire lentamente; **to o. out** trapelare.
oozy ['uːzi] *a* melmoso.
opal ['oupəl] *n* opale.
opaque [ou'peik] *a* opaco.
open ['oupən] *a* aperto; franco; libero; **in the o.** *ad* all'aperto; **o. air** l'aria aperta, l'aperto; *vti* aprir(si).
opener ['oupnə] *n* tin, can o. apriscatole; **bottle o.** apribottiglie.
open-eyed ['oupn'aid] *a ad* ad occhi aperti.
open-handed ['oupn'hændid] *a* generoso.
open-hearted ['oupən,hɑːtid] *a* cordiale, espansivo.
opening ['oupəniŋ] *a* che si apre, inaugurale, iniziale; *n* apertura, inaugurazione, inizio.
openly ['oupənli] *ad* apertamente; pubblicamente.
openness ['oupənnis] *n* (*fig*) franchezza.
opera ['ɔpərə] *pl* **operas** *n* opera.
operate ['ɔpəreit] *vti* operare; **operating room** (*or* **theatre**) *n* sala operatoria.
operation [,ɔpə'reiʃən] *n* operazione; azione.
operative ['ɔpərətiv] *a* efficace; operativo, operante; operatorio; attivo, *n* lavorante, operaio.
operator ['ɔpəreitə] *n* operatore.
Ophelia [ɔ'fiːliə] *nf pr* Ofelia.
ophthalmic [ɔf'θælmik] *a* oftalmico.
opiate ['oupiit] *a* oppiato; *n* narcotico.
opine [ou'pain] *vi* opinare, essere del parere.
opinion [ə'pinjən] *n* opinione, parere.
opinionated [ə'pinjəneitid] *a* ostinato, dogmatico.
opium ['oupiəm] *n* oppio.
opponent [ə'pounənt] *n* antagonista, rivale; *a* contrario, opposto.
opportune ['ɔpətjuːn] *a* opportuno.
opportunity [,ɔpə'tjuːniti] *n* occasione, opportunità.
oppose [ɔ'pouz] *vt* opporre, contrapporre, opporsi a.
opposite ['ɔpəzit] *a* contrario, opposto; *prep* dirimpetto a, di faccia a; *n* opposto.
opposition [,ɔpə'ziʃən] *n* opposizione.
oppress [ə'pres] *vt* opprimere.

oppression [ə'preʃən] n oppressione.
oppressive [ə'presiv] a oppressivo.
opprobrious [ə'proubriəs] a obbrobrioso.
opt [ɔpt] vi optare.
optic ['ɔptik] a ottico.
optical ['ɔptikəl] a ottico.
optician [ɔp'tiʃən] n ottico.
optics ['ɔptiks] n ottica.
optimism ['ɔptimizəm] n ottimismo.
optimist ['ɔptimist] n ottimista.
optimistic [ˌɔpti'mistik] a ottimistico.
option ['ɔpʃən] n opzione, scelta.
optional ['ɔpʃənl] a facoltativo.
opulence ['ɔpjuləns] n opulenza.
opulent ['ɔpjulənt] a opulento.
or [ɔː] cj o, oppure.
oracle ['ɔrəkl] n oracolo.
oral ['ɔːrəl] a orale.
orange ['ɔrindʒ] a di color arancio, arancione; n arancia; (tree, color) arancio.
oration [ɔː'reiʃən] n orazione; discorso.
orator ['ɔrətə] n oratore.
oratory ['ɔrətəri] n oratorio.
orb [ɔːb] n cerchio; globo; orbita.
orbit ['ɔːbit] n orbita.
Orcadian [ɔː'keidiən] a delle isole Orcadi; n abitante delle isole Orcadi.
orchard ['ɔːtʃəd] n frutteto.
orchestra ['ɔːkistrə] n orchestra; o. seat (theat) poltrona.
orchid ['ɔːkid] n orchidea.
ordain [ɔː'dein] vt ordinare; decretare.
ordeal [ɔː'diːl] n cimento, dura prova.
order ['ɔːdə] n ordine; (com) ordinazione; in o. that affinchè; vi ordinare.
orderliness ['ɔːdəlinis] n ordine, disciplina.
orderly ['ɔːdəli] a ordinato, disciplinato; n (mil) ordinanza.
ordinal ['ɔːdinl] a n ordinale.
ordinance ['ɔːdinəns] n decreto, ordinanza.
ordinary ['ɔːdnri] a ordinario, comune, solito.
ordination [ˌɔːdi'neiʃən] n (eccl) ordinazione.
ordnance ['ɔːdnəns] n (mil) artiglieria; sussistenza.
ore [ɔː] n minerale.
organ ['ɔːgən] n organo.
organic [ɔː'gænik] a organico.
organism ['ɔːgənizəm] n organismo.
organist ['ɔːgənist] n organista.
organization [ˌɔːgənai'zeiʃən] n organizzazione.
organize ['ɔːgənaiz] vt organizzare.
organizer ['ɔːgənaizə] n organizzatore.
orgasm ['ɔːgæzəm] n orgasmo, eccitazione.
orgy ['ɔːdʒi] n orgia.

oriel ['ɔːriəl] n (arch) finestra sporgente.
orient ['ɔːriənt] a n (poet) orientale, oriente; vti orientare, orientarsi.
oriental [ˌɔːri'entl] a orientale.
origin ['ɔridʒin] n origine.
original [ə'ridʒənl] a n originale; a originario.
originality [əˌridʒ'næliti] n originalità.
originate [ə'ridʒineit] vt originare, dare origine a; vi avere origine.
Orkney Islands ['ɔːkni'ailəndz] n Isole Orcadi.
ornament ['ɔːnəmənt] n ornamento; vt adornare, ornare.
ornamental [ˌɔːnə'mentl] a ornamentale.
ornate [ɔː'neit] a adorno, ornato, riccamente decorato.
ornithology [ˌɔːni'θɔlədʒi] n ornitologia.
ornithologist [ˌɔːni'θɔlədʒist] n ornitologo.
orphan ['ɔːfən] a n orfano; vt rendere orfano.
orphanage ['ɔːfənidʒ] n brefotrofio, orfanotrofio.
Orpheus ['ɔːfjuːs] nm pr Orfeo.
orthodox ['ɔːθədɔks] a ortodosso.
orthodoxy ['ɔːθədɔksi] n ortodossia.
orthography [ɔː'θɔgrəfi] n ortografia.
orthopedic [ˌɔːθou'piːdik] a ortopedico.
Oscar ['ɔskə] nm pr Oscar.
oscillate ['ɔsileit] vi oscillare; vt (far) oscillare.
oscillation [ˌɔsi'leiʃən] n oscillazione.
osier ['ouʒə] n vimine.
osprey ['ɔspri] n ossifraga.
Ostend [ɔs'tend] n Ostenda.
ostensible [ɔs'tensəbl] a apparente; finto.
ostensibly [ɔs'tensibli] ad apparentemente, con il pretesto di.
ostentation [ˌɔsten'teiʃən] n ostentazione; sfarzo.
ostentatious [ˌɔsten'teiʃəs] a ostentato; sfarzoso.
ostracism ['ɔstrəsizəm] n ostracismo.
ostracize ['ɔstrəsaiz] vt dare l'ostracismo a, bandire.
ostrich ['ɔstriʃ] n struzzo.
Othello [ou'θelou] nm pr Otello.
other ['ʌðə] a pron altro; every o. day ogni due giorni.
otherwise ['ʌðəwaiz] ad altrimenti.
otter ['ɔtə] n lontra.
ought [ɔːt] v aux impers (al condizionale) dovere.
ounce [auns] (abbr oz) oncia.
our ['auə] a (il) nostro etc; ours pron (il) nostro etc; ourselves pron ci, noi stessi.
oust [aust] vt espellere; soppiantare.
out [aut] ad fuori; o. of prep fuori da, fuori di; a motivo di, per; o. of date fuori moda; arcaico; o. of door(s) all'aperto, fuori di casa.

outbid [aut'bid] vt offrire un prezzo più alto.

outbreak ['aut'breik] n eruzione; scoppio; sommossa.

outburst ['aut'bə:st] n esplosione; (fig) scoppio, accesso.

outcast ['autka:st] a n abbandonato, reietto.

outcome ['autkʌm] n esito, risultato.

outcry ['autkrai] n clamore, grido; scalpore.

outdo [aut'du:] vt superare.

outdoor ['autdɔ:] a all'aperto.

outer ['autə] a esteriore; esterno.

outermost ['autəmoust] a estremo; il più remoto.

outfit ['autfit] n corredo, equipaggiamento.

outfitter ['autfitə] n fornitore (di articoli di abbigliamento).

outgoing [aut'gouiŋ] a uscente; in partenza; n uscita; pl spese.

outgrow [aut'grou] vt sorpassare in crescita, diventare troppo grande per.

outhouse ['authaus] n edificio annesso.

outing ['autiŋ] n passeggiata; gita, scampagnata.

outlandish [aut'lændiʃ] a strano; remoto.

outlaw ['aut'lɔ:] n bandito, fuori legge; vt bandire.

outlay ['aut'lei] n spesa.

outlet ['autlet] n sbocco, uscita.

outline ['autlain] n contorno, schizzo; vt schizzare, tracciare i contorni di.

outlive [aut'liv] vt sopravvivere a.

outlook ['autluk] n vista, prospettiva, modo di vedere.

outlying ['aut.laiiŋ] a fuori mano, periferico.

outnumber [aut'nʌmbə] vt superare in numero.

outpatient ['aut.peiʃənt] n malato esterno.

outplay [aut'plei] vt superare in un gioco, battere.

outpost ['autpoust] n (mil) avamposto.

outpouring [aut'pɔ:riŋ] n sfogo, effusione.

output ['autput] n produzione.

outrage ['autreidʒ] n oltraggio; vt oltraggiare; violare.

outrageous [aut'reidʒəs] a oltraggioso; atroce; eccessivo.

outright ['autrait] ad immediatamente, completamente, in blocco; a completo.

outrun [aut'rʌn] vt oltrepassare, superare.

outset ['autset] n inizio, principio.

outside ['aut'said] a esteriore, esterno, superficiale; prep fuori di; all'infuori di; ad all'esterno, esternamente, fuori, all'aperto; n l'esterno, apparenza esteriore; massimo.

outsider ['aut'saidə] n estraneo; (horse) cavallo non classificato.

outskirts ['autskə:ts] n pl periferia.

outspoken [aut'spoukən] a esplicito, franco.

outstanding [aut'stændiŋ] a prominente; di rilievo, eminente; (com) arretrato, in sospeso.

outstretched [aut'stretʃt] a disteso, spiegato, aperto.

outstrip [aut'strip] vt distanziare, vincere.

outward ['autwəd] a esterno; esteriore, o. **bound** (naut) diretto a un porto straniero; **outwards** esternamente.

outwear [aut'wɛə] vt durare più a lungo di, logorare con continuo uso.

outweigh [aut'wei] vt superare di peso; superare in importanza.

outwit [aut'wit] vt superare in furberia.

oval ['ouvəl] a n ovale.

ovary ['ouvəri] n (anat) ovaia; ovario.

ovation [ou'veiʃən] n ovazione.

oven ['ʌvn] n forno.

over ['ouvə] prep su, sopra, al di sopra; attraverso a; ad al di sopra; dall'altra parte; in aggiunta; di nuovo, completamente, dal principio alla fine; a eccessivo.

overall ['ouvərɔ:l] a completo, globale; n (usu pl) grembiule; tuta.

overbalance [.ouvə'bæləns] n eccedenza; vti superare di peso; (far) perdere l'equilibrio.

overbearing [.ouvə'bɛəriŋ] a imperioso, prepotente.

overboard ['ouvəbɔ:d] ad fuori bordo, in mare.

overburden [.ouvə'bə:dn] vt sovraccaricare.

overcast ['ouvəka:st] a coperto di nubi; vt offuscare; cucire a sopraggitto.

overcharge ['ouvə'tʃɑ:dʒ] n sovrapprezzo; vti sovraccaricare; chiedere troppo di prezzo.

overcloud [.ouvə'klaud] vti coprire di nubi, (r)annuvolarsi.

overcoat ['ouvəkout] n soprabito, cappotto.

overcome [.ouvə'kʌm] vt vincere, sopraffare.

overconfidence ['ouvə'kɔnfidəns] n presunzione; eccessiva sicurezza di sè.

overcrowd [.ouvə'kraud] vt affollare all'eccesso.

overdo [.ouvə'du:] vti esagerare; cuocere troppo; strafare; affaticare.

overdose ['ouvədous] n dose eccessiva.

overdraft ['ouvədra:ft] n (com) credito allo scoperto.

overdraw ['ouvə'drɔ:] vt (com) trarre allo scoperto; (fig) esagerare.

overdress ['ouvə'dres] vi vestire in modo troppo vistoso.

overdrive ['ouvə'draiv] *n* eccessivo sforzo; eccessivo sfruttamento; (*tec*) moltiplicatore di velocita; *vt* affaticare, sfruttare troppo.

overdue ['ouvə'dju:] *a* (*com*) in sofferenza, scaduto; in ritardo.

overeat ['ouvər'i:t] *vi* mangiare troppo.

overestimate ['ouvər'estimeit] *vt* sopravvalutare.

overexcited ['ouvərik'saitid] *a* sovraeccitato.

overflow ['ouvəflou] *n* traboccamento; [.ouvə'flou] *vt* inondare; *vi* straripare, traboccare.

overgrown ['ouvə'groun] *a* cresciuto troppo; coperto di.

overhang ['ouvəhæŋ] *vti* incombere su, sovrastare (a).

overhaul ['ouvəhɔ:l] *n* revisione, verifica, esame accurato; riparazione.

overhead ['ouvəhed] *a* superiore; *ad* di sopra, in alto; *n pl* spese generali *pl*.

overhear [.ouvə'hiə] *vt* udire per caso.

overlap [.ouvə'læp] *vti* sovrapporre, sovrapporsi.

overleaf ['ouvə'li:f] *ad* sul verso, sul retro (della pagina).

overload ['ouvəloud] *n* sovraccarico; *vt* sovraccaricare.

overlook [.ouvə'luk] *vt* guardare dall'alto, sorvegliare; passar sopra, trascurare, non accorgersi di.

overnight ['ouvə'nait] *a ad* durante la notte.

overpass ['ouvəpa:s] *n* soprappassaggio; *vt* [.ouvə'pa:s] sorpassare; trasgredire; ignorare.

overpay ['ouvə'pei] *vt* pagare più del dovuto.

overpower [.ouvə'pauə] *vt* sopraffare, vincere.

overpowering [.ouvə'pauəriŋ] *a* schiacciante, irresistibile.

overrate ['ouvə'reit] *vt* sopravvalutare.

overreach [.ouvə'ri:tʃ] *vti* oltrepassare, spingersi al di là di; **to o.** oneself fare il passo più lungo della gamba.

override ['ouvə'raid] *vti* far scorrerie; (*fig*) infrangere, annullare, non tener conto di.

overrun [.ouvə'rʌn] *vt* invadere; oltrepassare.

oversea(s) ['ouvə'si:(z)] *a* d'oltre mare; *ad* oltremare.

overseer ['ouvəsiə] *n* capo operaio, sopraintendente.

overshadow [.ovə'ʃædou] *vt* ombreggiare; (*fig*) oscurare, eclissare.

overshoe ['ouvəʃu:] *n* soprascarpa.

oversight ['ouvəsait] *n* svista; sorveglianza.

oversleep ['ouvə'sli:p] *vi* dormire oltre l'ora giusta.

overspill ['ouvəspil] *n* l'eccesso, l'in più.

overstate ['ouvə'steit] *vt* esagerare.

overstatement ['ouvə'steitmənt] *n* esagerazione.

overstrain ['ouvə'strein] *vti* sforzar (si) eccessivamente.

overt ['ouvə:t] *a* aperto, pubblico, visibile.

overtake [.ouvə'teik] *vt* raggiungere; sorpassare.

overtax ['ouvə'tæks] *vt* abusare di; gravare di imposte.

overthrow ['ouvəθrou] *n* rovesciamento, disfatta; *vt* [.ouvə'θrou] rovesciare, abbattere.

overtime ['ouvətaim] *n* lavoro straordinario.

overtire ['ouvə'taiə] *vt* stancare troppo, strapazzare.

overtop ['ouvə'tɔp] *vt* sovrastare, superare di altezza.

overture ['ouvətjuə] *n* offerta, proposta; (*mus*) preludio, sinfonia.

overturn ['ouvətə:n] *vti* capovolgere, rovesciar(si).

overweight ['ouvəweit] *a* che supera il peso; n eccedenza di peso.

overwhelm [.ouvə'welm] *vt* sopraffare, opprimere, schiacciare.

overwork ['ouvə'wə:k] *vti* (far) lavorare troppo.

overwrought ['ouvə'rɔ:t] *a* esausto; sovreccitato; troppo ornato.

owe [ou] *vt* dovere, essere in debito di.

owing ['ouiŋ] *a* dovuto, che resta da pagare; **o.** to *prep* a causa di.

owl [aul] *n* civetta; gufo.

own [oun] *a* proprio; *vti* possedere; confessare, riconoscere.

owner ['ounə] *n* possessore, proprietario.

ownership ['ounəʃip] *n* proprietà, possesso.

ox [ɔks] *pl* **oxen** *n* bue.

oxide ['ɔksaid] *n* ossido.

oxygen ['ɔksidʒən] *n* ossigeno.

oyster ['ɔistə] *n* ostrica.

P

pace [peis] *n* andatura, passo; *vt* misurare a passi; *vi* andare al passo.

Pacific [pə'sifik] *n* Pacifico.

pacific [pə'sifik] *a* pacifico.

pacifism ['pæsifizəm] *n* pacifismo.

pacifist ['pæsifist] *n* pacifista.

pacify ['pæsifai] *vt* pacificare.

pack [pæk] *n* pacco, involto; peso; (*mil*) zaino; (*hounds*) muta; (*cards*) mazzo; (*ice*) banchisa; (*thieves*) banda; *vt* imballare, impaccare, stipare; (*med*) fare impacchi a; **to p.** up fare le valigie.

package ['pækidʒ] *n* balla, collo, pacco; **p. holiday** (*or* **tour**) villeggiatura o gita turistica spesata in anticipo.

packet ['pækit] n pacchetto; **p.-boat** (naut) vapore postale.
packing ['pækiŋ] n imballaggio; fare le valigie; (of food) confezione.
pact [pækt] n patto.
pad [pæd] n blocco di carta; cuscinetto; imbottitura; zampa di animale; (med) tampone; vt imbottire; tamponare.
padding ['pædiŋ] n imbottitura.
paddle ['pædl] n (naut) pagaia; vt remare con la pagaia; sguazzare nell'acqua.
paddock ['pædək] n recinto per i cavalli da corsa; chiuso.
padlock ['pædlɔk] n lucchetto.
Padua ['pædjuə] n Padova; **Paduan** a n padovano.
pagan ['peigən] a n pagano.
page [peidʒ] n pagina; paggio; **pageboy** fattorino d'albergo.
pageant ['pædʒənt] n corteo o spettacolo storico.
pageantry ['pædʒəntri] n sfarzo, spettacolo sfarzoso.
pail [peil] n secchia, secchio.
pain [pein] n dolore, male, sofferenza, pena; vt affliggere, far soffrire.
painful ['peinful] a doloroso, penoso.
painfully ['peinfuli] ad dolorosamente, penosamente.
painless ['peinlis] a indolore.
painstaking ['peinz,teikiŋ] a coscienzioso.
paint [peint] n pittura; vernice; colore; belletto; vt dipinger(si).
painter ['peintə] n pittore; decoratore; imbianchino.
painting ['peintiŋ] n pittura; quadro.
pair [pɛə] n paio, coppia; vt accoppiare, appaiare; vi accoppiarsi.
pajamas [pə'dʒɑːməz] n pl pigiama.
Pakistan [,pɑːkis'tɑːn] n Pakistan.
Pakistani [,pɑːkis'tɑːni] a n pachistano.
palace ['pælis] n palazzo.
paladin ['pælədin] n paladino.
palatable ['pælətəbl] a gradevole.
palate ['pælit] n palato; gusto.
palaver [pə'lɑːvə] n discussione, chiacchiere.
pale [peil] a pallido, scialbo, chiaro; n palo; palizzata; vi impallidire.
paleness ['peilnis] n pallore.
Palestine ['pælistain] n Palestina.
Palestinian [,pæles'tiniən] a n palestinese.
palette ['pælit] n tavolozza.
palisade [,pæli'seid] n palizzata.
pall [pɔːl] n coltre funebre; vi diventare insipido, non essere più interessante.
pallet ['pælit] n giaciglio, pagliericcio.
palliate ['pælieit] vt mitigare.
palliative ['pæliətiv] a n palliativo.
pallid ['pælid] a pallido.
pallor ['pælə] n pallore.
palm [pɑːm] n (tree) palma; (hand) palmo.

palpable ['pælpəbl] a palpabile; evidente.
palpitate ['pælpiteit] vi palpitare.
palpitation [,pælpi'teiʃən] n palpitazione.
palsy ['pɔːlzi] n paralisi.
palter ['pɔːltə] vi tergiversare.
paltry ['pɔːltri] a di poco valore, meschino.
pamper ['pæmpə] vt trattare con soverchia indulgenza, viziare.
pamphlet ['pæmflit] n opuscolo.
pan [pæn] n padella, tegame.
pancake ['pænkeik] n frittella.
pandemonium ['pændi'mouniəm] n pandemonio.
pander ['pændə] n mezzano, ruffiano; vi fare il mezzano; (fig) accarezzare i gusti.
pane [pein] n vetro di finestra.
panegyric [,pæni'dʒirik] n panegirico.
panel ['pænl] n pannello; commissione; **p. doctor** dottore della mutua.
pang [pæŋ] n dolore acuto, spasimo.
panic ['pænik] n panico.
panorama [,pænə'rɑːmə] n panorama.
pansy ['pænzi] n viola del pensiero.
pant [pænt] n palpitazione, palpito; vi ansimare; desiderare ardentemente.
pantaloons [,pæntə'luːns] n pl pantaloni pl.
pantheism ['pænθiːizəm] n panteismo.
panther ['pænθə] n pantera.
pantomime ['pæntəmaim] n pantomima.
pantry ['pæntri] n dispensa.
pap [pæp] n pappa.
papa [pə'pɑː] n papà, babbo.
papacy ['peipəsi] n papato.
papal ['peipəl] a papale.
paper ['peipə] n carta; documento; giornale; dissertazione, saggio; vt tappezzare; **wrapping p.** carta da imballaggio; **waste p.** carta straccia.
paper-hanger ['peipə,hæŋə] n tappezziere.
paper-mill ['peipəmil] n cartiera.
papist ['peipist] n papista.
papyrus [pə'paiərəs] n papiro.
par [pɑː] n pari, parità.
parable ['pærəbl] n parabola.
parachute ['pærəʃuːt] n paracadute.
parachutist ['pærəʃuːtist] n paracadutista.
parade [pə'reid] n mostra; parata, sfilata, rivista; vt far mostra di; vi sfilare in parata.
paradise ['pærədais] n paradiso.
paradox ['pærədɔks] n paradosso.
paradoxical [pærə'dɔksikəl] a paradossale.
paraffin ['pærəfin] n paraffina, petrolio.
paragon ['pærəgən] n paragone, modello.

paragraph ['pærəgrɑ:f] n paragrafo, capoverso.
Paraguay ['pærəgwai] n Paraguai.
Paraguayan [,pærə'gwaiən] a n paraguaiano.
parallel ['pærəlel] a parallelo; n parallela; parallelo: confronto.
paralysis [pə'rælisis] n paralisi.
paralytic [,pærə'litik] a n paralitico.
paralyze ['pærəlaiz] vt paralizzare.
paramount ['pærəmaunt] a sovrano, supremo.
parapet ['pærəpit] n parapetto.
paraphernalia [,pærəfə'neiliə] n (fam) armamentario, roba.
paraphrase ['pærəfreiz] n parafrasi.
parapsychology ['pærəsai'kɔlədʒi] n metapsichica.
parasite ['pærəsait] n parassita.
parasol ['pærəsol] n ombrellino, parasole.
paratrooper ['pærətru:pə] n paracadutista.
paratyphoid ['pærə'taifɔid] n paratifo.
parboil ['pɑ:bɔil] vt bollire parzialmente.
parcel ['pɑ:sl] n pacco; pezzo di terra; vt to p. up impaccare.
parch [pɑ:tʃ] vt disseccare, inaridire; vi diventare riarso.
parchment ['pɑ:tʃmənt] n pergamena.
pardon ['pɑ:dn] n perdono, amnistia; vt perdonare.
pardonable ['pɑ:dnəbl] a perdonabile, scusabile.
pare [pɛə] vt (fruit) sbucciare; (nails) tagliare.
parent ['pɛərənt] n genitore m, genitrice f genitori pl.
parentage ['pɛərəntidʒ] n origini, natali pl.
parental [pə'rentl] a paterno, materno, di genitori.
parenthesis [pə'renθisis] n parentesi.
Paris ['pæris] n Parigi.
parish ['pæriʃ] n parrocchia.
parishioner [pə'riʃənə] n parrocchiano.
Parisian [pə'riziən] a n parigino.
park [pɑ:k] n parco; (aut) posteggio.
parking ['pɑ:kiŋ] n (aut) parcheggio, posteggio; aiuola spartitraffico; p. meter contatore per parcheggio; p. place, p. lot area per parcheggio, posteggio.
parlance ['pɑ:ləns] n parlata, gergo.
parley ['pɑ:li] n discussione, parlamento; vi discutere, parlamentare.
parliament ['pɑ:ləmənt] n parlamento.
parliamentary [,pɑ:lə'mentəri] a parlamentare.
parlor ['pɑ:lə] n salotto.
Parmesan [,pɑ:mi'zæn] a parmigiano.
parochial [pə'roukiəl] a parrocchiale.

parody ['pærədi] n parodia; vt parodiare.
paroxysm ['pærəksizəm] n parossismo.
parricide ['pærisaid] n parricida, parricidio.
parrot ['pærət] n pappagallo.
parry ['pæri] n parata; vt evitare; parare.
parse [pɑ:z] vt fare l'analisi (grammaticale o logica) di.
parsimonious [,pɑ:si'mouniəs] a parsimonioso, economo.
parsimony ['pɑ:siməni] n parsimonia, economia.
parsley ['pɑ:sli] n prezzemolo.
parsnip ['pɑ:snip] n pastinaca.
parson ['pɑ:sn] n parroco (anglicano); (fam) pastore.
part [pɑ:t] n parte; vti divider(si), separar(si).
partake [pɑ:'teik] vi partecipare.
partial ['pɑ:ʃəl] a parziale, propenso verso.
partiality [,pɑ:ʃi'æliti] n parzialità; favoritismo; predilezione.
participant [pɑ:'tisipənt] a partecipe; n partecipante.
participate [pɑ:'tisipeit] vi partecipare; prendere parte a.
participation [pɑ:,tisi'peiʃən] n partecipazione.
participle ['pɑ:tisipl] n (gram) participio.
particle ['pɑ:tikl] n particella; (eccl) particola.
particular [pə'tikjulə] a particolare, speciale; minuzioso; n particolare, dettaglio; informazione; in p. in particolare.
particularly [pə'tikjuləli] ad particolarmente, dettagliatamente.
parting ['pɑ:tiŋ] n separazione; congedo; (hair) scriminatura, divisa.
partisan [,pɑ:ti'zæn] a n partigiano.
partition [pɑ:'tiʃən] n divisione; spartizione; tramezzo.
partly ['pɑ:tli] ad in parte.
partner ['pɑ:tnə] n compagno, ballerina, -no, marito, moglie; (com) socio; **partnership** (com) società, associazione.
partridge ['pɑ:tridʒ] n pernice.
party ['pɑ:ti] n partito; brigata; trattenimento, festa, festicciola; (leg) parte in causa.
pass [pɑ:s] n passo, valico; situazione; passaggio; (mil) permesso, lasciapassare; vti passare; accadere; vt attraversare; superare; approvare (una legge); to p. away morire; to p. by passare davanti a; passare sotto silenzio.
passable ['pɑ:səbl] a discreto, passabile; attraversabile.
passage ['pæsidʒ] n passaggio; traversata; varco; corridoio; brano.
passenger ['pæsindʒə] n passeggiero, viaggiatore.

passer-by ['pɑːsə'bai] n passante.
passing ['pɑːsiŋ] a passante; passeggiero, casuale; n passaggio; trapasso, morte.
passion ['pæʃən] n passione.
passionate ['pæʃənit] a appassionato; passionale; irascibile.
passive ['pæsiv] a n passivo.
passport ['pɑːspɔːt] n passaporto.
password ['pɑːswəːd] n parola d'ordine.
past [pɑːst] a passato, scorso; finito; prep al di là di; ad oltre; n passato.
paste [peist] n pasta; colla; vt incollare.
pasteboard ['peistbɔːd] n cartone grosso.
pastel ['pæstəl] n pastello.
pastime ['pɑːstaim] n passatempo.
pastor ['pɑːstə] n (eccl) pastore.
pastoral ['pɑːstərəl] a n pastorale.
pastry ['peistri] n pasticceria; **p. board** asse per la pasta.
pasture ['pɑːstʃə] n pascolo, pastura; vti far pascolare.
pat [pæt] n colpetto, tocco leggero; panetto di burro; a pronto, adatto; ad a proposito; vt accarezzare, dare un piccolo colpo su, dare un buffetto a.
patch [pætʃ] n toppa; piccolo pezzo di terreno; macchia; vt rattoppare, mettere insieme alla meglio; **patchwork** rappezzatura, mescolanza, mosaico.
patent ['peitənt] a evidente, ovvio; brevettato, patentato; n brevetto; **p. leather** n cuoio verniciato; vt brevettare.
patentee [ˌpeitən'tiː] n detentore di brevetto.
paternal [pə'təːnl] a paterno.
paternity [pə'təːniti] n paternità.
path [pɑːθ] n sentiero, viottolo.
pathetic [pə'θetik] a commovente, patetico.
pathfinder ['pɑːθˌfaində] n esploratore, pioniere.
pathologic(al) [ˌpæθə'lɔdʒik(əl)] a patologico.
pathology [pə'θɔlədʒi] n patologia.
pathos ['peiθɔs] n pathos, commozione.
pathway ['pɑːθwei] n sentiero.
patience ['peiʃəns] n pazienza.
patient ['peiʃənt] a n paziente.
patriarch ['peitriɑːk] n patriarca.
patriarchal [ˌpeitri'ɑːkəl] a patriarcale.
Patricia [pə'triʃə] nf pr Patrizia.
patrician [pə'triʃən] a n patrizio.
Patrick ['pætrik] nm pr Patrizio.
patrimony ['pætriməni] n patrimonio.
patriot ['peitriət] n patriota.
patriotic [ˌpætri'ɔtik] a patriottico.
patriotism ['pætriətizəm] n patriottismo.
patrol [pə'troul] n (mil) pattuglia; vt perlustrare; vi pattugliare.

patrolman [pə'troulmæn] pl -men n poliziotto.
patron ['peitrən] n patrono, mecenate.
patronage ['pætrənidʒ] n patronato, patrocinio; (shop) concorso di avventori.
patronize ['pætrənaiz] vt patrocinare; trattare con aria condiscendente; essere cliente abituale di.
patter ['pætə] n picchiettio, scalpitio; (rain) ticchettio; parlata, cicaleccio; vi picchiettare; camminare con passetti rapidi; parlare meccanicamente.
pattern ['pætən] n campione, modello.
Paul [pɔːl] nm pr Paolo.
Pauline ['pɔːliːn] nf pr Paola, Paolina.
paunch ['pɔːntʃ] n pancia, pancione.
pauper ['pɔːpə] n povero, mendicante.
pauperism ['pɔːpərizəm] n indigenza.
pauperize ['pɔːpəraiz] vt impoverire.
pause [pɔːz] n pausa; vi fare una pausa, fermarsi.
pave [peiv] vt pavimentare; (fig) preparare il terreno.
pavement ['peivmənt] n marciapiede, selciato.
pavilion [pə'viljən] n padiglione.
paw [pɔː] n zampa.
pawn [pɔːn] n pegno; (chess) pedina; vt impegnare.
pawnbroker ['pɔːnˌbroukə] n chi presta denaro su pegno.
pawnshop ['pɔːnʃɔp] n monti di pegni.
pay [pei] n paga, salario, retribuzione; vt pagare, rimunerare; vi dar frutti, rendere.
payable ['peiəbl] a pagabile.
payment ['peimənt] n pagamento, saldo.
pea [piː] n pisello.
peace [piːs] n pace, ordine pubblico; **peacemaker** paciere.
peaceable ['piːsəbl] **peaceful** ['piːsful] a pacifico, tranquillo.
peach [piːtʃ] n pesca.
peacock ['piːkɔk] n pavone.
peak [piːk] n cima, picco; punta; visiera.
peal [piːl] n scampanio; salva d'artiglieria; scroscio; rombo; vi risuonare, scampanare, tuonare.
peanut ['piːnʌt] n arachide, nocciolina americana; **p. butter** pasta di arachidi.
pear [pɛə] n pera; **p. tree** pero.
pearl [pəːl] n perla.
peasant ['pezənt] n contadino; a contadinesco, rustico.
peasantry ['pezəntri] n contadini pl.
peat [piːt] n torba.
pebble ['pebl] n ciottolo, sassolino.
peck [pek] vti beccare.

peculiar [pi'kju:liə] *a* peculiare, particolare; strano.
peculiarity [pi.kju:li'æriti] *n* caratteristica.
peculiarly [pi'kju:liəli] *ad* particolarmente; stranamente.
pecuniary [pi'kju:niəri] *a* pecuniario.
pedagogue ['pedəgɔg] *n* pedagogo.
pedal ['pedl] *n* pedale.
pedant ['pedənt] *n* pedante.
pedantic [pe'dæntik] *a* pedantesco, pedante.
pedantry ['pedəntri] *n* pedanteria.
peddle ['pedl] *vt* vendere al minuto; *vi* fare il venditore ambulante.
peddler ['pedlə] *n* venditore ambulante.
pedestal ['pedistl] *n* piedistallo.
pedestrian [pi'destriən] *a* pedestre; *n* pedone.
pedigree ['pedigri:] *n* albero genealogico; (*animals*) pedigree.
peel [pi:l] *n* buccia; *vt* sbucciare.
peep [pi:p] *n* occhiata, sguardo furtivo o timido; *vi* far capolino, guardare furtivamente, lasciarsi intravedere, spuntare.
peer [piə] *n* pari; *vi* spuntare; scrutare.
peerage ['piəridʒ] *n* la nobiltà; almanacco nobiliare.
peevish ['pi:viʃ] *a* stizzoso, irritabile.
peewit ['pi:wit] *n* pavoncella.
peg [peg] *n* cavicchio, piuolo; molletta; (*fam*) bevanda alcoolica.
Pekinese [.pi:ki'ni:z] *a n* pechinese.
Peking [pi:'kiŋ] *n* Pechino.
pelf [pelf] *n* denaro, lucro.
pelican ['pelikən] *n* pellicano.
pellet ['pelit] *n* pallina; pallottola; pillola.
pell-mell ['pel'mel] *n* confusione, mischia; *ad* confusamente, alla rinfusa.
pelt [pelt] *n* pelle grezza; scroscio di pioggia; velocità; colpo di proiettile; *vt* colpire; *vi* (*of rain*) battere con violenza, correre.
pelvis ['pelvis] *n* (*anat*) pelvi, bacino.
pen [pen] *n* penna; piccolo recinto per animali; *vt* scrivere; chiudere (animali) in un recinto; **penpoint** pennino; **ballpoint p.** penna a sfera; **fountain p.** penna stilografica.
penal ['pi:nl] *a* penale.
penalize ['pi:nəlaiz] *vt* penalizzare.
penalty ['penlti] *n* penalità, punizione; **p. kick** (*football*) calcio di rigore; **p. stroke** (*golf*) colpo di ammenda.
penance ['penəns] *n* penitenza.
pencil ['pensl] *n* matita.
pendant ['pendənt] *n* ciondolo, pendente.
pending ['pendiŋ] *a* pendente; in sospeso; *prep* durante, fino a.
pendulum ['pendjuləm] *n* pendolo.
penetrate ['penitreit] *vti* penetrare.

penetration [.peni'treiʃən] *n* penetrazione, acutezza.
penguin ['peŋgwin] *n* pinguino.
penicillin [.peni'silin] *n* penicillina.
peninsula [pi'ninsjulə] *n* penisola.
peninsular [pi'ninsjulə] *a* peninsulare.
penitence ['penitəns] *n* penitenza.
penitent ['penitənt] *a n* penitente.
penitentiary [.peni'tenʃəri] *a* penitenziale; *n* riformatorio, penitenzario.
penknife ['pennaif] *n* temperino.
penniless ['penilis] *a* senza un soldo.
penny ['peni] *n* 'penny', soldo; **penny-farthing** bicicletta antiquata; **penny-worth** un soldo di.
pension ['penʃən] *n* pensione; *vt* pensionare.
pensioner ['penʃənə] *n* pensionato, pensionata.
pensive ['pensiv] *a* malinconico, pensoso.
pensiveness ['pensivnis] *n* malinconia.
Pentecost ['pentikɔst] *n* Pentecoste.
penthouse *n* tettoia; appartamento sul tetto di un edificio.
penurious [pi'njuəriəs] *a* bisognoso; avaro.
penury ['penjuri] *n* penuria.
peony ['piəni] *n* peonia.
people ['pi:pl] *n* popolo, nazione; (*costruzione pl*) gente, parenti *pl*; *vt* popolare.
pep [pep] *n* (*sl*) iniziativa, vigore.
pepper ['pepə] *n* pepe.
peppercorn ['pepəkɔ:n] *n* grano di pepe.
peppermint ['pepəmint] *n* menta peperita, caramella di menta.
peppery ['pepəri] *a* pepato; pungente; collerico.
perambulator ['præmbjuleitə]
pram [præm] *n* carrozzina per bambini.
perceive [pə'si:v] *vt* percepire, accorgersi di, scorgere.
percentage [pə'sentidʒ] *n* percentuale.
perceptible [pə'septəbl] *a* percettibile.
perceptibly [pə'septəbli] *ad* in modo percettibile.
perception [pə'sepʃən] *n* percezione; intuizione.
perceptiveness [pə'septivnis] *n* percettività.
perch [pə:tʃ] *n* (*bird's*) posatoio, gruccia; (*measure 25,293 sq meters*) pertica; pesce persico; *vi* appollaiarsi, posarsi.
perchance [pə'tʃɑːns] *ad* (*arc*) forse, per caso.
percolate ['pə:kəleit] *vti* filtrare.
percolator ['pə:kəleitə] *n* filtro; macchina per il caffè.
percussion [pə:'kʌʃən] *n* percussione.
perdition [pə:'diʃən] *n* perdizione.

peremptory [pə'remptəri] a perentorio.
perennial [pə'reniəl] a n (of plant) perenne.
perfect ['pə:fikt] a n perfetto; vt perfezionare.
perfection [pə'fekʃən] n perfezione.
perfectionist [pə'fekʃənist] n perfezionista.
perfidious [pə'fidiəs] a perfido.
perfidy ['pə:fidi] n perfidia.
perforate ['pə:fəreit] vti forare; penetrare; (mech) perforare.
perform [pə'fɔ:m] vt adempiere, compiere; eseguire; rappresentare.
performance [pə'fɔ:məns] a adempimento; rappresentazione, recita.
performer [pə'fɔ:mə] n esecutore, attore.
perfume ['pə:fju:m] n profumo; vt profumare.
perfunctory [pə'fʌŋktəri] a meccanico, superficiale.
perhaps [pə'hæps] ad forse.
peril ['peril] n pericolo.
perilous ['periləs] a pericoloso.
perilously ['periləsli] ad pericolosamente.
period ['piəriəd] n epoca, periodo.
periodic [,piəri'ɔdik] a periodico.
periodical [,piəri'ɔdikəl] a n periodico.
periphery [pə'rifəri] n periferia.
periscope ['periskoup] n periscopio.
perish ['periʃ] vti (far) perire.
perishable ['periʃəbl] a deperibile, perituro, deteriorabile.
periwinkle ['peri,wiŋkl] n pervinca.
perjure ['pə:dʒə] vr; **p. oneself** spergiurare.
perjury ['pə:dʒəri] n spergiuro.
perk [pə:k] vti **to p. up** drizzare; (fig) rallegrare.
perky ['pə:ki] a birichino; impertinente.
perm [pə:m] v **permanent wave.**
permanence ['pə:mənəns] n permanenza.
permanent ['pə:mənənt] a permanente; **p. wave** (ondulazione) permanente.
permeate ['pə:mieit] vt permeare.
permissible [pə'misəbl] a lecito.
permission [pə'miʃən] n permesso.
permissive [pə'misiv] a che permette, tollerante; permissivo.
permit ['pə:mit] n permesso, autorizzazione; vti [pə'mit] permettere.
pernicious [pə:'niʃəs] a pernicioso, nocivo.
peroration [,perə'reiʃən] n perorazione.
peroxide [pə'rɔksaid] n (chem) perossido.
perpendicular [,pə:pən'dikjulə] a n perpendicolare.
perpetrate ['pə:pitreit] vt perpetrare.
perpetual [pə'petjuəl] a perpetuo.
perpetuate [pə'petjueit] vt perpetuare.

perplex [pə'pleks] vt imbarazzare, rendere perplesso.
perplexity [pə'pleksiti] n perplessità.
perquisite ['pə:kwizit] n mancia; guadagno occasionale.
perquisition [,pə:kwi'ziʃən] n perquisizione.
persecute ['pə:sikju:t] vt perseguitare; importunare.
persecution [,pə:si'kju:ʃən] n persecuzione.
persecutor ['pə:sikju:tə] n persecutore.
perseverance [,pə:si'viərəns] n perseveranza.
persevere [,pə:si'viə] vi perseverare
Persia ['pə:ʃə] n Persia.
Persian ['pə:ʃən] a n persiano.
persist [pə'sist] vi persistere, durare.
persistence [pə'sistəns] n persistenza, perseveranza.
persistent [pə'sistənt] a persistente, tenace.
persistently [pə'sistəntli] ad persistentemente, tenacemente.
person ['pə:sn] n persona.
personage ['pə:snidʒ] n personaggio, personalità.
personal ['pə:snl] a personale; **p. business** questione personale.
personality [,pə:sə'næliti] n personalità.
personally ['pə:snəli] ad personalmente.
personification [pə:,sɔnifi'keiʃən] n personificazione.
personify [pə:'sɔnifai] vt personificare.
personnel [,pə:sə'nel] n personale.
perspective [pə'spektiv] n prospettiva.
perspicacious [,pə:spi'keiʃəs] a perspicace.
perspicacity [,pə:spi'kæsiti] n perspicacia.
perspiration [,pə:spə'reiʃən] n traspirazione, sudore.
perspire [pəs'paiə] vi sudare, traspirare.
persuade [pə'sweid] vt persuadere.
persuasion [pə'sweiʒən] n persuasione, fede.
persuasive [pə'sweisiv] a persuasivo; n motivo.
pert [pə:t] a impertinente; sveglio.
pertain [pə:'tein] vi concernere.
pertinacious [,pə:ti'neiʃəs] a pertinace.
pertinent ['pə:tinənt] a pertinente, proprio.
pertness ['pə:tnis] n impertinenza; vivacità.
perturb [pə'tə:b] vt perturbare, turbare.
perturbation [,pə:tə:'beiʃən] n turbamento.
Peru [pə'ru:] n Perù.
perusal [pə'ru:zəl] n lettura attenta.
peruse [pə'ru:z] vt leggere attentamente; esaminare.

Peruvian [pə'ruːviən] *a n* peruviano.
pervade [pəːˈveid] *vt* pervadere, permeare.
pervasive [pəːˈveisiv] *a* penetrante; invadente.
perverse [pəˈvəːs] *a* perverso.
perversion [pəˈvəːʃən] *n* perversione, pervertimento.
perversity [pəˈvəːsiti] *n* perversità.
pervert [pəˈvəːt] *vt* pervertire.
pessimism ['pesimizəm] *n* pessimismo.
pessimist ['pesimist] *n* pessimista.
pessimistic [ˌpesiˈmistik] *a* pessimistico.
pest [pest] *n* peste, individuo noiosissimo.
pester ['pestə] *vt* importunare, infastidire; infestare.
pestilence ['pestiləns] *n* pestilenza.
pestilent ['pestilənt] *a* pestilenziale.
pestle ['pesl] *n* pestello.
pet [pet] *a* favorito; vezzeggiato; *n* animale favorito, beniamino; cattivo umore, collera; *vt* vezzeggiare.
petal ['petl] *n* petalo.
Peter ['piːtə] *nm pr* Pietro.
petition [piˈtiʃən] *n* petizione, supplica; *vt* presentare una petizione a.
petitioner [piˈtiʃənə] *n* supplicante, postulante.
petrify ['petrifai] *vt* pietrificare.
petrol ['petrəl] *n* benzina.
petroleum [piˈtrouliəm] *n* petrolio.
petticoat ['petikout] *n* sottoveste, sottana.
petty ['peti] *a* piccolo, insignificante, meschino; **p. officer** sottufficiale di marina.
petulant ['petjulənt] *a* petulante.
petunia [piˈtjuːniə] *n* (*bot*) petunia.
pew [pjuː] *n* banco in chiesa.
pewter ['pjuːtə] *n* peltro.
phantom ['fæntəm] *n* fantasma.
Pharaoh ['fɛərou] *n* faraone.
Pharisee ['færisiː] *n* fariseo.
pharmacy ['fɑːməsi] *n* farmacia, scienza farmaceutica.
phase [feiz] *n* fase.
pheasant ['feznt] *n* fagiano.
phenomenon [fiˈnɔminən] *n* fenomeno.
phenomenal [fiˈnɔminl] *a* fenomenale; (*phil*) fenomenico.
phial ['faiəl] *n* fiala.
Philadelphia [ˌfiləˈdelfiə] *n* Filadelfia.
philanderer [fiˈlændərə] *n* donnaiolo.
philanthropic [ˌfilənˈθrɔpik] *a* filantropico.
philanthropist [fiˈlænθrəpist] *n* filantropo.
philanthropy [fiˈlænθrəpi] *n* filantropia.
philatelist [fiˈlætəlist] *n* filatelico.
philately [fiˈlætəli] *n* filatelia.
Philip ['filip] *nm pr* Filippo.
philologist [fiˈlɔlədʒist] *n* filologo.

philology [fiˈlɔlədʒi] *n* filologia.
philosopher [fiˈlɔsəfə] *n* filosofo.
philosophic(al) [ˌfiləˈsɔfik(l)] *a* filosofico.
philosophy [fiˈlɔsəfi] *n* filosofia.
philter ['filtə] *n* filtro.
phlegm [flem] *n* flemma.
phlegmatic [flegˈmætik] *a* flemmatico.
phobia ['foubiə] *n* fobia.
phoenix ['fiːniks] *n* fenice.
phonetic [fəˈnetik] *a* fonetico.
phonetics [fouˈnetiks] *n pl* fonetica.
phonograph ['founəgrɑːf] *n* fonografo.
phosphate ['fɔsfeit] *n* fosfato.
phosphorous ['fɔsfərəs] *n* fosforo.
photocopy ['foutoukɔpi] *n* fotocopia.
photoflash ['foutouflæʃ] *n* fotografia al lampo di magnesio.
photograph ['foutəgrɑːf] *n* fotografia; *vt* fotografare.
photographer [fəˈtɔgrəfə] *n* fotografo.
photographic [ˌfoutəˈgræfik] *a* fotografico.
photography [fəˈtɔgrəfi] *n* (*arte fotografica*) fotografia.
photostat ['foutoustæt] *n* apparecchio fotostatico; copia fotostatica.
phrase [freiz] *n* frase.
phraseology [ˌfreiziˈɔlədʒi] *n* fraseologia.
physical ['fizikəl] *a* fisico.
physician [fiˈziʃən] *n* medico.
physicist ['fizisist] *n* fisico.
physics ['fiziks] *n pl* fisica.
physiognomy [ˌfiziˈɔnəmi] *n* fisionomia.
physiotherapy [ˌfiziəˈθerəpi] *n* fisioterapia.
physique [fiˈziːk] *n* fisico, costituzione fisica.
pianist ['piənist] *n* pianista.
piano [piˈænou] *n* pianoforte.
pick [pik] *n* piccone; scelta; *vt* cogliere; **p. up** raccogliere; (*rad*) captare; scegliere.
picket ['pikit] *n* (*mil*) picchetto.
pickle ['pikl] *n* salamoia; situazione spiacevole.
pickpocket ['pikˌpɔkit] *n* borsaiolo.
pick-up ['pikʌp] *n* (*el*) riproduttore acustico, fonorivelatore, 'pick-up'; (*tv*) dispositivo di presa.
picnic ['piknik] *n* 'pic-nic', scampagnata.
pictorial [pikˈtɔːriəl] *a* pittorico, illustrato.
picture ['piktʃə] *n* dipinto, quadro, ritratto; **pictures** *pl* (*fam*) cinematografo.
picture ['piktʃə] *vt* dipingere, descrivere, figurarsi.
picturesque [ˌpiktʃəˈresk] *a* pittoresco.
pie [pai] *n* pasticcio di carne, torta di frutta; (*ornit*) gazza.
piece [piːs] *n* pezzo; (*material*) pezza;

(*mus*) composizione; **piecework** lavoro a cottimo.

piecemeal ['piːsmiːl] *ad* pezzo a pezzo, a pezzi e a bocconi.

Piedmont ['piːdmənt] *n* Piemonte; **piedmontese** *a n* piemontese.

pier [piə] *n* banchina, molo; pilastro.

pierce [piəs] *vti* penetrare, forare.

piercing ['piəsiŋ] *a* penetrante; *n* perforamento.

piety ['paiəti] *n* religiosità, pietà.

pig [pig] *n* maiale, porco.

pigeon ['pidʒin] *n* piccione, colombo.

pigeonhole ['pidʒinhoul] *n* nicchia di colombaia; casella; **set of pigeonholes** casellario; *vt* incasellare, archiviare.

pigtail ['pigteil] *n* treccina stretta di capelli, codino.

pike [paik] *n* picca; (*fish*) luccio.

pilchard ['piltʃəd] *n* sardella.

pile [pail] *n* ammasso, mucchio; pira; (*el*) pila; palafitta; (*nap*) pelo; **piles** *pl* (*med*) emorroidi.

pile [pail] *vt* accumulare, ammucchiare, esagerare.

pilfer ['pilfə] *vt* rubacchiare.

pilgrim ['pilgrim] *n* pellegrino.

pilgrimage ['pilgrimidʒ] *n* pellegrinaggio.

pill [pil] *n* pillola.

pillage ['pilidʒ] *n* saccheggio; *vt* saccheggiare.

pillar ['pilə] *n* colonna, pilastro.

pillory ['piləri] *n* berlina, gogna; *vt* mettere alla berlina.

pillow ['pilou] *n* guanciale, cuscino; (*mech*) cuscinetto.

pilot ['pailət] *n* pilota; *vt* pilotare.

pimple ['pimpl] *n* foruncolo.

pin [pin] *n* spillo; **pins and needles** (*fig*) formicolio.

pincers ['pinsəz] *n pl* pinze; tanaglie *pl*.

pinch [pintʃ] *n* pizzico; (*snuff*) presa; *vti* pizzicare; stringere; privare del necessario; far soffrire.

pincushion ['pin,kuʃin] *n* portaspilli.

pine [pain] *n* pino; *vi* languire, struggersi.

pink [piŋk] *a* rosa; *n* color rosa; garofano; (*fig*) fiore, modello, perfezione.

pinnacle ['pinəkl] *n* pinnacolo; (*fig*) apogeo.

pinpoint ['pinpɔint] *vt* localizzare, determinare con esattezza.

pint [paint] *n* pinta (*circa mezzo litro*).

pioneer [,paiə'niə] *n* pioniere.

pious ['paiəs] *a* pio, devoto.

pip [pip] *n* seme di frutto; (*cards etc*) macchia; (*officer's*) stelletta; (*sl*) malumore.

pipe [paip] *n* tubo; canna; cornamusa, zampogna; pipa; vena di minerale; *vi* suonare (la cornamusa etc).

piper ['paipə] *n* sonatore di cornamusa, pifferaio.

piquant ['piːkənt] *a* piccante.

pique [piːk] *n* picca, risentimento; *vt* ferire l'orgoglio di, offendere.

piracy ['paiərəsi] *n* pirateria.

pirate ['paiərit] *n* pirata.

pistol ['pistl] *n* pistola.

piston ['pistən] *n* pistone, stantuffo.

pit [pit] *n* abisso; buca, cava, cavità; miniera.

pitch [pitʃ] *n* pec (*degree*) grado; intensità; massimo punto; (*mus*) tono; *vt* lanciare, piantare, fissare al suolo; *vi* (*naut*) beccheggiare.

pitcher ['pitʃə] *n* brocca.

piteous ['pitiəs] *a* commovente, pietoso.

pitfall ['pitfɔːl] *n* trappola; (*fig*) inganno.

pith [piθ] *n* midollo, parte essenziale.

pitiable ['pitiəbl] *a* compassionevole.

pitiful ['pitiful] *a* pietoso, miserando.

pitiless ['pitilis] *a* crudele, spietato.

pittance ['pitəns] *n* elemosina, piccola parte o quantità, piccola somma.

pity ['piti] *n* pietà, compassione; **what a p.!** *interj* che peccato!; *vt* compiangere.

Pius ['paiəs] *nm pr* Pio.

pivot ['pivət] *n* pernio.

placard ['plækɑːd] *n* affisso, manifesto.

placate [plə'keit] *vt* placare.

place [pleis] *n* luogo, località, posto; *vt* collocare, mettere, posare.

placid ['plæsid] *a* placido.

plagiarize ['pleidʒəraiz] *vt* plagiare.

plague [pleig] *n* peste, pestilenza; *vt* tormentare, vessare.

plain [plein] *a* piano, liscio; chiaro, evidente, sincero; insignificante; *n* pianura, piano; **p. clothes** abiti borghesi.

plainly ['pleinli] *ad* chiaramente; semplicemente.

plaintiff ['pleintif] *a* querelante.

plaintive ['pleintiv] *a* lamentoso.

plait [plæt] *n* piega; treccia; *vt* pieghettare; intrecciare.

plan [plæn] *n* piano, progetto, disegno; (*building etc*) pianta; *vt* progettare, pianificare.

plane [plein] *a* piano; *n* piano, (*tool*); pialla; (*tree*) platano; aereo.

planet ['plænit] *n* pianeta.

plank [plæŋk] *n* asse, tavola.

plant [plɑːnt] *n* pianta, impianto; *vt* piantare.

plantation [plæn'teiʃən] *n* piantagione.

planter ['plɑːntə] *n* piantatore, colono.

plaque [plɑːk] *n* placca.

plaster ['plɑːstə] *n* cerotto; impiastro; gesso, intonaco, stucco; *vt* applicare un cerotto a; intonacare.

plasterer ['plɑːstərə] *n* imbianchino; gessaio.

plastic ['plæstik] *a* plastico; **plastics** *n sing* plastica.

plasticine ['plæstisiːn] *n* plastilina.

plate [pleit] *n* piatto; lamina; placca,

targa; argenteria; (book) tavola fuori testo; dentiera; vt placcare, rivestire.

plateau ['plætou] pl **plateaux**, **plateaus** n altipiano.

platform ['plætfɔːm] n piattaforma; pianoro; (rly) marciapiede.

platinum ['plætinəm] n platino.

platitude ['plætitjuːd] n banalità.

platonic [plə'tɔnik] a platonico.

platoon [plə'tuːn] n (mil) plotone.

platter ['plætə] n piatto grande.

plausibility [ˌplɔːzə'biliti] n plausibilità.

plausible ['plɔːzəbl] a plausibile.

play [plei] n gioco, divertimento; commedia, dramma; vti giocare, rappresentare; suonare; **playground** n cortile (di scuola) per la ricreazione; **playmate** compagno di giuochi; **plaything** giocattolo.

player ['pleiə] n giocatore; suonatore; attore.

playful ['pleiful] a giocoso, scherzoso.

plea [pliː] n difesa, scusa.

plead [pliːd] vti addurre come pretesto; dichiararsi; perorare, supplicare.

pleading ['pliːdiŋ] a supplichevole; n discussione d'una causa.

pleasant ['pleznt] a piacevole, simpatico.

please [pliːz] vti piacere (a).

pleasing ['pliːziŋ] a piacente, attraente, ameno, piacevole.

pleasure ['pleʒə] n piacere.

plebeian [pli'biːən] a n plebeo.

plebiscite ['plebisit] n plebiscito.

pledge [pledʒ] n pegno, garanzia; promessa; brindisi; vt impegnare; brindare a.

plenipotentiary [ˌplenipə'tenʃəri] a n plenipotenziario.

plentiful ['plentiful] a abbondante, copioso.

plenty ['plenti] n abbondanza.

pleurisy ['pluərisi] n pleurite.

pliable ['plaiəbl] **pliant** ['plaiənt] a pieghevole, flessibile; docile, influenzabile.

pliers ['plaiəz] n pl pinze pl.

plight [plait] n condizione, situazione.

plimsolls ['plimsəls] n pl scarpe di tela.

plod [plɔd] vi camminare con passi lenti e pesanti; sgobbare.

plodder ['plɔdə] n sgobbone.

plot [plɔt] n complotto, cospirazione; (novel etc) intreccio, trama; piccolo pezzo di terreno; vt fare la pianta di; vti complottare.

plotter ['plɔtə] n cospiratore.

plover ['plʌvə] n piviere, pavoncella.

plow [plau] n aratro; vti arare, solcare; **to put one's hand to the p.** intraprendere un lavore.

pluck [plʌk] n (fig) coraggio; frattaglie; vt strappare, pelare, tirare.

plucky ['plʌki] a coraggioso.

plug [plʌg] n tappo; tampone; (el) spina, tabacco compresso.

plum [plʌm] n prugna; susina.

plumage ['pluːmidʒ] n penne pl.

plumb [plʌm] vt misurare la profondità di, scandagliare; ad a piombo; (fig) esattamente; assolutamente.

plumber ['plʌmə] n idraulico.

plumbing ['plʌmiŋ] n impiombatura; impianto idraulico.

plume [pluːm] n piuma; (mil) pennacchio.

plump [plʌmp] a grassoccio, paffuto.

plumpness ['plʌmpnis] n rotondità di forme.

plunder ['plʌndə] n saccheggio, bottino; vt depredare, saccheggiare.

plunge [plʌndʒ] n immersione, tuffo; vti immerger(si), tuffar(si).

plural ['pluərəl] a n plurale.

plus [plʌs] a in più; n più, quantità addizionale, quantità positiva.

plush [plʌʃ] n felpa; a felpato; comodo, elegante.

ply [plai] vt maneggiare; occuparsi di; importunare; vi andare avanti e indietro regolarmente.

plywood ['plaiwud] n legno compensato.

pneumatic [nju:'mætik] a n pneumatico.

pneumonia [nju:'mouniə] n polmonite.

poach [poutʃ] vt cuocere (uova) in camicia; vi andare a caccia di frodo.

poacher ['poutʃə] n cacciatore di frodo; bracconiere.

pocket ['pɔkit] n tasca; vt intascare, appropriarsi di; **p.-book** taccuino, libro formato tascabile.

pod [pɔd] n baccello.

poem ['pouim] n poesia, poema.

poet ['pouit] n poeta.

poetic [pou'etik] a poetico.

poetics [pou'etiks] n poetica.

poetry ['pouitri] n poesia.

poignancy ['pɔinənsi] n (of grief) acutezza; commozione; mordacità.

poignant ['pɔinənt] a acuto, vivo, cocente; mordace.

point [pɔint] n punto, punta, promontorio; vt (sharpen) fare la punta a; (emphasize) dar rilievo a; **to p. at** additare; **to p. out** indicare, far osservare.

point-blank ['pɔint'blæŋk] a diretto; orizzontale; ad orizzontalmente; chiaro e tondo; a bruciapelo.

pointed ['pɔintid] a appuntito, aguzzo; (fig) evidente; mordace.

pointer ['pɔintə] n indicatore; lancetta; cane da ferma.

pointless ['pɔintlis] a senza punta; (fig) inutile.

poise [pɔiz] n equilibrio; portamento; vt equilibrare.

poison ['pɔizn] n veleno; vt avvelenare.

poisonous ['pɔiznəs] a velenoso.

poke [pouk] *n* spinta; *vt* spingere; (*fire*) attizzare; frugare; **to buy a pig in a p.** comperare la gatta nel sacco.
poker ['poukə] *n* attizzatoio.
Poland ['poulənd] *n* (*geogr*) Polonia.
polar ['poulə] *a* polare; (*el*) magnetico; (*fig*) opposto.
Pole [poul] *n* polacco.
pole [poul] *n* palo; pertica (misura di lunghezza uguale a m. 5 circa); polo.
polemic [pɔ'lemik] *n* polemica.
police [pə'liːs] *n* polizia.
policeman [pə'liːsmən] *n* poliziotto, agente di polizia, vigile urbano.
policy ['pɔlisi] *n* politica; linea di condotta; polizza.
poliomyelitis [ˌpoulioumaiə'laitis] *n* poliomielite.
Polish ['pouliʃ] *a n* polacco.
polish ['pɔliʃ] *n* lucidatura; lucido, vernice; raffinatezza; *vt* lucidare, lustrare; raffinare.
polite [pə'lait] *a* cortese, educato, gentile.
politeness [pə'laitnis] *n* cortesia, educazione.
political [pə'litikəl] *a* uomo politico, politicante.
politician [ˌpɔli'tiʃən] *n* uomo politico, politicante.
politics ['pɔlitiks] *n pl* politica, scienza politica.
poll [poul] *n* votazione; scrutinio; lista elettorale; voti; **polling** *a* votante; *n* votazione elettorale.
pollen ['pɔlin] *n* polline.
pollute [pə'luːt] *vt* contaminare; corrompere.
pollution [pə'luːʃən] *n* contaminazione.
polygamy [pɔ'ligəmi] *n* poligamia.
polyvinyl ['pɔli'vinl] *a* polivinilico; *n* polivinile.
poliphony [pə'lifəni] *n* (*mus*) polifonia.
polythene ['pɔliθiːn] *n* politene.
pomade [pə'mɑːd] *n* pomata.
pomegranate ['pɔmˌgrænit] *n* melagrana.
pomp [pɔmp] *n* pompa, fasto.
Pompeian [pɔm'piːən] *a* pompeiano.
Pompeii ['pɔmpiai] *n* Pompei.
pompous ['pɔmpəs] *a* pomposo.
pompousness ['pɔmpəsnis] *n* sussiego.
pond [pɔnd] *n* laghetto, stagno; vivaio.
ponder ['pɔndə] *vti* meditare, ponderare.
ponderous ['pɔndərəs] *a* ponderoso, pesante.
pontiff ['pɔntif] *n* pontefice, papa.
pontoon [pɔn'tuːn] *n* pontone.
pony ['pouni] *n* cavallino, "pony".
poodle ['puːdl] *n* cane barbone, barboncino.
pool [puːl] *n* stagno, pozzanghera; (*com*) fondo comune; (*com*) 'pool'; sindacato; **football p.** totocalcio; **p. room** sala del biliardo.

poop [puːp] *n* (*naut*) poppa.
poor [puə] *a* povero, scarso.
poorly ['puəli] *a* indisposto; *ad* poveramente, dimessamente.
pop [pɔp] *n* scoppio, sparo; *vti* (far) esplodere; entrare, uscire (di colpo); (*cork*) saltare.
Pope [poup] *n* papa; (*Russian priest*) pope.
popery ['poupəri] *n* papismo.
poplar ['pɔplə] *n* pioppo.
poppy ['pɔpi] *n* papavero.
populace ['pɔpjuləs] *n* plebaglia, popolaccio.
popular ['pɔpjulə] *a* popolare.
popularity [ˌpɔpju'læriti] *n* popolarità.
populate ['pɔpjuleit] *vt* popolare.
population [ˌpɔpju'leiʃən] *n* popolazione.
populous ['pɔpjuləs] *a* popoloso.
porcelain ['pɔːslin] *n* porcellana.
porch [pɔːtʃ] *n* portico, porticato.
porcupine ['pɔːkjupain] *n* porcospino.
pore [pɔː] *n* poro; *vi* studiare assiduamente.
pork [pɔːk] *n* carne di maiale.
pornographic [ˌpɔːnə'græfik] *a* pornografico.
porous ['pɔːrəs] *a* poroso.
porphyry ['pɔːfiri] *n* porfido.
porpoise ['pɔːpəs] *n* focena.
porridge ['pɔridʒ] *n* pappa di farina d'avena.
port [pɔːt] *n* porto; (*naut*) fianco sinistro della nave; vino d'Oporto.
portable ['pɔːtəbl] *a* portatile.
portal ['pɔːtl] *n* portale; **p. vein** vena porta.
portend [pɔː'tend] *vt* presagire.
portent ['pɔːtent] *n* portento; presagio.
porter ['pɔːtə] *n* facchino; portiere, portinaio.
porterage ['pɔːtəridʒ] *n* facchinaggio.
portfolio [pɔːt'fouliou] *n* cartella; portafoglio ministeriale.
portion ['pɔːʃən] *n* porzione, parte; destino.
portly ['pɔːtli] *a* corpulento; di portamento dignitoso.
portmanteau [pɔːt'mæntou] *n* baule armadio.
portrait ['pɔːtrit] *n* ritratto.
portray [pɔː'trei] *vt* ritrarre; rappresentare.
Portugal ['pɔːtjugəl] *n* Portogallo.
Portuguese [ˌpɔːtju'giːz] *a n* portoghese.
pose [pouz] *n* posa, affettazione.
position [pə'ziʃən] *n* posizione; condizione; impiego, posto.
positive ['pɔzətiv] *a* preciso, certo, reale, positivo; *n* cosa positiva, (il) positivo; (*phot*) positiva.
posse ['pɔsi] *n* manipolo di persone incaricate di far rispettare l'ordine pubblico.

possess [pə'zes] vt possedere.
possession [pə'zeʃən] n possesso, possedimento.
possessive [pə'zesiv] a possessivo.
possibility [,pɔsə'biliti] n possibilità.
possible ['pɔsəbl] a possibile.
possibly ['pɔsəbli] ad possibilmente, forse; (in the negative) assolutamente.
post [poust] n posta; impiego, posto; palo, pilastro; vt affiggere; impostare; imbucare;; pubblicare; (com) registrare, collocare; **p. office** ufficio postale.
postage ['poustidʒ] n affrancatura.
postal ['poustəl] a postale; **p. order** vaglia postale.
poster ['poustə] n affisso, manifesto pubblicitario, cartellone.
poste-restante ['poust'restãːnt] n fermo posta.
posterior [pɔs'tiəriə] a posteriore; n deretano, sedere.
posterity [pɔs'teriti] n posterità.
posthumous ['pɔstjuməs] a postumo.
postman ['poustmən] n portalettere, postino.
postpone [poust'poun] vt posporre, rimandare.
postponement [poust'pounmənt] n rinvio.
postscript ['pousskript] n poscritto.
postulate ['pɔstjuleit] vti richiedere; supporre.
posture ['pɔstʃə] n posizione, atteggiamento.
posy ['pouzi] n mazzo di fiori.
pot [pɔt] n vaso; pentola.
potash ['pɔtæʃ] n potasso.
potassium [pə'tæsiəm] n potassio.
potato [pə'teitou] pl **potatoes** n patata; **p. chips** patatine fritte; **mashed p.** pl purè di patate.
potent ['poutənt] a potente, forte.
potentate ['poutənteit] n potentato.
potential [pə'tenʃəl] a potenziale.
pother ['pɔðə] n confusione, pandemonio.
potion ['pouʃən] n pozione.
potted ['pɔtid] a conservato, in conserva.
pottery ['pɔtəri] n terraglie, stoviglie pl.
pouch [pautʃ] n bisaccia, borsa; carniera.
poulterer ['poultərə] n pollivendolo.
poultice ['poultis] n cataplasma.
poultry ['poultri] n pollame, gallinacei domestici pl.
pounce [pauns] n balzo; vti avventarsi, piombare (su).
pound [paund] (abbr **lb**) n libbra (uguale a grammi 453); (abbr **£**) lira sterlina; recinto per bestiame; vt pestare, frantumare.
pour [pɔə] vt versare; vi diluviare.
pout [paut] vi fare il broncio.
poverty ['pɔvəti] n miseria, povertà.
powder ['paudə] n polvere; cipria; vt incipriare; polverizzare; spolveriz-

zare; **p.-puff** piumino per la cipria; **powdery** a friabile; polveroso.
power ['pauə] n potere, potenza, forza, energia; **p. station** centrale elettrica.
powerful ['pauəful] a potente, possente.
powerless ['pauəlis] a impotente.
practical ['præktikəl] a pratico, fattibile.
practically ['præktikəli] ad praticamente; quasi, virtualmente.
practice ['præktis] n pratica, abitudine; esercizio; clientela; lavoro professionale.
practice ['præktis] vti esercitar(si), praticare.
practitioner [præk'tiʃnə] n professionista (medico); **general p.** medico generico.
prairie ['prɛəri] n prateria.
praise [preiz] n elogio, lode; vt lodare.
praiseworthy ['preiz,wəːði] a lodevole, degno di lode.
prance [prɑːns] vi (of horses) impennarsi; camminare con spavalderia.
prank [præŋk] n scherzo, tiro.
prattle ['prætl] n cicaleccio infantile; vi cianciare, cinguettare.
prawn [prɔːn] n gambero.
pray [prei] vti pregare.
prayer ['preiə] n preghiera; **p.-book** libro di preghiere.
preach [priːtʃ] vti predicare.
preacher ['priːtʃə] n predicatore.
precarious [pri'kɛəriəs] a precario.
precaution [pri'kɔːʃən] n precauzione.
precede [priː'siːd] vti precedere.
precedence [priː'siːdəns] n precedenza.
precedent ['presidənt] n precedente.
preceding [priː'siːdiŋ] a precedente.
precept ['priːsept] n precetto.
precinct ['priːsiŋkt] n recinto; **precincts** pl confini, limiti pl.
preciosity [,preʃi'ɔsiti] n preziosità, ricercatezza.
precious ['preʃəs] a prezioso, ricercato.
precipice ['presipis] n precipizio.
precipitate [pri'sipiteit] a precipitoso, avventato; vti precipitare.
precipitous [pri'sipitəs] a erto, scosceso.
precise [pri'sais] a preciso.
precisely [pri'saisli] ad precisamente, esattamente, in punto.
precision [pri'siʒən] n precisione.
preclude [pri'kluːd] vt precludere, escludere.
precocious [pri'kouʃəs] a precoce.
preconceived ['priːkən'siːvd] a preconcetto.
precursor [priː'kəːsə] n precursore.
predecessor ['priːdisesə] n predecessore.
predicament [pri'dikəmənt] n situazione difficile o pericolosa.

predict [pri'dikt] vt predire.
predilection [.pri:di'lekʃən] n predilezione.
predispose ['pri:dis'pouz] vt predisporre.
predominance [pri'dɔminəns] n predominio.
predominant [pri'dɔminənt] a predominante.
predominate [pri'dɔmineit] vi predominare.
pre-eminent [pri:'eminənt] a preminente.
prefab ['pri:'fæb] n (fam) casa prefabbricata.
prefabricate ['pri:'fæbrikeit] vt prefabbricare.
preface ['prefis] n prefazione; (eccl) prefazio.
prefect ['pri:fekt] n prefetto.
prefer [pri'fə:] vt preferire; **preferred shares** (com) azioni privilegiate (or preferenziali).
preferable ['prefərəbl] a preferibile.
preference ['prefərəns] n preferenza.
prefix ['pri:fiks] n prefisso.
pregnancy ['pregnənsi] n gravidanza.
pregnant ['pregnənt] a gravida, incinta; pregno, significativo.
prejudice ['predʒudis] n pregiudizio; vt compromettere, pregiudicare.
prejudicial [.predʒu'diʃəl] a pregiudizievole, dannoso.
prelate ['prelit] n prelato.
preliminary [pri'liminəri] a n preliminare.
prelude ['prelju:d] n preludio.
premature [.premə'tjuə] a prematuro.
premier ['premiə] a primo; n primo ministro.
premiere ['premjɛ:r] n (theat) prima.
premise ['premis] n premessa.
premise [pri'maiz] vt premettere.
premises ['premisiz] n pl edificio, locali pl.
premium ['pri:miəm] n (com) premio, aggio.
premonition [.pri:mə:'niʃən] n premonizione, presentimento.
preparation [.prepə'reiʃən] n preparazione, preparativo.
preparatory [pri'pærətəri] a preparatorio.
prepare [pri'pɛə] vti preparar(si).
prepay ['pri:'pei] vt pagare in anticipo.
preponderant [pri'pɔndərənt] a preponderante.
preponderate [pri'pɔndəreit] (over) vi predominare, prevalere.
preposition [.prepə'ziʃən] n preposizione.
prepossess [.pri:pə'zes] vt influenzare.
prepossessing [.pri:pə'zesiŋ] a simpatico, attraente.
prepossession [.pri:pə'zeʃən] n prevenzione; predisposizione.

preposterous [pri'pɔstərəs] a assurdo.
prerogative [pri'rɔgətiv] n prerogativa.
presage ['presidʒ] n presagio.
presbyterian [.prezbi'tiəriən] a n presbiteriano.
prescribe [pris'kraib] vti prescrivere.
prescription [pris'kripʃən] n ricetta medica.
presence ['prezns] n presenza.
present ['preznt] a presente; attuale; n presente, regalo, dono; vt presentare; regalare a.
presentation [.prezen'teiʃən] n presentazione; dono, omaggio.
presentiment [pri'zentimənt] n presentimento.
presently ['prezntli] ad tra poco, presto, poco dopo, di lì a poco.
preservation [.prezə:'veiʃən] n conservazione, preservazione.
preservative [pri'zə:vətiv] a n preservativo.
preserve [pri'zə:v] n conserva, marmellata; (game etc) riserva; vt preservare, conservare, mettere in conserva.
preside [pri'zaid] vi presiedere.
presidency ['prezidənsi] n presidenza.
president ['prezidənt] n presidente.
presidential [.prezi'denʃəl] a presidenziale.
press [pres] n torchio; pressione; folla; (mech) pressa; stampa; armadio; vti premere, comprimere, stringere; urgere, affollarsi.
pressing ['presiŋ] a pressante, insistente, urgente.
pressure ['preʃə] n pressione.
prestige [pres'ti:ʒ] n prestigio.
presume [pri'zju:m] vti presumere, supporre.
presumption [pri'zʌmpʃən] n presunzione; supposizione.
presumptive [pri'zʌmptiv] a presuntivo, presunto.
presumptuous [pri'zʌmptjuəs] a presuntuoso.
presuppose [.pri:sə'pouz] vt presupporre.
pretend [pri'tend] vt fingere, pretendere; vi aspirare, vantare diritti su.
pretense [pri'tens] n pretesa; pretesto, finzione.
pretension [pri'tenʃən] n pretensione, pretesa, diritto.
pretentious [pri'tenʃəs] a pretenzioso.
pretext ['pri:tekst] n pretesto.
prettiness ['pritinis] n grazia, leggiadria.
pretty ['priti] a grazioso, carino; ad discretamente, piuttosto, un po'.
prevail [pri'veil] vi prevalere; **to p. (up)on** persuadere.
prevalent ['prevələnt] a prevalente.

prevaricate [pri'værikeit] *vi* tergiversare; mentire.
prevarication [pri͵væri'keiʃən] *n* tergiversazione; menzogna.
prevent [pri'vent] *vt* impedire.
prevention [pri'venʃən] *n* impedimento; misura preventiva.
preventive [pri'ventiv] *a* preventivo; *n* misura preventiva.
preview ['priːvjuː] *n* visione privata, anteprima; 'prossimamente'.
previous ['priːviəs] *a* anteriore, precedente.
previously ['priːviəsli] *ad* precedentemente.
prevision [priː'viʒən] *n* previsione.
prey [prei] *n* preda; **p. upon** *vi* predare; consumare.
price [prais] *n* prezzo.
priceless ['praislis] *a* inestimabile; (*sl*) impagabile.
prick [prik] *n* puntura; (*fig*) pungolo, rimorso; *vt* pungere, punzecchiare; drizzare (gli orecchi).
prickle ['prikl] *n* pungiglione; puntura.
prickly ['prikli] *a* spinoso; **p. pear** fico d'India.
pride [praid] *n* orgoglio, superbia; **p. oneself on** gloriarsi di, vantarsi.
priest [priːst] *n* prete, sacerdote.
priesthood ['priːsthud] *n* sacerdozio.
prig [prig] *n* pedante, saccente.
priggish ['prigiʃ] *a* affettato, pedante.
prim [prim] *a* affettato, cerimonioso.
primacy ['praiməsi] *n* primato, supremazia.
primarily ['praimərili] *ad* in primo luogo, essenzialmente.
primary ['praiməri] *a* primario, originario, fondamentale, principale.
primate ['praimeit] *n* arcivescovo, primate.
prime [praim] *a* primo; di prima qualità; *n* fiore, rigoglio.
primeval [prai'miːvəl] *a* primitivo, primordiale.
primitive ['primitiv] *a* primitivo.
primordial [prai'mɔːdiəl] *a* primordiale.
primrose ['primrouz] *n* primula.
prince [prins] *n* principe.
princely ['prinsli] *a* principesco.
princess [prin'ses] *n* principessa.
principal ['prinsəpəl] *a* principale; *n* principale, capo, direttore, superiore, rettore; (*com*) capitale.
principality [͵prinsi'pæliti] *n* principato.
principle ['prinsəpl] *n* principio.
print [print] *n* impronta, orma, stampa; tessuto di cotone stampato; *vt* imprimere; pubblicare, stampare.
printer ['printə] *n* tipografo, stampatore.
printing ['printiŋ] *n* stampa, tiratura.
prior ['praiə] *a* antecedente, precedente; *n* priore; *ad* anteriormente, prima di.

priority [prai'ɔriti] *n* priorità.
prism ['prizəm] *n* prisma.
prison ['prizn] *n* prigione, penitenziario, carcere.
prisoner ['priznə] *n* prigioniero, detenuto.
pristine ['pristain] *a* pristino.
privacy ['praivəsi] *n* intimità, segreto, ritiro, vita privata.
private ['praivit] *n* soldato semplice; *a* privato; **p. business** questione personale.
privateer [͵privə'tiə] *n* nave corsara.
privation [prai'veiʃən] *n* privazione.
privet ['privit] *n* ligustro.
privilege ['privilidʒ] *n* privilegio.
privy ['privi] *a* privato; **p. to** a conoscenza di.
prize [praiz] *n* premio; *vt* apprezzare, valutare.
probability [͵prɔbə'biliti] *n* probabilità.
probable ['prɔbəbl] *a* probabile.
probate ['proubit] *n* verifica di testamento.
probation [prə'beiʃən] *n* prova; noviziato; libertà condizionata.
probationer [prə'beiʃnə] *n* apprendista; novizio; chi si trova in libertà condizionata.
probe [proub] *n* (*med*) sonda; *vt* sondare; scandagliare.
probity ['proubiti] *n* probità.
problem ['prɔbləm] *n* problema.
problematic [͵prɔbli'mætik] *a* problematico.
procedure [prə'siːdʒə] *n* procedimento; procedura.
proceed [prə'siːd] *vi* procedere, avanzare; derivare.
proceeding [prə'siːdiŋ] *n* atto, azione, condotta, procedimento.
proceeds ['prousiːdz] *n pl* provento, ricavo.
process ['prouses] *n* corso, processo; *vt* sottoporre a procedimento.
procession [prə'seʃən] *n* processione, corteo.
proclaim [prə'kleim] *vt* proclamare.
proclamation [͵prɔklə'meiʃən] *n* proclama(zione).
proclivity [prə'kliviti] *n* inclinazione, tendenza.
procrastinate [prou'kræstineit] *vti* procrastinare.
procrastination [prou͵kræsti'neiʃən] *n* indugio, procrastinazione.
procreate ['proukrieit] *vt* procreare.
procreation [͵proukri'eiʃən] *n* procreazione.
procure [prə'kjuə] *vt* procurar(si).
prod [prɔd] *n* pungolo, stimolo; *vt* stimolare.
prodigal ['prɔdigəl] *a n* prodigo.
prodigious [prə'didʒəs] *a* prodigioso.
prodigy ['prɔdidʒi] *n* prodigio.
produce ['prɔdjuːs] *n* prodotti *pl*; *vti* [prə'djuːs] produrre; presentare.
producer [prə'djuːsə] *n* produttore; (*theat*) regista, impresario.

product ['prɔdəkt] n prodotto.
production [prə'dʌkʃən] n produzione.
productive [prə'dʌktiv] a produttivo.
productivity [ˌprɔdʌk'tiviti] n produttività.
profanation [ˌprɔfə'neiʃən] n profanazione.
profane [prə'fein] a profano; vt profanare.
profess [prə'fes] vti professare; esercitare; insegnare.
profession [prə'feʃən] n professione.
professional [prə'feʃənl] a di professione, professionale; n professionista.
professor [prə'fesə] n professore; **professorship** professorato.
proffer ['prɔfə] vt offrire.
proficiency [prə'fiʃənsi] n abilità, perizia.
proficient [prə'fiʃənt] a n esperto, competente.
profile ['proufail] n profilo.
profit ['prɔfit] n guadagno, profitto, utile, vantaggio; vt giovare; vi (ap)profittare, trarre vantaggio.
profitable ['prɔfitəbl] a vantaggioso.
profiteer [ˌprɔfi'tiə] n profittatore; (fig) pescecane.
profligacy ['prɔfligəsi] n dissolutezza, licenziosità.
profligate ['prɔfligit] a n dissoluto.
profound [prə'faund] a profondo.
profuse [prə'fjuːs] a abbondante; prodigo.
profusion [prə'fjuːʒən] n profusione.
progeny ['prɔdʒini] n progenie.
prognosticate [prəg'nɔstikeit] vt pronosticare.
program ['prougræm] n programma.
progress ['prougres] n avanzata; corso; progresso; vi [prə'gres] progredire, fare progressi.
progressive [prə'gresiv] a progressivo.
prohibit [prə'hibit] vt proibire, vietare.
prohibition [ˌproui'biʃən] n proibizione, divieto.
prohibitive [prə'hibitiv] a proibitivo.
project ['prɔdʒekt] n progetto; vt [prə'djekt] proiettare; vi sporgere.
projectile ['prɔdʒiktail] n proiettile.
projection [prə'dʒekʃən] n proiezione; sporgenza.
proletariat [ˌproule'tɛəriət] n proletariato.
prolific [prə'lifik] a prolifico.
prolix ['prouliks] a prolisso.
prologue ['proulɔg] n prologo.
prolong [prə'lɔŋ] vt prolungare.
promenade [ˌprɔmi'naːd] n passeggiata; lungomare.
prominence ['prɔminəns] n prominenza, risalto.

prominent ['prɔminənt] a prominente, cospicuo.
promiscuity [ˌprɔmis'kjuːiti] n promiscuità.
promiscuous [prə'miskjuəs] a promiscuo.
promise ['prɔmis] n promessa; vti promettere.
promising ['prɔmisiŋ] a promettente.
promissory ['prɔmisəri] a che contiene una promessa, promettente.
promontory ['prɔməntri] n promontorio.
promote [prə'mout] vt incoraggiare, promuovere.
promotion [prə'mouʃən] n promozione.
prompt [prɔmpt] a pronto, sollecito; vt incitare; suggerire.
prompter ['prɔmptə] n (theat) suggeritore.
promptitude ['prɔmptitjuːd] n prontezza, sollecitudine.
promptness ['prɔmptnis] n prontezza.
promulgate ['prɔmələgeit] vt promulgare.
promulgation [ˌprɔməl'geiʃən] n promulgazione.
prone [proun] a incline, propenso; prono, prostrato.
proneness ['prounnis] n inclinazione, propensione.
prong [prɔŋ] n rebbio; punta.
pronoun ['prounaun] n pronome.
pronounce [prə'nauns] vt pronunciare, -ziare; dichiarare.
pronounced [prə'naunst] a pronunziato.
pronunciation [prəˌnʌnsi'eiʃən] n pronuncia, -zia.
proof [pruːf] n prova; (print) bozza di stampa.
prop [prɔp] n appoggio, puntello; (theat) attrezzo scenico; vt puntellare, sostenere.
propaganda [ˌprɔpə'gændə] n propaganda.
propagate ['prɔpəgeit] vti propagar (si).
propagation [ˌprɔpə'geiʃən] n propagazione.
propel [prə'pel] vt spingere avanti.
propeller [prə'pelə] n (mech) elica; propulsore.
propensity [prə'pensiti] n propensione, tendenza.
proper ['prɔpə] a proprio, appropriato, vero e proprio.
properly ['prɔpəli] ad per bene, come si deve. correttamente.
property ['prɔpəti] n proprietà, beni; qualità.
prophecy ['prɔfisi] n profezia.
prophesy ['prɔfisai] vti profetizzare.
prophet ['prɔfit] n profeta.
prophetic [prə'fetik] a profetico.
propinquity [prə'piŋkwiti] n vicinanza.
propitiate [prə'piʃieit] vt propiziare.

propitious [prə'pifəs] a propizio.
proportion [prə'pɔːʃən] n proporzione.
proportional [prə'pɔːʃənl] a proporzionale.
proportionate [prə'pɔːʃnit] a proporzionato.
proposal [prə'pouzəl] n proposta; proposta di matrimonio.
propose [prə'pouz] vt proporre; **p. a toast** to fare un brindisi a; vi proporre; fare una proposta di matrimonio.
proposition [,prɔpə'ziʃən] n asserzione; proposta; proposizione.
propound [prə'paund] vt proporre.
proprietor [prə'praiətə] n proprietario.
propriety [prə'praiəti] n correttezza, proprietà; opportunità.
prorogation [,prourə'geiʃən] n proroga, rinvio.
prosaic [prou'zeiik] a prosaico.
proscribe [prous'kraib] vt proscrivere.
proscription [prous'kripʃən] n proscrizione.
prose [prouz] n prosa; **p. writer** prosatore.
prosecute ['prɔsikjuːt] vti perseguire, proseguire; procedere contro, querelare.
prosecution [,prɔsi'kjuːʃən] n prosecuzione; (leg) processo.
prosecutor ['prɔsikjuːtə] n prosecutore; querelante; **public p.** pubblico ministero.
proselyte ['prɔsilait] n proselito.
proselytize ['prɔsilitaiz] vi fare proseliti.
prosody ['prɔsədi] n prosodia.
prospect ['prɔspekt] n vista; prospettiva, speranza; vt [prəs'pekt] esplorare.
prospective [prəs'pektiv] a eventuale, probabile.
prospectus [prəs'pektəs] n programma, prospetto.
prosper ['prɔspə] vi prosperare.
prosperity [prɔs'periti] n prosperità.
prosperous ['prɔspərəs] a prospero.
prostitute ['prɔstitjuːt] n prostituta.
prostitution [,prɔsti'tjuːʃən] n prostituzione.
prostrate ['prɔstreit] a prosternato; (fig) prostrato; vt [prɔs'treit] prosternare; (fig) prostrare.
prostration [prɔs'treiʃən] n prostrazione.
protagonist [prə'tægənist] n protagonista.
protect [prə'tekt] vt proteggere.
protection [prə'tekʃən] n protezione; salvacondotto.
protective [prə'tektiv] a protettivo.
protector [prə'tektə] n protettore.
protégé ['prouteʒei] n protetto.
protein ['proutiːn] n proteina.
protest ['proutest] n protesta; (com) rotesto; vti [prə'test] protestare.

protestant ['prɔtistənt] a n protestante.
Protestantism ['prɔtistəntizəm] n protestantesimo.
protocol ['proutəkɔl] n protocollo.
protoplasm ['proutə,plæzəm] n protoplasma.
prototype ['proutətaip] n prototipo.
protract [prə'trækt] vt protrarre.
protraction [prə'trækʃən] n protrazione; disegno su scala.
protrude [prə'truːd] vt sporgere, spingere avanti; vi proiettarsi, sporgere.
protuberance [prə'tjuːbərəns] n protuberanza.
proud [praud] a fiero, orgoglioso; superbo.
prove [pruːv] vt dimostrare, provare; vi mostrarsi, riuscire.
Provençal [,prɔvãːn'saːl] a n provenzale; lingua provenzale.
Provence [prɔ'vãːs] n Provenza.
provender ['prɔvində] n foraggio.
proverb ['prɔvəb] n proverbio.
proverbial [prə'vəːbiəl] a proverbiale.
provide [prə'vaid] vti provvedere, fornire; **to p. against** premunirsi contro.
provided [prə'vaidid] cj purchè, a patto che.
providence ['prɔvidəns] n provvidenza; previdenza.
provident ['prɔvidənt] a provvido; previdente.
providential [,prɔvi'denʃəl] a provvidenziale.
province ['prɔvins] n provincia; (fig) competenza, sfera d'azione.
provincial [prə'vinʃəl] a n provinciale.
provision [prə'viʒən] n preparativo, provvedimento; clausola; pl provviste, viveri; vt approvvigionare.
provisional [prə'viʒənl] a provvisorio.
provocation [,prɔvə'keiʃən] n provocazione.
provocative [prə'vɔkətiv] a provocante.
provoke [prə'vouk] vt provocare.
provoking [prə'voukiŋ] a provocante.
prow [prau] n (naut) prora, prua.
prowess ['prauis] n prodezza.
prowl [praul] vi vagare in cerca di preda.
proximity [prɔk'simiti] n prossimità.
proxy ['prɔksi] n procura; procuratore.
prude [pruːd] n donna eccessivamente pudica.
prudence ['pruːdəns] n prudenza.
prudent ['pruːdənt] a prudente, circospetto, giudizioso.
prudery ['pruːdəri] n eccessiva pudicizia.
prudish ['pruːdiʃ] a pudibondo; schifiltoso.

prune [pruːn] *n* prugna secca; *vt* potare, sfrondare.
prurient ['pruəriənt] *a* lascivo.
Prussia ['prʌʃə] *n* Prussia.
pry [prai] *vi* curiosare, ficcare il naso.
psalm [sɑːm] *n* salmo.
pseudonym ['sjuːdənim] *n* pseudonimo.
psychedelic [ˌsaikə'delik] *a* psichedelico.
psychiatrist [sai'kaiətrist] *n* psichiatra.
psychiatry [sai'kaiətri] *n* psichiatria.
psychic ['saikik] *a* psichico.
psychologic(al) [ˌsaikə'lɔdʒik(l)] *a* psicologico.
psychology [sai'kɔlədʒi] *n* psicologia.
psychosis [sai'kousis] *n* psicosi.
puberty ['pjuːbəti] *n* pubertà.
public ['pʌblik] *a n* pubblico; **p. convenience**, **p. comfort station** gabinetto pubblico; **p. house** spaccio di birra e bevande alcooliche.
publican ['pʌblikən] *n* oste; proprietario di bar.
publication [ˌpʌbli'keiʃən] *n* pubblicazione.
publicity [pʌb'lisiti] *n* pubblicità.
publish ['pʌbliʃ] *vt* pubblicare; promulgare.
publisher ['pʌbliʃə] *n* editore; (*of newspaper*) proprietario.
pucker ['pʌkə] *n* crespa, grinza; *vt* corrugare, increspare; *vi* raggrinzirsi.
pudding ['pudiŋ] *n* budino, dolce.
puddle ['pʌdl] *n* pozzanghera.
puerility [pjuə'riliti] *n* puerilità.
Puerto Rican ['pwəːtou'riːkən] *a n* portoricano.
Puerto Rico ['pwəːtou'riːkou] *n* Portorico.
puff [pʌf] *n* sbuffo; soffio; piumino da cipria, pubblicità con elogi esagerati; *vt* gonfiare soffiando; fare una pubblicità esagerata a; *vi* ansimare; sbuffare; soffiare; **p. pastry** pasta sfoglia.
pug [pʌg] *n* (*clay*) argilla; (*dog*) cagnolino; **p. nose** naso camuso.
pugilist ['pjuːdʒilist] *n* pugile.
pugnacious [pʌg'neiʃəs] *a* pugnace, battagliero.
pugnacity [pʌg'næsiti] *n* spirito battagliero.
pull [pul] *n* strattone, tirata; (*sl*) influenza; vantaggio; *vt* strappare, tirare.
pullet ['pulit] *n* pollastrella.
pulley ['puli] *n* (*mech*) puleggia.
pullover ['pulˌouvə] *n* 'pullover', golf.
pulmonary ['pʌlmənəri] *a* polmonare.
pulp [pʌlp] *n* polpa; (*paper making*) pasta.
pulpit ['pulpit] *n* pulpito.
pulsate [pʌl'seit] *vti* battere, pulsare.
pulsation [pʌl'seiʃən] *n* pulsazione.
pulse [pʌls] *n* polso, battito.

pulverize ['pʌlvəraiz] *vti* polverizzar(si).
pumice ['pʌmis] *n* pomice.
pump [pʌmp] *n* pompa; *vti* pompare; (*fam*) cercare di estrarre informazioni.
pumpkin ['pʌmpkin] *n* zucca.
pun [pʌn] *n* gioco di parole.
punch [pʌntʃ] *n* pugno; (*fam*) vigore; punzone; ponce; *vt* perforare; dare pugni a.
punctual ['pʌŋktjuəl] *a* puntuale.
punctuality [ˌpuŋktju'æliti] *n* puntualità.
punctuate ['puŋktjueit] *vt* punteggiare.
punctuation [ˌpuŋktju'eiʃən] *n* punteggiatura.
puncture ['pʌŋktʃə] *n* puntura; (*tire*) foratura.
pungent ['pʌndʒənt] *a* pungente, acuto, mordace.
punish ['pʌniʃ] *vt* punire.
punishable ['pʌniʃəbl] *a* punibile.
punishment ['pʌniʃmənt] *n* punizione.
punt [pʌnt] *n* chiatta, pontone; barchino; *vti* navigare su chiatta.
punter ['pʌntə] *n* puntatore (alle corse *etc*).
puny ['pjuːni] *a* piccolo e debole.
pup [pʌp] **puppy** ['pʌpi] *n* cucciolo.
pupil ['pjuːpil] *n* alunno, -na; scolaro, -ra, (*eye*) pupilla.
puppet ['pʌpit] *n* burattino, marionetta.
purchase ['pəːtʃəs] *n* acquisto; *vt* acquistare, comperare.
purchaser ['pəːtʃəsə] *n* acquirente, compratore.
pure [pjuə] *a* puro.
pureness ['pjuənis] *n* purezza.
purgative ['pəːgətiv] *a* purgativo; *n* purgante.
purgatory ['pəːgətəri] *n* purgatorio.
purge [pəːdʒ] *n* purga(nte); epurazione; *vti* purgar(si), purificar(si).
purification [ˌpjuərifi'keiʃən] *n* purificazione.
purify ['pjuərifai] *vt* purificare.
puritan ['pjuəritən] *a n* puritano.
puritanism ['pjuəritənizəm] *n* puritanismo.
purity ['pjuəriti] *n* purezza, purità.
purl [pəːl] *vi* mormorare, gorgogliare; **p. knitting** lavoro a punto rovescio.
purloin [pəː'lɔin] *vt* rubare, sottrarre.
purple ['pəːpl] *a* purpureo, violaceo; *n* porpora.
purport ['pəːpət] *n* significato; tenore; *vt* [pəː'pɔːt] significare.
purpose ['pəːpəs] *n* fine, proposito, scopo; *vti* proporsi, avere intenzione di.
purr [pəː] *vi* far le fusa.
purse [pəːs] *n* borsa, portamonete.
purser ['pəːsə] *n* (*naut*) commissario di bordo.

pursuance [pə'sjuːəns] n continuazione; esecuzione.
pursue [pə'sjuː] vti inseguire; continuare; perseguire.
pursuer [pə'sjuːə] n inseguitore; (Scots law) attore.
pursuit [pə'sjuːt] n inseguimento; occupazione.
purvey [pəː'vei] vti provvedere, fornire.
purveyor [pəː'veiə] n fornitore.
pus [pʌs] n (med) pus.
push [puʃ] n spinta; (el) pulsante; pressione; energia; momento critico; **p.-button switch** interruttore a pulsante; **p. cart** carretto a mano; passeggino; vt spingere, far pressioni su.
pushing ['puʃiŋ] a energico; intraprendente; invadente.
pusillanimous [ˌpjuːsi'læniməs] a pusillanime.
puss [pus] n micio; **pussy** micino.
put [put] vt mettere, porre; **p. off** differire; (fig) scoraggiare; distrarre; **p. on** indossare; **p. out** mettere fuori; spegnere; **p. up** contribuire; costruire; (cards) puntare; alloggiare; **p. up with** sopportare.
putrefaction [ˌpjuːtri'fækʃən] n putrefazione.
putrefy ['pjuːtrifai] vti putrefar(si).
putrid ['pjuːtrid] a putrido.
puttee ['pʌtiː] n mollettiera.
putty ['pʌti] n stucco; mastice.
puzzle ['pʌzl] n enigma, indovinello, rebus; perplessità; vt rendere perplesso.
puzzling ['pʌzliŋ] a sconcertante, imbarazzante.
pygmy ['pigmi] a n pigmeo.
pyjamas [pə'dʒɑːməz] n pl pigiama.
pylon ['pailɔn] n pilone.
pyramid ['pirəmid] n piramide.
pyre ['paiə] n pira, rogo.
pyrotechnic ['pairou'teknik] a pirotecnico.

Q

quack [kwæk] n ciarlatano; verso dell'anatra; vi (duck) schiamazzare.
quackery ['kwækəri] n ciarlataneria; empirismo.
quadrangle ['kwɔˌdræŋgl] n quadrangolo; corte quadrangolare interna.
quadrant ['kwɔdrənt] n quadrante.
quadrille [kwə'dril] n quadriglia.
quadruped ['kwɔdruped] a n quadrupede.
quadruple ['kwɔdrupl] a quadruplice, quadruplo; n quadruplo.
quaff [kwɑːf] vt tracannare.
quagmire ['kwægmaiə] n pantano, palude.
quail [kweil] n quaglia; vi scoraggiarsi.

quaint [kweint] a curioso, strano; caratteristico.
quaintness ['kweintnis] n bizzarria, singolarità.
quake [kweik] n scossa, tremito; vi tremare.
Quaker ['kweikə] a n quacquero.
qualification [ˌkwɔlifi'keiʃən] n requisito, titolo, qualifica; condizione.
qualify ['kwɔlifai] vt qualificare, abilitare; autorizzare; modificare; restringere; vi rendersi idoneo.
quality ['kwɔliti] n qualità.
qualm [kwɔːm] n nausea; (fig) scrupolo.
quandary ['kwɔndəri] n imbarazzo, incertezza, situazione difficile.
quantity ['kwɔntiti] n quantità.
quarantine ['kwɔrəntiːn] n quarantena.
quarrel ['kwɔrəl] n litigio, lite; vi litigare.
quarrelsome ['kwɔrəlsəm] a litigioso.
quarry ['kwɔri] n cava; preda.
quarryman ['kwɔrimən] n cavatore.
quart [kwɔːt] n quarto di gallone.
quarter ['kwɔːtə] n quarto; quartiere; direzione; località; trimestre; vt dividere in quarti; (mil) acquartierare.
quarter-deck ['kwɔːtədek] n (naut) cassero.
quarterly ['kwɔːtəli] a trimestrale; ad trimestralmente; n pubblicazione trimestrale.
quartermaster ['kwɔːtəˌmɑːstə] n (mil) furiere.
quartet [kwɔː'tet] n (mus) quartetto.
quartz [kwɔːts] n quarzo.
quash [kwɔʃ] vt schiacciare, annullare.
quatrain ['kwɔtrein] n quartina.
quaver ['kweivə] n trillo, tremolio, vibrazione; (mus) croma; vi tremolare, vibrare.
quay [kiː] n banchina, molo.
queasy ['kwiːzi] a delicato di stomaco; nauseato; scrupoloso.
queen [kwiːn] n regina.
queenly ['kwiːnli] a da (di) regina, regale.
queer [kwiə] a strano, bizzarro, eccentrico; dubbio, sospetto; debole, che ha le vertigini.
quell [kwel] vt reprimere, soffocare.
quench [kwentʃ] vt spegnere, estinguere, calmare.
querulous ['kwerjuləs] a querulo, lamentevole.
query ['kwiəri] n domanda, punto interrogativo; vt mettere in dubbio, interrogare.
quest [kwest] n ricerca, inchiesta.
question ['kwestʃən] n domanda; questione; vt interrogare, mettere in dubbio.
questionable ['kwestʃənəbl] a discutibile, dubbio.

questionnaire [‚kwestiə'nɛə] *n* questionario.
queue [kju:] *n* coda; *vi* to q. up fare la coda.
quibble ['kwibl] *n* gioco di parole, cavillo; *vi* far giochi di parole, cavillare.
quick [kwik] *a* rapido, svelto, pronto, vivace, vivo; *ad* presto, rapidamente; *n* vivo, parte vitale.
quicken ['kwikən] *vt* affrettare, stimolare; *vi* animarsi, affrettarsi..
quickness ['kwiknis] *n* rapidità, prontezza, acutezza.
quicksand ['kwiksænd] *n* sabbia mobile.
quicksilver ['kwik‚silvə] *n* mercurio, argento vivo.
quiet ['kwaiət] *a* quieto, tranquillo, dolce, sobrio; *n* quiete, tranquillità.
quiet(en) ['kwaiət(n)] *vti* acquietar (si), calmar(si).
quietness ['kwaiətnis] *n* quiete, riposo, silenzio.
quill [kwil] *n* penna, penna d'oca.
quilt [kwilt] *n* trapunta; *vt* trapuntare.
quince [kwins] *n* cotogna.
quinine [kwi'ni:n] *n* chinino.
quinsy ['kwinzi] *n* (*med*) tonsillite.
quintal ['kwintl] *n* quintale.
quintet [kwin'tet] *n* (*mus*) quintetto.
quip [kwip] *n* battuta spiritosa, motto pungente.
quire ['kwaiə] *n* quaderno, insieme di 24 fogli di carta da scrivere.
quirk [kwə:k] *n* arguzia; svolazzo.
quit [kwit] *a* sdebitato, libero; *vt* abbandonare, lasciare; *vi* andarsene.
quite [kwait] *ad* completamente, del tutto, proprio.
quits [kwits] *a* pari.
quiver ['kwivə] *n* brivido, fremito; faretra; *vi* fremere, tremare.
quiz [kwiz] *n* beffa, scherzo, indovinello, 'quiz'; *vt* burlare, porre quesiti, esaminare.
quizzical ['kwizikəl] *a* canzonatorio.
quoit [kɔit] *n* grosso anello piatto di metallo o di gomma.
quorum ['kwɔːrəm] *n* 'quorum'.
quota ['kwoutə] *n* quota.
quotation [kwou teiʃən] *n* citazione; (*com*) quotazione; q. marks virgolette.
quote [kwout] *vt* citare; (*com*) quotare.
quotidian [kwɔ'tidiən] *a* quotidiano.
quotient ['kwouʃənt] *n* quoziente.

R

rabbi ['ræbai] *n* rabbino.
rabbit ['ræbit] *n* coniglio; (*fam*) giocatore scadente; r.-warren conigliera.
rabble ['ræbl] *n* folla tumultuante, plebaglia.

rabid ['ræbid] *a* rabbioso, fanatico; r. dog cane idrofobo.
rabies ['reibi:z] *n* idrofobia.
race [reis] *n* corsa; razza, stirpe; racecourse, racetrack ippodromo; *vt* far andar a gran velocità, far correre; *vi* correre, gareggiare in velocità.
racehorse ['reishɔːs] *n* cavallo da corsa.
Rachel ['reitʃəl] *nf pr* Rachele.
racial ['reiʃəl] *a* razziale.
rack [ræk] *n* (*luggage, rly*) rete; (*fodder*) rastrelliera; (*plates etc*) scolapiatti; tortura della ruota; rovina; *vt* torturare; to r. one's brains scervellarsi.
racket ['rækit] *n* racchetta; chiasso.
racy ['reisi] *a* piccante; vigoroso; vivace.
radar ['reidaː] *n* radar.
radiance ['reidiəns] *n* splendore.
radiant ['reidiənt] *a* raggiante.
radiate ['reidieit] *vi* irradiare; brillare.
radiation [‚reidi'eiʃən] *n* radiazione, irradiazione.
radiator ['reidieitə] *n* radiatore, termosifone.
radical ['rædikəl] *a n* radicale.
radio ['reidiou] *pl* radios *n* radio; r. set apparecchio radio(fonico).
radioactive ['reidiou'æktiv] *a* radioattivo.
radiogram ['reidiougræm] *n* radiogramma; radiogrammofono.
radiography [‚reidi'ɔgrəfi] *n* radiografia.
radish ['rædiʃ] *n* ravanello.
radius ['reidiəs] *n* raggio.
raffle ['ræfl] *n* lotteria; *vt* estrarre a sorte.
raft ['raːft] *n* chiatta, zattera.
rafter ['raːftə] *n* trave, puntone.
rag [ræg] *n* cencio, straccio, brandello; (*sl*) baldoria.
ragamuffin ['rægə‚mʌfin] *n* piccolo straccione.
rage [reidʒ] *n* collera, rabbia; (*fam*) persona o cosa di gran moda; *vi* essere furibondo, infuriarsi.
ragged ['rægid] *a* cencioso, stracciato; imperfetto; senza uniformità.
raid [reid] *n* incursione, scorreria; *vt* razziare, fare un'incursione.
rail [reil] *n* inferriata, ringhiera; (*rly*) rotaia; sbarra; *vt* chiudere con, cingere di, cancellata o sbarre; to r. at ingiuriare.
railing ['reiliŋ] *n* ringhiera, parapetto di ferro, inferriata, cancellata.
raillery ['reiləri] *n* leggera satira.
railway ['reilwei] railroad [reilroud] *n* ferrovia, strada ferrata.
rain [rein] *n* pioggia; *vi* piovere; r. water acqua piovana.
rainbow ['reinbou] *n* arcobaleno.
raincoat ['reinkout] *n* impermeabile.
rainfall ['reinfɔ:l] *n* piovosità, caduta di pioggia.

rainy ['reini] *a* piovoso.

raise [reiz] *n* (di stipendio) aumento; *vt* alzare, levare, sollevare; allevare, coltivare; elevare, innalzare, aumentare; dare occasione a; raccogliere.

raisin ['reizn] *n* uva passa.

rake [reik] *n* rastrello; (*fig*) libertino; *vt* rastrellare; passare in rassegna; abbracciare con lo sguardo; (*mil*) colpire d'infilata.

rakish ['reikiʃ] *a* dissoluto.

rally ['ræli] *n* adunata; ricupero di forze; *vt* raccogliere; rianimare; *vi* rianimarsi, schierarsi.

ram [ræm] *n* ariete, montone; (*mil*) ariete; (*naut*) sperone; *vt* conficcare; (*naut*) speronare; sbattere contro.

ramble ['ræmbl] *n* passeggiata senza meta precisa; *vi* vagare; divagare.

rambler ['ræmblə] *n* chi passeggia senza meta; divagatore.

rambling ['ræmbliŋ] *a* errante, vagante; incoerente, sconnesso; (*plants*) rampicante.

ramification [ˌræmifi'keiʃən] *n* ramificazione.

ramify ['ræmifai] *vi* ramificar(si).

ramp [ræmp] *n* salita, rampa.

rampant ['ræmpənt] *a* aggressivo; violento; esuberante; rampante.

rampart ['ræmpɑːt] *n* bastione.

ramrod ['ræmrɔd] *n* bacchetta di fucile.

ramshackle ['ræmˌʃækl] *a* sgangherato.

ranch [rɑːntʃ] *n* 'ranch', grande fattoria con bestiame.

rancid ['rænsid] *a* rancido.

rancidity [ræn'siditi] *n* rancidezza.

rancor ['ræŋkə] *n* rancore.

Randolph ['rændɔlf] *nm pr* Rodolfo.

random ['rændəm] *a* fatto a caso; **at r.** *ad* a casaccio.

range [reindʒ] *n* serie; fila; (*mountains*) catena; distesa; campo, sfera; gamma; campo da tiro, raggio, gittata; cucina economica; *vt* collocare, disporre; *vi* (e)stendersi, distribuirsi; errare, vagare.

rank [ræŋk] *a* lussureggiante; rancido, puzzolente; indecente; *vt* classificare, assegnare un grado a; *vi* essere nel grado di; *n* rango, grado, fila.

rankle ['ræŋkl] *vi* inasprirsi, bruciare.

rankness ['ræŋknis] *n* esuberanza, rigoglio; rancidezza; indecenza.

ransack ['rænsæk] *vt* frugare, saccheggiare.

ransom ['rænsəm] *n* riscatto; *vt* riscattare.

rant [rænt] *vti* declamare, usare un linguaggio ampolloso.

rap [ræp] *n* colpo, colpetto, picchio; *vt* battere, colpire, picchiare.

rapacious [rə'peiʃəs] *a* rapace.

rape [reip] *n* ratto; stupro; *vt* rapire; stuprare; violentare.

Raphael ['ræfeiəl] *nm pr* Raffaele.

rapid ['ræpid] *a* rapido, veloce; erto; *n* rapida.

rapidity [ræ'piditi] *n* rapidità, velocità.

rapier ['reipiə] *n* stocco, spadino.

rapine ['ræpain] *n* rapina.

rapture ['ræptʃə] *n* estasi, rapimento.

rapturous ['ræptʃərəs] *a* estatico.

rare [reə] *a* raro; poco cotto.

rareness ['reənis] **rarity** ['reəriti] *n* rarità; rarefazione.

rascal ['rɑːskəl] *n* briccone, furfante.

rascality [rɑːs'kæliti] *n* furfanteria.

rash [ræʃ] *a* avventato, imprudente, sconsiderato; *n* eruzione cutanea.

rasher ['ræʃə] *n* fetta sottile di pancetta o prosciutto.

rashness ['ræʃnis] *n* avventatezza, imprudenza, sconsideratezza.

rasp [rɑːsp] *n* raspa, raschietto; *vt* raspare, raschiare; *vi* stridere.

raspberry ['rɑːzbəri] *n* lampone.

rat [ræt] *n* topo, ratto; (*pol*) disertore, girella; (*blackleg*) crumiro; *vi* andare alla caccia dei topi; (*pol*) defezionare.

rate [reit] *n* tasso; aliquota, prezzo, tariffa; (con)tributo; passo, velocità; *vt* calcolare, valutare; tassare, considerare; classificare; *vi* classificarsi.

rather ['rɑːðə] *ad* piuttosto, alquanto, un po'.

ratification [ˌrætifi'keiʃən] *n* ratifica.

ratify ['rætifai] *vt* ratificare.

rating ['reitiŋ] *n* valutazione, stima; classifica, posizione; classificazione.

ratio ['reiʃiou] *pl* **ratios** *n* rapporto, proporzione, ragione.

ration ['ræʃən] *n* razione; *vt* razionare.

rational ['ræʃənl] *a* razionale, ragionevole.

rattle ['rætl] *n* sonaglio; tintinnio; strepito, rumore; rantolo; chiacchierio vuoto; chiacchierone; *vi* produrre un rumore secco; ciarlare; *vt* (*sl*) innervosire.

raucous ['rɔːkəs] *a* rauco, aspro.

ravage ['rævidʒ] *n* danno, devastazione; *vt* devastare, saccheggiare.

rave [reiv] *n* delirio; infatuazione; *vi* delirare; (*fam*) andare in estasi; infuriare.

ravel ['rævəl] *vti* ingarbugliar(si), sfilacciarsi.

raven ['reivn] *a* corvino; *n* corvo.

ravenous ['rævinəs] *a* affamato, vorace.

ravine [ræ'viːn] *n* burrone.

raving ['reiviŋ] *a* delirante; *n* delirio.

ravish ['ræviʃ] *vt* rapire, violentare; (*fig*) estasiare.

ravishing ['ræviʃiŋ] *a* incantevole.

raw [rɔː] *a* crudo; greggio; (*wound*) scoperto, vivo; (*fig*) inesperto; (*weather*) freddo e umido.

rawness ['rɔːnis] *n* crudezza; inesperienza; (*weather*) rigore.

ray [rei] n raggio.
rayon ['reiɔn] n raion, seta artificiale.
Raymond ['reimənd] nm pr Raimondo.
raze, rase [reiz] vt radere al suolo, distruggere completamente.
razor ['reizə] n rasoio.
re- ['riː] prefisso usato davanti a verbi e sostantivi ri- (qualora non si trovasse il vocabolo sotto la forma composta si cerchi la forma senza prefisso).
reach [riːtʃ] n portata; possibilità; estensione; tiro; **out of r.** a irraggiungibile; vt arrivare a, (rag)giungere, tendere; vi estendersi.
react [riː'ækt] vi reagire.
reaction [riː'ækʃən] n reazione.
reactive [riː'æktiv] a reattivo, reagente.
reactor [riː'æktə] n reattore.
read [riːd] vt leggere; (of instruments) segnare.
readable ['riːdəbl] a interessante, piacevole.
reader ['riːdə] n lettore, lettrice; libro di lettura.
readily ['redili] ad prontamente; volentieri; facilmente.
readiness ['redinis] n prontezza, facilità.
reading ['riːdiŋ] n lettura, interpretazione; **r. desk** leggio; **r. room** sala di lettura.
ready ['redi] a pronto, preparato; facile, disinvolto; **r.-made** confezionato; **r. money** denaro in contanti.
real ['riːəl] a n reale; a autentico; vero; (leg) immobile.
realism ['riəlizəm] n realismo.
realist ['riəlist] n realista.
realistic [riə'listik] a realistico.
reality [riː'æliti] n realtà.
realization [ˌriəlai'zeiʃən] n percezione; realizzazione; compimento.
realize ['riəlaiz] vt accorgersi, capire, rendersi conto; realizzare; convertire in denaro.
really ['riəli] ad davvero, realmente.
realm [relm] n reame, regno.
ream [riːm] n risma.
reap [riːp] vti mietere, raccogliere.
reaper ['riːpə] n mietitore, mietitrice, (mech) mietitrice.
rear [riə] n (mil) retroguardia; coda, parte posteriore, retro; vt allevare, coltivare, educare; costruire, ergere; vi (horse) impennarsi; **r. admiral** (naut) contrammiraglio; **in the r., at the r.** indietro.
reason ['riːzn] n ragione, ragionevolezza; vi ragionare, persuadere.
reasonable ['riːznəbl] a ragionevole.
reasonableness ['riːznəblnis] n ragionevolezza.
reasoning ['riːzniŋ] n ragionamento, argomentazione.
reassure [ˌriːə'ʃuə] vt rassicurare.
rebate ['riːbeit] n (com) riduzione, sconto, rimborso.

rebel ['rebl] a n ribelle; vi [ri'bel] ribellarsi.
rebellion [ri'beljən] n ribellione, rivolta.
rebellious [ri'beljəs] a ribelle.
rebound [ri'baund] n reazione, rimbalzo; vi rimbalzare.
rebuff [ri'bʌf] n rifiuto; rabbuffo; vt respingere.
rebuke [ri'bjuːk] n rimprovero; vt rimproverare.
recall [ri'kɔːl] n richiamo; revoca; vt richiamare, ricordare; revocare.
recant [ri'kænt] vti abiurare, ritrattar(si).
recantation [ˌriːkæn'teiʃən] n abiura, ritrattazione.
recapitulate [ˌriːkə'pitjuleit] vt riassumere, ricapitolare.
recapitulation [ˌriːkəpitju'leiʃən] n ricapitolazione.
recede [riː'siːd] vt recedere; diminuire.
receding [riː'siːdiŋ] a rientrante, sfuggente; **r. chin** mento sfuggente; **r. hair** calvizie incipiente.
receipt [ri'siːt] n ricevimento, ricevuta, quietanza.
receive [ri'siːv] vti ricevere.
receiver [ri'siːvə] n ricevitore; (rad) apparecchio radioricevente.
recent ['riːsnt] a recente.
receptacle [ri'septəkl] n ricettacolo.
reception [ri'sepʃən] n ricevimento, accoglienza.
recess [ri'ses] n luogo appartato, nicchia, recesso; tregua; vacanza scolastica.
recipe ['resipi] n ricetta.
recipient [ri'sipiənt] n ricevente, chi riceve.
reciprocal [ri'siprəkl] a reciproco.
reciprocate [ri'siprəkeit] vt contraccambiare, ricambiare.
reciprocity [ˌresi'prɔsiti] n reciprocità.
recital [ri'saitl] n esposto, racconto, "recital", esibizione di un solista, di un attore.
recitation [ˌresi'teiʃən] n recitazione.
recite [ri'sait] vt recitare; (leg) esporre.
reckless ['reklis] a avventato, temerario.
reckon ['rekən] vti calcolare, contare, considerare, supporre, contare su.
reckoning ['rekəniŋ] n computo, calcolo, resa dei conti.
reclaim [ri'kleim] vt (land) bonificare, rivendicare.
reclamation [ˌreklə'meiʃən] n bonifica, rivendicazione.
recline [ri'klain] vi essere o mettersi in posizione inclinata.
recluse [ri'kluːs] n anacoreta.
recognition [ˌrekəg'niʃən] n riconoscimento.
recognize ['rekəgnaiz] vt riconoscere.
recoil [ri'kɔil] n indietreggiamento, rinculo; vi indietreggiare, rinculare.

recollect [ˌrekə'lekt] vt ricordare, ricordarsi.
recollection [ˌrekə'lekʃən] n reminiscenza, ricordo.
recommend [ˌrekə'mend] vt raccomandare.
recommendation [ˌrekəmen'deiʃən] n raccomandazione.
recompense ['rekəmpens] n ricompensa; vt ricompensare.
reconcile ['rekənsail] vt (ri)conciliare.
reconcilement [ˌrekən'sailmənt] **reconciliation** [ˌrekənsili'eiʃən] n (ri) conciliazione.
recondite [ri'kɔndait] a recondito.
reconstruct ['riːkəns'trʌkt] vt ricostruire.
reconstruction ['riːkəns'trʌkʃən] n ricostruzione.
record ['rekɔːd] n registrazione; documento; verbale, atto; archivio, (sport) record, primato; (gramophone) disco; **r.-player** giradischi, grammofono; vt [ri'kɔːd] mettere a verbale; registrare, riportare, notare; (disc) incidere.
recorder [ri'kɔːdə] n apparecchio registratore; (leg) cancelliere; (mus) flauto dolce; **tape r.** magnetofono, registratore a nastro.
recount [ri'kaunt] vt raccontare.
recourse [ri'kɔːs] n ricorso.
recover [ri'kʌvə] vt ricuperare, riprendere; vi riaversi, ricuperare la salute.
recovery [ri'kʌvəri] n guarigione; ricupero.
re-create ['riːkri'eit] vt ricreare.
recreate ['rekrieit] vt ricreare, divertire.
recreation [ˌrekri'eiʃən] n ricreazione, divertimento.
recruit [ri'kruːt] n recluta; (fig) novizio; vt reclutare; rinvigorire; vi ricuperare la salute.
rectangle ['rekˌtæŋgl] n rettangolo.
rectification [ˌrektifi'keiʃən] n rettificazione.
rectify ['rektifai] vt rettificare, correggere.
rectitude ['rektitjuːd] n rettitudine.
rector ['rektə] n parroco; rettore.
rectory ['rektəri] n canonica.
recumbent [ri'kʌmbənt] a appoggiato, semi-sdraiato.
recuperate [ri'kjuːpəreit] vti ricuperare, ristabilirsi.
recur [ri'kəː] vi ricorrere, ritornare.
recurrence [ri'kʌrəns] n ricorrenza, ritorno.
recurrent [ri'kʌrənt] a ricorrente, periodico.
red [red] a n rosso; **r.-hot** rovente; (fig) ardente.
redden ['redn] vti arrossare, arrossire.
reddish ['rediʃ] a rossastro, rossiccio.
redeem [ri'diːm] vt redimere, riabilitare, riscattare, salvare.

redeemer [ri'diːmə] n redentore.
redemption [ri'dempʃən] n redenzione, salvezza.
redness ['rednis] n rossore.
redolent ['redoulənt] a fragrante, profumato.
redouble [ri'dʌbl] vti raddoppiar(si), intensificar(si).
redoubt [ri'daut] n (mil) ridotta.
redoubtable [ri'dautəbl] a formidabile.
redound [ri'daund] vi ridondare.
redress [ri'dres] n atto di giustizia riparatrice, riparazione; vt riparare, raddrizzare.
reduce [ri'djuːs] vt ridurre.
reduction [ri'dʌkʃən] n riduzione.
redundant [ri'dʌndənt] a ridondante, sovrabbondante.
re-echo [riː'ekou] vt ripetere; vi riecheggiare.
reed [riːd] n canna; (poet) zampogna.
reef [riːf] n scoglio, scogliera, banco; (naut) terzaruolo.
reek [riːk] n fumo, esalazione, fetore; vi fumare, puzzare.
reel [riːl] n arcolaio, aspo, bobina, spoletta, rocchetto; rotolo, rullo; vacillamento; danza scozzese; vt avvolgere su un rocchetto; vi girare; vacillare.
re-election ['riːi'lekʃən] n rielezione.
refectory [ri'fektəri] n refettorio.
refer [ri'fəː] vt ascrivere, attribuire, riferire; rimandare a; vi alludere, riferire, rivolgersi a.
referee [ˌrefə'riː] n arbitro; vti fare da arbitro, arbitrare.
reference ['refrəns] n riferimento, allusione; referenza; competenza; **r. book** libro di consultazione.
refill ['riː'fil] n ricambio; vti riempire, riempirsi; ricaricare.
refine [ri'fain] vt ingentilire, (r)affinare; vi ingentilirsi, raffinarsi; sottilizzare.
refinement [ri'fainmənt] n raffinamento; (fig) raffinatezza, finezza.
reflect [ri'flekt] vt riflettere; vi riflettere, meditare; gettare biasimo.
reflection [ri'flekʃən] n riflessione; riflesso.
reflective [ri'flektiv] a riflessivo.
reflector [ri'flektə] n riflettore.
reflex ['riːfleks] a n riflesso.
reflexive [ri'fleksiv] a (gram) riflessivo.
reform [ri'fɔːm] n riforma; vti riformar(si).
reformation [ˌrefə'meiʃən] n riforma.
reformer [ri'fɔːmə] n riformatore.
refract [ri'frækt] vt rifrangere.
refraction [ri'frækʃən] n rifrazione.
refractor [ri'fræktə] n rifrattore.
refractory [ri'fræktəri] a refrattario, ribelle.
refrain [ri'frein] n ritornello; vi frenarsi, trattenersi.
refresh [ri'freʃ] vt ravvivare, riani-

mare, rinfrescare, rinvigorire; *vi* ristorarsi.

refreshing [ri'freʃiŋ] *a* rinfrescante, ristoratore.

refresher [ri'freʃə] *n* chi, cosa che rinfresca; **r. course** corso di aggiornamento.

refreshment [ri'freʃmənt] *n* rinfresco, ristoro.

refrigerator [ri'fridʒəreitə] *n* frigorifero.

refuel [ri'fjuəl] *vti* (*av*, *aut*) rifornire, rifornirsi di carburante.

refuge ['refju:dʒ] *n* rifugio.

refugee [ˌrefju:'dʒi:] *n* profugo, rifugiato.

refund ['ri:fʌnd] *n* rimborso; [ri'fʌnd] *vt* rifondere, rimborsare.

refusal [ri'fju:zəl] *n* rifiuto; diritto di opzione.

refuse ['refju:s] *n* rifiuti, scarti *pl*.

refuse [ri'fju:z] *vti* rifiutare, negare.

refute [ri'fju:t] *vt* confutare, ribattere.

regain [ri'gein] *vt* riguadagnare, riacquistare, ricuperare; raggiungere di nuovo.

regal ['ri:gəl] *a* regale.

regale [ri'geil] *vt* intrattenere.

regality [ri'gæliti] *n* regalità.

regard [ri'gɑ:d] *n* considerazione, stima; *vt* riguardare, considerare, concernere; **regards** *pl* ossequi, saluti; **with r. to**, **regarding** riguardo a, per quanto riguarda.

regardless [ri'gɑ:dlis] *a* incurante, senza riguardo; **r. of** a dispetto di, nonostante.

regatta [ri'gætə] *n* regata.

regency ['ri:dʒənsi] *n* reggenza.

regenerate [ri'dʒenəreit] *vti* rigenerare, rigenerarsi.

regent ['ri:dʒənt] *n* reggente.

regicide ['redʒisaid] *n* regicida, regicidio.

regime [rei'ʒi:m] *n* regime.

regiment ['redʒimənt] *n* reggimento.

regimental [ˌredʒi'mentl] *a* reggimentale.

Reginald ['redʒinld] *nm pr* Reginaldo.

region ['ri:dʒən] *n* regione.

regional ['ri:dʒənl] *a* regionale.

register ['redʒistə] *n* registro; registratore; (*mech*) valvola di regolazione; (*mus*, *type*) registro; *vt* registrare; (*post*) raccomandare; (*luggage*) assicurare; *vi* (far) iscrivere il proprio nome su un registro; **r. of voters** lista elettorale.

registrar [ˌredʒis'trɑ:] *n* archivista, ufficiale dello stato civile.

registration [ˌredʒis'treiʃən] *n* registrazione; iscrizione; (*post*) raccomandazione; (*luggage*) assicurazione.

registry ['redʒistri] *n* ufficio del registro, ufficio di stato civile; ufficio di collocamento.

regression [ri'greʃən] *n* regresso.

regret [ri'gret] *n* rammarico, rim-

pianto; *vt* rimpiangere, deplorare, rammaricarsi di.

regretful [ri'gretful] *a* dolente.

regrettable [ri'gretəbl] *a* deplorevole, increscioso.

regrettingly [ri'gretiŋli] *ad* con rammarico, con dispiacere.

regular ['regjulə] *a n* regolare.

regularity [ˌregju'læriti] *n* regolarità.

regulate ['regjuleit] *vt* regolare.

regulation [ˌregju'leiʃən] *a* regolamentare; *n* regolamento, regola.

regulator ['regjuleitə] *n* regolatore.

rehabilitation ['ri:əˌbili'teiʃən] *n* riabilitazione.

rehearsal [ri'hə:səl] *n* prova.

rehearse [ri'hə:s] *vt* provare.

reign [rein] *n* regno; *vi* regnare.

reimburse [ˌri:im'bə:s] *vt* rimborsare, rifondere.

rein [rein] *n* redine.

reindeer ['reindiə] *n* renna.

reinforce [ˌri:in'fɔ:s] *vt* rinforzare, rafforzare.

reinforcement [ˌri:in'fɔ:smənt] *n* rinforzo.

reinstate ['ri:in'steit] *vt* ricollocare, rimettere, reintegrare.

reiterate [ri:'itəreit] *vt* reiterare.

reiteration [ri:'itəreiʃən] *n* reiterazione.

reject [ri'dʒekt] *vt* rigettare, respingere; (*mil*) riformare.

rejection [ri'dʒekʃən] *n* rigetto, rifiuto.

rejoice [ri'dʒɔis] *vi* gioire, rallegrarsi; *vt* rallegrare.

rejoicing [ri'dʒɔisiŋ] *n* gioia, letizia; **rejoicings** *pl* festeggiamenti *pl*.

rejoin [ri'dʒɔin] *vt* raggiungere, riunire; *vi* ribattere, rispondere.

rejoinder [ri'dʒɔində] *n* risposta.

rejuvenate [ri'dʒu:vineit] *vti* ringiovanire.

relapse [ri'læps] *n* ricaduta; *vi* ricadere.

relate [ri'leit] *vt* narrare; *vi* aver rapporto, riferirsi.

relation [ri'leiʃən] *n* relazione, rapporto; parente.

relationship [ri'leiʃənʃip] *n* relazione, rapporto; parentela.

relative ['relətiv] *a* relativo; *n* parente.

relativity [ˌrelə'tiviti] *n* relatività.

relax [ri'læks] *vt* allentare, rilassare, diminuire; *vi* allentarsi, rilassarsi.

relaxation [ˌri:læk'seiʃən] *n* rilassamento, distensione, ricreazione, riposo, diminuzione.

relay ['ri:lei] *n* (*horses*) cavalli di ricambio, (*dogs*) muta di ricambio; **r. race** corsa a staffetta; *vt* sostituire; (*rad*) ritrasmettere.

release [ri'li:s] *n* liberazione; (*mech*) scarico; *vt* liberare, sciogliere.

relegate ['religeit] *vt* relegare.

relent [ri'lent] *vi* piegarsi, intenerirsi.

relentless [ri'lentlis] *a* inflessibile, rigido.

relevance ['relivəns] **relevancy** ['relivənsi] n attinenza, pertinenza.
relevant ['relivənt] a attinente, pertinente.
reliability [ri,laiə'biliti] n attendibilità; fidatezza.
reliable [ri'laiəbl] a fidato; attendibile.
reliance [ri'laiəns] n fiducia.
reliant [ri'laiənt] a fiducioso; che fa assegnamento.
relic ['relik] n reliquia; **relics** pl reliquie, avanzi, resti pl.
relief [ri'li:f] n sollievo; aiuto, soccorso; cambio; diversivo; rilievo.
relieve [ri'li:v] vt alleviare, mitigare, soccorrere, sollevare, liberare, dare il cambio a.
religion [ri'lidʒən] n religione.
religious [ri'lidʒəs] a religioso; a devoto, pio.
relinquish [ri'liŋkwiʃ] vt abbandonare, rinunziare a.
relish ['reliʃ] n gusto, sapore, piacere, condimento; vt (far) gustare, trovar piacere.
reluctance [ri'lʌktəns] n riluttanza.
reluctant [ri'lʌktənt] a riluttante.
rely [ri'lai] vi fare assegnamento (su), contare (su), fidarsi (di).
remain [ri'mein] vi restare, rimanere; avanzare.
remainder [ri'meində] n resto, rimanenza.
remaining [ri'meiniŋ] a restante, rimanente.
remains [ri'meins] n pl avanzi, resti, reliquie pl, resti mortali pl, spoglie pl.
remand [ri'mɑ:nd] vt rimandare in carcere.
remark [ri'mɑ:k] n commento, osservazione; vti notare, osservare.
remarkable [ri'mɑ:kəbl] a eccezionale, notevole.
remedy ['remidi] n rimedio, medicina; vt porre rimedio a.
remember [ri'membə] vt ricordare, ricordar(si di), rammentar(si di).
remembrance [ri'membrəns] n ricordo, memoria, rimembranza; **remembrances** pl saluti, ossequi pl.
remind [ri'maind] vt ricordare a, richiamare alla memoria di, rammentare a.
reminder [ri'maində] n ricordo, promemoria.
reminiscence [,remi'nisns] n reminiscenza.
reminiscent [,remi'nisnt] a che richiama alla memoria.
remiss [ri'mis] a negligente, trascurato.
remission [ri'miʃən] n remissione, condono.
remit [ri'mit] vt rimettere, perdonare.
remittance [ri'mitəns] n (com) rimessa.

remnant ['remnənt] n resto, scampolo.
remonstrance [ri'mɔnstrəns] n rimostranza.
remonstrate ['remənstreit] vi protestare, fare rimostranza.
remorse [ri'mɔ:s] n rimorso.
remorseful [ri'mɔ:sful] a pieno di rimorsi.
remorseless [ri'mɔ:slis] a spietato.
remote [ri'mout] a lontano, remoto.
removal [ri'mu:vəl] n rimozione, trasferimento, trasloco.
remove [ri'mu:v] vti rimuovere; levare; trasferirsi, traslocare.
remunerate [ri'mju:nəreit] vt rimunerare.
remuneration [ri,mju:nə'reiʃən] n rimunerazione.
remunerative [ri'mu:nərətiv] a rimunerativo.
renaissance, renascence [rə'neisəns] n rinascimento.
rend [rend] vt lacerare, strappare.
render [ri'rendə] vt rendere, tradurre; (fats) sciogliere; (oil) raffinare.
rendering ['rendəriŋ] n resa, traduzione, interpretazione.
rendezvous ['rɔndeivu:] n (mil) luogo di raduno; appuntamento; vi riunirsi.
renegade ['renigeid] n rinnegato, traditore.
renew [ri'nju:] vt rinnovare.
renewal [ri'nju:əl] n rinnovamento.
rennet ['renit] n caglio; mela ranetta.
renounce [ri'nauns] vt rinunciare a, ripudiare.
renouncement [ri'naunsmənt] n rinunzia.
renovate ['renouveit] vt rinnovare.
renovation [,renou'veiʃən] n rinnovamento.
renown [ri'naun] n fama, rinomanza.
renowned [ri'naund] a celebre, famoso.
rent [rent] n affitto, nolo; strappo; vt dare o prendere in affitto; vi venire affittato; **rental** canone d'affitto; **rental library** biblioteca circolante.
renunciation [ri,nʌnsi'eiʃən] n rinuncia.
repair [ri'pɛə] n riparazione, restauro; vt riparare, restaurare, rimediare a; vi recarsi, rifugiarsi; **in good r.** in buono stato.
reparation [,repə'reiʃən] n riparazione, risarcimento.
repartee [,repɑ:'ti:] n risposta pronta.
repast [ri'pɑ:st] n pasto.
repatriate [ri:'pætrieit] n rimpatriato; vti rimpatriare.
repay [ri:'pei] vt ripagare; restituire; ricompensare.
repayment [ri:'peimənt] n rimborso; ricompensa.
repeal [ri'pi:l] vt abrogare, revocare.
repeat [ri'pi:t] vt ripetere.

repel [ri'pel] *vt* respingere; ripugnare a.

repent [ri'pent] *vti* pentirsi (di).

repentance [ri'pentəns] *n* pentimento.

repentant [ri'pentənt] *a* pentito.

repertoire ['repətwɑː] *n* repertorio.

repertory ['repətəri] *n* repertorio.

repetition [‚repi'tiʃən] *n* ripetizione.

replace [ri'pleis] *vt* ricollocare, rimettere; sostituire.

replacement [ri'pleismənt] *n* ricollocamento; sostituzione.

replenish [ri'pleniʃ] *vt* riempire.

replete [ri'pliːt] *a* pieno, sazio.

repletion [ri'pliːʃən] *n* pienezza, sazietà.

replica ['replikə] *n* replica, copia.

reply [ri'plai] *n* risposta; *vi* rispondere.

report [ri'pɔːt] *n* rapporto, relazione, resoconto; detonazione; *vt* fare un rapporto di, riferire, fare la cronaca di; *vi* fare il cronista.

reporter [ri'pɔːtə] *n* corrispondente, cronista.

repose [ri'pouz] *n* riposo; *vi* riposarsi, basarsi.

repository [ri'pɔzitəri] *n* deposito, magazzino; (*fig*) confidente.

reprehensible [‚repri'hensəbl] *a* biasimevole.

represent [‚repri'zent] *vt* rappresentare.

representation [‚reprizen'teiʃən] *n* rappresentazione.

representative [‚repri'zentətiv] *a* rappresentativo; *n* rappresentante.

repress [ri'pres] *vt* reprimere, frenare.

repression [ri'preʃən] *n* repressione.

reprieve [ri'priːv] *n* dilazione; *vt* accordare una dilazione a.

reprimand ['reprimɑːnd] *n* rimprovero; *vt* rimproverare.

reprint ['riː'print] *n* ristampa; *vt* ristampare.

reprisal [ri'praizəl] *n* rappresaglia.

reproach [ri'proutʃ] *n* rimprovero, vergogna; *vt* rimproverare.

reproachful [ri'proutʃful] *a* di rimprovero.

reprobate ['reproubeit] *a n* reprobo; *vt* riprovare.

reproduce [‚riːprə'djuːs] *vti* riprodur(si).

reproduction [‚riːprə'dʌkʃən] *n* riproduzione.

reproductive [‚riːprə'dʌktiv] *a* riproduttivo.

reproof [ri'pruːf] *n* biasimo, rimprovero.

reprove [ri'pruːv] *vt* biasimare, rimproverare.

reptile ['reptail] *n* rettile.

republic [ri'pʌblik] *n* repubblica.

republican [ri'pʌblikən] *a n* repubblicano.

repudiate [ri'pjuːdieit] *vt* ripudiare, rinnegare.

repugnance [ri'pʌgnəns] *n* ripugnanza.

repugnant [ri'pʌgnənt] *a* ripugnante.

repulse [ri'pʌls] *n* ripulsa, rifiuto; *vt* respingere.

repulsion [ri'pʌlʃən] *n* repulsione.

repulsive [ri'pʌlsiv] *a* repellente, ripulsivo.

reputable ['repjutəbl] *a* rispettabile.

reputation [‚repjuː'teiʃən] *n* reputazione; rispettabilità.

repute [ri'pjuːt] *n* reputazione, fama; *vt* giudicare, reputare.

request [ri'kwest] *n* domanda, richiesta; *vt* domandare, pregare, richiedere.

require [ri'kwaiə] *vt* richiedere, esigere; aver bisogno di.

requirement [ri'kwaiəmənt] *n* richiesta, esigenza; bisogno; requisito.

requisite ['rekwizit] *a* necessario, richiesto; *n* requisito.

requisition [‚rekwi'ziʃən] *n* requisizione; *vt* requisire.

requital [ri'kwaitl] *n* contraccambio; ricompensa.

requite [ri'kwait] *vt* ricompensare; contraccambiare.

rescue ['reskjuː] *n* liberazione, salvezza, soccorso; *vt* liberare, salvare.

research [riː'səːtʃ] *n* indagine, ricerca; *r.* **worker** ricercatore, investigatore.

resemblance [ri'zembləns] *n* (ras) somiglianza.

resemble [ri'zembl] *vt* (as)somigliare a, rassomigliare.

resent [ri'zent] *vt* risentirsi di, risentire.

resentment [ri'zentmənt] *n* risentimento, rancore.

reservation [‚rezə'veiʃən] *n* riserva; prenotazione.

reserve [ri'zəːv] *n* reticenza, riserbo, riserva; *vt* riservare, prenotare.

reservoir ['rezəvwɑː] *n* serbatoio.

reside [ri'zaid] *vi* risiedere.

residence ['rezidəns] *n* residenza.

resident ['rezidənt] *a n* residente.

residential [‚rezi'denʃəl] *a* adatto per case di abitazione, residenziale.

residue ['rezidjuː] *n* residuo, resto.

resign [ri'zain] *vt* rinunziare a; *vi* dimettersi, rassegnare le dimissioni.

resignation [‚rezig'neiʃən] *n* dimissioni *pl*; rassegnazione.

resilience [ri'ziliəns] *n* elasticità, capacità di ricupero.

resilient [ri'ziliənt] *a* elastico, rimbalzante; che ha la capacità di ricupero.

resin ['rezin] *n* resina.

resist [ri'zist] *vt* resistere a; *vi* resistere.

resistance [ri'zistəns] *n* resistenza.

resistant [ri'zistənt] *a* resistente.

resolute ['rezəluːt] *a* risoluto.

resolution [‚rezə'luːʃən] *n* risolutezza, decisione; soluzione, risoluzione.

resolve [ri'zɔlv] *n* decisione; *vt*

risolvere, sciogliere; *vi* decidere, risolversi.

resonance ['reznəns] *n* risonanza.

resonant ['reznənt] *a* risonante.

resort [ri'zɔːt] *n* ricorso, risorsa; luogo di soggiorno; *vi* ricorrere a; affluire.

resound [ri'zaund] *vi* risuonare, echeggiare.

resource [ri'sɔːs] *n* risorsa, mezzo, espediente, ingegnosità.

resourceful [ri'sɔːsful] *a* pieno di risorse.

respect [ris'pekt] *n* rispetto, stima; riguardo, aspetto; *vt* rispettare, tenere in considerazione; **respects** *pl* ossequi *pl*.

respectability [ri,spektə'biliti] *n* rispettabilità.

respectable [ris'pektəbl] *a* rispettabile, per bene, considerevole.

respectably [ri'spektəbli] *ad* rispettabilmente; decentemente.

respectful [ris'pektful] *a* rispettoso.

respecting [ris'pektiŋ] *prep* riguardo a.

respective [ris'pektiv] *a* rispettivo, relativo.

respiration [,respə'reiʃən] *n* respirazione.

respirator ['respəreitə] *n* (*med*) respiratore; (*mil*) maschera anti-gas.

respite ['respait] *n* tregua, respiro.

resplendent [ris'plendənt] *a* (ri) splendente.

respond [ris'pɔnd] *vi* rispondere.

respondent [ris'pɔndənt] *n* (*leg*) convenuto, imputato.

response [ris'pɔns] *n* risposta, responso; reazione; (*eccl*) responsorio.

responsibility [ris,pɔnsə'biliti] *n* responsabilità.

responsible [ris'pɔnsəbl] *a* responsabile.

responsive [ris'pɔnsiv] *a* sensibile a.

responsiveness [ris'pɔnsivnis] *n* rispondenza, sensibilità.

rest [rest] *n* riposo; resto, rimanente; *pron pl* gli altri, le altre *pl*; *vt* posare, appoggiare; *vi* riposarsi, stare quieto.

restaurant ['restərɔ̃ːŋ] *n* ristorante; **r. car** vettura ristorante.

restful ['restful] *a* riposante, tranquillo.

restitution [,resti'tjuːʃən] *n* restituzione, risarcimento.

restive ['restiv] *a* restio, recalcitrante.

restless ['restlis] *a* irrequieto, agitato.

restlessness ['restlisnis] *n* irrequietezza, agitazione.

restoration [,restə'reiʃən] *n* restauro, restaurazione, restituzione, ricupero, ripristino.

restore [ris'tɔː] *vt* rimettere, restaurare, restituire, ricuperare, ripristinare.

restrain [ris'trein] *vt* reprimere, trattenere.

restraint [ris'treint] *n* controllo, freno, ritegno; detenzione.

restrict [ris'trikt] *vt* restringere, limitare.

restriction [ris'trikʃən] *n* restrizione.

restrictive [ris'triktiv] *a* restrittivo.

result [ri'zʌlt] *n* risultato, esito; *vi* risultare, risolversi.

resultant [ri'zʌltənt] *a n* risultante.

resume [ri'zjuːm] *vti* riprendere.

resumption [ri'zʌmpʃən] *n* ripresa.

resurrection [,rezə'rekʃən] *n* risurrezione.

resuscitate [ri'sʌsiteit] *vti* risuscitare.

retail ['riːteil] *n* vendita al minuto; *ad* al minuto; *vt* vendere al minuto; raccontare dettagliatamente.

retailer ['riːteilə] *n* venditore al minuto.

retain [ri'tein] *vt* mantenere; conservare.

retaliate [ri'tælieit] *vt* ricambiare; *vi* rendere la pariglia.

retaliation [ri,tæli'eiʃən] *n* rappresaglia.

retard [ri'tɑːd] *vt* ritardare.

retch [riːtʃ] *vi* avere conati di vomito.

retention [ri'tenʃən] *n* ritenzione, conservazione; memoria.

retentive [ri'tentiv] *a* ritentivo, tenace.

reticence ['retisəns] *n* reticenza.

reticent ['retisənt] *a* reticente, riservato.

retinue ['retinjuː] *n* seguito.

retire [ri'taiə] *vti* ritirar(si).

retirement [ri'taiəmənt] *n* ritiro, collocamento a riposo.

retort [ri'tɔːt] *n* ritorsione, risposta incisiva; (*chem*) storta; *vti* ritorcere, ribattere.

retrace [ri'treis] *vt* rintracciare, ripercorrere, tornare indietro.

retract [ri'trækt] *vt* ritrattare; *vi* disdirsi.

retreat [ri'triːt] *n* (*mil*) ritirata; ritiro; *vi* ritirarsi.

retrench [ri'trentʃ] *vt* diminuire, ridurre; *vi* economizzare.

retribution [,retri'bjuːʃən] *n* retribuzione, ricompensa.

retrieve [ri'triːv] *vt* ricuperare, riacquistare il possesso di, riparare; (*game*) riportare.

retriever [ri'triːvə] *n* cane da presa.

retrograde ['retrougreid] *a* retrogrado; inverso.

retrospect ['retrouspekt] *n* sguardo retrospettivo.

retrospective [,retrə'spektiv] *a* retrospettivo.

return [ri'təːn] *n* ritorno; restituzione; prospetto statistico; *usu pl* provento, guadagno; *vt* contraccambiare; restituire; rimandare; *vi* (ri)tornare; replicare, rispondere.

reunion ['riːˈjuːnjən] n riunione.
reveal [riˈviːl] vt rivelare.
revel ['revl] n baldoria, gozzoviglia; vi fare baldoria, gozzovigliare, dilettarsi.
revelation [ˌreviˈleiʃən] n rivelazione.
revenge [riˈvendʒ] n vendetta, rivincita; vti vendicar(si).
revengeful [riˈvendʒful] a vendicativo.
revenue ['revinjuː] n entrata; reddito; fisco; r. stamp marca da bollo; r. tax imposta sull'entrata.
reverberate [riˈvəːbəreit] vti riverberar(si), riecheggiare, rimbombare.
reverberation [riˌvəːbəˈreiʃən] n riverbero; riverberazione.
revere [riˈviə] vt riverire, venerare.
reverence ['revərəns] n riverenza, venerazione.
reverend ['revərənd] a n reverendo.
reverent ['revərənt] a riverente.
reverie ['revəri] n sogno ad occhi aperti, fantasticheria.
reversal [riˈvəːsəl] n rovesciamento, inversione.
reverse [riˈvəːs] a contrario, inverso, rovescio, opposto; n il rovescio, l'opposto, il contrario; vt rovesciare, capovolgere, invertire; vi girare in senso inverso.
reversible [riˈvəːsəbl] a reversibile, revocabile; (mech) a inversione di marcia.
reversion [riˈvəːʃən] n reversione, ritorno.
revert [riˈvəːt] vi ritornare.
review [riˈvjuː] n rivista, recensione; revisione; sguardo retrospettivo; vt passare in rivista; recensire; rivedere; vi scrivere recensioni.
reviewer [riˈvjuːə] n recensore, critico d'una rivista.
revile [riˈvail] vt ingiuriare, insultare; vi inveire.
revise [riˈvaiz] vt rivedere, correggere.
revision [riˈviʒən] n revisione, correzione.
revival [riˈvaivəl] n rinascita, risveglio, riesumazione.
revive [riˈvaiv] vt far rivivere, risvegliare, riesumare; vi riprendere i sensi, ritornare in uso, in vita.
revoke [riˈvouk] vt revocare, ritirare.
revolt [riˈvoult] n rivolta, insurrezione; senso di disgusto; vt rivoltare; vi ribellarsi, rivoltarsi; provar disgusto.
revolting [riˈvoultiŋ] a disgusting.
revolution [ˌrevəˈluːʃən] n rivoluzione; giro.
revolutionary [ˌrevəˈluːʃnəri] a n rivoluzionario.
revolve [riˈvɔlv] vt rivolgere; meditare; vi girare.
revolver [riˈvɔlvə] n rivoltella, "revolver".
revue [riˈvjuː] n (theat) rivista.
revulsion [riˈvʌlʃən] n revulsione, ripugnanza.

reward [riˈwɔːd] n compenso, ricompensa; vt (ri)compensare.
Reynold ['renld] nm pr Rinaldo.
rhapsody ['ræpsədi] n rapsodia.
rhetoric ['retərik] n retorica.
rhetorical [riˈtɔrikəl] a retorico.
rheumatic [ruːˈmætik] a reumatico; **rheumatics** n pl reumatismi pl.
rheumatism ['ruːmætizəm] n reumatismo.
Rhine [rain] n Reno.
rhinoceros [raiˈnɔsərəs] n rinoceronte.
Rhodes [roudz] n Rodi.
Rhodesia [rouˈdiːziə] n Rodesia.
Rhodesian [rouˈdiːziən] a n di Rodesia, della Rodesia.
rhododendron [ˌroudəˈdendrən] n rododendro.
Rhone [roun] n Rodano.
rhubarb ['ruːbaːb] n rabarbaro.
rhyme, rime [raim] n rima; vt mettere in rima; vi rimare.
rhythm ['riðəm] n ritmo.
rhythmic(al) ['riðmik(əl)] a ritmico.
rib [rib] n costola; (umbrella etc) stecca.
ribald ['ribəld] a osceno, sboccato.
ribaldry ['ribəldri] n linguaggio osceno.
ribbon ['ribən] n nastro; **to tear to ribbons** stracciare, far a brandelli.
rice [rais] n riso.
rich [ritʃ] a ricco.
Richard ['ritʃəd] nm pr Riccardo.
riches ['ritʃiz] n pl ricchezza, -ze.
richly ['ritʃli] ad riccamente; ampiamente.
richness ['ritʃnis] n ricchezza, sontuo sità.
rick [rik] n (of straw etc) cumulo, mucchio.
rickets ['rikits] n rachitismo.
rickety ['rikiti] a rachitico; sgangherato, traballante.
rid [rid] vt liberare, sbarazzare.
riddance ['ridəns] n liberazione.
riddle ['ridl] n enigma, indovinello; crivello; vaglio; vt crivellare; vagliare; vi proporre indovinelli.
ride [raid] n cavalcata, galoppata, corsa; vt cavalcare, percorrere a cavallo; vi cavalcare, andare a cavallo; in bicicletta etc; (naut) essere all'ancora; (fig) opprimere.
rider ['raidə] n cavaliere, cavallerizzo; aggiunta, codicillo.
ridge [ridʒ] n (of mountains) cresta, spartiacque; (agr) porca.
ridicule ['ridikjuːl] n ridicolo; vt mettere in ridicolo.
ridiculous [riˈdikjuləs] a ridicolo.
ridiculously [riˈdikjuləsli] ad ridicolamente; in modo assurdo.
riding ['raidiŋ] n cavalcata; equitazione; r. school scuola di equitazione, maneggio.
rife [raif] a comune; prevalente; rigoglioso.
riff-raff ['rifræf] n plebaglia.

rifle ['raifl] *n* fucile, carabina; **rifleman** fuciliere; *vt* derubare, vuotare.

rift [rift] *n* crepa, spaccatura.

rig [rig] *n* (*naut*) attrezzatura; (*fam*) abbigliamento; *vt* (*naut*) attrezzare.

right [rait] *a* giusto, retto, esatto; destro; corretto; *n* il giusto, il bene; il diritto; destra; *vt* correggere; (*rad*) drizzare; vendicare; *vi* raddrizzarsi; **to be r.** aver ragione; *ad* bene, direttamente; **a destra; r. away** immediatamente.

righteous ['raitʃəs] *a* retto, virtuoso.

rightful ['raitful] *a* legittimo, giusto.

rightly ['raitli] *ad* giustamente; esattamente.

rigid ['ridʒid] *a* rigido, inflessibile.

rigidity [ri'dʒiditi] *n* rigidezza, inflessibilità.

rigmarole ['rigməroul] *n* filastrocca.

rigor ['rigə] *n* rigore; intransigenza.

rigorous ['rigərəs] *a* rigido, rigoroso.

rill [ril] *n* ruscelletto.

rim [rim] *n* orlo, bordo, margine; (*wheel*) cerchione; (*spectacles*) montatura.

rind [raind] *n* buccia, corteccia; (*cheese, bread*) crosta.

ring [riŋ] *n* anello; cerchio; scampanellata; colpo di telefono; crocchio; (*boxing*) 'ring', quadrato; (*sport*) pista, recinto; *vt* accerchiare; suonare (il campanello); *vi* suonare, tintinnare; **to r. up** chiamare per telefono.

ringleader ['riŋ‚liːdə] *n* capo d'una sommossa.

ringlet ['riŋlit] *n* ricciolo.

rink [riŋk] *n* recinto per pattinaggio.

rinse [rins] *vt* risciacquare; *n* risciucquata.

riot ['raiət] *n* schiamazzo, tumulto, rivolta; *vi* tumultuare.

riotous ['raiətəs] *a* sedizioso, tumultuante; dissoluto.

rip [rip] *n* squarcio, strappo; persona dissoluta; *vt* squarciare, strappare; (*fam*) andare a tutta velocità.

ripe [raip] *a* maturo.

ripen ['raipən] *vti* maturare.

ripeness ['raipnis] *n* maturità.

ripple ['ripl] *n* increspatura, piccola onda; *vi* incresparsi.

rise [raiz] *n* (*sun*) levata; sorgere, ascesa, salita, aumento; *vi* alzarsi, levarsi, salire, sorgere, aumentare, insorgere.

risk [risk] *n* rischio; *vt* rischiare, mettere in pericolo.

risky ['riski] *a* arrischiato, rischioso.

rite [rait] *n* rito.

ritual ['ritjuəl] *a n* rituale.

rival ['raivəl] *a n* rivale; *vt* rivaleggiare.

rivalry ['raivəlri] *n* rivalità.

river ['rivə] *n* fiume.

rivet ['rivit] *n* chiodo, rivetto; *vt* inchiodare, ribadire, fissare.

rivulet ['rivjulit] *n* fiumicello.

roach [routʃ] *n* (*fish*) carpa; scarafaggio.

road [roud] *n* strada, via; (*naut*) rada; **r. detour** deviazione stradale; **r. haulier(s)** impresa autotrasporti.

roadhouse ['roudhaus] *n* albergo, locanda, trattoria sulla strada.

roadside ['roudsaid] *n* bordo della strada.

roam [roum] *vt* percorrere; *vi* girovagare, vagare.

roan [roun] *a n* roano.

roar [rɔ:] *n* mugghio, muggito; rombo; (*laughter, applause*) scroscio; *vti* mugghiare, ruggire; urlare.

roast [roust] *a n* arrosto; *vti* arrostir(si), (*coffee*) tostar(si).

rob [rɔb] *vt* (de)rubare, spogliare, svaligiare.

robber ['rɔbə] *n* ladro, rapinatore; ladrone.

robbery ['rɔbəri] *n* furto, rapina.

robe [roub] *n* lungo manto da cerimonie, toga; *vti* vestirsi.

Robert ['rɔbət] *nm pr* Roberto.

robin (redbreast) ['rɔbin('redbrest)] *n* pettirosso.

robot ['roubɔt] *n* 'robot', automa.

robust [rə'bʌst] *a* robusto, vigoroso.

rock [rɔk] *n* roccia, scoglio; rocca; *vti* cullar(si), dondolar(si).

rocket ['rɔkit] *n* razzo, missile; *vi* elevarsi come un razzo, (*of prices*) salire vertiginosamente.

rocking ['rɔkiŋ] *a* a dondolo, barcollante; **r. chair** sedia a dondolo.

rocky ['rɔki] *a* roccioso.

rod [rɔd] *n* bacchetta; verga; canna (da pesca), (*measure*) pertica.

rodent ['roudənt] *a n* roditore.

Roderick ['rɔdərik] *nm pr* Rodrigo.

roe [rou] *n* capriolo; (*fish*) uova di pesce.

Roger ['rɔdʒə] *nm pr* Ruggero.

rogue [roug] *n* briccone, furfante; birichino, bricconcello.

roguery ['rougəri] *n* furfanteria.

roguish ['rougiʃ] *a* furbo, malizioso.

roguishness ['rougiʃnis] *n* bricconeria; furberia, malizia.

roister ['rɔistə] *vi* far baccano.

Roland ['roulənd] *nm pr* Orlando.

role [roul] *n* ruolo.

roll [roul] *n* rotolo; rullo, elenco; (*naut*) rullio, (*thunder etc*) rombo; panino; *vt* avvolgere, rotolare; *vi* rotolare, ruzzolare, rullare; (*time*) scorrere.

roller ['roulə] *n* rullo, cilindro; (*sea*) maroso; **r. skates** pattini a rotelle.

rolling stock ['rouliŋstɔk] *n* (*rly*) materiale rotabile.

Roman ['roumən] *a n* romano.

romance [rə'mæns] *n* romanzo cavalleresco; (*mus*) romanza; romanticheria, idillio; *vi* romanzare; **R.** *a* romanzo.

Romanesque [ˌroumə'nesk] *a* romanico; *n* (*arch*) stile romanico.
romantic [rə'mæntik] *a* romantico; romanzesco.
romanticism [rə'mæntisizəm] *n* romanticismo.
Rome [roum] *n* Roma.
romp [rɔmp] *n* giuoco rumoroso; ragazza indiavolata; *vi* giocare rumorosamente.
Ronald ['rɔnld] *nm pr* Rinaldo.
roof [ru:f] *n* tetto; *vt* ricoprire con tetto, fare il tetto a.
rook [ruk] *n* cornacchia; (*chess*) torre.
room [rum] *n* camera, stanza; posto, spazio; possibilità.
roomy ['rumi] *a* spazioso, vasto.
roost [ru:st] *n* posatoio di uccelli; pollaio; *vi* appollaiarsi; (*fam*) andare a dormire.
rooster ['ru:stə] *n* gallo domestico.
root [ru:t] *n* radice; *vt* fissare saldamente; **to r. up** sradicare; *vi* radicarsi.
rope [roup] *n* corda, fune; (*pearls*) filo.
Rosalind ['rɔzəlind] *nf pr* Rosalinda.
rosary ['rouzəri] *n* rosario.
rose [rouz] *n* rosa.
rosemary ['rouzməri] *n* rosmarino.
rosy ['rouzi] *a* roseo.
rot [rɔt] *n* marciume, putrefazione; malattia delle pecore; (*sl*) sciocchezze; *vt* far marcire; *vi* imputridire, marcire.
rotate [rou'teit] *vti* (far) rotare; coltivare a rotazione.
rotation [rou'teiʃən] *n* rotazione, successione.
rote [rout] *n* memoria meccanica.
rotten ['rɔtn] *a* marcio, putrido; (*sl*) disgustoso; (*fig*) corrotto.
rotund [rou'tʌnd] *a* rotondo.
rotundity [rou'tʌnditi] *n* rotondità.
rouble ['ru:bl] *n* rublo.
rouge [ru:ʒ] *n* rossetto; *vt* imbellettare; *vi* mettersi il rossetto.
rough [rʌf] *a* (*ground*) accidentato; grossolano, rozzo, rude, ruvido; approssimativo; violento, (*sea*) agitato, (*weather*) tempestoso.
roughen ['rʌfən] *vti* irruvidir(si), diventare (rendere) rozzo.
roughly ['rʌfli] *ad* approssimativamente; ruvidamente, violentemente.
roughness ['rʌfnis] *n* rozzezza, ruvidezza; grossolanità, violenza.
Roumania [ru:'meiniə] *v* **Rumania**.
round [raund] *a* circolare, rotondo, tondo; *n* cerchio, sfera; (*tour*) giro; (*rung*) piolo; (*applause*) scoppio, ronda; *ad* all'intorno, in giro; *prep* intorno a; *vt* arrotondare; completare; girare; *vi* completarsi; **r.-up** raduno, accolta.
roundabout ['raundəbaut] *a* indiretto, tortuoso; *n* giostra.
roundly ['raundli] *ad* vigorosamente; chiaro e tondo.

rouse [rauz] *vt* destare, (ri)svegliare; incitare, provocare; *vi* svegliarsi.
rout [raut] *n* folla tumultuante, sommossa; (*mil*) rotta, sconfitta; *vt* (*mil*) mettere in rotta, sbaragliare; **to r. out** cacciar fuori, snidare.
route [ru:t] *n* via, rotta; (*mil*) (ordini di) marcia; **r. march** marcia d'allenamento.
routine [ru:'ti:n] *n* 'routine', pratica, abitudine meccanica.
rove [rouv] *vi* errare, vagabondare.
rover ['rouvə] *n* giramondo; (*scouts*) 'rover'; pirata.
row [rou] *n* (*fam*) baccano, lite rumorosa.
row [rou] *n* fila, filare; gita in barca a remi; *vt* far andare a forza di remi; *vi* remare, vogare.
rowdy ['raudi] *a* rumoroso, litigioso.
rowel ['rauəl] *n* stella di sperone.
royal ['rɔiəl] *a* reale, regale, regio; eccellente.
royalist ['rɔiəlist] *n* realista, monarchico.
royalty ['rɔiəlti] *n* regalità, sovranità; membro di famiglia reale; diritto d'autore.
rub [rʌb] *n* fregata, frizione; (*fig*) difficoltà, ostacolo; *vt* fregare, strofinare, lucidare; *vi* fregarsi, logorarsi.
rubber ['rʌbə] *n* gomma, caucciù; strofinaccio; (*cards*) partita tripla; *pl* soprascarpe di gomma.
rubbish ['rʌbiʃ] *n* rifiuti, scarti *pl*; cosa di nessun valore, sciocchezza.
rubble ['rʌbl] *n* pietrisco, frantumi di pietra.
Rubicon ['ru:bikən] *n pr* Rubicone.
rubric ['ru:brik] *n* rubrica.
ruby ['ru:bi] *n* rubino.
rudder ['rʌdə] *n* (*naut*) timone.
ruddy ['rʌdi] *a* rubicondo, vermiglio; rubizzo.
rude [ru:d] *a* rude, offensivo, sgarbato; vigoroso.
rudeness ['ru:dnis] *n* sgarbatezza, grossolanità.
rudiment ['ru:dimənt] *n* rudimento.
rudimental [ˌru:di'mentl] *a* rudimentale.
Rudolf, Rudolph ['ru:dɔlf] *n pr* Rodolfo.
rue [ru:] *n* (*bot*) ruta; *vt* pentirsi di.
rueful ['ru:ful] *a* lamentevole, triste.
ruff [rʌf] *n* gorgiera; (*of bird*) collare.
ruffian ['rʌfiən] *n* malfattore, ribaldo.
ruffle ['rʌfl] *n* guarnizione pieghettata; increspatura; *vt* arruffare, increspare; (*fig*) irritare.
rug [rʌg] *n* coperta (da viaggio); tappetino.
rugby ['rʌgbi] *n* (*sport*) 'rugby', pallaovale.
rugged ['rʌgid] *a* ruvido, scabro, irregolare; aspro, austero, inflessibile; vigoroso.
ruggedness ['rʌgidnis] *n* ruvidezza,

scabrosità, irregolarità; asprezza inflessibilità.

ruin ['ruin] n rovina, macerie, ruderi pl; vt rovinare.

ruinous ['ruinəs] a rovinoso; in rovina.

rule [ruːl] n regola, norma; regolo, riga; governo; vt dominare, governare, regolare; rigare; vi aver dominio.

ruler ['ruːlə] n sovrano, governatore; regolo, riga.

ruling ['ruːliŋ] a dominante, prevalente; n regolamento; governo; rigatura.

rum [rʌm] n rum.

Rumania [ruːˈmeiniə] n Romania.

Rumanian [ruːˈmeiniən] a n romeno.

rumble ['rʌmbl] n (thunder etc) rombo; brontolio; rumoreggiamento; vi brontolare; rumoreggiare.

ruminate ['ruːmineit] vti ruminare; meditare, rumiginare.

rumination [ˌruːmiˈneiʃən] n ruminazione.

rummage ['rʌmidʒ] vti frugare, rovistare.

rumor ['ruːmə] n diceria.

rump [rʌmp] n groppa, posteriore.

rumple ['rʌmpl] vt sgualcire; (hair) arruffare.

run [rʌn] n corsa, gita, giro; tragitto, corso; periodo, successione, serie; recinto di animali; vt far correre; condurre, gestire; vi correre; decorrere; scorrere; fuggire; diffondersi.

runaway ['rʌnəwei] n fuggiasco.

rung [rʌŋ] n piolo.

runner ['rʌnə] n corridore; messo; (mil) staffetta; passatoia; (millstone) macina; r. bean fagiolo rampicante; r.-up (sport) secondo arrivato.

runway ['rʌnwei] n pista di decollo, pista di lancio.

rupture ['rʌptʃə] n rottura; (med) ernia.

rural ['ruərəl] a rurale, campestre.

ruse [ruːz] n astuzia, stratagemma.

rush [rʌʃ] n giunco; afflusso, assalto, impeto; vt prendere d'assalto; vi affluire, precipitarsi.

rusk [rʌsk] n pane biscottato.

russet ['rʌsit] a color ruggine.

Russia ['rʌʃə] n Russia.

Russian ['rʌʃən] a n russo.

rust [rʌst] n ruggine; vt corrodere; vi arrugginire.

rustic ['rʌstik] a rustico, grezzo.

rusticate ['rʌstikeit] vt sospendere (studenti universitari); vi vivere in campagna.

rustle ['rʌsl] n fruscio, stormire; vti (far) frusciare, (far) stormire.

rusty ['rʌsti] a arrugginito, rugginoso.

rut [rʌt] n (groove) solco; (fig) abitudine inveterata; (of animals) fregola; vt solcare; vi essere in fregola, in calore.

ruthless ['ruːθlis] a spietato.

rye [rai] n segale.

S

Sabbath ['sæbəθ] n (Jewish) sabato, (Christian) domenica.

saber ['seibə] n sciabola.

sable ['seibl] a di zibellino; n zibellino.

sabotage ['sæbətɑːʒ] n sabotaggio; vt sabotare.

saccharine ['sækərin] n saccarina.

sack [sæk] n sacco; saccheggio; (sl) licenziamento; vt insaccare; saccheggiare; (sl) licenziare.

sacking ['sækiŋ] n tela da sacchi.

sacrament ['sækrəmənt] n sacramento.

sacred ['seikrid] a sacro, consacrato.

sacrifice ['sækrifais] n sacrificio; vt sacrificare.

sacrilege ['sækrilidʒ] n sacrilegio.

sacristan ['sækristən] n sagrestano.

sacristy ['sækristi] n sagrestia.

sad [sæd] a triste, doloroso, funesto.

sadden ['sædn] vt rattristare.

saddle ['sædl] n sella; vt sellare; (fig) addossare, gravare.

sadistic [səˈdistik] a sadico.

sadness ['sædnis] n tristezza.

safe [seif] a sano, salvo, sicuro, intatto, al sicuro, cauto; n cassaforte; (arms) sicura.

safe conduct ['seifˈkɔndəkt] n salvacondotto.

safeguard ['seifgɑːd] n salvaguardia, difesa.

safety ['seifti] n sicurezza, salvezza; s. belt cintura di sicurezza; s. pin spilla di sicurezza; s. island salvagente (stradale).

saffron ['sæfrən] n zafferano.

sag [sæg] vi curvarsi, piegarsi, (of prices) cedere.

saga ['sɑːgə] n saga; romanzo fiume.

sagacious [səˈgeiʃəs] a sagace.

sagacity [səˈgæsiti] n sagacia, perspicacia.

sage [seidʒ] a n saggio; n salvia.

sageness ['seidʒnis] n saggezza.

sail [seil] n vela, gita o viaggio su imbarcazione a vela; vti navigare, veleggiare, salpare, sorvolare.

sailer ['seilə] n veliero.

sailor ['seilə] n marinaio.

saint [seint] a n santo (abbr St).

saintly ['seintli] a santo.

sake [seik] n amore, causa, motivo.

salacious [səˈleiʃəs] a salace.

salad ['sæləd] n insalata.

salamander ['sæləˌmændə] n salamandra.

salary ['sæləri] n stipendio.

sale [seil] n vendita; svendita.

saleable ['seilabl] a smerciabile, vendibile.

salesman ['seilzmən] n venditore, viaggiatore commesso, piazzista.

salient ['seiliənt] a n saliente.

saliva [səˈlaivə] n saliva; **salivary** a salivare.

sallow ['sælou] *a* olivastro; *n* salice.
sally ['sæli] *n* sortita; battuta spiritosa; *vi* balzar fuori, fare una sortita.
salmon ['sæmən] *n* salmone.
salon ['sælɔ̃:ŋ] *n* salone; galleria d'arte.
saloon [sə'lu:n] *n* sala da ricevimenti; bar; **s. keeper** oste, proprietario di bar.
salt [sɔ:lt] *a* amaro, salato, salso; *n* sale; *vt* salare; **s.-cellar** saliera; **s. water** acqua salsa, acqua di mari.
saltiness ['sɔ:ltnis] *n* gusto di sale.
saltpeter ['sɔ:lt͵pi:tə] *n* salnitro.
salty ['sɔ:lti] *a* salato, salmastro; piccante.
salutary ['sæljutəri] *a* salutare.
salutation [͵sælju:'teiʃən] *n* saluto.
salute [sə'lu:t] *n* saluto; (*mil*) salva; *vt* salutare.
salvage ['sælvidʒ] *n* salvataggio, ricupero; *vt* salvare.
salvation [sæl'veiʃən] *n* salvezza.
salver ['sælvə] *n* vassoio.
salvo ['sælvou] *pl* **salvoes** *n* (*mil*) salva.
same [seim] *a pron* medesimo, stesso.
sameness ['seimnis] *n* identità, uniformità.
sample ['sɑ:mpl] *n* campione, modello, esemplare; **samples** *pl* campionario; *vt* assaggiare.
sanatorium [͵sænə'tɔ:riəm] *n* sanatorio.
sanctify ['sæŋktifai] *vt* santificare.
sanctimonious [͵sæŋkti'mouniəs] *a* santarello, bigotto, ipocrita.
sanction ['sæŋkʃən] *n* sanzione; *vt* autorizzare, ratificare, sanzionare.
sanctity ['sæŋktiti] *n* santità.
sanctuary ['sæŋktjuəri] *n* santuario, asilo.
sand [sænd] *n* sabbia, rena; **sandbank** banco di sabbia; **sandhill** duna; **sandpaper** cartavetrata.
sandal ['sændl] *n* sandalo.
sandwich ['sænwidʒ] *n* 'sandwich', panino ripieno; **open s.** tartina.
sandy ['sændi] *a* sabbioso; (*color*) giallo-rossastro.
sane [sein] *a* sano di mente, equilibrato.
sanguinary ['sæŋgwinəri] *a* sanguinario.
sanguine ['sæŋgwin] *a* sanguigno, rubicondo; ottimista.
sanitary ['sænitəri] *a* igienico, sanitario.
sanitation [͵sæni'teiʃən] *n* igiene.
sanity ['sæniti] *n* sanità di mente.
Santa Claus [͵sæntə'klɔ:z] *nm pr* Babbo Natale.
sap [sæp] *n* linfa, succo; (*mil*) scavo d'approccio, trincea; *vt* minare (*also fig*).
sapling ['sæpliŋ] *n* alberello.
sapper ['sæpə] *n* zappatore; (*mil*) geniere, genio.
sapphire ['sæfaiə] *n* zaffiro.

sappy ['sæpi] *a* ricco di linfa, succoso.
Saracen ['særəsn] *a n* saraceno.
Sarah ['seərə] *nf pr* Sara.
sarcasm ['sɑ:kæzəm] *n* sarcasmo.
sarcastic [sɑ:'kæstik] *a* sarcastico.
sardine [sɑ:'di:n] *n* sardina.
Sardinia [sɑ:'diniə] *n* Sardegna.
Sardinian [sɑ:'diniən] *a n* sardo.
sardonic [sɑ:'dɔnik] *a* sardonico.
sash [sæʃ] *n* cintura, sciarpa; telaio scorrevole di finestra.
Satan ['seitən] *nm pr* Satana.
satchel ['sætʃəl] *n* cartella di scolaro.
sate [seit] *vt* satollare, saziare.
satellite ['sætəlait] *a n* satellite.
satiate ['seiʃieit] *vt* saziare.
satiation [͵seiti'eiʃən] **satiety** [sə'taiəti] *n* sazietà.
satin ['sætin] *n* raso.
satire ['sætaiə] *n* satira.
satiric(al) [sə'tirik(əl)] *a* satirico.
satirist ['sætərist] *n* scrittore satirico.
satirize ['sætəraiz] *vt* satireggiare.
satisfaction [͵sætis'fækʃən] *n* soddisfazione.
satisfactorily [͵sætis'fæktərili] *ad* soddisfacentemente.
satisfactory [͵sætis'fæktəri] *a* soddisfacente.
satisfy ['sætisfai] *vt* soddisfare; convincere, persuadere.
saturate ['sætʃəreit] *vt* saturare.
saturation [͵sætʃə'reiʃən] *n* saturazione.
Saturday ['sætədi] *n* sabato.
saturnine ['sætə:nain] *a* cupo, taciturno, tetro.
sauce [sɔ:s] *n* intingolo, salsa; (*fig*) impertinenza.
saucepan ['sɔ:spən] *n* casseruola.
saucer ['sɔ:sə] *n* piattino, sottocoppa.
sauciness ['sɔ:sinis] *n* impertinenza.
saucy ['sɔ:si] *a* impertinente.
saunter ['sɔ:ntə] *vi* andare a zonzo.
sausage ['sɔsidʒ] *n* salsiccia, salame.
sauté ['soutei] *a* (*cook*) saltato in padella, fritto.
savage ['sævidʒ] *a n* selvaggio; *a* barbaro, brutale.
savageness ['sævidʒnis] **savagery** ['sævidʒəri] *n* brutalità, ferocia.
save [seiv] *prep* ad eccezione di, salvo; *vt* salvare, conservare, economizzare, risparmiare; *vi* fare economie.
saving ['seiviŋ] *a* economico; *n* risparmio, economia.
savior ['seivjə] *n* salvatore, redentore.
savor ['seivə] *n* gusto, sapore; *vi* sapere di, aver il gusto; *vt* assaporare, gustare; insaporire.
savory ['seivəri] *a* saporito, piccante; *n* salatino.
Savoy [sə'vɔi] *n* Savoia.
Savoyard [sə'vɔiɑ:d] *a n* savoiardo.
saw [sɔ:] *n* sega; massima, proverbio; *vt* segare.
sawdust ['sɔ:dʌst] *n* segatura.
sawmill ['sɔ:mil] *n* segheria.

sawyer ['sɔ:jə] n segatore.
Saxon ['sæksn] a n sassone.
Saxony ['sæksni] n Sassonia.
saxophone ['sæksəfoun] n sassofono.
say [sei] vti dire, affermare, asserire.
saying ['seiiŋ] n massima, proverbio.
scab [skæb] n crosta, scabbia; crumiro.
scabbard ['skæbəd] n fodero, guaina.
scabby ['skæbi] a pieno di croste, scabbioso.
scaffold ['skæfəld] n patibolo.
scaffolding ['skæfəldiŋ] n impalcatura, intelaiatura.
scald [skɔ:ld] n scottatura; vt scottare, ustionare.
scalding ['skɔ:ldiŋ] a bollente, scottante; n scottatura.
scale [skeil] n gradazione, scala; scaglia, squama; bilancia; vti scalare, graduare; vi squamarsi.
scalp [skælp] n cuoio capelluto; vt scotennare.
scalpel ['skælpəl] n (med) scalpello.
scaly ['skeili] a squamoso, coperto di incrostazioni.
scamp [skæmp] n birichino, mascalzoncello.
scamper ['skæmpə] vi correre; **s. away** svignarsela.
scan [skæn] vt scandire; scrutare attentamente; vi (verse) essere corretto.
scandal ['skændl] n scandalo.
scandalize ['skændəlaiz] vt scandalizzare.
scandalous ['skændələs] a scandaloso.
Scandinavia [ˌskændi'neiviə] n Scandinavia.
Scandinavian [ˌskændi'neiviən] a n scandinavo.
scansion ['skænʃən] n scansione.
scant [skænt] a esiguo, insufficiente, scarso.
scantiness ['skæntinis] n esiguità, scarsezza.
scanty ['skænti] a limitato, ristretto, scarso.
scapegoat ['skeipgout] n capro espiatorio.
scapegrace ['skeipgreis] n scapestrato.
scapular(y) ['skæpjulər(i)] n scapolare.
scar [skɑ:] n cicatrice, segno.
scarce [skeəs] a scarso, raro.
scarcely ['skeəsli] ad appena, a mala pena, a stento.
scarcity ['skeəsiti] n scarsezza, penuria.
scare [skeə] n panico, spavento; vt spaventare.
scarecrow ['skeəkrou] n spauracchio, spaventapasseri.
scarf [skɑ:f] n sciarpa.
scarlet ['skɑ:lit] a n rosso scarlatto.
scathing ['skeiðiŋ] a sarcastico, mordace.
scatter] 'skætə] vti sparger(si).

scavenger ['skævindʒə] n spazzino.
scene [si:n] n scena; scenata; spettacolo; **behind the scenes** dietro la scena; **to make a s.** fare una scenata; **the s. of the battle** il teatro del combattimento.
scenery ['si:nəri] n scenario, veduta, panorama, paesaggio.
scenic ['si:nik] a scenico, teatrale.
scent [sent] n odore, profumo; fiuto; vt fiutare; profumare.
scepter ['septə] n scettro.
schedule ['skedju:l] n inventario, lista; orario, programma.
scheme [ski:m] n piano, progetto; vt progettare; vi fare progetti, intrigare.
schism ['sizəm] n scisma.
schismatic [siz'mætik] a n scismatico.
schizophrenic [ˌskitsou'frenik] a n schizofrenico.
scholar ['skɔlə] n erudito, studioso, studente detentore d'una borsa di studio.
scholarly ['skɔləli] a dotto, erudito.
scholarship ['skɔləʃip] n dottrina, erudizione; borsa di studio.
scholastic [skə'læstik] a n scolastico.
school [sku:l] n scuola; vt disciplinare, domare; **schoolhouse** scuola.
schooling ['sku:liŋ] n insegnamento, istruzione.
schoolmaster ['sku:lˌmɑːstə] n insegnante, maestro, professore.
schoolroom ['sku:lrum] n aula scolastica.
schooner ['sku:nə] n (naut) goletta.
sciatica [sai'ætikə] n sciatica.
science ['saiəns] n scienza; **s. fiction** fantascienza.
scientific [ˌsaiən'tifik] a scientifico.
scientist ['saiəntist] n scienziato.
scimitar ['simitə] n scimitarra.
scintillate ['sintileit] vt scintillare, brillare.
scion ['saiən] n (plants) pollone; (fig) erede, rampollo.
scissors ['sizəz] n pl forbici pl.
scoff [skɔf] vti **s. at** beffare, deridere.
scold [skould] n donna bisbetica; vti rimproverare, sgridare.
scone [skɔn] n pastina da tè.
scoop [sku:p] n paletta, ramaiuolo; (fig, press) notizia, servizio in esclusiva; vt vuotare; (press) accapararrsi una notizia; **to s. up** raccogliere con la pala.
scooter ['sku:tə] n monopattino; 'scooter', motoretta.
scope [skoup] n portata, campo d'azione, prospettiva.
scorch [skɔ:tʃ] n scottatura; vt scottare.
score [skɔ:] n ventina; punto; punteggio; numero di punti; conto; scotto; tacca; (mus) spartito; vt intaccare, marcare, segnare; segnare punti, mettere in conto; (mus) orche-

strare; *vi* assicurarsi un vantaggio, aver fortuna.

scorn [skɔːn] *n* disprezzo, sdegno; *vt* disprezzare.

scornful ['skɔːnful] *a* sdegnoso.

scornfully ['skɔːnfuli] *ad* sprezzantemente, sdegnosamente.

scorpion ['skɔːpiən] *n* scorpione.

Scot [skɔt] *n* scozzese.

Scotch [skɔtʃ] **Scottish** ['skɔtiʃ] *a* scozzese.

Scotland ['skɔtlənd] *n* Scozia.

Scots [skɔts] *a* scozzese.

Scotsman [skɔtsmən] *n* scozzese.

scoundrel ['skaundrəl] *n* farabutto, mascalzone.

scour ['skauə] *vt* pulire fregando; perlustrare.

scourge [skəːdʒ] *n* frusta, sferza; *vt* fustigare, sferzare.

scout [skaut] *n* esploratore, vedetta; *vt* respingere con sdegno; *vi* esplorare.

scowl [skaul] *n* sguardo torvo; *vi* guardare torvo.

scrabble ['skræbl] *vi* frugare affannosamente.

scraggy ['skrægi] *a* ossuto, scarno.

scramble ['skræmbl] *n* parapiglia, lotta, confusione; *vi* affrettarsi, arrampicarsi con mani e piedi; *vt* arraffare, (*eggs*) strapazzare.

scrap [skræp] *n* frammento, pezzetto; rottame; *vt* scartare; **scrapbook** album di ritagli.

scrape [skreip] *n* raschiatura, graffio; (*fam*) impiccio, situazione difficile; *vt* raschiare, scrostare, sfregare; **to s. through** cavarsela.

scraper ['skreipə] *n* raschietto; (*mat*) pulisciscarpe.

scrapings ['skreipiŋz] *n pl* risparmi.

scrappy ['skræpi] *a* frammentario.

scratch [skrætʃ] *a* male assortito, eterogeneo; *n* graffio; linea di partenza; *vti* graffiare, grattare, raspare; **to start from s.** partire da zero; **to come up to s.** (*fig*) farsi onore; **s. pad** blocco per note, nòtes.

scratchy ['skrætʃi] *a* scarabocchiato; scricchiolante.

scrawl [skrɔːl] *n* scarabocchio; *vti* scarabocchiare.

scream [skriːm] *n* strillo, urlo; *vi* strillare, urlare.

screech [skriːtʃ] *n* strillo acuto; *vi* strillare.

screed [skriːd] *n* lunga filastrocca.

screen [skriːn] *n* parafuoco, paravento; difesa, riparo; (*cin*, *TV*) schermo; *vt* proteggere, riparare; proiettare.

screw [skruː] *n* vite; (*sl*) strozzino; (*naut*) elica; *vt* torcere; *vti* avvitare; (*fig*) opprimere.

screwdriver ['skruːˌdraivə] *n* cacciavite.

scribble ['skribl] *n* scarabocchio; *vti*

scarabocchiare; **scribbling block** blocco per note, nòtes.

scribbler ['skriblə] *n* imbrattacarte.

scribe [skraib] *n* copista, scriba.

scrimmage ['skrimidʒ] *n* schermaglia.

script [skript] *n* scrittura; (*typ*) corsivo; (*theat etc*) copione, sceneggiatura.

scripture ['skriptʃə] *n* sacra scrittura.

scroll [skroul] *n* pergamena; rotolo di carta; svolazzo; (*arch*) voluta.

scrub [skrʌb] *n* sottobosco, macchia; *vti* strofinare energicamente.

scruff [skrʌf] *n* (*of the neck*) collottola.

scruple ['skruːpl] *n* scrupolo; *vi* esitare, farsi scrupolo di.

scrupulosity [ˌskruːpjuˈlɔsiti] *n* scrupolosità.

scrupulous ['skruːpjuləs] *a* scrupoloso.

scrutinize ['skruːtinaiz] *vt* scrutinare.

scrutiny ['skruːtini] *n* esame minuzioso, scrutinio.

scud [skʌd] *n* fuga, rapida corsa; *vi* correre velocemente.

scuffle ['skʌfl] *n* baruffa, parapiglia; *vi* azzuffarsi.

scull [skʌl] *n* remo; *vti* vogare con remi corti.

scullery ['skʌləri] *n* retrocucina.

sculptor ['skʌlptə] *n* scultore.

sculptural ['skʌlptʃərəl] *a* di scultura, scultorio.

sculpture ['skʌlptʃə] *n* scultura; *vt* scolpire.

scum [skʌm] *n* schiuma, (*also fig*) feccia, scoria.

scurf [skəːf] *n* forfora.

scurrility [skʌˈriliti] *n* scurrilità.

scurrilous ['skʌriləs] *a* scurrile.

scurry ['skʌri] *n* corsa frettolosa; *vi* correre, affrettarsi.

scurvy ['skəːvi] *a* basso, vile; *n* scorbuto.

scuttle ['skʌtl] *n* recipiente per il carbone; fuga precipitosa; (*naut*) portello; *vt* (*naut*) affondare; *vi* svignarsela.

scythe [saið] *n* falce.

sea [siː] *n* mare; **s. level** livello del mare; **s. power** potenza navale; **s. shell** conchiglia; **s. voyage** viaggio per mare.

seafarer ['siːˌfɛərə] *n* navigatore.

seal [siːl] *n* sigillo, suggello, timbro; (*zool*) foca; *vt* bollare, sigillare, suggellare.

sealing wax ['siːliŋwæks] *n* ceralacca.

seam [siːm] *n* costura, cucitura; cicatrice; (*geol*) giacimento.

seaman ['siːmən] *n* marinaio.

seamstress ['semstris] *n* cucitrice.

seaplane ['siːplein] *n* idrovolante.

seaport ['siːpɔːt] *n* porto di mare.

sear [siə] *vt* bruciare, cauterizzare, dissecare; (*fig*) indurire.

search [səːtʃ] *n* ricerca, indagine, inchiesta; perquisizione; *vt* perquisire; *vi* cercare, fare ricerche, perlustrare.

searching ['sə:tʃiŋ] *a* indagatore, penetrante, minuzioso.

searchlight ['sə:tʃlait] *n* riflettore.

seaside ['si:'said] *n* spiaggia, mare; **s. resort** stazione balneare.

season ['si:zn] *n* stagione; epoca; tempo; *vt* condire; stagionare; acclimatare; *vi* divenire stagionato.

seasonable ['si:znəbl] *a* di stagione; tempestivo.

seasoning ['si:zniŋ] *n* condimento; stagionatura.

seat [si:t] *n* posto (a sedere), panca, sedia, sedile, seggio; sede; residenza; sedere, deretano; *vt* far sedere, offrire posti a sedere a; **four-seater** (*aut*) automobile a quattro posti.

seaweed ['si:wi:d] *n* alga.

Sebastian [si'bæstiən] *nm pr* Sebastiano.

secede [si'si:d] *vi* separarsi.

secession [si'seʃən] *n* secessione, separazione.

secluded [si'klu:did] *a* ritirato, appartato.

seclusion [si'klu:ʒən] *n* ritiro, solitudine, reclusione.

second ['sekənd] *a n* secondo; *vt* appoggiare, assecondare; **s.-hand** di seconda mano.

secondary ['sekəndəri] *a* secondario, subordinato.

secrecy ['si:krisi] *n* segretezza.

secret ['si:krit] *a n* segreto.

secretary ['sekrətri] *n* segretario, -a.

secrete [si'kri:t] *vt* secernere; nascondere.

secretion [si'kri:ʃən] *n* secrezione.

secretive ['si:kritiv] *a* riservato, poco comunicativo.

sect [sekt] *n* setta.

sectarian [sek'tɛəriən] *a n* settario.

section ['sekʃən] *n* sezione, paragrafo; parte.

sector ['sektə] *n* settore.

secular ['sekjulə] *a n* secolare.

secularization ['sekjulərai'zeiʃən] *n* secolarizzazione.

secularize ['sekjuləraiz] *vt* secolarizzare.

secure [si'kjuə] *a* sicuro, al sicuro, fiducioso, tranquillo; *vt* assicurare, garantire; procurarsi.

security [si'kjuəriti] *n* sicurezza, garanzia.

sedan [si'dæn] *n* portantina.

sedate [si'deit] *a* calmo, pacato.

sedateness [si'deitnis] *n* calma, pacatezza.

sedative ['sedətiv] *a n* sedativo, calmante.

sedentary ['sedntəri] *a n* sedentario.

sedge [sedʒ] *n* carice.

sediment ['sedimənt] *n* sedimento.

sedition [si'diʃən] *n* sedizione.

seditious [si'diʃəs] *a* sedizioso.

seduce [si'dju:s] *vt* sedurre.

seduction [si'dʌkʃən] *n* seduzione.

sedulous ['sedjuləs] *a* assiduo, diligente.

see [si:] *n* diocesi, sede; *vti* vedere; capire; visitare.

seed [si:d] *n* seme, semenza; *vi* produrre semi.

seedling ['si:dliŋ] *n* pianticella, alberello.

seedy ['si:di] *a* pieno di semi: (*fig*) male in arnese, indisposto.

seek [si:k] *vti* cercare, perseguire.

seem [si:m] *vi* sembrare, parere.

seeming ['si:miŋ] *a* apparente.

seemly ['si:mli] *a* di bell'aspetto, decoroso.

seep [si:p] *vi* filtrare, penetrare.

seer ['si:ə] *n* veggente, profeta.

seesaw ['si:sɔ:] *n* altalena.

seethe [si:ð] *vi* bollire; essere in fermento.

segment ['segmənt] *n* segmento.

segregate ['segrigeit] *vti* segregar(si).

segregation [,segri'geiʃən] *n* segregazione.

Seine [sein] *n* Senna.

seize [si:z] *vt* afferrare, impadronirsi di, confiscare, sequestrare.

seizure ['si:ʒə] *n* presa, confisca; (*med*) attacco.

seldom ['seldəm] *ad* di rado, raramente.

select [si'lekt] *a* scelto; *vt* scegliere, selezionare.

selection [si'lekʃən] *n* assortimento, scelta, selezione.

self [self] *n* l'io, l'individuo, se stesso.

self-command ['selfkə'ma:nd] *n* padronanza di sè.

self-conceit ['selfkən'si:t] *n* presunzione.

self-confidence ['self'kɔnfidəns] *n* sicurezza di sè.

self-conscious ['self'kɔnʃəs] *a* impacciato; (*phil*) autocosciente.

self-contained ['selfkən'teind] *a* riservato; autonomo, indipendente.

self-control ['selfkən'troul] *n* padronanza di sè.

self-defense ['selfdi'fens] *n* autodifesa.

self-denial ['selfdi'naiəl] *n* abnegazione.

self-government ['self'gʌvnmənt] *n* autonomia.

selfish ['selfiʃ] *a* egoista, egoistico.

selfishness ['selfiʃnis] *n* egoismo.

selfless ['selflis] *a* altruistico, disinteressato.

self-made ['self'meid] *a* che deve tutto a se stesso, che si è fatto da sè.

self-reliance ['selfri'laiəns] *n* fiducia in sè.

self-supporting ['selfsə'pɔ:tiŋ] *a* indipendente.

self-service ['self'sə:vis] *a n* 'self service', (di) locale in cui ci si serve da sè.

self-taught ['self'tɔ:t] *a* autodidatta.

sell [sel] *vt* vendere; *vi* trovare smercio, vendersi.

semaphore ['seməfɔ:] n semaforo.
semblance ['sembləns] n aspetto, apparenza; parvenza; somiglianza.
semicircle ['semi.sə:kl] n semicerchio.
seminar ['seminɑ:] n (university) seminario.
seminary ['seminəri] n seminario.
semolina [semə'li:nə] n semolino.
senate ['senit] n senato.
senator ['senətə] n senatore.
send [send] vt mandare, inviare, spedire; **to s. for** mandare a chiamare; **sender** mittente, speditore.
senile ['si:nail] a senile.
senility [si'niliti] n senilità.
senior ['si:niə] a n maggiore, più anziano, seniore, decano.
seniority [si:ni'ɔriti] n anzianità.
sensation [sen'seiʃən] n sensazione, scalpore.
sensational [sen'seiʃənl] a sensazionale.
sense [sens] n senso; conoscenza; buon senso; significato.
senseless ['senslis] a inanime; assurdo, senza significato.
sensibility [sensi'biliti] n sensibilità.
sensible ['sensəbl] a sensato, ragionevole, cosciente.
sensitive ['sensitiv] a sensibile, sensitivo, suscettibile.
sensitiveness ['sensitivnis] **sensitivity** [sensi'tiviti] n sensibilità, suscettibilità.
sensorial [sen'sɔ:riəl] a sensorio.
sensual ['sensjuəl] a sensuale, voluttuoso.
sensuality [sensju'æliti] n sensualità, voluttà.
sensuous ['sensjuəs] a dei sensi, sensitivo.
sentence ['sentəns] n sentenza, condanna; frase, periodo; massima; vt condannare.
sentiment ['sentimənt] n sentimento, idea; sentimentalità.
sentimental [senti'mentl] a sentimentale.
sentinel ['sentinl], **sentry** ['sentri] n (mil) sentinella.
sentry-box ['sentribɔks] n garitta.
separate ['sepəreit] vti divider(si), separar(si); ['sepərit] a separato, distinto.
separately ['sepəritli] ad separatamente, singolarmente.
separation [sepə'reiʃən] n separazione.
sepia ['si:piə] n seppia; color seppia.
September [səp'tembə] n settembre.
septic ['septik] a settico.
sepulcher ['sepəlkə] n sepolcro; **whited s.** sepolcro imbiancato, ipocrita.
sepulchral [si'pʌlkrəl] a sepolcrale.
sequel ['si:kwəl] n seguito.
sequence ['si:kwəns] n serie, successione.

sequestered [si'kwestəd] a remoto, solitario.
sequestrate [si'kwestreit] vt sequestrare.
sequestration [si:kwes'treiʃən] n sequestro.
serenade [seri'neid] n serenata.
serene [si'ri:n] a calmo, sereno.
serenity [si'reniti] n serenità.
serf [sə:f] n servo della gleba.
serge [sə:dʒ] n 'serge', saia.
sergeant ['sɑ:dʒənt] n sergente.
serial ['siəriəl] a periodico, a puntate; n romanzo a puntate, pubblicazione periodica.
series ['siəri:z] n serie.
serious ['siəriəs] a serio, grave.
seriously ['siəriəsli] ad seriamente, sul serio; gravemente.
seriousness ['siəriəsnis] n serietà, gravità.
sermon ['sə:mən] n predica, sermone, (fam) predicozzo.
serpent ['sə:pənt] n serpente.
serrated [se'reitid] a dentellato, seghettato.
servant ['sə:vənt] n domestico, -ca, servitore, servo, -va; funzionario.
serve [sə:v] vti servire.
service ['sə:vis] n servizio; ufficio (divino), funzione (religiosa), **s. flats** appartamenti d'affitto con servizio; **s. lift** montavivande.
serviceable ['sə:visəbl] a utile, pratico.
serviette [sə:vi'et] n tovagliolo.
servile ['sə:vail] a servile, abbietto.
servility [sə:'viliti] n servilità.
servitude ['sə:vitju:d] n servitù, schiavitù.
session ['seʃən] n sessione.
set [set] a fisso, stabilito, ostinato; n collezione, serie, servizio; cricca, crocchio; partita, gioco; (rad) apparecchio; (teeth) dentiera; vt disporre, mettere; fissare; montare; regolare; (type) comporre; vi applicarsi; disporsi, mettersi; solidificarsi; tramontare; **set up** sistemazione, situazione, stato di cose.
settee [se'ti:] n divano.
setter ['setə] n cane da ferma.
setting ['setiŋ] n montaggio; messa in scena; solidificazione; (gem) montatura; (typ) composizione; **hair s.** messa in piega.
settle ['setl] vt accomodare, fissare, stabilire, sistemare; calmare; pagare, saldare; vi fissarsi, sistemarsi, stabilirsi.
settlement ['setlmənt] n contratto, accordo, sistemazione; saldo; colonia, colonizzazione.
settler ['setlə] n colonizzatore, colono.
seven ['sevn] a n sette; **seventh** a settimo.
seventeen ['sevn'ti:n] a n diciassette; **seventeenth** a diciassettesimo.
seventy ['sevnti] a n settanta; **seventieth** a settantesimo.

sever ['sevə] *vti* staccar(si), separar (si).

several ['sevrəl] *a* diverso, separato; *a pron pl* parecchi(e) *pl*.

severance ['sevərəns] *n* distacco, separazione.

severe [si'viə] *a* severo, austero; rigido; violento.

severity [si'veriti] *n* severità; rigore.

Seville ['sevil] *n* Siviglia.

sew [sou] *vti* cucire.

sewage ['sju:idʒ] *n* acque di scolo *pl*.

sewer ['sjuə] *n* conduttura, fogna.

sex [seks] *n* sesso.

sexton ['sekstən] *n* sagrestano; becchino.

sexual ['seksjuəl] *a* sessuale.

shabbiness ['ʃæbinis] *n* l'essere male in arnese; grettezza.

shabby ['ʃæbi] *a* male in arnese; gretto.

shackle ['ʃækl] *n* anello di metallo; *vt* mettere in ceppi; (*fig*) ostacolare; **shackles** *pl* ceppi, manette, ferri *pl*.

shade [ʃeid] *n* ombra; paralume; riparo dalla luce; sfumatura; tinta; *vt* adombrare; ombreggiare; proteggere, riparare; sfumare.

shading ['ʃeidiŋ] *n* ombreggiatura, sfumatura.

shadow ['ʃædou] *n* ombra; fantasma; *vt* seguire come un'ombra.

shadowy ['ʃædoui] *a* ombroso; indistinto.

shady ['ʃeidi] *a* fresco, ombreggiato; (*fig*) equivoco, losco.

shaft [ʃɑ:ft] *n* lancia; fusto; freccia, strale; (*light*) raggio; manico; (*mine*) pozzo.

shag [ʃæg] *n* tabacco forte; cormorano crestato.

shaggy ['ʃægi] *a* irsuto, ispido, peloso.

shagreen [ʃæ'gri:n] *n* zigrino.

shake [ʃeik] *n* scossa, urto, tremore; (*mus*) trillo; *vt* scuotere, scrollare; turbare; *vi* tremare, vacillare, agitarsi; (*mus*) trillare; **milk s.** frappè.

shaky ['ʃeiki] *a* tremolante, vacillante; malsicuro; debole; precario.

shale [ʃeil] *n* argilla schistosa; **s. oil** olio minerale, olio di schisto.

shallow ['ʃælou] *a* basso, poco profondo; (*fig*) superficiale; *n* bassofondo, secca.

shallowness ['ʃælounis] *n* poca profondità, superficialità.

sham [ʃæm] *a* finto, simulato; *n* finta, inganno, impostura; *vti* fingere, simulare.

shamble ['ʃæmbl] *vi* avere, camminare con, una andatura goffa o strascicante.

shambles ['ʃæmblz] *n* carneficina, macello, disordine, confusione.

shame [ʃeim] *n* vergogna, obbrobrio, onta; *vt* svergognare, indurre, costringere (per vergogna) a.

shamefaced ['ʃeimfeist] *a* vergognoso; confuso.

shameful ['ʃeimful] *a* vergognoso, disonorevole.

shameless ['ʃeimlis] *a* svergognato, sfacciato, impudente.

shampoo [ʃæm'pu:] *n* lavatura dei capelli, 'shampoo'; *vt* lavare i capelli, fare lo 'shampoo'.

shamrock ['ʃæmrɔk] *n* trifoglio (emblema nazionale dell'Irlanda).

Shanghai [ʃæŋ'hai] *n* Sciangai.

shank [ʃæŋk] *n* gamba, stinco.

shape [ʃeip] *n* forma, figura, stampo; *vt* foggiare, formare, modellare; *vi* assumere forma, presentarsi.

shapeless ['ʃeiplis] *a* informe.

shapely ['ʃeipli] *a* ben fatto, ben proporzionato.

share [ʃeə] *n* parte, porzione, quota; (*com*) azione; **common s.** azione ordinaria; *vt* (con)dividere, spartire, distribuire; *vi* partecipare.

shareholder ['ʃeə,houldə] *n* azionista.

shark [ʃɑ:k] *n* pescecane, squalo; furfante, speculatore; *vti* truffare, vivere di truffe.

sharp [ʃɑ:p] *a* acuto, affilato, aguzzo, penetrante; improvviso; piccante; scaltro; vivace; *n* (*mus*) diesis; *ad* in punto, puntualmente.

sharpen ['ʃɑ:pən] *vt* affilare, aguzzare, eccitare.

sharpness ['ʃɑ:pnis] *n* acutezza, acume; astuzia; prontezza, vivacità.

shatter ['ʃætə] *vti* frantumar(si), fracassar(si).

shave [ʃeiv] *n* rasatura; sfioramento; *vt* radere, tagliare; *vti* rader(si), far(si) la barba; **to have a close s.** salvarsi per miracolo, scamparla bella.

shaving ['ʃeiviŋ] *n* il rader(si); truciolo.

shawl [ʃɔ:l] *n* scialle.

she [ʃi:] *pron* ella, lei, colei; *n* femmina.

sheaf [ʃi:f] *n* covone, fascio.

shear [ʃiə] *vti* tosare, pelare; spogliare.

shears [ʃiəz] *n pl* cesoie *pl*.

sheath [ʃi:θ] *n* astuccio, fodero, guaina.

sheathe [ʃi:ð] *vt* rimettere nel fodero, inguainare.

shed [ʃed] *n* capannone, rimessa; *vt* spargere, spogliarsi di, versare.

sheen [ʃi:n] *n* lustro, splendore.

sheep [ʃi:p] *pl* **sheep** *n* pecora.

sheepish ['ʃi:piʃ] *a* vergognoso, timido, impacciato.

sheer [ʃiə] *a* puro, semplice; a piombo, perpendicolare; *ad* a piombo, verticalmente.

sheet [ʃi:t] *n* lenzuolo; foglio; giornale; lamina; (*of ice*) lastra, (*of water*) specchio.

shelf [ʃelf] *n* scaffale; palchetto, ripiano; scoglio.

shell [ʃel] *n* conchiglia; guscio; involucro; proiettile; *vt* sgusciare;

sbucciare; bombardare; **shellfish** crostaceo.

shelter ['ʃeltə] n riparo, rifugio, difesa; vt mettere al coperto, riparare; vi rifugiarsi; **air-raid** s. rifugio antiaereo.

shelve [ʃelv] vt mettere sugli scaffali; (fig) differire, mettere in disparte.

shepherd ['ʃepəd] n pastore; **shepherdess** pastorella.

sheriff ['ʃerif] n sceriffo.

sherry ['ʃeri] n 'sherry', vino di Xeres.

shield [ʃi:ld] n scudo; difesa, protezione; vt difendere, proteggere.

shift [ʃift] n cambiamento; espediente; turno; abito da donna; vt cambiare, spostare, trasferire; vi cambiar di posto, cambiarsi, spostarsi.

shifty ['ʃifti] a volubile, furbo, ambiguo; s. **glance** sguardo sfuggente.

shilling ['ʃiliŋ] n scellino.

shimmer ['ʃimə] n luccichio, scintillio.

shin [ʃin] n stinco, coscia; (beef) garretto; s.-**bone** tibia.

shindy ['ʃindi] n (fam) chiasso, baccano.

shine [ʃain] n lucentezza, splendore; vi brillare, splendere.

shingle ['ʃiŋgl] n ghiaia; tegola di legno; **shingles** pl (med) fuoco di S. Antonio; vt tagliare (capelli) alla garçonne.

shiny ['ʃaini] a rilucente; lucido.

ship [ʃip] n nave, bastimento; vt imbarcare, spedire; vi imbarcarsi.

shipbroker ['ʃip.broukə] n sensale marittimo.

shipbuilding ['ʃip.bildiŋ] n costruzione navale.

ship-chandler ['ʃip'tʃɑːndlə] n fornitore navale.

shipmate ['ʃipmeit] n compagno di bordo.

shipment ['ʃipmənt] n imbarco, spedizione.

shipping ['ʃipiŋ] n imbarco, marina mercantile, forze navali pl.

shipwreck ['ʃiprek] n naufragio.

shipwright ['ʃiprait] n (naut) maestro d'ascia.

shipyard ['ʃipjɑːd] n cantiere navale, arsenale.

shire ['ʃaiə] n contea.

shirk [ʃəːk] vt schivare, sfuggire.

shirt [ʃəːt] n camicia da uomo; s. **front** sparato di camicia.

shiver ['ʃivə] n brivido; frantume, scheggia; vi rabbrividire, tremare; vti rompere (andare) in frantumi.

shoal [ʃoul] n secca, bassofondo; banco di pesci; folla, ressa.

shock [ʃɔk] n colpo, urto, forte emozione, scossa; massa di capelli incolti; vt offendere, scandalizzare, urtare.

shocker ['ʃɔkə] n cosa che colpisce, romanzo scandalistico.

shocking ['ʃɔkiŋ] a scandaloso.

shoddy ['ʃɔdi] a scadente e appariscente; n cascame; (fig) roba scadente e appariscente.

shoe [ʃuː] n scarpa; ferro da cavallo; vt calzare; ferrare.

shoemaker ['ʃuː.meikə] n calzolaio.

shoot [ʃuːt] n germoglio; partita di caccia; vt colpire, fucilare; vi andare a caccia, sparare; germogliare; lanciarsi.

shooting ['ʃuːtiŋ] n sparatoria; caccia; s. **pain** dolore lancinante; s. **star** stella cadente.

shop [ʃɔp] n bottega, negozio, spaccio; vi fare delle compere; s. **assistant** commesso; **to talk** s. parlare di affari; s. **window** vetrina.

shopkeeper ['ʃɔp.kiːpə] n negoziante.

shore [ʃɔː] n spiaggia, riva, sponda; puntello; vt puntellare.

short [ʃɔːt] a breve, corto, (height) basso; brusco, conciso, ristretto; ad di botto; s.-**cut** scorciatoia; s.-**sighted** miope.

shortage ['ʃɔːtidʒ] a scarsezza.

shorten ['ʃɔːtn] vti accorciar(si); diminuir(si).

shorthand ['ʃɔːthænd] n stenografia; s. **typist** stenodattilografo; s. **writer** stenografo.

shortly ['ʃɔːtli] ad in breve, tra poco.

shortness ['ʃɔːtnis] n brevità, cortezza; insufficenza.

shot [ʃɔt] n colpo; sparo; scarica; palla, proiettile; tiratore; tiro; portata.

shotgun ['ʃɔtgʌn] n fucile da caccia.

shoulder ['ʃouldə] n spalla; (of road) bordo della strada; vt addossarsi, prendere sulle spalle.

shout [ʃaut] n grido; vti gridare.

shove [ʃʌv] n spinta; vti spingere.

shovel ['ʃʌvl] n pala, palata; vt ammucchiare, spalare; rimpinzarsi la bocca di.

show [ʃou] n mostra, esibizione; esposizione; ostentazione, pompa; spettacolo; vt far vedere, mostrare.

shower ['ʃauə] n acquazzone, rovescio; doccia; vt far piovere; vi diluviare.

showery ['ʃauəri] a temporalesco.

showman ['ʃoumən] n imbonitore; direttore, capocomico.

showy ['ʃoui] a appariscente, vistoso.

shrapnel ['ʃræpnl] n shrapnel.

shred [ʃred] n brandello, pezzetto, ritaglio; vt sminuzzare, tagliuzzare.

shrew [ʃruː] n bisbetica.

shrewd [ʃruːd] a accorto, perspicace, scaltro.

shrewdness ['ʃruːdnis] n accortezza, perspicacia.

shriek [ʃriːk] n grido acuto, strillo; vti strillare, gridare.

shrike [ʃraik] n averla.

shrill [ʃril] a stridulo; vti stridere.
shrimp [ʃrimp] n gamberetto; (fig) omiciattolo.
shrine [ʃrain] n reliquario, santuario.
shrink [ʃriŋk] vt far restringere; vi restringersi, ritirarsi; indietreggiare.
shrivel ['ʃrivl] vti raggrinzar(si).
shroud [ʃraud] n sudario; velo; vt avvolgere, coprire, nascondere.
Shrove Tuesday ['ʃrouv'tjuːzdi] n martedì grasso.
shrub [ʃrʌb] n arbusto, cespuglio; bibita di succo di frutta.
shrug [ʃrʌg] n alzata di spalle; vi stringersi nelle spalle.
shudder ['ʃʌdə] n brivido; vi rabbrividire.
shuffle ['ʃʌfl] n andatura strascicata; il mescolare le carte; vt (cards) mescolare; muovere con fatica, strascicare; vi muoversi con fatica, strascicarsi; ricorrere a sotterfugi.
shun [ʃʌn] vt evitare, scansare.
shunt [ʃʌnt] n (rly) binario di smistamento; (el) derivazione; vt (rly) smistare; (el) derivare.
shut [ʃʌt] vti chiuder(si).
shutter ['ʃʌtə] n imposta, persiana; (phot) otturatore.
shuttle ['ʃʌtl] n navetta, spoletta.
shy [ʃai] a timido; diffidente, (horse) ombroso; vt lanciare; vi pigliar ombra.
shyness ['ʃainis] n timidezza.
Siamese [ˌsaiə'miːz] a n siamese.
Siberia [sai'biəriə] n Siberia.
Siberian [sai'biəriən] a n siberiano.
sibilant ['sibilənt] a n sibilante.
sibyl ['sibil] n sibilla.
Sicilian [si'siliən] a n siciliano.
Sicily ['sisili] n Sicilia.
sick [sik] a (am)malato, sofferente; nauseato; stanco.
sicken ['sikn] vt disgustare; vi ammalarsi, disgustarsi.
sickle ['sikl] n falcetto, falce.
sickly ['sikli] a di salute cagionevole, malaticcio; nauseante.
sickness ['siknis] n malattia; nausea.
sickroom ['sikrum] n camera per ammalati.
side [said] n fianco, lato; riva; parte, partito; vi parteggiare.
sideboard ['saidbɔːd] n credenza.
side-effect ['saidi'fekt] n effetto secondario.
sidelong ['saidlɔŋ] a obliquo; ad obliquamente.
sidewalk ['saidwɔːk] n marciapiede.
sideways ['saidweiz] ad lateralmente, a sghembo.
sidle ['saidl] vi camminare di sghembo; diportarsi untuosamente.
siding ['saidiŋ] n (rly) binario morto.
siege [siːdʒ] n assedio.
sieve [siv] n crivello, staccio; vt stacciare.
sift [sift] vt setacciare.
sigh [sai] n sospiro; vi sospirare.

sight [sait] n vista, occhi pl; (gun) mirino; spettacolo, visione; (fam) gran quantità; vt avvistare; prendere la mira di; s.-seeing visita turistica.
sightless ['saitlis] a cieco.
sightly ['saitli] a avvenente, bello.
Sigismond, Sigismund ['sigismənd] nm pr Sigismondo.
sign [sain] n segno, cenno; insegna; vti firmare, segnare.
signal ['signl] a cospicuo, notevole; n segnale, segnalazione, segno; vti segnalare.
signatory ['signətəri] n firmatario.
signature ['signitʃə] n firma; (typ) segnatura; (mus) indicazione.
signet ['signit] n sigillo.
significance [sig'nifikəns] n significato; espressione; importanza.
significant [sig'nifikənt] a significativo, importante.
signify ['signifai] vt significare, far sapere, voler dire; vi importare.
silence ['sailəns] n silenzio.
silencer ['sailənsə] n (aut) silenziatore.
silent ['sailənt] a silenzioso, muto.
silhouette [ˌsilu(ː)'et] n profilo; vti profilar(si).
silk [silk] a di seta; n seta.
silken ['silkən] a serico, di seta; (fig) insinuante.
silkiness ['silkinis] n morbidezza, lucentezza.
silkworm ['silkwəːm] n baco da seta.
silky ['silki] a di seta, serico; morbido.
sill [sil] n davanzale; soglia.
silliness ['silinis] n stupidità, sciocchezza.
silly ['sili] a sciocco, stupido.
silt [silt] n sedimento di fango o sabbia; vti ostruir(si) per fango o sabbia.
silver ['silvə] a d'argento; n argento.
silversmith ['silvəsmiθ] n argentiere.
silvery ['silvəri] a argenteo, -tato, -tino.
similar ['similə] a n simile; a somigliante, analogo.
similarity [ˌsimi'læriti] n somiglianza.
simile ['simili] n paragone, similitudine.
simmer ['simə] vti (far) bollire lentamente; (fig) essere sul punto di scoppiare per, ribollire di.
Simon ['saimən] nm pr Simone.
simony ['saiməni] n simonia.
simper ['simpə] n sorriso melenso; vi sorridere in modo melenso.
simple ['simpl] a semplice; n erba medicinale.
simpleton ['simpltən] n semplicione.
simplicity [sim'plisiti] n semplicità.
simplification [ˌsimplifi'keiʃən] n semplificazione.
simplify ['simplifai] vt semplificare.
simulate ['simjuleit] vt simulare.
simulation [ˌsimju'leiʃən] n simulazione.

simultaneous [ˌsiməl'teiniəs] *a* simultaneo.
simultaneously [ˌsiməl'teiniəsli] *ad* simultaneamente.
sin [sin] *n* peccato; *vi* peccare.
since [sins] *ad cj prep* d'allora in poi; da quando; poichè; da.
sincere [sin'siə] *a* sincero.
sincerity [sin'seriti] *n* sincerità.
sinecure ['sinikjuə] *n* sinecura.
sinew ['sinjuː] *n* nervo, tendine; nerbo.
sinewy ['sinjuːi] *a* nerboruto, gagliardo.
sinful ['sinful] *a* peccaminoso, colpevole.
sing [siŋ] *vti* cantare.
singe [sindʒ] *vt* bruciare, bruciacchiare.
singer ['siŋə] *n* cantante, cantore.
singing ['siŋiŋ] *a* cantante, canterino; *n* canto.
single ['siŋgl] *a* solo, unico; semplice; singolo, celibe, nubile; *vt* distinguere; scegliere; **s. ticket** (*rly*) biglietto d'andata.
singular ['siŋgjulə] *a n* singolare; *a* caratteristico, particolare.
singularity [ˌsiŋgju'læriti] *n* singolarità; stranezza.
singularly ['siŋgjuləli] *ad* singolarmente, particolarmente.
sinister ['sinistə] *a* sinistro, funesto.
sink [siŋk] *n* acquaio; sentina; *vt* affondare, immergere; nascondere; investire denaro a fondo perduto; *vi* affondare; declinare; sparire, tramontare.
sinless ['sinlis] *a* innocente, puro.
sinner ['sinə] *n* peccatore, -trice.
sinuous ['sinjuəs] *a* sinuoso.
sip [sip] *n* sorso; *vti* centellinare.
siphon ['saifən] *n* sifone.
sir [səː] *n* (*vocative*) signore, 'Sir', titolo premesso a nome proprio di cavaliere, baronetto.
sire ['saiə] *n* sire.
siren ['saiərin] *n* sirena.
sirloin ['səːlɔin] *n* lombo di manzo.
sister ['sistə] *n* sorella; suora; **s.-in-law** cognata.
sisterhood ['sistəhud] *n* comunità religiosa.
sisterly ['sistəli] *a* da (di) sorella.
sit [sit] *vi* sedere, stare seduto; **to s. down** mettersi a sedere.
site [sait] *n* sito, luogo, posizione.
sitting ['sitiŋ] *a* seduto; in seduta; *n* seduta; posa; riunione; **s. room** salotto, stanza di soggiorno.
situated ['sitjueitid] *a* posto, situato.
situation [ˌsitju'eiʃən] *n* posizione; situazione; condizioni *pl*; impiego, posto.
six [siks] *a n* sei; **sixth** *a* sesto.
sixpence ['sikspəns] *n* mezzo scellino.
sixteen ['siks'tiːn] *a n* sedici; **sixteenth** *a* sedicesimo.
sixty ['siksti] *a n* sessanta; **sixtieth** *a* sessantesimo.

sizable ['saizəbl] *a* piuttosto grande.
size [saiz] *n* grandezza, dimensione; formato; misura; **s. up** *vt* valutare, giudicare.
skate [skeit] *n* pattino; (*fish*) razza; *vi* pattinare; schettinare.
skating ['skeitiŋ] *n* pattinaggio.
skein [skein] *n* matassa.
skeleton ['skelitn] *n* scheletro; ossatura.
skeptic ['skeptik] *n* scettico.
skeptical ['skeptikəl] *a* scettico.
skepticism ['skeptisizəm] *n* scetticismo.
sketch [sketʃ] *n* abbozzo, bozzetto, schizzo; *vti* abbozzare, schizzare, fare degli schizzi.
skew [skjuː] *a* obliquo, sbieco.
skewer ['skjuə] *n* spiedo; *vt* infilare sullo spiedo.
ski [skiː] *n* sci; *vi* sciare.
skid [skid] *n* slittamento; (*av*) pattino di coda; **side s.** (*aut*) sbandamento; *vi* sbandare, slittare; scivolare.
skier ['skiːə] *n* sciatore.
skiff [skif] *n* (*naut*) schifo.
skill [skil] *n* abilità, destrezza, perizia.
skilled [skild] *a* esperto, specializzato.
skilful ['skilful] *a* abile, destro, esperto.
skim [skim] *vt* schiumare, scremare; sfiorare, dare un'occhiata a; **skimmed milk** latte scremato.
skimmer ['skimə] *n* schiumatoio.
skimp [skimp] *vt* lesinare, tenere a stecchetto.
skimpy ['skimpi] *a* scarso, misero.
skin [skin] *n* pelle; *vt* pelare; sbucciare, scorticare; **s. diver** nuotatore subacqueo, sommozzatore; **s. diving** nuoto subacqueo.
skinny ['skini] *a* magro, macilento.
skip [skip] *n* balzo; *vt* omettere, passare sopra; *vi* balzare, saltare.
skipper ['skipə] *n* capitano di nave mercantile o peschereccia.
skirmish ['skəːmiʃ] *n* scaramuccia; *vi* scaramucciare.
skirt [skəːt] *n* sottana, gonna; falda, lembo; *vt* costeggiare, rasentare, confinare con.
skit [skit] *n* parodia, frizzo.
skittish ['skitiʃ] *a* capriccioso, volubile, vivace.
skittle ['skitl] *n* birillo.
skulk [skʌlk] *vi* celarsi, nascondersi, sottrarsi al proprio dovere.
skull [skʌl] *n* cranio, teschio.
skunk [skʌŋk] *n* moffetta; (*fig*) individuo ignobile.
sky [skai] *n* cielo, volta del cielo.
skylark ['skailɑːk] *n* allodola.
skylight ['skailait] *n* lucernario.
skyline ['skailain] *n* orizzonte.
skyscraper ['skaiˌskreipə] *n* grattacielo.
slab [slæb] *n* grossa fetta; lastra.

slack [slæk] *a* allentato, fiacco, indolente; fermo, stagnante.

slacken ['slækən] *vti* allentar(si), moderar(si).

slackness ['slæknis] *n* fiacchezza, rilassatezza; (*com*) fermo.

slag [slæg] *n* scoria, -ie.

slake [sleik] *vt* estinguere; soddisfare.

slam [slæm] *n* sbatacchiamento; *vti* sbatacchiar(si), scaraventare.

slander ['slɑːndə] *n* calunnia; *vt* calunniare, diffamare.

slanderer [slɑːndərə] *n* calunniatore, diffamatore.

slanderous ['slɑːndərəs] *a* calunnioso, diffamatorio.

slang [slæŋ] *n* gergo.

slant [slɑːnt] *n* inclinazione, pendio; posizione obliqua; (*fig*) prospettiva; *vt* disporre obliquamente; *vi* inclinarsi.

slap [slæp] *n* colpo, schiaffo; *vt* colpire, schiaffeggiare; gettare, scaraventare.

slapdash ['slæpdæʃ] *a* impetuoso; affrettato, superficiale.

slapstick ['slæpstik] *n* farsa grossolana.

slash [slæʃ] *n* squarcio, taglio; *vt* squarciare, tagliare; criticare ferocemente.

slate [sleit] *n* ardesia; tegola d'ardesia; lavagna.

slattern ['slætəːn] *n* donna sciatta.

slaughter ['slɔːtə] *n* carneficina, macello; *vt* macellare, massacrare.

Slav [slɑːv] *a n* slavo.

slave [sleiv] *n* schiavo; *vi* sgobbare.

slaver ['sleivə] *n* negriero; nave negriera.

slaver ['slævə] *n* bava, saliva; *vi* sbavare.

slavery ['sleivəri] *n* schiavitù.

Slavic ['slævik] *a n* slavo, lingua slava.

slavish ['sleiviʃ] *a* abietto, servile.

slavishness ['sleiviʃnis] *n* servilismo.

Slavonic [slə'vɔnik] *a n* slavo, lingua slava.

slay [slei] *vt* ammazzare, trucidare.

sled [sled] *n* slitta.

sledge [sledʒ] *n* slitta; **s.-hammer** mazza da fabbro.

sleek [sliːk] *a* liscio; *vt* lisciare.

sleep [sliːp] *n* sonno; *vi* dormire.

sleeper ['sliːpə] *n* dormiente; (*rly*) traversa, -sina; cuccetta; (*av*) poltrona letto; (*rly*) vagone letto.

sleepiness ['sliːpinis] *n* sonnolenza.

sleepless ['sliːplis] *a* insonne.

sleeplessness ['sliːplisnis] *n* insonnia.

sleepwalker ['sliːp,wɔːkə] *n* sonnambulo.

sleepy ['sliːpi] *a* assonnato, sonnolento.

sleet [sliːt] *n* nevischio; *vi* cadere nevischio.

sleeve [sliːv] *n* manica.

sleigh [slei] *n* slitta.

slender ['slendə] *a* slanciato, snello, sottile; esiguo, piccolo, scarso.

slenderness ['slendənis] *n* snellezza; scarsità.

slice [slais] *n* fetta; parte, porzione; *vt* affettare, dividere.

slide [slaid] *n* scivolata; scivolo; (*phot*) diapositiva, lastra; vetrino per microscopio; *vt* far scorrere; *vi* scivolare, sdrucciolare; **sliding** scorrevole, mobile; **sliding scale** scala mobile.

slight [slait] *a* magro, esile, esiguo; insufficiente, scarso; superficiale; *n* affronto, mancanza di riguardo; *vt* mancare di rispetto a, non far caso di.

slim [slim] *a* esile, slanciato, sottile; *vi* dimagrire.

slime [slaim] *n* melma, sostanza viscida in genere.

slimness ['slimnis] *n* snellezza, esilità.

slimy ['slaimi] *a* melmoso, viscido.

sling [sliŋ] *n* fionda; striscia di tela per sostenere un braccio ammalato; **s. shot** fionda; *vt* scagliare con la fionda; sospendere.

slink [sliŋk] *vi* svignarsela, sgattaiolare.

slip [slip] *n* scivolone, sdrucciolone; errore, svista, passo falso; guinzaglio; federa; sottabito; *vt* far scivolare in; *vi* scivolare, sdrucciolare; andare furtivamente; sbagliare, scappare; **s. on** *vt* (*garment*) infilare.

slipper ['slipə] *n* pantofola, ciabatta.

slippery ['slipəri] *a* sdrucciolevole; viscido; (*fig*) incostante, poco scrupoloso.

slipshod ['slipʃɔd] *a* trasandato, trascurato.

slit [slit] *n* fessura, lunga incisione; *vt* fendere, tagliare a strisce.

sloe [slou] *n* prugnola.

slogan ['slougən] *n* grido di guerra; (*com*) motto pubblicitario, motto, "slogan".

sloop [sluːp] *n* (*naut*) scialuppa, corvetta.

slop [slɔp] *n* (*usu pl*) risciacquatura di piatti; liquidi sporchi.

slope [sloup] *n* pendenza, pendio; *vt* inclinare; *vi* essere in pendenza.

sloppy ['slɔpi] *a* bagnato; (*fig*) sciatto; sdolcinato.

slot [slɔt] *n* buco o foro oblungo; **s.-machine** distributore automatico.

sloth [slouθ] *n* pigrizia, ignavia.

slothful ['slouθful] *a* indolente, pigro.

slouch [slautʃ] *n* andatura dinoccolata; *vi* camminare in modo dinoccolato; **s. hat** cappello a cencio.

slough [slau] *n* palude, pantano; [slʌf] *vti* (*of snakes*) cambiare la pelle; (*fig*) liberarsi di.

sloven ['slʌvn] *n* persona trasandata.

slovenliness ['slʌvnlinis] *n* sudiceria, sciatteria.

slovenly ['slʌvnli] a disordinato, trasandato.

slow [slou] a lento; tardo; in ritardo; ad adagio; vti rallentare.

slowness ['slounis] n lentezza, indolenza.

slug [slʌg] n lumaca.

sluggard ['slʌgəd] n poltrone.

sluggish ['slʌgiʃ] a indolente, neghittoso, lento.

sluggishness ['slʌgiʃnis] n indolenza.

sluice [sluːs] n cateratta, chiusa; vt bagnare abbondantemente; vi scorrere violentemente.

slum [slʌm] n quartiere popolare e sudicio.

slumber ['slʌmbə] n sonno; vi dormire.

slump [slʌmp] n tracollo, brusco ribasso di prezzi, improvviso arresto nelle richieste di vendita; vi cadere, precipitare.

slur [sləː] n calunnia, insulto, macchia, pronuncia indistinta; (mus) legatura; vt pronunciare indistintamente; (mus) legare.

slush [slʌʃ] n fanghiglia, neve sciolta.

slut [slʌt] n donna trasandata, sudiciona.

sly [slai] a astuto, furbo, scaltro.

slyness ['slainis] n astuzia, furberia, scaltrezza.

smack [smæk] n schiaffo; schiocco; gusto, sapore di; peschereccio; vt schiaffeggiare; schioccare; vi aver sapore di, sapere di.

small [smɔːl] a piccolo; limitato; scarso; umile; meschino.

smallness ['smɔːlnis] n piccolezza.

smallpox ['smɔːlpɔks] n vaiolo.

smart [smɑːt] a acuto, intelligente, sveglio; elegante; n bruciore, dolore acuto; vi dolere, bruciare; soffrire.

smartness ['smɑːtnis] n vivacità, spirito; eleganza.

smash [smæʃ] n scontro, urto; rovina; fallimento; vt fracassare, frantumare; vi fracassarsi; fallire.

smattering ['smætəriŋ] n infarinatura.

smear [smiə] n macchia; vt imbrattare, macchiare.

smell [smel] n fiuto; odorato, olfatto; odore; vt fiutare, sentire l'odore di; (fig) sospettare; vi odorare, aver l'odore di.

smelt [smelt] vt fondere.

smelting ['smeltiŋ] n fusione.

smile [smail] n sorriso; vi sorridere.

smirk [sməːk] n sorriso affettato; vi sorridere affettatamente.

smith [smiθ] n fabbro.

smithy ['smiði] n fucina.

smock [smɔk] n grembiule da bambino; blusa da operaio.

smog [smɔg] n 'smog', caligine.

smoke [smouk] n fumo; vt fumare, affumicare; vi emettere fumo; **smoked herring** aringa affumicata.

smoker ['smoukə] n fumatore; (rly) carrozza per fumatori.

smoky ['smouki] a fumoso.

smolder ['smouldə] vi bruciare senza fiamma, covare sotto la cenere.

smooth [smuːð] a levigato, liscio; calmo; blando, mellifluo; vt levigare, lisciare, piallare, spianare; vi calmarsi, rasserenarsi.

smoothness ['smuːðnis] n levigatezza; scorrevolezza; calma.

smother ['smʌðə] n nuvola di polvere etc; vt asfissiare, soffocare; coprire; opprimere; spegnere.

smudge [smʌdʒ] n chiazza; sgorbio; vt chiazzare, macchiare.

smug [smʌg] a ipocrita, soddisfatto di sè.

smuggle ['smʌgl] vt far entrare di contrabbando; vi esercitare il contrabbando.

smuggler ['smʌglə] n contrabbandiere.

smut [smʌt] n macchia di fuliggine.

smutty ['smʌti] a fuligginoso, sporco; (fig) osceno.

snack [snæk] n spuntino.

snag [snæg] n nodo; sporgenza; (fig) intoppo, difficoltà.

snail [sneil] n chiocciola; lumaca.

snake [sneik] n serpe, serpente.

snap [snæp] n schiocco; rumore secco; (phot) istantanea; (fig) brio, vivacità; vt rompere con rumore secco; schioccare; fare l'istantanea a; vi fare un rumore secco, rompersi.

snappish ['snæpiʃ] a bisbetico, secco, stizzoso.

snapshot ['snæpʃɔt] n (phot) istantanea.

snare [snɛə] n insidia; laccio; trappola; vt prendere al laccio, in trappola.

snarl [snɑːl] n groviglio; ringhio; vt aggrovigliare; vi aggrovigliarsi, ringhiare.

snatch [snætʃ] vt afferrare, ghermire, strappare.

sneak [sniːk] n (fam) persona vile; (school sl) spia; vi strisciare.

sneaking ['sniːkiŋ] a basso, servile; nascosto.

sneer [sniə] n (sog)ghigno, sarcasmo; vi sogghignare, deridere.

sneeze [sniːz] n starnuto; vi starnutire; s. at disprezzare.

sniff [snif] n l'annusare, il fiutare; vti annusare, fiutare; aspirare.

snigger ['snigə] n risolino cinico; vi ridere sotto i baffi, ridacchiare.

snip [snip] n forbiciata, ritaglio; vti tagliuzzare, tagliare.

snipe [snaip] n beccaccino.

sniper ['snaipə] n chi caccia beccaccini; (mil) franco tiratore.

snippet ['snipit] n pezzettino, ritaglio.

snivel ['snivəl] vi piagnucolare; simulare contrizione, dolore.

snob [snɔb] *n* 'snob'.
snobbery ['snɔbəri] *n* snobismo.
snobbish ['snɔbiʃ] *a* snobistico, snob.
snooze [snuːz] *n* pisolino, sonnellino; *vi* fare un pisolino.
snore [snɔː] *n* il russare; *vi* russare.
snorkel ['snɔːkəl] *n* 'snorkel', presa d'aria per nuotatori e sommergibili.
snort [snɔːt] *n* sbuffo; *vi* sbuffare.
snout [snaut] *n* muso, grugno.
snow [snou] *n* neve; *vi* nevicare.
snowdrift ['snoudrift] *n* ammasso di neve, raffica di neve.
snowdrop ['snoudrɔp] *n* bucaneve.
snowflake ['snoufleik] *n* fiocco di neve.
snow-plow ['snouplau] *n* spazzaneve.
snowshoe ['snouʃuː] *n* racchetta per la neve.
snowstorm ['snoustɔːm] *n* tormenta.
snowy ['snoui] *n* nevoso, niveo, candido.
snub [snʌb] *a* (*nose*) camuso; *n* rimprovero, affronto; *vt* rimproverare, umiliare.
snuff [snʌf] *n* tabacco da fiuto; *vti* fiutare, annusare.
snuffers ['snʌfəz] *n pl* smoccolatoio.
snuffle ['snʌfl] *vi* respirare rumorosamente; parlare nel naso; parlare in tono piagnucoloso.
snug [snʌg] *a* comodo, riparato dalle intemperie.
snuggle ['snʌgl] *vi* rannicchiarsi.
so [sou] *ad* così, a questo modo, tanto, perciò, quindi; **s. as to** tanto . . . da; **s. that** *cj* così che, di modo che.
soak [souk] *vt* bagnare, immergere, inzuppare.
soap [soup] *n* sapone.
soapy ['soupi] *a* saponoso.
soar [sɔː] *vi* librarsi sulle ali, volare in alto.
sob [sɔb] *n* singhiozzo; *vi* singhiozzare.
sober ['soubə] *a* sobrio, moderato nel bere; equilibrato; sensato; serio.
soberness ['soubənis] **sobriety** [sou-'braiəti] *n* moderazione, temperanza.
sociable ['souʃəbl] *a* socievole.
social ['souʃəl] *a* sociale.
socialism ['souʃəlizəm] *n* socialismo.
socialist ['souʃəlist] *a n* socialista.
socialite ['souʃəlait] *n* membro dell'alta società.
society [sə'saiəti] *n* società, associazione, compagnia.
sociology [ˌsousi'ɔlədʒi] *n* sociologia.
sock [sɔk] *n* calzino, soletta; **s. suspender** giarrettiera.
socket ['sɔkit] *n* orbita, cavità; (*teeth*) alveolo.
sod [sɔd] *n* zolla erbosa.
soda ['soudə] *n* soda; **s.-water** (acqua di) seltz; **s. biscuit** galletta, 'cracker'.
sodden ['sɔdn] *a* impregnato d'acqua, fradicio; (*fig*) istupidito dal bere.

sodium ['soudiəm] *n* sodio.
sofa ['soufə] *n* sofa.
Sofia ['soufiə] *n* Sofia.
soft [sɔft] *a* morbido, molle, soffice; cedevole; delicato; mite, conciliante.
soften ['sɔfn] *vti* ammollir(si), mitigar(si), intenerir(si).
softly ['sɔftli] *ad* dolcemente; sommessamente, adagio.
softness ['sɔftnis] *n* morbidezza; delicatezza; mitezza.
soggy ['sɔgi] *a* bagnato; (*bread*) mal cotto.
soil [sɔil] *n* suolo, terra, terreno; macchia; sporcizia; *vt* insozzare, sporcare; *vi* sporcarsi.
sojourn ['sɔdʒəːn] *n* soggiorno; *vi* soggiornare.
solace ['sɔləs] *n* sollievo, consolazione; *vt* consolare, sollevare.
solar ['soulə] *a* solare.
solder ['sɔldə] *n* saldatura; *vt* saldare.
soldier ['souldʒə] *n* soldato, militare.
soldierly ['souldʒəli] *a* marziale, militare.
soldiery ['souldʒəri] *n* soldati *pl*, soldatesca.
sole [soul] *a* solo, unico; *n* pianta del piede; suola; (*fish*) sogliola; *vt* risolare.
solecism ['sɔlisizəm] *n* solecismo.
solemn ['sɔləm] *a* solenne.
solemnity [sə'lemniti] *n* solennità; rito solenne.
solemnize ['sɔləmnaiz] *vt* solennizzare.
solicit [sə'lisit] *vt* chiedere con insistenza.
solicitor [sə'lisitə] *n* avvocato, procuratore legale.
solicitous [sə'lisitəs] *a* premuroso, sollecito; desideroso.
solicitude [sə'lisitjuːd] *n* sollecitudine, premura.
solid ['sɔlid] *a* solido; compatto; massiccio; intero; pieno; posato, serio; (*com*) solvibile; *n* corpo solido.
solidarity [ˌsɔli'dæriti] *n* solidarietà.
solidify [sə'lidifai] *vti* solidificar(si).
solidity [sə'liditi] *n* solidità; (*com*) solvenza.
soliloquy [sə'liləkwi] *n* soliloquio.
solitary ['sɔlitəri] *a* solo, solitario.
solitude ['sɔlitjuːd] *n* solitudine.
solo ['soulou] *pl* **solos** *n* (*mus*) assolo; (*av*) volo solitario.
solstice ['sɔlstis] *n* solstizio.
soluble ['sɔljubl] *a* solubile.
solution [sə'ljuːʃən] *n* soluzione, risoluzione.
solve [sɔlv] *vt* risolvere, sciogliere, spiegare.
solvent ['sɔlvənt] *a n* solvente; *a* (*com*) solvibile.
Somali [sou'mɑːli] *n* somalo.
Somaliland [sou'mɑːlilænd] *n* Somalia.
somber ['sɔmbə] *a* fosco, tenebroso; triste.

some [sʌm] a pron qualche, alcuni, del; ne; un po' di; ad all'incirca, circa.

somebody ['sʌmbədi] pron qualcuno.

somehow ['sʌmhau] ad in qualche modo, in un modo o nell'altro.

someone ['sʌmwʌn] pron qualcuno.

somersault ['sʌməsɔːlt] n capriola, salto mortale.

something ['sʌmθiŋ] pron qual(che) cosa; ad un po'.

sometime ['sʌmtaim] a di un tempo, antico; ad un tempo, un giorno o l'altro; s. soon uno di questi giorni.

sometimes ['sʌmtaimz] ad talvolta.

somewhat ['sʌmwɔt] ad piuttosto, un po'.

somewhere ['sʌmwɛə] ad in qualche parte.

somnambulism [sɔm'næmbjulizəm] n sonnambulismo.

somnambulist [sɔm'næmbjulist] n sonnambulo.

somniferous [sɔm'nifərəs] a soporifero, sonnifero.

somnolent ['sɔmnələnt] a sonnolento.

son [sʌn] n figlio; s.-in-law genero.

song [sɔŋ] n canto, canzone; romanza.

songster ['sɔŋstə] n uccello canterino.

sonnet ['sɔnit] n sonetto.

sonorous ['sɔnərəs] a sonoro.

soon [suːn] ad fra poco, presto, tosto; sooner piuttosto.

soot [sut] n fuliggine.

soothe [suːð] vt calmare, placare; blandire.

soothing ['suːðiŋ] a calmante, lenitivo.

soothsayer ['suːθ͵seiə] n indovino.

sooty ['suti] a fuligginoso, nero.

sop [sɔp] n pezzo di pane o altro inzuppato; (fig) dono propiziatorio.

sophism ['sɔfizəm] n sofisma.

sophist ['sɔfist] n sofista.

sophisticate [sə'fistikeit] vti sofisticare.

sophisticated [sə'fistikeitid] a sofisticato, raffinato.

sophistry ['sɔfistri] n sofisticheria, cavilli pl.

soporific [͵sɔpə'rifik] a soporifero; n sonnifero, narcotico.

soprano [sə'prɑːnou] pl sopranos n soprano.

sorcerer ['sɔːsərə] n mago, stregone.

sorceress ['sɔːsəris] n strega, fattucchiera.

sorcery ['sɔːsəri] n magia, stregoneria.

sordid ['sɔːdid] a sordido, spilorcio; ignobile.

sordidness ['sɔːdidnis] n sordidezza, grettezza.

sore [sɔː] a dolorante; infiammato; addolorato, irritato; grave; n piaga, ulcera.

sorely ['sɔːli] ad gravemente, fortemente.

soreness ['sɔːnis] n dolore, irritazione.

sorrel ['sɔrəl] n acetosa; cavallo sauro; a di color sauro.

sorrow ['sɔrou] n afflizione, dolore; sventura; vi addolorarsi, rattristarsi.

sorrowful ['sɔrəful] a addolorato, doloroso.

sorry ['sɔri] a dispiacente, dolente; meschino, misero.

sort [sɔːt] n sorta, genere, specie, tipo; vt selezionare, classificare, smistare.

sortie ['sɔːtiː] n (mil) sortita.

so-so ['sousou] a discreto; ad così così.

sot [sɔt] n ubriacone inveterato.

sough [sau] vi gemere; (wind) sussurrare.

soul [soul] n anima, spirito; (fig) incarnazione.

soulful ['soulful] a pieno di sentimento.

sound [saund] n rumore, suono; sonda; (geogr) stretto; a giusto, logico; profondo; sano, solido, ben fondato; ad profondamente; vt suonare, far risonare; sondare, scandagliare; vi sembrare; suonare, risonare.

sounding ['saundiŋ] n sonorità; (med) auscultazione; (naut) scandaglio.

soundness ['saundnis] n sanità, solidità.

soup [suːp] n minestra, brodo, zuppa.

sour ['sauə] a acido, agro, aspro, amaro; (of soil) sterile; vt fare inacidire; (fig) esacerbare; vi inacidire, inasprirsi.

source [sɔːs] n fonte, origine, sorgente.

sourish ['sauəriʃ] a acidulo.

sourness ['sauənis] n acidità, asprezza; (fig) acrimonia.

souse [saus] n salamoia; vt marinare.

south [sauθ] n mezzogiorno, sud; a del sud, meridionale; ad a sud.

South Africa [͵sauθ'æfrikə] n Sud Africa.

southerly ['sʌðəli] a del sud, meridionale; ad a sud.

southern ['sʌðən] a del sud.

southerner ['sʌðənə] n meridionale.

southward ['sauθwəd] a verso sud; **southwards** ad verso sud.

south-west ['sauθ'west] a di sudovest; n sud-ovest; ad verso sudovest.

souvenir [͵suːvə'niə] n ricordo.

sovereign ['sɔvrin] a sovrano, supremo; n sovrano; sterlina d'oro.

sovereignty ['sɔvrənti] n sovranità.

sow [sou] vt seminare, spargere.

sow [sau] n scrofa.

spa [spɑː] n stazione termale.

space [speis] n spazio, estensione, luogo; periodo di tempo; a spaziale; vt disporre ad intervalli.

space-craft ['speiskrɑːft] **space-ship** ['speisʃip] n astronave.

spacious ['speiʃəs] a ampio, spazioso.
spaciousness ['speiʃəsnis] n ampiezza, spaziosità.
spade [speid] n badile, vanga; (cards) picche.
Spain [spein] n Spagna.
span [spæn] n spanna, palmo; apertura; breve durata, periodo; vt abbracciare, misurare, estendersi attraverso.
spangle ['spæŋgl] n lustrino.
Spaniard ['spænjəd] n spagnolo.
spaniel ['spænjəl] n 'spaniel', cane spagnolo; (fig) persona servile.
Spanish ['spæniʃ] a spagnolo.
spank [spæŋk] vt sculacciare.
spanner ['spænə] n (mech) chiave.
spar [spɑː] n (naut) alberatura; pugilato; vi allenarsi nel pugilato; avere un battibecco.
spare [spɛə] a magro; parco, frugale; disponibile, libero; di ricambio, di riserva; n pezzo di ricambio; vt fare a meno di; risparmiare, mettere da parte; vi essere risparmiatore.
sparing ['spɛəriŋ] a economo, parco.
sparingly ['spɛəriŋli] ad in moderazione; limitatamente.
spark [spɑːk] n favilla, scintilla, barlume; (fig) bellimbusto; vi emettere scintille; **spark plug** (aut) candela.
sparkle ['spɑːkl] n bagliore, scintillio, vivacità; vi brillare, scintillare.
sparkling ['spɑːkliŋ] a scintillante, brillante; (wine) spumante.
sparrow ['spærou] n passero.
sparse [spɑːs] a rado, sparso, che si trova ad intervalli irregolari.
sparsely ['spɑːsli] ad scarsamente, poco; qui e là.
spasm ['spæzəm] n contrazione, spasimo.
spasmodic [spæs'mɔdik] a spasmodico.
spastic ['spæstik] a spastico.
spat [spæt] n ghetta.
spate [speit] n piena, straripamento.
spatter ['spætə] vti impillaccherare, spruzzare.
spawn [spɔːn] n (of fish etc) uova pl; micelio; vt generare, produrre; vi deporre le uova.
speak [spiːk] vi parlare; vt pronunziare.
speaker ['spiːkə] n parlatore, oratore; **S. of the House** Presidente della Camera; **loud-s.** alto parlante.
spear [spiə] n arpione, lancia; vt trafiggere con arpione; o lancia.
special ['speʃəl] a speciale, particolare; n treno speciale; edizione straordinaria di giornale.
specialist ['speʃəlist] n specialista.
speciality [,speʃi'æliti] n specialità.
specialize ['speʃəlaiz] vti specializzar(si).
species ['spiːʃiz] pl **species** n specie, genere, sorta.

specific [spi'sifik] a n specifico; a caratteristico.
specification [,spesifi'keiʃən] n specificazione.
specify ['spesifai] vt specificare.
specimen ['spesimin] n campione, esemplare, saggio.
specious ['spiːʃəs] a specioso.
speck [spek] n macchiolina; punto; vt chiazzare, macchiare.
speckle ['spekl] n macchiolina; vt segnare con macchioline, variegare.
spectacle ['spektəkl] n spettacolo, vista; **spectacles** pl occhiali pl.
spectacular [spek'tækjulə] a spettacolare, spettacoloso.
spectator [spek'teitə] n spettatore.
specter ['spektə] n fantasma, spettro.
spectral ['spektrəl] a spettrale.
speculate ['spekjuleit] vi speculare.
speculation [,spekju'leiʃən] n speculazione, congettura, meditazione.
speculator ['spekjuleitə] n speculatore.
speech [spiːtʃ] n discorso, orazione; favella, linguaggio.
speechless ['spiːtʃlis] a muto, senza parole; sbalordito.
speed [spiːd] n velocità, rapidità, sveltezza; vti affrettar(si); **to s. up** accelerare.
speedometer [spi'dɔmitə] n (aut) tachimetro.
speedway ['spiːdwei] n pista, circuito; autostrada.
speedy ['spiːdi] a pronto, rapido, veloce.
spell [spel] n incantesimo, magia, fascino; breve periodo; vti compitare; significare.
spellbound ['spelbaund] a affascinato, incantato.
spelling ['speliŋ] n ortografia.
spend [spend] vt spendere; impiegare, passare, trascorrere; vi consumarsi; spendere.
spendthrift ['spendθrift] a n prodigo.
sperm [spəːm] n sperma.
spew [spjuː] vti vomitare.
sphere [sfiə] n sfera; ambiente.
spherical ['sferikəl] a sferico.
sphinx [sfiŋks] n sfinge.
spice [spais] n spezie pl; aroma, sapore.
spick-and-span ['spikən'spæn] a lucido come uno specchio, lindo e ordinato.
spicy ['spaisi] a aromatico, piccante.
spider ['spaidə] n ragno.
spigot ['spigət] n zipolo; rubinetto.
spike [spaik] n aculeo, chiodo, punta; spiga.
spiky ['spaiki] a munito di aculei, irto; (fig) di carattere difficile, spinoso.
spill [spil] n atto del versare; (fam) caduta, rovesciamento, (pipe light) legnetto; vt rovesciare, versare, spargere; vi cadere, rovesciarsi.

spin [spin] n giro, giretto; rotazione; vt filare, far girare, raccontare (una storia); vi girare, roteare.
spinach ['spinidʒ] n spinaci $pl.$
spindle ['spindl] n fuso; perno; a **s.-shanked** dalle gambe lunghe e sottili.
spin-drier ['spin'draiə] n asciugatrice automatica.
spine [spain] n spina (dorsale).
spineless ['spainlis] a senza spina dorsale; molle, senza carattere.
spinet ['spinit] n (mus) spinetta.
spinning ['spiniŋ] n filatura; **s. wheel** filatoio.
spinster ['spinstə] n zitella.
spiral ['spaiərəl] a spirale.
spire ['spaiə] n spira, spirale; guglia.
spirit ['spirit] n spirito.
spirited ['spiritəd] a brioso, vivace, ardente.
spiritless ['spiritlis] a avvilito, senz'energia.
spiritual ['spiritjuəl] a spirituale; n canto religioso dei negri degli S.U.
spiritualism ['spiritjuəlizəm] n spiritismo.
spiritualist ['spiritjuəlist] n spiritualista; spiritista.
spirt [spəːt] n getto, zampillo improvviso.
spit [spit] n spiedo; lingua di terra che avanza nel mare; sputo; padella, vanga; vt infilzare nello spiedo; sputare; pronunciare con violenza; vi sputare; piovigginare; mandar faville.
spite [spait] n dispetto, rancore; vt contrariare, vessare; **in s. of** $prep$ a dispetto di, malgrado.
spiteful ['spaitful] a dispettoso, malevolo.
spitefully ['spaitfuli] ad per dispetto; con astio.
spitefulness ['spaitfulnis] n dispetto, malevolenza.
spittle ['spitl] n saliva, sputo.
spittoon [spi'tuːn] n sputacchiera.
splash [splæʃ] n spruzzo, tonfo; pillacchera; vt impillaccherare; spruzzare; vi sollevare spruzzi; cadere nell'acqua con un tonfo; **to make a s.** fare un effetone, fare colpo, far furore.
splay [splei] a largo e piatto; voltato verso l'esterno; obliquo; vti ($arch$) svasare; essere in posizione obliqua; slogare.
spleen [spliːn] n milza; bile, ipocondria.
splendid ['splendid] a splendido.
splendor ['splendə] n splendore.
splice [splais] n unione, intrecciatura; ($naut$) impiombatura; vt congiungere, unire; impiombare.
splint [splint] n scheggia; (med) stecca.
splinter ['splintə] n scheggia.
split [split] a spaccata; n fenditura,

spaccatura; scisma; vti fender(si), spaccar(si), scheggiar(si).
splutter ['splʌtə] vti barbugliare; ($in speech$) sputacchiare; ($of pen$) spruzzare.
spoil [spɔil] n usu pl bottino; vti deteriorar(si), guastar(si), viziare.
spoke [spouk] n raggio.
spokesman ['spouksmən] n portavoce.
spoliation [,spouli'eiʃən] n spoliazione.
sponge [spʌndʒ] n spugna; spugnatura; **s. cake** biscotto spugnoso; **sponger** (fig) parassita, scroccone; vt cancellare, lavare con la spugna; vi vivere a scrocco.
spongy ['spʌndʒi] a spugnoso, poroso.
sponsor ['spɔnsə] n garante, madrina f, padrino m.
spontaneity [,spɔntə'niːiti] n spontaneità.
spontaneous [spɔn'teiniəs] a spontaneo.
spool [spuːl] n bobina, rocchetto.
spoon [spuːn] n cucchiaio.
spoonful ['spuːnful] n cucchiaiata.
sporadic [spə'rædik] a sporadico.
spore [spɔː] n spora.
sport [spɔːt] n gioco, divertimento; sport; (fig) persona di spirito; vi divertirsi, giocare; vt ostentare; **sports requisites** (or **sports goods**) articoli sportivi.
sporting ['spɔːtiŋ] a sportivo; **s. goods** articoli sportivi.
sportive ['spɔːtiv] a gioviale, sportivo.
sportsman ['spɔːtsmən] n sportivo; giocatore d'azzardo.
spot [spɔt] n luogo, posto, punto; macchia, (fam) piccola quantità; vti macchiar(si); vt (fam) individuare, scoprire.
spotless ['spɔtlis] a immacolato, senza macchia.
spotlight ['spɔtlait] n luce della ribalta, riflettore.
spouse [spauz] n coniuge, marito m, moglie f.
spout [spaut] n becco; ($of teapot etc$) beccuccio; ($of liquid$) getto; tubo di scarico; vi gettare, spruzzare; vti scaricare, scaturire, zampillare; (fig) declamare.
sprain [sprein] n storta; vt storcere.
sprat [spræt] n spratto; (fam) bimbetto.
sprawl [sprɔːl] vi sdraiarsi, stare sdraiato, in modo scomposto.
spray [sprei] n schiuma, spruzzo; rametto, ramoscello; vt spruzzare.
spread [spred] n distesa, estensione; (fam) banchetto; vt diffondere, propagare, spargere, spiegare, stendere; vi spargersi, spiegarsi, stendersi.
spree [spriː] n (fam) baldoria.
sprig [sprig] n rametto; (fig) giovincello.

sprightliness ['spraitlinis] n spirito, vivacità.

sprightly ['spraitli] a spiritoso, vivace.

spring [spriŋ] n balzo, salto; molla; fonte, sorgente; (*season*) primavera; vt far scattare; vi balzare; derivare, provenire; sorgere.

springtime ['spriŋtaim] n tempo di primavera.

springy ['spriŋi] a elastico.

sprinkle ['spriŋkl] n aspersione, spruzzatina; vt aspergere, spruzzare.

sprinkling ['spriŋkliŋ] n spruzzamento; spruzzatina; aspersione; (*fig*) pizzico, infarinatura.

sprint [sprint] n (*sport*) scatto finale, 'sprint'; vi correre alla massima velocità.

sprite [sprait] n folletto, spiritello.

sprout [spraut] n germoglio; (*vegetable*) cavolino di Bruxelles; vi germogliare, spuntare.

spruce [spruːs] a azzimato, attillato; n abete rosso.

spry [sprai] a arzillo, vivace.

spur [spəː] n sprone, sperone; (*fig*) incitamento; vt incitare, spronare, stimolare.

spurious ['spjuəriəs] a falso, spurio.

spuriousness ['spjuəriəsnis] n contraffazione, falsità.

spurn [spəːn] vt respingere a calci; (*fig*) disprezzare, rifiutare con sdegno.

spurt [spəːt] n breve sforzo violento; vti fare un breve sforzo violento, scattare; schizzare.

sputter ['spʌtə] vi parlare incoerentemente, barbugliare, sputacchiare.

spy [spai] n spia; vti spiare.

squab [skwɔb] n piccioncino; cuscinetto.

squabble ['skwɔbl] n bisticcio; vi bisticciar(si).

squad [skwɔd] n squadra.

squadron ['skwɔdrən] n (*mil*) squadra, squadrone; (*naut, av*) squadriglia.

squalid ['skwɔlid] a squallido, sordido.

squall [skwɔːl] n raffica, turbine; (*fig*) litigio.

squalor ['skwɔlə] n squallore, miseria.

squander ['skwɔndə] vt scialacquare.

square [skwɛə] a quadro, quadrato; robusto; giusto, onesto; preciso; sostanzioso; n quadrato; piazza; (*instrument*) squadra; ad angolo retto, direttamente; vt quadrare; elevare al quadrato; (*fam*) corrompere; vi adattarsi, conformarsi.

squash [skwɔʃ] n spremuta; cosa schiacciata; (*fam*) ressa; melopopone; **Italian s.** zucchino; vti schiacciar(si), spremere; vt (*fam*) stroncare, soffocare.

squat [skwɔt] a tarchiato, tozzo; rannicchiato; vi accosciarsi, rannicchiarsi.

squawk [skwɔːk] n grido rauco; vti

emettere un grido rauco; lamentarsi.

squeak [skwiːk] n grido acuto, squittio, stridore; vi squittire, stridere, cigolare; parlare con voce stridula.

squeaky ['skwiːki] a (*voice*) acuto; che squittisce; cigolante, stridente.

squeal [skwiːl] n strillo, squittio; vi strillare.

squeamish ['skwiːmiʃ] a delicato di stomaco; schizzinoso.

squeamishness ['skwiːmiʃnis] n delicatezza di stomaco; schizzinosità.

squeeze [skwiːz] n compressione, spremitura, stretta; ressa; vti spremere, spremersi, stringere, stringersi; estorcere.

squelch [skweltʃ] vti fare il rumore del piede tirato su dal fango molle; diguazzare; (*fig*) soffocare, sopprimere.

squib [skwib] n petardo, razzo; pasquinata, satira.

squid [skwid] n seppia.

squint [skwint] n strabismo; sguardo furtivo; vi guardare obliquamente; essere strabico; aver tendenza verso.

squire ['skwaiə] n gentiluomo di campagna; (*hist*) scudiero.

squirm [skwəːm] vi contorcersi; provare imbarazzo, o umiliazione.

squirrel ['skwirəl] n scoiattolo.

squirt [skwəːt] n schizzetto; siringa; vti schizzare.

stab [stæb] n pugnalata; vt pugnalare.

stability [stə'biliti] n stabilità.

stabilize ['steibilaiz] vt stabilizzare.

stable ['steibl] a fermo, stabile; n scuderia, stalla.

stack [stæk] n ammasso, mucchio, catasta; pagliaio, gruppo di camini sul tetto; (*fam*) grande quantità; vt ammucchiare, accatastare.

stadium ['steidiəm] pl **stadia** n stadio, campo sportivo.

staff [staːf] n appoggio, sostegno; bastone; personale; corpo insegnante, (*mil*) stato maggiore; vt fornire di personale.

stag [stæg] n cervo, cerbiatto; **s. beetle** cervo volante.

stage [steidʒ] n palcoscenico, teatro; tappa; fase; periodo; scena; vt (*theat*) mettere in scena.

stagger ['stægə] n barcollamento, passo incerto; vt far barcollare; (*fig*) sbalordire; vi barcollare, vacillare.

stagnant ['stægnənt] a stagnante.

stagnate ['stægneit] vi stagnare, subire una stasi ristagnare.

stagnation [stæg'neiʃən] n ristagno; stasi.

staid [steid] a posato, serio.

stain [stein] n macchia; onta; colore, tinta; vt macchiare; dipingere.

stainless ['steinlis] a senza macchia; **s. steel** acciaio inossidabile.

stair [stɛə] n gradino, scalino; pl scala.

staircase ['stɛəkeis] n scala, tromba delle scale.

stake [steik] n palo; rogo; posta, premio; vt sostenere, delimitare con pali; rischiare; scommettere.

stale [steil] a raffermo, stantio; spossato, trito; vti rendere, diventare stantio.

stalemate ['steil'meit] n (chess) stallo; (fig) punto morto; vt fare stallo a; (fig) portare a un punto morto.

stalk [stɔːk] n gambo, stelo; andatura maestosa; inseguimento di selvaggina; vi camminare maestosamente; inseguire selvaggina.

stall [stɔːl] n stalla; stallo; bancherella; chiosco, edicola; scanno; vr fermarsi; vi non andare innanzi, posporre.

stallion ['stæljən] n stallone.

stalwart ['stɔlwət] a robusto, vigoroso.

stammer ['stæmə] n balbettamento, balbuzie; vi balbettare, tartagliare.

stamp [stæmp] n francobollo; bollo, marchio, timbro; impronta; vt affrancare; bollare, timbrare; imprimere; vi pestare i piedi.

stampede [stæm'piːd] n fuga precipitosa e tumultante.

stanch [staːntʃ] v **staunch.**

stanchion ['staːnʃən] n puntello; sbarra.

stand [stænd] n arresto, pausa; posizione; posteggio; posto; banco, edicola; palco, tribuna; leggio, piedistallo; (exhibition) "stand"; vt appoggiare, mettere in piedi; affrontare, resistere a, sopportare; vi stare ritto, stare in piedi; fermarsi.

standard ['stændəd] n bandiera, stendardo; modello, livello; a classico, normale.

standardize ['stændədaiz] vt standardizzare.

standing ['stændiŋ] n posizione, riputazione.

standpoint ['stændpɔint] n punto di vista.

standstill ['stændstil] n punto morto, ristagno.

stanza ['stænzə] n (poet) stanza, strofa.

staple ['steipl] a principale; n (com) prodotto principale.

star [staː] n stella, astro; asterisco; (theat etc) divo, -va; vt segnare con l'asterisco; ornare di stelle; vi essere attore di cartello.

starboard ['staːbəd] n (naut) tribordo.

starch [staːtʃ] n amido; (fig) formalismo; vt inamidare.

stare [stɛə] n sguardo fisso; vi fissare, guardare fisso.

starfish ['staːfiʃ] n stella di mare.

stark [staːk] a rigido; completo; ad del tutto, completamente.

starling ['staːliŋ] n stornello.

starlit ['staːlit] a stellato.

starry ['staːri] a stellato; scintillante.

start [staːt] n partenza, avvio, inizio; sobbalzo, sussulto; vantaggio; vt mettere in moto, iniziare; vi partire; sobbalzare, trasalire.

starter ['staːtə] n iniziatore, fondatore, (aut) avviamento.

startle ['staːtl] vt far trasalire.

startling ['staːtliŋ] a impressionante, sensazionale.

starvation [staːˈveiʃən] n fame, inedia.

starve [staːv] vti (far) morire di fame; vi agognare.

state [steit] n stato, nazione; condizioni pl; grado, qualità, dignità; pompa; vt affermare, asserire, formulare, specificare, stabilire.

stateliness ['steitlinis] n imponenza, maestosità.

stately ['steitli] a imponente, maestoso, solenne.

statement ['steitmənt] n affermazione, dichiarazione; deposizione testimoniale; rendiconto.

statesman ['steitsmən] pl -men n statista, uomo di stato; **statesmanship** arte di governo.

static ['stætik] a statico.

station ['steiʃən] n stazione; grado; posto, posizione sociale; vt assegnare un posto a, collocare.

stationary ['steiʃnəri] a stazionario, fisso.

stationer ['steiʃnə] n cartolaio.

stationery ['steiʃnəri] n cartoleria.

statistic [stəˈtistik] a statistico; n pl statistica.

statuary ['stætjuəri] a statuario; n scultura, statuaria.

statue ['stætjuː] n statua.

statuesque [ˌstætjuˈesk] a statuario.

stature ['stætʃə] n statura.

status ['steitəs] n stato, condizione sociale, situazione; s. **symbol** simbolo di posizione sociale.

statute ['stætjuːt] n statuto, legge.

statutory ['stætjutəri] a statutario, fissato dalla legge.

staunch [stɔːntʃ] a fedele, leale; solido; vt (med) tamponare.

stave [steiv] n doga; strofa, stanza; (mus) rigo; vt praticare un foro in; to s. **off** allontanare, stornare.

stay [stei] n permanenza, soggiorno; sostegno; (leg) sospensione; vt trattenere, arrestare, ritardare; vi rimanere, stare, soggiornare; n pl busto, corsetto.

stead [sted] n luogo, vece.

steadfast ['stedfəst] a costante, risoluto.

steadiness ['stedinis] n costanza, fermezza.

steady ['stedi] a costante, fermo, posato, stabile.

steak [steik] n fetta di carne o pesce.

steal [stiːl] vt rubare, sottrarre; vi rubare; muoversi furtivamente.

stealth [stelθ] n movimento, o atto, furtivo.

stealthily ['stelθili] ad furtivamente, di nascosto.

stealthy [ˈstelθi] a clandestino, furtivo.

steam [stiːm] n vapore; vt esporre a vapore; cuocere a vapore; vi emettere vapore, fumare; **s. roller** rullo compressore.

steamboat ['stiːmbout] n battello a vapore.

steamer ['stiːmə] n piroscafo, vapore.

steamship ['stiːmʃip] n piroscafo, vapore.

steed [stiːd] n destriero, corsiero.

steel [stiːl] n acciaio; vt ricoprire, rivestire di acciaio; (fig) fortificare; indurire; **steelwork** lavoro in acciaio, pl acciaierie.

steely ['stiːli] a di acciaio; (fig) duro, inflessibile, di ferro.

steep [stiːp] a erto, ripido, scosceso; (fam) esorbitante; n erta, precipizio.

steeple ['stiːpl] n campanile.

steeplechase ['stiːpltʃeis] n corsa ad ostacoli.

steepness ['stiːpnis] n ripidezza.

steer [stiə] vti dirigere, guidare, governare, dirigersi.

steer [stiə] n (zool) giovenco.

steerage ['stiəridʒ] n governo del timone; parte della nave riservata ai passeggeri di 3ª classe.

steersman ['stiəzmən] pl -men n timoniere.

stem [stem] n gambo; stelo; ramo, rampollo, stirpe; (gram) tema, radicale; vt arginare, arrestare, contenere.

stench [stentʃ] n fetore, tanfo.

stencil ['stensl] n stampino, decorazione fatta con stampino; **s. copy** copia a ciclostile.

stenographer [steˈnɔgrəfə] n stenografo m, stenografa f.

stenography [steˈnɔgrəfi] n stenografia.

step [step] n passo; gradino, scalino; piolo, provvedimento; pl scalinata; scala a mano; vt misurare a passi; vi andare, venire, camminare.

stepbrother ['step,brʌðə] n fratellastro; **stepdaughter** n figliastra; **stepfather** n patrigno; **stepmother** n matrigna; **stepsister** n sorellastra; **stepson** n figliastro.

Stephen ['stiːvn] nm pr Stefano.

stepping-stone ['stepiŋstoun] n pietra per guadare; (fig) trampolino.

stereophonic [ˌsteriəˈfɔnik] a stereofonico.

stereoscope ['stiəriəskoup] n stereoscopio.

stereoscopic [ˌsteriəˈskɔpik] a stereoscopico.

stereotype ['stiəriətaip] n stereotipo.

sterile ['sterail] a sterile.

sterility [steˈriliti] n sterilità.

sterling ['stəːliŋ] a genuino, puro, di

buona lega; **pound s.** (lira) sterlina.

stern [stəːn] a austero, rigido, severo; n (naut) poppa; deretano.

sternness ['stəːnnis] n austerità, severità.

stertorous ['stəːtərəs] a affannoso.

stew [stjuː] n ragù, stufato; vivaio di pesci; vti cuocere a fuoco lento.

steward ['stjuəd] n amministratore; dispensiere; cameriere di bordo; **stewardess** cameriera di bordo.

stick [stik] n bacchetta; bastone; ramo, stecco; vt ficcare, conficcare; appiccicare, incollare; vi aderire, rimanere attaccato; **s.-in-the-mud** persona priva di iniziativa.

sticker ['stikə] n attacchino; scocciatore; etichetta gommata.

stickler ['stiklə] n sostenitore accanito; pignolo.

sticky ['stiki] a appiccicoso, viscido; (fig) poco accomodante.

stiff [stif] a duro, inflessibile, rigido; intorpidito; (price) caro; difficile; impacciato.

stiffen ['stifn] vt indurire, irrigidire; inamidare; indolenzire; vi irrigidirsi, rassodarsi.

stiffness ['stifnis] n rigidezza; intorpidimento, indolenzimento; difficoltà.

stifle ['staifl] vti soffocare; vt estinguere.

stifling ['staifliŋ] s soffocante.

stigma ['stigmə] n marchio, segno (d'infamia).

stigmatize ['stigmətaiz] vt stigmatizzare.

stiletto [stiˈletou] pl -os, -oes n stiletto; **s. heels** tacchi a spillo.

still [stil] a calmo; fermo, immobile; tranquillo, silenzioso; ad ancora, tuttora, tuttavia; n silenzio, quiete; alambicco; vt calmare, far tacere.

stillness ['stilnis] n calma, quiete, tranquillità.

stilt [stilt] n trampolo.

stilted ['stiltid] a ricercato, affettato, privo di naturalezza.

stimulant ['stimjulənt] a n stimolante.

stimulate ['stimjuleit] vt stimolare.

stimulating ['stimjuleitiŋ] a stimolante, eccitante.

stimulation [ˌstimjuˈleiʃən] n stimolo.

stimulus ['stimjuləs] n stimolo; pungolo.

sting [stiŋ] n pungiglione; puntura; (insect) pungolo; (fig) frecciata, sarcasmo; vt pungere; (fig) irritare, far arrabbiare.

stinginess ['stindʒinis] n spilorceria, tirchieria.

stingy ['stindʒi] a spilorcio, tirchio.

stink [stiŋk] n fetore, puzzo; vi puzzare.

stint [stint] n limite, restrizione; compito; vt lesinare, limitare, tenere a stecchetto.

stipend ['staipend] n (eccl) stipendio.
stipulate ['stipjuleit] vti pattuire, stipolare.
stipulation [.stipju'leiʃən] n patto, stipolazione.
stir [stəː] n il rimescolare, l'attizzare; trambusto, movimento; vt agitare, muovere, rimescolare; vi muoversi; **to s. up** stimolare, eccitare.
stirrup ['stirəp] n staffa.
stitch [stitʃ] n punto (di cucitura); maglia; vt cucire.
stoat [stout] n ermellino.
stock [stɔk] n riserva, scorta; bestiame; famiglia, stirpe; ceppo, tronco; (rifle) calcio; (com) azioni pl; **s. market** mercato finanziario; **common s.** azioni ordinarie; **stocks and shares** valori di borsa, titoli; vt tenere in magazzino; provvedere, rifornire.
stockbroker ['stɔk.broukə] a agente di cambio.
stockfish ['stɔkfiʃ] n stoccafisso.
Stockholm ['stɔkhoum] n Stoccolma.
stocking ['stɔkiŋ] n calza (lunga).
stockist ['stɔkist] n (com) grossista; fornitore.
stocky ['stɔki] a tarchiato.
stodgy ['stɔdʒi] a indigesto, pesante.
stoic ['stouik] a n stoico; **stoically** stoicamente.
stoke [stouk] vt attizzare (il fuoco), alimentare (la caldaia); vi fare il fuochista.
stoker ['stoukə] n fuochista.
stole [stoul] n stola.
stolid ['stɔlid] a stolido, imperturbabile.
stolidity [stɔ'liditi] n stolidezza, stolidità.
stomach ['stʌmək] n stomaco; (fig) coraggio; vt ingoiare, subire, tollerare.
stone [stoun] n pietra, sasso; (fruit) nocciolo; misura di peso (≡ 14 libbre, kg 6,45); (med) calcolo; vt lapidare; togliere il nocciolo a.
stony ['stouni] a pietroso; (fig) duro, freddo.
stool [stuːl] n sgabello; escremento, feci pl.
stoop [stuːp] n curvatura, inclinazione del corpo in avanti; vi curvarsi, chinarsi; umiliarsi; essere curvo.
stop [stɔp] n arresto, fermata; punto d'interpunzione; vt arrestare, sospendere; ostruire; (ot)turare; vi fermarsi, cessare.
stoppage ['stɔpidʒ] n arresto, cessazione; ostruzione; (med) occlusione.
stopper ['stɔpə] n tampone, tappo, turacciolo.
storage ['stɔːridʒ] n immagazzinamento, deposito, (com) magazzinaggio.
store [stɔː] n grande magazzino, emporio, negozio; provvista, pl provvigioni, abbondanza; vt approvvigionare, immagazzinare;

storehouse magazzino deposito; **s. clerk** commesso.
stork [stɔːk] n cicogna.
storm [stɔːm] n burrasca, tempesta, temporale; scoppio; vi essere violento, infuriare; vt prendere d'assalto.
stormily ['stɔːmili] ad violentemente.
stormy ['stɔːmi] a tempestoso; (fig) violento.
story ['stɔːri] n storia, novella, racconto, favola, frottola; **storyteller** narratore; (fam) bugiardo; n piano (d'una casa).
stout [staut] a forte, robusto, ben piantato, corpulento; n birra scura.
stout-hearted ['staut'haːtid] a coraggioso, intrepido.
stoutness ['stautnis] n corpulenza.
stove [stouv] n fornello, stufa, cucina.
stow [stou] vt collocare accuratamente, stivare; (sl) smettere.
stowage ['stouidʒ] n (naut) stivaggio.
stowaway ['stouəwei] n passeggero clandestino.
straddle ['strædl] vti stare a cavalcioni di, cavalcare, divaricare, stare a gambe divaricate.
straggle ['strægl] vi disperdersi, sbandarsi, sparpagliarsi.
straggler ['stræglə] n ritardatario; soldato sbandato.
straggling ['strægliŋ] a sparso, isolato; **s. beard** barba rada.
straight [streit] a diritto; retto; (drinks) liscio; ad direttamente.
straighten ['streitn] vti raddrizzar (si).
straightforward [streit'fɔːwəd] a franco, leale, retto; semplice, facile.
straightforwardness [streit'fɔːwədnis] n franchezza, rettitudine; semplicità, chiarezza.
straightness ['streitnis] n dirittura.
strain [strein] n tensione, sforzo, strappo muscolare; tono; razza, pl melodia; vt sforzare, mettere a dura prova; filtrare; vi sforzarsi; filtrare; procedere faticosamente.
strainer ['streinə] n colino.
strait [streit] n (geogr) stretto; difficoltà, imbarazzo; **s.-jacket** camicia di forza; **in straitened circumstances** in difficoltà, in strettezze.
strand [strænd] n filo di corda, fune; riva, spiaggia; vt far arenare; vi arenarsi.
strange [streindʒ] a strano, bizzarro; estraneo; insolito, nuovo; forestiero, sconosciuto.
strangeness ['streindʒnis] n stranezza, singolarità, novità.
stranger ['streindʒə] n estraneo, sconosciuto, forestiero.
strangle ['stræŋgl] vt strangolare, soffocare; (fig) reprimere.
strap [stræp] n cinghia, correggia; vt legare con una cinghia.
strapping ['stræpiŋ] a robusto, ben piantato.

stratagem ['strætidʒəm] n stratagemma.

strategic [strə'tiːdʒik] a strategico.

strategist ['strætidʒist] n stratega.

strategy ['strætidʒi] n strategia.

stratum ['straːtəm] pl **strata** n strato; strato sociale.

straw [strɔː] n paglia; festuca; pagliuzza; (fig) cosa da nulla; **the last s.** il colmo, la goccia che fa traboccare il vaso.

strawberry ['strɔːbəri] n fragola.

stray [strei] a smarrito; casuale, sporadico; vi smarrirsi, sviarsi, errare.

streak ['striːk] n striscia, stria; (fig) vena; vt striare; vi muoversi velocemente.

streaky ['striːki] a striato, a strisce.

stream [striːm] n corrente, corso d'acqua, fiotto, fiume; vt versare a fiotti; vi fluire, scorrere.

streamer ['striːmə] n banderuola; nastro; (newspaper) testata.

streamline ['striːmlain] n (aut, av) linea aerodinamica; vt dare linea aerodinamica; (fig) ordinare, semplificare.

street [striːt] n via, strada; **streetcar** tram.

strength [streŋθ] n forza, forze pl, robustezza, vigore.

strengthen ['streŋθən] vt fortificare, rafforzare.

strengthless ['streŋθlis] a debole, senza forza.

strenuous ['strenjuəs] a strenuo; vigoroso; arduo.

strenuousness ['strenjuəsnis] n accanimento.

stress [stres] n sforzo, tensione; accento, enfasi; importanza; vt mettere l'accento su, mettere in rilievo, sottolineare.

stretch [stretʃ] n distesa, tratto; stiramento; vt (e)stendere; sgranchire; esagerare; vi (e)stendersi, stirarsi.

stretcher ['stretʃə] n barella.

strew [struː] vt cospargere, disseminare.

strict [strikt] a stretto, esatto; (fig) severo.

strictness ['striktnis] n esattezza, severità.

stricture ['striktʃə] n censura, critica.

stride [straid] n passo lungo; vt scavalcare; vi camminare a gran passi.

strident ['straidənt] a stridente, stridulo.

strife [straif] n conflitto.

strike [straik] n sciopero; scoperta di giacimento minerario; vt battere, colpire; accendere; impressionare; vi colpire; scioperare; (clock) suonare.

striker ['straikə] n scioperante; battitore.

striking ['straikiŋ] a sorprendente, impressionante, rimarchevole.

string [striŋ] n corda, spago, stringa; serie; fila, filza; vt (pearls etc) infilare; **to s. up** (violin etc) accordare.

stringent ['strindʒənt] a rigoroso, severo.

stringy ['striŋi] a filamentoso; fibroso.

strip [strip] n striscia; vt denudare, privare, spogliare; vi spogliarsi, svestirsi.

stripe [straip] n striscia; (mil) gallone.

strive [straiv] vi sforzarsi, lottare.

stroke [strouk] n colpo; battuta; (med) colpo; sferzata; tratto; carezza; vt accarezzare, lisciare.

stroll [stroul] n giretto, passeggiata; vi andare a zonzo, bighellonare.

strong [strɔŋ] a forte, robusto, saldo.

stronghold ['strɔŋhould] n roccaforte, cittadella.

strop [strɔp] n coramella; vt affilare un rasoio.

strophe ['stroufi] n strofa.

structure ['strʌktʃə] n struttura, costruzione.

struggle ['strʌgl] n combattimento, lotta; vi lottare, divincolarsi.

strum [strʌm] n strimpellamento; vti strimpellare.

strut [strʌt] vi pavoneggiarsi, camminare impettito.

stub [stʌb] n troncone; mozzicone; (cheque book etc) matrice; vt sradicare; sbattere; spegnere.

stubble ['stʌbl] n stoppia, stoppie pl; barba ispida.

stubborn ['stʌbən] a ostinato, testardo.

stubbornness ['stʌbənnis] n ostinazione, testardaggine.

stucco ['stʌkou] n stucco.

stud [stʌd] n borchia; bottoncino da colletto; allevamento di cavalli da corsa.

student ['stjudənt] n studente, studentessa.

studio ['stjudiou] n (artist's) studio; (cin) teatro di posa.

studious ['stjudiəs] a studioso.

study ['stʌdi] n studio; applicazione; premura; vt studiare, esaminare attentamente; vi studiare, darsi la pena.

stuff [stʌf] n materia; roba; sostanza; stoffa, tessuto; cosa di nessun valore; vt imbottire, infarcire, rimpinzare; impagliare; vi rimpinzarsi.

stuffing ['stʌfiŋ] n imbottitura; (cook) ripieno.

stuffy ['stʌfi] a chiuso, senz'aria; (of weather) afoso, (fam) di idee antiquate; noioso.

stultify ['stʌltifai] vt infirmare, neutralizzare.

stumble ['stʌmbl] n passo falso; (fig) errore; vi incespicare, inciampare, fare errori.

stump [stʌmp] n ceppo, tronco;

moncherino; mozzicone; *vt* confondere, mettere nell'imbarazzo; *vi* camminare goffamente.

stumpy ['stʌmpi] *a* tarchiato, tozzo.

stun [stʌn] *vt* assordare, stordire; far perdere i sensi a.

stunning ['stʌniŋ] *a* stordente, assordante; (*sl*) meraviglioso.

stunt [stʌnt] *n* (*sl*) bravata; trovata pubblicitaria, notizia sensazionale; (*av*) acrobazia; *vt* arrestare lo sviluppo di.

stupefy ['stjupifai] *vt* istupidire.

stupendous [stju'pendəs] *a* stupendo.

stupid ['stjupid] *a* stupido.

stupidity [stju'piditi] *n* stupidità.

stupor ['stjupə] *n* stupore; (*med*) torpore.

sturdiness ['stə:dinis] *n* gagliardia, vigore.

sturdy ['stə:di] *a* robusto, vigoroso, gagliardo.

sturgeon ['stə:dʒən] *n* storione.

stutter ['stʌtə] *n* balbuzie; *vi* essere balbuziente.

sty [stai] *n* porcile.

sty(e) [stai] *n* orzaiolo.

style [stail] *n* stile; distinzione; titolo; stilo; (*com*) ragion sociale.

stylish ['stailiʃ] *a* elegante, distinto, alla moda.

stylus ['stailəs] *n* stilo, puntina per grammofono.

suave [swɑ:v] *a* mellifluo; garbato.

subaltern ['sʌbltən] *a n* subalterno.

subdue [səb'dju:] *vt* domare, soggiogare, vincere.

sub-editor ['sʌb'editə] *n* redattore aggiunto, revisore di stampa.

subject ['sʌbdʒikt] *a* soggetto; suscettibile; *n* argomento; soggetto; materia di studio; suddito; *vt* [səb'dʒekt] assoggettare, sottoporre.

subjection [səb'dʒekʃən] *n* soggezione, sottomissione.

subjective [səb'dʒektiv] *a n* soggettivo.

subjugate ['sʌbdʒugeit] *vt* soggiogare.

subjunctive [səb'dʒʌŋktiv] *n* (*gram*) congiuntivo.

sub-let ['sʌb'let] *vt* subaffittare.

sublime [sə'blaim] *a* sublime.

submarine ['sʌbmərin] *a* sottomarino; *n* sommergibile.

submerge [səb'mə:dʒ] *vti* sommerger(si), immerger(si).

submersion [səb'mə:ʃən] *n* sommersione.

submission [səb'miʃən] *n* sottomissione.

submissive [səb'misiv] *a* remissivo, sottomesso.

submit [səb'mit] *vt* sottomettere, sottoporre; *vi* cedere, rassegnarsi.

subordinate [sə'bɔ:dnit] *a* subordinato; *n* subalterno; *vt* subordinare.

suborn [sʌ'bɔ:n] *vt* subornare.

subscribe [səb'skraib] *vt* sottoscrivere a; *vi* aderire, sottoscriversi.

subscriber [səb'skraibə] *n* sottoscritto; (*com*) contraente; abbonato.

subscription [səb'skripʃən] *n* abbonamento; quota d'iscrizione.

subsequent ['sʌbsikwənt] *a* successivo, susseguente.

subservient [səb'səviənt] *a* ossequiente, servile; subordinato.

subside [səb'said] *vi* abbassarsi, (*waters*) decrescere; cedere, (*ground*) sprofondare; calmarsi, diminuire.

subsidence [səb'saidəns] *n* abbassamento, cedimento.

subsidiary [səb'sidjəri] *a* sussidiario, accessorio, supplementare.

subsidize ['sʌbsidaiz] *vt* sussidiare, sovvenzionare.

subsidy ['sʌbsidi] *n* sussidio, sovvenzione.

subsist [səb'sist] *vi* sussistere.

subsistence [səb'sistəns] *n* sussistenza, sostentamento.

substance ['sʌbstəns] *n* sostanza.

substantial [səb'stænʃəl] *a* sostanzioso; sostanziale.

substantiate [səb'stænʃieit] *vt* provare, dar fondamento a.

substitute ['sʌbstitju:t] *n* sostituto, surrogato; *vt* sostituire.

substitution [,sʌbsti'tju:ʃən] *n* sostituzione.

subterfuge ['sʌbtəfju:dʒ] *n* sotterfugio.

subterranean ['sʌbtə'reiniən] *a* sotterraneo.

subtle ['sʌtl] *a* sottile, delicato, tenue, indefinibile; astuto, ingegnoso.

subtlety ['sʌtlti] *n* sottigliezza; astuzia.

subtract [səb'trækt] *vt* sottrarre.

subtraction [səb'trækʃən] *n* sottrazione.

suburb ['sʌbə:b] *n* sobborgo.

suburban [sə'bə:bən] *a* suburbano, della periferia.

subversive [sʌb'və:siv] *a* sovversivo, sovvertitore.

subvert [sʌb'və:t] *vt* sovvertire.

subway ['sʌbwei] *n* sottopassaggio; metropolitana.

succeed [sək'si:d] *vt* succedere a; *vi* riuscire, aver successo, salire a.

success [sək'ses] *n* successo, fortuna.

successful [sək'sesful] *a* fortunato.

successfully [sək'sesfuli] *ad* con successo, felicemente.

succession [sək'seʃən] *n* successione; serie.

successive [sək'sesiv] *a* successivo, consecutivo.

successor [sək'sesə] *n* successore.

succinct [sək'siŋkt] *a* conciso, succinto.

succor ['sʌkə] *n* soccorso; *vt* aiutare, soccorrere.

succulent ['sʌkjulənt] *a* succulento; squisito.

succumb [sə'kʌm] *vi* soccombere.
such [sʌtʃ] *a pron* tale; questo; simile.
suck [sʌk] *vt* succhiare; poppare; assorbire.
sucker ['sʌkə] *n* (*of insect*) succhiatoio; (*of leech*) ventosa ; (*fig*) credulone; parassita.
suckle ['sʌkl] *vt* allattare.
suckling ['sʌkliŋ] *n* lattante, poppante.
suction ['sʌkʃən] *n* succhiamento; aspirazione.
sudden ['sʌdn] *a* improvviso, imprevisto.
suddenly ['sʌdnli] *ad* (tutt')ad un tratto, improvvisamente.
suddenness ['sʌdnnis] *n* subitaneità.
suds [sʌdz] *n* saponata.
sue [sjuː] *vt* citare in giudizio.
suède [sweid] *n* pelle scamosciata.
suet ['sjuit] *n* grasso, sugna.
suffer ['sʌfə] *vt* soffrire, subire, tollerare; *vi* soffrire, patire.
sufferance ['sʌfərəns] *n* sopportazione, tolleranza.
suffering ['sʌfəriŋ] *a* sofferente; *n* sofferenza.
suffice [sə'fais] *vt* essere sufficiente per; *vi* bastare.
sufficient [sə'fiʃənt] *a* bastevole, sufficiente; *n* quantità sufficiente.
suffix ['sʌfiks] *n* (*gram*) suffisso.
suffocate ['sʌfəkeit] *vt* soffocare, asfissiare.
suffocation [,sʌfə'keiʃən] *n* soffocazione, asfissia.
suffrage ['sʌfridʒ] *n* suffragio, diritto di voto.
suffragette [,sʌfrə'dʒet] *n* suffragetta.
suffuse [sə'fjuːz] *vt* diffondersi su, coprire.
sugar ['ʃugə] *n* zucchero; (*fig*) parole dolci *pl*; **icing s.** zucchero a velo; **powdered s.** zucchero in polvere.
suggest [sə'dʒest] *vt* suggerire, proporre.
suggestion [sə'dʒestʃən] *n* suggerimento, proposta.
suggestive [sə'dʒestiv] *a* che richiama alla mente; allusivo; suggestivo.
suicidal [sui'saidl] *a* suicida; (*fig*) disastroso.
suicide ['sjuisaid] *n* suicida; suicidio.
suit [sjuːt] *n* abito completo; petizione, supplica; causa; (*cards*) colore, seme; *vt* soddisfare, convenire a, giovare a; donare a; *vi* addirsi, andar bene, convenire.
suitable ['sjuːtəbl] *a* adatto, conveniente.
suitably ['sjuːtəbli] *ad* appropriatamente; opportunamente.
suite [swiːt] *n* sèguito; serie.
suitor ['sjuːtə] *n* aspirante, corteggiatore; (*leg*) attore in una causa.
sulk [sʌlk] *vi* tenere il broncio.
sulky ['sʌlki] *a* imbronciato, scontroso.

sullen ['sʌlən] *a* cupo, imbronciato.
sullenness ['sʌlənnis] *n* umor nero, intrattabilità.
sully ['sʌli] *vt* macchiare, disonorare.
sulphur ['sʌlfə] *n* zolfo.
sulphuric [sʌl'fjuərik] *a* solforico.
sultan ['sʌltən] *n* sultano.
sultana [səl'taːnə] *n* sultana, uva sultanina.
sultry ['sʌltri] *a* afoso, soffocante.
sum [sʌm] *n* addizione, somma; *vt* addizionare, sommare; **s. up** riassumere.
summary ['sʌməri] *n* riassunto; *a n* sommario.
summer ['sʌmə] *n* estate.
summery ['sʌməri] *a* estivo.
summit ['sʌmit] *n* sommità, vetta, apice.
summon ['sʌmən] *vt* chiamare, mandare a chiamare, convocare; (*leg*) citare.
summons ['sʌmənz] *n* (*leg*) citazione; convocazione; (*mil*) chiamata.
sump [sʌmp] *n* pozzo nero; (*aut*) coppa.
sumptuous ['sʌmptjuəs] *a* sontuoso.
sun [sʌn] *n* sole.
sunbeam ['sʌnbiːm] *n* raggio di sole.
sunburnt ['sʌnbəːnt] *a* abbronzato.
Sunday ['sʌndi] *n* domenica.
sunder ['sʌndə] *vt* scindere, separare.
sundry ['sʌndri] *a* parecchi, diversi; **sundries** *n* *pl* bagatelle *pl*; spese varie *pl*.
sunlight ['sʌnlait] *n* luce del sole; **s. treatment** elioterapia.
sunny ['sʌni] *a* pieno di sole, solatio, assolato; (*fig*) allegro.
sunrise ['sʌnraiz] *n* alba, levata del sole.
sunset ['sʌnset] *n* tramonto.
sunshine ['sʌnʃain] *n* (luce del) sole; (*fig*) gioia, felicità.
sup [sʌp] *vi* cenare.
superb [sjuː'pəːb] *a* superbo, magnifico, splendido.
supercilious [,sjuːpə'siliəs] *a* arrogante, sdegnoso.
superficial [,sjuːpə'fiʃəl] *a* superficiale.
superfluous [sjuː'pəːfluəs] *a* superfluo.
superhuman [,sjuːpə'hjumən] *a* sovrumano.
superintend [,sjuːprin'tend] *vti* sovrintendere (a).
superintendent [,sjuːprin'tendənt] *n* sovrintendente.
superior [sjuː'piəriə] *a n* superiore.
superiority [sjuː,piəri'ɔriti] *n* superiorità.
superlative [sjuː'pəːlətiv] *a* superlativo, eccellente; *n* superlativo.
supermarket ['sjuːpə,maːkit] *n* 'supermarket', supermercato.
supernatural [,sjuːpə'nætʃrəl] *a* sovrannaturale.
supersede [,sjuːpə'siːd] *vt* rimpiazzare, sostituire, sostituirsi(a).

supersonic ['sju:pə'sɔnik] *a* ultrasonoro; (*av*) supersonico.

superstition [,sju:pə'stiʃən] *n* superstizione.

superstitious [,sju:pə'stiʃəs] *a* superstizioso.

superstructure ['sju:pə,strʌktʃə] *n* sovrastruttura.

supervene [,sju:pə'vi:n] *vi* sopravvenire.

supervise ['sju:pəvaiz] *vt* sorvegliare, sovrintendere a.

supervision [,sju:pə'viʒən] *n* sorveglianza, sovrintendenza.

supine ['sju:pain] *a* supino; inerte.

supper ['sʌpə] *n* cena.

supplant [sə'plɑ:nt] *vt* soppiantare.

supple ['sʌpl] *a* flessibile, pieghevole, agile; (*fig*) docile.

supplement ['sʌplimənt] *n* supplemento; ['sʌpliment] *vt* aggiungere a, completare, integrare.

suppleness ['sʌplnis] *n* flessibilità, pieghevolezza.

suppliant ['sʌpliənt] *a* supplichevole; *n* supplicante, supplice.

supplicate ['sʌplikeit] *vt* supplicare.

supplication [,sʌpli'keiʃən] *n* supplica(zione).

supplier [sə'plaiə] *n* fornitore, fornitrice.

supply [sə'plai] *n* approvvigionamento, fornitura, rifornimento, scorta; *vt* approvvigionare, (ri)fornire, provvedere; supplire.

support [sə'pɔ:t] *n* sostegno, appoggio, aiuto, mantenimento; *vt* sostenere, mantenere; assecondare.

supportable [sə'pɔ:təbl] *a* sopportabile.

supporter [sə'pɔ:tə] *n* fautore, sostenitore; (*sport*) tifoso.

suppose [sə'pouz] *vt* supporre, ritenere.

supposedly [sə'pouzidli] *ad* presumibilmente, per ipotesi.

supposition [,sʌpə'ziʃən] *n* supposizione, ipotesi.

suppress [sə'pres] *vt* sopprimere; (*fig*) soffocare, nascondere.

suppression [sə'preʃən] *n* soppressione.

suppurate ['sʌpjuəreit] *vi* (*med*) suppurare.

supremacy [sju'preməsi] *n* supremazia.

supreme [sju'pri:m] *a* supremo.

surcharge ['sə:tʃɑ:dʒ] *n* soprattassa, soprapprezzo.

sure [ʃuə] *a* certo, sicuro; *ad* (*fam*) sicuro.

surely ['ʃuəli] *ad* sicuramente, senza dubbio, certo, certamente.

sureness ['ʃuənis] *n* certezza, sicurezza.

surety ['ʃuəti] *n* garanzia; garante, mallevadore.

surf [sə:f] *n* frangente, risacca; **s.-boat** barca piatta per navigare tra i frangenti; **s.-riding** sport dell'acquaplano.

surface ['sə:fis] *n* superficie.

surfeit ['sə:fit] *n* sovrabbondanza, sazietà.

surge [sə:dʒ] *n* onda, onde *pl*; *vi* ondeggiare.

surgeon ['sə:dʒən] *n* chirurgo.

surgery ['sə:dʒəri] *n* chirurgia; gabinetto medico; ambulatorio.

surgical ['sə:dʒikəl] *a* chirurgico.

surliness ['sə:linis] *n* scontrosità, villania.

surly ['sə:li] *a* scontroso, villano.

surmise ['sə:maiz] *n* congettura; *vt* congetturare, sospettare.

surmount [sə'maunt] *vt* sormontare, sorpassare.

surname ['sə:neim] *n* cognome.

surpass [sə'pɑ:s] *vt* sorpassare, superare.

surplice ['sə:pləs] *n* (*eccl*) cotta.

surplus ['sə:pləs] *n* eccedenza, sovrappiù.

surprise [sə'praiz] *n* sorpresa; *vt* sorprendere.

surprisingly [sə'praiziŋli] *ad* sorprendentemente, tra la sorpresa generale.

surrealism [sə'riəlizəm] *n* surrealismo.

surrender [sə'rendə] *n* resa; cessione, consegna; (*com*) riscatto; *vt* cedere; rinunziare a, abbandonare; *vi* arrendersi, sottomettersi.

surreptitious [,sʌrəp'tiʃəs] *a* clandestino.

surround [sə'raund] *vt* attorniare, circondare.

surroundings [sə'raundiŋz] *n pl* dintorni *pl*, ambiente.

survey ['sə:vei] *n* esame; rilevamento topografico; sguardo generale; indagine; [sə'vei] *vt* esaminare, dare uno sguardo generale a, rilevare.

surveyor [sə'veiə] *n* ispettore; agrimensore, geometra.

survival [sə'vaivəl] *n* sopravvivenza.

survive [sə'vaiv] *vt* sopravvivere (a).

survivor [sə'vaivə] *n* superstite.

Susan ['suzn] *nf pr* Susanna.

susceptibility [sə,septi'biliti] *n* suscettibilità.

susceptible [sə'septəbl] *a* suscettibile, sensibile.

suspect ['sʌspekt] *a* sospetto; *n* persona sospetta; *vt* sospettare, diffidare di.

suspend [səs'pend] *vt* sospendere, differire.

suspender [səs'pendə] *n* giarrettiera; *pl* bretelle.

suspense [səs'pens] *n* ansietà, indecisione, sospensione d'animo, incertezza; **in s.** nell'incertezza, in sospeso.

suspension [səs'penʃən] *n* sospensione.

suspicion [səs'piʃən] *n* sospetto.

suspicious [səs'piʃəs] *a* sospettoso, diffidente.

sustain [səs'tein] *vt* sostenere; prolungare; subire; mantenere.

sustenance ['sʌstinəns] *n* nutrimento, vitto, sostentamento.

swab [swɔb] *n* strofinaccio; (*naut*) radazza; (*med*) tampone.

swaddling clothes ['swɔdliŋklouðz] *n* fasce *pl.*

swagger ['swægə] *n* fanfaronata, spavalderia; *vi* camminare con sussiego, vantarsi.

swaggerer ['swægərə] *n* fanfarone.

swain [swein] *n* (*poet*) contadino, rustico innamorato.

swallow ['swɔlou] *n* rondine; *vt* inghiottire, ingoiare.

swamp ['swɔmp] *n* palude.

swampy ['swɔmpi] *a* paludoso.

swan [swɔn] *n* cigno.

swap [swɔp] *n* scambio, baratto; *vt* barattare.

sward [swɔːd] *n* distesa erbosa.

swarm [swɔːm] *n* sciame, frotta, gran numero; *vi* sciamare, brulicare.

swarthy ['swɔːði] *a* bruno, di carnagione scura.

swastika ['swɔstikə] *n* svastica, croce uncinata.

swathe [sweið] *n* benda, fascia; *vt* fasciare, bendare.

sway [swei] *n* oscillazione; influenza, dominio; *vt* far oscillare; influenzare; *vi* oscillare.

swear [swɛə] *vti* (far) giurare; *vi* bestemmiare, imprecare.

sweat [swet] *n* sudore; *vti* sudare; (*fig*) sfruttare.

sweater ['swetə] *n* chi suda; maglione di lana.

Swede [swiːd] *n* svedese; **swede** rapa svedese.

Sweden ['swiːdn] *n* Svezia.

Swedish ['swiːdiʃ] *a* svedese.

sweep [swiːp] *n* scopata, spazzata; spazzacamino; distesa; movimento circolare; (*mil*) rastrellamento; *vt* scopare, spazzare; (*mil*) rastrellare; *vi* muoversi rapidamente.

sweeper ['swiːpə] *n* chi scopa; spazzino.

sweeping ['swiːpiŋ] *a* vasto, sconfinato; impetuoso; assoluto.

sweepings ['swiːpiŋz] *n pl* spazzatura.

sweet [swiːt] *a* dolce, profumato, tenero, amabile; *n* dolce, dolciume.

sweetbread ['swiːtbred] *n* animella.

sweeten ['swiːtn] *vt* addolcire, inzuccherare.

sweetheart ['swiːthɑːt] *n* innamorato, -a.

sweetmeat ['swiːtmiːt] *n* (*usu pl*) dolciumi, frutta candita.

sweetness ['swiːtnis] *n* dolcezza, tenerezza, profumo.

swell [swel] *n* il sollevarsi delle acque; (*sl*) elegantone; *a* (*fam*) elegante; *vti* gonfiar(si), ingrossar(si).

swelling ['sweliŋ] *n* gonfiamento, gonfiore.

swelter ['sweltə] *vi* essere oppresso dal caldo, sudare; *n* afa, caldo opprimente.

sweltering ['sweltəriŋ] *a* soffocante; molle di sudore.

swerve [swəːv] *vi* deviare, fare uno scarto.

swift [swift] *a* agile, rapido, svelto, veloce; *n* rondine.

swiftness ['swiftnis]*n* agilità, rapidità, velocità.

swill [swil] *n* risciacquatura; *n* risciacquata; *vt* risciacquare; *vi* bere all'eccesso.

swim [swim] *n* nuotata; (*fig*) corrente degli affari, della vita sociale; *vi* nuotare.

swimmer ['swimə] *n* nuotatore.

swimming ['swimiŋ] *n* nuoto; **s. pool** piscina.

swindle ['swindl] *n* truffa; *vti* truffare, imbrogliare.

swindler ['swindlə] *n* imbroglione, truffatore.

swine [swain] *n pl* maiali *pl*, suini *pl*; (*fig*) porco.

swing [swiŋ] *n* dondolio; oscillazione; altalena; ritmo; *vt* dondolare; *vi* dondolare; oscillare; pendere; (*of boat*) muoversi sull'ancora.

swipe [swaip] *n* colpo violento, manata; *vt* colpire violentemente; (*sl*) rubacchiare.

swirl [swəːl] *n* vortice, turbine.

swish [swiʃ] *n* fruscio; sibilo; sferzata.

Swiss [swis] *a n* svizzero.

switch [switʃ] *n* (*mech*) interruttore; commutatore; (*rly*) scambio; bastoncino, verga; treccia finta.

Switzerland ['switsələnd] *n* Svizzera.

swivel ['swivl] *n* (*mech*) perno.

swoon [swuːn] *n* deliquio, svenimento; *vi* svenire, venir meno.

swoop [swuːp] *n* calata improvvisa, attacco; *vt* **to s. down** piombare su.

swop *v* **swap.**

sword [sɔːd] *n* spada; **s.-cane** stocco; **s. fish** pesce spada; **s. hilt** elsa della spada; **s. thrust** stoccato.

swordsman ['sɔːdzmən] *pl* **-men** *n* spadaccino.

sycamore ['sikəmɔː] *n* sicomoro.

syllable ['siləbl] *n* sillaba.

syllabus ['siləbəs] *n* programma scolastico, prospetto.

syllogism ['silədʒizəm] *n* sillogismo.

sylvan ['silvən] *a* silvano, silvestre.

Sylvia ['silviə] *nf pr* Silvia.

symbol ['simbəl] *n* simbolo.

symbolic [sim'bɔlik] *a* simbolico.

symbolize ['simbəlaiz] *vt* simboleggiare.

symmetrical [si'metrikəl] *a* simmetrico.

symmetry ['simitri] *n* simmetria.

sympathetic [ˌsimpə'θetik] *a* sensibile, comprensivo.

sympathetically [ˌsimpə'θetikli] *ad* con comprensione.

sympathize ['simpəθaiz] *vi* condividere i sentimenti altrui, aver comprensione, compassione.

sympathy ['simpəθi] *n* comprensione, partecipazione ai sentimenti altrui, compassione.

symphony ['simfəni] *n* sinfonia.

symposium [sim'pouziəm] *n* simposio.

symptom ['simptəm] *n* sintomo.

symptomatic [ˌsimptə'mætik] *a* sintomatico.

synagogue ['sinagɔg] *n* sinagoga.

synchronize ['siŋkrənaiz] *vti* sincronizzare.

syndicate ['sindikit] *n* sindacato.

synod ['sinəd] *n* sinodo.

synonym ['sinənim] *n* sinonimo.

synonymous [si'nɔniməs] *a* sinonimo.

syntax ['sintæks] *n* (*gram*) sintassi.

synthesis ['sinθisis] *n* sintesi.

synthetic [sin'θetik] *a* sintetico.

syphilis ['sifilis] *n* (*med*) sifilide.

Syracuse ['saiərəkjuːz] *n* Siracusa.

Syria ['siriə] *n* Siria.

Syriac ['siriæk] *a* *n* siriaco, lingua siriaca.

Syrian ['siriən] *a* *n* siriano.

syringe [si'rindʒ] *n* (*med*) siringa; *vt* (*med*) siringare.

syrup ['sirəp] *n* sciroppo, melassa.

system ['sistim] *n* sistema; organizzazione; metodo.

systematic [ˌsisti'mætik] *a* sistematico, metodico.

T

tab [tæb] *n* linguetta, (*mil*) mostrina; cartellino; (*av*) aletta compensatrice.

tabernacle ['tæbənækl] *n* tabernacolo.

table ['teibl] *n* tavola, -lo; prospetto, tabella; **t. of contents** *n* indice; **t. d'hôte** pasto a prezzo fisso.

table-cloth ['teiblklɔθ] *n* tovaglia.

tablet ['tæblit] *n* tavoletta; lapide; pastiglia.

taboo [tə'buː] *a* tabù, proibito; *n* tabù, interdizione.

tabulate ['tæbjuleit] *vt* ordinare in tavole sinottiche; catalogare.

tabulator ['tæbjuleitə] *n* (*mech*) tabulatore, incolonnatore.

tacit ['tæsit] *a* implicito, sottinteso, tacito.

taciturn ['tæsitəːn] *a* taciturno.

tack [tæk] *n* bulletta, chiodo; (*fig*) linea di condotta, tattica; *vt* inchiodare; imbastire; *vi* (*naut*) virare.

tackle ['tækl] *n* (*naut*) sartiame; attrezzi; *vt* affrontare, mettere mano a.

tacky ['tæki] *a* appiccicaticcio.

tact [tækt] *n* tatto.

tactful ['tæktful] *a* pieno di tatto.

tactical ['tæktikəl] *a* tattico.

tactics ['tæktiks] *n* *pl* tattica; espedienti *pl*.

tactless ['tæktlis] *a* senza tatto.

tadpole ['tædpoul] *n* girino.

taffy ['tæfi] *n* caramella.

tag [tæg] *n* punta metallica; puntale; cartellino di spedizione, etichetta; frase o luogo comune; ritornello.

tail [teil] *n* coda, estremità; *vt* mettere la coda a; (*sl*) pedinare; *vi* essere in coda a.

tailor ['teilə] *n* sarto.

taint [teint] *n* infezione; marchio; *vti* corromper(si), infettar(si).

take [teik] *vti* prendere, afferrare; acquistare; accettare; condurre, portare; catturare; rubare; considerare, ritenere; attaccare; **t. in** ricevere; capire; ingannare; **t. off** togliere; (*av*) decollare; fare la caricatura a; **t. on** assumere, intraprendere; **t. over** succedere in.

take-off ['teikɔf] *n* (*av*) decollo; (*sport*) linea di partenza; caricatura.

taking ['teikiŋ] *a* attraente, piacevole; contagioso; *n* presa; *pl* (*com*) incasso.

talcum ['tælkʌm] *n* talco.

tale [teil] *n* racconto, novella.

talent ['tælənt] *n* talento, attitudine.

talk [tɔːk] *n* abboccamento, colloquio, conversazione, discorso, chiacchiere *pl*; *vti* parlare, conversare; chiacchierare, discorrere (su, di).

talkative ['tɔːkətiv] *a* loquace.

talkies ['tɔːkiz] *n* *pl* (*sl*) film sonoro.

tall [tɔːl] *a* alto; grande; incredibile.

tallow ['tælou] *n* sego.

tally ['tæli] *n* tacca; conto; piastrina di contrassegno; *vi* concordare corrispondere a; *vt* calcolare; spuntare.

talon ['tælən] *n* artiglio.

tamarind ['tæmərind] *n* tamarindo.

tamarisk ['tæmərisk] *n* tamerice, tamarisco.

tame [teim] *a* domestico, addomesticato; docile, mansueto; insipido; *vt* domare, addomesticare.

tameness ['teimnis] *n* docilità.

tamper ['tæmpə] *vi* immischiarsi; (*fig*) corrompere, falsificare.

tan [tæn] *n* concia; abbronzatura; tanè; *vt* conciare (*skins*), abbronzare.

tandem ['tændəm] *n* tandem.

tang [tæŋ] *n* sapore; asprigno piccante; odore penetrante; accento speciale.

tangent ['tændʒənt] *n* tangente.

tangerine [ˌtændʒə'riːn] *n* mandarino.

tangible ['tændʒəbl] *a* tangibile.

Tangier [tæn'dʒiə] *n* Tangeri.

tangle ['tæŋgl] *n* complicazione, garbuglio; *vti* complicar(si), ingarbugliar(si).

tank [tæŋk] *n* cisterna, serbatoio, vasca; (*mil*) carro armato.

tankard ['tæŋkəd] n grosso boccale.
tanker ['tæŋkə] n nave cisterna.
tanner ['tænə] n conciatore, conciapelli.
tannery ['tænəri] n conceria.
tannin ['tænin] n tannino.
tantalize ['tæntəlaiz] vt tormentare, lusingare.
tantamount ['tæntəmaunt] a equivalente.
tantrum ['tæntrəm] n furie, nervi pl.
tap [tæp] n spina; rubinetto; qualità di birra; colpetto, picchio; vt spillare; battere, picchiare leggermente; intercettare.
tape [teip] n nastro, passamano, fettuccia; t.-recorder registratore a nastro.
taper ['teipə] vt affusolar(si); n candela, stoppino.
tapering ['teipəriŋ] a affusolato, a punta.
tapestry ['tæpistri] n arazzi pl; tappezzeria.
tapeworm ['teipwə:m] n tenia.
tar [ta:] n catrame; vt incatramare.
tardiness ['ta:dinis] n lentezza; riluttanza.
tardy ['ta:di] a lento, tardo; riluttante.
tare [tɛə] n tara; veccia.
target ['ta:git] n bersaglio; (fig) obiettivo, mira.
tariff ['tærif] n tariffa.
tarmac ['ta:mæk] n macadam al catrame; (av) pista di decollo, di atterraggio.
tarnish ['ta:niʃ] vti appannar(si), offuscar(si), ossidar(si); (fig) macchiar(si).
tarpaulin [ta:'pɔ:lin] n copertone impermeabile, tessuto incerato.
tarry ['ta:ri] a incatramato, bituminoso; ['tæri] vi indugiare, ritardare.
tart [ta:t] a agro, aspro; n torta di frutta; (sl) sgualdrina.
tartan ['ta:tən] n tessuto di ana scozzese; (naut) tartana.
tartar ['ta:tə] n tartaro.
tartaric [ta:'tærik] a tartarico.
tartness ['ta:tnis] n asprezza; (fig) mordacità.
task [ta:sk] n compito, mansione, lavoro, incarico; vt mettere a prova, affaticare.
tassel ['tæsəl] n fiocco, nappa.
taste [teist] n gusto, sapore, assaggio; vt assaggiare; vi avere gusto di, sapere di.
tasteful ['teistful] a di buon gusto.
tasteless ['teistlis] a senza gusto, insipido.
tasty ['teisti] a saporito.
tatter ['tætə] n brandello, straccio; vt ridurre a brandelli, stracciare.
tattle ['tætl] n chiacchierio, ciarla; vi chiacchierare, ciarlare.
tattler ['tætlə] n chiacchierone, pettegolo.
tattoo [tə'tu:] n tatuaggio; (mil)

ritirata; (il) tamburellare; vt tatuare.
taunt [tɔ:nt] n sarcasmo, scherno, rimprovero; vt rinfacciare; ingiuriare, schernire.
taut [tɔ:t] a teso, rigido.
tavern ['tævən] n osteria, trattoria.
tawdry ['tɔ:dri] a vistoso e di cattivo gusto.
tawny ['tɔ:ni] a abbronzato, fulvo, tanè.
tax [tæks] n imposta, tassa, gravame, onere; vt tassare, mettere a dura prova; accusare, tacciare.
taxable ['tæksəbl] a tassabile.
taxation [tæk'seiʃən] n tassazione, tasse pl.
taxi ['tæksi] n auto pubblica, tassì; **taximeter** tassametro; t.-stand posteggio di tassì.
tea [ti:] n tè; **teacup** tazza da tè; **teapot** teiera; **teaspoon** cucchiaino da tè.
teach [ti:tʃ] vt insegnare, istruire, ammaestrare; t.-in 'teach-in'.
teacher ['ti:tʃə] n insegnante.
teaching ['ti:tʃiŋ] n insegnamento, dottrina.
teak [ti:k] n tek (albero, legno).
team [ti:m] n (horses) tiro; squadra.
tear [tɛə] vti lacerar(si), strappar(si); vi correre precipitosamente.
tear [tiə] n lacrima, lagrima.
tearful ['tiəful] a lacrimoso, piangente.
tearless ['tiəlis] a senza lacrime.
tease [ti:z] n importuno, seccatore; vt stuzzicare, tormentare; (textiles) cardare.
teasel, teazle ['ti:zl] n cardo; (mech) scardasso.
teat [ti:t] n capezzolo.
technical ['teknikəl] a tecnico.
technicality [ˌtekni'kæliti] n tecnicismo, particolare tecnico.
technician [tek'niʃən] n tecnico.
technique [tek'ni:k] n tecnica.
technology [tek'nɔlədʒi] n tecnologia.
tedious ['ti:diəs] a tedioso, noioso.
tedium ['ti:diəm] n tedio, noia.
teem [ti:m] vi abbondare, brulicare di.
teenager ['ti:nˌeidʒə] n chi ha meno di vent'anni, adolescente.
teens [ti:nz] n pl età da 13 a 19 anni.
teething ['ti:ðiŋ] n dentizione.
teetotal(er) [ti:'toutl(ə)] a n astemio.
telecast ['telika:st] vt teletrasmettere; n trasmissione televisiva.
telegram ['teligræm] n telegramma.
telegraph ['teligra:f] n telegrafo; vti telegrafare.
telegraphic [teli'græfik] a telegrafico.
telepathy [ti'lepəθi] n telepatia.
telephone ['telifoun] n telefono; vti telefonare.
telephonic [ˌteli'fɔnik] a telefonico.
telephonist [ti'lefənist] n telefonista.

telescope ['teliskoup] *n* telescopio; cannocchiale.

televiewer ['telivjuə] *n* telespettatore, telespettatrice.

televise ['telivaiz] *vt* teletrasmettere

television ['teli,viʒən] *n* televisione.

tell [tel] *vt* dire; informare; raccontare; ingiungere, ordinare.

teller ['telə] *n* chi riferisce; (*com*) cassiere.

telltale ['telteil] *a n* pettegolo; *a* indiscreto.

temerity [ti'meriti] *n* temerità.

temper ['tempə] *n* carattere, indole; umore; collera; (*metal*) tempera; *vt* mitigare, modificare, temperare, temprare; *vi* (*metal*) temprarsi.

temperament ['tempərəmənt] *n* temperamento, carattere.

temperance ['tempərəns] *n* temperanza, moderazione, astinenza dall'alcool.

temperate ['tempərit] *a* (*climate*) temperato, moderato, sobrio.

temperature ['tempritʃə] *n* temperatura, febbre.

tempest ['tempist] *n* tempesta.

tempestuous [tem'pestjuəs] *a* tempestoso, violento.

templar ['templə] *n* templare.

temple ['templ] *n* tempia; tempio.

temporal ['tempərəl] *a* temporale.

temporary ['tempərəri] *a* temporaneo, transitorio.

temporize ['tempəraiz] *vi* temporeggiare.

tempt [tempt] *vt* tentare, indurre.

temptation [temp'teiʃən] *n* tentazione.

tempter ['temptə] *n* tentatore; **the t.** il Diavolo.

tempting ['temptiŋ] *a* allettante, seducente.

ten [ten] *a n* dieci; **tenth** *a n* decimo.

tenable ['tenəbl] *a* difendibile, che si può tenere, sostenibile.

tenacious [ti'neiʃəs] *a* tenace, adesivo.

tenacity [ti'næsiti] *n* tenacia.

tenancy ['tenənsi] *n* affitto, locazione.

tenant ['tenənt] *n* affittuario, locatario, inquilino.

tend [tend] *vi* tendere, essere diretto; *vt* curare, sorvegliare.

tendency ['tendənsi] *n* tendenza .

tender ['tendə] *a* tenero, delicato, sensibile; *n* (*com*) offerta; (*rly*) tender; (*naut*) lancia; *vt* offrire, porgere; *vi* (*com*) concorrere ad un appalto.

tenderness ['tendənis] *n* tenerezza.

tendon ['tendən] *n* tendine.

tenement ['tenimənt] *n* abitazione, appartamento; **t. house** casa popolare; casamento.

tennis ['tenis] *n* tennis.

tenor ['tenə] *n* tenore.

tense [tens] *a* teso; *n* (*gram*) tempo.

tension ['tenʃən] *n* tensione.

tent [tent] *n* tenda.

tentacle ['tentəkl] *n* tentacolo.

tentative ['tentətiv] *a* sperimentale, di prova.

tenuous ['tenjuəs] *a* tenue, sottile.

tenure ['tenjuə] *n* possesso, diritto di possesso, durata di possesso.

tepid ['tepid] *a* tiepido.

term [təːm] *n* termine, periodo di tempo; trimestre; (*leg*) sessione; *vt* chiamare, denominare; **terms** *pl* condizioni, patti; rapporti *pl*.

termagant ['təːməgənt] *n* bisbetica, virago.

terminate ['təːmineit] *vti* finire, terminare.

termination [,təːmi'neiʃən] *n* conclusione, fine; (*gram*) desinenza.

terminology [,təːmi'nɔlədʒi] *n* terminologia.

terminus ['təːminəs] *n* capolinea.

termite ['təːmait] *n* termite.

terrace ['terəs] *n* terrazzo, terrapieno; terrazza; fila di case.

terrestrial [ti'restriəl] *a* terrestre.

terrible ['terəbl] *a* terribile.

terrier ['teriə] *n* cane terrier.

terrific [tə'rifik] *a* terrificante; (*fam*) magnifico.

terrify ['terifai] *vt* atterrire, terrificare.

territorial [,teri'tɔːriəl] *a* territoriale; *n* soldato della milizia territoriale.

territory ['teritəri] *n* territorio.

terror ['terə] *n* terrore.

terrorist ['terərist] *n* terrorista.

terse [təːs] *a* conciso, incisivo.

terseness ['təːsnis] *n* concisione.

test [test] *n* prova, esperimento, saggio; (*chem*) reagente; *vt* collaudare, provare; (*chem*) analizzare.

testament ['testəmənt] *n* testamento.

testify ['testifai] *vt* testimoniare.

testimonial [,testi'mouniəl] *a* testimoniale; *n* benservito, certificato di servizio, attestato.

testimony ['testiməni] *n* testimonianza.

testy ['testi] *a* irritabile, risentito.

tetanus ['tetənəs] *n* tetano.

tether ['teðə] *n* pastoia; *vt* impastoiare; **at the end of one's t.** all'estremo delle proprie risorse, al limite della pazienza.

Teutonic [tjuˈtɔnik] *a* teutonico.

text [tekst] *n* testo, argomento.

textile ['tekstail] *a* tessile; *n* tessuto, fibra tessile.

textual ['tekstjuəl] *a* testuale.

texture ['tekstʃə] *n* tessitura; tessuto; trama.

Thames [temz] *n* Tamigi.

than [ðæn] *cj prep* di, che, di quello che (non), di quanto.

thank [θæŋk] *vt* ringraziare.

thankful ['θæŋkful] *a* grato, riconoscente.

thankfulness ['θæŋkfulnis] *n* gratitudine, riconoscenza.

thankless ['θæŋklis] *a* ingrato.

thanklessness ['θæŋklisnis] *n* ingratitudine.
thanks [θæŋks] *n pl* grazie, ringraziamenti *pl*.
thanksgiving ['θæŋks giviŋ] *n* ringraziamento solenne; **T. (Day)** (*US*) giorno del ringraziamento.
that [ðæt] *pl* **those** [ðouz] *a pron* quello *etc*, ciò; che, il quale, la quale *etc*; *cj* che; *ad* (*fam*) così, a tal segno, tanto.
thatch [θætʃ] *n* tetto di paglia; *vt* coprire di paglia.
thaw [θɔ:] *n* (di)sgelo; *vti* disgelar(si), scioglier(si); (*fig*) commuover(si).
the [ðə, ði] *def art* il, lo, la, i, gli, le; *ad* (*before comparatives*) quanto . . . tanto.
theater ['θiətə] *n* teatro.
theatrical [θi'ætrikəl] *a* scenico, teatrale; (*fig*) affettato, manierato.
theft [θeft] *n* furto.
their [ðɛə] *poss a* il loro *etc*; **theirs** *poss pron* il loro *etc*.
them [ðem] *pron* li, le, loro; **themselves** *pron pl* se stessi, si *etc*.
theme [θi:m] *n* tema, argomento.
then [ðen] *ad* allora, poi, in sèguito; dunque, perciò, quindi; *a* di allora.
thence [ðens] *ad* di là; quindi, pertanto.
thenceforth ['ðens'fɔ:θ] *ad* d'allora in poi
Theodore ['θiədɔ:] *nm pr* Teodoro.
theologian [θiə'loudʒjən] *n* teologo.
theological [θiə'lɔdʒikəl] *a* teologico.
theology [θi'ɔlədʒi] *n* teologia.
theorem ['θiərəm] *n* teorema.
theoretical [θiə'retikəl] *a* teorico.
theory ['θiəri] *n* teoria.
therapeutic [ˌθerə'pju:tik] *a* terapeutico.
therapist ['θerəpist] *n* terapeuta.
therapy ['θerəpi] *n* terapia.
there [ðɛə] *ad* là, vi, lì, ci.
thereby ['ðɛə'bai] *ad* così, perciò.
thereabout(s) ['ðɛərəbaut(s)] *ad* all'incirca, a un dipresso, nei dintorni *pl*.
therefore ['ðɛəfɔ:] *ad* perciò.
Theresa [ti'ri:zə] *nf pr* Teresa.
thereupon ['ðɛərə'pɔn] *ad* al che.
thermometer [θə'mɔmitə] *n* termometro.
thermos ['θə:mɔs] *n* termos.
thesis ['θi:sis] *pl* **theses** *n* tesi.
they [ðei] *pron pl* essi, esse, loro.
thick [θik] *a* denso, fitto, folto, grosso, spesso.
thicken ['θikən] *vti* condensar(si), infittire, infoltire.
thicket ['θikit] *n* boschetto, macchia.
thickness ['θiknis] *n* densità, foltezza; spessore, strato.
thief [θi:f] *n* ladro.
thieve [θi:v] *vi* fare il ladro.
thievish ['θi:viʃ] *a* ladresco.
thigh [θai] *n* coscia.
thimble ['θimbl] *n* ditale.
thin [θin] *a* magro, delicato, fine,

leggero, rado, sparso sottile; *vti* assottigliar(si), diradar(si).
thing [θiŋ] *n* cosa, coso.
think [θiŋk] *vti* pensare, credere, ritenere.
thinker ['θiŋkə] *n* pensatore.
thinness ['θinnis] *n* magrezza, sottigliezza, tenuità.
third [θə:d] *a* terzo.
thirst [θə:st] *n* sete; (*fig*) avidità, brama.
thirsty ['θə:sti] *a* assetato, avido; **be t.** aver sete.
thirteen ['θə:'ti:n] *a n* tredici; **thirteenth** *a n* tredicesimo.
thirty ['θə:ti] *a n* trenta; **thirtieth** *a n* trentesimo.
this [ðis] *pl* **these** [ði:z] *dem a pron* questo *etc*.
thistle ['θisl] *n* cardo.
thither ['ðiðə] *ad* là, in quella direzione; **hither and t.** qua e là.
Thomas ['tɔməs] *nm pr* Tommaso.
thong [θɔŋ] *n* cinghia, correggia.
thorn [θɔ:n] *n* spina.
thorny ['θɔ:ni] *a* spinoso.
thorough ['θʌrə] *a* completo, intero; perfetto, esauriente.
thoroughbred ['θʌrəbred] *a* purosangue, che ha stile; *n* purosangue.
thoroughfare ['θʌrəfɛə] *n* arteria di gran traffico, strada principale.
thoroughness ['θʌrənis] *n* perfezione.
thou [ðau] *pron* tu.
though [ðou] *cj* benché, quantunque, sebbene.
thought [θɔ:t] *n* pensiero.
thoughtful ['θɔ:tful] *a* pensieroso, pensoso; attento; previdente.
thoughtfully ['θɔ:tfuli] *ad* pensosamente, pensierosamente; premurosamente.
thoughtfulness ['θɔ:tfulnis] *n* meditazione; attenzione; previdenza; premura.
thoughtless ['θɔ:tlis] *a* irriflessivo, sconsiderato.
thoughtlessly ['θɔ:tlisli] *ad* sventatamente; negligentemente, trascuratamente.
thoughtlessness ['θɔ:tlisnis] *n* sconsideratezza, mancanza di riguardo.
thousand ['θauzənd] *a n* mille; **thousandth** *a n* millesimo.
thrall [θrɔ:l] *n* schiavo, schiavitù.
thrash [θræʃ] *vt* bastonare, battere.
thrashing ['θræʃiŋ] *n* bastonatura, legnate.
thread [θred] *n* filo; *vt* infilare, (far) passare attraverso.
threadbare ['θredbɛə] *a* consumato, logoro; (*fig*) vieto, trito.
threat [θret] *n* minaccia.
threaten ['θretn] *vt* minacciare.
three [θri:] *a n* tre.
threefold ['θri:fould] *a* triplice, triplo.
threshold ['θreʃhould] *n* soglia.
thrice [θrais] *ad* tre volte.
thrift [θrift] *n* economia, frugalità.
thrifty ['θrifti] *a* economico, frugale.

thrill [θril] *n* fremito, palpito; *vt* elettrizzare, far rabbrividire; *vi* fremere, vibrare.
thriller ['θrilə] *n* dramma, film poliziesco, libro, film giallo.
thrive [θraiv] *vi* crescere, prosperare, svilupparsi vigorosamente.
throat [θrout] *n* gola.
throb [θrɔb] *n* pulsazione, vibrazione; *vi* battere, pulsare, vibrare.
throes [θrouz] *n pl* sofferenza acuta.
throne [θroun] *n* trono.
throng [θrɔŋ] *n* calca, folla, ressa; *vt* affollare, ingombrare; *vi* affollarsi, affluire.
throttle ['θrɔtl] *n* (*mech*) valvola; (*aut*) acceleratore; *vt* strangolare.
through [θru:] *a* diretto; *prep* attraverso, per; per mezzo di; *ad* da parte a parte.
throughout [θru'aut] *prep* da un capo all'altro di; per tutta la durata di; *ad* completamente, dappertutto.
throw [θrou] *n* getto, lancio, tiro; *vt* buttare, gettare, lanciare.
thrush [θrʌʃ] *n* tordo.
thrust [θrʌst] *n* pressione, spinta; *vti* cacciar(si), conficcar(si), introdur(si) a viva forza.
thud [θʌd] *n* rumore sordo, tonfo.
thug [θʌg] *n* teppista, furfante.
thumb [θʌm] *n* pollice; *vt* sfogliare; lasciar ditate su; **thumbtack** puntina da disegno; **to t. a lift** chiedere un passaggio facendo l'autostop.
thump [θʌmp] *n* rumore sordo, colpo; *vt* battere, percuotere.
thunder ['θʌndə] *n* tuono, -ni *pl*; *vt* pronunciare con voce tonante; *vi* tuonare.
thunderbolt ['θʌndəboult] *n* fulmine.
thunderstruck ['θʌndəstrʌk] *a* fulminato; sbalordito.
Thursday ['θəːzdi] *n* giovedì.
thus [ðʌs] *ad* così, in tal modo.
thwart [θwɔːt] *n* (*naut*) banco di rematore; *vt* contrariare, frustrare.
thy [ðai] *a poss* tuo, tua, tuoi, tue.
thyme [taim] *n* timo.
tiara [ti'ɑːrə] *n* tiara; diadema.
tick [tik] *n* battito; ticchettio; (*fam*) attimo; (*insect*) zecca; (*fam*) credito; *vi* battere, fare tic-tac.
ticket ['tikit] *n* biglietto, cartellino; **t. agent** (*rly*) bigliettario; **t. office** (*rly*) biglietteria.
tickle ['tikl] *n* solletico; *vt* solleticare; stuzzicare; divertire; *vt* far solletico.
ticklish ['tikliʃ] *a* che sente molto il solletico; (*fig*) delicato, scabroso.
tidal ['taidl] *a* della marea; **t. wave** onda di marea; (*fig*) impulso travolgente.
tide [taid] *n* marea; (*fig*) corrente.
tidings ['taidiŋz] *n pl* notizie, nuove.
tidy ['taidi] *a* ordinato, preciso, lindo; (*fam*) considerevole; **to t. up** *vt* rassettare, mettere in ordine.

tie [tai] *n* cravatta; legame, vincolo; (*sport*) pareggio; (*rly*) traversina; *vt* legare, unire; *vi* (*sport*) pareggiare; **cup-t.** eliminatoria di torneo; **t.-up** ingorgo stradale.
tier [tiə] *n* fila; ordine graduato (di posti).
tiff [tif] *n* (*fam*) bisticcio.
tiger ['taigə] **tigress** (*f*) *n* tigre.
tight [tait] *a* aderente, attillato, stretto; teso; (*sl*) brillo; *n pl* calzamaglia.
tighten ['taitn] *vti* serrar(si), stringer(si), tirare.
tightness ['taitnis] *n* strettezza; tensione; oppressione di petto.
tile [tail] *n* mattonella, piastrella; tegola; *vt* coprire di tegole *etc.*
till [til] *n* cassa; *prep* fino a, sino a; *cj* finchè (non); *vt* coltivare (la terra).
tillage ['tilidʒ] *n* coltivazione.
tilt [tilt] *n* inclinazione, giostra, torneo; copertone; *vti* (far) inclinare; giostrare.
timber ['timbə] *n* alberi *pl* di alto fusto, legname da costruzione.
time [taim] *n* tempo; epoca; ora; volta; *vt* cronometrare, scegliere il momento giusto per.
timeless ['taimlis] *a* eterno, infinito; senza tempo; fuori del tempo.
timely ['taimli] *a* opportuno, tempestivo.
timid ['timid] *a* timido.
timidity [ti'miditi] *n* timidezza.
timorous ['timərəs] *a* timoroso.
Timothy ['timəθi] *nm pr* Timoteo.
tin [tin] *n* stagno; latta; scatola, barattolo di latta.
tincture ['tiŋktʃə] *n* tintura; tinta; leggero aroma; (*fig*) infarinatura.
tinder ['tində] *n* (per fuoco) esca.
tinfoil ['tinfɔil] *n* lamina di stagno, stagnola.
tinge [tindʒ] *n* lieve coloritura, sfumatura; *vt* colorire leggermente, sfumare.
tingle ['tiŋgl] *vi* sentire un formicolio; fremere.
tinker ['tiŋkə] *n* stagnino; **to t. with** affaccendarsi.
tinkle ['tiŋkl] *n* tintinnio.
tinkle ['tiŋkl] *vti* (far) tintinnare.
tinsel ['tinsəl] *n* 'lamè'; orpello.
tint [tint] *n* tinta; sfumatura; *vt* colorire; sfumare.
tiny ['taini] *a* minuscolo.
tip [tip] *n* punta; cima; puntale; mancia; informazione segreta, suggerimento; *vt* mettere la punta; (far) inclinare; dare la mancia; avvisare; *vi* ribaltare.
tipple ['tipl] *n* (*fam*) forte bevanda alcoolica; *vi* bere parecchio.
tippler ['tiplə] *n* bevitore abituale.
tipsy ['tipsi] *a* alticcio, brillo.
tiptoe ['tiptou] *n* punta dei piedi; **on t.** *ad* in punta di piedi.
tirade [tai'reid] *n* tirata, filippica.

tire ['taiə] _n_ cerchione di ruota, pneumatico; _vti_ stancar(si).
tired ['taiəd] _a_ stanco.
tiredness ['taiədnis] _n_ stanchezza.
tiresome ['taiəsəm] _a_ faticoso, noioso.
tissue ['tisjuː] _n_ tessuto; **t. paper** carta velina.
titbit ['titbit] **tidbit** ['tidbit] _n_ boccone delicato, leccornia.
tithe [taið] _n_ decima, tassa.
Titian ['tiʃiən] _nm pr_ Tiziano.
title ['taitl] _n_ titolo; appellativo; **t. page** frontespizio.
titter ['titə] _vi_ ridacchiare.
titular ['titjulə] _a n_ titolare; **t. saint** santo patrono.
to [tuː] _prep_ a; per; rispetto a; verso, in; fino a; contro.
toad [toud] _n_ rospo.
toady ['toudi] _vt_ adulare; _n_ parassita.
toast [toust] _n_ pane abbrustolito; brindisi; _vt_ abbrustolire; fare un brindisi a; _vi_ brindare.
toaster ['toustə] _n_ graticola; tostino; tostapane.
tobacco [tə'bækou] _n_ tabacco.
tobacconist [tə'bækənist] _n_ tabaccaio; **t.'s shop** tabaccheria.
toboggan [tə'bɔgən] _n_ toboga; _vi_ andare in toboga; (_of prices_) calare.
today [tə'dei] _n ad_ oggi.
toddle ['tɔdl] _vi_ fare i primi passi.
toddler ['tɔdlə] _n_ infante ai primi passi.
toe [tou] _n_ dito del piede.
toffee ['tɔfi] _n_ caramella.
together [tə'geðə] _ad_ insieme, assieme.
toil [tɔil] _n_ fatica, lavoro faticoso; _vi_ faticare.
toilet ['tɔilit] _n_ toeletta; gabinetto
toilsome ['tɔilsəm] _a_ faticoso, laborioso.
token ['toukən] _n_ segno, pegno.
Toledo [tɔ'leidou] _n_ Toledo.
tolerable ['tɔlərəbl] _a_ tollerabile, sopportabile; discreto.
tolerance ['tɔlərəns] _n_ tolleranza, sopportazione, indulgenza.
tolerant ['tɔlərənt] _a_ tollerante, indulgente.
tolerate ['tɔləreit] _vt_ tollerare, sopportare.
toleration [.tɔlə'reiʃən] _n_ tolleranza.
toll [toul] _n_ gabella, pedaggio, tassa; rintocco di campana; _vti_ suonare a rintocco.
tomato [tə'maːtou] _n_ pomodoro.
tomb [tuːm] _n_ tomba.
tombstone ['tuːmstoun] _n_ pietra sepolcrale.
tom-cat ['tɔm'kæt] _n_ gatto (maschio).
tomorrow [tə'mɔrou] _n ad_ domani.
ton [tʌn] _n_ tonnellata.
tone [toun] _n_ tono; _vt_ dare il tono a; _vi_ armonizzare, intonarsi.
tongs [tɔŋz] _n pl_ molle, mollette _pl_.

tongue [tʌŋ] _n_ lingua; linguaggio; (_of bell_) battaglio; (_strip_) linguetta.
tonic ['tɔnik] _a n_ tonico, ricostituente.
tonight [tə'nait] _n ad_ stanotte; stasera.
tonnage ['tʌnidʒ] _n_ tonnellaggio.
tonsil ['tɔnsl] _n_ tonsilla.
tonsure ['tɔnʃə] _n_ tonsura.
too [tuː] _ad_ troppo; anche; inoltre, per di più; pure.
tool [tuːl] _n_ arnese, attrezzo, strumento, utensile.
tooth [tuːθ] _n_ dente.
toothache ['tuːθeik] _n_ mal di dente.
toothless ['tuːθlis] _a_ senza denti, sdentato.
top [tɔp] _n_ cima, culmine; coperchio; (_toy_) trottola; _vt_ coprire, coronare, raggiungere la sommità di; sorpassare.
topaz ['toupæz] _n_ topazio.
topic ['tɔpik] _n_ argomento, soggetto.
topical ['tɔpikəl] _a_ d'attualità.
topmost ['tɔpmoust] _a_ (il) più alto.
topographic(al) [.tɔpə'græfik(l)] _a_ topografico.
topography [tə'pɔgrəfi] _n_ topografia.
topsyturvy ['tɔpsi'təːvi] _ad_ sossopra, a soqquadro.
torch [tɔːtʃ] _n_ torcia, fiaccola; lampadina tascabile.
torment ['tɔːment] _n_ tormento; [tɔː'ment] _vt_ tormentare.
tornado [tɔː'neidou] _n_ tornado, ciclone.
torpedo [tɔː'piːdou] _n_ torpedine, siluro.
torpid ['tɔːpid] _a_ torpido, apatico, inerte.
torpor ['tɔːpə] _n_ torpore, apatia.
torrent ['tɔrənt] _n_ torrente.
torrid ['tɔrid] _a_ torrido.
tortoise ['tɔːtəs] _n_ tartaruga, testuggine.
tortuous ['tɔːtjuəs] _a_ tortuoso.
torture ['tɔːtʃə] _n_ tortura; _vt_ torturare.
Tory ['tɔːri] _a n_ (_pol_) conservatore.
toss [tɔs] _n_ lancio; moto brusco; beccheggio; _vt_ buttare in aria; sballottare, scuotere; _vi_ dimenarsi; giocare a testa o croce.
tot [tɔt] _n_ piccino; bicchierino.
total ['toutl] _a n_ totale.
totter ['tɔtə] _vi_ barcollare, vacillare.
touch [tʌtʃ] _n_ tatto, tocco, colpetto; contatto; leggero attacco; accenno; un po' di; _vt_ toccare; commuovere; riguardare; _vi_ toccarsi; **to t. at** (_naut_) far scalo; **to t. up** ritoccare.
touching ['tʌtʃiŋ] _a_ commovente.
touchstone ['tʌtʃstoun] _n_ pietra di paragone.
touchy ['tʌtʃi] _a_ suscettibile, permaloso.
tough [tʌf] _a_ duro, difficile, resistente, tenace; (_of meat_) tiglioso.
toughen ['tʌfn] _vti_ indurir(si).

toughness ['tʌfnis] n durezza, tenacia; difficoltà.

tour [tuə] n giro, gita, viaggio; vi fare un viaggio, una gita, un giro, visitare.

tourism ['tuərizəm] n turismo.

tourist ['tuərist] n turista.

tournament ['tuənəmənt] n torneo.

tousle ['tauzl] vt scarmigliare.

tout [taut] vi sollecitare ordini; (com) fare la piazza.

tow [tou] n stoppa; rimorchio; vt rimorchiare.

toward(s) [tə'wɔːd(z)] prep verso; a favore di.

towel ['tauəl] n asciugamano.

tower ['tauə] n torre; vi torreggiare.

town [taun] n città; **town hall** municipio.

toy [tɔi] n balocco, giocattolo; vi giocherellare, trastullarsi.

trace [treis] n traccia, orma, impronta; residuo; vt tracciare; rintracciare; seguire le tracce.

track [træk] n traccia, cammino, pista; sentiero; binario; rotta; scia; vt seguire la traccia di; snidare.

tract [trækt] n tratto, distesa; trattato, opuscolo.

tractable ['træktəbl] a trattabile, docile.

traction ['trækʃən] n trazione.

tractor ['træktə] n (mech) trattore, trattrice.

trade [treid] n commercio, traffico; mestiere, occupazione; vti commerciare, trattare; scambiare; **T. Union** sindacato; **t. winds** (venti) alisei pl.

trader ['treidə] n commerciante; nave mercantile.

tradesman ['treidzmən] n commerciante, negoziante.

tradition [trə'diʃən] n tradizione.

traditional [trə'diʃənl] a tradizionale.

traduce [trə'djuːs] vt calunniare, diffamare.

traffic ['træfik] n traffico; circolazione; vti trafficare, commerciare; **t. lights** semaforo.

tragedian [trə'dʒiːdiən] n tragediografo; attore tragico.

tragedy ['trædʒidi] n tragedia.

tragic(al) ['trædʒik(əl)] a tragico.

trail [treil] n traccia, scia, strascico, pista; vt seguire la traccia di, strascicare; vi strisciare, trascinarsi.

trailer ['treilə] n rimorchio; roulotte; (cin) 'prossimamente'.

train [trein] n treno; sèguito; strascico; serie; vt allenare, ammaestrare, allevare; vi allenarsi.

trainer ['treinə] n allenatore.

training ['treiniŋ] n allenamento, ammaestramento, esercitazione.

trait [treit] n tratto, caratteristica.

traitor ['treitə] n traditore.

tram(car) ['træm(kɑː)] n tram.

trammel ['træməl] n tramaglio; pl

impedimenti, ostacoli pl; vt impedire, impastoiare.

tramp [træmp] n viaggio a piedi; calpestio; vagabondo; vt attraversare a piedi; vi camminare con passo pesante.

trample ['træmpl] n calpestio; vti calpestare.

trance [trɑːns] n trance, catalessi ipnotica.

tranquil ['træŋkwil] a tranquillo.

tranquillity [træŋ'kwiliti] n tranquillità.

transact [træn'zækt] vt eseguire, trattare, negoziare.

transaction [træn'zækʃən] n affare, operazione; (leg) transazione; pl atti, verbali di società.

transatlantic ['trænzət'læntik] a transatlantico.

transcend [træn'send] vti trascendere.

transcendent [træn'sendənt] a trascendente; **transcendental** a trascendentale.

transcribe [træns'kraib] vt trascrivere.

transcript ['trænskript] n copia; riproduzione.

transfer ['trænsfəː] n trasferimento; cessione; (com) storno; decalcomania.

transfer [træns'fəː] vt trasferire; (com) stornare; decalcare.

transferable [træns'fəːrəbl] a trasferibile.

transfiguration ['trænsfigju'reiʃən] n trasfigurazione.

transfigure [træns'figə] vt trasfigurare.

transfix [træns'fiks] vt trafiggere, trapassare; pietrificare.

transform [træns'fɔːm] vt trasformare.

transformation [‚trænsfə'meiʃən] n trasformazione, metamorfosi.

transformer [træns'fɔːmə] n trasformatore.

transfuse [træns'fjuːz] vt travasare; (fig) trasfondere.

transfusion [træns'fjuːʒən] n trasfusione.

transgress [træns'gres] vt contravvenire a, trasgredire.

transgression [træns'greʃən] n trasgressione.

transgressor [træns'gresə] n trasgressore.

transient ['trænziənt] a transitorio, fugace.

transistor [træn'sistə] n transistor.

transit ['trænsit] n transito.

transition [træn'siʒən] n transizione, passaggio.

transitive ['trænsitiv] a transitivo.

transitory ['trænsitəri] a transitorio.

translatable [træns'leitəbl] a traducibile.

translate [træns'leit] vt tradurre.

translation [træns'leiʃən] n traduzione.

translator [træns'leitə] *n* traduttore.
translucent [træns'luːsnt] *a* traslucido, trasparente, diafano.
transmigration [ˌtrænzmai'greiʃən] *n* trasmigrazione.
transmission [trænz'miʃən] *n* trasmissione.
transmit [trænz'mit] *vt* trasmettere.
transmitter [trænz'mitə] *n* trasmettitore.
transparency [træns'pɛərənsi] *n* trasparenza; (*phot*) diapositiva.
transparent [træns'pɛərənt] *a* trasparente.
transpire [træns'paiə] *vi* trasparire, trapelare.
transplant [træns'plɑːnt] *vt* trapiantare.
transport ['trænspɔːt] *n* trasporto, mezzo di trasporto; violenta emozione; estasi; [træns'pɔːt] *vt* trasportare, rapire.
transportation [ˌtrænspɔː'teiʃən] *n* trasporto, deportazione.
transpose [træns'pouz] *vi* trasporre, spostare.
trans-ship [træns'ʃip] *vt* (*naut*) trasbordare.
transubstantiation ['trænsəbˌstænʃi'eiʃən] *n* transubstanziazione.
trap [træp] *n* trappola; botola; calesse; *vt* prendere in trappola.
trap-door ['træp'dɔːr] *n* botola.
trapeze [trə'piːz] *n* trapezio.
trapper ['træpə] *n* cacciatore di pelli.
trappings ['træpiŋz] *n pl* bardatura, finimenti *pl*.
trash [træʃ] *n* robaccia; sciocchezze.
traumatic [trɔː'mætik] *a* traumatico.
travel ['trævl] *n* viaggi *pl*; *vi* viaggiare.
traveler ['trævlə] *n* viaggiatore.
traverse ['trævəːs] *a* trasversale; *n* traversa; *vt* attraversare; contestare.
travesty ['trævisti] *n* parodia; *vt* parodiare.
trawl [trɔːl] *n* rete a strascico; *vti* pescare con strascico.
trawler ['trɔːlə] *n* motopeschereccio a strascico.
tray [trei] *n* vassoio; (*of a trunk*) scompartimento.
treacherous ['tretʃərəs] *a* traditore, sleale.
treachery ['tretʃəri] *n* tradimento, slealtà.
treacle ['triːkl] *n* melassa.
tread [tred] *n* passo; parte di suola che tocca la terra; (*of tire*) battistrada; (*of stair step*) pedata; *vt* calpestare; *vi* mettere il piede, camminare.
treadle ['tredl] *n* pedale.
treason ['triːzn] *n* tradimento.
treasonable ['triːznəbl] *a* proditorio.
treasure ['treʒə] *n* tesoro; *vt* custodire, tener caro.
treasurer ['treʒərə] *n* tesoriere.
treasury ['treʒəri] *n* tesoreria, tesoro.

treat [triːt] *n* festa, trattenimento; piacere; *vt* trattare; offrire un trattenimento a; (*med*) curare; *vi* negoziare, trattare.
treatise ['triːtiz] *n* trattato, dissertazione.
treatment ['triːtmənt] *n* trattamento, cura.
treaty ['triːti] *n* trattato, patto.
treble ['trebl] *a n* triplo; (*mus*) soprano; *vti* triplicar(si).
tree [triː] *n* albero.
trefoil ['trefɔil] *n* trifoglio.
trellis ['trelis] *n* traliccio; graticcio.
tremble ['trembl] *n* trèmito, tremore; *vi* tremare.
tremendous [tri'mendəs] *a* tremendo, terribile; (*fam*) straordinario.
tremor ['tremə] *n* tremore.
tremulous ['tremjuləs] *a* tremulo.
trench [trentʃ] *n* trincea, fosso.
trenchant ['trentʃənt] *a* tagliente, incisivo.
trend [trend] *n* orientamento, direzione, tendenza; *vi* tendere a, dirigersi.
Trent [trent] *n* Trento.
trepidation [ˌtrepi'deiʃən] *n* trepidazione.
trespass ['trespəs] *n* trasgressione, infrazione; violazione di proprietà; *vi* commettere un'infrazione, trasgredire, abusare di.
trespasser ['trespəsə] *n* trasgressore, contravventore.
tress [tres] *n* treccia.
trestle ['tresl] *n* cavalletto, trespolo.
trial ['traiəl] *n* esperimento, prova; processo; *pl* tribolazione.
triangle ['traiæŋgl] *n* triangolo.
triangular [trai'æŋgjulə] *a* triangolare.
tribe [traib] *n* tribù.
tribulation [ˌtribju'leiʃən] *n* tribolazione.
tribunal [trai'bjuːnl] *n* tribunale.
tribune ['tribjuːn] *n* tribuno; tribuna.
tributary ['tribjutəri] *n* affluente; *a n* tributario.
tribute ['tribjuːt] *n* tributo.
trice [trais] *n* istante; **in a t.** in un batter d'occhio.
trick [trik] *n* tiro; trucco; abitudine; espediente; *vt* ingannare; *vi* giocar tiri.
trickery ['trikəri] *n* inganno, stratagemma.
trickle ['trikl] *n* gocciolio; ruscelletto; *vi* gocciolare.
trickster ['trikstə] *n* raggiratore.
tricky ['triki] *a* furbo, ingannevole; difficile.
tricolor ['trikələ] *a n* tricolore.
tricycle ['traisikl] *n* triciclo.
trident ['traidənt] *n* tridente.
triennial [trai'eniəl] *a* triennale.
trifle ['traifl] *n* bagattella, bazzecola; (*cook*) zuppa inglese; *vti* gingillarsi, scherzare.
trifler ['traiflə] *n* persona frivola.

trifling ['traiflin] *a* insignificante; frivolo.

trigger ['trigə] *n* grilletto; **to t. off** *vt* dare inizio a.

trigonometry [.trigə'nɔmitri] *n* trigonometria.

trill [tril] *n* trillo; *vti* trillare.

trim [trim] *a* accurato, azzimato; *n* ordine, assetto, stato; *vt* aggiustare, rassettare; guarnire; tagliare.

trimming ['trimiŋ] *n* guarnizione.

Trinity ['triniti] *n* trinità.

trinket ['triŋkit] *n* gingillo, ninnolo.

trio ['triou] *pl* **trios** *n* (*mus*) trio, terzetto.

trip [trip] *n* gita, viaggio; incespicamento, passo falso, sgambetto; *vt* far inciampare, far sbagliare; *vi* inciampare, far un passo falso; **to t. along** saltellare.

tripe [traip] *n* trippa; (*sl*) sciocchezze *pl*.

triple ['tripl] *a* triplice; *vti* triplicar(si).

triplet ['triplit] *n* terzina; bimbo nato di parto trigemino.

triplicate ['triplikit] *a* triplicato; triplice; ['triplikeit] *vt* triplicare.

tripod ['traipɔd] *n* treppiedi; tripode.

Tripoli ['tripəli] *n* Tripoli.

trite [trait] *n* trito, banale, comune.

triteness ['traitnis] *n* banalità.

triton ['traitn] *n* tritone.

triumph ['traiəmf] *n* trionfo; *vi* trionfare.

triumphant [trai'ʌmfənt] *a* trionfante.

trivet ['trivit] *n* treppiedi.

trivial ['triviəl] *a* insignificante, banale, senza importanza.

triviality [.trivi'æliti] *n* banalità, cosa di nessuna importanza.

troll [troul] *vi* pescare con esca girante.

trolley ['trɔli] *n* carrello; (*el*) rotella di presa; **t. bus** filobus; **t. car** vettura tranviaria.

trombone [trɔm'boun] *n* (*mus*) trombone.

troop [tru:p] *n* (*mil*) truppa; frotta; compagnia teatrale; *vti* radunar(si), sfilare.

trooper ['tru:pə] *n* (*mil*) soldato di cavalleria; cavallo di truppa; (*naut*) nave per il trasporto di truppe.

trophy ['troufi] *n* trofeo.

tropic ['trɔpik] *n* tropico.

tropical ['trɔpikəl] *a* tropicale.

trot [trɔt] *n* trotto, trottata; *vi* trottare.

trotter ['trɔtə] *n* trottatore, zampa, zampino.

troubadour ['trubəduə] *n* trovatore.

trouble ['trʌbl] *n* disturbo, guaio, seccatura, imbroglio, disordine; *vt* disturbare, turbare, importunare, affliggere; *vi* preoccuparsi prendersi la briga di.

troubled ['trʌbld] *a* agitato, inquieto.

troublesome ['trʌblsəm] *a* fastidioso, molesto, noioso.

trough [trɔf] *n* trogolo.

trousers ['trauzəz] *n* *pl* calzoni pantaloni *pl*.

trout [traut] *n* trota.

trowel ['trauəl] *n* cazzuola; trapiantatoio.

truant ['truənt] *a* *n* pigro, svogliato, vagabondo; **play t.** marinare la scuola.

truce [tru:s] *n* tregua, armistizio.

truck [trʌk] *n* baratto; roba, robaccio; carro, carretto, autocarro; **t. farmer** ortolano, orticoltore; **t. line** impresa autotrasporti; **t. trailer** rimorchio di autocarro.

truckle ['trʌkl] *vi* mostrarsi servile.

truculent ['trʌkjulənt] *a* truculento.

trudge [trʌdʒ] *vt* percorrere faticosamente; *vi* camminare faticosamente.

true [tru:] *a* vero, fedele, leale.

truffle ['trʌfl] *n* tartufo.

truism ['truizəm] *n* truismo, verità lapalissiana.

truly ['tru:li] *ad* veramente, sinceramente; **yours t.** vostro devotissimo.

trump [trʌmp] *n* (*cards*) briscola, atout; (*fam*) persona eccellente; *vti* giocare una briscola, degli atouts.

trumpery ['trʌmpəri] *a* senza valore; *n* chincaglieria, orpello.

trumpet ['trʌmpit] *n* tromba; *vi* strombazzare, suonare la tromba; (*elephant*) barrire.

trumpeter ['trʌmpitə] *n* trombettiere.

truncate ['trʌŋkeit] *vt* troncare, mozzare.

truncheon ['trʌntʃən] *n* bastone, randello.

trundle ['trʌndl] *vti* (far) correre, ruzzolare.

trunk [trʌŋk] *n* tronco; baule; proboscide; *pl* calzoni corti, calzoncini.

truss [trʌs] *n* fascio, fastello, (*building*) travatura; (*med*) cinto erniario; *vt* (*of chicken etc, before cooking*) legare le ali; immobilizzare.

trust [trʌst] *n* fede, fiducia; custodia; (*com*) credito; *vt* aver fiducia in, fidarsi di; *vi* sperare vivamente.

trustee [trʌs'ti:] *n* fiduciario, amministratore.

trusteeship [trʌs'ti:ʃip] *n* amministrazione fiduciaria.

trustful ['trʌstful] *a* fiducioso.

trustworthy ['trʌst.wəði] *a* fidato, attendibile.

trusty ['trʌsti] *a* fedele, fidato.

truth [tru:θ] *n* verità.

truthful ['tru:θful] *a* veritiero, verace.

truthfully ['tru:θfuli] *ad* sinceramente; fedelmente, esattamente.

truthfulness ['tru:θfulnis] *n* veracità, sincerità

try [trai] *vt* provare, tentare, mettere alla prova, saggiare; (*leg*) processare; *vi* provare, sforzarsi.

trying ['traiiŋ] a difficile, penoso.
tsar [tsɑː] n zar.
tub [tʌb] n tino, tinozza, vasca da bagno; (naut) barcaccia.
tubby ['tʌbi] a tondo e grasso.
tube [tjuːb] n tubo; (London) ferrovia sotterranea; (US rad) valvola; test t. provetta.
tubercle ['tjuːbəkl] n tubercolo.
tubercular [tju(ː)'bəːkjulə] a tubercolare; tubercoloso.
tuberculosis [tju(ː),bəːkju'lousis] n tuberculosi.
tuberculous [tju'bəːkjuləs]a tubercoloso, tubercolotico.
tubular ['tjuːbjulə] a tubolare.
tuck [tʌk] n piega, basta; (sl) cibo; vt fare pieghe in; t. in ripiegare; (fam) mangiare avidamente; t. up rimboccare.
Tuesday ['tjuːzdi] n martedì.
tuft [tʌft] n ciuffo, fiocco, cespuglio.
tug [tʌg] n strappo, sforzo; strazio; (naut) rimorchiatore; vti tirare con forza, rimorchiare.
tuition [tju'iʃən] n insegnamento, istruzione.
tulip ['tjuːlip] n tulipano.
tumble ['tʌmbl] n capitombolo; vt buttar giù, rovesciare; vi cadere, capitombolare, fare acrobazie.
tumbler ['tʌmblə] n acrobata; bicchiere.
tumour ['tjuːmə] n tumore.
tumult ['tjuːmʌlt] n tumulto.
tumultuous [tju'mʌltjuəs] a tumultuoso.
tun [tʌn] n botte, tino.
tuna ['tuːnə] n tonno.
tune [tjuːn] n aria, melodia; accordo; vt accordare; to t. in (rad) sintonizzare.
tuneful ['tjuːnful] a armonioso, melodioso.
tunic ['tjuːnik] n tunica.
tunnel ['tʌnl] n galleria, traforo, tunnel.
tunny ['tʌni] n tonno.
turban ['təːbən] n turbante.
turbid ['təːbid] a torbido.
turbine ['təːbin] n turbina.
turbot ['təːbət] n rombo.
turbulence ['təːbjuləns] n turbolenza, agitazione.
turbulent ['təːbjulənt] a turbolento.
tureen [tə'riːn] n zuppiera.
turf [təːf] n zolla erbosa, tappeto, erboso.
turgid ['təːdʒid] a turgido; (fig) ampolloso.
Turin [tjuːˈrin] n Torino; **Turinese** a n torinese.
Turk [təːk] n turco.
Turkey ['təːki] n Turchia.
turkey ['təːki] n tacchino.
Turkish ['təːkiʃ] a n turco.
turmoil ['təːmɔil] n baccano, tumulto.
turn [təːn] n giro, curva, voltata, piega; turno; passeggiata; inclina-

zione; vt cambiare; girare; trasformare; voltare; tornire; tradurre; vi girare; divenire, farsi; rivolgersi, voltarsi; trasformarsi. **turntable** (rly) piattaforma girevole, (of record player) piatto, giradischi.
turncoat ['təːnkout] n girella.
turncock ['təːnkɔk] n fontaniere.
turner ['təːnə] n tornitore.
turning ['təːniŋ] a girevole; n svolta, voltata; t. point n svolta decisiva.
turnip ['təːnip] n rapa.
turnover ['təːn,ouvə] n rovesciamento; (com) giro di affari; torta.
turpentine ['təːpəntain] n trementina, acqua ragia.
turquoise ['təːkwɑːz] n turchese.
turret ['tʌrit] n torre, torretta.
turtle ['təːtl] n tartaruga; t.-dove n tortora.
Tuscan ['tʌskən] a n toscano.
Tuscany ['tʌskəni] n Toscana.
tusk [tʌsk] n zanna.
tussle ['tʌsl] n rissa, zuffa; vi azzuffarsi.
tutor ['tjuːtə] n istitutore, precettore; tutore; vt istruire, essere il precettore di.
tutorial [tju'tɔːriəl] a tutorio; n lezione a un piccolo gruppo di studenti.
twang [twæŋ] n suono acuto, suono nasale; vt pronunciare con tono nasale; vi fare un suono acuto o nasale.
tweed [twiːd] n tessuto di lana cardata, "tweed".
tweezers ['twiːzəz] n pl pinze, pinzette pl.
twelfth [twelfθ] a n dodicesimo.
twelve [twelv] a n dodici.
twenty ['twenti] a n venti; **twentieth** a n ventesimo.
twice [twais] ad due volte.
twig [twig] n rametto, ramoscello.
twilight ['twailait] n crepuscolo.
twin [twin] a n gemello.
twine [twain] n cordicella, spago; vti attorcigliar(si), intracciar(si), torcer(si).
twinge [twindʒ] n dolore lancinante, fitta; (fig) rimorso.
twinkle ['twiŋkl] n luccichio, scintillio; vi luccicare, scintillare; ammiccare, strizzare l'occhio.
twinkling ['twiŋkliŋ] n scintillio, balenio; in the t. of an eye in un baleno, in un batter d'occhio.
twirl [twəːl] n ghirigoro, piroetta.
twist [twist] n filo ritorto; rotolo di tabacco; filoncino (di pane); torsione; tendenza; capriccio; (dance) "twist"; vti contorcer(si), intrecciar(si), torcer(si).
twister ['twistə] n torcitore; (sl) truffatore; compito difficile, situazione ingarbugliata; **tongue-t.** scioglilingua.
twit [twit] vt rinfacciare.

twitch ['twitʃ] n contrazione spasmodica; vt dare uno strattone a; vi contorcersi spasmodicamente.
twitter ['twitə] n cinguettio, pigolio; (fam) agitazione; vi cinguettare, pigolare.
two [tuː] a n due.
twofold ['tuːfould] a doppio, duplice.
tycoon [tai'kuːn] n (sl) capitalista, magnate.
type [taip] n tipo, modello, genere; carattere tipografico.
typewrite ['taiprait] vt dattilografare.
typewriter ['taip.raitə] n macchina per scrivere.
typhoid ['taifɔid] a tifoide; n febbre tifoidea.
typhoon [tai'fuːn] n tifone.
typhus ['taifəs] n (med) tifo.
typical ['tipikəl] a tipico.
typify ['tipifai] vt rappresentare, simboleggiare, esemplificare.
typist ['taipist] n dattilografo, -fa.
typographer [tai'pɔgrəfə] n tipografo.
typography [tai'pɔgrəfi] n tipografia.
tyrannical [ti'rænikəl] a tirannico, dispotico.
tyrannize ['tirənaiz] vti tiranneggiare.
tyranny ['tirəni] n tirannia.
tyrant ['taiərənt] n tiranno.
tyro ['tairou] n novizio.
Tyrol ['tiroul] n Tirolo.
Tyrolean [ti'rouliən] **Tyrolese** [.tiri-'liːz] a n tirolese.

U

ubiquitous [ju'bikwitəs] a onnipresente.
ubiquity [ju'bikwiti] n ubiquità.
udder ['ʌdə] n mammella.
Uganda [ju'gændə] n Uganda.
ugliness ['ʌglinis] n bruttezza.
ugly ['ʌgli] a brutto.
Ukraine [ju'krein] n Ucraina.
ulcer ['ʌlsə] n ulcera.
ulcerate ['ʌlsəreit] vti ulcerare.
ulceration [.ʌlsə'reiʃən] n ulcerazione.
Ulster ['ʌlstə] n Ulster.
ulterior [ʌl'tiəriə] a ulteriore.
ultimate ['ʌltimit] a finale, fondamentale.
ultimatum [.ʌlti'meitəm] n ultimatum.
ultraviolet ['ʌltrə'vaiəlit] a ultravioletto.
umbrage ['ʌmbridʒ] n (fig) ombra, sospetto; offesa.
umbrella [ʌm'brelə] n ombrello.
Umbria ['ʌmbriə] n Umbria; **Umbrian** a n umbro.
umpire ['ʌmpaiə] n arbitro; vti arbitrare.
un- [ʌn] prefisso (avente significato negativo se unito ad aggettivi,

avverbi e sostantivi, indicante i contrario o l'annullamento dell'azione, se unito a verbi; qualora non si trovasse il vocabolo sotto la forma composta, si cerchi la forma senza prefisso).
unable ['ʌn'eibl] a inabile, incapace.
unabridged ['ʌnə'bridʒd] a non abbreviato, intero; **u. edition** edizione integrale.
unaccountable ['ʌnə'kauntəbl] a inesplicabile; irresponsabile.
unaccustomed ['ʌnə'kʌstəmd] a insolito; non abituato.
unacquainted ['ʌnə'kweintid] a **to be u. with** non conoscere.
unadulterated [.ʌnə'dʌltəreitid] a non adulterato, genuino.
unaffected ['ʌnə'fektid] a semplice, senz'affettazione, non influenzato.
unanimity [.junə'nimiti] n unanimità.
unanimous [ju'næniməs] a unanime.
unanswerable [ʌn'ɑːnsərəbl] a irrefutabile.
unassuming ['ʌnə'sjuːmiŋ] a modesto, senza pretese.
unattended ['ʌnə'tendid] a solo, incustodito.
unaware ['ʌnə'wɛə] a inconsapevole, inconscio; **unawares** ad all'improvviso, di sorpresa.
unbearable [ʌn'bɛərəbl] a insopportabile.
unbecoming ['ʌnbi'kʌmiŋ] a sconveniente; che non sta bene, che non si addice.
unbelief ['ʌnbi'liːf] n incredulità, scetticismo.
unbeliever [.ʌnbi'liːvə] n persona incredula, miscredente.
unbend ['ʌn'bend] vt raddrizzare; vi raddrizzarsi, rilassarsi; (fig) farsi affabile.
unbending ['ʌn'bendiŋ] a inflessibile.
unbidden ['ʌn'bidn] a spontaneo, non invitato.
unblemished [ʌn'blemiʃt] a senza macchia, perfetto.
unborn ['ʌn'bɔːn] a non ancora nato, futuro.
unbridled [ʌn'braidld] a sfrenato.
unburden [ʌn'bəːdn] vt alleggerire; **u. oneself** confidarsi con qlcu.
unbutton ['ʌn'bʌtn] vti sbottonare, sbottonarsi.
uncanny [ʌn'kæni] a misterioso, strano; inquietante.
uncertain [ʌn'səːtn] a incerto, poco sicuro.
uncertainty [ʌn'səːtnti] n incertezza.
unchangeable [ʌn'tʃeindʒəbl] a immutabile, invariabile.
uncle ['ʌŋkl] n zio.
unclean ['ʌn'kliːn] a impuro, sporco.
uncomfortable [ʌn'kʌmfətəbl] a scomodo, spiacevole.
uncommon [ʌn'kɔmən] a raro.
uncompromising [ʌn'kɔmprəmaiz-

iŋ] *a* intransigente, inflessibile, assoluto.

unconcerned ['ʌnkən'sə:nd] *a* indifferente.

unconditional ['ʌnkən'diʃənl] *a* incondizionato, assoluto.

unconquered ['ʌn'kɔŋkəd] *a* invitto.

unconscious [ʌn'kɔnʃəs] *a* inconscio, inconsapevole, privo di sensi.

uncouth [ʌn'kuθ] *a* goffo, rozzo.

uncouthness [ʌn'kuθnis] *n* goffaggine, rozzezza.

uncover [ʌn'kʌvə] *vt* scoprire, svelare; *vi* scoprirsi.

unction ['ʌnkʃən] *n* unzione, parole melliflue *pl.*

unctuous ['ʌŋktjuəs] *a* untuoso, mellifluo.

undaunted [ʌn'dɔːntid] *a* imperterrito, intrepido.

undecided ['ʌndi'saidid] *a* indeciso, indefinito.

under ['ʌndə] *prep* sotto, al di sotto di; in corso di; *ad* sotto.

underclothes ['ʌndəklouðz] *n pl,* **underclothing** ['ʌndəklouðiŋ] *n* biancheria personale, intima.

undercurrent ['ʌndə,kʌrənt] *n* corrente sottomarina, corrente nascosta.

underdeveloped ['ʌndədi'veləpt] *a* sottosviluppato.

underdone ['ʌndə'dʌn] *a* poco cotto, al sangue.

underfed ['ʌndə'fed] *a* denutrito.

undergo [,ʌndə'gou] *vt* subire, sottoporsi a, sopportare.

undergraduate [,ʌndə'grædjuit] *n* studente universitario.

underground ['ʌndəgraund] *a* sotterraneo; *n* sottosuolo; movimento clandestino; metropolitana, ferrovia sotterranea; *ad* sotto terra.

undergrowth ['ʌndəgrouθ] *n* sottobosco.

underhand ['ʌndəhænd] *a* clandestino, subdolo.

underlie [,ʌndə'lai] *vt* costituire la base di.

underline ['ʌndəlain] *vt* sottolineare.

undermine [,ʌndə'main] *vt* minare.

underneath [,ʌndə'niːθ] *ad prep* sotto, al di sotto (di).

underrate [,ʌndə'reit] *vt* sottovalutare.

undersell ['ʌndə'sel] *vt* vendere sotto prezzo.

undersigned ['ʌndəsaind] *a* sottoscritto.

understand [,ʌndə'stænd] *vti* capire, comprendere; dedurre; sottintendere; apprendere.

understandable [,ʌndə'stændəbl] *a* comprensibile.

understanding [,ʌndə'stændiŋ] *a* comprensivo; intelligente.

understatement ['ʌndə'steitmənt] *n* attenuazione dei fatti.

undertake [,ʌndə'teik] *vti* intraprendere, impegnarsi a.

undertaker ['ʌndə,teikə] *n* imprenditore di pompe funebri.

undertaking [,ʌndə'teikiŋ] *n* impresa.

undervalue ['ʌndə'væljuː] *vt* sottovalutare.

underwrite ['ʌndərait] *vt* sottoscrivere; (*com*) assicurare.

underwriter ['ʌndə,raitə] *n* firmatario; (*com*) assicuratore.

undisturbed ['ʌndis'təːbd] *a* indisturbato, imperturbato.

undo ['ʌn'duː] *vt* disfare, sciogliere, annullare, rovinare.

undoing ['ʌn'duiŋ] *n* rovina.

undone ['ʌn'dʌn] *a* slacciato, disfatto, rovinato, incompiuto, intentato.

undress ['ʌn'dres] *vti* svestire, svestirsi, spogliar(si).

undue ['ʌn'djuː] *a* indebito, eccessivo.

undulate ['ʌndjuleit] *vi* ondeggiare, fluttuare.

undulation [,ʌndju'leiʃən] *n* ondulazione.

unearth ['ʌn'əːθ] *vt* dissotterrare.

unearthly ['ʌn'əːθli] *a* soprannaturale, spettrale; (*fam*) impossibile.

uneasiness [ʌn'iːzinis] *n* disagio, inquietudine, ansia.

uneasy [ʌn'iːzi] *a* ansioso, inquieto.

unequal ['ʌn'iːkwəl] *a* ineguale, impari, non all'altezza di.

unequaled ['ʌn'iːkwəld] *a* senza pari.

unerring ['ʌn'əːriŋ] *a* infallibile.

uneven ['ʌn'iːvən] *a* ineguale; dispari; irregolare, accidentato.

unevenness ['ʌn'iːvənnis] *n* disuguaglianza; natura accidentata, irregolarità.

unexpected ['ʌniks'pektid] *a* inatteso, imprevisto.

unfair ['ʌn'fɛə] *a* ingiusto.

unfairness ['ʌn'fɛənis] *n* ingiustizia.

unfaithful ['ʌn'feiθful] *a* infedele, sleale; inesatto.

unfavorable ['ʌn'feivərəbl] *a* sfavorevole.

unfeeling [ʌn'fiːliŋ] *a* insensibile, spietato.

unfinished ['ʌn'finiʃt] *a* incompiuto, non rifinito.

unfit ['ʌn'fit] *a* inadatto, inabile; indegno.

unfold ['ʌn'fould] *vt* aprire, spiegare; svelare; svolgere.

unforgettable ['ʌnfə'getəbl] *a* indimenticabile.

unfortunate [ʌn'fɔːtʃnit] *a* sfortunato, infelice; **unfortunately** sfortunamente.

unfrock ['ʌn'frɔk] *vt* spretare.

ungainly [ʌn'geinli] *a* goffo.

ungrateful [ʌn'greitful] *a* ingrato.

unguent ['ʌŋgwənt] *n* unguento.

unhappiness [ʌn'hæpinis] *n* infelicità.

unhappy [ʌn'hæpi] *a* infelice, poco felice; inopportuno.

unhealthy [ʌn'helθi] *a* malsano; malaticcio.
unheard of [ʌn'həːdɔv] *a* inaudito.
unhurt ['ʌn'həːt] *a* illeso, incolume.
unicorn ['junikɔːn] *n* unicorno.
uniform ['junifɔːm] *a* uniforme; *n* divisa, uniforme.
uniformity [,juni'fɔːmiti] *n* uniformità.
unilateral ['juni'lætərəl] *a* unilaterale.
unimpaired ['ʌnim'pɛəd] *a* non danneggiato, intatto.
unintelligence ['ʌnin'telidʒəns] *n* mancanza di intelligenza.
unintelligent ['ʌnin'telidʒənt] *a* ottuso, stupido.
union ['junjən] *n* unione, accordo, alleanza; **u. suit** combinazione.
unique [juː'niːk] *a* unico, solo.
unison ['juːnizn] *a n* unisono.
unit ['juːnit] *n* unità, unità di misura.
unitarian [,juːni'tɛəriən] *a n* unitario.
unite [juː'nait] *vti* congiunger(si), unir(si).
United States [ju,naitid'steits] *n pl* Stati Uniti (d'America).
unity ['juːniti] *n* unità, uniformità, armonia.
universal ['juːni'vəːsəl] *a n* universale.
universality [,juːnivəː'sæliti] *n* universalità.
universe ['juːnivəːs] *n* universo.
university [,juni'vəːsiti] *n* università.
unjust ['ʌn'dʒʌst] *a* ingiusto.
unkempt ['ʌn'kempt] *a* spettinato, incolto.
unkind [ʌn'kaind] *a* scortese, cattivo.
unkindness [ʌn'kaindnis] *n* scortesia, cattiveria.
unknown ['ʌn'noun] *a* sconosciuto, ignoto; *n* ignoto.
unless [ən'les] *cj* a meno che non, se non.
unlike ['ʌn'laik] *a* dissimile; *prep* diversamente da.
unlikely [ʌn'laikli] *a* inverosimile, improbabile.
unload ['ʌn'loud] *vt* scaricare, (*fin*) liberarsi di.
unlock ['ʌn'lɔk] *vt* aprire, disserrare.
unlooked-for [ʌn'luktfɔː] *a* inaspettato, inatteso.
unlucky [ʌn'lʌki] *a* sfortunato; sinistro.
unmake ['ʌn'meik] *vt* disfare.
unman ['ʌn'mæn] *vt* scoraggiare, snervare.
unmannerly [ʌn'mænəli] *a* sgarbato.
unmistakable ['ʌnmis'teikəbl] *a* chiaro, indubbio.
unmoved ['ʌn'muːvd] *a* immobile, impassibile.
unnatural [ʌn'nætʃrəl] *a* contro natura, artificioso.
unnecessary [ʌn'nesisəri] *a* inutile, superfluo.

unnerve ['ʌn'nəːv] *vt* snervare.
unobtrusive ['ʌnəb'truːsiv] *a* discreto, modesto, riservato.
unpleasant [ʌn'pleznt] *a* sgradevole, spiacevole.
unpopular ['ʌn'pɔpjulə] *a* impopolare.
unpretending ['ʌnpri'tendiŋ] **unpretentious** ['ʌnpri'tenʃəs] *a* modesto, senza pretese.
unpublished ['ʌn'pʌbliʃt] *a* inedito.
unquestionable [ʌn'kwestʃənəbl] *a* indiscutibile, indubitabile.
unreadable ['ʌn'riːdəbl] *a* (*of writing, of a book*) illeggibile.
unreasonable [ʌn'riːznəbl] *a* irragionevole.
unreasonableness [ʌn'riːznəblnis] *n* irragionevolezza, assurdità.
unrequited ['ʌnri'kwaitid] *a* non corrisposto, non compensato.
unrest ['ʌn'rest] *n* fermento, agitazione.
unruly [ʌn'ruːli] *a* sregolato, indisciplinato.
unsavory ['ʌn'seivəri] *a* (*fig*) ripugnante, disgustoso.
unscripted ['ʌn'skriptid] *a* improvvisato, estemporaneo.
unseemly [ʌn'siːmli] *a* indecoroso, sconveniente.
unseen ['ʌn'siːn] *a* non visto; **u. (sight) translation** traduzione a prima vista.
unselfish ['ʌn'selfiʃ] *a* disinteressato, altruista.
unsettle ['ʌn'setl] *vt* sconvolgere, turbare.
unsightly [ʌn'saitli] *a* brutto, deforme.
unspeakable [ʌn'spiːkəbl] *a* indicibile, inqualificabile.
unsteady ['ʌn'stedi] *a* vacillante, instabile, variabile.
unsure [ʌn'ʃuə] *a* malsicuro, incerto.
untidy [ʌn'taidi] *a* disordinato, sciatto.
until [ən'til] *prep* fino a, prima di; *cj* finchè (non).
untimely [ʌn'taimli] *a* prematuro, intempestivo.
untiring [ʌn'taiəriŋ] *a* instancabile.
untold ['ʌn'tould] *a* indicibile; innumerevole.
unusual [ʌn'juʒuəl] *a* insolito.
unwary [ʌn'wɛəri] *a* imprudente, incauto.
unwelcome [ʌn'welkəm] *a* malaccolto, sgradito.
unwell ['ʌn'wel] *a* indisposto, sofferente.
unwilling ['ʌn'wiliŋ] *a* riluttante.
unworthy ['ʌn'wəːði] *a* indegno.
up [ʌp] *prep* su per; *ad* in alto; in piedi; su, in su; **up to** fino a; *a* che va verso l'alto.
upbraid [ʌp'breid] *vt* rimproverare.
upbraiding [ʌp'breidiŋ] *n* rimproveri *pl*.

upbringing ['ʌp̩briŋiŋ] n educazione.

upheaval [ʌp'hiːvəl] n sollevamento, subbuglio, scompiglio.

uphill ['up'hil] a erto, faticoso; ad in salita, in su.

uphold [ʌp'hould] vt sostenere, mantenere.

upholsterer [ʌp'houlstərə] n tappezziere.

upholstery [ʌp'houlstəri] n tappezzeria, imbottitura.

upkeep ['ʌpkiːp] n mantenimento, manutenzione.

upland ['ʌplənd] a alto, montagnoso; n altipiano.

uplift ['ʌplift] n incoraggiamento; vt [ʌp'lift] alzare, sollevare.

upon [ə'pɔn] prep sopra, su; al momento di.

upper ['ʌpə] a più in alto, più elevato, superiore.

uppermost ['ʌpəmoust] a ad il più alto, il più importante, sopra a tutti.

upright ['ʌp'rait] a diritto, eretto, in piedi; (fig) onesto, retto; ad in posizione verticale.

uprightness ['ʌp'raitnis] n perpendicolarità; rettitudine.

uproar ['ʌp̩rɔː] n tumulto, baraonda.

uproarious [ʌp'rɔːriəs] a rumoroso, fragoroso; tumultuoso.

uproariously [ʌp'rɔːriəsli] ad rumorosamente; tumultuosamente.

uproot [ʌp'ruːt] vt estirpare, sradicare, svellere.

upset [ʌp'set] n capovolgimento, rovesciamento; vt capovolgere, rovesciare, sconvolgere.

upshot ['ʌpʃɔt] n esito, risultato finale.

upside-down ['ʌpsaid'daun] ad in disordine, sottosopra; capovolto.

upstairs ['ʌp'stɛəz] a del piano superiore; ad su, al piano di sopra.

upstart ['ʌpstɑːt] n villano rifatto, nuovo ricco.

up-to-date ['ʌptu'deit] a aggiornato; alla moda.

upward ['ʌpwəd] a che si muove verso l'alto; **upwards** ad in alto, verso l'alto.

urban ['əːbən] a urbano, di città.

urbane [əː'bein] a urbano, cortese.

urbanity [əː'bæniti] n urbanità, cortesia.

urchin ['əːtʃin] n monello; **sea u.** riccio di mare.

urge [əːdʒ] n stimolo, impulso; sprone; vt incalzare, spingere.

urgency ['əːdʒənsi] n urgenza.

urgent ['əːdʒənt] a urgente.

urine ['juərin] n orina.

urn [əːn] n urna; bricco.

Uruguay ['urugwai] n Uruguay.

us [ʌs] pron noi, ci.

usage ['juːzidʒ] n uso, trattamento, usanza.

use [juːs] n uso, impiego; utilità;

abitudine, usanza; [juːz] vt usare, servirsi di, utilizzare, adoperare.

useful ['juːsful] a utile, vantaggioso.

usefulness ['juːsfulnis] n utilità.

useless ['juːslis] a inutile, vano, inefficace.

uselessness ['juːslisnis] n inutilità.

user ['juːzə] n chi usa, utente; (leg) usufruttuario.

usher ['ʌʃə] n usciere; **to u. in** vt introdurre, annunciare.

usual ['juːʒuəl] a usuale, solito; **as u.** ad come al solito.

usurer ['juːʒərə] n usuraio.

usurp [juː'zəːp] vt usurpare.

usurpation [̩juːzə'peiʃən] n usurpazione.

usurper [juː'zəːpə] n usurpatore.

usury ['juːʒuri] n usura.

utensil [ju'tensl] n utensile, arnese, strumento.

uterus ['juːtərəs] n utero.

utilitarian [̩juːtili'tɛəriən] a utilitario; n (phil) utilitarista.

utility [juː'tiliti] n utilità, vantaggio.

utilization [̩juːtilai'zeiʃən] n utilizzazione.

utilize ['juːtilaiz] vt utilizzare.

utmost ['ʌtmoust] a n massimo, estremo.

utter ['ʌtə] a assoluto, completo; vt emettere, pronunciare.

utterance ['ʌtərəns] n pronuncia modo di parlare; espressione, sfogo.

V

vacancy ['veikənsi] n posto vacante, vuoto; (fig) vacuità.

vacant ['veikənt] a vacante, vuoto, libero; vacuo.

vacate [və'keit] vt lasciar libero.

vacation [və'keiʃən] n vacanza, -ze pl; **vacationist** villeggiante.

vaccinate ['væksineit] vt vaccinare.

vaccination [̩væksi'neiʃən] n vaccinazione.

vaccine ['væksiːn] n vaccino.

vacillate ['væsileit] vi vacillare.

vacillation [̩væsi'leiʃən] n vacillamento, irresolutezza.

vacuity [væ'kjuiti] n vacuità.

vacuous ['vækjuəs] a vacuo, vuoto, privo di espressione.

vacuum ['vækjuəm] n vuoto, vuoto pneumatico.

vagabond ['vægəbənd] a n vagabondo.

vagary ['veigəri] n capriccio, ghiribizzo.

vagrant ['veigrənt] a ambulante, vagabondo; n vagabondo, accattone.

vague [veig] a vago, impreciso.

vain [vein] a vano, vanitoso.

vainglorious [vein'glɔːriəs] a vanaglorioso.

vainglory [vein'glɔːri] n vanagloria.

vale [veil] n (poet) valle, vallata.

Valentine ['væləntain] *nm pr* Valentino.

valentine ['væləntain] *n* innamorato, fidanzato; biglietto amoroso (che si invia il giorno di S. Valentino).

valet ['vælit] *n* cameriere personale.

valiant ['væliənt] *a* valoroso, prode.

valid ['vælid] *a* valido.

validity [və'liditi] *n* validità.

valley ['væli] *n* valle.

valor ['vælə] *n* valore, coraggio.

valuable ['væljuəbl] *a* costoso, prezioso; *n* oggetto di valore.

valuation [‚vælju'eiʃən] *n* valutazione, stima.

value ['væljuː] *n* valore, pregio; *vt* valutare, stimare.

valueless ['væljulis] *a* di nessun valore.

valve [vælv] *n* (*mech, anat*) valvola.

vamp [væmp] *n* (*shoe*) tomaia, rimonta; (*mus*) accompagnamento improvvisato; (*sl*) donna fatale; *vt* fare la rimonta; (*mus*) improvvisare; (*sl*) adescare.

vampire ['væmpaiə] *n* vampiro.

van [væn] *n* camioncino, furgoncino; avanguardia.

vanadium [və'neidiəm] *n* vanadio.

vandal ['vændəl] *a n* vandalo.

vandalism ['vændəlizəm] *n* vandalismo.

vane [vein] *n* banderuola.

vanguard ['væŋɡɑːd] *n* avanguardia.

vanilla [və'nilə] *n* vaniglia.

vanish ['væniʃ] *vi* svanire, sparire, dileguarsi.

vanity ['væniti] *n* vanità.

vanquish ['væŋkwiʃ] *vt* sopraffare, vincere.

vantage ['vɑːntidʒ] *n* (*tennis*) vantaggio; **v. ground** posizione elevata.

vapor ['veipə] *n* vapore.

vaporize ['veipəraiz] *vti* vaporizzar(si).

vaporous ['veipərəs] *a* vaporoso.

variable ['vɛəriəbl] *a* variabile; *n* (*math*) quantità variabile.

variance ['vɛəriəns] *n* disaccordo; **at v.** *ad* in disaccordo con.

variation [‚vɛəri'eiʃən] *n* variazione.

varicose ['værikous] *a* varicoso.

varied ['vɛərid] *a* vario, variato.

variegate ['vɛərigeit] *vt* screziare, variegare.

variety [və'raiəti] *n* varietà; **v. theatre** teatro di varietà.

various ['vɛəriəs] *a* diverso, vario, parecchi.

varnish ['vɑːniʃ] *n* vernice; *vt* verniciare.

vary ['vɛəri] *vt* variare, modificare; *vi* variare, essere diverso.

vase [vɑːz] *n* vaso.

vaseline ['væsilin] *n* vasellina.

vassal ['væsəl] *n* vassallo.

vast [vɑːst] *a* vasto, immenso.

vastness ['vɑːstnis] *n* vastità, immensità.

vat [væt] *n* tino, tinozza.

Vatican ['vætikən] *n* Vaticano.

vaudeville ['voudəvil] *n* 'vaudeville', operetta, spettacolo di varietà; **v. theater** teatro di varietà.

vault [vɔːlt] *n* (*arch*) volta; cantina; sotterraneo; tomba; volteggio, salto; *vt* costruire a volta; *vti* saltare.

vaulting ['vɔltiŋ] *n* salto, volteggio; **pole v.** salto con l'asta.

vaunt [vɔːnt] *n* vanteria, vanto; *vti* vantarsi di.

veal [viːl] *n* vitello.

veer [viə] *vi* (*wind*) cambiar direzione; (*fig*) cambiar opinione.

vegetable ['vedʒitəbl] *a* vegetale; *n pl* verdura; ortaggio, legume; **v. marrow** zucchino.

vegetarian [‚vedʒi'tɛəriən] *a n* vegetariano.

vegetate ['vedʒiteit] *vi* vegetare.

vegetation [‚vedʒi'teiʃən] *n* vegetazione.

vehemence ['viːiməns] *n* veemenza.

vehement ['viːimənt] *a* veemente.

vehicle ['viːikl] *n* veicolo.

veil [veil] *n* velo; *vt* velare.

vein [vein] *n* vena; (*fig*) umore.

vellum ['veləm] *n* pergamena.

velocity [vi'lɔsiti] *n* velocità.

velvet ['velvit] *a n* (di) velluto.

venal ['viːnl] *a* venale.

vendor ['vendɔː] *n* venditore.

veneer [vi'niə] *n* impiallacciatura; (*fig*) vernice.

venerable ['venərəbl] *a* venerabile.

venerate ['venəreit] *vt* venerare.

veneration [‚venə'reiʃən] *n* venerazione.

venereal [vi'niəriəl] *a* venereo.

Venetian [vi'niːʃən] *a n* veneziano.

Venezuela [‚vene'zweilə] *n* Venezuela.

vengeance ['vendʒəns] *n* vendetta.

venial ['viniəl] *a* veniale.

Venice ['venis] *n* Venezia.

venison ['venzn] *n* carne di cervo, di daino.

venom ['venəm] *n* veleno.

venomous ['venəməs] *a* velenoso; (*fig*) malevolo.

vent [vent] *n* buco, foro; sbocco; conduttura di camino; (*fig*) sfogo; *vt* dare sfogo a.

ventilate ['ventileit] *vt* ventilare.

ventilation [‚venti'leiʃən] *n* ventilazione.

ventilator ['ventileitə] *n* ventilatore.

ventriloquism [ven'triləkwizəm] *n* ventriloquio.

ventriloquist [ven'triləkwist] *n* ventriloquo.

venture ['ventʃə] *n* impresa, avventura; rischio; speculazione; *vti* arrischiarsi, avventurarsi, osare.

venturesome ['ventʃəsəm] *a* avventuroso, ardito.

Venus ['viːnəs] *n pr* Venere.

veracious [və'reiʃəs] *a* verace, veridico.

veracity [və'ræsiti] *n* veracità.

verb [vəːb] *n* (*gram*) verbo.
verbal ['vəːbəl] *a* verbale.
verbatim [vəː'beitim] *a* testuale; *ad* testualmente.
verbose [vəː'bous] *a* verboso.
verbosity [və'bɔsiti] *n* verbosità.
verdant ['vəːdənt] *a* verdeggiante.
verdict ['vəːdikt] *n* verdetto.
verdure ['vəːdʒə] *n* vegetazione, verde, verzura.
verge [vəːdʒ] *n* bordo, limite, orlo; punto estremo; *vi* confinare; declinare, tendere verso.
verger ['vəːdʒə] *n* sagrestano.
Vergil ['vəːdʒil] *n* Virgilio.
verification [ˌverifi'keiʃən] *n* verifica.
verify ['verifai] *vt* verificare, controllare.
verity ['veriti] *n* verità.
vermilion [vəː'miljən] *n* cinabro, vermiglione; (*color*) vermiglio.
vermin ['vəːmin] *n* *pl* animali nocivi, insetti parassiti *pl*.
verminous ['vəːminəs] *a* infestato da animali nocivi, da insetti parassiti.
vermouth ['vəːməθ] *n* vermut, vermouth.
vernacular [vəː'nækjulə] *a n* vernacolo.
vernal ['vəːnl] *a* primaverile.
Verona [vi'rounə] *n* Verona; **Veronese** *a n* veronese.
versatile ['vəːsətail] *a* versatile.
versatility [ˌvəːsə'tiliti] *n* versatilità.
verse [vəːs] *n* verso, -si *pl*, poesia.
versed [vəːst] *a* versato, abile.
version ['vəːʃən] *n* versione.
vertex ['vəːteks] *pl* **vertices** *n* vertice.
vertical ['vəːtikəl] *a* verticale.
vertigo ['vəːtigou] *n* vertigine, -ni *pl*.
vervain ['vəː'vein] *n* verbena.
verve [vəːv] *n* 'verve', brio; energia, vigore.
very ['veri] *a* stesso, proprio; *ad* molto, assai.
Vespers ['vespəz] *n* *pl* vespri *pl*.
vessel ['vesl] *n* recipiente; nave, vascello; (*anat*) vaso.
vest [vest] *n* maglia; panciotto.
vestibule ['vestibjuːl] *n* vestibolo.
vestige ['vestidʒ] *n* vestigio, orma, traccia.
vestment ['vestmənt] *n* (*eccl*) paramento sacerdotale.
vestry ['vestri] *n* sagrestia; consiglio d'amministrazione d'una parrocchia.
veteran ['vetərən] *a n* veterano.
veterinary ['vetərinəri] *a n* veterinario.
veto ['viːtou] *pl* **vetoes** *n* veto; diritto di veto.
vex [veks] *vt* irritare.
vexation [vek'seiʃən] *n* irritazione.
vexatious [vek'seiʃəs] *a* irritante, fastidioso.
via [vaiə] *prep* per la via di, via.
viaduct ['vaiədʌkt] *n* viadotto.
vial ['vaiəl] *n* fiala.

viand ['vaiənd] *n* (*usu* *pl*) cibo, provvista.
vibrant ['vaibrənt] *a* vibrante.
vibrate [vai'breit] *vi* vibrare.
vibration [vai'breiʃən] *n* vibrazione.
vicar ['vikə] *n* parroco, vicario.
vicarage ['vikəridʒ] *n* canonica, dignità di parroco.
vicarious [vi'kɛəriəs] *a* sopportato per un altro, vicario.
vice [vais] *n* vizio; sostituto, vice; **v.-president** vice presidente.
viceroy ['vaisrɔi] *n* viceré.
vicinity [vi'siniti] *n* vicinanza.
vicious ['viʃəs] *a* vizioso, cattivo; (*style* *etc*) scorretto.
vicissitude [vi'sisitjuːd] *n* vicissitudine, vicenda.
victim ['viktim] *n* vittima.
victimize ['viktimaiz] *vt* far vittima di.
victor ['viktə] *n* vincitore.
Victor ['viktə] *nm* *pr* Vittorio.
Victoria [vik'tɔːriə] *nf* *pr* Vittoria.
victorious [vik'tɔːriəs] *a* vittorioso.
victory ['viktəri] *n* vittoria.
victual ['vitl] *vt* vettovagliare.
victuals ['vitlz] *n* *pl* vettovaglie *pl*.
video ['vaidiou] *a* (*tv*) video; *n* televisione.
vie [vai] *vi* gareggiare, rivaleggiare.
Vienna [vi'enə] *n* Vienna; **Viennese** *a n* viennese.
view [vjuː] *n* vista, veduta, paesaggio; visione; opinione; *vt* guardare attentamente, considerare.
vigil ['vidʒil] *n* veglia; vigilia.
vigilance ['vidʒiləns] *n* vigilanza.
vigilant ['vidʒilənt] *a* vigilante.
vigor ['vigə] *n* vigore.
vigorous ['vigərəs] *a* vigoroso.
Viking ['vaikiŋ] *n* vichingo.
vile [vail] *a* vile, abietto.
vileness ['vailnis] *n* viltà, abiezione.
villa ['vilə] *n* villa.
village ['vilidʒ] *n* villaggio, paese.
villager ['vilidʒə] *n* villico, abitante di villaggio.
villain ['vilən] *n* mascalzone, furfante.
villainous ['vilənəs] *a* scellerato, infame.
villainy ['viləni] *n* scelleratezza, infamia.
Vincent ['vinsənt] *nm* *pr* Vincenzo.
vindicate ['vindikeit] *vt* rivendicare.
vindication [ˌvindi'keiʃən] *n* rivendicazione.
vindictive [vin'diktiv] *a* vendicativo.
vine [vain] *n* vite.
vinegar ['vinigə] *n* aceto.
vineyard ['vinjəd] *n* vigna, vigneto.
vintage ['vintidʒ] *n* vendemmia, raccolto.
vinyl ['vainil] *n* vinile.
viola [vi'oulə] *n* viola.
violate ['vaiəleit] *vt* violare; trasgredire, infrangere.
violation [ˌvaiə'leiʃən] *n* violazione, infrazione.

violence ['vaiələns] n violenza.
violent ['vaiələnt] a violento.
violet ['vaiəlit] a violetto, di color viola; n violetta, viola mammola; color viola.
violin [,vaiə'lin] n (mus) violino.
violinist ['vaiəlinist] n violinista.
viper ['vaipə] n vipera.
virago [vi'rɑːgou] n virago, donna violenta.
Virgil ['vəːdʒil] nm pr Virgilio.
virgin ['vəːdʒin] a n vergine.
virginity [vəː'dʒiniti] n verginità.
virile ['virail] a virile.
virility [vi'riliti] n virilità.
virtual ['vəːtjuəl] a virtuale, di fatto.
virtue ['vəːtjuː] n virtù.
virtuous ['vəːtjuəs] a virtuoso.
virulence ['viruləns] n virulenza.
virulent ['virulənt] a virulento.
virus ['vaiərəs] n virus.
visa ['viːzə] n visto consolare; vt vistare.
visage ['vizidʒ] n viso.
viscount(ess) ['vaikaunt(is)] n visconte(ssa).
viscous ['viskəs] a viscoso.
vise [vais] n morsa.
visibility [,vizi'biliti] n visibilità.
visible ['vizəbl] a visibile.
vision ['viʒən] n visione; (sight) vista.
visionary ['viʒnəri] a n visionario; a immaginario, chimerico.
visit ['vizit] n visita; vt visitare, far visita a.
visitation [,vizi'teiʃən] n visita ufficiale; (eccl) visitazione.
visitor ['vizitə] n visitatore, ospite.
visor ['vaizə] n visiera.
vista ['vistə] n vista, scorcio panoramico, lunga serie; **v. dome car** (rly) carrozza panoramica.
visual ['vizjuəl] a visuale, visivo.
visualize ['vizjuəlaiz] vti immaginare; rendere visibile.
vital ['vaitl] a vitale, (fig) essenziale, importante; **v. statistics** statistiche anagrafiche; (fam) misure femminili.
vitality [vai'tæliti] n vitalità.
vitamin ['vitəmin] n vitamina.
vitiate ['viʃieit] vt viziare; corrompere; invalidare.
vitreous ['vitriəs] a vitreo.
vitriol ['vitriəl] n vetriolo.
vituperate [vi'tjupəreit] vt vituperare.
vituperation [vi,tjupə'reiʃən] n vituperazione.
vivacious [vi'veiʃəs] a vivace.
vivacity [vi'væsiti] n vivacità.
vivid ['vivid] a vivace, vivo, vivido.
vividness ['vividnis] n vivezza, vivacità.
vivify ['vivifai] vt vivificare.
vivisection [,vivi'sekʃən] n vivisezione.
vixen ['viksn] n volpe femmina.
vizier [vi'ziə] n visir.
vocabulary [və'kæbjuləri] n vocabolario.

vocal ['voukəl] a vocale.
vocalist ['voukəlist] n cantante.
vocation [vou'keiʃən] n vocazione.
vocative ['vɔkətiv] n vocativo.
vociferate [vou'sifəreit] vi vociferare, vociare.
vociferous [və'sifərəs] a vociferante, clamoroso.
vogue [voug] n voga, moda.
voice [vɔis] n voce; grido; (of animals) verso; vt esprimere, intonare.
void [vɔid] a n vuoto; a privo, nullo.
volatile ['vɔiətail] a volatile.
volatility [,vɔlə'tiliti] n volatilità.
volatilize [vɔ'lætilaiz] vti volatilizzar(si).
volcanic [vɔl'kænik] a vulcanico.
volcano [vɔl'keinou] n vulcano.
volition [vou'liʃən] n volizione.
volley ['vɔli] n raffica, scarica, salva.
volt [voult] n (el) volt.
voltage ['voultidʒ] n (el) voltaggio.
voluble ['vɔljubl] a fluente, loquace.
volume ['vɔljuːm] n volume.
voluminous [və'ljuːminəs] a voluminoso.
voluntary ['vɔləntəri] a volontario.
volunteer [,vɔlən'tiə] n soldato volontario; vti offrir(si) volontariamente.
voluptuary [və'lʌptjuəri] n individuo sensuale.
voluptuous [və'lʌptjuəs] a voluttuoso.
voluptuousness [və'lʌptjuəsnis] n voluttà.
vomit ['vɔmit] vti vomitare.
voracious [və'reiʃəs] a vorace.
voracity [vɔ'ræsiti] n voracità.
vortex ['vɔːteks] n vortice.
votary ['voutəri] n devoto, seguace fedele.
vote [vout] n voto, votazione; vti votare.
voter ['voutə] n votante, elettore.
votive ['voutiv] a votivo.
vouch [vautʃ] vt attestare, confermare; **to v. for** rispondere di, garantire per.
voucher ['vautʃə] n documento giustificativo, pezza d'appoggio; buono, tagliando; (com) ricevuta.
vouchsafe [vautʃ'seif] vt accordare, concedere.
vow [vau] n promesso, voto; vt far voto di, giurare.
vowel ['vauəl] n vocale.
voyage ['vɔidʒ] n viaggio (per mare); vi navigare, fare una traversata.
vulgar ['vʌlgə] a volgare.
vulgarity [vʌl'gæriti] n volgarità.
vulnerable ['vʌlnərəbl] a vulnerabile.
vulture ['vʌltʃə] n avvoltolo.

W

wad [wɔd] n batuffolo; stoppaccio; (sl) denaro.

wadding ['wɔdiŋ] n imbottitura, ovatta.

waddle ['wɔdl] vi camminare dondolandosi (come le anitre).

wade [weid] vti attraversare a guado; procedere faticosamente.

wafer ['weifə] n wafer, cialda, ostia.

waft [wɑːft] n soffio, alito, zaffata; vt diffondere, spandere.

wag [wæg] n burlone; vti scodinzolare.

wage(s) ['weidʒ(iz)] n (usu pl) paga, salario; **to w. war** muover guerra.

wager ['weidʒə] n scommessa; vt scommettere.

waggle ['wægl] n dimenamento, dondolamento; vt dimenare, dondolare.

wagon ['wægən] n carro.

wagtail ['wægteil] n cutrettola.

waif [weif] n trovatello; **waifs and strays** relitti, oggetti smarriti pl.

wail [weil] n lamento, gemito; vi lamentarsi; (of baby) vagire.

wainscot ['weinskət] n rivestimento in legno; zoccolo (di parete).

waist [weist] n vita, cintola.

waistcoat ['weiskout] n panciotto, gilè.

wait [weit] n attesa; vi aspettare, attendere; servire a tavola; **to w. upon** servire.

waiter ['weitə] **waitress** ['weitris] n (d'albergo etc) cameriere, -ra.

waive [weiv] vt rinunziare a, desistere da.

wake [weik] n scia; veglia; vti risvegliar(si), svegliar(si); vegliare.

wakeful ['weikful] a sveglio, insonne, vigile.

wakefulness ['weikfulnis] n insonnia, vigilanza.

waken ['weikən] vti svegliar(si).

Wales [weilz] n Galles.

walk [wɔːk] n passeggiata; percorso; passo; viale; **w. of life** professione, mestiere; ceto; **sidewalk** marciapiede; vt far camminare, percorrere; vi camminare, passeggiare, andare a piedi.

walker ['wɔːkə] n camminatore, pedone.

walking ['wɔːkiŋ] a che cammina, ambulante; n il camminare; **w. stick** bastone da passeggio.

wall [wɔːl] n muro; mura pl; parete; vt cingere di mura.

wallet ['wɔlit] n portafoglio; borsa.

wallow ['wɔlou] vi avvoltolarsi, sguazzare.

wallpaper ['wɔːl,peipə] n tappezzeria, carta da parato.

walnut ['wɔːlnət] n noce.

walrus ['wɔːlrəs] n tricheco.

Walter ['wɔːltə] nm pr Walter, Gualtiero.

waltz [wɔls] n valzer; vi ballare il valzer.

wan [wɔn] a pallido, smorto.

wand [wɔnd] n bacchetta.

wander ['wɔndə] vi vagabondare, errare, vagare; divagare; vaneggiare.

wanderer ['wɔndərə] n vagabondo.

wane [wein] n declino, decrescenza; vi declinare, decrescere; (moon) calare.

want [wɔnt] n bisogno, deficienza, mancanza, miseria; vt desiderare, volere; aver bisogno di, mancare di; vi occorrere, mancare.

wanton ['wɔntən] a licenzioso, lascivo; capriccioso; senza scopo.

wantonness ['wɔntənnis] n licenziosità; leggerezza.

war [wɔː] n guerra; vi guerreggiare, far guerra.

warble ['wɔːbl] vti gorgheggiare, trillare, cantare.

ward [wɔːd] n custodia, guardia; tutela; pupillo; (of town) quartiere; (hospital) corsia; **to w. off** schivare, evitare, parare, respingere.

warden ['wɔːdn] n custode, guardiano; (of school, prison etc) direttore.

warder ['wɔːdə] n carceriere.

wardrobe ['wɔːdroub] n armadio, guardaroba.

warehouse ['wɛəhaus] n magazzino.

wares [wɛəz] n pl merce, mercanzia, articoli pl.

warfare ['wɔːfɛə] n guerra, stato di guerra.

wariness ['wɛərinis] n cautela, prudenza.

warlike ['wɔːlaik] a bellicoso, marziale.

warm [wɔːm] a caldo; caloroso, cordiale; vti riscaldar(si), scaldar(si); eccitar(si).

warmth [wɔːmθ] n calore.

warn [wɔːn] vt avvertire, ammonire, mettere in guardia, avvisare.

warning ['wɔːniŋ] n ammonimento, avvertimento, preavviso; (leg) diffida.

warp [wɔːp] n ordito; (of wood) curvatura; (fig) pervertimento; vt curvare, pervertire; vi curvarsi, deformarsi.

warrant ['wɔrənt] n autorizzazione, mandato, ordine; garanzia; vt autorizzare, garantire.

warranty ['wɔrənti] n garanzia.

warren ['wɔrin] n conigliera.

warrior ['wɔriə] n guerriero.

wart [wɔːt] n verruca.

wary ['wɛəri] a cauto, guardingo.

wash [wɔʃ] n lavata, lavatura, (linen) bucato; (art) acquerello; (waves) sciabordio; (slops) risciacquatura di piatti; (walls etc) mano di colore; vti lavar(si); vt imbiancare; metallizzare; bagnare; **to w. away** trascinar via, lavar via; **to w. up** lavare i piatti, rigovernare; **w.-out** (fig) un fallimento completo; **washday** giorno di bucato.

washer ['wɔʃə] n lavatore, -trice; **dishwasher** lavastoviglie.

washing ['wɔʃiŋ] n bucato, lavata;

w. day giorno di bucato; **w. machine** lavatrice; **w. powder** detersivo.

wasp [wɔsp] n vespa.

wastage ['weistidʒ] n consumo, sciupio.

waste [weist] a deserto, desolato; n rifiuti pl; spreco, perdita; consumo; vt sprecare, dissipare; vi consumarsi, deperire.

wasteful ['weistful] a prodigo, spendereccio, dissipatore, rovinoso.

wastefulness ['weistfulnis] n prodigalità, sciupio.

wasting ['weistiŋ] a che consuma, che indebolisce; n sciupio, spreco, devastazione, deperimento.

watch [wɔtʃ] n orologio; veglia; guardia, sentinella; osservazione; vt osservare, sorvegliare, spiare; vi vegliare, vigilare; **watchdog** cane da guardia; **w.-post** posto di guardia; **watchword** parola d'ordine.

watchful ['wɔtʃful] a guardingo, vigilante.

watchfulness ['wɔtʃfulnis] n vigilanza, cautela.

watchman ['wɔtʃmən] pl -men n guardia (notturna), guardiano.

water ['wɔːtə] n acqua; vt innaffiare; (horse) abbeverare; (drink) diluire; vi (eyes) piangere; **w. bottle** bottiglia per acqua, borraccia; **hot-w. bottle** bottiglia dell'acqua calda.

water-closet ['wɔːtə,klɔzit] n gabinetto.

water-color ['wɔːtə,kʌlə] n acquarello.

watercourse ['wɔːtəkɔːs] n corso d'acqua, canale.

waterfall ['wɔːtəfɔːl] n cascata.

watering-can ['wɔːtəriŋkæn] n annaffiatoio.

waterpipe ['wɔːtəpaip] n conduttura d'acqua.

watering-place ['wɔːtəriŋ,pleis] n abbeveratoio, luogo di rifornimento d'acqua; stazione balneare, termale.

water-lily ['wɔːtə,lili] n ninfea.

waterproof ['wɔːtəpruːf] a n impermeabile.

waterskiing ['wɔːtəskiiŋ] n sci nautico.

watertight ['wɔːtətait] a impermeabile, stagno.

waterway ['wɔːtəwei] n canale navigabile.

water-wheel ['wɔːtəwiːl] n (mech) turbina idraulica.

waterworks ['wɔːtəwəːks] n impianto idrico.

watery ['wɔːtəri] a acquoso.

wattle ['wɔtl] n canniccio, graticcio; (birds) bargiglio; (fish) barbetta.

wave [weiv] n onda, flutto; (hand) cenno; (wand) colpo; vt agitare; ondulare; vi ondeggiare, fluttuare; far segno di.

waver ['weivə] vi vacillare.

wavy ['weivi] a ondulato; ondoso; ondeggiante.

wax [wæks] n cera; ceralacca; cerume; vt incerare; dare la cera a.

waxen ['wæksən] a di cera, cereo.

way [wei] n via, strada; mezzo, modo; abitudine; passaggio; direzione; stato; **by the w.** strada facendo; (fig) a proposito.

wayfarer ['wei,fɛərə] n viandante.

wayside ['weisaid] n margine della strada.

wayward ['weiwəd] a ostinato; capriccioso.

waywardness ['weiwədnis] n ostinazione; capricciosità.

we [wiː] pron pl noi.

weak [wiːk] a debole.

weaken ['wiːkən] vti indebolir(si).

weakling ['wiːkliŋ] n creatura debole; debole, inetto.

weakly ['wiːkli] a di debole costituzione; ad debolmente.

weakness ['wiːknis] n debolezza.

wealth [welθ] n ricchezza, -ze pl.

wealthy ['welθi] a ricco.

wean [wiːn] vt svezzare; (fig) togliere il vezzo di.

weapon ['wepən] n arma.

wear [wɛə] n uso, consumo; durata; abbigliamento; vt portare, indossare, avere; vti consumar(si); durare; **to w. on** passare lentamente.

weariness ['wiərinis] n stanchezza, tedio, disgusto.

wearisome ['wiərisəm] a stancante, faticoso, tedioso.

weary ['wiəri] a stanco; vti stancar(si).

weasel ['wiːzl] n donnola.

weather ['weðə] n (atmosferico) tempo; vt esporre alle intemperie, resistere a, sopportare; **w. bureau** ufficio metereologico.

weathercock ['weðəkɔk] n banderuola.

weave [wiːv] vt tessere; (fig) unbastire, ordire.

weaver ['wiːvə] n tessitore.

weaving ['wiːviŋ] n tessitura.

web [web] n tela, tessuto; (bird's foot) membrana; (spider's) ragnatela; (fig) trama.

wed [wed] vti sposar(si).

wedding ['wediŋ] n nozze pl, sposalizio, matrimonio.

wedge [wedʒ] n cuneo, bietta; vt incuneare, incastrare; vi incunearsi.

wedlock ['wedlɔk] n matrimonio, stato coniugale.

Wednesday ['wenzdi] n mercoledì.

wee [wiː] a (fam) piccolo, minuscolo.

weed [wiːd] n erbaccia, mala erba; vt sarchiare; **to w. out** estirpare; (fig) eliminare.

weeds [wiːdz] n pl gramaglie pl.

weedy ['wiːdi] a pieno di erbacce; (fig) magro, sparuto.

week [wiːk] n settimana.

weekday ['wiːkdei] n giorno feriale, giorno lavorativo.

weekend ['wiːk'end] *n* 'weekend', (vacanza di) fine settimana.
weekly ['wiːkli] *a n* settimanale; *ad* ogni settimana.
weep [wiːp] *vti* piangere; trasudare.
weeping ['wiːpiŋ] *a* piangente; trasudante; *n* pianto, lacrime.
weft [weft] *n* (*di tessuto*) trama.
weigh [wei] *vti* pesare; (*naut*) levare l'ancora.
weight [weit] *n* peso; importanza; **lightweight** (*sport*) peso leggero; (*US sl*) persona di nessuna importanza.
weighty ['weiti] *a* pesante, gravoso; importante.
weir [wiə] *n* diga, sbarramento.
weird [wiəd] *a* misterioso, soprannaturale; (*fam*) bizzarro.
welcome ['welkəm] *a* gradito, ben accetto; *n* benvenuto, buona accoglienza; *vt* accogliere cordialmente, dare il benvenuto a; gradire; **w.!** benvenuto!
weld [weld] *vt* saldare.
welding ['weldiŋ] *n* saldatura.
welfare ['welfeə] *n* benessere, prosperità.
well [wel] *n* pozzo, fonte; tromba delle scale; *vi* scaturire.
well [wel] *a* bene, buono, in buona salute; *ad* bene; **w.-off**, **w.-to-do** *a* agiato, benestante.
Welsh [welʃ] *a* gallese; *n* (lingua) gallese; **Welshman** *n* gallese.
welt [welt] *n* (*shoe*) tramezza.
welter ['weltə] *n* tumulto, confusione; *vi* avvoltolarsi; essere sballottato; essere immerso; **welterweight** (*sport*) peso medio-leggero.
wen [wen] *n* natta, gozzo.
wench [wentʃ] *n* (*arc*) ragazza; ragazzotta, popolana, donna di servizio.
west [west] *n* occidente, ovest, ponente.
westerly ['westəli] *a* occidentale; *ad* da (verso) ovest.
western ['westən] *a* occidentale.
westward ['westwəd] *a* volto ad ovest; **westwards** *ad* verso ovest.
wet [wet] *a* bagnato; umido, piovoso; (*of paint*) fresco; *n* umidità, pioggia, tempo piovoso; *vt* bagnare, inumidire; **w. blanket** guastafeste; **w. nurse** balia.
wether ['weðə] *n* castrato.
wetness ['wetnis] *n* umidità.
whack [wæk] *n* bastonata, colpo; (*sl*) parte.
whale [weil] *n* balena.
whaler ['weilə] *n* baleniere, (*naut*) baleniera.
wharf [wɔːf] *n* banchina, molo.
wharfage ['wɔːfidʒ] *n* diritti di banchina *pl*.
what [wɔt] *a rel interrog* che, quale; *pron interrog rel indef* che cosa, ciò che, quello che.
whatever [wɔt'evə] *a* qualunque,

qualsiasi; *pron rel indef* qualunque cosa, tutto ciò che.
whatsoever [‚wɔtsou'evə] *a pron* (*arc*) qualunque cosa.
wheat [wiːt] *n* grano, frumento.
wheedle ['wiːdl] *vt* ottenere con le moine, persuadere con le moine.
wheel [wiːl] *n* ruota; (*naut*) ruota del timone; (*aut*) volante; *vti* spingere o tirare (veicolo); (far) girare, turbinare.
wheelbarrow ['wiːl‚bærou] *n* carriola.
wheeze [wiːz] *n* respiro affannoso; *vi* ansimare.
whelk [welk] *n* buccina.
when [wen] *ad cj* quando.
whence [wens] *cj ad* da dove, donde, da che cosa; *n* origine.
whenever [wen'evə] *ad* tutte le volte che, in qualunque momento.
where [wɛə] *ad* dove.
whereabouts ['wɛərəbauts] *ad* dove, in che parte.
whereas [wɛər:'æz] *cj* mentre, (*leg*) siccome.
whereby [wɛə'bai] *ad* per la qual cosa.
wherefore ['wɛəfɔː] *ad* perciò; (*interrog*) perchè; *n* causa, motivo.
wherein [wɛər'in] *ad* nel quale; (*interrog*) in che cosa.
whereupon [‚wɛərə'pɔn] *ad* al che, in conseguenza di che.
wherever [wɛər'evə] *ad* dovunque, in qualunque luogo.
whet [wet] *vt* affilare; stimolare.
whether ['weðə] *cj* se, sia che.
whetstone ['wetstoun] *n* cote.
which [witʃ] *pron rel* (*riferito ad animali o cose*) che, il quale *etc*; *a pron interrog* (*riferito a persone, animali e cose*) quale.
whichever [witʃ'evə] *a pron indef* qualunque.
whiff [wif] *n* boccata (d'aria *etc*).
whig [wig] *a n* liberale, membro del partito liberale.
while [wail] *n* momento, tempo; *cj* mentre; finchè; sebbene.
whilst [wailst] *cj* mentre.
whim [wim] *n* capriccio.
whimper ['wimpə] *n* piagnucolio; *vi* piagnucolare.
whimsical ['wimzikəl] *a* capriccioso, stravagante.
whimsy ['wimzi] *n* capriccio.
whine [wain] *n* (*of dogs*) uggiolio, piagnucolio; *vi* uggiolare, piagnucolare.
whip [wip] *n* frusta, scudiscio; *vt* frustare, sferzare; battere; cucire a sopraggitto; (*of cream*) montare, frullare; **w. hand** vantaggio; **to w. out** cacciar fuori; **to w. around** girarsi bruscamente.
whirl [wəːl] *n* turbine, vortice; *vt* roteare; *vi* girare, roteare, turbinare, susseguirsi vorticosamente.
whirligig ['wəːligig] *n* giostra; carosello; girandola.

whirlpool ['wə:lpu:l] *n* vortice d'acqua, gorgo.

whirlwind ['wə:lwind] *n* turbine di vento.

whisk [wisk] *n* frullino; movimento rapido; scopetta; *vt* frullare; spazzolare, (*eggs etc*) sbattere; *vti* muover(si) rapidamente, spazzar via.

whisker ['wiskə] *n* basetta; (*cat*) baffo.

whiskey, whisky ['wiski] *n* whisky.

whisper ['wispə] *n* bisbiglio, mormorio; *vti* bisbigliare, mormorare.

whist [wist] *n* 'whist', gioco di carte.

whistle ['wisl] *n* fischio, fischietto; *vti* fischiare.

whit [wit] *n* quantità minima; **W. Sunday** domenica di Pentecoste.

white [wait] *a n* bianco; **w.-collar worker** impiegato.

whiten ['waitn] *vti* imbiancare.

whiteness ['waitnis] *n* bianchezza.

whitewash ['waitwɔʃ] *n* calce per imbiancare, intonaco; (*sport*) vittoria schiacciante; *vt* imbiancare; (*fig*) riabilitare.

whiting ['waitiŋ] *n* merlano.

whittle ['witl] *vt* tagliuzzare; **to w. down** assottigliare.

whiz(z) [wiz] *n* sibilo; *vi* sibilare, passare sibilando.

who [hu:] *pron interrog* chi; *rel* chi, che, il quale *etc*.

whoever [hu'evə] *pron indef* chiunque.

whole [houl] *a* intero, tutto; *n* il tutto, l'intero, il totale; **on the w.** nel complesso, tutto considerato.

whole-hearted ['houl'hɑ:tid] *a* caloroso, cordiale.

whole-heartedly ['houl'hɑ:tidli] *ad* calorosamente, cordialmente.

wholesale ['houlseil] *n* vendita all'ingrosso; *a ad* all'ingrosso.

wholesome ['houlsəm] *a* sano, salubre.

wholly ['houlli] *ad* completamente, del tutto.

whom [hu:m] *pron rel interrog* che, chi, il quale, la quale, i quali, le quali.

whooping cough ['hupiŋkɔf] *n* pertosse.

whore [hɔ:] *n* prostituta.

whortleberry ['wə:tl,beri] *n* mirtillo.

whose [hu:z] *pron rel interrog* di cui, il cui, del quale *etc*, di chi? a chi?

whosoever [,husou'evə] *pron indef* chiunque.

why [wai] *ad interrog* perchè; *interj* ma, ma certo, ma via; *n* il perchè, motivo, causa.

wick [wik] *n* lucignolo, stoppino.

wicked ['wikid] *a* maligno, malvagio, perfido, perverso.

wickedness ['wikidnis] *n* malignità, malvagità, perfidia, perversità.

wicker ['wikə] *n* vimine; **wickerwork** lavoro in vimini.

wicket ['wikit] *n* cancellino, porticina; (*cricket*) porta.

wide [waid] *a* largo, vasto; (*of material*) alto; *ad* bene, completamente; **w.-open** spalancato; **w.-awake** completamente sveglio; **widely** *ad* largamente, molto.

widen ['waidn] *vti* allargar(si), ampliar(si).

widespread ['waidspred] *a* esteso, diffuso.

widow ['widou] *n* vedova.

widower ['widouə] *n* vedovo.

width [widθ] *n* larghezza; (*of material*) altezza.

wield [wi:ld] *vt* tenere, maneggiare, reggere.

wieldy ['wi:ldi] *a* maneggevole.

wife [waif] *n* moglie.

wig [wig] *n* parrucca.

wigwam ['wigwæm] *n* 'wigwam', tenda di pellirosse.

wild [waild] *a* selvaggio, selvatico; tempestoso, violento.

wilderness ['wildənis] *n* deserto, landa solitaria, luogo selvaggio.

wildfire ['waild,faiə] *n* fuoco greco; lampo di caldo.

wildness ['waildnis] *n* selvatichezza, ferocia.

wile [wail] *n* astuzia, inganno; *vt* ingannare, adescare.

Wilhelmina [,wilhel'mi:nə] *nf pr* Guglielmina.

wiliness ['wailinis] *n* astuzia.

will [wil] *n* volontà; (*leg*) testamento; *vti* volere; disporre, lasciare per testamento; costringere.

willful ['wilful] *a* caparbio, ostinato; (*leg*) premeditato.

wilfullness ['wilfulnis] *n* ostinazione, caparbietà.

William ['wiljəm] *nm pr* Guglielmo.

willing ['wiliŋ] *a* disposto (a), volonteroso; volontario.

willingly ['wiliŋli] *ad* volontieri.

willingness ['wiliŋnis] *n* buona volontà.

willow ['wilou] *n* salice.

willy-nilly ['wili'nili] *ad* volente o nolente.

Wilma ['wilmə] *nf pr* Vilma.

wilt [wilt] *vt* far appassire; *vi* appassire, languire.

wily ['waili] *a* astuto, malizioso.

wimple ['wimpl] *n* soggolo.

win [win] *n* successo, vittoria; *vt* vincere, conquistare, ottenere; persuadere; *vi* vincere.

wince [wins] *vi* ritrarsi improvvisamente, trasalire.

winch [wintʃ] *n* (*mech*) argano, manovella.

wind [waind] *vt* avvolgere; (*watch etc*) caricare; *vi* serpeggiare.

wind [wind] *n* vento; fiato; soffio; sentore.

windfall ['windfɔ:l] *n* frutto fatto cadere dal vento; (*fig*) fortuna inaspettata.

windlass ['windləs] n (mech) argano.
windmill ['winmil] n mulino a vento.
window ['windou] n finestra; vetrina.
windpipe ['windpaip] n trachea.
windshield ['windʃi:ld] n (aut) parabrezza; **w. wiper** tergicristallo.
windward ['windwəd] n parte da cui spira il vento; a situato dalla parte da cui spira il vento; ad contro vento.
windy ['windi] a ventoso, esposto al vento; (fig) verboso, vuoto.
wine [wain] n vino; **wineglass** bicchiere da vino; **wineshop** osteria, spaccio di vini.
wing [wiŋ] n ala; volo; pl (theat) quinte.
winged [wiŋd] a alato.
wink [wiŋk] n batter d'occhio, ammicco, cenno; vi ammiccare, strizzar l'occhio, batter le palpebre; brillare con intermittenza.
winkle ['wiŋkl] n chiocciola di mare.
winner ['winə] n vincitore.
winning ['winiŋ] a vincente, vincitore; avvincente, attraente; n pl vincita.
winnow ['winou] vt vagliare, spulare, ventilare.
winsome ['winsəm] a (poet) pieno di grazia, amabile.
winter ['wintə] n inverno; a d'inverno, invernale; vi passare l'inverno, svernare.
wintry ['wintri] a invernale, freddo.
wipe [waip] n strofinata, asciugatura, spolverata; vt asciugare, pulire, strofinare.
wire ['waiə] n filo metallico; telegrafo, telegramma; vti assicurare con filo metallico; (el) installare fili elettrici; telegrafare.
wireless ['waiəlis] a senza fili; n radio; **w. valve** valvola.
wiry ['waiəri] a magro e nerboruto.
wisdom ['wizdəm] n saggezza, sapienza, prudenza, giudizio.
wise [waiz] a saggio, savio, prudente, avveduto; **none the wiser** senza saperne più di prima.
wish [wiʃ] n desiderio; augurio; cosa desiderata; vti desiderare, volere; augurare.
wishful ['wiʃful] a desideroso, bramoso; **w. thinking** un pio desiderio.
wisp [wisp] n ciuffo, ciuffetto, striscia; **will-o'-the-w.** fuoco fatuo.
wistaria [wis'tɛəriə] n glicine.
wistful ['wistful] a nostalgico, pensoso, preoccupato.
wit [wit] n spirito, arguzia; intelligenza; pl ingegno, cervello.
witch [witʃ] n strega, ammaliatrice.
witchcraft ['witʃkrɑːft] n magia, stregoneria.
witchery ['witʃəri] n incantesimo, fascino.
with [wið] prep con, insieme a; da;

presso; di, per; **to be w. it** essere aggiornato.
withdraw [wið'drɔ:] vti ritirar(si).
wither ['wiðə] vt far avvizzire; vi avvizzire, inaridirsi.
withhold [wið'hould] vt trattenere; rifiutare, negare.
within [wi'ðin] prep entro, dentro; in meno di, fra; ad dentro, all'interno.
without [wi'ðaut] prep senza (di), fuori di; ad fuori; n esterno.
withstand [wið'stænd] vt resistere a, opporsi a, sostenere.
witness ['witnis] n testimone, teste, testimonianza; vti testimoniare, essere presente a, firmare come teste; **w. box, w. stand** banco dei testi.
witticism ['witisizəm] n frizzo, motto di spirito.
witty ['witi] a spiritoso.
wizard ['wizəd] n mago, stregone.
wizardry ['wizədri] n magia, stregoneria.
wizened ['wiznd] a raggrinzito.
wobble ['wɔbl] vi barcollare, dondolare.
woe [wou] n (poet) dolore, sventura.
woeful ['wouful] a doloroso, triste.
wolf [wulf] n lupo; vt divorare.
wolfish ['wulfiʃ] a da lupo, crudele, vorace.
woman ['wumən] pl **women** ['wimin] n donna, -ne.
womanhood ['wumənhud] n condizione di donna, maturità della donna.
womanish ['wuməniʃ] a effeminato.
womanly ['wumənli] a femminile, di donna.
womb [wu:m] n grembo, utero.
wonder ['wʌndə] n meraviglia, miracolo, prodigio; vi meravigliarsi, domandarsi.
wonderful ['wʌndəful] a meraviglioso, prodigioso.
wonderland ['wʌndəlænd] n paese delle meraviglie.
woo [wu:] vt corteggiare, fare la corte a.
wood [wud] n bosco; legno; botte.
woodcut ['wudkʌt] n incisione su legno, xilografia.
wooded ['wudid] a boschivo, coperto di boschi.
wooden ['wudn] a di legno, legnoso; senz'espressione.
woodland ['wudlənd] n luogo boscoso.
woodman ['wudmən] pl **-men** n guarda boschi, guardia forestale, taglialegna.
woodpecker ['wud,pekə] n picchio.
woodwork ['wudwə:k] n lavoro in legno.
woodworm ['wudwə:m] n tarlo.
woody ['wudi] a boscoso; legnoso.
woof [wu:f] n tessitura, trama.
wool [wul] n lana.

woolen ['wulin] *a* di lana; *n* articolo di lana.

woolly ['wuli] *a* lanoso; *n* indumento di lana.

word [wə:d] *n* parola; *vt* esprimere con parole, mettere in parole.

wordy ['wə:di] *a* verboso; consistente di parole.

work [wə:k] *n* lavoro; *pl* opere, lavori *pl*; meccanismo; macchinario; fabbrica, officina, stabilimento; *vt* lavorare; azionare; *vi* lavorare; funzionare; **to w. out** esaurire; calcolare; **t. w. up** eccitare.

workable ['wə:kəbl] *a* eseguibile, praticabile, realizzabile.

worker ['wə:kə] *n* lavoratore, operaio.

workhouse ['wə:khaus] *n* ospizio di mendicità.

workman ['wə:kmən] *pl* **-men** *n* operaio, artigiano.

workmanship ['wə:kmənʃip] *n* abilità, tecnica, fattura.

workshop ['wə:kʃɔp] *n* laboratorio, officina.

world [wə:ld] *n* mondo; **worldwide** mondiale.

worldliness ['wə:ldlinis] *n* mondanità.

worldly ['wə:ldli] *a* terreno, mondano.

worm [wə:m] *n* verme, baco, lombrico; *vti* muoversi insidiosamente; **w.-eaten** tarlato.

wormwood ['wə:mwud] *n* assenzio; (*fig*) mortificazione.

worn-out ['wɔ:n'aut] *a* logoro; (*fig*) esausto, sfinito.

worry ['wʌri] *n* inquietudine, fastidio, preoccupazione; *vt* infastidire, importunare; *vi* preoccuparsi, tormentarsi.

worse [wə:s] *a* peggiore; *n* (il) peggio; *ad* peggio.

worsen ['wə:sn] *vti* peggiorare, aggravare, aggravarsi.

worship ['wə:ʃip] *n* adorazione, culto; *vt* adorare, venerare; *vi* prestare culto.

worshipper ['wə:ʃipə] *n* adoratore; *pl* i fedeli *pl*.

worst [wə:st] *a* (il) peggiore; *ad* (il) peggio; *vt* sopraffare.

worsted ['wə:stid] *n* pettinato di lana; *a* di lana pettinata.

worth [wə:θ] *a* degno di, meritevole di; del valore di; *n* valore, merito; **to be w.** valere; **to be worthwhile** valere la pena.

worthiness ['wə:ðinis] *n* merito, rispettabilità.

worthless ['wə:θlis] *a* senza valore, indegno.

worthlessness ['wə:θlisnis] *n* mancanza di valore, indegnità.

worthy ['wə:ði] *a* meritevole, degno; *n* persona illustre, personaggio.

would-be ['wudbi:] *a* sedicente; aspirante.

wound [wu:nd] *n* ferita; *vt* ferire.

wraith [reiθ] *n* fantasma, spettro.

wrangle ['ræŋgl] *n* alterco, rissa; *vi* altercare, azzuffarsi.

wrangler ['ræŋglə] *n* attaccabrighe; guardiano di cavalli.

wrangling ['ræŋgliŋ] *n* disputazione, litigio.

wrap [ræp] *n* scialle; *vt* avvolgere; **w. up** *vi* avvolgersi, imbacuccarsi.

wrapper ['ræpə] *n* accappatoio; fascia, copertina di libro; carta da imballo.

wrath [rɔ:θ] *n* collera, ira.

wrathful ['rɔ:θful] *a* furioso, irato.

wreak [ri:k] *vt* sfogare, soddisfare il desiderio di.

wreath [ri:θ] *n* ghirlanda, corona (funeraria).

wreathe [ri:ð] *vti* inghirlandare, intrecciare, attorcigliarsi.

wreck [rek] *n* naufragio, rovina, relitti *pl*; persona che ha ricevuto gravi colpi; *vt* far naufragare, rovinare, distruggere; *vi* naufragare, andare in pezzi.

wreckage ['rekidʒ] *n* naufragio, relitti, rottami *pl*.

wren [ren] *n* scricciolo.

wrench [rentʃ] *n* violento strappo, slogatura, storta; (*fig*) dolore, strazio; (*mech*) chiave inglese; *vt* strappare violentemente, (con)torcere, slogare; (*fig*) svisare.

wrest [rest] *vt* strappare.

wrestle ['resl] *vi* lottare, fare la lotta.

wrestling ['resliŋ] *n* lotta, (*sport*) lotta libera.

wrestler ['reslə] *n* lottatore.

wretch [retʃ] *n* miserabile, sciagurato.

wretched ['retʃid] *a* miserabile, misero, spregevole.

wretchedness ['retʃidnis] *n* infelicità, miseria, squallore.

wriggle ['rigl] *vi* contorcersi, dimenarsi.

wring [riŋ] *vti* torcere, torcersi, stringere, strizzare, spremere; estorcere.

wringer ['riŋə] *n* asciugatrice meccanica.

wrinkle ['riŋkl] *n* ruga, grinza; *vti* corrugare, increspare.

wrist [rist] *n* polso.

wristband ['ristbænd] *n* polsino.

writ [rit] *n* citazione, mandato, ordine.

write [rait] *vti* scrivere.

writer ['raitə] *n* scrivente, scrittore.

writhe [raið] *vi* contorcersi.

writing ['raitiŋ] *n* scrittura, calligrafia, lo scrivere; *pl* scritti *pl*; **w. paper** carta da lettera, carta da scrivere.

wrong [rɔŋ] *a* sbagliato, erroneo, inesatto, scorretto; ingiusto; *n* torto, danno, male; *vt* far torto a, giudicare erroneamente; **be w.** aver torto; *ad* male, erroneamente;

w.-doer peccatore, trasgressore, offensore.
wrongful ['rɔŋful] *a* ingiusto.
wrought [rɔːt] *a* (*di ferro*) battuto, lavorato; **w.-up** nervoso, agitato.
wry [rai] *a* contorto, storto; ironico.

X

Xanthippe [zæn'θipi] *n* *pr* Santippe; moglie bisbetica.
Xmas ['krisməs] *see* **Christmas.**
X-ray ['eks'rei] *a* di raggi X; **X-ray photograph** radiografia; *vt* sottoporre a raggi X.
X-rays ['eks'reiz] *n* *pl* raggi X *pl*.
xylography [zai'lɔgrəfi] *n* xilografia.
xylophone ['zailəfoun] *n* (*mus*) xilofono.

Y

yacht [jɔt] *n* panfilo, yacht.
yankee ['jæŋki] *a n* (*fam*) americano.
yap [jæp] *vi* guaire, uggiolare, abbaiare.
yard [jɑːd] *n* iarda (*misura di lunghezza=cm 91 circa*); cortile, recinto.
yarn [jɑːn] *n* filato; (*tale*) racconto, storia; *vi* (*fam*) raccontare storie.
yawn [jɔːn] *n* sbadiglio; *vi* sbadigliare.
ye [jiː] *pron* (*poet*) voi; *def art* (*arc*) il *etc*.
year [jəː] *n* anno, annata; età.
yearling ['jəːliŋ] *n* animale di un anno.
yearly ['jəːli] *a* annuale, annuo; *ad* annualmente.
yearn [jəːn] *vi* **y. for** agognare, struggersi di.
yearning ['jəːniŋ] *n* desiderio ardente, struggimento.
yeast [jiːst] *n* lievito.
yell [jel] *n* urlo; *vi* urlare.
yellow ['jelou] *a n* giallo.
yellowish ['jelouiʃ] *a* giallastro, giallognolo.
yellowness ['jelounis] *n* color giallastro.
yelp [jelp] *n* guaito; *vi* guaire.
yeoman ['joumən] *n* piccolo proprietario terriero.
yeomanry ['joumənri] *n* classe dei piccoli proprietari terrieri; corpo di cavalleria volontaria.
yes [jes] *ad* sì.
yesterday ['jestədi] *n* *ad* ieri.
yet [jet] *ad* ancora, finora, tuttora; eppure, ciononondimeno; *cj* tuttavia.

yew (tree) ['juː(triː)] *n* tasso.
yield [jiːld] *n* raccolto, produzione; *vt* produrre, rendere; *vi* arrendersi, cedere.
yoghurt ['jɔgə(ː)t] *n* yogurt.
yoke [jouk] *n* giogo; coppia, paio; *vt* aggiogare, soggiogare.
yolk [jouk] *n* rosso d'uovo, tuorlo.
yonder ['jɔndə] *a* quello là; *ad* laggiù, lassù.
yore [jɔː] *n* (*poet*) tempo passato; **of y.** *ad* anticamente.
you [juː] *pron* tu, voi, ti, te, vi, ve, Lei, Loro.
young [jʌŋ] *a* giovane; *n* piccolo, piccoli, (*of animals*) prole.
youngster ['jʌŋstə] *n* ragazzo, giovane.
your [jɔː] *a* (il) tuo *etc*, (il) vostro *etc*; **yours** *pron* (il) tuo *etc*, (il) vostro *etc*; **yourself** *pron* tu stesso, te stesso, ti; **yourselves** *pl* *pron* voi stessi, vi *etc* *pl*.
youth [juːθ] *n* giovane, gioventù, giovinezza.
youthful ['juːθful] *a* giovanile.
youthfulness ['juːθfulnis] *n* aspetto, spirito giovanile.
Yugoslavia ['jugou'slɑːviə] *n* Jugoslavia.
Yule [juːl] *n* Natale, feste natalizie; **y. log** ceppo di Natale.

Z

Zagreb ['zɑːgreb] *n* Zagabria.
zany ['zeini] *n* buffone, zanni.
zeal [ziːl] *n* zelo.
zealot ['zelət] *n* fanatico, zelatore.
zealous ['zeləs] *a* zelante.
zebra ['ziːbrə] *n* zebra.
zenith ['zeniθ] *n* zenit; (*fig*) culmine, apice.
zephyr ['zefə] *n* zeffiro, brezza.
zero ['ziərou] *n* zero.
zest [zest] *n* sapore piccante; (*fig*) gusto, interesse.
zigzag ['zigzæg] *n* zig-zag; *a ad* a zig-zag; *vi* andare a zig-zag, zigzagare.
zinc [ziŋk] *n* zinco.
zip [zip] *n* chiusura lampo.
zither ['ziðə] *pl* **zithern** *n* (*mus*) cetra tirolese.
zodiac ['zoudiæk] *n* zodiaco.
zodiacal [zou'daiəkəl] *a* zodiacale.
zone [zoun] *n* zona.
zoo [zuː] *n* giardino zoologico, zoo.
zoologist [zou'ɔlədʒist] *n* zoologo.
zoology [zou'ɔlədʒi] *n* zoologia.
Zulu ['zuːluː] *a n* Zulù.
Zurich ['zjuərik] *n* Zurigo.

Italian Grammar—Grammatica Italiana

GENDER OF NOUNS

In Italian there are two genders: masculine and feminine.

Masculine { nouns ending in **o** (exceptions: **la màno** etc.)
nouns ending in **i** (exceptions: nouns of Greek origin, like **la crísi, la diòcesi, la tèsi** etc.)

Feminine { nouns ending in **a** (exceptions: some words ending in **ta** and **ma** of Greek origin, like **il telegràmma, il dràmma, il poèma** etc.)

Nouns ending in **e** are sometimes masculine, sometimes feminine.

The following are masculine: nouns referring to male human beings and animals, names of fruit trees (whose corresponding fruit is feminine) names of months, days, mountains, lakes.

The following are feminine: nouns referring to female human beings and animals; names of fruits (whose corresponding tree is masculine); names of islands, abstract nouns indicating quality.

PLURAL OF NOUNS AND ADJECTIVES

The plural of masculine nouns and adjectives is **i**: **artísta, artísti; càne, càni; pòrto, pòrti.**

The plural of feminine nouns and adjectives is **e** if the word in the singular ends in **a: pàtria, pàtrie.** It is **i** if the singular ends in **e: nàve, nàvi.** Exceptions: **àla** (wing), **àli.** The word **màno** (hand) is feminine and its plural is **màni.**

Note:—

1. Nouns and adjectives ending in the singular in **ca** and **ga** end in the plural in **che** and **ghe** if they are feminine; in **chi** and **ghi** if they are masculine: **amíca** (lady friend), **amíche; dúca** (duke), **dúchi; stréga** (witch), **stréghe; collèga** (colleague), **collèghi.** Exception: **bèlga** (Belgian), **bèlgi** (m.)
2. Nouns and adjectives ending in the singular in **cia** and **gia** end in the plural in **e** keeping the **i** if it is stressed, omitting it if it is not: **bugía** (lie), **bugíe; fàccia** (face) **fàcce.** Sometimes—to avoid ambiguity— the unaccented **i** is kept, as in the noun **audàcia** (daring), **audàcie,** to distinguish it from the adjective **audàce** (bold).

396

3. Nouns and adjectives ending in the singular in **io** end in the plural in **ii** if the **i** of **io** is stressed; if it is unstressed the plural is simply **i**: **zío** (uncle), **zíi**; **fàggio** (beech tree), **fàggi**. Again, to avoid ambiguity the **i**, even if unstressed, is sometimes retained: **òdio** (hatred), **òdii**, to distinguish it from **òde** (ode), **òdi**.

4. Nouns and adjectives consisting of two syllables and ending in the singular in **co** and **go** end in the plural in **chi** and **ghi**: **biànco** (white) **biànchi**; **làgo** (lake) **làghi**. Exceptions: **pòrco** (pig), **pòrci**; **grèco** (Greek), **grèci**.

5. Nouns and adjectives of more than two syllables, ending in the singular in **co** and **go** end in the plural in **chi** and **ghi** if **co** and **go** are preceded by a consonant: **almanàcco** (almanac) **almanàcchi**; **albèrgo** (hotel), **albèrghi**. They end in **ci** and **gi** if **co** and **go** are preceded by a vowel: **amíco** (friend), **amíci** etc. This category, however, presents a considerable number of exceptions. To help the student we have indicated in the Dictionary all the exceptions concerning (2) and (3) and the plural of all the words—regular or exceptions —concerning (4) and (5).

6. Some nouns change their gender in the plural: singular **uòvo** (egg), **uòva**; **díti** (finger), **díta** etc. There are nouns which have two plurals with different meanings: **úrlo** (shout), **úrli** (cries of animals), **úrla** (shouts of human beings). Such irregularities and peculiarities have been indicated in the Dictionary.

7. Some nouns are used only in the singular (**pròle**, **sàngue**, **mièle**, **fàme**); some only in the plural (**esèquie**, **fòrbici**, **occhiàli**, **nòzze**, etc.)

8. Some nouns have the same form both for the singular and for the plural. They are: words accented on the last syllable; *e.g.* la **città**, le **città** (city, cities); monosyllables, *e.g.* il **re**, i **re** (king, kings); surnames; words ending in a consonant, *e.g.* il **gas**, i **gas** (gas, gasses); compounds made of a verb and of a plural noun, *e.g.* il **portalèttere**, i **portalèttere** (postman, postmen); nouns ending in **ie**, *e.g.* **progènie** (progeny). Exceptions to this are **superfície** (surface) and **móglie** (wife) which in the plural become **superfíci** and **mógli**.

9. Compounds, other than those mentioned in (8), form their plural as follows: some change into plural only the second part of the word, *e.g.* **cartapècora** (parchment) **cartapècore**. Some have both parts in plural form *e.g.* **mezzanòtte** (midnight) **mezzenòtti**.

397

Compounds of **càpo** either change both parts *e.g.* **capocuòco** (chef), **capicuòchi**, or use the plural only in the first part, *e.g.* **caposquàdra** (foreman, group-leader), **capisquàdra**, or only in the second, *e.g.* **capolavóro** (masterpiece), **capolavóri**. These plurals are duly indicated in their place in the Dictionary.

10. Some words have an entirely irregular plural: **uòmo** (man), **uòmini**; **dío** (god), **dèi**; **búe** (ox), **buoi**; **mílle** (one thousand), **míla**.

FEMININE OF NOUNS AND ADJECTIVES

When the masculine noun or adjective ends in **o** the feminine ends in **a**: **il maéstro, la maéstra**.

When the masculine noun or adjective ends in **e** the feminine ends in **e**: **il nipóte, la nipóte**.

When the masculine noun or adjective ends in **a** the feminine ends in **a**: **un artísta, un' artísta**.

When the masculine noun or adjective ends in **ière** the feminine ends in **ièra**: **il consiglière, la consiglièra**.

When the masculine noun or adjective ends in **tóre** the feminine ends in **tríce**: **il pittóre, la pittríce**. Exception: **il fattóre** (the land agent), **la fattóra**, or **la fattoréssa**.

There are some exceptions like: **studènte, studentéssa** (student); **avvocàto, avvocatéssa** (lawyer, lady lawyer) etc. These are indicated in the Dictionary. Names of animals ending in **e** and **u** are common: *e.g.* **il lèpre, la lèpre** (the hare); **il gru, la gru** (the crane). Some have no feminine: *e.g.* **il tòpo** (the mouse), **il coníglio** (the rabbit). Some have no masculine: *e.g.* **la vòlpe** (the fox), **l'àquila** (the eagle). In these cases the word **fémmina** (female) or the word **màschio** (male) is added as explicatory: *e.g.* **il tòpo fémmina** (or **la fémmina del tòpo**), **la vòlpe màschio**, etc.

Italian Verbs—Verbi Italiani

PROGRESSIVE FORM

In Italian there are three progressive tenses: the present, the past and the future, formed respectively by the Present Indicative, the Imperfect and the Future of **stàre** and less frequently **andàre**; *e.g.* he is sleeping, **sta dormèndo**; he was sleeping, **stava dormèndo**; he will be sleeping, **starà dormèndo**. These tenses can be rendered in Italian by the simple tense; *e.g.* he is sleeping, **dorme**.

ORTHOGRAPHIC CHANGES OF SOME VERBS IN–ÀRE

1. Verbs ending in **càre** and **gàre**, as **pagàre, cercàre,** when the **c** or **g** is followed by **e** or **i**, take in **h** in order to preserve the hard sound of the consonant; *e.g.* **paghiàmo, cercherò**.
2. Verbs in **ciàre** and **giàre**, as **cominciàre, mangiàre,** drop the **i** before **e** or **i**; *e.g.* **màngi, mangerò**.
3. Verbs in **iàre** having a sounded **i**, as **spiàre, inviàre,** retain the **i** except before **iàmo** and **iàte**; *e.g.* **invíi, spierémo, inviàmo, spiàte**.
4. Verbs in **iàre** where the **i** is not sounded, as **pigliàre, invecchiàre, annoiàre,** drop the **i** when followed by another **i**; *e.g.* **pígli, píglio, invècchi**.

NOTE ON THE VERBS IN–ÍRE

Verbs in –íre take the terminations **ísco, ísci, ísce, íscono** in the 1st, 2nd, and 3rd singular, and in the 3rd plural of the Indicative. Similarly in the Present Subjunctive and in the Imperative.

Regular Verbs

Conjugation 1	Conjugation 2	Conjugation 3
	INFINITIVE	
Parlàre. to speak	Temére, to fear	Sentíre, to hear
	PRESENT INDICATIVE	
I speak	*I fear*	*I hear*
io pàrl-o	tém-o	sènt-o
tu pàrl-i	tém-i	sènt-i
egli pàrl-a	tém-e	sènt-e
noi parl-iàmo	tem-iàmo	sent-iàmo
voi parl-àte	tem-éte	sent-íte
essi pàrl-ano	tém-ono	sènt-ono

399

IMPERFECT

I used to speak	*I used to fear*	*I used to hear*
io parl-àvo	tem-évo	sent-ívo
tu parl-àvi	tem-évi	sent-ívi
egli parl-àva	tem-éva	sent-íva
noi parl-avàmo	tem-evàmo	sent-ivàmo
voi parl-avàte	tem-evàte	sent-ivàte
essi parl-àvano	tem-évano	sent-ívano

GERUND

parl-àndo, *speaking*   tem-èndo, *fearing*   sent-èndo, *hearing*

PAST PARTICIPLE

parl-àto, *spoken*   tem-úto, *feared*   sent-íto, *heard*

Subjunctive

PRESENT

that I speak	*that I fear*	*that I hear*
ch'io-pàrl-i	ch'io tém-a	ch'io sènt-a
che tu pàrl-i	che tu tém-a	che tu sènt-a
ch'egli pàrl-i	ch'egli tém-a	ch'egli sènt-a
che noi parl-iàmo	che noi tem-iàmo	che noi sent-iàmo
che voi parl-iàte	che voi tem-iàte	che voi sent-iàte
ch'essi pàrl-ino	che essi tém-ano	ch'essi sènt-ano

IMPERFECT

if I spoke	*if I feared*	*if I heard*
se io parl-àssi	tem-éssi	sent-íssi
se tu parl-àssi	tem-éssi	sent-íssi
se egli parl-àsse	tem-ésse	sent-ísse
se noi parl-àssimo	tem-éssimo	sent-íssimo
se voi parl-àste	tem-éste	sente-íste
se essi parl-àssero	tem-éssero	sent-íssero

Compound Tenses

Perfect	io ho	⎫ parlàto	*I have*	⎫ *spoken,*
Pluperfect	io avévo		*I had*	
2nd Pluperf.	io èbbi		*I had*	
2nd Future	io avrò	or	*I shall have*	or
2nd Condit.	io avrèi		*I should have*	
		⎬ temúto,		⎬ *feared,*
Subj. Perfect.	ch'io àbbia		*that I have*	
Subj. Pluperf.	se io avéssi	or	*if I had*	or
Past Infin.	avér(e)		*to have*	
Past Gerund	avèndo	⎭ sentíto	*having*	⎭ *heard*

PAST DEFINITE

I spoke	*I feared*	*I heard*
io parl-ài	tem-éi or -étti	sent-íi
tu parl-àsti	tem-ésti	sent-isti
egli parl-ò	tem-è or -ètte	sent-í
noi parl-àmmo	tem-émmo	sent-ímmo
voi parl-àste	tem-éste	sent-íste
essi parl-àrono	tem-érono or -èttero	sent-írono

FUTURE

I shall speak	*I shall fear*	*I shall hear*
io parl-erò	tem-erò	sent-irò
tu parl-erài	tem-erài	sent-irài
egli parl-erà	tem-erà	sent-irà
noi parl-erémo	tem-erémo	sent-irémo
voi parl-eréte	tem-eréte	sent-iréte
essi parl-erànno	tem-erànno	sent-irànno

CONDITIONAL

I should speak	*I should fear*	*I should hear*
io parl-erèi	tem-erèi	sent-irèi
tu parl-erésti	tem-erésti	sent-irésti
egli parl-erèbbe	tem-erèbbe	sent-irèbbe
noi parl-erèmmo	tem-erèmmo	sent-irèmmo
voi parl-eréste	tem-eréste	sent-iréste
essi parl-erèbbero	tem-erèbbero	sent-irèbbero

IMPERATIVE

speak	*fear*	*hear*
pàrl-a	tém-i	sènt-i
pàrl-i	tém-a	sènt-a
parl-iàmo	tem-iàmo	sent-iàmo
parl-àte	tem-éte	sent-íte
pàrl-ino	tém-ano	sént-ano

PRESENT INFINITIVE

parl-àre, *to speak*	tem-ére, *to fear*	sent-íre, *to hear*

PRESENT PARTICIPLE

parl-ànte, *speaking*	tem-ènte, *fearing*	sent-ènte, *hearing*

Auxiliary Verbs

NOTE: **Veníre** and **andàre** may be used as auxiliaries instead of **èssere** with a past participle or with a gerund.

Èssere, to be   **Avére, to have**

PRESENT INDICATIVE

I am	*I have*
io sóno	io ho
tu sèi	tu hai
egli } è essa	egli } ha essa
noi siàmo	noi abbiàmo
voi siète	voi avéte
essi } sóno esse	essi } hànno esse

401

IMPERFECT

I was	*I had*
io èro	io avévo
tu èri	tu avévi
egli èra	egli avéva
noi eravàmo	noi avevàmo
voi eravàte	voi avevàte
essi èrano	essi avévano

PAST DEFINITE

I was	*I had*
io fúi	io èbbi
tu fósti	tu avésti
egli fu	egli èbbe
noi fúmmo	noi avémmo
voi fóste	voi avéste
essi fúrono	essi èbbero

FUTURE

I shall be	*I shall have*
io sarò	io avrò
tu sarài	tu avrài
egli sarà	egli avrà
noi sarémo	noi avrémo
voi saréte	voi avréte
essi sarànno	essi avrànno

CONDITIONAL

I should be	*I should have*
io sarèi	io avrèi
tu sarésti	tu avrésti
egli sarèbbe	egli avrèbbe
noi sarèmmo	noi avrémmo
voi saréste	voi avréste
essi sarèbbero	essi avrèbbero

IMPERATIVE

be	*have*
síi	àbbi
sía	àbbia
siàmo	abbiàmo
siàte	abbiàte
síano	àbbiano

INFINITIVE

èssere, *to be*   avére, *to have*

GERUND

essèndo, *being*   avèndo, *having*

PAST PARTICIPLE

stàto, stàta ⎱ been   avúto, avúta ⎱ had
stàti, stàte ⎰   avúti, avúte ⎰

402

Compound Tenses

PERFECT

I have been
io sóno stàto
tu sèi stàto
egli è stàto ⎫
essa è stàta ⎭
noi siàmo stàti
voi siète stàti
essi sóno stàti ⎫
esse sóno stàte ⎭

I have had
io ho avúto
tu hai avúto
egli ⎫ ha avúto
essa ⎭
noi abbiàmo avúto
voi avéte avúto
essi ⎫ hànno avúto
esse ⎭

PLUPERFECT

I had been
io èro stàto
tu èri stàto
egli èra stàto ⎫
essa èra stàta ⎭
noi eravàmo stàti
voi eravàte stàti
essi èrano stàti ⎫
esse èrano stàte ⎭

I had had
io avévo avúto
tu avévi avúto
egli ⎫ avéva avúto
essa ⎭
noi avevàmo avúto
voi avevàte avúto
essi ⎫ avévano avúto
esse ⎭

SECOND PLUPERFECT

I had been
io fúi stàto
tu fósti stàto
egli fu stàto ⎫
essa fu stàta ⎭
noi fúmmo stàti
voi fóste stàti
essi fúrono stàti ⎫
esse fúrono stàte ⎭

I had had
io èbbi avúto
tu avésti avúto
egli ⎫ èbbe avúto
essa ⎭
noi avémmo avúto
voi avéste avúto
essi ⎫ èbbero avúto
esse ⎭

FUTURE PERFECT

I shall have been
io sarò stàto
tu sarài stàto
egli sarà stàto ⎫
essa sarà stàta ⎭
noi sarémo stàti
voi saréte stàti
essi sarànno stàti ⎫
esse sarànno stàte ⎭

I shall have had
io avrò avúto
tu avrài avúto
egli ⎫ avrà avúto
essa ⎭
noi avrémo avúto
voi avréte avúto
essi ⎫ avrànno avúto
esse ⎭

PERFECT CONDITIONAL

I should have been
io sarèi stàto
tu sarésti stàto
egli sarèbbe stàto ⎫
essa sarèbbe stàta ⎭

I should have had
io avrèi avúto
tu avrésti avúto
egli ⎫ avrèbbe avúto
essa ⎭

noi sarèmmo stàti
voi saréste stàti
essi sarèbbero stàti }
esse sarèbbero stàte }

noi avrémmo avúto
voi avréste avúto
essi }
esse }avrèbbero avúto

PERFECT INFINITIVE

to have been
èssere stàto
èssere stàta

to have had
avére avúto
avére avúta

PERFECT GERUND

having been
essèndo stàto
essèndo stàta

having had
avèndo avúto
avèndo avúta

PRESENT SUBJUNCTIVE

that I be
ch'io sía
che tu sía
che egli sía
che noi siàmo
che voi siàte
che essi síano

that I have
ch'io àbbia
che tu àbbia
che egli àbbia
che noi abbiàmo
che voi abbiàte
che essi àbbiano

IMPERFECT

if I were
se io fóssi
se tu fóssi
se egli fósse
se noi fóssimo
se voi fóste
se essi fóssero

if I had
se io avéssi
se tu avéssi
se egli avésse
se noi avéssimo
se voi avéste
se essi avéssero

PERFECT

that I have been
ch'io sía stàto
che tu sía stàto
che egli sía stàto }
che essa sía stàta }
che noi siàmo stàti
che voi siàte stàti
che essi síano stàti }
che esse síano stàte }

that I have had
ch'io àbbia avúto
che tu àbbia avúto
che egli }àbbia avúto
che essa }
che noi abbiàmo avúto
che voi abbiàte avúto
che essi }àbbiano avúto
che esse }

PLUPERFECT

if I had been
se io fóssi stàto
se tu fóssi stàto
se egli fósse stàto }
se essa fósse stàta }
se noi fóssimo stàti
se voi fóste stàti
se essi fóssero stàti }
se esse fóssero stàte }

if I had had
se io avéssi avúto
se tu avéssi avúto
se egli avésse avúto }
se essa avésse avúto }
se noi avéssimo avúto
se voi avéste avúto
se essi avéssero avúto }
se esse avéssero avúto }

404

The following regular verbs in –íre do not insert isc:

apríre	to open	àpro	dormíre	to sleep	dòrmo
copríre	to cover	còpro	fuggíre	to escape	fúggo
cucíre	to sew	cúcio	partíre	to depart	pàrto
pentírsi	to repent	mi pènto	servíre	to serve	sèrvo
seguíre	to follow	séguo	vestíre	to dress	vèsto
sentíre	to hear, feel	sènto			

Bollíre (to boil) when used intransitively prefers not to insert isc.

Nutríre (to nourish) uses either form.

Irregular Verbs

Accèndere *to light*
past   accesi, accendesti, accese, accendemmo, accendeste, accésero
past part.   acceso

Acclúdere *to enclose*
past   acclusi, accludesti, accluse, accludemmo, accludeste, acclúsero
past part.   accluso

Addúrre *to adduce*
past   addussi, adducesti, addusse, adducemmo, adduceste, addússero
fut.   addurrò
cond.   addurrei
past part.   addotto

Adémpiere, Adempíre *to accomplish*
pres. ind.   adempio, adempi, adempie, adempiamo, adempite, adémpiono
pres. sub.   adempia
imper.   adempi, adempia, adempite, adémpiano
past   adempii, adempisti, adempí, adempimmo, adempiste, adempirono
past part.   adempito *or* adempiuto

Afflíggere *to afflict*
past   afflissi, affliggesti, afflisse, affliggemmo, affliggeste, afflíssero
past part.   afflitto

Allúdere *to allude*
past   allusi, alludesti, alluse, alludemmo, alludeste, allúsero
past part.   alluso

Andàre *to go*
pres. ind.   vado, vai, va, andiamo, andate, vanno
pres. sub.   vada, vada, vada, andiamo, andiate, vàdano
imp.   vai *or* va', vada, andiamo, andate, vàdano
fut.   andrò
cond.   andrei

Annèttere *to annex*
past   annessi, annettesti, annesse, annettemmo,
               annetteste, annèssero
past part.   annesso

Apparíre *to appear*
pres. ind.   apparisco *or* appaio, apparisci *or* appari, appa-
               risce *or* appare, appariamo, apparite, appa-
               ríscono *or* appàiono
past   apparvi *or* apparii, apparisti, apparve *or* apparí
               or apparse, apparimmo, appariste, appàrvero
               or apparírono *or* appàrsero
pres. sub.   apparisca *or* appaia, apparisca *or* appaia,
               apparisca *or* appaia, appariamo, appariate,
               apparíscano *or* appàiano
imper.   apparisci *or* appari, apparisca *or* appaia,
               apparite, apparíscano *or* appàiano
past. part. apparso

Appèndere *to hang*
past   appesi, appendesti, appese, appendemmo,
               appendeste, appésero
past. part. appeso

Apríre *to open*
pres. ind.   apro, apri, apre, apriamo, aprite, àprono
past   aprii, *or* apersi, apristi, aprí *or* aperse, aprimmo,
               apriste, aprírono *or* apèrsero
past. part. aperto

Àrdere *to burn*
past   arsi, ardesti, arse, ardemmo, ardeste, àrsero
past. part. arso

Aspèrgere *to sprinkle*
past   aspersi, aspergesti, asperse, aspergemmo, asper-
               geste, aspèrsero
past. part. asperso

Assalíre *to assail*
pres. ind.   assalgo *or* assalisco, assali *or* assalisci, assale *or*
               assalisce, assaliamo, assalite, assàlgono *or*
               assalíscono

406

past assalii *or* assalsi, assalisti, assalí *or* assalse, assalimmo, assaliste, assalírono *or* assàlsero

pres. sub. assalga *or* assalisca, assalga *or* assalisca, assalga *or* assalisca, assaliamo, assaliate, assàlgano *or* assalíscano

Assídersi *to take one's seat*

past mi assisi, ti assidesti, si assise, ci assidemmo, vi assideste, si assísero

past part. assiso

Assístere *to assist*

past assistei *or* assistetti, assistesti, assistè *or* assistette, assistemmo, assisteste, assistérono or assistèttero

past part. assistito

Assòlvere *to absolve*

past assolsi *or* assolvei *or* assolvetti, assolvesti, assolse *or* assolvette, assolvemmo, assolveste, assòlsero *or* assolvèttero

past part. assolto *or* assoluto

Assorbíre *to absorb*

pres. assorbo *or* assorbisco, assorbi *or* assorbisci, assorbe *or* assorbisce, assorbiamo, assorbite, assòrbono *or* assorbíscono

past part. assorbito *or* assorto

Assúmere *to assume*

past assunsi, assumesti, assunse, assumemmo, assumeste, assúnsero

past part. assunto

Assúrgere *to rise*

past assursi, assurgesti, assurse, assurgemmo, assurgeste, assursero

past part. assurto

Bére *to drink*

pres. ind. bevo, bevi, beve, beviamo, bevete, bévono

imp. ind. bevevo, bevevi, beveva, bevevamo, bevevate, bevévano

past bevvi *or* bevei, bevesti, bevve *or* bevè *or* bevette, bevemmo, beveste, bèvvero *or* bevérono *or* bevèttero

fut. berrò

cond. berrei

pres. sub. beva

imp. sub. bevessi

imper. bevi, beva, bevete, bévano

past part. bevuto

407

Cadére *to fall*
past caddi, cadesti, cadde, cademmo, cadeste, càddero
fut. cadrò
cond. cadrei
Cèdere *to give*
past cedei *or* cedetti, cedesti, cedè *or* cedette, cedemmo, cedeste, cedérono *or* cedèttero
Chiédere *to ask*
past chiesi, chiedesti, chiese, chiedemmo, chiedeste, chiésero
past part. chiesto
Chiúdere *to close*
past chiusi, chiudesti, chiuse, chiudemmo, chiudeste, chiúsero
past part. chiuso
Cíngere *to gird*
past cinsi, cingesti, cinse, cingemmo, cingeste, cínsero
past part. cinto
Cògliere *to gather*
pres. ind. colgo, cogli, coglie, cogliamo, cogliete, còlgono
past colsi, cogliesti, colse, cogliemmo, coglieste, còlsero
pres. sub. colga, colga, colga, cogliamo, cogliate, còlgano
past part. colto
Còmpiere, Compíre *to complete*
pres. ind. cómpio, compi, cómpie, compiamo, compite, cómpiono
past compii, compisti, compí, compimmo, compiste, compírono
pres. sub. compia
imper. compi, cómpia, compite, cómpiano
past part. compìto *or* compiúto
Comprímere *to compress*
past compressi, comprimesti, compresse, comprimemmo, comprimeste, comprèssero
past part. compresso
Conóscere *to know*
past conobbi, conoscesti, conobbe, conoscemmo, conosceste, conòbbero
Contúndere *to bruise*
past contusi, contundesti, contuse, contundemmo, contundeste, contúsero
past part. contuso

408

Convèrgere *to converge*
past   conversi *or* convergei, convergesti, converse *or* convergè, convergemmo, convergeste, convèrsero *or* convergèrono
past part. converso

Copríre *to cover*
pres. ind. copro, copri, copre, copriamo, coprite, còprono
past   coprii *or* copersi, copristi, coprí *or* coperse, coprimmo, copriste, coprírono *or* copèrsero
past part. coperto

Córrere *to run*
past   corsi, corresti, corse, corremmo, correste, córsero
past part. corso

Créscere *to grow*
past   crebbi, crescesti, crebbe, crescemmo, cresceste, crébbero

Cuòcere *to cook*
pres. ind. cuocio, cuoci, cuoce, cociamo, cocete, cuòciono
past   cossi, cocesti, cosse, cocemmo, coceste, còssero
past part. cotto

Dàre *to give*
pres. ind. do, dài, dà, diamo, date, dànno
imp. ind. davo
past   diedi, desti, diede, demmo, deste, dièdero
fut.   darò
pres. sub. dia
imp. sub. dessi
cond.   darei
imper. da, dia, date, díano
pres. part. dando
past part. dato

Decídere *to decide*
past   decisi, decidesti, decise, decidemmo, decideste, decísero
past part. deciso

Devòlvere *to devolve*
past   devolvei *or* devolvetti, devolvesti, devolvè *or* devolvette, devolvemmo, devolveste, devolvérono *or* devolvèttero
past part. devoluto

Difèndere *to defend*
past   difesi, difendesti, difese, difendemmo, difendeste, difésero
past part. difeso

Díre *to say*
pres. ind. dico, dici, dice, diciamo, dite, dícono
imp. ind. dicevo
past   dissi, dicesti, disse, dicemmo, diceste, díssero
fut.   dirò
pres. sub. dica
imp. subj. dicesse
cond.   direi
imper.   di', dica, dite, dìcano
pres. part. dicendo
past part. detto

Dirígere *to direct*
past   diressi, dirigesti, diresse, dirigemmo, dirigeste, dirèssero
past part. diretto

Discútere *to discuss*
past   discussi *or* discutei, discutesti, discusse *or* discutè, discutemmo, discuteste, discússero *or* discutérono
past part. discusso

Distínguere *to distinguish*
past   distinsi, distinguesti, distinse, distinguemmo, distingueste, distínsero
past part. distinto

Divídere *to divide*
past   divisi, dividesti, divise, dividemmo, divideste, divísero
past part. diviso

Dolérsi *to regret*
pres. ind. mi dolgo, ti duoli, si duole, ci doliamo *or* dogliamo, vi dolete, si dólgono
past   mi dolsi, ti dolesti, si dolse, ci dolemmo, vi doleste, si dólsero
fut.   mi dorrò
pres. sub. mi dolga, ti dolga, si dolga, ci doliamo, vi doliate, si dólgano
imp. sub. mi dolessi
cond.   mi dorrei
imper.   duoliti, si dolga, doletevi, si dólgano
pres. part. dolente
past part. dolutosi

Dovére *to have to*
pres. ind. devo *or* debbo, devi, deve, dobbiamo, dovete, dévono *or* dèbbono
past dovei *or* dovetti, dovesti, dovè *or* dovette, dovemmo, doveste, dovérono *or* dovèttero
fut. dovrò
pres. sub. deva *or* debba, deva *or* debba, deva *or* debba, dobbiamo, dobbiate, dévano *or* dèbbono
imper. devi, deve, dovete, dévono
past part. dovuto

Emèrgere *to emerge*
past emersi, emergesti, emerse, emergemmo, emergeste, emèrsero
past part. emerso

Émpiere *to fill: conjugate like* **empíre**

Empíre *to fill*
pres. ind. empio, empi, empie, empiamo, empite, émpiono
pres. sub. empia, empia, empia, empiamo, empiate, émpiano
imper. empi, empia, empite, émpiano
pres. part. empiente

Èrgere *to raise*
past ersi, ergesti, erse, ergemmo, ergeste, èrsero
past part. erto

Esauríre *to exhaust*
past part. esaurito *or* esàusto

Esígere *to exact*
past esigei *or* esigetti, esigesti, esigè *or* esigette, esigemmo, esigeste, esigérono *or* esigèttero
past part. esatto

Esímere *to exempt*
past esimei *or* esimetti, esimesti, esimè *or* esimette, esimemmo, esimeste, esimérono *or* esimèttero
past part. Not used. Use esente or esentato

Espèllere *to expel*
past espulsi, espellesti, espulse, espellemmo, espelleste, espúlsero
past part. espulso

Esplòdere *to explode*
past esplosi, esplodesti, esplose, esplodemmo, esplodeste, esplòsero
past part. esploso

411

Evàdere *to escape*
past   evasi, evadesti, evase, evademmo, evadeste, evàsero
past part.   evaso
Fàre *to do, make*
pres. ind.   faccio *or* fo, fai, fa, facciamo, fate, fanno
imp. ind.   facevo
past   feci, facesti, fece, facemmo, faceste, fécero
fut.   farò
cond.   farei
pres. sub.   faccia
imp. sub.   facessi
imper.   fai *or* fa', faccia, fate, fàcciano
pres. part.   facente
past part.   fatto
Fèndere *to split*
past   fendei *or* fendetti, fendesti, fendè *or* fendette, fendemmo, fendeste, fendérono *or* fendèttero
past part.   fesso *or* fenduto
Fíggere *to fix*
past   fissi, figgesti, fisse, figgemmo, figgeste, físsero
past part.   fitto
Flèttere *to bend*
past   flettei *or* flessi, flettesti, flettè *or* flesse, flettemmo, fletteste, flettérono *or* flèssero
past part.   flesso
Fóndere *to melt*
past   fusi, fondesti, fuse, fondemmo, fondeste, fúsero
past part.   fuso
Fràngere *to break*
past   fransi, frangesti, franse, frangemmo, frangeste, frànsero
past part.   franto
Fríggere *to fry*
past   frissi, friggesti, frisse, friggemmo, friggeste, físsero
past part.   fritto
Giacére *to lie*
pres. ind.   giaccio, giaci, giace, giacciamo *or* giaciamo, giacete, giàcciono
past   giacqui, giacesti, giacque, giacemmo, giaceste, giàcquero
pres. sub.   giaccia
past part.   giaciuto

412

Indúlgere *to indulge*
past indulsi, indulgesti, indulse, indulgemmo, indulgeste, indúlsero
past part. indulto
Inferíre *to infer*
past inferii *or* infersi, inferisti, inferí *or* inferse, inferimmo, inferiste, inferírono *or* infèrsero
past part. inferito *or* inferto
Inseríre *to insert*
past part. inserito *or* (*rare*) inserto
Intrúdere *to intrude*
past intrusi, intrudesti, intruse, intrudemmo, intrudeste, intrúsero
past part. intruso
Lèdere *to offend*
past lesi, ledesti, lese, ledemmo, ledeste, lèsero
past part. leso
Lèggere *to read*
past lessi, leggesti, lesse, leggemmo, leggeste, lèssero
past part. letto
Méscere *to pour*
pres. ind. mesco, mesci, mesce, mesciamo, mescete, méscono
pres. sub. mesca, mesca, mesca, mesciamo, mesciate, méscano
past part. mesciuto *or* misto
Méttere *to place*
past misi, mettesti, mise, mettemmo, metteste, mísero
past part. messo
Mòrdere *to bite*
past morsi, mordesti, morse, mordemmo, mordeste, mòrsero
past part. morso
Moríre *to die*
pres. ind. muoio, muori, muore, moriàmo, morite, muòiono
fut. morirò *or* morrò, morirai *or* morrai, morirà *or* morrà, moriremo *or* morremo, morirete *or* morrete, morirànno *or* morrànno
cond. morirei *or* morrei, moriresti *or* morresti, morirebbe *or* morrebbe, moriremmo *or* morremmo, morireste *or* morreste, morirèbbero *or* morrèbbero

413

pres. sub.   muoia, muoia, muoia, moriamo, moriate, muòiano
imper.   muori, muoia, morite, muòiano
past part.   morto

Múngere   *to milk*
past   munsi, mungesti, munse, mungemmo, mungeste, múnsero
past part.   munto

Muòvere   *to move*
past   mossi, movesti, mosse, movemmo, moveste, mòssero
past part.   mosso

Nàscere   *to be born*
past   nacqui, nascesti, nacque, nascemmo, nasceste, nàcquero
past part.   nato

Nascóndere   *to hide*
past   nascosi, nascondesti, nascose, nascondemmo, nascondeste, nascósero
past part.   nascosto

Nuòcere   *to harm*
pres. ind.   nuoccio *or* noccio, nuoci, nuoce, nociamo, nocete, nuòcciono *or* nòcciono
past   nocqui, nocesti, nocque, nocemmo, noceste, nòcquero
pres. subj.   noccia, noccia, noccia, nociamo, nociate, nòcciano
imper.   nuoci, noccia, nocete, nocciano
past part.   nociuto

Offríre   *to offer*
past   offrii *or* offersi, offristi, offrí *or* offerse, offrimmo, offriste, offrírono *or* offèrsero
past part.   offerto

Parére   *to seem*
pres. ind.   paio, pari, pare, paiamo, parete, pàiono
past   parvi, paresti, parve, paremmo, pareste, pàrvero
fut.   parrò
pres. sub.   paia, paia, paia, pariamo, pariate *or* paiate, pàiano
cond.   parrei
imper.   *lacking*
pres. part.   parvente
past part.   parso

Pèrdere *to lose*
past persi *or* perdetti, perdesti, perse *or* perdette, perdemmo, perdeste, pèrsero *or* perdèttero
past part. perso *or* perduto

Persuadére *to persuade*
past persuasi, persuadesti, persuase, persuademmo, persuadeste, persuàsero
past part. persuaso

Piacére *to please*
pres. ind. piaccio, piaci, piace, piacciamo, piacete, piàcciono
past piacqui, piacesti, piacque, piacemmo, piaceste, piàcquero
pres. sub. piaccia
past part. piaciuto

Piàngere *to weep*
past piansi, piangesti, pianse, piangemmo, piangeste, piànsero
past part. pianto

Piòvere *to rain*
past piovvi, piovesti, piovve, piovemmo, pioveste, piòvvero

Pòrgere *to offer*
past porsi, porgesti, porse, porgemmo, porgeste, pòrsero
past part. porto

Pórre *to place*
pres. ind. pongo, poni, pone, poniamo, ponete, póngono
imp. ind. ponevo
past posi, ponesti, pose, ponemmo, poneste, pósero
fut. porrò
cond. porrei
pres. sub. ponga, ponga, ponga, poniamo, poniate, póngano
imp. sub. ponessi
imper. poni, ponga, ponete, póngano
pres. part. ponente
past part. posto

Potére *to be able*
pres. ind. posso, puoi, può, possiamo, potete, pòssono
fut. potrò
cond. potrei
pres. sub. possa
past part. potuto

Prediligere   *to prefer*
past   predilessi, prediligesti, predilesse, predili-
                  gemmo, prediligeste, predilessero
past part.   prediletto

Prèndere   *to take*
past   presi, prendesti, prese, prendemmo, prendeste,
                  présero
past part.   preso

Prescíndere   *to leave out of consideration*
past   prescindei *or* prescissi, prescindesti, pres-
                  cindè *or* prescisse, prescindemmo, prescindeste,
                  prescindérono *or* prescíssero
past part.   prescisso

Prevedére   *to foresee*
                  see **vedere**

Proferíre   *to utter*
past   proferii, proferisti, proferí, proferimmo, pro-
                  feriste, proferírono
past part.   proferito

Profferíre   *to proffer*
past   proffersi, profferisti, profferse, profferimmo,
                  profferiste, proffèrsero
past part.   profferto

Protèggere   *to protest*
past   protessi, proteggesti, protesse, proteggemmo,
                  proteggeste, protèssero
past part.   protetto

Púngere   *to prick*
past   punsi, pungesti, punse, pungemmo, pungeste,
                  púnsero
past part.   punto

Ràdere   *to shave*
past   rasi, radesti, rase, rademmo, radeste, ràsero
past part.   raso

Redígere   *to draw up*
past   redassi, redigesti, redasse, redigemmo, re-
                  digeste, redàssero
past part.   redatto

Redímere   *to redeem*
past   redensi, redimesti, redense, redimemmo, re-
                  dimeste, redénsero
past part.   redento

Règgere *to support*
past ressi, reggesti, resse, reggemmo, reggeste, rèssero
past part. retto

Rèndere *to give back*
past resi, rendesti, rese, rendemmo, rendeste, résero
past part. reso

Restríngere *to restrict*
past part. ristretto

Rídere *to laugh*
past risi, ridesti, rise, ridemmo, rideste, rísero
past part. riso

Riflèttere *to reflect*
past riflettei *or* riflessi, riflettesti, riflettè *or* riflesse, riflettemmo, rifletteste, riflettérono *or* riflèssero
past part. riflettuto *or* riflesso

Rifúlgere *to shine*
past rifulsi, rifulgesti, rifulse, rifulgemmo, rifulgeste, rifúlsero
past part. rifulso

Rilúcere *to shine*
past rilucei, rilucesti, rilucè, rilucemmo, riluceste, rilucérono
past part. lacking

Rimanére *to remain*
pres. ind. rimango, rimani, rimane, rimaniamo, rimanete, rimàngono
past rimasi, rimanesti, rimase, rimanemmo, rimaneste, rimàsero
fut. rimarrò
cond. rimarrei
pres. sub. rimanga, rimanga, rimanga, rimaniamo, rimaniate, rimàngano
imper. rimani, rimanga, rimanete, rimàngano
past part. rimasto

Rispóndere *to reply*
past risposi, rispondesti, rispose, rispondemmo, rispondeste, rispósero
past part. risposto

Ródere *to gnaw*
past rosi, rodesti, rose, rodemmo, rodeste, rósero
past part. roso

417

Rómpere *to break*
past   ruppi, rompesti, ruppe, rompemmo, rompeste,
                 rúppero
past part.   rotto

Salíre *to climb*
pres. ind.   salgo, sali, sale, saliamo, salite, sàlgono
pres. sub.   salga, salga, salga, saliamo, saliate, sàlgano
imper.   sali, salga, salite, sàlgano

Sapére *to know*
pres. ind.   so, sai, sa, sappiamo, sapete, sanno
past   seppi, sapesti, seppe, sapemmo, sapeste,
                 sèppero
fut.   saprò
cond.   saprei
pres. sub.   sappia
imper.   sappi, sappia, sappiate, sàppiano
pres. part.   sapiente

Scégliere *to choose*
pres. ind.   scelgo, scegli, sceglie, scegliamo, scegliete,
                 scélgono
past   scelsi, scegliesti, scelse, scegliemmo, sceglieste
                 scélsero
pres. sub.   scelga, scelga, scelga, scegliamo, scegliate,
                 scélgano
imper.   scegli, scelga, scegliete, scélgano
past part.   scelto

Scéndere *to descend*
past   scesi, scendesti, scese, scendemmo, scendeste,
                 scésero
past part.   sceso

Scèrnere *to choose*
past   scernei *or* scernetti, scernesti, scernè *or* scer-
                 nette, scernemmo, scernérono *or* scernèttero
past part.   *lacking*

Scíndere *to cut*
past   scissi, scindesti, scisse, scindemmo, scindeste,
                 scíssero
past part.   scisso

Sciògliere *to melt*
past   sciolsi, sciogliesti, sciolse, sciogliemmo, sciogli-
                 este, sciòlsero
past part.   sciolto

Scolpíre *to carve*
past   scolpii, scolpisti, scolpì, scolpimmo, scolpiste,

418

	scolpírono; *poet.* sculsi, scolpisti, sculse, scolpimmo, scolpiste, scúlsero
past part.	scolpito; *poet.* sculto

Scòrgere *to perceive*
past scorsi, scorgesti, scorse, scorgemmo, scorgeste, scòrsero
past part. scorto

Scrívere *to write*
past scrissi, scrivesti, scrisse, scrivemmo, scriveste, scríssero
past part. scritto

Scuòtere *to shake*
past scossi, scotesti, scosse, scotemmo, scoteste, scòssero
past part. scosso

Sedére *to sit*
pres. ind. siedo *or* seggo, siedi, siede, sediamo, sedete, sièdono *or* sèggono
past sedei *or* sedetti, sedesti, sedè *or* sedette, sedemmo, sedeste, sedérono *or* sedèttero
pres. sub. sieda *or* segga, sieda *or* segga, sieda *or* segga, sediamo, sediate, sièdano *or* sèggano
imper. siedi, sieda *or* segga, sedete, sièdano *or* sèggano

Seppellíre *to bury*
past part. seppellito *or* sepolto

Soddisfàre *to satisfy*
pres. ind. soddisfo *or* soddisfaccio, soddisfi *or* soddisfai, soddìsfa, soddisfiamo *or* soddisfacciamo, soddisfate, soddísfano *or* soddisfànno
pres. sub. soddisfi *or* soddisfaccia, soddisfi *or* soddisfaccia, soddisfi *or* soddisfaccia, soddisfacciamo, soddisfacciate, soddísfino *or* soddisfàcciano
imper. soddisfa, soddisfi *or* soddisfaccia, soddisfate, soddísfino *or* soddisfàcciano
past part. soddisfatto

Solére *to be used to*
pres. ind. soglio, suoli, suole, sogliamo, solete, sògliono; *or* sono sòlito, sei sòlito è sòlito, siamo sòliti, siete sòliti, sono sòliti
fut. *lacking*
cond. *lacking*
pres. sub. soglia
imp. sub. solessi

past   solei, solesti, solè, solemmo, soleste, solérono (*rare*); *now most commonly*: fui sòlito, fosti sòlito, fu sòlito, fummo sòliti, foste sòliti, fúrono sòliti

imper.   lacking

pres. part. lacking

past. part. sòlito

Sórgere *to rise*

past   sorsi, sorgesti, sorse, sorgemmo, sorgeste, sórsero

past part. sorto

Spàndere *to spread*

past   spandei *or* spansi, spandesti, spandè *or* spanse, spandemmo, spandeste, spandérono *or* spànsero

past part. Not used. Use Sparso (pp. of spargere)

Spàrgere *to scatter*

past   sparsi, spargesti, sparse, spargemmo, spargeste, spàrsero

past part. sparso

Sparíre *to disappear*

past   sparii *or* sparvi, sparisti, sparí *or* sparve, sparimmo, spariste, sparírono *or* spàrvero

Spégnere *or* **Spéngere** *to extinguish*

pres. ind. spengo, spegni *or* spengi, spegne *or* spenge, spegniamo *or* spengiamo, spegnete *or* spengete, spéngono

past   spensi, spegnesti *or* spengesti, spense, spegnemmo *or* spengemmo, spegneste *or* spengeste, spénsero

pres. sub. spenga, spenga, spenga, spegniamo *or* spengiamo, spegniate *or* spengiate, spéngano

imper.   spegni *or* spengi, spenga, spegnete *or* spengete, spéngano

past part. spento

Stàre *to stay*

pres. ind. sto, stai, sta, stiamo, state, stanno

past   stetti, stesti, stette, stemmo, steste, stéttero

fut.   starò

cond.   starei

pres. sub. stia

imp. sub. stessi

imper.   stai *or* sta', stia, state, stíano

past part. stato

Stríngere *to press*
past strinsi, stringesti, strinse, stringemmo, stringeste, strínsero
past part. stretto

Strúggere *to melt*
past strussi, struggesti, strusse, struggemmo, struggeste, strússero
past part. strutto

Svèllere *to eradicate*
pres. ind. svelgo *or* svello, svelli, svelle, svelliamo, svellete, svèlgono *or* svèllono
past svelsi, svellesti, svelse, svellemmo, svelleste, svèlsero
past part. svelto

Tacére *to be silent*
pres. ind. taccio, taci, tace, taciamo, tacete, tàcciono
past. tacqui, tacesti, tacque, tacemmo, taceste, tàcquero
pres. sub. taccia
imper. taci, taccia, tacete, tacciano

Tèndere *to stretch out*
past tesi, tendesti, tese, tendemmo, tendeste, tésero
past part. teso

Tenére *to hold*
pres. ind. tengo, tieni, tiene, teniamo, tenete, tèngono
past tenni, tenesti, tenne, tenemmo, teneste, tènnero
fut. terrò
cond. terrei
pres. sub. tenga, tenga, tenga, teniamo, teniate, tèngano
imper. tieni, tenga, tenete, tèngano

Tèrgere *to dry*
past tersi, tergesti, terse, tergemmo, tergeste, tèrsero
past part. terso

Tíngere *to dye*
past tinsi, tingesti, tinse, tingemmo, tingeste, tínsero
past part tinto

Tògliere *to take away*
pres. ind. tolgo, togli, toglie, togliamo, togliete, tòlgono
past tolsi, togliesti, tolse, togliemmo, toglieste, tòlsero
pres. sub. tolga, tolga, tolga, togliamo, togliate, tòlgano
imper. togli, tolga, togliete, tòlgano
cond. toglierei *or* torrei, toglieresti *or* torresti, toglierebbe *or* torrebbe, toglieremmo *or* torremmo,

togliereste *or* torreste, toglierèbbero *or* rèbbero

fut. toglierò *or* torrò, toglierai *or* torrai, toglierà *or* torrà, toglieremo *or* torremo, toglierete *or* torrete, toglieranno *or* torranno

past part. tolto

Tòrcere *to twist*

past torsi, torcesti, torse, torcemmo, torceste, tòrsero

past part. torto

Tràrre *to draw*

pres. ind. traggo, trai, trae, traiamo, traete, tràggono

imp. ind. traevo

fut. trarrò

past trassi, traesti, trasse, traemmo, traeste, tràssero

cond. trarrei

pres. sub. tragga, tragga, tragga, traiamo, traiate, tràggano

imp. sub. traessi

imper. trai, tragga, traete, tràggano

pres. part. traente

past part. tratto

Uccídere *to kill*

past uccisi, uccidesti, uccise, uccidemmo, uccideste, uccísero

past part ucciso

Udíre *to hear*

pres. ind. odo, odi, ode, udiamo, udite, òdono

fut. udirò *or* udrò, udirai *or* udrai, udirà *or* udrà, udiremo *or* udremo, udirete *or* udrete, udiranno *or* udranno

pres. sub. oda, oda, oda, udiamo, udiate, òdano

imper. odi, oda, udite, òdano

pres. part. udente *or* udiente

Uscíre *to go out*

pres. ind. esco, esci, esce, usciamo, uscite, éscono

pres. sub. esca, esca, esca, usciamo, usciate, éscano

imper. esci, esca, uscite, éscano

Valére *to be worth*

pres. ind. valgo, vali, vale, valiamo, valete, vàlgono

past valsi, valesti, valse, valemmo, valeste, vàlsero

fut. varrò

cond. varrei

pres. sub. valga, valga, valga, valiamo, valiate, vàlgano

imper. vali, valga, valete, vàlgano

past part. valso

422

Vedére *to see*
past   vidi, vedesti, vide, vedemmo, vedeste, vídero
fut.   vedrò
cond.   vedrei
pres. part.   vedente *or* veggente
past part.   visto *or* veduto

Veníre *to come*
pres. ind.   vengo, vieni, viene, veniamo, venite, vèngono
past   venni, venisti, venne, venimmo, veniste,
                vènnero
fut.   verrò
cond.   verrei
pres. sub.   venga, venga, venga, veniamo, veniate, vèngano
imper.   vieni, venga, venite, vèngano
pres. part.   veniente
past part.   venuto

Víncere *to win*
past   vinsi, vincesti, vinse, vincemmo, vinceste,
                vínsero
past part.   vinto

Vívere *to live*
past   vissi, vivesti, visse, vivemmo, viveste, víssero
fut.   vivrò
cond.   vivrei
past part.   vissuto

Volére *to want*
pres. ind.   voglio, vuoi, vuole, vogliamo, volete, vògliono
past   volli, volesti, volle, volemmo, voleste, vòllero
fut.   vorrò
cond.   vorrei
pres. sub.   voglia
past part.   voluto

Vòlgere *to turn*
past   volsi, volgesti, volse, volgemmo, volgeste,
                vòlsero
past part.   volto

Grammatica Inglese—English Grammar

IL PLURALE DEI SOSTANTIVI

1. Normalmente il plurale si forma aggiungendo –s: **chair** (sedia), **chairs**; **table** (tavolo), **tables**.
2. **–ch, –s, –sh, –x, –z.** I sostantivi terminanti in questo modo aggiungono **–es**, che costituisce una sillaba extra: **arch** (arco), **arches**; **kiss** (bacio), **kisses**; **dish** (piatto), **dishes**; **box** (scatola), **boxes**; **buzz** (ronzio), **buzzes**.
3. **–y.** Se la **–y** è preceduta da vocale, il plurale si forma normalmente: **boy** (ragazzo), **boys**. Se la **–y** è precuduto da consonante, il plurale si forma in **–ies**: **lady** (signora), **ladies**.
4. **–fe, –f.** I sostantivi in **–fe**, e molti in **–f**, formano il plurale in **–ves**: **wife** (moglie), **wives**; **leaf** (foglia), **leaves**.
5. **–o.** Alcuni sostantivi formano il plurale in **–oes**: **hero** (eroe), **heroes**; altri in **–os**: **piano** (pianoforte), **pianos**.
6. Molti sostantivi di origine latina o greca fanno il plurale come in latino o in greco, specialmente nel caso di termini scientifici: **radius** (raggio), **radii**; **thesis** (tesi), **theses**; **medium** (mezzo), **media**.
7. Alcuni nomi di animali non cambiano nel plurale: **sheep** (pecora); **deer** (cervo).
8. Alcuni sostantivi hanno il plurale irregolare: **man** (uomo), **men**; **woman** (donna), **women**; **child** (bambino), **children**; **foot** (piede), **feet**; **tooth** (dente), **teeth**; **goose** (oca), **geese**; **mouse** (sorcio), **mice**; **louse** (pidocchio), **lice**; **ox** (bue), **oxen**.

Nel dizionario il plurale è indicato dei sostantivi che entrano nelle categorie trattate nelle note 4-8.

Verbi Inglesi—English Verbs

Verbi Ausiliari

To be, *essere*   **To have,** *avere*

INDICATIVO PRESENTE

Sono, ecc   *Ho, ecc*
I am   I have
You are (thou art)   You have (thou hast)
He ⎫   He ⎫
She ⎬ is   She ⎬ has
It ⎭   It ⎭
We are   We have
You are   You have
They are   They have

INDICATIVO PASSATO

Ero, fui, ecc   *Avevo, ebbi, ecc*
I was   I had
You were (thou wert)   You had (thou hadst)
He ⎫   He ⎫
She ⎬ was   She ⎬ had
It ⎭   It ⎭
We were   We had
You were   You had
They were   They had

FUTURO

sarò, ecc   *Avrò, ecc*
I shall be   I shall have
You will (thou wilt) be   You will (thou wilt) have
He ⎫   He ⎫
She ⎬ will be   She ⎬ will have
It ⎭   It ⎭
We shall be   We shall have
You will be   You will have
They will be   They will have

CONDIZIONALE

Sarei, ecc   *Avrei, ecc*
I should be   I should have
You would (thou wouldst) be   You would (thou wouldst)
                                                          have
He ⎫   He ⎫
She ⎬ would be   She ⎬ would have
It ⎭   It ⎭
We should be   We should have
You would be   You would have
They would be   They would have

IMPERATIVO

[*Ch'io sia*], *sii*	[*Ch'io abbia*], *abbi*
Let me be	Let me have
Be	Have
Let him ⎫	Let him ⎫
her ⎬ be	her ⎬ have
it ⎭	it ⎭
Let us be	Let us have
Be	Have
Let them be	Let them have

INFINITO

To be, *essere*   To have, *avere*

GERUNDIO E PARTICIPIO PRESENTE

Being, *essendo*   Having, *avendo, avente*

PARTICIPIO PASSATO

Been, *stato*   Had, *avuto*

Tempi Composti
PERFETTO

Sono stato, ecc	*Ho avuto, ecc*
I have been	I have had
You have been	You have had
He ⎫	He ⎫
She ⎬ has been	She ⎬ has had
It ⎭	It ⎭
We have been	We have had
You have been	You have had
They have been	They have had

PIUCCHEPERFETTO

Ero, fui stato, ecc	*Avevo, ebbi avuto, ecc*
I had been	I had had
You had been	You had had
He ⎫	He ⎫
She ⎬ had been	She ⎬ had had
It ⎭	It ⎭
We had been	We had had
You had been	You had had
They had been	They had had

FUTURO PERFETTO

Sarò stato, ecc	*Avrò avuto, ecc*
I shall have been	I shall have had
You will have been	You will have had
He ⎫	He ⎫
She ⎬ will have been	She ⎬ will have had
It ⎭	It ⎭
We shall have been	We shall have had
You will have been	You will have had
They will have been	They will have had

CONDIZIONALE PERFETTO

Sarei stato, ecc
I should have been
You would have been
He ⎫
She ⎬ would have been
It ⎭
We should have been
You would have been
They would have been

Avrei avuto, ecc
I should have had
You would have had
He ⎫
She ⎬ would have had
It ⎭
We should have had
You would have had
They would have had

INFINITO PASSATO

Essere stato
To have been

Avere avuto
To have had

GERUNDIO PASSATO

Essendo stato
Having been

Avendo avuto
Having had

CONGIUNTIVO PRESENTE

Ch'io sia, ecc
That I be
That you be
That he ⎫
    she ⎬ be
    it ⎭
That we be
That you be
That they be

Ch'io abbia, ecc
That I have
That you have
That he ⎫
    she ⎬ have
    it ⎭
That we have
That you have
That they have

N.B.—Il congiuntivo presente non si usa ormai più in inglese, se non in qualche frase idiomatica

CONGIUNTIVO PASSATO

Se io fossi, ecc
If I were
If you were
If he ⎫
    she ⎬ were
    it ⎭
If we were
If you were
If they were

Se io avessi, ecc
If I had
If you had
If he ⎫
    she ⎬ had
    it ⎭
If we had
If you had
If they had

Verbi Irregolari Inglesi
English Irregular Verbs

Infinito		Passato	Part. passato
abide	dimorare	abode	abode
arise	alzarsi	arose	arisen
awake	svegliare, svegliarsi	awoke	awaked*
bear	portare	bore	borne
beat	battere	beat	beaten

Infinito		Passato	Part. passato
begin	cominciare	began	begun
bend	piegare	bent	bent
bereave	orbare	bereft	bereft*
beseech	implorare	besought	besought
bid	ordinare	bade (bid)	bidden (bid)
bind	legare	bound	bound
bite	mordere	bit	bitten
bleed	sanguinare	bled	bled
blow	soffiare	blew	blown
break	rompere	broke	broken
breed	generare, allevare	bred	bred
bring	portare	brought	brought
build	costruire	built	built
burn	bruciare	burned	burned*
burst	scoppiare	burst	burst
buy	comperare	bought	bought
cast	gettare	cast	cast
catch	afferrare	caught	caught
chide	sgridare	chid	chidden, chid*
choose	scegliere	chose	chosen
cleave	fendere	cleft, clove	cleft, cloven*
cling	aggrapparsi	clung	clung
come	venire	came	come
cost	costare	cost	cost
creep	strisciare	crept	crept
crow	cantare (del gallo)	crew	crowed
cut	tagliare	cut	cut
dare	osare	(durst)	dared*
deal	trattare	dealt	dealt
dig	scavare	dug	dug
do	fare	did	done
draw	disegnare, trarre	drew	drawn
dream	sognare	dreamt	dreamt*
drink	bere	drank	drunk
drive	guidare	drove	driven
dwell	abitare	dwelled	dwelled*
eat	mangiare	ate	eaten
fall	cadere	fell	fallen
feed	nutrire	fed	fed
feel	sentire	felt	felt
fight	combattere	fought	fought
find	trovare	found	found
flee	fuggire	fled	fled
fling	lanciare	flung	flung
fly	volare	flew	flown
forsake	abbandonare	forsook	forsaken
freeze	gelare	froze	frozen
get	acquisire	got	got, gotten
gild	dorare	gilt	gilt*
gird	cingere	girt	girt*
give	dare	gave	given
go	andare	went	gone

428

grind	macinare	ground	ground
grow	crescere	grew	grown
hang	appendere	hung	hung (=impiccare)*
hear	udire	heard	heard
hew	spaccare	hewed	hewn
hide	nascondere	hid	hidden, hid
hit	colpire	hit	hit
hold	tenere	held	held
hurt	dolere	hurt	hurt
keep	conservare	kept	kept
kneel	inginocchiarsi	knelt	knelt*
know	conoscere, sapere	knew	known
lay	deporre	laid	laid
lead	guidare	led	led
leave	lasciare	left	left
lend	prestare	lent	lent
let	lasciare, affittare	let	let
lie	giacere	lay	lain (=mentire*)
light	accendere, illuminare	lit	lit*
lose	perdere	lost	lost
make	fare	made	made
mean	significare	meant	meant
meet	incontrare	met	met
mow	mietere	mowed	mown
pay	pagare	paid	paid
put	mettere	put	put
read	leggere	read	read
rend	strappare	rent	rent
rid	liberare	rid	rid
ride	cavalcare	rode	ridden
ring	suonare	rang, rung	rung
rise	alzarsi, sorgere	rose	risen
rive	spaccare	rived	riven
run	correre	ran	run
say	dire	said	said
see	vedere	saw	seen
seek	cercare	sought	sought
sell	vendere	sold	sold
send	mandare	sent	sent
set	mettere	set	set
shake	scuotere	shook	shaken
shear	tosare	sheared	shorn
shed	versare	shed	shed
shine	brillare	shone	shone
shoe	calzare, ferrare	shod	shod
shoot	sparare	shot	shot
show	mostrare	showed	shown
shrink	ritirarsi	shrank	shrunk
shut	chiudere	shut	shut
sing	cantare	sang	sung
sink	affondare	sank	sunk

Infinito		*Passato*	*Part. passato*
sit	sedere	sat	sat
slay	uccidere	slew	slain
sleep	dormire	slept	slept
slide	slittare	slid	slid
sling	lanciare, appendere	slung	slung
slink	sgattaiolare	slunk	slunk
slit	fendere	slit	slit
smell	fiutare	smelled	smelled*
smite	colpire	smote	smitten
sow	seminare	sowed	sown*
speak	parlare	spoke	spoken
spend	spendere	spent	spent
spill	versare	spilled	spilled*
spin	filare	span, spun	spun
spit	sputare	spat, spit	spit
split	spaccare, dividere	split	split
spread	spandere	spread	spread
spring	balzare, scaturire	sprang	sprung
stand	stare in piedi	stood	stood
steal	rubare	stole	stolen
stick	attaccare	stuck	stuck
sting	pungere	stung	stung
stink	puzzare	stank, stunk	stunk
stride	camminare a grandi passi	strode	stridden
strike	colpire	struck	struck
string	infilare	strung	strung
strive	sforzarsi	strove	striven
swear	giurare, imprecare	swore	sworn
sweep	scopare	swept	swept
swell	gonfiarsi	swelled	swollen
swim	nuotare	swam	swum
swing	dondolare	swung	swung
take	prendere	took	taken
teach	insegnare	taught	taught
tear	stracciare	tore	torn
tell	dire, raccontare	told	told
think	pensare	thought	thought
thrive	prosperare	throve	thriven*
throw	gettare	threw	thrown
thrust	spingere	thrust	thrust
tread	camminare, calpestare	trod	trod, trodden
wear	indossare	wore	worn
weave	tessere	wove	woven
weep	piangere	wept	wept
win	vincere	won	won
wind	attorcigliare	wound	wound
work	lavorare	(wrought)	(wrought)*
wring	torcere	wrung	wrung
write	scrivere	wrote	written

NOTE: I verbi contrassegnati da asterisco si coniugano anche regolarmente.

430

Numerals - Numerali

NUMERI CARDINALI		CARDINAL NUMBERS
uno	1	one
due	2	two
tre	3	three
quattro	4	four
cinque	5	five
sei	6	six
sette	7	seven
otto	8	eight
nove	9	nine
dieci	10	ten
undici	11	eleven
dodici	12	twelve
tredici	13	thirteen
quattordici	14	fourteen
quindici	15	fifteen
sedici	16	sixteen
diciassette	17	seventeen
diciotto	18	eighteen
diciannove	19	nineteen
venti	20	twenty
ventuno	21	twenty-one
ventidue	22	twenty-two
ventitre etc.	23	twenty-three etc.
trenta	30	thirty
trentuno	31	thirty-one
trentadue	32	thirty-two
quaranta	40	forty
cinquanta	50	fifty
sessanta	60	sixty
settanta	70	seventy
ottanta	80	eighty
novanta	90	ninety
cento	100	one hundred
centouno	101	one hundred and one
centodue	102	one hundred and two
duecento	200	two hundred
trecento	300	three hundred
quattrocento	400	four hundred
cinquecento	500	five hundred
mille	1,000	one thousand
mille e cento	1,100	one thousand one hundred
mille e duecento	1,200	one thousand two hundred
duemila	2,000	two thousand
tremila	3,000	three thousand

431

diecimila	10,000	ten thousand
centomila	100,000	one hundred thousand
un milione	1,000,000	one million
due milioni	2,000,000	two million

NUMERI ORDINALI		ORDINAL NUMBERS
primo	1st	the first
secondo	2nd	the second
terzo	3rd	the third
quarto	4th	the fourth
quinto	5th	the fifth
sesto	6th	the sixth
settimo	7th	the seventh
ottavo	8th	the eighth
nono	9th	the ninth
decimo	10th	the tenth
undicesimo	11th	the eleventh
dodicesimo	12th	the twelfth
tredicesimo	13th	the thirteenth
quattordicesimo	14th	the fourteenth
quindicesimo	15th	the fifteenth
sedicesimo	16th	the sixteenth
diciasettesimo	17th	the seventeenth
diciottesimo	18th	the eighteenth
dicianovesimo	19th	the nineteenth
ventesimo	20th	the twentieth
ventesimoprimo	21st	the twenty-first
ventesimosecondo etc.	22nd	the twenty-second etc.
trentesimo	30th	the thirtieth
quarantesimo	40th	the fortieth
cinquantesimo	50th	the fiftieth
sessantesimo	60th	the sixtieth
settantesimo	70th	the seventieth
ottantesimo	80th	the eightieth
novantesimo	90th	the ninetieth
centesimo	100th	the hundredth
centesimoprimo	101st	the hundred and first
centocinquantesimo	150th	the hundred and fiftieth
centonovantesimo	190th	the hundred and ninetieth
ducentesimo	200th	the two hundredth
millesimo	1,000th	the thousandth
duemillesimo	2,000th	the two thousandth
diecimillesimo	10,000th	the ten thousandth
centomillesimo	100,000th	the hundred thousandth
milionesimo	1,000,000th	the millionth

Italian Measures and Weights
Misure e Pesi Italiani

LUNGHEZZA—LENGTH
1 Millimetro	$=\cdot 001$ Metro	$=\cdot 0394$ inch
1 Centimetro	$=\cdot 01$ Metro	$=\cdot 394$ inch
1 Metro	$=39\cdot 4$ inches	$=*1$ yard
1 Chilometro	$=1000$ Metri	$=*1094$ yards or $\frac{5}{8}$ mile
8 Chilometri	$=5$ miles	

SUPERFICIE—AREA
| 1 Ettaro | $=11960\cdot 11$ square yards |
| 1 Quadrachilometro | $=247\cdot 11$ acres |

CAPACITÀ—CAPACITY
1 Centilitro	$=\cdot 01$ Litro	$=\cdot 0176$ pint	
1 Litro	$=*1\frac{3}{4}$ pints	$=\cdot 2201$ gallon	
1 Ettolitro	$=100$ Litri	$=*22$ gallons	$=2\frac{3}{4}$ bushels
1 Chilolitro	$=1000$ Litri	$=*220$ gallons	$=27\frac{1}{2}$ bushels

PESI—WEIGHTS
1 Milligrammo	$=\cdot 001$ Grammo	$=\cdot 0154$ grain
1 Centigrammo	$=\cdot 01$ Grammo	$=\cdot 1543$ grain
1 Grammo		$=15\cdot 43$ grains
1 Ettogrammo	$=1000$ Grammi	$=*3\frac{1}{2}$ oz
1 Tonnellata	$=1000$ Chilogrammi	$=*1$ ton

IL TERMOMETRO—THE THERMOMETER
Punto di Congelamento	$=$Centigrade $0°$
Freezing Point	$=$Fahrenheit $32°$
Punto d'Ebollizione	$=$Centigrade $100°$
Boiling Point	$=$Fahrenheit $212°$

*roughly

433

Misure e Pesi Americani
American Weights and Measures

LENGTH—LUNGHEZZA
Inch (in)	=25 Millimetri
Foot (ft) (12 in)	=304 Millimetri
Yard (yd) (3 ft)	=913 Millimetri (quasi 1 Metro)
Fathom (fthm) (2 yards)	=1 Metro 828 Millimetri
Mile (8 furlongs, 1760 yards)	=1609 Metri
Nautical mile, knot	=1853 Metri
5 miles	=8 Chilometri

AREA—SUPERFICIE
Square inch	=6,45 Centimetri quadrati (cm^2)
Square foot	=929 cm^2
Square yard	=0,8360 Metri quadrati (m^2)
Acre	=4047 m^2

CAPACITY—CAPACITÀ
Pint	=0,567 Litro
Quart (2 pints)	=1,136 Litri
Gallon (4 quarts)	=4,53 Litri
Peck (2 gallons)	=9,086 Litri
Bushel (8 gallons)	=36,348 Litri
Quarter (8 bushels)	=290,8 Litri

WEIGHTS (AVOIRDUPOIS)—PESI
Ounce (oz)	=28,35 Grammi
Pound (lb) (16 oz)	=453,59 Grammi
Stone (st) (14 lb)	=6,35 Chili
Quarter (qr) (28 lb)	=12,7 Chili
Hundredweight (cwt) (112 lb)	=50,8 Chili
Ton (T) (20 cwts)	=1016 Chili

THE THERMOMETER—IL TERMOMETRO
Freezing Point	=Fahrenheit 32°
Punto di Congelamento	=Centigrade 0°
Boiling Point	=Fahrenheit 212°
Punto d'Ebollizione	=Centigrade 100°

Italian Abbreviations—Abbreviazioni Italiane

AA	Accademia Aeronautica (*Air Force Academy*); Assistenza Automobilistica (*organization for assisting motorists*)
aC	avanti Cristo (*before Christ*)
ACDG	Associazione Cristiana dei Giovani (*Young Men's Christian Association*)
ACI	Automobile Club d'Italia (*Italian Automobile Association*); Azione Cattolica Italiana (*Italian Catholic Action*)
ACIS	Alto Commissariato per l'Igiene e la Sanità (*Public Health Board*)
AGIP	Azienda Generale Italiana Petroli (*National Italian Oil Company*)
ago	agosto (*August*)
AI	Aeronautica Italiana (*Italian Air Force*)
ALITALIA	Aerolinee Italiane Internazionali (*Italian International Airlines*)
all	allegato (*enclosure*)
alt	altezza (*height*); altitudine (*altitude*)
ANAS	Azienda Nazionale Autonoma della Strada (*National Road Board*)
ANSA	Agenzia Nazionale Stampa Associata (*Associated Press*)
apr	aprile (*April*)
AR	Altezza Reale (*Royal Highness*); andata e ritorno (*round trip*)
ASC	Associazione Scoutistica Cattolica (*Catholic Scout Movement*)
ATM	Azienda Tranviaria Municipale (*Municipal Tram Company*)
AVIS	Associazione Volontari Italiani del Sangue (*Association of Italian Blood Donors*)
avv	avverbio (*adverb*); avvocato (*lawyer*)
BI	Banca d'Italia (*Bank of Italy*)
brev	brevetto (*patent*)
c	capitolo (*chapter*); circa (*about*); codice ((*leg*) code); corpo (*type-size*)
cabl	cablogramma (*cable*)
cad	cadauno (*each*)
CAI	Club Alpino Italiano (*Italian Alpine Club*)
Cap	Capitano (*Captain*); capitolo (*chapter*)
Cav	Cavaliere (*Knight*)
cc	conto corrente (*current account*)
CC	Corpo Carabinieri (*Carabiniere Corps*); Corte di Cassazione (*Supreme Court of Appeal*)
CCI	Camera di Commercio Internazionale (*International Chamber of Commerce*)
ccp	conto corrente postale (*current postal account*)
Cd'A	Corte d'Assise (*Court of Assizes*)
CdL	Camera del Lavoro (*Trade Union*)
CdS	Circolo della Stampa (*Press Club*); Codice della Strada (*Highway Code*); Consiglio di Sicurezza (*Security Council*)
CECA	Comunità Europea per il Carbone e l'Acciaio (*European Coal and Steel Community*)
CERN	Consiglio Europeo per le Ricerche Nucleari (*European Council for Nuclear Research*)

435

CGIL Confederazione Generale Italiana del Lavoro (*Federation of Italian Trade Unions*)
CIT Compagnia Italiana Turismo (*Italian Travel Agency*)
CLN Comitato di Liberazione Nazionale (*Resistance Movement Committee* (*World War II*))
cm corrente mese (*present month*)
CONFINDUSTRIA Confederazione Generale dell'Industria Italiana (*General Confederation of Italian Industry*)
CONI Comitato Olimpico Nazionale Italiano (*Italian Olympic Games Committee*)
CP Casella Postale (*Post Office Box*)
CRI Croce Rossa Internazionale (*International Red Cross*)
Croce Rossa Italiana (*Italian Red Cross*)
c. to conto (*account*)
CV cavallo vapore (*horse power*)
dC dopo Cristo (*Anno Domini, in the year of the Lord*)

DC Democrazia Cristiana (*Christian Democrat Party*)
devmo devotissimo ((*in letters*) *yours truly*)
dic dicembre (*December*)
dott Dottore (*Doctor*)
dr Dottore (*Doctor*)
dr.ssa Dottoressa (*Doctor*)

ecc eccetera (*et cetera*)
Ecc Eccellenza (*Excellency*)
Egr.Sig. Egregio Signore ((*in addresses*) *Mr.*; (*in letters*) Dear Sir)
ENAL Ente Nazionale Assistenza Lavoratori (*National Association for Assistance to Workers*)
ENIC Ente Nazionale Industrie Cinematografiche (*National Association of the Cinema Industry*)
ENIT Ente Nazionale Industrie Turistiche (*National Tourist Office*)

feb febbraio (*February*)
ferr ferrovia (*railway*)
FFSS Ferrovie dello Stato (*State Railways*)
FIAT Fabbrica Italiana Automobili Torino (*Italian Automobile Works Torino*)
FIGC Federazione Italiana Giuoco Calcio (*Italian Football Association*)
FIT Federazione Italiana Tennis (*Italian Lawn Tennis Association*)
Flli Fratelli ((*com*) *Brothers*)
FPI Federazione Pugilistica Italiana (*Italian Boxing Association*)
Fr b franco belga (*Belgian franc*)
Fr f franco francese (*French franc*)
Fr s franco svizzero (*Swiss franc*)

GB Gran Bretagna (*Great Britain*)
GdF Guardia di Finanza (*Revenue Guard*)
GEI Giovani Esploratori Italiani (*Italian Boy Scouts*)
gen genitivo (*genitive*); gennaio (*January*)
GU Gazzetta Ufficiale (*Official Gazette*)

h ora (*hour*)
HF alta frequenza (*high frequency*)

IGE Imposta Generale sull'Entrata (*Income Tax*)
INA Istituto Nazionale Assicurazioni (*National Insurance*)
INAM Istituto Nazionale per l'Assicurazione contro le malattie (*National Health Insurance*)

436

INCOM	Industria Cortometraggi (*Short-Film Industry*)
INPI	Istituto Nazionale per la Prevenzione degli Infortuni (*National Institute for the Prevention of Accidents*)
INPS	Istituto Nazionale Previdenza Sociale (*National Institute of Social Security*)
IPS	Istituto Poligrafico dello Stato (*Stationery Office*)
Italcable	Compagnia Italiana dei Cavi Telegrafici e Telefonic Sottomarini (*Italian Cable Company*)
kg	chilogrammo (*kilogram*)
lett.	letterario (*literary*); letteratura (*literature*)
LF	bassa frequenza (*low frequency*)
Lit	Lire italiane (*Italian lire*)
LLPP	Lavori Pubblici (*Public Works*)
lm	livello del mare (*sea level*)
Lsr	lira sterlina (*£ pound* (*sterling*))
lug	luglio (*July*)
M	Monte (*Mount*)
mag	maggio (*May*)
mar	marzo (*March*)
MAS	motoscafo antisommergibile (*motor torpedo-boat*)
MCD	massimo comun divisore (*highest common factor*)
mcm	minimo comune multiplo (*lowest common multiple*)
ME	Medio Evo (*Middle Ages*)
MEC	Mercato Europeo Comune ((*European*) *Common Market*)
MM	Marina Militare (*Royal Navy*)
M/N	motonave (*motorship*)
Mo	Maestro ((*mus*) *maestro*)
MPPTT	Ministero delle Poste e delle Telecomunicazioni (*Post Office*)
Msa	Marchesa (*Marchioness*)
Mse	Marchese (*Marquis*)
MSI	Movimento Sociale Italiano (*neo-Fascist Party*)
n	nato (*born*); neutro (*neuter*)
ND	Nobil Donna (*lady of a noble family*)
NdA	Nota dell'Autore (*author's note*)
NdE	Nota dell'Editore (*publisher's note*)
NdT	Nota del Traduttore (*translator's note*)
NH	Nobil Uomo (*member of a noble family*)
NN	(L. *Nescio nomen*) di paternità ignota (*name of father unknown*)
nov	novembre (*November*)
NU	Nazioni Unite (*United Nations*)
OdG	ordine del giorno (*agenda*)
OECE	Organizzazione Economica per la Cooperazione Europea (*Organization for European Economic Co-operation*)
OIL	Organizzazione Internazionale del Lavoro (*International Labour Organization*)
OMR	Ordine al Merito della Repubblica (*Order of Merit of the Republic*)
ONMI	Opera Nazionale per il Mezzogiorno d'Italia (*National Board for the South of Italy*); Opera Nazionale per la Protezione della Maternità e dell'Infanzia (*National Board for Maternity and Child Welfare*)
ONU	Organizzazione delle Nazioni Unite (*United Nations Organization*)

OSSSA	Ordine Supremo della Santissima Annunziata (*Supreme Order of the Holy Annunciation*)
ott	ottobre (*October*)
OVRA	Opera Volontaria per la Repressione dell'Antifascismo (*Fascist Secret Police*)
P	Padre (*eccl*) *Father*)
pag	pagina (*page*)
pcc	per copia conforme (*certified copy*)
PCI	Partito Comunista Italiano (*Italian Communist Party*)
PdA	Partito d'Azione (*Action Party*)
PDC	Partito Democratico Cristiano (*Christian Democrat Party*)
PDI	Partito Democratico Italiano (*Italian Democratic Party*)
pes	per esempio (*for example*)
pf	per favore (*please*)
PG	Procuratore Generale (*Attorney General*)
PI	Pubblica Istruzione (*Public Education*)
PLI	Partito Liberale Italiano (*Italian Liberal Party*)
PM	Polizia Militare (*Military Police*); Pubblico Ministero (*Public Prosecutor*)
PNF	Partito Nazionale Fascista (*National Fascist Party*)
pp	pacco postale (*parcel post*)
pr	per ringraziamento (*with thanks*)
PRI	Partito Repubblicano Italiano (*Italian Republican Party*)
Proc Gen	Procuratore Generale (*Attorney General*)
profsta	professionista (*professional man*)
PSDI	Partito Socialista Democratico Italiano (*Italian Socialist Democratic Party*)
PSI	Partito Socialista Italiano (*Italian Socialist Party*)
PT	Poste e Telegrafi (*Post and Telegraph Service*)
PTP	Posto Telefonico Pubblico (*public telephone*)
pza	piazza (*square*)
q	quadrato (*square*)
qb	quanto basta (*a sufficient quantity*)
QG	Quartier Generale (*Headquarters*)
R	raccomandata (*registered letter*)
racc	raccomandata (*registered letter*)
rag	ragioniere (*certified accountant*)
RAI	Radio Audizioni Italiane (*Italian Broadcasting Corporation*)
RAU	Repubblica Araba Unita (*United Arab Republic*)
RI	Repubblica Italiana (*Italian Republic*)
RU	Regno Unito (*United Kingdom*)
S	Santo (*Saint*); Sud (*South*)
SA	Sua Altezza (*His, Her Highness*)
SAR	Sua Altezza Reale (*His, Her Royal Highness*)
sbf	salvo buon fine ((*com*) *under usual reserve*)
SCV	Stato della Città del Vaticano (*Vatican City*)
SEDI	Società Editrice Documentari Italiani (*Italian Newsreel Company*)
SEO	salvo errori ed omissioni (*com*) (*errors and omissions excepted*)
serg	sergente (*sergeant*)
sett	settembre (*September*)
sfr	sotto fascia raccomandata (*registered printed matter*)
sfs	sotto fascia semplice (*unregistered printed matter*)
Sig	Signore (*Mr, Mister*)
Siga	Signora (*Mrs, Mistress*)
Sigg	Signori (*Messrs, Messieurs*)

Signa Signorina (*Miss*)
SISAL Società Italiana Sistemi a Lotto (*Italian Society of State Lottery Systems*)
SMG Stato Maggiore Generale (*General Staff*)
SMOM Sovrano Militare Ordine di Malta (*Sovereign Military Order of Malta*)
SNDA Società Nazionale Dante Alighieri (*National Dante Alighieri Society*)
SO Sud-Ovest (*South-West*)
Soc Società (*Society*)
Sottte Sottotenente (*Sub-Lieutenant*)
SpA Società per Azioni (*joint-stock company or limited liability company*)
SPA Società Protettrice degli Animali (*Society for the Prevention of Cruelty to Animals*)
Spett Spettabile (honorable)
SPM sue proprie mani (*personal (for addressee)*)
SRC Santa Romana Chiesa (*Holy Roman Church*)
Srl Società a responsabilità limitata (*Limited Company*)
SSPP Santi Padri (*Holy Fathers*)
STIPEL Società Telefonica Interregionale Piemonte e Lombardia (*Telephone Company (Piedmont and Lombardy)*)
SU Stati Uniti (*United States*)
SUA Stati Uniti d'America (*United States of America*)
SVP (*German* Südtiroler Volkspartei) Partito Popolare Sudtirolese (*People's Party of South Tyrol*)
tbc, TBC tubercolosi (*tuberculosis*)
TCI Touring Club Italiano (*Italian Touring Club*)
tel telefono (*telephone*)
Ten Tenente (*Lieutenant*)
TOTIP Totalizzatore Ippico (*horse-race pools*)
TOTOCALCIO Totalizzatore Calcistico (*Football Pools*)
tr tratta (*draft*)

UCDG Unione Cristiana delle Giovani (*Young Women's Christian Association*)
UCI Unione Ciclistica Internazionale (*International Cycling Union*)
UDE Unione Doganale Europea (*European Customs Union*)
UDI Unione Donne Italiane (*Association of Italian Women*)
urg urgente (*urgent*)
URSS Unione Repubbliche Socialiste Sovietiche (*Union of Soviet Socialist Republics*)
US Ufficio Stampa (*Press Agency*); Uscita di Sicurezza (*Emergency Exit*)

V Via (*Street*)
Vat Vaticano (*Vatican*)
VE Vostra Eccellenza (*Your Excellency*)
VEm Vostra Eminenza (*Your Eminence*)
Vle Viale (*avenue*)
VM Vostra Maestà (*Your Majesty*)
vr vedi retro (*please turn over*)
vs vostro (*your, yours*)

W viva! (*long live*); watt (*watt*)
WL (F. *wagon-lit*) carrozza-letto (*sleeping car*)
YCI Yacht Club Italia (*Italian Yacht Club*)

439

Abbreviazioni Americani—American Abbreviations

A	adults (*adulti*)
AA	Automobile Association (*Automobile Club*); Alcoholics Anonymous (*Alcoolizzati Anonimi*)
AAA	American Automobile Association (*Automobile Club d'America*)
a/c	account (current) *conto* (*corrente*)
AEC	Atomic Energy Commission (*Commissione per l'Energia Atomica*)
AFL-CIO	American Federation of Labor and Congress of Industrial Organizations (*Confederazione Generale Americana del Lavoro*)
A1	first class (*Prima Categoria*)
AID	Artificial Insemination by Donor (*Fecondazione Artificiale da parte di Donatore*)
AMA	American Medical Association (*Ordine Americano dei Medici*)
anon	anonymous (*anonimo*)
AP	Associated Press (*Stampa Associata*)
approx	approximate(ly) (*approssimato, approssimativamente*)
ARC	American Red Cross (*Croce Rossa Americana*)
arr	arrives (*arrivo*)
assn, assoc	association (*associazione*)
asst	assistant (*assistente*)
av	average (*medio*)
Ave	Avenue (*viale*)
b	born (*nato*)
BA	Bachelor of Arts (*Diplomato in Lettere*); British Academy (*Accadèmia Britannica*); British Association (For the Advancement of Sciences) (*Associazione Britannica (per il Progresso della Scienza*))
Bart	Baronet (*Baronetto*)
BBC	British Broadcasting Corporation (*Ente Radiofonico Britannico*)
BC	before Christ (*avanti Cristo*); British Columbia (*Colombia Britannica*)
BD	Bachelor of Divinity (*Diplomato in Teologia*)
Bd	Board (*Commissione, Consiglio, Ministero*)
BDS	Bachelor of Dental Surgery (*Diplomato in Odontoiatria*); bomb disposal squad (*gruppo addetto al disinnestamento delle bombe*)
be, B/E	bill of exchange (*cambiale*)
BEA	British European Airways (*Compagnia Britannica delle Linee Europee*)
bibl.	biblical (*biblico*); bibliographical (*bibliografica*)
B Litt	Bachelor of Letters (*Diplomato in Lettere*)
BM	British Museum (*Museo Britannico*); Bachelor of Medicine (*Diplomato in Medicina*)
B. Mus	Bachelor of Music (*Diplomato in Musica*)
BOAC	British Overseas Airways Corporation (*Compagnia Britannica delle Linee Transoceaniche*)
B of A	Bank of America (*Banca d'America*)
B of E	Bank of England (*Banca d'Inghilterra*); Board of Education (*Ministero della Pubblica Istruzione*)
B of T	Board of Trade (*Ministero del Commercio e dell'Industria*)

Brit	Britain ((*Gran*) *Bretagna*); British (*Britannico*)
Bros	Brothers (*com*) (*Fratelli*)
B/S	Bill of Sale (*nota di vendita, fattura*)
BSA	Boy Scouts of America (*Giovani Exploratori Americani*)
BSc	Bachelor of Science (*Diplomato in Scienze*)
Bt	Baronet (*Baronetto*)
BTU	British Thermal Unit (*unità* (*inglese*) *de misura de calore*)
BUP	British United Press (*Stampa Unita Britannica*)
C	Cape (*Capo*); centigrade (*centigrado*); Central (*Centrale*); Conservative (*Conservatore*)
c	cent (*centesimo*); century (*secolo*); about (*L. circa*) (*circa*); chapter (*capitolo*)
Cantab	Cambridge (*cantabrigense*)
cap	capital letter (*lettera maiuscola*); chapter (*capitolo*)
Capt	Captain (*Capitano*)
CBS	Columbia Broadcasting System (*Rete Radiofonica Colombia*)
CD	Civil Defense (*Difesa Civile*)
cf .	compare (*confronta*)
CIA	Central Intelligence Agency (*Agenzia Centrale Informazioni* (*Servizio Segreto*))
CID	Criminal Investigation Department (*Polizia Giudiziaria*)
cif	cost, insurance, freight (*costo compreso il nolo e l'assicurazione*)
CND	Campaign for Nuclear Disarmament (*Campagna per il Disarmo Nucleare*)
CO	Commanding Officer (*Ufficiale Comandante*); conscientious objector (*obiettore di coscienza*)
Co	Company (*Compagnia*)
c/o	care of (*presso*)
COD	cash on delivery (*pagamento alla consegna*)
C of E	Church of England (*Chiesa d'Inghilterra*)
C of S	Chief of Staff (*capo di stato maggiore*)
Col	Colonel (*Colonnello*)
cont	continued (*continuazione*)
Co-op	Co-operative (*Cooperativa*)
CPA	certified public accountant (*ragioniere*)
Cpl	Corporal (*caporale*)
CUP	Cambridge University Press (*Edizioni dell'Università di Cambridge*)
CWS	Co-operative Wholesale Society (*Società Cooperativa all' Ingrosso*)
cwt	hundredweight(s)
d	died (*morta*); date (*data*); daughter (*figlia*); penny
DC	District of Columbia (*Distretto di Colombia*); (*mus*) (*da capo*); Direct Current (*corrente continua*)
DD	Doctor of Divinity (*Dottore in Teologia*)
Dem	Democrat, Democratic (*Democratico, Democratico*)
dep	departs (*partenza*); deputy (*vice*)
dept	department (*reparto*); deponent (*deponente*)
DG	*Deo gratias, Dei gratia,* thanks to God, by the grace of God (*grazie a Dio, per grazia di Dio*)
diam	diameter (*diametro*)
dim	diminuendo (*diminuendo*); diminutive (*diminutivo*)
D. Litt.	Doctor of Letters (*Dottore in Lettere*)
DM	Doctor of Medicine (*Dottore in Medicina*)
do	ditto (the same) (*suddetto*)

doz	dozen (*dozzina*)
Dr.	Doctor (*dottore, dottoressa*)
DSC	Distinguished Service Cross (*Croce per Meriti Speciali*)
DSM	Distinguished Service Medal (*Medaglia per Meriti Speciali*)
DSO	Distinguished Service Order (*Ordine dei Meriti Speciali*)
DST	Daylight Saving Time (*ora estiva*)
E	East (*Est*); Eastern (*Orientale*)
EEC	European Economic Community (Common Market) (*Comunità Economica Europea* (*Mercato Comune*)
EFTA	European Free Trade Association (*Associazione Europea di Libero Scambio*)
eg	for example (L. *exempli gratia*) (*per esempio*)
EP	Extended Play (gramophone record)
ESP	extra sensory perception (*percezione metapsìchica*)
esp	especially (*specialmente*)
Esq	Esquire (*Signore*)
est	established (*fondato*)
et al.	and others (L. *et alia*) (*e altri*)
etc	and the rest (L. *et cetera*) (*eccetera*)
FA	Football Association (*Associazione Calcistica*)
FAO	Food and Agriculture Organization (*Organizzazione Alimenti e Agricoltura*)
FBI	Federal Bureau of Investigation (*Polizia Federale Statunitense*)
FC	Football Club (*Club Calcistico*)
fig	figurative (*figurato*)
fin	financial (*finanziario*)
FO	Foreign Office (*Ministero degli Affari Esteri*)
fob	free on board (*franco a bordo*)
FRAM	Fellow of the Royal Academy of Music (*Membro della Reale Accadèmia di Musica*)
FRCS	Fellow of the Royal College of Surgeons (*Membro del Reale Collegio dei Chirurghi*)
FRS	Fellow of the Royal Society (*Membro della "Royal Society"*)
ft	foot (*piede*); feet (*piedi*); fort (*forte*); fortification (*fortificazione*)
FTC	Federal Trade Commission (*Commissione Federale di Commercio*)
gal	gallon(s) (*gallone, galloni*)
GATT	General Agreement on Tariffs and Trade (*Accordo Generale Tariffe e Commercio*)
GB	Great Britain (*Gran Bretagna*)
gen	gender (*genere*); general (*generale*); genitive (*genitivo*)
GHQ	General Headquarters (*Quartier Generale*)
GI	Government Issue (American private soldier) (*soldato semplice*)
Gib	(*fam*) Gibraltar (*Gibilterra*)
gm	gram (*grammo*)
GMT	Greenwich Mean Time (*Ora di Greenwich*)
GOP	(Grand Old Party) Republican Party (*Partito Repubblicano*)
Govt	Government (*Governo*)
GP	General Practitioner (*medico generico*)
GPO	General Post Office (*Posta Centrale*)

h & c	hot and cold (water) (*acqua calda e fredda*)
HCF	highest common factor *massimo commun divisore*)
HE	high-explosive (*alto esplosivo*); His Eminence (*Sua Eminenza*); His Excellency (*Sua Eccellenza*)
HEW	(Department of) Health, Education and Welfare (*Ministero di Sanità, Educazione e Salute Pubblica*)
HH	His (Her) Highness (*Sua Altezza*); His Holiness (*Sua Santità*)
HF	high frequency (*alta frequenza*)
HM	His (Her) Majesty (*Sua Maestà*)
Hon	Honorary (*Onorario*); Honorable (*Onorevole*)
HP	Houses of Parliament (*Palazzo del Parlamento*); House Physician (*medico interno (di ospedale*))
hp	horse-power (*potenza in cavalli vapore*)
HQ	headquarters (*Quartier Generale*)
hr	hour (*ora*)
HRH	His (Her) Royal Highness (*Sua Altezza Reale*)
I, Is	Island(s) (*Isola (Isole*))
ib, ibid	in the same place (L. *ibidem*) (*nello stesso luogo*)
i/c	in charge (*incaricato, addetto*)
ICBM	Inter-Continental Ballistic Missile (*Missile Balistico Intercontinentale*)
ICC	Interstate Commerce Commission (*Commissione di Commercio Interstatale*)
Ice	Iceland(*Islanda*)
id	the same (L. *idem*) (*lo stesso*)
ie	that is, namely (L. *id est*) (*cioè*)
ILO	International Labour Organization (*Organizzazione Internazionale del Lavoro*)
IMF	International Monetary Fund (*Fondo Monetario Internazionale*)
in	inch (*pollice*); inches (*pollici*)
Inc	incorporated (*incorporato*)
incl	included, including, inclusive (*incluso, compreso*)
incog	incognito (*incognito*)
INS	International News Service (*Agenzia Stampa Internazionale*)
Inst	Institute (*Istituto*); inst, instant, the present month (*corrente mese*)
IOU	I owe you (*com*) (*pagherò*)
IQ	Intelligence Quotient (*coefficiente di intelligenza*)
IRA	Irish Republican Army (*Esercito della Repubblica Irlandese*)
IS	Island(s) (*isola, isole*)
JP	Justice of the Peace (*Giudice di Pace*)
jr	junior
KBE	Knight Commander of the British Empire (*Cavaliere dell'Impero Britannico*)
KC	King's Counsel (*Avvocato di Corte suprema*)
KCB	Knight Commander of the Bath (*Cavaliere Maestro (dell'Ordine) del Bagno*))
KG	Knight of the Garter (*Cavaliere (dell'Ordine) della Giarrettiera*)
KKK	Ku Klux Klan
KO	(*boxing*) knock out; kick off (*calcio d'inizio*)
Kt	Knight (*Cavaliere*)

kw   kilowatt (*chilowatt*)

L   Latin (*Latino*); Law (*Legge*); Learner (on motor cars); Liberal (*Liberale*)

l   lake (*lago*); left (*sinistra*); lira

£   pound (*sterlina*)

lab   laboratory (*laboratorio*); Labor (*laburista*)

Lat   Latin (*Latino*)

lb   pound (*libbra*)

LC   Library of Congress (*Biblioteca del Congresso*)

LCM   lowest common multiple (*minimo commune multiplo*)

LF   low frequency (*bassa frequenza*)

Lib   Library (*Biblioteca*); Liberal (*Liberale*)

lit   literal (*letterale*); literally (*letteralmente*); literature (*letteratura*); litre (*litro*)

LLB   Bachelor of Laws (*Diplomato in Legge*)

log   logarithm (*logaritmo*)

LP   Labour Party (*Partito Laburista*); Long Playing (gramophone record) (*disco lunga durata*)

LSD   lysergic acid diethylamide (*acido lisergico dietilamidico*)

£sd   Pounds Shillings Pence (*L librae, solidi, denarii*) (*sterline, scellini, pence*)

LSE   London School of Economics (*Instituto di Economia di Londra*)

Ltd (Co)   Limited (Company) (*Società a responsabilità limitata*)

Lw   Long wave (*onda lunga*)

m   meter (*metro*); married (*coniugato*); male (*sesso maschile*); masculine (*maschile*); mile (*miglio*); minute (*minuto*); month (*mese*)

MA   Master of Arts (*Dottore in Lettere*)

MB, ChB   Bachelor of Medicine; Bachelor of Surgery (*Dottore in Medicina*)

MBE   Member of the Order of the British Empire (*Membro dell'Ordine dell'Impero Britannico*)

MC   Master of Ceremonies (*Cerimoniere*); Member of Congress (*Membro del Congresso*); Military Cross (*Croce di Guerra*)

MD   Doctor of Medicine (*Dottore in Medicina*); mentally deficient (*deficiente mentale*)

memo   memorandum (*memorandum*)

Messrs   the plural of Mr. (*Signori*); (*com*) Ditta (*in indirizzi*))

Mgr   Monsignor (*Monsignore*)

MI   Military Intelligence (*Controspionaggio*)

MO   Medical Officer (*Ufficiale Medico*)

MOH   Medical Officer of Health (*Ufficiale Medico d'Igiene*)

MP   Member of Parliament (*Deputato al Parlamento*); Military Police (*Polizia Militare*); Metropolitan Police (*Polizia Metropolitana*)

mpg   miles per gallon (*miglia per gallone*)

mph   miles per hour (*miglia all'ora*)

Mr   Mister (*Signore*)

MRCP   Member of Royal College of Physicians (*Membro del Reale Collegio dei Medici*)

Mrs   Mistress (*Signora*)

Mt   Mount, mountain (*monte*)

Mw   medium wave (*onda media*)

444

N	North (*Nord*); Northern (*Settentrionale*)
n	name (*nome*); noun (*sostantivo*); neuter (*neutro*); noon (*mezzogiorno*); born (L. *natus*) (*nato*); nephew (*nipote*)
NAS	National Academy of Sciences (*Academia Nazionale delle Scienze*)
NASA	National Aeronautics and Space Administration (*Ministero Nazionale di Aeronautica e Spazio*)
Nat	National (*nazionale*); nationalist (*nazionalista*)
NBC	National Broadcasting Company (*Ente Radiofonico Nazionale*)
NCO	Non-commissioned officer (*sottufficiale*)
NE	New England (*Nuova Inghilterra*); Northeast(ern) (*Nord-Est, Nord-Orientale*); new edition (*nuova edizione*)
NFL	National Football League (*Associazione Nazionale Calcistica*)
neg	negative (*negativo*)
NSC	National Security Council (*Censiglio di Sicurezza Nazionale*)
NSPCC	National Society for the Prevention of Cruelty to Children (*Società Nazionale per la Protezione dell' Infanzia*)
NW	Northwest (*Nord-Ovest*); Northwestern (*Nord-Occidentale*)
NY	New York
NZ	New Zealand (*Nuova Zelanda*)
OAS	Organization of American States (*Organizzazione Stati Americani*); Organisation Armée Secrète (*Organiz-i zazione Armata segreta*)
OBE	Order of the British Empire (*Ordine dell'Impero Britannico*)
OECD	Organization for Economic Co-operation and Development (*Organizzazione per la Cooperazione e lo Sviluppo Economici*)
OEEC	Organization for European Economic Co-operation (*Organizzazione Economica per la Cooperazione Europea*)
OED	Oxford English Dictionary (*Dizionario Inglese di Oxford*)
OM	Order of Merit (*ordine di merito*)
op	out of print (*esaurito*)
OT	Old Testament (*Antico Testamento*)
OUP	Oxford University Press (*Edizioni dell'Università di Oxford*)
OXFAM	Oxford Committee for Famine Relief
Oxon	Oxford, of Oxford (L. *Oxoniensis*) (*di Oxford, Ossoniano*)
oz	ounce(s) (*oncia, once*)
p	page (*pagina*); participle (*participio*)
pa	per annum, by the year (*all'anno*)
PAA	Pan American Airways (*Linee Aeree Pan Americane*)
P & O	Peninsular and Oriental (Steam Navigation Company) (*Compagnia di Navigazione Peninsulare-Orientale*)
PAYE	Pay as you earn (Income Tax) (*trattenuta imposte su paghe da parte del datore di lavoro*)
PC	police constable (*agente di polizia*); Privy Council (*Consiglio Privato*); Privy Councillor (*Consigliere Privato*); postcard (*cartolina postale*)
pd	paid (*pagato*)
PhD	Doctor of Philosophy (*Dottore in Filosofia*)
PM	Prime Minister (*Primo Ministro*)
PMG	Postmaster-General (*Direttore Generale delle Poste*)

445

PO	Petty Officer (*naut*) (*sottufficiale*); Pilot Officer (*Ufficiale Pilota*); Post Office (*Ufficio postale*); Postal Order (*Vaglia Postale*)
POB	post office box (*cassetta postale*)
POW	Prisoner of War (*Prigioniero di Guerra*)
p.p.	on behalf of (L. *per procurationem*) (*per procura*); parcel post (*pacco postale*)
Pres	President (*Presidente*); Presbyterian (*Presbiteriano*)
PRO	Public Relations Officer (*Addetto alla Pubblicità*)
PT	Physical Training (*Educazione Fisica*)
pt	part (*parte*); pint(s) (*pinta, pinte*)
PTO	Please Turn Over (*vedi retro*)
PVC	Polyvinyl chloride (*cloruro di polivinile* (*plastica*))
QMG	Quartermaster-General (*mil*) (*capo del dipartimento amministrazione e alloggi*)
qr	Quarter(s)
qt	quart
qv	which see (L. *Quod vide*) (*vedi*)
RA	Royal Academy (*Accademia Reale*)
RADA	Royal Academy of Dramatic Art (*Accademia Reale d'Arte Drammatica*)
RAF	Royal Air Force (*Regia Aeronautica*)
RC	Roman Catholic (*Cattolico Apostolico Romano*); Red Cross (*Croce Rossa*)
Rd	Road (*Via, Corso*)
ref	reference (*riferimento*)
regd	registered (*raccomandato*)
rel	relative (*relativo*); related (*riferentesi*); religion (*religione*)
Rep	Representative (*Rappresentante*); Republic (*Repubblica*) Republican (*Repubblicano*); Repertory (*Repertorio*) Reporter (*cronista, corrispondente*)
Repub	Republic (*Repubblica*)
Rev	Reverend (*Reverendo*); Revelations (*Rivelazioni*); Revised (*riveduto*)
RN	Registered Nurse (*Infermiera Diplomata*)
rpm	revolutions per minute (*giri al minuto*)
Rt. Hon	Right Honorable (*Molto Onorevole*)
S	South (*Sud*); Saint (*Santo*); Socialist (*Socialista*); Society (*Società*)
s	second (*secondo*); shilling (*scellino*); son (*figlio*); singular (*singolare*); substantive (*sostantivo*); solubility (*solubilità*)
SA	South Africa (*Sud-Africa*)
s.a.e.	stamped addressed envelope (*busta indirizzata e affrancata*)
Sch	School (*scuola*)
SE	Southeast (*Sud-Est*); Southeastern (*Sud-Orientale*)
Sec, Secy	Secretary (*segretario*)
SHAPE	Supreme Headquarters Allied Powers, Europe (*Supremo Quartier Generale delle Truppe Alleate in Europa*)
SPCA	Society for the Prevention of Cruelty to Animals) (*Società per la protezione degli animali*)
SS	steamship (*piroscafo*); Social Security (*Previdensa Sociale*)
St	Saint (*Santo*); Strait (*Stretto*); Street (*strada, via*)

SW	Southwest (*Sud-Ovest*); Southwestern (*Sud-Occidentale*)
TB	Tuberculosis (*Tuberculosi*)
TNT	trinitrotoluene (explosive) (*trinitrotoluolo*)
TT	total abstainer (teetotal) (*astemio*); Tourist Trophy; tuberculin tested
TU	Trade Union (*Sindacato*)
TUC	Trade Union Congress (*Congresso dei Sindacati*)
TWA	Trans World Airlines (*Linee Aeree Intercontinentali*)
UAR	United Arab Republic (*Repubblica Araba Unita*)
UDI	Unilateral Declaration of Independence (*Dichiarazione Unilaterale d'Indipendenza*)
UK	United Kingdom (*Regno Unito*)
ult	(L. *ultimo*) last (month) (*ultimo scorso*)
UN(O)	United Nations (Organization) ((*Organizzazione delle Nazioni Unite*)
UNA	United Nations Association (*Associazione delle Nazioni Unite*)
UNICEF	United Nations International Children's Emergency Fund (*fondo di emergenza delle Nazioni Unite per l'Infanzia*)
UP	United Press (*Stampe Associate*)
US	United States (*Stati Uniti*)
USA	United States of America (*Stati Uniti d'America*)
USAF	United States Air Force (*Aeronautica Militare Statunitense*)
USIS	United States Information Service (*Ufficio Informazioni per gli Stati Uniti d'America*)
USLTA	United States Lawn Tennis Association (*Federazione Statunitense Tennis*)
USN	United States Navy (*Marina Militare Statunitense*)
USSR	Union of Soviet Socialist Republics (*Unione delle Repubbliche Socialiste Sovietiche*)
v	(L. *vide*) see (*vedi*); versus (*contro*)
VA	Veterans Administration (*Amministrazione dei Veterani*)
VC	Victoria Cross (*Croce della Regina Vittoria*)
VD	Venereal Disease (*Malattie veneree*)
Vet	Veterinary Surgeon (*veterinario*)
vg	very good (*molto bene, ottimo, lodevole*)
VIP	(*fam*) very important person (*pezzo grosso, persona molto importante*)
viz	(L. *videlicet*) namely (*vale a dire*)
W	West (*Ovest*); Western (*Occidentale*); Welsh (*gallese*)
WD	War Department (*Ministero della Guerra*)
WHO	World Health Organization (*Organizzazione Mondiale della Sanità*)
wk	week (*settimana*)
wp	weather permitting (*tempo permettendo*)
wt	weight (*peso*)
yd	yard(s) (*iarda, iarde*)
YHA	Youth Hostels Association (*Associazione degli Ostelli della Gioventù*)
YMCA	Young Men's Christian Association (*Associazione Cristiana dei Giovani*)

447

yr   year (*anno*); younger (*più giovane*); your (*vostro*)
YWCA   Young Women's Christian Association (*Unione Cristiana delle Giovani*)